PENGUIN ⓟ CLASSICS

GENERAL EDITOR, POETRY: CHRISTOPHER RICKS

THE CANTERBURY TALES

GEOFFREY CHAUCER was born in London, the son of a wine-merchant, in about 1340, and as he spent his life in royal and government service his career happens to be unusually well documented. By 1357 Chaucer was a page to the wife of Prince Lionel, second son of Edward III, and it was while in the prince's service that Chaucer was ransomed when captured during the English campaign in France in 1359–60. Chaucer's wife Philippa, whom he married *c.* 1365, was the sister of Katherine Swynford, the mistress (*c.* 1370) and third wife (1396) of John of Gaunt, Duke of Lancaster, whose first wife Blanche (d. 1368) is commemorated in Chaucer's earliest major poem, *The Book of the Duchess*.

From 1374 Chaucer worked as controller of customs on wool in the port of London, but between 1366 and 1378 he made a number of trips abroad on official business, including two trips to Italy in 1372–3 and 1378. The influence of Chaucer's encounter with Italian literature is felt in the poems he wrote in the late 1370s and early 1380s – *The House of Fame*, *The Parliament of Fowls* and a version of *The Knight's Tale* – and finds its fullest expression in *Troilus and Criseyde*.

In 1386 Chaucer was member of parliament for Kent, but in the same year he resigned his customs post, although in 1389 he was appointed Clerk of the King's Works (resigning in 1391). After finishing *Troilus* and his translation into English prose of Boethius' *De consolatione philosophiae*, Chaucer started his *Legend of Good Women*. In the 1390s he worked on his most ambitious project, *The Canterbury Tales*, which remained unfinished at his death. In 1399 Chaucer leased a house in the precincts of Westminster Abbey but died in 1400 and was buried in the Abbey.

JILL MANN took her BA from the University of Oxford and her PhD from the University of Cambridge. She taught medieval literature at Cambridge from 1972 onwards and from 1988 to

1998 was Professor of Medieval and Renaissance English. From 1999 to 2004 she was Notre Dame Professor of English at the University of Notre Dame. She is the author of *Chaucer and Medieval Estates Satire* (1973) and *Feminizing Chaucer* (2002), and co-editor (with Piero Boitani) of *The Cambridge Chaucer Companion* (2nd edition, 2003). She has also published on medieval Latin and has written many articles on medieval literature. She is a Fellow of the British Academy, an Honorary Fellow of St Anne's College, Oxford, and a Life Fellow of Girton College, Cambridge.

GEOFFREY CHAUCER

The Canterbury Tales

Edited with an Introduction and Notes by
JILL MANN

PENGUIN BOOKS

PENGUIN BOOKS

Published by the Penguin Group
Penguin Books Ltd, 80 Strand, London WC2R ORL, England
Penguin Group (USA) Inc., 375 Hudson Street, New York, New York 10014, USA
Penguin Books Canada Ltd, 10 Alcorn Avenue, Toronto, Ontario, Canada M4V 3B2
(a division of Pearson Penguin Canada Inc.)
Penguin Ireland, 25 St Stephen's Green, Dublin 2, Ireland
(a division of Penguin Books Ltd)
Penguin Books Australia Ltd, 250 Camberwell Road, Camberwell, Victoria 3124, Australia
(a division of Pearson Australia Group Pty Ltd)
Penguin Books India (P) Ltd, 11 Community Centre, Panchsheel Park, New Delhi – 110 017, India
Penguin Group (NZ), cnr Airborne and Rosedale Roads, Albany, Auckland 1310, New Zealand
(a division of Pearson New Zealand Ltd)
Penguin Books (South Africa) (Pty) Ltd, 24 Sturdee Avenue, Rosebank 2196, South Africa

Penguin Books Ltd, Registered Offices: 80 Strand, London WC2R ORL, England

www.penguin.com

This edition first published 2005

028

Text and editorial matter copyright © Jill Mann, 2005;
Chronology copyright © Barry Windeatt, 2003
All rights reserved

The moral right of the editor has been asserted

Set in 10.25/12.25 pt PostScript Adobe Sabon
Typeset by Rowland Phototypesetting Ltd, Bury St Edmunds, Suffolk
Printed and bound in Great Britain by Clays Ltd, Elcograf S.p.A.

ISBN-13: 978-0-140-42234-4

www.greenpenguin.co.uk

Contents

The Canterbury Tales

Fragment I (Group A)

Fragment II (Group B¹)

Acknowledgements

This edition has been longer in the making than anyone connected with it will care to recall. My first thanks must therefore go to Christopher Ricks, who has shown the patience of Griselda in seeing the project through to completion, and has been a constant source of encouragement, helpful criticism and wise advice. I am also grateful to Lindeth Vasey and Laura Barber at Penguin for their counsel and support. Over the years I have incurred many other debts to scholars and friends who have responded generously to questions falling within their particular area of expertise: for help of this sort, I am grateful to Caroline Barron, Richard Beadle, Larry Benson, Pat Boyde, the late David Burnley, Helen Cooper, John Davies, Peter Dronke, Chris Dyer, Robert Hardy, Sir James Holt, George Kane, Ruth Mazo Karras, Henry Ansgar Kelly, Robert Markus, Ludo Milis, James Murray, J. D. North, Oliver Padel, Christopher Page, Richard Partington, Peter Spufford, Matthew Strickland and Siegfried Wenzel. I am grateful to Barry Windeatt, editor of the companion edition of *Troilus and Criseyde* in this series, for permission to use his Chronology of Chaucer's life in this volume, and for friendly discussion of our parallel enterprises. Michael Lapidge has provided me with constant support, the benefits of his learning and practical assistance.

Girton College, Cambridge, provided a grant to pay for the initial typing of the Glossary. Long ago, Chris Cannon assisted with making the glossary entries consistent; more recently, his comments have improved the Introduction and the Note on the Text. My three Notre Dame graduate research assistants, Patrick Jehle, Ben Fischer and Sian White, have given invaluable assistance in the final stages of the project. To the University of Notre Dame I am grateful for the extremely generous amount of research time that the terms of my contract afforded during the last five years; without this arrangement, the edition would have taken even longer.

Like all editors of Chaucer, I am deeply indebted to the labours of former editors, especially to W. W. Skeat, and to Larry Benson and all those who contributed to the *Riverside Chaucer*. If I have been able on occasion to correct or supplement the latter, I am aware that I have doubtless created a new crop of errors all my own, which are well-nigh inevitable in a project of this scope, and for which I ask the reader's indulgence. That there are not more is due to the eagle-eyed proof-reading of Sophia Kingshill, and above all to the meticulous copy-editing of Monica Schmoller, whose perceptive eye for detail and tireless concern for accuracy have given the final touches to the volume.

Editor's Note

The text of the *Canterbury Tales* in this edition is accompanied by glosses, at the foot of each page, of those words and phrases with which modern readers may need immediate help. Since readers will not necessarily read the tales in sequence, it has not been assumed that knowledge of the meaning of words will be acquired cumulatively, and they are, as far as possible, glossed afresh within each individual tale. For definitions of parts of speech, and for fuller indications of a word's possible range of meanings in the *Tales*, readers should consult the Glossary. For a brief explanation of grammatical forms, they are referred to the section on Chaucer's Language. For the modern spelling of proper names, readers should usually consult the Notes, but where there is no relevant note, the modern spelling is given in an on-page gloss. Where entries in the Notes or the Glossary provide fuller linguistic information, this is indicated in the on-page gloss by 'n.' and 'g.' respectively, but information of other kinds contained in the Notes is not signalled in this way. For the abbreviations used for the individual Canterbury tales in the Notes, the Glossary and elsewhere in this edition, see Abbreviations of the *Canterbury Tales*. The list of Abbreviated References provides full details of frequently cited works. A select list of Further Reading has also been provided as a guide to some contemporary criticism devoted to Chaucer's *Canterbury Tales*.

Chronology

c. 1340 Born in London, son of John Chaucer, a well-to-do wine-merchant, and his wife Agnes. John Chaucer holds office (1347–9) as the king's deputy-butler in the port of Southampton, supervising wine shipments from Bordeaux for the royal cellars.

1357 In service as a young 'page' in the household of Elizabeth, Countess of Ulster, wife of Prince Lionel, second surviving son of Edward III. (The Countess's household expense accounts record payments to Chaucer at Easter 1357 for a paltock (short cloak), a pair of black and red hose and a pair of shoes, and at Whitsun and Christmas for other necessities.)

1359–60 In service as a *valettus* or yeoman in Prince Lionel's retinue in France; captured at the siege of Rheims and ransomed for £16 (payment from the King's Wardrobe, 1 March 1360); see 15 October 1386, below.

1360 *October*: Paid by Prince Lionel for carrying letters to England from Calais.

1361–6 Prince Lionel in Ireland as Viceroy; Chaucer's life in these years is unrecorded; presumably in service in a royal household.

1365/6 Marries Philippa, eldest daughter of Paon de Roet (of the household of Queen Philippa) and sister of Katherine Swynford, who became mistress (*c.* 1370) and third wife (1396) of John of Gaunt, Duke of Lancaster.

1366 Chaucer's father dies; his mother remarries.

February–May: receives a safe-conduct from the King of Navarre; possibly on pilgrimage to Santiago, or on diplomatic business. Perhaps previously in Aquitaine with the Black Prince.

1367 *20 June*: granted an annuity of 20 marks as an esquire of the royal household.

c. **1367** Chaucer's son Thomas born.

late 1360s Translates (part of) the *Roman de la Rose*.

1368 *July–September*: abroad on the king's service.

12 September: death of Blanche, Duchess of Lancaster, John of Gaunt's first wife. *The Book of the Duchess* written not long after.

1369 *September*: in France with John of Gaunt's expeditionary force.

1370 *June–September*: in France again, presumably in connection with the annual military campaign.

1372 *30 August*: Philippa Chaucer granted an annuity of £10 by John of Gaunt for service in the household of his second wife, Constance of Castille (through whose right he claimed the throne of Castille).

1371–3 Payments for winter and summer robes to Chaucer as an 'esquire of the King's chamber', i.e. Edward III's inner household.

1372–3 *1 December–23 May*: in Italy (Genoa and Florence), as a member of a trading and diplomatic mission.

1373 *20 August*: Chaucer receives a royal commission to travel to Dartmouth to arrange for the restoration to its master of an arrested Genoese merchant ship.

1374 *23 April*: granted a pitcher of wine a day for life by the king (commuted in 1378 for an exchequer annuity of 20 marks).

10 May: granted lease for life of rent-free dwelling above the city gate at Aldgate.

8 June: appointed controller of the customs of hides, skins and wools in the port of London (annual income £16 13s 4d), with requirement to keep the records in his own hand.

13 June: receives an annuity of £10 from John of Gaunt.

1375–7 Writing *The House of Fame*; probably completed by 1378.

1376–7 In France on several occasions, deputed from the

customs to serve on diplomatic commissions negotiating for peace and for the marriage of Richard II.

late 1370s Writing *Anelida and Arcite*.

1378 *May–September*: in Lombardy on diplomatic business to Bernabò Visconti, lord of Milan, and Sir John Hawkwood (an English mercenary adventurer in Italy).

1380 Birth of Chaucer's son Lewis (said to be aged eleven when Chaucer writes the *Treatise on the Astrolabe* for him in 1391).

4 May: released by Cecily Champain from any legal action in respect of what the deed of release terms her *raptus* (a term used in legal documents to refer to both abduction and/or rape).

c. **1380** Writes *The Parliament of Fowls*.

c. **1380–81** Writes *Palamon and Arcite* (later *The Knight's Tale*).

1381 Chaucer's mother dies.

c. **1381–6** Writing *Troilus and Criseyde*; perhaps simultaneously with, or shortly after, the *Boece*, his prose translation of Boethius.

1382 Appointed controller of the petty custom in the port of London.

1383 *23 June–1 November*: obtains permission to appoint a deputy in his principal controllership (pleading pressure of unspecified other business).

1385 The French poet Eustache Deschamps sends a poem of praise to Chaucer with the refrain 'Grand translateur, noble Geoffroy Chaucier!'.

17 February: obtains permission to have a permanent deputy at the wool customs.

10 September: Receives livery of mourning as an esquire of the King's Household upon the death of the king's mother, Joan of Kent.

12 October: Appointed a member of the commission of the peace in Kent; appointment renewed 28 June 1386, possibly with occasional service until 1389; probably now living in Kent.

c. **1385** *The Complaint of Mars* written.

1386 *1 October–28 November*: Member of Parliament for Kent at one session, the 'Wonderful Parliament' (held in the chapter-house of Westminster Abbey); one minor petition presented by the Commons requested that life-appointed controllers of customs be removed from office, on suspicion of financial irregularities, and that in future no such life appointments be made.

By 5 October: gives up lease on Aldgate dwelling.

15 October: a witness before the High Court of Chivalry (meeting in the refectory of Westminster Abbey) in the Scrope–Grosvenor trial, a dispute over the right to bear certain arms. Chaucer gives evidence that he saw the said arms borne by Sir Richard Scrope when he was himself in arms before the town of Rethel, near Rheims, during the campaign of 1359–60. Testifies to being forty years of age 'and more'.

4 December: resigns his two controllerships at the customs.

c. 1386–7 Writing *The Legend of Good Women*.

1387 Philippa Chaucer dies.

c. 1387 Begins *The Canterbury Tales*.

1388 *3 February–4 June*: the 'Merciless Parliament', hostile to the King's Household and personal patronage, and to the practice of granting life annuities.

1 May: transfers his two exchequer annuities to John Scalby.

1389 *12 July*: appointed Clerk of the King's Works.

1390s Appointed deputy-forester of North Petherton in Somerset (possibly a legal appointment while the estate's owner was a minor).

1390 *3 September*: Robbed by highwaymen of his horse and of £20 6s 8d of the king's money at the 'Fowle Ok', Hatcham, in Deptford, probably on his way to pay workmen's wages at the royal manor of Eltham. (Also recorded as the victim on 6 September of further robberies of £10 in Westminster and of £9 and 43d at Hatcham.)

1391 Writes *Treatise on the Astrolabe*; continues work on *The Canterbury Tales*.

17 June: resigns as Clerk of the King's Works.

1392 *The Equatorie of the Planetis*, possibly by Chaucer.

1394 *28 February*: granted royal annuity of £20 for life.

Death of Anne of Bohemia (Queen Consort of Richard II).

1394–5 Revises Prologue to *The Legend of Good Women* (and removes a reference to Queen Anne).

1395/6 Receives a gown of scarlet with fur trimming from Henry, Earl of Derby (the future Henry IV).

1396? *Envoy to Bukton* (mentioning the Wife of Bath).

1397 *1 December*: royal grant of a tun (a large cask) of wine per year.

1398 Moves back to London from Kent? (Responsibility for collecting from Chaucer a debt incurred in 1389 is transferred from the Sheriff of Kent to the Sheriff of London.)

1399 *24 December*: takes 53-year lease on a house in precincts of Westminster Abbey.

1400 *The Complaint of Chaucer to his Purse* with an envoy to Henry IV, who became king upon the deposition of Richard II on 30 September 1399; Henry IV renews payment of Chaucer's annuities.

25 October: Chaucer's death, according to a now illegible inscription on his tomb, recorded in 1606 (*Life-Records*, p. 548); buried in Westminster Abbey at the entrance to St Benedict's Chapel; moved in 1556 to a new tomb set against the east wall of the south transept, in what has subsequently become 'Poets' Corner'.

Introduction

In 1635, one Brian Walker, a resident of Bishop Auckland in County Durham, was found guilty of numerous instances of blasphemy by the High Commission Court (an ecclesiastical court). One of the witnesses to these blasphemies, William Hutchinson, reported that he 'did hear Walker confer and speak of "the book called Chaucer", which book he very much commended, and said he did believe the same as well as he did the Bible, or words to the same effect.'[1] Nothing further is known of Walker, but to judge from the occupations of the associates and relatives who witnessed his words he was a tradesman of some sort – not, that is, a member of an obviously literate or book-owning class. For that very reason, a spontaneous and genuine admiration for 'the book called Chaucer' seems to make itself felt in his words. No particular work of Chaucer's is named in Walker's remark, but it is reasonable to assume that it is the *Canterbury Tales* that most merit comparison with the Bible, in terms of the breadth and variety of experience that they represent. Like the Bible, this is a work that presents the reader with an autonomous narrative universe, richly and diversely peopled, in which truth is inseparable from the storial experience in which it is embedded. Divided from Chaucer by almost as many centuries as divide him from us, Walker is an unexpected witness to the affection and unforced respect that Chaucer has inspired in his readers over the years and the central place that his writings occupy in the English imagination.

The success of the *Canterbury Tales* in establishing itself as a national monument and one of the great classics of English literature is all the more remarkable when one considers that at Chaucer's death in 1400 it was (like several of his other works) left unfinished. It might at that point have seemed no more than a series of brilliant fragments,[2] its final shape and meaning forever inaccessible. If the work was known at all to Chaucer's contemporaries, it was most probably in the form of individual tales, passed around among his friends or perhaps read aloud to entertain a court audience.[3] In the Prologue to the *Legend of Good Women*, Chaucer refers to himself as having written 'the love of Palamon and Arcite | Of Thebes' and 'the lyf . . . of Seynt Cecile', narratives which were later to be included in the Canterbury collection as the Knight's Tale and the Second Nun's Tale respectively.[4] In his *Envoy to Bukton*, Chaucer refers to the Wife of Bath in a way that suggests she was a familiar figure (to Bukton and others).[5] Yet soon after Chaucer's death, the *Canterbury Tales* began to circulate as a complete collection. The two manuscripts on which the present edition is based – known as Ellesmere and Hengwrt (see the Note on the Text) – were written in the first years of the fifteenth century, and are probably very early attempts to gather together the fragments of the *Tales* and present the work as a whole for the first time. Many other manuscripts of the *Canterbury Tales* followed in the course of the century, their rapid multiplication testifying to Chaucer's high reputation and popularity. The first attempt at a 'collected Chaucer' (containing *Troilus and Criseyde*, the *Legend of Good Women*, the *Parliament of Fowls* and some shorter poems as well as the *Canterbury Tales*), Cambridge, University Library, MS Gg.4.27, was made early in the 1420s. When, towards the end of the century, printing in England began, the *Canterbury Tales* was among the first works to issue from the presses.[6]

This initial success proved to be long lasting. Chaucer was both an inspiration and a model to the generations of writers who followed him: Lydgate, Hoccleve, Hawes, Henryson, Dunbar, Skelton.[7] Spenser called him the 'pure well-head of Poesie'; Shakespeare drew on the Knight's Tale as well as *Troilus and Criseyde*.[8] Dryden praised the 'most wonderful comprehensive Nature' that characterized the *Canterbury*

Tales; Pope called him 'the first tale teller in the true enlivened natural way',[9] and both poets tried their hand at new versions of the tales. Dryden rewrote the tales of the Knight, Wife of Bath and Nun's Priest, while Pope recast the Wife of Bath's Prologue and Merchant's Tale (as well as the *House of Fame*). To Wordsworth, who translated the Prioress's Tale, he was the 'great Precursor, genuine morning Star'.[10] In describing his engraving of the Canterbury pilgrims, Blake called Chaucer 'the great poetical observer of men, who in every age is born to record and eternize its acts'.[11] In modern times, his reputation lives on not only in schools and universities, but in popular culture, through adaptations of the *Tales* on the stage, in film and on television. Monumentalized by the veneration both of his immediate successors and of later writers, and encircled by scholarly commentary and academic criticism, he has nevertheless retained the power to speak directly to his audience, commanding admiration for the scope of his vision, the acuteness of his observation and the undiminished force of his pathos and his comedy.

Tales and Tellers

The *Canterbury Tales* was the last in a series of experiments that Chaucer made with narratives of different kinds: from the simple narratives that hold together his early dream-visions, to the greatly extended single narrative of *Troilus and Criseyde*, with its complexities of tone and brilliant naturalistic rendering of human speech and psychology, and finally a move in the opposite direction with the *Legend of Good Women*, an experiment with a series of brief narratives, united by a single theme.[12] The *Canterbury Tales* marks a radically new departure: a collection of tales that vary in length, subject-matter, genre affiliation, verse-form and mood. Some of the tales have obvious sources, some do not, but almost without exception they are reshaped by Chaucer's telling in such a way that their meaning and literary effect are utterly transformed.[13] And in addition, the tales are given an extra dimension of meaning by the narrative frame that Chaucer devised: a pilgrimage to Canterbury, with a company of pilgrims as narrators and himself as one of their number.

The Canterbury pilgrims and the tales they tell are so familiar a part of English culture that it is easy to forget how stunningly original a work this was. The rich variety of the tales themselves, their sophistication of language and tone, can be matched only in Boccaccio's *Decameron*, which Chaucer may have been attempting to emulate and surpass.[14] But the pilgrimage-frame of the *Canterbury Tales* is quite different from the frame narrative of the *Decameron*. Boccaccio's narrators are not on a journey; they have retreated from plague-stricken Florence in order to pass ten days of recreation in a beautiful villa in the countryside. Their stories represent a holiday from serious concerns; young, well-born and well-bred, they understand the role of literature as a pleasurable exercise for the mind and the emotions, a subject for witty discussion and polite emulation. Charles Singleton has called the art of the *Decameron* an 'art of escape', 'an art which simply in order to be, to exist, required the moment free of all other cares, the willingness to stop *going anywhere* (either toward God or toward philosophical truth).'[15] Chaucer's pilgrims, in contrast, are perpetually in motion, both physically and mentally. Yet their motion does not represent a reinstatement of the transcendental goal abandoned by Boccaccio. The gradual approach to Canterbury is fitfully apparent in occasional references to place-names, but the pilgrims never reach their goal (and in any case, in the original plan, the ultimate goal was a secular one: a festive dinner at the Tabard Inn). Travelling becomes more important than arrival. The pilgrims also represent a much greater diversity than Boccaccio's young people in terms of social class; drawn from a wide spectrum of English society, they are formed into a temporary 'compaignie' only by their common journey and the tale-telling game to which they have agreed, accepting the Host as their temporary 'governour'. Literature as social contract, one might say. But this fragile accord is constantly threatened by jealousies, quarrels and class enmities. The pilgrims interrupt each other, insult each other and tell tales specifically designed to show each other in a bad light. Though their tale-telling is represented as a 'game', it is always hovering on the brink of becoming 'earnest', and dissolving into chaos.[16]

The dynamic interactions between the Canterbury pilgrims show us literature as part of the texture of everyday life, as moulding and being moulded by human experiences, ideas and emotions. The tales represent the imaginative and linguistic frameworks through which human beings make sense of their lives, their place in the cosmos and their relationships with each other. The interests that they serve can sometimes be narrowly sectarian, as when the Summoner and the Friar use their tales as direct attacks on each other, or when the Merchant tries to express his personal disillusionment with marriage. The responses they provoke can be equally self-oriented, as when the Host responds to stories about women by comparing them with his own wife.[17] But the tales are manifestly larger than the immediate purposes of their tellers or the immediate responses of their hearers. The paired tales of the Summoner and the Friar, for example, contain an exploration of the various relationships between language and 'the real' (as I shall indicate later) that forms no part of the quarrel between them; the Merchant's Tale has as much to say about the selfish folly of men as about the deceitful wiles of women. The tales say *more* than their tellers can know; they illustrate the wisdom of the saying 'never trust the teller, trust the tale'.

An earlier generation of critics liked to see the *Canterbury Tales* as a collection of dramatic monologues. As George Lyman Kittredge famously put it, 'the Pilgrims do not exist for the sake of the story, but *vice versa*. Structurally regarded, the stories are merely long speeches expressing, directly or indirectly, the characters of the several persons. They are more or less comparable, in this regard, to the soliloquies of Hamlet or Iago or Macbeth.'[18] For many years, Chaucer critics responded enthusiastically to this notion by interpreting each tale as a subtle delineation of its teller's character. Problems with this approach are, however, fairly readily apparent.[19] Sometimes a tale seems quite at odds with the character of the pilgrim that is suggested by the description in the General Prologue: the jovial Monk, with his love of hunting and good food, tells a relentlessly gloomy set of 'tragedies' emphasizing the fragility of human happiness. Are we to assume that his jovial exterior hides a deep despair? Sometimes, as with the Nun's Priest or the Second Nun, there is no description at all in the General Prologue which might serve as a guide in interpreting character traits revealed in the tale, and to deduce them from the tale alone is to enter into a process of circular reasoning of the purest sort. Sometimes the tale extends the General Prologue portrait in unexpected ways: we might have expected to hear about the Merchant's unhappy marriage when he is first introduced rather than later on when he is about to tell his tale. The signs that Chaucer switched tales from one teller to another as he worked are also evidence that he did not think the tales were indissolubly linked to a particular psychology.[20]

In the two cases that most nearly resemble dramatic soliloquies, the Prologues of the Wife of Bath and the Pardoner, it is significant that the social status and/or occupation of the pilgrim looms far larger than individual psychology or experience. The Wife of Bath speaks as a woman, grappling with the antifeminist writings through which men try to contain and control womankind.[21] The Pardoner describes his professional activities, frankly revealing the tricks of his trade and giving a sample of his preaching style. Whatever the vividness with which their speech and behaviour are realized for us, they are conceived at the level of the general rather than the individual. Each represents a class, a mass of experience that is widely shared. It is significant that Chaucer does not refer to the pilgrims by their personal names (which in most cases we are never told), but by the names of their professions or occupations. They are the Knight, the Squire, the Prioress, the Friar, and so on, not Peter, Richard, Eglantine or Hubert. (The last two names are assigned to the Prioress and the Friar in the General Prologue, but – significantly – are never mentioned again.) Modern printed editions create the impression of personal names by giving capital letters to these titles, but the manuscripts do not reserve capitals for the pilgrims and are likely to capitalize prominent nouns of any type; lower-case titles such as 'the knight', 'the merchant', and so on, would give a more accurate impression of the way the pilgrims are referred to.[22] Through these occupational names, the individual merges into the general. It is the social, rather than the psychological, aspects of the Canterbury pilgrims that are the focus of interest.

Shaking the Kaleidoscope: the Proverbial, the Individual and the General

The tales that the pilgrims tell likewise draw on and feed back into a general social experience. One of the markers of this orientation towards general experience is the high proportion of proverbial phrases in the *Canterbury Tales*. Chaucer's language is threaded through with the commonplace phraseology of everyday speech – with proverbial similes (as brown as a berry, busy as bees, true as steel, white as a lily, still as stone, drunk as a mouse, light as a leaf on the tree, glad as a bird is of day, to pass like a shadow on the wall, to clack like a mill) and popular sayings (better late than never, murder will out, you need a long spoon to eat with the devil, old poachers make the best gamekeepers, strike while the iron is hot, old fish and young flesh).[23] The easy inventiveness of popular speech is also evident in the frequent expressions of 'negative worth', as when something is said to be not worth an oyster, a mite, a leek, an old shoe, a hen, a bean, a fly, a turd, a straw, a gnat, a butterfly or a rake handle.[24] Out of this bedrock of common speech emerge proverbs that become the special focus of narrative experience, realizing it as at once general and individual. Individual experience both revalidates the generalizing truth of the proverb and makes contact with the common experience that has brought it into being. So, Theseus's speech at the close of the Knight's Tale bases a philosophical disquisition on the universal experience of decay – the tree dying, the stone wearing away, the river running dry – and rediscovers the meaning of the proverb 'make virtue of necessity' (3041–2). The events of the Franklin's Tale pour a rich human meaning into the apparently threadbare proverb 'Patience conquers' (773–4). Like other kinds of social experience in the *Canterbury Tales*, the proverbial can shift in tone and mood: if the Man of Law's Tale observes in deadly earnest that joy always ends in woe ('Wo occupieth the fin [end] of oure gladnesse': 424), in the Nun's Priest's Tale, this observation is seen as comically banal: 'evere the latter ende of joye is wo' could be quoted by a rhetorician as 'a soverein notabilitee' (3205–9). If the Knight's Tale and the Franklin's Tale provide narrative contexts that fill time-worn proverbs with new depths of feeling, the Nun's Priest's Tale moves in the opposite direction. Its ballooning rhetoric rehearses various clichéd interpretations of a simple barnyard incident – destiny, Fortune, women's influence, vulnerability to flattery – to settle on two banal morals of its own: keep your eyes open and keep your mouth shut. While this trajectory is comic in effect, in the Manciple's Tale it is with a sense of bleakness that the moral 'keep your mouth shut' is hammered home with a series of proverbs that act like so many nails in the coffin of verbal creativity. Yet no tale, whether it comes early or late in the *Canterbury Tales*, can claim a final perspective; the kaleidoscope is always ready to shift into a new pattern.

Proverbs are part of a rich body of social wisdom that makes up the mental furniture of the tales and, by implication, their tellers. Chaucer's own Tale of Melibee – often passed over by modern readers – plays a central role as representative of this body of collective wisdom. The arguments by which Prudence seeks to persuade her husband Melibee not to take vengeance on his enemies are a dense synthesis of quotations, drawn from the Bible (especially the Solomonic books) and secular wisdom texts, both classical and medieval. Many of these prosaic commonplaces are absorbed into the other narratives of the *Canterbury Tales* and there take on the colour of their surroundings. Solomon's 'Werk ... by conseil', for example, is used by Prudence to initiate the long process of counselling in the Tale of Melibee (1003), but is also invoked by Nicholas in the Miller's Tale in order to deceive his landlord (3530), and by Placebo in order to flatter January in the Merchant's Tale (1485). Solomon's statement that he never found a good woman is part of a serious debate in Melibee (1057, 1076–80), but part of a comic marital quarrel in the Merchant's Tale (2242–8, 2286–90). The line in which Arcite plangently expresses the isolation of the grave – 'Allone, withouten any compaignye' (Knight's Tale 2779) – reappears shortly afterwards as a purely factual description of Nicholas's life as a lodger (Miller's Tale 3204). The echo has been interpreted as a deliberate signalling of the shift of mood from heroic seriousness to mundane practicality; yet the phrase also appears in the Tale of Melibee (1560), where Chaucer introduces it as his own embellishment of a quoted maxim to the effect that if you are poor, you will find yourself 'allone withouten any compaignye'. And this last instance is in a way the most significant, for it shows that the phrase was for Chaucer a quasi-proverbial unit that acquired emotional resonances only from the context in which it was used: carrying an implicit moral force in Melibee, expressing a neutral fact in the Miller's Tale and a tragic bleakness in the Knight's Tale. Similarly, the maxim that 'pitee renneth soone in gentil herte' is applied in all seriousness to Theseus's response to finding Palamon and Arcite fighting in the grove (Knight's Tale 1761), to Alla's compassion for the accused Constance (Man of Law's Tale 660), and to Canacee's sympathy for the grieving falcon (Squire's Tale 479), but when it is used to comment on the lightning speed with which May succumbs to Damian's advances in the Merchant's Tale (1986), it is freighted with comic sarcasm. In the world of the latter tale, that is, 'pitee' is no more than a sham, and to believe in it as a motivator of human behaviour is to be as blind a dupe as January.

The careful reader of the *Canterbury Tales* learns to recognize a series of echoes, reminiscences and internal allusions that link the tales together without ever settling into a definitive or fixed pattern. Rather, they suggest that life itself is repetitive, constantly offering new variations on recurring themes, and through such repetitions we can see how narrative context creates individual meanings. In some other, transcendental, world, where the ceaseless process of change that characterizes human life could be arrested, a final and all-encompassing meaning might take shape. In the life we know, however, the kaleidoscope is all we have, and ultimate meaning appears only as a tantalizing possibility suggested in the motifs on which the constantly varying patterns seem to converge.

The repetitions and reminiscences that run through the *Canterbury Tales* point the reader towards the major themes suggested by these motifs. In the rest of this Introduction, I shall briefly sketch out the most important of these themes and the key words that serve to focus them. Once again, their different narrative embodiments give the reader a sense of simultaneous sameness and difference, of plural versions of experience, each providing a perspective that is distinct and yet somehow in touch with the rest.

'Aventure'

At the core of the Chaucerian vision of the world is the notion of chance, for which Chaucer most often uses the word 'aventure'; other words associated with this idea are the nouns 'hap', 'cas', 'grace', and the verbs 'felle' and 'befelle'. The role of chance in human affairs is a major obstacle in the way of determining a satisfactory meaning for the vicissitudes of life, since it challenges both the notion that men and women can control their destinies by their own agency, and the notion that a divine ruler dispenses happiness or unhappiness in just proportion to human deserts. The Knight's Tale focuses on the problem of chance with particular sharpness. Chaucer continually emphasizes the role of 'aventure' in the events of the narrative, altering his Boccaccian source to this end.[25] It thus seems entirely arbitrary that Arcite ends up dead, while Palamon is happily married to Emily; the reader may well agree with Egeus that life is merely a random succession of joy and woe (2841). Theseus's speech at the end of the tale both is and is not an answer to this problem: he asserts that the First 'Moevere', who, in this pagan universe, takes the place of the Christian God, has 'of his wise purveiaunce' ordained life in such a way that all earthly things must have an end (2994–3016). Change is an ineradicable part of life.

The word 'purveiaunce' (providence) implicitly invokes

Boethius's *Consolation of Philosophy*, a philosophical work that Chaucer translated and whose influence is apparent throughout his writings.[26] It takes the form of a debate between Boethius, at the point of his life when he was disgraced and imprisoned, and the personified figure of Philosophy. Like Palamon and Arcite, Boethius complains of the injustice of human life and the arbitrary malevolence of Fortune. Palamon's anguished question – 'What governaunce is in this prescience | That giltelees tormenteth innocence?' (1313–14) – directly echoes the complaint that drives Boethius's work. If God is 'governor' of the world, why does he allow Fortune to hold sway, so that the innocent suffer and the guilty prosper (I m.5)? Lady Philosophy's long answer to Boethius's complaint ultimately rests on a discrimination between the divine and the human perspectives. Divine providence, she explains, surveys all things together in an eternal present; this eternal whole is, however, executed in the world of time by an 'ordinance' that she calls 'destiny' (IV pr.6). Destiny is to providence as the line is to the circle; through the linear process of time it weaves the pattern that is eternally contemplated in its entirety by the divine intelligence. God does not 'foresee' events, he merely 'sees' them in his atemporal present, and his knowledge does not, therefore, constrain human freedom to act. Similarly, 'destiny' does not predetermine the course of events; it is simply the name given to the shape into which events fall. The apparently random changeability that is all that human beings can see from their narrower perspective is the stuff from which this larger pattern is made. So, in the Knight's Tale, the 'aventures' that make up the lives of Palamon and Arcite link themselves into a final pattern, joyful in one case and tragic in the other. Chance too is a matter of perspective, as Philosophy explains: 'hap', or 'aventure of fortune', is merely the name we give to events that are unforeseen by human agents. So if a man finds some gold in a field, the event has a cause, in that some other man buried it there, but because the burying was unknown to the finder, he sees the event as 'chance' (V pr.1–m.1).

In Boethius, Lady Philosophy's explanation answers the problem of chance on a philosophical level, but it does not greatly help in telling people how they should live their lives. For the divine perspective that will weave all causes together and reveal a meaningful pattern in human existence is necessarily and by definition unavailable to the human beings who are bound to the world of time. It is for this reason that the disruptive effects of chance, and the arbitrary see-sawing of joy and woe, remain problems not only in the pagan world of the Knight's Tale but also in the Christian world of the Man of Law's Tale. In this tale, Boethius's complaint that humankind is 'turmented in this see of fortune' (I m.5) is realized in the narrative, as Constance is twice cast out to sea in a rudderless boat and carried where 'aventure' takes her (465). The constable who is forced to consign her to the second of these journeys echoes Boethius's questioning of God's justice, given the suffering of the innocent and the prosperity of the wicked (813–16). Divine agency directly intervenes in this tale, miraculously protecting Constance from death and striking down her accuser (668–76), but the operations of this miraculous power are as shrouded in mystery as the workings of chance. If the Chaucerian narrator insists on God's 'mighty werkes', he also insists that what God does is often 'ful derk' to human comprehension; his 'prudent purveiaunce' is unknown and unknowable (478–83).

The workings of 'aventure' are not always disruptive, however. In the Franklin's Tale, Dorigen too questions God's 'purveiance' and 'governance' of the world (865–6) as she contemplates the black rocks that threaten her husband's life, and Aurelius might well complain of the 'aventure' (940) that causes him to fall in love with a woman already married. Yet in the happy resolution of the tale, when Aurelius releases Dorigen from her promise to give herself to him and renounces his love for her, 'aventure' plays a benign role. Twice within the space of a few lines, Chaucer emphasizes that their meeting on the way to the garden took place by chance ('Of aventure happed hir to meete': 1501; 'thus they mette, of aventure or grace': 1508). Since the coincidence is not so *very* extraordinary (Aurelius has been watching for her to leave the house, and is following her to the garden), the emphasis on chance seems to attach itself to the transformation that the meeting brings about: Aurelius's miraculously gratuitous change of heart. The workings of chance – as Theseus too acknowledges – leave open the possibilities of fresh beginnings, of openings towards happiness as well as lapses into disaster. If joy is not inevitable, neither is woe.

And then again, like all serious notions in the *Canterbury Tales*, 'aventure' can appear in comic, bathetic or travestied forms. The word does not appear in the Miller's Tale and the Reeve's Tale, and it may seem that in the everyday world of these tales human beings are able to dictate the course of their own lives, calculating the means to achieve the ends they desire. 'Purveiaunce' here refers to human, rather than divine, activity, and is downscaled to refer only to practical preparations for an envisaged event (Miller's Tale 3566). But in both tales – with Nicholas's cry of 'Water!' in the Miller's Tale, and the moving of the cradle in the Reeve's Tale – chance intervenes to send events spiralling out of human control as surely as in the Knight's Tale or the Man of Law's Tale. The neatness of the denouement does not bring with it any revelation of a deeper meaning (poetic justice, say); the clockwork precision with which the narrative logic moves to its inevitable con-clusion expresses nothing other than the ability of 'aventure' to produce comic chaos. Travesty of the notion is to be found in the Clerk's Tale, where Walter cruelly disguises his own willed actions as the effects of chance, parodying Lady Philosophy when he advises the suffering Griselda to endure with equa-nimity 'The strook of Fortune or of aventure' (811–12). (And yet, of course, his mysteriously irrational impulse to cruelty *is*, in its effects on Griselda, a 'stroke of chance'.) In the Merchant's Tale, 'aventure' forms part of the list of possible causes for May's instantaneous capitulation to Damian's amorous ad-vances. Destiny, 'aventure', planetary influence, pity running soon in 'gentil herte' – the elements that make up the fabric of narrative action in the Knight's Tale – are here introduced only to be discarded (1967–86). In a moment of self-reflexive comedy, Chaucer seems to suggest that his own narrative frameworks are superfluous and indeed misleading: in this tale, if you want to account for human behaviour, sexual appetite is enough.

Patience and Pity

Since human knowledge and human control are both of necessity limited, wise action takes on a responsive rather than a directive character. For this reason Chaucer's tales often focus on the virtues of patience and pity. Patience is central to Chaucer's Tale of Melibee: Prudence persuades Melibee to bear the wrongs that have been done to him because 'pacience is a greet vertu of perfeccioun' (1517). The Parson's Tale adds a Christian dimension to the concept, offering Christ as an example of patient suffering, and quoting a variation of the proverb 'Patience conquers': 'If thow wolt venquisse [vanquish] thin enemy, lerne to suffre' (661). The Franklin's Tale and the Clerk's Tale offer different narrative explorations of this paradox. The long eulogy of patience that appears near the beginning of the Franklin's Tale incorporates both the proverb 'Patience conquers' and the admonition 'Lerneth to suffre' (773–5, 777). It is a passage that presents patience as a response to the ceaseless changes of life, the internal and external disturbances (miniature 'aventures', one could say) that threaten to destroy stability and happiness. Patience does not involve spiritual or psychological immobility (Patience on a monument, as it were), but rather a process of constant adaptation, or 'temperaunce', as Chaucer calls it. It is from this 'temperaunce', not from the forcible imposition of one's will, that good 'governaunce' issues (785–6). The tale translates this notion into practice. It is through the exercise of patience – the surrender to the 'aventure' (1483) that is constituted by Dorigen's promise to Aurelius – that Arveragus sets in motion the events that create the unexpected resolution of the narrative problem. In the Clerk's Tale too, the exercise of patience is tied to the keeping of a promise – in this case Griselda's promise to comply with her husband's will in both deed and thought, without 'grucching' (grudging/grumbling). If patience is, in the Franklin's Tale, exercised by Arveragus and Aurelius as well as Dorigen, in the Clerk's Tale it becomes a predominantly female quality; women's patience, claims the Clerk, outdoes even Job's (932–8). The religious resonances of the tale give Griselda's suffering a Christ-like quality. Her long and arduous trials make it seem that patience is here forced into the immobility that is rejected in the Franklin's Tale, yet the stasis is finally broken and here too patience conquers; it is Walter who breaks under the pressure of Griselda's unchanging steadfastness and is forced to realize the human appetite for change in himself.

In both the Franklin's Tale and the Clerk's Tale it is pity that responds to patience and breaks the narrative deadlock. Aurelius is overcome by 'compassioun' and 'routhe' (pity) for Dorigen and Arveragus (1515, 1520); Walter is finally moved to take pity ('rewen') on Griselda (1050). Pity, that is, resembles patience in its responsive quality; it submerges the beholder in the experience of the sufferer ('Feelinge his similitude in peines smerte', as the Squire's Tale puts it: 480), obliterating the distinction between them. So, in the Knight's Tale, pity is the quality that prompts Theseus to respond to the unexpected 'aventures' that confront him – the line of weeping widows who interrupt his triumphal procession to Athens, the discovery of his enemies Palamon and Arcite fighting in the grove (952–6, 1760–81). In the Man of Law's Tale, Alla likewise responds to Constance's anguish, when she is accused of murder, with the pity that distinguishes the 'gentil herte' (659–60). Yet if in this instance pity averts disaster, the happy resolution is not a final conclusion but only one more stage in the endless succession of joy and sorrow. Even more clearly than in the Clerk's Tale, pity and suffering take on a religious dimension, emblematized in the Cross, 'Reed of the Lambes blood, ful of pitee' (452). In Constance's prayer to the Virgin, in which she both asks for Mary's pity and expresses her own pity for Mary's sufferings at the death of her child, the divine and the human converge at the level of shared experience (841–54). Pity and cruelty circulate, incomprehensibly, within the same divine economy; if God 'suffers' (allows) innocents to die (815), he also suffers, in the most literal sense, the same kind of death. The Physician's Tale offers one narrative image of the nexus that binds together cruelty and pity, as Virginius cuts off his daughter's head with 'pitous hand', begging her to take her death 'in pacience' (226, 223). As this pagan story adumbrates God's loving sacrifice of his son, so the Prioress's Tale recapitulates the Crucifixion in the Jewish murder of an innocent. This tale too focuses on pity, but its relation to cruelty and to divine 'governaunce' is even more problematic. Fathers, both human and divine, are conspicuous by their absence, leaving mothers and children vulnerable in a hostile universe. Yet the tender feelings focused on mother and child have as their backwash new waves of cruelty, as the murderous Jews are tortured and killed. The cruel God of the Old Testament persists alongside the suffering God of the New.[27]

Like 'aventure', however, patience and pity have their comic forms. As we have seen, the 'pitee' that 'renneth soone' in May's 'gentil herte' is a thinly disguised sexual appetite. And the Wife of Bath thinks patience is an excellent means of dominating her old husbands. Since they (she claims) praise Job's patience, they should imitate it (434–6). Echoing the Franklin's serious admonition – 'Lerneth to suffre, or elles, so moot I goon, | Ye shul it lerne, wherso ye wole or noon' – she comically twists it into a threat of wifely nagging: 'Suffreth alwey, sin ye so wel kan preche; | And but ye do, certein we shal yow teche | That it is fair to have a wif in pees' (437–9). Whereas the Clerk had praised woman's patience, the Wife stands the gender roles on their head: since a man is more 'resonable' than a woman, then *he* is the one who must be 'suffrable' (441–2). The end of the Wife of Bath's Prologue shows us patience in a form that is at once comic and serious: the violent quarrel between the Wife and her fifth husband is resolved by their own mundane version of patience. It is through shamelessly milking pathos ('Er I be deed, yet wol I kisse thee': 802), rather than through persisting in aggression, that she manages to get the upper hand and induces him to surrender 'the governaunce of hous and lond' (814). Their resulting harmony and happiness is yet another illustration of the dictum that 'Patience conquers', even in this apparently inauspicious environment.

Anger, 'Grucching', 'Maistrye' and 'Glosinge'

Alongside patience and pity, the *Canterbury Tales* explores their opposites. The most important of these is anger or ire (for which the Parson's Tale prescribes patience as the remedy: 659). Another is 'grucching' (a combination of 'grudging' and 'grumbling'), which the Parson's Tale represents as the fruit of 'inpacience agains God, and som time agains man' (499). The 'Boethian question' (why do the innocent suffer and the guilty prosper?) is, it would seem, a kind of 'grucching': 'Agains God is it whan a man gruccheth again the pine of helle, or agains poverte or los of catel [property], or again rein or tempest, or elles gruccheth that shrewes [wicked people] han prosperitee, or elles for that goode men han adversitee' (500) – all of these being things that humankind should 'suffre paciently' (501). Griselda's promise to Walter is an undertaking 'nevere . . . to grucche' against what he commands her (Clerk's Tale 354); the religious resonances of this tale translate this renunciation of 'grucching' against man into a narrative exploration of the level of trust required to renounce 'grucching' against God, who, like Walter, may take away one's children, but, unlike Walter, will not give them back in this life. In the pagan setting of the Knight's Tale, Theseus likewise urges that 'grucching' against the necessity of death is 'folye' and 'wilfulnesse' (3045, 3057–8, 3062) and a rebellion against Jupiter's rule (3046).

While the Clerk's Tale claims for women pre-eminence in patience, medieval antifeminist literature associated them with anger. The friar of the Summoner's Tale, despite his fondness for female company, assures Thomas that no serpent is so cruel when one treads on his tail as a woman is 'whan she hath caught an ire' (2003). The portrait of the Wife of Bath in the General Prologue accords with this stereotype, representing her as 'so wrooth' if anyone usurps her social rank in the church procession at the Offertory that she is 'out of alle charitee' (451–2). Her Prologue enlarges this detail, showing the Wife

shrilly scolding her first three old husbands, and finally, in a
paroxysm of fury, tearing three leaves out of her fifth husband
Jankin's book, just after he has quoted Solomon's proverb
about the torments of life with an 'angry wif' (775–81). But in
this instance, Chaucer gives the old stereotype a new twist,
by showing that antifeminist literature (implicit in the list of
accusations that the Wife claims her old husbands made against
her, and explicit in the contents of Jankin's book) *produces* the
angry woman that it purports only to describe.

The Wife's quarrel with Jankin also indicates the opposition
between patience and 'maistrye' (dominance/mastery), particularly when the relations between the sexes are in question. The
Wife's tale goes on to show male 'maistrye' in extreme and ugly
form in the knight's rape of a young girl; fittingly, the Loathly
Lady's lecture stresses the benefits of poverty 'To him that
taketh it in pacience', and leads into the voluntary surrender of
'maistrye' by the newly submissive knight (1198, 1236–8).
The Franklin's Tale too links the masculine renunciation of
'maistrye' with the exercise of patience in marriage (747, 764–
75), and shows how rape is, this time, averted by Aurelius's
pity. In the Manciple's Tale, however, we see the dark obverse
of this happy resolution. Beginning with an idyllic picture of
the god Phoebus, handsome, brave and supremely gifted in
music, the tale then surprises us with the information that he
was, like any aged husband in a medieval fabliau,[28] jealous of
his wife (144) – jealousy being, as the Franklin's Tale makes
clear, the manifestation of a desire for 'maistrye' (747–8). The
changeability that the eulogy of patience in the Franklin's Tale
teaches us to recognize as an indelible part of human nature
here manifests itself as the wife's 'newfangelnesse' (193; cf. Sq
610, 618) – the ineradicable appetite for something or someone
new. Told of his wife's infidelity by his talking crow, Phoebus
is overwhelmed by anger, 'And in his ire his wif thanne hath he
slain' (265). The destruction of the idyll is symbolized in his
breaking of his musical instruments and the irrational vengeance that he takes on the crow, turning his colour from
white to black and depriving him of his song. Anger represents

Phoebus's refusal to accept the 'aventure' of his wife's infidelity; he eradicates it by eradicating *her*. Yet this is not the only way that the infidelity is eradicated. Having killed his wife, Phoebus resurrects her in transformed image, lamenting her as 'to me so sad [constant] and eek so trewe', and 'Ful giltelees – that dorste I swere, iwys [for sure]' (275–7).

Melodramatically, he launches into a rhetorical denunciation of his own 'ire recchelees', underscoring the thematic prominence of anger in the tale (278–90). Renouncing 'ire', he substitutes rhetoric, which here becomes simply an alternative way of refusing to accept reality. Earlier in the tale, the Manciple had insisted on the virtues of plain unadorned language: 'The word moot nede acorde with the dede' (208). Camouflaging lust by describing it as romantic passion is, he suggests, to use language to obscure an underlying reality. But it is the bluntness with which the crow announces to Phoebus that he has been cuckolded – 'Cokkow! Cokkow! Cokkow!' (243) – that the god is unable to bear; having obliterated the adultery by killing his wife, he then obliterates it a second time by rendering the truth-telling crow speechless and re-creating his illusions in his own cocoon of words.

The Summoner's Tale about a friar shows us that Chaucer's name for this kind of deceptive rhetoric is 'glosinge'; in this tale too it is linked with anger.[29] Responding to the claim (which is, as far as we can see, unjustified) by Thomas's wife that her husband is 'as angry as a pissemire [ant]' (1825), the visiting friar throws up an extempore sermon on anger which is a brilliant demonstration of his skill in 'glosinge'. 'Glosing', he has earlier assured Thomas, 'is a glorious thing, certein, | For lettre sleeth, so as we clerkes seyn' (1793–4). The Pauline contrast between the letter that kills and the spirit that gives life (2 Corinthians 3:6) is co-opted to justify the friar's abandonment of 'the text of Holy Writ' (1790) in favour of a 'glose' that will instruct people to give generously to friars (1795–6), or that proves that Christ was referring to friars when he said, 'Blessed are the poor in spirit' (1919–23). The friar's sermon links 'glosinge' and anger in that the first is its method and the second is its content. But the link between them is closer than that. The illustrative anecdotes in the friar's sermon show that anger resembles 'glosinge' in that both are at bottom refusals to accept an external other – in the case of anger, an event or 'aventure'; in the case of 'glosinge', the (literal meaning of the) text. In the first anecdote (2017–42), a judge who has sentenced a man to death for murder refuses to alter his judgement when the supposedly murdered man turns out to be alive. Instead of altering his verbal pronouncement to fit an external reality, he forces reality into the shape of his words. The original sentence must therefore hold good, and the supposed murderee must also be executed in order to justify it, while the executioner too must die as punishment for failing to carry out the original command. The second anecdote shows 'irous' Cambises reacting to the lord who reproves his drunkenness by shooting the lord's son in order to prove that his hand and eye are unimpaired (2043–73). As in the Manciple's Tale, plain speaking is shown to be perilous; truth must be well disguised (2074–8). Finally, the story of Cyrus ordering his soldiers to obliterate the river Gyndes by dispersing it into a multitude of channels, simply because one of his horses had accidentally drowned in it, again shows anger as the opposite of patience, a refusal to accept 'aventure' (2079–84).

The friar's sermon on anger paradoxically (like Jankin's quotations about angry women) has the effect of producing violent anger in its listener, the sick man Thomas, who becomes 'wel neigh wood for ire' (2121). Thomas takes his revenge on the friar by pretending that he will give him a treasure hidden in the cleft of his buttocks, and when he feels the friar's groping hand, letting fly an enormous fart. At this, the preacher of the sermon against anger himself becomes violently angry, leaping up like a raging lion (2152) and storming out 'with a ful angry cheere' (2158), grinding his teeth in fury (2161). The ineffectuality of mendicant 'glosinge', its lack of connection with reality at any point, could hardly be better demonstrated.

Words, Deeds, 'Entente' and 'Termes'

The friar's sermon is a superb example of free-floating rhetoric, a glorious verbal balloon whose main function is to demonstrate the ability of language to take on a life of its own. The fart with which Thomas answers it is not a randomly chosen insult, but a reminder that the basic physical definition of the word is 'broken air'.[30] The fart, that is, represents the bodily aspect of language, without which it cannot exist. Thomas's riposte empties the friar's sermon of semantic content and implicitly reduces it to 'hot air', to be answered only with more hot air. The implicit parody of the 'mighty wind' that signals the coming of the Holy Ghost at Pentecost (Acts 2:2) reinforces this comic reduction; instead of the linguistic empowerment bestowed on the apostles (the gift of tongues), we have a linguistic emptying-out of the sign.[31] This reductive response to verbal elaboration is also evident, although in less extreme form, in the Manciple's insistence that 'the word moot cosin be to the werking [deed]' (210); to call someone who plunders countries a conqueror rather than a thief is to use language to disguise reality (223–34). Yet in the Manciple's Tale, delusive rhetoric and blunt truth-telling are presented as equally dispiriting options, and the tale concludes with a lengthy series of admonitions to say as little as possible and keep one's mouth shut whenever one can. Speech, in whatever form, is a snare and a delusion.

The delusive aspects of language, and the question of how it connects with reality, are subjects explored throughout the *Canterbury Tales*. Perhaps surprisingly, it is in Chaucer's fabliau tales that elaborate verbal constructions of the type represented by the friar's sermon predominate, while in his romances and other serious tales we find a strong pull towards literalism. In the Franklin's Tale, Dorigen is held to the strict letter of her promise, and the meaning that it conveys, which is flatly contradictory to the literal sense of the words, is of no account in saving her from Aurelius's claim. In the Knight's Tale, Arcite and Palamon are each given exactly and literally what they asked for (victory in Arcite's case, Emily in

Palamon's), even though they both clearly intend to ask for the same thing. The arbitrariness of cosmic 'governaunce' seems to be evident in this demonstration of the way a small difference in verbal formulation can so dramatically alter one's fate. In the Clerk's Tale, Griselda is bound to obedience, not by her duty as a wife, but by the words of her promise to Walter. In such cases, words exercise a quasi-magical power, binding those who utter them to suffer unimagined consequences. In the Friar's Tale, in contrast, the devil refuses to take the literal form of words as decisive: when the summoner urges him to take the carter's curses literally and seize the horses, cart and hay that he has consigned to the devil, the fiend declines, on the grounds that the carter's 'entente' was not behind his words. 'The carl spak o [one] thing, but he thoghte another' (1568). In the world of the Friar's Tale, Dorigen would have had no problems.

In the fabliau tales, words and intentions have to be carefully discriminated. Only fools would dream of taking words at face-value; for the worldly-wise, they are a mask behind which one can work towards one's own ends. So, in the Shipman's Tale, the wife and the monk weave a complicated verbal dance, at the end of which she has agreed to have sex with him in reward for the sum of 100 francs,[32] although this has at no point been explicitly stated (98–203). In the Miller's Tale, Nicholas's fantastic story of Noah's flood lures the carpenter into willing collaboration in his own cuckolding. Overwhelmed by 'imaginacioun', the power of words to conjure up pictures that work on the mind and so create their own reality, the carpenter thinks he sees Noah's flood, billowing like the sea, coming to drown his wife (3611–17).

Professional jargon, for which Chaucer uses the word 'termes', is another potential means of manipulating reality. Legal jargon, or 'termes queinte of lawe' (Man of Law's Epilogue 1189), is used by both the Sergeant of Law and the Summoner as a way to impress (General Prologue 323, 639). Scientific jargon is the foundation of deception in the Canon's Yeoman's Tale: the cascade of 'termes' deployed in the descriptions of the alchemist's activities (752, 980, 1398) dazzles the mind, creating the illusion of a real command of natural processes (just as the magician's removal of the rocks in the Franklin's Tale uses 'termes of astrologye' (1266) to create in the reader's mind the illusion that something real has been accomplished). As the concluding anecdote of Plato and his disciple shows, these words are locked in a hermeneutic circle that never connects with reality: asked what is 'the stoon that Titanos men name', Plato simply renames the stone as 'Magnasia', provoking the exasperated comment that he is explaining *'ignotum per ignocius'* (the unknown by the more unknown). Further questioning leads only to a void: Plato asserts that at the centre of the alchemical art is a secret that can be known only by divine inspiration (1448–71). Yet if alchemy cannot make gold, words can; 'termes' are the true tools of the alchemist, possessing the fertile power of 'multiplicacioun' that he claims to find in metals.

The suspicion that 'termes' may be merely a cover for deception accounts for their rejection, not only by the virtuous Virginia in the Physician's Tale, whose speech is said to be devoid of 'countrefeted termes' which might give her a specious appearance of wisdom (51), but also by the Host, who has the plain man's distrust of language that is anything other than basic. Fearing that the Clerk might speak over his head, he urges him to forget his 'termes', the 'colours' and 'figures' of rhetoric, and to speak plainly enough to be understood (Clerk's Prologue 16–20). Both the Miller's Tale and the Reeve's Tale pit university clerks against practical labouring men, and both the carpenter in the former tale and the miller in the latter ridicule the insubstantial world of the intellectual and pride themselves on their own down-to-earth sense of reality (Miller's Tale 3457–61, Reeve's Tale 4049–56). The miller sarcastically pretends that the sophisticated verbal logic of the clerks can prove his house to be many times bigger than it is (4123–6). Yet it is a trust in the world of solid objects that leads to his own downfall. In the Reeve's Tale, the simple shifting of the cradle has its own devastating semantic charge: if this is the cradle, then this is my bed. Objects can be as deceptive as words. It is Alein who first falls victim to this semantic illusion, showing that the clerkly manipulation of reality has its limits. So too in the Miller's

Tale, Nicholas overreaches himself and loses control of the plot that he has initiated when he attempts to repeat Alison's trick and is branded by Absalon. As in the Summoner's Tale, a fart (released by Nicholas as a derisive response to Absalon's request that he should speak: 3805) seems to mark the lowest common denominator of the verbal, a retreat from the elaborations of clerical rhetoric. But in this tale as in the Summoner's, this retreat is the prelude only to a triumphant reascendancy of the verbal/intellectual. The squire's ingenious application of the techniques of university logic to solve the 'inpossible' question of how to divide a fart into thirteen brings the bodily back under the control of the intellect (2243–86). And Nicholas's cry of 'Water, water', so far from being a retreat to linguistic basics, shows the power and complexity of meaning in a single word: paradoxically underwriting his own (by now forgotten) story of the Flood, it leaps from one linguistic context to another where it is instantly charged with a whole new world of significance, translating itself into action and sending the carpenter hurtling to the ground. In the Shipman's Tale, multiple meaning in the form of a pun provides a comic solution to the wife's predicament, as she wriggles out of the trap sprung on her by the monk by asking her husband to score the debt of 100 francs 'upon my taille' (416). The pun on 'tail' and 'tally' suggests that language, like sex, has a miraculous and beneficent fecundity; this is a bank that will never run out of funds.

The Pardoner's Prologue also quasi-miraculously turns words into money. In a dazzling deployment of clerical rhetoric (his own version of 'glosinge'), the Pardoner transforms his collection of rags and bones into a collection of holy relics, imbued with magical powers, and persuades his hearers to give him money and goods in return for their illusory benefits. The Prologue also shows a particularly complicated relationship between the verbal construct, the 'entente' that motivates it, and its effect on those who hear it: the Pardoner's sermon warns against avarice, but avarice is his motivation in preaching it (400–404, 423–8, 432–3). Yet whereas the sermon against anger in the Summoner's Tale paradoxically *produces* anger in its listener, by an equal but opposite paradox this avariciously motivated sermon actually makes people repent of avarice (429–31) – and the more they do so, the more the Pardoner's avarice is satisfied. The power of words is quasi-autonomous, not dependent on the honest 'entente' of the speaker. This notion is extended in the Pardoner's Tale. Blind to the semantic content of the word 'death', the three revellers seek death and, by a strange inevitability of narrative logic, find it. Even stranger is the way that their nonsensical oath, 'Deeth shal be deed [dead]' (710), evokes a biblical text in which the paradox is a sign of religious mystery rather than illogical nonsense. 'O death, I will be thy death' (Hosea 13:14) is a prophetic text that was held to find its fulfilment in Christ's Crucifixion and Redemption. Prophecy implies that linguistic constructs, so far from attaining the highest level of truth when they slavishly follow reality, can make their own reality, in advance of the events that will validate it. The Pardoner's Prologue and Tale explore the complex relations between language and the sacred: at one extreme, language is a tool for religious trickery, at the other, an opening into another dimension of truth.

Words are, however, the stock-in-trade of the poet as well as of the cleric. If Nicholas in the Miller's Tale achieves his ends by virtue of his gifts as a master-narrator, an even greater master-narrator is Chaucer himself, whose picture-making words conjure up Nicholas, Alison and the whole world of fourteenth-century Oxford. So the question of whether to give credence to verbal fictions applies not just to the gullible dupes of the fabliau, but also to the reader of the *Canterbury Tales*. How can we be sure that the *poet*'s words are cousin to the deed? In the Manciple's Tale, as suggested earlier, Chaucer creates a kind of double vision, in which rhetoric offers us romantic passion, a lady, a conqueror and an innocent wife wrongfully slain, while reality offers us lust, a wench, a thief and a self-deluded husband (205–34). The Merchant's Tale similarly offers a double vision of the affair between May and Damian, oscillating between the language of romantic love and the bald physical reality of sexual appetite ('in he throng [thrust]': 2353). It is, we realize, the words in which the tale is told that define the way we interpret reality. January's blindness, which at the end of the tale is voluntarily continued even when his sight is restored, becomes the symbol of a larger human blindness, which hides the simple workings of human appetite under the cloak of grandiose conceptions.

This bleak conclusion might also seem to apply to the Nun's Priest's Tale, where human dignity, noble aspirations and intellectual pretensions are mocked by being grafted on to a story about a pair of chickens. But the comic atmosphere of the tale makes the inexhaustible flow of rhetoric an occasion for amusement, not pessimism. As in the Miller's Tale and the Summoner's Tale, the narrative denouement brings language back to its basic physical aspect, as the cock tricks the fox into forgetting that in order to utter verbal insults he must *open his mouth*. But this reductive moment does not signal a final disillusionment with the verbal. If the fox, like the Manciple's Tale, draws a moral condemning anyone who 'jangleth whan he sholde holde his pees' (3435), we remember that his 'jangling' has been the saving of Chauntecleer. And rhetoric can cope with this happy ending just as easily as it can with disaster: Fortune, as so often, is invoked to explain everything; 'Lo, how Fortune turneth sodeinly | The hope and pride eek of hir enemy!' (3403–4). As with the pun on 'taille' at the end of the Shipman's Tale, the inexhaustible fecundity of language and of poetic rhetoric becomes a matter for comic celebration. The poet can find meaning in everything and has a set of words for every occasion.

The Links

The themes that I have been tracing through the tales also appear in the prologues, epilogues and links that make up the pilgrimage-frame. The exercise of patience holds the company together, expressing itself as obedience ('obeisaunce') to the Host's 'governaunce'.[33] But their fragile accord is constantly threatened by outbreaks of anger, usually provoked by one pilgrim's belief that he has been mocked or attacked in the tale of another. So the Reeve – who identifies anger as one of the 'four sparks' left in the embers of old age – has 'a litel ire' in his heart and 'gan to grucche' at the Miller's Tale because he thinks the carpenter husband is a surrogate for himself (3862–3, 3913–20). He therefore seeks to take vengeance on the Miller with his own tale about a cuckolded miller. The Friar and the Summoner have a brief quarrel at the end of the Wife of Bath's Prologue (829–49), in which the Summoner comments on the Friar's loss of patience (849). When the Wife's tale is over, the Friar hastens to take his revenge by telling his tale about a summoner. This throws the pilgrim-Summoner into a paroxysm of rage: standing in his stirrups, he shakes like an aspen-leaf (1665–7), and launches into his own tale about a cheating friar. The Summoner's Tale is thus not only *about* anger, it is also *produced by* anger. From these instances it appears that anger is a creative impulse; it fuels the urge to tell tales. Tale-telling is not a neutral and dispassionate activity; it is motivated by the desire to affect the world.

Oddly enough, the other creative stimulus identified in the links is strong drink. It is the 'ale of Southwerk' (3140) that impels the Miller to thrust himself forward before his turn and tell his story of the carpenter. The Pardoner insists on seeking inspiration for his tale in 'a draghte of moiste and corny ale' (315). Anger and drink have parallel effects: the Host tells the quarrelling Friar and Summoner that they act like 'folk that dronken ben of ale' (Wife of Bath's Prologue 852). Yet as the pilgrimage progresses, anger and drink at times threaten to close off the tale-telling instead of stimulating it. At the end of the Pardoner's Tale, the Host's vigorous rejection of the Pardoner's invitation to kiss his relics makes the Pardoner so 'wrooth' that he is speechless; 'no word ne wolde he seye' (957). His anger threatens to disrupt the 'pleye' that binds the pilgrims together. ' "Now," quod oure Hoost, "I wol no lenger pleye | With thee, ne with noon oother angry man" ' (958–9). A similar threat emerges in the Manciple's Prologue, where drink and anger are combined. The Manciple jeers at the drunken Cook, who waxes 'wrooth [wrathful] and wraw [angry]', but is *so* drunk that he cannot speak (46–8). Disaster is averted by the Host, who reconciles the two; the Manciple promises that he will not 'wrathe' the Cook, and appeases him by giving him yet more to drink (76–93). The Host blesses Bacchus, 'That so kanst turnen ernest into game' (99–100).

In the end it is not anger that ends the tale-telling, but the Parson's rejection of 'fables and swich wrecchednesse' (34). Like the Nun's Priest, he offers corn rather than chaff (35–6; cf. Nun's Priest's Tale 3443), but the grindingly dull prose of his treatise on penance is poles apart from the rhetorical exuberance of Chauntecleer and Pertelote. The Manciple's concluding admonitions to hold one's tongue seem well designed to lead into this prosaic world, which neatly slices up human behaviour on the dissecting-table of moral categorization.

Chaucer in the Tales

To emphasize the continuity of themes between the tales and the links is not to deprive the pilgrim-tellers of their robust humanity; on the contrary, it is to stress that the tale-telling is a very human activity, enmeshed in the moment-by-moment oscillations from patience to anger, from pathos to ribald game, from seriousness to flippancy, that the pilgrims experience. Essential to this sense of literature as enmeshed in the texture of life is Chaucer's inclusion of himself in the pilgrim-company, a brilliantly original stroke which transforms the meaning of the *Canterbury Tales*. For whereas other authors might express opinions about the human figures in their works, Chaucer organizes the central moment of his work as the point where his pilgrims express their opinions of *him*. His spectacularly bad tale of Sir Thopas is interrupted by the Host, who can bear no more of this 'drasty speche' (923). The joke is taken a stage further by Chaucer's protestation that this is the only verse tale he knows (708–9, 928), so that he is obliged to switch to the prose tale of Melibee. The irony by which the poet who created the pilgrims and all their richly various tales is represented as able only to tell a rather unexciting tale in prose is, as G. K. Chesterton long ago pointed out, comedy on the grand scale, a joke so large that it threatens to escape notice.[34] But its effects go farther than the joke. The Thopas–Melibee sequence represents

Chaucer's own manifestation of patience. Surrendering his claims to authority and to creative superiority, the author puts himself on the same level as the other pilgrims, as simultaneously real and insubstantial as they are. The tales they tell not only have tellers, they have an audience, and it is for the audience to say what significance they will allow the tales to have in their lives. So Chaucer hands the *Canterbury Tales* over to its audience, to make of it what they will.[35] It is his master stroke, as endearing as it is witty, and profound in its implications for our notion of the relation between the literary creator and his creation.

NOTES

1. The case is reported in *The Acts of the High Commission Court within the Diocese of Durham*, Surtees Society 30 (Durham, 1858), pp. 115–19; the passage quoted is on p. 116, and is also reproduced in Derek Brewer, ed., *Chaucer: The Critical Heritage*, 2 vols. (London and New York, 1978), I, 152.

2. I follow current editorial convention in distinguishing ten fragments (see Contents), but it should be noted that the separation of Fragments IV and V depends on creating a break between the Merchant's Epilogue and Squire's Prologue which has no support in the manuscripts where this stretch of text appears; see note on Mch 2419–40/Sq 1–8.

3. However, the older view that the frontispiece to Cambridge, Corpus Christi College, MS 61 shows Chaucer reading aloud to the court of Richard II is now no longer accepted; see Derek Pearsall, 'The *Troilus* Frontispiece and Chaucer's Audience', *Yearbook of English Studies*, 7 (1977), 68–74.

4. The quotation is from the F version of the Prologue (generally thought to be earlier than the G version), lines 420–21, 426.

5. The addressee of this short poem is probably Sir Peter Bukton; for his connections with Chaucer, see Derek Pearsall, *The Life of Geoffrey Chaucer* (London, Boston, MA, and Sydney, 1985), p. 184, and cf. the note to Sum 1710 in this volume.

6. William Caxton set up his printing press in Westminster in 1476; scholars are agreed that the *Canterbury Tales* was among the first items that he published. A second edition appeared

c. 1483. (Since neither edition bears a date, it is not possible to be precise.)

7.   For a study of the reception of Chaucer's writings in fifteenth-century England, see Seth Lerer, *Chaucer and His Readers* (Princeton, NJ, 1993). A comprehensive collection of references to Chaucer and his works up to the twentieth century can be found in C. F. E. Spurgeon, *Five Hundred Years of Chaucer Criticism and Allusion*, 3 vols. (Cambridge, 1925; repr. 1961); a more selective collection, which goes up to 1933, is Brewer, *Geoffrey Chaucer: The Critical Heritage*. J. A. Burrow, *Geoffrey Chaucer: A Critical Anthology* (Harmondsworth, 1969) extends from the fourteenth century to 1968, and contains much useful material.

8.   See Brewer, *Critical Heritage*, I, 116 (Spenser), and Ann Thompson, *Shakespeare's Chaucer: A Study in Literary Origins* (Liverpool, 1978).

9.   Brewer, *Critical Heritage*, I, 166, 173.

10.   Ibid., I, 248.

11.   Ibid., I, 252.

12.   See Robert Worth Frank, Jr, *Chaucer and the Legend of Good Women* (Cambridge, MA, 1972), esp. pp. 8–10.

13.   Further information on the sources and analogues (or lack of them) for each tale is given in the Headnote to each tale, with bibliographical references. For general surveys, see *Sources and Analogues of Chaucer's Canterbury Tales*, ed. W. F. Bryan and Germaine Dempster (Chicago, 1941; repr. New York, 1958), and *Sources and Analogues of the Canterbury Tales*, ed. Robert M. Correale and Mary Hamel, 2 vols. (Cambridge, 2002–5).

14.   See note to GP 792–4.

15.   Charles S. Singleton, 'On Meaning in the *Decameron*', *Italica*, 21 (1944), 117–27 (pp. 118, 119).

16.   From the first, the tale-telling is represented as a 'game' or 'pley' that excludes 'ernest' and diffuses the aggressive potential of 'sooth [truth]' (see GP 853, Mil 3117, 3186, Co 4354–7, WB 192), but the maintenance of this game becomes increasingly precarious as the pilgrimage goes on (see especially Mcp 81, 100, and p. xliii above).

17.   For the Host's reactions, see Cl 1212a–d, Mch 2419–40, Mk 1891–1923. For discussion, see Alan T. Gaylord, '*Sentence* and *Solaas* in Fragment VII of the *Canterbury Tales*: Harry Bailly as Horseback Editor', *PMLA*, 82 (1967), 226–35.

18. George Lyman Kittredge, *Chaucer and his Poetry* (Cambridge, MA, 1915), p. 155.

19. For some discussions of these problems, see David Lawton, *Chaucer's Narrators* (London, 1986), esp. pp. 90, 97; A. C. Spearing, 'Narrative Voice: The Case of Chaucer's *Man of Law's Tale*', *New Literary History*, 32 (2001), 715–46; C. David Benson, 'The *Canterbury Tales*: Personal Drama or Experiments in Poetic Variety?', in *The Cambridge Companion to Chaucer*, ed. Piero Boitani and Jill Mann, 2nd edn (Cambridge, 2003), pp. 126–42.

20. See notes to ML 96, 1163–90, Sh 12.

21. I use the term 'antifeminist' in the sense traditional among medievalists – that is, to refer to the traditional body of medieval literature that is 'hostile to women' rather than 'hostile to feminism' (which would of course be anachronistic at this period). I prefer 'antifeminist' to the term 'misogynistic' as a designation for the literary tradition that overtly satirizes or attacks women, since misogyny may appear in other genres and take more subtle or covert forms.

22. The Hengwrt manuscript, for example, gives capital letters to some of the pilgrims listed in the General Prologue (Squyer, Prioresse, Monk, Marchant, and so on), but not to others (knyght, frere, haberdasshere, wyf, persoun, and so on). Capital letters are also given to perfectly ordinary words, such as Monthe, Pecock, Mous, Oystre. The scribe's aim seems to be to improve the look of the page, rather than to give the pilgrims' names a quasi-individual character. Early printed editions share this habit of alternating lower-case letters and capitals, and though a growing tendency towards regularization can be observed over the centuries, it is not until F. N. Robinson's first edition (*The Complete Works of Geoffrey Chaucer* (Oxford, 1933)) that capital letters are consistently given to the pilgrims and withheld from other persons designated by their occupation (e.g., the carpenter in the Miller's Tale).

    For a chronological list of the principal editions of the *Canterbury Tales*, see D. Pearsall, *The Canterbury Tales* (London, Boston, MA, and Sydney, 1985), pp. 325–6.

23. Some of these sayings have of course not passed into modern English, and I have also slightly modernized some in this list of examples for the sake of easier recognition. The proverbial phrases used by Chaucer (some of which he seems to have

brought into the written language for the first time) are recorded in the Notes.

24. For examples, see GP 182 (oyster); Kn 1558, Sum 1961, SN 511, CY 633, 698 (mite); WB 572 (leek); WB 708 (old shoe); GP 177, WB 1112 (hen); Mch 1263, 1854 (bean); Fkl 1132, Sh 171, CY 1150 (fly); Mel 930 (turd); Pars 601 (straw); Mcp 255 (gnat); Mk 2790 (butterfly); WB 949 (rake-handle). For other expressions of this sort, with examples from Chaucer and other Middle English texts, see B. J. Whiting, *Proverbs, Sentences, and Proverbial Phrases From English Writings Mainly Before 1500* (London and Cambridge, MA, 1968), Index, s.vv. Not count, Not give, Not the mountance, Not reck, Not set, Not worth.

25. The primary example is Palamon's escape from prison, which in Boccaccio is motivated by his discovery that Arcite is serving Emily in disguise; he then makes for the grove outside Athens because he knows he will find Arcite there. In Chaucer, these events are the result of chance. See also Kn 1663–9 and note. For discussion, see Jill Mann, 'Chance and Destiny in *Troilus and Criseyde* and the *Knight's Tale*', in *The Cambridge Companion to Chaucer*, pp. 93–111, at pp. 106–9.

26. Citations of the *Consolation* in this Introduction are given in parenthesis in the body of the text. The work is divided into five Books (signalled by Roman numerals) and each Book is subdivided into alternating sections of verse (metres) and prose; citation is by Book and metre (m.) or prose (pr.) For a modern English translation, see *Boethius: The Consolation of Philosophy*, tr. P. G. Walsh (Oxford, 1999).

27. For the relation of these aspects of the tale to the anti-Semitism with which it has often been charged, see Headnote to the Prioress's Tale.

28. Most fabliaux are in medieval French; they are comic verse narratives, usually concerning sexual deception and trickery, often at the expense of an old husband. The tales of the Miller, Merchant and Shipman are good examples of the typical fabliau-plot, although they are longer and more elaborate than most fabliaux.

29. For fuller discussion, see Jill Mann, 'Anger and "Glosynge" in the *Canterbury Tales*', *PBA*, 86 (1990), 203–23.

30. See note to Sum 2149.

31. See note to Sum 2253–77.

32. For the value of this sum, see the note to Sh 181.

33. See GP 813, 851, Cl 23–4, Fkl 703–5.

34. G. K. Chesterton, *Chaucer* (London, 1932; repr. 1962), pp. 21–2.
35. See Jill Mann, 'The Authority of the Audience in Chaucer', in *Poetics: Theory and Practice in Medieval English Literature*, ed. Piero Boitani and Anna Torti (Cambridge, 1991), pp. 1–12.

Further Reading

Useful Websites

The Chaucer MetaPage: http://www.unc.edu/depts/chaucer an umbrella site organizing access to Chaucer resources on the World Wide Web.

The Harvard Chaucer Page:
http://www.courses.fas.harvard.edu/~chaucer
accessed via the Chaucer MetaPage (via Chaucer Pages), it has a wealth of information about Chaucer, and provides guidance on his language and the pronunciation of Middle English (with accompanying sound recordings).

The Chaucer Bibliography Online: http://uchaucer.utsa.edu searchable bibliography of Chaucer studies, with useful summaries of each item.

Books and articles

The following is a highly selective list of some works of Chaucer criticism; a fuller list, together with helpful comments, can be found in Joerg Fichte, 'Further Reading: A Guide to Chaucer Studies', in *The Cambridge Companion to Chaucer*, ed. Boitani and Mann, pp. 290–306.

Andrew, Malcolm, ed., *Critical Essays on Chaucer's Canterbury Tales* (Toronto, 1991).
Benson, C. David, *Chaucer's Drama of Style: Poetic Variety and Contrast in the Canterbury Tales* (Chapel Hill, NC, and London, 1986).

Benson, C. David, and Elizabeth Robertson, eds., *Chaucer's Religious Tales* (Cambridge, 1990).

Boitani, Piero, and Jill Mann, eds., *The Cambridge Companion to Chaucer*, 2nd edn (Cambridge, 2003).

Brewer, Derek, ed., *Writers and Their Background: Geoffrey Chaucer* (London, 1974).

—, ed., *Chaucer: The Critical Heritage*, 2 vols. (London and New York, 1978).

—, *A New Introduction to Chaucer*, 2nd edn (London and New York, 1998).

—, *The World of Chaucer* (Woodbridge, 2000).

Brown, Peter, ed., *A Companion to Chaucer* (Oxford, 2000).

Burnley, J. D., *Chaucer's Language and the Philosophers' Tradition* (Cambridge, 1979).

—, *The Language of Chaucer* (London, 1989).

Cannon, Christopher, *The Making of Chaucer's English: A Study of Words* (Cambridge, 1998).

Cooper, Helen, *The Structure of the Canterbury Tales* (London, 1983).

—, *Oxford Guides to Chaucer: The Canterbury Tales* (Oxford and New York, 1989).

Crane, Susan, *Gender and Romance in Chaucer's Canterbury Tales* (Princeton, NJ, 1994).

Dinshaw, Carolyn, *Chaucer's Sexual Poetics* (Madison, WI, 1989).

Donaldson, E. Talbot, *Speaking of Chaucer* (London and New York, 1970).

Gaylord, A. T., 'Scanning the Prosodists: An Essay in Meta-criticism', *Chaucer Review*, 11 (1976), 22–82.

Kolve, V. A., *Chaucer and the Imagery of Narrative: The First Five Canterbury Tales* (London, 1984).

Lawton, David, *Chaucer's Narrators* (London, 1986).

Mann, Jill, *Chaucer and Medieval Estates Satire: The Literature of Social Classes and the General Prologue of the Canterbury Tales* (Cambridge, 1973).

—, *Feminizing Chaucer* (Cambridge, 2002).

Minnis, A. J., *Chaucer and Pagan Antiquity* (Cambridge, 1982).

Muscatine, Charles, *Chaucer and the French Tradition* (Berkeley and Los Angeles, CA, 1975).

Patterson, Lee, *Chaucer and the Subject of History* (Madison, WI, 1991).

Pearsall, Derek, *The Canterbury Tales* (London, Boston, MA, and Sydney, 1985).

—, *The Life of Geoffrey Chaucer: A Critical Biography* (Oxford, 1992).

Robertson, D. W., Jr, *A Preface to Chaucer: Studies in Medieval Perspectives* (Princeton, NJ, 1962).

Strohm, Paul, *Social Chaucer* (Cambridge, 1989).

Wallace, David, *Chaucerian Polity: Absolutist Lineages and Associational Forms in England and Italy* (Stanford, CA, 1997).

Chaucer's Language

These notes are an elementary guide to Chaucer's grammar. Further information may be found in the Glossary, which gives full details of irregular verb conjugations and includes comments on other features of grammar and syntax.

Nouns

The plural ending is normally *-es* (sometimes spelled *-is* or *-ez*), or *-s* when the word ends in *-e*. When the word ends in *-t*, the plural ending is spelled *-z*. A few nouns have a plural ending in *-(e)n*: *asshen, been, doghtren, eyen, hosen, oxen, shoon, sustren, toon* (but also *asshes, bees, doghtres, hoses, shoes, sustres, toos*). As in modern English, some nouns form their plurals by changing the main vowel: *men, wommen, feet, gees, teeth*. Some nouns are unchanged in the plural: *deer, hors, neet, sheep*; these include nouns following numerals in expressions indicating value, or extent of space or time (*twenty foot, five mile, ten pound, forty night, a thousand winter, twenty yeer*) and words of French origin ending in *-s* (*ca(a)s, pa(a)s*).

The genitive singular ending is also *-(e)s*. Some nouns are unchanged in the genitive: *lady grace, herte blood, fader kin, brother sone, Venus temple*.

Occasionally in prepositional phrases an *-e* may be added to a noun (with a change, in some cases, from an unvoiced to a voiced consonant or with doubling of the final consonant after a short vowel): *lif/on live, fir/on fire, bed/to bedde, lond/in londe*.

Adjectives

Monosyllabic adjectives ending in a consonant have a final -e
in the plural, and also in the singular in 'weak' positions, as
follows: after 'the'; after 'that' or 'this'; after a noun in the
genitive or a possessive pronoun (my, thy, his, your, etc.); in
vocative expressions (O *leeve brother*); before a proper name,
including God and Fortune.

The comparative form of the adjective ends in -er and the
superlative in -est (sometimes -re, -este).

Adverbs

Adverbial endings are -liche, -ly, or simply -e. Thus words such
as *hoote, loude* or *wide* may be adverbs as well as adjectives.

Personal Pronouns

SINGULAR	Nominative	Accusative/Dative	Genitive
1st person	I, ich, ik	me	my
2nd person	thou, thow	the(e)	thy
3rd person	he, she, it	him, hir(e), it	his, hir(e), his

PLURAL	Nominative	Accusative/Dative	Genitive
1st person	we	us	oure
2nd person	ye	yow	youre
3rd person	they	hem	hir(e)

The plural form of the second person pronoun is often used as
a polite form, as in modern French or German, even when only
one person is addressed. The singular form 'thou, thow' is often
combined with the verb (*wiltow* = thou wilt).

The genitive forms 'my, thy' have an ending in -n when they
precede a vowel or *h*: *min armes, min heed*.

Reflexive pronouns usually have the same forms (i.e. they do
not necessarily add -self): *he cladde him* = he dressed himself.

Relative and Interrogative Pronouns

The most frequent relative pronouns are *that* and *which (that)* (used for persons as well as things). *Who* is not found as a relative pronoun in the nominative case, though it is frequent as an interrogative pronoun (i.e. in questions). However, the accusative/dative and genitive forms *whom*, *whos* are found as relative pronouns.

The relative pronoun is often omitted, not only when it is the object of the relative clause (as in modern English 'the sorrow ^ I suffered'), but also when it is its subject: 'he hadde found a corn ^ lay in the yerde'.

Verbs

The infinitive form of the verb ends in *-en* or simply *-e*: *callen*, *calle*. (The form with final *-e* is the one used as headword for verbs in the Glossary.)

Present Tense

Present indicative endings are as follows:

> *SINGULAR*
> *1st person* (I)   calle
> *2nd person* (thou)   callest
> *3rd person* (he/she/it)   calleth
>
> *PLURAL*
> *1st/2nd/3rd person* (we/ye/they)   calle(n)

The present participle ends in *-ing(e)*: **calling(e)**.

In monosyllabic verbs with a stem ending in *-d*, *-t*, *-th* or *-s*, the third person ending *-eth* is often absorbed into the stem, forming an ending in *-t* or *-th*: e.g. *bit* for *biddeth*, *list* for *listeth*, *rist* for *riseth*, *rit* for *rideth*, *slit* for *slideth, worth* for *wortheth*.

Past Tense

The past tense is formed in two different ways: so-called 'weak' verbs add a past tense ending, while so-called 'strong' verbs change their main vowel.

	Weak	Strong
SINGULAR		
1st person (I)	called(e)	**sang, song**
2nd person (thou)	calledest	**songe**
3rd person (he/she/it)	called(e)	**sang, so(o)ng**
PLURAL		
1st/2nd/3rd person (we/ye/they)	call**ede(n)**	**songe(n)**
Past participle	**(y)called**	**(y)songe(n)**

The medial -*e*- may be elided (*ledde* = *ledede*), and *d* may be replaced by a *t* after unvoiced consonants (*f, k, p, s, t*), liquids (*l, r*), or nasals (*m, n*): *caste* (from *caste*), *gretto* (from *grete*), *sighte* (from *sike*), *slepte* (from *slepe*), *felte* (from *fele*), *mente* (from *mene*). The past participle of 'weak' verbs may also end in -*t*: *ybrent*, *yclept* (as well as *ybrend*, *ycleped*).

Perfect and Pluperfect Tense

The perfect and pluperfect tenses are formed by a combination of the past participle and the verbs 'to have' or 'to be'. So, *hath perced* = has pierced, *hath yronne* = has run. The pluperfect uses 'hadde' instead of 'hath'. Forms of the verb 'to be' are used instead of 'to have' when the main verb is intransitive (that is, incapable of taking an object): *been they went* = they have gone, *he was come* = he had come.

The present and past forms of the verbs 'to be' and 'to have' are as follows:

Present

SINGULAR

1st person (I)	am	have
2nd person (thou)	art	hast
3rd person (he/she/it)	is	hath

PLURAL

1st/2nd/3rd person (we/ye/they)	be(e)(n), beth, arn, are	han, have

Past

SINGULAR

1st person (I)	was	had(de)
2nd person (thou)	were	haddest
3rd person (he/she/it)	was	had(de)

PLURAL

1st/2nd/3rd person (we/ye/they)	were(n)	hadde(n)

Future Tense and Future-in-the-Past

These tenses are formed with the present and past tenses of the auxiliaries *shal* ('shall') and *wille* ('will'), whose forms follow:

Present

SINGULAR

1st person (I)	shal	wil, wol(e)
2nd person (thou)	shalt	wolt
3rd person (he/she/it)	shal	wil, wol(e)

PLURAL

1st/2nd/3rd person (we/ye/they)	shal, shul(n), shulle(n)	wil, wol(e)

Past

SINGULAR

1st person (I)	sholde	wolde
2nd person (thou)	sholdest	woldest
3rd person (he/she/it)	sholde	wolde

PLURAL

1st/2nd/3rd person (we/ye/they)	sholde(n)	wolde(n)

The use of 'shall' and 'will' is not governed by formal consider-
ations, as it is in modern English, where 'shall' is used for the
first person and 'will' for the second and third; instead, the
choice is most often determined by the original meanings of
these words, which imply obligation in the case of 'shall', and
desire in the case of 'will'. For further details, see the Glossary
entries for these words.

The Passive

The passive is formed by combining the past participle and
appropriate forms of the verb 'to be'.

Imperative

The imperative has both singular and plural forms; as in the
indicative, the plural is used as a polite form.

SINGULAR	calle	be
PLURAL	calleth	beth

Subjunctive and Subjunctive-Equivalents

The subjunctive mood is used in certain syntactical situations
(e.g., in wishes, in curses, in adverbial clauses of condition or
concession, in generalizing clauses beginning with such words
as 'wherever' or 'whenever', to indicate that something is being
considered as a hypothesis rather than as a fact. Only a few of
the Old English subjunctive endings survive into Middle English. In the present tense, the second and third person singular
have subjunctive endings in -e (calle) instead of -est and -eth.
In the present tense of the verb 'to be', all three persons of the
singular have a subjunctive form be (instead of am, art, is), and
in the past tense they have a subjunctive form were (instead of
was, were, was). In the present tense of the verb 'to have',
the second and third persons singular have a subjunctive form
have (instead of hast, hath). Examples are italicized in the

following lines: This cok ... | ... seide, 'Sire, if that I *were* as ye, | Yit sholde I seyn, as wis God *helpe* me, | "Turneth again, ye proude cherles alle! | A verray pestilence upon yow *falle*!"' (NP 3405–10).

In the second and third of these examples, modern English uses the auxiliary 'may' as a subjunctive-equivalent ('*may* God help', '*may* a pestilence fall'), and Middle English also uses auxiliary verbs in this way. The principal verbs used thus are *mowe* ('may'), *mote* ('must, may'), and the past forms of 'shall' and 'will', *sholde* and *wolde*. The use of *sholde* and *wolde* in this way should be distinguished from their use as auxiliaries of future-in-the-past: e.g., at Kn 2078: 'Wexinge it was and sholde wanie soone', 'It was waxing and would soon wane', corresponding to 'It is waxing and will soon wane', a straightforward future tense with no hypotheticality about it. In contrast, '*sholde* I seyn' expresses hypotheticality. As in modern English, the past tense is also used to indicate or reinforce the notion of hypotheticality: 'I dar wel seyn, if she *had been* a mous | And he a cat, he *wolde* hir *hente* [would have seized her] anon' (Mil 3346–7).

In addition to the regular subjunctive forms described above, isolated examples of past subjunctive forms of strong verbs survive in Chaucer; see, e.g., the entries in the Glossary for *breek*, *fille*, *songe*, *tooke*, *write*.

Negation

Negative sentences are formed by adding *ne* before the verb or *nat* after it, or both. Before verbs beginning with a vowel, *h* or *w*, '*ne*' may be combined with the verb (*nam = ne am*, *nadde = ne hadde*, *nolde = ne wolde*, *noot = ne woot*). Other negative adverbs, such as *nevere*, *nowher*, *nothing* (= not at all), *in no cas*, may be used with or without *ne*. In Middle English, multiple negatives do not cancel each other out but reinforce each other: 'Ne nevere yet no vileinye he saide | In al his lif unto no maner wight' (GP 70–71).

Impersonal constructions

Some verbs that have personal subjects in modern English ('I like', 'I think') are often used impersonally in Middle English, with the personal pronoun as indirect object, and often no expressed grammatical subject. So, *me thinketh/thoughte* = it seems/seemed to me, *me list* or *me liketh* = it pleases me.

Word Order

Both because Middle English is more flexible in this respect and because of the requirements of metre and rhyme, Chaucer's word order often diverges from the patterns conventional in modern English. So, 'he that Hermengild slow' (ML 627) does not mean, as it would in modern English, 'he whom Hermengild killed', but 'he who slew Hermengild'. It is not possible to illustrate every possible variation, but some characteristic patterns are these:

Object–Verb–Subject God loved he best
Object–Subject–Verb Frenssh she spak
Adverb–Verb–Subject soore wepte she
Subject–Past Participle–Auxiliary Verb whan she dronken hadde
Complement–Verb–Subject Ful fetis was hir cloke
Complement–Subject–Verb Curteis he was

Prepositions often follow the nouns they govern: *him aboute* = about him, *him bifore* = before him. They are often placed directly before or after a verb: 'That I *of* woot' (ML 1021) = that I know of, 'to shorte *with* oure weye' (GP 791) = to shorten our journey with/with which to shorten our journey.

A Note on the Text

Previous Editions

There are some 55 surviving manuscripts of the (more or less) complete *Canterbury Tales*, and a further 28 or so excerpted or fragmentary copies.[1] The eight-volume edition of the *Canterbury Tales* by John M. Manly and Edith Rickert published in 1940, which occupied a large portion of the working life of both scholars, is the only full-scale attempt to record all the readings of all these manuscripts, to try to establish their relation to an original common ancestor (which they dubbed O^1), and so to produce a fully critical text of the work. Unfortunately, the defects of Manly and Rickert's editorial assumptions and methods, which have been analysed with devastating thoroughness by George Kane,[2] deprive it of the authoritative status to which it might seem to be entitled. As Manly and Rickert themselves recognized, a vernacular text such as the *Canterbury Tales* is subject both to contamination between manuscripts (which may be the result of deliberate comparison between texts by scribes, or the unintentional and unconscious effects of scribal memory), and to coincident variation (the independent occurrence of the same scribal errors in manuscripts unrelated by descent). The operations of these two processes blur the lines of textual affiliation beyond recovery, and make it impossible to construct a satisfactory stemma (a 'family tree' representing the relations between the manuscripts) which could be used as a guide in determining the most probable readings of the author's original. In these circumstances, editors have returned to the practice of selecting a good manuscript as base text and emending it eclectically after comparison with selected others. The two most favoured candidates for such a base text are the manuscripts known as Hengwrt (Hg), now Aberystwyth, National Library of Wales, MS Peniarth 392, and Ellesmere (El), now San Marino, California, Huntington Library, MS EL 26 C 9, which are generally considered the earliest and best copies of the work.[3] Most student editions of the *Canterbury Tales* – and also more ambitious editions, such as the *Variorum Chaucer*[4] – are based on one of these two manuscripts, borrowing readings from other manuscripts only in the case of manifest errors of sense or gross lapses in metre. The *Riverside Chaucer*, like the second edition of F. N. Robinson,[5] of which it is a revised version, takes El as its base text, although it admits an even larger number of Hg readings than Robinson did, and also takes into account the readings of manuscripts which Manly and Rickert's analysis established as important either in their own right or as representative of larger groups.[6]

The Present Edition

The choice of either El or Hg as base text has the disadvantage of allowing the selected manuscript to take over the work of editorial decision in the multitude of smaller, humdrum instances of variant readings. For this reason, the present edition does not privilege either manuscript against the other (whether on the basis of a presumption of their position in a hypothetical stemma or on the basis of a presumption as to their relative accuracy in reproducing the original), but is squarely based on both. I have compared all their readings afresh, weighing each case of manuscript variance on its own merits, in the light of sense, metrical quality, knowledge of common types of scribal error and probable direction of scribal error (that is, which reading is more likely to have been the source, and which the result, of miscopying). George Kane's pioneering work on the habits of Middle English scribes has been of great help to me in the last two respects.[7] The collation of El and Hg has been accomplished with the aid of the *Facsimile and Transcription of the Hengwrt Manuscript*, edited by Paul G. Ruggiers (Norman,

OK, 1979), which prints all Ellesmere variants as marginal annotations to the transcription of the Hengwrt text, and the *Working Facsimile* of the Ellesmere manuscript (Cambridge, 1989). In order to identify and emend places where both El and Hg are likely to be wrong, I have also taken into account the wider manuscript tradition as it is represented in the *Riverside Chaucer*, and in Manly and Rickert's three-volume Corpus of Variants.[8] Restrictions of space have prohibited complete documentation of every emendation made as a result of this comparison, but textual matters of particular importance or interest are discussed in the Notes. If an emendation is supported by the readings in other manuscripts of the *Canterbury Tales*, this is indicated by an asterisk against the headword (lemma); full details of these readings may be found in the Corpus of Variants contained in vols. V–VIII of Manly and Rickert's edition.

On numerous occasions I have also emended the text on metrical grounds. For discussion of the kind of quasi-unconscious scribal variations in morphology, spelling and grammar that frequently impair the metre in El and Hg, see my article on 'Chaucer's Meter and the Myth of the Ellesmere Editor'.[9] The following is a sample list of commonly emended forms, illustrated by selected examples (my emended form of the text is followed after the square bracket by the El/Hg readings):

1. Presence or absence of final -*n* in verbal inflexions and in such words as bitwixe(n), ofte(n), sithe(n), withoute(n). E.g. GP 40: weren] were El; weere Hg. GP 326: pinche] pinchen El Hg.
2. Presence or absence of final -*e* in the past tense endings of weak verbs (touched/e). E.g. GP 756: lakkede] lakked El Hg.
3. Presence or absence of a *y*-prefix in the past participle. E.g. GP 396: ydrawe] drawe El Hg.
4. Presence or absence of 'ne' or 'nat'. E.g. GP 320: ne mighte] mighte El Hg.
5. Contraction or expansion of endings in *d/t/th* (depeinted/depeint). E.g. Kn 2049: depeint] depeinted El Hg.

6. Variation between syncopated and unsyncopated forms of the verb (preyed/preyd). E.g. Kn 2108: preyed] preyd El; prayd Hg.

7. Variation between 'muche' and 'muchel'. E.g. GP 132: muche] ful muchel El; muchel Hg.

8. Variation between 'made' and 'maked'. E.g. Fri 1642: maked] made El Hg.

9. Presence or absence of a final -e in certain nouns and adjectives (hoost/e, Seint/e,[10] Oxenford/e). E.g. GP 509: Seinte] Seint El Hg.

10. Presence or absence of medial -e- in such words as Bromeholm, chaunterye, chivetein, cloisterer, faierye, giltelees, lichewake, mottelee. E.g. GP 259: cloisterer] cloistrer El Hg.

11. Omission or addition of 'that' after conjunctions or relatives. E.g. Kn 1848: wher that] where El Hg.

12. Repetition or omission of prepositions or articles in parallel constructions ('for gold or [for] silver'). E.g. GP 558: A swerd and bokeler] a swerd and a bokeler El Hg.

13. Simple changes in word order. E.g. GP 516: to sinful men noght] nat to sinful men El; noght to sinful men Hg.

It should also be noted that the definite article 'the' or the negative 'ne' may be written out in full by the scribes even though the metre requires them to be elided with a following word beginning with a vowel or *h*; e.g. GP 110: th'usage] the usage El Hg. Similarly, verbs ending in -*eth*, such as bereth, cometh, falleth, maketh, speketh, taketh, thinketh (whether third person singular present indicative or imperative plural), are frequently pronounced as monosyllables (e.g., 'Maketh' at ML 898), and scribes will not necessarily indicate this by using a contracted form (berth, comth). Conversely, they may use a contracted form where a dissyllable is called for by the metre.

In emending the El/Hg text on metrical grounds, I have made no attempt to indicate manuscript support for the adopted readings, not only because Manly and Rickert's Corpus of Variants avowedly excludes this sort of detail, but also because these are among the features most subject to coincidental variation, and the readings of other manuscripts have in consequence no confirmatory value even if they happen to agree with the reading preferred. Even if the emendations I have made do not restore exactly what Chaucer wrote (given the possibility of alternative emendations that would fit the metrical requirements equally well), they produce what Peter Shillingsburg has called a 'less unsatisfactory text',[11] in that it at least respects Chaucer's ability to write good metre.

Versification

Emendations on metrical grounds are based on the assumption, confirmed by my own experience of reading Chaucer and working with the text, that Chaucer uses a five-stress (rather than ten-syllable) line.[12] The stress pattern is normally rising (that is, a weak stress is followed by a strong one). (The term 'iambic' is often used but is misleading, since it is borrowed from classical metre, which is constructed in a quite different way from English verse. The classical notion of metrical 'feet' is particularly inappropriate to English prosody.) Strong stress falls on syllables that would bear stress in normal speech, but verse also makes use of the fact that in a succession of syllables, the balance of strong and weak stress is determined by the relative strength of neighbouring syllables. So, in the following line of the Merchant's Tale: 'He háth it pút, and léid it át his hérte', the word 'at' stands in a stressed position, but in the subsequent line, 'The móone, thát at nóon was thílke dáy', it does not. Final -e is sometimes pronounced (as in the words 'moone' and 'thilke' in the line just quoted), and sometimes not, as the metre requires;[13] it is elided before a following vowel or h. Final -e is always pronounced in the following instances: (1) at the end of monosyllabic adjectives in a weak position (that is, following a definite article, demonstrative adjective, possessive adjective or noun in the vocative case), unless the following noun is stressed on the second syllable;[14] (2) in monosyllabic strong adjectives in the plural.[15] Variations in the general stress pattern which occur with some frequency are: the inversion of weak and strong stress at the opening of a line or after the mid-line break;

the absence of a weak stress at the opening of a line (a so-called
'headless' line); and the absence of a weak stress between two
strong stresses, especially at the mid-line break, where the per-
ception of a tiny pause between the two strong stresses takes
its place.

Spelling

Since neither El nor Hg is used as the base text of this edition,
I have followed the spelling of the Manly–Rickert edition, very
occasionally altering it to an El or Hg form for the sake of
greater accessibility (e.g., 'saugh' instead of 'say').[16] However,
with the aim of making the text more accessible to modern
readers, I have regularized use of *i/j*, *i/y* and *u/v* so that the
spelling of a word is always as close as possible to modern
practice.[17] In recording readings in El and Hg in the Notes,
differences between them involving capital letters and variable
word division in words such as 'upon' are ignored, and the
spelling of *i/j*, *i/y* and *u/v* follows the rules adopted for the
edited text.

Tale Order

Despite having been written by the same scribe, El and Hg
present very different pictures as far as the ordering of the
Canterbury Tales is concerned. In Hengwrt, the order of the
tales is confused and uncertain, and there are clear indications
(spaces left to be filled later) that the scribe did not have all the
material in front of him as he copied, but was receiving it –
from whatever source – piecemeal. This meant that he occasionally had to alter the names of tellers in the links, since he had
already copied the tales in the wrong order, leaving space for
the link to be inserted later. The Canon's Yeoman's Prologue
and Tale never reached him at all. Ellesmere, in contrast, confidently presents the tales in a smooth and plausible order. Whatever the problems with which the scribe was initially dealing, it
looks as if, by the time he copied Ellesmere, they had been
authoritatively cleared away. The present edition follows the

Ellesmere order, as being the nearest we can get to Chaucer's likely intentions.[18]

Line-numbering

Those early editors who accepted the validity of the 'Bradshaw shift' (see note to the Wife of Bath's Tale 847), carried the line-numbering of the tales straight through from the end of the Man of Law's Tale to the end of the Nun's Priest's Tale (that is, through the fragment that they labelled B^2). This numbering is used, for example, in the editions of Skeat and of Manly and Rickert (see Abbreviated References), in the Tatlock and Kennedy *Concordance*,[19] and in the *Chaucer Glossary* edited by Norman Davis et al.[20] The *Riverside Chaucer*, which leaves fragment B^2 in its Ellesmere position, starts the main line-numbering afresh with the Shipman's Tale, but gives the alternative numbering as well (indicated by an asterisk after the line-number). The present edition follows the Ellesmere order, and therefore likewise starts the numbering afresh with the Shipman's Tale; anyone who needs to convert these line-numbers to their counterparts in the 'Bradshaw shift' system should add 1190 to the number in question.

Headings and Verse Paragraphs

The headings that mark the beginning and ending of tales are taken from El, and printed in italics. Latin headings marking internal divisions in certain tales have been translated into English, and are likewise printed in italics. The small indentations marking minor narrative breaks are editorial.

NOTES

1. For a complete list, see Derek Pearsall, *The Canterbury Tales* (London, 1985), pp. 321–5.
2. George Kane, 'John M. Manly (1865–1940) and Edith Rickert (1871–1938)', in *Editing Chaucer: The Great Tradition*, ed. Paul

G. Ruggiers (Norman, OK, 1984), pp. 207–29. For a defence of the Manly and Rickert edition, and a moving account of the difficulties they faced, see Roy Vance Ramsey, *The Manly–Rickert Text of the Canterbury Tales* (Lewiston, NY, 1994).

3. Modern palaeographers agree that El and Hg were written by the same scribe; because of the scribe's problems with tale-order in Hg (see below), it is generally assumed that it was copied after Chaucer's death, and because these problems have been resolved in El, it is generally assumed that El was copied later than Hg, but both manuscripts date from the first decade of the fifteenth century.

4. This series aims to provide an analysis of the textual history of Chaucer's individual works, and to offer a comprehensive survey of all aspects of critical commentary on his work. For individual volumes cited in the Notes to this edition, see notes to GP 164, Sq 110, Pri 518 and NP 2771–90. For a full list of published volumes and an update on the project, see the Variorum website: http://www.ou.edu/variorum/

5. F. N. Robinson, ed., *The Works of Geoffrey Chaucer*, 2nd edn (Boston, 1957).

6. See the *Riverside Chaucer*, Textual Notes, pp. 1120–21.

7. For examples and discussion, see George Kane, ed., *Piers Plowman: The A Version* (London, 1960; rev. edn 1988), pp. 115–65; *The Legend of Good Women*, ed. Janet Cowen and George Kane (East Lansing, 1995), pp. 43–111.

8. Examples include (1) cases where El and Hg have inaccurate forms of proper names (e.g. 'Risus/Rusus' for 'Rufus' at GP 430; 'Pavik' for 'Panik' at Cl 590; 'Neptimus' for 'Neptunus' at Fkl 1047; 'Onedake' for 'Odenake' at Mk 2272); (2) lines present in other manuscripts but absent from El and Hg (see, e.g., the notes to Kn 2681–2; ML 1163–90; WB 44a–f; Mel 1335–6, 1777); (3) cases where deficiencies of sense, often in conjunction with deficiencies of metre, suggest scribal corruption in El and Hg (see, e.g., the notes to Kn 1252, 1376, 1906, 1945, 2202; ML 289; Mch 2229–33, 2240; Sh 214, 228; Pri 564, 676; Mk 2467; NP 2855, 3422, 3444–6).

9. *Studies in the Age of Chaucer*, 23 (2001), 71–107.

10. For an explanation of the use of 'Seinte' before masculine names, see E. Talbot Donaldson, *Studia Neophilologica*, 21 (1948–9), 222–30.

11. P. L. Shillingsburg, *Scholarly Editing in the Computer Age: Theory and Practice*, 3rd edn (Ann Arbor, MI, 1996), p. 63.

12. The most helpful account of Chaucer's metre is Morris Halle and Samuel Jay Keyser, 'Chaucer and the Study of Prosody', *College English*, 28 (1966), 187–219. A refinement of their theory proposed by Dudley L. Hascall, 'Some Contributions to the Halle-Keyser Theory of Prosody', *College English*, 30 (1968), 357–65, was accepted by Halle and Keyser in the section on iambic pentameter in their book *English Stress: Its Form, Its Growth, and Its Role in Verse* (New York, 1971); see p. 172, n. 15. Further modifications to the Halle and Keyser theory are discussed in Gilbert Youmans, 'Reconsidering Chaucer's Prosody', in *English Historical Metrics*, ed. C. B. McCully and J. J. Anderson (Cambridge, 1996), pp. 185–209. For a helpful survey of theories of English metre, which includes a measured assessment of the advantages and disadvantages of the Halle–Keyser theory (pp. 34–46), see Derek Attridge, *The Rhythms of English Poetry* (London, 1982).

13. For an analysis of the evidence, see Charles Barber and Nicholas Barber, 'The Versification of *The Canterbury Tales*: A Computer-Based Statistical Study', *Leeds Studies in English*, n.s. 21 (1990), 81–103, and n.s. 22 (1991), 57–83, and the introductory section on 'The Grammar of Chaucer's Final *E* in Relation to Editorial Problems of Metre', in the Cowen and Kane edition of Chaucer's *Legend of Good Women*, pp. 112–23.

14. Derek Pearsall, 'The Weak Declension of the Adjective and its Importance in Chaucerian Metre', in *Chaucer in Perspective: Middle English Essays in Honour of Norman Blake*, ed. Geoffrey Lester (Sheffield, 1999), pp. 178–93, at p. 182.

15. See J. D. Burnley, 'Inflexion in Chaucer's Adjectives', *Neuphilologische Mitteilungen*, 83 (1982), 169–77; Cowen and Kane, *Legend of Good Women*, pp. 115–16; and the article by Pearsall cited in the preceding note.

16. The spelling in the Manly-Rickert edition is a regularized version of that found in El and Hg. See Manly-Rickert I, x, 151. M. L. Samuels has argued that editors should base their spellings on the Hengwrt manuscript since its spellings are closest to Chaucer's own usage ('Chaucer's Spelling', *Middle English Studies Presented to Norman Davis*, ed. Douglas Gray and E. G. Stanley (Oxford, 1983), pp. 17–37; reprinted in *The English of Chaucer and his Contemporaries: Essays by M. L. Samuels and J. J. Smith*, ed. J. J. Smith (Aberdeen, 1988), pp. 23–37), but Larry Benson has (to my mind) convincingly dismantled Samuels's case ('Chaucer's Spelling Reconsidered', *English*

Manuscript Studies 1100–1700, 3 (1992), 1–28; reprinted in L. Benson, *Contradictions: From Beowulf to Chaucer*, ed. Theodore M. Andersson and Stephen A. Barney (Aldershot, 1995), pp. 70–99).

17. Thus, for example, martyr, tyraunt, crye, seye are spelled with a *y*, whereas veine, ride, wide, cride, seide are spelled with an *i*, and 'wis' and 'wisely', meaning 'wise', 'wisely', are spelled with a medial *-i-* to distinguish them from 'iwys', 'wysly', meaning 'indeed', 'surely'.

18. For further discussion and bibliography, see the note to WB 847.

19. *A Concordance to the Complete Works of Geoffrey Chaucer*, ed. John S. P. Tatlock and Arthur G. Kennedy (Washington, 1927; repr. Gloucester, MA, 1963). Though still useful, this concordance has now been replaced by *A Glossarial Concordance to the Riverside Chaucer*, ed. Larry D. Benson (New York, 1993).

20. *A Chaucer Glossary*, ed. Norman Davis, Douglas Gray, Patricia Ingham and Anne Wallace-Hadrill (Oxford, 1979).

Abbreviations of the *Canterbury Tales*

Cl The Clerk's Prologue and Tale
Co The Cook's Prologue and Tale
CY The Canon's Yeoman's Prologue and Tale
Fri The Friar's Prologue and Tale
Fkl The Squire–Franklin Link, The Franklin's Prologue and Tale
GP The General Prologue
Kn The Knight's Tale
Mch The Merchant's Prologue, Tale, and Epilogue
Mcp The Manciple's Prologue and Tale
Mel The Thopas–Melibee Link and The Tale of Melibee
Mil The Miller's Prologue and Tale
Mk The Monk's Prologue and Tale
ML The Man of Law's Prologue, Tale [and Epilogue]
NP The Nun's Priest's Prologue, Tale [and Epilogue]
Pard The Physician–Pardoner Link, The Pardoner's Prologue and Tale
Pars The Parson's Prologue and Tale
Phys The Physician's Tale
Pri The Shipman–Prioress Link, The Prioress's Prologue and Tale
Retr Chaucer's Retractions
Rv The Reeve's Prologue and Tale
Sh The Shipman's Tale
SN The Second Nun's Prologue and Tale
Sq The Squire's Prologue and Tale
Sum The Summoner's Prologue and Tale

Th The Prioress–Sir Thopas Link and Sir Thopas
WB The Wife of Bath's Prologue and Tale

Where necessary, Prologue or Tale is specified by adding Pr or T to the above abbreviations.

The
Canterbury
Tales

THE GENERAL PROLOGUE

Whan that Aprill with his shoures soote
The droghte of March hath perced to the roote,
And bathed every veine in swich licour
Of which vertu engendred is the flour,
Whan Zephirus eek with his sweete breeth   5
Inspired hath in every holt and heeth
The tendre croppes, and the yonge sonne
Hath in the Ram his halve cours yronne,
And smale foweles maken melodye,
That slepen al the night with open eye –   10
So priketh hem nature in hir corages –
Than longen folk to goon on pilgrimages,
And palmeres for to seken straunge strondes,
To ferne halwes, kouthe in sondry londes;
And specially from every shires ende   15
Of Engelond to Caunterbury they wende,
The holy blisful martyr for to seke
That hem hath holpen whan that they were seeke.
   Bifel that in that sesoun on a day,
In Southwerk at the Tabard as I lay,   20
Redy to wenden on my pilgrimage
To Caunterbury with ful devout corage,
At night was come into that hostelrye
Wel nine and twenty in a compaignye

1 **his shoures soote** its sweet showers   3 **veine** sap-vessel **licour** liquid, sap
4 **Of which vertu** by whose power   5 **Zephirus** the West Wind **eek** also
6 **Inspired** blown on, breathed life into **holt and heeth** wood and field
7 **croppes** buds, shoots **yonge sonne** new sun (n.)   8 Has completed its half
course in Aries (n.)   9 **foweles** birds   11 **corages** hearts, spirits
13 **palmeres** pilgrims (n.) **strondes** shores, countries
14 **ferne halwes** distant shrines **kouthe** renowned, famous
17 **blisful martyr** blessed martyr (St Thomas Becket) (n.)   18 **holpen** helped
seeke ill   21 **wenden** go   22 **corage** spirit

25 Of sondry folk, by aventure yfalle
In felaweshipe, and pilgrimes were they alle,
That toward Caunterbury wolden ride.
The chambres and the stables weren wide,
And wel we weren esed atte beste;
30 And shortly, whan the sonne was to reste,
So hadde I spoken with hem everychon
That I was of hir felaweshipe anon,
And made forward erly for to rise,
To take oure wey theras I yow devise.
35   But nathelees, whil I have time and space,
Er that I ferther in this tale pace,
Me thinketh it acordant to resoun
To telle yow al the condicioun
Of ech of hem, so as it semed me,
40 And whiche they weren and of what degree,
And eek in what array that they were inne;
And at a knight than wol I first biginne.
        A KNIGHT ther was, and that a worthy man,
That fro the time that he first bigan
45 To riden out, he loved chivalrye,
Trouthe and honour, fredom and curteisye.
Ful worthy was he in his lordes werre,
And therto hadde he riden, no man ferre,
As wel in Cristendom as hethenesse,
50 And evere honoured for his worthinesse.
At Alisaundre he was whan it was wonne;
Ful ofte time he hadde the bord bigonne

---

25 **by aventure** by chance   **yfalle** fallen   27 **wolden** intended to
29 **esed atte beste** accommodated to our heart's content
31 **everychon** every one   32 **anon** immediately   33 **made forward** made an
agreement   34 **theras** where   **devise** tell   35 **nathelees** nevertheless
36 **pace** proceed   37 It seems reasonable to me   40 **degree** rank
41 **array** clothing   44 **fro** from   46 **Trouthe** loyalty, fidelity
fredom magnanimity, generosity   **curteisye** courtly behaviour
47 **werre** war   48 **ferre** further   49 **hethenesse** heathen countries
51 **Alisaundre** Alexandria (n.)   52 **the bord bigonne** sat in the place of
honour at the head of the table (n.)

Aboven alle nacions in Pruce;
In Lettow hadde he reised and in Ruce,
No Cristen man so ofte of his degree.   55
In Gernade at the seege eek hadde he be
Of Algezir, and riden in Belmarye;
At Lyeys was he and at Satalye
Whan they were wonne, and in the Grete See
At many a noble armee hadde he be.   60
At mortal batailles hadde he been fiftene,
And foghten for oure feith at Tramissene
In listes thries, and ay slain his foo.
This ilke worthy knight hadde been also
Somtime with the lord of Palatye   65
Again another hethen in Turkye,
And everemoore he hadde a soverein pris.
And though that he were worthy he was wis,
And of his port as meke as is a maide,
Ne nevere yet no vileinye he saide   70
In al his lif unto no maner wight.
He was a verray parfit gentil knight.
But for to tellen yow of his array,
Hise hors were goode but he was nat gay.
Of fustian he wered a gipoun,   75
Al bismotered with his habergeoun,
For he was late ycome from his viage,
And wente for to doon his pilgrimage.
   With him ther was his sone, a yong SQUIER,
A lovere and a lusty bacheler,   80

54 **reised** campaigned (n.)   56 **be** been   59 **the Grete See** the
Mediterranean   60 **armee** military expedition   62 **foghten** fought
63 **listes** jousts (n.)   **ay** always   66 **Again** against   67 **everemoore** at all
times   **soverein pris** outstanding reputation
68 **though that he were worthy** though he was doughty   69 **port** bearing,
manner   70 **vileinye** discourtesy   71 **no maner wight** any kind of person
72 **gentil** noble   75 **fustian** fustian, a kind of cloth (not necessarily coarse or
poor)   **gipoun** padded tunic worn under a coat of chain-mail (n.)
76 **bismotered** stained   **habergeoun** mail-coat (n.)   77 **was late ycome** had
recently come   79 **SQUIER** squire (n.)   80 **lusty** lively   **bacheler** young
man in knightly service

With lokkes crulle as they were leid in presse;
Of twenty yeer of age he was, I gesse.
Of his stature he was of evene lengthe,
And wonderly delivere and of greet strengthe;
85   And he hadde been somtime in chivachye
In Flaundres, in Artois and Picardye,
And born him wel, as of so litel space,
In hope to stonden in his lady grace.
Embrouded was he, as it were a meede,
90   Al ful of fresshe floures white and reede.
Singinge he was, or floitinge, al the day;
He was as fressh as is the monthe of May.
Short was his gowne, with sleves longe and wide;
Wel koude he sitte on hors and faire ride.
95   He koude songes make and wel endite,
Juste and eek daunce, and wel purtreye and write.
So hoote he lovede, that by nightertale
He slepte namoore than dooth a nightingale.
Curteis he was, lowely and servisable,
100   And carf biforn his fader at the table.
        A YEMAN hadde he (and servantz namo
At that time, for him liste ride so),
And he was clad in coote and hood of grene.
A sheef of pecok arwes, bright and kene,
105   Under his belt he bar ful thriftily –
Wel koude he dresse his takel yemanly;
His arwes drouped noght with fetheres lowe –
And in his hand he bar a mighty bowe.

81 **crulle** curly **as they were leid in presse** as if they had been put in a
curling-press 83 **stature** height **of evene lengthe** of moderate height
84 **wonderly** wonderfully **delivere** agile, athletic 85 **chivachye** cavalry
expedition 87 **as of so litel space** in so brief a period of time
88 **his lady grace** his lady's favour 89 **Embrouded** embroidered
meede meadow 91 **floitinge** playing the flute 95 **endite** write, compose
96 **Juste** joust **purtreye** draw 97 **by nightertale** at night 100 **carf** carved
101 **YEMAN** yeoman (n.) 102 **him liste** (= *listede*) it pleased him
103 **coote** tunic 104 **sheef** sheaf **pecok arwes** peacock arrows **kene** sharp
105 **thriftily** properly 106 **dresse** prepare **takel** equipment **yemanly** as a
yeoman does 107 **lowe** trailing 108 **bar** bore

A not-heed hadde he, with a broun visage;
Of wodecraft wel koude he al th'usage.   110
Upon his arm he bar a gay bracer,
And by his side a swerd and a bokeler,
And on that oother side a gay daggere,
Harneised wel and sharp as point of spere;
A Cristofre on his brest of silver shene.   115
An horn he bar, the bawdrik was of grene.
A forster was he soothly, as I gesse.

   Ther was also a nonne, a PRIORESSE,
That of hir smiling was ful simple and coy;
Hir gretteste ooth was but 'by Seinte Loy',   120
And she was cleped Madame Eglentine.
Ful wel she soong the service divine,
Entuned in hir nose ful semely,
And Frenssh she spak ful faire and fetisly,
After the scole of Stratford-atte-Bowe,   125
For Frenssh of Paris was to hire unknowe.
At mete wel ytaught was she withalle;
She leet no morsel from hir lippes falle,
Ne wette hir fingres in hir sauce depe.
Wel koude she carye a morsel and wel kepe   130
That no drope ne fille upon hir brest;
In curteisye was set ful muche hir lest.
Hir over-lippe wiped she so clene
That in hir coppe ther was no ferthing sene
Of grece, whan she dronken hadde hir draughte;   135
Ful semely after hir mete she raughte.

---

109 **not-heed** close-cropped head   110 **koude** knew   111 **bracer** arm guard
used by archers   112 **bokeler** small shield   114 **Harneised** ornamented
115 **Cristofre** an image of St Christopher **shene** bright
116 **bawdrik** baldric, sash worn over the shoulder for carrying a horn
117 **forster** forester (n.)   119 **simple and coy** ingenuous and demure
120 **but** only   121 **cleped** called   123 **Entuned** intoned
124 **fetisly** elegantly   125 **After** according to   126 **unknowe** unknown
127 **At mete** at meals **withalle** besides   129 **wette** (= *wetede*) wetted, wet
130 **kepe** take care   131 **fille** fell   132 **lest** pleasure, enjoyment
133 **over-lippe** upper lip   134 **ferthing** particle   135 **grece** grease
136 **after hir mete she raughte** she reached for her food

And sikerly she was of greet desport,
And ful plesaunt and amiable of port,
And peined hire to countrefete cheere
140 Of court, and been estatlich of manere,
And to been holden digne of reverence.
But for to speken of hir conscience,
She was so charitable, and so pitous,
She wolde wepe if that she sawe a mous
145 Caught in a trappe, if it were deed or bledde.
Of smale houndes hadde she, that she fedde
With rosted flessh, or milk and wastel breed;
But soore wepte she if oon of hem were deed,
Or if men smoot it with a yerde smerte,
150 And al was conscience and tendre herte.
Ful semely hir wimpel pinched was;
Hir nose tretis, hir eyen greye as glas,
Hir mouth ful smal, and therto softe and reed.
But sikerly she hadde a fair forheed –
155 It was almoost a spanne brood, I trowe,
For hardily she was nat undergrowe.
Ful fetis was hir cloke, as I was war;
Of smal coral aboute hir arm she bar
A peire of bedes, gauded al with grene,
160 And theron heng a brooch of gold ful shene,
On which ther was first write a crowned A,
And after, '*Amor vincit omnia*'.

137 **desport** pleasant behaviour, fun   138 **port** manner   139–40 And tried
to imitate courtly behaviour, and to be dignified in manner
141 **holden digne of reverence** considered worthy of respect
147 **rosted flessh** roast meat **wastel breed** fine white bread
148 **soore** bitterly   149 **yerde** switch **smerte** severely
150 **conscience** feeling   151 **wimpel** wimple, headcloth covering the chin
and sides of face **pinched** pleated   152 **tretis** well-shaped, long
154 **sikerly** assuredly   155 **spanne** hand's breadth
156 **undergrowe** undergrown, short   157 **fetis** elegant   158 **smal** fine
159 A set of beads (i.e. a rosary), adorned with large green ornamental
beads (n.)   161 **crowned** surmounted by the figure of a crown
162 *Amor vincit omnia* Love conquers all (n.)

Another NONNE with hire hadde she,
That was hir chapeleine, and preestes thre.
A MONK ther was, a fair for the maistrye,   165
An outridere, that lovede venerye,
A manly man, to been an abbot able.
Ful many a deintee hors hadde he in stable,
And whanne he rood, men mighte his bridel
          heere
Ginglen in a whistlinge wind as cleere   170
And eek as loude as dooth the chapel belle.
Theras this lord was kepere of the celle,
The reule of Seint Maure or of Seint Beneit,
Bicause that it was old and somdel streit,
This ilke monk leet olde thinges pace,   175
And heeld after the newe world the space.
He yaf nat of that text a pulled hen
That seyth that hunters been nat holy men,
Ne that a monk, whan he is recchelees,
Is likned til a fissh that is waterlees –   180
This is to seyn, a monk out of his cloistre –
But thilke text heeld he nat worth an oystre.
And I seide his opinioun was good:
What sholde he studye, and make himselven
          wood,
Upon a book in cloistre alwey to poure,   185
Or swinken with his handes and laboure,
As Austin bit? How shal the world be served?
Lat Austin have his swink to him reserved!

164 **chapeleine** chaplain (n.)   165 **for the maistrye** in the highest degree
166 **outridere** agent of a monastery who rides out to administer its
affairs (n.) **venerye** hunting   168 **deintee** excellent   170 **Ginglen** jingle
cleere clearly   172 **Theras** where **kepere of the celle** monk in charge of a
monastic cell which is dependent on a larger monastery   173 The Rule of
St Maurus or of St Benedict (n.)   174 **somdel streit** rather strict
175 **leet . . . pace** allowed to go by   176 And followed the custom of the
modern world   177 **pulled** plucked   179 **recchelees** negligent   180 **til** to
waterlees without water   182 **thilke** that   184 **What** why **wood** mad
185 **Upon a book . . . to poure** to pore over a book   186 **swinken** labour
187 **Austin** Augustine (n.) **bit** (= *biddeth*) bids

Therfore he was a prikasour aright.
190 Grehoundes he hadde, as swift as fowel in flight;
Of priking and of hunting for the hare
Was al his lust; for no cost wolde he spare.
I seigh his sleves purfiled at the hond
With gris, and that the fineste of a lond;
195 And for to festne his hood under his chin
He hadde of gold ywroght a curious pin;
A love-knotte in the gretter ende ther was.
His heed was balled, that shoon as any glas,
And eek his face, as he hadde been enoint;
200 He was a lord ful fat and in good point.
Hise eyen stepe, and rollinge in his heed,
That stemed as a forneis of a leed;
His bootes souple, his hors in greet estat.
Now certeinly he was a fair prelat;
205 He was nat pale as a forpined goost.
A fat swan loved he best of any roost;
His palfrey was as broun as is a berye.
    A FRERE ther was, a wantowne and a merye,
A limitour, a ful solempne man.
210 In alle the ordres foure is noon that kan
So muche of daliaunce and fair langage.
He hadde maad ful many a mariage
Of yonge wommen, at his owene cost.
Unto his ordre he was a noble post.

189 **prikasour** huntsman   190 **Grehoundes** greyhounds
191 **priking** tracking   192 **lust** pleasure   193 **seigh** saw **purfiled** trimmed
at the edge   194 **gris** grey fur **fineste of a lond** finest in the country
195 **festne** fasten   196 **curious** elaborate   197 **love-knotte** knot-shaped
ornament **gretter** larger   199 **as** as if   200 **in good point** in good
condition   201 **stepe** prominent   202 **stemed** glowed
forneis of a leed furnace under a cauldron   203 **souple** supple
in greet estat in excellent condition   204 **prelat** church dignitary
205 **forpined goost** tormented soul (of dead person)   206 **roost** roast
207 **palfrey** saddle-horse   208 **FRERE** friar **wantowne** jovial (with pun on
'wanton')   209 **limitour** friar who begs within territorial limits (n.)
solempne cheerful/dignified (punning)   210 **ordres foure** four orders of
friars (n.) **kan** knows   211 **daliaunce** conversation

Ful wel biloved and famulier was he   215
With frankeleins overal in his contree,
And eek with worthy wommen of the toun;
For he hadde power of confessioun –
As seide himself – moore than a curat,
For of his ordre he was licenciat.   220
Ful swetely herde he confessioun,
And plesaunt was his absolucioun.
He was an esy man to yeve penaunce
Theras he wiste to have a good pitaunce.
For unto a povre ordre for to yive   225
Is signe that a man is wel yshrive;
For if he yaf, he dorste make avaunt
He wiste that a man was repentaunt.
For many a man so hard is of his herte,
He may nat wepe, althogh him soore smerte.   230
Therfore, in stede of wepinge and preyeres,
Men moote yeve silver to the povre freres.
His tipet was ay farsed ful of knives
And pinnes, for to yeven faire wives.
And certeinly he hadde a murye note;   235
Wel koude he singe and pleyen on a rote;
Of yeddinges he bar outrely the pris.
His nekke whit was as the flour-de-lis;
Therto he strong was as a champioun.
He knew the tavernes wel in al the toun,   240
And every hostiler and tappestere,
Bet than a lazar or a beggestere.

216 **frankeleins** franklins, landowners **overal** everywhere   219 **curat** parish
priest   220 **was licenciat** had an official licence from the bishop to preach or
hear confession   224 **Theras he wiste to have** where he knew he would
have **pitaunce** donation, alms (n.)   225 **povre** poor   226 **yshrive** confessed
227 **make avaunt** boast   230 **him soore smerte** he may suffer greatly
232 **moote** may   233 **tipet** hanging part of a sleeve **farsed** stuffed
234 **yeven** give   235 **murye** sweet-sounding   236 **rote** zither (n.)
237 **yeddinges** songs **bar outrely the pris** surpassed everyone
238 **flour-de-lis** fleur-de-lis, lily   241 **tappestere** barmaid   242 **Bet** better
lazar leper **beggestere** beggar

For unto swich a worthy man as he
Acorded nat, as by his facultee,
245   To have with sike lazars aqueintaunce.
It is nat honeste – it may nat avaunce –
For to deelen with no swich poraille,
But al with riche and selleres of vitaille.
And overal, theras profit sholde arise,
250   Curteis he was and lowely of servise;
Ther was no man nowher so vertuous.
He was the beste beggere in his hous
252a   – And yaf a certein ferme for the graunt;
252b   Noon of his bretheren cam ther in his haunt –
For thogh a widwe hadde noght a sho,
So plesant was his 'In principio',
255   Yet wolde he have a ferthing er he wente.
His purchas was wel bettre than his rente,
And rage he koude, as it were right a whelpe.
In love-dayes ther koude he muchel helpe,
For ther he was nat lik a cloisterer,
260   With a thredbare cope, as is a povre scoler,
But he was lik a maister or a pope;
Of double worstede was his semicope,
That rounded as a belle out of the presse.
Somwhat he lipsed for his wantownesse,
265   To make his Englissh sweete upon his tonge;
And in his harping, whan that he hadde songe,
Hise eyen twinkled in his heed aright
As doon the sterres in the frosty night.

---

244 **Acorded nat** it was not fitting **facultee** profession   247 **deelen** have
dealings **poraille** poor people   248 **vitaille** food   249 **overal** everywhere
251 **vertuous** virtuous   252a **ferme** payment, rent   252b **haunt** territory
253 **sho** shoe   256 His 'perks' were worth more than his regular
income (n.)   257 **rage** play, frolic **whelpe** puppy   258 **love-dayes** meetings
to settle disputes out of court (n.)   261 **maister** MA (n.)
262 **double worstede** heavy worsted cloth **semicope** short cloak
263 **rounded** swelled out **presse** cupboard, closet   264 **lipsed** lisped
wantownesse affectation, conscious charm   268 **sterres** stars

This worthy limitour was cleped Huberd.
    A MARCHANT was ther, with a forked 270
    berd,
In mottelee, and hye on hors he sat.
Upon his heed a Flaundrissh bevere hat,
His bootes clasped faire and fetisly.
Hise resons spak he ful solempnely,
Sowninge alwey th'encrees of his winning. 275
He wolde the see were kept, for any thing,
Bitwixen Middelburgh and Orewelle.
Wel koude he in eschaunge sheeldes selle.
This worthy man ful wel his wit bisette;
Ther wiste no wight that he was in dette, 280
So estatly was he of his governaunce,
With his bargaines and with his chevisaunce.
For sothe, he was a worthy man withalle,
But sooth to seyn, I noot how men him calle.
    A CLERK ther was of Oxenford also, 285
That unto logik hadde longe ygo.
As leene was his hors as is a rake,
And he was nat right fat, I undertake,
But looked holwe and therto sobrely.
Ful thredbare was his overeste courtepy; 290
For he hadde gete him yet no benefice,
Ne was so worldly for to have office.
For him was levere have at his beddes heed
Twenty bookes, clad in blak or reed,

---

269 **cleped** called   271 **mottelee** cloth of mixed colour (n.)   272 **bevere** of
beaver fur   273 **fetisly** neatly   274 **resons** remarks, statements
275 Constantly harping on the growth of his profits   276 **were kept** should
be protected (n.) **for any thing** at all costs   278 **eschaunge** money-changing
sheeldes *écus* (n.)   279 **his wit bisette** used his head
281 **governaunce** demeanour   282 **chevisaunce** borrowing or lending money
at interest, wheeler-dealing   284 **noot** (= *ne woot*) do not know
285 **CLERK** university student   286 Who had long devoted himself to
logic (n.)   287 **leene** lean   289 **therto** as well   290 **overeste** uppermost
courtepy short woollen jacket   291 **gete** got **benefice** ecclesiastical
living (n.)   292 **office** secular employment (n.)   293 **him was levere have** he
preferred to have

295 Of Aristotle and his philosophye,
   Than robes riche, or fithele, or gay sautrye.
   But al be that he was a philosophre,
   Yet hadde he but litel gold in cofre!
   But al that he mighte of his frendes hente,
300 On bookes and on lerninge he it spente,
   And bisily gan for the soules preye
   Of hem that yaf him wherwith to scoleye.
   Of studye took he moost cure and moost heede.
   Noght oo word spak he moore than was neede,
305 And that was seid in forme and reverence,
   And short, and quik, and ful of heigh sentence.
   Sowninge in moral vertu was his speche,
   And gladly wolde he lerne and gladly teche.
    A SERGEANT OF THE LAWE, war and wis,
310 That often hadde been at the Parvis,
   Ther was also, ful riche of excellence.
   Discreet he was and of greet reverence –
   He semed swich, hise wordes weren so wise.
   Justice he was ful often in assise,
315 By patente and by plein commissioun.
   For his science, and for his heigh renoun,
   Of fees and robes hadde he many oon.
   So greet a purchasour was nowher noon;
   Al was fee simple to him in effect.
320 His purchasing ne mighte nat been infect.

296 **fithele** fiddle **sautrye** psaltery (n.) 298 **cofre** coffer, chest
299 **of . . . hente** acquire from 301 **gan . . . preye** prayed
302 **scoleye** study 303 **moost cure** greatest concern 304 **oo** one
305 **in forme** properly, with decorum 306 **quik** pithy **heigh sentence** great
wisdom 307 **Sowninge in** consonant with
309 **SERGEANT OF THE LAWE** serjeant at law, member of a superior
order of barristers (n.) 310 **Parvis** porch? of St Paul's Cathedral in
London (n.) 314 **assise** assize court (n.) 315 **patente** letters patent (n.)
plein commissioun full authority (invested in an officer) (n.)
316 **For** because of 318 **purchasour** conveyancer, buyer of land
319 **fee simple** unrestricted ownership (n.) **in effect** in fact, actually
320 **purchasing** conveyancing **infect** invalidated, brought into question

Nowher so bisy a man as he ther nas,
And yet he semed bisier than he was.
In termes hadde he caas and doomes alle
That from the time of King William were falle.
Therto he koude endite and make a thing,   325
Ther koude no wight pinche at his writing;
And every statut koude he plein by roote.
He rood but hoomly in a medlee coote,
Girt with a ceint of silk, with barres smale;
Of his array telle I no lenger tale.   330

    A FRANKELEIN was in his compaignye;
Whit was his berd as is the daiesye.
Of his complexioun he was sangwin;
Wel loved he by the morwe a sop in win.
To liven in delit was evere his wone,   335
For he was Epicurus owene sone,
That heeld opinioun that plein delit
Was verray felicitee parfit.
An housholdere, and that a greet, was he;
Seint Julian he was in his contree.   340
His breed, his ale, was alweys after oon;
A bettre envined man was nowher noon.
Withoute bake-mete was nevere his hous,
Of fissh and flessh, and that so plentevous

323 **In termes** in the correct jargon **caas and doomes** legal cases and
judgments   324 **King William** William the Conqueror (n.)
325 **endite** draft, draw up **thing** legal document   326 **pinche at** find fault
with   327 **plein** completely **by roote** by heart   328 **hoomly** simply, plainly
medlee coote a striped robe (n.)   329 **ceint** belt **barres smale** thin bars of
metal   330 **telle . . . tale** give an account
331 **FRANKELEIN** franklin (n.)   332 **daiesye** daisy   333 His
temperament was sanguine (n.)   334 **by the morwe** in the morning
sop in win piece of bread dipped in wine (n.)   335 **wone** custom
336 **Epicurus owene sone** own son to Epicurus (n.)
337 **plein delit** unalloyed pleasure   340 **Seint Julian** patron saint of
hospitality   341 **after oon** of the same standard   342 **envined** stocked with
wine   343 **bake-mete** pie, pastry dish   344 **plentevous** plentiful

345   It snewed in his hous of mete and drinke,
       Of alle deintees that men koude thinke.
       After the sondry sesons of the yeer,
       So chaunged he his mete and his soper.
       Ful many a fat partrich hadde he in muwe,
350   And many a breem and many a luce in stuwe.
       Wo was his cook but if his sauce were
       Poinaunt and sharp, and redy al his geere!
       His table dormaunt in his halle alway
       Stood redy covered al the longe day.
355   At sessions ther was he lord and sire;
       Ful ofte time he was knight of the shire.
       An anlaas and a gipser al of silk
       Heeng at his girdel, whit as morne milk.
       A shirreve hadde he been, and a countour;
360   Was nowher swich a worthy vavasour.
           An HABERDASSHERE and a CARPENTER,
       A WEBBE, a DYERE, and a TAPICER,
       And they were clothed alle in oo liveree
       Of a solempne and a greet fraternitee.
365   Ful fressh and newe hir geere apiked was;
       Hir knives were chaped noght with bras,
       But al with silver, wroght ful clene and wel,
       Hir girdles and hir pouches everydel.

345 **snewed** snowed   347 **After** according to   348 **mete** dinner
soper supper   349 **partrich** partridge **muwe** coop (for fattening poultry)
350 **breem** bream **luce** pike **stuwe** fish-pond   351–2 It was the worse for
his cook if his sauce was not pungent and tasty **geere** utensils
353 **table dormaunt** permanent, fixed-frame table (n.)   355 He presided
over court sessions (n.)   356 **knight of the shire** Member of Parliament (n.)
357 **anlaas** two-edged dagger **gipser** ornamental purse   358 **Heeng** hung
359 **shirreve** sheriff **countour** lawyer, pleader in court (n.)
360 **vavasour** gentleman, landowner (n.)   362 **WEBBE** weaver
TAPICER tapestry-maker   363 **liveree** uniform costume worn by members
of a guild (n.)   364 **solempne** important **fraternitee** fraternity, guild
365 **geere** clothes **apiked** adorned   366 **chaped** mounted, trimmed
367 **clene** handsomely   368 **everydel** in every respect

Wel semed ech of hem a fair burgeis
To sitten in a yeldehalle on a deis. 370
Everich, for the wisdom that he kan,
Was shaply for to been an alderman,
For catel hadde they inogh and rente,
And eek hir wives wolde it wel assente.
And elles, certein, were they to blame; 375
It is ful fair to been ycleped 'madame',
And goon to vigilies al bifore,
And have a mantel royalliche ybore.
　A COOK they hadde with hem for the
　　nones,
To boille the chiknes with the marybones, 380
And poudre-marchaunt tart and galingale.
Wel koude he knowe a draughte of Londoun ale;
He koude rooste and sethe and broille and frye,
Maken mortreux and wel bake a pie.
But greet harm was it, as it thoughte me, 385
That on his shine a mormal hadde he.
For blankmanger, that made he with the beste.
　A SHIPMAN was ther, woning fer by weste –
For aught I woot he was of Dertemouthe.
He rood upon a rouncy, as he kouthe, 390
In a gowne of falding to the knee.
A daggere hanginge on a laas hadde he,

369 **burgeis** citizen   370 **yeldehalle** guildhall **deis** dais   371 **kan** knows
372 **shaply** fit   373 **catel** property **rente** income
375 **elles ... were they** otherwise they would be   377 **vigilies** vigil in church
the night before an important religious occasion (n.)
378 **royalliche ybore** carried like royalty   379 **for the nones** for the
occasion   380 **chiknes** chickens **marybones** marrow-bones
381 **poudre-marchaunt tart** tart flavouring powder **galingale** galingale (a
spice)   383 **sethe** boil **broille** grill   384 **mortreux** thick soup, casserole
dish   386 **mormal** inflamed sore   387 **blankmanger** dish of chopped
chicken or fish boiled with rice, fricassee **with the beste** superbly
388 **woning fer by weste** living far in the west   389 **For aught I woot** for all
I know **Dertemouthe** Dartmouth   390 **rouncy** hackney (a kind of horse)
as he kouthe as best he could (n.)   391 **falding** coarse woollen cloth (g.)
392 **laas** cord

Aboute his nekke, under his arm adoun;
The hoote somer had maad his hewe al broun.

395 And certeinly he was a good felawe;
Ful many a draughte of win hadde he ydrawe
Fro Burdeuxward whil that the chapman sleep.
Of nice conscience took he no keep:
If that he faught and had the hyer hond,

400 By water he sente hem hoom to every lond.
But of his craft to rekene wel his tides,
His stremes, and his daungers him bisides,
His herberwe and his moone, his lodemenage,
Ther nas noon swich from Hulle to Cartage.

405 Hardy he was, and wis to undertake;
With many a tempest hadde his berd been shake.
He knew alle the havenes as they were
Fro Gootland to the cape of Finistere,
And every crike in Britaigne and in Spaine.

410 His barge ycleped was the Mawdelaine.
        With us ther was a DOCTOUR OF PHYSIK.
In al this world ne was ther noon him lik
To speke of physik and of surgerye,
For he was grounded in astronomye.

415 He kepte his pacient a ful greet deel
In houres by his magik natureel.
Wel koude he fortunen the ascendent
Of hise images for his pacient.

---

394 **hewe** complexion   397 **Fro Burdeuxward** from the direction of
Bordeaux (n.)   **chapman** merchant   **sleep** slept   398 **nice** scrupulous
took he no keep he did not bother about   400 i.e. he drowned his prisoners
401 **craft to rekene** skill in calculating   402 **him bisides** near to him
403 **herberwe** harbours   **moone** position of the moon
lodemenage navigational skills   408 From Gotland to Cape Finisterre (n.)
409 **crike** creek, inlet   **Britaigne** Brittany   411 **PHYSIK** medicine
414 **grounded** learned   415 **kepte** watched over   **a ful greet deel** to a great
extent   416 **houres** hours of astrological significance (n.)
magik natureel 'white magic' (g.)   417 **fortunen the ascendent** choose a
favourable ascendant (n.)   418 **images** metal talismans (n.)

He knew the cause of every maladye,
Were it of hoot or coold or moiste or drye,   420
And where engendred and of what humour;
He was a verray parfit practisour.
The cause yknowe, and of his harm the roote,
Anon he yaf the sike man his boote.
Ful redy hadde he hise apothecaries,   425
To sende him drogges, and his letuaries,
For ech of hem made oother for to winne –
Hir frendshipe nas nat newe to biginne.
Wel knew he the olde Esculapius,
And Deiscorides, and eek Rufus,   430
Old Ipocras, Haly, and Galien,
Serapion, Razis, and Avicen,
Averrois, Damascien, and Constantin,
Bernard, and Gatesden, and Gilbertin.
Of his diete mesurable was he,   435
For it was of no superfluitee,
But of greet norissinge and digestible.
His studye was but litel on the Bible.
In sangwin and in pers he clad was al,
Lined with taffata and with sendal.   440
And yet he was but esy of dispence;
He kepte that he wan in pestilence.
For gold in physik is a cordial;
Therfore he loved gold in special.

   A good WIF was ther of biside BATHE,   445
But she was somdel deef, and that was scathe.

---

420 see n. to GP 333   421 **humour** bodily fluid (n.)
422 **practisour** practitioner   424 **boote** remedy   426 **drogges** drugs,
medicines **letuaries** potions   427 **to winne** to profit
428 **newe to biginne** to be created for the first time   429–34 On these
medical authorities, see n.   435 **mesurable** moderate   439 **sangwin** red
(cloth) **pers** blue (cloth)   440 **taffata** taffeta, shiny silk **sendal** a thin rich
silk   441 **esy of dispence** parsimonious   442 **that he wan in pestilence** what
he gained in time of plague   443 **cordial** invigorating medicine
445 **biside** near   446 **scathe** a pity

Of clooth-making she hadde swich an haunt,
She passed hem of Ypres and of Gaunt.
In al the parisshe wif ne was ther noon
450   That to the offringe bifore hire sholde goon –
And if ther dide, certein, so wrooth was she
That she was out of alle charitee.
Hir coverchiefs ful fine were of ground;
I dorste swere they weyeden ten pound
455   That on a Sonday weren upon hir heed.
Hir hosen weren of fin scarlet reed,
Ful streite yteyd, and shoes ful moiste and newe.
Boold was hir face, and fair, and reed of hewe.
She was a worthy womman al hir live;
460   Housbondes at chirche-dore she hadde five,
Withouten oother compaignye in youthe –
But therof nedeth nat to speke as nouthe.
And thries hadde she been at Jerusalem;
She hadde passed many a straunge strem.
465   At Rome she hadde been and at Boloine,
In Galice at Seint Jame, and at Coloine –
She koude muche of wandringe by the weye.
Gat-tothed was she, soothly for to seye.
Upon an amblere esily she sat,
470   Ywimpled wel, and on hir heed an hat
As brood as is a bokeler or a targe;
A foot-mantel aboute hir hipes large,

447 **hadde swich an haunt** was so expert in   448 **passed** surpassed
hem those   450 **offringe** Offertory (n.)   453 **coverchiefs** head cloths
ground texture, material   454 **dorste swere** dare swear
456 **hosen** stockings   457 **streite** tightly **yteyd** tied
458 **hewe** complexion   460 **chirche-dore** church-door (n.)
461 **Withouten** besides **compaignye** relationships   462 **nedeth nat** it is not
necessary **as nouthe** at the moment   464 **straunge strem** foreign river
466 **Seint Jame** Santiago de Compostela (n.)   467 **koude muche of** knew a
lot about   468 **Gat-tothed was she** her teeth were set wide apart
469 **amblere** saddle-horse   470 **Ywimpled** wearing a wimple
471 **bokeler** small shield **targe** shield   472 **foot-mantel** over-skirt coming
down to the feet (to protect the dress in riding) **large** broad

And on hir feet a peire of spores sharpe.
In felawshipe wel koude she laughe and carpe;
Of remedies of love she knew par chaunce,   475
For she koude of that art the olde daunce.
    A good man was ther of religioun,
And was a povre PERSOUN of a toun,
But riche he was of holy thoght and werk.
He was also a lerned man, a clerk,   480
That Cristes gospel trewely wolde preche;
His parisshens devoutly wolde he teche.
Benigne he was and wonder diligent,
And in adversitee ful pacient,
And swich he was ypreved ofte sithes.   485
Ful looth were him to cursen for his tithes,
But rather wolde he yeven, out of doute,
Unto his povre parisshens aboute
Of his offringe and eek of his substaunce;
He koude in litel thing have suffisaunce.   490
Wid was his parisshe, and houses fer asonder,
But he ne lafte nat, for rein ne thonder,
In siknesse nor in meschief to visite
The ferreste in his parisshe, muche and lite,
Upon his feet, and in his hond a staf.   495
This noble ensample to his sheep he yaf,
That first he wroghte, and afterward he taughte.
Out of the gospel he tho wordes caughte;
And this figure he added eek therto,
That if gold ruste, what sholde iren do?   500

473 **spores** spurs   474 **carpe** talk, gossip   475 **par chaunce** as it happened
476 **koude** knew **the olde daunce** all the old tricks   477 **of religioun** in holy
orders   478 **PERSOUN** parson   483 **wonder** wonderfully
485 **ypreved** proved to be **ofte sithes** many times
486 **cursen** excommunicate (n.)   487 **out of doute** doubtless
488 **aboute** round about   489 From the donations made at the Offertory
and also from his own possessions   490 **suffisaunce** sufficiency
493 **meschief** affliction   494 **ferreste** furthest **muche and lite** great and
small   495 **staf** staff   496 **yaf** gave   498 **tho** those   499 **figure** metaphor,
figure of speech **therto** in addition

For if a preest be foule, on whom we truste,
No wonder is a lewed man to ruste!
And shame it is, if a preest take keep,
A shiten shepherde and a clene sheep.
505　Wel oghte a preest ensample for to yive
By his clennesse, how that his sheep sholde live.
He sette nat his benefice to hire,
And leet his sheep encombred in the mire,
And ran to Londoun unto Seinte Poules
510　To seken him a chaunterye for soules,
Or with a bretherhede to been withholde,
But dwelte at hoom and kepte wel his folde,
So that the wolf ne made it nat miscarye;
He was a shepherde and noght a mercenarye.
515　And thogh he hooly were and vertuous,
He was to sinful men noght despitous,
Ne of his speche daungerous ne digne,
But in his teching discreet and benigne;
To drawen folk to hevene by fairnesse,
520　By good ensample – this was his bisinesse.
But it were any persone obstinat,
Whatso he were, of heigh or lowe estat,
Him wolde he snibben sharply, for the nonis.
A bettre preest I trowe that nowher noon is.
525　He waited after no pompe and reverence,
Ne maked him a spiced conscience,
But Cristes loore, and his apostles twelve,
He taughte, but first he folwed it himselve.

502 It is not surprising if a layman turns rusty   503 **take keep** takes note
504 **shiten** covered with shit   507 He did not farm out his parish (n.)
508 **leet** left **encombred** bogged down   510 **chaunterye** see n.
511 **bretherhede** guild, fraternity **withholde** retained   513 **miscarye** suffer
harm   514 **mercenarye** hireling   516 **despitous** scornful
517 **daungerous ne digne** haughty or proud   519 **fairnesse** gentleness
520 **bisinesse** endeavour   521 **But** unless   522 **Whatso** whatever
estat rank   523 **snibben** rebuke, reprimand   525 **waited after** looked for
526 **spiced conscience** (over-)fastidiousness

With him ther was a PLOWMAN, was his
    brother,
That hadde ylad of donge ful many a fother.   530
A trewe swinkere and a good was he,
Livinge in pees and parfit charitee.
God loved he best with al his hoole herte
At alle times, thogh him gamed or smerte,
And thanne his neighebore right as himselve.   535
He wolde thresshe, and therto dike and delve,
For Cristes sake, for every povre wight
Withouten hire, if it lay in his might.
His tithes payede he ful faire and wel,
Bothe of his propre swink and his catel.   540
In a tabard he rood upon a mere.

    Ther was also a REVE, and a MILLERE,
A SOMNOUR, and a PARDONER also,
A MAUNCIPLE, and myself – ther were namo.

    The MILLER was a stout carl for the nones;   545
Ful big he was of brawn and eek of bones.
That proved wel, for overal ther he cam
At wrastlinge he wolde have alwey the ram.
He was short-sholdred, brood, a thikke knarre;
Ther was no dore that he nolde heve of harre,   550
Or breke it at a renning with his heed.
His berd as any sowe or fox was reed,
And therto brood as though it were a spade.
Upon the cop right of his nose he hade
A werte, and theron stood a tuft of heris,   555
Reed as the bristles of a sowes eris.

530 **ylad** carried **fother** cart-load   531 **swinkere** labourer
534 **him gamed or smerte** it pleased him or pained him
536 **thresshe** thresh **therto** also **dike** make ditches **delve** dig
537 **wight** person   539 **faire and wel** conscientiously
540 **propre swink** own labour (n.)   541 **tabard** loose tunic (n.) **mere** mare
544 **namo** no others   545 **stout** strong, powerful **for the nones** indeed
546 **big** strong **brawn** muscle   547 **overal ther** everywhere that
548 **wrastlinge** wrestling   549 **short-sholdred** short in the upper arm
knarre thick-set man   550 **heve of harre** heave off its hinges
551 **renning** run   554 **cop** tip   555 **werte** wart

His nosethirles blake were and wide;
A swerd and bokeler bar he by his side.
His mouth as greet was as a greet fourneis.
560 He was a jangler and a goliardeis,
And that was moost of sinne and harlotries.
Wel koude he stelen corn and tollen thries;
And yet he hadde a thombe of gold, pardee!
A whit cote and a blew hood wered hee;
565 A bagge-pipe wel koude he blowe and sowne,
And therwithal he broghte us out of towne.

A gentil MAUNCIPLE was ther of a temple,
Of which achatours mighte take exemple
For to be wis in byinge of vitaille;
570 For wheither that he paide or took by taille,
Algate he waited so in his achaat,
That he was ay biforn and in good staat.
Now is nat that of God a ful fair grace,
That swich a lewed mannes wit shal pace
575 The wisdom of an heep of lerned men?
Of maistres hadde he mo than thries ten,
That weren of lawe expert and curious,
Of whiche ther were a dozeine in that hous
Worthy to been stiwardes of rente and lond
580 Of any lord that is in Engelond,
To make him live by his propre good
In honour detteles, but he were wood,

---

558 **bokeler** small shield   559 **fourneis** furnace   560 **jangler** loudmouth
goliardeis ribald story-teller   561 **harlotries** obscenities   562 **tollen** collect
a toll (n.)   563 **thombe of gold** see n.   564 **blew** blue
567 **MAUNCIPLE** manciple (n.) **temple** Inn of Court
568 **achatours** buyers of provisions   569 **byinge of vitaille** buying food
570 **taille** tally, a scored wooden stick kept by a creditor as a record of sums
owed   571 **waited so in his achaat** took such precautions in his purchasing
572 **ay biforn** always ahead   574 **lewed** uneducated **pace** surpass
576 **mo** more   577 **of lawe expert** learned in law **curious** skilled
581 **by his propre good** off his own property   582 **but he were wood** unless
he was mad

Or live as scarsly as him list desire,
And able for to helpen al a shire
In any caas that mighte falle or happe –   585
And yet this maunciple sette hir aller cappe.
    The REVE was a sclendre colerik man.
His berd was shave as neigh as ever he kan;
His heer was by his eris ful round yshorn;
His top was dokked lik a preest biforn.   590
Ful longe were his legges, and ful lene,
Ilik a staf – ther was no calf ysene.
Wel koude he kepe a gerner and a binne;
Ther was noon auditour koude on him winne.
Wel wiste he by the droghte and by the rein   595
The yeldinge of his seed and of his grein.
His lordes sheep, his neet, his daierye,
His swin, his hors, his stoor, and his pultrye
Was hoolly in this Reves governinge,
And by his covenant yaf the rekeninge   600
Sin that his lord was twenty yeer of age;
Ther koude no man bringe him in arrerage.
Ther nas baillif, ne hierde, nor oother hine,
That he ne knew his sleighte and his covine;
They were adrad of him as of the deeth.   605
His woning was ful faire upon an heeth;
With grene trees yshadwed was his place.
He koude bettre than his lord purchace;

583 **him list** it pleased him   586 **sette hir aller cappe** made fools of them all
587 **REVE** reeve (n.) **sclendre** slender **colerik** irascible, choleric (n.)
588 **as neigh as ever he kan** as closely as possible   589 **yshorn** cut
590 **dokked** cut short **biforn** in front   593 **gerner** garner, granary
binne bin (for grain)   594 **on him winne** get the better of him
595 **wiste he** he knew   596 **yeldinge** yield   597 **neet** cattle **daierye** dairy
herd   598 **swin** pigs **stoor** livestock **pultrye** poultry
599 **governinge** control   600 **by his covenant** according to his contract
601 **Sin that** since   602 **bringe him in arrerage** find him short in his
accounts   603 **hierde** herdsman **hine** servant   604 **sleighte** trickery
covine fraud   605 **adrad** afraid   606 **woning** dwelling-place
607 **yshadwed** shadowed   608 **purchace** acquire wealth

Ful riche he was astored prively.

610   His lord wel koude he plesen subtilly,
To yeve and lene him of his owene good,
And have a thank, and yet a coote and hood.
In youthe he lerned hadde a good mister:
He was a wel good wrighte, a carpenter.

615   This Reve sat upon a ful good stot
That was al pomely grey and highte Scot.
A long surcote of pers upon he hade,
And by his side he baar a rusty blade.
Of Northfolk was this Reve of which I telle,

620   Biside a toun men clepen Baldeswelle.
Tukked he was as is a frere aboute,
And evere he rood the hindreste of oure route.

    A SOMNOUR was ther with us in that place,
That hadde a fir-reed cherubinnes face,

625   For saucefleem he was with eyen narwe.
As hoot he was and lecherous as a sparwe,
With scaled browes blake and piled berd;
Of his visage children were aferd.
Ther nas quiksilver, litarge, ne brimstoon,

630   Boras, ceruce, ne oille of tartre noon,
Ne oinement that wolde clense and bite,
That him mighte helpen of his whelkes white,
Nor of the knobbes sittinge on his chekes.
Wel loved he garlek, oinons and eek lekes,

---

609 **astored** stocked up   611 **lene** lend   612 **yet** in addition **coote** tunic
613 **mister** trade   615 **stot** farm-horse   616 **pomely** dappled **highte** was
called   617 **surcote** (outer) coat **pers** blue (cloth)   619 **Northfolk** Norfolk
620 **clepen** call   621 His gown was tucked up on all sides (over his girdle),
like a friar's   622 **hindreste** rearmost   623 **SOMNOUR** summoner (n.)
624 **a fir-reed cherubinnes face** the fire-red face of a cherub (n.)
625 **saucefleem** covered with pimples (as a result of a disease called 'salt
phlegm') (n.)   627 **scaled** scabby **piled** scrubby   628 **aferd** afraid
629 **quiksilver** mercury **litarge** lead monoxide **brimstoon** sulphur
630 **Boras** borax **ceruce** white lead **oille of tartre** saturated solution of
potassium carbonate   632 **him ... helpen of** cure him of **whelkes** pimples
633 **knobbes** lumps

And for to drinke strong win, reed as blood; 635
Thanne wolde he speke and crye as he were
    wood.
And whan that he wel dronken hadde the win,
Thanne wolde he speke no word but Latin.
A fewe termes hadde he, two or thre,
That he had lerned out of som decre – 640
No wonder is, he herde it al the day,
And eek ye knowen wel how that a jay
Kan clepen 'Watte' as wel as kan the pope –
But whoso koude in oother thing him grope,
Thanne hadde he spent al his philosophye; 645
Ay '*Questio quid iuris*' wolde he crye.
He was a gentil harlot and a kinde;
A bettre felawe sholde men noght finde.
He wolde suffre, for a quart of win,
A good felawe to have his concubin 650
A twelf-monthe, and excuse him atte fulle;
Ful prively a finch eek koude he pulle.
And if he foond owher a good felawe,
He wolde techen him to have noon awe
In swich caas of the ercedekenes curs, 655
But if a mannes soule were in his purs,
For in his purs he sholde ypunisshed be.
'Purs is the ercedekenes helle,' seide he.
But wel I woot he lied right in dede;
Of cursing oghte ech gilty man him drede, 660
For curs wol slee right as assoilling savith,
And also war him of a *significavit*.

---

636 **as he were wood** as if he were mad   640 **decre** decree, edict
643 **clepen 'Watte'** say 'Walter'   644 **grope** question   645 Then he had
used up all his learning   646 **Questio quid iuris** The question is, what
(point) of law (is relevant)   647 **gentil harlot** noble rogue
649 **suffre** allow   650 **concubin** mistress   651 **atte fulle** completely
652 Secretly he could also cheat a dupe (n.)   653 **owher** anywhere
655 **ercedekenes curs** archdeacon's excommunication (n.)
656 **But if** unless   661 **assoilling** absolution   662 *significavit* see n.

In daunger hadde he at his owene gise
The yonge gerles of the diocise,
665   And knew hir counseil, and was al hir reed.
A gerland hadde he set upon his heed,
As greet as it were for an ale-stake;
A bokeler hadde he maad him of a cake.
    With him ther rood a gentil PARDONER
670   Of Rouncival, his freend and his comper,
That streight was comen fro the court of Rome.
Ful loude he soong 'Com hider, love, to me!'
This somnour bar to him a stif burdoun;
Was nevere trompe of half so greet a soun.
675   This Pardoner hadde heer as yelow as wex,
But smothe it heeng as dooth a strike of flex.
By ounces henge his lokkes that he hadde,
And therwith he his shuldres overspradde;
But thinne it lay, by colpons, oon and oon.
680   But hood, for jolitee, ne wered he noon,
For it was trussed up in his walet –
Him thoughte he rood al of the newe jet;
Dischevelee, save his cappe, he rood al bare.
Swiche glaringe eyen hadde he as an hare.
685   A vernicle hadde he sowed upon his cappe;
His walet lay biforn him in his lappe,

663 He had in his power, to do as he pleased   664 **gerles** youngsters (of
either sex) **diocise** diocese   665 **counseil** private affairs **was al hir reed** was
their exclusive adviser   667 **greet** big **ale-stake** inn-sign (g.)   668 **him** for
himself   670 **Rouncival** St Mary Roncevall (n.) **comper** intimate
671 **streight** directly **court of Rome** papal court
673 **stif burdoun** powerful bass accompaniment (see n. to GP 691)
674 **trompe** trumpet   676 **smothe** smoothly **heeng** hung **strike of flex** hank
of flax   677 **By ounces** in thin clusters   678 **overspradde** spread over
679 **thinne** thinly **by colpons** in hanks **oon and oon** one by one
680 **jolitee** attractiveness   681 **trussed up** bundled up **walet** bag
682 **Him thoughte** it seemed to him **al of the newe jet** in the latest fashion
683 **Dischevelee** bareheaded **save** except for   684 **glaringe** staring
685 **vernicle** pilgrim badge bearing an image of Christ's face (n.)

Bret-ful of pardoun, come from Rome al hoot.
A vois he hadde as smal as hath a goot;
No berd hadde he, ne nevere sholde have;
As smothe it was as it were late yshave –   690
I trowe he were a gelding or a mare.
But of his craft, fro Berwik into Ware
Ne was ther swich another pardoner.
For in his male he hadde a pilwe-beer,
Which that he seide was Oure Lady veil;   695
He seide he hadde a gobet of the seil
That Seinte Peter hadde, whan that he wente
Upon the see, til Jesu Crist him hente.
He hadde a crois of latoun ful of stones,
And in a glas he hadde pigges bones.   700
But with thise relikes, whan that he fond
A povre persoun dwelling upon lond,
Upon a day he gat him moore moneye
Than that the persoun gat in monthes tweye.
And thus with feined flaterye and japes   705
He made the persoun and the peple his apes.
But trewely to tellen atte laste,
He was in chirche a noble ecclesiaste.
Wel koude he rede a lessoun or a storye,
But alderbest he song an offertorye.   710
For wel he wiste, whan that song was songe,
He moste preche and wel affile his tonge
To winne silver, as he ful wel koude;
Therfore he song the murierly and loude.

687 **Bret-ful** brimful **from Rome al hoot** fresh from Rome
690 **smothe** smooth **as it were late yshave** as if it had just been shaved
691 see n.   694 **male** bag **pilwe-beer** pillow-case   696 **gobet** fragment
seil sail 698 **hente** (= *hentede*) summoned   699 **latoun** brass
701 **fond** found   702 **persoun** parson **upon lond** in the country
703 **Upon a day** in one day   704 **tweye** two   706 **made . . . his apes** made
fools of   710 **alderbest** best of all   **offertorye** offertory (anthem sung at
Mass while people's offerings are being collected)   712 **moste** had to
affile his tonge polish his speech   713 **koude** knew how to
714 **murierly** more sweetly

715   Now have I told yow soothly, in a clause,
           Th'estaat, th'array, the nombre, and eek the cause
           Why that assembled was this compaignye,
           In Southwerk, at this gentil hostelrye
           That highte the Tabard, faste by the Belle.
720   But now is time to yow for to telle
           How that we baren us that ilke night,
           Whan we were in that hostelrye alight;
           And after wol I telle of oure viage,
           And al the remenant of oure pilgrimage.
725   But first I pray yow, of youre curteisye,
           That ye n'arette it nat my vileinye,
           Thogh that I pleinly speke in this matere,
           To telle yow hir wordes and hir cheere,
           Ne thogh I speke hir wordes properly;
730   For this ye knowen also wel as I,
           Whoso shal telle a tale after a man,
           He moot reherce as neigh as evere he kan
           Everich a word, if it be in his charge,
           Al speke he nevere so rudeliche and large,
735   Or ellis he moot telle his tale untrewe,
           Or feine thing or finde wordes newe.
           He may nat spare, althogh he were his brother;
           He moot as wel seye o word as another.
           Crist spak himself ful brode in holy writ,
740   And wel ye woot no vileinye is it.
           Eek Plato seyth, whoso kan him rede,
           The wordes mote be cosin to the dede.

715 **in a clause** briefly   716 **estaat** social condition   718 **gentil** noble
719 **highte** was called   721 **baren us** behaved   722 **were ... alight** had
alighted   726 **n'arette it nat** do not attribute it to **vileinye** boorishness
728 **cheere** behaviour   729 **proprely** literally   731 **telle a tale after** repeat a
tale after   732 **moot reherce** must repeat   733 **Everich a** every
if it be in his charge if it is in his power   734 However coarsely or broadly
he speaks   735 **untrewe** inaccurately   736 **finde** invent   738 **o** one
739 **brode** plainly, frankly   740 **ye woot** you know
742 **mote be cosin to** must be akin to, match

Also I pray yow to foryeve it me
Al have I nat set folk in hir degree
Here in this tale, as that they sholde stonde;   745
My wit is short, ye may wel understonde.
   Greet cheere made oure HOOST us
      everychon,
And to the soper sette he us anon.
He served us with vitaille at the beste;
Strong was the win and wel to drinke us leste.   750
A semely man oure Hooste was withalle
For to been a marchal in an halle.
A large man he was, with eyen stepe;
A fairer burgeis was ther noon in Chepe.
Boold of his speche, and wis, and wel ytaught,   755
And of manhode him lakkede right naught.
Eke therto he was right a murye man;
And after soper pleyen he bigan,
And spak of mirthe amonges othere thinges,
Whan that we hadde maad oure rekeninges,   760
And seide thus: 'Now, lordinges, trewely
Ye been to me right welcome, hertely!
For by my trouthe, if that I shal nat lie,
I saugh nat this yeer so murye a compaignye
Atones in this herberwe as is now.   765
Fain wolde I doon yow mirthe, wiste I how,
And of a mirthe I am right now bithoght,
To doon yow ese, and it shal coste noght.
   Ye goon to Caunterbury – God yow spede!
The blisful martyr quite yow youre mede! –   770

744 **Al have I** if I have not   746 **wit** intelligence
747 **Greet cheere made ... us** treated us very hospitably   749 **vitaille** food
750 **us leste** gave us pleasure   752 **marchal in an halle** see n.
753 **stepe** prominent   755 **Boold of his speche** ready of speech
757 **therto** in addition   758 **pleyen** to joke   764 **murye** pleasant
765 **Atones** together **herberwe** lodgings   766 **doon yow mirthe** entertain
you **wiste I how** if I knew how   767 And I have just thought of an
entertainment   768 **doon yow ese** amuse you
770 **quite yow youre mede** reward you

And wel I woot, as ye goon by the weye
Ye shapen yow to talen and to pleye.
For trewely, confort ne mirthe is noon
To ride by the weye domb as the stoon.
775   And therfore wol I maken yow disport,
As I seide erst, and doon yow som confort.
And if yow liketh alle by oon assent
For to stonden at my juggement,
And for to werken as I shal yow seye,
780   Tomorwe whan ye riden by the weye,
Now, by my fader soule that is deed,
But ye be murye, I wol yeve yow min heed!
Hoold up youre hondes, withouten moore speche.'
    Oure conseil was nat longe for to seche:
785   Us thoughte it was nat worth to make it wis,
And graunted him, withouten moore avis,
And bad him seye his voirdit as him leste.
'Lordinges,' quod he, 'now herkneth for the beste –
But taak it nat, I pray yow, in desdein –
790   This is the point, to speken short and plein:
That ech of yow, to shorte with oure weye
In this viage, shal tellen tales tweye
To Caunterburyward, I mene it so,
And homward he shall tellen othere two,
795   Of aventures that whilom have bifalle.
And which of yow that berth him best of alle –

---

772 **Ye shapen yow to talen** you plan to talk (n.)   775 **disport** amusement
776 **erst** before   777 **yow liketh** it pleases you   780 **Tomorwe** tomorrow
782 **But ye be murye** if you are not cheerful
783 **hoold up youre hondes** promise   784 Our decision didn't have to be
requested for long   785 **make it wis** deliberate, hesitate
786 **avis** deliberation   787 **voirdit** opinion   788 **herkneth** listen
789 **taak it nat . . . in desdein** do not take offence at it   791 **shorte** shorten
793 **To Caunterburyward** towards Canterbury   794 **othere two** another
two   795 **aventures** notable events **whilom** formerly
796 **berth him** performs

That is to seyn, that telleth in this caas
Tales of best sentence and moost solaas –
Shal have a soper at oure aller cost,
Here in this place, sitting by this post,   800
Whan that we come again fro Caunterbury.
And for to make yow the moore mury,
I wol myself goodly with yow ride,
Right at min owene cost, and be your gide.
And whoso wole my juggement withseye   805
Shal paye al that we spende by the weye.
And if ye vouchesauf that it be so,
Tel me anoon, withouten wordes mo,
And I wol erly shape me therfore.'

    This thing was graunted, and oure othes swore   810
With ful glad herte, and preyden him also
That he wolde vouchesauf for to do so,
And that he wolde been oure governour,
And of oure tales juge and reportour,
And sette a soper at a certain pris,   815
And we wol reuled been at his devis
In heigh and lough; and thus by oon assent
We been acorded to his juggement.
And therupon the win was fet anoon;
We dronken and to reste wente echon,   820
Withouten any lenger taryinge.

    Amorwe, whan that day bigan to springe,
Up roos oure Hoost and was oure aller cok,
And gadred us togidre in a flok;

798 **sentence** serious meaning **solaas** pleasure, entertainment
799 **at oure aller cost** at the expense of all of us   803 **goodly** gladly
807 **vouchesauf** agree   809 **shape me therfore** get ready for it
810 **swore** sworn   811 **preyden** requested   813 **governour** leader
814 **reportour** reporter, recorder   816 **devis** desire
817 **In heigh and lough** in everything   818 **We been acorded to** we agreed
to   819 **fet anoon** fetched immediately   820 **echon** each one
822 **Amorwe** next morning **springe** dawn, break
823 **was oure aller cok** woke us all up (*lit.* was our cock)
824 **togidre** together

825   And forth we riden, a litel moore than pas,
       Unto the watering of Seint Thomas.
       And there oure Hoost bigan his hors areste,
       And seide, 'Lordinges, herkneth if yow leste!
       Ye woot youre forward, and it yow recorde.
830   If evensong and morwe-song acorde,
       Lat se now who shal telle the firste tale.
       As evere moot I drinke win or ale,
       Whoso be rebel to my juggement
       Shal paye for al that by the wey is spent.
835   Now draweth cut, er that we ferrer twinne;
       He which that hath the shorteste shal biginne.
       Sire knight,' quod he, 'my maister and my lord,
       Now draweth cut, for that is min acord.
       Comth neer,' quod he, 'my lady prioresse,
840   And ye, sire clerk, lat be youre shamefastnesse,
       Ne studyeth noght – ley hond to, every man!'
          Anoon to drawen every wight bigan;
       And shortly for to tellen as it was,
       Were it by aventure or sort or cas,
845   The sothe is this: the cut fil to the Knight,
       Of which ful blithe and glad was every wight.
       And telle he moste his tale as was resoun,
       By forward and by composicioun,
       As ye han herd – what nedeth wordes mo?
850   And whan this goode man saugh that it was so,
       As he that wis was and obedient
       To kepe his forward by his free assent,

---

825 **riden** rode **a litel moore than pas** at little more than walking-pace
826 **watering of Seint Thomas** St Thomas Watering (n.)
827 **bigan his hors areste** brought his horse to a halt   829 You know your
agreement, if you remember it   830 **morwe-song** morning-song
acorde agree with each other   832 **As evere moot I** so may I
833 **Whoso be** whoever is   835 **draweth cut** draw straws **ferrer twinne** go
further   838 **acord** agreement   841 **Ne studyeth noght** don't deliberate
844 Whether it was by chance or fate or accident   845 **fil** fell
847 **moste** had to **as was resoun** as was right
848 **composicioun** agreement

He seide, 'Sin I shal biginne the game,
What, welcome be the cut, a Goddes name!
Now lat us ride, and herkneth what I seye.'   855
And with that word we riden forth oure weye,
And he bigan with right a murye cheere
His tale anoon, and seide as ye may heere.

THE KNIGHT'S TALE

*Iamque domos patrias Scithice post aspera gentis
    prelia laurigero etc.*

Heere biginneth the Knightes Tale.

Whilom, as olde stories tellen us,
Ther was a duc that highte Theseus.   860
Of Atthenes he was lord and governour,
And in his time swich a conqueror
That gretter was ther noon under the sonne.
Ful many a riche contree hadde he wonne,
What with his wisdom and his chivalrye.   865
He conquered al the regne of Femenye,
That whilom was ycleped Scythia,
And weddede the queene Ypolita,
And broghte hir hoom with him in his contree
With muchel glorye and greet solempnitee,   870
And eek hir yonge suster Emelye.
And thus with victorye and with melodye

853 **Sin** since   857 **murye cheere** cheerful expression

Iamque domos . . . etc. And now, after the fierce battles with the Scythian
people, (Theseus approaches) his native land in his laurel-crowned
(chariot) . . .

859 **Whilom** once upon a time   860 **highte** was called
866 **Femenye** land of the Amazons   867 **ycleped** called
868 **Ypolita** Hippolyta   870 **solempnitee** festivity

Lete I this noble duc to Atthenes ride,
And al his hoost in armes him biside.

875   And certes, if it nere to long to heere,
I wolde have toold yow fully the manere
How wonnen was the regne of Femenye
By Theseus and by his chivalrye,
And of the grete bataille for the nones
880   Bitwixen Atthenes and Amazones,
And how asseged was Ypolita,
The faire hardy queene of Scythia,
And of the feste that was at hir weddinge
And of the tempest at hir hom-cominge;
885   But al that thing I moot as now forbere.
I have, God woot, a large feeld to ere,
And waike been the oxen in my plough.
The remenant of the tale is long inough.
I wol nat letten eek noon of this route;
890   Lat every felawe telle his tale aboute,
And lat se now who shal the soper winne!
– And ther I lefte, I wol ayein biginne.

This duc of whom I make mencioun,
Whan he was come almost unto the toun,
895   In al his wele and in his mooste pride,
He was war, as he caste his eye aside,
Wher that ther kneled in the hye weye
A compaignye of ladies, tweye and tweye,
Ech after oother, clad in clothes blake.
900   But swich a cry and swich a wo they make
That in this world nis creature livinge
That herde swich another waimentinge.

---

873 **Lete ... ride** leave ... riding   875 **certes** certainly **if it nere** if it were
not   879 **for the nones** on the occasion   881 **asseged** besieged
882 **hardy** brave   885 **moot ... forbere** must omit   886 **God woot** God
knows **ere** plough   887 **waike** weak   889 **letten** delay
892 **ther I lefte** where I left off   895 **wele** splendour **mooste** greatest
896 **war** aware   897 **hye weye** high road   898 **tweye and tweye** two by
two   902 **waimentinge** lamentation

And of this cry they nolde nevere stenten
Til they the reines of his bridel henten.
   'What folk been ye, that at min hom-cominge   905
Perturben so my feste with cryinge?'
Quod Theseus. 'Have ye so greet envye
Of min honour, that thus compleine and crye?
Or who hath yow misboden or offended?
And telleth me if it may been amended,   910
And why that ye been clothed thus in blak.'
   The eldeste lady of hem alle spak,
Whan she hadde swowned with a deedly cheere
That it was routhe for to seen and here,
And seide, 'Lord, to whom Fortune hath yeven   915
Victorye, and as a conquerour to liven,
Noght greveth us youre glorye and youre honour,
But we biseken mercy and socour.
Have mercy on oure wo and oure distresse!
Som drope of pitee thurgh thy gentillesse   920
Upon us wrecched wommen lat thow falle.
For certes, lord, ther is noon of us alle
That she nath been a duchesse or a queene.
Now be we caitives, as it is wel seene,
Thanked be Fortune and hir false wheel,   925
That noon estaat assureth to be weel.
And certes, lord, t'abiden youre presence
Here in this temple of the goddesse Clemence
We have been waitinge al this fourtenight.
Now help us, lord, sith it is in thy might!   930
   I, wrecche, which that wepe and waille thus
Was whilom wif to king Cappaneus

---

903 **stenten** cease   904 **henten** seized   906 **Perturben** disturb
909 **misboden** maltreated   913 **swowned** fainted   **deedly cheere** death-like
face   914 **routhe** a pity   915 **yeven** given   917 **Noght greveth us** we do
not begrudge   918 **biseken** beseech   920 **gentillesse** graciousness
924 **caitives** wretches   926 Who guarantees prosperity to no social rank
928 **Clemence** Clementia (the deified principle of mercy)   930 **sith** since
might power   932 **Cappaneus** see n.

That starf at Thebes – cursed be that day! –
And alle we that been in this array
935   And maken al this lamentacioun,
We losten alle oure housbondes at that toun,
Whil that the sege theraboute lay.
And yet now the olde Creon, weilaway,
That lord is now of Thebes the citee,
940   Fulfild of ire and of iniquitee,
He for despit, and for his tyrannye,
To do the dede bodies vileinye
Of alle oure lordes whiche that been yslawe,
Hath alle the bodies on an heep ydrawe,
945   And wol nat suffren hem by noon assent
Neither to been yburied nor ybrent,
But maketh houndes ete hem in despit.'
And with that word, withouten moore respit,
They fillen gruf and criden pitously:
950   'Have on us wrecched wommen som mercy,
And let oure sorwe sinken in thin herte!'
        This gentil duc doun from his courser sterte
With herte pitous, whan he herde hem speke.
Him thoughte that his herte wolde breke
955   Whan he saugh hem so pitous and so maat,
That whilom weren of so greet estaat.
And in his armes he hem alle up hente
And hem conforteth in ful good entente,
And swoor his ooth, as he was trewe knight,
960   He wolde doon so ferforthly his might

933 **starf** died   937 **theraboute** about that place   938 **yet now** in addition
940 **Fulfild of** filled with   941 **despit** malice   942 **vileinye** dishonour
943 **yslawe** slain   945 **suffren** allow **by noon assent** on no account
946 **ybrent** burned   947 **houndes** dogs **in despit** in spite   948 **respit** delay
949 **fillen gruf** fell on their faces **pitously** pitifully   952 **gentil** noble
courser charger, battle-horse **sterte** leaped   953 **pitous** compassionate
955 **pitous** sorrowful **maat** helpless   957 **up hente** took up
958 **in ful good entente** with great good will   960 **so ferforthly** to such an
extent that

Upon the tyraunt Creon hem to wreke
That al the peple of Grece sholde speke
How Creon was of Theseus yserved,
As he that hadde his deeth ful wel deserved.
And right anoon, withouten moore abood,   965
His baner he desplayeth and forth rood
To Thebesward, and al his hoost biside.
Ne neer Atthenes wolde he go ne ride,
Ne take his ese fully half a day,
But onward on his wey that night he lay,   970
And sente anoon Ypolita the queene,
And Emelye hir yonge suster sheene,
Unto the toun of Atthenes to dwelle,
And forth he rit; ther is namoore to telle.

   The rede statue of Mars, with spere and targe,   975
So shineth in his white baner large
That alle the feeldes gliteren up and doun,
And by his baner born is his penoun
Of gold ful riche, in which ther was ybete
The Minotaur, which that he wan in Crete.   980
Thus rit this duc, thus rit this conquerour,
And in his hoost of chivalrye the flour,
Til that he cam to Thebes and alighte,
Faire in a feeld, theras he thoghte fighte.

   But shortly for to speken of this thing,   985
With Creon, which that was of Thebes king,
He faught, and slough him manly as a knight
In plein bataille, and putte the folk to flight.
And by assaut he wan the citee after,
And rente adoun bothe wal and sparre and rafter;   990

961 **wreke** avenge   963 **of Theseus yserved** dealt with by Theseus
965 **right anoon** straight away   **abood** delay   967 **To Thebesward** towards
Thebes   968 **neer** nearer   972 **sheene** beautiful   974 **rit** (= *rideth*) rides
975 **targe** shield   976 **large** broad   978 **penoun** pennon
979 **ybete** embossed   980 **wan** overcame   983 **alighte** dismounted
984 **theras he thoghte fighte** where he planned to fight
988 **plein bataille** open war   990 **sparre** beam

And to the ladies he restored again
The bones of hir freendes that were slain,
To doon obsequies as was tho the gise.
But it were al to long for to devise
995   The grete clamour and the waimentinge
That the ladies made at the brenninge
Of the bodies, and the grete honour
That Theseus the noble conquerour
Doth to the ladies, whan they from him wente;
1000   But shortly for to telle is min entente.

    Whan that this worthy duc, this Theseus,
Hath Creon slain and wonne Thebes thus,
Stille in that feeld he took al night his reste,
And dide with al the contree as him leste.

1005   To ransake in the taas of bodies dede,
Hem for to strepe of harneis and of wede,
The pilours diden bisinesse and cure,
After the bataille and disconfiture.
And so bifel that in the taas they founde,
1010   Thurgh-girt with many a grevous blody wounde,
Two yonge knightes, ligginge by and by,
Both in oon armes wroght ful richely;
Of whiche two, Arcita highte that oon,
And that oother knight highte Palamon.
1015   Nat fully quik ne fully dede they were,
But by hir cote-armures and by hir gere
The heraudes knew hem best in special,
As they that weren of the blood royal

---

992 **freendes** kinsfolk   993 **tho the gise** then the custom
994 But it would be too long to recount   995 **waimentinge** lamentation
1000 **entente** intention   1003 **Stille** quietly   1004 **as him leste** as it pleased
him   1005 **taas** heap   1006 **strepe** strip **harneis** armour **wede** clothing
1007 The scavengers exerted themselves   1008 **disconfiture** defeat
1010 **Thurgh-girt** pierced through   1011 **ligginge by and by** lying side by
side   1012 **oon armes** identical armour   1015 **quik** alive
1016 **cote-armures** outer tunics bearing heraldic arms (n.)
1017 **in special** in particular

Of Thebes, and of sustren two yborn.
Out of the taas the pilours han hem torn   1020
And han hem caried softe unto the tente
Of Theseus, and he ful soone hem sente
To Atthenes, to dwellen in prisoun
Perpetuelly; he nolde no raunsoun.
    And whan this worthy duc hath thus   1025
        ydoon,
He took his hoost and hom he rit anoon,
With laurer crowned as a conquerour;
And ther he liveth in joye and in honour
Terme of his lif; what nedeth wordes mo?
And in a tour, in angwissh and in wo,   1030
Dwellen this Palamon, and eek Arcite,
For everemoore; ther may no gold hem quite.
    This passeth yeer by yeer and day by day,
Til it fil ones, in a morwe of May,
That Emelye, that fairer was to sene   1035
Than is the lilye upon his stalke grene,
And fressher than the May with floures newe –
For with the rose colour stroof hir hewe;
I noot which was the finer of hem two –
Er it were day, as was hir wone to do,   1040
She was arisen and al redy dight.
For May wol have no slogardye a-night;
The sesoun priketh every gentil herte,
And maketh it out of his sleep to sterte,
And seyth, 'Aris, and do thin observaunce!'   1045
This maked Emelye have remembraunce

1019 **sustren** sisters   1021 **softe** gently   1024 **nolde no raunsoun** did not
want any ransom   1027 **laurer** laurel   1029 **Terme of his lif** for the rest of
his life   1030 **tour** tower   1032 **quite** release   1033 **This** thus
1034 **fil ones** befell one day   **morwe** morning   1035 **sene** behold
1038 For her complexion vied with the colour of the rose
1039 **noot** (= *ne woot*) do not know   **finer** purer, more radiant
1040 **wone** custom   1041 **dight** dressed   1042 **slogardye** slothfulness
1043 **priketh** stimulates   **gentil** noble   1044 **sterte** start
1045 **do thin observaunce** pay tribute to the occasion

To doon honour to May, and for to rise.
Yclothed was she fressh for to devise;
Hir yelow heer was broided in a tresse
1050   Bihinde hir bak, a yerde long, I gesse.
And in the gardin, at the sonne-upriste,
She walketh up and doun, and as hir liste
She gadreth floures, party white and rede,
To make a subtil gerland for hir hede,
1055   And as an aungel hevenisshly she song.
        The grete tour, that was so thikke and strong,
Which of the castel was the chief dongeoun,
Theras the knightes weren in prisoun
Of which I tolde yow and tellen shal,
1060   Was evene joinant to the gardin wal
Theras this Emelye hadde hir pleyinge.
Bright was the sonne and cleer that morweninge,
And Palamon, this woful prisoner,
As was his wone, by leve of his gailer,
1065   Was risen and romed in a chambre an heigh,
In which he al the noble citee seigh,
And eek the gardin, ful of braunches grene,
Theras this fresshe Emelye the shene
Was in hir walk, and romed up and doun.
1070   This sorweful prisoner, this Palamoun,
Gooth in the chambre roming to and fro
And to himself compleining of his wo;
That he was born ful ofte he seide 'allas!'
And so bifel, by aventure or cas,

1048 She was clothed (so that she was) beautiful to look upon
1049 **broided in a tresse** braided in a plait   1050 **yerde** yard
1051 **sonne-upriste** sunrise   1052 **as hir liste** as it pleased her
1053 **party** parti-coloured   1054 **subtil** intricate   1055 **hevenisshly** in a
heavenly manner   1057 **dongeoun** keep-tower (n.)   1058 **Theras** where
1060 **evene joinant** immediately adjoining   1061 **pleyinge** amusement
1064 **leve** permission   1065 **an heigh** up above   1066 **seigh** saw
1074 **by aventure or cas** by chance or accident

That thurgh a window, thikke of many a barre   1075
Of iren greet and square as any sparre,
He caste his eye upon Emelya,
And therwithal he bleinte and cride 'A!'
As thogh he stongen were unto the herte.
And with that cry Arcite anoon up sterte   1080
And seide, 'Cosin min, what eileth thee,
That art so pale and deedly on to see?
Why cridestow? Who hath the doon offence?
For Goddes love, take al in pacience
Oure prisoun, for it may noon oother be!   1085
Fortune hath yeven us this adversitee.
Som wikke aspect or disposicioun
Of Saturne, by som constellacioun,
Hath yeven us this, althogh we hadde it sworn;
So stood the hevene whan that we were born.   1090
We mote endure; this is the short and plain.'
    This Palamon answerde and seide again:
'Cosin, for sothe, of this opinioun
Thou hast a vein imaginacioun.
This prisoun caused me nat for to crye,   1095
But I was hurt right now, thurghout min eye
Into min herte, that wol my bane be.
The fairnesse of that lady that I se
Yond in the gardin romen to and fro
Is cause of al my crynge and my wo.   1100

1075 **thikke of** thickly set with   1078 **bleinte** blenched, winced
1079 **stongen** stung   1080 **up sterte** leapt up   1081 **eileth** ails
1082 **deedly** death-like   1083 **cridestow** did you cry out
hath the doon offence has harmed you   1087 **aspect** the relative position of
one planet or sign to another at a particular time
1088 **constellacioun** planetary conjunction
1089 **althogh we hadde it sworn** even if we had sworn the contrary
1091 **mote** must   1092 **again** in answer   1094 **vein imaginacioun** deluded
assumption   1096 **thurghout** through   1097 **my bane be** be the death of
me   1099 **Yond** over there

I noot wher she be womman or goddesse,
But Venus is it soothly, as I gesse.'
And therwithal on knees doun he fil
And seide, 'Venus, if it be thy wil
1105   Yow in this gardin thus to transfigure
Bifore me, sorweful wrecched creature,
Out of this prisoun help that we may scape.
And if so be my destinee be shape
By eterne word to dien in prisoun,
1110   Of oure linage have som compassioun,
That is so lowe ybroght by tyrannye.'
And with that word Arcite gan espye
Wheras this lady romed to and fro,
And with that sighte hir beautee hurte him so,
1115   That if that Palamon was wounded soore,
Arcite is hurt as muche as he or moore.
And with a sigh he seide pitously:
'The fresshe beautee sleeth me sodeinly
Of hire that rometh in the yonder place,
1120   And but I have hir mercy and hir grace,
That I may seen hire at the leeste weye,
I nam but deed; ther is namoore to seye.'
This Palamon, whan he tho wordes herde,
Despitously he loked, and answerde:
1125   'Wher seystow this in ernest, or in pley?'
'Nay,' quod Arcite, 'in ernest, by my fey!
God help me so, me list ful ivele pleye.'
This Palamon gan knitte his browes tweye.

1101 **noot** (= *ne woot*) **wher** do not know whether   1103 **fil** fell
1108 **be shape** is determined   1110 **linage** lineage, family
1112 **gan espye** caught sight of   1115 **soore** severely
1117 **pitously** pitifully   1119 **yonder** over there   1120 **but** unless
1121 **at the leeste weye** at least   1122 **I nam but deed** I am as good as dead
1123 **tho** those   1124 **Despitously** angrily
1125 **Wher seystow** (= *seyest thow*) do you say this
1127 **me list ful ivele pleye** I have no inclination to joke

'It nere to thee', quod he, 'no greet honour
For to be fals, ne for to be traitour   1130
To me, that am thy cosin and thy brother
Ysworn ful depe, and ech of us til oother,
That nevere, for to dien in the peine,
Til that the deeth departe shal us tweine,
Neither of us in love to hindre oother,   1135
Ne in noon other caas, my leeve brother,
But that thow sholdest trewely forthre me
In every caas, as I shal forthre thee.
This was thin ooth, and min also, certein;
I woot right wel thou darst it nat withseyn.   1140
Thus artow of my counseil, out of doute.
And now thow woldest falsly been aboute
To love my lady, whom I love and serve
And evere shal, til that min herte sterve.
Now certes, false Arcite, thow shalt nat so!   1145
I loved hire first, and tolde thee my wo
As to my counseil and my brother sworn,
To forthre me, as I have told biforn.
For which thou art ybounden as a knight
To helpe me, if it lay in thy might,   1150
Or elles artow fals, I dar wel seyn!'
     This Arcite ful proudly spak agein:
'Thou shalt', quod he, 'be rather fals than I.
And thou art fals, I telle thee outrely;
For *par amour* I loved hire first er thow.   1155
What wiltow seyn? Thow wistest nat yet now

1129 **It nere to thee ... no greet honour** it would not be very honourable for
you   1132 **til** to   1133 **for to dien in the peine** even if we were tortured to
death   1134 **departe** separate   1136 **in noon other caas** in any other
situation **leeve** dear   1137 **forthre** assist   1140 **withseyn** gainsay
1141 **of my counseil** my confidant   1142 **been aboute** be intent on
1144 **sterve** dies   1147 **counseil** counsellor   1150 **might** power
1152 **agein** in answer   1154 **outrely** plainly   1155 *par amour* as a lover
1156 **wistest nat** did not know

Wheither she be a womman or goddesse!
Thin is affeccioun of holinesse,
And min is love as to a creature,
1160 For which I tolde thee min aventure,
As to my cosin and my brother sworn.
I pose that thow lovedest hire biforn:
Wostow nat wel the olde clerkes sawe,
That "who shal yeve a lovere any lawe?"
1165 Love is a gretter lawe, by my pan,
Than may be yeve to any erthely man.
And therfore positif lawe and swich decree
Is broke al day for love, in ech degree.
A man moot nedes love, maugree his heed;
1170 He may nat fleen it thogh he sholde be deed,
Al be she maide, widwe, or ellis wif.
And eek it is nat likly al thy lif
To stonden in hir grace; namoore shal I.
For wel thow woost thyselven, verraily,
1175 That thow and I be dampned to prisoun
Perpetuelly; us gaineth no raunsoun.
We strive as dide the houndes for the boon:
They foghte al day, and yet hir part was noon.
Ther cam a kite, whil that they were so wrothe,
1180 And bar awey the boon bitwixe hem bothe.
And therfore, at the kinges court, my brother,
Ech man for himself; ther is noon oother.

1158 **affeccioun of holinesse** religious devotion   1160 **min aventure** what
happened to me   1162 **pose** put the case   1163 Do you not know well the
old saying of learned men   1165 **pan** head   1166 **yeve** given
1167 **positif lawe** the law specific to an individual society, as distinguished
from the 'natural law' which governs human kind as a whole
1168 **al day** all the time   1169 **moot nedes** must of necessity
maugree his heed in spite of himself   1171 **Al be she** whether she is
1174 **verraily** truly   1175 **dampned** condemned
1176 **us gaineth no raunsoun** no ransom is of any use to us
1178 **noon** nothing (*lit*. none)   1179 **wrothe** angry
1182 **noon oother** nothing else for it

Love if thee list; for I love, and ay shal.
And soothly, leve brother, this is al:
Here in this prisoun moote we endure,   1185
And everich of us take his aventure.'
    Greet was the strif and long bitwixe hem
        tweye,
If that I hadde leiser for to seye.
But to th'effect: it happed on a day,
To telle it yow as shortly as I may,   1190
A worthy duc that highte Perotheus,
That felawe was unto duc Theseus
Sin thilke day that they were children lite,
Was come to Atthenes, his felawe to visite,
And for to pleye as he was wont to do;   1195
For in this world he loved no man so,
And he loved him as tendrely agein.
So wel they loved, as olde bookes seyn,
That whan that oon was deed, soothly to telle,
His felawe wente and soghte him doun in helle.   1200
But of that storye list me nat to write.
Duc Perotheus loved wel Arcite,
And hadde him knowe at Thebes yeer by yere,
And finally, at requeste and prayere
Of Perotheus, withoute any raunsoun,   1205
Duc Theseus him leet out of prisoun,
Frely to goon wher that him liste overal,
In swich a gise as I yow tellen shal.
    This was the forward, pleinly for t'endite,
Bitwixen Theseus and him Arcite: 1210

1183 **if thee list** if it pleases you **ay** always   1185 **moote** must
1186 **everich** each **take his aventure** take his chance
1188 **leiser for to seye** leisure to relate (it)   1189 **to th'effect** to get to the
point   1191 **Perotheus** Pirithous   1193 **Sin thilke day** since the time
1195 **pleye** amuse himself **wont** accustomed   1199 **that oon** one
1201 **list me nat to write** I do not want to write   1203 **yeer by yere** for years
on end   1206 **leet** let   1207 **wher that him liste overal** anywhere he
pleased   1208 **gise** manner   1209 **forward** agreement **endite** write

That if so were that Arcite were yfounde,
Evere in his lif, by day or night, o stounde,
In any contree of this Theseus,
And he were caught, it was acorded thus:
1215 That with a swerd he sholde lese his heed.
Ther nas noon other remedye ne reed;
But takth his leve, and homward he him spedde.
Lat him be war; his nekke lith to wedde.
    How greet a sorwe suffreth now Arcite!
1220 The deeth he feeleth thurgh his herte smite.
He wepeth, waileth, cryeth pitously;
To sleen himself he waiteth prively.
He seide, 'Allas that day that I was born!
Now is my prisoun worse than biforn;
1225 Now is me shape eternally to dwelle,
Noght in purgatorye, but in helle.
Allas that evere knew I Perotheus!
For elles hadde I dwelled with Theseus,
Yfetered in his prisoun everemo;
1230 Thanne hadde I been in blisse and nat in wo.
Oonly the sight of hire whom that I serve,
Thogh that I nevere hir grace may deserve,
Wolde have suffised right inogh for me.
O deere cosin Palamon,' quod he,
1235 'Thin is the victorye of this aventure!
Ful blisfully in prisoun maystow dure –
In prisoun? nay, certes, but in paradis.
Wel hath Fortune yturned thee the dis,
That hast the sight of hire, and I th'absence.
1240 For possible is, sin thow hast hir presence,

1212 **o stounde** for an instant   1214 **acorded** agreed   1215 **lese** lose
1216 **reed** course of action   1217 **him spedde** (= *spedede*) hastened
1218 **lith to wedde** is a pledge (for his behaviour)   1222 **sleen** kill
waiteth prively secretly looks for a chance   1225 **is me shape** I am destined
1228 **elles** otherwise   1229 **Yfetered** fettered   1230 **hadde I been** I would
have been   1235 **aventure** chance event   1236 **dure** remain
1238 **yturned thee the dis** thrown the dice for you   1240 **sin** since

And art a knight, a worthy and an able,
That by som caas, sin Fortune is chaungeable,
Thow mayst to thy desir som time atteine.
But I, that am exiled and bareine
Of alle grace, and in so greet despeir   1245
That ther nis erthe, water, fir, ne eir,
Ne creature that of hem maked is,
That may me helpe or doon confort in this,
Wel oghte I sterve in wanhope and distresse.
Farewel, my lif, my lust, and my gladnesse!   1250
    Allas, why pleinen folk so in comune
On purveiaunce of God or on Fortune,
That yeveth hem ful ofte in many a gise
Wel bettre than they kan hemself devise?
Som man desireth for to have richesse,   1255
That cause is of his moerdre, or greet siknesse.
And som man wolde out of his prisoun fain,
That in his hous is of his meinee slain.
Infinite harmes been in this matere;
We witen nat what thing we prayen heere.   1260
We fare as he that dronke is as a mous:
A dronke man woot wel he hath an hous,
But he noot which the righte wey is thider,
And to a dronke man the wey is slider.
And certes in this world so faren we: 1265
We seken fast after felicitee,
But we goon wrong ful often, trewely.
Thus may we seyen alle, and nameliche I,

1242 **caas** chance   1244 **bareine** destitute   1246 **nis** (= *ne is*) is neither
1249 **sterve** to die **wanhope** despair   1250 **lust** source of joy
1251–2 **pleinen ... On** complain about **in comune** in general
1253 **gise** fashion   1254 **devise** conceive   1256 **moerdre** murder
1257 **wolde ... fain** would gladly (be)   1258 **of his meinee** by his
household   1260 **witen** know   1261 **fare** behave
1263 **noot** (= *ne woot*) does not know   1264 **slider** slippery
1266 **seken fast after** search earnestly for   1268 **nameliche** especially

That wende and hadde a greet opinioun
1270   That if I mighte escapen from prisoun,
Than hadde I been in joye and parfit heele,
Ther now I am exiled fro my wele,
Sin that I may nat seen yow, Emelye.
I nam but deed; ther nis no remedye.'
1275   Upon that oother side Palamon,
Whan that he wiste Arcite was agon,
Swich sorwe he maketh that the grete tour
Resouneth of his yowling and clamour.
The pure fettres on his shines grete
1280   Were of his bittre salte teres wete.
'Allas,' quod he, 'Arcita, cosin min,
Of al oure strif, God woot, the fruit is thin!
Thou walkest now in Thebes at thy large,
And of my wo thou yevest litel charge.
1285   Thou mayst, sin thou hast wisdom and manhede,
Assemblen alle the folk of oure kinrede,
And make a werre so sharp in this citee
That by som aventure, or som tretee,
Thou mayst have hire to lady and to wif
1290   For whom that I moste nedes lese my lif.
For, as by wey of possibilitee,
Sith thou art at thy large, of prisoun free,
And art a lord, greet is thin avauntage,
Moore than is min, that sterve here in a cage.
1295   For I moot wepe and waille whil I live,
With al the wo that prisoun may me yeve,
And eek with peine that love me yeveth also,
That doubleth al my torment and my wo.'

1269 **wende** imagined   1271 **parfit heele** perfect happiness
1272 **Ther** whereas   1274 **I nam but deed** I am as good as dead
1275 **that oother** the other   1278 **Resouneth of** echoes with
yowling wailing   1279 **pure fettres** very fetters   1283 **at thy large** at liberty
1284 And you care little about my sorrow   1285 **manhede** valour
1287 **werre** war   1288 **aventure** chance event **tretee** negotiation
1289 **to** as   1290 **moste nedes lese my lif** must inevitably lose my life
1294 **sterve** die   1295 **moot** must

Therwith the fir of jalousye up sterte
Withinne his brest, and hente him by the herte,   1300
So woodly that he lik was to biholde
The box-tree, or the asshen dede and colde.
　　Thanne seide he, 'O cruel goddes, that governe
This world with binding of youre word eterne,
And writen in the table of atthamaunt   1305
Youre parlement and youre eterne graunt,
What is mankinde moore unto yow holde
Than is the sheep that rowketh in the folde?
For slain is man right as another beest,
And dwelleth eek in prisoun and areest,   1310
And hath siknesse and greet adversitee,
And ofte times giltelees, pardee.
What governaunce is in this prescience
That giltelees tormenteth innocence?
And yet encreseth this al my penaunce: 1315
That man is bounden to his observaunce,
For Goddes sake, to letten of his wille,
Theras a beest may al his lust fulfille.
And whan a beest is deed he hath no peine,
But man after his deeth moot wepe and pleine,   1320
Though in this world he have care and wo;
Withouten doute, it may stonden so.
The answere of this lete I to divinis;
But wel I woot that in this world greet pine is.
Allas, I se a serpent or a theef,   1325
That many a trewe man hath doon mescheef,

1299 **up sterte** sprang up   1300 **hente** (= *hentede*) seized   1301–2 So
furiously that to look at he was like the box-tree, or like dead, cold ashes
1305 **atthamaunt** adamant (a mythical rock of great hardness)
1306 **parlement** decision **graunt** decree   1307 In what way is mankind
more obligated to you   1308 **rowketh** huddles, cowers
1310 **areest** confinement   1313 What (kind of) government exists in this
(divine) foresight   1315 **penaunce** suffering, distress
1316 **observaunce** duty   1317 **letten of** refrain from
1318 **Theras** whereas **lust** pleasure   1320 **pleine** lament
1323 **lete I to divinis** I leave to theologians   1326 Who has done harm to
many an honest man

Goon at his large, and wher him list may turne,
But I moot been in prisoun thurgh Saturne,
And eek thurgh Juno, jalous and eek wood,
1330   That hath destroyed wel ny al the blood
Of Thebes, with his waste walles wide.
And Venus sleeth me on that oother side,
For jalousye and feere of him Arcite.'
        Now wol I stinte of Palamon a lite,
1335   And lete him in his prisoun stille dwelle,
And of Arcita forth I wol yow telle.

        The somer passeth, and the nightes longe
Encresen double wise the peines stronge,
Bothe of the lovere and the prisoner.
1340   I noot which hath the wofuller mister:
For, shortly for to seyn, this Palamoun
Perpetuelly is dampned to prisoun,
In cheines and in fettres to been deed;
And Arcite is exiled, upon his heed,
1345   For everemo as out of that contree,
Ne neveremo he shal his lady see.
        Yow loveris axe I now this questioun:
Who hath the worse, Arcite or Palamoun?
That oon may seen his lady day by day,
1350   But in prisoun moot he dwelle alway;
That oother wher him list may ride or go,
But seen his lady shal he neveremo.
Now demeth as yow liste, ye that kan,
For I wol telle forth as I bigan.

1328 **thurgh** through the agency of   1329 **eek wood** also furious
1330 **wel ny** very nearly   1331 **waste** ruined   1332 **sleeth** slays
1334 **stinte of** cease speaking about   1335 **stille** quietly
1340 **mister** plight   1343 **to been deed** until death
1344 **upon his heed** on pain of death   1347 **axe** ask   1349 **That oon** the
one   1350 **moot** must   1353 **demeth as yow liste** judge as it pleases you

[Part Two]

Whan that Arcite to Thebes comen was,	1355
Ful ofte a day he swelte and seide 'allas!',	
For seen his lady shal he neveremo.	
And shortly to concluden al his wo,	
So muchel sorwe had nevere creature	
That is or shal whil that the world may dure.	1360
His sleep, his mete, his drinke, is him biraft,	
That lene he wex and drye as is a shaft;	
Hise eyen holwe and grisly to biholde,	
His hewe falow and pale as asshen colde.	
And solitarye he was and evere allone,	1365
And waillinge al the night, makinge his mone.	
And if he herde song or instrument,	
Thanne wolde he wepe; he mighte nat be stent.	
So feble eek were his spiritz, and so lowe,	
And chaunged so that no man koude knowe	1370
His speche, nor his vois, though men it herde.	
And in his gere for al the world he ferde	
Nat oonly lik the loveris maladye	
Of hereos, but rather lik manye,	
Engendred of humour malencolik	1375
Biforen, in his celle fantastik.	
And shortly, turned was al up-so-doun	
Bothe habit and eek disposicioun	
Of him, this woful lovere, daun Arcite;	
What sholde I al day of his wo endite?	1380

1356 **Ful ofte a day** many times in a day **swelte** (= *sweltede*) fainted
1358 **concluden** sum up   1360 **shal** shall be **dure** last   1362 **That** so that
wex grew **shaft** shaft (of an arrow or spear)   1364 **falow** sallow
1366 **mone** lamentation   1368 **stent** stopped   1372 **gere** behaviour
ferde acted   1374 **hereos** lovesickness (n.) **manye** mania
1375 **humour malencolik** melancholic humour (see n. to GP 333)
1376 **Biforen** in front **celle fantastik** part of the brain controlling ideas and
the imagination   1377 **up-so-doun** upside-down   1378 **habit** bodily
condition   1379 **daun** sir   1380 **What** why **endite** write

Whan he endured hadde a yeer or two
This cruel torment and this peine and wo,
At Thebes in his contree, as I seide,
Upon a night, in sleep as he him leide,
1385   Him thoughte how that the winged god Mercurye
Biforn him stood and bad him to be murye.
His slepy yerde in honde he bar uprighte;
An hat he wered upon his heres brighte.
Arrayed was this god, as he took keep,
1390   As he was whan that Argus took his sleep;
And seide him thus: 'To Atthenes shaltow wende,
Ther is thee shapen of thy wo an ende.'
And with that word Arcite wook and sterte.
'Now trewely, how sore that me smerte,'
1395   Quod he, 'to Atthenes right now wol I fare.
Ne for the drede of deeth shal I nat spare
To see my lady that I love and serve;
In hir presence I recche nat to sterve.'
And with that word he caughte a greet mirour,
1400   And saugh that chaunged was al his colour,
And saugh his visage al in another kinde.
And right anoon it ran him in his minde
That, sith his face was so disfigured
Of maladye the which he hadde endured,
1405   He mighte wel, if that he bar him lowe,
Live in Atthenes everemoore unknowe,
And seen his lady wel ny day by day.
And right anoon he chaunged his array,
And cladde him as a povre laborer;
1410   And al allone, save oonly a squier

1387 **slepy yerde** sleep-inducing staff (n.)   1388 **wered** wore
1389 **as he took keep** as he (Arcite) took note   1391 **wende** go
1392 **thee shapen** ordained for you
1394 **how sore that me smerte** however severely it pains me   1395 **fare** go
1398 **I recche nat to sterve** I do not care if I die   1403 **sith** since
1404 **Of** by   1405 **bar him lowe** lived in a humble fashion
1407 **wel ny** almost   1409 **cladde him** clothed himself

That knew his privetee and al his cas,
Which was disgised povrely as he was,
To Atthenes is he goon the nexte way.
And to the court he wente upon a day,
And at the gate he profreth his servise,   1415
To drugge and drawe, whatso men wol devise.
And shortly of this matere for to seyn,
He fil in office with a chamberlein,
The which that dwelling was with Emelye,
For he was wis and koude soone espye   1420
Of every servant which that serveth here.
Wel koude he hewen wode and water bere,
For he was yong and mighty for the nones,
And therto he was long and big of bones
To doon that any wight kan him devise.   1425
A yeer or two he was in this servise,
Page of the chambre of Emelye the brighte,
And Philostrate he seide that he highte.
But half so wel biloved a man as he
Ne was ther nevere in court of his degree.   1430
He was so gentil of condicioun
That thurghout al the court was his renoun.
They seiden that it were a charitee
That Theseus wolde enhauncen his degree,
And putten him in worshipful servise,   1435
Theras he mighte his vertu excercise.
And thus withinne a while his name is spronge,
Bothe of his dedes and his goode tonge,
That Theseus hath taken him so ner
That of his chambre he made him a squier,   1440

1411 **privetee** private affairs   1413 **nexte way** quickest way
1415 **profreth** offers   1416 **drugge and drawe** labour and draw water
devise direct   1418 **fil in office** got employment   1420–21 **espye Of** find
out about   1424 **long** tall **big** strong   1430 **degree** rank
1431 **gentil** noble **condicioun** character   1433 **were** would be
1435 **worshipful** honourable   1436 **his vertu excercise** put his ability to
good use   1437 **is spronge** has spread abroad
1439 **taken him so ner** placed him in a position of such intimacy

And gaf him gold to maintene his degree.
And eek men broghte him out of his contree
Fro yeer to yeer ful prively his rente.
But honestly and sleighly he it spente,
1445   That no man wondred how that he it hadde.
And thre yeer in this wise his lif he ladde,
And bar him so in pees and eek in werre,
Ther was no man that Theseus hath derre.
And in this blisse lete I now Arcite,
1450   And speke I wol of Palamon a lite.

      In derknesse and horrible and strong prisoun
This seven yeer hath seten Palamoun
Forpined, what for wo and for distresse.
Who feeleth double soor and hevinesse
1455   But Palamon, that love destreineth so
That wood out of his wit he gooth for wo?
And eek therto he is a prisoner
Perpetuelly, nat oonly for a yer.
Who koude ryme in Englissh proprely
1460   His martyrdom? For sothe, it am noght I!
Therfore I passe as lightly as I may.

      It fil that in the seventhe yeer, of May
The thridde night (as olde bokes seyn,
That al this storye tellen moore plein),
1465   Were it by aventure or destinee –
As whan a thing is shapen it shal be –
That soone after the midnight, Palamoun
By helping of a freend brak his prisoun,
And fleeth the citee faste as he may go.
1470   For he had yeve his gailler drinke so,
Of a clarree maad of a certein win,
With nercotikes and opie of Thebes fin,

1443 **rente** income   1444 **honestly** suitably **sleighly** secretly
1447 **bar him** behaved   1448 **hath derre** holds dearer   1452 **seten** sat
1453 **Forpined** wasted away   1455 **destreineth** torments   1456 **wood** mad
1461 **passe** proceed   1462 **fil** happened   1465 **aventure** chance
1466 **shapen** destined   1468 **brak** broke out of   1471 **clarree** spiced and
sweetened wine   1472 **nercotikes** narcotics **opie** opium

That al that night, thogh that men wolde him
          shake,
The gailler sleep; he mighte noght awake.
And thus he fleeth as faste as evere he may.   1475
The night was short and faste by the day,
That nedes-cost he moste himselven hide.
And til a grove faste therbiside
With dreedful foot thanne stalketh Palamoun.
For, shortly, this was his opinioun,   1480
That in that grove he wolde him hide al day,
And in the night thanne wolde he take his way
To Thebesward, his freendes for to preye
On Theseus to helpe him to werreye.
And shortly, outher he wolde lese his lif,   1485
Or winnen Emelye unto his wif.
This is th'effect and his entente plein.
     Now wol I turne to Arcite agein,
That litel wiste how neigh that was his care,
Til that Fortune had broght him in the snare.   1490
     The bisy larke, messager of day,
Salueth in hir song the morwe gray,
And firy Phebus riseth up so brighte
That al the orient laugheth of the lighte,
And with his stremes dryeth in the greves   1495
The silver dropes hanginge on the leves.
And Arcita, that in the court royal
With Theseus is squier principal,
Is risen and looketh on the murye day,
And for to doon his observaunce to May,   1500

1473 **wolde** were to   1474 **sleep** slept   1476 **faste by** close at hand
1477 **nedes-cost** of necessity   **moste** had to   1479 **dreedful** fearful
stalketh steals   1483 **To Thebesward** towards Thebes   1484 **werreye** make
war   1485 **outher** either   1487 **entente plein** whole purpose
1489 **neigh** near   **care** misfortune   1493 **Phebus** Phoebus, the sun
1494 **orient** east   1495 **greves** bushes   1499 **murye** beautiful
1500 **doon his observaunce to** pay tribute to

Remembringe on the point of his desir,
He on a courser, startlinge as the fir,
Is riden into the feeldes him to pleye,
Out of the court, were it a mile or tweye;
1505   And to the grove of which that I yow tolde
By aventure his wey he gan to holde,
To maken him a gerland of the greves,
Were it of wodebinde or hawethorn leves.
And loude he song ayein the sonne shene:
1510   'May, with alle thy floures and thy grene,
Welcome be thow, faire fresshe May,
In hope that I som grene gete may.'
And from his courser, with a lusty herte,
Into the grove ful hastily he sterte,
1515   And in a path he rometh up and doun,
Theras by aventure this Palamoun
Was in a bussh, that no man mighte him se,
For soore afered of his deeth was he.
Nothing knew he that it was Arcite;
1520   God woot he wolde have trowed it ful lite!
But sooth is seid, go sithen many yeres,
That 'feeld hath eyen and the wode hath eres'.
It is ful fair a man to bere him evene,
For al day meeten men at unset stevene.
1525   Ful litel woot Arcite of his felawe,
That was so neigh to herknen al his sawe,
For in the bussh he sitteth now ful stille.
    Whan that Arcite hadde romed al his fille,

1501 **point** object   1502 **startlinge** prancing   1506 **By aventure** by chance
gan to holde held   1507 **gerland** garland   1508 **wodebinde** woodbine,
honeysuckle   1509 **ayein the sonne** in the sun
1512 **I som grene gete may** I may get some greenery   1513 **lusty** cheerful
1514 **sterte** plunged   1519 **Nothing** Not at all   1520 **trowed** believed
lite little   1521 **go sithen many yeres** for many a year   1523 It is a good
thing for a man to conduct himself with equanimity
1524 **unset stevene** unarranged rendezvous   1526 **sawe** speech

And songen al the roundel lustily,
Into a studye he fil sodeinly,   1530
As doon thise loveres in hir queinte geres –
Now in the croppe, now doun in the breres,
Now up, now doun, as boket in a welle;
Right as the Friday, soothly for to telle:
Now it shineth, now it reineth faste.   1535
Right so kan gery Venus overcaste
The hertes of hir folk; right as hir day
Is gerful, right so chaungeth she array.
Selde is the Friday al the wike ilike.
   Whan that Arcite hadde songe, he gan to sike,   1540
And sette him doun withouten any moore.
'Allas', quod he, 'that day that I was bore!
How longe, Juno, thurgh thy crueltee
Woltow werreyen Thebes the citee?
Allas, ybroght is to confusioun   1545
The blood royal of Cadme and Amphioun –
Of Cadmus, which that was the firste man
That Thebes bulte, or first the toun bigan,
And of the citee first was crowned king.
Of his linage am I, and his ofspring,   1550
By verray ligne as of the stok royal.
And now I am so caitif and so thral
That he that is my mortal enemy,
I serve him as his squier povrely.
And yet doth Juno me wel moore shame,   1555
For I dar noght biknowe min owene name;

1529 **roundel** rondeau (n.) **lustily** gaily   1530 **studye** reverie
1531 **hir queinte geres** their strange moods   1532 **croppe** tree-top
breres briars   1533 **boket** bucket   1535 **reineth** rains
1536 **gery** capricious, changeable   1538 **gerful** changeable **array** her state
1539 Friday is seldom like the rest of the week   1540 **sike** sigh
1544 **Woltow** will you **werreyen** make war on   1548 **bulte** built **or** before
1551 **verray ligne** true line of descent **stok** stock   1552 **caitif** enslaved
1556 **biknowe** acknowledge

But theras I was wont to highte Arcite,
Now highte I Philostrate, noght worth a mite.
Allas, thou felle Mars, allas Juno!
1560   Thus hath youre ire oure linage al fordo,
Save oonly me and wrecched Palamoun,
That Theseus martyreth in prisoun.
And over al this, to sleen me outrely,
Love hath his firy dart so brenningly
1565   Ystiked thurgh my trewe careful herte,
That shapen was my deeth erst than my sherte.
Ye sleen me with youre eyen, Emelye!
Ye been the cause wherfore that I die.
Of al the remenant of min oother care
1570   Ne sette I noght the mountaunce of a tare,
So that I koude doon aught to youre plesaunce.'
And with that word he fil doun in a traunce
A longe time, and after he up sterte.
     This Palamoun, that thoughte that thurgh his herte
1575   He felte a cold swerd sodeinliche glide,
For ire he quook; no lenger wolde he bide.
And whan that he had herd Arcites tale,
As he were wood, with face deed and pale,
He sterte him up out of the buskes thikke,
1580   And seide, 'Arcite, false traitour wikke!
Now artow hent, that lovest my lady so,
For whom that I have al this peine and wo,
And art my blood and to my counseil sworn,
As I ful ofte have told thee herbiforn,

1559 **felle** cruel   1560 **fordo** destroyed   1562 **martyreth** torments
1563 **outrely** utterly   1564 **brenningly** burningly   1565 **Ystiked** thrust
careful sorrowful   1566 **shapen** determined   **erst than my sherte** before my
shirt (i.e. before I was born)   1568 **wherfore** for which
1570 **mountaunce of a tare** value of a tare (i.e. not a jot)
1571 **So that** provided that   **to youre plesaunce** to please you
1573 **up sterte** sprang up   1576 **quook** trembled   1577 **tale** words
1578 **As he were wood** as if he were mad   1579 **buskes** bushes
1580 **wikke** wicked   1581 **hent** caught   1583 **to my counseil sworn** sworn
to be my supporter

And hast bijaped here duc Theseus,   1585
And falsly chaunged hast thy name thus!
I wol be deed, or elles thow shalt die;
Thow shalt nat love my lady Emelye,
But I wol love hire oonly and namo.
For I am Palamon, thy mortal foo,   1590
And thogh that I no wepne have in this place,
But out of prisoun am astert by grace,
I drede noght that outher thou shalt die,
Or thou ne shalt noght loven Emelye.
Chees which thow wolt, or thow shalt noght   1595
        asterte!'
    This Arcite, with ful despitous herte,
Whan he him knew and hadde his tale herd,
As fiers as leoun pulled out his swerd
And seide thus: 'By God that sit above,
Nere it that thow art sik and wood for love,   1600
And eek that thow no wepne hast in this place,
Thow sholdest nevere out of this grove pace
That thow ne sholdest dien of my hond.
For I diffye the seuretee and the bond
Which that thow seyst that I have maad to thee.   1605
What, verray fool, think wel that love is free,
And I wol love hire, maugree al thy might!
But forasmuche thow art a worthy knight,
And wilnest to darreine hire by bataille,
Have here my trouthe: tomorowe I wol nat   1610
        faille,
Withoute witing of any oother wight,
That here I wol be founden as a knight,

1585 **bijaped** tricked   1589 **namo** no one else   1591 **wepne** weapon
1592 **am astert** have escaped **by grace** by good fortune   1593 **drede** doubt
1595 **Chees** choose **asterte** escape   1596 **despitous** scornful
1599 **sit** (= *sitteth*) sits   1600 **Nere it** were it not   1603 **of** by
1604 **diffye** reject **seuretee** pledge   1606 **verray fool** fool that you are
1607 **maugree al thy might** in spite of everything you can do
1609 **wilnest to darreine hire** wish to lay claim to her   1610 **trouthe** word
1611 **witing** knowledge **wight** person

And bringen harneis right inogh for thee,
And chees the beste, and leve the worste for me.

1615 And mete and drinke this night wol I bringe,
Inogh for thee, and clothes for thy beddinge.
And if so be that thow my lady winne
And slee me in this wode ther I am inne,
Thow mayst wel have thy lady, as for me.'

1620   This Palamon answerde, 'I graunte it thee.'
And thus they been departed til amorwe,
Whan ech of hem had leid his feith to borwe.
     O Cupide, out of alle charitee!
O regne that wolt no felawe have with thee!

1625 Ful sooth is seid, that love ne lordshipe
Wol noght, his thankes, have no felaweshipe;
Wel finden that Arcite and Palamoun.
Arcite is riden anon unto the toun;
And on the morwe, er it were dayes light,

1630 Ful prively two harneis hath he dight,
Bothe suffisaunt and mete to darreine
The bataille in the feeld bitwix hem tweine.
And on his hors, allone as he was born,
He caryeth al this harneis him biforn.

1635 And in the grove, at time and place yset,
This Arcite and this Palamon been met.
     To chaungen gan the colour in hir face,
Right as the hunters in the regne of Trace,
That stondeth at the gappe with a spere,

1640 Whan hunted is the leoun or the bere,
And hereth him come russhing in the greves,
And breketh bothe bowes and the leves,

1613 **harneis** armour   1615 **mete** food   1618 **slee** slay **ther** where
1622 **leid his feith to borwe** pledged his word
1623 **out of alle charitee** lacking all brotherly love   1624 **regne** power
1626 **his thankes** willingly   1630 **dight** prepared
1631–2 **mete to darreine The bataille** fit to engage in combat
1635 **yset** arranged   1638 **regne of Trace** kingdom of Thrace
1639 **stondeth** stand **gappe** gap, opening in the forest   1641 **greves** thicket

And thinketh, 'Here comth my mortal enemy!
Withoute faille he moot be deed, or I;
For outher I moot sleen him at the gappe,   1645
Or he moot sle me, if that me mishappe.'
So ferden they in chaunging of hir hewe.

   As fer as everich of hem oother knewe,
Ther nas no 'good day' ne no saluinge,
But streight, withouten word or rehersinge,   1650
Everich of hem heelp for to armen other,
As frendly as he were his owene brother;
And after that with sharpe speres stronge
They foinen ech at other, wonder longe.
Thou mightest wene that this Palamoun   1655
In his fighting were a wood leoun,
And as a cruel tigre was Arcite.
As wilde bores gonnen they to smite,
That frothen whit as foom for ire wood;
Up to the anclee foghte they in hir blood.   1660
And in this wise I lete hem fighting dwelle,
And forth I wol of Theseus yow telle.

   The destinee, ministre general,
That executeth in the world overal
The purveiaunce that God hath sein biforn,   1665
So strong it is, that thogh the world had sworn
The contrarye of a thing by ye or nay,
Yet somtime it shal fallen on a day
That falleth nat eft withinne a thousand yeer.
For certeinly, oure appetites heer,   1670
Be it of werre, or pees, or hate, or love,
Al is this ruled by the sighte above.

1646 **me mishappe** I should meet with misfortune   1647 **ferden** acted
hewe complexion   1648–9 Since they both knew each other, there was no
'Good day' nor salutation   1650 **rehersinge** repetition (of what had been
said before)   1651 **heelp** helped   1654 **foinen** thrust **wonder longe** for an
amazingly long time   1655 **wene** think   1656 **wood** furious
1659 **frothen** foam at the mouth   1660 **anclee** ankle
1661 **lete hem . . . dwelle** leave them to continue   1663–9 see n.
1669 **eft** afterwards   1671 **Be it** whether they are

This mene I now by mighty Theseus,
That for to hunten is so desirus,
1675 And namely at the grete hert in May,
That in his bed ther daweth him no day
That he nis clad and redy for to ride,
With hunte and horn, and houndes him biside.
For in his hunting hath he swich delit
1680 That it is al his joye and appetit
To been himself the grete hertes bane;
For after Mars he serveth now Diane.

  Cleer was the day, as I have told er this,
And Theseus, with alle joye and blis,
1685 With his Ypolita, the faire quene,
And Emelye, clothed al in grene,
On hunting be they riden royally.
And to the grove that stood ful faste by,
In which ther was an hert, as men him tolde,
1690 Duc Theseus the streighte wey hath holde,
And to the launde he rideth him ful right,
For thider was the hert wont have his flight,
And over a brook, and so forth on his weye.
This duc wol han a cours at him or tweye,
1695 With houndes swiche as that him list comaunde.
And whan this duc was come unto the launde,
Under the sonne he loketh, and anon
He was war of Arcite and Palamon,
That foghten breme, as it were boles two.
1700 The brighte swerdes wenten to and fro,
So hidously, that with the leeste strook
It semed as it wolde felle an ook.

1673 **by** concerning   1675 **hert** stag   1676 **daweth** dawns
1678 **hunte** huntsman   1681 **bane** slayer   1682 **Mars** god of war
Diane Diana, goddess of hunting   1683 **er** before   1688 **ful faste by** very
near   1690 **the streighte wey hath holde** has taken the direct route
1691 **launde** clearing   1692 **wont have** accustomed to take
1694 **han a cours at** hunt   1697 **Under the sonne** all around (n.)
1699 **breme** fiercely   **boles** bulls   1702 **ook** oak

But what they were, nothing he ne woot.
This duc his courser with his spores smoot,
And at a stert he was bitwix hem two,   1705
And pulled out a swerd and cried 'Ho!
Namoore, up peine of lesing of youre heed!
By mighty Mars, he shal anon be deed
That smiteth any strook that I may seen.
But telleth me what mister men ye been,   1710
That been so hardy for to fighten here
Withouten juge or oother officere,
As it were in a listes, royally.'
This Palamon answerede hastily
And seide, 'Sire, what nedeth wordes mo?   1715
We have the deeth disserved bothe two.
Two woful wrecches been we, two caitives,
That been encombred of oure owene lives;
And as thow art a rightful lord and juge,
Ne yeve us neither mercy ne refuge;   1720
But slee me first, for seinte charitee!
But slee my felawe eek, as wel as me –
Or slee him first; for thogh thow knowe it lite,
This is thy mortal foo, this is Arcite,
That fro thy lond is banisshed on his heed,   1725
For which he hath deserved to be deed.
For this is he that cam unto thy gate,
And seide that he highte Philostrate.
Thus hath he japed thee ful many a yeer,
And thow hast maked him thy chief squier.   1730
And this is he that loveth Emelye.
For sith the day is come that I shal die,
I make pleinly my confessioun
That I am thilke woful Palamoun

1703 **nothing** not at all   1704 **smoot** struck   1705 **at a stert** at a bound
1706 **Ho** stop   1707 **lesing** loss   1710 **what mister men** what kind of men
1715 **what nedeth** what need is there of   **mo more**   1717 **caitives** captives
1718 **encombred of** burdened by   1720 **refuge** protection
1721 **seinte** holy   1723 **thow knowe it lite** you don't know it
1725 **on his heed** on pain of death   1729 **japed** tricked

1735   That hath thy prisoun broken wikkedly.
        I am thy mortal foo, and it am I
        That loveth so hoote Emelye the brighte,
        That I wol dien present in hir sighte.
        Wherfore I axe deeth and my juwise.
1740   But slee my felawe in the same wise,
        For bothe have we deserved to be slain.'
            This worthy duc answerde anoon again
        And seide, 'This is a short conclusioun!
        Youre owene mouth, by youre confessioun,
1745   Hath dampned yow, and I wol it recorde.
        It nedeth noght to pine yow with the corde!
        Ye shul be deed, by mighty Mars the rede!'
            The queen anoon, for verray wommanhede,
        Gan for to wepe, and so dide Emelye,
1750   And alle the ladies in the compaignye.
        Greet pitee was it, as it thoughte hem alle,
        That evere swich a chaunce sholde falle,
        For gentil men they were, of greet estaat,
        And nothing but for love was this debaat;
1755   And sawe hir blody woundes wide and soore,
        And alle criden, bothe lasse and moore,
        'Have mercy, lord, upon us wommen alle!'
        And on hir bare knees adoun they falle,
        And wolde have kist his feet theras he stood;
1760   Til at the last aslaked was his mood,
        For pitee renneth soone in gentil herte.
        And thogh he first for ire quook and sterte,

1735 **broken** broken out of   1737 **hoote** passionately   1739 **axe** ask
juwise punishment   1743 **conclusioun** decision
1745 **dampned** condemned **recorde** confirm   1746 There is no need to
torture you with a cord   1748 **wommanhede** womanliness
1752 **falle** befall   1753 **gentil** noble   1754 **nothing but for love** only for
love   1756 **bothe lasse and moore** both the greater and the less (i.e. of all
ranks)   1759 **theras** where   1760 **aslaked** grown calm
1761 **renneth soone** is quick to arise   1762 **quook** trembled **sterte** quivered

He hath considered shortly, in a clause,
The trespas of hem bothe, and eek the cause,
And althogh that his ire hir gilt accused,   1765
Yet in his resoun he hem bothe excused,
As thus: he thoghte wel that every man
Wol helpe himself in love if that he kan,
And eek delivere himself out of prisoun;
And eek his herte had compassioun   1770
Of wommen, for they wepen evere in oon;
And in his gentil herte he thoghte anoon,
And softe unto himself he seide, 'Fy
Upon a lord that wol have no mercy,
But be a leoun, bothe in word and dede,   1775
To hem that been in repentaunce and drede
As wel as to a proud despitous man,
That wol maintene that he first bigan.
That lord hath litel of discrecioun
That in swich caas kan no divisioun,   1780
But weyeth pride and humblesse after oon.'
    And shortly, whan his ire is thus agoon,
He gan to loken up with eyen lighte,
And spak thise same wordes al on highte:
'The God of love, a, *benedicitee*!   1785
How mighty and how greet a lord is he!
Agains his might ther gaineth none obstacles.
He may be cleped a god for his miracles,
For he kan maken at his owene gise
Of everich herte as that him list devise.   1790
Lo here, this Arcite and this Palamoun,
That quitly weren out of my prisoun,

1763 **in a clause** briefly   1764 **trespas** offence
1771 **wepen evere in oon** wept constantly   1773 **softe** quietly
1777 **despitous** haughty   1778 **maintene** persist in
1780 **kan no divisioun** recognizes no distinction   1781 **weyeth** weighs
after oon equally   1784 **on highte** aloud   1785 **a** ah   1787 No obstacles
are effective against his power   1788 **cleped** called
1789 **at his owene gise** as he pleases   1790 **as that him list devise** as he is
pleased to direct   1792 **quitly** at liberty

And mighte have lived in Thebes royally,
And witen I am hir mortal enemy,
1795   And that hir deeth lith in my might also,
And yet hath love, maugree hir eyen two,
Broght hem hider bothe for to die!
Now looketh, is nat that an heigh folye?
Who may been a fool but if he love?
1800   Bihoold, for Goddes sake that sit above,
Se how they blede! Be they noght wel arrayed?
Thus hath hir lord, the God of love, ypayed
Hir wages and hir fees for hir servise!
And yet they wenen for to be ful wise
1805   That serven love, for aught that may bifalle.
But this is yet the beste game of alle,
That she for whom they have this jolitee
Kan hem therfore as muche thank as me!
She woot namoore of al this hoote fare,
1810   By God, than woot a cokkow or an hare!
But al moot been assayed, hoot and coold;
A man moot been a fool, or yong or oold.
I woot it by myself, ful yore agoon,
For in my time a servant was I oon.
1815   And therfore, sin I knowe of loves peine,
And woot how sore it kan a man distreine,
As he that hath been caught ofte in his laas,
I yow foryeve al hoolly this trespaas,
At requeste of the queene that kneleth here,
1820   And eek of Emelye, my suster dere.

1794 **witen** know   1795 **lith** lies   1796 **maugree hir eyen two** in spite of
themselves   1799 **but if he love** unless he loves   1800 **sit** (= *sitteth*) sits
1801 **Be they noght wel arrayed** are they not in a fine condition
1804 **wenen for to be** think they are
1805 **for aught that may bifalle** whatever happens   1806 **game** joke
1807 **jolitee** sport   1808 **Kan . . . thank** owes . . . thanks
1809 **woot** knows **this hoote fare** these passionate goings-on
1810 **cokkow** cuckoo   1811 **assayed** tried out   1812 **or . . . or** either . . .
or   1813 I know it from my own experience, long ago
1816 **distreine** torment   1817 **laas** net   1818 **trespaas** offence

And ye shal bothe anoon unto me swere
That neveremo ye shal my contree dere,
Ne make werre upon me, night nor day,
But been my freendes in al that ye may,
I yow foryeve this trespas everydel.'   1825
    And they him swore his axing faire and wel,
And him of lordshipe and of mercy preyde;
And he hem graunteth grace, and thus he seide:
'To speke of royal linage and richesse,
Thogh that she were a queen or a princesse,   1830
Ech of yow bothe is worthy, doutelees,
To wedden whan time is; but nathelees –
I speke as for my suster Emelye,
For whom ye have this strif and jalousye –
Ye woot yourself she may nat wedden two   1835
Atones, thogh ye fighten everemo.
That oon of yow, al be him looth or lief,
He moot go pipen in an ivy-leef.
This is to seyn, she may nat now have bothe,
Al be ye nevere so jalous ne so wrothe.   1840
And forthy I yow putte in this degree,
That ech of yow shal have his destinee
As him is shape, and herkneth in what wise;
Lo here, youre ende, of that I shal devise.
My wil is this, for plat conclusioun,   1845
Withouten any replicacioun –
If that yow liketh, take it for the beste:
That everich of yow shal goon wher that him leste,

1821 **And if**   1822 **dere** harm   1825 **everydel** completely
1826 **axing** request **faire** willingly   1827 **of lordshipe** for patronage
1829 **To speke of** in terms of   1836 **Atones** at once
1837 **al be him looth or lief** whether he likes it or not
1838 **pipen in an ivy-leef** 'jump in the lake' (*lit.* whistle in an ivy leaf)
1840 However jealous or angry you are   1841 **forthy** therefore
degree condition   1843 **him is shape** it is ordained for him
1844 **devise** contrive   1845 **for plat conclusioun** with finality, definitely
1846 Without protest   1847 **take it for the beste** adopt it as the best course
1848 **wher that him leste** where he pleases

Frely, withouten raunsoun or daunger,
1850   And this day fifty wikes, fer ne ner,
Everich of yow shal bringe an hundred knightes,
Armed for listes up at alle rightes,
Al redy to darreine hire by bataille.
And this bihote I yow, withouten faille,
1855   Upon my trouthe, and as I am a knight,
That wheither of yow bothe that hath might –
This is to seyn that wheither he or thou –
May with his hundred, as I spak of now,
Sleen his contrarye, or out of listes drive,
1860   Thanne shal I yeve Emelya to wive
To whom that Fortune yeveth so faire a grace.
The listes shal I maken in this place;
And God so wysly on my soule rewe
As I shal evene juge been and trewe!
1865   Ye shul noon oother ende with me maken,
That oon of yow ne shal be deed or taken.
And if yow thinketh this is wel ysaid,
Sey youre avis, and holdeth yow apaid.
This is youre ende and youre conclusioun.'
1870   Who looketh lightly now but Palamoun?
Who springeth up for joye but Arcite?
Who koude telle, or who koude it endite,
The joye that is maked in the place,
Whan Theseus hath doon so fair a grace?
1875   But doun on knees wente every maner wight,
And thonken him with al hir herte and might,

1849 **daunger** resistance   1850 **fer ne ner** neither later nor sooner
1851 **Everich** each   1852 **listes** (jousting in) the lists (n.)
up at alle rightes in every respect   1853 **darreine** lay claim to
1854 **bihote** promise   1856 **wheither** whichever   1858 **spak** spoke
1859 **Sleen** slay **contrarye** opponent   1860 **to wive** as a wife
1861 **grace** stroke of luck   1863 **rewe** have mercy   1864 **evene** impartial
1866 **taken** captured   1868 **avis** opinion **holdeth yow apaid** be content
1869 **conclusioun** fate   1870 **lightly** cheerfully
1874 **doon so fair a grace** granted such a favour

And namely the Thebans ofte sithe.
And thus with good hope, and with herte blithe,
They take hir leve and homward gonne they ride
To Thebes with hise olde walles wide.   1880

[Part Three]

I trowe men wolde deme it necligence
If I foryete to tellen the dispence
Of Theseus, that gooth so bisily
To maken up the listes royally,
That swich a noble theatre as it was,   1885
I dar wel seyen, in this world ther nas.
The circuit a mile was aboute,
Walled of stoon and diched al withoute.
Round was the shap, in maner of compas,
Ful of degrees, the heighte of sixty paas,   1890
That whan a man was set on o degree,
He letted noght his felawe for to see.

Estward ther stood a gate of marbul whit;
Westward right swich another in th'oposit.
And shortly to concluden, swich a place   1895
Was noon in erthe, as in so litel space.
For in the lond ther was no crafty man
That geometrye or ars-metrik kan,
Ne purtreyour ne kerver of images,
That Theseus ne yaf him mete and wages   1900
The theatre for to maken and devise.
And for to doon his rite and sacrifise,

1877 **namely** especially **ofte sithe** often   1880 **hise** its   1881 **trowe** believe
deme think   1882 **dispence** expenditure   1884 **maken up** build
1887 **circuit** circumference   1888 **diched** surrounded by a trench
1889 **compas** a circle   1890 **degrees** steps (for sitting on) **paas** paces
1891 **o** one   1892 **letted noght** did not prevent   1893 **marbul** marble
1894 **th'oposit** the opposite point   1895 **place** arena   1896 **space** time
1897 **crafty man** craftsman   1898 **ars-metrik** arithmetic **kan** knows
1899 **purtreyour** painter **kerver** carver   1900 **mete** food
1901 **devise** construct

He estward hath upon the gate above,
In worship of Venus, goddesse of love,
1905   Doon make an auter and an oratorye;
And on the westward gate, in memorye
Of Mars, he maked hath right swich another,
That coste largely of gold a fother.
And northward in a touret on the wal,
1910   Of alabastre whit and reed coral
An oratorye, riche for to see,
In worship of Diane of chastitee,
Hath Theseus doon wroght in noble wise.
    But yet hadde I forgeten to devise
1915   The noble kerving and the purtreitures,
The shap, the contenance, and the figures,
That weren in thise oratories thre.
    First in the temple of Venus maystow se
Wroght on the wal, ful pitous to biholde,
1920   The broken slepes and the sikes colde,
The sacred teeris, and the waimentinge,
The firy strokes of the desiringe
That loves servantz in this lif enduren;
The othes that hir convenantz assuren,
1925   Plesance, and Hope, Desir, Foolhardinesse,
Beautee and Youthe, Bauderye, Richesse,
Charmes and Force, Lesinges, Flaterye,
Despense, Bisinesse, and Jalousye,
That wered of yelowe gooldes a gerland,
1930   And a cokkow sitting on hir hand,

1905 **Doon make** had made **auter** altar   1908 **largely of gold a fother** a
good heap of gold   1909 **touret** turret   1913 **Hath . . . doon wroght** has
had made   1914 **devise** describe   1915 **kerving** carving
purtreitures paintings   1916 **contenance** appearance   1919 **pitous** pitiful
1920 **sikes** sighs   1921 **waimentinge** lamentation
1924 **hir covenantz assuren** guarantee their promises
1926 **Bauderye** Gaiety   1927 **Charmes** Spells **Lesinges** Lies
1928 **Despense** Expense **Bisinesse** Trouble   1929 **gooldes** marigolds

Festes, instrumentz, caroles, daunces,
Lust and array, and alle the circumstaunces
Of love, whiche that I rekned and rekne shal,
By ordre weren peinted on the wal,
And mo than I kan make of mencioun.   1935
For soothly, al the mount of Citheroun,
Ther Venus hath hir principal dwellinge,
Was shewed on the wal in purtreyinge,
With al the gardin and the lustinesse.
Nat was foryeten the porter Idelnesse,   1940
Ne Narcisus the faire of yore agon,
Ne yet the folye of king Salomon,
Ne yet the grete strength of Ercules,
Th'enchauntementz of Medea and Circes,
Ne Turnus with the hardy fiers corage,   1945
The riche Cresus, caitif in servage.
Thus may ye seen that wisdom ne richesse,
Beautee ne sleighte, strengthe, hardinesse,
Ne may with Venus holde champartie,
For as hir lust the world than may she gye.   1950
Lo, al thise folk so caught were in hir laas,
Til they for wo ful ofte seide 'allas!'
Suffiseth here ensamples oon or two,
And though I koude rekne a thousand mo.

   The statue of Venus, glorious for to see,   1955
Was naked, fleting in the large see,
And fro the navele doun al covered was
With wawes grene and brighte as any glas.

1931 **caroles** carols (round dances accompanied by singing)
1932 **Lust** pleasure **array** adornment   1934 **By ordre** in order
1935 **mo** more   1936 **Citheroun** see n.   1938 **purtreyinge** painting
1939 **lustinesse** pleasure   1941 **yore agon** long ago
1945 **hardy fiers corage** bold valiant spirit   1946 **caitif** wretched
1948 **sleighte** cleverness   1949 **holde champartie** contend successfully
1950 **as hir lust** as it pleases her **gye** govern   1951 **laas** net
1956 **fleting** floating   1958 **wawes** waves

A citole in hir right hand hadde she,
1960   And on hir heed, ful semely for to se,
A rose gerland, fressh and wel smellinge;
Above hir heed hir dowves flikeringe.
Biforn hire stood hir sone Cupido;
Upon his shuldres winges hadde he two,
1965   And blind he was, as it is ofte sene;
A bowe he bar, and arwes brighte and kene.

Why sholde I nat as wel eek telle yow al
The purtreiture that was upon the wal
Withinne the temple of mighty Mars the rede?
1970   Al peinted was the wal in lengthe and brede,
Lik to the estres of the grisly place
That highte the grete temple of Mars in Trace,
In thilke colde frosty regioun
Theras Mars hath his soverein mansioun.

1975   First on the wal was peinted a forest,
In which ther dwelleth neither man ne best,
With knotty knarry bareine trees olde,
Of stubbes sharpe, and hidouse to biholde,
In which ther ran a rumbel and a swough,
1980   As thogh a storm sholde bresten every bough.
And dounward from an hil, under a bente,
Ther stood the temple of Mars armipotente,
Wroght al of burned steel, of which th'entree
Was long and streit and gastly for to see.
1985   And therout cam a rage and swich a veze
That it made al the gate for to rese.

1959 **citole** a stringed instrument, plucked with the fingers (n.)
1961 **wel smellinge** beautifully scented   1962 **dowves** doves
flikeringe fluttering   1966 **bar** bore **kene** sharp   1970 **brede** breadth
1971 **estres** interior   1974 **soverein** principal   1977 **knarry** gnarled
1978 **stubbes** stumps   1979 **rumbel** rumble **swough** sough, sighing sound
1980 **sholde bresten** were going to break   1981 **under a bente** at the bottom
of a grassy slope   1982 **armipotente** mighty in battle
1983 **burned** burnished   1984 **streit** narrow **gastly** terrible
1985 **rage** blast of wind **veze** gust   1986 **rese** shake

The northren light in at the dores shoon,
For window on the wal ne was ther noon
Thurgh which men mighten any light discerne.
The dore was al of athamant eterne,   1990
Yclenched overthwart and endelong
With iren togh, and, for to make it strong,
Every piler, the temple to sustene,
Was tonne-greet, of iren bright and shene.
      Ther saugh I first the derke imagininge   1995
Of felonye, and al the compassinge;
The cruel Ire, reed as any gleede,
The pikepurs, and eek the pale Drede;
The smilere with the knif under the cloke;
The shepne brenning with the blake smoke;   2000
The tresoun of the mordring in the bed;
The open werre with woundes al bibled;
Contek with blody knif, and sharp Manace;
Al ful of chirking was that sory place.
The sleere of himself yet saugh I ther,   2005
His herte-blood hath bathed al his heer;
The nail ydriven in the shode a-night;
The colde deeth, with mouth gaping upright.
Amiddes of the temple sat Meschaunce,
With disconfort and sory contenaunce.   2010
      Yet saugh I Woodnesse laughing in his rage,
Armed Compleint, Outhees, and fiers Outrage.
The caroine in the bussh, with throte ycorve;
A thousand slain, and noght of qualm ystorve;

1987 **northren** northern   1990 **athamant** adamant (a mythical rock of great
hardness)   1991 Riveted crosswise and lengthwise   1992 **togh** strong
1993 **piler** pillar **sustene** hold up   1994 **tonne-greet** as thick as a barrel
1995 **derke imagininge** secret planning   1996 **compassinge** conspiring
1997 **gleede** coal   1998 **pikepurs** pickpurse **Drede** Fear
2000 **shepne** cowshed   2001 **mordring** murdering   2002 **bibled** blood-
covered   2003 **Contek** Strife   2004 **chirking** creaking noises **sory** dismal
2005 **sleere** slayer   2006 **heer** hair   2007 **shode** crown of the head
2008 **upright** upwards   2011 **Woodnesse** Madness   2012 **Outhees** Outcry,
Clamour **Outrage** Excess   2013 **caroine** corpse **ycorve** cut
2014 **of qualm ystorve** dead from plague

2015   The tyraunt with the praye by force yraft;
        The toun destroyed – ther was nothing laft.
        Yet saugh I brent the shippes hoppesteres;
        The hunte strangled with the wilde beres;
        The sowe freten the child right in the cradel;
2020   The cook yscalded, for al his longe ladel.
        Naught was forgeten, by th'infortune of Marte,
        The cartere over-riden with his carte;
        Under the wheel ful lowe he lay adoun.
        Ther were also of Martes devisioun
2025   The barbour, and the bochier, and the smith,
        That forgeth sharpe swerdes on his stith.
        And al above, depeinted in a tour,
        Saugh I Conquest, sitting in greet honour,
        With the sharpe swerd over his heed,
2030   Hanginge by a subtil twines threed.
        Depeinted was the slaughtre of Julius,
        Of grete Nero, and of Anthonius;
        Al be that thilke time they were unborn,
        Yet was hir deeth depeinted therbiforn,
2035   By manasinge of Mars, right by figure.
        So was it shewed in that purtreiture,
        As is depeinted in the sterres above
        Who shal be slain, or ellis deed for love.
        Suffiseth oon ensample in stories olde;
2040   I may nat rekne hem alle, thogh I wolde.
            The statue of Mars upon a carte stood,
        Armed, and loked grim as he were wood.

2015 **yraft** seized   2017 **brent** burned **shippes hoppesteres** dancing ships
2018 **hunte** huntsman   2019 **freten** gnaw **right in the cradel** in the very
cradle   2020 **for al** in spite of   2021 **infortune of Marte** malign influence of
Mars   2022 **over-riden with** run over by   2024 **devisioun** clan
2025 **barbour** barber **bochier** butcher   2026 **stith** anvil
2027 **depeinted** painted   2030 **subtil twines threed** fine thread of string
2033 **Al be that** although   2035 **manasinge** threatening **figure** stellar
configuration   2040 **thogh I wolde** even if I wanted to
2041 **carte** war-chariot   2042 **as he were wood** as if he were mad

And over his heed ther shinen two figures
Of sterres, that been cleped in scriptures
That oon Puella, that oother Rubeus.   2045
This god of armes was arrayed thus:
A wolf ther stood bifore him at his feet,
With eyen rede, and of a man he eet.
With subtil pencel was depeint this storye,
In redoutinge of Mars and of his glorye.   2050
   Now to the temple of Diane the chaste
As shortly as I kan I wol me haste,
To telle yow al the descripcioun.
Depeinted been the walles, up and doun,
Of hunting and of shamfast chastitee.   2055
Ther saw I how woful Calistopee,
Whan that Diane agreved was with here,
Was turned from a womman til a bere,
And after was she maad the lodesterre.
Thus was it peinted; I kan seye yow no ferre.   2060
Hir sone is eek a sterre, as men may see.
Ther saw I Dane yturned to a tree;
I mene nat the goddesse Diane,
But Penneus doghter, which that highte Dane.
Ther saw I Attheon an hert ymaked,   2065
For vengeaunce that he saw Diane al naked.
I saugh how that his houndes have him caught,
And freten him for that they knewe him naught.
Yet peinted was a litel forther moor
How Atthalante hunted the wilde boor,   2070
And Meleagree, and many another mo,
For which Diane wroghte him care and wo.

2044 **been cleped** are called **scriptures** writings   2048 **eet** ate
2049 **pencel** brush **depeint** depicted   2050 **redoutinge** reverence
2054 **Depeinted** painted   2055 **Of** with   2057 **agreved** angry   2058 **til** to
2059 **lodesterre** pole star   2060 **ferre** further   2062 **Dane** Daphne
2064 **highte** was called   2068 **freten** eat **for that** because
2069 **forther moor** further on   2072 **wroghte him care and wo** caused him
hardship and sorrow

Ther saugh I many another wonder storye,
The which me list nat drawen to memorye.

2075   This goddesse on an hert ful hye seet,
With smale houndes al aboute hir feet,
And undernethe hir feet she hadde a moone;
Wexinge it was and sholde wanie soone.
In gaude grene hir statue clothed was,
2080 With bowe in honde, and arwes in a cas.
Hir eyen caste she ful lowe adoun,
Ther Pluto hath his derke regioun.
A womman travailling was hir biforn;
But, for hir child so longe was unborn,
2085 Ful pitously Lucina gan she calle,
And seide, 'Help, for thow mayst best of alle!'
Wel koude he peinten lifly that it wroghte;
With many a florin he the hewes boghte.
    Now been thise listes maad, and Theseus,
2090 That at his grete cost arrayed thus
The temples and the theatre every del,
Whan it was doon, him liked wonder wel.
But stinte I wol of Theseus a lite,
And speke of Palamon and of Arcite.

2095   The day approcheth of hir retourninge,
That everich sholde an hundred knightes bringe,
The bataille to darreine, as I yow tolde.
And til Atthenes, hir covenant for to holde,
Hath everich of hem broght an hundred knightes,
2100 Wel armed for the werre at alle rightes.

2074 Which I do not care to call to mind   2075 **seet** sat
2077 **undernethe** beneath   2078 **sholde wanie soone** was soon to wane
2079 **gaude grene** yellowish green   2083 **travailling** in labour
2085 **pitously** pitifully **gan she calle** she called on
2086 **thow mayst best of alle** you are best able to   2087 **lifly** in a life-like
manner   2088 **hewes** colours   2090 **arrayed** adorned   2091 **every del** in
their entirety   2092 **him liked** it pleased him   2093 **stinte . . . of** cease to
speak of   2097 **The bataille to darreine** to engage in combat   2098 **til** to
hir covenant their promise   2100 **at alle rightes** in every respect

And sikerly, ther trowed many a man
That nevere, sithen that the world bigan,
As for to speke of knighthod of hir hond,
As fer as God hath maked see and lond,
Nas of so fewe so noble a compaignye.   2105
For every wight that loved chivalrye,
And wolde his thankes han a passant name,
Hath preyed that he mighte been of that game,
And wel was him that therto chosen was.
For if ther fille tomorwe swich a cas,   2110
Ye knowen wel that every lusty knight
That loveth paramours and hath his might,
Were it in Engelond or elleswhere,
They wolde hir thankes wilnen to be there.
To fighten for a lady, *benedicitee*! –   2115
It were a lusty sighte for to see.
      And right so ferden they with Palamon.
With him ther wenten knightes many oon;
Som wol ben armed in an haubergeoun,
And in a brestplate and a light gipoun,   2120
And som wol have a peire plates large,
And som wol have a Pruce sheeld, or a targe,
Som wol be armed on his legges weel
And have an ax, and som a mace of steel.
Ther nis no newe gise that it nas old!   2125
Armed were they as I have yow told,
Everich after his opinioun.
      Ther maystow seen cominge with Palamoun

2101 **sikerly** assuredly **trowed** believed   2102 **sithen** since
2103 **knighthod of hir hond** fighting ability   2105 There was no company
made up of such small numbers that was so noble   2107 And would gladly
have a distinguished reputation   2108 **been of that game** participate
2109 **therto** for it   2110 **fille** befell   2112 **loveth paramours** is in love
2113 **Were it** whether it was   2114 **wilnen** wish   2116 **were** would be
lusty fine   2119 **Som wol ben** one wishes to be **haubergeoun** mail-coat
2120 **gipoun** surcoat (n.)   2121 **a peire plates** a set of plate armour
2122 **Pruce** Prussian   2125 There is no new fashion that isn't an old one
2127 Each one as he thought best

Lygurge himself, the grete king of Trace.
2130   Blak was his berd and manly was his face.
The cercles of his eyen in his heed,
They gloweden bitwixen yelow and reed,
And lik a griffoun loked he aboute,
With kempe heres on his browes stoute.
2135   His limes grete, his brawnes harde and stronge,
His shuldres brode, his armes rounde and longe.
And as the gise was in his contree,
Ful hye upon a chaar of gold stood he,
With foure white boles in the trais.
2140   In stede of cote-armure over his harnais,
With nailes yelwe and brighte as any gold,
He hadde a beres skin, col-blak for old.
His longe heer was kembd bihinde his bak;
As any ravenes fethere it shoon for blak.
2145   A wrethe of gold, arm-greet, of huge wighte,
Upon his heed, set ful of stones brighte,
Of fine rubies and of diamauntz.
Aboute his chaar ther wenten white alauntz,
Twenty and mo, as grete as any steer,
2150   To hunten at the leoun or the deer,
And folwed him, with mosel faste ybounde,
Colered of gold and turrettes filed rounde.
An hundred lordes hadde he in his route,
Armed ful wel, with hertes sterne and stoute.

2133 **griffoun** griffin (mythical beast with the body of a lion and head of an eagle)   2134 **kempe** shaggy   **stoute** menacing   2135 **grete** massive
brawnes muscles   2137 **gise** custom   2138 **chaar** chariot
2139 **boles** bulls   **trais** traces   2140 **cote-armure** surcoat (g.)
harnais armour   2141 **yelwe** yellow   2142 **col-blak for old** coal-black with age   2143 **kembd** combed   2144 **for blak** for blackness
2145 **wrethe** circlet   **arm-greet** as thick as one's arm   **wighte** weight
2147 **diamauntz** diamonds   2148 **alauntz** hunting dogs   2149 **mo** more
steer bullock   2151 **mosel** muzzle   2152 **Colered** with collars
turrettes rings on a dog's collar (by which a leash can be attached)
filed rounde filed into a circle   2153 **route** company   2154 **stoute** valiant

With Arcita, in stories as men finde,   2155
The grete Emetreus, the king of Inde,
Upon a steede bay, trapped in steel,
Covered in clooth of gold diapred weel,
Cam ridinge lik the god of armes, Mars.
His cote-armure was of clooth of Tars,   2160
Couched with perles white and rounde and
          grete.
His sadel was of brend gold newe ybete,
A mantelet upon his shulder hanginge,
Bret-ful of rubies rede, as fir sparklinge.
His crispe heer lik ringes was yronne,   2165
And that was yelow and glitred as the sonne.
His nose was heigh, his eyen bright citrin,
His lippes rounde, his colour was sangwin.
A fewe fraknes in his face yspreind,
Bitwixen yelow and somdel blak ymeind,   2170
And as a leoun he his looking caste.
Of five-and-twenty yeer his age I caste.
His berd was wel bigonne for to springe;
His vois was as a trompe thonderinge.
Upon his heed he wered of laurer grene   2175
A gerland, fressh and lusty for to sene.
Upon his hand he bar for his deduit
An egle tame, as any lilye whit.
An hundred lordes hadde he with him there,
Al armed, save hir heddes, in al hir gere,   2180

2156 **Inde** India   2157 **steede bay** bay horse   **trapped** covered with
trappings   2158 **diapred** of patterned weave   2160 **clooth of Tars** Tharsian
silk (?from Turkestan)   2161 **Couched** ornamented   2162 **brend gold** pure
gold   **newe ybete** freshly hammered   2163 **mantelet** short cloak
2164 **Bret-ful** crammed full   2165 **yronne** clustered
2167 **heigh** prominent   **citrin** brownish yellow, orange
2168 **sangwin** ruddy   2169 **fraknes** freckles   **yspreind** sprinkled
2170 **somdel** partly   **ymeind** mixed   2171 **his looking caste** gazed around
2172 **caste** estimate   2173 **springe** grow   2174 **thonderinge** thundering
2175 **wered** wore   2176 **lusty** delightful   2177 **deduit** pleasure
2180 **save** except for

Ful richely in alle manere thinges.
For trusteth wel that dukes, erles, kinges,
Were gadred in this noble compaignye,
For love and for encrees of chivalrye.

2185   Aboute this king ther ran on every part
Ful many a tame leoun and leopart.
And in this wise thise lordes, alle and some,
Been on the Sonday to the citee come
Aboute prime, and in the toun alight.

2190   This Theseus, this duc, this worthy knight,
Whan he had broght hem into his citee,
And inned hem, everich at his degree,
He festeth hem, and dooth so gret labour
To esen hem and doon hem al honour,

2195   That yet men wenen that no mannes wit
Of noon estaat ne koude amenden it.
    The minstralcye, the service at the feeste,
The grete yiftes to the meeste and leeste,
The riche array of Theseus paleis,

2200   Ne who sat first ne last upon the deis,
What ladies fairest been, or best daunsinge,
Or which of hem kan chaunten best and singe,
Ne who moost felingly speketh of love,
What haukes sitten on the perche above,

2205   What houndes liggen on the floor adoun –
Of al this make I now no mencioun,
But al th'effect; that thinketh me the beste.
Now comth the point, and herkneth if yow leste.

2182 **trusteth** be assured   2183 **gadred** assembled   2185 **part** side
2186 **leopart** leopard   2187 **alle and some** one and all
2189 **prime** 9 a.m. (g.) **alight** dismounted   2192 **inned** provided with
lodging **at his degree** according to his rank   2193 **festeth** feasts
dooth so gret labour makes such an effort   2194 **esen** entertain
2195 **yet men wenen** people still think   2196 **amenden** improve on
2198 **meeste** greatest   2199 **array** splendour   2203 **moost felingly** most
sympathetically   2205 **liggen** lie   2207 **th'effect** the essentials
thinketh me seems to me   2208 **if yow leste** if it pleases you

The Sonday night, er day bigan to springe,
Whan Palamon the larke herde singe –   2210
Althogh it nere nat day by houres two
Yet song the larke – and Palamon right tho,
With holy herte and with an heigh corage,
He roos to wenden on his pilgrimage
Unto the blisful Citherea benigne;   2215
I mene Venus, honurable and digne.
And in hir hour he walketh forth a paas,
Unto the listes ther hir temple was,
And doun he kneleth, and with humble cheere
And herte soor, he seide as ye shal heere: 2220
    'Faireste of faire, O lady min Venus,
Doghter to Jove and spouse to Vulcanus,
Thow gladere of the mount of Citheron,
For thilke love thow haddest to Adoon,
Have pitee of my bittre teeres smerte,   2225
And taak min humble prayere at thin herte.
Allas, I ne have no langage to telle
Th'effectes, ne the tormentz of min helle,
Min herte may mine harmes nat biwreye;
I am so confus that I kan noght seye   2230
But "mercy, lady bright, that knowest wele
My thoght, and seest what harmes that I feele!"
Considre al this and rewe upon my soore,
As wysly as I shal for everemoore,
Emforth my might, thy trewe servaunt be,   2235
And holden werre alwey with chastitee.

2211 **it nere nat day** it was not daylight   2212 **tho** then
2213 **heigh corage** solemn frame of mind   2215 **Citherea** Venus (see n. to
Kn 1936)   2216 **digne** revered   2217 **a paas** at walking speed
2218 **ther** where   2219 **cheere** expression   2220 **soor** aching
2223 **gladere** one who gladdens or cheers **Citheron** Mount Cithaeron in
Greece (see n. to Kn 1936)   2225 **smerte** painful   2226 **at** to
2229 **biwreye** reveal   2230 **confus** confounded   2231 **But** except
2233 **rewe** have pity **soore** suffering   2234 **wysly** surely
2235 **Emforth my might** to the extent of my power

That make I min avow, so ye me helpe!
I kepe noght of armes for to yelpe,
Ne I n'axe noght tomorwe to have victorye,
2240 No renoun in this cas, ne veine glorye
Of pris of armes blowen up and doun;
But I wolde have fully possessioun
Of Emelye, and die in thy servise.
Find thow the maner how and in what wise;
2245 I recche nat, but it may bettre be,
To have victorye of hem, or they of me,
So that I have my lady in min armes.
For thogh so be that Mars is god of armes,
Youre vertu is so greet in hevene above,
2250 That if yow list, I shal wel have my love.
Thy temple wol I worshipe everemo,
And on thin auter, wher I ride or go,
I wol doon sacrifice and fires beete.
And if ye wol noght so, my lady sweete,
2255 Than praye I thee tomorwe with a spere
That Arcita me thurgh the herte bere.
Thanne rekke I noght, whan I have lost my lif,
Thogh that Arcita winne hire to his wif.
This is th'effect and ende of my prayere:
2260 Yif me my love, thow blisful lady deere!'
    Whan th'orisoun was doon of Palamon,
His sacrifice he dide, and that anon,
Ful pitously, with alle circumstaunces,
Al telle I nat as now his observaunces.
2265 But at the laste the statue of Venus shook,
And made a signe, wherby that he took

2237 **so** provided that   2238 **kepe noght** do not care   **yelpe** boast
2241 **pris** renown   **blowen** proclaimed   2245–6 see n.   2247 **So that** so
long as   2248 **thogh so be** though it is the case   2249 **vertu** power
2252 **auter** altar   **wher** wherever   2253 **beete** kindle   2257 **rekke** care
2259 **effect** purport   **ende** aim   2260 **Yif** give   **blisful** blessed
2261 **orisoun** prayer   2262 **anon** immediately   2263 Very devoutly, with
every formality   2264 **Al telle I nat** although I do not relate
2266 **took** understood

That his prayere accepted was that day.
For thogh the signe shewed a delay,
Yet wiste he wel that graunted was his boone,
And with glad herte he wente him hoom ful   2270
  soone.
  The thridde hour inequal that Palamon
Bigan to Venus temple for to gon,
Up roos the sonne, and up roos Emelye,
And to the temple of Diane gan hie.
Hir maidens that she thider with hire ladde,   2275
Ful redily with hem the fir they hadde,
Th'encens, the clothes, and the remenant al
That to the sacrifice longen shal,
The hornes ful of meeth, as was the gise;
Ther lakked noght to doon hir sacrifise,   2280
Smokinge the temple, ful of clothes faire.
This Emelye, with herte debonaire,
Hir body wessh with water of a welle.
But how she dide hir rite I dar nat telle,
But it be anything in general –   2285
And yet it were a game to heren al!
To him that meneth wel it were no charge;
But it is good a man been at his large.
Hir brighte heer was kembd, untressed al;
A corone of a grene ook cerial   2290
Upon hir heed was set, ful fair and meete.
Two fires on the auter gan she beete,
And dide hir thinges, as men may biholde
In Stace of Thebes, and thise bokes olde.

2269 **wiste** knew **boone** prayer   2271 **The thridde hour inequal** see n.
2274 **gan hie** hastened   2275 **ladde** led   2277 **clothes** hangings
2278 **longen** belong   2279 **meeth** mead **gise** custom
2281 **Smokinge** reeking with incense   2282 **debonaire** meek
2283 **wessh** washed   2285 Unless in very general terms
2287 **were no charge** would be no trouble   2288 **been at his large** to be
unencumbered (by the duty of narrating it)   2289 **untressed** unplaited
2290 **ook cerial** Turkey oak   2291 **meete** fitting
2292 **gan . . . beete** kindled   2293 **dide hir thinges** performed her rites

2295   Whan kindled was the fir, with pitous cheere
       Unto Diane she spak, as ye may heere:
          'O chaste goddesse of the wodes grene,
       To whom bothe hevene and erthe and see is sene,
       Queene of the regne of Pluto, derk and lowe,
2300   Goddesse of maidens, that min herte hast knowe
       Ful many a yeer, and woost what I desire,
       As keep me fro thy vengeaunce and thin ire,
       That Attheon aboughte cruelly!
       Chaste goddesse, wel wostow that I
2305   Desire to been a maiden al my lif,
       Ne nevere wol I be no love ne wif.
       I am, thow woost, yet of thy compaignye,
       A maide, and love hunting and venerye,
       And for to walken in the wodes wilde,
2310   And noght to been a wif and be with childe.
       Noght wol I knowe compaignye of man.
       Now help me, lady, sith ye may and kan,
       For tho thre formes that thow hast in thee,
       And Palamon, that hath swich love to me,
2315   And eek Arcite, that loveth me so soore.
       This grace I preye thee, withoute moore:
       As sende love and pees bitwix hem two,
       And fro me turne awey hir hertes so,
       That al hir hote love and hir desir,
2320   And al hir bisy torment and hir fir
       Be queint, or turned in another place.
       And if so be thow wolt noght do me grace,
       Or if my destinee be shapen so
       That I shal nedes have oon of hem two,

2295 **pitous cheere** pitiful expression   2298 **sene** visible
2301 **woost** know   2302 **As keep me fro** preserve me from
2303 **Attheon** Actaeon (see n. to Kn 2065) **aboughte** paid for
2307 **yet** still   2308 **venerye** hunting   2311 **compaignye of man** sexual
relations   2312 **sith ye may** since you are able   2313 **tho** those
thre formes see n. to Kn 2297–9   2315 **soore** deeply   2319 **That** so that
2320 **bisy** anxious   2321 **Be queint** may be quenched   2323 **be shapen** is
ordained   2324 **nedes** of necessity

As send me him that moost desireth me.   2325
Bihoold, goddesse of clene chastitee,
The bittre teeres that on my chekes falle!
Sin thow art maide and kepere of us alle,
My maidenhode thow kepe and wel conserve,
And whil I live, a maide I wol thee serve.'   2330
    The fires brenne upon the auter clere
Whil Emelye was thus in hir prayere,
But sodeinly she saugh a sighte queinte.
For right anon oon of the fires queinte,
And quiked again, and after that anon   2335
That oother fir was queint and al agon.
And as it queinte, it made a whistelinge,
As doon thise wete brondes in hir brenninge,
And at the brondes ende out ran anoon
As it were blody dropes, many oon.   2340
For which so soore agast was Emelye
That she was wel neigh mad, and gan to crye;
For she ne wiste what it signified,
But oonly for the fere thus hath she cried,
And weep that it was pitee for to heere.   2345
    And therwithal Diane gan appeere,
With bowe in honde, right as an hunteresse,
And seide, 'Doghter, stint thin hevinesse!
Among the goddes hye it is affermed,
And by eterne word write and confermed,   2350
Thou shalt be wedded unto oon of tho
Than han for thee so muchel care and wo;
But unto which of hem I may nat telle.
Farewel, for I ne may no lenger dwelle.

2330 **a maide** as a virgin   2331 **brenne** burn **clere** brightly
2333 **queinte** strange   2334 **queinte** died   2335 **quiked** kindled
2336 **agon** extinguished   2338 **brondes** firebrands
2341 **so soore agast** so deeply afraid   2342 **gan to crye** cried out
2345 **weep** wept   2346 **gan appeere** appeared
2348 **stint thin hevinesse** put an end to your sorrow   2350 **write** written
2352 **care** sorrow   2354 **dwelle** remain

2355   The fires whiche that on min auter brenne
        Shul thee declaren, er that thow go henne,
        Thin aventure of love, as in this cas.'
        And with that word, the arwes in the caas
        Of the goddesse clateren faste and ringe,
2360   And forth she wente, and made a vanisshinge,
        For which this Emelye astoned was,
        And seide, 'What amounteth this, allas?
        I putte me in thy proteccioun,
        Diane, and in thy disposicioun.'
2365   And hoom she gooth anoon the nexte weye.
        This is th'effect; ther is namoore to seye.

            The nexte houre of Mars folwinge this,
        Arcite unto the temple walked is
        Of fierse Mars, to doon his sacrifise,
2370   With alle the rites of his payen wise.
        With pitous herte and heigh devocioun,
        Right thus to Mars he seide his orisoun:
            'O stronge god, that in the regnes colde
        Of Trace honoured art and lord yholde,
2375   And hast in every regne and every lond
        Of armes al the bridel in thin hond,
        And hem fortunest as thee list devise –
        Accepte of me my pitous sacrifise.
        If so be that my youthe may deserve,
2380   And that my might be worthy for to serve
        Thy godhede, that I may be oon of thine,
        Thanne praye I thee to rewe upon my pine,
        For thilke peine and thilke hote fir
        In which thow whilom brendest for desir,

2356 **henne** hence   2357 **Thin aventure** what is to happen to you
2359 **clateren** clatter   2360 **made a vanisshinge** vanished
2366 **th'effect** the long and the short of it   2367 **houre of Mars** see n. to
Kn 2217   2370 **payen** pagan   2371 **pitous** devout   2373 **stronge** mighty
2374 **yholde** considered as   2377 **hem fortunest** control their destiny
2381 **thine** your servants   2382 **rewe** have pity on **pine** suffering
2383 **For** for the sake of **thilke** the same   2384 **whilom brendest** once
burned

Whan that thow usedest the beautee   2385
Of faire yonge fresshe Venus free,
And haddest hire in armes at thy wille –
Although thee ones on a time misfille,
Whan Vulcanus had caught thee in his laas
And foond thee ligging by his wif, allas!   2390
For thilke sorwe that was in thin herte,
Have routhe as wel upon my peines smerte.
I am yong and unkonning, as thow woost,
And as I trowe, with love offended moost
That evere was any lives creature;   2395
For she that dooth me al this wo endure
Ne reccheth nevere wher I sinke or fleete.
And wel I woot, er she me mercy heete,
I moot with strengthe winne hire in the place;
And wel I woot, withouten help or grace   2400
Of thee ne may my strengthe noght availle.
Thanne help me, lord, tomorwe in my bataille,
For thilke fir that whilom brente thee,
As wel as thilke fir now brenneth me,
And do that I tomorwe have victorye.   2405
Min be the travaille and thin be the glorye!
Thy soverein temple wol I moost honouren
Of any place, and alwey moost labouren
In thy plesaunce, and in thy craftes stronge.
And in thy temple I wol my baner honge,   2410
And alle the armes of my compaignye;
And everemo, unto that day I die,
Eterne fir I wol bifore thee finde.
And eek to this avow I wol me binde:

2385 usedest enjoyed   2388 thee . . . misfille it turned out badly for you
2389 laas net   2390 ligging lying   2392 smerte bitter
2393 unkonning ignorant, untutored   2395 lives living
2396 dooth me . . . endure causes me to suffer   2397 Ne reccheth does not
care wher whether fleete float   2398 heete promises   2399 moot must
place arena   2405 do bring it about   2407 soverein principal
2409 In thy plesaunce to please you craftes stronge mighty arts
2413 finde provide

2415   My berd, min heer, that hangeth long adoun,
That nevere yet ne felte offensioun
Of rasour ne of shere, I wol thee yive,
And been thy trewe servaunt whil I live.
Now, lord, have routhe upon my sorwes soore;
2420   Yif me the victorye! I axe thee namoore!'
      The prayere stint of Arcita the stronge.
The ringes on the temple dore that honge,
And eek the dores, clatereden ful faste,
Of which Arcita somwhat him agaste.
2425   The fires brende upon the auter brighte,
That it gan al the temple for to lighte.
A swete smel anoon the ground up yaf,
And Arcita anoon his hand up haf,
And moore encens into the fir he caste,
2430   With othere rites mo; and at the laste
The statue of Mars bigan his hauberk ringe,
And with that soun he herde a murmuringe
Ful lowe and dim, and seide thus: 'Victorye!'
– For which he yaf to Mars honour and glorye.
2435   And thus with joye, and hope wel to fare,
Arcite anoon unto his in is fare,
As fain as fowel is of the brighte sonne.
      And right anoon swich strif ther is bigonne
For thilke graunting, in the hevene above,
2440   Bitwixen Venus, the goddesse of love,
And Mars the sterne god armipotente,
That Juppiter was bisy it to stente,
Til that the pale Saturnus the colde,
That knew so many of aventures olde,

2416 **offensioun** violation   2417 **shere** shears   2419 **routhe** pity
2421 **stint** having ended (n.)   2423 **faste** vigorously   2424 **him agaste** was
afraid   2426 **That** so that   **gan . . . for to lighte** illuminated
2427 **up yaf** yielded up   2428 **haf** raised   2431 **hauberk** mail-coat
2433 **dim** faint, muffled   2436 **unto his in is fare** went to his lodging
2437 **fain** glad   **fowel** bird   2439 **graunting** grant
2441 **armipotente** mighty in battle   2442 **bisy** concerned   **stente** put an end
to   2444 **aventures** vicissitudes

Foond in his olde experience an art   2445
That he ful soone hath plesed every part;
As sooth is seid, 'elde hath greet avantage'.
In elde is bothe wisdom and usage;
Men may the olde atrenne and nat atrede.
Saturne anoon, to stinten strif and drede,   2450
Al be it that it is again his kinde,
Of al this strif he gan remedye finde.
    'My deere doghter Venus,' quod Saturne,
'My cours, that hath so wide for to turne,
Hath moore power than woot any man.   2455
Min is the drenching in the see so wan;
Min is the prisoun in the derke cote;
Min is the strangling and hanging by the throte,
The murmur and the cherles rebelling,
The groining, and the privee empoisoning.   2460
I do vengeance and plein correccioun
Whil I dwelle in the signe of the Leoun.
Min is the ruine of the hye halles,
The falling of the toures and of the walles
Upon the minour or the carpenter.   2465
I slow Sampson shaking the piler,
And mine be the maladies colde,
The derke tresons and the castes olde;
My loking is the fader of pestilence.
Now weep namoore; I shal doon diligence   2470
That Palamon, that is thin owene knight,
Shal have his lady as thow hast him hight.

2447 **elde** age   2448 **usage** experience   2449 **atrenne** out-run
atrede outwit   2451 **kinde** nature   2454 My (planetary) course, which
makes such a wide revolution (n.)   2455 **woot** knows
2456 **drenching** drowning **wan** dark   2457 **cote** hovel
2460 **groining** grumbling **privee** secret   2461 **plein correccioun** complete
punishment   2462 **sign of the Leoun** sign of Leo (in the zodiac) (n.)
2463 **ruine** toppling, falling   2465 **minour** miner (under walls)
2466 **slow** killed   2468 **castes** plots   2469 **loking** (astrological) aspect
2470 **doon diligence** take pains   2472 **hight** promised

Thogh Mars shal helpe his knight, yet nathelees
Bitwixe yow ther moot be som time pees,
2475   Al be ye noght of o complexioun;
That causeth al day swich divisioun.
I am thin aiel, redy at thy wille.
Weep now namoore; I wol thy lust fulfille.'
    Now wol I stinten of the goddes above,
2480   Of Mars, and of Venus, goddesse of love,
And telle yow as pleinly as I kan
The grete effect, for which that I bigan.

[*Part Four*]

Greet was the feeste in Atthenes that day;
And eek the lusty sesoun of that May
2485   Made every wight to been in swich plesaunce
That al that Monday justen they and daunce,
And spenden it in Venus heigh servise.
And by the cause that they sholde rise
Erly for to seen the grete fight,
2490   Unto hir reste wenten they at night.
And on the morwe, whan that day gan springe,
Of hors and harneis noise and clateringe
Ther was in hostelries al aboute.
And to the paleis rood ther many a route
2495   Of lordes, upon steedes and palfreys.
Ther maystow seen devisinge of harneis,
So unkouth and so riche, and wroght so weel,
Of goldsmithrye, of browding, and of steel;

2474 **Bitwixe** between **moot** must **pees** peace
2475 **complexioun** temperament, character (as produced by the
predominance of one of the four humours) (n.)   2476 **divisioun** dissension
2477 **aiel** grandfather   2478 **lust** desire   2479 **stinten** cease speaking of
2482 **The grete effect** the main point   2484 **lusty** delightful
2486 **justen** joust   2488 **by the cause** because   2492 **harneis** armour
2494 **route** company   2495 **palfreys** saddle-horses
2496 **devisinge** workmanship   2497 **unkouth** strange, exotic
2498 **goldsmithrye** goldsmith's work **browding** embroidering

The sheldes brighte, testeres and trappures,
Gold-hewen helmes, hauberkes, cote-armures,   2500
Lordes in parementz on hir coursers,
Knightes of retenue, and eek squiers,
Nailinge the speres, and helmes bokelinge,
Gigginge of sheeldes, with lainers lasinge.
Theras nede is they weren nothing idel.   2505
The fomy steedes on the golden bridel
Gnawinge, and faste the armurers also
With file and hamer priking to and fro.
Yemen on foote, and communes many oon,
With shorte staves, thikke as they may goon;   2510
Pipes, trompes, nakers, clariounes,
That in the bataille blowen blody sounes;
The paleis ful of peple up and doun,
Heer thre, ther ten, holdinge hir questioun,
Divininge of thise Thebane knightes two.   2515
Somme seiden thus, somme seide it shal be so;
Somme helden with him with the blake berd,
Somme with the balled, somme with the
          thikke-herd.
Somme seide he looked grim, and he wolde
          fighte;
He hath a sparth of twenty pound of wighte.   2520
Thus was the halle ful of devininge,
Longe after that the sonne gan to springe.
   The grete Theseus, that of his sleep awaked
With minstralcye and noise that was maked,

2499 **testeres** head-pieces, casques **trappures** trappings   2500 Helmets
inlaid with gold, mail-coats, surcoats (see n. to Kn 1016)
2501 **parementz** rich clothing **coursers** battle-horses   2502 **of retenue** in
service   2503 **bokelinge** buckling   2504 Fitting shields with straps and
fastening of thongs   2505 **Theras** where **nothing** not at all
2506 **fomy** frothing (at the mouth)   2507 **Gnawinge** champing
armurers armourers   2510 **thikke as they may goon** as thickly crowded as
they can walk   2511 **nakers** kettle-drums   2514 **questioun** discussion
2515 **Divininge of** speculating about   2518 **balled** bald
thikke-herd thick-haired   2519 **he . . . he** this one . . . that one
2520 **sparth** battle-axe **wighte** weight

2525   Held yet the chambre of his paleis riche,
        Til that the Thebane knightes, bothe iliche
        Honoured, were into the paleis fet.
        Duc Theseus was at a window set,
        Arrayed right as he were a god in trone.
2530   The peple preeseth thiderward ful soone
        Him for to seen, and doon heigh reverence,
        And eek to herkne his heste and his sentence.
            An heraud on a scaffold made an 'Oo!'
        Til al the noise of peple was ydo;
2535   And whan he say the peple of noise al stille,
        Thus shewed he the mighty dukes wille:
        'The lord hath, of his heigh discrecioun,
        Considered that it were destruccioun
        To gentil blood to fighten in the gise
2540   Of mortal bataille now in this emprise.
        Wherfore to shapen that they shal noght die,
        He wol his firste purpos modifye.
        No man, therefore, up peine of los of lif,
        No maner shot ne polax ne short knif
2545   Into the listes sende or thider bringe,
        Ne short swerd, for to stoke with point bitinge,
        No man ne drawe, ne bere it by his side.
        Ne no man shal unto his felawe ride
        But o cours with a sharp ygrounde spere;
2550   Foine, if him list, on foote, himself to were.
        And he that is at meschief shal be take,
        And noght slain, but be broght unto the stake
        That shal ordeined been on either side.
        But thider he shal by force, and ther abide.

2525 **Held** remained in   2526 **iliche** equally   2527 **fet** brought
2528 **set** seated   2530 **preeseth** crowd **thiderward** in that direction
2532 **heste** command **sentence** judgement   2534 **ydo** finished
2538 **were** would be   2540 **emprise** enterprise   2541 **shapen** ensure
2543 **up** upon   2544 **No maner shot** no kind of arrow
polax (short-handled) axe   2546 **stoke** thrust   2549 **But o cours** more than
one charge   2550 **Foine** let him fence **were** defend
2551 **at meschief** defeated   2554 **abide** remain

And if so falle the chivetein be take   2555
On either side, or ellis sleen his make,
No lenger shal the turneyinge laste.
God spede yow; go forth and ley on faste.
With long swerd and with maces fighte your
        fille!
Go now youre way; this is the lordes wille.'   2560
    The vois of peple touchede the hevene,
So loude cride they with mury stevene:
'God save swich a lord that is so good!
He wilneth no destruccioun of blood.'
    Up goon the trompes and the melodye,   2565
And to the listes rit the compaignye,
By ordinaunce thurghout the citee large,
Hanged with clooth of gold and noght with sarge.
Ful lik a lord this noble duc gan ride,
Thise two Thebanes upon either side,   2570
And after rood the queene and Emelye,
And after that another compaignye
Of oon and oother, after hir degree.
And thus they passen thurghout the citee,
And to the listes come they bitime –   2575
It nas nat of the day yet fully prime.
    Whan set was Theseus ful riche and hye,
Ypolita the queene, and Emelye,
And othere ladies in degrees aboute,
Unto the setes preeseth al the route;   2580
And westward thurgh the gates, under Marte,
Arcite, and eek the hundred of his parte,

2555 **if so falle** if it happens that **chivetein** leader
2556 **make** opposite number   2557 **turneyinge** tournament
2558 **spede yow** give you success   2560 **Go now youre way** proceed
2562 **mury stevene** glad voice   2564 **wilneth** desires
2566 **rit** (= *rideth*) rides   2567 **By ordinaunce** in due order **large** wide
2568 **sarge** serge, coarse cloth   2569 **gan ride** rode   2573 Of all and
sundry, according to their rank   2575 **bitime** in good time
2576 **prime** 9 a.m. (g.)   2577 **set** seated **riche** splendidly
2579 **in degrees** in tiers (of seats)   2580 **route** crowd   2582 **parte** party

With baner reed is entred right anon,
And in that selve moment Palamon
2585   Is under Venus, estward in the place,
With baner whit and hardy cheere and face.
In al the world to seken up and doun,
So evene, withouten variacioun,
Ther nere swiche compaignyes tweye;
2590   For ther was noon so wis that koude seye
That any hadde of oother avauntage,
Of worthinesse, ne of estaat, ne age;
So evene were they chosen, for to gesse.
And in two renges faire they hem dresse.

2595   Whan that hir names rad were everychon,
That in hir nombre gile were ther noon,
Tho were the gates shet, and cried was loude:
'Do now your devoir, yonge knightes proude!'
        The heraudes lefte hir priking up and doun;
2600   Now ringen trompes loude and clarioun.
Ther is namoore to seyn, but west and est
In goon the speres ful sadly in arest;
In gooth the sharpe spore into the side.
Ther seen men who kan juste and who kan ride;
2605   Ther shiveren shaftes upon sheeldes thikke;
He feeleth thurgh the herte-spoon the prikke.
Up springen speres twenty foot on highte;
Out goon the swerdes, as the silver brighte.
The helmes they to-hewen and to-shrede;
2610   Out brest the blood with sterne stremes rede.

2584 **selve** same   2586 **hardy cheere** bold expression   2588 **evene** equal
variacioun difference   2592 **worthinesse** prowess **estaat** rank   2593 So
equally excellent were they, in everyone's estimation   2594 **renges** rows
hem dresse take up their positions   2595 **rad** read out   2596 So that there
should be no cheating as to their number   2597 **shet** shut
2598 **Do . . . your devoir** do your best   2599 **lefte** left off **priking** riding
2602 **sadly** firmly **arest** hook on the side of the breastplate on which the butt
of the lance rested when ready for a charge   2603 **spore** spur
2605 **shiveren** shiver, break   2606 **herte-spoon** midriff
2609 **to-hewen and to-shrede** hew to pieces and cut to shreds
2610 **brest** bursts

With mighty maces the bones they to-breste;
He thurgh the thikkest of the throng gan threste.
Ther stomblen steedes stronge, and doun gooth al;
He rolleth under foot as dooth a bal;
He foineth on his feet with his tronchoun,   2615
And he him hurtleth with his hors adoun.
He thurgh the body is hurt, and sithe ytake,
Maugree his heed, and broght unto the stake;
As forward was, right ther he moste abide.
Another lad is on that oother side.   2620
And somtime dooth hem Theseus to reste,
Hem to refresshe, and drinken if hem leste.

    Ful ofte a day have thise Thebanes two
Togidre ymet, and wroght his felawe wo;
Unhorsed hath ech oother of hem tweye.   2625
Ther nas no tigre in the vale of Galgopheye,
Whan that hir whelp is stole whan it is lite,
So cruel on the hunte as is Arcite,
For jalous herte, upon this Palamoun;
N'in Belmarye ther nis so fel leoun,   2630
That hunted is, or for his hunger wood,
Ne of his praye desireth so the blood
As Palamon to sleen his foo Arcite.
The jalous strokes on hir helmes bite;
Out renneth blood on bothe hir sides rede.   2635

    Somtime an ende ther is of every dede;
For er the sonne unto the reste wente,
The stronge king Emetreus gan hente

2611 **to-breste** shatter   2612 **threste** thrust   2613 **stomblen** stumble
2615 **foineth** fences **tronchoun** broken spear-shaft
2616 **hurtleth . . . adoun** knocks down   2617 **sithe ytake** afterwards
captured   2618 **Maugree his heed** in spite of all he can do
2619 **forward** agreement   2621 **dooth hem . . . to reste** makes them rest
2622 **if hem leste** if it pleases them   2623 **Ful ofte a day** many times in that
day   2624 **wroght . . . wo** done harm to   2626 **Galgopheye** Gargaphia (in
Greece)   2627 **whelp** cub **stole** stolen   2628 **hunte** hunter
2630 **Belmarye** Benmarin (Morocco) **fel** fierce   2631 **wood** mad
2633 **sleen** kill   2634 **jalous** fierce   2638 **gan hente** seized

This Palamon, as he faught with Arcite
2640 And made his swerd depe in his flessh to bite,
And by the force of twenty is he take
Unyolden, and ydrawen to the stake.
And in the rescus of this Palamoun
The stronge king Lygurge is born adoun,
2645 And king Emetrius, for al his strengthe,
Is born out of his sadel a swerdes lengthe,
So hitte him Palamon er he were take.
But al for noght; he was broght to the stake.
His hardy herte mighte him helpe naught;
2650 He moste abide, whan that he was caught,
By force, and eek by composicioun.

  Who sorweth now but woful Palamoun,
That moot namoore goon again to fighte?
And whan that Theseus had seen this sighte,
2655 Unto the folk that foghten thus echon
He cride 'Hoo! Namoore, for it is doon!
I wol be trewe juge and no partie:
Arcite of Thebes shal have Emelye,
That by his fortune hath hir faire ywonne.'
2660 Anon ther is a noise of peple bigonne
For joye of this, so loude and heigh withalle,
It semed that the listes sholde falle.

  What kan now faire Venus doon above?
What seyth she now? What dooth this queene of love,
2665 But wepeth so, for wanting of hir wille,
Til that hir teeres in the listes fille.
She seide, 'I am ashamed, doutelees.'

  Saturnus seide, 'Doghter, hoold thy pees!
Mars hath his wille; his knight hath al his boone.
2670 And, by min heed, thow shalt been esed soone.'

2642 **Unyolden** without having surrendered **ydrawen** dragged
2643 **rescus** rescue 2644 **born adoun** overthrown 2650 **moste abide** had
to remain 2651 **composicioun** agreement 2656 **Hoo** stop
2657 **partie** partial judge, partisan 2661 **heigh** loudly
2665 **wanting** lack 2666 **fille** fell 2667 **ashamed** disgraced
2669 **boone** prayer 2670 **esed** consoled

The trompours with the loude minstralcye,
The heraudes that ful loude yelle and crye,
Been in hir wele for joye of daun Arcite.
But herkneth me, and stinteth noise a lite,
Which a miracle ther bifel anon.   2675

This fierse Arcite hath of his helm ydon,
And on a courser, for to shewe his face,
He priketh endelong the large place,
Loking upward upon Emelye;
And she again him caste a freendlich eye   2680
(For wommen, as to speken in comune,
They folwen al the favour of Fortune),
And she was al his cheere as in his herte.

Out of the ground a furye infernal sterte,
From Pluto sent at requeste of Saturne;   2685
For which his hors for feere gan to turne,
And leep aside, and foundred as he leep,
And er that Arcite may taken keep
He pighte him on the pomel of his heed,
That in the place he lay as he were deed,   2690
His brest to-brosten with his sadel-bowe.
As blak he lay as any cole or crowe,
So was the blood yronnen in his face.
Anon he was yborn out of the place,
With herte soor, to Theseus paleis.   2695
Tho was he corven out of his harneis,
And in a bed ybroght ful faire and blive,
For he was yet in memorye and alive,

2671 **trompours** trumpeters   2673 **Been in hir wele** are in their element
2674 **stinteth** cease   2676 **of his helm ydon** taken off his helmet
2677 **courser** swift horse   2678 **place** arena   2680 **again** towards
freendlich friendly   2681 **in comune** in general   2683 **cheere** (source of)
happiness   2686 **gan to turne** turned   2687 **leep** leapt **foundred** stumbled
2688 **taken keep** be on his guard   2689 **pighte him** pitched, fell
pomel crown (n.)   2691 **to-brosten** shattered   2694 **yborn** carried
2695 **soor** aching   2696 **Tho** then **corven** cut   2697 **blive** quickly
2698 **yet in memorye** still conscious

And alwey crying after Emelye.
2700   Duc Theseus, with al his compaignye,
Is comen hoom to Atthenes his citee,
With alle blisse and greet solempnitee.
Al be it that this aventure was falle,
He nolde noght disconforten hem alle.
2705   Men seide eek that Arcite shal nat die;
He shal been heled of his maladye.
And of another thing they were as fain:
That of hem alle was ther noon yslain,
Al were they sore yhurt, and namely oon,
2710   That with a spere was thirled his brest-boon.
To oothere woundes, and to broken armes,
Somme hadden salves, and somme hadden charmes;
Fermacies of herbes, and eek save
They dronken, for they wolde hir limes have.
2715   For which this noble duc, as he wel kan,
Conforteth and honoureth every man,
And made revel al the longe night
Unto the straunge lordes, as was right.
Ne ther was holden no disconfitinge,
2720   But as a justes or a tourneyinge.
For soothly ther was no disconfiture,
For falling nis nat but an aventure;
Ne to be lad by force unto the stake,
Unyolden, and with twenty knightes take,
2725   O persone allone, withouten mo,
And haried forth by arm, foot, and too,

2699 **crynge after** calling for   2702 **solempnitee** pomp   2703–4 Although
this mishap had occurred, he didn't want to dishearten them all
2707 **fain** glad   2709 **Al** although **sore** severely **namely** especially
2710 **thirled** pierced   2713 **Fermacies** purgatives **save** a decoction of herbs
2714 **wolde hir limes have** wanted to preserve their limbs
2719 **disconfitinge** defeat   2720 **justes** joust **tourneyinge** tournament
2722 **aventure** accident   2724 **Unyolden** without having surrendered
take captured   2725 **O** one   2726 **haried** dragged

And eek his steede driven forth with staves,
With footmen, bothe yemen and eek knaves –
It nas arretted him no vileinye;
Ther may no man clepe it cowardye.   2730
For which anoon duc Theseus leet crye,
To stinten alle rancour and envye,
The gree as wel of oo side as of oother,
And either side ilik as otheres brother.
And yaf hem yiftes after hir degree,   2735
And fully heeld a feeste dayes three,
And conveyed the kinges worthily
Out of his toun a journee largely.
And hoom wente every man the righte way;
Ther was namoore but 'Farewel, have good   2740
     day!'
Of this bataille I wol namoore endite,
But speke of Palamon and of Arcite.
   Swelleth the brest of Arcite, and the soore
Encreeseth at his herte moore and moore.
The clothered blood, for any lechecraft,   2745
Corrupteth, and is in his bouk ylaft,
That neither veine-blood, ne ventusinge,
Ne drinke of herbes, may been his helpinge.
The vertu expulsif, or animal,
Fro thilke vertu cleped natural   2750
Ne may the venim voiden ne expelle.
The pipes of his longes gan to swelle,

2728 **yemen** yeomen **knaves** fighters on foot   2729 It was not counted as a
disgrace for him   2730 **cowardye** cowardice   2731 **leet crye** had
proclaimed   2732 **stinten** put an end to   2733 **gree** victory
oo ... oother the one ... the other   2735 **after hir degree** according to their
rank   2737 **conveyed** escorted   2738 **journee largely** good day's journey
2739 **the righte way** by the direct route   2741 **endite** write
2745 **clothered** clotted **for any lechecraft** in spite of any medical treatment
2746 **bouk** trunk (of the body)   2747 **veine-blood** blood-letting
ventusinge cupping, drawing blood by the use of a cupping-glass
2749–50 **vertu expulsif** natural faculty of expelling toxic matter from the
body **vertu ... animal ... natural** see n. to Kn 2743–56
2751 **voiden** evacuate   2752 **longes** lungs

And every lacerte in his brest adoun
Is shent with venim and corrupcioun.
2755   Him gaineth neither, for to gete his lif,
Vomit upward, ne dounward laxatif.
Al is to-brosten thilke regioun;
Nature hath now no dominacioun.
And certainly, ther Nature wol nat werche,
2760   Farewel physik! Go ber the man to cherche!
This al and som: that Arcite moot die.
For which he sendeth after Emelye,
And Palamon that was his cosin deere.
Thanne seide he thus, as ye shal after heere:
2765   'Nat may the woful spirit in min herte
Declare o point of alle my sorwes smerte
To yow, my lady, that I love moost.
But I biquethe the service of my goost
To yow aboven every creature,
2770   Sin that my lif may no lenger dure.
Allas, the wo! Allas, the peines stronge
That I for yow have suffred, and so longe!
Allas, the deeth! Allas, min Emelye!
Allas, departing of oure compaignye!
2775   Allas, min hertes queene! Allas, my wif,
Min hertes lady, endere of my lif!
What is this world? What axeth men to have?
Now with his love, now in his colde grave,
Allone, withouten any compaignye.
2780   Farewel, my swete foo, min Emelye!

2753 **lacerte** muscle   2754 **shent** damaged   2755 **Him gaineth** helps him
gete save   2757 **to-brosten** shattered   2758 **dominacioun** power
2759 **ther** where   2760 **physik** medicine   2761 **This al and som** this is the
long and the short of it   **moot** must   2762 **sendeth after** sends for
2765 **Nat may** cannot   2766 **point** particle   **smerte** bitter
2768 **goost** spirit   2770 **Sin that** since   **dure** last
2774 **departing** separation   2777 **axeth** asks
2779 **withouten any compaignye** without a companion   2780 **foo** enemy

And softe take me in your armes tweye,
For love of God, and herkneth what I seye.
  I have heer with my cosin Palamon
Had strif and rancour, many a day agon,
For love of yow, and for my jalousye.   2785
And Juppiter so wys my soule gye,
To speken of a servaunt proprely,
With circumstances alle, trewely –
That is to seyn, trouthe, honour, knighthede,
Wisdom, humblesse, estaat, and heigh kinrede,   2790
Fredom, and al that longeth to that art –
So Juppiter have of my soule part,
As in this world right now ne knowe I non
So worthy to ben loved as Palamon,
That serveth yow, and wol doon al his lif.   2795
And if that evere ye shal been a wif,
Foryet nat Palamon, the gentil man.'
And with that word his speche faille gan,
For from his feet up to his brest was come
The coold of deeth, that hadde him overcome.   2800
And yet mooreover, for in his armes two
The vital strengthe is lost and al ago.
Oonly the intellect, withoute moore,
That dwelled in his herte sik and soore,
Gan faillen whan the herte felte deeth.   2805
Dusked his eyen two and failled breeth,
But on his lady yet caste he his eye;
His laste word was 'Mercy, Emelye!'
His spirit chaunged hous and wente ther,
As I cam nevere, I kan nat tellen wher.   2810

2781 **softe** gently   2786 And, as Jupiter may protect my soul
2791 **Fredom** generosity **art** way of life   2792 **of my soule part** concern for
my soul   2797 **gentil** noble   2798 **faille gan** failed
2801 **And yet mooreover** and that is not all   2802 **ago** gone
2804 **soore** suffering   2806 **Dusked** darkened   2807 **yet** still
2809 **ther** to that place

Therfore I stinte; I nam no divinistre.
Of soules finde I nat in this registre,
Ne me ne list thilke opinions to telle
Of hem, thogh that they writen wher they dwelle.
2815   Arcite is coold; ther Mars his soule gye!
Now wol I speken forth of Emelye.

Shrighte Emelye, and howleth Palamon,
And Theseus his suster took anon
Swowninge, and baar hire fro the corps away.
2820   What helpeth it to taryen forth the day,
To tellen how she weep bothe eve and morwe?
For in swich caas wommen have swich sorwe,
Whan that hir housbond is from hem ago,
That for the moore part they sorwen so,
2825   Or ellis fallen in swich maladye,
That at the laste certeinly they die.

Infinite been the sorwes and the teeres
Of olde folk, and folk of tendre yeeres,
In al the toun for deeth of this Theban.
2830   For him ther wepeth bothe child and man.
So greet weping was ther noon, certain,
Whan Ector was ybroght al fressh yslain
To Troye. Allas, the pitee that was ther! –
Cracchinge of chekes, renting eek of heer.
2835   'Why woldestow be deed?' thise wommen crye,
'And haddest gold inow, and Emelye?'
No man mighte gladen Theseus,
Saving his olde fader Egeus,
That knew this worldes transmutacioun,
2840   As he hadde seyn it chaunge, bothe up and doun,

2811 **nam no divinistre** am no theologian   2812 **registre** record, narrative
2815 **ther Mars his soule gye** may Mars protect his soul
2817 **Shrighte** shrieked   2820 **taryen forth the day** waste the day
2821 **weep** wept   2824 **for the moore part** mostly   2832 **fressh** newly
2834 **Cracchinge** scratching **renting** tearing **heer** hair
2836 **gold inow** plenty of gold   2838 **Saving** except **Egeus** Aegeus
2839 **transmutacioun** mutability

Joye after wo, and wo after gladnesse;
And shewed hem ensample and liknesse.
    'Right as ther deyed nevere man,' quod he,
'That he ne lived in erthe in som degree,
Right so ther lived nevere man,' he seide,   2845
'In al this world, that somtime he ne deide.
This world nis but a thurghfare ful of wo,
And we been pilgrimes passinge to and fro.
Deeth is an ende of every worldly soore.'
And over al this yet seide he muchel moore   2850
To this effect, ful wisely to enhorte
The peple, that they sholde hem reconforte.
    Duc Theseus, with al his bisy cure,
Caste now wher that the sepulture
Of good Arcite may best ymaked be,   2855
And eek moost honurable in his degree.
And at the laste he took conclusioun
That theras first Arcite and Palamoun
Hadden for love the bataille hem bitwene,
That in the selve grove swoote and grene   2860
Theras he hadde his amorouse desires,
His compleinte, and for love his hote fires,
He wolde make a fir in which th'office
Funeral he mighte al acomplice.
And leet anoon comaunde to hakke and hewe   2865
The okes olde and leye hem on a rewe,
In colpons wel arrayed for to brenne.
His officers with swifte feet they renne

2842 **ensample** example **liknesse** story, parable 2844 **in som degree** to
some extent 2849 **soore** suffering 2851 **enhorte** urge
2852 **hem reconforte** take heart, be consoled 2853 **bisy cure** diligent care
2854 **Caste** deliberated 2856 **in his degree** according to his rank
2857 **took conclusioun** decided 2858 **theras** where 2860 **selve** same
swoote sweet 2862 **compleinte** lament 2864 **acomplice** perform
2865 **leet ... comaunde** ordered 2866 **rewe** row 2867 **colpons** separate
pieces **brenne** burn

And ride anoon at his comandement.
2870 And after this, Theseus hath ysent
After a beere, and it al overspradde
With clooth of gold, the richeste that he hadde.
And of the same suite he cladde Arcite;
Upon his handes hadde he gloves white,
2875 Eek on his heed a croune of laurer greene,
And in his hand a swerd ful bright and keene.
He leide him, bare the visage, on the beere;
Therwith he weep that pitee was to heere.
And for the peple sholde seen him alle,
2880 Whan it was day he broghte him to the halle,
That roreth of the crying and the soun.
   Tho cam this woful Theban Palamoun,
With flotry berd and ruggy asshy heeris,
In clothes blake ydropped al with teeris,
2885 And, passing othere of weping, Emelye,
The rufulleste of al the compaignye.
Inasmuche as the service sholde be
The moore noble and riche in his degree,
Duc Theseus leet forth thre steedes bringe
2890 That trapped were in steel al gliteringe,
And covered with the armes of daun Arcite.
Upon thise steedes, that were grete and white,
Ther seten folk, of which oon baar his sheeld,
Another his spere up in his hondes heeld;
2895 The thridde bar with him his bowe Turkeis –
Of brend gold was the caas and eek the harneis –
And riden forth a paas with sorweful cheere
Toward the grove, as ye shul after heere.

2870–71 **ysent After a beere** sent for a bier   2873 **of the same suite** of the
same cloth   2875 **laurer** laurel   2876 **keene** sharp
2877 **bare the visage** with face uncovered   2881 **roreth of** echoes with
2883 **flotry** fluttering **ruggy** shaggy **asshy** sprinkled with ashes (as a sign of
mourning)   2884 **ydropped** sprinkled   2885 **passing othere of** exceeding
others in   2886 **rufulleste** saddest   2889 **leet forth . . . bringe** had brought
forth   2891 **armes** heraldic arms   2893 **seten** sat   2895 **Turkeis** Turkish
2896 **brend** pure   2897 **a paas** at a footpace **cheere** expression

The nobleste of the Grekes that ther were
Upon hir shuldres carieden the beere,   2900
With slakke paas, and eyen rede and wete,
Thurghout the citee by the maister strete,
That sprad was al with blak, and wonder hye
Right of the same is the strete ywrye.
Upon the right hand wente olde Egeus,   2905
And on that oother side duc Theseus,
With vessels in hir hand of gold ful fin,
Al ful of hony, melk, and blood, and win;
Eek Palamon, with ful greet compaignye,
And after that cam woful Emelye,   2910
With fir in hande, as was that time the gise,
To do th'office of funeral servise.
   Heigh labour and greet apparaillinge
Was at the service and the fir-makinge,
That with his grene top the hevene raughte,   2915
And twenty fadme of brede the armes straughte –
This is to seyn, the bowes were so brode.
Of stree first was ther leid ful many a lode –
But how the fir was maked upon highte,
Ne eek the names how the trees highte –   2920
As ook, fir, birch, asp, alder, holm, popler,
Wilow, elm, plane, assh, box, chestain, linde,
      laurer,
Mapul, thorn, beech, hasil, ew, whippultree,
How they were feld – shal nat been told for me;
Ne how the goddes ronnen up and doun,   2925
Disherited of hir habitacioun,

2901 **slakke** slow   2902 **maister strete** main street   2903 **sprad** spread
wonder amazingly   2904 **Right of the same** of the very same (colour)
ywrye covered   2908 **melk** milk   2911 **gise** custom
2913 **apparaillinge** preparation   2915 **his** its **raughte** reached
2916 **fadme of brede** fathoms wide   2918 **stree** straw **lode** load
2920 **highte** were called   2921 **asp** aspen **holm** holm-oak
2922 **chestain** chestnut **linde** linden, lime   2923 **Mapul** maple **hasil** hazel
ew yew **whippultree** ?cornel-tree   2925 **ronnen** ran

In which they woneden in reste and pees –
Nymphes, fawnes, and amadrydes –
Ne how the beestes and the briddes alle
2930   Fledden forfered whan the wode was falle;
Ne how the ground agast was of the light,
That was nat wont to seen the sonne bright;
Ne how the fir was couched first with stree,
And than with drye stikkes cloven a-three,
2935   And thanne with grene wode and spicerye,
And thanne with clooth of gold and with perrye,
And gerlandes hanginge, ful of many a flour,
The myrre, th'encens, with al so greet savour;
Ne how Arcite lay among al this;
2940   Ne what richesse aboute his body is;
Ne how that Emelye, as was the gise,
Putte in the fir of funeral servise;
Ne how she swowned whan men made the fir;
Ne what she spak, ne what was hir desir,
2945   Ne what juels in the fir men caste,
Whan that the fir was greet and brente faste;
Ne how somme caste hir sheeld, and somme hir spere,
And of hir vestimentz whiche that they were,
And coppes ful of milk and win and blood
2950   Into the fir, that brente as it were wood;
Ne how the Grekes with an huge route
Thries riden al the fir aboute
Upon the left hand, with a loud shoutinge,
And thries with hir speres clateringe,
2955   And thries how the ladies gonne crye,
And how that lad was homward Emelye;

2927 **woneden** dwelled   2928 **fawnes** fauns **amadrydes** hamadryads,
wood-nymphs   2930 **forfered** in fright   2931 **agast** afraid
2932 **wont** accustomed   2933 **couched** laid   2934 **cloven a-three** split in
three   2935 **spicerye** spices   2936 **perrye** jewellery   2938 **myrre** myrrh
savour smell   2945 **juels** precious objects   2948 **vestimentz** robes
2950 **as it were wood** as if it were mad   2951 **route** company
2952 **Thries** three times   2955 **gonne crye** cried out

Ne how Arcite is brent to asshen colde;
Ne how that lichewake was yholde
Al thilke night; ne how the Grekes pleye
The wake-pleyes, ne kepe I noght to seye –   2960
Who wrastleth best, naked with oille enoint,
Ne who that baar him best, in no disjoint;
I wol nat tellen al how that they goon
Hoom til Atthenes whan the pleye is doon,
But shortly to the point than wol I wende,   2965
And maken of my longe tale an ende.

   By proces, and by lengthe of certein yeris,
Al stinted is the moorninge and the teris
Of Grekes, by oon general assent.
Thanne semed me ther was a parlement   2970
At Atthenes, upon certein pointes and caas,
Among the whiche pointes yspoken was
To have with certein contrees alliaunce,
And have fully of Thebans obeisaunce.
For which this noble Theseus anon   2975
Leet senden after gentil Palamon,
Unwist of him what was the cause and why.
But in his blake clothes sorwefully
He cam at his comandement in hie;
Tho sente Theseus for Emelye.   2980

   Whan they were set, and hust was al the place,
And Theseus abiden hadde a space
Er any word cam from his wise brest,
His eyen sette he theras was his lest,
And with a sad visage he siked stille,   2985
And after that, right thus he seide his wille:

2958 **lichewake** wake, watch over a corpse **yholde** held
2960 **wake-pleyes** funeral games   2961 **enoint** anointed
2962 **baar him** performed **in no disjoint** in no difficulty   2967 **certein** a
certain number of   2968 **stinted** ended   2970 **parlement** council
2974 **obeisaunce** obedience   2976 Had noble Palamon sent for
2977 **Unwist of** unknown to   2979 **in hie** in haste   2981 **hust** hushed
2982 **abiden** waited   2984 **sette** rested **lest** desire   2985 **sad visage** grave
face **siked stille** sighed quietly   2986 **seide his wille** spoke his mind

'The Firste Moevere of the cause above,
Whan he first made the faire cheine of love,
Greet was th'effect and heigh was his entente.
2990 Wel wiste he why, and what therof he mente;
For with that faire cheine of love he bond
The fir, the eir, the water, and the lond,
In certein boundes, that they may nat flee.
That same prince and that Moevere', quod he,
2995 'Hath stabliced in this wrecched world adoun
Certeine dayes and duracioun
To al that is engendred in this place,
Over the whiche day they may nat pace,
Al mowe they yet tho dayes wel abregge.
3000 Ther nedeth noon auctoritee t'allegge,
For it is proved by experience,
But that me list declaren my sentence.
Thanne may men by this ordre wel discerne
That thilke Moevere stable is and eterne.
3005 Wel may men knowe, but it be a fool,
That every part diriveth from his hool;
For nature hath nat take his biginning
Of no partie or cantel of a thing,
But of a thing that parfit is and stable,
3010 Descendinge so til it be corrumpable.
And therfore, of his wise purveiaunce,
He hath so wel biset his ordinaunce,
That speces of thinges and progressiouns
Shullen enduren by successiouns,

2987 **Firste Moevere** see n.   2989 **th'effect** the purpose **entente** wisdom
2993 **certein** fixed   2995 **stabliced** established   2996 **Certeine** limited
2998 **pace** pass   2999–3000 Although they may well shorten those days.
There is no need to cite written evidence   3002 **declaren my sentence** make
my meaning clear   3005 **but** unless   3006 **diriveth** derives **his hool** its
whole   3007 **his** its   3008 **cantel** portion   3010 **corrumpable** corruptible,
subject to decay   3011 **purveiaunce** providence
3012 **biset his ordinaunce** ordered his plan   3013 **speces** species
progressiouns processes, developments   3014 **by successiouns** successively,
in succession

And noght eterne, withouten any lie.   3015
This maystow understonde and seen at eye.
   'Lo, the ook, that hath so long a norisshinge,
From time that it first biginneth springe,
And hath so long a lif, as we may see,
Yet at the laste wasted is the tree.   3020
   'Considereth eek how that the harde stoon,
Under oure feet on which we ride and goon,
Yit wasteth it as it lith by the weye.
The brode river somtime wexeth dreye;
The grete townes se we wane and wende.   3025
Than may ye se that al this thing hath ende.
   'Of man and womman se we wel also,
That nedes in oon of thise termes two –
This is to seyn, in youthe or elles age –
He moot be deed, the king as shal a page.   3030
Som in his bed, som in the depe see,
Som in the large feeld, as ye may se.
Ther helpeth noght – al gooth that ilke weye.
Thanne may I seyn that al this thing moot
     deye.
   'What maketh this but Juppiter the king,   3035
That is prince and cause of alle thing,
Converting al unto his propre welle
From which it is derived, sooth to telle?
And heeragains no creature on live,
Of no degree, availleth for to strive.   3040
   'Thanne is it wisdom, as it thinketh me,
To maken vertu of necessitee,
And take it wel that we may nat eschue,
And nameliche that to us alle is due.

3020 **wasted** destroyed   3024 **wexeth** becomes   3025 **wende** pass away
3028 **nedes** of necessity **termes** states   3030 **page** commoner
3031 **Som ... som** one ... one   3033 There's no help for it – everything
goes the same way   3037 Turning back everything to its own source
3039 **heeragains** in opposition to this **on live** alive   3042 To make the best
of what is unavoidable   3043 **eschue** avoid   3044 **nameliche** especially

3045 And whoso gruccheth oght, he dooth folye,
And rebel is to him that al may gye.
And certeinly, a man hath moost honour
To dien in his excellence and flour,
Whan he is siker of his goode name.
3050 Thanne hath he doon his freend ne him no shame,
And gladder oghte his freend been of his deeth,
Whan with honour up yolden is his breeth,
Than whan his name appalled is for age,
For al forgeten is his vasselage.
3055 Thanne is it best, as for a worthy fame,
To dien whan that he is best of name.
    'The contrarye of al this is wilfulnesse.
Why grucchen we? Why have we hevinesse,
That goode Arcite, of chivalrye flour,
3060 Departed is with duetee and honour
Out of this foule prisoun of this lif?
Why grucchen heere his cosin and his wif
Of his welfare that loved hem so weel?
Kan he hem thank? Nay, God wot, never a deel!
3065 – That bothe his soule and eek hemself offende,
And yet they mowe hir lustes nat amende.
    'What may I conclude of this longe serye,
But after wo I rede us to be merye,
And thanken Juppiter of al his grace?
3070 And er that we departen from this place,
I rede that we make of sorwes two
O parfit joye, lastinge everemo.
And loketh now, wher moost sorwe is herinne,
Ther wol I first amenden and biginne.

3045 **grucceth oght** grumbles at all **dooth folye** acts foolishly
3046 **gye** rule   3049 **siker** sure   3050 **him** himself
3052 **up yolden** relinquished   3053 **appalled** enfeebled
3054 **vasselage** knightly prowess   3058 **hevinesse** sorrow
3060 **with duetee** as is due   3064 **Kan he him thank** does he owe them
thanks **never a deel** not at all   3066 **hir lustes . . . amende** increase their
own happiness   3067 **serye** process   3068 **rede** advise

'Suster,' quod he, 'this is my ful assent,   3075
With al th'avis heer of my parlement,
That gentil Palamon, youre owene knight,
That serveth yow with wille, herte, and might,
And evere hath doon, sin ye first him knewe,
That ye shul of youre grace upon him rewe,   3080
And taken him for housbonde and for lord.
Lene me youre hond, for this is oure accord;
Lat se now of youre wommanly pitee.
He is a kinges brother sone, pardee;
And thogh he were a povre bachiler,   3085
Sin he hath served yow so many a yeer,
And had for yow so greet adversitee,
It moste been considered, leveth me,
For gentil mercy oghte to passen right.'

 Thanne seide he thus to Palamon the knight: 3090
'I trowe ther nedeth litel sermoning
To make yow assente to this thing!
Com neer, and taak youre lady by the hond.'
 Bitwixen hem was maad anon the bond
That highte matrimoigne or mariage,   3095
By al the conseil and the baronage.
And thus with alle blisse and melodye
Hath Palamon ywedded Emelye;
And God, that al this wide world hath wroght,
Sende him his love, that hath it deere aboght!   3100
For now is Palamon in alle wele,
Livinge in blisse, in richesse, and in hele.
And Emelye him loveth so tendrely,
And he hir serveth so gentilly,

3075 **ful assent** whole-hearted opinion   3076 **th'avis** the opinion
parlement council   3080 **of youre grace** graciously   **rewe** take pity
3082 **accord** agreement   3083 **Lat se** show   3088 **moste been** would have
to be   **leveth** believe   3089 **to passen right** to go beyond justice
3091 **sermoning** lecturing   3094 **Bitwixen** between
3095 **matrimoigne** matrimony   3096 **conseil** council
3100 **deere aboght** paid dearly for   3101 **wele** prosperity
3102 **hele** health   3104 **gentilly** considerately

3105 That nevere was ther no word hem bitwene
Of jalousye, or any oother tene.
Thus endeth Palamon and Emelye,
And God save al this faire compaignye! Amen.

Heere is ended the Knightes Tale.

THE MILLER'S PROLOGUE

*Heere folwen the wordes bitwene the
Hoost and the Millere.*

Whan that the Knight had thus his tale ytold,
3110 In al the route ne was ther yong ne old
That he ne seide it was a noble storye
And worthy for to drawen to memorye,
And namely the gentils everychon.
Oure Hooste lough, and swoor, 'So moot I gon,
3115 This gooth aright; unbokeled is the male!
Lat se now who shal telle another tale,
For trewely the game is wel bigonne.
Now telleth ye, sire Monk, if that ye konne,
Somwhat to quite with the Knightes tale.'
3120   The Miller, that for dronken was al pale,
So that unnethe upon his hors he sat,
He nolde avalen neither hood ne hat,

3106 **tene** vexation, annoyance

3110 **route** company   3112 **drawen to memorye** recall
3113 **gentils** well-born people   3114 **lough** laughed **So moot I gon** as I live
3115 **unbokeled is the male** the bag is unbuckled (i.e. we have made a start)
3119 **to quite with** to requite   3120 **for dronken** because of being drunk
3121 **unnethe** with difficulty   3122 **avalen** take off

N'abiden no man for his curteisye,
But in Pilates vois he gan to crye
And swoor, 'By armes, and by blood and bones,   3125
I kan a noble tale for the nones,
With which I wol now quite the Knightes tale!'
Oure Hooste saugh that he was dronke of ale,
And seide, 'Abide, Robin, leeve brother;
Som bettre man shal telle us first another.   3130
Abide, and lat us werken thriftily.'
      'By Goddes soule,' quod he, 'that wol nat I!
For I wol speke, or elles go my wey.'
Oure Hoost answerde, 'Tel on, a devel wey!
Thow art a fool; thy wit is overcome.'   3135
      'Now herkneth,' quod the Millere, 'alle and
            some!
But first I make a protestacioun
That I am dronke – I knowe it by my soun.
And therfore, if that I misspeke or seye,
Wite it the ale of Southwerk, I yow preye.   3140
For I wol telle a legende and a lif
Both of a carpenter and of his wif,
How that a clerk hath set the wrightes cappe.'
      The Reve answerde and seide, 'Stint thy clappe!
Lat be thy lewed dronken harlotrye!   3145
It is a sinne and eek a greet folye
To apeiren any man, or him defame,
And eek to bringen wives in swich fame.
Thow mayst inow of othere thinges seyn.'
      This dronken Millere spak ful sone agein   3150

3123 abiden wait for   3126 kan know   for the nones for the occasion
3129 leeve dear   3131 werken thriftily proceed in a seemly fashion
3134 a devel wey in the devil's name   3136 alle and some one and all
3138 soun sound   3139 misspeke speak amiss   3140 Wite it blame it on
3143 set the wrightes cappe made a fool of the carpenter
3144 clappe noise   3145 lewed coarse   harlotrye dirty story
3147 apeiren slander   3148 And also to bring women into such repute
3149 inow enough   3150 agein in answer

And seide, 'Leve brother Osewold,
Who hath no wif, he is no cokewold;
But I seye nat therfore that thow art oon.
Ther been ful goode wives many oon,
3155   And evere a thousand goode ayeins oon badde;
That knowestow wel thyself but if thow madde.
Why artow angry with my tale now?
I have a wif, pardee, as wel as thow,
Yet nolde I, for the oxen in my plough,
3160   Take upon me moore than inough,
As demen of myself that I were oon.
I wol bileve wel that I am noon.
An housbonde shal noght been inquisitif
Of Goddes privetee, nor of his wif.
3165   So he may finde Goddes foison there,
Of the remenant nedeth noght enquere.'
        What sholde I moore seyn, but this Millere
He nolde his wordes for no man forbere,
But tolde his cherles tale in his manere.
3170   M'athinketh that I shal reherce it here;
And therfore every gentil wight I preye,
Demeth noght, for Goddes love, that I seye
Of ivel entente, but for I moot reherse
Hir tales alle, be they bet or werse,
3175   Or elles falsen som of my matere.
And therfore, whoso list it noght ihere,
Turne over the leef and chese another tale,
For he shal finde inowe, grete and smale,

3152 **cokewold** cuckold   3155 **ayeins oon badde** for every bad one
3156 **but if thow madde** unless you are mad   3161 **As demen** by believing
3164 **privetee** secrets   3165 **foison** abundance   3166 There is no need to
enquire about the rest   3168 **his wordes . . . forbere** spare his language
3170 **M'athinketh** I regret   **reherce** repeat   3171 **wight** person
3172 **Demeth noght** do not believe   3173 **entente** intention   **for** because
3174 **be they bet** whether they are better   3175 **falsen** falsify
3177 **chese** choose

Of storial thing that toucheth gentillesse,
And eek moralitee and holinesse.   3180
Blameth noght me, if that ye chese amis.
The Millere is a cherl; ye knowe wel this.
So was the Reve eek, and othere mo,
And harlotrye they tolden bothe two.
Aviseth yow, and put me out of blame –   3185
And eek men shal noght make ernest of game.

THE MILLER'S TALE

Heere biginneth the Millere his Tale.

Whilom ther was dwelling in Oxenford
A riche gnof, that gestes held to bord,
And of his craft he was a carpenter.
With him ther was dwellinge a povre scoler   3190
Had lerned art, but al his fantasye
Was turned for to lerne astrologye,
And koude a certein of conclusions,
To demen by interrogacions,
If that men axed him in certein houres   3195
Whan that men sholde have droghte, or ellis
      shoures,
Or if men axed him what sholde bifalle
Of everything – I may nat rekene hem alle.

3179 **storial** historical **toucheth gentillesse** concerns noble behaviour
3181 **amis** wrongly   3185 **Aviseth yow** reflect
3186 **make ernest of game** take a joke seriously

3187 **Oxenford** Oxford   3188 **gnof** churl, fellow **gestes** lodgers
held to bord boarded   3190 **povre scoler** poor student
3191 **Had lerned art** who had studied the arts course **fantasye** inclination
3193 **a certein of conclusions** a certain number of principles
3194 **interrogacions** investigations   3196 **droghte** drought

This clerk was cleped hende Nicholas.
3200 Of derne love he koude, and of solas,
And therto he was sleigh and ful privee,
And lik a maiden meke for to see.
A chambre hadde he in that hostelrye,
Allone, withouten any compaignye,
3205 Ful fetisly ydight with herbes swoote;
And he himself as swete as is the roote
Of licoris, or any cetewale.
His Almageste, and bokes grete and smale,
His astrelabye, longinge for his art,
3210 His augrim-stones, layen faire apart
On shelves couched at his beddes heed;
His presse ycovered with a falding reed.
And al above ther lay a gay sautrye,
On which he made a-nightes melodye
3215 So swetely that al the chambre rong;
And *Angelus ad virginem* he song,
And after that he song the kinges note.
Ful often blessed was his murye throte.
And thus this swete clerk his time spente,
3220 After his frendes finding and his rente.
    This carpenter had wedded newe a wif,
Which that he loved moore than his lif.
Of eighteteene yeer she was of age.
Jalous he was, and heeld hire narwe in cage,
3225 For she was yong and wilde, and he was old,
And demed himself been lik a cokewold.

3199 **cleped** called **hende** courtly   3200 **derne love** clandestine love
solas fun   3201 **sleigh** clever **privee** discreet   3205 **fetisly ydight** elegantly
garnished **swoote** sweet   3207 **licoris** liquorice **cetewale** zedoary (a spice)
3209 **astrelabye** astrolabe (n.) **longinge for** belonging to
3210 **augrim-stones** counters used in arithmetic (n.)   3211 **couched** placed
3212 **presse** cupboard (n.) **falding reed** red cloth (g.)
3213 **sautrye** psaltery (n.)   3214 **a-nightes** at night   3215 **rong** echoed
3217 **kinges note** the name of a song (n.)   3218 **murye throte** musical voice
3220 **frendes finding** what his friends provided **rente** income
3221 **newe** recently   3224 **narwe** closely   3226 And thought himself likely
to be a cuckold

He knew nat Catoun – for his wit was rude –
That bad men sholde wedde his similitude.
Men sholde wedden after hir estaat,
For youthe and elde is often at debaat.   3230
But sith that he was fallen in the snare,
He moste endure, as oother folk, his care.
    Fair was this yonge wif, and therwithal
As any wesele hir body gent and smal.
A ceint she wered, barred al of silk;   3235
A barmecloth, as whit as morne milk,
Upon hir lendes, ful of many a goore.
Whit was hir smok and broiden al bifore
And eek bihinde, on hir coler aboute,
Of col-blak silk, withinne and eek withoute.   3240
The tapes of hir white voluper
Were of the same sute of hir coler;
Hir filet brood of silk, and set ful hye.
And sikerly she hadde a likerous eye.
Ful smale ypulled were hir browes two,   3245
And tho were bent and blake as any slo.
She was ful moore blisful on to see
Than is the newe pere-jonette tree,
And softer than the wolle is of a wether;
And by hir girdel heng a purs of lether,   3250
Tasseled with grene and perled with latoun.
In al this world, to seken up and doun,

3227 **rude** uneducated   3228 **wedde his similitude** marry someone like
himself   3229 **after hir estaat** according to their condition in life
3230 **is . . . at debaat** are at odds with each other   3232 **care** sorrow
3234 **wesele** weasel **gent** shapely   3235 **ceint** belt **barred al of silk** striped
with silk   3236 **barmecloth** apron **morne** morning   3237 **lendes** hips
goore gore, inset panel in a skirt (to make it flare out)
3238 **broiden** embroidered   3241 **voluper** cap
3242 **of the same sute of** matching, of the same cloth as
3243 **filet brood** broad headband   3244 **likerous** flirtatious
3245 **Ful smale ypulled** plucked very finely   3246 **tho** they **slo** sloe
3247 **blisful** lovely   3248 **pere-jonette** an early-ripening kind of pear
3249 **wether** (male) sheep   3251 **perled with latoun** decorated with
pearl-shaped bits of brass

Ther nis no man so wis that koude thenche
So gay a popelote, or swich a wenche.
3255 Ful brighter was the shining of hir hewe
Than in the Tour the noble yforged newe.
But of hir song, it was as loude and yerne
As any swalwe sitting on a berne.
Therto she koude skippe and make game,
3260 As any kide or calf folwinge his dame.
Hir mouth was swete as bragot or the meeth,
Or hoord of apples leid in hey or heeth.
Winsing she was, as is a joly colt,
Long as a mast, and upright as a bolt.
3265 A broche she bar upon hir loue coler,
As brood as is the boos of a bokeler.
Hir shoes were laced on hir legges hye.
She was a primerole, a piggesnye,
For any lord to leggen in his bedde,
3270 Or yet for any good yeman to wedde.
   Now sire, and eft sire, so bifel the cas,
That on a day this hende Nicholas
Fil with this yonge wif to rage and pleye,
Whil that hir housbonde was at Oseneye –
3275 As clerkes been ful subtil and ful queinte.
And prively he caughte hire by the queinte,
And seide, 'Iwys, but if ich have my wille,
For derne love of thee, lemman, I spille!'

3253 **thenche** imagine   3254 **popelote** pet, darling   3255 **shining** radiance
3256 **Tour** Tower of London (the site of the principal London Mint)
noble gold coin (g.) **yforged newe** freshly minted   3257 **yerne** lively
3258 **swalwe** swallow   3259 **make game** frolic   3260 **dame** mother
3261 **bragot** drink made of ale and honey **meeth** mead
3262 **heeth** heather   3263 **Winsing** skittish **joly** frisky
3264 **upright as a bolt** straight as an arrow   3265 **broche** brooch
loue coler low-cut collar   3266 **boos of a bokeler** boss of a shield
3268 **primerole** primrose, cowslip **piggesnye** darling, pet   3269 **leggen** lay
3273 **Fil . . . to rage and pleye** began to fool about and have fun
3275 **queinte** clever   3276 **queinte** crotch (n.)   3277 **Iwys** for sure
but if unless   3278 **derne** secret **lemman** sweetheart **spille** die

And heeld hire harde by the haunche-bones,
And seide, 'Lemman, love me al atones,   3280
Or I wol dien, also God me save!'
And she sprong as a colt doth in the trave,
And with hir heed she wryed faste awey.
She seide, 'I wol nat kisse thee, by my fey!
Why, lat be,' quod she, 'lat be, Nicholas!   3285
Or I wol crye "out, harrow!" and "allas!"
Do wey youre handes, for youre curteisye!'
        This Nicholas gan mercy for to crye,
And spak so faire, and profred him so faste,
That she hir love him graunted atte laste,   3290
And swoor hir ooth, by Seint Thomas of Kent,
That she wolde been at his comaundement,
Whan that she may hir leiser wel espye.
'Min housbonde is so ful of jalousye
That, but ye waite wel and been privee,   3295
I woot right wel I nam but deed,' quod she.
'Ye moste been ful derne as in this cas.'
        'Nay, therof care thee noght,' quod Nicholas,
'A clerk had litherly biset his while
But if he koude a carpenter bigile.'   3300
And thus they been acorded and ysworn
To waite a time, as I have told biforn.
        Whan Nicholas had doon thus everydel,
And thakked hire aboute the lendes wel,
He kiste hir swete, and taketh his sautrye   3305
And pleyeth faste, and maketh melodye.

3279 **haunche-bones** thigh-bones   3281 **also** as   3282 **trave** frame in which
a frisky horse is placed to be shod   3283 **wryed faste** turned vigorously
3285 **lat be** leave off   3287 **Do wey** take away **for youre curteisye** kindly, if
you please   3288 **gan mercy for to crye** begged forgiveness
3289 **profred him** offered himself **faste** earnestly
3293 **hir leiser wel espye** see her chance   3295 **but** unless **waite** watch
3296 **I nam but deed** I am as good as dead   3297 **derne** secret
3298 **therof care thee noght** don't worry about it   3299 A student would
have spent his time poorly   3300 **But if he koude** if he could not
3304 **thakked** patted **lendes** buttocks

Thanne fil it thus, that to the parissh chirche,
Cristes owene werkes for to wirche,
This goode wif wente on an haliday.
3310   Hir forheed shoon as bright as any day,
So was it wasshen whan she leet hir werk.
    Now was ther of that chirche a parissh clerk,
That which that was ycleped Absolon.
Crul was his heer, and as the gold it shoon,
3315   And strouted as a fanne large and brode.
Ful streight and evene lay his joly shode;
His rode was reed, his eyen greye as goos.
With Poules window corven on his shoos,
In hoses rede he wente fetisly.
3320   Yclad he was ful smal and proprely
Al in a kirtel of a light waget;
Ful faire and thikke been the pointes set.
And therupon he hadde a gay surplis,
As whit as is the blosme upon the ris.
3325   A mery child he was, so God me save!
Wel koude he laten blood and clippe and shave,
And make a chartre of lond or aquitaunce.
In twenty manere koude he trippe and daunce,
After the scole of Oxenforde tho,
3330   And with his legges casten to and fro,
And pleyen songes on a smal rubible;
Therto he song somtime a loud quinible,

3308 **wirche** perform   3309 **haliday** holy day   3311 **leet** left off
3314 **Crul** curly   3315 **strouted** stuck out **fanne** fan   3316 **evene** straight
joly shode handsome parting (of hair)   3317 **rode** complexion
3318 **Poules window corven** the window of St Paul's cut out (n.)
3319 **fetisly** elegantly   3320 **ful smal** in very close-fitting clothes
3321 **kirtel** tunic **waget** light-blue cloth   3322 **pointes** laces (n.)
3323 **therupon** over that   3324 **blosme** blossom **ris** spray, branch
3325 **child** youth   3326 **laten blood** let blood (n.)
3327 **chartre of . . . aquitaunce** document in evidence of a transaction
3328 **manere** ways   3330 **casten** leap   3331 **rubible** ribible, two-stringed
fiddle (n.)   3332 **quinible** high treble part (*lit.* one octave above the treble)

And as wel koude he pleye on a giterne.
In al the toun nas brewhous ne taverne
That he ne visited with his solas,   3335
Ther any gailard tappestere was.
But sooth to seyn, he was somdel squaimous
Of farting, and of speche daungerous.
    This Absolon, that joly was and gay,
Goth with a sencer on the haliday,   3340
Sensinge the wives of the parisshe faste;
And many a lovely look on hem he caste,
And namely on this carpenteres wif.
To loke on hire him thoughte a mery lif,
She was so propre and swete and likerous.   3345
I dar wel seyn, if she had been a mous
And he a cat, he wolde hir hente anon.
This parisshe clerk, this joly Absolon,
Hath in his herte swich a love-longinge
That of no wif ne took he noon offringe;   3350
For curteisye, he seide, he wolde noon.
    The moone, whan it was night, ful brighte
        shoon,
And Absolon his giterne hath ytake;
For paramours he thoghte for to wake.
And forth he goth, jolif and amorous,   3355
Til he cam to the carpenteres hous,
A litel after cokkes hadde ycrowe,
And dressed him up by a shot-windowe

3333 **giterne** gittern, a lute-like instrument (n.)   3334 **nas** there was no
3335 **solas** powers of entertaining   3336 **gailard tappestere** gaily dressed
barmaid   3337–8 **somdel squaimous Of** somewhat squeamish about
daungerous fastidious   3339 **joly** gallant   3340 **sencer** censer
3341 **Sensinge** censing **faste** vigorously   3342 **lovely** fond, amorous
3345 **propre** good-looking **likerous** delectable   3347 **hente** catch
3351 **wolde noon** did not want any   3354 **paramours** love
3357 **ycrowe** crowed   3358 **dressed him** took up his position
shot-windowe casement window (n.)

That was upon the carpenteres wal.
3360 He singeth in his vois gentil and smal:
'Now dere lady, if thy wille be,
I preye yow that ye wol rewe on me',
Ful wel acordant to his giterninge.
This carpenter awook and herde him singe,
3365 And spak unto his wif and seide anon,
'What, Alison, herestow noght Absolon,
That chaunteth thus under oure boures wal?'
And she answerde hir housbonde therwithal:
'Yis, God wot, John, I here it everydel.'
3370   This passeth forth; what wol ye bet than wel?
Fro day to day this joly Absolon
So woweth hire that him is wo bigon.
He waketh al the night and al the day;
He kembed his lokkes brode and made him gay;
3375 He woweth hire by menes and brocage,
And swoor he wolde been hir owene page;
He singeth, brokking as a nightingale;
He sente hir piment, meeth and spiced ale,
And wafres, piping hoot out of the glede;
3380 And for she was of towne, he profred mede.
For som folk wol be wonnen for richesse,
And som for strokes, and som for gentilesse.
Som time, to shewe his lightnesse and maistrye,
He pleyeth Herodes upon a scaffold hye.
3385 But what availleth him as in this cas?
She loveth so this hende Nicholas

3360 **gentil and smal** refined and high-pitched   3362 **rewe** take pity
3363 **acordant to his giterninge** in harmony with his accompaniment on the
gittern   3367 **boures wal** bedroom wall   3369 **everydel** all   3370 So this
goes on; what more do you want   3372 **woweth** woos **him is wo bigon** he
is overcome with sadness   3374 **made him gay** made himself handsome
3375 **menes** intermediaries **brocage** employment of a go-between
3376 **page** servant   3377 **brokking** ?warbling   3378 **piment** wine
sweetened with honey and flavoured with spices   3379 **wafres** wafers, thin
cakes **glede** fire   3380 **of town** from the town **mede** payment
3382 **strokes** blows   3383 **lightnesse** agility   3384 **scaffold** stage (n.)

That Absolon may blowe the bukkes horn;
He ne had for his labour but a scorn.
And thus she maketh Absolon hir ape,
And al his ernest turneth til a jape.   3390
Ful sooth is this proverbe, it is no lie,
Men seyth right thus: 'Alwey the nye slye
Maketh the ferre leeve to be looth.'
For thogh that Absolon be wood or wrooth,
Bicause that he fer was from hir sighte,   3395
This nye Nicholas stood in his lighte.
Now bere thee wel, thow hende Nicholas!
For Absolon may waille and singe 'allas!'
    And so bifel it, on a Saterday
This carpenter was goon til Osenay;   3400
And hende Nicholas and Alisoun
Acorded been to this conclusioun,
That Nicholas shal shapen hem a wile
This sely jalous housbonde to bigile.
And if so be the game wente aright,   3405
She sholde slepen in his arm al night;
For this was hir desir and his also.
And right anoon, withouten wordes mo,
This Nicholas no lenger wolde tarye,
But doth ful softe unto his chambre carye   3410
Bothe mete and drinke for a day or tweye;
And to hir housbonde bad hir for to seye,
If that he axed after Nicholas,
She sholde seye she niste wher he was;

3387 **blowe the bukkes horn** go and twiddle his thumbs (*lit.* to idle away
time blowing a goat's horn, like a shepherd)
3389 **maketh . . . hir ape** makes her dupe   3390 **jape** joke
3391 **sooth** true   3392 **nye slye** rogue who is close by   3393 Makes the
loved one who is further off fall out of favour   3394 **wood** angry
3396 **stood in his lighte** put him at a disadvantage   3397 **bere thee** bear
yourself   3402 **conclusioun** decision   3403 **shapen hem a wile** devise a
trick for them   3404 **sely** simple   3410 **softe** unobtrusively
3414 **niste** did not know

3415 Of al that day she seigh him noght with eye.
      She trowed that he was in maladye,
      For for no cry hir maide koude him calle;
      He nolde answere, for thing that mighte falle.
          This passeth forth al thilke Saterday,
3420 That Nicholas stille in his chambre lay,
      And eet and sleep, or dide what him leste,
      Til Sonday, that the sonne gooth to reste.
      This sely carpenter hath greet mervaille
      Of Nicholas, or what thing mighte him aille,
3425 And seide, 'I am adrad, by Seint Thomas,
      It stondeth nat aright with Nicholas.
      God shilde that he deide sodeinly!
      This world is now ful tikel sikerly;
      I saugh today a corps yborn to chirche
3430 That now, a Monday last, I saugh him wirche.
      Go up,' quod he unto his knave anoon,
      'Clepe at his dore, or knokke with a stoon.
      Loke how it is, and tel me boldely.'
          This knave gooth him up ful sturdily,
3435 And at the chambre-dore whil that he stood,
      He cride and knokked as that he were wood.
      'What how! what do ye, maister Nicholay?
      How may ye slepen al the longe day?'
      – But al for noght; he herde nat a word.
3440 An hole he fond, ful lowe upon a bord,
      Theras the cat was wont in for to crepe,
      And at that hole he looked in ful depe,

3416 **trowed** believed **in maladye** ill   3418 **for thing that mighte falle** in
spite of anything that might happen   3419 **passeth forth** continues
3420 **stille** quietly   3421 And ate and slept, or did what pleased him
3423–4 **hath greet mervaille Of** wonders greatly about **him aille** be wrong
with him   3425 **adrad** afraid   3426 **It stondeth nat aright** all is not well
3427 **shilde** forbid   3428 **tikel** changeable, unreliable
3430 **That . . . him** whom **wirche** work   3431 **knave** servant
3432 **Clepe** call   3436 **wood** mad   3438 **may ye** can you
al the longe day all day long   3440 **fond** found   3441 **Theras** where
wont accustomed   3442 **depe** far inside

And atte laste he hadde of him a sighte.
This Nicholas sat caping evere uprighte,
As he had kiked on the newe moone.   3445
Adoun he gooth, and tolde his maister soone
In what array he saugh this ilke man.

    This carpenter to blessen him bigan,
And seide, 'Help us, Seinte Frideswide!
A man woot litel what him shal bitide.   3450
This man is falle, with his astromye,
In som woodnesse, or in som agonye.
I thoghte ay wel how that it sholde be;
Men sholde noght knowe of Goddes privetee.
Ye, blessed be alwey a lewed man,   3455
That noght but oonly his bileve kan!
So ferde another clerk with astromye;
He walked in the feeldes for to prye
Upon the sterres, what ther sholde bifalle,
Til he was in a marle-pit yfalle;   3460
He saw nat that! But yet, by Seint Thomas,
Me reweth sore of hende Nicholas.
He shall be rated of his studying,
If that I may, by Jesus hevene king!
Get me a staf, that I may under-spore,   3465
Whil that thow, Robin, hevest of the dore.
He shal out of his studying, as I gesse.'
And to the chambre-dore he gan him dresse.
His knave was a strong carl for the nones,
And by the haspe he haf it of atones;   3470

3444 **caping evere uprighte** continually staring upwards
3445 **kiked on** gazed at   3446 **soone** straightaway   3447 **array** state
3448 **blessen him** cross himself   3452 **woodnesse** madness **agonye** fit
3454 **privetee** secrets   3455 **Ye** yes **lewed** uneducated   3456 **bileve** creed
kan knows   3458 **prye** gaze   3460 **marle-pit** lime-pit
3462 **Me reweth sore of** I am deeply sorry for   3463 **rated of** scolded for
3465 **under-spore** lever from beneath   3466 **hevest of** lift off
3468 **gan him dresse** turned his attention   3470 **haf it of** lifted it off

Into the floor the dore fil anoon.
    This Nicholas sat ay as stille as stoon,
And evere caped up into the eir.
This carpenter wende he were in despeir,

3475   And hente him by the shuldres mightily
And shook him harde, and cride spitously.
'What, Nicholay, what how! What, loke adoun!
Awake, and thenk on Cristes passioun!
I crouche thee from elves and fro wightes.'

3480   – Therwith the night-spel seide he anon-rightes
On foure halves of the hous aboute,
And on the thresshfold of the dore withoute.
'Jesu Crist, and Seinte Benedight,
Blesse this hous from every wikked wight,

3485   For nightes verye, the white *Pater noster*!
Where wentestow, Seinte Petres soster?'
    And atte laste this hende Nicholas
Gan for to sike soore, and seide, 'Allas!
Shal al the world be lost eftsones now?'

3490   This carpenter answerde, 'What seystow?
What, thenk on God, as we doon, men that swinke!'
This Nicholas answerde, 'Fecche me drinke,
And after wol I speke in privetee,
Of certein thing that toucheth me and thee;

3495   I wol telle it noon oother man, certain.'
    This carpenter gooth doun and comth again,
And broghte of mighty ale a large quart.
And whan that ech of hem had dronke his part,

3472 **stille** silent   3473 **caped** gawped **eir** air
3474 **wende he were** thought he was   3476 **spitously** vehemently
3479 **crouche . . . fro wightes** guard from supernatural beings by making the
sign of the cross   3480 **night-spel** see n.   3481 **halves** sides
3482 **withoute** outside   3484 **wight** creature   3485 see n. to 3480–86
3486 **wentestow** did you go **soster** sister   3488 **sike soore** sigh deeply
3489 **eftsones now** right now   3491 **swinke** labour
3494 **toucheth** concerns

This Nicholas his dore faste shette,
And doun the carpenter by him he sette,   3500
And seide, 'John, min hooste lief and deere,
Thou shalt upon thy trouthe swere me heere
That to no wight thou shalt this counseil wreye;
For it is Cristes counseil that I seye,
And if thou telle it man, thou art forlore,   3505
For this vengeaunce thow shalt have therfore,
That if thow wreye me, thow shalt be wood.'
'Nay, Crist forbede it, for his holy blood!'
Quod tho this sely man, 'I nam no labbe,
Ne, thogh I seye, I am nat lief to gabbe.   3510
Sey what thow wolt; I shal it nevere telle
To child ne wif, by him that harwed helle!'
    'Now John,' quod Nicholas, 'I wol noght lie;
I have yfounde in min astrologye,
As I have looked in the moone bright,   3515
That now a Monday next, at quarter night,
Shal falle a rein, and that so wilde and wood
That half so greet was nevere Noes flood.
This world', he seide, 'in lasse than an hour
Shal al be dreint, so hidous is the shour.   3520
Thus shal mankinde drenche and lese hir lif.'
    This carpenter answerde, 'Allas, my wif!
And shal she drenche? Allas, min Alisoun!'
For sorwe of this he fil almoost adoun,
And seide, 'Is ther no remedye in this cas?'   3525
'Why yis, for Gode!' quod hende Nicholas.

3499 **shette** shut   3500 **sette** seated   3501 **lief** beloved
3503 **this counseil wreye** reveal this secret   3505 **man** to anyone
art forlore will be destroyed   3509 **sely** simple **labbe** loudmouth
3510 **lief to gabbe** fond of blabbing   3512 **harwed helle** harrowed hell (n.)
3516 **at quarter night** a quarter of the way through the night
3517 **wood** furious   3518 **Noes** Noah's   3520 **dreint** drowned
3521 **drenche** drown **lese** lose   3526 **for Gode** by God

'– If thow wolt werken after loore and reed.
Thow mayst noght werken after thin owene heed;
For thus seyth Salomon, that was ful trewe:
3530   "Werk al by conseil, and thow shalt noght rewe."
And if thow werken wolt by good consail,
I undertake, withouten mast or sail,
Yit shal I saven hire, and thee, and me.
Hastow nat herd how saved was Noe,
3535   Whan that oure Lord had warned him biforn
That al the world with water sholde be lorn?'
'Yis,' quod this carpenter, 'ful yore ago.'

       'Hastow nat herd,' quod Nicholas, 'also
The sorwe of Noe, with his felaweshipe,
3540   Er that he mighte gete his wif to shipe?
Him hadde levere, I dar wel undertake,
At thilke time than al hise wetheres blake
That she hadde had a ship hirself allone!
And therfore wostow what is best to done?
3545   This axeth haste, and of an hastif thing
Men may noght preche or maken tarying;
       'Anon go gete us faste into this in
A kneding-trogh, or ellis a kemelin,
For ech of us – but looke that they be large –
3550   In which we mowen swimme as in a barge,
And han therinne vitaille suffisaunt
But for a day – fy on the remenaunt!
The water shal aslake and goon away
Aboute prime upon the nexte day.

3527 If you are willing to act according to instruction and advice
3528 **after thin owene heed** according to your own judgement
3530 **Werk al by conseil** always act after consultation **rewe** be sorry
3536 **lorn** destroyed   3537 **ful yore ago** long ago
3541 **Him hadde levere** he would have preferred   3542 **wetheres** (male)
sheep   3544 **wostow** do you know   3547 **in** house
3548 **kneding-trogh** trough in which bread was kneaded **kemelin** trough
(used in cooking or brewing)   3550 **mowen** may
3551 **vitaille suffisaunt** enough food   3553 **aslake** subside
3554 **prime** 9 a.m. (g.)

But Robin may nat wite of this, thy knave,   3555
Ne eek thy maide Gille I may nat save.
Axe noght why, for thogh thou axe me,
I wol noght tellen Goddes privetee.
Suffiseth thee, but if thy wittes madde,
To han as greet a grace as Noe hadde.   3560
Thy wif shal I wel saven out of doute.
Go now thy wey, and speed thee heeraboute.
      'But whan thou hast for hire, and thee, and me,
Ygeten us thise kneding-tubbes thre,
Thanne shaltow hange hem in the roof ful hye,   3565
That no man of oure purveiaunce espye.
And whan thow thus hast doon as I have seid,
And hast oure vitaille faire in hem yleid,
And eek an ax to smite the corde atwo
Whan that the water comth, that we may go   3570
And breke an hole an heigh, upon the gable,
Unto the gardinward over the stable,
That we may frely passen forth oure wey,
Whan that the grete shour is goon awey.
Thanne shaltow swimme as murye, I undertake,   3575
As doth the white doke after his drake.
Thanne wol I clepe, "How, Alison! how, John!
Be murye, for the flood wol passe anon!"
And thou wolt seyn, "Hail, maister Nicholay!
Good morwe, I see thee wel, for it is day."   3580
And thanne shal we be lordes al oure lif
Of al the world, as Noe and his wif.
      'But of o thing I warne thee ful right:
Be wel avised, on that ilke night

3555 wite know   3559 but if thy wittes madde unless your wits are
deranged   3562 speed thee make haste heeraboute about this
3564 Ygeten got   3566 purveiaunce preparations   3568 faire carefully
3569 atwo in two   3571 an heigh high up
3572 Unto the gardinward towards the garden   3576 doke duck
3577 How hello, hi   3578 passe anon soon be over   3583 o one
3584 Be wel avised take good care ilke same

3585   That we been entred into shippes bord,
That noon of us ne speke noght a word,
Ne clepe ne crye, but been in his preyere,
For it is Goddes owene heste deere.
Thy wif and thow mote hange fer atwinne,
3590   For that bitwixe yow shal be no sinne,
Namoore in looking than ther shal in dede.
   'This ordinaunce is seid; go, God thee spede!
Tomorwe at night, whan folk been alle aslepe,
Into oure kneding-tubbes wol we crepe,
3595   And sitten ther, abiding Goddes grace.
Go now thy wey; I have no lenger space
To make of this no lenger sermoning.
Men seyn thus: "Sende the wise and sey nothing."
Thow art so wis, it nedeth thee nat teche.
3600   Go, save oure lif, and that I thee biseche!'
   This sely carpenter gooth forth his wey;
Ful ofte he seide 'allas!', and 'weilawey!'
And to his wif he tolde his privetee;
And she was war, and knew it bet than he,
3605   What al this queinte cast was for to seye.
But nathelees she ferde as she wolde deye,
And seide, 'Allas, go forth thy wey anon!
Help us to scape, or we been dede echon!
I am thy trewe verray wedded wif;
3610   Go, deere spouse, and help to save oure lif.'
   Lo, which a greet thing is affeccioun!
Men may die of imaginacioun,

3585 **into shippes bord** on board ship   3587 **Ne clepe ne crye** nor call nor cry out   3588 **heste** command   3589 **mote hange fer atwinne** must hang far apart   3592 **ordinaunce** order **spede** prosper   3595 **abiding** waiting for   3596 **space** time   3599 **it nedeth thee nat teche** there is no need to teach you   3603 **privetee** secret   3604 **bet** better   3605 What all this ingenious contrivance signified   3606 **ferde as** acted as if
3611 **which a** what a **affeccioun** emotion   3612 **imaginacioun** fantasy, hallucination

So depe may impressioun be take.
This sely carpenter biginneth quake;
Him thinketh verrailiche that he may se   3615
Noes flood come walwing as the see
To drenchen Alison, his hony deere.
He wepeth, waileth, maketh sory cheere;
He siketh with ful many a sory swogh;
He gooth and geteth him a kneding-trogh,   3620
And after that a tubbe and kimelin;
And prively he sente hem to his in,
And heeng hem in the roof in privetee.
His owene hand he made laddres thre
To climben by the ronges and the stalkes   3625
Unto the tubbes hanging in the balkes,
And hem vitailled, bothe trogh and tubbe,
With breed and chese, and good ale in a jubbe,
Suffisinge right inogh as for a day.

But er that he had maad al this array,   3630
He sente his knave and eek his wenche also
Upon his nede to Londoun for to go.
And on the Monday, whan it drogh to night,
He shette his dore withouten candel-light
And dressed alle thing as it sholde be;   3635
And shortly up they clomben alle thre.
They seten stille, wel a furlong way.
'Now, *Pater noster*, clum!' seide Nicholay,
And 'clum!' quod John, and 'clum!' seide Alisoun.

This carpenter seide his devocioun,   3640

3613 So deeply may the mental image be imprinted   3614 **quake** to tremble
3616 **walwing** surging   3618 **maketh sory cheere** acts sorrowfully
3619 **siketh** sighs **swogh** groan   3622 **prively** secretly **in** house
3623 **heeng** hung   3624 **His owene hand** with his own hands
3625 **ronges** rungs **stalkes** uprights (of a ladder)   3626 **balkes** rafters
3627 **vitailled** stocked with food   3628 **jubbe** jar   3629 **right inogh** amply
3630 **array** preparation   3631 **wenche** serving-maid   3632 **nede** business
3633 **drogh to** drew towards   3635 **dressed** arranged
3636 **clomben** climbed   3637 **seten** sat **wel a furlong way** a good two or
three minutes   3638 *Pater noster*, **clum** (say) the Lord's Prayer, (then) hush
3640 **devocioun** prayer

And stille he sit and biddeth his prayere,
Awaitinge on the rein, if he it heere.
The dede sleep, for wery bisinesse,
Fil on this carpenter right (as I gesse)
3645   Aboute corfew-time, or litel moore.
For travaille of his goost he groneth soore,
And eft he routeth, for his heed mislay.
Doun of the laddre stalketh Nicholay,
And Alisoun, ful softe adoun she spedde.
3650   Withouten wordes mo they goon to bedde
Theras the carpenter is wont to lie;
Ther was the revel and the melodye.
And thus lith Alison and Nicholas
In bisinesse of mirthe and of solas,
3655   Til that the belle of laudes gan to ringe,
And freres in the chauncel gonne singe.
      This parissh clerk, this amorous Absolon,
That is for love alwey so wo-bigon,
Upon the Monday was at Oseneye
3660   With compaignye, him to disporte and pleye,
And axed upon cas a cloisterer
Ful prively after John the carpenter.
And he drogh him apart out of the cherche,
And seide, 'I noot; I saugh him here noght werche
3665   Sith Saterday. I trowe that he be went
For timber, ther oure abbot hath him sent;

3641 **sit** (= *sitteth*) sits **biddeth** prays   3642 **Awaitinge on** waiting for
3643 **bisinesse** activity   3645 **corfew-time** curfew (n.)
3646 **travaille** trouble **goost** spirit **soore** deeply   3647 **routeth** snores
mislay lay in an uncomfortable position   3648 **of** from **stalketh** steals
3649 **spedde** hastened   3651 **Theras** where
3654 Occupied with pleasure and fun   3655 **laudes** Lauds (n.)
3656 **chauncel** chancel (the part of the church containing altar and choir
seats, separated from the nave by a screen)
3658 **wo-bigon** overwhelmed with suffering   3661 **upon cas** by chance
cloisterer canon   3663 **drogh** drew   3664 **werche** work
3665 **be went** has gone   3666 **ther** where

For he is wont for timber for to go
And dwellen at the graunge a day or two –
Or ellis he is at his hous, certein.
Wher that he be, I kan noght soothly seyn.'   3670
   This Absolon ful joly was and light,
And thoughte, 'Now is time to wake al night,
For sikerly I saugh him noght stiringe
Aboute his dore sin day bigan to springe.
So mote I thrive, I shal at cokkes crowe   3675
Ful prively knokken at his windowe,
That stant ful lowe upon his boures wal.
To Alison now wol I tellen al
My love-longing, for yit I shal nat misse
That at the leeste wey I shal hir kisse.   3680
Som maner confort shal I have, parfay.
My mouth hath icched al this longe day;
That is a signe of kissing, atte leeste.
Al night me mette eek I was at a feeste.
Therfore I wol go slepe an houre or tweye,   3685
And al the night than wol I wake and pleye.'
   Whan that the firste cok hath crowe, anon
Up rist this joly lovere Absolon,
And him arrayeth gay, at point devis.
But first he cheweth grein and likoris,   3690
To smellen swete, er he hadde kembd his heer.
Under his tonge a trewe-love he beer,
For therby wende he to be gracious.
He rometh to the carpenteres hous,

3668 **graunge** farm (n.)   3671 **joly** cheerful **light** light-hearted
3674 **sin** since   3675 **So mote I thrive** as I may prosper
3677 **stant** (= *standeth*) stands **boures wal** bedroom wall   3679 **misse** fail
3681 **parfay** truly   3682 **icched** itched   3684 **me mette** I dreamed
3687 **crowe** crowed   3688 **rist** (= *riseth*) rises **joly** gallant
3689 And dresses himself finely, to the pitch of perfection
3690 **grein** cardamom **likoris** liquorice   3691 **kembd** combed
3692 **trewe-love** Herb Paris (a plant with four leaves arranged around a
central flower or berry, resembling a true-love knot)
3693 **gracious** attractive, alluring

3695   And stille he stant under the shot-windowe –
        Unto his brest it raughte, it was so lowe –
        And softe he cougheth with a semi-soun:
        'What do ye, honycomb, swete Alisoun?
        My faire brid, my swete cinamome!
3700   Awaketh, lemman min, and speketh to me!
        Wel litel thinken ye upon my wo,
        That for youre love I swete ther I go.
        No wonder is thogh that I swelte and swete;
        I moorne as dooth a lamb after the tete.
3705   Iwys, lemman, I have swich love-longing
        That lik a turtel trewe is my moorning;
        I may nat ete namoore than a maide.'
              'Go fro the window, Jakke fool,' she saide.
        'As help me God, it wol nat be "com pa me"!
3710   I love another – and ellis I were to blame –
        Wel bet than thee, by Jesu, Absolon.
        Go forth thy wey, or I wol caste a stoon,
        And lat me slepe, a twenty devel wey!'
              'Allas,' quod Absolon, 'and weilawey,
3715   That trewe love was evere so ivel biset!
        Thanne kis me, sin that it may be no bet,
        For Jesus love, and for the love of me.'
              'Woltow thanne go thy wey therwith?' quod she.
        'Ye, certes, lemman,' quod this Absolon.
3720   'Thanne make thee redy,' quod she, 'I come anon.'
        And unto Nicholas she seide stille,
        'Now hust, and thou shalt laughen al thy fille!'

3695 **stant** (= *standeth*) stands   3696 **raughte** reached
3697 **cougheth** clears his throat **semi-soun** slight, gentle sound
3699 **brid** bird, 'baby' **cinamome** cinnamon, 'honey'
3700 **lemman** sweetheart   3702 **swete ther I go** sweat as I walk
3703 **swelte** grow faint   3704 **moorne . . . after** yearn for **tete** teat
3706 **turtel** turtle-dove   3709 **com pa me** come and kiss me (n.)
3711 **bet** better   3713 **a twenty devel wey** in the devil's name
3715 **ivel biset** badly bestowed   3721 **stille** quietly   3722 **hust** hush

This Absolon doun sette him on his knees,
And seide, 'I am a lord at alle degrees,
For after this I hope ther cometh moore.   3725
Lemman, thy grace, and swete brid, thin oore!'
    The window she undoth, and that in haste.
'Have do,' quod she, 'com of, and speed thee
        faste,
Lest that oure neighebores thee espye.'
    This Absolon gan wipe his mouth ful drye.   3730
Derk was the night as pich or as the cole,
And at the window out she putte hir hole,
And Absolon, him fil no bet ne wers,
But with his mouth he kiste hir naked ers
Ful savourly, er he were war of this.   3735
Abak he sterte, and thoghte it was amis,
For wel he wiste a womman hath no berd.
He felte a thing al rogh and long yherd,
And seide, 'Fy, allas! what have I do?'
'Tehee!' quod she, and clapte the window to,   3740
And Absolon gooth forth a sory paas.
'A berd, a berd!' quod hende Nicholas,
'By Goddes corpus, this gooth faire and wel!'
    This sely Absolon herde every del,
And on his lippe he gan for anger bite,   3745
And to himself he seide, 'I shal thee quite!'
Who rubbeth now, who froteth now his lippes,
With dust, with sond, with straw, with clooth,
        with chippes,

3724 **lord at alle degrees** lord to the highest degree
3726 **oore** mercy, favour   3727 **undoth** opens
3728 **Have do . . . com of** have done, get on with it **speed thee** hurry up
3731 **pich** pitch   3733 And Absalon had no better or worse fate
3734 **ers** arse   3735 **savourly** with relish   3736 **sterte** sprang
3738 **rogh** rough **long yherd** covered with long hairs
3740 **clapte . . . to** banged shut   3741 **a sory paas** with dejected steps
3743 **Goddes corpus** God's body   3744 **sely** poor **every del** every bit
3746 **quite** pay back   3747 **froteth** rubs

But Absolon, that seyth ful ofte 'Allas!
3750 My soule bitake I unto Sathanas,
But me were levere than al this toun', quod he,
'Of this despit awreken for to be.
Allas,' quod he, 'allas, I nadde ybleint!'
His hote love was coold and al yqueint,
3755 For fro that time that he had kist hir ers
Of paramours he sette noght a kers,
For he was heeled of his maladye.
Ful ofte paramours he gan defye,
And weep as dooth a child that is ybete.
3760 A softe paas he wente over the strete,
Until a smith men clepen daun Gerveis,
That in his forge smithed plough-harneis;
He sharpeth shaar and cultour bisily.
This Absolon knokketh al esily,
3765 And seide, 'Undo, Gerveis, and that anon!'
'What, who artow?' 'It am I, Absolon.'
'What, Absolon! for Cristes swete tree,
Why rise ye so rathe? Ey, *benedicitee*,
What eileth yow? Som gay gerl, God it woot,
3770 Hath broght yow thus upon the viritoot;
By Seinte Note, ye woot wel what I mene!'
This Absolon ne roghte nat a bene
Of al his pley; no word again he yaf.
He hadde moore tow on his distaf

3750 bitake consign Sathanas Satan, the devil   3751-2 But I would rather
be avenged for this humiliation than (own) all this town
3753 ybleint blenched, moved away   3754 yqueint quenched
3756 paramours love kers cress (a worthless object)
3758 gan defye renounced   3760 A softe paas at a leisurely pace
3761 Until to   3762 smithed plough-harneis forged harness or fittings for a
plough   3763 sharpeth sharpens shaar ploughshare cultour coulter (blade
of plough-share)   3764 esily softly   3765 Undo open up   3767 tree cross
3768 rathe early   3769 eileth is wrong with gay gerl loose woman
3770 Has set you spinning (n.)   3772-3 ne roghte nat a bene Of did not
care a bean for pley fun again he yaf returned   3774 He had more business
in hand

Than Gerveis knew, and seide, 'Freend so   3775
    deere,
That hoote cultour in the chimenee heere,
As lene it me; I have therwith to doone,
And I wol bringe it thee again ful soone.'
Gerveis answerde, 'Certes, were it gold,
Or in a poke nobles al untold,   3780
Thow sholdest have, as I am trewe smith!
Ey, Cristes foo, what wol ye do therwith?'
'Therof', quod Absolon, 'be as be may;
I shal wel telle it thee another day' –
And caughte the cultour by the colde stele.   3785

    Ful softe out at the dore he gan to stele,
And wente unto the carpenteres wal.
He cogheth first, and knokketh therwithal
Upon the windowe, right as he dide er.
This Alison answerde, 'Who is ther,   3790
That knokketh so? I warante it a theef!'
'Why nay,' quod he, 'God woot, my swete lief;
I am thin Absolon, my dereling.
Of gold', quod he, 'I have thee broght a ring.
My moder yaf it me, so God me save.   3795
Ful fin it is, and therto wel ygrave;
This wol I yeven thee, if thow me kisse.'

    This Nicholas was risen for to pisse,
And thoughte he wolde amenden al the jape:
He sholde kisse his ers, er that he scape.   3800
And up the window dide he hastily,
And out his ers he putteth prively,
Over the buttok, to the haunche-bon.
And therwith spak this clerk, this Absolon:

3777 Lend it to me; I have (something) to do with it   3780 poke bag
untold uncounted   3782 Cristes foo the devil   3783 Therof as to that
be as be may let it be as it may   3785 stele handle
3788 therwithal as well   3789 er before   3792 lief beloved
3793 dereling darling   3796 ygrave engraved   3798 was risen had got up
3799 amenden al the jape improve on the joke   3801 up ... dide raised

3805 'Spek, swete brid; I noot noght wher thow art.'
           This Nicholas anoon leet fle a fart,
      As greet as it hadde been a thonder-dent,
      That with the strook he was almoost yblent;
      And he was redy with his iren hoot,
3810 And Nicholas amidde the ers he smoot.
      Of gooth the skin, an hande-brede aboute;
      The hoote cultour brende so his toute
      That for the smert he wende for to die.
      As he were wood, for wo he gan to crye:
3815 'Help! Water, water, help, for Goddes herte!'
      This carpenter out of his slomber sterte,
      And herde oon cryen 'Water!' as he were wood,
      And thoghte, 'Allas, now comth Nowelis flood!'
      He sette him up withouten wordes mo,
3820 And with his ax he smoot the corde atwo,
      And doun gooth al – he fond neither to selle,
      Ne breed ne ale, til he cam to the celle
      Upon the floor, and there aswowne he lay.
           Up stirte hire Alison and Nicholay,
3825 And criden 'out!' and 'harrow!' in the strete.
      The neighebores, bothe smale and grete,
      In ronnen for to gauren on this man,
      That yet aswowne lay, bothe pale and wan,
      For with the fal he brosten hadde his arm.
3830 But stonde he moste unto his owene harm,
      For whan he spak, he was anon bore doun
      With hende Nicholas and Alisoun.

3805 **noot noght** do not know   3807 **thonder-dent** thunder-clap
3808 **yblent** blinded   3809 **hoot** hot   3810 **smoot** struck   3811 **Of** off
an hand-brede aboute a hand's breadth all round   3812 **brende** burned
toute rump, arse   3813 **smert** pain **wende for to die** thought he would die
3814 **wood** mad   3816 **sterte** started   3817 **oon** someone
3818 **Nowelis** Noah's   3819 **sette him up** sat up   3820 **atwo** in two
3821-2 **he fond neither to selle, Ne breed ne ale** he did not stop (n.)
celle floor   3823 **aswowne** in a swoon   3824 **Up stirte hire** up jumped
3827 **ronnen** ran **gauren on** stare at   3829 **brosten** broken
3830 **stonde he moste unto** he had to submit to
3831 **bore doun** borne down   3832 **With** by

They tolden every man that he was wood;
He was agast so of Nowelis flood
Thurgh fantasye, that of his vanitee   3835
He hadde yboght him kneding-tubbes thre,
And hadde hem hanged in the roof above,
And that he preyed hem, for Goddes love,
To sitten in the roof, *par compaignye.*

The folk gan laughen at his fantasye;   3840
Into the roof they kiken and they cape,
And turned al his harm unto a jape.
For whatso that this carpenter answerde
It was for noght; no man his reson herde.
With othes grete he was so sworn adoun   3845
That he was holden wood in al the toun,
For every clerk anon-right heeld with oother.
They seide, 'The man was wood, my leve
       brother!'
And every wight gan laughen at this strif.

Thus swived was the carpenteres wif,   3850
For al his keping and his jalousye;
And Absolon hath kist hir nether eye,
And Nicholas is scalded in the toute.
This tale is doon, and God save al the route!

Heere endeth the Millere his Tale.

3834 **agast** afraid   3835 **fantasye** delusion **vanitee** folly
3839 *par compaignye* for company   3841 **kiken** gaze **cape** stare
3844 **reson** explanation, account   3847 **anon-right** immediately
3849 **strif** quarrel   3850 **swived** laid (sexual sense)
3851 **For al his keping** in spite of all his guarding   3852 **nether eye** arsehole

THE REEVE'S PROLOGUE

The Prologe of the Reves Tale.

3855   Whan folk had laughen at this nice cas
      Of Absolon and hende Nicholas,
      Diverse folk diversely they seide,
      But for the moore part they loughe and pleyde;
      Ne at this tale I saugh no man him greve
3860   But it were oonly Osewold the Reve.
      Bicause he was of carpenteres craft,
      A litel ire is in his herte ylaft;
      He gan to grucche, and blamed it a lite.
        'So thee'k,' quod he, 'ful wel koude I thee quite,
3865   With blering of a proud milleres eye,
      If that me liste speke of ribaudye!
      But ik am oold; me list nat pleye for age.
      Gras time is doon; my fodder is now forage.
      This white top writeth mine olde yeris;
3870   Min herte is also mowled as mine heris,
      But if I fare as dooth an openers –
      That ilke fruite is ever lenger the wers
      Til it be roten, in mullok or in stree.
      We olde men, I drede, so fare we:
3875   Til we be roten kan we noght be ripe.
      We hoppe alwey whil that the world wol pipe;

3855 **nice cas** ludicrous incident   3858 **moore part** greater part
pleyde joked   3859 **him greve** get angry   3860 **But it were** unless it was
3862 **ylaft** left   3863 **gan to grucche** grumbled
3864 **So thee'k** (= *So thee ik*) as I prosper **quite** pay back   3865 With the
hoodwinking of a proud miller   3867 **ik** I   3869 **writeth** proclaims
3870 **also mowled** as mouldy   3871 **openers** medlar, 'open-arse'
3872 **ever lenger the wers** always the longer, the worse
3873 **mullok** rubbish-heap **stree** straw   3876 **hoppe** dance

For in oure wil ther stiketh evere a nail,
To have an hoor heed and a grene tail,
As hath a leek; for thogh oure might be goon,
Oure wil desireth folye evere in oon.   3880
For whan we may noght doon, than wol we
        speke;
Yet in oure asshen olde is fir yreke.
    'Foure gleedes have we, whiche I shal devise:
Avaunting, lying, anger, coveitise.
Thise foure sparkles longen unto eelde.   3885
Oure olde limes mowe wel been unweelde,
But wil ne shal noght faillen; that is sooth.
And yet ik have alwey a coltes tooth,
As many a yeer as it is passed henne,
Sin that my tappe of lif bigan to renne.   3890
For sikerlik, whan I was bore, anon
Deeth drough the tappe of lif and leet it goon;
And evere sith hath so the tappe yronne
Til that almoost al empty is the tonne.
The streem of lif now droppeth on the chimbe.   3895
The sely tonge may wel ringe and chimbe
Of wrecchednesse that passed is ful yoore!
With olde folk, save dotage, is namoore.'
    Whan that oure Hoost had herd this
        sermoning,
He gan to speke, as lordly as a king.   3900
He seide, 'What amounteth al this wit?
What shal we speke al day of holy writ?

3878 **hoor** white   3879 **might** capacity   3880 **evere in oon** constantly
3882 **yreke** raked up   3883 **gleedes** live coals   **devise** name
3884 **Avaunting** boastfulness   **coveitise** covetousness   3885 **sparkles** sparks
eelde age, old age   3886 **limes** limbs   **unweelde** impotent
3888 **have alwey a coltes tooth** still have youthful desires   3889 Though
many years have passed since then   3891 **sikerlik** certainly
3892 **drough the tappe** pulled out the stopper (n.)   3894 **tonne** barrel
3895 **chimbe** rim (of a barrel)   3896 **sely** innocent   **chimbe** chime, ring out
3897 **ful yoore** long ago   3901 What is the meaning of this display of
wisdom   3902 **What** why

The devel made a reve for to preche,
Or of a soutere, a shipman or a leche!
3905   Sey forth thy tale, and tarye noght the time.
Lo, Depeford, and it is half wey prime!
Lo, Grenewich, ther many a shrewe is inne!
It were al time thy tale to biginne.'
      'Now, sires,' quod this Osewold the Reve,
3910   'I pray yow alle that ye noght yow greve,
Thogh I answere and somdel sette his howve;
For leveful is, with force force of-showve.
This dronken millere hath ytold us heer
How that bigiled was a carpenter,
3915   Paraventure in scorn, for I am oon.
And by youre leve, I shal him quite anoon.
Right in his cherles termes wol I speke.
I pray to God his nekke mote to-breke!
He kan wel in min eye seen a stalke,
3920   But in his owene he kan noght seen a balke.'

THE REEVE'S TALE

Heere biginneth the Reves Tale.

At Trompingtoun, nat fer fro Cantebrigge,
Ther gooth a brook, and over that a brigge,
Upon the whiche brook ther stant a melle;
And this is verray sooth that I yow telle.

3904 **soutere** cobbler **leche** doctor   3906 **half wey prime** half-way between
6 and 9 a.m., 7.30 a.m.   3907 **ther** where **shrewe** rascal
3908 **It were al time** it is high time   3910 **yow greve** take offence
3911 **somdel** in some degree **sette his howve** mock him
3912 **leveful** lawful **of-showve** repel   3915 **Paraventure** perhaps
3917 **cherles termes** boorish language   3918 **to-breke** break
3919 **stalke** straw (n.)   3920 **balke** beam

3922 **brigge** bridge   3923 **melle** mill   3924 **sooth** truth

A millere was ther dwelling many a day.   3925
As any pecok he was proud and gay;
Pipen he koude, and fisshe, and nettes beete,
And turne coppes, and wel wrastle and sheete.
Ay by his belt he baar a long panade,
And of a swerd ful trenchaunt was the blade.   3930
A joly poppere baar he in his pouche;
Ther was no man for peril dorste him touche.
A Sheffeld thwitel baar he in his hose.
Round was his face, and camuse was his nose;
As piled as an ape was his skulle.   3935
He was a market-betere atte fulle.
Ther dorste no wight hand upon him legge,
That he ne swoor he sholde anon abegge.
A theef he was, forsothe, of corn and mele,
And that a sleigh, and usant for to stele.   3940
His name was hoten deinous Simkin.
    A wif he hadde, ycome of noble kin:
The person of the toun hir fader was.
With hire he yaf ful many a panne of bras,
For that Simkin sholde in his blood allye.   3945
She was yfostred in a nonnerye,
For Simkin wolde no wif, as he saide,
But she were wel ynorisshed and a maide,
To saven his estaat of yemanrye.
And she was proud, and peert as is a pie.   3950

3927 **beete** repair   3928 **turne coppes** turn (wooden) cups (on a lathe)
sheete shoot   3929 **panade** large knife   3930 **trenchaunt** sharp-edged
3931 **poppere** small dagger   3932 **dorste** dared   3933 **thwitel** knife
3934 **camuse** pug   3935 **piled** bald   3936 **market-betere** a swaggerer in the
market **atte fulle** to the hilt   3937 **legge** lay   3938 **abegge** pay for it
3940 **sleigh** cunning **usant** accustomed   3941 **His name was hoten** he was
called **deinous** scornful, haughty   3943 **person** parson
3944 **panne of bras** brass pan   3946 **nonnerye** nunnery   3948–9 Unless
she was well brought up and a virgin, to preserve his standing as a yeoman
3950 **peert** spirited, uppity **pie** magpie

A ful fair sighte was it upon hem two;
On halidayes biforn hire wolde he go,
With his tipet wounde aboute his heed,
And she cam after in a gite of reed,
3955 And Simkin hadde hosen of the same.
Ther dorste no wight clepen hire but 'dame';
Was noon so hardy that wente by the weye
That with hire dorste rage, or ones pleye,
But if he wolde be slain of Simkin,
3960 With panade, or with knif or boidekin.
For jalous folk been perilouse everemo –
Algate they wolde hir wives wenden so.
And eek, for she was somdel smoterlich,
She was as digne as water in a dich,
3965 And ful of hoker and of bisemare.
Hir thoghte that a lady sholde hir spare,
What for hir kinrede and hir nortelrye
That she hadde lerned in the nonnerye.

A doghter hadde they bitwix hem two
3970 Of twenty yeer, withouten any mo,
Saving a child that was of half yeer age;
In cradel it lay, and was a propre page.
This wenche thikke and wel ygrowen was,
With camuse nose and eyen greye as glas,
3975 With buttokes brode, and brestes rounde and hye;
But right fair was hir heer, I wol nat lie.
The person of the toun, for she was feir,
In purpos was to maken hir his heir,

3952 **halidayes** (religious) feast days   3953 **tipet** hanging part of a hood
3954 **gite** gown   3956 **but 'dame'** anything but 'my lady'
3957 **hardy** bold   3958 **rage** banter   3960 **boidekin** dagger
3962 **Algate** at any rate   **wenden** thought   3963 **somdel smoterlich** of rather
doubtful reputation   3964 **digne** proud   3965 **hoker** scorn
bisemare disdain   3966 **Hir thoghte** it seemed to her   **hir spare** hold herself
aloof   3967 **nortelrye** education   3972 **propre page** fine boy
3976 **heer** hair   3978 **In purpos was** intended

Bothe of his catel and his mesuage;
And straunge he made it of hir mariage.   3980
His purpos was for to bistowe hir hye
Into som worthy blood of auncetrye,
For holy chirches good moot been despended
On holy chirches blood that is descended.
Therfore he wolde his holy blood honoure,   3985
Thogh that he holy chirche sholde devoure.

Greet soken hath this millere, out of doute,
With whete and malt of al the land aboute.
And nameliche ther was a greet collegge
Men clepe the Soler Halle at Cantebregge;   3990
Ther was hir whete and eek hir malt ygrounde.
And on a day it happed in a stounde,
Sik lay the maunciple on a maladye;
Men wenden wysly that he sholde die.
For which this millere stal bothe mele and corn   3995
An hundred time moore than biforn;
For therbiforn he stal but curteisly,
But now he was a theef outrageously,
For which the wardein chidde and made fare.
But therof sette the millere noght a tare;   4000
He craked boost, and swoor it was noght so.

Thanne were ther yonge povre scolers two,
That dwelten in the halle of which I seye.
Testif they were, and lusty for to pleye,
And, oonly for hir mirthe and reverye,   4005
Upon the warden bisily they crye

3979 **catel** property **mesuage** house   3980 **straunge he made it of** he was
fussy about   3981 **hye** into high position   3982 **auncetrye** ancestry
3983 **despended** spent   3987 **Greet soken** a thriving trade
3992 **in a stounde** at one time   3993 **maunciple** see n. to GP 567
3994 **wysly** for sure   3995 **stal** stole   3997 **therbiforn** previously
curteisly 'decently' (in ironic sense)   3998 **outrageously** flagrantly, without
restraint   3999 **wardein** head of the college **chidde** complained
made fare made a fuss   4000 **sette . . . noght a tare** did not care a jot
4001 **craked boost** blustered   4004 **Testif** headstrong **lusty** keen
4005 **mirthe** fun **reverye** amusement   4006 **Upon . . . crye** entreat
bisily eagerly

To yeve hem leve, but a litel stounde,
To go to mille and seen hir corn ygrounde,
And hardily they dorste leye hir nekke,
4010   The millere sholde noght stele hem half a pekke
Of corn by sleighte, ne by force hem reve;
And at the laste the wardein yaf hem leve.
John highte that oon, and Alein highte that oother;
Of oon toun were they born, that highte Strother,
4015   Fer in the north – I kan noght telle where.
        This Alein maketh redy al his gere,
And on an hors the sak he caste anon.
Forth gooth Alein the clerk, and also John,
With good swerd and with bokeler by hir side.
4020   John knew the wey – hem nedede no gide –
And at the mille the sak adoun he layth.
Alein spak first: 'Al hail, Simond, i'faith!
How fares thy faire doghter and thy wif?'
        'Alein, welcome,' quod Simkin, 'by my lif!
4025   And John also; how now, what do ye here?'
'By God,' quod John, 'Simond, nede has na peere;
Him boes serve himself that has na swain,
Or ellis he is a fool, as clerkes sayn.
Oure maunciple, I hope he wil be deed,
4030   Swa werkes ay the wanges in his heed.
And forthy is I come, and eek Alain,
To grinde oure corn and carye it ham again.
I pray yow speed us heithen that ye may.'
        'It shal be doon,' quod Simkin, 'by my fay!
4035   What wol ye doon whil that it is in hande?'
'By God, right by the hoper wil I stande,'

4007 **stounde** while   4009 **hardily** boldly **leye** wager   4010 **pekke** peck (a
quarter of a bushel)   4011 **sleighte** cunning **reve** rob   4013 **highte** was
called **that oon . . . that oother** one . . . the other   4016 **gere** things
4019 **bokeler** small shield   4022 **Al hail** good health to you
4026 **nede has na peere** necessity has no fellow   4027 He who has no
servant must serve himself   4029 **hope** fear   4030 The molar-teeth in his
head ache so much   4031 **forthy** therefore   4032 **ham** home   4033 I beg
you to send us away as quickly as you can   4036 **hoper** hopper (n.)

Quod John, 'and se howgat the corn gas in.
Yet saw I nevere, by my fader kin,
How that the hoper wagges til and fra.'
    Alein answerde: 'John, and wiltow swa?'   4040
Thanne wol I be binethen, by my croun,
And se howgat the mele falles doun
Into the trogh; that sal be my desport.
For John, i'faith, I may been of youre sort;
I is as ille a millere as ar ye.'   4045
    This millere smiled of hir nicetee,
And thoghte, 'Al this nis doon but for a wile;
They wene that no man may hem bigile.
But by my thrift yet shal I blere hir eye,
For al the sleighte in hir philosophye.   4050
The moore queinte crekes that they make,
The moore wol I stele whan I take;
In stede of flour yet wol I yeve hem bren.
The grettest clerkes been noght the wisest men –
As whilom to the wolf thus spak the mare.   4055
Of al hir art ne counte I noght a tare!'
    Out at the dore he gooth ful prively,
Whan that he saugh his time, softely.
He looketh up and doun til he hath founde
The clerkes hors, ther as it stood ybounde   4060
Bihinde the mille, under a levesel.
And to the hors he gooth him faire and wel;
He strepeth of the bridel right anon,
And whan the hors was laus, he ginneth gon

4037 **howgat** how, in what way **gas in** goes in   4039 **til and fra** to and fro
4040 **wiltow swa** will you do so   4041 **croun** crown, top of head
4042 **mele** meal   4043 **sal** shall **desport** amusement   4045 **ille** bad,
incompetent   4046 **of hir nicetee** at their foolishness
4047 **but for a wile** only for a trick   4048 **wene** think
4049 **by my thrift** as I prosper **blere hir eye** hoodwink them
4050 **sleighte** cleverness   4051 **queinte crekes** clever stratagems
4053 **bren** bran   4055 **whilom** once upon a time   4056 I care not a jot for
all their learning   4057 **prively** secretly   4058 **softely** stealthily
4060 **ybounde** tied   4061 **levesel** arbour of leaves   4062 **faire** cheerfully
4063 **strepeth of** strips off   4064 **laus** loose

4065 Toward the fen, ther wilde mares renne,
And forth with 'wehe!' gooth thurgh thikke and thenne.
     This millere gooth again; no word he seide,
But dooth his note and with the clerkes pleyde
Til that hir corn was faire and wel ygrounde.
4070 And whan the mele was sakked and ybounde,
This John gooth out and fint his hors away,
And gan to crye 'harrow!' and 'weilaway!'
'Oure hors is lost! Alein, for Goddes banes,
Step on thy feet! Com of, man, al at anes!
4075 Allas, oure wardein has his palfrey lorn!'
This Alein al forgat, bothe mele and corn;
Al was out of his minde his housbondrye.
'What, whilk wey is he gane?' he gan to crye.
     The wif cam leping inward with a ren.
4080 She seide, 'Allas, youre hors gooth to the fen
With wilde mares, as faste as he may go.
Unthank come on his hand that bond him so,
And he that bettre sholde have knit the reine!'
'Allas,' quod John, 'Alein, for Cristes peine,
4085 Lay doun thy swerd, and I wol min alswa.
I is ful wight, God wat, as is a ra;
By Goddes hert, he sal nat scape us bathe!
Why nad thow pit the capul in the lathe?
Il hail, by God, Alein, thow is a fonne!'
4090   Thise sely clerkes han ful faste yronne
Toward the fen, bothe Alein and eek John.
And whan the millere saugh that they were gon,

4065 **fen** see n.   4066 **wehe** a whinnying noise
thurgh thikke and thenne through thick and thin   4067 **gooth again** returns
4068 **note** business **pleyde** joked   4070 **sakked** put in a sack
4071 **fint** (= *findeth*) finds   4073 **banes** bones   4074 **Step on thy feet** step
on it **Com of** hurry up **at anes** at once   4075 **lorn** lost
4077 **housbondrye** household affairs   4078 **whilk** which **gane** gone
4079 **ren** run   4082 **Unthank** a curse   4083 **knit** tied   4085 **alswa** also
4086 **wight** agile, swift **wat** knows **ra** roe   4087 **bathe** both   4088 Why
did you not put the horse in the barn   4089 **Il hail** curse it **fonne** fool
4090 **sely** poor

He half a busshel of hir flour hath take,
And bade his wif go knede it in a cake.
He seide, 'I trowe the clerkes were aferd!   4095
Yet kan a millere make a clerkes berd,
For al his art; now lat hem goon hir weye!
Lo, where he gooth; ye, lat the children pleye!
They gete him noght so lightly, by my croun.'

Thise sely clerkes rennen up and doun,   4100
With 'Keep, keep! stand, stand! Jossa, warderere!
Ga whistle thow, and I sal kepe him here!'
But shortly, til that it was verray night,
They koude noght, though they dide al hir might,
Hir capul cacche, he ran alwey so faste;   4105
Til in a dich they caughte him at the laste.

Wery and weet, as beest is in the rein,
Comth sely John, and with him comth Alein.
'Allas,' quod John, 'the day that I was born!
Now ar we drive til hething and til scorn.   4110
Oure corn is stoln; men wil us fooles calle,
Bathe the wardein and oure felawes alle,
And namely the millere, weilawey!'
Thus pleineth John as he gooth by the wey
Toward the mille, and Bayard in his hond.   4115
The millere sitting by the fir he fond,
For it was night, and ferther mighte they noght;
But for the love of God they him bisoght
Of herberwe and of ese, as for hir peny.

The millere seide again: 'If ther be eny,   4120
Swich as it is, yet shal ye have youre part.
Min hous is streit, but ye han lerned art;

4094 **knede** knead   4095 **aferd** suspicious   4096 **make a clerkes berd** get
the better of a clerk   4097 **art** study   4099 **lightly** easily
4101 **Keep** stand **Jossa** a call used in rounding up horses
warderere (= *ware derere*) ?look out behind   4102 **Ga** go
4105 **capul** horse   4110 **til** to **hething** mockery   4113 **namely** especially
4114 **pleineth** laments   4115 **Bayard** traditional name for a horse, as
'Dobbin'   4116 **fond** found   4118 **bisoght** asked   4119 **herberwe** lodging
ese hospitality   4122 **streit** confined, restricted in space **art** logic

Ye kan by argumentes make a place
A mile brood of twenty foot of space!

4125   Lat se now if this place may suffise,
Or make it rowm with speche, as is youre gise.'
'Now Simond,' seide this John, 'by Seint Cutberd,
Ay is thou mirye, and this is faire answerd.
I have herd seye, men sal taa, of twa thinges,

4130   Slik as he findes, or taa slik as he bringes.
But specially I pray thee, hooste deere,
Get us som mete and drink, and make us cheere,
And we wol payen trewely atte fulle.
With empty hand men may na haukes tulle;

4135   Lo here, oure silver, redy for to spende.'
This millere into toun his doghter sende
For ale and breed, and rosted hem a goos,
And bond hir hors; it sholde namoore go loos.
And in his owene chambre hem made a bed,

4140   With shetes and with chalons faire yspred,
Noght from his owene bed ten foot or twelve.
His doghter hadde a bed al by hirselve,
Right in the same chambre, by and by.
It mighte be no bet, and cause why?

4145   Ther was no rowmer herberwe in the place.
They soupen and they speke, hem to solace,
And drinken evere strong ale at the beste;
Aboute midnight wente they to reste.
Wel hath this millere vernisshed his heed;

4150   Ful pale he was for dronken, and noght reed.

4126 **rowm** roomy **gise** practice   4128 **Ay is thou mirye** you are always
humorous   4129 **taa** take **twa** two   4130 **Slik** such
4132 **make us cheere** give us hospitality   4134 **tulle** lure
4136 **sende** (= *sendede*) sent   4138 **bond** tied up   4140 **chalons** a kind of
tapestry bedspread made of a figured woollen material named after Chalons-
sur-Marne   4143 **by and by** alongside   4145 **rowmer herberwe** roomier
accommodation   4146 **hem to solace** to entertain themselves
4147 **at the beste** to their heart's content   4149 **vernisshed** given a shine to
4150 **for dronken** because of being drunk

He yexeth and he speketh thurgh the nose,
As he were on the quake or on the pose.
To bedde he gooth, and with him goth his wif;
As any jay she light was and jolif,
So was hir joly whistle wel ywet.   4155
The cradel at hir beddes feet is set,
To rokken and to yeve the child to sowke.
And whan that dronken al was in the crowke,
To bedde wente the doghter right anon.
To bedde gooth Alein and also John;   4160
Ther nas namoore; hem nedede no dwale.
This millere hath so wysly bibbed ale
That as an hors he fnorteth in his sleep;
Ne of his tail bihinde he took no keep.
His wif bar him a burdon, a ful strong;   4165
Men mighte hir routing heren a furlong.
The wenche routeth eek, *par compaignye*.
    Alein the clerk, that herde this melodye,
He poked John, and seide, 'Slepestow?
Herd thow evere slik a sang er now?'   4170
Lo, whilk a complin is imel hem alle!
A wilde fir upon thair bodies falle!
Wha herkned evere slik a ferly thing?
Ye, they sal have the flour of il ending!
This lang night ther tides me na reste.   4175
But yet na force; al sal be for the beste!

4151 **yexeth** hiccups   4152 **on the quake** hoarse **on the pose** suffering from
a cold   4154 **light** merry **jolif** gay   4155 So much had she drunk
4157 **sowke** suck   4158 **crowke** crock, jug   4161 **dwale** sleeping-potion
4162 **wysly** heavily **bibbed** tippled   4163 **fnorteth** snores, snorts
4165 **burdon** accompaniment   4166 **routing** snoring
4167 *par compaignye* in accompaniment   4170 **slik** such **sang** song
4171 **whilk a** what a **complin** compline, the last of the seven daily services
sung by monks and priests (jokingly applied to the miller's family snoring in
concert) **imel** among   4172 **wilde fir** destructive fire   4173 **Wha** who
ferly frightful   4174 **sal** shall **flour of il ending** worst possible fate
4175 This long night I shall meet with no rest   4176 **na force** no matter

For, John,' seide he, 'als evere moot I thrive,
If that I may, yon wenche wol I swive.
Som esement has lawe shapen us;
4180   For, John, ther is a lawe that sayes thus:
That gif a man in a point be agreved,
That in another he sal be releved.
Oure corn is stoln – soothly, it is na nay –
And we han had an il fit al this day;
4185   And sin I sal have nan amendement
Again my los, I wil have esement.
By Goddes saule, it sal nan other be!'
        This John answerde, 'Alein, avise thee.
The millere is a perilous man,' he saide,
4190   And gif that he out of his sleep abraide,
He mighte doon us bathe a vileinye.'
        Alein answerde, 'I counte him noght a flye.'
And up he rist, and by the wenche he crepte.
This wenche lay upright, and faste slepte,
4195   Til he so neigh was, er she mighte espye,
That it hadde been to late for to crye;
And shortly for to seyn, they were at oon.
Now pley, Alein, for I wol speke of John.
        This John lith stille, a furlong wey or two,
4200   And to himself he maketh routhe and wo.
'Allas,' quod he, 'this is a wikked jape!
Now may I seyn that I is but an ape.
Yet has my felawe somwhat for his harm:
He has the milleris doghter in his arm.

4177 **als evere moot I thrive** as I prosper   4178 **swive** lay (sexual sense)
4179 **esement** compensation   **shapen us** devised for us   4181 **gif** if
4182 **releved** compensated   4183 **it is na nay** it cannot be denied
4184 **il fit** unlucky time   4185 **nan** no   4186 **Again** in return for
4187 **saule** soul   4188 **avise thee** take thought   4190 **gif** if   **abraide** wake
suddenly   4191 **vileinye** injury   4193 **rist** (= *riseth*) rises   4194 **upright** on
her back   **faste** deeply   4196 **hadde been** would have been   4197 **at oon** in
agreement   4199 **a furlong wey** two or three minutes
4200 **maketh routhe and wo** laments   4201 **wikked jape** bad joke
4202 **ape** fool   4203 **somwhat for his harm** something in return for the
injury done him

He auntred him and has his nedes sped,   4205
And I lie as a draf-sek in my bed.
And whan this jape is tald another day,
I sal been halden a daffe, a cokenay!
I wil arise and auntre it, by my faith!
"Unhardy is unsely", thus men saith.'   4210
And up he roos, and softely he wente
Unto the cradel, and in his hand it hente,
And baar it softe unto his beddes feet.
  Soone after this, the wif hir routing leet,
And gan awake, and wente hir out to pisse,   4215
And cam again and gan hir cradel misse,
And groped heer and ther; but she fond noon.
'Allas,' quod she, 'I hadde almoost misgoon!
I hadde almoost goon to the clerkes bed.
Ey, *benedicite*, thanne had I foule ysped!'   4220
And forth she gooth til she the cradel fond.
She gropeth alwey forther with hir hond
And fond the bed, and thoghte noght but good,
Bicause that the cradel by it stood,
And niste wher she was, for it was derk;   4225
But faire and wel she creep in to the clerk,
And lith ful stille, and wolde have caught a sleep.
Withinne a while this John the clerk up leep,
And on this goode wif he leyth on soore.
So mury a fit ne hadde she nat ful yoore;   4230
He priketh harde and depe as he were mad.
This joly lif han thise two clerkes lad
Til that the thridde cok bigan to singe.
  Alein wax wery in the daweninge,

4205 He took a chance and has got what he wanted   4206 **as a draf-sek** like
a sack of chaff or rubbish   4207 **tald** told   4208 I shall be considered a
fool and a wimp   4210 **Unhardy** cowardly   **unsely** unfortunate
4212 **hente** seized   4213 **baar it softe** carried it quietly   4214 **leet** left off
4218 **misgoon** gone astray   4220 **foule ysped** made a mess of it
4222 **alwey forther** still further   4225 **niste** did not know
4226 **creep** crept   4227 **caught a sleep** gone to sleep   4228 **leep** leapt
4230 **fit** bout   4233 **singe** crow   4234 Alein grew weary at dawn

4235   For he had swonken al the longe night,
    And seide, 'Farewel, Malin, swete wight!
    The day is come; I may no lenger bide.
    But everemo, wherso I go or ride,
    I is thin awen clerk, swa have I sel.'
4240   'Now, deere lemman,' quod she, 'go, farewel!
    But er thow go, o thing I wol thee telle:
    Whan that thow wendest homward by the melle,
    Right at the entree of the dore bihinde
    Thow shalt a cake of half a busshel finde
4245   That was ymaked of thin owene mele,
    Which that I heelp my fader for to stele.
    And, goode lemman, God thee save and kepe!'
    And with that word almoost she gan to wepe.
      Alein uprist and thoghte, 'Er that it dawe,
4250   I wol go crepen in by my felawe.'
    And fond the cradel with his hond anon.
    'By God,' thoghte he, 'al wrang I have misgon!
    Min heed is toty of my swink tonight;
    That maketh me that I go noght aright.
4255   I woot wel by the cradel I have misgo;
    Here lith the millere and his wif also.'
    And forth he gooth, a twenty devel way,
    Unto the bed theras the millere lay.
    He wende have cropen by his felawe John;
4260   And by the millere in he creep anoon,
    And caughte him by the nekke, and softe he spak.
    He seide, 'Thou John, thow swines-hed, awak,
    For Cristes saule, and here a noble game!
    For by that lord that called is Seint Jame,

4235 **swonken** laboured   4237 **bide** stay   4239 **awen** own
swa have I sel as I prosper   4240 **lemman** sweetheart   4242 **wendest** go
melle mill   4243 **dore bihinde** back door   4246 **heelp** helped
4249 **uprist** (= *upriseth*) gets up   **dawe** grows light   4252 **wrang** wrong
4253 **toty** dizzy   **swink** labour   4257 **a twenty devel way** devil take it
4259 **wende have cropen** intended to creep   4262 **swines-hed** numbskull
4263 **saule** soul

As I have thries in this shorte night   4265
Swived the milleris doghter bolt-upright,
Whil thow hast, as a coward, been agast.'
  'Ye, false harlot,' quod the millere, 'hast?
A, false traitour, false clerk,' quod he,
'Thou shalt be deed, by Goddes dignitee!   4270
Who dorste be so bold to disparage
My doghter, that is come of swich linage?'
And by the throte-bolle he caughte Alain,
And he hente him despitously again,
And on the nose he smoot him with his fest.   4275
Doun ran the blody streem upon his brest,
And in the floor, with nose and mouth to-broke,
They walwe as doon two pigges in a poke.
And up they goon, and doun again anoon,
Til that the millere sporned at a stoon,   4280
And doun he fil bakward upon his wif,
That wiste nothing of this nice strif,
For she was falle aslepe a litel wight,
With John the clerk, that waked hadde al night.
And with the fal out of hir sleep she breide;   4285
'Help, holy cros of Bromeholm!' she seide.
'*In manus tuas!* Lord, to thee I calle!
Awake, Simond, the feend is on me falle!
Min herte is broken; help, I nam but ded!
Ther lith oon on my wombe and on min heed.   4290
Help, Simkin, for the false clerkes fighte!'
  This John sterte up as faste as evere he mighte,

4266 **Swived** laid (sexual sense) **bolt-upright** flat on her back
4268 **hast** have you   4271 **disparage** disgrace   4273 **throte-bolle** Adam's
apple   4274 **hente** seized **despitously** violently **again** in turn
4275 **smoot** struck   4277 **to-broke** bashed in   4278 **walwe** thrash about
poke bag   4280 **sporned** stumbled   4282 **wiste** knew **nice strif** foolish
quarrel   4283 **a litel wight** for a short time   4285 **breide** awoke suddenly
4286 **cros** cross   4287 **In manus tuas** into thy hands (n.)
4288 **is on me falle** has fallen on me   4290 **oon** someone **wombe** stomach
4292 **sterte up** jumped up

And graspeth by the walles to and fro,
To finde a staf; and she sterte up also,
4295   And knew the estres bet than dide this John,
And by the wal a staf she fond anon,
And saugh a litel shimering of a light,
For at an hole in shoon the moone bright;
And by that light she saugh hem bothe two,
4300   But sikerly she niste who was who,
But as she saugh a whit thing in hir eye.
And whan she gan this white thing espye,
She wende the clerk hadde wered a voluper,
And with the staf she drow ay ner and ner
4305   And wende han hit this Alein atte fulle,
And smoot the millere on the piled skulle
That doun he gooth, and cride, 'Harrow, I die!'
    Thise clerkes bette him wel and lete him lie,
And greithen hem, and took hir hors anon,
4310   And eke hir mele, and on hir wey they gon,
And at the mille yet they toke hir cake
Of half a busshel flour, ful wel ybake.
    Thus is the proude millere wel ybete,
And hath ylost the grinding of the whete,
4315   And payed for the soper everydel
Of Alein and of John, that bette him wel;
His wif is swived, and his doghter als.
Lo, swich it is a millere to be fals!
And therfore this proverbe is seid ful sooth:
4320   Him thar nat wene wel that ivele dooth.

4293 **graspeth** gropes   4295 **estres** interior   4297 **shimering** glimmer
4300 **sikerly** assuredly   4303 **voluper** night-cap   4304 **ay ner and ner** ever
nearer and nearer   4305 Intended to hit Alein fairly and squarely
4306 **smoot** struck **piled** bald   4307 **That** so that   4308 **bette** beat
lete him lie left him lying there   4309 **greithen hem** get ready
4312 **ybake** baked   4313 **ybete** beaten   4317 **swived** fucked
4320 Anyone who does evil need not expect good (in return)

A gilour shal himself bigiled be.
And God, that sitteth heighe in magestee,
Save al this compaignye, grete and smale.
– Thus have I quit the Millere in my tale.

Heere is ended the Reves Tale.

THE COOK'S PROLOGUE

The Prologe of the Cokes Tale.

The Cook of Londoun, whil the Reve spak,   4325
For joye him thoughte he clawed him on the bak.
'Ha, ha!' quod he, 'for Cristes passioun,
This millere hadde a sharp conclusioun
Upon his argument of herbergage!
Wel seide Salomon in his langage: 4330
"Ne bring nat every man into thin hous."
For herberwing by nighte is perilous.
Wel oghte a man avised for to be
Whom that he broghte into his privetee.
I pray to God, so yeve me sorwe and care,   4335
If ever, sith I highte Hogge of Ware,
Herde I a millere bettre yset a-werk.
He hadde a jape of malice in the derk!
But God forbede that we stinten heere;
And therfore, if ye vouchesauf to heere   4340

4321 **gilour** trickster   4322 **heighe** on high

4326 **clawed** scratched   4328 **sharp** unpleasant   4329 **herbergage** lodgings
4332 **herberwing** taking in guests   4333 **avised for to be** to take care
4334 **privetee** private environment   4336 **sith I highte** since I was named
4337 **yset a-werk** set to work   4338 **jape** trick   4339 **stinten** leave off

A tale of me, that am a povre man,
I wol yow telle, as wel as evere I kan,
A litel jape that fil in oure citee.'
    Oure Hoost answerde and seide, 'I graunte it
      thee.

4345   Now tel on, Roger, look that it be good!
For many a pastee hastow laten blood,
And many a Jakke of Dover hastow soold,
That hath been twies hoot and twies coold.
Of many a pilgrim hastow Cristes curs,
4350   For of thy persely yet they fare the wors,
That they han eten with thy stubbul goos;
For in thy shoppe is many a flye loos.
Now telle on, gentil Roger, by thy name!
But yet I praye thee, be nat wrooth for game;
4355   A man may seye ful sooth in game and pley.'
    'Thow seyst ful sooth,' quod Roger, 'by my fey!
But "sooth pley, quade pley", as the Fleming seyth.
And therfore Herry Bailly, by thy feith,
Be thou nat wrooth, er we departen heer,
4360   Thogh that my tale be of an hostileer.
But nathelees I wol nat telle it yit;
But er we parte, ywis, thow shalt be quit.'
And therwithal he lough and made cheere,
And seide his tale, as ye shal after heere.

4343 **fil** happened   4346 **pastee** pasty, pie **laten blood** let blood, i.e.
drained (n.)   4347 **Jakke of Dover** see n.   4349 **Of** from
4350 **of . . . fare the wors** are the worse for **persely** parsley
4351 **stubbul goos** fatted goose (i.e. one fed in the stubble-fields)
4354 **wrooth for game** angry at a joke   4355 **seye ful sooth** speak truly
4357 **sooth pley, quade pley** a true joke is a bad joke (n.)   4362 **quit** paid
back

THE COOK'S TALE

Heere biginneth the Cookes Tale.

A prentis whilom dwelled in oure citee,   4365
And of a craft of vitaillers was he.
Gaillard he was as goldfinch in the shawe;
Broun as a berye, a propre short felawe,
With lokkes blake, ykembd ful fetisly.
Dauncen he koude so wel and jolily   4370
That he was cleped Perkin Revelour.
He was as ful of love and paramour
As is the hive ful of hony swete;
Wel was the wenche that with him mighte mete.
At every bridale wolde he singe and hoppe.   4375
He loved bet the taverne than the shoppe,
For whan ther any riding was in Chepe,
Out of the shoppe thider wolde he lepe;
Til that he hadde al the sighte yseyn
And daunced wel, he wolde noght come agein.   4380
And gadred him a meinee of his sort,
To hoppe and singe, and maken swich disport.
And ther they setten stevene for to meete,
To pleyen at the dis in swich a streete;
For in the toune nas ther no prentis   4385
That fairer koude caste a paire of dis

4365 **prentis** apprentice **whilom** once   4366 **craft of vitaillers** guild of
victuallers   4367 **Gaillard** gay **shawe** copse, wood   4368 **propre** fine
4369 **ykembd** combed **fetisly** elegantly   4370 **jolily** friskily
4371 **Perkin Revelour** Fun-Loving Pete   4372 **paramour** amorousness
4375 **hoppe** dance   4377 **riding** procession   4381 **meinee** retinue
4382 **disport** amusement   4383 **setten stevene** arranged a rendezvous
4384 **dis** dice

Than Perkin koude; and therto he was free
Of his dispense, in place of privetee.
That fond his maister wel in his chaffare;
4390   For ofte time he foond his box ful bare.
For sikerly a prentis revelour
That haunteth dis, riot, or paramour,
His maister shal it in his shoppe abye,
Al have he no part of the minstralcye.
4395   For thefte and riot, they been convertible.
Al konne he pleye on giterne or ribible,
Revel and trouthe, as in a lowe degree,
They been ful wrothe al day, as men may see.
    This joly prentis with his maister bood
4400   Til he were neigh out of his prentishood,
Al were he snibbed bothe erly and late,
And somtime lad with revel to Newgate.
But atte laste his maister him bithoghte,
Upon a day whan he his paper soghte,
4405   Of a proverbe that seyth this same word:
'Wel bet is roten appul out of hord
Than that it rotie al the remenaunt.'
So fareth it by a riotous servaunt;
It is ful lasse harm to lete him pace,
4410   Than he shende al the servantz in the place.
Therfore his maister yaf him acquitaunce,
And bad him go, with sorwe and with
       meschaunce!

4387–8 **free Of his dispense** generous in spending **in place of privetee** in a
private place   4389 **chaffare** trade   4390 **box** strong-box
4392 **haunteth** indulges in **riot** debauchery   4393 **abye** pay for
4394 **no part of** no share in   4395 **convertible** interchangeable
4396 see n. to Mil 3331–3   4397 **trouthe** honesty   4398 **ful wrothe** at
odds with each other   4399 **bood** remained
4400 **prentishood** apprenticeship   4401 **snibbed** reprimanded
4403–5 **him bithoghte . . . Of** called to mind **paper** accounts, papers
4407 **rotie** rot   4408 This is the case with a dissolute servant
4409 **pace** go   4410 **shende** ruin   4411 **yaf him acquitaunce** discharged
him   4412 **with sorwe and with meschaunce** curse him

And thus this joly prentis hadde his leve.
Now lat him riote al the night, or leve!
And, for ther is no theef withoute a lowke,   4415
That helpeth him to wasten and to sowke
Of that he bribe kan or borwe may,
Anon he sente his bed and his array
Unto a compeer of his owene sort,
That loved dis and revel and disport,   4420
And hadde a wif that held for contenaunce
A shoppe, and swived for hir sustenaunce.

4414 He can riot all night or not (as he pleases)   4415 **lowke** accomplice
4416 **sowke** squeeze out   4417 **bribe** pilfer   4418 **array** clothes
4419 **compeer** companion, intimate   4421 **for contenaunce** for
appearance's sake   4422 **swived for hir sustenaunce** earned her living by
prostitution

THE MAN OF
LAW'S PROLOGUE

*The wordes of the Hoost to
the compaignye.*

Oure Hoost saugh wel that the brighte sonne
The ark of his artificial day hath ronne
The ferthe part, and half an houre and moore,
And thogh he were nat depe ystert in loore,
5   He wiste it was the eightetethe day
Of Aprill, that is messager to May,
And saw wel that the shadwe of every tree
Was as in lengthe the same quantitee
That was the body erect that caused it,
10   And therfore by the shadwe he took his wit
That Phebus, which that shoon so clere and brighte,
Degrees was five and fourty clombe on highte,
And for that day, as in that latitude,
It was ten at the clokke, he gan conclude;
15   And sodeinly he plighte his hors aboute.
     'Lordinges,' quod he, 'I warne yow, al this route,
The ferthe party of this day is goon.
Now, for the love of God, and of Seint John,
Leseth no time, as ferforth as ye may.
20   Lordinges, the time wasteth night and day,

---

2 **ark of his artificial day** semicircle of its daytime course (n.)
3 **ferthe** fourth   4 **depe ystert in loore** far advanced in knowledge
5 **eightetethe** eighteenth   7 **shadwe** shadow   10 **took his wit** derived his
opinion   11 **Phebus** Phoebus, the sun   12 **was . . . clombe** had climbed
15 **plighte** snatched, pulled   16 **route** company   17 **ferthe party** fourth
part, portion   19 **Leseth** lose **as ferforth as** as far as

And steleth from us, what prively slepinge,
And what thurgh necligence in oure wakinge,
As dooth the streem that turneth nevere again,
Descendinge fro the montaigne into plain.
Wel kan Senec, and many a philosophre,   25
Biwaillen time moore than gold in cofre;
"For los of catel may recovered be,
But los of time shendeth us," quod he.
It wol nat come again, withouten drede,
Namoore than wol Malkins maidenhede,   30
Whan she hath lost it in hir wantownesse.
Lat us nat mowlen thus in idelnesse!

   'Sire Man of Lawe,' quod he, 'so have ye blis,
Tel us a tale anon, as forward is.
Ye been submitted thurgh youre free assent   35
To stonden in this cas at my juggement.
Acquiteth yow nowe of youre biheste;
Thanne have ye doon youre devoir, atte leste.'

   'Hoost,' quod he, '*depardieux*, ich assente!
To breke forward is nat min entente.   40
Biheste is dette, and I wol holde fain
Al my biheste; I kan no bettre sayn.
For swich lawe as a man yeveth another wight,
He sholde himselven usen it by right –
Thus wol oure text. But nathelees, certein,   45
I kan right now no thrifty tale seyn
That Chaucer, thogh he kan but lewedly
On metres and on ryming craftily,
Hath seid hem, in swich Englissh as he kan,
Of olde time, as knoweth many a man.   50

---

21 **what** partly   22 **wakinge** period of wakefulness   27 **catel** wealth
28 **shendeth** destroys   29 **drede** doubt   32 **mowlen** grow mouldy
34 **forward** agreement   37 Now fulfil your promise   38 **devoir** duty
39 *depardieux* certainly   40 **breke forward** break an agreement
entente intention   41 **Biheste is dette** see n. **fain** gladly   43 **wight** person
45 **Thus wol oure text** so the saying goes   46 **thrifty** respectable
47–8 **kan but lewedly On** knows little about

And if he have nat seid hem, leeve brother,
In o book, he hath seid hem in another.
For he hath told of lovers up and doun
Mo than Ovide made of mencioun
55   In his Episteles, that been ful olde.
What sholde I tellen hem, sin they been tolde?
      'In youthe he made of Ceys and Alcyone,
And sithen hath he spoke of everychone,
Thise noble wives, and thise loveres eke.
60   Whoso that wol his large volume seke
Cleped the Seintes Legende of Cupide,
Ther maystow seen the large woundes wide
Of Lucresse and of Babilan Tesbee,
The swerd of Dido for the false Enee,
65   The tree of Phillis for hir Demophon,
The pleinte of Dianire, and Hermion,
Of Adriane, and of Isiphilee,
The bareine ile stondinge in the see,
The dreinte Leandre for his Erro,
70   The teeris of Eleine, and eke the wo
Of Brixseide, and of the, Ladomia;
The crueltee of the queene Medea –
The litel children hanging by the hals,
For thy Jason, that was of love so fals.
75   O Ypermystra, Penolopee, Alceste,
Youre wifhode he comendeth with the beste!
      'But certeinly no word ne writeth he
Of thilke wikke ensample of Canacee,
That loved hir owene brother sinfully.
80   Of swiche cursed stories I sey "fy!"
Or ellis of Tyro Appollonius –
How that the cursed king Antiochus

---

51 leeve dear   54 made of mencioun mentioned   56 What why sin since
58 sithen afterwards   59 eke also   61 Cleped called   66 pleinte lament
69 dreinte drowned   73 hals neck   76 with the beste among the finest

Birafte his doghter of hir maidenhede.
That is so horrible a tale for to rede,
Whan he hir threw upon the pavement!   85
And therfore he, of ful avisement,
Nolde nevere write in noon of his sermons
Of swiche unkinde abhominacions,
Ne I wol noon reherce, if that I may.
  'But of my tale how shal I doon this day?   90
Me were looth be likned, doutelees,
To Muses that men clepe Pierides –
Methamorphosios woot what I mene.
But nathelees I recche noght a bene,
Thogh I come after him with hawe-bake.   95
I speke in prose, and lat him rymes make.'
And with that word he with a sobre cheere
Bigan his tale, as ye shal after heere.

The Prologe of the Mannes Tale of Lawe.

O hateful harm, condicion of poverte,
With thurst, with cold, with hunger so   100
    confoundid!
To asken help thee shameth in thin herte;
If thou noon aske, so soore artow ywoundid
That verray nede unwrappeth al thy wounde hid.
Maugree thin heed, thou most for indigence
Or stele, or begge, or borwe thy despence.   105

---

83 **Birafte** deprived   85 **pavement** (paved) floor
86 **of ful avisement** deliberately   87 **sermons** writings
88 **unkinde** unnatural   89 **reherce** repeat   90 **doon** act
91 **Me were looth be likned** I would not want to be compared
94 **recche noght a bene** do not care a bean   95 **hawe-bake** baked haws, i.e.
meagre fare   97 **cheere** expression   101 **thee shameth** makes you ashamed
104 **Maugree thin heed** in spite of all you can do   105 Either steal, beg or
borrow your means of subsistence

Thou blamest Crist, and seyst ful bitterly
He misdeparteth richesse temporal.
Thy neighebore thow witest sinfully,
And seyst thow hast to lite, and he hath al.
110   'Parfay,' seystow, 'somtime he rekne shal,
Whan that his tail shal brennen in the gleede,
For he noght helpeth nedefulle in hir nede!'

Herke what is the sentence of the wise:
'Bet is to dien than have indigence.
115   Thy selve neighebore wol thee despise.'
If thow be povre, farewel thy reverence!
Yet of the wise man tak this sentence:
'Alle the dayes of povre men been wikke.'
Be war, therfore, er thow come to that prikke.

120   If thou be povre, thy brother hateth thee,
And alle thy freendes fleen from thee, allas!
O riche marchauntz, ful of wele been ye!
O noble, o prudent folk, as in this cas!
Youre bagges been noght filled with *ambes as*,
125   But with *sis cink* that renneth for youre chaunce.
At Cristemasse murye may ye daunce!

Ye seken lond and see for youre winninges.
As wise folk ye knowen al th'estat
Of regnes; ye been fadres of tidinges
130   And tales, bothe of pees and of debat.

---

107 **misdeparteth** distributes unfairly   108 **witest** blame   109 **to lite** too
little   110 **rekne** render an account   111 **brennen in the gleede** burn in the
fire (of hell)   112 **nedefulle** the needy   113 **sentence** maxim
115 **selve** very   116 **thy reverence** the respect shown to you
117 **sentence** saying   118 **wikke** wretched   119 **prikke** condition
122 **wele** wealth   124 *ambes as* two ones, a double ace (n.)   125 **But** with
'six-five' that runs in your favour (n.)   127 **seken** explore   128 **th'estat** the
condition   129 **fadres** fathers, originators   130 **debat** war

I were right now of tales desolat,
Nere that a marchaunt, goon is many a yere,
Me taughte a tale, which that ye shal heere.

THE MAN OF LAW'S TALE

*Heere biginneth the
Man of Lawe his Tale.*

In Surrye whilom dwelte a compaignye
Of chapmen riche, and therto sadde and trewe,   135
That wide-where senten hir spicerye,
Clothes of gold and satins riche of hewe.
Hir chaffare was so thrifty and so newe
That every wight hath deintee to chaffare
With hem, and eek to sellen hem hir ware.   140

Now fil it that the maistres of that sort
Han shapen hem to Rome for to wende.
Were it for chapmanhode or for disport,
Noon oother message wolde they thider sende,
But comen hemself to Rome; this is the ende.   145
And in swich place as thoughte hem avauntage
For hir entente, they take hir herbergage.

131 **were** would be **desolat** destitute of   132 **Nere** were it not
goon is many a yere many years ago

134 **Surrye** Syria **whilom** once   135 **chapmen** merchants
sadde and trewe dignified and honest   136 **wide-where** far and wide
spicerye spices   138 **chaffare** merchandise **thrifty** high-quality
139 **hath deintee to chaffare** is delighted to do business   141 **sort** company
142 **Han shapen hem** determined **wende** go   143 Whether it was for
business or pleasure   144 **message** messenger   145 **the ende** the long and
short of it   146 **avauntage** convenient   147 **herbergage** lodging

Sojourned han thise marchauntz in that toun
A certein time, as fil to hir plesaunce.
150 And so bifel that th'excellent renoun
Of th'Emperoures doghter, dame Custaunce,
Reported was, with every circumstaunce,
Unto thise Surrien marchauntz in swich wise,
Fro day to day, as I shal yow devise.

155 This was the commune vois of every man:
'Oure Emperour of Rome, God him se!
A doghter hath that, sin the world bigan,
To rekne as wel hir goodnesse as beautee,
Nas nevere swich another as is she.
160 I pray to God in honour hir sustene,
And wolde she were of al Europe the queene!

'In hire is heigh beautee withoute pride,
Youthe, withouten grenehede or folye;
To alle hir werkes vertu is hir gide;
165 Humblesse hath slain in hir al tyrannye.
She is mirour of alle curteisye;
Hir herte is verray chambre of holinesse,
Hir hand, ministre of fredam for almesse.'

And al this vois was sooth, as God is trewe;
170 But now to purpos lat us turne again.
Thise marchauntz han doon fraught hir shippes newe,
And whan they han this blisful maiden sayn,

149 **fil to hir plesaunce** suited their pleasure   151 **Custaunce** Constance
152 **with every circumstaunce** in full detail   154 **devise** relate
155 **vois** opinion   156 **God him se** may God protect him
158 **rekne** evaluate   160 **sustene** sustain   161 **wolde** would wish
163 **grenehede** immaturity   168 **fredam** generosity **almesse** alms-giving
170 **to purpos** to the matter in hand
171 **han doon fraught hir shippes newe** had their ships loaded afresh
172 **blisful** blessed **sayn** seen

Hom to Surrye been they went ful fain,
And doon hir nedes as they han doon yoore,
And liven in wele; I kan sey yow namoore.   175

Now fil it that thise marchauntz stode in grace
Of him that was the Sowdan of Surrye;
For whan they come from any straunge place,
He wolde, of his benigne curteisye,
Make hem good cheere and bisily espye   180
Tidinges of sondry regnes, for to leere
The wondres that they mighte seen or heere.

Amonges othere thinges, specially,
Thise marchauntz han him told of dame
          Custaunce
So greet noblesse, in ernest, ceriously,   185
That this Sowdan hath caught so greet plesaunce
To han hir figure in his remembraunce,
That al his lust and al his bisy cure
Was for to love hire, whil his lif may dure.

Paraventure, in thilke large book   190
Which that men clepe the hevene, ywriten was
With sterres, whan that he his birthe took,
That he for love sholde han his deth, allas!
For in the sterres, clerer than is glas,
Is writen, God woot, whoso koude it rede,   195
The deeth of every man, withouten drede.

---

174 **doon hir nedes** perform their business **yoore** formerly
175 **wele** prosperity   176 **stode in grace** enjoyed the favour
177 **Sowdan** Sultan   178 **straunge** foreign   179 **curteisye** kindness
180 Entertain them well and eagerly seek to discover   181 **sondry** different
leere learn about   183 **specially** in particular   185 **ceriously** minutely, in
detail   186 **caught so greet plesaunce** experienced such great pleasure
187 **figure** image   188 **lust** delight **bisy cure** earnest concern
190 **Paraventure** perhaps   191 **clepe** call   196 **drede** doubt

In sterres many a winter therbiforn
Was write the deeth of Ector, Achilles,
Of Pompey, Julius, er they were born;
200   The strif of Thebes, and of Hercules,
Of Sampson, Turnus, and of Socrates
The deeth; but mennes wittes been so dulle,
That no wight kan wel rede it atte fulle.

This Sowdan for his privee conseil sente,
205   And shortly of this matere for to pace,
He hath to hem declared his entente,
And seide hem, certein, but he mighte have grace
To han Custaunce withinne a litel space,
He nas but deed, and charged hem in hie
210   To shapen for his lif som remedye.

Diverse men diverse thinges seiden;
They argumenten, casten up and doun.
Many a subtil reson forth they leiden;
They speke of magik and abusioun.
215   But finally, as in conclusioun,
They kan nat seen in that noon avauntage,
Ne in noon oother wey, save mariage.

Thanne sawe they therinne swich difficultee,
By wey of reson, for to speke al plain,
220   Bicause that ther was swich diversitee
Bitwene hir bothe lawes, that they seyn

---

197 **therbiforn** beforehand   198 **write** written   203 **atte fulle** in full
204 **privee conseil** confidential advisers   205 **of . . . pace** pass over
207 **but he mighte have grace** unless he had the good fortune
208 **space** time   209 **He nas but deed** he was as good as dead **hie** haste
210 **shapen** devise   212 **argumenten** argue **casten** deliberate
213 **forth . . . leiden** produced   214 **abusioun** deception
219 **By wey of reson** on rational consideration   221 **hir bothe** of both of
them

They trowe that 'no Cristen prince wolde fain
Wedden his child under oure lawe swete
That us was taught by Mahoun, oure prophete.'

And he answerde, 'Rather than I lese   225
Custaunce, I wol be cristned, doutelees.
I moot been hires; I may noon oother chese.
I pray yow, hold youre argumentz in pees;
Saveth my lif, and beth noght recchelees
To geten hire that hath my lif in cure,   230
For in this wo I may nat longe endure.'

What nedeth gretter dilatacioun?
I seye, by tretis and embassadrye,
And by the Popes mediacioun,
And al the chirche, and al the chivalrye,   235
That in destruccioun of Maumetrye,
And in encrees of Cristes lawe deere,
They been acorded, so as ye shal heere:

How that the Sowdan and his baronage
And alle his lieges sholde ycristned be,   240
And he shal han Custaunce in mariage,
And certein gold – I noot what quantitee;
And heerto founde sufficient seuretee.
This same acord was sworn on either side.
Now, faire Custaunce, almighty God thee gide!   245

222 **trowe** believe **fain** gladly   224 **Mahoun** Mohammed   225 **lese** lose
227 **moot** must **hires** hers **chese** choose   228 **hold ... in pees** cease
229 **recchelees** negligent   230 **hath ... in cure** has in her power
232 **dilatacioun** amplification   233 **tretis** negotiation
embassadrye diplomacy   236 **Maumetrye** Mohammedanism   242 **noot** do
not know   243 And adequate security provided for this

Now wolde som men waiten, as I gesse,
That I sholde tellen al the purveiaunce
That th'Emperour, of his grete noblesse,
Hath shapen for his doghter, dame Custaunce.
250 Wel may men knowe that so greet ordinaunce
May no man tellen in a litel clause,
As was arrayed for so heigh a cause.

Bisshopes been shapen with hire for to wende,
Lordes, ladies, knightes of renoun,
255 And oother folk inowe – this is th'ende.
And notified is thurghout the toun
That every wight with greet devocioun
Sholde preyen Crist that he this mariage
Receive in gree, and spede this viage.

260 The day is comen of hir departinge –
I seye the woful day fatal is come,
That ther may be no lenger taryinge,
But forthward they hem dressen, alle and some.
Custaunce, that was with sorwe al overcome,
265 Ful pale arist, and dresseth hire to wende,
For wel she seeth ther is noon oother ende.

Allas, what wonder is it thogh she wepte,
That shal be sent to straunge nacioun,
Fro freendes that so tendrely hir kepte,
270 And to be bounde under subjeccioun

246 **waiten** expect   247 **purveiaunce** preparations   249 **shapen** devised
250 **ordinaunce** arrangements   251 **in a litel clause** briefly
252 **heigh** important   253 **shapen** appointed   255 **inowe** plenty of
256 **notified** proclaimed   259 **Receive in gree** may look favourably on
spede this viage give prosperity to this undertaking   263 **hem dressen** ready
themselves (to go) **alle and some** one and all   265 **arist** (= *ariseth*) rises
dresseth hire prepares   268 **straunge** foreign   269 **freendes** kinsfolk

Of oon, she knoweth noght his condicioun?
Housbondes been alle goode, and han been yoore;
That knowen wives – I dar sey yow namoore.

'Fader,' she seide, 'thy wrecched child
    Custaunce,
Thy yonge doghter fostred up so softe,   275
And ye, my moder, my soverein plesaunce
Over alle thing, out-taken Crist on-lofte,
Custaunce youre child hir recomaundeth ofte
Unto youre grace, for I shal to Surrye,
Ne shal I nevere seen yow moore with eye.   280

'Allas, unto the Barbre nacioun
I moste anon, sin that it is youre wille!
But Crist, that starf for oure redempcioun,
So yeve me grace his hestes to fulfille.
I, wrecche womman, no fors thogh I spille.   285
Wommen are born to thraldom and penaunce,
And to been under mannes governaunce.'

I trowe at Troye, whan Pirrus brak the wal
Or Ilion brende, at Thebes the citee,
N'at Rome for the harm thurgh Hanibal,   290
That Romains hath venquisshed times thre,
Nas herd swich tendre weping, for pitee,
As in the chambre was for hir departinge!
But forth she moot, wherso she wepe or singe.

272 **han been yoore** have long been so   275 **fostred up** brought up
276 **soverein plesaunce** chief delight   277 **out-taken** except **on-lofte** above
278 **hir recomaundeth** commends herself   279 **shal to** must go to
281 **Barbre** heathen   283 **starf** died   284 **hestes** commands
285 **no fors thogh I spille** no matter if I die   286 **thraldom** servitude
penaunce suffering   287 **governaunce** control   289 **Or** before
brende burned   293 **departinge** departure   294 **wherso** whether

295　　O Firste Moeving, cruel firmament!
　　　With thy diurnal sweigh that crowdest ay
　　　And hurlest al from est til occident
　　　That naturelly wolde holde another way,
　　　Thy crowding set the hevene in swich array
300　　At the biginning of this fiers viage,
　　　That cruel Mars hath slain this mariage.

　　　Infortunat ascendent tortuous,
　　　Of which the lord is helplees falle, allas,
　　　Out of his angle into the derkest hous!
305　　O Mars, o atazir, as in this cas!
　　　O fieble moone, unhappy been thy pas!
　　　Thow knittest thee ther thow art nat received;
　　　Ther thow were wel, fro thennes artow weived.

　　　Inprudent Emperour of Rome, allas!
310　　Was ther no philosophre in al thy toun?
　　　Is no time bet than oother in swich cas?
　　　Of viage is ther noon eleccioun,
　　　Namely to folk of heigh condicioun,
　　　Nat whan a roote is of a burthe yknowe?
315　　Allas, we been to lewed or to slowe!

295 **Firste Moeving** Primum Mobile (n.) **firmament** sphere
296 **diurnal sweigh** daily rotation **crowdest** drive　297 **est til occident** east
to west　299 **crowding** driving force　300 **fiers viage** dangerous voyage
302 see n.　304 **derkest** most inauspicious **hous** one of twelve segments into
which astrologers divided the ecliptic or annual pathway of the sun (n.)
305 **atazir** birth-sign (n.)　306 **unhappy** unlucky **pas** steps, motion
307 **knittest thee** are in conjunction **received** acceptable
308 **were wel** would be in a good position **weived** removed
310 **philosophre** astrologer　312 **eleccioun** choice, on astrological grounds,
of the proper time for some undertaking　313 **Namely** especially
314 **roote . . . of a burthe** position of the heavens at the time of birth (n.)
315 **lewed** ignorant

To ship is broght this woful faire maide,
Solempnely, with every circumstance.
'Now Jesu Crist be with yow alle,' she saide.
Ther nis namoore but 'farewel, faire Custaunce!'
She peineth hire to make good contenaunce;   320
And forth I lete hir saille in this manere,
And turne I wol again to my matere.

The moder of the Sowdan, welle of vices,
Espied hath hir sones plein entente,
How he wol lete his olde sacrifices,   325
And right anon she for hir conseil sente,
And they ben come to knowen what she mente.
And whan assembled was this folk in-feere,
She sette hir doun, and seide as ye shal heere:

'Lordes,' quod she, 'ye knowen, everychon,   330
How that my sone in point is for to lete
The holy lawes of oure Alkaron,
Yeven by Goddes message Makomete.
But oon avow to grete God I hete:
The lif shal rather out of my body sterte,   335
Or Makometes lawe out of min herte!

'What sholde us tiden of this newe lawe
But thraldom to oure bodies and penaunce,
And afterward in helle to be drawe
For we reneyed Mahoun oure creaunce?   340

317 **Solempnely** in state **every circumstance** careful attention to propriety
320 She strives to keep her composure   323 **welle** source
325 **lete** abandon   326 **conseil** council   328 **in-feere** together
329 **sette hir doun** seated herself   331 **in point is** is about to
332 **Alkaron** Koran   333 **message Makomete** messenger Mohammed
334 **hete** promise   335 **rather** sooner **sterte** depart   336 **Or** before
337 **tiden** betide **of** from   338 **thraldom** servitude **penaunce** suffering
339 **drawe** dragged   340 **reneyed** renounced **creaunce** belief

But lordes, wol ye maken assuraunce
As I shal seyn, assenting to my loore,
And I shal make us sauf for everemoore?'

They sworen and assenten, every man,
345   To live with hire and die, and by hir stonde,
And everich, in the beste wise he kan,
To strengthen hire shal alle his freendes fonde.
And she hath this emprise ytake on honde
Which ye shal heren that I shal devise,
350   And to hem alle she spak right in this wise:

'We shul first feine us Cristendom to take –
Coold water shal nat greve us but a lite!
And I shal swich a feste and revel make
That, as I trowe, I shal the Sowdan quite.
355   For, thogh his wif be cristned never so white,
She shal have nede to wasshe awey the rede,
Thogh she a font-ful water with hir lede.'

O Sowdanesse, roote of iniquitee,
Virago, thow Semirame the secounde!
360   O serpent under femininitee,
Lik to the serpent depe in helle ybounde!
O feined womman, al that may confounde
Vertu and innocence, thurgh thy malice,
Is bred in thee, as nest of every vice!

365   O Sathan, envious sin thilke day
That thow were chaced from oure heritage,
Wel knowestow to wommen the olde way!
Thow madest Eva bringe us in servage.

---

341 **assuraunce** pledge   342 **loore** advice   343 **sauf** safe   346 **wise** way
347 **fonde** sound out   348 **emprise** enterprise   349 **devise** relate
351 **feine us** pretend   352 **lite** little   354 **quite** pay back   357 **lede** bring
360 **femininitee** woman's shape   362 **confounde** destroy
366 **chaced from** deprived of   368 **servage** servitude

Thow wolt fordoon this Cristen mariage.
Thin instrument – so weilawey the while! –   370
Makestow of wommen, whan thou wolt bigile.

This Sowdanesse, whom I thus blame and
        warie,
Leet prively hir conseil goon hir way.
What sholde I in this tale lenger tarye?
She rideth to the Sowdan on a day,   375
And seide him that she wolde reneye hir lay,
And Cristendom of preestes handes fonge,
Repentinge hir she hethen was so longe,

Biseking him to doon hire that honour,
That she moste han the Cristen folk to feste.   380
'To plesen hem I wol do my labour.'
The Sowdan seyth, 'I wol doon at youre heste,'
And, knelinge, thanketh hire of that requeste.
So glad he was, he niste what to seye.
She kiste hir sone, and hom she gooth hir weye.   385

[Part Two]

Arrived been this Cristen folk to londe
In Surrye, with a gret solempne route,
And hastily this Sowdan sente his sonde,
First to his moder, and al the regne aboute,
And seide his wif was comen, out of doute.   390
And preide hire for to ride again the queene,
The honour of his regne to sustene.

369 **fordoon** destroy   370 **so weilawey the while** alas the day
372 **warie** curse   373 **goon hir way** go away   376 **reneye** renounce
lay law   377 **fonge** receive   379 **Biseking** beseeching   380 **moste** might
381 **do my labour** do my best   382 **at youre heste** as you desire
384 **niste** did not know   387 **solempne** splendid   388 **sonde** message
391 **again** to meet

Greet was the prees, and riche was th'array
Of Surriens and Romains met ifeere.
395   The moder of the Sowdan, riche and gay,
Receiveth hire with also glad a cheere
As any moder mighte hir doghter deere.
And to the nexte citee therbiside
A softe paas solempnely they ride.

400   Naught trowe I the triumphe of Julius,
Of which that Lucan maketh swich a boost,
Was royaller ne moore curius
Than was th'assemblee of this blisful oost.
But this scorpion, this wikked goost,
405   The Sowdanesse, for al hir flateringe,
Caste under this ful mortally to stinge.

The Sowdan comth himself soone after this,
So royally, that wonder is to telle.
He welcomth hire with alle joye and blis.
410   And thus in mirthe and joye I lete hem dwelle;
The fruit of this matere is that I telle.
Whan time cam, men thoughte it for the beste
That revel stinte, and men go to hir reste.

The time cam, this olde Sowdanesse
415   Ordeined hath this feste of which I tolde,
And to the feste Cristen folk hem dresse
In general, ye, bothe yonge and olde.
Heer may men feste and royaltee biholde,
And deintees mo than I kan yow devise –
420   But al to deere they boghte it er they rise.

393 **prees** throng   394 **ifeere** together   395 **riche and gay** richly and
beautifully dressed   396 **also glad a cheere** as glad a face
399 **A softe paas** at a leisurely pace   **solempnely** in state
402 **curius** splendid   403 **oost** company   406 **Caste** planned
413 **stinte** should cease   416 **hem dresse** make their way   417 **In general** in
a body, without exception   419 **mo** more   420 **boghte** paid for

O sodein wo, that evere art successour
To worldly blisse, spreind with bitternesse!
Th'ende of the joye of oure worldly labour!
Wo occupieth the fin of oure gladnesse.
Herke this conseil for thy sikernesse: 425
'Upon thy glade day have in thy minde
The unwar wo or harm that comth bihinde.'

For shortly for to tellen, at o word,
The Sowdan and the Cristen everychone
Been al to-hewe and stiked at the bord,   430
But it were oonly dame Custaunce allone.
This olde Sowdanesse, cursed crone,
Hath with hir freendes doon this cursed dede,
For she hirself wolde al the contree lede.

Ne ther nas Surrien noon that was converted,   435
That of the conseil of the Sowdan woot,
That he nas al to-hewe er he asterted.
And Custaunce han they take anon, foot-hoot,
And in a ship al sterelees, God woot,
They han hir set, and bidde hir lerne saille   440
Out of Surrye againward to Itaille.

A certein tresor that she thider ladde,
And, sooth to seyn, vitaille gret plentee,
They han hir yeven, and clothes eek she hadde;
And forth she sailleth in the salte see.   445

422 **spreind** mingled   424 **fin** end   425 **conseil** advice **sikernesse** security
426 **Upon thy glade day** in your prosperity   427 **unwar** unexpected
428 **at o word** in a word   430 **to-hewe** hacked to pieces **stiked** stabbed
bord table   431 **But it were** except for   434 **wolde . . . lede** wanted to rule
437 **asterted** escaped   438 **foot-hoot** straightaway
439 **sterelees** rudderless   440 **lerne saille** learn to sail
441 **againward** back **Itaille** Italy   443 **vitaille** food

O my Custaunce, ful of benignitee,
O emperoures yonge doghter deere,
He that is lord of Fortune be thy steere!

She blisseth hire, and with ful pitous vois,
450   Unto the crois of Crist thus seide she:
'O clere, o weleful auter, holy crois,
Reed of the Lambes blood, ful of pitee,
That wesshe the world fro th'olde iniquitee,
Me fro the feend and fro his clawes kepe,
455   That day that I shal drenchen in the depe!

'Victorious tree, proteccion of trewe,
That oonly worthy were for to bere
The king of hevene, with his woundes newe,
The white Lamb, that hurt was with a spere;
460   Flemere of feendes out of him and here
On which thy limes feithfully extenden,
Me kepe, and yeve me might my lif t'amenden!'

Yeres and dayes fleet this creature
Thurghout the See of Grece, unto the Straite
465   Of Marrok, as it was hir aventure.
On many a sory meel now may she baite!
After hir deth ful often may she waite,
Er that the wilde wawes wol hir drive
Unto the place ther she shal arrive.

446 **benignitee** gentleness   448 **steere** rudder, guide
449 **blisseth hire** crosses herself   **pitous** pitiful   451 **clere** glorious
weleful joyful   **auter** altar   452 **Reed of** red with   453 **wesshe** washed
455 **drenchen** drown   456 **trewe** the faithful   460 **Flemere** banisher
him and here (every) man and woman   461 Over whom your arms
faithfully spread (i.e. who have been marked with the sign of the Cross)
463 **fleet** (= *fleteth*) floats   465 **aventure** lot   466 **sory** wretched **baite** feed
467 **After ... waite** expect   469 **arrive** touch land

Men mighten asken why she was noght slain   470
Eek at the feste? who mighte hir body save?
And I answere to that demaunde again,
Who saved Daniel in the horrible cave,
Ther every wight save he, maister and knave,
Was with the leoun frete er he asterte?   475
No wight but God, that he bar in his herte.

God liste to shewe his wonderful miracle
In hire, for we sholde seen his mighty werkes.
Crist, which that is to every harm triacle,
By certein menes ofte, as knowen clerkes,   480
Dooth thing for certein ende that ful derk is
To mannes wit, that for oure ignoraunce
Ne konne noght knowe his prudent purveiaunce.

Now, sith she was nat at the feste yslawe,
Who kept hire fro the drenching in the see?   485
Who kepte Jonas in the fisshes mawe,
Til he was spouted up at Ninivee?
Wel may men knowe it was no wight but he
That kepte peple Ebraik from hir drenchinge,
With drye feet thurghout the see passinge.   490

Who bad the foure spiritz of tempest
That power han t'anoyen lond and see,
Bothe north and south and also west and est,
'Anoyeth neither see ne land ne tree'?
Soothly, the comandour of that was he   495
That fro the tempest ay this womman kepte,
As wel whan she wook as whan she slepte.

---

472 **demaunde** question   474 **Ther** where **knave** servant   475 **with** by
frete eaten **asterte** (= *astertede*) escaped   479 **triacle** remedy
481 **derk** obscure   483 Cannot have knowledge of his wise providence
484 **yslawe** slain   489 **peple Ebraik** the Hebrew people
drenchinge drowning   492 **t'anoyen** to disturb

Wher mighte this womman mete and drinke have
Thre yeer and moore? how lasteth hir vitaille?
500   Who fedde th'Egipcien Marie in the cave
Or in desert? No wight but Crist, *sanz faille.*
Five thousand folk it was as greet mervaille
With loves five and fisshes two to fede.
God sente his foison at hir grete nede.

505   She driveth forth into oure occian
Thurghout the wilde see, til at the laste
Under an hoold that nempnen I ne kan,
Fer in Northumberland, the wawe hir caste.
And in the sond hir ship stiked so faste
510   That thennes wolde it noght of al a tide;
The wil of Crist was that she sholde abide.

The constable of the castel doun is fare
To seen this wrak, and al the ship he soghte,
And foond this wery womman ful of care;
515   He foond also the tresor that she broghte.
In hir langage mercy she bisoghte,
The lif out of hir body for to twinne,
Hir to delivere of wo that she was inne.

A maner Latin corrupt was hir speche,
520   But algates therby was she understonde.
This constable, whan him liste no lenger seche,
This woful womman broghte he to the londe.

---

501 *sanz faille* without doubt   503 **loves** loaves
504 **foison** plenty   507 **hoold** castle **nempnen** name   508 **wawe** wave
510 **of al a tide** during the whole ebb and flow of a tide
512 **constable** governor **doun is fare** came down   513 **wrak** wreck
soghte searched   514 **care** sorrow   517 **twinne** sever
519 **A maner Latin corrupt** a kind of corrupt Latin
520 **algates** nevertheless   521 **whan him liste no lenger seche** when he did
not wish to search any further

She kneleth doun, and thanketh Goddes sonde;
But what she was, she wolde no man seye,
For foul ne fair, thogh that she sholde deye.   525

She seide, she was so mazed in the see
That she forgat hir minde, by hir trouthe.
The constable hath of hire so greet pitee,
And eek his wif, that they wepe for routhe.
She was so diligent, withouten slouthe,   530
To serve and plesen everich in that place
That alle hir loven that looken on hir face.

This constable, and dame Hermengild his wif,
Were payens, and that contree everywhere.
But Hermengild loved hire right as hir lif,   535
And Custaunce hath so longe sojourned there,
In orisons, with many a bitter teere,
Til Jesu hath converted thurgh his grace
Dame Hermengild, constablesse of that place.

In al that land no Cristen dorste route;   540
Alle Cristen folk been fled fro that contree,
Thurgh payens that conquereden al aboute
The plages of the north, by land and see.
To Walis fledde the Cristianitee
Of olde Britons dwelling in this ile;   545
Ther was hir refut for the mene-while.

523 **sonde** dispensation   525 **For foul ne fair** on no account
526 **mazed** bewildered   527 **forgat hir minde** had lost her memory
by hir trouthe on her honour   529 **routhe** pity   530 **slouthe** sloth
534 **payens** pagans   537 **orisons** prayers   539 **constablesse** wife of a castle
governor   540 **dorste route** dared to make a move   543 **plages** regions
544 **Walis** Wales **Cristianitee** Christian people   546 **refut** refuge

But yet nere Cristen Britons so exiled
That ther nere somme that in hir privetee
Honoured Crist, and hethen folk bigiled;
550   And neigh the castel swiche ther dwelten thre.
That oon of hem was blind and mighte nat se,
But it were with thilke eyen of his minde,
With whiche men seen whan that they been blinde.

Bright was the sonne as in that someres day,
555   For which the constable and his wif also
And Custaunce han ytake the righte way
Toward the see, a furlong wey or two,
To pleyen and to romen to and fro.
And in hir walk this blinde man they mette,
560   Croked and old, with eyen faste yshette.

'In name of Crist,' cride this blinde Britoun,
'Dame Hermengild, yif me my sighte again!'
This lady weex affrayed of the soun,
Lest that hir housbounde, shortly for to sayn,
565   Wolde hire for Jesu Cristes love han slain;
Til Custaunce made hir boold, and bad hir wirche
The wil of Crist, as doghter of his chirche.

The constable weex abasshed of that sight,
And seide, 'What amounteth al this fare?'
570   Custaunce answerde, 'Sire, it is Cristes might,
That helpeth folk out of the feendes snare.'
And so ferforth she gan oure lay declare,
That she the constable, er that it was eve,
Converteth, and on Crist made him bileve.

548 in hir privetee secretly   549 bigiled deceived
552 But it were except   556 the righte way the direct route
558 pleyen take recreation romen roam   560 yshette shut
563 weex affrayed was alarmed soun sound   566 wirche work
568 weex abasshed of was disturbed by   569 amounteth is the meaning of
fare commotion   572 And she explained our law to the extent that

This constable was nothing lord of this place 575
Of which I speke, ther he Custaunce fond,
But kepte it strongly, many wintres space,
Under Alla, king of al Northumberlond,
That was ful wis and worthy of his hond
Again the Scottes, as men may wel heere. 580
But turne I wol again to my matere.

Sathan, that evere us waiteth to bigile,
Saugh of Custaunce al hir perfeccioun,
And caste anon how he mighte quite hir while,
And made a yong knight that dwelte in that toun 585
Love hire so hote, of foul affeccioun,
That verraily him thoughte he sholde spille,
But he of hire mighte ones have his wille.

He woweth hire, but it availleth noght –
She wolde do no sinne by no weye. 590
And for despit, he compassed in his thoght
To maken hire on shameful deeth to deye.
He waiteth whan the constable was aweye,
And prively upon a night he crepte
In Hermengildes chambre whil she slepte. 595

Wery, forwaked in hir orisons,
Slepeth Custaunce, and Hermengild also.
This knight, thurgh Sathanas temptacions,
Al softely is to the bed ygo,

575 **nothing** not   577 **many wintres space** for a period of many years
579 **worthy of his hond** redoubtable in combat   580 **Again** against
582 **waiteth** lies in wait   584 **caste** (= *castede*) plotted **quite hir while** pay
her back   586 **hote** hotly   587 **sholde spille** would die
588 **But he . . . mighte** if he could not **ones** once   589 **woweth** woos
591 **for despit** out of malice **compassed** planned
593 **waiteth whan** watches for a time when   596 **forwaked** worn out by
wakefulness   598 **Sathanas** of Satan   599 Went stealthily to the bed

600   And kitte the throte of Hermengild atwo,
        And leide the blody knif by dame Custaunce
        And wente his wey – ther God yeve him meschaunce!

        Soone after comth this constable hom again,
        And eek Alla, that king was of that lond,
605   And saw his wif despitously yslain,
        For which ful ofte he weep and wrong his hond.
        And in the bed the blody knif he fond
        By dame Custaunce. Allas, what mighte she seye?
        For verray wo hir wit was al aweye.

610   To King Alla was told al this meschaunce,
        And eek the time, and where and in what wise
        That in a ship was founden this Custaunce,
        As herbiforn that ye han herd devise.
        The kinges herte of pitee gan agrise,
615   Whan he saw so benigne a creature
        Falle in disese and in misaventure.

        For as the lomb toward his deeth is broght,
        So stant this innocent bifore the king.
        This false knight that hath this treson wroght
620   Bereth hire on hond that she hath doon this thing.
        But nathelees ther was greet moorning
        Among the peple, and seyn they kan nat gesse
        That she had doon so greet a wikkednesse.

600 **kitte** cut   602 **God yeve him meschaunce** May God curse him
605 **despitously** cruelly   606 **weep** wept   609 **aweye** gone
613 **herbiforn** previously   **herd devise** heard related   614 **gan agrise** melted
616 **disese** suffering   **misaventure** misfortune   617 **lomb** lamb
618 **stant** (= *standeth*) stands   620 **Bereth hire on hond** accuses her
622 **seyn** say

For they han seyn hire evere so vertuous,
And loving Hermengild right as hir lif;   625
Of this baar witnesse everich in that hous,
Save he that Hermengild slow with his knif.
This gentil king hath caught a gret motif
Of this witnesse, and thoghte he wolde enquere
Depper in this, a trouthe for to lere.   630

Allas, Custaunce, thow hast no champioun,
Ne fighte kanstow noght, so weilawey!
But he that starf for oure redempcioun
And bond Sathan (and yet lith ther he lay),
So be thy stronge champion this day!   635
For but if Crist open miracle kithe,
Withouten gilt thow shalt been slain as swithe.

She sette hir doun on knees, and thus she saide:
'Inmortal God, that savedest Susanne
Fro fals blame, and thow, merciful maide,   640
Marye I mene, doghter to Seint Anne,
Biforn whos child aungeles singe Osanne,
If I be giltlees of this felonye,
My socour be, for ellis shal I die!'

Have ye nat seyn somtime a pale face   645
Among a prees, of him that hath be lad
Toward his deeth, wheras him gat no grace,
And swich a colour in his face hath had,
Men mighte knowe his face that was bistad
Amonges alle the faces in that route?   650
So stant Custance, and looketh hire aboute.

624 seyn seen   627 he that Hermengild slow the one who killed
Hermengild   628–9 hath caught a gret motif Of was greatly impressed by
630 Depper more deeply lere learn   632 so weilawey alas   633 starf died
634 bond bound yet lith he (Satan) still lies   636 but if unless
kithe performs   637 as swithe without delay   642 Osanne Hosanna
644 My socour be be my help   645 seyn seen   646 prees crowd
647 him gat no grace he obtained no mercy   649 bistad hard beset

O queenes, livinge in prosperitee,
Duchesses, and ye ladies everychone,
Haveth som routhe on hir adversitee!
655   An emperoures doghter stant allone;
She hath no wight to whom to make hir mone.
O blood royal, that stondest in this drede,
Fer ben thy freendes at thy grete nede!

This Alla king hath swich compassioun,
660   As gentil herte is fulfild of pitee,
That from his eyen ran the water doun.
'Now hastily do fecche a book,' quod he,
'And if this knight wol sweren how that she
This womman slow, yet wol we us avise
665   Whom that we wole that shal been oure justise.'

A Briton book, writen with Evangiles,
Was fet, and on this book he swoor anoon
She gilty was, and in the mene-whiles
An hand him smoot upon the nekke-boon,
670   That doun he fel atones as a stoon,
And bothe his eyen broste out of his face,
In sighte of everybody in that place.

A vois was herd in general audience,
And seide: 'Thow hast disclaundred, giltelees,
675   The doghter of holy chirche in heigh presence.
Thus hastow doon, and yet holde I my pees!'

654 Haveth . . . routhe have pity   656 mone plea
662 do fecche have fetched   664 us avise consider   665 Whom we want to
be our judge   666 Evangiles the Gospels   667 fet fetched
anoon immediately   668 in the mene-whiles meanwhile   670 atones at a
stroke as like   671 broste burst   673 in general audience in the hearing of
everyone   674 disclaundred slandered   675 in heigh presence in solemn
assembly

Of this mervaille agast was al the prees;
As mazed folk they stoden everychone
For drede of wreche, save Custance allone.

Greet was the drede, and eek the repentaunce,   680
Of hem that hadden wrong suspecioun
Upon this sely innocent Custaunce.
And for this miracle, in conclusioun,
And by Custances mediacioun,
The king, and many another in that place,   685
Converted was, thanked be Cristes grace!

This false knight was slain for his untrouthe
By juggement of Alla, hastily,
And yet Custaunce hadde of his deeth greet
        routhe.
And after this Jesus of his mercy   690
Made Alla wedden ful solempnely
This holy maide, that is so bright and shene.
And thus hath Crist ymaad Custance a queene.

But who was woful, if I shal nat lie,
Of this wedding, but Donegild and namo,   695
The kinges moder, ful of tyrannye?
Hir thoughte hir cursed herte brast atwo;
She wolde noght hir sone had doon so.
Hir thoughte a despit that he sholde take
So straunge a creature unto his make.   700

677 **agast** afraid   678 **mazed** bewildered   679 **drede of wreche** fear of
vengeance   **save** except   682 **sely** poor   687 **untrouthe** treachery
691 **ful solempnely** with great pomp   692 **shene** radiant
695 **and namo** alone   697 **brast atwo** would break in two   699 **a despit** an
insult   700 **unto his make** as his spouse

Me list nat of the chaf ne of the stree
Maken so long a tale as of the corn.
What sholde I tellen of the royaltee
At mariage, or which cours gooth biforn,
705   Who bloweth in the trompe or in an horn?
The fruit of every tale is for to seye:
They ete, and drinke, and daunce, and singe,
        and pleye.

They goon to bedde, as it was skile and right,
For though that wives been ful holy thinges,
710   They moste take in pacience at night
Swich maner necessaries as been plesinges
To folk that han ywedded hem with ringes,
And leye a lite hir holinesse aside
As for the time – it may no bet bitide.

715   On hire he gat a knave child anon;
And to a bisshop, and his constable eke,
He took his wif to kepe whan he is gon
To Scotlondward, his foomen for to seke.
Now faire Custaunce, that is so humble and
        meke,
720   So longe is goon with childe til that stille
She halt hir chambre, abiding Cristes wille.

701 **Me list nat** I do not want **stree** straw   702 **corn** i.e. the best, most
important, part (as opposed to 'chaf')   703 **What** why
royaltee magnificence   704 **gooth biforn** comes first   708 **skile** reasonable
711 **necessaries** necessities **plesinges** sources of pleasure   713 **a lite** a little
714 **As for the time** on this occasion **bet** better   715 **gat** begot **knave** boy
717 **took** gave **to kepe** for protection
718 **Scotlondward** towards Scotland **foomen** enemies
720 **goon with childe** pregnant **stille** calmly   721 **halt** keeps to

The time is come a knave child she beer;
Mauricius at the font-stoon they him calle.
This constable dooth forth come a messager,
And wroot unto his king that cleped was Alle   725
How that this blisful tidinge is bifalle,
And othere tidinges speedful for to seye.
He tath the lettre, and forth he goth his weye.

This messager, to doon his avauntage,
Unto the kinges moder rideth swithe,   730
And salueth hire ful faire in his langage.
'Madame,' quod he, 'ye may be glad and blithe,
And thanketh God an hundred thousand sithe:
My lady queene hath child, withouten doute,
To joye and blisse of al this regne aboute.   735

'Lo here, the lettres seled of this thing,
That I moot bere with al the haste I may.
If ye wol aught unto youre sone the king,
I am youre servaunt, bothe night and day.'
Donegild answerde, 'As now at this time, nay.   740
But here al night I wol thow take thy reste;
Tomorwe wol I seye thee what me leste.'

This messager drank sadly ale and win,
And stolen were his lettres prively
Out of his box, whil he sleep as a swin.   745
And countrefeted was ful subtilly
Another lettre, wroght ful sinfully,
Unto the king direct of this matere
Fro his constable, as ye shal after heere.

---

722 **beer** gave birth to   723 **font-stoon** font
724 **dooth forth come** summons   725 **wroot** wrote
726 **blisful tidinge** happy event   727 **speedful** expedient   728 **tath** takes
729 **doon his avauntage** win himself favour   730 **swithe** with all speed
733 **sithe** times   737 **moot bere** must carry   738 **wol aught** want (to send)
anything   742 **me leste** pleases me   743 **sadly** heavily
745 **sleep as a swin** slept like a pig   748 **direct** directed, addressed

750 The lettre spak the queene delivered was
Of so horrible a fendlich creature
That in the castel noon so hardy was
That any while dorste ther endure.
The moder was an elf, by aventure
755 Ycome, by charmes or by sorcerye,
And everich wight hateth hir compaignye.

Wo was this king whan he this lettre had seyn,
But to no wight he tolde his sorwes soore,
But of his owene hond he wroot agein:
760 'Welcome the sonde of Crist for everemoore
To me that am now lerned in his loore!
Lord, welcome be thy lust and thy plesaunce;
My lust I putte al in thin ordinaunce.

'Kepeth this child, al be it foul or feir,
765 And eek my wif, unto min hom-cominge.
Crist, whan him list, may sende me an heir
Moore agreable than this to my likinge.'
This lettre he seleth, prively wepinge,
Which to the messager was take soone,
770 And forth he goth; ther is namoore to doone.

O messager, fulfild of dronkenesse,
Strong is thy breeth, thy limes faltren ay,
And thow biwreyest alle secrenesse.
Thy minde is lorn, thou janglest as a jay;

751 **fendlich** fiendish   752 **hardy** brave   753 **endure** remain
754 **aventure** chance   756 **everich wight** everyone   757 **seyn** seen
758 **soore** bitter   759 **of** with   **agein** in reply   760 **the sonde of Crist** what
Christ sends   761 **loore** teaching   762 **lust** pleasure
763 **in thin ordinaunce** at your disposal   764 **al be it** whether it is
768 **prively** secretly   769 **take** given   771 **fulfild of** filled with
772 **limes faltren ay** limbs are constantly shaky   773 **biwreyest** betray
secrenesse secrets   774 **lorn** destroyed **janglest as** chatter like

Thy face is turned in a new array.   775
Ther dronkenesse regneth in any route
Ther is no conseil hid, withouten doute.

O Donegild, I ne have noon Englissh digne
Unto thy malice and thy tyrannye,
And therfore to the feend I thee resigne;   780
Lat him enditen of thy traitorye!
Fy, mannissh, fy – O nay, by God, I lie! –
Fy, feendlich spirit! for I dar wel telle,
Thogh thow heere walke, thy spirit is in helle.

This messager comth fro the king again,   785
And at the kinges modres court he lighte,
And she was of this messager ful fain,
And plesed him in al that evere she mighte.
He drank and wel his girdel underpighte;
He slepeth and he fnorteth in his gise   790
Al night, til that the sonne gan arise.

Eft were his lettres stolen everychon,
And countrefeted lettres in this wise:
'The king comaundeth his constable anon,
Up peine of hanging and on heigh juise,   795
That he ne sholde suffren in no wise
Custance inwith his regne for t'abide
Thre dayes and a quarter of a tide;

775 **array** state   776 **Ther** where   777 **conseil** secret   778 **digne** suitable
781 **enditen of** write about   **traitorye** treachery   786 **lighte** dismounted
789 **wel his girdel underpighte** padded out his belt well, filled his belly
790 **fnorteth** snores   **in his gise** in his own fashion   792 **Eft** again
795 **heigh juise** severe punishment   796 **suffren** allow   797 **inwith** within
798 **tide** duration of a tide's ebb and flow

'But in the same ship as he hir fond,
800   Hire and hir yonge sone and al hir geere
He sholde putte, and crowde hir fro the lond,
And charge hire that she nevere eft come there.'
O my Custaunce, wel may thy goost have fere,
And sleping in thy dreem been in penaunce,
805   Whan Donegild caste al this ordinaunce!

This messager on morwe, whan he wook,
Unto the castel halt the nexte wey,
And to the constable he the lettre took.
And whan that he this pitous lettre sey,
810   Ful ofte he seide 'allas!' and 'weilawey!'
'Lord Crist,' quod he, 'how may this world endure,
So ful of sinne is many a creature?

'O mighty God, if that it be thy wille,
Sith thow art rightful juge, how may it be
815   That thow wolt suffren innocentz to spille,
And wikked folk regne in prosperitee?
O goode Custaunce, allas, so wo is me,
That I moot be thy tormentour, or deye
On shames deeth; ther is noon oother weye.'

820   Wepen bothe yonge and olde in al that place,
Whan that the king this cursed lettre sente.
And Custaunce, with a dedly pale face,
The ferthe day toward hir ship she wente.
But nathelees she taketh in good entente
825   The wil of Crist, and kneling on the stronde,
She seide, 'Lord, ay welcome be thy sonde!

800 geere possessions   801 crowde push   803 goost spirit
804 penaunce distress   805 caste (= castede) determined on
ordinaunce plan   806 on morwe in the morning   807 nexte quickest
808 took gave   809 pitous pitiful sey saw   815 suffren allow spille die
817 wo is me sorrow overcomes me   823 ferthe fourth
824 in good entente cheerfully   825 stronde shore   826 thy sonde what
you send

'He that me kepte fro the false blame
Whil I was on the lond amonges yow,
He kan me kepe from harm and eek fro shame
In salte see, althogh I se noght how.   830
As strong as evere he was, he is yet now.
In him triste I, and in his moder deere,
That is to me my sail and eek my steere.'

Hir litel child lay weping in hir arm,
And kneling, pitously to him she seide,   835
'Pees, litel sone, I wol do thee noon harm.'
With that hir coverchief of hir hed she breide,
And over his litel eyen she it leide,
And in hir arm she lulleth it ful faste,
And into hevene hir eyen up she caste.   840

'Moder,' quod she, 'and maide bright, Marye,
Sooth is, that thurgh wommans eggement
Mankinde was lorn and dampned ay to die,
For which thy child was on a crois yrent.
Thy blisful eyen sawe al his torment;   845
Thanne is ther no comparison bitwene
Thy wo, and any wo man may sustene.

'Thow saw thy child yslain bifore thine eyen,
And yet now liveth my litel child, parfay.
Now lady bright, to whom alle woful cryen,   850
Thow glorye of wommanhod, thow faire may,
Thow haven of refut, brighte sterre of day,
Rewe on my child, that of thy gentillesse
Rewest on every rewful in distresse.

---

833 **steere** helm   835 **pitously** compassionately   837 **coverchief** head cloth
breide pulled   839 **lulleth** rocks   842 **Sooth** true **eggement** instigation
843 **lorn** ruined **dampned** condemned   844 **yrent** torn
845 **blisful** blessed   847 **sustene** endure   851 **may** maiden
852 **refut** refuge **sterre of day** morning star   853 **Rewe** have pity
854 **rewful** pitiable person

855   'O litel child, allas, what is thy gilt,
       That nevere wroghtest sinne as yet, pardee?
       Why wil thin harde fader han thee spilt?
       O mercy, deere constable,' quod she,
       'As lat my litel child dwelle here with thee!
860   And if thow darst noght saven him for blame,
       So kis him ones in his fadres name!'

       Therwith she looketh bakward to the londe,
       And seide, 'Farewel, housbonde routhelees!'
       And up she rist and walketh doun the stronde
865   Toward the ship; hir folweth al the prees.
       And evere she prayeth hir child to holde his pees,
       And taketh hir leve, and with an holy entente
       She blesseth hire, and into ship she wente.

       Vitailled was the ship, it is no drede,
870   Habundantly for hire ful longe space;
       And othere necessaries that sholde nede
       She hadde inow, heried be Goddes grace!
       For wind and weder almighty God purchace,
       And bringe hir hom! I kan no bettre seye;
875   But in the see she driveth forth hir weye.

[Part Three]

       Alla the king comth hom soone after this
       Unto his castel, of the which I tolde,
       And axeth where his wif and his child is.
       The constable gan aboute his herte colde,

856 **wroghtest** committed   857 **spilt** killed   859 **As lat** let
863 **routhelees** pitiless   864 **rist** (= *riseth*) rises   865 **prees** throng
867 **entente** spirit   868 **blesseth hire** crosses herself
869 **it is no drede** without doubt   870 **space** time
871 **necessaries** necessities   872 **heried** praised   873 May almighty God see
to the wind and weather   875 **driveth forth hir weye** makes her way
878 **axeth** asks   879 **gan . . . colde** turned cold

And pleinly al the manere he him tolde –   880
As ye han herd; I kan telle it no bettre –
And sheweth the king his seel and eek his lettre,

And seide, 'Lord, as ye comaunded me
Up peine of deeth, so have I doon, certein.'
This messager tormented was til he   885
Moste biknowe and tellen, plat and plein,
Fro night to night in what place he had lein.
And thus by wit and subtil enqueringe
Imagined was by whom this harm gan springe.

The hond was knowe that the lettre wroot,   890
And al the venim of this cursed dede,
But in what wise, certeinly I noot.
Th'effect is this: that Alla, out of drede,
His moder slow – that may men pleinly rede –
For that she traitour was to hir ligeaunce.   895
Thus endeth olde Donegild, with meschaunce!

The sorwe that this Alla night and day
Maketh for his wif and for his child also,
Ther is no tonge that it telle may.
But now wol I unto Custaunce go,   900
That fleteth in the see, in peine and wo,
Five yeer and moore, as liked Cristes sonde,
Er that hir ship approched unto londe.

884 Up upon   885 tormented tortured   886 Moste biknowe had to
confess plat bluntly   888 wit reasoning   889 gan springe originated
890 knowe recognized   892 noot (= *ne woot*) do not know
893 Th'effect the essential point out of drede without doubt
895 ligeaunce allegiance   896 with meschaunce curse her   901 fleteth drifts
902 as liked Cristes sonde as was pleasing to Christ's ordinance

Under an hethen castel atte laste,
905   Of which the name in my text noght I finde,
Custaunce and eek hir child the see up caste.
Almighty God, that saveth al mankinde,
Have on Custaunce and on hir child som minde,
That fallen is in hethen hand eftsoone,
910   In point to spille, as I shal telle yow soone.

Doun from the castel comth ther many a wight
To gauren on this ship, and on Custaunce;
But shortly, from the castel on a night
The lordes stiward – God yeve him meschaunce! –
915   A theef that hadde reneyed oure creaunce,
Cam into ship allone and seide he sholde
Hir lemman be, wherso she wolde or nolde.

Wo was this wrecched womman tho bigon;
Hir child cride, and she cride pitously.
920   But blisful Marye heelp hire right anon;
For with hir strogeling wel and mightily
The theef fil overbord al sodeinly,
And in the see he dreinte for vengeaunce.
And thus hath Crist unwemmed kept Custaunce.

925   O foule lust of luxurye, lo, thin ende!
Nat oonly that thow faintest mannes minde,
But verraily thow wolt his body shende.
Th'ende of thy werk or of thy lustes blinde

908 **Have on ... som minde** remember   909 **eftsoone** a second time
910 **In point to spille** on the brink of death   912 **gauren on** gaze at
915 **reneyed** abjured   **creaunce** faith   917 Have sex with her, whether she
liked it or not   918 **Wo ... bigon** overwhelmed with misery
920 **heelp** helped   921 **strogeling** struggling   923 **dreinte** drowned
924 **unwemmed** undefiled   925 **lust** delight   **luxurye** lechery
926 **faintest** enfeeble   927 **shende** destroy

Is compleining. How many oon may men finde,
That noght for werk somtime, but for th'entente   930
To doon this sinne, been outher slain or shente?

How may this waike womman han this strengthe
Hir to defende again this renegat?
O Golias, unmesurable of lengthe,
How mighte David make thee so maat,   935
So yong and of armure so desolat?
How dorste he looke upon thy dredful face?
Wel may men seen, it was but Goddes grace.

Who yaf Judith corage or hardinesse
To sleen him Olofernus in his tente,   940
And to deliveren out of wrecchednesse
The peple of God? I sey for this entente,
That right as God spirit of vigour sente
To hem, and saved hem out of meschaunce,
So sente he might and vigour to Custaunce.   945

Forth gooth hir ship thurghout the narwe mouth
Of Jubaltare and Septe, driving ay
Somtime west, and somtime north and south,
And somtime est, ful many a wery day.
Til Cristes moder – blessed be she ay! –   950
Hath shapen thurgh hir endelees goodnesse
To make an ende of al hir hevinesse.

Now lat us stinte of Custaunce but a throwe,
And speke we of the Romain Emperour,
That out of Surrye hath by lettres knowe   955
The slaughtre of Cristen folk, and dishonour

929 **compleining** lamentation   930 **werk** the deed   932 **waike** weak
933 **renegat** renegade   934 **lengthe** height   935 **maat** helpless
936 **desolat** destitute   939 **hardinesse** bravery
944 **out of meschaunce** from misfortune   946 **narwe** narrow
947 **driving** rushing   951 **shapen** determined   952 **hevinesse** sorrow
953 **stinte of** cease speaking of **but a throwe** only for a short time

Doon to his doghter by a fals traitour;
I mene the cursed wikked Sowdanesse,
That at the feeste leet sleen bothe moore and lesse.

960 For which this Emperour hath sent anon
His senatour, with royal ordinaunce,
And othere lordes, God woot, many oon,
On Surriens to taken heigh vengeaunce.
They brennen, sleen, and bringe hem to meschaunce
965 Ful many a day; but shortly, this is th'ende:
Homward to Rome they shapen hem to wende.

This senatour repaireth with victorye
To Romeward, sailinge ful royally,
And mette the ship drivinge, as seyth the storye,
970 In which Custaunce sit ful pitously.
Nothing ne knew he what she was, ne why
She was in swich array, ne she nil seye
Of hir estaat, althogh she sholde deye.

He bringeth hire to Rome, and to his wif
975 He yaf hire, and hir yonge sone also,
And with the senatour she ladde hir lif.
Thus kan Oure Lady bringen out of wo
Woful Custaunce, and many another mo;
And longe time dwelled she in that place,
980 In holy werkes evere, as was hir grace.

The senatoures wif hir aunte was,
But for al that she knew hir never the moore.
I wol no lenger taryen in this cas,
But to King Alla, which I spak of yoore,

959 **leet sleen** caused to be killed   961 **ordinaunce** decree
964 **brennen** burn   966 **shapen hem to wende** prepare to go
967 **repaireth** returns   970 **sit** (= *sitteth*) sits   972 **nil seye** will not speak
973 About her condition in life, were she to die for it
982 **never the moore** not at all

That wepeth for his wif and siketh soore,   985
I wol retourne, and lete I wole Custaunce
Under the senatoures governaunce.

King Alla, which that hadde his moder slain,
Upon a day fil in swich repentaunce
That, if I shortly tellen shal and plein,   990
To Rome he comth, to receiven his penaunce,
And putte him in the Popes ordinaunce
In heigh and logh, and Jesu Crist bisoghte
Foryeve his wikked werkes that he wroghte.

The fame anon thurgh Rome toun is born   995
How Alla king shal come in pilgrimage,
By herbergeours that wenten him biforn;
For which the senatour, as was usage,
Rood him agains, and many of his linage,
As wel to shewe his heighe magnificence,   1000
As to doon any king a reverence.

Greet cheere dooth this noble senatour
To King Alla, and he to him also;
Everich of hem dooth oother greet honour.
And so bifel, that in a day or two,   1005
This senatour is to King Alla go
To feste, and shortly, if I shal nat lie,
Custaunces sone wente in his compaignye.

Som men wolde seyn at requeste of Custaunce
This senatour hath lad this child to feste.   1010
I may nat tellen every circumstaunce;
Be as be may, ther was he atte leste.

---

985 **siketh** sighs **soore** deeply   986 **lete** leave   987 **governaunce** control
991 **penaunce** penance   992 **ordinaunce** control   994 **werkes** deeds
997 **herbergeours** harbingers, king's officers who arrange for lodgings
998 **as was usage** as was customary   999 **agains** to meet
1002–3 **Greet cheere dooth . . . To** entertains lavishly   1004 **Everich** each
1010 **lad** brought   1012 **Be as be may** however that may be

But sooth is this, that at his modres heste
Biforn Alla, during the metes space,
1015   The child stood, looking in the kinges face.

This Alla king hath of this child greet wonder,
And to the senatour he seide anon:
'Whos is that faire child that stondeth yonder?'
'I noot,' quod he, 'by God and by Seint John!
1020   A moder he hath, but fader hath he non
That I of woot' – and shortly, in a stounde,
He tolde Alla how that this child was founde.

'But God wot,' quod this senatour also,
'So vertuous a livere in my lif
1025   Ne saw I nevere as she, ne herde of mo,
Of worldly wommen, maide ne of wif.
I dar wel seyn hir hadde levere a knif
Thurghout hir brest than been a womman wikke;
Ther is no man koude bringe hire to that prikke.'

1030   Now was this child as lik unto Custaunce
As possible is a creature to be.
This Alla hath the face in remembraunce
Of dame Custaunce, and theron mused he,
If that the childes moder were aught she
1035   That is his wif, and prively he sighte,
And spedde him fro the table that he mighte.

'Parfay,' thoughte he, 'fantome is in min heed!
I oghte deme, of skilful jugement,
That in the salte see my wif is deed.'
1040   And afterward he made his argument:

1013 **heste** bidding   1014 **metes space** course of the meal
1017 **anon** immediately   1021 **of woot** know of   **in a stounde** in a short
while   1027 **hir hadde levere** she would prefer   1029 **prikke** condition
1034 **aught** by any means   1035 **sighte** sighed   1036 **spedde him** hastened
that he mighte as best he could   1037 **fantome** illusion   1038 **deme** believe
skilful rational

'What woot I if that Crist have hider sent
My wif by see, as wel as he hir sente
To my contree fro thennes that she wente?'

And after noon, hom with the senatour
Goth Alla, for to seen this wonder chaunce.   1045
This senatour dooth Alla greet honour
And hastily he sente after Custaunce.
But trusteth wel, hir liste noght to daunce
Whan that she wiste wherfore was that sonde;
Unnethe upon hir feet she mighte stonde.   1050

Whan Alla saugh his wif, faire he hir grette,
And weep that it was routhe for to se;
For at the firste look he on hir sette
He knew wel verraily that it was she.
And she for sorwe as domb stant as a tree,   1055
So was hir herte shet in hir distresse,
Whan she remembred his unkindenesse.

Twies she swowneth in his owene sighte,
He weep and him excuseth pitously.
'Now God,' quod he, 'and alle his halwes   1060
    brighte,
So wysly on my soule as have mercy,
That of youre harm as giltelees am I
As is Maurice my sone, so lik youre face –
Ellis the feend me fecche out of this place!'

1045 **wonder chaunce** wondrous occurrence   1047 **after** for
1048 **hir liste noght to daunce** she did not feel like dancing   1049 When she
knew the reason for that message   1050 **Unnethe** hardly
1051 **grette** greeted   1052 **weep** wept **routhe** pity   1056 **shet** closed up
1057 **unkindenesse** unnatural behaviour, cruelty   1060 **halwes** saints
1061 **So wysly** as surely   1064 **Ellis the feend me fecche** otherwise may the
devil take me

1065   Long was the sobbing and the bitter peine
        Er that hir woful hertes mighte cesse.
        Greet was the pitee for to heere hem pleine,
        Thurgh whiche pleintes gan hir wo encresse.
        I pray yow al my labour to relesse;
1070   I may nat telle hir wo until tomorwe –
        I am so wery for to speke of sorwe.

        But finally, whan that the sooth is wist,
        That Alla giltelees was of hir wo,
        I trowe an hundred times been they kist,
1075   And swich a blisse is ther bitwix hem two
        That, save the joye that lasteth everemo,
        Ther is noon lik that any creature
        Hath seyn or shal, whil that the world may dure.

        Tho preyde she hir housbond mekely,
1080   In relief of hir longe pitous pine,
        That he wolde preye hir fader specially,
        That of his magestee he wolde encline
        To vouchesauf som day with him to dine.
        She preyde him eek he sholde by no weye
1085   Unto hir fader no word of hir seye.

        Som men wolde seyn how that the child Maurice
        Dooth this message unto this Emperour;
        But, as I gesse, Alla was noght so nice,
        To him that was of so soverein honour –
1090   As he that is of Cristen folk the flour –
        Sente any child; but it is bet to deme
        He wente himself, and so it may wel seme.

1066 **cesse** grow calm   1067 **pleine** lament   1069 **relesse** discharge
1070 **until tomorwe** all day and all night long   1072 **wist** known
1078 **seyn** seen   1080 **pine** suffering   1083 **vouchesauf** grant
1088 **nice** foolish   1089 **soverein** supreme   1091 **Sente** (that he) sent (n.)
deme believe

This Emperour hath graunted gentilly
To come to diner as he him bisoghte;
And wel rede I he looked bisily   1095
Upon this child, and on his doghter thoghte.
Alla gooth to his in, and as him oghte
Arrayed for this feste in every wise,
As ferforth as his konning may suffise.

The morwe cam, and Alla gan him dresse,   1100
And eek his wif, this Emperour to meete,
And forth they ride in joye and in gladnesse.
And whan she saugh hir fader in the strete,
She lighte doun and falleth him to feete.
'Fader,' quod she, 'youre yonge child   1105
          Custaunce
Is now ful clene out of youre remembraunce.

'I am youre doghter Custance,' quod she,
'That whilom ye han sent unto Surrye.
It am I, fader, that in the salte see
Was put allone, and dampned for to die.   1110
Now goode fader, mercy I yow crye!
Sende me namoore unto noon hethenesse,
But thonke my lord heere of his kindenesse.'

Who kan the pitous joye tellen al
Bitwix hem thre, sin they be thus ymette?   1115
But of my tale make an ende I shal;
The day goth faste, I wol no lenger lette.
This glade folk to diner they hem sette;
In joye and blisse at mete I lete hem dwelle,
A thousand fold wel moore than I kan telle.   1120

1093 **gentilly** courteously   1095 **bisily** intently   1097 **in** lodging   1099 To
the full extent of his ability   1100 **gan him dresse** got ready
1104 **lighte doun** dismounted **him to feete** at his feet
1106 **ful clene** completely   1108 **whilom** formerly   1109 **It am I** it is I
1110 **dampned** condemned   1117 **lette** delay   1119 **mete** dinner **lete** leave

This child Maurice was sithen emperour
Maad by the Pope, and lived cristenly;
To Cristes chirche he dide greet honour.
But I lete al his story passen by;
1125   Of Custaunce is my tale specially.
In th'olde Romain gestes may men finde
Maurices lif; I bere it noght in minde.

This King Alla, whan he his time say,
With his Custaunce, his holy wif so swete,
1130   To Engelond been they come the righte way,
Wheras they live in joye and in quiete.
But litel while it lasteth, I yow heete,
Joye of this world, for time wol nat abide;
Fro day to night it chaungeth as the tide.

1135   Who lived evere in swich delit o day
That him ne moeved outher conscience,
Or ire, or talent, or som kinnes affray,
Envye, or pride, or passion, or offence?
I ne seye but for this ende this sentence,
1140   That litel while in joye or in plesaunce
Lasteth the blisse of Alla with Custaunce.

For deeth, that taketh of heigh and logh his rente,
Whan passed was a yeer, evene as I gesse,
Out of this world this King Alla he hente,
1145   For whom Custance hath ful greet hevinesse.
Now lat us prayen God his soule blesse!
And dame Custaunce, finally to seye,
Toward the toun of Rome gooth hir weye.

1121 **sithen** afterwards   1122 **cristenly** in a Christian manner
1126 **gestes** chronicles   1128 **say** saw   1130 **the righte way** by the direct
route   1132 **heete** promise   1133 **abide** stay still   1134 **as** like
1135 **o** one   1136 **conscience** feelings   1137 **talent** passion
som kinnes affray some kind of disturbance   1139 **sentence** saying
1142 **taketh . . . his rente** takes his toll   1143 **evene** just
1144 **hente** (= *hentede*) took   1145 **hevinesse** sorrow

To Rome is come this holy creature,
And findeth hire freendes hoole and sounde;   1150
Now is she scaped al hir aventure.
And whan that she hir fader hath yfounde,
Doun on hir knees falleth she to grounde;
Wepinge for tendrenesse in herte blithe,
She herieth God an hundred thousand sithe.   1155

In vertu and in holy almes-dede
They liven alle, and nevere asonder wende;
Til deeth departeth hem this lif they lede.
And fareth now wel, my tale is at an ende.
Now Jesu Crist, that of his might may sende   1160
Joye after wo, governe us in his grace,
And kepe us alle that been in this place! Amen.

Heere endeth the Tale of the Man of Lawe.

THE EPILOGUE TO THE
MAN OF LAW'S TALE

Our Hoost upon his stiropes stood anoon,
And seide, 'Gode men, herkneth everychoon!
This was a thrifty tale for the nones!   *1165*
Sire parisshe prest,' quod he, 'for Goddes bones,
Tel us a tale, as was thy forward yore.
I sel wel that ye lerned men in lore

1151 **aventure** vicissitudes   1155 **herieth** praises **sithe** times
1157 **asonder wende** part   1158 **departeth** separates

1165 **thrifty** excellent   1166 **prest** priest   1167 **forward yore** former
agreement   1168 **lore** knowledge

Kan muche good, by Goddes dignitee.'

1170   The Persoun him answerde, 'Benedicite!
What eileth the man, so sinfully to swere?'
    Our Hoost answerde, 'O Jankin, be ye there?
I smelle a Loller in the wind!' quod he.
'Now, gode men,' quod our Hooste, 'herkeneth me!

1175   Abide, for Goddes digne passioun,
For we shal han a predicacioun –
This Loller heer will prechen us somwhat.'
    'Nay, by my fader soule, that shal he nat!'
Seide the Shipman, 'Heer shal he nat preche.

1180   He shal no gospel glosen heer ne teche.
We leven alle in the grete God,' quod he,
'He wolde sowen som difficultee,
Or springen cokkel in our clene corn.
And therfor, Hoost, I warne thee biforn,

1185   My joly body shal a tale telle,
And I shal clinken yow so mery a belle
That I shal waken al this compaignye.
But it shal nat be of philosophye,
Ne phislyas, ne termes queinte of lawe.

1190   Ther is but litel Latin in my mawe!'

1169 **Kan muche good** know what you are about   1171 **eileth** is the matter
with   1175 **digne** noble   1176 **predicacioun** piece of preaching
1180 **glosen** interpret (n.)   1181 **leven** believe   1183 **springen** scatter
cokkel tares, weed growing in corn (n.)   1184 **warne** notify
1185 **joly body** fine person   1186 I shall sound so lively a note
1189 **phislyas** see n. **queinte** esoteric   1190 **mawe** gullet

THE WIFE OF
BATH'S PROLOGUE

The Prologe of the Wives Tale of Bathe.

'Experience, thogh noon auctoritee
Were in this world, is right inogh for me
To speke of wo that is in mariage.
For, lordinges, sith I twelve yeer was of age,
Thonked be God that is eterne on live,   5
Housbondes at chirche-dore I have had five –
If I so ofte mighte han wedded be –
And alle were worthy men in hir degree.
But me was told, certein, noght longe agon is,
That sith that Crist ne wente nevere but onis   10
To wedding in the Cane of Galilee,
That by the same ensample taughte he me
That I ne sholde wedded be but ones.
Herke eek, lo, which a sharp word for the nones
Biside a welle, Jesus, God and man,   15
Spak in repreeve of the Samaritan:
"Thow hast yhad five housbondes," quod he,
"And that ilke man which now hath thee
Is nat thin housbonde" – thus seide he, certein.
What that he mente therby, I kan nat seyn;   20
But that I axe why that the fifthe man
Was noon housbonde to the Samaritan?
How manye mighte she have in mariage?
Yet herde I nevere tellen in min age

---

1 **auctoritee** written authority   5 **is eterne on live** has eternal life
8 **hir degree** their social station   10 **onis** once   16 **repreeve** reproof
18 **ilke** same   21 **axe** ask

25   Upon this nombre diffinicioun.
        Men may divine and glosen, up and doun,
        But wel I woot, expres, withouten lie,
        God bad us for to wexe and multiplye.
        That gentil text kan I wel understonde!
30   Eek wel I woot, he seide that min housbonde
        Sholde lete fader and moder and take to me;
        But of no nombre mencioun made he,
        Of bigamye, or of octogamye.
        Why sholde men thanne speke of it vileinye?
35   'Lo, here, the wise king, daun Salomon,
        I trowe he hadde wives mo than oon!
        As wolde God it leveful were to me
        To be refresshed half so ofte as he!
        Which yifte of God hadde he for alle his wivis!
40   No man hath swich that in this world alive is.
        God woot, this noble king, as to my wit,
        The firste night had many a murye fit
        With ech of hem, so wel was him on live!
        Blessed be God, that I have wedded five,
44a   Of whiche I have ypiked out the beste,
        Bothe of here nether purs and of here cheste.
        Diverse scoles maken parfit clerkes,
        And diverse practik in many sondry werkes
        Maketh the werkman parfit, sekirly.
44f   Of five husbondes scoleying am I;
45   Welcome the sixte, whan that evere he shal!
        For sothe, I wol nat kepe me chaast in al;

25 **diffinicioun** definition   26 **divine** speculate **glosen** interpret
27 **woot** know **expres** explicitly   31 **lete** leave   33 **octogamye** marrying
eight times   34 **speke of it vileinye** speak ill of it   36 **trowe** am sure that
37 **leveful** legitimate   39 **Which** what a **for** in spite of   41 **as to my wit** in
my opinion   42 **murye fit** merry bout, session
43 **so wel was him on live** so happy was his life   44a **ypiked** picked
44b **here nether purs** their balls, testicles   44d **practik** practice
44e **parfit** perfect **sekirly** certainly   44f **scoleying** studying
45 **whan that evere** whenever   46 **chaast** chaste

Whan min housbonde is fro the world ygon,
Som Cristen man shal wedde me anon.
For thanne th'Apostle seyth that I am free
To wedde, a Goddes half, wher liketh me.   50
He seyth that to be wedded is no sinne;
"Bet is to be wedded than to brinne."
What rekketh me, theigh folk seye vileinye
Of shrewed Lameth and his bigamye?
I woot wel Abraham was an holy man,   55
And Jacob eek, as fer as evere I kan,
And ech of hem hadde wives mo than two,
And many another holy man also.
Where kan ye seye, in any maner age,
That heighe God defended mariage   60
By expres word? I pray yow, telleth me.
Or where comanded he virginitee?
I woot as wel as ye, it is no drede,
Th'Apostle, whan he speketh of maidenhede,
He seide that precept therof hadde he noon.   65
Men may conseille a womman to be oon,
But conseilling nis no comandement;
He put it in oure owene juggement.
For hadde God comanded maidenhede,
Thanne hadde he dampned wedding with the dede.   70
And certes, if ther were no seed ysowe,
Virginitee, thanne wherof sholde it growe?
Poul dorste nat comanden, at the leeste,
A thing of which his maister yaf noon heeste.
The dart is set up for virginitee;   75
Cacche whoso may, who renneth best lat se!

---

50 **a Goddes half** in God's name **liketh me** it pleases me   52 **brinne** burn
53 Why do I care if people speak ill   54 **shrewed** wicked
56 **as fer as evere I kan** to the best of my knowledge   61 **expres** explicit
63 **drede** doubt   64 **maidenhede** virginity   66 **oon** single
70 **with the dede** in doing so   71 **ysowe** sown   72 **wherof** from what
73 **Poul** St Paul   74 **yaf** gave **heeste** command   75 **dart** spear used as prize
in a race   76 **Cacche whoso may** let him obtain it who can

'But this word is noght take of every wight,
But theras God list yeve it of his might.
I woot wel that th'Apostle was a maide,
But nathelees, thogh that he wroot and saide
He wolde that every wight were swich as he,
Al nis but conseil to virginitee.
And for to been a wif he yaf me leve
Of indulgence; so nis it no repreve
To wedde me, if that my make die,
Withoute excepcioun of bigamye,
Al were it good no womman for to touche –
He mente as in his bed or in his couche –
For peril is bothe fir and tow t'assemble –
Ye knowe what this ensample may resemble!
This al and som: he heeld virginitee
Moore parfit than wedding in freletee.
Freletee clepe I, but if that he and she
Wolde leden al hir lif in chastitee.
I graunte it wel, I have noon envye,
Thogh maidenhede preferre bigamye.
Hem liketh to be clene, in body and goost.
Of min estat ne wol I make no boost;
For wel ye knowe, a lord in his houshold
Ne hath nat every vessel al of gold.
Somme been of tree, and doon hir lord servise.
God clepeth folk to him in sondry wise,
And everich hath of God a propre yifte,
Som this, som that, as him liketh shifte.

80
85
90
95
100

---

77 **take of** understood (as being) about **wight** person   78 **list yeve** is pleased
to grant   79 **maide** virgin   82 **Al nis but** it is all no more than
84 **Of indulgence** as a concession   85 **make** spouse
86 **excepcioun of** objection on the grounds of   87 **Al were it good** although
it would be a good thing   90 **ensample** metaphor   91 **This al and som** this
is the long and the short of it   92 **freletee** frailty   93 **clepe** call
but if that unless   96 **preferre** takes precedence over   97 **goost** spirit
98 **boost** boast   101 **tree** wood   102 **clepeth** calls **sondry wise** different
ways   103 **propre** peculiar (to the individual)   104 **shifte** to determine

'Virginitee is greet perfeccioun   105
And continence eek with devocioun.
But Crist, that of perfeccioun is welle,
Bad nat every wight he sholde go selle
Al that he hadde, and yeve it to the poore,
And in swich wise folwe him and his foore.   110
He spak to hem that wolde live parfitly;
And lordinges, by youre leve, that am nat I!
I wol bistowe the flour of al min age
In th'actes and in fruit of mariage.

'Telle me also, to what conclusioun   115
Were membres maad of generacioun,
And of so parfit wis a wright ywroght?
Trusteth right wel, they were nat maad for
        noght.
Glose whoso wole, and seye bothe up and doun
That they were maad for purgacioun   120
Of urine, and oure bothe thinges smale
Was eek to knowe a femele from a male,
And for noon oother cause – sey ye no?
Th'experience woot wel it is noght so.
So that the clerkes be nat with me wrothe,   125
I sey this: that they beth made for bothe –
That is to seye, for office and for ese
Of engendrure, ther we nat God displese.
Why sholde men ellis in hir bokes sette
That man shal yelde to his wif hir dette?   130
Now wherwith sholde he make his paiement,
If he ne used his sely instrument?

---

107 **welle** source   110 **foore** footsteps   113 **the flour of al min age** my
prime of life   115 **conclusioun** purpose
116 **membres . . . of generacioun** genitals   117 And fashioned by so
perfectly wise a Maker   119 Let anyone who wants to, spin an argument,
and say on all sides   120 **purgacioun** discharge   122 **femele** female
125 **So that** provided that   **wrothe** angry   126 **beth** are
127 **office** function (of urination)   128 **engendrure** procreation   **ther** in
circumstances when   130 **yelde** pay   132 **sely instrument** blessed tool

Thanne were they maad upon a creature
To purge urine, and eek for engendrure.
135   'But I seye noght that every wight is holde,
That hath swich harneis as I to yow tolde,
To goon and usen hem in engendrure –
Thanne sholde men take of chastitee no cure.
Crist was a maide, and shapen as a man,
140 And many a seint sith that the world bigan,
Yet lived they evere in parfit chastitee.
I nil envye no virginitee;
Lat hem be breed of pured whete-seed,
And lat us wives hoten barly-breed –
145 And yet with barly-breed, Mark telle kan,
Oure Lord Jesu refresshed many a man.
In swich estat as God hath cleped us
I wol persevere; I nam nat precius.
In wifhode wol I use min instrument
150 As frely as my makere hath it sent.
If I be daungerous, God yeve me sorwe!
Min housbonde shal it have bothe eve and morwe,
Whan that him list com forth and paye his dette.
An housbonde wol I have, I wol nat lette,
155 Which shal be bothe my dettour and my thral,
And have his tribulacioun withal
Upon his flessh, whil that I am his wif.
I have the power during al my lif
Upon his propre body, and nat he.
160 Right thus th'Apostle tolde it unto me,
And bad oure housbondes for to love us wel;
Al this sentence me liketh everydel.'

---

135 **holde** obliged   136 **harneis** equipment   138 **take … no cure** have no
concern   139 **shapen** created   142 **nil** (= *ne wil*) will not
143 **pured** refined   144 **hoten** be called   148 **precius** fastidious, hard to
please   149 **wifhode** the married state   150 **frely** generously
151 **daungerous** niggardly   153 **him list** it pleases him   154 **lette** delay,
hang back   155 **thral** slave   156 **withal** besides   162 **sentence** saying
everydel in every respect

Up stirte the Pardoner, and that anon:
'Now, dame,' quod he, 'by God and by Seint John,
Ye been a noble prechour in this cas!   165
I was aboute to wedde a wif, allas!
What! sholde I bye it on my flessh so deere?
Yet hadde I levere wedde no wif to-yeere!'
    'Abide,' quod she, 'my tale is nat bigonne.
Nay, thow shalt drinken of another tonne,   170
Er that I go, shal savoure wors than ale.
And whan that I have toold thee forth my tale
Of tribulacioun in mariage,
Of which I am expert in al min age –
This is to seye, myself hath been the whippe –   175
Thanne maystow chese whether thow wolt sippe
Of thilke tonne that I shal abroche.
Be war of it, er thow to neigh approche!
For I shal telle ensamples mo than ten.
"Whoso that nil be war by othere men,   180
By him shal othere men corrected be."
Thise same wordes writeth Ptholome;
Rede in his Almageste, and take it there.'
    'Dame, I wolde praye yow, if youre wil it were,'
Seide this Pardoner, 'as ye bigan,   185
Telle forth youre tale; spareth for no man,
And teche us yonge men of youre praktike.'
    'Gladly,' quod she, 'sith it may yow like.
But yet I praye to al this compaignye,
If that I speke after my fantasye,   190
As taketh nat agrief of that I seye,
For min entente nis but for to pleye.

---

163 **Up stirte** up leapt   165 **prechour** preacher   167 **bye** pay for
deere dearly   168 **hadde I levere** I would rather   **to-yeere** this year
170 **of another tonne** from another barrel   171 **shal savoure** which will
taste   174 **expert** experienced   176 **chese** choose   177 **abroche** tap
178 **to neigh** too near   180 **nil be war by** will not take warning from
186 **spareth** hold back   187 **praktike** practices   188 **like** please
190 **after my fantasye** according to my whim
191 **As taketh nat agrief of** do not be upset by

'Now sire, thanne wol I telle yow forth my tale.
As evere moot I drinken win or ale,
I shal seye sooth: tho housbondes that I hadde,
As three of hem were goode, and two were badde.
The thre men were goode, and riche, and olde.
Unnethe mighte they the statut holde
In which that they were bounden unto me –
Ye woot wel what I mene of this, pardee!
As help me God, I laughe whan I thinke
How pitously a-night I made hem swinke.
And by my fey, I tolde of it no stoor.
They hadde me yeven hir land and hir tresoor;
Me neded nat do lenger diligence
To winne hir love, or doon hem reverence.
They loved me so wel, by God above,
That I ne tolde no deintee of hir love.
A wis womman wol bisye hire evere in oon
To gete hir love, ye, theras she hath noon.
But sith I hadde hem hoolly in min hond,
And sith they hadde me yeven al hir lond,
What sholde I taken kepe hem for to plese,
But it were for my profit and min ese?
I sette hem so a-werke, by my fey,
That many a night they songen "weilawey!"
The bacon was nat fet for hem, I trowe,
That som men han in Essex at Donmowe.
I governed hem so wel after my lawe,
That ech of hem ful blisful was and fawe
To bringe me gaye thinges fro the feire.
They were ful glad whan I spak to hem feire,

195 **tho** those   198 With difficulty could they fulfil the obligation
200 **of** by   202 **swinke** labour   203 **fey** faith **tolde of it no stoor** set no
store by it   204 **yeven** given   206 **doon hem reverence** show them respect
208 **ne tolde no deintee of** set no store by   209 A wise woman will
continually exert herself   210 **hir** for herself   213 **What** why
taken kepe be concerned   214 **But** unless   215 **a-werke** to work
217 **fet** fetched   220 **fawe** eager   221 **feire** fair   222 **feire** kindly

For God it woot, I chidde hem spitously.
   'Now herkneth how I bar me proprely.
Ye wise wives that konne understonde,   225
Thus sholde ye speke and bere hem wrong on
        honde,
For half so boldely kan ther no man
Sweren and lien as a womman kan.
I sey nat this by wives that ben wise,
But if it be whan they hem misavise.   230
A wis wif, if that she kan hir good,
Shal beren him on hond the cow is wood,
And take witnesse of hir owene maide
Of hir assent – but herkneth how I saide.
   '"Sir olde kainard, is this thin array?   235
Why is my neighebores wif so gay?
She is honoured overal ther she goth;
I sitte at hoom; I have no thrifty cloth.
What dostow at my neighebores hous?
Is she so fair? artow so amorous?   240
What rowne ye with oure maide, *benedicite*?
Sire olde lechour, lat thy japes be!
And if I have a gossib or a freend,
Withouten gilt, thou chidest as a feend
If that I walke or pleye unto his hous.   245
Thow comest hoom as dronken as a mous,
And prechest on thy bench, with ivel preef!
Thow seyst to me, it is a greet meschief

---

223 **chidde hem spitously** scolded them mercilessly   224 **bar me** behaved
proprely characteristically   226 **bere hem wrong on honde** make false
assertions against them   229 **by** with respect to   230 **But if it be** except
hem misavise are misguided   231 **kan hir good** knows what is to her
advantage   232 Will maintain that the chough is mad (n.)
234 **Of hir assent** with her connivance   235 **kainard** dotard **array** way of
behaving   236 **gay** finely dressed   237 **overal ther** wherever
238 **thrifty cloth** decent clothes   241 **What rowne ye** why do you whisper
242 **japes** tricks   243 **gossib** intimate friend   244 **chidest as** nag like
247 **with ivel preef** bad luck to you   248 **meschief** calamity

To wedde a povre womman, for costage,
250   And if that she be riche, of heigh parage,
Thanne seystow that it is a tormentrye
To suffre hir pride and hir malencolye.
And if that she be fair, thow verray knave,
Thow seyst that every holour wol hire have.
255   She may no while in chastitee abide,
That is assailed upon ech a side.
   '"Thow seyst, som folk desire us for richesse,
Somme for oure shap, and somme for oure fairnesse,
And somme for she kan either singe or daunce,
260   And somme for gentillesse and daliaunce,
Somme for hir handes and hir armes smale –
Thus goth al to the devel, by thy tale!
Thow seyst men may nat kepe a castel wal,
It may so longe assailled been overal.
265   And if that she be foul, thow seyst that she
Coveiteth every man that she may se,
For as a spaniel she wol on him lepe
Til that she finde som man hir to chepe;
Ne noon so grey goos goth ther in the lake
270   As, seystow, wol be withoute make.
And seyst it is an hard thing for to welde
A thing that no man wol, his thankes, helde.
Thus seystow, lorel, whan thow goost to bedde,
And that no wis man nedeth for to wedde,
275   Ne no man that entendeth unto hevene –
With wilde thonder-dint and firy levene

249 **costage** expense   250 **heigh parage** high birth
251 **tormentrye** torment   252 **malencolye** spleen   254 **holour** lecher
256 **ech a** every   260 **daliaunce** flirtation   261 **smale** slender
262 **by thy tale** by your account   265 **foul** ugly   268 **hir to chepe** to do
business with her   270 **make** mate   271 **welde** control
272 **his thankes** willingly **helde** own, keep   273 **lorel** rogue
275 **entendeth unto** strives after   276 **thonder-dint** thunderbolt
levene lightning

Moote thy welked nekke be to-broke!
'"Thow seyst that dropping houses, and eek
    smoke,
And chiding wives maken men to flee
Out of hir owene house – a, *benedicitee*,   280
What eileth swich an old man for to chide?
'"Thow seyst we wives wil oure vices hide
Til we be fast, and thanne we wol hem shewe.
Wel may that be a proverbe of a shrewe!
'"Thow seyst that oxen, asses, hors, and   285
    houndes,
They been assayed at diverse stoundes,
Bacines, lavours, er that men hem bye;
Spoones, stooles, and al swich housbondrye,
And so be pottes, clothes, and array,
But folk of wives maken noon assay   290
Til they be wedded, olde dotard shrewe!
And thanne, seystow, we wil oure vices shewe.
'"Thow seyst also that it displeseth me
But if that thow wolt preise my beautee,
And but thow poure alwey upon my face,   295
And clepe me 'faire dame' in every place,
And but thow make a feeste on thilke day
That I was born, and make me fressh and gay,
And but thow do to my norice honour,
And to my chamberere withinne my bour,   300
And to my fadres folk and his allies;
Thus seystow, olde barel-ful of lies!
'"And yet of oure apprentice, Janekin,
For his crispe heer, shining as gold so fin,

---

277 **welked** withered **to-broke** broken   278 **dropping** leaking
283 **fast** tied down (by marriage)   284 **shrewe** rascal   286 **stoundes** times
287 **Bacines** basins **lavours** bowls **er** before   288 **housbondrye** household
goods   289 **array** finery   290 But people do not try out wives
294 **But if** if not   295 **poure ... upon** gaze intently at   296 **clepe** call
299 **norice** nurse   300 **chamberere** chambermaid **bour** room
301 **allies** kinsfolk   302 **lies** lees, dregs *or* lies (punning?)   304 **crispe** curly

305 And for he squiereth me bothe up and doun,
    Yet hastow caught a fals suspecioun;
    I wil him nat, thogh thow were deed tomorwe!
        '"But tel me this, why hidestow, with sorwe,
    The keyes of thy cheste awey fro me?

310 It is my good as wel as thin, pardee!
    What, wenestow make an idiot of oure dame?
    Now, by that lord that called is Seint Jame,
    Thou shalt noght bothe, thogh that thow were wood,
    Be maister of my body and of my good.

315 That oon thow shalt forgo, maugree thine eyen.
    What nedeth thee of me enquere or spyen?
    I trowe thow woldest loke me in thy chiste!
    Thow sholdest seye, 'Wif, go wher thee liste.
    Taak youre disport; I nil nat leve no talis.

320 I knowe yow for a trewe wif, dame Alis.'
    We love no man that taketh kepe or charge
    Wher that we goon; we wol been at oure large.
        '"Of alle men yblessed moot he be,
    The wise astrologen, daun Ptholome,

325 That seyth this proverbe in his Almageste:
    'Of alle men his wisdom is hieste
    That rekketh nat who hath the world in honde.'
    By this proverbe thow shalt understonde,
    Have thow inogh, what thar thee rekke or care

330 How mirily that othere folkes fare?
    For certes, olde dotard, by youre leve,
    Ye shal han queinte right inogh at eve.

---

305 **squiereth** escorts   307 **wil him nat** do not want him **thogh** even if
308 **with sorwe** bad luck to you   311 **wenestow make** do you expect to
make   313 **wood** furious   315 **maugree thine eyen** in spite of yourself
316 **What nedeth thee** why do you need to **of me** about me
317 **woldest loke** would like to lock **chiste** strongbox   319 **leve** believe
talis tales   321 **taketh kepe or charge** is concerned about
322 **at oure large** at liberty   324 **astrologen** astronomer
327 **rekketh nat** does not care **in honde** in his control   329 If you have
enough, why do you need to care   332 **queinte right inogh** your fill of sex

He is to greet a nigard that wil werne
A man to lighte a candel at his lanterne;
He shal han never the lasse light, pardee!   335
Have thow inogh, thee thar nat pleine thee.
  ' "Thow seyst also, that if we make us gay
With clothing and with precious array,
That it is peril of oure chastitee.
And yet – with sorwe – thow most enforce thee,   340
And seye thise wordes in th'Apostles name:
'In habit maad with chastitee and shame
Ye wommen shal apparaille yow,' quod he,
'And nat in tressed heer and gay perree,
As perles, ne with gold, ne clothes riche.'   345
After thy text, ne after thy rubriche,
I wol nat werke as muchel as a gnat!
  ' "Thow seidest this, that I was lik a cat,
For whoso wolde senge a cattes skin,
Than wolde the cat wel dwellen in his in;   350
And if the cattes skin be slik and gay,
She wol nat dwelle in house half a day.
But forth she wole, er any day be dawed,
To shewe hir skin and goon a-caterwawed.
This is to seye, if I be gay, sire shrewe,   355
I wol renne out, my borel for to shewe.
  ' "Sire, olde fool, what helpeth thee t'espyen?
Thogh thow preye Argus with his hundred eyen
To be my warde-corps, as he kan best,
In feith, he shal nat kepe me but me lest.   360

333 **werne** refuse to allow   336 **pleine thee** complain
340 **with sorwe** curse it **enforce thee** wind yourself up   342 **habit** clothing
343 **apparaille yow** dress yourself   344 **tressed heer** plaited hair
perree jewellery   345 **As** such as   346 **After** in accordance with
rubriche direction   349 **senge** singe   350 **in** house   351 **slik** sleek
353 **be dawed** has dawned   354 **a-caterwawed** caterwauling
355 **shrewe** rascal   356 **borel** coarse cloth   357 **what helpeth thee** what
good does it do you   359 **warde-corps** bodyguard   360 **but me lest** unless
it pleases me

Yet koude I make his berd, so moot I thee!
   ' "Thow seidest eek that ther ben thinges three,
The whiche thinges troublen al this erthe,
And that no wight may endure the ferthe –
365   O leeve sire shrewe, Jesu shorte thy lif!
Yet prechestow and seyst an hateful wif
Yrekened is for oon of thise mischaunces.
Been ther noone othere manere resemblaunces
That ye may likne youre parables to,
370   But if a sely wif be oon of tho?
   ' "Thow liknest eek wommanes love to helle,
To bareine lond, ther water may nat dwelle.
Thow liknest it also to wilde fir:
The moore it brenneth, the moore it hath desir
375   To consume every thing that brent wol be.
Thow seyst, right as wormes shende a tree,
Right so a wif destroyeth hir housbonde;
This knowen they that been to wives bonde."
   'Lordinges, right thus, as ye han understonde,
380   Bar I stifly mine olde housbondes on honde
That thus they seiden in hir dronkenesse;
And al was fals, but that I took witnesse
On Janekyn and on my nece also.
O Lord, the peine I dide hem and the wo,
385   Ful giltelees, by Goddes swete pine!
For as an hors I koude bite and whine.
I koude pleine and I was in the gilt,
Or elles often time I hadde been spilt.
Whoso that first to mille comth, first grint;
390   I pleined first, so was oure werre ystint.

---

361 Still I could get the better of him, as I live   364 **ferthe** fourth
365 **Jesu shorte** may Jesus shorten   370 Without a poor wife being one of
them   373 **wilde fir** Greek fire (inflammable material used in warfare)
374 **brenneth** burns   375 **brent** burned   376 **shende** destroy
378 **bonde** bound   380 I vigorously accused my old husbands
385 **pine** suffering   386 **whine** whinny   387 **pleine** complain **in the gilt** in
the wrong   388 **hadde been spilt** would have been ruined
389 **grint** (= *grindeth*) grinds   390 **werre** strife **ystint** ended

They were ful glad t'excusen hem ful blive
Of thing of which they nevere agilte hir live.
　　'Of wenches wolde I beren hem on honde,
Whan that for sik they mighte unnethe stonde.
Yet tikled I his herte, for that he   395
Wende that I hadde of him so greet chiertee.
I swoor that al my walking out by nighte
Was for t'espye wenches that he dighte;
Under that colour hadde I many a mirthe.
For al swich wit is yeven us in oure birthe;   400
Deceite, weping, spinning, God hath yeve
To wommen kindely, whil they may live.
And thus of o thing I avaunte me:
Atte ende I hadde the bet in ech degree,
By sleighte, or force, or by som maner thing,   405
As by continuel murmur or grucching.
Namely abedde hadden they meschaunce;
Ther wolde I chide and do hem no plesaunce.
I wolde no lenger in the bed abide,
If that I felte his arm over my side,   410
Til he hadde maad his raunceon unto me;
Thanne wolde I suffre him do his nicetee.
And therfore every man this tale I telle,
Winne whoso may, for al is for to selle!
With empty hond men may none haukes lure.   415
For winning wolde I al his lust endure,
And make me a feined appetit –
And yet in bacoun hadde I nevere delit.

391 **ful blive** very quickly　　392 **agilte** were guilty　**hir live** in their lives
394 **for sik** for illness　**unnethe** hardly　　396 **Wende** believed
chiertee affection　　398 **dighte** had it off with　　399 **colour** pretext
400 **wit** cunning　　401 **yeve** given　　402 **kindely** by nature　　403 **o** one
avaunte me boast　　404 **Atte ende** in the end　**the bet in ech degree** the better
in every way　　405 **sleighte** cunning　　406 **As** such as　**grucching** grumbling
407 **abedde** in bed　　411 Until he had bought me off　　412 **suffre** allow
do his nicetee to have his fun　　415 **lure** call back to the hand (n.)
416 **winning** profit

That made me that evere I wolde hem chide;
420 For thogh the pope had seten hem biside,
     I wolde noght spare hem at hir owene bord,
     For, by my trouthe, I quitte hem word for word.
     As help me verray God omnipotent,
     Thogh I right now sholde make my testament,
425 I n'owe hem nat a word that it nis quit!
     I broghte it so aboute by my wit
     That they moste yeve it up, as for the beste,
     Or elles hadde we nevere been in reste.
     For thogh he looked as a wood leoun,
430 Yet sholde he faille of his conclusioun.
          'Thanne wolde I seye, "Goode lief, taak keep
     How mekely looketh Wilkin, oure sheep!
     Com neer, my spouse, lat me ba thy cheke.
     Ye sholden be al pacient and meke,
435 And han a swete spiced conscience,
     Sith ye so preche of Jobes pacience.
     Suffreth alwey, sin ye so wel kan preche;
     And but ye do, certein we shal yow teche
     That it is fair to have a wif in pees.
440 Oon of us two moste bowen, doutelees,
     And sith a man is moore resonable
     Than womman is, ye mosten been suffrable.
     What eileth yow, to grucche thus and grone?
     Is it for ye wolde have my queinte allone?
445 Wy, taak it al; lo, have it every del!
     Peter, I shrewe you but ye love it wel!

---

420 **thogh** even if **seten** sat   421 **bord** table   422 **quitte hem** paid them
back   424 **testament** will   425 I do not owe them a word that has not been
repaid   426 **wit** cleverness   429 **wood** furious
430 **faille of his conclusioun** fall short of his goal   431 **Goode lief** my dear
taak keep take note   433 **ba** kiss   435 **swete spiced conscience** see n.
437 **Suffreth** practise endurance   438 **but ye do** if you do not
442 **suffrable** long-suffering   443 **grucche** grumble
444 **for** because **queinte** fanny (vagina)   445 **del** bit   446 By St Peter,
damn you if you don't enjoy it

For if I wolde selle my *bele chose*,
I koude walke as fressh as is a rose;
But I wol kepe it for youre owene tooth.
Ye be to blame, by God; I sey yow sooth."   450
Swiche manere wordes hadde we on honde.
Now wol I speken of my ferthe housbonde.

  'My ferthe housbonde was a revelour;
This is to seyn, he hadde a paramour.
And I was yong, and ful of ragerye,   455
Stibourne and strong, and joly as a pie.
How koude I daunce to an harpe smale,
And sing, iwys, as any nightingale,
Whan I had dronke a draughte of swete win.
Metellius, the foule cherl, the swin,   460
That with a staf birafte his wif hir lif
For she drank win, though I hadde been his wif,
Ne sholde nat han daunted me fro drinke!
And after win on Venus moste I thinke,
For also siker as coold engendreth hail,   465
A likerous mouth moste han a likerous tail.
In womman vinolent is no defence;
This knowen lechours by experience.

  'But, Lord Crist, whan that it remembreth me
Upon my youthe and on my jolitee,   470
It tikeleth me aboute min herte-roote.
Unto this day it dooth min herte boote,
That I have had my world as in my time.
But age, allas, that al wole envenime,

447 *bele chose* thingummy (vagina)   450 **I sey yow sooth** I am telling you
the truth   451 **hadde we on honde** we were occupied with
453 **revelour** reveller   454 **paramour** mistress   455 **ragerye** high spirits
456 **joly** lively   **pie** magpie   461 **birafte his wif** deprived his wife of
463 **daunted me fro** frightened me away from   465 **also siker** as surely
466 **likerous** gluttonous   **likerous** lecherous   467 **vinolent** bibulous
defence resistance   469 **it remembreth me** I remember
471 **min herte-roote** the bottom of my heart   472 **boote** good
474 **envenime** poison

475 Hath me biraft my beautee and my pith.
     Lat go, farwel; the devel go therwith!
     The flour is goon; ther is namoore to telle.
     The bren, as I best kan, now moste I selle.
     But yet to be right murye wol I fonde!
480 Now wol I tellen of my ferthe housbonde.
          'I seye, I hadde in herte gret despit
     That he of any oother had delit;
     But he was quit, by God and by Seint Joce!
     I made him of the same wode a croce –
485 Nat of my body, in no foul manere,
     But certeinly, I made folk swich cheere
     That in his owene grece I made him frye,
     For angre and for verray jalousye.
     By God, in erthe I was his purgatorye!
490 For which I hope his soule be in glorye.
     For, God it woot, he sat ful ofte and song,
     Whan that his shoo ful bitterly him wrong.
     Ther was no wight save God and he that wiste
     In many wise how soore I him twiste.
495 He deide whan I cam fro Jerusalem,
     And lith ygrave under the roode-beem,
     Al is his toumbe noght so curious
     As was the sepulcre of him Darius,
     Which that Appelles wroghte subtilly;
500 It nis but wast to burye him preciously.
     Lat him far wel, God give his soule reste!
     He is now in his grave and in his cheste.
          'Now of my fifthe housbonde wol I telle.
     God lat his soule nevere come in helle!

---

475 **me biraft** taken away from me **pith** vigour   478 **bren** bran
479 **fonde** try   481 **hadde . . . despit** resented   483 **quit** paid back
484 **croce** stick   486 **made folk swich cheere** acted in such a friendly way to
people   487 **grece** grease   492 see n.   493 **no wight** no one
494 **soore** painfully   496 **ygrave** buried **roode-beem** beam supporting a
cross (n.)   497 **toumbe** tomb **curious** elaborate   499 **subtilly** skilfully
500 It is only a waste to give him an expensive tomb
501 **Lat him far wel** bless him   502 **cheste** coffin

And yet was he to me the mooste shrewe –   505
That feele I on my ribbes al by rewe,
And evere shal, unto min ending day.
But in oure bed he was so fressh and gay,
And therwithal so wel koude he me glose,
Whan that he wolde han my *bele chose*,   510
That thogh he hadde me bet on every bon,
He koude winne again my love anon.
I trowe I loved him best, for that he
Was of his love daungerous to me.
We wommen han, if that I shal nat lie,   515
In this matere a queinte fantasye:
Waite what thing we may nat lightly have,
Therafter wol we crye al day and crave.
Forbede us thing, and that desiren we;
Preesse on us faste, and thanne wol we fle.   520
With daunger oute we al oure chaffare;
Greet prees at market maketh deere ware,
And to greet cheep is holde at litel pris.
This knoweth every womman that is wis.
  'My fifthe housbonde – God his soule blesse! –   525
Which that I took for love, and no richesse,
He somtime was a clerk of Oxenford,
And hadde laft scole and wente at hom to bord
With my gossib, dwelling in oure toun –
God have hir soule! Hir name was Alisoun.   530
She knew min herte, and eek my privetee,
Bet than oure parissh preest, so mote I thee.

505 shrewe wicked   506 by rewe in a row   507 ending day dying day
509 glose cajole   511 bet beaten   512 anon immediately
513 trowe believe   514 daungerous niggardly
516 queinte fantasye strange fantasy   517 Waite what whatever
lightly easily   518 Therafter for that   520 Preesse on urge   521 We
display our wares reluctantly (n.)   522 prees crowd deere ware expensive
goods   523 greet cheep inexpensive at litel pris of little value
528 wente at hom to bord lodged at home   531 privetee secrets
532 Bet better so mote I thee as I may prosper

To hire biwreyed I my conseil al;
For hadde min housbonde pissed on a wal,
535   Or doon a thing that sholde have cost his lif,
To hire, and to another worthy wif,
And to my nece, which that I loved wel,
I wolde han toold his conseil everydel.
And so I dide ful often, God it woot.
540   That made his face ful often reed and hoot
For verray shame, and blamed himself for he
Hadde toold to me so greet a privetee.
    'And so bifel, that ones in a Lente –
So often times I to my gossib wente,
545   For evere yet I loved to be gay,
And for to walke in March, Averill, and May,
From hous to hous to here sondry tales –
That Jankin clerk and my gossib, dame Alis,
And I myself into the feeldes wente.
550   Min housbonde was at Londoun al that Lente;
I hadde the bettre leiser for to pleye,
And for to se, and eek for to be seye
Of lusty folk. What wiste I wher my grace
Was shapen for to be, or in what place?
555   Therfore I made my visitacions
To vigilies, and to processions,
To preching eek, and to thise pilgrimages,
To pleyes of miracles, and to mariages,
And wered upon my gaye scarlet gites.
560   Thise wormes, ne thise moththes, ne thise mites,

533 **biwreyed** revealed **conseil** secrets   543 **ones** once   545 **gay** finely
dressed   551 **leiser for to pleye** opportunity to amuse myself
552 **seye** seen   553 By pleasure-loving people. How did I know where my
good luck   554 **shapen** destined   555 **visitacions** visits
556 **vigilies** watches kept in church on the evening before a religious
festival (n.)   558 **pleyes of miracles** miracle-plays   559 **wered upon** wore
gites gowns   560 **mites** insects

Upon my peril, frete hem nevere a del;
And wostow why? for they were used wel.
  'Now wol I tellen forth what happed me:
I seye that in the feeldes walked we,
Til trewely we hadde swich daliaunce,   565
This clerk and I, that of my purveiaunce
I spak to him, and seide him how that he,
If I were widewe, sholde wedde me.
For certeinly, I seye for no bobaunce,
Yet was I nevere withouten purveiaunce   570
Of mariage, n'of othere thinges eek.
I holde a mouses herte nat worth a leek
That hath but oon hole for to sterte to,
And if that faille, thanne is al ydo.
  'I bar him on honde he hadde enchanted me;   575
My dame taughte me that soutiltee.
And eek I seide, I mette of him al night;
He wolde han slain me as I lay upright,
And al my bed was ful of verray blood –
"But yet I hope that ye shal do me good,   580
For blood bitokeneth gold, as me was taught."
And al was fals; I dremed of it right naught,
But as I folwed ay my dames loore,
As wel of that as othere thinges moore.
  'But now, sire – lat me se – what shal I seyn?   585
A ha! by God, I have my tale agein!
  'Whan that my fourthe housbonde was on beere,
I weep algate, and made sory cheere –

---

561 **Upon my peril** may I be damned otherwise **frete** (= *fretede*) gnawed
nevere a del not at all   562 **wostow** do you know **for** because
565 **daliaunce** flirtation   566 **of my purveiaunce** by my foresightedness
569 **bobaunce** boast   570 **purveiaunce** provision   573 **sterte** escape
574 **is al ydo** everything is over   575 **bar him on honde** maintained
576 **dame** mother **soutiltee** trick   577 **mette** dreamed   578 **upright** on my
back   583 **loore** teaching   587 **beere** bier   588 I wept continually and put
on a sorrowful expression

As wives mooten, for it is usage –
590   And with my coverchief covered my visage.
But for that I was purveyed of a make,
I wepte but smal, and that I undertake.
To chirche was min housbonde born amorwe,
With neghebores that for him maden sorwe,
595   And Janekin, oure clerk, was oon of tho.
As help me God, whan that I saw him go
After the beere, me thoughte he hadde a paire
Of legges and of feet so clene and faire,
That al min herte I yaf unto his hoold.
600   He was, I trowe, a twenty winter oold,
And I was fourty, if I shal seye sooth,
But yet I hadde alwey a coltes tooth.
Gat-tothed I was, and that bicam me weel;
I hadde the preente of Seinte Venus seel.
605   As help me God, I was a lusty oon,
And fair, and riche, and yong, and wel bigoon!
And trewely, as mine housbondes tolde me,
I hadde the beste *quoniam* mighte be.
For certes, I am al Venerien
610   In feeling, and min herte is Marcien.
Venus me yaf my lust, my likerousnesse,
And Mars yaf me my sturdy hardinesse.
Min ascendent was Taur and Mars therinne –
Allas, allas, that evere love was sinne!

589 **mooten** must **usage** customary   591 **purveyed of** provided with
make spouse   592 **smal** little **undertake** warrant   593 **amorwe** next
morning   594 **With** by **maden sorwe** mourned   595 **oon of tho** one of
them   598 **clene** shapely   599 **unto his hoold** into his possession
600 **winter** years   602 **hadde ... a coltes tooth** had youthful desires
603 **Gat-tothed** gap-toothed **bicam** suited   604 **preente** print (n.)
605 **lusty** lively   606 **wel bigoon** in good spirits   608 *quoniam* 'what-for'
(vagina) (n.)   609 **Venerien** a child of Venus   610 **Marcien** dominated by
the influence of Mars   611 **lust** appetite for pleasure
likerousnesse lasciviousness   612 **sturdy** rebellious **hardinesse** boldness
613 **ascendent** dominant sign of the zodiac (n.)

I folwed ay min inclinacioun,   615
By vertu of my constellacioun.
That made me I koude noght withdrawe
My chambre of Venus from a good felawe.
Yet have I Martes mark upon my face,
And also in another privee place.   620
For, God so wysly be my savacioun,
I loved nevere by no discrecioun,
But evere folwed I min appetit,
Al were he short, or long, or blak, or whit.
I took no kepe, so that he liked me,   625
How povre he was, ne eek of what degree.
  'What sholde I seye, but at the monthes ende,
This joly clerk, Jankin, that was so hende,
Hath wedded me with greet solempnitee,
And to him yaf I al the lond and fee   630
That evere was me yeven therbifore.
But afterward repented me ful sore;
He nolde suffre nothing of my list.
By God, he smoot me ones on the list,
For that I rente out of his book a leef,   635
That of the strook min ere wex al deef.
Stibourne I was, as is a leonesse,
And of my tonge a verray jangleresse,
And walke I wolde, as I hadde doon biforn,
From hous to hous, althogh he hadde it sworn.   640
For which he often times wolde preche,
And me of olde Romain gestes teche –

---

615 **inclinacioun** natural disposition (as influenced by the planets at birth)
616 **By vertu of** in consequence of   618 **chambre of Venus** 'love-chamber'
(vagina)   619 **Martes** of Mars (n.)   622 **by no discrecioun** in moderation
624 **Al were he** whether he was   625 I did not care, provided that he
pleased me   628 **joly** gallant **hende** handsome   629 **solempnitee** festivity
630 **fee** property   632 **repented me ful sore** I repented bitterly
633 **suffre** tolerate **list** pleasure   634 **list** ear   635 **rente** tore
636 **of the strook** from the blow **wex** became   637 **leonesse** lioness
638 **jangleresse** nagger   640 **althogh he hadde it sworn** although he had
sworn the contrary   642 And tell me about old Roman stories

How he Simplicius Gallus lafte his wif,
And hire forsook for terme of al his lif,
645 Noght but for open-heveded he hir say,
Loking out at his dore upon a day.
    'Another Romain tolde he me by name,
That, for his wif was at a someres game
Withoute his witing, he forsook hire eke.
650 And thanne wolde he upon his Bible seke
That ilke proverbe of Ecclesiaste,
Where he comandeth and forbedeth faste
"Man shal nat suffre his wif go roule aboute."
Thanne wolde he seye right thus, withouten doute:
655 "Whoso that buildeth his hous al of salwes,
And priketh his blinde hors over the falwes,
And suffreth his wif to go seken halwes,
Is worthy to ben hanged on the galwes!"
But al for noght – I sette noght an hawe
660 Of his proverbes, n'of his olde sawe,
Ne I wolde nat of him corrected be.
I hate him that my vices telleth me;
And so doo mo, God woot, of us than I!
This made him with me wood al outrely;
665 I nolde noght forbere him in no cas.
    'Now wol I sey yow sooth, by Seint Thomas,
Why that I rente out of his book a leef,
For which he smoot me so that I was deef.
    'He hadde a book that gladly, night and day,
670 For his disport he wolde rede alway.
He cleped it "Valerie and Theofraste" –
At which book he lough alwey ful faste.

645 Only because he saw her with uncovered head
648 **someres game** Midsummer revels (n.)   649 **witing** knowledge
653 **roule aboute** gad about   655 **salwes** willows   656 **priketh** spurs
falwes fallow land   657 **halwes** saints' shrines   658 **galwes** gallows
659 **hawe** hawthorn berry   663 **mo** more   664 **wood al outrely** extremely
angry   665 I would not put up with him under any circumstances
670 **disport** amusement   672 **lough** laughed **ful faste** very heartily

And eek ther was somtime a clerk at Rome,
A cardinal, that highte Seint Jerome,
That made a book again Jovinian;   675
In which book eek ther was Tertulan,
Crisippus, Trotula, and Helowis,
That was abbesse nat fer fro Paris,
And eek the Parables of Salomon,
Ovides Art, and bokes many on.   680
And alle thise were bounde in o volume,
And every night and day was his custume,
Whan he hadde leiser and vacacioun
From oother worldly occupacioun,
To reden in this book of wikked wives.   685
He knew of hem mo legendes and lives
Than been of goode wives in the Bible.
For trusteth wel, it is an inpossible
That any clerk wol speke good of wives,
But if it be of holy seintes lives,   690
Ne of noon oother womman neverthemo.
Who peinted the leoun, tel me who?
By God, if wommen hadde writen stories,
As clerkes han withinne hir oratories,
They wolde han write of men moore wikkednesse   695
Than al the mark of Adam may redresse!
The children of Mercurye and of Venus
Been in hir wirking ful contrarius:
Mercurye loveth wisdam and science,
And Venus loveth riot and dispence.   700
And for hir diverse disposicioun,
Ech falleth in otheres exaltacioun;

673 **clerk** scholar   681 **o** one   683 **vacacioun** spare time
688 **inpossible** impossibility   691 **neverthemo** at all   695 **write** written
696 **mark** race **redresse** make amends for   697 **children of Mercurye** those
born under the influence of the planet Mercury   698 **wirking** behaviour
contrarius opposed   699 **science** knowledge   700 **riot** debauchery
dispence expenditure   702 Each one loses influence in the sign of the zodiac
where the other gains it most (n.)

And thus, God woot, Mercurye is desolat
In Pisces, wher Venus is exaltat,
705   And Venus falleth ther Mercurye is reised.
Therfore no womman of no clerk is preised.
The clerk, whan he is old, and may noght do
Of Venus werkes worth his olde sho,
Thanne sit he doun and writ in his dotage
710   That wommen kan nat kepe hir mariage!
       'But now to purpos, why I tolde thee
That I was beten for a book, pardee.
Upon a night, Jankin, that was oure sire,
Redde on his book, as he sat by the fire,
715   Of Eva first, that for hir wikkednesse
Was al mankinde ybroght to wrecchednesse,
For which that Jesu Crist himself was slain,
That boghte us with his herte-blood again.
Lo here, expres of wimmen may ye finde,
720   That womman was the los of al mankinde!
       'Tho redde he me how Sampson loste his heres:
Slepinge, his lemman kitte it with hir sheres,
Thurgh which tresoun loste he bothe his eyen.
       'Tho redde he me, if that I shal nat lien,
725   Of Hercules, and of his Dianire,
That caused him to sette himself afire.
       'Nothing forgat he the sorwe and wo
That Socrates hadde with his wives two –
How Xantippa caste pisse upon his heed.
730   This sely man sat stille as he were deed.
He wipte his heed; namoore dorste he seyn,
But "Er that thonder stinte, comth a rein!"

---

703 **desolat** helpless   704 **exaltat** in the position of greatest influence (n.)
708 **Venus werkes** sexual activity   709 **sit** (= *sitteth*) sits
writ (= *writeth*) writes   711 **to purpos** to the point
716 **wrecchednesse** misery   719 **expres** explicitly   721 **Tho** then
heres hair   722 **lemman** mistress **kitte** cut   727 **Nothing** not at all
730 **sely** poor **as** as if   731 **wipte** wiped   732 **stinte** ceases

– Of Phasipha, that was the queen of Crete;
For shrewednesse him thoughte the tale swete –
Fy, spek namoore, it is a grisly thing,   735
Of hir horrible lust and hir liking!
– Of Clitermystra, for hir lecherye
That falsly made hir housbonde for to die;
He redde it with ful good devocioun.

    'He tolde me eek for what occasioun   740
Amphiorax at Thebes loste his lif;
Min housbonde hadde a legende of his wif,
Eriphilem, that for an ouche of gold
Hath prively unto the Grekes told
Wher that hir housbonde hidde him in a place,   745
For which he hadde at Thebes sory grace.

    'Of Livia tolde he me, and of Lucye:
They bothe made hir housbondes for to die,
That oon for love, that oother was for hate.
Livia hir housbonde on an even late   750
Empoisoned hath, for that she was his fo.
Lucia, likerous, loved hir housbonde so
That, for he sholde alwey upon hir thinke,
She yaf him swich a maner love-drinke
That he was deed er it were by the morwe –   755
And thus algates housbondes han sorwe.

    'Thanne tolde he me how oon Latumius
Compleined unto his felawe Arrius,
That in his gardin growed swich a tree,
On which he seide how that his wives thre   760
Honged hemself, for herte despitus.
"O leeve brother," quod this Arrius,
"Yif me a plante of thilke blessed tree,
And in my gardin planted shal it be!"

734 **shrewednesse** maliciousness   736 **liking** pleasure   742 **legende** story
743 **ouche** jewelled ornament (n.)   744 **prively** secretly
746 **sory grace** misfortune   750 **even** evening   752 **likerous** amorous
754 **maner** kind of   756 **algates** continually   **han sorwe** come to grief
761 **herte despitus** recalcitrant spirit   762 **leeve** dear   763 **Yif** give

765   'Of latter date of wives hath he red,
That somme han slain hir housbondes in hir bed,
And lete hir lechour dighte hire al the night,
Whan that the corps lay in the floor upright;
And somme han driven nailes in hir brain,
770   Whil that they sleepe, and thus they han hem slain.
Somme han hem yeven poisoun in hir drinke.
He spak moore harm than herte may bithinke;
And therwithal he knew of mo proverbes
Than in this world ther growen gras or herbes.
775   "Bet is", quod he, "thin habitacioun
Be with a leoun or a foul dragoun,
Than with a womman using for to chide.
Bet is", quod he, "hye in the roof abide,
Than with an angry wif doun in the hous.
780   They been so wikked and contrarious;
They haten that hir housbondes loveth ay."
He seide, "A womman cast hir shame away
Whan she cast of hir smok," and forthermo,
"A fair womman, but she be chaast also,
785   Is lik a gold ring in a sowes nose."
Who wolde wene, or who wolde suppose
The wo that in min herte was, and pine?
       'And whan I say he wolde nevere fine
To reden on this cursed book al night,
790   Al sodeinly thre leves have I plight
Out of his book, right as he radde, and eke
I with my fist so took him on the cheke
That in oure fir he fil bakward adoun.
And he up stirte as dooth a wood leoun,

---

765 **Of latter date** from more recent times   767 And let her lover pleasure
her all night   768 **upright** on its back   772 **bithinke** imagine
775 **habitacioun** dwelling   777 **using** accustomed   778 **hye** high
781 **that** that which   783 **cast of** takes off   784 **but** unless
786 **wene** imagine   787 **pine** distress   788 **fine** cease   790 **plight** plucked
794 **wood** furious

And with his fest he smoot me on the heed,   795
That in the floor I lay as I were deed.
And whan he saugh how stille that I lay,
He was agast, and wolde han fled his way,
Til atte laste out of my swough I braide.
"O, hastow slain me, false theef?" I saide,   800
"And for my land thus hastow mordred me?
Er I be deed, yet wol I kisse thee!"
     'And neer he cam, and kneled faire adoun,
And seide, "Deere suster Alisoun,
As help me God, I shal thee nevere smite.   805
That I have doon, it is thyself to wite;
Foryeve it me, and that I thee biseke."
And yet eftsoones I hitte him on the cheke,
And seide, "Theef, thus muchel am I wreke!
Now wol I die; I may no lenger speke."   810
But at the laste, with muchel care and wo,
We fille acorded by us selven two.
He yaf me al the bridel in min hond,
To han the governaunce of hous and lond,
And of his tonge and of his hond also,   815
And made him brenne his book anon-right tho.
And whan that I hadde geten unto me
By maistrye al the soverainetee,
And that he seide, "Min owene trewe wif,
Do as thee lust the terme of al thy lif;   820
Keep thin honour, and keep eek min estaat,"
After that day we hadden nevere debaat.
God help me so, I was to him as kinde
As any wif from Denmark unto Inde,

795 **fest** fist   798 He was afraid and wanted to run away
799 **out of my swough I braide** I recovered consciousness   806 **to wite** to be
blamed   807 **biseke** beseech   808 **eftsoones** a second time
809 **wreke** avenged   811 **care** sorrow   812 **fille acorded** came to an
agreement   813 **bridel** bridle   814 **governaunce** management
816 **anon-right tho** right away   818 **maistrye** skilfulness
soverainetee supremacy   820 Do as it pleases you, for the rest of your life
821 **estaat** social standing   822 **debaat** strife   824 **Inde** India

825   And also trewe, and so was he to me.
       I pray to God that sit in magestee,
       So blesse his soule, for his mercy deere!
       Now wol I seye my tale, if ye wol here.'

            Biholde the wordes bitwene the
               Somonour and the Frere.

       The Frere logh whan he hadde herd al this;
830   'Now dame,' quod he, 'so have I joye or blis,
       This is a long preamble of a tale!'
       And whan the Somnour herde the Frere gale,
       'Lo,' quod the Somnour, 'Goddes armes two,
       A frere wol entremette him everemo!
835   Loo, goode men, a flye and eek a frere
       Wol falle in every dissh and eek matere!
       What spekestow of preambulacioun?
       What, amble, or trotte, or paas, or go sit doun!
       Thow lettest oure disport in this manere.'
840   'Ye, woltow so, sir Somnour?' quod the Frere.
       'Now, by my feith, I shal, er that I go,
       Telle of a somnour swich a tale or two
       That al the folk shal laughen in this place.'
           'Now elles, Frere, I bishrewe thy face,'
845   Quod this Somnour, 'and I bishrewe me,
       But if I telle tales two or three
       Of freres, er I come to Sidingborne,
       That I shal make thin herte for to morne,
       For wel I woot thy pacience is gon.'
850   Oure Hooste cride, 'Pees, and that anon!'
       And seide, 'Lat the womman telle hir tale.
       Ye fare as folk that dronken ben of ale.

829 **logh** laughed   830 **so have I joye or blis** on my hope of bliss
832 **gale** make an outcry   834 **entremette him everemo** constantly interfere
836 **matere** (piece of) business   837 Why do you talk about preambling
838 **paas** (go at) walking-speed (n.)   839 **lettest** hinder **disport** amusement
840 **woltow so** will you do so   844 **bishrewe** curse   846 **But if I** if I do not
848 **morne** grieve   852 **fare as** behave like

Do, dame, tel forth youre tale, and that is best.'
   'Al redy, sire,' quod she, 'right as yow lest,
If I have licence of this worthy frere.'   855
'Yis, dame,' quod he, 'tel forth, and I wol here.'

Heere endeth the Wif of Bathe hir
Prologe and biginneth hir Tale.

THE WIFE OF BATH'S TALE

In th'olde dayes of the king Arthour,
Of which that Britons speken greet honour,
Al was this land fulfild of faierye.
The elf-queene with hir joly compaignye   860
Daunced ful ofte in many a grene mede.
This was the olde opinioun, as I rede –
I speke of many hundred yeres ago.
But now kan no man se none elves mo,
For now the grete charitee and prayeres   865
Of limitours and othere holy freres,
That serchen every lond and every streem
As thikke as motes in the sonne-beem,
Blessinge halles, chambres, kichenes, boures,
Citees, burghes, castels, hye toures,   870
Thropes, bernes, shipnes, daieryes –
This maketh that ther been no faieryes.
For ther as wont to walken was an elf,
Ther walketh now the limitour himself

856 **here** listen   858 **which that** whom   859 **faierye** fairy creatures
860 **joly** beautiful   861 **mede** meadow   866 **limitours** friars who begged
within territorial limits (see n. to GP 209)   867 **serchen** scour
868 **sonne-beem** sunbeam   869 **boures** bedrooms   870 **burghes** towns
871 Villages, barns, cattle-sheds, dairies   873 For where an elf used to walk

875 In undermeles and in morweninges,
     And seyth his matins and his holy thinges
     As he gooth in his limitacioun.
     Wommen may go saufly up and doun;
     In every bussh or under every tree,
880 Ther is noon oother incubus but he,
     And he ne wol doon hem but dishonour.
         And so bifel that this king Arthour
     Hadde in his hous a lusty bacheler
     That on a day cam riding fro river,
885 And happed that, allone as he was born,
     He saugh a maide walkinge him biforn,
     Of which maide anoon, maugree hir hed,
     By verray force he rafte hir maidenhed;
     For which oppressioun was swich clamour
890 And swich pursuite unto the king Arthour
     That dampned was this knight for to be deed
     By cours of lawe, and sholde han lost his heed –
     Paraventure, swich was the statut tho –
     But that the queene and othere ladies mo
895 So longe preyeden the king of grace
     Til he his lif him graunted in the place,
     And yaf him to the queene, al at hir wille,
     To chese wher she wolde him save or spille.
         The queene thanketh the king with al hir might;
900 And after this thus spak she to the knight,
     Whan that she saugh hir time upon a day,
     'Thow standest yet', quod she, 'in swich array

875 At noon-time and morning   876 **thinges** prayers
877 **in his limitacioun** on his begging rounds   878 **saufly** safely
880 **incubus** demon which has sex with women in their sleep (n.)
881 **but** only   883 **lusty bacheler** lively young knight   884 **river** hawking
887 **maugree hir hed** in spite of all she could do   888 **rafte** ravished
889 **oppressioun** rape   890 **pursuite** petition   891 **dampned** condemned
895 **of grace** for mercy   898 **spille** put to death   901 One day when she
saw an appropriate moment   902 **yet** still **array** situation

That of thy lif yet hastow no suretee.
I graunte thee lif, if thow kanst tellen me
What thing is it that wommen moost desiren.   905
Be war and keep thy nekke-boon from iren!
And if thow kanst nat tellen it anon,
Yet wol I yeve thee leve for to gon
A twelf-monthe and a day, to seche and lere
An answere suffisant in this matere.   910
And suretee wol I han, er that thow pace,
Thy body for to yelden in this place.'

  Wo was this knight, and sorwefully he siketh,
But what! he may nat doon al as him liketh.
And at the laste he chees him for to wende,   915
And come again, right at the yeres ende,
With swich answere as God wolde him purveye;
And taketh his leve, and wendeth forth his weye.

  He seketh every hous and every place
Whereas he hopeth for to finde grace,   920
To lerne what thing wommen loven moost;
But he ne koude arriven in no coost
Whereas he mighte finde in this matere
Two creatures acording in-feere.
Somme seiden wommen loven best richesse;   925
Somme seide honour, somme seide jolynesse;
Somme riche array, somme seiden lust abedde,
And ofte time to be widwe and wedde.
Somme seide that oure herte is moost esed
Whan that we been yflatered and yplesed.   930

---

903 **suretee** assurance   906 **Be war** be wary **iren** iron (of an axe-blade)
907 **anon** immediately   909 **seche** seek **lere** learn
910 **suffisant** satisfactory   911 And I will have some security (bail) before
you go   912 **Thy body for to yelden** that you will deliver yourself in person
913 **siketh** sighs   915 **chees him for to wende** chose to depart
917 **purveye** provide   918 **wendeth forth his weye** sets out
920 **finde grace** have good fortune   922 **coost** region
924 **acording in-feere** agreeing with each other   926 **jolynesse** gallantry
927 **riche array** finery **lust** pleasure   928 **widwe** widowed
929 **esed** soothed

(He gooth ful ny the sothe, I wol nat lie!
A man shal winne us best with flaterye;
And with attendaunce and with bisinesse
Been we ylimed, bothe moore and lesse.)
935   And somme seyen that we loven best
For to be free, and do right as us lest,
And that no man repreve us of oure vice,
But seye that we be wise, and nothing nice.
For trewely, ther is noon of us alle,
940 If any wight wol clawe us on the galle,
That we nil kike for he seyth us sooth.
Assay, and he shal finde it, that so dooth.
For be we nevere so vicious withinne,
We wol be holden wise and clene of sinne.
945   And somme seyn that greet delit han we
For to be holden stable, and eek secree,
And in o purpos stedefastly to dwelle,
And nat biwreye thing that men us telle –
But that tale is nat worth a rake-stele!
950 Pardee, we wommen konne no thing hele;
Witnesse on Mida – wol ye heere the tale?
    Ovide, amonges othere thinges smale,
Seide Mida hadde, under his longe heres,
Growinge upon his heed two asses eres;
955 The whiche vice he hidde as he best mighte
Ful sotilly from every mannes sighte,
That, save his wif, ther wiste of it namo.
He loved hire moost, and trusted hire also;

931 **He gooth ful ny the sothe** he gets very near to the truth
933 **bisinesse** attentiveness   934 **ylimed** snared (as birds are trapped with bird-lime)   936 **as us lest** as it pleases us   937 **repreve . . . of** reprove for 938 **nothing nice** not at all foolish   940 If anyone rubs us on a sore spot
941 **kike** kick **for** because   942 **Assay** make trial
944 **wol be holden** want to be considered as   946 **secree** discreet
948 **biwreye** disclose   949 **rake-stele** rake-handle   950 **Pardee** by God
hele conceal   951 **wol ye heere** do you want to hear   952 **smale** trivial
956 **sotilly** cleverly   957 So that . . . nobody knew of it

He preyed hire that to no creature
She sholde tellen of his disfigure.   960
   She swoor him 'nay', for al this world to winne
She nolde do that vileinye or sinne,
To make hir housbonde han so foul a name;
She nolde nat telle it, for hir owene shame.
But nathelees hir thoughte that she dide   965
That she so longe sholde a conseil hide.
Hir thoughte it swal so soore aboute hir herte
That nedely som word hir moste asterte.
And sith she dorste telle it to no man,
Doun to a maris faste by she ran –   970
Til she cam there hir herte was afire –
And as a bitore bombleth in the mire,
She leide hir mouth unto the water doun.
'Biwrey me nat, thow water, with thy soun!'
Quod she, 'To thee I telle it, and namo: 975
Min housbonde hath longe asses eris two!
Now is min herte al hool; now is it oute.
I mighte no lenger kepe it, out of doute.'
Heere may ye see, thogh we a time abide,
Yet out it moot; we kan no conseil hide.   980
The remenant of the tale, if ye wol heere,
Redeth Ovide, and ther ye may it leere.
   This knight of which my tale is specially,
Whan that he saugh he mighte nat come therby –
This is to seye, what wommen loven moost –   985
Withinne his brest ful sorweful was the goost.

960 **disfigure** disfigurement   961 **for al this world to winne** even to gain the
whole world   962 **vileinye** wickedness   964 **for** for fear of
965 **dide** would die   966 **conseil** secret   967 **swal so soore** swelled so
painfully   968 That necessarily some word would have to slip from her
970 **maris** marsh   972 **bitore** bittern (a marsh-bird, which makes a booming
sound in the breeding-season) **bombleth** booms   974 **Biwrey** betray
soun sound   975 **namo** nobody else   977 **hool** healed   979 **abide** wait
980 **out it moot** it must come out   982 **leere** learn about   983 **specially** in
particular   984 **come therby** come by it   986 **goost** spirit

But hom he gooth; he mighte nat sojourne;
The day was come that homward moste he tourne.
And in his wey it happed him to ride,
990   In al this care, under a forest side,
Wheras he saugh upon a daunce go
Of ladies foure and twenty, and yet mo.
Toward the whiche daunce he drow ful yerne,
In hope that som wisdom sholde he lerne.
995   But certeinly, er he cam fully there,
Vanisshed was this daunce; he niste where.
No creature ne saugh he that bar lif,
Save on the grene he saugh sittinge a wif –
A fouler wight ther may no man devise.
1000   Again the knight this olde wif gan rise
And seide, 'Sire knight, heerforth ne lith no wey.
Tel me what that ye seken, by youre fey!
Paraventure it may the bettre be;
Thise olde folk konne muchel thing,' quod she.
1005   'My leeve moder,' quod this knight, 'certein
I nam but deed, but if that I kan seyn
What thing it is that wommen moost desire.
Koude ye me wisse, I wolde wel quite youre hire.'
'Plight me thy trouthe, here in min hand,' quod she,
1010   'The nexte thing that I requere thee
Thow shalt it do, if it lie in thy might,
And I wol telle it yow er it be night.'
'Have here my trouthe!' quod the knight, 'I
graunte.'
'Thanne,' quod she, 'I dar me wel avaunte

987 **sojourne** stay   989 **it happed him** he chanced   990 **care** sorrow
under by, beside   993 **drow ful yerne** went eagerly   996 **niste** did not
know   998 **Save** except that **wif** woman   999 **wight** creature
devise imagine   1000 **Again . . . gan rise** stood up to meet
1001 **heerforth** in this direction **lith** lies   1003 **Paraventure** perhaps
1004 **muchel thing** many things   1005 **leeve** dear   1006 **but if that** unless
1008 If you could give me guidance, I would repay you handsomely
1009 **Plight me thy trouthe** pledge me your faith   1010 **requere** ask of
1014 **me . . . avaunte** boast

Thy lif is sauf, for I wol stonde therby.   1015
Upon my lif, the queene wol seye as I.
Lat see which is the proudeste of hem alle
That wereth on a coverchief or a calle
That dar seye nay of that I shal thee teche.
Lat us go forth withouten lenger speche.'   1020
Tho rowned she a pistel in his ere,
And bad him to be glad and have no fere.
   Whan they be comen to the court, this knight
Seide he hadde holde his day as he had hight,
And redy was his answere, as he saide.   1025
Ful many a noble wif and many a maide
And many a widwe – for that they ben wise –
The queene hirself, sitting as justise,
Assembled been his answere for to here;
And afterward this knight was bode appere.   1030
   To every wight comanded was silence,
And that the knight sholde telle in audience
What thing that worldly wommen loven best.
This knight ne stood nat stille as dooth a best,
But to his questioun anon answerde   1035
With manly vois, that al the court it herde.
   'My lige lady, generally,' quod he,
'Wommen desiren to have sovereintee
As wel over hir housbonde as hir love,
And for to been in maistrye him above.   1040
This is youre mooste desir, thogh ye me kille;
Dooth as yow list; I am at youre wille.'
In al the court ne was ther wif ne maide
Ne widwe that contraried that he saide,

1015 **stonde therby** make it good   1017 **Lat** let   1018 Who wears a
head-cloth or a hairnet   1019 **seye nay of** contradict
1021 **rowned** whispered **pistel** message   1024 **holde** kept **hight** promised
1028 **justise** judge   1030 **bode** ordered   1036 **that** so that
1037 **generally** universally, without exception   1038 **sovereintee** mastery
1040 **maistrye** dominance   1041 **mooste** greatest

1045   But seiden he was worthy han his lif.
            And with that word up stirte the olde wif
        Which that the knight saugh sitting on the grene.
        'Mercy,' quod she, 'my soverein lady queene;
        Er that youre court departe, do me right.
1050   I taughte this answere unto the knight,
        For which he plighte me his trouthe there,
        The firste thing that I wolde him requere,
        He wolde it do, if it laye in his might.
        Bifore the court thanne preye I thee, sire knight,'
1055   Quod she, 'that thow me take unto thy wif,
        For wel thow woost that I have kept thy lif.
        If I seye fals, sey nay, upon thy fey.'
            This knight answerde, 'Allas and weilawey!
        I woot right wel that swich was my biheste.
1060   For Goddes love, as chees a newe requeste!
        Taak al my good, and lat my body go.'
            'Nay, thanne,' quod she, 'I shrewe us bothe two!
        For thogh that I be foul and old and poore,
        I nolde, for al the metal ne for oore
1065   That under erthe is grave or lith above,
        But if thy wif I were, and eek thy love.'
            'My love!' quod he, 'nay, my dampnacioun!
        Allas, that any of my nacioun
        Sholde evere so foule disparaged be!'
1070   But al for noght: th'ende is this, that he
        Constreined was; he nedes moste hir wedde,
        And taketh his olde wif, and goth to bedde.
            Now wolden som men seye, paraventure,
        That for my necligence I do no cure

1045 **han** to have   1046 **stirte** jumped   1049 **departe** breaks up
right justice   1056 **kept** saved   1057 **fey** faith   1059 **biheste** promise
1060 **as chees** choose   1061 **good** property   1062 **shrewe** curse
1064 **nolde** would not wish   **oore** ore   1065 **grave** buried   **lith** lies
1066 **But if thy wif I were** anything other than to be your wife
1067 **dampnacioun** ruin   1068 **nacioun** family
1069 **disparaged** disgraced by a misalliance   1071 **nedes moste** of necessity
had to   1074 **do no cure** take no pains

To tellen yow the joye and al th'array   1075
That at the feste was that ilke day.
To which thing shortly answere I shal:
I seye, ther nas no joye ne feste at al;
Ther nas but hevinesse and muche sorwe.
For prively he wedded hire on morwe,   1080
And al day after hidde him as an owle;
So wo was him – his wif looked so foule.

 Greet was the wo the knight hadde in his thoght
Whan he was with his wif abedde ybroght;
He walweth and he turneth to and fro.   1085
His olde wif lay smiling everemo,
And seide, 'O deere housbonde, *benedicite!*
Fareth every knight thus with his wif as ye?
Is this the lawe of King Arthures hous?
Is every knight of his thus daungerous?   1090
I am youre owene love and eek youre wif;
I am she which saved hath youre lif,
And, certes, yet ne dide I yow unright.
Why fare ye thus with me this firste night?
Ye faren lik a man hadde lost his wit!   1095
What is my gilt? For Goddes love, tel it,
And it shal ben amended, if I may.'

 'Amended!' quod this knight, 'Allas, nay, nay!
It wol nat ben amended neveremo.
Thow art so loothly, and so old also,   1100
And therto comen of so lowe a kinde,
That litel wonder is thogh I walwe and winde.
So wolde God min herte wolde breste!'

 'Is this', quod she, 'the cause of youre unreste?'
'Ye, certeinly,' quod he, 'no wonder is.'   1105

1075 **array** splendour   1079 **nas but hevinesse** was nothing but gloom
1080 **prively** privately   **on morwe** next morning   1081 **as** like
1085 **walweth** thrashes about   1086 **everemo** all the time
1090 **daungerous** hard to please   1093 **unright** wrong   1094 **fare** behave
1095 **hadde** who had   1100 **loothly** ugly   1101 **kinde** family
1102 **winde** twist   1103 **So wolde God** would to God (that)   **breste** break
1105 **no wonder is** it is not surprising

'Now, sire,' quod she, 'I koude amende al this,
If that me liste, er it were dayes thre,
So wel ye mighte bere yow unto me.
        'But for ye speken of swich gentilesse
1110   As is descended out of old richesse,
That therfore sholden ye be gentil men,
Swich arrogance nis nat worth an hen.
Looke who that is moost vertuous alway,
Privee and apert, and moost entendeth ay
1115   To do the gentil dedes that he kan,
Taak him for the gretteste gentil man.
Crist wol we claime of him oure gentillesse,
Nat of oure eldres, for hir old richesse.
For thogh they yeve us al hir heritage,
1120   For which we claime to been of heigh parage,
Yet may they nat biquethe for nothing
To noon of us hir vertuous living,
That made hem gentil men ycalled be,
And bad us folwen hem in swich degree.
1125   'Wel kan the wise poete of Florence,
That highte Dant, speken in this sentence –
Lo, in swich maner rim is Dantes tale:
"Ful selde up riseth by his braunches smale
Prowesse of man, for God, of his goodnesse,
1130   Wol that of him we claime oure gentillesse."
For of oure eldres may we nothing claime
But temporel thing, that man may hurte and maime.
        'Eek every wight woot this as wel as I:
If gentillesse were planted naturelly
1135   Unto a certein linage doun the line,
Privee and apert thanne wolde they nevere fine

1108 **bere yow** behave   1109 **for** since **gentilesse** nobility
1110 **richesse** wealth   1114 Privately and in public, and always strives the
most   1117 **wol** wishes   1119 **heritage** inheritance   1120 **parage** lineage
1121 **for nothing** not at all   1124 **degree** condition
1126 **sentence** maxim   1127 **rim** rhyme, verse   1129 **Prowesse** excellence
1132 **maime** destroy   1136 **fine** cease

To doon of gentilesse the faire office;
They mighte do no vileinye or vice.
    'Taak fir, and bere it in the derkeste hous
Bitwix this and the mount of Kaukasous,   1140
And lat men shette the dores and go thenne,
Yet wol the fir as faire lie and brenne
As twenty thousand men mighte it biholde.
His office naturel ay wol it holde,
Up peril of my lif, til that it die.   1145
    'Here may ye se wel how that gentrye
Is nat annexed to possessioun,
Sith folk ne doon hir operacioun
Alwey, as dooth the fir, lo, in his kinde.
For, God it woot, men may wel often finde   1150
A lordes sone do shame and vileinye.
And he that wol han pris of his gentrye
For he was boren of a gentil hous,
And hadde his eldres noble and vertuous,
And nil himselven do no gentil dedis,   1155
Ne folwe his gentil auncestre that deed is,
He nis nat gentil, be he duc or erl,
For vileins sinful dedes make a cherl.
For gentilesse nis but renomee
Of thin auncestres for hir heigh bountee,   1160
Which is a straunge thing to thy persone;
Thy gentilesse cometh fro God allone.
Thanne comth oure verray gentilesse of grace;
It was nothing biquethe us with oure place.

1137 To carry out the excellent practice of nobility   1138 **vileinye** shameful
action   1141 **shette** shut **thenne** thence   1142 **lie** blaze **brenne** burn
1143 **As** as if   1144 It will still maintain its natural function
1145 **Up peril of my lif** as I live   1147 Is not linked to wealth
1148 **doon hir operacioun** perform their function   1149 **Alwey** in all
circumstances **in his kinde** according to its nature
1152 **wol han pris of** wants to be esteemed for   1153 **boren** born
1155 **nil** is unwilling   1158 **vileins** base **cherl** serf   1159 **renomee** renown
1161 **straunge** external   1163 **verray** true   1164 It was in no way
bequeathed to us with our rank

1165   'Thenketh how noble, as seyth Valerius,
Was thilke Tullius Hostillius,
That out of poverte roos to heigh noblesse.
Redeth Senek, and redeth eek Boece,
Ther shul ye seen expres, that it no drede is
1170   That he is gentil that dooth gentil dedis.
And therfore, leve housbonde, I conclude:
Al were it that mine auncestres were rude,
Yet may the hye God – and so hope I –
Graunte me grace to liven vertuously.
1175   Thanne am I gentil, whan that I biginne
To liven vertuously, and weive sinne.
    'And theras ye of poverte me repreve,
The hye God on whom that we bileve
In wilful poverte chees to live his lif.
1180   And certes, every man, maiden or wif
May understonde that Jesus, hevene king,
Ne wolde nat chese a vicious living.
Glad poverte is an honeste thing, certein:
This wol Senek and othere clerkes seyn.
1185   Whoso that halt him paid of his poverte,
I holde him riche, al hadde he nat a sherte.
He that coveiteth is a povre wight,
For he wolde han that is nat in his might.
But he that noght hath, ne coveiteth have,
1190   Is riche, althogh ye holde him but a knave.
    'Verray poverte, it singeth proprely.
Juvenal seyth of poverte mirily:
"The povre man, whan he gooth by the weye,
Biforn the theves he may singe and pleye."
1195   Poverte is hateful good, and, as I gesse,

1169 **expres** explicitly **drede** doubt   1172 **rude** uncultivated
1176 **weive** shun   1177 **theras** whereas **repreve** reproach
1179 **wilful** voluntary **chees** chose   1183 **honeste** honourable
1185 **halt him paid of** considers himself satisfied with
1186 **al hadde he nat** even if he did not have   1188 **might** power
1189 **noght hath** has nothing   1190 **knave** commoner
1192 **mirily** appositely

A ful greet bringere out of bisinesse;
A greet amendere eek of sapience,
To him that taketh it in pacience.
Poverte is this, althogh it seme alenge:
Possessioun that no wight wol chalenge.   1200
Poverte ful often, whan a man is lowe,
Maketh his God and eek himself to knowe.
Poverte a spectacle is, as thinketh me,
Thurgh which he may his verray freendes se.
And therfore, sire, sin that I noght yow greve,   1205
Of my poverte namoore ye me repreve.

'Now, sire, of elde ye repreve me;
And certes, sire, thogh noon auctoritee
Were in no book, ye gentils of honour
Seyn that men sholde an old wight doon favour,   1210
And clepe him fader, for youre gentilesse;
And auctours shal I finden, as I gesse.

'Now ther ye seye that I am foul and old,
Thanne drede yow noght to been a cokewold.
For filthe and elde, also mote I thee,   1215
Been grete wardeins upon chastitee.

'But nathelees, sin I knowe youre delit,
I shal fulfille youre worldly appetit.
Chees now', quod she, 'oon of thise thinges
      tweye:
To han me foul and old til that I deye,   1220
And be to yow a trewe humble wif,
And nevere yow displese in al my lif,
Or elles ye wol han me yong and fair,
And take youre aventure of the repair

1196 **bringere out of** release from **bisinesse** anxiety
1197 **amendere** increaser **sapience** wisdom   1199 **alenge** wretched
1200 **chalenge** dispute   1203 **spectacle** lens, eye-glass
1205 **sin that I noght yow greve** since I do you no harm   1207 **of elde** for
old age   1208 **auctoritee** written authority   1209 **gentils** nobles
1212 **auctours** authors   1214 **cokewold** cuckold   1215 **also mote I thee** as
I may prosper   1216 **wardeins** guardians   1217 **delit** pleasure
1224 **take youre aventure** accept the risk **repair** flocking of people

1225   That shal be to youre hous bicause of me,
         Or in som oother place, may wel be.
         Now chees yourselven, wheither that yow liketh.'
             This knight aviseth him, and soore siketh,
         But atte laste he seide in this manere:
1230   'My lady and my love, and wif so deere,
         I putte me in youre wise governaunce.
         Cheseth youreself which may be moost plesaunce,
         And moost honour to yow and me also.
         I do no fors the wheither of the two,
1235   For as yow liketh, it suffiseth me.'
             'Thanne have I gete of yow maistrye,' quod she,
         'Sin I may chese and governe as me lest?'
         'Ye, certes, wif,' quod he, 'I holde it best.'
             'Kis me,' quod she, 'we be no lenger wrothe.
1240   For, by my trouthe, I wol be to yow bothe –
         This is to seyn, ye, bothe fair and good.
         I pray to God that I mote sterven wood,
         But I to yow be also good and trewe
         As evere was wif, sin that the world was newe.
1245   And but I be to-morn as fair to sene
         As any lady, emperice or queene,
         That is bitwix the est and eek the west,
         Do with my lif and deth right as yow lest.
         Cast up the curtin; looke how that it is.'
1250   And whan the knight saugh verraily al this,
         That she so fair was, and so yong therto,
         For joye he hente hire in his armes two.
         His herte bathed in a bath of blisse;
         A thousand time a-rewe he gan hir kisse,

1227 **wheither** which of the two   1228 **aviseth him** reflects
soore siketh sighs deeply   1231 **governaunce** control
1232 **plesaunce** pleasure   1234 **do no fors** do not care
1235 **suffiseth** satisfies   1236 **gete of yow maistrye** won mastery over you
1237 **as me lest** as it pleases me   1239 **wrothe** angry
1242 **sterven wood** die insane   1243 **also** as   1245 **but I be** if I am not
sene see   1249 **Cast up** lift up   **curtin** curtain   1252 **hente** took
1254 **a-rewe** in a row

And she obeyed him in every thing   1255
That mighte do him plesance or liking.
    And thus they live unto hir lives ende
In parfit joye – and Jesu Crist us sende
Housbondes meke, yonge, and fressh abedde,
And grace t'overbide hem that we wedde.   1260
And eek I praye Jesu shorte hir lives
That noght wol be governed by hir wives,
And olde and angry nigardes of dispence,
God sende hem soone verray pestilence!

Heere endeth the Wives Tale of Bathe.

THE FRIAR'S PROLOGUE

The Prologe of the Freres Tale.

This worthy limitour, this noble Frere,   1265
He made alwey a maner louring cheere
Upon the Somnour, but for honestee
No vileins word as yet to him spak he.
But atte laste he seide unto the Wif:
'Dame,' quod he, 'God yeve yow right good lif!   1270
Ye han heer touched, also mote I thee,
In scole-matere greet difficultee.
Ye han seid muche thing right wel, I seye.
But dame, here as we riden by the weye,

1260 **overbide** outlive   1261 **shorte** shorten   1263 **of dispence** in expenditure   1264 **pestilence** plague

1265 **limitour** see n. to GP 209   1266 **maner louring cheere** kind of scowling expression   1267 **Somnour** see n. to GP 623   1270 **yeve** give 1272 **scole-matere** questions for scholastic debate   1273 **muche thing** many a thing

1275 Us nedeth nat to speken but of game,
     And lete auctoritees, on Goddes name,
     To preching and to scoles of clergye.
     But if it like to this compaignye,
     I wol yow of a somnour telle a game.
1280 Pardee, ye may wel knowe by the name
     That of a somnour may no good be said –
     I praye that noon of yow be ivel apaid.
     A somnour is a rennere up and doun
     With mandementz for fornicacioun,
1285 And is ybet at every tounes ende.'
         Oure Hoost tho spak: 'A, sire, ye sholde be hende
     And curteis, as a man of youre estaat!
     In compaignye we wol no debaat.
     Telleth youre tale, and lat the Somnour be!'
1290   'Nay,' quod the Somnour, 'lat him seye to me
     Whatso him list; whan it comth to my lot,
     By God, I shal him quiten every grot!
     I shal him tellen which a gret honour
     It is to be a flateringe limitour,
1295 And of many another manere crime
     Which nedeth nat rehercen at this time,
     And his office I shal him telle, iwys!'
         Oure Hoost answerde, 'Pees, namoore of this!'
     And after this he seide unto the Frere:
1300 'Tel forth youre tale, leeve maister deere.'

1275 **game** fun   1276 **lete auctoritees** leave learned quotations
1277 **scoles of clergye** schools of higher learning (i.e. the universities)
1279 **game** joke   1282 **ivel apaid** displeased   1283 **rennere** runner
1284 **mandementz** writs   1285 **ybet** beaten   1286 **hende** polite
1291 **Whatso him list** whatever pleases him   1292 **quiten** pay back **grot** bit
1297 And I shall tell him what he does, you bet   1300 **leeve** dear

THE FRIAR'S TALE

Heere biginneth the Freres Tale.

Whilom ther was dwellinge in my contree
An erchedekene, a man of heigh degree,
That boldely dide execucioun
In punisshinge of fornicacioun,
Of wicchecraft, and eek of bawderye,   1305
Of diffamacioun and avoutrye,
Of chirche reves, and of testamentz,
Of contractes, and of lakke of sacramentz,
Of usure, and of simonye also.
But certes, lecchours dide he grettest wo;   1310
They sholde singen if that they were hent.
And smale titheres weren foule yshent,
If any persone wolde upon hem pleine.
Ther mighte asterte him no pecunial peine;
For smale tithes and for smal offringe   1315
He made the peple pitously to singe.
For er the bisshop caughte hem with his hook,
They weren in the erchedekenes book,
And thanne hadde he, thurgh his jurisdiccioun,
Power to doon on hem correccioun.   1320
He hadde a somnour redy to his hond;
A slyer boy nas noon in Engelond.

1303 **dide execucioun** executed sentences   1305 **wicchecraft** witchcraft
bawderye pimping   1306 **diffamacioun** defamation, slander
avoutrye adultery   1307 **chirche reves** church robberies
1308 **lakke of sacramentz** failure to receive the sacraments
1311 **singen** squeal **hent** caught   1312 **titheres** tithe-payers
yshent punished   1313 **persone** parson **pleine** make a complaint
1314 No pecuniary penalty could elude him   1316 **pitously** pitifully
1317 **er** before **hook** curved end of a bishop's staff
1320 **doon . . . correccioun** inflict punishment   1322 **boy** rascal

For subtilly he hadde his espiaille
That taughte him wher that him mighte availle.
He koude spare of lecchours oon or two

1325

To techen him to foure and twenty mo.
For theigh this somnour wood were as an hare,
To telle his harlotrye I wol nat spare;
For we been out of his correccioun.

1330

They han of us no jurisdiccioun,
Ne nevere shullen, terme of alle hir lives.
    'Peter! so been wommen of the stives',
Quod the Somnour, 'yput out of oure cure!'
    'Pees, with mischaunce and with misaventure!'

1335

– Thus seide oure Hoost – 'and lat him telle his tale.
Now telleth forth, thogh that the Somnour gale;
Ne spareth nat, min owene maister deere.'
    This false theef, this somnour, – quod the Frere –
Hadde alwey baudes redy to his hond

1340

As any hauk to lure in Engelond,
That tolde him al the secree that they knewe,
For hir aqueintance was nat come of newe;
They weren hise approwours prively.
He took himself a greet profit therby;

1345

His maister knewe nat alwey what he wan.
Withouten mandement a lewed man
He koude somne, on peine of Cristes curs,
And they were glade for to fille his purs
And make him grete festes atte nale.

1350

And right as Judas hadde purses smale

1323 **espiaille** body of spies   1324 **wher that him mighte availle** where his
profit might lie   1325 **spare** have mercy on   1326 **techen . . . to** direct to
1327 **theigh** though   1328 **harlotrye** wickedness
1329 **correccioun** authority   1331 **shullen** shall   **terme of alle hir lives** all
their lives long   1332 **stives** brothels   1333 **cure** control   1334 Peace, bad
luck to you   1336 **gale** protests   1339 **baudes** pimps   1340 **lure** see n. to
WB 415   1341 **secree** secrets   1342 **come of newe** recently created
1343 **approwours** agents   1345 **wan** acquired   1346 **lewed man** layman
1347 **somne** summon   **Cristes curs** excommunication   1349 **atte nale** at the
ale-house

And was a theef, right swich a theef was he.
His maister hadde but half his duetee.
He was, if I shal yeven him his laude,
A theef, and eek a somnour, and a baude.
He hadde eek wenches at his retenue   1355
That, wheither that Sir Robert or Sir Hewe,
Or Jakke, or Rauf, or whoso that it were
That lay by hem, they tolde it in his ere.
Thus was the wenche and he of oon assent.
And he wolde fecche a feined mandement,   1360
And somne hem to chapitre bothe two,
And pile the man and lete the wenche go.
    Thanne wolde he seye: 'Freend, I shal for thy
        sake
Do striken hire out of oure lettres blake.
Thee thar namoore as in this cas travaille;   1365
I am thy freend, ther I thee may availle.'
Certein he knew of briberies mo
Than possible is to telle in yeres two.
For in this world nis dogge for the bowe
That kan an hurt deer from an hool iknowe   1370
Bet than this somnour knewe a sly lecchour,
Or an avouter or a paramour.
And for that was the fruit of al his rente,
Therfore on it he sette al his entente.
    And so bifel that ones on a day,   1375
This somnour, evere waiting on his pray,

1352 his duetee what was due to him   1353 laude (due) praise
1355 at his retenue in his service   1359 of oon assent in league with each
other   1360 feined forged   1361 chapitre ecclesiastical court
1362 pile fleece   1364 Have her struck out of our document
1365 Thee thar you need travaille exert yourself   1366 ther where
1367 briberies swindles   1369 nis there is no   dogge for the bowe hunting
dog trained to track game wounded by archers   1372 avouter adulterer
paramour lover   1373 fruit of al his rente bulk of his income
1374 sette al his entente was completely devoted
1376 waiting on his pray watching out for his prey

Rood for to somne an old widwe, a ribibe,
Feininge a cause, for he wolde bribe;
Happed that he saugh bifore him ride
1380   A gay yeman under a forest side.
A bowe he bar, and arwes bright and kene;
He hadde upon a courtepy of grene,
An hat upon his heed with frenges blake.
        'Sire,' quod this somnour, 'Hail, and wel atake!'
1385   'Welcome,' quod he, 'and every good felawe!
Where ridestow under this grene-wode shawe?'
Seide this yeman, 'Wiltow fer today?'
        This somnour him answerde and seide 'Nay;
Here faste by', quod he, 'is min entente
1390   To riden, for to reisen up a rente
That longeth to my lordes duetee.'
        'Artow thanne a bailly?' 'Ye,' quod he.
He dorste nat, for verray filthe and shame,
Seye that he was a somnour, for the name.
1395   'Depardieux,' quod this yeman, 'deere brother,
Thow art a bailly, and I am another.
I am unknowen as in this contree;
Of thin aqueintance I wolde praye thee,
And eek of bretherhede, if that yow leste.
1400   I have gold and silver in my cheste;
If that thee happe to comen in oure shire,
Al shal be thin, right as thow wolt desire.'
        'Graunt mercy,' quod this somnour, 'by my feith!'
Everich in ootheres hond his trouthe leyth

1377 **ribibe** hag (metaphorical use of 'ribible', a two-stringed fiddle)
1378 **Feininge** inventing **bribe** practise extortion   1379 **Happed** it chanced
1380 **gay** well-dressed   1382 **courtepy** short woollen jacket
1383 **frenges** fringes   1384 **wel atake** well met   1386 **shawe** copse
1387 **Wiltow fer** are you going far   1390 **reisen up** collect
1391 **duetee** dues   1392 **bailly** bailiff (n.)   1393 **dorste nat** did not dare
1395 *Depardieux* by God   1398 **Of** for   1399 And also for brotherhood,
if it pleases you   1401 **thee happe** you chance   1402 **thin** yours, at your
service   1403 *Graunt mercy* thank you   1404 **Everich** each one
leyth pledges

For to be sworn bretheren til they deye.   1405
In daliaunce they riden forth and pleye.
   This somnour, which that was as ful of jangles
As ful of venim been thise wariangles,
And evere enquering upon every thing,
'Brother,' quod he, 'where is now youre   1410
        dwelling,
Another day if that I sholde yow seche?'
This yeman him answerde in softe speche:
'Brother,' quod he, 'fer in the north contree,
Whereas I hope som time I shal thee see.
Er we departe, I shal thee so wel wisse   1415
That of min hous ne shaltow nevere misse.'
   'Now, brother,' quod this somnour, 'I yow
        preye,
Teche me, whil that we riden by the weye –
Sin that ye been a baillif as am I –
Som subtiltee, and tel me feithfully   1420
In min office how I may moost winne;
And spareth nat for conscience ne sinne,
But as my brother tel me how do ye.'
   'Now, by my trouthe, brother deere,' seide he,
'As I shal tellen thee a feithful tale: 1425
My wages been ful streite and eke ful smale.
My lord is hard to me and daungerous,
And min office is ful laborous,
And therfore by extorcions I live;
For sothe, I take al that men wol me yeve.   1430
Algate, by sleighte, or by violence,
Fro yeer to yeer I winne al my dispence.

1406 **daliaunce** chat   1407 **jangles** idle chatter
1408 **wariangles** shrikes (n.)   1409 **enquering upon** asking about
1411 **yow seche** look for you   1415 **departe** separate **wisse** instruct
1416 **of . . . misse** fail to find   1420 **subtiltee** trickery   1423 **do ye** you act
1425 **feithful tale** true account   1426 **streite** scanty
1427 **daungerous** niggardly   1431 **Algate** in any way **sleighte** cunning
1432 **dispence** expenditure

I kan no bettre tellen, feithfully.'
   'Now, certes,' quod this somnour, 'so fare I!
1435   I spare nat to taken, God it woot,
But if it be to hevy or to hoot.
What I may gete in conseil prively,
No manere conscience of that have I.
Nere min extorcioun, I mighte nat liven.
1440   Ne of swich japes wol I nat be shriven;
Stomak ne conscience ne knowe I noon.
I shrewe thise shrifte-fadres everychon!
Wel be we met, by God and by Seint Jame!
But, leeve brother, tel me thanne thy name,'
1445   Quod this somnour. In this mene-while,
This yeman gan a litel for to smile.
   'Brother,' quod he, 'woltow that I thee telle?
I am a feend; my dwelling is in helle.
And here I ride aboute my purchasing,
1450   To wite wher men wol yeve me anything.
My purchas is th'effect of al my rente.
Looke how thow ridest for the same entente,
To winne good – thow rekkest nevere how –
Right so fare I, for ride I wolde right now
1455   Unto the worldes ende for a preye.'
   'A,' quod this somnour, '*benedicite!* what sey ye?
I wende ye were a yeman, trewely;
Ye han a mannes shape as wel as I.
Han ye a figure thanne determinat
1460   In helle, ther ye been in youre estat?'

1434 **so fare I** I do the same   1435 **God it woot** God knows
1436 **to hevy or to hoot** too heavy or too hot (to carry away) (n.)
1437 **in conseil** on the sly   1438 **conscience** scruples
1439 **Nere min extorcioun** were it not for my extortion   1440 **japes** tricks
shriven confessed   1441 **Stomak** emotion   1442 **shrewe** curse
shrifte-fadres confessors   1448 **feend** devil   1449 **purchasing** gain
1450 **wite wher** learn whether   1451 My perks comprise my whole income
(see n. to GP 256)   1452 **entente** purpose   1453 **good** profit
rekkest nevere do not care   1456 **A** ah   1457 **wende** thought
1459 **figure . . . determinat** fixed shape   1460 **in youre estat** in your (true)
state

'Nay, certeinly,' quod he, 'ther have we noon.
But whan us liketh we kan take us oon,
Or elles make yow seme we ben shape.
Somtime lik a man, or lik an ape,
Or lik an aungel kan I ride or go.   1465
It is no wonder thing thogh it be so;
A lousy jogelour kan deceive thee,
And pardee, yet kan I moore craft than he.'
   'Why', quod this somnour, 'ride ye thanne or
      goon
In sondry shap, and nat alwey in oon?'   1470
'For we', quod he, 'wol us swiche formes make
As moost able is oure preyes for to take.'
   'What maketh yow to han al this labour?'
'Ful many a cause, leve sire somnour,'
Seide this feend, 'but alle thing hath time.   1475
The day is short, and it is passed prime,
And yet ne wan I nothing in this day.
I wol entende to winning, if I may,
And nat entende oure wittes to declare;
For, brother min, thy witte is al to bare   1480
To understonde, althogh I tolde hem thee.
But for thow axest why labouren we:
For somtime we been Goddes instrumentz
And meenes to doon his comandementz,
Whan that him list, upon his creatures,   1485
In divers art and in diverse figures.
Withouten him we have no might, certain,
If that him list to stonden theragain.

1466 **no wonder thing** not surprising   1467 **lousy jogelour** lice-ridden
conjurer   1468 **kan I moore craft** I have greater skill   1469 **goon** walk
1470 **In sondry shap** in different forms **in oon** in the same way
1472 **able** effective   1476 **prime** 9 a.m. (g.)   1478 **entende to** pay attention
to   1479 **oure wittes to declare** to reveal our strategies
1481 **althogh I tolde hem thee** even if I were to tell you them
1482 **for thow axest** since you ask   1483 **For** because
1484 **meenes** agents   1486 **divers art** various ways
1488 **stonden theragain** withstand it

And somtime at oure preyere han we leve
1490 Oonly the body and nat the soule greve;
Witnesse on Job, whom that we diden wo.
And somtime han we might of bothe two:
This is to seyn, of soule and body eke.
And somtime be we suffred for to seke
1495 Upon a man and do his soule unreste,
And nat his body, and al is for the beste,
Whan he withstandeth oure temptacioun;
It is a cause of his savacioun,
Al be it that it was nat oure entente
1500 He sholde be sauf, but that we wolde him hente.
And somtime be we servant unto man,
As to the erchebisshop Seint Dunstan;
And to the apostles servant eek was I.'
 'Yet tel me', quod the somnour, 'feithfully,
1505 Make ye yow newe bodyes thus alway
Of elementz?' The feend answerde 'Nay.
Somtime we feine, and somtime we arise
With dede bodies in ful sondry wise,
And speke as renably and faire and wel
1510 As to the Phitonissa dide Samuel.
(And yet wol som men seye it was nat he –
I do no fors of youre divinitee.)
But o thing warne I thee, I wol nat jape:
Thow wolt algates wite how we be shape;
1515 Thow shalt herafterwardes, my brother deere,
Come there thee nedeth nat of me to lere!
For thow shalt, by thin owene experience,
Konne in a chaier rede of this sentence

1490 **greve** to harm 1494–5 **be we suffred for to seke Upon** we are
allowed to attack **unreste** disturbance 1499 **Al be it** although
1500 **wolde him hente** wanted to get possession of him
1502 **erchebisshop** archbishop 1507 **feine** counterfeit
1509 **renably** fluently 1512 I attach no importance to your theology
1513 **o** one **jape** joke 1514 **algates** at any rate 1516 **there** where
lere learn 1518 Be able to lecture on this topic from a professorial
chair (n.)

Bet than Virgile whil he was on live,
Or Dant also. Now lat us ride blive,   1520
For I wol holde compaignye with thee
Til it be so that thow forsake me.'
    'Nay,' quod this somnour, 'that shal nat bitide!
I am a yeman, knowen is ful wide;
My trouthe wol I holde as in this cas.   1525
For though thow were the devel Sathanas,
My trouthe wol I holde to thee, my brother,
As I am sworn, and ech of us til oother,
For to be trewe brother in this cas.
And bothe we goon abouten oure purchas;   1530
Taak thow thy part, what that men wol thee yeve,
And I shal min; thus may we bothe live.
And if that any of us have moore than oother,
Lat him be trewe, and parte it with his brother.'
    'I graunte,' quod the devel, 'by my fey!'   1535
And with that word they riden forth hir wey,
And right at th'entring of the tounes ende
To which this somnour shoop him for to wende,
They saugh a cart that charged was with hey,
Which that a cartere droof forth in his wey.   1540
Deep was the wey, for which the carte stood;
This cartere smoot and cride as he were wood.
'Hait, Brok, hait, Scot! What, spare ye for the
        stones?
The feend', quod he, 'yow fecche, body and bones,
As ferforthly as evere were ye foled,   1545
So muchel wo as I have with yow tholed!
The devel have al, bothe hors and cart and hey!'
    This somnour seide, 'Heer shul we have a pley!'

1520 **blive** quickly   1526 **Sathanas** Satan, the devil   1530 **purchas** profit
1531 **part** share   1534 **parte** share   1535 **fey** faith
1538 **shoop him** planned   **wende** go   1539 **charged** laden   **hey** hay
1541 **Deep** deep in mud   **stood** stood still   1543 **Hait** gee up
spare ye for are you holding back because of   1545 As sure as ever you
were born   1546 **tholed** suffered   1548 **pley** joke

And neer the feend he drough, as noght ne were,
1550   Ful prively, and rowned in his ere:
'Herkne, my brother, herkne, by thy feith!
Herestow nat how that the cartere seyth?
Hent it anon, for he hath yeve it thee,
Bothe hey and cart, and eek his caples thre.'
1555   'Nay,' quod the devel, 'God woot, never a del!
It is nat his entente, trust thow me wel.
Axe him thyself, if thow nat trowest me,
Or ellis stint a while and thow shalt se.'
This cartere thakketh his hors upon the croupe,
1560   And they bigonne to drawen and to stoupe.
'Heit, now,' quod he, 'ther Jesu Crist yow blesse,
And al his handwerk, bothe moore and lesse!
That was wel twight, min owene liard boy!
I pray God save thee, and Seinte Loy.
1565   Now is my cart out of the slow, pardee!'
'Lo, brother,' quod the feend, 'what tolde I thee?
Heer may ye se, min owene deere brother,
The carl spak o thing, but he thoghte another.
Lat us go forth abouten oure viage;
1570   Heere winne I nothing upon cariage.'
Whan that they comen somwhat out of toune,
This somnour to his brother gan to roune:
'Brother,' quod he, 'here woneth an old rebekke,
That hadde almoost as leef to lese hir nekke
1575   As for to yeve a peny of hir good.
I wol han twelf pens, thogh that she be wood,

1549 And he drew nearer to the devil, as if nothing was going on
1550 **rowned** whispered   1553 **Hent** take   **yeve** given   1554 **caples** horses
1555 **never a del** not at all   1558 **stint** stand still   1559 **thakketh** pats
croupe rump   1560 **stoupe** lean forward (in order to pull better)
1561 **Heit** gee up   1562 **handwerk** handiwork   1563 **twight** pulled
liard grey   1565 **slow** mire   1568 **carl** fellow   **o** one
1569 **viage** enterprise   1570 **upon cariage** in the way of carriage-service (g.)
1572 **roune** whisper   1573 **woneth** lives   **rebekke** old woman (literally, the
name of a stringed instrument)   1574 **hadde . . . as leef to lese** would as
soon lose   1576 **wood** furious

Or I wol somne hire unto oure office –
And yet, God wot, of hire knowe I no vice.
But for thow kanst nat as in this contree
Winne thy cost, taak heer ensample of me.'   1580
   This somnour clappeth at the widwes gate.
'Com out,' quod he, 'thow olde viritrate!
I trowe thow hast som frere or preest with thee.'
   'Who clappeth?' seide this wif, '*benedicite!*
God save yow, sire; what is youre swete wille?'   1585
   'I have', quod he, 'of somonance a bille.
Up peine of cursing, looke that thow be
To-morn bifore the erchedeknes knee
T'answere to the court of certein thinges.'
   'Now, Lord,' quod she, 'Crist Jesu, king of   1590
      kinges,
So wysly helpe me, as I ne may!
I have been sik, and that ful many a day;
I may nat go so fer,' quod she, 'ne ride,
But I be deed, so priketh it in my side.
May I nat axe a libel, sire somnour,   1595
And answere there by my procuratour
To swich thing as men wole opposen me?'
   'Yis,' quod this somnour, 'pay anon – lat see –
Twelf pens to me, and I wol thee acquite.
I shal no profit han therby but lite.   1600
My maister hath the profit, and nat I.
Com of, and lat me riden hastily;
Yif me twelf pens, I may no lenger tarye.'
   'Twelf pens!' quod she, 'Now, lady Seinte Marye

1579 **for** since   1581 **clappeth** knocks   1582 **viritrate** hag
1586 **of somonance a bille** a writ of summons
1587 **Up peine of cursing** on pain of excommunication   1588 Tomorrow
before the archdeacon   1591 **ne may** cannot   1594 **But I be deed** without
dying **so priketh it** there is such a pain   1595 **libel** written statement of
charges (n.)   1596 **procuratour** proctor, legal representative (n.)
1597 **thing** charge **opposen me** lay to my charge   1599 **thee acquite** let you
off   1600 **lite** little   1602 **Com of** get a move on

1605   So wysly help me out of care and sinne,
This wide world thogh that I sholde winne,
Ne have I nat twelf pens withinne min hoold.
Ye knowen wel that I am povre and oold;
Kithe youre almesse on me, povre wrecche.'
1610   'Nay, thanne', quod he, 'the foule feend me fecche,
If I th'excuse, though thow shul be spilt!'
'Allas,' quod she, 'God woot, I have no gilt!'
    'Pay me,' quod he, 'or by the swete Seinte Anne,
As I wol bere awey thy newe panne
1615   For dette which thow owest me of oold,
Whan that thow madest thin housbonde cokewold;
I paide at hom for thy correccioun.'
    'Thow lixt!' quod she, 'By my savacioun,
Ne was I nevere er now, widwe ne wif,
1620   Somoned unto youre court in al my lif,
Ne nevere I nas but of my body trewe.
Unto the devel blak and rough of hewe
Yeve I thy body, and my panne also!'
    And whan the devel herde hire cursen so
1625   Upon hir knees, he seide in this manere:
'Now, Mabely, min owene moder dere,
Is this youre wil in ernest that ye seye?'
    'The devel', quod she, 'so fecche him er he deye,
And panne and al, but he wol him repente!'
1630   'Nay, olde stot, that is nat min entente,'
Quod this somnour, 'for to repente me
For anything that I have had of thee.
I wolde I hadde thy smok and every clooth!'
    'Now, brother,' quod the devel, 'be noght wrooth:
1635   Thy body and this panne been mine by right.
Thow shalt with me to helle yet tonight,

1607 **min hoold** my possession   1609 **Kithe** show **almesse** charity
1611 **spilt** ruined   1616 **cokewold** cuckold
1617 **correccioun** punishment   1618 **lixt** lie   1622 **hewe** appearance
1629 **but he wol** if he will not   1630 **stot** bawd   1633 **clooth** piece of
clothing   1634 **wrooth** angry

Wher thow shalt knowen of oure privetee
Moore than a maister of divinitee.'
And with that word this foule feend him hente;
Body and soule he with the devel wente   1640
Wheras that somnours han hir heritage.
And God, that maked after his image
Mankinde, save and gide us, alle and some,
And leve thise somnours goode men bicome!

 Lordinges, I koude han tolde yow – quod this   1645
  Frere –
Hadde I had leiser for this Somnour heere,
After the text of Crist, Poul and John,
And of oure othere doctours many oon,
Swich peines that youre hertes mighte agrise;
Albeit so no tonge may it devise,   1650
Thogh that I mighte a thousand winter telle
The peines of thilke cursed hous of helle.
But for to kepe us fro that cursed place,
Waketh and preyeth Jesu for his grace;
So kepe us fro the temptour Sathanas.   1655
Herketh this word – beth war, as in this cas:
'The leoun sit in his await alway
To sle the innocent, if that he may.
Disposeth ay youre hertes to withstonde
The feend, that yow wolde make thral and bonde.'   1660
He may nat tempte yow over youre might,
For Crist wol be youre champion and knight.
And prayeth that thise somnoures hem repente
Of hir misdedes, er that the feend hem hente!

Heere endeth the Freres Tale.

1637 **privetee** secrets 1638 **divinitee** theology 1641 To the place where
summoners get their inheritance (i.e. what is coming to them)
1643 **alle and some** one and all 1644 **leve** allow 1646 **leiser** leisure
1647 **After** according to 1649 **agrise** shudder 1650 **devise** describe
1651 **winter** years 1655 **temptour** tempter **Sathanas** Satan, the devil
1656 **Herketh** listen to **beth war** take warning 1657 **in his await** in
ambush 1658 **sle** slay 1660 The devil, who would like to enslave you

THE SUMMONER'S PROLOGUE

The Prologe of the Somonours Tale.

1665   This Somnour in his stiropes hye stood;
Upon this Frere his herte was so wood
That lik an aspen leef he quook for ire.
'Lordinges,' quod he, 'but o thing I desire:
I yow biseke that, of youre curteisye,
1670   Sin ye han herd this false Frere lie,
As suffreth me I may my tale telle!
This Frere bosteth that he knoweth helle,
And God it woot, that it is litel wonder;
Freres and feendes been but lite asonder.
1675   For, pardee, ye han ofte time herd telle
How that a frere ravisshed was to helle
In spirit ones by a visioun,
And as an aungel ladde him up and doun
To shewen him the peines that ther were,
1680   In al the place saugh he nat a frere;
Of oother folk he saugh inowe in wo.
Unto this aungel spak the frere tho:
"Now, sire," quod he, "han freres swich a grace,
That noon of hem shal come to this place?"
1685   "Yis," quod this aungel, "many a milioun!"
And unto Sathanas he ladde him doun.
"And now hath Sathanas", seyth he, "a tail
Brodder than of a carrik is the sail.

1665 **Somnour** see n. to GP 623   1666 **wood** angry   1667 **quook** shook
1668 **o** one   1671 **As suffreth me** allow me   1678 **ladde** led
1681 **inowe** plenty   1683 **grace** good fortune   1685 **Yis** yes
1686 **Sathanas** Satan, the devil   1688 **Brodder** broader **carrik** type of large
ship

Hold up thy tail, thow Sathanas!" quod he,
"Shewe forth thin ers, and lat the frere se   1690
Where is the nest of freres in this place."
And er that half a furlong wey of space,
Right so as bees out swarmen from an hive,
Out of the develes ers ther gonne drive
Twenty thousand freres on a route,   1695
And thurghout helle swarmeden aboute,
And comen again as faste as they may gon
And in his ers they crepten everychon;
He clapte his tail again and lay ful stille.
This frere, whan he looked hadde his fille   1700
Upon the tormentz of this sory place,
His spirit God restored, of his grace,
Unto his body again, and he awook.
But nathelees for fere yet he quook,
So was the develes ers ay in his minde;   1705
That is his heritage of verray kinde.
God save yow alle, save this cursed Frere!
My prologe wol I ende in this manere.'

THE SUMMONER'S TALE

Heere biginneth the Somonour his Tale.

Lordinges, ther is in Yorkshire, as I gesse,
A mersshy contree called Holdernesse,   1710
In which ther wente a limitour aboute
To preche, and eek to begge, it is no doute.

1690 **ers** arse   1692 And in less than a minute (g. 'furlong')
1694 **drive** rush   1695 **on a route** in a throng
1699 **clapte . . . again** closed up   1706 **of verray kinde** by virtue of his
profession   1710 **mersshy** marshy   1711 **limitour** friar (g.)
1712 **it is no doute** it is certain

And so bifel that on a day this frere
Hadde preched at a chirche in his manere,
1715   And specially, aboven every thing,
Excited he the peple in his preching
To trentals, and to yeve for Goddes sake
Wherwith men mighten holy houses make,
Theras divine service is honoured –
1720   Nat theras it is wasted and devoured,
Ne ther it nedeth nat for to be yeve,
As to possessioners, that mowen live,
Thanked be God, in wele and habundaunce!
'Trentals', seide he, 'deliveren fro penaunce
1725   Hir freendes soules, as wel olde as yonge,
Ye, whan that they been hastily ysonge –
Nat for to holde a preest joly and gay;
He singeth nat but o masse in a day.
Delivereth out', quod he, 'anon the soules!
1730   Ful hard it is with flessh-hook or with oules
To been yclawed, or to brenne or bake.
Now spede yow hastily, for Cristes sake!'
And whan this frere hadde seid al his entente,
With *qui cum patre* forth his wey he wente.
1735   Whan folk in chirche hadde yeve him what hem
leste,
He wente his wey – no lenger wolde he reste –
With scrippe and tipped staf, ytukked hye.
In every hous he gan to poure and prye,
And beggeth mele and chese, or ellis corn.
1740   His felawe hadde a staf, tipped with horn,

1716 **Excited** urged   1717 **trentals** sets of thirty masses (n.)
1719 **Theras** where   1721 **yeve** given   1722 **possessioners** clerics endowed
with a living (n.)   **mowen** may   1723 **wele** prosperity
1724 **penaunce** purgatory   1727 **joly** fine   **gay** well-dressed
1730 **flessh-hook** metal hook for lifting meat from a pot   **oules** awls
1731 **brenne** burn   1733 **seid al his entente** spoken his mind
1734 *qui cum patre* who with the Father (n.)   1735 **what hem leste** what
they pleased   1737 **scrippe** small bag   **tipped** metal-tipped   **ytukked** with
gown tucked up (n.)   1738 **poure** gaze intently   1739 **mele** ground corn

A peire of tables, al of ivory,
And a pointel, polisshed fetisly,
And wroot the names alwey, as he stood,
Of alle folk that yaf hem any good,
Ascaunces that he wolde for hem preye.   1745
'Yif us a busshel whete, malt or reye,
A Goddes kechil, or a trip of chese,
Or ellis what yow list; we may nat chese.
A Goddes halfpeny, or a masse-peny,
Or yif us of youre brawn, if ye have any;   1750
A dagoun of youre blanket, leeve dame,
Oure suster deere – lo, heere I write youre name –
Bacoun or beef, or swich thing as ye finde.'
    A sturdy harlot wente ay hem bihinde,
That was hir hostes man, and baar a sak,   1755
And what men yaf hem, leide it on his bak;
And whan that he was out at dore, anon
He planed awey the names everychon
That he biforn had writen in his tables;
He served hem with nifles and with fables.   1760
    'Nay, ther thow lixt, thow Somnour!' quod the
        Frere.
'Pees!' quod oure Hoost, 'for Cristes moder deere!
Tel forth thy tale, and spare it nat at al.'
'So thrive I,' quod this Somnour, 'so I shal.'
    So longe he wente hous by hous, til he   1765
Cam til an hous ther he was wont to be
Refresshed moore than in an hundred placis.
Sik lay the goode man whos the place is;

1741 **peire of tables** set of writing-tables (n.)   1742 **pointel** stylus
fetisly elegantly   1745 **Ascaunces** as if   1746 **reye** rye
1747 **Goddes kechil** a little cake given in charity   **trip** piece
1748 **what yow list** whatever pleases you   **chese** choose
1749 **Goddes halfpeny** halfpenny given in charity   **masse-peny** penny for a
mass   1751 **dagoun** scrap   **blanket** undyed woollen cloth
1754 **harlot** servant   1755 **hostes man** inn-servant (n.)   **baar** carried
1758 **planed** scraped   1760 **nifles** trifling stories   1761 **lixt** lie
1763 **spare** hold back   1768 **goode man** master of the house

Bedred upon a couche lowe he lay.
1770   'Deus hic!' quod he, 'O Thomas, freend, good day!'
Seide this frere curteisly and softe.
'Thomas,' quod he, 'God yelde yow, ful ofte
Have I upon this bench faren ful wel!
Heere have I eten many a murye mel.'
1775   And fro the bench he droof awey the cat,
And leide adoun his potente and his hat,
And eek his scrippe, and sette him softe adoun.
His felawe was go walked into toun,
Forth with his knave, into that hostelrye
1780   Wheras he shoop him thilke night to lie.
       'O deere maister,' quod this sike man,
'How han ye fare, sith that March bigan?
I saw yow noght this fourtenight or moore.'
'God woot,' quod he, 'laboured I have ful soore,
1785   And specially, for thy savacioun
Have I seid many a precious orisoun,
And for oure othere freendes, God hem blesse!
I have today been at youre chirche at messe,
And seid a sermon after my simple wit –
1790   Nat al after the text of holy writ,
For it is hard to yow, as I suppose,
And therfore wol I teche yow al the glose.
Glosing is a glorious thing, certein,
For lettre sleeth, so as we clerkes seyn.
1795   Ther have I taught hem to be charitable,
And spende hir good ther it is resonable;
And ther I saugh our dame – a, where is she?'
       'Yond in the yerd I trowe that she be,'

1769 **Bedred** bedridden   1770 *Deus hic* God be here   1771 **softe** quietly
1772 **yelde** reward   1774 **mel** meal   1776 **potente** staff
1777 **softe** gently   1778 **felawe** companion **was go walked** had gone
walking   1780 **shoop him** planned   1782 **How han ye fare** how have you
been   1784 **soore** hard   1786 **orisoun** prayer   1788 **messe** mass
1790 **after** according to   1793 **Glosing** see n. to ML 1180
1794 **lettre sleeth** 'the letter kills' (n.)   1798 **yerd** garden

Seide this man, 'and she wol come anon.'

'Ey, maister, welcome be ye, by Seint John!'   1800
Seide this wif, 'How fare ye, hertely?'

The frere ariseth up ful curteisly,
And hire embraceth in his armes narwe,
And kiste hir swete and chirketh as a sparwe
With his lippes. 'Dame,' quod he, 'right wel,   1805
As he that is youre servant everydel,
Thanked be God that yow yaf soule and lif!
Yet saugh I nat this day so fair a wif
In al the chirche, God so save me!'

'Ye, God amende defautes, sire,' quod she.   1810
'Algates welcome be ye, by my fey!'

'*Graunt mercy*, dame, this have I founde alwey.
But of youre grete goodnesse, by youre leve,
I wolde pray yow that ye nat yow greve:
I wol with Thomas speke a litel throwe.   1815
Thise curatz been ful necligent and slowe
To grope tendrely a conscience.
In shrift, in preching, is my diligence,
And studye in Petres wordes and in Poules.
I walke and fisshe Cristen mennes soules,   1820
To yelden Jesu Crist his propre rente;
To sprede his word is set al min entente.'

'Now, by youre leeve, O deere sire,' quod she,
'Chideth him wel, for seinte Trinitee!
He is as angry as a pissemire,   1825
Thogh that he have al that he kan desire.
Thogh I him wrye a-night and make him warm,
And over him leye my leg outher min arm,

1801 **hertely** in all sincerity   1803 **narwe** tightly   1804 **chirketh** chirps
1806 **everydel** entirely   1810 **God amende defautes** may God correct (my)
defects   1811 **Algates** at any rate   1814 **yow greve** take offence
1815 **throwe** while   1817 **grope** probe   1818 **shrift** confession
1819 **Petres wordes ... Poules** Peter and Paul's words, i.e. the New
Testament   1821 **yelden** give   **rente** tribute   1824 **Chideth** scold
seinte Trinitee the holy Trinity   1825 **pissemire** ant   1827 **wrye** cover

He groneth lik oure boor, lith in oure sty.
1830   Oother disport right noon of him have I;
        I may nat plese him in no maner cas.'
            'O Thomas, *je vous dy*, Thomas, Thomas!
        This maketh the feend, this moste been amended!
        Ire is a thing that hye God defended,
1835   And therof wol I speke a word or two.'
            'Now, maister,' quod the wif, 'er that I go,
        What wol ye dine? I wol go theraboute.'
            'Now, dame,' quod he, 'now *je vous dy sanz doute*,
        Have I nat of a capoun but the livere,
1840   And of youre softe breed nat but a shivere,
        And after that a rosted pigges heed –
        But that I nolde no beest for me were deed –
        Thanne hadde I with yow homly suffisaunce.
        I am a man of litel sustenaunce;
1845   My spirit hath his fostring in the Bible.
        The body is ay so redy and penible
        To wake, that my stomak is destroyed.
        I pray yow, dame, ye be nat anoyed,
        Thogh I so freendly yow my conseil shewe.
1850   By God, I wolde nat telle it but a fewe!'
            'Now, sire,' quod she, 'but o word er I go:
        My child is deed withinne thise wikes two,
        Soone after that ye wente out of this toun.'
            'His deeth saugh I by revelacioun,'
1855   Seide this frere, 'at hom in oure dortour.
        I dar wel seyn that, er that half an hour

1829 **boor** male pig **lith** which lies   1830 **disport** pleasure
1831 **no maner cas** any circumstances   1832 *je vous dy* I say to you
1834 **defended** forbade   1837 **dine** eat for dinner **theraboute** about it
1838 *je vous dy sanz doute* I tell you truly   1839 **Have I nat ... but** if I
have only **capoun** chicken   1840 **shivere** sliver
1843 **suffisaunce** sufficiency   1845 **fostring** nourishment
1846 **penible** conscientious   1847 **wake** keep watch **stomak** appetite
1849 **yow my conseil shewe** confide in you   1850 **but a fewe** except to a few
people   1851 **but o** only one   1852 **wikes** weeks   1855 **dortour** dormitory

After his deeth, I saugh him born to blisse
In min avisioun, so God me wisse!
So dide oure sextein and oure fermerer,
That han been trewe freres fifty yeer;   1860
They may now, God be thanked of his lone,
Maken hir jubilee and walke allone.
And up I roos, and al oure covent eke,
With many a tere trikling on my cheke,
Withouten noise or clatering of belles.   1865
Te deum was oure song, and nothing elles,
Save that to Crist I seide an orisoun,
Thankinge him of his revelacioun.
For, sire and dame, trusteth me right wel,
Oure orisons been moore effectuel,   1870
And moore we seen of Cristes secree thinges
Than burel folke, althogh they weren kinges.
We live in poverte and in abstinence,
And burel folk in richesse and dispence
Of mete and drink, and in hir foul delit.   1875
We han this worldes lust al in despit.
Lazar and Dives liveden diversly,
And diverse guerdoun hadden they therby.
Whoso wol praye, he moot faste and be clene,
And fatte his soule, and make his body lene.   1880
We fare as seyth th'Apostle: clooth and foode
Suffiseth us, thogh they be nat ful goode.
The clennesse and the fasting of us freres
Maketh that Crist accepteth oure prayeres.

1857 **born to blisse** carried to heaven   1858 **wisse** guide
1859 **sextein** sacristan (g.) **fermerer** infirmarer, friar in charge of the convent
infirmary   1861 **lone** gift   1862 **jubilee** jubilee, 50th anniversary (n.)
1863 **covent** convent (g.)   1865 **clatering** clanging   1866 *Te deum* see n.
1868 **of** for   1872 **burel folke** laymen **althogh** even if
1874 **dispence** expenditure   1876 We completely despise the pleasure of this
world   1877 **diversly** differently   1878 **guerdoun** reward **therby** because of
that   1879 **wol** wants to   1880 **fatte** fatten
1881 **fare** live **clooth** clothing   1882 **Suffiseth** are enough for
1883 **clennesse** purity   1884 **Maketh** brings it about

1885   'Lo, Moises fourty dayes and fourty night
          Fasted, er that the heighe God of might
          Spak with him in the mountaine of Sinai;
          With empty wombe, fastinge many a day,
          Received he the lawe that was writen
1890   With Goddes finger; and Elie, wel ye witen,
          In Mount Oreb er he hadde any speche
          With hye God, that is oure lives leche,
          He fasted longe and was in contemplaunce.
             'Aaron, that hadde the temple in governaunce,
1895   And eek the othere preestes everychon,
          Into the temple whan they sholde gon
          To preye for the peple and do servise,
          They nolden drinken in no maner wise
          No drinke which that mighte hem dronke make,
1900   But there in abstinence preye and wake,
          Lest that they deiden. Tak hede what I seye:
          But they be sobre that for the peple preye,
          War that I seye; namoore, for it suffiseth!
             'Oure Lord Jesu, as holy writ deviseth,
1905   Yaf us ensample of fasting and prayeres.
          Therfore we mendinantz, we sely freres,
          Been wedded to poverte and continence,
          To charitee, humblesse, and abstinence,
          To persecucioun for rightwisnesse,
1910   To weping, misericorde, and clennesse.
          And therfore may ye se that oure prayeres –
          I speke of us, we mendinantz, we freres –
          Be to the hye God moore acceptable
          Than youres, with youre festes at the table.
1915   Fro Paradis first, if I shal nat lie,
          Was man out chaced for his glotonye,

1888 **wombe** stomach   1890 **witen** know   1892 **leche** healer
1893 **contemplaunce** contemplation   1894 **in governaunce** under his
control   1898 **in no maner wise** at all   1902 If they who pray for the
people are not sober   1903 **War** take note of   1904 **deviseth** relates
1906 **mendinantz** mendicants **sely** poor   1910 **misericorde** charity
1916 **out chaced** expelled

And chaast was man in Paradis, certein.
   'But herkne now, Thomas, what I shal seyn:
– I ne have no text of it, as I suppose,
But I shal finde it in a maner glose –   1920
That specially oure swete Lord Jesus
Spak this by freres, whan he seide thus:
"Blessed be they that povre in spirit been."
And so forth al the gospel may ye seen,
Wher it be likker oure professioun,   1925
Or hirs that swimmen in possessioun.
Fy on hir pompe and on hir glotonye!
And for hir lewednesse I hem diffye.
   'Me thinketh they been lik Jovinian,
Fat as a whale, and walking as a swan,   1930
Al vinolent as botel in the spence.
Hir preyere is of ful greet reverence,
Whan they for soules seye the Psalm of Davit:
"Lo, buf!" they seye, *cor meum eructavit!*"
Who folweth Cristes gospel and his foore,   1935
But we that humble been and chaast and poore,
Werkers of Goddes word, nat auditours?
Therfore, right as an hauk up at a sours
Up springeth into th'eir, right so prayeres
Of charitable and chaste bisy freres   1940
Maken hir sours to Goddes eres two.
Thomas, Thomas, so mote I ride or go,
And by that lord that clepid is Seint Ive,
Nere thow oure brother, sholdestow nat thrive.

1920 **maner glose** kind of gloss   1925 Whether it is more like our religious
practice 1926 **hirs** theirs **swimmen** wallow **possessioun** property
1928 **lewednesse** sinfulness **diffye** scorn   1929 **Me thinketh** it seems to me
1930 **as** like   1931 **vinolent** wine-filled **spence** pantry
1933 **Davit** David   1934 **buf** sound of a belch (n.)   1935 **foore** footsteps
1937 **auditours** hearers   1938 **at a sours** in swift upward flight
1941 **eres** ears   1942 **so mote I ride or go** as I live   1944 If you were not
our brother (n.), you would not prosper

1945   In oure chapitre praye we day and night
        To Crist, that he thee sende heele and might
        Thy body for to welden hastily.'
            'God woot,' quod he, 'nothing therof feele I!
        As help me Crist, as I in fewe yeres
1950   Have spended upon diverse manere freres
        Ful many a pound, yet fare I nevere the bet.
        Certein, my good have I almoost biset;
        Farwel my gold, for it is al ago!'
            The frere answerde, 'O Thomas, dostow so?
1955   What nedeth yow diverse freres seche?
        What nedeth him that hath a parfit leche
        To sechen othere leches in the toun?
        Youre inconstance is youre confusioun!
        Holde ye than me, or ellis oure covent,
1960   To preye for yow been insufficient?
        Thomas, that jape nis nat worth a mite!
        Youre maladye is for we han to lite.
        A, yif that covent half a quarter otes!
        A, yif that covent foure and twenty grotes!
1965   A, yif that frere a peny and lat him go!
        Nay, nay, Thomas, it may nothing be so!
        What is a ferthing worth parted in twelve?
        Lo, ech thing that is oned in himselve
        Is moore strong than whan it is to-scatered.
1970   Thomas, of me thow shalt nat been yflatered:
        Thow woldest han oure labour al for noght.
        The hye God, that al this world hath wroght,

1945 **chapitre** chapter, assembly of members of a religious house
1946 **heele** health   1947 **welden** have the use of   1951 **bet** better
1952 **biset** spent   1953 **al ago** all gone   1955 Why do you need to seek out
different (orders of) friars   1956 **leche** doctor
1958 **inconstance** inconstancy **confusioun** ruin   1959 **Holde ye** do you
consider   1961 **jape** piece of foolishness **mite** farthing
1962 **for we han to lite** because we have too little   1963 **otes** oats
1964 **grotes** groats (g.)   1966 **nothing** not at all   1967 **ferthing** farthing
1968 **oned** united   1969 **to-scatered** dispersed   1970 **of** by

Seyth that the werkman worthy is his hire.
Thomas, noght of youre tresor I desire
As for myself, but that al oure covent   1975
To praye for yow is ay so diligent,
And for to builden Cristes owene chirche.
Thomas, if ye wol lernen for to wirche,
Of building up of chirches may ye finde,
If it be good, in Thomas lif of Inde.   1980
Ye lie heere ful of anger and of ire
With which the devel set youre herte afire,
And chiden heere the sely innocent,
Youre wif, that is so meke and pacient.
And therfore Thomas – trowe me if thee leste –   1985
Ne strive nat with thy wif, as for thy beste.
And bere this word awey now, by thy feith,
Touchinge swich thing – lo, what the wise seyth:
"Withinne thin hous ne be thow no leoun;
To thy subgitz do noon oppressioun,   1990
Ne make thine aqueintance nat for to flee."
And Thomas, yet eftsoones I charge thee:
Be war from hire that in thy bosom slepeth!
War fro the serpent that so sleighly crepeth
Under the gras, and stingeth subtilly.   1995
Be war, my sone, and herkne paciently,
That twenty thousand men han lost hir lives
For striving with hir lemmans and hir wives.
Now sith ye han so holy meke a wif,
What nedeth yow, Thomas, to maken strif?   2000
Ther nis, iwys, no serpent so cruel
Whan man tret on his tail, ne half so fel,

1978 **for to wirche** to do good works   1980 **If it be good** whether it is a
good thing   1982 **set** (= *setteth*) sets   1983 **sely** poor
1986 **as for thy beste** in your own best interests
1988 **Touchinge** concerning **the wise** the wise man
1990 **subgitz** subordinates   1992 **eftsoones** a second time
1993 **hire** see n.   1994 **sleighly** stealthily   1995 **subtilly** treacherously
1998 **lemmans** lovers   2001 **iwys** truly   2002 **tret** (= *tredeth*) treads
fel fierce

As womman is whan she hath caught an ire.
Vengeance is thanne al that they desire.
2005 Ire is a sinne, oon of the grete of sevene,
Abhominable unto the God of hevene,
And to himself it is destruccioun.
This every lewed viker or persoun
Kan seye, how ire engendreth homicide.
2010 Ire is, in sooth, executour of pride.
I koude of ire seye so muche sorwe
My tale sholde laste til tomorwe;
And therfore praye I God, bothe day and night,
An irous man, God sende him litel might!
2015 It is greet harm, and certes greet pitee,
To sette an irous man in heigh degree.
       'Whilom ther was an irous potestat,
As seyth Senek, that during his estat,
Upon a day out riden knightes two.
2020 And as Fortune wolde that it were so,
That oon of hem cam hoom, that oother noght.
Anon the knight bifore the juge is broght,
That seide thus: "Thow hast thy felawe slain,
For which I deme thee to the deeth, certein."
2025 And to another knight comanded he:
"Go lede him to the deeth, I charge thee."
And happed, as they wente by the weye
Toward the place ther he sholde deye,
The knight cam which men wenden had be deed.
2030 Thanne thoghten they it were the beste reed
To lede hem bothe to the juge again.
They seiden, "Lord, the knight ne hath nat slain
His felawe; heere he standeth, hool alive."
"Ye shul be deed," quod he, "so moot I thrive!

2008 **lewed viker** ignorant vicar **persoun** parson
2010 **is . . . executour of pride** puts pride into action (n.)
2014 **might** power   2017 **Whilom** once **irous potestat** wrathful potentate
2018 **estat** term of office   2021 **That oon** one   2024 **deme** sentence
2027 **happed** it happened   2028 **ther** where **sholde deye** was to die
2029 **wenden had be deed** thought was dead   2030 **reed** plan

This is to seyn, bothe oon and two and thre." 2035
And to the firste knight right thus spak he:
"I dampned thee; thou most algate be deed.
And thow also most nedes lese thin heed,
For thow art cause why thy felawe deyth."
And to the thridde knight right thus he seyth: 2040
"Thow hast nat doon that I comanded thee" –
And thus he dide do sleen hem alle thre.

'Irous Cambises was eek dronkelewe,
And ay delited him to been a shrewe.
And so bifel, a lord of his meinee, 2045
That loved vertuous moralitee,
Seide on a day bitwix hem two right thus:
'"A lord is lost if he be vicious,
And dronkenesse is eek a foul record
Of any man, and namely in a lord. 2050
Ther is ful many an eighe and many an ere
Awaiting on a lord, and he noot where.
For Goddes love, drink moore attemprely!
Win maketh man to lesen wrecchedly
His minde, and eek his limes everychon." 2055
'"The revers shaltow se," quod he, "anon,
And preve it by thin owene experience,
That win ne dooth to folk no swich offence.
Ther is no win bireveth me my might
Of hond ne foot, ne of mine eyen sight." 2060
And for despit he drank ful muchel moore
An hundred part than he hadde doon bifore.
And right anon this irous cursed wrecche
Leet this knightes sone bifore him fecche,

2037 **dampned** condemned **algate** in any case   2038 **nedes** inevitably
2042 **dide do sleen hem** had them killed   2043 **dronkelewe** given to drink
2044 And always took pleasure in wickedness   2045 **meinee** household
2049 **record** reputation   2051 **eighe** eye   2052 **Awaiting on** watching
noot does not know   2053 **attemprely** moderately   2054 **lesen** lose
2055 **limes** limbs   2058 **offence** harm   2061 **for despit** out of resentment
2062 **An hundred part** a hundred times   2064 **Leet . . . fecche** had fetched

2065   Comandinge him he sholde bifore him stonde,
        And sodeinly he took his bowe in honde,
        And up the streng he pulled to his ere,
        And with an arwe he slow the child right there.
        "Now wheither have I a siker hand or noon?"
2070   Quod he. "Is al my might and minde agoon?
        Hath win bireved me min eyen sight?"
            'What sholde I telle th'answere of the knight?
        His sone was slain; ther is namoore to seye.
        Beth war, therfore, with lordes how ye pleye.
2075   Singeth "*Placebo*", and "I shal if I kan",
        But if it be unto a povre man.
        To a povre man men sholde his vices telle,
        But nat to a lord, thogh he sholde go to helle.
            'Lo, irous Cirus, thilke Percien,
2080   How he destroyed the river of Gisen,
        For that an hors of his was dreint therinne,
        Whan that he wente Babiloine to winne.
        He made that the river was so smal
        That wommen mighte wade it overal.
2085   Lo, what seide he that so wel teche kan:
        "Ne be no felawe to an irous man,
        Ne with no wood man walke by the weye
        Lest thee repente; I wol no ferther seye."
            'Now, Thomas, leeve brother, leve thin ire.
2090   Thow shalt me finde as just as is a squire.
        Hoold nat the develes knif ay at thin herte –
        Thin angre dooth thee al to soore smerte –
        But shewe to me al thy confessioun.'
            'Nay,' quod the sike man, 'by Seint Simoun,

2067 **streng** string   2068 **slow** killed   2069 **wheither have I** do I have
2074 **Beth war** beware   2075 *Placebo* see n.   2076 **But if** unless
2079 **Percien** Persian   2081 **dreint** drowned   2082 **Babiloine to winne** to
capture Babylon   2085 **so wel teche kan** can teach so well (n.)
2090 **as just as is a squire** as true as a (carpenter's) square
2092 **dooth thee al to soore smerte** causes you to suffer too deeply
2093 **shewe ... confessioun** make confession

I have be shriven this day at my curat.   2095
I have him toold al hoolly min estat;
Nedeth namoore to speke of it, seyth he,
But if me list, of min humilitee.'
    'Yif me thanne of thy gold to make oure
        cloistre,'
Quod he, 'for many a muscle and many an oystre,   2100
Whan othere men han been ful wel at eise,
Hath been oure foode, oure cloistre for to reise.
And yet, God woot, unnethe the fundement
Parfourmed is, ne of oure pavement
Nis nat a tile yet withinne oure wones.   2105
By God, we owen fourty pound for stones!
Now help, Thomas, for him that harwed helle,
Or ellis mote we oure bookes selle.
And if yow lakke oure predicacioun,
Thanne gooth the world al to destruccioun.   2110
For whoso fro this world wolde us bireve,
So God me save, Thomas, by youre leve,
He wolde bireve out of this world the sonne.
For who kan teche and werchen as we konne?
And that is nat of litel time,' quod he,   2115
'But sith Elie was, or Elise,
Han freres been, that finde I of record,
In charitee, ythanked be oure Lord!
Now, Thomas, help, for seinte charitee!'
And doun anon he set him on his knee.   2120
    This sike man wex wel neigh wood for ire;
He wolde that the frere hadde been afire,

2095 **be shriven** been confessed   2096 **al hoolly** absolutely all
2098 **But if me list** unless it pleases me   2100 **muscle** mussel
2101 **eise** ease   2102 **reise** erect   2103 **unnethe** hardly
fundement foundation (n.)   2104 **Parfourmed** completed **pavement** paved
floor   2105 **wones** buildings   2107 **harwed** harrowed (see n. to Mil 3512)
2109 **predicacioun** preaching   2111 **bireve** take away   2113 **sonne** sun
2114 **werchen** do good works   2116 But since the time of Elijah or
Elisha (n.)   2117 **of record** recorded   2120 At once he kneeled down
2121 **wex wel neigh wood** became almost mad

With his false dissimulacioun.
'Swich thing as is in my possessioun,'
2125   Quod he, 'that may I yeven, and noon oother.
Ye sey me thus, how that I am youre brother?'
     'Ye, certes,' quod the frere, 'trusteth wel;
I took oure dame oure lettre with oure seel.'
     'Now wel,' quod he, 'and somwhat shal I yeve
2130   Unto youre holy covent whil I live.
And in thin hand thow shalt it han anon –
On this condicioun, and oother noon:
That thow departe it so, my deere brother,
That every frere have as muche as oother.
2135   This shaltow swere, on thy professioun,
Withouten fraude or cavelacioun.'
     'I swere it,' quod this frere, 'upon my feith!'
And therwithal his hand in his he leyth.
'Lo here my feith; in me shal be no lak.'
2140   'Now thanne, put in thin hand doun by my bak,'
Seide this man, 'and grope wel bihinde,
Binethe my buttok; ther shaltow finde
A thing that I have hid in privetee.'
     'A!' thoghte this frere, 'that shal go with me!'
2145   And doun his hand he launcheth to the clifte,
In hope for to finde there a yifte.
And whan this sike man felte this frere
Aboute his tuwel grope there and heere,
Amidde his hand he leet the frere a fart.
2150   Ther nis no capul drawing in a cart
That mighte han late a fart of swich a soun.
     The frere up stirte as dooth a wood leoun.
'A, false cherl!' quod he, 'for Goddes bones,
This hastow for despit doon for the nones!

2128 **took oure dame** gave to the lady of the house **lettre** document
2133 **departe it** share it out   2135 **professioun** religious vows
2136 **cavelacioun** quibbling   2138 **therwithal** with that **leyth** places
2139 **lak** failure   2143 **privetee** secret   2145 **launcheth** thrusts **clifte** cleft
between the buttocks   2148 **tuwel** anus   2149 **leet** let out
2150 **capul** horse   2151 **late** let out   2152 **up stirte** leapt up

Thow shalt abye this fart, if that I may!'   2155
    His meinee, which that herden this affray,
Cam leping in and chaced out the frere,
And forth he gooth with a ful angry cheere,
And fette his felawe theras lay his stoor.
He looked as it were a wilde boor;   2160
He grinte with his teeth, so was he wrooth.
A sturdy paas doun to the court he gooth,
Wheras ther woned a man of greet honour,
To whom that he was alwey confessour;
This worthy man was lord of that village.   2165
This frere cam as he were in a rage
Whereas this lord sat eting at his bord.
Unnethes mighte the frere speke a word,
Til atte laste he seide, 'God yow see!'
    This lord gan looke, and seide, '*Benedicitee!*   2170
What, Frere John, what maner world is this?
I se wel that somthing ther is amis.
Ye loken as the wode were ful of thevis!
Sit doun anon, and tel me what youre grief is,
And it shal been amended, if I may.'   2175
    'I have', quod he, 'had a despit today,
God yelde yow, adoun in youre village,
That in this world is noon so povre a page
That he nolde have abhominacioun
Of that I have received in youre toun.   2180
And yet ne greveth me nothing so soore
As that this olde cherl with lokkes hoore

2155 **abye** pay for   2156 **meinee** servants **affray** commotion
2158 **cheere** face   2159 And fetched his companion from where his hoard
(of goods) was   2161 **grinte** (= *grindede*) **with** ground **wrooth** angry
2162 **A sturdy paas** with determined strides, at a great rate
court manor-house   2163 **woned** lived   2167 **bord** table
2168 **Unnethes** hardly   2169 **God yow see** may God protect you
2171 **what maner world is this** what is going on   2174 **grief** trouble
2176 **had a despit** been insulted   2179 **abhominacioun** disgust
2180 **that** that which   2182 **lokkes hoore** white hair

Blasphemed hath oure hooly covent eke.'
　　'Now, maister,' quod this lord, 'I yow biseke –'
2185 'No maister, sire,' quod he, 'but servitour;
Thogh I have had in scole that honour,
God liketh nat that "Raby" men us calle,
Neither in market, ne in youre large halle.'
'No force,' quod he, 'but tel me al youre grief.'
2190 　　'Sire,' quod this frere, 'an odious meschief
This day bitid is to min ordre and me,
And so, *per consequens*, to ech degree
Of Holy Chirche, God amende it soone!'
　　'Sire,' quod the lord, 'ye woot what is to doone.
2195 Distempre yow noght; ye be my confessour.
Ye been the salt of th'erthe and the savour;
For Goddes love, youre pacience ye holde.
Tel me youre grief.' And he anon him tolde
As ye han herd biforn – ye woot wel what.
2200 　　The lady of the hous ay stille sat
Til she hadde herd what the frere saide.
'Ey, Goddes moder,' quod she. 'blisful maide!
Is ther aught elles? Tel me feithfully.'
　　'Madame,' quod he, 'how thinketh yow therby?'
2205 'How that me thinketh?' quod she. 'So God me spede,
I seye a cherl hath doon a cherles dede.
What sholde I seye? God lat him nevere thee!
His sike heed is ful of vanitee.
I holde him in a manere frenesye.'
2210 　　'Madame,' quod he, 'by God I shal nat lie,

2185 **servitour** servant   2186 **in scole** at university   2187 **Raby** Rabbi,
master (n.)   2189 **No force** no matter   2190 **meschief** calamity
2191 **bitid is** has befallen   2192 *per consequens* in consequence
2194 **to doone** to be done   2195 **Distempre yow noght** do not upset
yourself   2200 **stille** silent   2204 **therby** about it
2205 **So God me spede** as God may prosper me   2206 **cherl** boor
2207 **thee** prosper   2209 I consider him to be in some kind of frenzy

But I on oother wise may be wreke,
I shal diffame him overal wher I speke,
The false blasphemour that charged me
To parte that wol nat departed be,
To every man iliche, with meschaunce!'   2215
    The lord sat stille as he were in a traunce,
And in his herte he rolled up and doun:
'How hadde this cherl imaginacioun
To shewe swich a probleme to the frere?
Nevere erst er now herde I of swich matere;   2220
I trowe the devel putte it in his minde!
In ars-metrik shal ther no man finde
Biforn this day of swich a questioun.
Who sholde make a demonstracioun
That every man sholde han ilike his part   2225
As of the soun or savour of a fart?
O nice proude cherl, I shrewe his face!
Lo, sires,' quod the lord, 'with harde grace,
Who evere herde of swich a thing er now?
To every man ilike – tel me how!   2230
It is an inpossible, it may nat be.
Ey, nice cherl, God lat him nevere thee!
The rumbling of a fart, and every soun,
Nis but of eir reverberacioun,
And evere it wasteth lite and lite awey.   2235
Ther nis no man kan demen, by my fey,
If that it were departed equally.
What, lo my cherl, lo yet how shrewedly

2211 If I cannot be avenged on him in any other way
2212 **diffame** slander **overal wher** everywhere that   2214 **parte** share
2215 **iliche** alike **with meschaunce** curse it   2218 **imaginacioun** ingenuity
2220 **erst er now** before now   2222 **ars-metrik** arithmetic (n.)
2224 **make a demonstracioun** demonstrate by logical reasoning
2225 **ilike his part** an equal share   2227 **nice** foolish **shrewe** curse
2228 **with harde grace** bad luck to him   2231 **inpossible** impossibility (n.)
2234 **eir** air   2235 **evere** continually **lite and lite** little by little
2236 **demen** judge   2238 **shrewedly** maliciously

Unto my confessour today he spak!
2240 I holde him certein a demoniak.
Now ete youre mete, and lat the cherl go pleye;
Lat him go hange himself, a devel weye!'

The wordes of the lordes squier and
his kervere for departinge of the
fart on twelve.

Now stood the lordes squier at the bord,
That carf his mete, and herde word by word
2245 Of alle thing of which I have yow said.
'My lord,' quod he, 'be ye nat ivele apaid;
I koude telle, for a gowne-clooth,
To yow, sire frere, so ye be nat wrooth,
How that this fart sholde evene ydeled be
2250 Among youre covent, if it liked me.'
'Tel,' quod the lord, 'and thow shalt have anon
A gowne-clooth, by God and by Seint John!'
'My lord,' quod he, 'whan that the weder is fair,
Withouten wind or parturbinge of air,
2255 Lat bringe a cartwheel heere into this halle.
But looke that it have his spokes alle –
Twelve spokes hath a cartwheel comunly.
And bringe me thanne twelve freres – woot ye why?
For thrittene is a covent, as I gesse.
2260 Youre confessour heere, for his worthinesse,
Shal perfourne up the nombre of this covent.
Thanne shal they knele adoun by oon assent,

2240 **demoniak** madman   2241 **pleye** joke   2242 **a devel weye** in the
devil's name   2244 **carf** carved   2246 **ivele apaid** displeased
2247 **gowne-clooth** length of cloth sufficient to make a gown
2248 **so** provided that   2249 **evene ydeled** divided equally
2250 **if it liked me** if I wanted to   2253 **weder** weather
2254 **parturbinge** disturbance   2255 **Lat bringe** have brought
2259 **thrittene** thirteen **covent** convent (n.)   2261 **perfourne up** make up

And to every spokes ende in this manere
Ful sadly leye his nose shal a frere.
Youre noble confessour, ther God him save,   2265
Shal holde his nose upright under the nave.
Thanne shal this cherl, with baly stif and toght
As any tabour, hider been ybroght,
And sette him on the wheel right of this cart,
Upon the nave, and make him lete a fart.   2270
And ye shal seen, up peril of my lif,
By preeve which that is demonstratif,
That equally the soun of it wol wende,
And eek the stink, unto the spokes ende.
Save that this worthy man, youre confessour,   2275
Bicause he is a man of greet honour,
Shal han the firste fruit, as reson is.
The noble usage of freres yet is this,
The worthy men of hem shul first be served,
And certeinly he hath it wel disserved.   2280
He hath today taught us so muchel good,
With preching in the pulpit ther he stood,
That I may vouchesauf, I seye for me,
He hadde the firste smel of fartes three.
And so wolde al his covent hardily;   2285
He bereth him so faire and holily.'
    The lord, the lady, and ech man save the frere,
Seiden that Jankin spak in this matere
As wel as Euclide dide or Ptholomee.
Touchinge the cherl, they seide subtiltee   2290

2264 **sadly** firmly   2266 **nave** hub   2267 **baly** belly   **toght** taut
2268 **tabour** drum   2272 **preeve ... demonstratif** proof based on logic,
conclusive proof   2273 **wende** travel   2277 **as reson is** as is right
2278 **usage** custom   2282 **ther** where   2283 **vouchesauf** grant
2284 **hadde** should have   2285 **hardily** to be sure
2286 **bereth him** behaves   2290 **subtiltee** cleverness

And heigh wit made him speken as he spak;
He nis no fool ne no demoniak.
And Jankin hath ywonne a newe gowne.
My tale is doon; we been almoost at towne.

Heere endeth the Somonours Tale.

2291 **heigh wit** deep intelligence

THE CLERK'S PROLOGUE

'Sire Clerk of Oxenford,' oure Hooste saide,
'Ye ride as coy and stille as dooth a maide
Were newe spoused, sitting at the bord.
This day ne herde I of youre tonge a word;
I trowe ye studye aboute som sophime.   5
But Salomon seyth "every thing hath time".
For Goddes sake, as beth of bettre cheere!
It is no time for to studyen heere.
Tel us som murye tale, by youre fey;
For what man that is entred in a pley,   10
He nedes moot unto the pley assente.
But precheth nat, as freres doon in Lente,
To make us for oure olde sinnes wepe,
Ne that thy tale make us nat to slepe.
   'Tel us som murye thing of aventures!   15
Youre termes, youre colours, and youre figures,
Kepe hem in stoor til so be ye endite
Heigh style, as whan that men to kinges write.
Speketh so plein at this time, we yow preye,
That we may understonde what ye seye.'   20
   This worthy clerk benignely answerde:
'Hoost,' quod he, 'I am under youre yerde.

2 **coy** quiet **stille** silent   3 **Were newe spoused** who had just been married
bord table   5 **sophime** sophism, question of logic
7 **as beth of bettre cheere** be in a better mood, cheer up   10 **pley** game
11 **nedes moot** must of necessity   15 **murye thing of aventures** entertaining
tale of notable events   16 **termes** technical terms **colours** rhetorical
embellishments (n.) **figures** figures of speech   17–18 **in stoor** stored away
endite Heigh style write in elevated style (n.)   22 **under youre yerde** under
your authority

Ye han of us as now the governaunce,
And therfore wol I do yow obeisaunce,
25   As fer as reson asketh, hardily.
I wol yow telle a tale which that I
Lerned at Padwe of a worthy clerk,
As preved by his wordes and his werk.
He is now deed and nailed in his cheste;
30   I pray to God so yeve his soule reste!
       'Fraunceis Petrak, the laureat poete,
Highte this clerk, whos rethorik swete
Enlumined al Itaille of poetrye
As Linian dide of philosophye,
35   Or lawe, or oother art particuler.
But deeth, that wol nat suffre us dwellen heer
But as it were a twinkling of an eye,
Hem bothe hath slain, and alle shul we die.
       'But forth to tellen of this worthy man
40   That taughte me this tale, as I bigan,
I seye that first with heigh style he enditeth,
Er he the body of his tale writeth,
A prohemie in which discriveth he
Pemond, and of Saluces the contree,
45   And speketh of Appenin, the hilles hye
That been the boundes of West Lumbardye,
And of Mount Vesulus in special
Wheras the Poo out of a welle smal
Taketh his firste springing and his sours,
50   That estward ay encresseth in his cours
To Emeleward, to Ferare and Venise,
The which a long thing were to devise.

---

24 **do yow obeisaunce** obey you   25 **hardily** certainly   32 **Highte** was
called   33 **Enlumined** made illustrious   35 **art particuler** specialized area of
university study   36 **suffre** allow   43 **prohemie** preface
discriveth describes   46 **boundes** boundaries   47 **in special** in particular
48 **welle** spring   49 **his firste springing** its source
51 **To Emeleward** towards Emilia   52 Which would be a lengthy matter to
relate

And trewely, as to my juggement
Me thinketh it a thing inpartinent,
Save that he wole conveyen his matere.   55
But this his tale, which that ye shal heere.'

THE CLERK'S TALE

*Heere biginneth the Tale of
the Clerk of Oxenford.*

Ther is, at the west side of Itaille,
Doun at the roote of Vesulus the colde,
A lusty plaine, habundant of vitaille,
Wher many a tour and toun thow mayst biholde   60
That founded were in time of fadres olde,
And many another delitable sighte;
And Saluces this noble contree highte.

A markis whilom lord was of that lond,
As were his worthy eldres him bifore,   65
And obeisant, ay redy to his hond,
Were alle his liges, bothe lasse and moore.
Thus in delit he liveth, and hath doon yoore,
Biloved and drad, thurgh favour of Fortune,
Bothe of his lordes and of his commune.   70

54 **inpartinent** irrelevant   55 **Save** except   **wole conveyen** wishes to
introduce

58 **roote** foot   59 **lusty** delightful   **of vitaille** in agricultural produce
61 **fadres olde** ancestors   64 **markis** marquis   **whilom** in earlier days
66 **obeisant** obedient   **ay** always   67 **liges** subjects   **bothe lasse and moore** of
greater or lesser rank   68 **yoore** for a long time
69 **drad** feared   70 **of** by   **commune** people

Therwith he was, to speke as of linage,
The gentileste yborn of Lumbardye;
A fair persone, and strong, and yong of age,
And ful of honour and of curteisye,

75   Discret inogh his contree for to gye –
Save in somme thinges that he was to blame.
And Walter was this yonge lordes name.

I blame him thus, that he considered noght
In time cominge what him mighte bitide,

80   But on his lust present was al his thoght,
As for to hauke and hunte on every side.
Wel neigh alle oothere cures leet he slide.
And eek he nolde – and that was worst of alle –
Wedde no wif, for noght that may bifalle.

85   Oonly that point his peple bar so soore
That flokmele on a day they to him wente;
And oon of hem that wisest was of loore –
Or ellis that the lord best wolde assente
That he sholde telle him what his peple mente,

90   Or ellis koude he shewe wel swich matere –
He to the markis seide as ye shal heere:

'O noble markis, youre humanitee
Assureth us and yeveth us hardinesse,
As ofte as time is of necessitee,

95   That we to yow mowe telle oure hevinesse.
Accepteth, lord, now, of youre gentillesse,
That we with pitous herte unto yow pleine,
And lat youre eris noght my vois desdeine.

72 **gentileste** noblest   75 **gye** govern   79 **bitide** befall
80 **lust present** immediate pleasure   82 **cures** cares   83 **nolde** was not
willing to   85 **bar** bore **soore** ill   86 **flokmele** in a flock
87 **loore** wisdom   90 **shewe** explain   93 **Assureth us** makes us confident
95 **hevinesse** sorrow   96 **gentillesse** graciousness   97 **pitous** sorrowful
pleine express our unhappiness

'Al have I noght to doone in this matere
Moore than another man hath in this place, 100
Yet, forasmuche as ye, my lord so deere,
Han alwey shewed me favour and grace,
I dar the bettre aske of yow a space
Of audience, to shewen oure requeste;
And ye, my lord, to doon right as yow leste. 105

'For certes, lord, so wel us liketh yow
And al youre werk, and evere han doon, that we
Ne kouden nat us self devisen how
We mighte liven in moore felicitee,
Save o thing, lord, if it youre wille be: 110
That for to been a wedded man yow leste –
Thanne were youre peple in soverein hertes reste!

'Boweth youre nekke under that blisful yok
Of sovereinetee, noght of servise,
Which that men clepe spousaille or wedlok. 115
And thenketh, lord, among youre thoghtes wise,
How that oure dayes passe in sondry wise;
For thogh we slepe, or wake, or rome, or ride,
Ay fleeth the time; it nil no man abide.

'And thogh youre grene youthe floure as yit, 120
In crepeth age alwey, as stille as stoon.
And deth manaceth every age, and smit
In ech estat, for ther escapeth noon.

99 Although I have no (personal) interest in this matter   103 **space** interval
105 **as yow leste** as it may please you   106 **us liketh yow** you please us
107 **werk** actions   108 **devisen** imagine   110 **o** one   111 **yow leste** it
might please you   112 **soverein** complete   113 **yok** yoke
115 **spousaille** marriage   117 **sondry wise** different ways   118 **rome** walk
about   119 **Ay fleeth** always flies   **abide** wait for   120 **as yit** still
121 **stille** quietly   122 **manaceth** threatens   **smit** (= *smiteth*) strikes
123 **estat** social condition

And also certein as we knowe echon
125   That we shul die, as uncertein we alle
Been of that day whan deth shal on us falle.

'Accepteth thanne of us the trewe entente,
That nevere yet refuseden thin heste.
And we wol, lord, if that ye wol assente,
130   Chese yow a wif, in short time at the leeste,
Born of the gentileste and of the meeste
Of al this lond, so that it oghte seme
Honour to God and yow, as we kan deme.

'Delivere us out of al this bisy drede,
135   And tak a wif, for hye Goddes sake!
For if it so bifelle, as God forbede,
That thurgh youre deeth youre line sholde slake,
And that a straunge successour sholde take
Youre heritage, O, wo were us alive!
140   Wherfore we pray yow hastily to wive.'

Hir meke prayere and hir pitous cheere
Maked the markis herte han pitee.
'Ye wol,' quod he, 'min owene peple deere,
To that I nevere erst thoghte streine me.
145   I me rejoised of my libertee,
That selde time is founde in mariage.
Ther I was free, I moot been in servage.

'But nathelees, I se youre trewe entente,
And truste upon youre wit, and have doon ay.
150   Wherfore, of my free wil I wol assente

125 **uncertein** uncertain   127 **trewe entente** loyal intention
128 **heste** command   130 **Chese** choose   131 **meeste** greatest
133 **deme** judge   134 **bisy drede** anxious fear   137 **slake** fail
139 **wo were us alive** how wretched our life would be   140 **wive** take a
wife   141 **pitous cheere** pitiable looks   143 **wol** wish   144 **erst** before
thoghte intended **streine** to constrain   145 **me rejoised of** delighted in
146 **selde time** seldom   147 **Ther** where   149 **wit** understanding

To wedde me, as soone as evere I may.
But theras ye han profred me today
To chese me a wif, I yow relesse
That chois, and pray yow of that profre cesse.

'For God it woot, that children ofte ben   155
Unlik hir worthy eldres hem bifore.
Bountee comth al of God, nat of the stren
Of which they been engendred and ybore.
I truste in Goddes bountee, and therfore
My mariage and min estat and reste   160
I him bitake; he may doon as him leste.

'Lat me allone in chesing of my wif;
That charge upon my bak I wol endure.
But I yow pray, and charge upon youre lif,
That what wif that I take, ye me assure   165
To worshipe hire whil that hir lif may dure,
In word and werk, bothe here and everywhere,
As she an emperoures doghter were.

'And ferthermoore, this shal ye swere: that ye
Again my chois shal neither grucche ne strive.   170
For sith I shal forgoon my libertee
At your requeste, as evere mote I thrive,
Theras min herte is set, ther wol I wive.
And but ye wol assente in swich manere,
I pray yow, speketh namoore of this matere.'   175

With hertly wil they sworen and assenten
To al this thing – ther seide no wight nay –
Bisekinge him of grace, er that they wenten,

152 profred offered   153 relesse discharge from   154 cesse cease
157 Bountee goodness stren lineage   161 him bitake entrust to him
166 worshipe honour dure last   167 werk deed   170 grucche grumble
171 sith since   172 as evere mote I thrive as I prosper   173 Theras where
174 but unless   176 hertly heartfelt   178 Bisekinge beseeching

That he wolde graunten hem a certein day
180 Of his spousaille, as soone as evere he may.
For yet alwey the peple somwhat dredde
Lest that the markis no wif wolde wedde.

He graunted hem a day, swich as him leste,
On which he wolde be wedded sikerly,
185 And seide he dide al this at hir requeste.
And they, with humble entente, buxomly,
Knelinge upon hir knees ful reverently,
Him thanken alle; and thus they han an ende
Of hir entente, and hom again they wende.

190 And herupon he to his officers
Comaundeth for the feste to purveye,
And to his privee knightes and squiers
Swich charge yaf as him liste on hem leye.
And they to his comandement obeye,
195 And ech of hem dooth al his diligence
To doon unto the feste reverence.

[Part Two]

Noght fer fro thilke paleis honurable
Wheras this markis shoop his mariage,
Ther stood a throop, of site delitable,
200 In which that povre folk of that village
Hadden hir bestes and hir herbergage,
And of hir labour toke hir sustenance,
After that the erthe yaf hem habundance.

181 dredde (= *dredede*) feared   184 sikerly of a certainty
186 buxomly obediently   188–9 they han an ende Of hir entente their
purpose is fulfilled   190 herupon thereupon officers servants
191 purveye provide   192 his privee knightes and squiers the knights and
squires who were his personal servants   193 Gave such duties as he wished
to assign them   198 shoop prepared   199 throop village site situation
201 herbergage home   202 sustenance food   203 After that according as

Among thise povre folk ther dwelte a man
Which that was holden povrest of hem alle;   205
But hye God som time senden can
His grace into a litel oxes stalle.
Janicula men of that throop him calle.
A doghter hadde he, fair inogh to sighte,
And Grisildis this yonge maiden highte.   210

But for to speke of vertuous beautee,
Thanne was she oon the faireste under sonne.
For povreliche yfostred up was she;
No likerous lust was thurgh hir herte yronne.
Wel ofter of the welle than of the tonne   215
She drank, and for she wolde vertu plese,
She knew wel labour, but noon idel ese.

But thogh this maide tendre were of age,
Yet in the brest of hir virginitee
Ther was enclosed ripe and sad corage.   220
And in greet reverence and charitee
Hir olde povre fader fostred she.
A fewe sheepe, spinninge, on feld she kepte;
She wolde noght been idel til she slepte.

And whan she homward cam, she wolde bringe   225
Wortes or othere herbes, times ofte,
The whiche she shredde and seeth for hir livinge,
And made hir bed ful hard and nothing softe.

205 **holden** considered to be **povrest** poorest   209 **fair inogh to sighte** very
beautiful to behold   212 She was the most beautiful in the world
213 **povreliche yfostred** brought up in poverty   214 **likerous lust** luxurious
pleasure   215 **tonne** (wine-)barrel   216 **for** because **plese** satisfy the
demands of   220 **ripe and sad corage** mature and serious spirit
222 **fostred** looked after   223 **spinninge** while she span
226 **Wortes** greens   227 **shredde** cut up **seeth** boiled   228 **nothing** not at
all

And ay she kepte hir fadres lif on-lofte,
230   With every obeisance and diligence
That child may doon to fadres reverence.

Upon Grisilde, this povre creature,
Ful ofte sithe this markis sette his eye
As he on hunting rood, paraventure;
235   And whan it fil that he mighte hire espye,
He noght with wantowne looking of folye
His eyen caste on hire, but in sad wise
Upon hir cheere he wolde him ofte avise,

Commendinge in his herte hir wommanhede,
240   And eek hir vertu, passing any wight
Of so yong age, as wel in cheere as dede.
For thogh the peple hath no greet insight
In vertue, he considered ful right
Hir bountee, and disposed that he wolde
245   Wedde hire oonly, if evere he wedden sholde.

The day of wedding cam, but no wight kan
Telle what womman that it sholde be.
For which merveille wondred many a man,
And seiden, whan they were in privetee,
250   'Wol nat oure lord yet leve his vanitee?
Wol he nat wedde? Allas, allas the while!
Why wol he thus himself and us bigile?'

But nathelees, this markis hath doon make
Of gemmes, set in gold and in asure,
255   Broches and ringes, for Grisildis sake.
And of hir clothing took he the mesure

229 on-lofte flourishing   233 ofte sithe often   235 fil chanced
espye observe   236 wantowne lascivious   237 sad wise sober manner
238 cheere face   him . . . avise ponder   240 passing surpassing
wight creature   244 bountee virtue   disposed resolved
249 privetee private   250 vanitee folly   251 allas the while alas the day
252 bigile trick   253 hath doon make has had made   254 asure lapis lazuli

By a maide lik to hir stature,
And eek of othere ornamentes alle
That unto swich a wedding sholde falle.

The time of undren of the same day   260
Approcheth, that this wedding sholde be.
And al the paleis put was in array,
Bothe halle and chambres, ech in his degree.
Houses of office stuffed with plentee
Ther maystow seen, of deintevous vitaille   265
That may be founde as fer as last Itaille.

This royal markis, richely arrayed,
Lordes and ladies in his compaignye,
The whiche that to the feste were yprayed,
And of his retenue the bachelrye,   270
With many a soun of sondry melodye,
Unto the village of the which I tolde
In this array the righte wey han holde.

Grisilde, of this, God woot, ful innocent,
That for hire shapen was al this array,   275
To fecchen water at a welle is went,
And cometh hoom as soone as ever she may;
For wel she hadde herd seid, that thilke day
The markis sholde wedde, and if she mighte,
She wolde fain han seyn som of that sighte.   280

She thoghte, 'I wole with othere maidens stonde,
That been my felawes, in oure dore and se
The markisesse, and therfore wol I fonde

257 **stature** build   259 **unto . . . sholde falle** might be appropriate to
260 **undren** mid-morning (g.)   262 **put was in array** was made to look nice
263 **in his degree** in order   264 **Houses of office** kitchens and pantries
265 **deintevous vitaille** delicious food   266 **as fer as last Itaille** throughout
all Italy   269 **yprayed** invited   270 **bachelrye** knights in attendance
273 **the righte wey** the direct route   275 **shapen** devised   276 **is went** has
gone   280 **fain** gladly   283 **markisesse** marchioness **fonde** try

To doon at hoom as soone as it may be
285 The labour which that longeth unto me,
And thanne I may at leiser hir biholde,
If she this wey unto the castel holde.'

And as she wolde over hir thresshfold gon,
The markis cam and gan hire for to calle,
290 And she set doun hir water-pot anon
Biside the thresshfold, in an oxes stalle,
And doun upon hir knees she gan to falle,
And with sad contenance kneleth stille
Til she hadde herd what was the lordes wille.

295 This thoghtful markis spak unto this maide
Ful sobrely, and seide in this manere:
'Where is youre fader, O Grisildis?' he saide.
And she with reverence, in humble cheere,
Answerde, 'Lord, he is al redy heere.'
300 And in she goth withouten lenger lette,
And to the markis she hir fader fette.

He by the hand than took this olde man,
And seide thus, whan he him hadde aside:
'Janicula, I neither may ne kan
305 Lenger the plesance of min herte hide.
If that thow vouchesauf, whatso bitide,
Thy doghter wol I take, er that I wende,
As for my wif, unto my lives ende.

'Thow lovest me, I woot it wel, certein,
310 And art my feithful lige man ybore,
And al that liketh me, I dar wel seyn,
It liketh thee, and specially therfore,

288 **thresshfold** threshold   292 **gan to falle** fell   293 **sad** serious   **stille** in
silence   295 **thoghtful** pensive   298 **cheere** manner   300 **lette** delay
301 **fette** fetched   305 **Lenger** longer   306 **vouchesauf** agree
310 **lige man** vassal   **ybore** born

Tel me that point that I have seid bifore –
If that thow wolt unto that purpos drawe,
To take me as for thy sone-in-lawe.'   315

The sodein cas this man astoneyd so
That reed he wax, abaist, and al quaking
He stood; unnethe seide he wordes mo
But oonly thus: 'Lord,' quod he, 'my willing
Is as ye wole, ne ayeins youre liking   320
I wol nothing; ye be my lorde so deere.
Right as yow list governeth this matere.'

'Yet wol I', quod this markis softely,
'That in thy chambre I and thow and she
Have a collacioun; and wostow why?   325
For I wol aske if it hir wille be
To be my wif and rule hire after me.
And al this shal be doon in thy presence;
I wol noght speke out of thin audience.'

And in the chambre whil they were aboute   330
Hir tretis, which as ye shal after heere,
The peple cam unto the hous withoute,
And wondred hem in how honeste manere
And tentifly she kepte hir fader deere.
But outrely Grisildis wondre mighte,   335
For nevere erst ne saw she swich a sighte.

314 unto . . . drawe fall in with   316 cas occurrence astoneyd amazed
317 reed he wax he turned red abaist perplexed   318 unnethe hardly
319 willing desire   320 wole wish ayeins against
325 collacioun consultation   327 rule hire after be guided by
329 audience hearing   331 tretis marriage treaty   332 withoute outside
333 wondred hem marvelled how honeste manere what a respectable
manner   334 tentifly attentively   335 outrely in the extreme
336 erst before

No wonder is thogh that she were astoned,
To seen so greet a gest come in that place.
She nevere was to swiche gestes woned,
340   For which she looked with ful pale face.
But shortly forth this matere for to chace,
Thise arn the wordes that the markis saide
To this benigne, verray, feithful maide:

'Grisilde,' he seide, 'ye shal wel understonde
345   It liketh to youre fader and to me
That I yow wedde; and eek it may so stonde,
As I suppose, ye wol that it so be.
But thise demandes aske I first,' quod he,
'That sith it shal be doon in hastif wise,
350   Wol ye assente, or ellis yow avise?

'I sey this, be ye redy with good herte
To al my lust, and that I frely may,
As me best thinketh, do yow laughe or smerte,
And nevere ye to grucche it, night ne day,
355   And eek whan I sey "ye", ne sey nat "nay",
Neither by word ne frowning contenance?
Swere this, and here I swere oure alliance.'

Wondringe upon this word, quaking for drede,
She seide, 'Lord, undigne and unworthy
360   Am I to thilke honour that ye me bede.
But as ye wol yourself, right so wol I.
And heere I swere that nevere willingly
In werk ne thoght I nil yow disobeye,
For to be deed, thogh me were looth to deye.'

337 **astoned** amazed   338 **place** house   339 **woned** accustomed
341 **forth . . . for to chace** to pursue   343 **verray** true   346 **so stonde** be the
case   350 **yow avise** take further thought   352 **lust** pleasure
353 **do yow laughe or smerte** cause you to laugh or feel pain
354 **grucche** grumble at   358 **upon** at   360 **bede** offer   361 **wol** wish
363 **werk** deed   364 Were I to die I for it, though I would be reluctant to die

'This is inogh, Grisilde min,' quod he;   365
And forth he goth with a ful sobre cheere
Out at the dore, and after that cam she,
And to the peple he seide in this manere:
'This is my wif', quod he, 'that standeth heere.
Honureth hire and loveth hire, I preye,   370
Whoso me loveth; ther is namoore to seye.'

And for that nothing of hir olde gere
She sholde bringe into his hous, he bad
That wommen sholde dispoilen hir right there;
Of which thise ladies were noght right glad   375
To handle hir clothes wherinne she was clad.
But nathelees, this maide bright of hewe
Fro foot to heed they clothed han al newe.

Hir heris han they kembd, that laye untressed
Ful rudely, and with hir fingres smale   380
A corone on hir heed they han ydressed,
And sette hire ful of nowches grete and smale.
Of hir array what sholde I make a tale?
Unnethe the peple hir knew for hir fairnesse
Whan she translated was in swich richesse.   385

This markis hath hire spoused with a ring
Broght for the same cause, and thanne hir sette
Upon an hors snow-whit and wel ambling,
And to his paleis, er he lenger lette,

372 **gere** clothes   374 **dispoilen** undress   376 **wherinne** in which
377 **bright of hewe** of radiant complexion   378 **newe** newly
379 **kembd** combed **untressed** loose   380 **rudely** untidily **hir** their
smale slender   381 **hir** her **ydressed** placed   382 **nowches** jewels
383 **what** why   384 **fairnesse** beauty   385 **translated** transformed
388 **wel ambling** gentle-paced   389 **er he lenger lette** without delaying
further

390   With joyful peple that hir ladde and mette,
       Conveyed hire; and thus the day they spende
       In revel, til the sonne gan descende.

       And shortly forth this tale for to chace,
       I seye, that to this newe markisesse
395   God hath swich favour sent hire of his grace
       That it ne semed nat by liklinesse
       That she was born and fed in rudenesse,
       As in a cote or in an oxe-stalle,
       But norissed in an emperoures halle.

400   To every wight she woxen is so deere
       And worshipful, that folk ther she was bore,
       That from hir birthe knewe hire yeer by yeere,
       Unnethe trowed they, but dorste han swore,
       That to Janicle, of which I spak bifore,
405   She doghter were, for as by conjecture
       Hem thoughte she was another creature.

       For thogh that evere vertuous was she,
       She was encressed in swich excellence
       Of thewes goode, yset in heigh bountee,
410   And so discreet and fair of eloquence,
       So benigne and so digne of reverence,
       And koude so the peples herte embrace,
       That ech hir lovede that looked on hir face.

390 **hir ladde and mette** went before her and came to meet her
392 **gan descende** went down   393 **for to chace** to pursue
396 **by liklinesse** according to the probabilities   397 **rudenesse** rusticity
398 **cote** cottage   400 **woxen is** has become   401 **worshipful** deserving of
respect **ther** where   403 **trowed** believed   408 **encressed** improved
409 **thewes goode** good qualities   412 **embrace** have a hold on

Noght oonly of Saluces in the toun
Publissed was the bountee of hir name,   415
But eek biside in many a regioun.
If oon seide wel, another seide the same.
So spradde of hir heighe bountee the fame
That men and wommen, as wel yonge as olde,
Goon to Saluce upon hire to biholde.   420

Thus Walter, lowely – nay, but royally –
Wedded with fortunat honestetee,
In Goddes pees liveth ful esily
At hom, and outward grace inow hadde he.
And for he saugh that under lowe degree   425
Was ofte vertu hid, the peple him helde
A prudent man, and that is seyn ful selde.

Noght oonly this Grisildis thurgh hir wit
Koude al the feet of wifly hoomlinesse,
But eek, whan that the cas required it,   430
The commune profit koude she redresse.
Ther nas discord, rancour, ne hevinesse
In al that land that she ne koude apese,
And wisely bringe hem alle in reste and ese.

Thogh that hir housbond absent were, anon,   435
If gentil men or othere of hir contree
Were wrothe, she wolde bringen hem aton.
So wise and ripe wordes hadde she,
And juggementz of so greet equitee,
That she from hevene sent was, as men wende,   440
Peple to save and every wrong t'amende.

416 **biside** nearby   418 **spradde** spread   422 **fortunat honestetee** honour
that augurs well   424 **inow** plenty of   427 **selde** seldom
429 **Koude** knew **feet** practice, duties **hoomlinesse** domesticity
431 **redresse** restore   432 **nas** was no **hevinesse** sorrow
433 **apese** alleviate   437 **bringen hem aton** reconcile them
438 **ripe** mature   440 **wende** thought

Nat longe time after that this Grisild
Was wedded, she a doghter hath ybore.
Al had hir levere have born a knave child,
445   Glad was the markis and the folk therfore.
For thogh a maide child coome al bifore,
She may unto a knave child atteine
By liklihede, sin she nis nat bareine.

[Part Three]

Ther fil, as it bifalleth times mo,
450   Whan that this child had souked but a throwe,
This markis in his herte longeth so
To tempte his wif, hir sadnesse for to knowe,
That he ne mighte out of his herte throwe
This merveillous desir, his wif t'assaye;
455   Nedelees, God woot, he thoghte hire for t'affraye!

He hadde assayed hire inow bifore,
And fond hire evere good; what neded it
Hir for to tempte, and alwey moore and moore,
Thogh som men preise it for a subtil wit?
460   But as for me, I seye that ivele it sit
T'assaye a wif whan that it is no nede,
And putten hire in angwyssh and in drede.

For which this markis wroghte in this manere:
He cam allone a-night theras she lay,
465   With steerne face, and with ful trouble cheere,
And seide thus: 'Grisilde,' quod he, 'that day

443 **ybore** given birth to   444 **Al had hir levere** although she would rather
447 **unto . . . atteine** succeed in having   448 **bareine** barren
449 **times mo** at other times too   450 **had souked but a throwe** had been
breast-feeding for only a short while   452 **sadnesse** constancy
454 **assaye** make trial of   455 **affraye** harass   456 **inow** enough
457 **fond** found   459 **subtil wit** clever strategy   460 **ivele it sit** it is wrong
461 **it is no nede** there is no need   463 **wroghte** acted
465 **trouble cheere** troubled expression

That I yow took out of youre povre array,
And putte yow in estat of heigh noblesse –
Ye have nat that forgeten, as I gesse?

'I seye, Grisilde, this present dignitee,   470
In which that I have put yow, as I trowe,
Maketh yow nat foryetful for to be
That I yow took in povre estat ful lowe,
For any wele ye mote yourselven knowe.
Tak hede of every word that I yow seye;   475
Ther is no wight that hereth it but we tweye.

'Ye woot yourself wel how that ye cam heere
Into this hous; it is nat longe ago.
And thogh to me that ye be lief and deere,
Unto my gentils ye be nothing so.   480
They seyn, to hem it is greet shame and wo
For to be subgetz and been in servage
To thee, that born art of a smal village.

'And namely sith thy doghter was ybore
Thise wordes han they spoken, doutelees.   485
But I desire, as I have doon bifore,
To live my lif with hem in reste and pees.
I may nat in this cas be recchelees;
I moot doon with thy doghter for the beste,
Nat as I wolde, but as my peple leste.   490

'And yet, God woot, this is ful looth to me.
But nathelees, withouten youre witing
I wol nat doon, but this wol I,' quod he,
'That ye to me assente as in this thing.

468 **noblesse** nobility   471 **trowe** believe   474 As far as concerns any
wealth that you can call your own   480 **gentils** high-born vassals
482 **servage** servitude   484 **namely** especially
488 **recchelees** unresponsive   491 **looth** disagreeable
492 **witing** knowledge

495   Shewe now youre pacience in youre wirking
     That ye me highte and swore in youre village,
     That day that maked was oure mariage.'

     Whan she hadde herd al this, she noght ameved,
     Neither in word or cheere or contenaunce,
500   For, as it semed, she was nat agreved.
     She seide, 'Lord, al lith in youre plesance.
     My child and I, with hertly obeisance,
     Been youres al, and ye mowe save or spille
     Youre owene thing; werketh after youre wille.

505   'Ther may nothing, God so my soule save,
     Liken to yow that may displese me;
     Ne I desire nothing for to have
     Ne drede for to lese, save oonly ye.
     This wil is in min herte and ay shal be;
510   No lengthe of time or deth may this deface,
     Ne chaunge my corage to another place.'

     Glad was this markis of hir answering,
     But yet he feined as he were nat so.
     Al drery was his cheere and his looking
515   Whan that he sholde out of the chambre go.
     Soone after this, a furlong wey or two,
     He prively hath told al his entente
     Unto a man, and to his wif him sente.

     A maner sergeant was this privee man,
520   The which that feithful ofte he founden hadde
     In thinges grete, and eek swich folk wel kan

495 **wirking** behaviour   496 **highte** promised   498 **noght ameved** did not
change   500 **agreved** distressed   501 **lith** lies   502 **hertly** sincere
503 **spille** destroy   504 **after** according to   508 **lese** lose
510 **deface** obliterate   511 **corage** mind   513 **feined** pretended
516 **a furlong wey or two** about five minutes (g.)   517 **prively** secretly
al his entente everything he had in mind   519 **sergeant** serving-man
privee man confidant

Doon execucioun in thinges badde;
The lord knew wel that he him loved and dradde.
And whan this sergeant wiste his lordes wille,
Into the chambre he stalked him ful stille.   525

'Madame,' he seide, 'ye mote foryeve it me,
Thogh I do thing to which I am constreined.
Ye ben so wis that ful wel knowe ye
That lordes hestes mowe nat ben yfeined.
They mowe wel been biwailled or compleined,   530
But men mote nede unto hir lust obeye.
And so wol I; ther is namoore to seye.

'This child I am comaunded for to take.'
– And spak namoore, but out the child he hente
Despitously, and gan a cheere make   535
As thogh he wolde han slain it er he wente.
Grisildis moot al suffren and consente,
And as a lamb she sitteth meke and stille,
And leet this cruel sergeant doon his wille.

Suspecious was the diffame of this man,   540
Suspect his face, suspect his word also,
Suspect the time in which he this bigan.
Allas, hir doghter that she loved so,
She wende he wolde han slawen it right tho!
But nathelees, she neither weep ne siked,   545
Conforminge hire to that the markis liked.

523 **dradde** feared   525 **stalked him** stole **stille** quietly
529 **hestes** commands **yfeined** evaded   531 **lust** will   535 Cruelly, and
made a gesture   537 **moot** has to   540 **diffame** reputation
541 **Suspect** suspicious   544 **wende** believed **slawen** slain **right tho** at that
very minute   545 **weep** wept **siked** sighed   546 Acquiescing in what
pleased the marquis

But at the laste to speken she bigan,
And mekely she to the sergeant preyde,
So as he was a worthy gentil man,
550   That she moste kisse hir child er that it deide.
And in hir barm this litel child she leide
With ful sad face, and gan the child to blisse,
And lulled it, and after gan it kisse.

And thus she seide, in hir benigne vois:
555   'Farewel, my child! I shal thee nevere see.
But sith I thee have marked with the crois
Of thilke fader – blessed mote he be –
That for us deide upon a crois of tree,
Thy soule, litel child, I him bitake,
560   For this night shaltow dien for my sake.'

I trowe that to a norice in this cas
It hadde been hard this routhe for to se;
Wel mighte a moder than han cryd 'allas!'
But nathelees, so sad stedefast was she
565   That she endured al adversitee;
And to the sergeant mekely she saide,
'Have here again youre litel yonge maide.

'Goth now,' quod she, 'and doth my lordes heste.
But o thing wol I pray yow, of youre grace,
570   That, but my lord forbad yow, at the leste
Burieth this litel body in som place
That bestes ne no briddes it to-race.'
But he no word wol to that purpos seye,
But took the child and wente upon his weye.

---

550 **moste** might   551 **barm** lap   552 **sad** unshaken   **gan . . . blisse** made
the sign of the cross over   558 **tree** wood   559 **bitake** entrust
561 **norice** nurse   562 **routhe** pitiful sight   564 **sad** constantly
570 **but** unless   572 **to-race** tear in pieces

This sergeant cam unto his lord again,   575
And of Grisildis wordes and hir cheere
He tolde him, point for point, in short and plain,
And him presenteth with his doghter deere.
Somwhat this lord hadde routhe in his manere,
But nathelees his purpos held he stille,   580
As lordes doon whan they wol han hir wille.

And bad this sergeant that he prively
Sholde this child softe winde and wrappe,
With alle circumstances tendrely,
And carye it in a cofre or in a lappe –   585
But, upon peine his heed of for to swappe,
That no man sholde knowe of his entente,
Ne whennes he cam, ne whider that he wente –

But at Boloigne, to his suster deere,
That thilke time of Panik was countesse,   590
He sholde it take and shewe hire this matere,
Bisekinge hire to doon hir bisinesse
This child to fostre in al gentilesse.
And whos child that it was, he bad hire hide
From every wight, for aught that may bitide.   595

The sergeant goth, and hath fulfild this thing;
But to this markis now retourne we.
For now goth he ful faste imagining
If by his wives cheere he mighte se,
Or by hir word aperceive, that she   600
Were chaunged; but he nevere hir koude finde
But evere in oon ilike sad and kinde.

576 **cheere** behaviour   577 **point for point** every detail   579 **routhe** pity
583 **softe winde** wrap up gently   584 **With alle circumstances** with every
care   585 **cofre** cradle **lappe** fold of a garment   586 **swappe** strike
588 **whennes** whence   591 **shewe** explain   592 **doon hir bisinesse** do her
best   593 **in al gentilesse** in a manner suited to noble birth
598 **imagining** wondering   602 **evere in oon ilike sad** always unvaryingly
steadfast

As glad, as humble, as bisy in servise,
And eek in love, as she was wont to be,
605   Was she to him in every maner wise.
Ne of hir doghter noght a word spak she.
Noon accident for noon adversitee
Was seyn in hire, ne nevere hir doghter name
Ne nempned she, in ernest ne in game.

[Part Four]

610   In this estat ther passed ben foure yeer
Er she with childe was, but, as God wolde,
A knave child she bar by this Walter,
Ful gracious and fair for to biholde.
And whan that folk it to his fader tolde,
615   Nat oonly he, but al his contree merye
Was for this child, and God they thanke and herie.

Whan it was two yeer old, and fro the brest
Departed of his norice, on a day
This markis caughte yet another lest
620   To tempte his wif yet ofter, if he may.
O nedelees was she tempted in assay!
But wedded men ne knowe no mesure
Whan that they finde a pacient creature.

'Wif,' quod this markis, 'ye han herd er this
625   My peple sikly berth oure mariage;
And namely sith my sone yboren is,
Now is it worse than evere in al oure age.

604 **wont** accustomed   607 **accident** outward sign
608 **doghter name** daughter's name   609 **nempned** named **game** play
613 **gracious** beautiful   616 **herie** praise   618 **Departed** weaned
619 **lest** whim, fancy   620 **yet ofter** even more often   621 **assay** trial
622 **mesure** moderation   625 **sikly berth** resent   627 **age** life

The murmur sleeth min herte and my corage,
For to min eris comth the vois so smerte
That it wel neigh destroyed hath min herte.   630

'Now sey they thus: "Whan Walter is agon,
Thanne shal the blood of Janicle succede
And been oure lord, for oother have we noon."
Swiche wordes seyth my peple, out of drede.
Wel oghte I of swich murmur taken hede,   635
For certeinly I drede swich sentence,
Though they nat plein speke in min audience.

'I wolde live in pees, if that I mighte.
Wherfore I am disposed outrely,
As I his suster servede by nighte,   640
Right so thenke I to serve him prively.
This warne I yow, that ye nat sodeinly
Out of yourself for no wo sholde outraye;
Beth pacient, and therof I yow praye.'

'I have', quod she, 'seid thus, and evere shal: 645
I wol no thing, ne nil no thing, certein,
But as yow list; noght greveth me at al
Thogh that my doghter and my sone be slein –
At youre comandement, this is to seyn.
I have nat had no part of children tweine   650
But first, siknesse, and after, wo and peine.

'Ye ben oure lord; dooth with youre owene thing
Right as yow list; axeth no reed of me.
For as I lefte at hom al my clothing,
Whan I first cam to yow, right so,' quod she,   655

628 **sleeth** destroys **corage** spirit   629 **vois** rumour **smerte** painfully
634 **out of drede** without a doubt   636 **sentence** opinion
637 **audience** hearing   639 **disposed outrely** fully resolved
640 **servede** dealt with   643 **Out of yourself . . . outraye** lose control of
yourself   647 **noght greveth me** it does not displease me
650 **had no part of** had no share in **tweine** two   653 **reed** advice

'Lefte I my wil and al my libertee,
And took youre clothing. Wherfore I yow preye,
Dooth youre plesance; I wol youre lust obeye.

'And certes if I hadde prescience
660 Youre wil to knowe er ye youre lust me tolde,
I wolde it doon withouten necligence.
But now I woot youre lust and what ye wolde,
Al youre plesance ferme and stable I holde.
For wiste I that my deeth wolde doon yow ese,
665 Right gladly wolde I dien, yow to plese.

'Deeth may nat make no comparisoun
Unto youre love.' And whan this markis say
The constance of his wif, he caste adoun
His eyen two, and wondreth that she may
670 In pacience suffre al this array.
And forth he goth with drery contenance,
But to his herte it was ful gret plesance.

This ugly sergeant, in the same wise
That he hir doghter caughte, right so he –
675 Or worse, if men worse kan devise –
Hath hent hir sone that ful was of beautee.
And evere in oon so pacient was she,
That she no cheere made of hevinesse,
But kiste hir sone, and after gan it blesse.

680 Save this: she preyede him that if he mighte
Hir litel sone he wolde in erthe grave,
His tendre limes, delicat to sighte,

658 lust desire, will   659 prescience foreknowledge   663 I comply
unswervingly with everything that pleases you   664 wiste I if I knew
667 say saw   670 suffre endure   array treatment   675 devise imagine
676 hent taken   678 cheere appearance   hevinesse sorrow
679 gan it blesse made the sign of the cross over it   681 grave bury
682 delicat delightful

Fro foweles and fro bestes for to save.
But she noon answere of him mighte have;
He wente his wey as him nothing ne roghte.   685
But to Boloigne he tendrely it broghte.

This markis wondreth, ever lenger the moore,
Upon hir pacience, and if that he
Ne hadde soothly knowen therbifoore
That parfitly hir children loved she,   690
He wolde have wend that of som subtiltee,
And of malice, or of cruel corage,
That she hadde suffred this with sad visage.

But wel he knew that next himself, certain,
She loved hir children best in every wise.   695
But now of wommen wolde I asken fain
If thise assayes mighte nat suffise?
What koude a sturdy housbond moore devise
To preve hir wifhod and hir stedfastnesse,
And he continuinge evere in sturdinesse?   700

But ther ben folk of swich condicioun,
That whan they have a certein purpos take,
They kan nat stinte of hir entencioun,
But right as they were bounden to a stake,
They wol nat of that firste purpos slake.   705
Right so, this markis fulliche hath purposed
To tempte his wif, as he was first disposed.

He waiteth if by word or contenance
That she to him was chaunged of corage.
But nevere koude he finde variance;   710

---

683 **foweles** birds   685 **as him nothing ne roghte** as if he did not care (about it)   690 **parfitly** whole-heartedly   691 **wend** believed   **subtiltee** treachery
693 **sad visage** unmoved expression   696 **fain** gladly   698 **sturdy** harsh
700 **sturdinesse** sternness   703 **stinte of** leave off   705 **of ... slake** desist
from   706 **fulliche** fully   708 **waiteth** watches to see   709 **of corage** in
spirit

She was ay oon in herte and in visage.
And ay the ferther that she was in age,
The moore trewe, if that it were possible,
She was to him in love, and moore penible.

715   For which it semed thus, that of hem two
Ther nas but o wil, for as Walter leste,
The same lust was hir plesance also.
And, God be thanked, al fil for the beste.
She shewed wel, for no worldly unreste
720   A wif, as of hirself, nothing ne sholde
Wille in effect, but as hir housbond wolde.

The sclaundre of Walter ofte and wide spradde,
That of a cruel herte he wikkedly,
For he a povre womman wedded hadde,
725   Hath mordred bothe his children prively.
Swich murmur was among hem comunly.
No wonder is, for to the peples ere
Ther cam no word, but that they mordred were.

For which, wheras his peple therbifore
730   Hadde loved him wel, the sclaundre of his diffame
Made hem that they hated him therfore.
To ben a mordrere is an hateful name;
But nathelees, for ernest ne for game,
He of his cruel purpos nolde stente;
735   To tempte his wif was set al his entente.

711 **ay oon** always the same   714 **penible** devoted   716 There was only
one will, for what Walter desired   718 **fil** turned out
719 **for no worldly unreste** in spite of any worldly vexation
721 **in effect** in substance   722 **sclaundre** evil report **spradde** spread
724 **For** because   727 **ere** ear   730 **diffame** disgrace
732 **mordrere** murderer   733 **for ernest ne for game** on no account
734 **of . . . stente** desist from   735 His mind was completely set on tempting
his wife

Whan that his doghter twelve yeer was of age,
He to the court of Rome, in subtil wise
Enformed of his wil, sente his message,
Comaundinge hem swiche bulles to devise
As to his cruel purpos may suffise: 740
How that the Pope, as for his peples reste,
Bad him to wedde another, if him leste.

I seye, he bad they sholde contrefete
The Popes bulles, making mencioun
That he hath leve his firste wif to lete,   745
As by the Popes dispensacioun,
To stinte rancour and dissencioun
Bitwixe his peple and him; thus seide the bulle,
The which they han publissed at the fulle.

The rude peple, as it no wonder is,   750
Wenden ful wel that it hadde ben right so.
But whan thise tidinges cam to Grisildis,
I deme that hir herte was ful wo,
But she, ilike sad for everemo,
Disposed was, this humble creature,   755
Th'adversitee of Fortune al t'endure,

Abidinge evere his lust and his plesance
To whom that she was yeven, herte and al,
As to hir verray worldly suffisance.
But shortly if this storye telle I shal,   760
This markis writen hath in special
A lettre in which he sheweth his entente,
And secrely he to Boloigne it sente.

737 **subtil** secret   738 **message** messenger   739 **bulles** papal
documents (n.)   743 **contrefete** forge   745 **lete** leave   747 **stinte** put an
end to   749 **publissed** made public   750 **rude** common   **no wonder** not
surprising   751 **Wenden** believed   753 **deme** think   **wo** sorrowful
754 **ilike sad** unvaryingly steadfast   757 **Abidinge** awaiting   759 As her
true source of contentment in this world   761 **in special** particularly
762 **sheweth** explains

To the Erl of Panik, which that hadde tho
765 Wedded his suster, preyde he specially
To bringen hom again his children two,
In honurable estat al openly.
But o thing he him prayede outrely,
That he to no wight, thogh men wolde enquere,
770 Sholde nat telle whos children that they were,

But seye the maiden sholde ywedded be
Unto the Markis of Saluce anon.
And as this erl was preyed, so dide he,
For at day set he on his wey is gon
775 Toward Saluce, and lordes many oon
In riche array, this maiden for to gide,
Hir yonge brother riding hir biside.

Arrayed was toward hir mariage
This fresshe maide, ful of gemmes clere.
780 Hir brother, which that seven yeer was of age,
Arrayed eek ful fressh in his manere.
And thus in gret noblesse and with glad cheere,
Toward Saluces shaping hir journey,
Fro day to day they riden in hir wey.

[Part Five]

785 Among al this, after his wikke usage,
This markis, yet his wif to tempte moore
To the outreste preve of hir corage,
Fully to han experience and loore

765 **preyde** requested   774 **at day set** on the appointed day
776 **riche array** splendid finery   778 **Arrayed** adorned **toward** in
preparation for   779 **clere** glittering   782 **cheere** demeanour
783 **shaping** directing   785 **Among al this** meanwhile **after** according to
787 **outreste preve** ultimate test   788 **experience** demonstration, proof
loore knowledge

If that she were as stedefast as bifore,
He on a day in open audience   790
Ful boistously hath seid hire this sentence:

'Certes, Grisilde, I hadde inogh plesance
To han yow to my wif for youre goodnesse,
As for youre trouthe and youre obeisance –
Noght for youre linage ne for youre richesse.   795
But now knowe I in verray sothfastnesse
That in gret lordshipe, if I wel avise,
Ther is gret servitute in sondry wise.

'I may nat do as every plowman may;
My peple me constreineth for to take   800
Another wif, and cryen day by day.
And eek the Pope, rancour for to slake
Consenteth it, that dar I undertake.
And trewely, thus muche I wol yow seye:
My newe wif is cominge by the weye.   805

'Be strong of herte, and voide anon hir place.
And thilke dowere that ye broghten me,
Tak it again; I graunte it of my grace.
Retourneth to youre fadres hous,' quod he.
'No man may alwey han prosperitee;   810
With evene herte I rede yow t'endure
The strook of Fortune or of aventure.'

And she again answerde in pacience:
'My lord,' quod she, 'I woot, and wiste alway,
How that bitwixen youre magnificence   815
And my poverte no wight kan ne may

791 **boistously** bluntly **sentence** decision   792 **plesance** complaisance
796 **sothfastnesse** truth   797 **avise** consider   801 **cryen** complain
802 **slake** decrease   805 **cominge by the weye** on her way here
806 **voide** vacate   807 **dowere** dowry   811 **evene** calm, steady **rede** advise
812 **aventure** chance

Maken comparisoun, it is no nay.
I ne heeld me nevere digne in no manere
To be youre wif – no, ne youre chambrere.

820   'And in this hous ther ye me lady made –
The heighe God take I for my witnesse,
And also wysly he my soule glade –
I nevere heeld me lady ne maistresse,
But humble servant to youre worthinesse,
825   And evere shal, whil that my lif may dure,
Aboven every worldly creature.

'That ye so longe of youre benignitee
Han holden me in honour and nobleye,
Whereas I was noght worthy for to be,
830   That thonke I God and yow, to whom I preye
Foryelde it yow; ther is namoore to seye.
Unto my fader gladly wol I wende,
And with him dwelle unto my lives ende.

'Ther I was fostred of a child ful smal,
835   Til I be deed my lif ther wol I lede,
A widwe clene in body, herte and al.
For sith I yaf to yow my maidenhede,
And am youre trewe wif, it is no drede,
God shilde swich a lordes wif to take
840   Another man to housbond or to make!

'And of youre newe wif God of his grace
So graunte yow wele and prosperitee;
For I wol gladly yelden hire my place,
In which that I was blisful wont to be.

817 **it is no nay** there is no denying it   818 I never considered myself at all
worthy   819 **chambrere** chambermaid   822 And as surely as he may give
my soul bliss   824 **youre worthinesse** your honour   828 **nobleye** noble
condition   831 **Foryelde it yow** to repay you for it   834 **of a child** from
childhood   837 **maidenhede** virginity   838 **it is no drede** without doubt
839 **shilde** forbid   840 **to make** as spouse   842 **wele** happiness

For sith it liketh yow, my lord,' quod she,   845
'That whilom weren al min hertes reste,
That I shal goon, I wol goon whan yow leste.

'But theras ye me profre swich dowaire
As I first broghte, it is wel in my minde
It were my wrecched clothes, nothing faire,   850
The whiche to me were hard now for to finde.
O goode God, how gentil and how kinde
Ye semed, by youre speche and youre visage,
The day that maked was oure mariage!

'But sooth is seid – algate I finde it trewe,   855
For in effect it proved is on me –
Love is noght old as whan that it is newe.
But certes, lord, for noon adversitee,
To dien in the cas, it shal nat be
That evere in word or werk I shal repente   860
That I yow yaf min herte in hool entente.

'My lord, ye woot that in my fadres place
Ye dide me strepe out of my povre wede,
And richely me cladden of youre grace.
To yow broght I noght ellis, out of drede,   865
But feith, and nakednesse, and maidenhede.
And here again youre clothing I restore,
And eek youre wedding ring for everemoore.

---

846 **whilom** once   848 In so far as you offer me such dowry
855 **sooth is seid** it is said with truth   **algate** at any rate   856 **on me** in my
case   858 **for noon adversitee** in spite of any adversity
859 **To dien in the cas** though death were the result
861 **in hool entente** wholeheartedly   862 **place** house
863 **Ye dide me strepe** you had me undressed   **wede** garment
864 **cladden** clothed   867 **restore** give back

'The remenant of youre jewels redy be
870   Inwith youre chambre, dar I saufly sayn.
Naked out of my fadres hous', quod she,
'I cam, and naked moot I turne again.
Al youre plesance wol I folwen fain.
But yet I hope it be nat youre entente
875   That I smoklees out of youre paleis wente.

'Ye koude nat doon so dishoneste a thing
That thilke wombe in which youre children leye
Sholde biforn the peple in my walking
Be seyn al bare; wherfore I yow preye,
880   Lat me nat lik a worm go by the weye.
Remembre yow, min owene lord so deere,
I was youre wif, thogh I unworthy weere.

'Wherfore in gerdoun of my maidenhede,
Which that I broghte, and noght again I bere,
885   As vouchethsauf to yeve me to my mede
But swich a smok as I was wont to were,
That I therwith may wrye the wombe of here
That was youre wif; and here take I my leve
Of yow, min owene lord, lest I yow greve.'

890   'The smok', quod he, 'that thow hast on thy bak,
Lat it be stille, and bere it forth with thee.'
But wel unnethes thilke word he spak,
But wente his wey, for routhe and for pitee.
Biforn the folk hirselven strepeth she,
895   And in hir smok, with heed and foot al bare,
Toward hir fader hous forth is she fare.

---

870 **Inwith** within **saufly** confidently   873 **fain** gladly
875 **smoklees** without a smock   876 **dishoneste** shameful   879 **seyn** seen
883 **in gerdoun of** as recompense for   884 **noght again I bere** I don't carry
back   885 **As vouchethsauf** grant **mede** recompense   886 **were** wear
887 **wrye** cover   892 **unnethes** with difficulty   896 **is she fare** she went

The folk hir folwen, wepinge in hir weye,
And Fortune ay they cursen as they goon.
But she fro weping kepte hir eyen dreye,
Ne in this time word ne spak she noon.   900
Hir fader, that this tidinge herd anon,
Curseth the day and time that Nature
Shoop him to been a lives creature.

For out of doute this olde povre man
Was evere in suspect of hir mariage.   905
For evere he demed, sith that it bigan,
That whan the lord fulfild hadde his corage
Him wolde thinke it were a disparage
To his estat so lowe for t'alighte,
And voiden hire as soone as evere he mighte.   910

Agains his doghter hastiliche goth he,
For he by noise of folk knew hir cominge.
And with hir olde cote, as it mighte be,
He covered hire, ful sorwefully wepinge.
But on hir body mighte he it nat bringe,   915
For rude was the clooth, and she moore of age
By dayes fele than at hir mariage.

Thus with hir fader, for a certein space,
Dwelleth this flour of wifly pacience,
That neither by hir wordes ne hir face   920
Biforn the folk, ne eek in hir absence,
Ne shewed she that hir was doon offence;
Ne of hir heighe estat no remembrance
Ne hadde she, as by hir contenance.

903 **Shoop** created **lives** living   904 **out of doute** without doubt
905 **Was evere in suspect of** was always suspicious of   907–8 That when
the lord had accomplished his desire, it would seem to him a dishonour
909 **alighte** descend   910 **voiden** send away   911 **Agains** to meet
913 **cote** tunic   916 **rude** coarse **moore of age** of greater age
917 **fele** many   922 **hir was doon offence** injury had been done to her
924 **contenance** behaviour

925 No wonder is, for in hir grete estat
Hir goost was evere in plein humilitee;
No tendre mouth, noon herte delicat,
No pompe, no semblant of realtee,
But ful of pacient benignitee,
930 Discreet and pridelees, ay honurable,
And to hir housbonde evere meke and stable.

Men speke of Job, and moost for his humblesse,
As clerkes whan hem lest kan wel endite,
Namely of men, but as in soothfastnesse,
935 Thogh clerkes preise wommen but a lite,
Ther kan no man in humblesse him acquite
As womman kan, ne kan be half so trewe
As wommen been, but it be falle of newe.

Fro Boloigne is this Erl of Panik come,
940 Of which the fame up sprong to moore and lesse;
And to the peples eres, alle and some,
Was kouth eek that a newe markisesse
He with him broghte, in swich pompe and richesse
That nevere was ther seyn with mannes eye
945 So noble array in al West Lumbardye.

The markis, which that shoop and knew al this,
Er that this erl was come sente his message
For thilke sely povre Grisildis,
And she with humble herte and glad visage,

926 **goost** spirit   927 **delicat** voluptuous   928 **semblant of realtee** display
of magnificence   930 **pridelees** without pride   933 **endite** write
934 **soothfastnesse** truth   935 **but a lite** very little
936 **him acquite** behave   938 **but it be falle of newe** unless it is of recent
occurrence   940 **fame up sprong** news spread abroad
941 **alle and some** one and all   942 **kouth** made known   944 **seyn** seen
946 **shoop** devised   948 **sely** innocent

Nat with no swollen thoght in hir corage,   950
Cam at his heste, and on hir knees hir sette,
And reverently and wisely she him grette.

'Grisilde,' quod he, 'my wille is outrely
This maiden, that shal wedded been to me,
Received be tomorwe as really   955
As it possible is in min hous to be;
And eek that every wight in his degree
Have his estat, in sitting and servise
And heigh plesance, as I kan best devise.

'I have no wommen suffisant, certain,   960
The chambres for t'arraye in ordinance
After my lust, and therfore wolde I fain
That thin were al swich manere governance.
Thow knowest eek of old al my plesance.
Though thin array be badde and ivel biseye,   965
Do thow thy devoir, at the leeste weye.'

'Nat oonly, lord, that I am glad', quod she,
'To doon youre lust, but I desire also
Yow for to serve and plese in my degree,
Withouten feinting, and shal everemo.   970
Ne nevere, for no wele ne no wo,
Ne shal the goost withinne min herte stente
To love yow best, with al my trewe entente.'

950 **swollen** puffed-up   952 **grette** (= *gretede*) greeted
953 **outrely** entirely   955 **really** royally   958 **Have his estat** should be
treated according to his rank   **sitting** seating, place at table
959 **devise** contrive   960 **suffisant** capable   961 **arraye in ordinance** put in
order   962 **After my lust** according to my wishes   963 That every
arrangement of this sort was in your hands   965 **ivel biseye** of poor
appearance   966 **Do thow thy devoir** do your best
969 **in my degree** according to my social station   970 **feinting** flagging
971 **no wele ne no wo** any joy or sorrow   972 **stente** cease

And with that word she gan the hous to dighte,
975   And tables for to sette and beddes make,
And peined hire to doon al that she mighte,
Preyinge the chambreres, for Goddes sake,
To hasten hem, and faste swepe and shake.
And she, the mooste servisable of alle,
980   Hath every chambre arrayed and his halle.

Abouten undren gan this erl alighte,
That with him broghte thise noble children tweye,
For which the peple ran to seen the sighte
Of hire array, so richely biseye.
985   And thanne at erst amonges hem they seye
That Walter was no fool, thogh that him leste
To chaunge his wif, for it was for the beste.

For she is fairer, as they demen alle,
Than is Grisilde, and moore tendre of age,
990   And fairer fruit bitwene hem sholde falle,
And moore plesant, for hire heigh linage.
Hir brother eek so fair was of visage
That hem to seen the peple hath caught plesance,
Commendinge now the markis governance.

995   O stormy peple, unsad and evere untrewe,
Ay undiscreet and chaunginge as a vane,
Delitinge evere in rumbul that is newe,
For lik the moone ay wexe ye and wane!

---

974 **dighte** get ready   976 **peined hire** made an effort
977 **chambreres** chambermaids   978 **faste** busily   979 **servisable** willing to
serve   981 **undren** mid-morning (g.) **gan . . . alighte** dismounted
984 **richely biseye** of splendid appearance   985 **at erst** for the first time
986 **him leste** it pleased him   994 **governance** conduct
995 **unsad** unstable   996 **undiscreet** undiscerning **vane** weather-vane
997 **rumbul** rumour   998 **wexe** wax

Ay ful of clapping, deere inow a jane!
Youre doom is fals, youre constance ivele   1000
    preveth;
A ful greet fool is he that on yow leveth.

– Thus seiden sadde folk in that citee,
Whan that the peple gazed up and doun,
For they were glad, right for the noveltee,
To han a newe lady of hir toun.   1005
Namoore of this make I now mencioun,
But to Grisilde again wol I me dresse,
And telle hir constance and hir bisinesse.

Ful bisy was Grisilde in everything
That to the feste was apertinent.   1010
Right noght was she abaist of hir clothing,
Thogh it were rude, and somdel eek to-rent,
But with glad cheere to the yate is went
With oother folk, to greete the markisesse,
And after that dooth forth hir bisinesse.   1015

With so glad cheere his gestes she receiveth,
And so konningly, everich in his degree,
That no defaute no man aperceiveth.
But ay they wondren what she mighte be
That in so povre array was for to se,   1020
And koude swich honour and reverence,
And worthily they preisen hir prudence.

---

999 **clapping** noisy chatter **deere inow a jane** not worth a halfpenny
1000 **doom** judgement **ivele preveth** is found wanting
1001 **on . . . leveth** trusts in   1002 **sadde** serious   1004 **noveltee** novelty
1007 **me dresse** turn   1008 **bisinesse** diligence
1010 **apertinent** appropriate   1011 **abaist of** embarrassed by
1012 **rude** coarse **somdel** partly **to-rent** torn   1013 **yate** gate **is went** went
1015 **dooth forth hir bisinesse** continues to perform her tasks
1017 **konningly** skilfully   1021 **koude** was capable of

In al this mene-while she ne stente
This maide and eek hir brother to commende
1025   With al hir herte, in ful benigne entente,
So wel that no man koude hir pris amende.
But at the laste, whan that thise lordes wende
To sitten doun to mete, he gan to calle
Grisilde, as she was bisy in his halle.

1030   'Grisilde,' quod he, as it were in his pley,
'How liketh thee my wif and hir beautee?'
'Right wel,' quod she, 'my lord, for, in good fey,
A fairer saw I nevere noon than she.
I prey to God yeve hire prosperitee;
1035   And so hope I that he wol to yow sende
Plesance inogh, unto youre lives ende.

'O thing biseke I yow, and warne also,
That ye ne prike with no tormentinge
This tendre maiden, as ye han don mo;
1040   For she is fostred in hir norissinge
Moore tendrely, and to my supposinge,
She koude nat adversitee endure
As koude a povre fostred creature.'

And whan this Walter saw hir pacience,
1045   Hir glade cheere, and no malice at al,
And he so ofte had doon to hire offence,
And she ay sad and constant as a wal,
Continuinge evere hir innocence overal,
This sturdy markis gan his herte dresse
1050   To rewen upon hir wifly stedfastnesse.

1023 stente ceased   1026 hir pris amende improve on her praise
1030 in his pley jokingly   1036 Plesance inogh an abundance of pleasure
1037 biseke entreat   1038 prike goad   1039 mo others
1040 norissinge upbringing   1041 to my supposinge as I believe
1043 povre poorly   1045 cheere expression   1047 sad steadfast
1048 Continuinge maintaining   1049 sturdy stern gan . . . dresse disposed
1050 rewen take pity

'This is inogh, Grisilde min,' quod he;
'Be now namoore agast ne ivele apaied.
I have thy feith and thy benignitee,
As wel as evere womman was, assayed,
In greet estat, and povreliche arrayed.   1055
Now knowe I, deere wif, thy stedfastnesse!'
And hire in armes took and gan hir kesse.

And she for wonder took of it no keep;
She herde nat what thing he to hir seide.
She ferde as she hadde stirt out of a sleep,   1060
Til she out of hir mazednesse abreide.
'Grisilde,' quod he, 'by God that for us deide,
Thow art my wif, ne noon oother I have,
Ne nevere hadde, as God my soule save!

'This is thy doghter, which thow hast supposed   1065
To be my wif; that oother, feithfully,
Shal be min heir, as I have ay disposed;
Thow bare him in thy body, trewely.
At Boloigne have I kept hem prively;
Tak hem again, for now maystow nat seye   1070
That thow hast lorn noon of thy children tweye.

'And folk that ootherweys han seid of me,
I warne hem wel, that I have doon this dede
For no malice, ne for no crueltee,
But for t'assaye in thee thy wommanhede,   1075
And nat to sleen my children – God forbede! –
But for to kepe hem prively and stille,
Til I thy purpos knewe and al thy wille.'

1052 **agast** afraid **ivele apaied** dissatisfied   1057 **gan . . . kesse** kissed
1058 And she, for amazement, did not take it in   1060 **ferde** behaved
stirt (= *stirted*) started   1061 **mazednesse** bewilderment **abreide** recovered
1067 **disposed** intended   1071 **lorn** lost   1072 **ootherweys** otherwise
1076 **sleen** kill   1077 **stille** secretly

Whan she this herde, aswowne doun she falleth
1080   For pitous joye, and after hir swowninge,
She bothe hir yonge children to hire calleth,
And in hir armes, pitously wepinge,
Embraceth hem, and tendrely kissinge,
Ful lik a moder, with hir salte teres
1085   She batheth bothe hir visage and hir heres.

O, which a pitous thing it was to se
Hir swowning and hir humble vois to heere!
'*Graunt mercy*, lord, God thanke it yow,' quod she,
'That ye han saved me my children deere!
1090   Now rekke I nevere to been ded right heere;
Sith I stonde in youre love and in youre grace,
No fors of deeth, ne whan my spirit pace.

'O tendre, o deere, o yonge children mine,
Youre woful moder wende stedfastly
1095   That cruel houndes, or som foul vermine,
Hadde eten yow; but God, of his mercy,
And youre benigne fader tendrely
Hath doon yow kept!' – and in that same stounde
Al sodeinly she swapte adoun to grounde.

1100   And in hir swough so sadly holdeth she
Hir children two, whan she gan hem t'embrace,
That with greet sleighte and greet difficultee
The children from hir arm they gonne arace.
O, many a teer on many a pitous face
1105   Doun ran of hem that stoden hir biside;
Unnethe aboute hire mighte they abide.

1079 **aswowne** in a swoon   1085 **hir** their **heres** hair   1086 **which** what
1089 **saved** preserved   1090 **rekke** care   1092 **No fors** no matter
pace may depart   1098 **doon yow kept** caused you to be preserved
stounde moment   1099 **swapte** dropped   1100 **swough** swoon
sadly firmly, tightly   1102 **sleighte** ingenuity   1103 **gonne arace** prised
loose   1106 **Unnethe** with difficulty **abide** remain

Walter hir gladeth, and hir sorwe slaketh;
She riseth up, abaised, from hir traunce,
And every wight hir joye and feste maketh,
Til she hath caught again hir contenaunce.   1110
Walter hir dooth so feithfully plesaunce
That it was deintee for to seen the cheere
Bitwix hem two, now they ben met ifeere.

Thise ladies, whan that they hir time say,
Han taken hire and into chambre goon,   1115
And strepen hire out of hir rude array,
And in a clooth of gold that brighte shoon,
With a coroune of many a riche stoon
Upon hir heed, they into halle hir broghte,
And ther she was honured as hir oghte.   1120

Thus hath this pitous day a blisful ende,
For every man and womman dooth his might
This day in murthe and revel to dispende,
Til on the welkne shoon the sterres light.
For moore solempne in every mannes sight   1125
This feste was, and gretter of costage,
Than was the revel of hir mariage.

Ful many a yeer in heigh prosperitee
Liven this two, in concord and in reste,
And richely his doghter maried he   1130
Unto a lord, oon of the worthieste
Of al Itaille; and thanne in pees and reste
His wives fader in his court he kepeth,
Til that the soule out of his body crepeth.

1107 **hir gladeth** comforts her **slaketh** relieves   1108 **abaised** confused
1109 **hir joye and feste maketh** makes much of her
1110 **caught again hir contenaunce** recovered her composure
1111 **dooth . . . plesaunce** attends to   1112 **cheere** happiness
1113 **ifeere** together   1114 **hir** their **say** saw   1116 **rude** coarse
1123 **murthe** merriment **dispende** pass   1124 **welkne** sky
1125 **solempne** sumptuous   1126 **costage** expense   1130 **richely** splendidly

1135   His sone succedeth in his heritage
        In reste and pees, after his fader day,
        And fortunat was eek in mariage –
        Al putte he nat his wif in gret assay.
        This world is nat so strong, it is no nay,
1140   As it hath been in olde times yore.
        And herkneth what this auctour seyth therfore:

        This storye is seid, nat for that wives sholde
        Folwen Grisilde as in humilitee,
        For it were inportable, thogh they wolde;
1145   But for that every wight, in his degree,
        Sholde be constant in adversitee
        As was Grisilde – therfore Petrak writeth
        This storye, which with heigh style he enditeth.

        For, sith a womman was so pacient
1150   Unto a mortal man, wel moore us oghte
        Receiven al in gree that God us sent.
        For greet skile is, he preve that he wroghte;
        But he ne tempteth no man that he boghte,
        As seyth Seint Jame, if ye his pistel rede.
1155   He preveth folk alday, it is no drede,

        And suffreth us, as for oure excercise,
        With sharpe scourges of adversitee
        Ful ofte to be bete in sondry wise;
        Nat for to knowe oure wil, for certes he,

1135 **heritage** inheritance   1136 **fader** father's   1138 **Al** although
1140 **olde times yore** times gone by   1144 **inportable** unendurable
1148 **enditeth** writes   1151 **Receiven . . . in gree** accept willingly
sent (= *sendeth*) sends   1152 For it is very reasonable that he should test
what he created   1153 **boghte** redeemed   1154 **pistel** Epistle
1155 **alday** constantly **drede** doubt   1156 **suffreth** allows
excercise training

Er we were born, knew al oure freletee.   1160
And for oure beste is al his governance;
Lat us thanne live in vertuous suffrance.

But o word, lordinges, herkneth, er I go:
It were ful hard to finde nowadayes
In al a toun Grisildis thre or two;   1165
For, if that they were put to swiche assayes,
The gold of hem hath now so badde alayes
With bras, that thogh the coine be fair at eye,
It wolde rather breste atwo than plye.

For which heere, for the Wives love of Bathe –   1170
Whos lif and al hir secte God maintene
In heigh maistrye, and elles were it scathe –
I wol with lusty herte, fressh and grene,
Seye yow a song, to glade yow, I wene;
And lat us stinte of ernestful matere.   1175
Herkneth my song, that seyth in this manere:

L'envoy de Chaucer.

Grisilde is deed, and eek hir pacience,
And bothe atones buried in Itaille.
For which I crye in open audience,
No wedded man so hardy be t'assaille   1180
His wives pacience, in trust to finde
Grisildis, for in certein he shal faille.

1160 **freletee** frailty   1161 **governance** government
1162 **suffrance** forbearance   1164 **were** would be
1166 **put to swiche assayes** put to the trial in this way   1167 **alayes** alloys
1168 **at eye** to the eye   1169 **breste atwo** break in two   **plye** bend
1170 **for the Wives love of Bathe** for love of the Wife of Bath
1171 **secte** sex   1172 **maistrye** dominance   **scathe** a pity
1174 **glade yow** make you glad   1175 **stinte of** cease to speak of
ernestful serious   1176 *L'envoy* the epilogue   1178 **atones** together
1179 **in open audience** publicly   1180 **hardy** rash

O noble wives, ful of heigh prudence,
Lat noon humilitee youre tonge naile!
1185   Ne lat no clerk have cause or diligence
To write of yow a storye of swich mervaille
As of Grisildis, pacient and kinde,
Lest Chichevache yow swelwe in hir entraille!

Folweth Ekko, that holdeth no silence,
1190   But evere answereth at the countretaille.
Beth nat bidaffed for youre innocence,
But sharply tak on yow the governaille.
Emprenteth wel this lessoun in youre minde,
For commune profit sith it may availle.

1195   Ye archewives, stondeth at defense,
Sin ye be strong as is a greet camaille;
Ne suffreth nat that men yow doon offense.
And sklendre wives, fieble as in bataille,
Beth egre as is a tigre yond in Inde;
1200   Ay clappeth as a mille, I yow consaille!

Ne dreed hem nat, dooth hem no reverence;
For thogh thin housbond armed be in maille,
The arwes of thy crabbed eloquence
Shal perce his brest and eek his aventaille.
1205   In jalousye I rede eek thow him binde,
And thow shalt make him couche as dooth a quaille.

1188 **swelwe** swallow **entraille** entrails   1190 **at the countretaille** in reply
1191 **bidaffed** made a fool of, cowed   1192 **governaille** mastery
1193 **Emprenteth** impress   1194 **may availle** may be of use   1195 You
viragoes, defend yourselves   1196 **camaille** camel   1197 **suffreth** allow
1199 **egre** fierce **Inde** India   1200 **clappeth** clack away **consaille** counsel
1202 **maille** chain mail   1203 **arwes** arrows **crabbed** spiteful
1204 **aventaille** piece of chain mail protecting neck and upper chest
1205 **rede** advise **binde** imprison   1206 **couche** cower

If thow be fair, ther folk ben in presence
Shewe thow thy visage, and thin apparaille.
If thow be foul, be fre of thy dispence;
To gete thee freendes ay do thy travaille.   1210
Be ay of cheere as light as leef on linde,
And lat him care, and wepe, and wringe, and waille!

Bihoold the murye wordes of the Hoost.

This worthy Clerk, whan ended was his tale,   1212a
Oure Hoost seide and swoor, 'By Goddes bones,
Me were levere than a barel ale
My wif at hom had herd this legend ones!
This is a gentil tale, for the nones,
As to my purpos, wiste ye my wille.
But thing that wol nat be, lat it be stille.'   1212g

Heere endeth the Tale of the
Clerk of Oxenford.

THE MERCHANT'S PROLOGUE

The Prologe of the Marchantes Tale.

'Weping and wailing, care and oother sorwe
I knowe inogh, on even and amorwe,'
Quod the Marchant, 'and so doon othere mo   1215
That wedded been; I trowe that it be so,

1207 **in presence** in company   1208 **apparaille** clothes
1209 **dispence** expenditure   1210 **do thy travaille** exert yourself
1211 **as light as leef on linde** as light-hearted as a leaf on the tree
1212 **care** grieve **wringe** wring his hands   1212c **Me were levere** I would rather

1214 **inogh** in plenty **on even and amorwe** night and morning
1216 **trowe** believe

For wel I woot, it fareth so with me.
I have a wif, the worste that may be;
For thogh the feend to hire ycoupled were,
1220   She wolde him overmacche, I dar wel swere.
What sholde I yow reherce in special
Hir hye malice? She is a shrewe at al!
Ther is a long and large difference
Bitwix Grisildis grete pacience,
1225   And of my wif the passing crueltee.
Were I unbounden, also moot I thee,
I wolde nevere eft come in the snare.
We wedded men live in sorwe and care.
Assaye whoso wol, and he shal finde
1230   That I seye sooth, by Seint Thomas of Inde! –
As for the moore part; I sey nat alle.
God shilde that it sholde so bifalle!

    A, goode sire Hoost, I have ywedded be
Thise monthes two, and moore nat, pardee;
1235   And yet I trowe, he that al his live
Wiflees hath been, though that men wolde him rive
Unto the herte, ne koude in no manere
Tellen so muchel sorwe as I now heere
Koude tellen of my wives cursednesse!'
1240   'Now,' quod oure Hoost, 'Marchaunt, so God yow
                    blesse,
Sin ye so muchel knowen of that art,
Ful hertely I pray yow, telle us part.'
    'Gladly,' quod he, 'but of min owene soore
For sory herte I telle may namoore.'

1217 **it fareth so** this is the case   1219 **feend** devil **ycoupled** wedded
1220 **overmacche** be more than a match for   1221 **What** why
reherce in special recount in detail   1222 **at al** in every respect
1225 **passing** excessive   1226 **unbounden** at liberty **thee** prosper
1227 **eft** again   1229 **Assaye whoso wol** let whoever wishes, make trial
1231 **moore** greater   1232 **shilde** forbid   1236 **Wiflees** wifeless **rive** stab
1239 **cursednesse** perversity, 'cussedness'   1243 **soore** suffering
1244 **telle may** can say

THE MERCHANT'S TALE

Heere biginneth the Marchantes Tale.

Whilom ther was dwelling in Lumbardye   1245
A worthy knight, that born was of Pavie,
In which he livede in greet prosperitee.
And sixty yeer a wiflees man was he,
And folwed ay his bodily delit
On wommen, theras was his appetit,   1250
As doon thise fooles that been seculer.
And whan that he was passed sixty yeer,
Were it for holinesse or for dotage
I kan nat seye, but swich a greet corage
Hadde this knight to been a wedded man   1255
That day and night he dooth al that he kan
T'espyen where he mighte wedded be,
Preyinge oure lord to graunten him that he
Mighte ones knowe of thilke blisful lif
That is bitwix an housbonde and his wif,   1260
And for to live under that holy bond
With which that first God man and womman bond.
'Noon oother lif', seide he, 'is worth a bene;
For wedlok is so esy and so clene
That in this world it is a paradis.'   1265
– Thus seide this olde knight that was so wis.
   And certeinly, as sooth as God is king,
To take a wif it is a glorious thing,
And namely whan a man is old and hoor;
Thanne is a wif the fruit of his tresor.   1270

1245 **Whilom** once   1249 **delit** pleasure   1251 **seculer** laymen
1254 **corage** desire   1257 **T'espyen** to seek to discover   1262 **bond** bound
1264 **esy** comfortable **clene** pure   1269 **hoor** white-haired

Thanne sholde he take a yong wif and a feir,
On which he mighte engendren him an heir,
And lede his lif in joye and in solas,
Wheras thise bacheleres singe 'allas!',
1275   Whan that they finden any adversitee
In love, which nis but childissh vanitee.
And trewely, it sit wel to be so,
That bachileres have ofte peine and wo.
On brotil grounde they bilde, and brotilnesse
1280   They finde, whan they wene sikernesse.
They live but as a brid or as a beest,
In libertee and under noon areest,
Theras a wedded man in his estat
Liveth a lif blisful and ordinat,
1285   Under this yok of mariage ybounde.
Wel may his herte in joye and blisse habounde;
For who kan be so buxom as a wif?
Who is so trewe, and eek so ententif
To kepe him, sik and hool, as is his make?
1290   For wele or wo she wol him nat forsake.
She nis nat wery him to love and serve,
Thogh that he lie bedrede til he sterve.
And yet som clerkes seyn it nis nat so,
Of whiche he Theofraste is oon of tho.
1295   What force thogh Theofraste liste lie?
'Ne take no wif', quod he, 'for housbondrye,
As for to spare in houshold thy dispence.
A trewe servant dooth moore diligence
Thy good to kepe than thin owene wif,
1300   For she wol claime half part al hir lif.

1271 **feir** fair one   1273 **solas** pleasure   1276 **nis but** is nothing but
1277 **it sit wel** it is befitting   1279 **brotil** brittle   **bilde** build
1280 **wene sikernesse** expect security   1282 **areest** restraint
1284 **ordinat** orderly   1287 **buxom** obedient   1288 **ententif** eager
1289 **hool** healthy   **make** spouse   1290 **wele or wo** joy or sorrow
1292 **bedrede** bedridden   **sterve** dies   1295 **What force** what does it matter
liste lie wants to lie   1296 **housbondrye** thrifty housekeeping
1297 **dispence** expenditure

And if that thow be sik, so God me save,
Thy verray freendes, or a trewe knave,
Wol kepe thee bet than she that waiteth ay
After thy good, and hath doon many a day.
And if thow take a wif unto thin hoold,   1305
Ful lightly maystow been a cokewold.'
This sentence, and an hundred thinges worse,
Writeth this man, ther God his bones curse!
But take no kepe of al swich vanitee;
Diffye Theofraste, and herke me.   1310
     A wif is Goddes yifte, verraily.
Alle othere manere yiftes, hardily –
As londes, rentes, pasture, or comune,
Or moebles – alle been yiftes of Fortune,
That passen as a shadwe upon the wal.   1315
But drede nat, if pleinly speke I shal,
A wif wol laste, and in thin hous endure,
Wel lenger than thee list, paraventure!
     Mariage is a ful greet sacrament;
He which that hath no wif, I holde him shent;   1320
He liveth helplees and al desolat –
I speke of folk in seculer estat.
And herke why – I sey nat this for noght –
That womman is for mannes help ywroght.
The hye God, whan he hadde Adam maked,   1325
And saugh him al allone, bely-naked,
God of his grete goodnesse seide than:
'Lat us now make an help unto this man,
Lik to himself' – and thanne he made him Eve.
Here may ye see, and hereby may ye preeve,   1330

1302 **knave** servant   1303–4 **bet** better **waiteth ay After thy good** is always
out for your property   1306 **Ful lightly** very easily **cokewold** cuckold
1307 **sentence** maxim   1309 **kepe** notice   1312 **hardily** certainly
1313 **rentes** revenues **comune** right to use common land
1314 **moebles** movable property   1318 **thee list** it pleases you
paraventure perhaps   1320 **shent** ruined   1321 **desolat** deserted, lonely
1324 **ywroght** created   1326 **bely-naked** stark naked   1330 **preeve** prove

That wif is mannes help and his confort,
His paradis terrestre and his disport.
So buxom and so vertuous is she,
They moste nedes live in unitee.

1335 O flessh they been, and o flessh, as I gesse,
Hath but oon herte, in wele and in distresse.
      A wif – a, Seinte Marye, *benedicite!*
How mighte a man han any adversitee
That hath a wif? Certes, I kan nat seye.

1340 The blisse which that is bitwix hem tweye
Ther may no tonge telle or herte thinke.
If he be povre, she helpeth him to swinke;
She kepeth his good, and wasteth never a del.
Al that hir housbonde lust, hir liketh wel.

1345 She seyth nat ones 'nay' whan he seyth 'ye'.
'Do this', seyth he; 'al redy, sire', seyth she.
O blisful ordre of wedlok precious,
Thow art so murye and eek so vertuous,
And so commended and approved eek,

1350 That every man that halt him worth a leek
Upon his bare knees oghte al his lif
Thanken his God that him hath sent a wif,
Or ellis preye to God him for to sende
A wif to laste unto his lives ende,

1355 For thanne his lif is set in sikernesse.
He may nat be deceived, as I gesse,
So that he werke after his wives reed;
Thanne may he boldely kepen up his heed.
They been so trewe, and therwithal so wise.

1360 For which, if thow wolt werken as the wise,
Do alwey so as wommen wol thee rede.
      Lo, how that Jacob, as thise clerkes rede,

1332 **terrestre** earthly **disport** solace   1333 **buxom** obedient   1335 **O** one
1336 **wele** prosperity   1342 **swinke** labour   1343 **good** property
never a del not a bit   1344 **lust** pleases   1348 **murye** happy
1350 **halt** (= *holdeth*) **him** considers himself   1355 **sikernesse** security
1357 **So that** provided that **after his wives reed** in accordance with his wife's
advice   1361 **rede** advise   1362 **rede** read

By good conseil of his moder Rebekke,
Boond the kides skin aboute his nekke,
For which his fadres benisoun he wan.   1365
    Lo, Judith, as the storye eek telle kan,
By wis conseil she Goddes peple kepte,
And slow him Olofernus whil he slepte.
    Lo, Abigail, by good conseil how she
Saved hir housbonde Nabal, whan that he   1370
Sholde han ben slain; and looke, Ester also
By good conseil delivered out of wo
The peple of God, and made him Mardochee
Of Assuere enhaunced for to be.
    Ther nis no thing in gree superlatif,   1375
As seyth Senek, above an humble wif.
    Suffre thy wives tonge, as Caton bit;
She shal comaunde, and thow shalt suffren it –
And yet she wol obeye of curteisye.
A wif is kepere of thin housbondrye;   1380
Wel may the sike man biwaille and wepe
Theras ther nis no wif the hous to kepe.
I warne thee, if wisely thow wolt wirche,
Love wel thy wif, as Crist loved his chirche.
If thow lovest thyself, thow lovest thy wif.   1385
No man hateth his flessh, but in his lif
He fostreth it; and therfore bidde I thee,
Cherisse thy wif, or thow shalt nevere thee.
Housbonde and wif, whatso men jape or pleye,
Of worldly folk holden the siker weye.   1390
They been so knit, ther may noon harm bitide,
And namely upon the wives side.
For which this Januarye, of whom I tolde,
Considered hath, inwith his dayes olde,

1364 **Boond** tied   1365 **benisoun** blessing   1368 **slow** killed   1374 **Of** by
enhaunced elevated   1375 **gree superlatif** superlative degree
1377 **Suffre** put up with   **bit** (= *biddeth*) bids   1380 **housbondrye** household
affairs   1383 **wirche** act   1388 **thee** prosper   1389 **jape** jest
1390 **siker weye** safe way   1394 **inwith** in

1395 The lusty lif, the vertuous quiete,
  That is in mariage hony-swete,
  And for his freendes on a day he sente
  To tellen hem th'effect of his entente.
   With face sad this tale he hath hem told:
1400 He seide, 'Freendes, I am hoor and old,
  And almoost, God woot, on my pittes brinke;
  Upon my soule somwhat moste I thinke.
  I have my body folily despended –
  Blessed be God that it shal been amended!
1405 For I wol be, certein, a wedded man,
  And that anon, in al the haste I kan.
  Unto som maide fair and tendre of age,
  I pray yow, shapeth for my mariage
  Al sodeinly, for I wol nat abide.
1410 And I wol fonde t'espyen, on my side,
  To whom I may be wedded hastily.
  But forasmuche as ye been mo than I,
  Ye shullen rather swich a thing espyen
  Than I, and where me beste were to allyen.
1415 'But o thing warne I yow, my freendes deere,
  I wol noon old wif han in no manere.
  She shal nat passe twenty yeer, certein.
  Old fissh and yong flessh wolde I have fein;
  Bet is', quod he, 'a pik than a pikerel,
1420 And bet than old boef is the tendre veel.
  I wol no womman thritty yeer of age;
  It is but benestraw and greet forage.
  And eek thise olde widwes, God it woot,

1395 **lusty** pleasant 1398 **effect** gist 1399 **sad** serious
1400 **hoor** white-haired 1401 **my pittes brinke** the edge of my grave
1403 **folily despended** used wantonly 1408 **shapeth** prepare
1409 **abide** wait 1410 **fonde t'espyen** try to discover
1414 **me beste were to allyen** it would be best for me to ally myself
1416 **in no manere** at all 1418 **fein** gladly 1419 **pik** pike **pikerel** young
pike 1420 **boef** beef **veel** veal 1422 **benestraw** refuse of bean plants
(after the beans have been picked) **greet** coarse

They konne so muchel craft on Wades boot,
So muchel broken harm, whan that hem leste,   1425
That with hem sholde I nevere live in reste.
For sondry scoles maken subtile clerkis;
Womman of many scoles half a clerk is.
But certeinly, a yong thing may men gye,
Right as men may warm wex with handes plye.   1430
Wherfore I sey yow pleinly, in a clause,
I wol noon old wif han, right for this cause.
For if so were I hadde swich meschaunce
That I in hire ne koude han no plesaunce,
Thanne sholde I lede my lif in avoutrye,   1435
And go streight to the devel whan I die.
Ne children sholde I noon upon hire geten;
Yet were me levere houndes hadde me eten
Than that min heritage sholde falle
In straunge hand, and this I telle yow alle.   1440
        'I dote nat; I woot the cause why
Men sholde wedde, and ferthermoore woot I
Ther speketh many a man of mariage
That woot namoore of it than woot my page
For whiche causes man sholde take a wif –   1445
If he ne may nat liven chast his lif –
Take him a wif with greet devocioun
Bicause of leveful procreacioun
Of children, to th'onour of God above,
And nat oonly for paramour or love;   1450
And for they sholde lecherye eschue,
And yelde hir dette whan that it is due;

1424 They are so good at telling you tall stories (n.)
1425 **broken harm** mischief-making (n.)   1427 **sondry** diverse   1428 A
woman trained in many schools is half learned   1429 **gye** guide
1430 **plye** mould   1435 **avoutrye** adultery   1437 **geten** beget
1438 **were me levere** I would rather   1440 **straunge** a stranger's
1441 **dote nat** am not a fool **woot** know   1444 **page** serving-boy
1448 **leveful** lawful   1450 **paramour** romantic passion
1451 **eschue** avoid   1452 **yelde** pay

Or for that ech of hem sholde helpen oother
In meschief, as a suster shal the brother,
1455   And live in chastitee ful holily.
But sires, by youre leve, that am nat I;
For, God be thanked, I dar make avaunt
I feele my limes stark and suffisaunt
To do al that a man bilongeth to.
1460   I woot myselven best what I may do.
Thogh I be hoor, I fare as dooth a tree
That blosmeth er that fruit ywoxen be;
And blosmy tree nis neither drye ne deed.
I feele me nowher hoor but on min heed.
1465   Min herte and alle my limes been as grene
As laurer thurgh the yeer is for to sene.
And sin that ye han herd al min entente,
I pray yow to my wil ye wol assente.'
        Diverse men diversely him tolde
1470   Of mariage manye ensamples olde.
Somme blamed it, somme preised it certein;
But at the laste, shortly for to seyn,
As alday falleth altercacioun
Bitwixen freendes in disputisoun,
1475   Ther fil a strif bitwix his bretheren two;
Of which that oon was cleped Placebo,
Justinus soothly called was that oother.
        Placebo seide, 'O Januarye, brother,
Ful litel nede hadde ye, my lord so deere,
1480   Conseil to axe of any that is heere,
But that ye been so ful of sapience
That yow ne liketh, for youre heighe prudence,
To weiven fro the word of Salomon.
This word seide he unto us everychon:

1454 **meschief** affliction   1457 **avaunt** boast   1458 **stark** strong
suffisaunt capable   1462 **blosmeth** blossoms **ywoxen be** has grown
1463 **blosmy tree** tree in blossom   1466 **laurer** laurel-tree
1473 **alday** constantly   1475 **fil** befell   1480 **axe** ask
1481 **sapience** wisdom   1483 **weiven fro** forsake

"Werk alle thing by conseil" – thus seide he –   1485
"And thanne shaltow nat repenten thee."
But thogh that Salomon spak swich a word,
Min owene deere brother and my lord,
So wysly God my soule bringe at reste,
I holde your owene conseil is the beste.   1490
For, brother min, of me tak this motif:
I have now been a court-man al my lif,
And God it woot, thogh I unworthy be,
I have stonden in ful greet degree
Abouten lordes of ful heigh estat,   1495
Yet hadde I nevere with noon of hem debat.
I nevere hem contraried, trewely;
I woot wel that my lord kan moore than I.
What that he seyth, I holde it ferme and stable;
I seye the same, or ellis thing semblable.   1500
A ful greet fool is any conseillour
That serveth any lord of heigh honour,
That dar presume, or ellis thenken it,
That his conseil sholde passe his lordes wit.
Nay, lordes been no fooles, by my fay!   1505
Ye han yourselven shewed heer today
So heigh sentence, so holily and weel,
That I consente and conferme everydeel
Youre wordes alle and youre opinioun.
By God, ther nis no man in al this toun,   1510
Ne in Itaille, that koude bet han said!
Crist halt him of this conseil wel apaid.

1489 **So wysly** as surely as   1491 **motif** proposition
1492 **court-man** courtier   1494 **in ful greet degree** in very high position
1496 **debat** strife   1497 **contraried** contradicted   1498 **kan** knows
1499 **holde it ferme and stable** support it   1500 **or ellis thing semblable** or
else something similar   1504 **conseil** advice   **passe** surpass, be better than
wit understanding   1507 **So heigh sentence** such lofty wisdom
holily piously   1508 **conferme everydeel** endorse completely
1512 **halt** (= *holdeth*) **him** considers himself   **wel apaid** very satisfied

And trewely, it is an heigh corage
Of any man that stapen is in age
1515 To take a yong wif; by my fader kin,
Youre herte hangeth on a joly pin!
Dooth now in this matere right as yow leste,
For, finally, I holde it for the beste.'
Justinus, that ay stille sat and herde,
1520 Right in this wise to Placebo answerde:
'Now, brother min, be pacient I preye,
Sin ye han seid, and herkneth what I seye.

'Senek, amonges othere wordes wise,
Seyth that a man oghte him right wel avise
1525 To whom he yeveth his lond or his catel.
And sin I oghte avisen me right wel
To whom I yeve my good awey fro me,
Wel muchel moore I oghte avised be
To whom I yeve my body for alwey.
1530 I warne yow wel, it is no childes pley
To take a wif withoute avisement.
Men moste enquere – this is min assent –
Wher she be wis, or sobre, or dronkelewe,
Or proud, or ellis ootherweys a shrewe,
1535 A chidester, or wastour of thy good,
Or riche, or povre, or ellis mannissh wood –
Albeit so that no man finden shal
Noon in this world that trotteth hool in al,
Ne man ne beest, swich as men koude devise.
1540 But nathelees, it oghte inogh suffise
With any wif, if so were that she hadde
Mo goode thewes than hir vices badde.

1513 **heigh corage** noble desire   1514 **stapen** advanced
1515 **fader** father's   1516 You have plenty of spirit   1519 **ay stille** all the
while silent   1524 **him . . . avise** consider   1525 **catel** property
1531 **avisement** reflection   1532 **assent** opinion   1533 **Wher** whether
dronkelewe a drunkard   1534 **ootherweys** in some other way
1535 **chidester** scold   1536 **mannissh wood** virago-like
1538 **hool** soundly   1539 **devise** imagine   1541 **if so were** if it were the
case   1542 **thewes** qualities

And al this axeth leiser for t'enquere.
For, God it woot, I have wept many a teere
Ful prively, sin I have had a wif.   1545
Preise whoso wole a wedded mannes lif,
Certein, I finde in it but cost and care,
And observances of alle blisses bare.
And yet, God woot, my neighebores aboute,
And namely of wommen many a route,   1550
Seyn that I have the mooste stedefast wif,
And eek the mekeste oon that bereth lif.
But I woot best where wringeth me my sho.
Ye mowe, for me, right as yow liketh do.
Aviseth yow – ye been a man of age –   1555
How that ye entren into mariage,
And namely with a yong wif and a feir.
By him that made water, erthe, and eir,
The yongeste man that is in al this route
Is bisy inough to bringen it aboute   1560
To han his wif allone. Trusteth me,
Ye shul nat plese hire fully yeres thre –
This is to seyn, to doon hire ful plesance.
A wif axeth ful many an observance.
I pray yow that ye be nat ivele apaid.'   1565
    'Wel,' quod this Januarye, 'and hastow said?
Straw for thy Senek and for thy proverbes!
I counte nat a panier ful of herbes
Of scole-termes! Wiser men than thow,
As thow hast herd, assenteden right now   1570

1543 **axeth** requires **leiser** leisure   1545 **prively** secretly
1546 **wole** desires   1547 **care** sorrow   1548 **observances** duties
bare devoid   1549 **aboute** round about   1550 **route** band
1552 **bereth lif** lives   1553 **wringeth** pinches **sho** shoe (see n. to WB 492)
1554 **for me** as far as I am concerned   1555 **Aviseth yow** take thought
1557 **namely** especially   1559 **route** company   1560 **bisy inough** hard put
1561 **allone** to himself   1563 **doon hire ful plesance** give her complete
satisfaction   1565 **ivele apaid** displeased   1568 **panier** basket
1569 **scole-termes** learned formulae

To my purpos. Placebo, what sey ye?'
   'I seye it is a cursed man', quod he,
'That letteth matrimoigne, sikerly.'
And with that word they risen sodeinly,
1575   And been assented fully that he sholde
Be wedded whan him liste, and wher he wolde.
   Heigh fantasye and curious bisinesse
Fro day to day gan in the soule impresse
Of Januarye aboute his mariage.
1580   Many fair shap and many a fair visage
Ther passeth thurgh his herte, night by night,
As whoso tooke a mirour, polisshed bright,
And sette it in a commune market-place,
Thanne sholde he se ful many a figure pace
1585   By his mirour; and in the same wise
Gan Januarye inwith his thoght devise
Of maidens whiche that dwelten him biside.
He wiste nat wher that he mighte abide;
For if that oon have beautee in hir face,
1590   Another stant so in the peples grace
For hir sadnesse and hir benignitee
That of the peple grettest vois hath she;
And somme were riche, and hadden badde name.
But nathelees, bitwix ernest and game,
1595   He atte laste apointed him on oon,
And leet alle othere from his herte goon,
And chees hire of his owene auctoritee;
For love is blind alday, and may nat see.
And whan that he was in his bed ybroght,

1573 **letteth** hinders   1575 **been assented** agree   1577 Powerful imaginings
and agitated anxiety   1578 **gan . . . impresse** became fixed
1582 **As whoso tooke** as if one were to take
1586-7 **Gan . . . devise . . . Of** thought about **inwith** within
1588 **abide** settle   1589 **that oon** one   1590 **stant** (= *standeth*) stands
grace favour   1591 **sadnesse** soberness   1592 **vois** praise
1594 **bitwix ernest and game** half seriously and half playfully
1595 **apointed him** decided   1597 **chees** chose   1598 **alday** always

He purtreyde in his herte and in his thoght   1600
Hir fresshe beautee and hir age tendre,
Hir middel smal, hir armes longe and sklendre,
Hir wise governance, hir gentilesse,
Hir wommanly bering and hir sadnesse.
And whan that he on hire was condescended,   1605
Him thoughte his chois ne mighte nat ben
          amended.
For whan that he himself concluded hadde,
Him thoughte ech oother mannes wit so badde
That impossible it were to replye
Again his chois; this was his fantasye.   1610
His freendes sente he to at his instance,
And preyed hem to doon him that plesance
That hastily they wolden to him come;
He wolde abregge hir labour, alle and some.
Nedeth namoore for him to go ne ride;   1615
He was apointed ther he wolde abide.

     Placebo cam, and eek his freendes soone,
And alderfirst he bad hem alle a boone,
That noon of hem none argumentes make
Again the purpos which that he hath take;   1620
Which purpos was plesant to God, seide he,
And verray ground of his prosperitee.
     He seide ther was a maiden in the toun,
Which that of beautee hadde greet renoun,
Al were it so she were of smal degree,   1625
Suffiseth him hir youthe and hir beautee;

1600 **purtreyde** pictured   1602 **middel smal** slender waist
1603 **governance** behaviour **gentilesse** nobility   1604 **sadnesse** soberness
1605 **was condescended** had settled   1607 **concluded** made up his mind
1608 **wit** opinion   1609–10 **replye Again** object to **fantasye** fancy
1611 **instance** urging, request   1612 **doon him that plesance** do him the
favour   1614 **abregge** shorten   1615 **Nedeth namoore** there is no more
need   1616 **was apointed** had resolved **ther** where   1618 **alderfirst** first of
all **bad . . . a boone** made a request   1625 **Al were it so** although it was the
case **of smal degree** of lowly rank   1626 **Suffiseth him** are enough for him

Which maide, he seide, he wolde han to his wif,
To lede in ese and holinesse his lif,
And thanked God that he mighte han hire al,
1630   That no wight his blisse parten shal,
And preyde hem to labouren in this nede,
And shapen that he faille nat to spede,
For thanne, he seide, his spirit was at ese.
'Thanne is', quod he, 'no thing may me displese,
1635   Save o thing priketh in my conscience,
The which I wol reherce in youre presence.

        'I have', quod he, 'herd seid, ful yoore ago,
Ther may no man han parfite blisses two –
This to seye, in erthe and eek in hevene.
1640   For thogh he kepe him fro the sinnes sevene,
And eek from every branche of thilke tree,
Yet is ther so parfit felicitee
And so greet ese and lust in mariage,
That evere I am agast now in min age
1645   That I shal lede now so murye a lif,
So delicat, withouten wo and strif,
That I shal have min hevene in erthe heere.
For sith that verray hevene is boght so deere,
With tribulacioun and greet penance,
1650   How sholde I thanne, that live in swich plesance
As alle wedded men doon with hir wivis,
Come to the blisse ther Crist eterne on live is?
This is my drede; and ye, my bretheren tweye,
Assoileth me this question, I preye.'
1655   Justinus, which that hated his folye,
Answerde anon-right in his japerye;

1628 **ese** comfort   1630 **parten** share   1631 **nede** exigency
1632 **shapen** ensure   **spede** be successful   1636 **reherce** recount
1637 **ful yoore ago** very long ago   1638 **parfite** perfect   1643 **ese** pleasure
lust enjoyment   1644 **agast** afraid   1645 **murye** happy
1646 **delicat** luxurious   1649 **penance** suffering   1654 **Assoileth** resolve
1656 **anon-right** at once   **japerye** jest

And for he wolde his longe tale abregge,
He wolde noon auctoritee allegge,
But seide, 'Sire, so ther be noon obstacle
Oother than this, God, of his hye miracle   1660
And of his mercy, may so for yow werche,
That er ye have your right of holy cherche
Ye may repente of wedded mannes lif,
In which ye seyn ther is no wo ne strif.
And elles, God forbede but he sente   1665
A wedded man him grace to repente
Wel ofte rather than a sengle man!
And therfore, sire, the beste reed I kan:
Dispeire yow noght, but have in youre memorye
Paraunter she may be youre purgatorye.   1670
She may be Goddes mene and Goddes whippe;
Thanne shal youre soule up to hevene skippe
Swifter than dooth an arwe out of a bowe.
I hope to God heerafter shul ye knowe
That ther nis noon so greet felicitee   1675
In mariage, ne neveremo shal be,
That yow shal lette of youre salvacioun,
So that ye use, as skile is and resoun,
The lustes of youre wif attemprely,
And that ye plese hire nat to amorously,   1680
And that ye kepe yow eek from oother sinne.
My tale is doon, for my wit is thinne.
Beth nat agast herof, my brother deere,
But lat us waden out of this matere.

1657 **abregge** curtail   1658 **noon auctoritee allegge** cite any written
authority   1659 **so** provided that   1662 **right of holy cherche** see n.
1665 **God forbede but he sente** God forbid that he should do other than
send   1668 **the beste reed I kan** the best suggestion I have   1669 Do not
despair, but bear in mind   1670 **Paraunter** perhaps
1671 **mene** instrument   1677 **lette of** deprive of   1678–9 Provided that
you enjoy the physical attractions of your wife moderately, as is proper and
right   1682 **wit** understanding   1684 **waden out of** move away from

1685   The Wif of Bathe, if ye han understonde,
        Of mariage, which we have on honde,
        Declared hath ful wel in litel space.
        Fareth now wel; God have yow in his grace.'
            And with that word this Justin and his brother
1690   Han take hir leve, and ech of hem of oother.
        For whan they sawe that it moste nedes be,
        They wroghten so, by sly and wis tretee,
        That she, this maiden, which that Mayus highte,
        As hastily as ever that she mighte
1695   Shal wedded be unto this Januarye.
        I trowe it were to longe yow to tarye,
        If I yow tolde of every scrit and bond
        By which that she was feffed in his lond,
        Or for to herknen of hir riche array.
1700   But finally, ycomen is the day
        That to the chirche bothe be they went
        For to receive the holy sacrament.
        Forth comth the preest, with stole aboute his nekke,
        And bad hire be lik Sarra and Rebekke
1705   In wisdom and in trouthe of mariage,
        And seide his orisons, as is usage,
        And croucheth hem, and bad God sholde hem blesse,
        And made al siker inow with holinesse.
            Thus been they wedded with solempnitee,
1710   And at the feste sitteth he and she
        With oother worthy folk upon the deis.
        Al ful of joye and blisse is the paleis,
        And ful of instrumentz and of vitaille,
        The mooste deintevous of al Itaille.

1686 **have on honde** are occupied with   1687 **Declared** told
1690 **leve** leave   1692 **wroghten** contrived **sly** skilful **tretee** negotiation
1696 **tarye** delay   1697 **scrit** written document, deed
1698 **feffed in** endowed with   1699 **riche array** splendid finery
1706 **orisons** prayers **usage** the custom   1707 **croucheth** makes the sign of
the cross over   1708 **inow** enough   1709 **solempnitee** ceremony
1711 **deis** dais   1713 **vitaille** food   1714 **deintevous** delicious

Biforn hem stooden instrumentz of swich soun   1715
That Orpheus, n'of Thebes Amphioun,
Ne maden nevere swich a melodye.
At every cours thanne cam loud minstralcye
That nevere tromped Joab for to heere,
Ne he Theodamas, yet half so cleere,   1720
At Thebes whan the citee was in doute.
Bacus the win hem shenketh al aboute,
And Venus laugheth upon every wight,
For Januarye was bicome hir knight,
And wolde bothe assayen his corage   1725
In libertee and eek in mariage,
And with hir firbrond in hir hand aboute
Daunceth bifore the bride and al the route.
And certeinly, I dar right wel sey this:
Imeneus, that god of wedding is,   1730
Say nevere his lif so murye a wedded man.
Hoold thow thy pees, thou poete Marcian,
That writest us that ilke wedding murye
Of hire Philologye and him Mercurye,
And of the songes that the Muses songe!   1735
To smal is bothe thy penne, and eek thy tonge,
For to discriven of this mariage.
Whan tendre youthe hath wedded stouping age,
Ther is swich murthe that it may nat be writen.
Assayeth it yourself; than may ye witen   1740
If that I lie or noon in this matere.
    Mayus, that sit with so benigne a cheere,
Hir to biholde it semed faierye.
Queene Ester looked nevere with swich an eye

1716 n'of Thebes Amphioun nor Amphion of Thebes   1719 tromped blew
the trumpet   1720 cleere loudly   1721 doute danger
1722 shenketh pours out   1725 assayen his corage test his spirit
1727 firbrond brand, torch   1728 route company   1731 Say saw his lif in
his life   1735 songe sang   1736 smal weak   1737 discriven of write
about   1738 stouping stooping   1740 witen know   1741 noon not
1742 sit (= sitteth) sits   1743 faierye magic, enchantment

1745   On Assuer, so meke a look hath she.
        I may yow nat devise al hir beautee;
        But thus muche of hir beautee telle I may,
        That she was lik the brighte morwe of May,
        Fulfild of alle beautee and plesaunce.
1750   This Januarye is ravisshed in a traunce
        At every time he looked on hir face.
        But in his herte he gan hir to manace
        That he that night in armes wolde hire streine
        Harder than evere Paris dide Eleine.
1755   But nathelees, yet hadde he gret pitee
        That thilke night offenden hire moste he,
        And thoghte, 'Allas, o tendre creature,
        Now wolde God ye mighte wel endure
        Al my corage, it is so sharp and kene.
1760   I am agast ye shul it nat sustene.
        But God forbede that I dide al my might!
        Now wolde God that it were woxen night,
        And that the night wolde lasten everemo.
        I wolde that al this peple were ago!'
1765   And finally he dooth al his labour,
        As he best mighte, saving his honour,
        To haste hem fro the mete in subtil wise.
            The time cam that reson was to rise,
        And after that men daunce and drinken faste,
1770   And spices al aboute the hous they caste,
        And ful of joye and blisse is every man –
        Al but a squier highte Damian,
        Which carf biforn the knight ful many a day.
        He was so ravisshed on his lady May

1746 **devise** describe   1752 **manace** threaten   1753 **streine** clasp
1756 **offenden** hurt   1759 **corage** desire   1760 **sustene** bear
1761 **al my might** everything I am capable of   1762 **were woxen night** was
night-time   1764 **ago** gone   1765 **dooth al his labour** does his best
1767 **mete** meal   **in subtil wise** by devious means   1768 **reson was** it was
right   1769 **faste** heartily   1772 **highte** who was called   1773 **carf** carved

That for the verray peine he was ny wood.   1775
Almoost he swelte and swowned ther he stood,
So sore hath Venus hurt him with hir brond,
As that she bar it dauncing in hir hond.
And to his bed he wente him hastily;
Namoore of him at this time speke I,   1780
But ther I lete him wepe inow and pleine,
Til fresshe May wol rewen on his peine.

O perilous fir, that in the bedstraw bredeth!
O famulier foo, that his service bedeth!
O servant traitour, false homly hewe,   1785
Lik to the neddre in bosom sly untrewe!
God shilde us alle from youre aqueintance.
O Januarye, dronken in plesance
In mariage, se how thy Damian,
Thin owene squier and thy borne man,   1790
Entendeth for to do thee vileinye.
God grante thee thin homly fo t'espye!
For in this world nis worse pestilence
Than homly fo alday in thy presence.

Parfourned hath the sonne his ark diurne;   1795
No lenger may the body of him sojurne
On th'orisonte as in that latitude.
Night with his mantel that is derk and rude
Gan oversprede the hemisperie aboute,
For which departed is this lusty route   1800
Fro Januarye, with thank on every side.

1775 **wood** mad   1776 **swelte** fainted **ther** where   1781 But there I leave
him to weep copiously and lament   1782 **rewen** take pity
1783 **bedstraw** straw used in a mattress **bredeth** breeds
1784 **famulier foo** enemy in the household **bedeth** offers
1785 **homly hewe** domestic servant   1786 **neddre** adder **sly** deceitful
untrewe faithless   1790 **borne man** servant from birth
1791 **Entendeth** intends **vileinye** wrong   1794 **alday** constantly
1795 **Parfourned** completed **ark diurne** daily course through the sky (g.)
1796 **sojurne** stay   1797 **orisonte** horizon   1798 **rude** rough
1799 **hemisperie** hemisphere   1800 **lusty route** gay company

Hom to hir houses lustily they ride,
Wheras they doon hir thinges as hem leste,
And whan they say hir time, go to reste.

1805   Soone after that, this hastif Januarye
Wol go to bedde; he wol no lenger tarye.
He drinketh ipocras, clarree and vernage
Of spices hoote, t'encressen his corage,
And many a letuarye hath he ful fin,

1810   Swich as the cursed monk daun Constantin
Hath writen in his book *De Coitu*;
To ete hem alle he nas nothing eschu.
And to his privee freendes thus seide he:
'For Goddes love, as soone as it may be,

1815   Lat voiden al this hous in curteis wise.'
And they han doon right as he wol devise;
Men drinken, and the travers drawe anon.
The bride was broght abedde, as stille as stoon;
And whan the bed was with the preest yblessed,

1820   Out of the chambre hath every wight him dressed.
And Januarye hath faste in armes take
His fresshe May, his paradis, his make.
He lulleth hire, he kisseth hire ful ofte;
With thikke bristles of his berd unsofte,

1825   Lik to the skin of houndfissh, sharp as brere –
For he was shave al newe in his manere –
He rubbeth hire aboute hir tendre face,
And seide thus: 'Allas, I moot trespace
To yow, my spouse, and yow gretly offende,

1830   Er time come that I wol doun descende.

1802 **lustily** gaily   1803 Where they go about their business as it pleases
them   1804 **say** saw   1807 **ipocras, clarree** spiced wines **vernage** sweet
wine   1808 **corage** desire   1809 **letuarye** potion   1812 **eschu** loath
1813 **privee** intimate   1815 **Lat voiden** cause to be cleared
1816 **wol devise** wishes to direct   1817 **travers** curtain used to partition a
room   1820 **him dressed** went   1822 **make** spouse   1823 **lulleth** cuddles
1824 **unsofte** harsh   1825 **houndfissh** dogfish **brere** briar
1828 **moot trespace** must do injury   1829 **offende** hurt

But natheles, considereth this,' quod he,
'Ther nis no werkman, whatsoevere he be,
That may bothe werke wel and hastily.
This wol be doon at leiser, parfitly.
It is no fors how longe that we pleye;   1835
In trewe wedlok coupled be we tweye.
And blessed be the yok that we been inne,
For in oure actes we mow do no sinne.
A man may do no sinne with his wif,
Ne hurte himselven with his owene knif,   1840
For we han leve to pleye us by the lawe.'
Thus laboureth he til that the day gan dawe,
And thanne he taketh a sop in fin clarree,
And upright in his bed thanne sitteth he,
And after that he song ful loude and clere,   1845
And kiste his wif, and made wantown cheere.
He was al coltissh, ful of ragerye,
And ful of jargon as a flekked pie.
The slakke skin aboute his nekke shaketh
Whil that he song, so chaunteth he and craketh.   1850
But God woot what that May thoghte in hir herte,
Whan she him saw up sitting in his sherte,
In his night-cappe, and with his nekke lene;
She preiseth nat his pleying worth a bene.
      Thanne seide he thus: 'My reste wol I take   1855
Now day is come; I may no lenger wake.'
And doun he leide his heed, and sleep til prime.
And afterward, whan that he saw his time,
Up riseth Januarye; but fresshe May
Heeld hir chambre unto the fourthe day,   1860

1835 **no fors** of no importance   1841 **han leve to pleye us** have permission
to enjoy ourselves   1842 **gan dawe** dawned   1843 **sop in fin clarree** piece
of bread dipped in spiced wine   1845 **song** sang
1846 **made wantown cheere** fooled around (sexually)
1847 **coltissh** coltish, playful **ragerye** high spirits   1848 **jargon** chatter
pie magpie   1849 **slakke** slack   1850 **chaunteth** sings **craketh** bawls
1854 **pleying** love-play   1857 **sleep til prime** slept until 9 a.m. (g.)
1860 **Heeld** remained in

As usage is of wives for the beste.
For every labour somtime moot han reste,
Or ellis longe may he nat endure –
This is to seyn, no lives creature,
1865   Be it of fissh or brid or beest or man.
        Now wol I speke of woful Damian,
That langwisseth for love, as ye shul heere.
Therfore I speke to him in this manere:
I seye, 'O sely Damian, allas!
1870   Answere to my demaunde as in this cas:
How shaltow to thy lady, fresshe May,
Telle thy wo? She wol alwey sey nay.
Eek if thow speke, she wol thy wo biwreye.
God be thin help! I kan no bettre seye.'
1875   This sike Damian in Venus fir
So brenneth that he dieth for desir,
For which he putte his lif in aventure.
No lenger mighte he in this wise endure;
But prively a penner gan he borwe,
1880   And in a letter wroot he al his sorwe,
In manere of a compleint or a lay
Unto his faire fresshe lady May.
And in a purs of silk heng on his sherte
He hath it put, and leid it at his herte.
1885   The moone, that at noon was thilke day
That Januarye hath wedded fresshe May,
In two of Taur, was into Cancre gliden,
So longe hath Mayus in hir chambre abiden,
As custume is unto thise nobles alle.
1890   A bride shal nat eten in the halle
Til dayes foure, or thre dayes atte leeste,
Ypassed ben; thanne lat hir go to feeste.

1861 **usage** the custom   1864 **lives** living   1870 **demaunde** question
1873 **biwreye** disclose   1876 **brenneth** burns   1877 **in aventure** at risk
1879 But secretly he borrowed a pen-case   1881 **compleint** poetic lament
1883 **heng** which hung   1888 **abiden** remained

The fourthe day complet from noon to noon,
Whan that the heighe masse was ydoon,
In halle sit this Januarye and May,   1895
As fressh as is the brighte someres day.
And so bifel how that this goode man
Remembred him upon this Damian,
And seide, 'Seinte Marye, how may this be,
That Damian entendeth nat to me?   1900
Is he ay sik, or how may this bitide?'
His squiers, whiche that stooden therbiside,
Excused him bicause of his siknesse,
Which letted him to doon his bisinesse;
Noon oother cause mighte make him tarye.   1905
    'That me forthinketh,' quod this Januarye,
'He is a gentil squier, by my trouthe.
If that he deide, it were harm and routhe.
He is as wis, discret and as secree
As any man I woot of his degree,   1910
And therto manly and eek servisable,
And for to be a thrifty man right able.
But after mete, as soone as evere I may,
I wol myself visite him, and eek May,
To do him al the confort that I kan.'   1915
And for that word him blessed every man,
That of his bountee and his gentilesse
He wolde so conforten in siknesse
His squier, for it was a gentil dede.
    'Dame,' quod this Januarye, 'tak good hede,   1920
At after-mete ye with youre wommen alle,
Whan ye han been in chambre out of this halle,

1893 **complet** completed   1894 **heighe masse** solemn mass
1900 **entendeth nat to** does not attend on   1901 **ay sik** ill all this time
1904 Which prevented him from performing his duties
1906 **That me forthinketh** I am sorry for that   1908 **routhe** a pity
1909 **secree** discreet   1910 **degree** rank   1911 **servisable** willing to serve
1912 **thrifty** worthy   1913 **mete** dinner   1917 **bountee** kindness
1919 **gentil** noble   1921 **At after-mete** in the afternoon

That alle ye go see this Damian.
Dooth him disport; he is a gentil man.
1925   And telleth him that I wol him visite,
Have I nothing but rested me a lite.
And spede yow faste, for I wol abide
Til that ye slepe faste by my side.'
And with that word he gan to him calle
1930   A squier that was marchal of his halle,
And tolde him certein thinges, what he wolde.
   This fresshe May hath streight hir wey yholde,
With alle hir wommen, unto Damian.
Doun by his beddes side sit she than,
1935   Conforting him as goodly as she may.
This Damian, whan that his time he say,
In secree wise his purs and eek his bille,
In which that he ywriten hadde his wille,
Hath put into hir hand withouten moore,
1940   Save that he siketh wonder depe and soore,
And softely to hire right thus seide he:
'Mercy, and that ye nat discovere me,
For I am deed if that this thing be kid!'
This purs hath she inwith hir bosom hid,
1945   And wente hir wey – ye gete namoore of me!
But unto Januarye ycomen is she,
That on his beddes side sit ful softe
And taketh hire and kisseth hire ful ofte,
And leide him doun to slepe, and that anon.
1950   She feined hire as that she moste gon
Theras ye woot that every wight moot nede.
And whan she of this bille hath taken hede,

1924 **Dooth him disport** cheer him up   1926 When I have just rested a
little   1927 **spede yow** make haste   1928 **faste** soundly
1930 **marchal** marshal (g.)   1932 **hir wey yholde** taken her course
1935 **as goodly as** as well as   1936 **say** saw   1937 **bille** petition
1938 **wille** desire   1940 **siketh** sighs **wonder** wonderfully **soore** earnestly
1942 **discovere** expose   1943 **kid** known   1947 **softe** comfortably
1950 **feined hire** pretended **moste gon** had to go   1951 **moot nede** must of
necessity

She rente it al to cloutes at the laste,
And in the privee softely it caste.
    Who studyeth now but faire fresshe May?   1955
Adoun by olde Januarye she lay,
That sleep til that the coughe hath him awaked.
Anon he preide hire strepen hire al naked;
He wolde of hire, he seide, han som plesaunce;
He seide hir clothes dide him encombraunce.   1960
And she obeyeth, be hir lief or looth.
But lest that precious folk be with me wrooth,
How that he wroghte I dar nat to yow telle,
Or wheither hir thoughte it paradis or helle,
But heere I lete hem werken in hir wise,   1965
Til evensong rong and that they moste arise.
    Were it by destinee or aventure,
Were it by influence, or by nature,
Or constellacioun, that in swich estat
The hevene stood that time fortunat   1970
Was for to putte a bille of Venus werkes –
For alle thing hath time, as seyn thise clerkes –
To any womman for to gete hir love,
I kan nat seye; but grete God above,
That knoweth that noon act is causelees,   1975
He deme of al, for I wol holde my pees.
But sooth is this, how that this fresshe May
Hath taken swich impressioun that day
Of pitee on this sike Damian,
That from hir herte she ne drive kan   1980

1953 **rente** tore **cloutes** pieces   1954 **privee** lavatory **softely** quietly
1955 **studyeth** deliberates   1958 **strepen hire** strip herself
1960 **dide him encombraunce** got in his way
1961 **be hir lief or looth** whether she likes it or not   1962 **precious** prudish
1963 **wroghte** acted   1965 **lete** leave   1967 **aventure** chance
1968 **influence** influence of the stars   1969 **constellacioun** a configuration of
stars and planets **estat** aspect   1970 **fortunat** propitious   1971 It was to
present a petition concerning affairs of love   1972 **alle thing hath time** every
thing has its season (n.)   1976 **He deme** let him judge
1978 **taken swich impressioun** received so strong a mental image

The remembrance for to doon him ese.
'Certein,' thoghte she, 'whom that this thing displese,
I rekke nat; for here I him assure
To love him best of any creature,
1985   Thogh he namoore hadde than his sherte.'
Loo, pitee renneth soone in gentil herte!

    Heere may ye se how excellent franchise
In wommen is, whan they hem narwe avise.
Som tyraunt is, as ther be many oon,
1990   That hath an herte as hard as any stoon,
Which wolde han lete him sterven in the place
Wel rather than han graunted him hir grace,
And hem rejoisen in hir cruel pride,
And rekke nat to been an homicide.

1995   This gentil May, fulfilled of pitee,
Right of hir hand a lettre maked she,
In which she graunteth him hir verray grace.
Ther lakketh noght but oonly day and place,
Wher that she mighte unto his lust suffise;
2000   For it shal be right as he wol devise.
And whan she saw hir time upon a day,
To visite this Damian goth May,
And subtilly this lettre doun she threste
Under his pilwe – rede it if him leste.

2005   She taketh him by the hand and harde him twiste,
So secrely that no wight of it wiste,
And bad him be al hool; and forth she wente
To Januarye whan that he for hir sente.

    Up riseth Damian the nexte morwe;
2010   Al passed was his siknesse and his sorwe.

1981 doon . . . ese comfort   1983 rekke care   1986 renneth flows
gentil noble   1987 franchise generosity   1988 hem narwe avise take careful
consideration   1991 sterven die in the place on the spot   1994 And do not
care about being a murderer   1999 unto his lust suffise satisfy his desire
2000 devise direct   2001 time opportunity   2003 subtilly surreptitiously
threste thrust   2004 pilwe pillow rede let him read
2005 twiste (= twistede) squeezed   2006 wiste knew

He kembeth him; he preineth him and piketh;
He dooth al that his lady lust and liketh.
And eek to Januarye he goth as lowe
As evere dide a dogge for the bowe.
He is so plesant unto every man –   2015
For craft is al, whoso that do it kan –
That every wight is fain to speke him good,
And fully in his lady grace he stood.
Thus lete I Damian aboute his nede,
And in my tale forth I wil procede.   2020
    Somme clerkes holden that felicitee
Stant in delit, and therfore certein he,
This noble Januarye, with al his might,
In honeste wise, as longeth to a knight,
Shoop him to live ful deliciously.   2025
His housing, his array, as honestly
To his degree was maked as a kinges.
Amonges othere of his honeste thinges,
He made a gardin, walled al with stoon;
So fair a gardin woot I nowher noon.   2030
For out of doute, I verraily suppose
That he that wroot the *Romance of the Rose*
Ne koude of it the beautee wel devise;
Ne Priapus ne mighte nat suffise,
Thogh he be god of gardins, for to telle   2035
The beautee of the gardin and the welle
That stood under a laurer, alwey grene.
Ful ofte time he Pluto and his queene

2011 He combs his hair, grooms himself and makes himself neat
2012 **lust** pleases   2013 **lowe** meekly   2014 **dogge for the bowe** dog
trained to hunt game, with an archer   2017 **fain** eager
2018 **lady grace** lady's favour   2019 **lete** leave **nede** business
2022 **Stant** (= *standeth*) consists   2024 **honeste** respectable
longeth to befits   2025 **Shoop him** planned **deliciously** luxuriously
2026 **array** clothes **honestly** finely   2028 **honeste** fine
2033 **devise** describe   2034 **suffise** be adequate   2037 **laurer** laurel-tree

Proserpina, and al hir faierye,
2040   Disporten hem and maken melodye
Aboute that welle, and daunced, as men tolde.
    This noble knight, this Januarye the olde,
Swich deintee hath in it to walke and pleye,
That he wol no wight suffre bere the keye
2045   Save he himself; for of the smal wiket
He bar alwey of silver a cliket,
With which, whan that him leste, he it unshette.
And whan he wolde paye his wif hir dette
In somer seson, thider wolde he go,
2050   And May his wif, and no wight but they two.
And thinges whiche that were nat doon abedde,
He in the gardin parfourned hem and spedde.
And in this wise many a murye day
Lived this Januarye and fresshe May.
2055   But worldly joye may nat alwey dure,
To Januarye, ne to no creature.
    O sodein hap, o thow Fortune unstable,
Lik to the scorpion so deceivable,
That flaterest with thin heed whan thow wolt stinge,
2060   Thy tail is deeth, thurgh thin enveniminge!
O brotil joye, o swete venim queinte!
O monstre, that so subtilly kanst peinte
Thy yiftes under hewe of stedefastnesse,
That thow deceivest bothe moore and lesse!
2065   Why hastow Januarye thus deceived,
That haddest him for thy fulle freend received,
And now thow hast biraft him bothe his eyen? –
For sorwe of which desireth he to dien.

2039 **hir faierye** their fairy company   2040 **Disporten hem** amuse
themselves   2043 **deintee** delight   2044 **suffre bere** allow to carry
2045 **wiket** wicket-gate   2046 **cliket** latch-key   2047 **unshette** unlocked
2052 **spedde** (= *spedede*) accomplished   2057 **sodein hap** sudden chance
2058 **deceivable** deceitful   2060 **enveniminge** poisoning
2061 **queinte** subtle   2062 **peinte** camouflage   2063 **hewe** appearance
2064 **moore and lesse** rich and poor   2067 **biraft him** deprived him of

Allas, this noble Januarye free,
Amidde his lust and his prosperitee   2070
Is woxen blind, and that al sodeinly.
He wepeth and he waileth pitously;
And therwithal the fir of jalousye,
Lest that his wif sholde falle in som folye,
So brente his herte that he wolde fain   2075
That som man bothe hire and him had slain.
For neither after his deeth nor in his lif
Ne wolde he that she were love ne wif,
But evere live as widwe in clothes blake,
Soul as the turtle that hath lost hir make.   2080
But atte laste, after a monthe or tweye,
His sorwe gan aswage, sooth to seye.
For whan he wiste it may noon oother be,
He paciently took his adversitee;
Save, out of doute, he may nat forgoon   2085
That he nas jalous everemoore in oon.
Which jalousye it was so outrageous,
That neither in halle, ne in noon oother hous,
Ne in noon oother place neverthemo,
He nolde suffre hire for to ride or go   2090
But if that he hadde hond on hir alway.
For which ful ofte wepeth fresshe May,
That loveth Damian so benignely,
That she moot outher dien sodeinly,
Or ellis she moot han him as hir leste;   2095
She waiteth whan hir herte wolde breste!
    Upon that oother side Damian
Bicomen is the sorwefulleste man

2069 **free** worthy   2070 **lust** pleasure   2071 **Is woxen** has become
2072 **pitously** piteously   2075 **brente** burned   2079 **widwe** a widow
2080 **Soul** solitary **turtle** turtle-dove **make** mate
2082 **gan aswage** subsided   2085–6 Except . . . he cannot refrain from
being jealous all the time   2087 **outrageous** excessive
2089 **neverthemo** neither   2090 **suffre** allow **go** walk   2094 That she must
either die immediately   2096 She expects her heart to break any minute

That evere was, for neither night ne day
2100 Ne mighte he speke a word to fresshe May,
As to his purpos, of no swich matere,
But if that Januarye moste it heere,
That hadde an hand upon hire everemo.
But nathelees, by writing to and fro,
2105 And privee signes, wiste he what she mente,
And she knew eek the fin of his entente.

O Januarye, what mighte it thee availle
Thogh thow mighte se as fer as shippes saille?
For as good is, blind deceived be
2110 As be deceived whan a man may se.

Lo, Argus, which that hadde an hundred eyen,
For al that evere he koude poure or pryen,
Yet was he blent; and God woot, so been mo,
That weneth wysly that it be nat so.
2115 Passe over is an ese; I seye namoore.

This fresshe May, that I spak of so yoore,
In warm wex hath emprented the cliket,
That Januarye bar, of the smale wiket,
By which into his gardin ofte he wente.
2120 And Damian, that knew al hir entente,
The cliket countrefeted prively.
Ther nis namoore to seye, but hastily
Som wonder by this cliket shal bitide,
Which ye shul heren, if ye wol abide.

2125 O noble Ovide, ful sooth seystow, God woot!
What sleighte is it, thogh it be long and hoot,
That love nil finde it out in som manere?
By Piramus and Thesbe may men lere:

2102 Without January being able to hear it   2106 **fin** goal
2112 **poure** gaze   2113 **blent** (= *blended*) blinded
2114 **weneth wysly** believe for a certainty   2115 **Passe over is an ese** it is a
relief to move on (to the next topic)   2116 **so yoore** so long ago
2117 **emprented** imprinted   2118 **bar** carried   2121 **countrefeted** made a
copy of   2123 **bitide** befall   2124 **abide** wait   2126 **sleighte** stratagem
hoot difficult

Thogh they were kept ful longe streite overal,
They been acorded, rowning thurgh a wal,   2130
Ther no wight koude han founde out swich a
    sleighte.
    But now to purpos: er that dayes eighte
Were passed, er the monthe of Juil, bifil
That Januarye hath caught so greet a wil
Thurgh egging of his wif, him for to pleye   2135
In his gardin, and no wight but they tweye,
That in a morwe unto his May seyth he:
'Ris up, my wif, my love, my lady free!
The turtles vois is herd, my dowve swete;
The winter is goon, with alle his reines wete.   2140
Com forth, now, with thine eyen columbin!
How fairer been thy brestes than is win!
The gardin is enclosed al aboute;
Com forth, my white spouse! Out of doute,
Thow hast me wounded in min herte, o wif;   2145
No spot of thee ne knew I al my lif.
Com forth, and lat us taken oure disport;
I chees thee for my wif and my confort.'
– Swiche olde lewed wordes used he.
    On Damian a signe made she   2150
That he sholde go biforn with his cliket.
This Damian thanne hath opened the wiket,
And in he stirte, and that in swich manere
That no wight mighte it se neither iheere;
And stille he sit under a bussh anon.   2155
    This Januarye, as blind as is a stoon,
With Mayus in his hand, and no wight mo,
Into his fresshe gardin is ago,

2129 **streite** strictly **overal** on all sides   2130 **been acorded** came to an
agreement **rowning** whispering   2133 **Juil** July   2134 **wil** desire
2135 **egging** instigation **him for to pleye** to have fun   2138 **free** noble
2139 **dowve** dove   2140 **reines wete** wet rains   2141 **columbin** dove-like
2142 **win** wine   2148 **chees** chose   2149 **lewed** coarse   2150 **On** to
2153 **stirte** slid   2154 **iheere** hear   2155 **stille** quietly **sit** (= *sitteth*) sits
2157 **no wight mo** no one else

And clapte to the wiket sodeinly.

2160   'Now, wif,' quod he, 'here nis but thow and I,
That art the creature that I best love.
For, by that lord that sit in hevene above,
Levere ich hadde to dien on a knif
Than thee offende, trewe deere wif!

2165   For Goddes sake, thenk how I thee chees,
Noght for no coveitise, doutelees,
But oonly for the love I hadde to thee.
And thogh that I be old and may nat see,
Beth to me trewe, and I wol telle yow why.

2170   Thre thinges, certes, shal ye winne therby:
First, love of Crist, and to yourself honour,
And al min heritage, toun and tour,
I yeve it yow – maketh chartres as yow leste.
This shal be doon tomorwe, er sonne reste,

2175   So wysly God my soule bringe in blisse!
I pray yow first in covenant ye me kisse.
And thogh that I be jalous, wite me noght;
Ye been so depe enprented in my thoght
That whan that I considere youre beautee,

2180   And therwithal the unlikly elde of me,
I may nat, certes, thogh I sholde die,
Forbere to been out of youre compaignye
For verray love; this is withouten doute.
Now kis me, wif, and lat us rome aboute.'

2185   This fresshe May, whan she thise wordes herde,
Benignely to Januarye answerde;
But first and forward she bigan to wepe.
'I have', quod she, 'a soule for to kepe

2159 **clapte to** banged shut   2163 **Levere ich hadde** I would rather
2164 **offende** harm   2166 **coveitise** covetousness   2173 **chartres** charters,
deeds transferring property **as yow leste** as it please you   2174 **reste** goes
down   2176 **in covenant** as a sign of agreement   2177 **wite** blame
2178 **enprented** imprinted   2180 **unlikly elde** disproportionate age
2187 **first and forward** first of all

As wel as ye, and also min honour,
And of my wifhod thilke tendre flour,   2190
Which that I have assured in youre hond,
Whan that the preest to yow my body bond.
Wherfore I wol answere in this manere,
By the leve of yow, my lord so deere:
I pray to God that nevere dawe the day   2195
That I ne sterve as foule as womman may,
If evere I do unto my kin that shame,
Or ellis I empeire so my name,
That I be fals; and if I do that lakke,
Do strepe me and put me in a sakke,   2200
And in the nexte river do me drenche.
I am a gentil womman and no wenche!
Why speke ye thus? – but men been evere
        untrewe,
And wommen have repreve of yow ay newe.
Ye han noon oother contenance, I leve,   2205
But speke to us of untrust and repreve.'
    And with that word she saw wher Damian
Sat in the bussh, and coughen she bigan,
And with hir finger signes made she
That Damian sholde climbe upon a tree   2210
That charged was with fruit, and up he wente;
For verraily he knew al hir entente,
And every signe that she koude make,
Wel bet than Januarye, hir owene make,
For in a lettre she hadde told him al,   2215
Of this matere how he werken shal.

2191 **assured** entrusted   2192 **bond** united   2194 **By the leve of yow** by
your leave   2195 **dawe** may dawn   2196 **sterve** die **foule** shamefully
2198 **empeire** impair **name** reputation   2199 **do that lakke** commit that
fault   2200 **Do strepe me** have me stripped   2201 **do me drenche** have me
drowned   2204 **repreve** reproach **ay newe** over and over again
2205 **contenance** way of behaving   2206 **But speke** except speaking
untrust distrust   2211 **charged** laden   2214 **make** spouse
2216 **Of** concerning

And thus I lete him sitte upon the pirie,
And Januarye and May rominge mirye.
    Bright was the day, and blew the firmament;
2220 Phebus of gold doun hath his stremes sent
To gladen every flour with his warmnesse.
He was that time in Geminis, as I gesse,
But litel fro his declinacioun
Of Cancer, Jovis exaltacioun.
2225 And so bifel, that brighte morwe-tide,
That in that gardin in the ferther side
Pluto, that is king of faierye,
And many a lady in his compaignye,
Folwinge his wif, the queene Proserpina,
2230 Which that he ravisshed out of Ethna,
Whil that she gadered floures in the mede –
In Claudian ye may the storye rede,
How in his grisly carte he hire fette –
This king of fairye thanne adoun him sette
2235 Upon a bench of turves, fressh and grene.
And right anon thus seide he to his queene:
    'My wif,' quod he, 'ther may no wight sey nay;
Th'experience so preveth every day
The treson which that womman dooth to man.
2240 Ten hundred thousand tales telle I kan,
Notable of youre untrouthe and brotelnesse.
O Salomon, wis and richest of richesse,
Fulfild of sapience and of worldly glorye,
Ful worthy been thy wordes to memorye,
2245 To every wight that wit and reson kan!
Thus preiseth he yet the bountee of man:

2217 **lete him sitte** leave him sitting **pirie** pear-tree   2218 **mirye** happily
2219 **blew** blue **firmament** sky   2223–4 **his declinacioun Of Cancer** the
summer solstice (n.) **exaltacioun** place of greatest influence (n.)
2225 **morwe-tide** morning   2226 **ferther side** opposite side
2227 **faierye** fairyland   2231 **mede** meadow   2233 **fette** fetched
2237 **sey nay** deny it   2238 **preveth** proves   2241 **Notable** historically
attested **untrouthe** unfaithfulness   2243 **sapience** wisdom
2244 **worthy . . . to memorye** memorable   2245 **kan** commands
2246 **bountee** goodness

"Amonges a thousand men yet foond I oon,
But of wommen alle foond I noon."
– Thus seyth the king that knoweth youre
        wikkednesse.
And Jesus, *filius Sirak*, as I gesse,   2250
Ne speketh of yow but selde reverence.
A wilde fir and corrupt pestilence
So falle upon youre bodies yet tonight!
Ne se ye noght this honurable knight,
Bicause, allas, that he is blind and old,   2255
His owene man shal make him cokewold?
Lo, where he sit, the lechour in the tree!
Now wol I graunten, of my magestee,
Unto this olde, blinde, worthy knight,
That he shal have ayein his eyen sight,   2260
Whan that his wif wolde doon him vileinye.
Thanne shal he knowen al hir harlotrye,
Bothe in repreve of hire, and othere mo.'
    'Ye shal?' quod Proserpine, 'wol ye so?
Now by my modres sires soule I swere   2265
That I shal yeve hire suffisant answere,
And alle wommen after, for hir sake –
That thogh they be in any gilt ytake,
With face bold they shul hemself excuse,
And bere hem doun that wolden hem accuse.   2270
For lakke of answere noon of hem shal dien.
Al hadde man seyn a thing with bothe his eyen,
Yet shal we wommen visage it hardily,
And wepe, and swere, and chide subtilly,
So that ye men shul been as lewed as gees.   2275
    'What rekketh me of youre auctoritees?

2247 **foond** found   2251 **selde** seldom   2252 **wilde fir** erysipelas
corrupt infectious   2260 **ayein** back   2261 **vileinye** wrong
2262 **harlotrye** lechery   2263 **repreve** reproach   2266 **suffisant** sufficient
2268 **in any gilt ytake** caught in any wrongdoing   2269 **excuse** exonerate
2270 **bere . . . doun** talk down   2273 **visage it** put a bold face on it
2275 **lewed** stupid   2276 **What rekketh me** what do I care
auctoritees written testimonies

I woot wel that this Jew, this Salomon,
Fand of us wommen fooles many oon.
But thogh that he ne fand no good womman,
2280   Yet hath ther founde many another man
Wommen ful trewe, ful goode, and vertuous.
Witnesse on hem that dwelle in Cristes hous:
With martyrdom they preved hir constaunce.
The Romain geestes eek make remembraunce
2285   Of many a verray, trewe wif also.
But sire, ne be nat wrooth al be it so,
Thogh that he seide he foond no good womman;
I pray yow, take the sentence of the man:
He mente thus, that in soverain bountee
2290   Nis noon but God, but neither he ne she.
        'Ey, for verray God that nis but oon,
What make ye so muche of Salomon?
What thogh he made a temple, Goddes hous?
What thogh he were riche and glorious?
2295   So made he eek a temple of false goddis!
How mighte he do a thing that moore forbode is?
Pardee, as faire as ye his name emplastre,
He was a lechour and an idolastre,
And in his elde he verray God forsook.
2300   And if God ne hadde, as seyth the book,
Yspared him for his fadres sake, he sholde
Have lost his regne rather than he wolde.
I sette right noght, of al the vileinye
That ye of wommen write, a boterflye!
2305   I am a womman; nedes moot I speke,
Or ellis swelle til min herte breke.

2278 **Fand** found   2280 Yet many other men have found
2284–5 **geestes** chronicles **make remembraunce Of** record
2286 **al be it so** although it is the case   2287 **foond** found
2288 **sentence** meaning   2289 **soverain** supreme   2290 **he ne she** man nor
woman   2296 **forbode** forbidden   2297 **emplastre** plaster over, whitewash
2298 **idolastre** idolater   2299 **elde** old age   2302 **regne** kingdom
rather than he wolde sooner than he might wish   2303 **sette right noght** do
not value

For sithe he seide that we been jangleresses,
As evere hool I mote brouke my tresses,
I shal nat spare for no curteisye
To speke him harm that wolde us vileinye.'   2310
     'Dame,' quod this Pluto, 'be no lenger wrooth;
I yeve it up! But sith I swoor min ooth
That I wolde graunten him his sighte agein,
My word shal stonde, I warne yow certein.
I am a king; it sit me noght to lie.'   2315
     'And I,' quod she, 'a queene of faierye!
Hir answere shal she have, I undertake.
Lat us namoore wordes herof make;
For sothe, I wol no lenger yow contrarye.'

     Now lat us turne again to Januarye,   2320
That in the gardin with his faire May
Singeth ful murier than the papejay,
'Yow love I best, and shal, and oother noon.'
So longe aboute the aleyes is he goon
Til he was come agains thilke pirie   2325
Wheras this Damian sitteth ful mirye,
An heigh among the fresshe leves grene.

     This fresshe May, that is so bright and shene,
Gan for to sike, and seide, 'Allas, my side!
Now sire,' quod she, 'for aught that may bitide,   2330
I moste han of the peris that I se,
Or I moot die; so sore longeth me
To eten of the smale peris grene.
Help, for hir love that is of hevene queene!
I telle yow wel, a womman in my plit   2335
May han to fruit so gret an appetit

2307 **jangleresses** scolds   2308 As I live (*lit.* as I may have the use of my
hair unharmed)   2310 **wolde us vileinye** would wish shame on us
2315 **sit me noght** does not befit me   2319 **contrarye** oppose
2322 **murier** more sweetly **papejay** parrot   2324 **aleyes** garden-walks
2325 **agains** in front of **pirie** pear-tree   2326 **mirye** pleasantly
2328 **shene** radiant   2329 **Gan for to sike** sighed   2331 **of the peris** some
of the pears   2332 **longeth me** I long   2335 **plit** condition

That she may dien but she of it have.'
        'Allas!' quod he, 'that I nadde here a knave
That koude climbe! Allas, allas!' quod he,
2340   'For I am blind.' 'Ye, sire, no fors,' quod she;
'But wolde ye vouchesauf, for Goddes sake,
The pirie inwith youre armes for to take –
For wel I woot that ye mistruste me –
Thanne sholde I climbe wel inow,' quod she,
2345   'So I my foot mighte sette upon youre bak.'
        'Certes,' quod he, 'theron shal be no lak,
Mighte I yow helpen with min herte-blood.'
He stoupeth doun, and on his bak she stood,
And caughte hir by a twiste, and up she goth –
2350   Ladies, I pray yow that ye be nat wroth;
I kan nat glose, I am a rude man –
And sodeinly anon this Damian
Gan pullen up the smok and in he throng.
        And whan that Pluto saugh this grete wrong,
2355   To Januarye he yaf again his sighte,
And made him see as wel as evere he mighte.
And whan that he hadde caught his sighte again,
Ne was ther nevere man of thing so fain.
But on his wif his thoght was everemo;
2360   Up to the tree he caste his eyen two,
And saugh that Damian his wif had dressed
In swich manere, it may nat ben expressed,
But if I wolde speke uncurteisly.
And up he yaf a roring and a cry,
2365   As doth the moder whan the child shal die.
        'Out, help! allas! harrow!' he gan to crye,

2337 **but** unless   2338 **knave** servant   2340 **no fors** no matter
2341 **vouchesauf** be so good as   2344 **inow** enough   2345 **So** provided
that   2349 **twiste** branch   2351 **glose** use euphemisms   **rude** uncultured
2353 **Gan pullen up** pulled up   **throng** thrust
2357 **caught ... again** recovered   2361 **dressed** dealt with   2363 Unless I
were willing to speak improperly   2364 **up ... yaf** uttered

'O stronge lady stoore, what dostow?'
   And she answerde, 'Sire, what eileth yow?
Have pacience and reson in youre minde.
I have yow holpe on bothe youre eyen blinde;   2370
Up peril of my soule, I shal nat lien,
As me was taught, to heele with youre eyen,
Was nothing bet to make yow to se,
Than strugle with a man upon a tree.
God woot, I dide it in ful good entente.'   2375
   'Strugle!' quod he, 'ye, algate in it wente!
God yeve yow bothe on shames deth to dien!
He swived thee, I saw it with mine eyen,
And ellis be I hanged by the hals!'
'Thanne is', quod she, 'my medicine fals;   2380
For certeinly, if that ye mighte se,
Ye wolde nat seyn thise wordes unto me.
Ye han som glimsinge, and no parfit sighte.'
   'I se', quod he, 'as wel as evere I mighte,
Thonked be God, with bothe mine eyen two!   2385
And by my trouthe, me thoughte he dide thee so.'
'Ye maze, maze, goode sire,' quod she,
'This thank have I for I have maad yow se!
Allas,' quod she, 'that evere I was so kinde!'
   'Now, dame,' quod he, 'lat al passe out of   2390
      minde.
Com doun, my lief, and if I have missaid,
God helpe me so as I am ivele apaid.
But by my fader soule, I wende have seyn
How that this Damian hadde by thee lein,
And that thy smok hadde lein upon thy brest.'   2395
'Ye, sire,' quod she, 'ye may wene as yow lest.

2367 **stronge** brazen **stoore** bold   2368 **what eileth yow** what is the matter
with you   2370 **holpe** helped   2372 **heele** heal   2373 **bet** better
2376 **algate** nevertheless   2377 **yeve** grant   2378 **swived** fucked
2379 **hals** neck   2383 **glimsinge** blurred vision   2387 **maze** are confused
2388 **for** because   2391 **lief** dear **missaid** spoken out of turn
2392 **ivele apaid** sorry   2393 **wende have seyn** thought I saw

But sire, a man that waketh out of his sleep,
He may nat sodeinly wel taken keep
Upon a thing, ne seen it parfitly,
2400　Til that he be adawed verraily.
Right so a man that longe hath blind ybe
Ne may nat sodeinly so wel ise
First whan his sighte is newe come agein,
As he that hath a day or two yseyn.
2405　Til that youre sighte ysatled be a while,
Ther may ful many a sighte yow bigile.
Beth war, I prey yow, for by hevene king,
Ful many a man weneth to se a thing,
And it is al another than it semeth.
2410　He that misconceiveth, he misdemeth.'
　– And with that word, she leep doun fro the tree.
　　This Januarye, who is glad but he?
He kisseth hire and clippeth hire ful ofte,
And on hir wombe he stroketh hire ful softe,
2415　And to his palais hom he hath hire lad.
Now goode men, I pray yow to be glad;
Thus endeth here my tale of Januarye;
God blesse us, and his moder Seinte Marye!

Heere is ended the
Marchantes Tale of Januarye.

2398–9 **taken keep Upon a thing** take something in
2400 **adawed** awakened 2402 **ise** see 2404 **yseyn** seen
2405 **ysatled** settled 2406 **bigile** deceive 2410 **misconceiveth** perceives
wrongly **misdemeth** misjudges 2411 **leep** leapt 2413 **clippeth** hugs

THE MERCHANT'S
EPILOGUE

'Ey, Goddes mercy,' seide oure Hooste tho,
'Now swich a wif I prey God kepe me fro!   2420
Lo, whiche sleightes and subtilitees
In wommen ben; for ay as bisy as bees
Ben they, us sely men for to deceive.
And from a sooth evere wol they weive;
By this Marchauntes tale it preveth weel.   2425
But doutelees, as trewe as any steel
I have a wif, thogh that she poore be.
But of hir tonge a labbing shrewe is she;
And yit she hath an heep of vices mo.
Therof no fors – lat alle swiche thinges go!   2430
But wite ye what? – in conseil be it seid –
Me reweth soore I am unto hire teid.
For, and I sholde rekenen every vice
Which that she hath, ywis I were to nice.
And cause why? It sholde reported be,   2435
And toold to hire, of somme of this meinee –
Of whom, it nedeth nat for to declare,
Sin wommen konnen outen swich chaffare.
And eek my wit suffiseth nat therto
To tellen al; wherfore my tale is do.'   2440

2421 **whiche sleightes** what tricks **subtilitees** stratagems
2423 **sely** innocent   2424 And they will always deviate from the truth
2425 **preveth weel** is very evident   2428 **labbing** blabbing
2430 **no fors** no matter   2431 **wite ye** do you know **in conseil** in
confidence   2432 **Me reweth soore** I bitterly regret **teid** tied, bound
2433 **and I sholde** if I were to   2434 **I were to nice** I would be too foolish
2436 **of somme** by some **meinee** company
2438 **konnen outen swich chaffare** can display goods of this sort
2439 **therto** for it   2440 **my tale is do** I have said my piece

THE SQUIRE'S PROLOGUE

'Squier, com neer, if it youre wille be,
And sey somwhat of love, for certes ye
Konnen theron as muche as any man.'
'Nay, sire,' quod he, 'but I wol seye as I kan
With hertly wil, for I wol nat rebelle
Again youre lust; a tale wol I telle.
Have me excused, if I speke amis.
My wil is good; and lo, my tale is this.'

THE SQUIRE'S TALE

Heere biginneth the Squieres Tale.

At Sarray, in the land of Tartarye,
Ther dwelte a king that werreyed Russie,
Thurgh which ther deide many a doghty man.
This noble king was cleped Cambiuskan,
Which in his time was of so greet renoun
That ther was nowher in no regioun
So excellent a lord in alle thing.
Him lakked noght that longeth to a king.
As of the secte of which that he was born,
He kepte his lay to which that he was sworn;

3 **Konnen theron** know about it   5 **hertly** sincere   6 **lust** wish

10 **werreyed** made war on   11 **doghty** brave   13 **Which** who
16 **longeth to** befits   17 **As of** as regards   **secte** sect, faith   18 **lay** law

And therto he was hardy, wis, and riche,
And pietous and just alwey iliche,   20
Sooth of his word, benigne and honurable,
Of his corage as any centre stable,
Yong, fressh, and strong, in armes desirous
As any bachiler of al his hous.
A fair persone he was, and fortunat,   25
And kepte alwey so wel royal estat
That ther was nowher swich another man.
     This noble king, this Tartre Cambiuskan,
Hadde two sones on Elpheta his wif;
Of whiche the eldeste highte Algarsif,   30
That oother sone was cleped Cambalo.
A doghter hadde this worthy king also,
That yongest was, and highte Canacee.
But for to telle yow al hir beautee,
It lith nat in my tonge n'in my konning.   35
I dar nat undertake so heigh a thing;
Min Englissh eek is insufficient.
It moste been a rethor excellent,
That koude hise colours longing for that art,
If he sholde hire discriven every part.   40
I am noon swich; I moot speke as I kan.
     And so bifel, that whan this Cambiuskan
Hath twenty winter born his diademe,
As he was wont fro yeer to yeer, I deme,
He leet the feste of his nativitee   45
Doon crien thurghout Sarray his citee,

19 **therto** also **hardy** brave   20 **pietous** merciful **iliche** unvaryingly
21 **Sooth** truthful   22 In temperament as stable as the centre of any circle
23 **in armes desirous** keen in battle   24 **bachiler** young knight
26 **kepte . . . royal estat** maintained regal splendour   30 **highte** was called
31 **cleped** called   35 **lith** lies **konning** ability   38 **moste been** would have
to be **rethor** rhetorician   39 **colours** stylistic embellishments (see n. to Cl
16–18) **longing for** belonging to   40 **discriven** describe   43 **born** worn
45–6 **leet . . . Doon crien** had proclaimed **nativitee** birthday

The laste Idus of March, after the yeer.
Phebus the sonne ful jolif was and cleer,
For he was ny his exaltacioun,
50   In Martes face, and in his mansioun
In Aries, the colerik hote signe.
Ful lusty was the weder and benigne,
For whiche the foweles again the sonne shene –
What for the sesoun and the yonge grene –
55   Ful loude songen hir affeccions.
Hem semed han geten hem proteccions
Again the swerd of winter, kene and cold.
    This Cambiuskan, of which I have yow told,
In royal vestiment sit on his deis,
60   With diademe, ful hye in his paleis,
And halt his feste, so solempne and so riche
That in this world ne was ther noon it liche.
Of which if I shal tellen al th'array,
Thanne wolde it occupye a someres day;
65   And eek it nedeth nat for to devise
At every cours the ordre of hir servise.
I wol nat tellen of hir straunge sewes,
Ne of hir swannes, n'of hir heronsewes.
Eek in that land, as tellen knightes olde,
70   Ther is som mete that is ful deintee holde
That in this land men recche of it but smal.
Ther nis no man that may reporten al;
I wol nat taryen yow, for it is prime,
And for it is no fruit, but los of time;

47 **The laste Idus of March** March 15   48 **jolif** gay   **cleer** bright
49 **ny** near   **exaltacioun** position of greatest influence (n.)
50 **face ... mansioun** see n.   51 **colerik** choleric (n.)   52 **lusty** pleasant
benigne mild   53 **again** in   **shene** bright   54 **grene** greenery
55 **loude** loudly   56 **geten hem** got themselves   59 **sit** (= *sitteth*) sits
deis dais   61 **halt** (= *holdeth*) holds   **solempne** splendid   62 **liche** like
65 **devise** recount   67 **straunge sewes** exotic concoctions
68 **heronsewes** young herons   70 **ful deintee holde** considered very
delicious   71 **recche of it but smal** think but little of it   73 **taryen** delay
prime 9 a.m. (g.)   74 **no fruit** nothing essential

Unto my firste I wol have my recours.   75
    And so bifel that, after the thridde cours,
Whil that this king sit thus in his nobleye,
Herkninge his minestrals hir thinges pleye
Biforn him at the bord deliciously,
In at the halle-dore al sodeinly   80
Ther cam a knight upon a steede of bras,
And in his hand a brood mirour of glas;
Upon his thombe he hadde of gold a ring,
And by his side a naked swerd hanging,
And up he rideth to the heighe bord.   85
In al the halle ne was ther spoke a word
For merveille of this knight; him to biholde
Ful bisily they waiten, yonge and olde.
    This straunge knight, that cam thus sodeinly,
Al armed, save his heed, ful richely,   90
Salueth king and queene and lordes alle,
By ordre, as they seten in the halle,
With so heigh reverence and obeisaunce,
As wel in speche as in his contenaunce,
That Gawain, with his olde curteisye,   95
Thogh he were come again out of fairye,
Ne koude him nat amende with a word.
And after this, biforn the hye bord,
He with a manly vois seide his message,
After the forme used in his langage,   100
Withouten vice of sylable or of lettre.
And for his tale sholde seme the bettre,
Acordant to his wordes was his cheere,
As techeth art of speche hem that it leere.
Albeit that I kan nat sowne his style,   105
Ne kan nat climben over so heigh a stile,

75 **firste** first subject **have my recours** return   77 **nobleye** splendour
78 **thinges** compositions   79 **deliciously** delightfully   85 **bord** table
88 **bisily** eagerly **waiten** watch   91 **Salueth** greets   92 **seten** sat
94 **contenaunce** behaviour   96 **fairye** fairyland   97 **amende** excel
100 **After** according to   101 **vice** defect **sylable** syllable   102 **for** in order
that   103 **cheere** expression   104 **leere** learn   105 **sowne** echo, imitate

Yet seye I this: as to commune entente,
Thus muche amounteth al that evere he mente –
If it be so that I have it in minde.
110   He seide, 'The king of Arabe and of Inde,
My lige lord, on this solempne day
Salueth yow as he best kan and may,
And sendeth yow, in honour of youre feste,
By me, that am al redy at youre heste,
115   This steede of bras, that esily and weel
Kan in the space of o day naturel –
This is to seyn, in foure and twenty houres –
Wherso yow list, in droghte or ellis shoures,
Beren youre body into every place
120   To which youre herte wilneth for to pace,
Withouten wem of yow, thurgh foul or fair.
Or if yow list to flee as hye in th'air
As dooth an egle whan him list to soore,
This same steede shal bere yow everemoore,
125   Withouten harm, til ye be ther yow leste,
Though that ye slepen on his bak or reste,
And turne again with writhing of a pin.
He that it wroghte koude ful many a gin;
He waited many a constellacioun
130   Er he hadde doon this operacioun,
And knew ful many a seel and many a bond.
        'This mirour eek, that I have in my hond,
Hath swich a might that men may in it see
Whan ther shal fallen any adversitee

---

107 **as to commune entente** as far as the general meaning is concerned
108 **al that evere** everything that   111 **lige** liege **solempne** festive
112 **as he best kan and may** to the best of his ability   114 **heste** command
116 **o day naturel** one 24-hour day   118 **Wherso yow list** wherever pleases
you   120 **wilneth** wishes **pace** go   121 **wem** harm **thurgh foul or fair** over
rough and smooth   122 **flee** fly   123 **soore** soar   124 **everemoore** all the
time   125 **ther yow leste** where you want to be   127 **turne again** return
writhing turning   128 The man who made it knew many contrivances
129 **waited** observed   131 **seel** seal **bond** ?legal document (n.)
133 **a might** power

Unto youre regne, or to youreself also,   135
And openly who is youre freend or fo.
   'And over al this, if any lady bright
Hath set hir herte on any maner wight,
If he be fals, she shal his tresoun see –
His newe love and al his subtiltee –   140
So openly, that ther shal nothing hide.
Wherfore, again this lusty someres tide,
This mirour and this ring that ye may see
He hath sent to my lady Canacee,
Youre excellente doghter that is heere.   145
   'The vertu of the ring, if ye wol heere,
Is this: that if hir list it for to were
Upon hir thombe, or in hir purs it bere,
Ther is no fowel that fleeth under the hevene
That she ne shal wel understonde his stevene,   150
And knowe his mening openly and plein,
And answere him in his langage agein;
And every gras that groweth upon roote,
She shal eek knowe, and whom it wol do boote,
Al be his woundes nevere so depe and wide.   155
   'This naked swerd that hangeth by my side
Swich vertu hath, that, what man so ye smite,
Thurghout his armure it wol kerve and bite,
Were it as thikke as is a braunched ook.
And what man that is wounded with the strook,   160
Shal nevere be hool til that yow list, of grace,
To stroke him with the platte in thilke place
Ther he is hurt; this is as muche to seyn
Ye moote with the platte swerd agein

135 regne kingdom   140 subtiltee treachery   141 hide be hidden
142 again this lusty someres tide at the approach of this fine summer
146 vertu power   147 hir list it it pleases her   were wear   148 bere carry
149 fowel bird   fleeth flies   150 stevene tongue   154 do boote heal
157 what man so ye smite whatever man you strike   158 kerve cut
161 hool healed   of grace as a favour   162 platte flat side   thilke the same

165   Stroke him in the wounde and it wol close.
        This is a verray sooth, withouten glose;
        It failleth nat whiles it is in youre hold.'
            And whan this knight hath thus his tale ytold,
        He rideth out of halle and doun he lighte.
170   His steede, which that shoon as sonne brighte,
        Stant in the court, as stille as any stoon.
        This knight is to his chambre lad anoon,
        And is unarmed, and to mete yset.
            The presentes been ful realliche yfet –
175   This is to seyn, the swerd and the mirour –
        And born anon into the heighe tour,
        With certein officers ordeined therfore.
        And unto Canacee the ring is bore
        Solempnely, ther she sit at the table.
180   But sikerly, withouten any fable,
        The hors of bras, that may nat be remewed,
        It stant as it were to the ground yglewed.
        Ther may no man out of the place it drive
        For noon engin of windas or polive.
185   And cause why? – for they kan nat the craft.
        And therfore in the place they han it laft,
        Til that the knight hath taught hem the manere
        To voiden him, as ye shal after heere.
            Greet was the prees that swarmeth to and fro
190   To gauren on this hors that stondeth so,
        For it so heigh was, and so brood and long,
        So wel proporcioned for to ben strong,
        Right as it were a steede of Lumbardye;
        Therwith so horsly, and so quik of eye,

166 **withouten glose** plainly, without word-spinning   167 **hold** possession
169 **doun . . . lighte** dismounted   171 **court** courtyard **stille** silent
173 **to mete yset** seated at dinner   174 **realliche** royally **yfet** fetched
177 **therfore** for that purpose   178 **bore** carried
179 **Solempnely** ceremoniously **ther** where   181 **remewed** removed
182 **yglewed** glued   184 **engin** contrivance **windas** windlass **polive** pulley
185 **kan nat the craft** don't know the art   188 **voiden** remove
189 **prees** crowd   190 **gauren on** stare at   194 **horsly** horse-like **quik** lively

As it a gentil Poileis courser were.   195
For certes, fro his tail unto his ere,
Nature ne art ne koude him nat amende
In no degree, as al the peple wende.
But everemoore hir mooste wonder was
How that it koude goon, and was of bras.   200
It was a fairye, as the peple semed.
Diverse folk diversely they demed;
As many heddes, as many wittes ther been.
They murmured as dooth a swarm of been,
And maden skiles after hir fantasies,   205
Rehersynge of thise olde poetries,
And seiden it was lik the Pegasee,
The hors that hadde winges for to flee;
Or ellis it was the Grekes hors Sinoun,
That broghte Troye to destruccioun,   210
As men mowe in thise olde gestes rede.
　　'Min herte', quod oon, 'is everemoore in drede;
I trowe som men of armes been therinne,
That shapen hem this cite for to winne.
It were right good that al swich thing were   215
　　knowe.'
Another rowned to his felawe lowe
And seide, 'He lieth, for it is rather lik
An apparence ymaad by som magik,
As jogelours pleyen at thise festes grete.'
Of sondry doutes thus they jangle and trete,   220

195 **gentil** well-bred **courser** steed   197 **amende** improve on
198 **In no degree** in any way **wende** thought   199 **everemoore** always
mooste greatest   200 **goon** move   201 It was a magic contrivance, as it
seemed to the people   202 **Diverse** different **demed** thought
203 **wittes** opinions   204 **been** bees   205 And invented arguments
according to their own fancies   206 **Rehersynge** repeating **poetries** poems
209 **the Grekes hors Sinoun** the horse of the Greek Sinon (n.)
211 **gestes** stories   212 **everemoore** continually   213 **therinne** inside
214 **shapen hem** plan   216 **rowned** whispered **lowe** softly
218 **apparence** illusion   219 **jogelours** conjurers   220 **jangle** chatter
trete discuss

As lewed peple demeth comunly
Of thinges that been maad moore subtilly
Than they kan in hir lewednesse comprehende;
They demen gladly to the badder ende.
225   And somme of hem wondred on the mirour,
That born was up unto the maister tour,
How men mighte in it swiche thinges se.
Another answerde and seide it mighte wel be
Naturelly, by composiciouns
230 Of anglis, and of sly reflexiouns,
And seiden that in Rome was swich oon.
They speke of Alocen and Vitulon,
And Aristotle, that writen in hir lives
Of queinte mirours and of perspectives,
235 As knowen they that han hir bookes herd.
    And oother folk han wondred on the swerd
That wolde percen thurghout every thing,
And fille in speche of Thelophus the king,
And of Achilles with his queinte spere,
240 For he koude with it bothe heele and dere,
Right in swich wise as men may with the swerd,
Of which right now ye han yourselven herd.
They speke of sondry harding of metal,
And speke of medicines therwithal,
245 And how and whanne it sholde yharded be,
Which is unknowe – algates unto me.
    Tho speeke they of Canacees ring,
And seiden alle that swich a wonder thing

---

221 **lewed** ignorant   223 **lewednesse** ignorance
224 **demen . . . to the badder ende** adopt the worst interpretation
226 **maister tour** principal tower   229 **composiciouns** combinations
230 **anglis** angles (of reflection)   **sly reflexiouns** skilful reflections
233 **writen in hir lives** wrote while they lived   234 **queinte** ingenious
perspectives optical lenses   238 **fille in speche of** began talking about
239 **queinte** curious   240 **dere** harm   243 **harding** hardening, tempering
244 **medicines** transmuting agents   245 **yharded** hardened   246 **algates** at
any rate

Of craft of ringes herde they nevere non,
Save that he Moises and king Salomon   250
Hadde a name of konning in swich art;
Thus seyn the peple, and drawen hem apart.

   But natheless, somme seiden that it was
Wonder to maken of fern-asshen glas,
And yet is glas nat lik asshen of fern,   255
But for they han yknowen it so fern,
Therfore cesseth hir jangling and hir wonder.
As soore wondren somme on cause of thonder,
On ebbe and flood, on gossomer, and on mist,
And alle thing, til that the cause is wist.   260
Thus janglen they and demen and devise,
Til that the king gan fro the bord arise.

   Phebus hath laft the angle meridional,
And yet ascending was the beest royal,
The gentil Leon, with his Aldiran,   265
Whan that this Tartre king, Cambiuskan,
Roos fro his bord theras he sat ful hye.
Biforn him gooth the loude minstralcye
Til he cam to his chambre of parementz
Thereas they sownen diverse instrumentz   270
That it is lik an hevene for to heere.
Now dauncen lusty Venus children deere,
For in the Fissh hir lady sat ful hye,
And looketh on hem with a freendly eye.

   This noble king is set upon his trone;   275
This straunge knight is fet to him ful soone,

---

249 **nevere non** none of them   251 **name of** reputation for
252 **drawen hem apart** move away   254 **fern-asshen** ashes made by burning
ferns (n.)   256 **for** because **so fern** for so long a time   257 **cesseth** ceases
jangling chatter   258 **soore** earnestly   259 **gossomer** gossamer
260 **wist** known   261 **demen** express opinions **devise** talk
263 **angle meridional** see n.   264 **yet** still   269 **chambre of parementz** state
room (hung with tapestries)   270 **sownen** play   272 **lusty** pleasure-loving
Venus children those born under Venus (n.)   273 **Fissh** Pisces
276 **straunge** stranger **fet** brought

And on the daunce he gooth with Canacee.
Here is the revel and the jolitee
That is nat able a dul man to devise!
280　He moste han knowen love and his servise,
And been a festlich man, as fressh as May,
That sholde yow devisen swich array.
　　Who koude telle yow the forme of daunces
So unkouthe, and swiche fresshe contenaunces,
285　Swich subtil looking and dissimulinges,
For drede of jalous mennes aperceivinges?
No man but Launcelot, and he is deed.
Therfore I passe of al this lustiheed;
I seye namoore, but in this jolynesse
290　I lete hem, til men to the soper dresse.
　　The stiward biddeth spices for to hie,
And eek the win, in al this melodye.
The usshers and the squiers been ygon;
The spices and the win is come anon.
295　They ete and drinke, and whan this hadde an
　　　　　ende,
Unto the temple, as reson was, they wende.
The service doon, they soupen al by day.
What nedeth yow rehercen hir array?
Ech man woot wel, that a kinges feste
300　Hath plentee to the meeste and to the leeste,
And deintees mo than been in my knowing.
At after-soper gooth this noble king
To seen this hors of bras, with al a route
Of lordes and of ladies him aboute.

279 **devise** describe　280 **his** its　281 **festlich** convivial
284 **unkouthe** unusual　**contenaunces** faces
285 **dissimulinges** dissimulations　286 **aperceivinges** perceptions
288 **passe of** pass over　**lustiheed** gaiety　289 **jolynesse** gaiety
290 **lete** leave　**dresse** turn their attention to　291 **biddeth** orders
hie be brought quickly　293 **usshers** door-keepers　296 **as reson was** as was
right　**wende** go　297 **soupen** eat supper　**by day** in daylight
298 **rehercen** describe　**array** splendour　300 **to** for　**meeste** greatest
303 **route** company

Swich wondring was ther on this hors of bras   305
That, sin the grete sege of Troye was,
Theras men wondreden on an hors also,
Ne was ther swich a wondring as was tho.
But finally, the king axeth this knight
The vertu of this courser and the might,   310
And preyed him to telle his governaunce.

This hors anon bigan to trippe and daunce,
Whan that this knight leide hand upon his reine,
And seide, 'Sire, ther is namoore to seyne
But, whan yow list to riden anywhere,   315
Ye moten trille a pin stant in his ere,
Which I shal telle yow bitwix us two.
Ye mote nempne him to what place also,
Or to what contree, that yow list to ride.
And whan ye come theras yow list abide,   320
Bid him descende, and trille another pin –
For therinne lith th'effect of al the gin –
And he wol doun descende and doon youre wille.
And in that place he wol abiden stille;
Though al the world the contrarye hadde yswore,   325
He shal nat thennes be ydrawe nor bore.
Or if yow liste bidde him thennes gon,
Trille this pin, and he wol vanisshe anon
Out of the sighte of every maner wight,
And come again, be it by day or night,   330
Whan that yow list to clepen him agein
In swich a gise as I shal to yow seyn
Bitwixen yow and me, and that ful soone.
Ride whan yow lust; ther is namoore to doone.'

---

307 **Theras** where   308 **tho** then   310 **vertu** abilities
311 **his governaunce** how to control him   312 **trippe** frisk
316 **moten** must **trille** turn **stant** (= *standeth*) which stands
318 **nempne** name   320 **abide** remain   322 **gin** device
325 **yswore** sworn   326 **ydrawe** dragged **bore** carried
329 **every maner wight** everybody   331 **clepen** call   332 **gise** manner
334 **namoore** nothing more

335   Enformed whan the king was of that knight,
        And hath conceived in his wit aright
        The manere and the forme of al this thing,
        Ful glad and blithe, this noble doghty king
        Repeireth to his revel as biforn.
340   The bridel is unto the tour yborn,
        And kept among his jewels leeve and deere;
        The hors vanisshed – I noot in what manere –
        Out of hir sighte; ye gete namoore of me!
        But thus I lete, in lust and jolitee,
345   This Cambiuskan his lordes festeyinge,
        Til wel neigh the day bigan to springe.

[Part Two]

        The norice of digestioun, the sleep,
        Gan on hem winke, and bad hem taken keep
        That muchel drink and labour wol have reste.
350   And with a galping mouth hem alle he keste,
        And seide that it was time to lie adoun,
        For blood was in his dominacioun.
        'Cherisseth blood, natures freend,' quod he.
        They thanken him, galpinge, by two, by three,
355   And every wight gan drawe him to his reste,
        As sleep hem bad; they tooke it for the beste.
           Hir dremes shul nat now been told for me;
        Ful were hir hedes of fumositee,
        That causeth dreem of which ther nis no charge.
360   They slepen til that it was prime large,

335 **of** by   336 **wit** mind   338 **doghty** excellent   339 **Repeireth** returns
340 **yborn** carried   341 **jewels** precious artefacts, treasures **leeve** prized
342 **noot** (= *ne woot*) do not know   344 **lete** leave **lust** pleasure
345 **festeyinge** feasting   346 **springe** dawn   347 **norice** nurse
348 **taken keep** take note   350 **galping** yawning **keste** kissed
352 **in his dominacioun** dominant (n.)   355 **gan drawe him** went
356 **bad** urged   358 **fumositee** vapour (g.)   359 **charge** significance
360 **prime large** fully 9 o'clock (g.)

The mooste part – but it were Canacee.
She was ful mesurable, as wommen be;
For of hir fader hadde she take leve
To goon to reste soone after it was eve –
Hir liste nat appalled for to be,   365
Nor on the morwe unfestlich for to se –
And slepte hir firste sleep and thanne awook.
For swich a joye she in hir herte took,
Bothe of hir queinte ring and hir mirour,
That twenty time she chaunged hir colour.   370
And in hir sleep, right for impressioun
Of hir mirour, she hadde a visioun.
Wherfore, er that the sonne gan up glide,
She cleped on hir maistresse hir biside,
And seide that hir liste for to rise.   375
    Thise olde wommen that been gladly wise,
As is hir maistresse, answerde hir anon,
And seide, 'Madame, whider wole ye gon
Thus erly, for the folk been alle on reste?'
'I wol', quod she, 'arise, for me leste   380
No lenger for to slepe, and walke aboute.'
    Hir maistresse clepith wommen a gret route,
And up they risen, wel a ten or twelve.
Up riseth fresshe Canacee hirselve,
As rody and bright as dooth the yonge sonne   385
That in the Ram is foure degrees up ronne –
Noon hyer was he whan she redy was.
And forth she walketh esily a pas,
Arrayed, after the lusty seson soote,
Lightly, for to pleye and walke on foote,   390

361 **but it were** except for   362 **mesurable** temperate   365 **Hir liste nat** she
did not want   **appalled** wan   366 Nor to look jaded next day
369 **queinte** curious   371 **impressioun** the emotional effect
373 **gan up glide** rose   374 **maistresse** governess
376 **been gladly wise** like to be wise   382 **route** band   385 **rody** ruddy
386 **the Ram** Aries (n.)   387 **Noon hyer** no higher   388 **esily a pas** in a
leisurely way   389 **lusty** pleasant **soote** sweet

Nat but with five or sixe of hir meinee,
And in a trench forth in the park goth she.
      The vapour which that fro the erthe glood
Made the sonne to seme rody and brood;
But nathelees it was so fair a sighte
That it made al hir hertes for to lighte,
What for the seson and the morweninge,
And for the fowles that she herde singe,
For right anon she wiste what they mente
Right by hir song, and knew al hir entente.
      The knotte why that every tale is told,
If it be taried til that lust be cold
Of hem that han it after herkned yoore,
The savour passeth, ever lenger the moore,
For fulsomnesse of his prolixitee.
And by the same reson, thinketh me,
I sholde to the knotte condescende,
And maken of hir walking soone an ende.
      Amidde a tree, for drye as whit as chalk,
As Canacee was pleyinge in hir walk,
Ther sat a fawkon over hir heed ful hye,
That with a pitous vois so gan to crye
That al the wode resowned of hir cry.
Ybeten hadde she hirself so pitously
With bothe hir winges, til the rede blood
Ran endelong the tree theras she stood.
And evere in oon she cride alwey and shrighte,
And with hir beek hirselven so she prighte

395

400

405

410

415

392 **trench** path cut through a wood   393 **vapour** mist **glood** rose
396 **lighte** be lightened   398 **fowles** birds   400 **entente** meaning
401 **knotte** nub (of story)   402 **taried** delayed **lust** pleasure
403 **after herkned** listened out for **yoore** for a long time
405 **fulsomnesse** abundance   406 **thinketh me** it seems to me
407 **condescende** proceed   409 **for drye** for dryness   411 **fawkon** falcon
412 **gan to crye** cried out   413 **resowned of** echoed with
416 **endelong** from top to bottom of   417 **shrighte** shrieked
418 **beek** beak **prighte** pricked, stabbed

That ther nis tigre ne so cruel beest
That dwelleth outher in wode or in forest   420
That nolde han wept, if that he wepe koude,
For sorwe of hire, she shrighte alwey so loude.
For ther nas nevere man yet on live –
If that I koude a faukon wel discrive –
That herde of swich another of fairnesse,   425
As wel of plumage as of gentillesse
Of shap, of al that mighte yrekened be.
A faukon peregrin thanne semed she,
Of fremde land; and everemoore, as she stood,
She swowned now and now for lakke of blood,   430
Til wel neigh is she fallen fro the tree.

    This faire kinges doghter, Canacee,
That on hir finger baar the queinte ring
Thurgh which she understood wel everything
That any fowl may in his ledene sayn,   435
And koude answere him in his ledene again,
Hath understonden what this faukon seide,
And wel neigh for the routhe almoost she deide.
And to the tree she goth ful hastily,
And on this faukon looketh pitously,   440
And heeld hir lappe abroad, for wel she wiste
The faukon moste fallen fro the twiste
Whan that it swowned next, for lakke of blood.
A longe while to waiten hir she stood,
Til at the laste she spak in this manere   445
Unto the hauk, as ye shal after heere:
    'What is the cause, if it be for to telle,
That ye been in this furial pine of helle?'

420 **outher** either   421 **nolde** would not   423 **on live** alive
426 **gentillesse** elegance   427 **yrekened** valued
428 **faukon peregrin** peregrine falcon   429 **fremde** foreign
430 **now and now** from time to time   433 **baar** wore **queinte** ingenious
435 **ledene** language   438 **routhe** pity   440 **pitously** pityingly
441 **heeld hir lappe abroad** stretched out her skirt   442 **twiste** branch
444 **waiten hir** watch her   448 **furial pine of helle** hellish torment, like that
of the Furies (see n. to Fkl 950)

Quod Canacee unto this hauk above.
450   'Is this for sorwe of deeth or los of love?
– For as I trowe, thise been causes two
That causen moost a gentil herte wo.
Of oother harm it nedeth nat to speke,
For ye yourself upon yourself yow wreke,
455   Which proveth wel that outher ire or drede
Moot been encheson of youre cruel dede,
Sin that I se noon oother wight yow chace.
For love of God, as dooth yourselven grace,
Or what may been youre help? – for west nor est
460   Ne saw I nevere er now no brid ne beest
That ferde with himself so pitously.
Ye sleen me with youre sorwe, verraily,
I have of yow so greet compassioun.
For Goddes love, com fro the tree adoun,
465   And as I am a kinges doghter trewe,
If that I verraily the cause knewe
Of youre disese, if it laye in my might,
I wolde amende it, er that it were night,
As wysly helpe me grete God of kinde!
470   And herbes shal I right inowe ifinde,
To heele with youre hurtes hastily.'
      Tho shrighte this faukon yet moore pitously
Than ever she dide, and fil to ground anon,
And lith aswowne, deed and lik a ston,
475   Til Canacee hath in hir lappe hir take,
Unto the time she gan of swow awake.
And after that she of hir swow gan breide,
Right in hir haukes ledene thus she seide:

---

452 **a gentil herte wo** distress to a noble heart   454 **yow wreke** take
vengeance   456 **encheson** cause   457 **chace** harass
458 **as dooth yourselven grace** have pity on yourself
461 **ferde with himself** behaved toward itself   462 **sleen** slay
467 **disese** suffering   468 **amende** remedy   469 **kinde** nature
470 **right inowe** in plenty   472 **pitously** pitiably   474 **lith aswowne** lies in a
swoon   476 **swow** swoon   477 **gan breide** awoke

'That pitee renneth soone in gentil herte,
Feelinge his similitude in peines smerte,   480
Is preved alday, as men may it see,
As wel by werk as by auctoritee,
For gentil herte kitheth gentillesse.
I se wel that ye han of my distresse
Compassion, my faire Canacee,   485
Of verray wommanly benignitee
That Nature in youre principles hath set.
But for noon hope for to fare the bet,
But for t'obeye unto youre herte free,
And for to maken othere be war by me,   490
As by the whelp is chasted the leoun,
Right for that cause and that conclusioun,
Whil that I have a leiser and a space,
Min harm I wol confessen, er I pace.'

     And evere whil that oon hir sorwe tolde,   495
That oother weep, as she to water wolde,
Til that the faukon bad hire to be stille;
And with a sik right thus she seide hir wille.
'Ther I was bred – allas, that ilke day! –
And fostred in a roche of marbul gray,   500
So tendrely that nothing eiled me,
I niste nat what was adversitee
Til I koude fle ful hye under the sky.
Tho dwelte a tercelet me faste by,
That semed welle of alle gentillesse.   505
Al were he ful of treson and falsnesse,

480 Recognizing its likeness in bitter sufferings   481 **alday** constantly
482 **by werk** in practice **auctoritee** written testimony
483 **kitheth gentillesse** displays noble behaviour   486 **benignitee** kindness
488 **the bet** better   489 **free** gracious   490 **be war** take warning   491 As
the lion learns from the dog's punishment (n.)   492 **conclusioun** purpose
493 **a leiser** time **a space** opportunity   494 **pace** die   495 **that oon** the one
496 The other wept, as if she would turn to water   497 **stille** silent
498 **sik** sigh   499 **Ther** where   500 **roche** rock   501 **eiled** ailed
502 **niste nat** did not know   503 **fle** fly   504 **tercelet** male falcon
505 **welle** source

It was so wrapped under humble cheere
And under hewe of trouthe in swich manere,
Under plesaunce, and under bisy peine,
510   That no wight wolde han wend he koude feine,
So depe in grein he dyed his colours.
Right as a serpent hit him under floures
Til he may se his time for to bite,
Right so this God of Loves ypocrite
515   Dooth so his cerimonies and obeisaunces,
And kepeth in semblaunt alle hise observaunces
That sownen into gentilesse of love.
As in a tombe is al the faire above,
And under is the corps, swich as ye woot,
520   Swich was this ypocrite, bothe cold and hoot.
And in this wise he served his entente,
That, save the feend, noon wiste what he mente,
Til he so longe hadde wopen and compleined,
And many a yeer his service to me feined,
525   Til that min herte, to pitous and to nice,
Al innocent of his corouned malice,
Forfered of his deeth, as thoughte me,
Upon his othes and his seuretee
Graunted him love, on this condicioun:
530   That everemo min honour and renoun
Were saved, bothe privee and apert.
This is to seyn, that after his desert
I yaf him al min herte and al my thoght –
God woot, and he, that ootherwise noght –

507 **cheere** behaviour   508 **hewe** appearance   509 **bisy peine** diligent
endeavour   510 **wend** believed **feine** dissemble   511 So fast did he dye his
colours (n.)   512 **hit** (= *hideth*) **him** hides   515–16 Performs so well his
polite formalities and respectful attentions, and in appearance pays all the
attentions   517 **sownen into** are consistent with   518 **faire** beauty
521 **served his entente** furthered his purpose   522 **feend** devil
523 **wopen** wept **compleined** lamented   525 **nice** foolish
526 **corouned** consummate   527 **Forfered** afraid   528 **seuretee** pledge
530 **everemo** always   531 **privee and apert** in private and in public
532 **after** according to

And took his herte in chaunge of min for ay.   535
'But sooth is seid, goon sithen many a day,
A trewe wight and a theef thenken nat oon.
And whanne he saw the thing so fer ygon
That I hadde graunted him fully my love,
In swich a gise as I have seid above,   540
And yeven him my trewe herte as fre
As he swoor he yaf his herte to me,
Anoon this tigre, ful of doublenesse,
Fil on his knees, with so devout humblesse,
With so heigh reverence, and, as by his cheere,   545
So lik a gentil lovere of manere,
So ravisshed, as it semed, for the joye
That nevere Jason ne Paris of Troye –
Jason? certes, ne noon oother man
Sin Lameth was, that alderfirst bigan   550
To loven two, as writen folk biforn –
Ne nevere, sin the firste man was born,
Ne koude man by twenty thousand part
Countrefete the sophimes of his art,
Ne were worthy unbokele his galoche,   555
Ther doublenesse or feining sholde approche,
Ne so koude thanke a wight as he did me!
His manere was an hevene for to see
Til any womman, were she never so wis;
So peinted he and kembde at point devis   560
As wel his wordes as his contenaunce.
'And I so loved him for his obeisaunce,

535 **chaunge of** exchange for   536 **goon sithen many a day** long ago
537 **wight** person   540 **gise** manner   541 **fre** freely   545 **heigh** solemn
cheere demeanour   547 **ravisshed** enraptured   550 **alderfirst** first of all
551 **writen** wrote **biforn** earlier   553 **by twenty thousand part** multiplied
twenty thousand times   554 **Countrefete** imitate **sophimes** sophistries
555 **unbokele** to unbuckle **galoche** shoe   556 **approche** be involved
559 **Til** to   560 **kembde** polished (*lit.* combed) **at point devis** to perfection
562 **obeisaunce** obedience

And for the trouthe I demed in his herte,
That if so were that anything him smerte,
565   Al were it never so lite, and I it wiste,
Me thoughte I felte deeth min herte twiste.
And shortly, so ferforth this thing is went,
That my wil was his willes instrument;
This is to seyn, my wil obeyed his wil
570   In alle thing, as fer as reson fil,
Kepinge the boundes of my worship evere,
Ne nevere hadde I thing so lief, ne levere,
As him, God woot, ne nevere shal namo.
      'This laste lenger than a yeer or two,
575   That I supposed of him noght but good.
But finally, thus at the laste it stood,
That Fortune wolde that he moste twinne
Out of that place which that I was inne.
Wher me was wo, that is no questioun;
580   I kan nat make of it discripcioun,
For o thing dar I tellen boldely,
I knowe what is the peine of deeth therby.
Swich harm I felte, for he ne mighte bileve.
      'So on a day of me he took his leve,
585   So sorwefully eek, that I wende verraily
That he hadde felt as muche harm as I,
Whan that I herde him speke and saw his hewe.
But nathelees, I thoughte he was so trewe,
And eek that he repeire sholde again
590   Withinne a litel while, sooth to sayn –

563 **demed** believed to be   564 **him smerte** (= *smertede*) caused him pain
565 **Al were it never so lite** however little it was   566 **twiste** squeeze
567 **so ferforth** so far **is went** went   570 **as fer as reson fil** as far as was
reasonable   571 **worship** honour   572 **lief** dear **levere** dearer
573 **namo** anyone else   574 **laste** (= *lastede*) lasted   577 **moste twinne** had
to depart   579 **Wher me was wo** whether I was unhappy
580 **discripcioun** description   581 **o** one   582 **therby** by it
583 **for he ne mighte bileve** because he could not remain
585 **verraily** truly   587 **hewe** facial colour   589 **repeire** return

And reson wolde eek that he moste go
For his honour, as ofte happeth so –
That I made vertu of necessitee,
And took it wel, sin that it moste be.
As I best mighte, I hidde from him my sorwe,   595
And took him by the hand, Seint John to borwe,
And seide him thus: "Lo, I am youres al.
Beth swich as I to yow have been and shal."
What he answerde, it nedeth nat reherse.
Who kan seyn bet than he? Who kan doon   600
      werse?
Whan he hath al wel seid, thanne hath he doon!
Therfore bihoveth hire a ful long spoon
That shal ete with a feend; thus herde I seye.
So at the laste he moste forth his weye,
And forth he fleeth, til he cam ther him leste   605
Whan it cam him to purpos for to reste.
      'I trowe he hadde thilke text in minde
That "alle thing repeiring to his kinde
Gladeth himself" – thus seyn men, as I gesse.
Men loven of propre kinde newfangelnesse,   610
As briddes doon that men in cages fede;
For though thow night and day take of hem hede,
And strawe hir cage faire and softe as silk,
And yeve hem sugre, hony, breed, and milk,
Yet, right anon as that his dore is uppe,   615
He with his feet wol sporne adoun his cuppe,

591 **wolde** required   592 **happeth so** is the case
593 **made vertu of necessitee** bore cheerfully what was unavoidable
594 **moste** had to   595 **mighte** could   596 **Seint John to borwe** under the
protection of St John (expression used in saying farewell)
599 **it nedeth nat reherse** there is no need to repeat   600 **doon** act
602 **bihoveth hire** she needs   604 **moste forth his weye** had to go on his
way   605 **ther him leste** where it pleased him   606 **it cam him to purpos** he
decided   608 **repeiring to his kinde** reverting to its nature
609 **Gladeth himself** rejoices   610 **of propre kinde** by their very nature
newfangelnesse novelty   613 **strawe** cover the floor of   614 **sugre** sugar
615 **right anon as** as soon as **uppe** open (outwards)   616 **sporne** spurn, kick

And to the wode he wole and wormes ete.
So newefangel been they of hir mete,
And love novelries of propre kinde;
620   No gentilesse of blood ne may hem binde.
          'So ferde this tercelet, allas the day!
Thogh he were gentil born, and fressh and gay,
And goodlich for to seen, and humble and free,
He saw upon a time a kite flee,
625   And sodeinly he loved this kite so
That al his love is clene fro me ago,
And hath his trouthe falsed in this wise.
Thus hath the kite my love in hir servise,
And I am lorn withouten remedye!'
630   And with that word this faukon gan to crye,
And swowned eft in Canacees barm.
          Greet was the sorwe for the haukes harm
That Canacee and alle hir wommen made.
They niste how they mighte the faukon glade;
635   But Canacee hom bereth hire in hir lappe,
And softely in plastres gan hir wrappe,
Theras she with hir beek hadde hurt hirselve.
Now kan nat Canacee but herbes delve
Out of the ground, and maken saves newe
640   Of herbes preciouse and fin of hewe
To heelen with this hauk; fro day to night
She dooth hir bisinesse and al hir might.
And by hir beddes heed she made a mewe,
And covered it with veluettes blewe,

617 **wole** will go   618 **mete** food   619 **novelries** novelties
620 **gentilesse** nobility   621 **ferde** behaved   622 **gentil born** of noble birth
gay handsome   623 **goodlich** handsome **free** generous   624 **flee** fly
626 **clene** completely **ago** gone   627 **his trouthe falsed** broken his word
629 **lorn** lost   630 **gan to crye** cried out   631 **eft** again **barm** lap
634 **niste** did not know **glade** cheer up   636 **plastres** bandages
637 **Theras** in the place where   638 **but** anything other than **delve** dig
639 **saves** decoctions of herbs   642 She tries hard and does all she can
643 **mewe** cage   644 **veluettes** pieces of velvet

In signe of trouthe that is in wommen sene.   645
And al withoute the mewe is peinted grene,
In which were peinted alle thise false fowles,
As been thise tidives, tercelettes, and owles,
And pies, on hem for to crye and chide,
Right for despit were peinted hem biside.   650
    Thus lete I Canacee hir hauk keping.
I wol namoore as now speke of hir ring
Til it come eft to purpos for to seyn
How that this faukon gat hir love agein
Repentant, as the storye telleth us,   655
By mediacioun of Cambalus,
The kinges sone of which that I yow tolde.
But hennesforth I wol my proces holde,
To speke of aventures and of batailles,
That nevere yet was herd so grete mervailles.   660
    First wol I telle yow of Cambiuskan,
That in his time many a citee wan;
And after wol I speke of Algarsif,
How that he wan Theodora to wif,
For whom ful ofte in greet peril he was,   665
Nadde he been holpen by the steede of bras;
And after wol I speke of Cambalo,
That faught in listes with the bretheren two
For Canacee, er that he mighte hir winne.
And ther I lefte, I wol ayein biginne.   670

[*Part Three*]

Appollo whirleth up his chaar so hye,
Til that the god Mercurius hous, the slye –

---

646 **withoute** on the outside   648 **tidives** small birds, ?titmice
649 **pies** magpies   **chide** screech   652 **as now** just now
653 **come eft to purpos** becomes relevant again   657 **which that** whom
658 **proces** narrative   662 **wan** captured   664 **to wif** as wife
666 **Nadde he been holpen** if he had not been helped   671 **chaar** chariot
672 **the god Mercurius hous** the mansion of the god Mercury (n.)
slye clever, cunning

THE SQUIRE –
FRANKLIN LINK

Heere folwen the wordes of the
Frankelein to the Squier and
the wordes of the Hoost to
the Frankelein.

'In feith, Squier, thow hast thee wel yquit
And gentilly; I preise wel thy wit,'
675   Quod the Frankelein, 'consideringe thy youthe,
So feelingly thow spekest, sire, I allowthe!
As to my doom, ther is noon that is heere
Of eloquence that shal be thy peere,
If that thow live; God yeve thee good chaunce,
680   And in vertu sende thee continuance,
For of thy speche I have gret deintee.
I have a sone, and by the Trinitee,
I hadde levere than twenty pound worth lond,
Thogh it right now were fallen in min hond,
685   He were a man of swich discrecioun
As that ye ben. Fy on possessioun,
But if a man be vertuous withal!
I have my sone snibbed, and yit shal,
For he to vertu listeth nat entende,
690   But for to pleye at dees, and to despende

673 **thee wel yquit** acquitted yourself well   674 **wit** understanding
676 **feelingly** sensitively **I allowthe** I applaud you   677 **As to my doom** in
my opinion   678 **peere** equal   679 **yeve** grant **good chaunce** good luck
681 Because I take great pleasure in your speech   683 **hadde levere** would
rather   686 **possessioun** wealth   687 **But if** unless
688 **snibbed** reprimanded **yit shal** shall in the future
689 **listeth nat entende** does not want to pay any attention   690 **dees** dice
despende spend

And lese al that he hath, is his usage.
And he hath levere talken with a page
Than to commune with any gentil wight,
Wher he mighte lerne gentillesse aright.'
   'Straw for youre gentillesse!' quod oure Hoost.   695
'What, Frankelein! pardee sire, wel thow woost
That ech of yow moot tellen atte leste
A tale or two, or breken his biheste.'
   'That knowe I wel, sire,' quod the Frankelein,
'I prey yow, haveth me nat in desdein,   700
Thogh to this man I speke a word or two.'
   'Telle on thy tale, withouten wordes mo!'
'Gladly, sire Hoost,' quod he, 'I wol obeye
Unto youre wil; now herkneth what I seye.
I wol yow nat contraryen in no wise,   705
As fer as that my wittes wol suffise.
I prey to God that it may plesen yow;
Thanne woot I wel that it is good inow.'

THE FRANKLIN'S PROLOGUE

The Prologe of the Frankeleins Tale.

Thise olde gentil Britons in hir dayes
Of diverse aventures maden layes,   710
Rymeyed in hir firste Briton tonge,
Whiche layes with hir instrumentz they songe,
Or elles redden hem for hir plesaunce;
And oon of hem have I in remembraunce,

---

691 **lese** lose **usage** custom 692 **page** peasant 696 **woost** know
698 **biheste** promise 700 **haveth me nat in desdein** don't be offended with
me 705 **contraryen** antagonize 706 **wittes** abilities

709 **Britons** Bretons 710 **aventures** events 711 **Rymeyed** rhymed
713 **redden** read 714 **have ... in remembraunce** remember

715 Which I shal seyn with good wil, as I kan.
        But sires, bicause I am a burel man,
    At my biginning first I yow biseche,
    Have me excused of my rude speche.
    I lerned nevere rethorik, certein;
720 Thing that I speke, it moot be bare and plein.
    I sleep nevere on the mount of Parnaso,
    Ne lerned Marcus Tullius Scithero.
    Colours ne knowe I none, withouten drede,
    But swich colours as growen in the mede,
725 Or ellis swiche as men dye or peinte.
    Colours of rethorik ben to me queinte;
    My spirit feeleth nat of swich matere.
    But if yow list, my tale shul ye heere.

THE FRANKLIN'S TALE

Heere biginneth the Frankeleins Tale.

    In Armorik, that called is Britaine,
730 Ther was a knight that loved and dide his paine
    To serve a lady in his beste wise.
    And many a labour, many a gret emprise
    He for his lady wroghte er she were wonne;
    For she was oon the faireste under sonne,
735 And eek therto come of so heigh kinrede
    That wel unnethes dorste this knight, for drede,

716 **burel man** uneducated man   718 **rude** unpolished   720 **moot** must
721 **sleep** slept   723 **Colours** stylistic embellishments (n.)
724 **mede** meadow   726 **queinte** strange   727 **feeleth** knows

730 **dide his paine** did his utmost   731 **in his beste wise** as best he could
732 **emprise** exploit   733 **wroghte** performed
734 **oon the faireste under sonne** the most beautiful in the world
736 **wel unnethes** hardly **dorste** dared

Telle hire his wo, his peine, and his distresse.
But atte laste she, for his worthinesse,
And namely for his meke obeisaunce,
Hath swich a pitee caught of his penaunce   740
That prively she fel of his acord
To take him for hir housbonde and hir lord,
Of swich lordshipe as men han over hir wives.
And for to lede the moore in blisse hir lives,
Of his fre wil he swoor hire as a knight   745
That nevere in al his lif he, day ne night,
Ne sholde upon him take no maistrye
Again hir wil, ne kithe hire jalousye,
But hire obeye, and folwe hir wil in al,
As any lovere to his lady shal;   750
Save that the name of soverainetee,
That wolde he have, for shame of his degree.
    She thanked him, and with ful gret humblesse
She seide, 'Sire, sith, of youre gentilesse,
Ye profre me to have so large a reine,   755
Ne wolde nevere God bitwix us tweine,
As in my gilt, were outher werre or strif.
Sire, I wol be youre humble trewe wif;
Have heer my trouthe, til that min herte breste.'
Thus been they bothe in quiete and in reste.   760
    For o thing, sires, saufly dar I seye,
That freendes everich oother moot obeye,
If they wol longe holden compaignye.
Love wol nat be constreined by maistrye;

738 **worthinesse** noble qualities   739 **namely** especially
740 **penaunce** suffering   741 **prively** inwardly   **fel of his acord** came to an
agreement with him   747 **maistrye** dominance   748 **kithe** show
751–2 Except that he would keep the title of authority, to preserve the
honour of his rank   754 **sith** since   755 **so large a reine** so free a rein
756 **tweine** two   757 **As in my gilt** through any fault of mine   **outher** either
759 **trouthe** pledge   **breste** may break   761 **o** one   **saufly** confidently
762 **everich** each   764 **maistrye** dominance

765 Whan maistrye comth, the God of Love anon
    Beteth hise winges, and farwel, he is gon!
    Love is a thing as any spirit free.
    Wommen, of kinde, desiren libertee,
    And nat to been constreined as a thral,
770 And so doon men, if I sooth seyen shal.
    Looke who that is moost pacient in love,
    He is at his avantage al above.
    Pacience is an heigh vertu, certein,
    For it venquisseth, as thise clerkes seyn,
775 Thinges that rigour sholde nevere atteine.
    For every word men may nat chide or pleine;
    Lerneth to suffre, or elles, so moot I gon,
    Ye shul it lerne, wherso ye wole or non.
    For in this world, certein, ther no wight is,
780 That he ne dooth or seyth somtime amis.
    Ire, siknesse, or constellacioun,
    Win, wo, or chaunging of complexioun
    Causeth ful ofte to doon amis or speken.
    On every wrong a man may nat be wreken;
785 After the time moste be temperaunce
    To every wight that kan on governaunce.
    And therfore hath this wise, worthy knight,
    To live in ese, suffraunce hire bihight,
    And she to him ful wysly gan to swere
790 That nevere sholde ther be defaute in here.
        Heere may men seen an humble, wis acord!
    Thus hath she take hir servant and hir lord –
    Servant in love, and lord in mariage;
    Thanne was he bothe in lordshipe and servage.

---

768 **of kinde** by nature   774 **venquisseth** conquers   775 **atteine** achieve
776 **pleine** complain   777 **so moot I gon** as I live
778 **wherso ye wole or non** whether you want to or not
780 **amis** wrongly   782 **complexioun** the balance of the bodily
'humours' (g.)   784 **wreken** avenged   785 **After** according to
temperaunce modification, adaptation   786 **kan on** knows about
788 **suffraunce** patience, forbearance **bihight** promised
789 **wysly** earnestly **gan to swere** swore   790 **defaute** shortcoming

Servage? – nay, but in lordshipe above,   795
Sith he hath bothe his lady and his love;
His lady, certes, and his wif also,
The which that lawe of love acordeth to.

And whan he was in this prosperitee,
Hom with his wif he gooth to his contree,   800
Nat fer fro Penmark, ther his dwelling was,
Wheras he liveth in blisse and in solas.

Who koude telle, but he hadde wedded be,
The joye, the ese, and the prosperitee
That is bitwix an housbonde and his wif?   805
A yeer and moore lasted this blisful lif,
Til that the knight of which I speke of thus,
That of Kairrud was cleped Arveragus,
Shoop him to goon and dwelle, a yeer or twaine,
In Engelond, that cleped was eek Britaine,   810
To seke in armes worship and honour,
For al his lust he sette in swich labour,
And dwelled ther two yeer; the book seyth thus.

Now wol I stinte of this Arveragus,
And speke I wole of Dorigene his wif,   815
That loveth hir housbonde as hir hertes lif.
For his absence wepeth she and siketh,
As doon thise noble wives whan hem liketh.
She moorneth, waketh, waileth, fasteth, pleineth;
Desir of his presence hir so destreineth   820
That al this wide world she set at noght.
Hir freendes, whiche that knewe hir hevy thoght,
Conforten hire in al that ever they may.
They prechen hire, they telle hire, night and day,

---

798 **acordeth to** is in harmony with   801 **ther** where   802 **solas** delight
803 **but** unless   **be** been   808 **cleped** called   809 **Shoop him** determined
811 **worship** honour, reputation   812 **lust** pleasure   814 **stinte of** cease
speaking of   817 **siketh** sighs   818 **hem liketh** it pleases them
819 **pleineth** laments   820 **destreineth** torments   821 **set at noght** counts as
nothing   822 **hevy** sorrowful   823 **Conforten** comfort

825   That causelees she sleeth hirself, allas!
        And every confort possible in this cas
        They doon to hire, with al hir bisinesse,
        Al for to make hire leve hir hevinesse.

            By proces, as ye knowen everychoon,
830   Men may so longe graven in a stoon
        Til som figure therinne emprented be.
        So longe han they conforted hire til she
        Received hath, by hope and by resoun,
        Th'emprenting of hir consolacioun,
835   Thurgh which hir grete sorwe gan aswage;
        She may nat alwey duren in swich rage.

            And eek Arveragus, in al this care,
        Hath sent hire lettres hom of his welfare,
        And that he wol come hastily again;
840   Or ellis hadde this sorwe hir herte slain.

            Hir freendes sawe hir sorwe gan to slake,
        And preyede hire on knees, for Goddes sake,
        To come and romen hire in compaignye,
        Awey to drive hir derke fantasye.
845   And finally she graunted that requeste,
        For wel she saw that it was for the beste.

            Now stood hir castel faste by the see,
        And often with hir freendes walketh she,
        Hir to disporte, upon the bank an heigh,
850   Wheras she many a ship and barge seigh,
        Seillinge hir cours, wheras hem liste go.
        But thanne was that a parcel of hir wo,
        For to hirself ful ofte 'Allas!' seyth she,
        'Is ther no ship, of so manye as I se,

---

825 **sleeth** is killing   827 **bisinesse** endeavour   830 **graven** engrave
833 **resoun** reasonableness   834 **hir** their   836 She cannot remain
continually in such anguish   840 **hadde** would have   841 **gan to slake** was
abating   843 **romen hire** take a stroll   844 **derke fantasye** gloomy
imaginings   847 **faste by** close by   849 **Hir to disporte** to amuse herself
850 **barge** boat **seigh** saw   851 **Seillinge** sailing **hem liste go** they wanted to
go   852 **parcel** part

Wol bringen hom my lord? Thanne were min 855
    herte
Al warisshed of hise bittre peines smerte.'
   Another time there wolde she sitte and thinke,
And caste hir eyen dounward fro the brinke.
But whan she seigh the grisly rokkes blake,
For verray fere so wolde hir herte quake, 860
That on hir feet she mighte hir noght sustene.
Thanne wolde she sitte adoun upon the grene,
And pitously in to the see biholde,
And seyn right thus, with sorweful sikes colde:
   'Eterne God, that thurgh thy purveiance 865
Ledest the world by certein governance,
In idel, as men seyn, ye nothing make.
But, Lord, thise grisly feendly rokkes blake,
That semen rather a foul confusioun
Of werk than any fair creacioun 870
Of swich a parfit wis God and a stable,
Why han ye wroght this werk unresonable?
For by this werk, south, north, ne west ne est,
Ther nis yfostred man ne brid ne beest.
It doth no good, to my wit, but anoyeth. 875
Se ye nat, Lord, how mankinde it destroyeth?
An hundred thousand bodies of mankinde
Han rokkes slain, al be they nat in minde;
Which mankinde is so fair part of thy werk
That thow it madest lik to thin owene merk. 880
Thanne semed it ye hadde a greet chiertee
Toward mankinde; but how thanne may it be
That ye swich menes make it to destroyen?
– Whiche menes do no good, but evere anoyen.

856 **warisshed** cured **hise** its **smerte** severe 860 **quake** tremble
863 **pitously** pitifully 864 **sikes** sighs 865 **purveiance** providence
866 **certein governance** unfaltering control 867 **In idel** in vain
871 **a stable** a steadfast one 874 **yfostred** nourished 875 **anoyeth** is
harmful 880 **merk** image 881 **chiertee** love

885   I woot wel, clerkes wol seyn as hem leste,
By argumentz, that al is for the beste,
Thogh I ne kan the causes nat iknowe.
But thilke God that made wind to blowe
As kepe my lord! – this my conclusioun.
890   To clerkes lete I al disputisoun.
But wolde God that alle thise rokkes blake
Were sonken into helle, for his sake.
Thise rokkes sleen min herte for the feere!'
– Thus wolde she seyn, with many a pitous teere.

895   Hir freendes sawe that it was no disport
To romen by the see, but disconfort,
And shopen for to pleyen somwher elles.
They leden hire by rivers and by welles,
And eek in othere places delitables;
900   They dauncen, and they pleyen at ches and tables.
So on a day, right in the morwe-tide,
Unto a gardin that was therbiside,
In which that they hadde maad hir ordinance
Of vitaille and of oother purveiance,
905   They goon and pleye hem al the longe day.
And this was on the sixte morwe of May,
Which May hadde peinted with his softe shoures
This gardin, ful of leves and of floures;
And craft of mannes hond so curiously
910   Arrayed hadde this gardin, trewely,
That nevere was ther gardin of swich pris,
But if it were the verray Paradis.
The odour of floures and the fresshe sighte
Wolde han maked any herte lighte

---

890 **lete** leave   **disputisoun** debate   892 **sonken** sunk   895 **disport** source of
pleasure   896 **disconfort** source of distress   897 **shopen** planned
899 **delitables** delightful   900 **ches** chess   **tables** backgammon
901 **morwe-tide** morning   903 **ordinance** arrangements   904 **vitaille** food
purveiance preparations   909 **curiously** skilfully   910 **Arrayed** set out
911 **pris** excellence   912 **But if** unless   914 **lighte** grow lighter

That evere was born, but if to greet siknesse   915
Or to greet sorwe helde it in distresse,
So ful it was of beautee with plesaunce.
At after-diner gonne they to daunce
And singe also, save Dorigen allone,
Which made alwey hir compleint and hir mone,   920
For she ne saugh him on the daunce go
That was hir housbonde and hir love also.
But nathelees she moste a time abide,
And with good hope lete hir sorwe slide.

   Upon this daunce, amonges othere men,   925
Daunced a squier bifore Dorigen,
That fressher was and jolier of array,
As to my doom, than is the monthe of May.
He singeth, daunceth, passing any man
That is, or was, sith that the world bigan.   930
Therwith he was, if men sholde him discrive,
Oon of the beste faringe man on live;
Yong, strong, right vertuous, and riche, and wis,
And wel biloved, and holden in gret pris.
And shortly, if the sothe I tellen shal,   935
Unwiting of this Dorigen at al,
This lusty squier, servant to Venus,
Which that ycleped was Aurelius,
Hadde loved hire best of any creature
Two yeer and moore, as was his aventure,   940
But nevere dorste he telle hire his grevance;
Withouten coppe he drank al his penance.

915 **but if** unless   920 **alwey** continually **compleint** lament
mone lamentation   923 **she moste a time abide** she had to wait a while
924 **slide** pass away   927 **jolier of array** more gaily clothed
928 **As to my doom** in my opinion   929 **passing** surpassing   932 One of
the handsomest men alive   934 **holden in gret pris** highly esteemed
935 **sothe** truth   936 **Unwiting of** unknown to **at al** completely
937 **lusty** gallant **servant to Venus** devotee of love   940 **aventure** lot,
fortune   941 **grevance** sorrow   942 He suffered intensely (n.)

He was despeired; nothing dorste he seye,
Save in his songes somwhat wolde he wreye
945   His wo, as in a general compleining.
He seide he lovede, and was biloved nothing.
Of swich matere made he many layes,
Songes, compleintes, roundels, virelayes,
How that he dorste nat his sorwe telle,
950   But langwisseth as a Furye dooth in helle;
And die he moste, he seide, as dide Ekko
For Narcisus, that dorste nat telle hir wo.
In oother manere than ye heere me seye
Ne dorste he nat to hire his wo biwreye;
955   Save that, paraventure, somtime at daunces,
Ther yonge folk kepen hir observaunces,
It may wel be he looked on hir face
In swich a wise as man that asketh grace,
But nothing wiste she of his entente.
960   Nathelees it happed, er they thennes wente,
Bicause that he was hir neighebour,
And was a man of worship and honour,
And hadde yknowen him of time yoore,
They fille in speche, and forth moore and moore
965   Unto his purpos drough Aurelius.
And whan he saugh his time, he seide thus:
        'Madame,' quod he, 'by God that this world
            made,
So that I wiste it mighte youre herte glade,
I wolde that day that youre Arveragus
970   Wente over the see, that I, Aurelius,
Hadde went ther nevere I sholde have come again.
For wel I woot my service is in vain;

944 **wreye** reveal   945 **compleining** lament   946 **nothing** not at all
948 **roundels . . . virelayes** short poems (n.)   949 **dorste** dared
950 **langwisseth** suffers   954 **biwreye** reveal   955 **paraventure** perhaps
956 **kepen hir observaunces** practise their social customs   959 **wiste** knew
962 **worship** good repute   963 **of time yoore** for a long time
965 **drough** drew   968 **So that** provided that   **glade** gladden

My gerdon is but bresting of min herte.
Madame, reweth upon my peines smerte,
For with a word ye may me sleen or save.   975
Here at youre feet God wolde that I were grave!
I ne have as now no leiser moore to seye;
Have mercy, swete, or ye wol do me deye.'
    She gan to looke upon Aurelius.
'Is this youre wil,' quod she, 'and sey ye thus?   980
Nevere erst', quod she, 'ne wiste I what ye mente.
But now, Aurelie, I knowe youre entente,
By thilke God that yaf me soule and lif,
Ne shal I nevere been untrewe wif
In word ne werk, as fer as I have wit;   985
I wol been his to whom that I am knit.
Taak this for final answere as of me.'
But after that in pleye thus seide she:
    'Aurelie,' quod she, 'by heighe God above,
Yet wolde I graunte yow to been youre love,   990
Sin I yow se so pitously complaine.
Looke what day that endelong Britaine
Ye remoeve alle the rokkes, stoon by stoon,
That they ne lette ship ne boot to goon –
I seye, whan ye han maad the coost so clene   995
Of rokkes, that ther nis no stoon ysene –
Thanne wol I love yow best of any man.
Have heer my trouthe, in al that evere I kan.'
    'Is there noon oother grace in yow?' quod he.
'No, by that Lord', quod she, 'that maked me,   1000
For wel I woot that it shal nevere bitide.
Lat swiche folies out of youre herte slide!
What deintee sholde a man han in his lif
For to go love another mannes wif,

---

973 gerdon reward bresting breaking   974 reweth have pity smerte bitter
975 sleen slay   976 grave buried   977 leiser power
978 do me deye cause me to die   985 In word or deed, as far as I am
capable of it   991 pitously pitifully   992 endelong along the length of
994 So that they do not prevent the movements of ships or boats
995 clene empty   1001 bitide come about   1003 deintee pleasure

1005   That hath hir body whan so that him liketh?'
       Aurelius ful ofte soore siketh;
    Wo was Aurelie, whan that he this herde,
    And with a sorweful herte he thus answerde:
    'Madame,' quod he, 'this were an inpossible!
1010   Thanne moot I die of sodein deth horrible.'
    – And with that word he turned him anon.
    Tho coome hir othere freendes many oon,
    And in the aleyes romeden up and doun,
    And nothing wiste of this conclusioun.
1015   But sodeinly bigonne revel newe,
    Til that the brighte sonne loste his hewe,
    For th'orisonte hath reft the sonne his light –
    This is as muche to seye as it was night.
    And hoom they goon, in joye and in solas,
1020   Save oonly wrecche Aurelius, allas!
    He to his hous is goon, with sorweful herte.
    He seeth he may nat from his deeth asterte;
    Him semed that he felte his herte colde.
    Up to the hevene his handes he gan holde,
1025   And on his knowes bare he sette him doun,
    And in his raving seide his orisoun.
    For verray wo out of his wit he breide;
    He niste what he spak, but thus he seide.
    With pitous herte his pleint hath he bigonne
1030   Unto the goddes, and first unto the sonne.
      He seide, 'Appollo, god and governour
    Of every plaunte, herbe, tree, and flour,
    That yevest, after thy declinacioun,
    To ech of hem his time and his sesoun,

1006 **soore siketh** sighs bitterly   1009 **were an inpossible** would be an impossibility   1010 **moot** must   1011 **word** speech   1012 **coome** came
1013 **aleyes** garden-walks   1014 **conclusioun** outcome   1016 **his hewe** its colour   1017 **th'orisonte** the horizon **reft** deprived of   1022 **asterte** escape
1025 **knowes** knees   1026 **orisoun** prayer   1027 **out of his wit he breide** he lost his senses   1029 **pleint** lament   1031 **governour** keeper
1033 **declinacioun** seasonal position in the sky (n.)

As thin herberwe chaungeth, lowe or heighe,   1035
Lord Phebus, cast thy merciable eighe
On wrecche Aurelie, which that am but lorn!
Lo, lord, my lady hath my deeth ysworn
Withouten gilt, but thy benignitee
Upon my dedly herte have som pitee.   1040
For wel I woot, lord Phebus, if yow lest,
Ye may me helpen, save my lady, best.
Now voucheth sauf that I may yow devise
How that I may been holpe, and in what wise.

'Youre blisful suster, Lucina the shene,   1045
That of the see is chief goddesse and queene,
(Thogh Neptunus have deitee in the see,
Yet emperesse aboven him is she),
Ye knowen wel, lord, that right as hir desir
Is to be quiked and lighted of youre fir,   1050
For which she folweth yow ful bisily,
Right so the see desireth naturelly
To folwen hire, as she that is goddesse
Bothe in the see and rivers, moore and lesse.
Wherfore, lord Phebus, this is my requeste –   1055
Do this miracle, or do min herte breste –
That now next at this opposicioun,
Which in the signe shal be of the Leoun,
As preyeth hire so greet a flood to bringe
That five fadme at the leeste it overspringe   1060
The hyeste rok in Armorik Britaine,
And lat this flood endure yeres twaine.

1035 **herberwe** position   1036 **merciable** merciful   1037 **lorn** lost
1039 **but** unless   1040 **dedly** dying, doomed   1041 **if yow lest** if it pleases
you   1043 **voucheth sauf** grant **devise** describe   1044 **holpe** helped
1045 **shene** bright   1047 **deitee** divine power   1050 **quiked** kindled
lighted of illuminated by   1051 **bisily** diligently   1054 **moore and lesse** big
and small   1056 **do min herte breste** make my heart break
1057 **opposicioun** see n.   1058 **the signe . . . of the Leoun** the sign of Leo in
the zodiac   1059 **As preyeth hire** ask her   1060 **fadme** fathoms
overspringe may rise above   1062 **twaine** two

Thanne, certes, to my lady may I seye,
"Holdeth youre heste; the rokkes been aweye."
1065   'Lord Phebus, dooth this miracle for me:
Prey hire she go no faster cours than ye.
I seye, preyeth youre suster that she go
No faster cours than ye thise yeres two.
Thanne shal she been evene at the fulle alway,
1070   And spring flood lasten bothe night and day.
And but she vouchesauf in swich manere
To graunte me my soverein lady deere,
Pray hire to sinken every rok adoun
In to hir owene dirke regioun
1075   Under the ground, ther Pluto dwelleth inne,
Or neveremo shal I my lady winne.
Thy temple in Delphos wol I barfoot seke.
Lord Phebus, se the teeris on my cheke,
And of my peine have som compassioun!'
1080   And with that word in swowne he fil adoun,
And longe time he lay forth in a traunce.
His brother, which that knew of his penaunce,
Up caughte him, and to bedde he hath him broght.
Dispeired in this torment and this thoght
1085   Lete I this woful creature lie;
Chese he, for me, wher he wol live or die!
Arveragus, with heele and greet honour,
As he that was of chivalrye the flour,
Is comen hom, and othere worthy men.
1090   O blisful artow now, thow Dorigen,
That hast thy lusty housbonde in thin armes,
The fresshe knight, the worthy man of armes,
That loveth thee as his owene hertes lif!
Nothing list him to been imaginatif

1064 **Holdeth youre heste** keep your promise   1069 **evene** exactly
1070 **spring flood** spring-tide   1071 **but she vouchesauf** if she does not
agree   1074 **dirke** dark   1080 **swowne** a swoon
1082 **penaunce** suffering   1084 **Dispeired** in despair   1085 **Lete** leave
1086 **Chese he** let him choose   **wher** whether   1087 **heele** health
1091 **lusty** gallant   1094 He was not at all suspicious

If any wight hadde spoke, whil he was oute,   1095
To hire of love; he hadde of it no doute.
He noght entendeth to no swich matere,
But daunceth, justeth, maketh hir good cheere.
And thus in joye and blisse I lete hem dwelle,
And of the sike Aurelius wol I telle.   1100
    In langour and in torment furius
Two yeer and moore lay wrecche Aurelius,
Er any foot he mighte on erthe gon.
Ne confort in this time hadde he noon,
Save of his brother, which that was a clerk.   1105
He knew of al this wo and al this werk;
For to noon oother creature, certein,
Of this matere he dorste no word seyn.
Under his brest he baar it moore secree
Than evere dide Pamphilus for Galathee.   1110
His brest was hool, withoute for to sene,
But in his herte ay was the arwe kene;
And wel ye knowe that of a sursanure
In surgerye is perilous the cure
But men mighte touche the arwe, or come therby.   1115
    His brother weep and wailed prively,
Til at the laste him fil in remembraunce
That whiles he was at Orliens in Fraunce –
As yonge clerkes, that been likerous
To reden artes that been curious,   1120
Seken in every halke and every herne
Particuler sciences for to lerne –
He him remembred that, upon a day,
At Orliens in studye a book he say

1096 **doute** apprehension   1097 **noght entendeth to** gives no thought to
1098 **maketh hir good cheere** makes much of her   1101 **langour** sickness
furius intense   1105 **of** from **clerk** university student   1109 **secree** secret
1111 **withoute** outwardly   1112 **arwe** arrow   1113 **sursanure** a wound
healed outwardly but not inwardly   1115 **But** unless **come therby** get at it
1116 **weep** wept **prively** in private   1119 **likerous** eager
1120 **curious** abstruse, recondite   1121 **every halke . . . herne** every nook
and cranny   1122 **Particuler** specialized   1124 **studye** college **say** saw

1125 Of magik naturel, which his felawe
      That was that time a bacheler of lawe,
      Al were he ther to lerne another craft,
      Hadde prively upon his desk ylaft.
      Which book spak muchel of the operaciouns
1130 Touchinge the eighte and twenty mansiouns
      That longen to the moone, and swich folye
      As in oure dayes is nat worth a flye;
      For holy chirches feith in oure bileve
      Ne suffreth noon illusioun us to greve.

1135 And whan this book was in his remembraunce,
      Anon for joye his herte gan to daunce,
      And to himself he seide prively:
        'My brother shal be warisshed hastily;
      For I am siker that ther be sciences
1140 By whiche men make diverse apparences,
      Swiche as thise subtile tregetoures pleye.
      For ofte at festes have I wel herd seye
      That tregetours withinne an halle large
      Have maad come in a water and a barge,
1145 And in the halle rowen up and doun.
      Somtime hath semed come a grim leoun,
      And somtime floures springe as in a mede,
      Somtime a vine and grapes white and rede,
      Somtime a castel, al of lim and stoon,
1150 And whan hem liked, voided it anoon;
      Thus semed it to every mannes sighte.
        'Now thanne conclude I thus, that if I mighte
      At Orliens som old felawe ifinde
      That hadde thise moones mansions in minde,

1125 **magik naturel** 'white' magic (g.) **felawe** companion
1127 **Al were he** although he was **craft** subject, discipline
1130 **mansiouns** see n.   1134 **Ne suffreth** does not allow
1138 **warisshed** cured   1139 **siker** sure   1140 **apparences** illusions
1141 **tregetoures** conjurers   1144 **barge** boat   1149 **lim** mortar
1150 **voided** removed

Or oother magik naturel above,   1155
He sholde wel make my brother han his love.
For with an apparence a clerk may make,
To mannes sighte, that alle the rokkes blake
Of Britaigne were yvoided everychon,
And shippes by the brinke come and gon,   1160
And in swich forme endure a wowke or two.
Thanne were my brother warisshed of his wo;
Thanne moste she nedes holden hir biheste,
Or ellis he shal shame hire at the leeste.'
    What sholde I make a lenger tale of this?   1165
Unto his brotheres bed he comen is,
And swich confort he yaf him for to gon
To Orliens, that he up stirte anon,
And on his wey forthward thanne is he fare,
In hope for to been lissed of his care.   1170
    Whan they were come almoost to that citee,
But if it were a two furlong or thre,
A yong clerk, roming by himself, they mette,
Which that in Latin thriftily hem grette,
And after that he seide a wonder thing: 1175
'I knowe', quod he, 'the cause of youre coming.'
And er they ferther any foote wente,
He tolde hem al that was in hir entente.
    This Britoun clerk him asked of felawes
The whiche that he hadde knowe in olde dawes,   1180
And he answerde him that they dede were,
For which he weep ful ofte many a teere.
    Doun of his hors Aurelius lighte anon,
And with this magicien forth is he gon
Hom to his hous, and made hem wel at ese.   1185
Hem lakked no vitaille that mighte hem plese;

1155 **above** in addition   1159 **yvoided** removed   1161 **wowke** week
1162 **were** would be   1163 **nedes holden hir biheste** necessarily keep her
promise   1165 **What** why   1168 **up stirte** leaped up   1169 **is he fare** he
went   1170 **lissed** relieved   1174 **thriftily** politely
grette (= *gretede*) greeted   1178 **entente** mind   1179 **of** about
1180 **dawes** days   1183 **Doun . . . lighte** dismounted

So wel arrayed hous as ther was oon
Aurelius in his lif saw nevere noon.

He shewed him, er he wente to sopeer,
1190 Forestes, parkes, ful of wilde deer;
Ther saw he hertes with hir hornes hye,
The gretteste that evere were seyn with eye.
He saw of hem an hundred slain with houndes,
And somme with arwes blede of bittre woundes.
1195 He saw, whan voided were thise wilde deer,
Thise fauconers upon a fair river,
That with hir haukes han the heron slain.
Tho saugh he knightes justing in a plain;
And after this he dide him swich plesaunce
1200 That he him shewed his lady on a daunce,
On which himself he daunced, as him thoughte.
And whan this maister that this magik wroughte
Saugh it was time, he clapte his handes two,
And farwel, al oure revel was ago!
1205 And yet remoeved they nevere out of the hous,
Whil they saugh al this sighte merveillous,
But in his studye, theras his bookes be,
They seten stille, and no wight but they thre.

To him this maister called his squier
1210 And seide him thus: 'Is redy oure soper?
Almoost an hour it is, I undertake,
Sith I yow bad oure soper for to make,
Whan that thise worthy men wenten with me
Into my studye, theras my bookes be.'
1215   'Sire,' quod this squier, 'whan it liketh yow,
It is al redy, thogh ye wol right now.'
'Go we thanne soupe,' quod he, 'as for the beste.
This amorous folk somtime mote han hir reste!'

1187 **arrayed** equipped 1189 **sopeer** supper 1195 **voided** removed
1196 **fauconers** falconers **river** river-bank 1199 **swich plesaunce** such a
service 1205 **remoeved** moved 1207 **theras** where 1208 **seten** sat
1218 **mote** must

At after-soper fille they in tretee
What somme sholde this maistres gerdoun be   1220
To remoeven alle the rokkes of Britaine,
And eek from Gerounde to the mouth of Saine.
    He made it straunge, and swoor, so God him
        save,
Lasse than a thousand pound he wolde nat have,
Ne gladly for that somme he wolde nat gon.   1225
    Aurelius with blisful herte anon
Answerde thus: 'Fy on a thousand pound!
This wide world, which that men seye is round,
I wolde it yeve, if I were lord of it!
This bargain is ful drive, for we ben knit;   1230
Ye shal be payed trewely, by my trouthe.
But looketh now, for no necligence or slouthe
Ye tarye us heer no lenger than tomorwe.'
'Nay,' quod this clerk, 'have heer my feith to
        borwe.'

    To bedde is goon Aurelius whan him leste,   1235
And wel neigh al that night he hadde his reste.
What for his labour and his hope of blisse,
His woful herte of penaunce hadde a lisse.
    Upon the morwe, whan that it was day,
To Britaine tooke they the righte way,   1240
Aurelius and this magicien biside,
And been descended ther they wolde abide.
And this was, as thise bookes me remembre,
The colde frosty seson of Decembre.
    Phebus wax old, and hewed lik latoun,   1245
That in his hote declinacioun

1219 **tretee** negotiation   1220 **gerdoun** reward
1223 **made it straunge** showed reluctance   1230 **ful drive** concluded
knit agreed   1233 **tarye** delay   1234 **have heer my feith to borwe** I pledge
my word   1235 **him leste** it pleased him   1238 **penaunce** suffering
lisse respite   1240 **righte way** direct route   1241 **biside** in addition
1242 **been descended** dismounted   1243 **me remembre** remind me
1245 **wax** grew **hewed lik latoun** coloured like brass
1246 **hote declinacioun** summer solstice (n.)

Shoon as the burned gold with stremes brighte;
But now in Capricorn adoun he lighte,
Wheras he shoon ful pale, I dar wel seyn.
1250 The bittre frostes, with the sleet and rein,
Destruyed hath the grene in every yerd.
Janus sit by the fir with double berd,
And drinketh of his bugle horn the win.
Biforn him stant brawen of the tusked swin,
1255 And 'Nowel!' cryeth every lusty man.
    Aurelius in al that evere he kan
Dooth to this maister cheere and reverence,
And preyeth him to doon his diligence
To bringen him out of his peines smerte,
1260 Or with a swerd that he wolde slitte his herte.
    This subtil clerk swich routhe hadde of this man
That night and day he spedde him that he kan
To waite a time of his conclusioun.
This is to seyn, to make illusioun
1265 By swich an apparence or jogelrye –
I ne kan no termes of astrologye –
That she and every wight sholde wene and seye
That of Britaine the rokkes were aweye,
Or ellis they were sonken under grounde.
1270 So at the laste he hath his time yfounde
To make his japes and his wrecchednesse
Of swich a supersticious cursednesse.
His tables Tolletanes forth he broght,
Ful wel corrected, ne ther lakked noght,

1247 **burned** burnished   1248 **lighte** (= *lightede*) descended
1251 **yerd** garden   1253 **bugle horn** drinking-horn   1254 **brawen** brawn,
cooked meat **tusked swin** boar   1255 **Nowel** 'Noel', a cry of joy uttered on
the day of Christ's birth (*dies natalis*)   1256 **in al that evere he kan** to the
best of his ability   1257 **Dooth . . . cheere and reverence** offers hospitality
and honour   1261 **routhe** pity   1262 **spedde him that he kan** made as
much haste as he could   1263 **waite** watch for **conclusioun** successful
result   1265 **apparence** illusion **jogelrye** conjuring trick   1266 **ne kan** do
not know   1267 **wene** think   1271 **japes** tricks
1273 **tables Tolletanes** (astronomical) tables made in Toledo (n.)

Neither his collect ne his expans yeris, 1275
Ne hise rootes, ne hise othere geris,
As been his centris and hise argumentz,
And hise proporcionels convenientz
For hise equacions in everything.
And by his eighte speere in his wirking 1280
He knew ful wel how fer Alnath was shove
Fro the heed of thilke fixe Aries above,
That in the ninthe speere considered is;
Ful subtilly he kalkuled al this.

Whan he hadde founde his firste mansioun, 1285
He knew the remenaunt by proporcioun,
And knew the arising of his moone wel,
And in whos face, and terme, and everydel,
And knew ful wel the moones mansioun
Acordaunt to his operacioun, 1290
And knew also hise othere observaunces
For swiche illusiouns and swiche meschaunces
As hethen folk useden in thilke dayes.
For which no lenger maked he delayes,
But thurgh his magik, for a wike or tweye, 1295
It semed that alle the rokkes were aweye.

Aurelius, which that yet despeired is
Wher he shal han his love or fare amis,
Awaiteth night and day on this miracle.
And whan he knew that ther was noon obstacle – 1300

1275 **collect ... expans yeris** computations of the changes of a planet's position over periods of varying length (n.) 1276 **rootes** positions of the heavens at specific moments in time (used as a basis for astrological calculations) (n.) **geris** equipment 1277 **centris ... argumentz** see n. 1278 **proporcionels** see n. **convenientz** suitable 1279 **equacions** see n. 1280 **eighte speere** eighth sphere **wirking** calculation 1281 **shove** driven 1282 **thilke fixe Aries** the first point of Aries (n.) 1284 **kalkuled** calculated 1286 **proporcioun** proportionate reckoning 1288 **face** one of the three parts of ten degrees into which each sign of the zodiac was divided (n.) **terme** a subdivision of a sign of the zodiac defining a period within which the influence of a planet is increased (n.) 1291 **observaunces** procedures 1295 **wike or tweye** week or two 1298 **Wher** whether **fare amis** fail 1299 **Awaiteth ... on** waits for

That voided were thise rokkes everychon –
Doun to his maistres feet he fil anon,
And seide, 'I, woful wrecche, Aurelius,
Thanke yow, lord, and lady min Venus,
1305   That me han holpen fro my cares colde!'
And to the temple his wey forth hath he holde,
Wheras he knew he sholde his lady se.
And whan he saugh his time, anon-right he
With dredful herte and with ful humble cheere
1310   Salued hath his soverain lady deere.

　　　'My righte lady,' quod this woful man,
'Whom I moost drede and love as I best kan,
And lothest were of al this world displese,
Nere it that I for yow have swich disese
1315   That I moste die heer at youre foot anon,
Noght wolde I telle how me is wo-bigon.
But certes outher moste I die or pleine;
Ye sleen me giltelees, for verray peine.
But of my deeth thogh that ye have no routhe,
1320   Aviseth yow er that ye breke youre trouthe.
Repenteth yow, for thilke God above,
Er ye me sleen bicause that I yow love.
For, madame, wel ye woot what ye han hight –
Nat that I chalange anything of right
1325   Of yow, my soverein lady, but youre grace –
But in a gardin, yond at swich a place,
Ye woot right wel what ye bihighten me,
And in my hand youre trouthe plighten ye
To love me best – God woot, ye seide so,
1330   Al be that I unworthy am therto.

1302 **fil** fell   1305 **holpen fro** helped out of **cares colde** anguish
1308 **anon-right** at once   1309 **dredful** fearful **cheere** expression
1310 **Salued** greeted **soverain** sovereign   1313 **lothest** most reluctant
1314 **disese** suffering   1317 **pleine** express my unhappiness   1318 You kill
me, guiltless, with true suffering   1320 **Aviseth yow** take thought
1324 **chalange** claim **of right** by right   1327 **bihighten** promised
1328 **plighten** pledged

Madame, I speke it for the honour of yow
Moore than to save min hertes lif right now:
I have do so as ye comaunded me,
And if ye vouchesauf, ye may go se.
Dooth as yow list; have youre biheste in minde,　　1335
For quik or deed, right ther ye shal me finde.
In yow lith al, to do me live or deye;
But wel I woot, the rokkes been aweye.'
　　He taketh his leve, and she astoned stood.
In al hir face nas a drope of blood.　　1340
She wende nevere have come in swich a trappe.
'Allas!' quod she, 'that evere this sholde happe!
For wende I nevere by possibilitee
That swich a monstre or merveille mighte be!
It is agains the proces of nature.'　　1345
And hom she gooth, a sorweful creature;
For verray feere unnethe may she go.
She wepeth, waileth, al a day or two,
And swowneth that it routhe was to se.
But why it was to no wight tolde she,　　1350
For out of towne was goon Arveragus.
But to hirself she spak and seide thus,
With face pale and with ful sorweful cheere,
In hir compleinte, as ye shal after heere.

　　'Allas!' quod she, 'on thee, Fortune, I pleine,　　1355
That unwar wrapped hast me in thy cheine,
Fro which t'escape woot I no socour,
Save oonly deeth or elles dishonour;
Oon of thise two bihoveth me to chese.
But nathelees, yet have I levere lese　　1360
My lif, than of my body have a shame,
Or knowe myselven fals, or lese my name.

1333 **do** done　1334 **vouchesauf** agree　1336 **quik** alive　1337 **lith** lies
1338 **been aweye** are gone　1340 **nas** there was not　1341 **wende** thought
1342 **happe** come about　1347 **unnethe** with difficulty　**go** walk
1355 **on thee . . . I pleine** I complain of you　1356 **unwar** unexpectedly
1357 **socour** help　1359 **chese** choose　1360 **have I levere lese** I prefer to
lose

And with my deeth I may be quit, ywis.
Hath ther nat many a noble wif er this,
1365   And many a maide, yslain hirself, allas,
Rather than with hir body doon trespas?
        'Yis, certes; lo, thise stories bere witnesse.
Whan thritty tyrauntz, ful of cursednesse,
Hadde slain Phidon in Atthenes atte feste,
1370   They comaunded his doghtren for t'areste
And bringen hem biforn hem in despit
Al naked, to fulfille hir foul delit,
And in hir fadres blood they made hem daunce
Upon the pavement – God yeve hem mischaunce!
1375   For which thise woful maidens, ful of drede,
Rather than they wolde lese hir maidenhede,
They prively been stirt into a welle
And dreinte hemselven, as the bokes telle.
        'They of Mecene leete enquere and seke
1380   Of Lacedomye fifty maidens eke,
On whiche they wolden doon hir lecherye.
But was ther noon of al that compaignye
That she nas slain, and with a good entente
Chees rather for to die than assente
1385   To been oppressed of hir maidenhede.
Why sholde I thanne to die been in drede?
Lo, eek, the tyraunt Aristoclides,
That loved a maiden heet Stimphalides,
Whan that hir father slain was on a night,
1390   Unto Dianes temple gooth she right,
And hente the image in hir handes two,
Fro which image wolde she nevere go.

1363 **quit** free   1366 **doon trespas** do wrong   1370 **doghtren** daughters
for t'areste to be seized   1371 **despit** humiliation
1376 **maidenhede** virginity   1377 **been stirt** leaped   1378 **dreinte** drowned
1379 The people of Messene caused to be sought out
1383 **with a good entente** cheerfully   1384 **Chees** chose   1385 To be
robbed of their virginity   1388 **heet** who was called
1391 **hente** (= *hentede*) seized

No wight ne mighte hir handes of it arace
Til she was slain, right in the selve place.
   'Now sith that maidens hadden swich despit   1395
To been defouled with mannes foul delit,
Wel oghte a wif rather hirselven slee
Than be defouled, as it thinketh me.
What shal I seyn of Hasdrubales wif,
That at Cartage birafte hirself hir lif?   1400
For whan she saw that Romains wan the toun,
She took hir children alle and skipte adoun
Into the fir, and chees rather to die
Than any Romain dide hire vileinye.
Hath nat Lucresse yslain hirself, allas,   1405
At Rome whan that she oppressed was
Of Tarquin, for hir thoughte it was a shame
To liven whan she hadde lost hir name?
The sevene maidens of Milesie also
Han slain hemself for verray drede and wo,   1410
Rather than folk of Gawle hem sholde oppresse.
Mo than a thousand stories, as I gesse,
Koude I now telle as touching this matere.
Whan Habradate was slain, his wif so deere
Hirselven slow, and leet hir blood to glide   1415
In Habradates woundes depe and wide,
And seide, "My body, at the leeste way,
Ther shal no wight defoulen, if I may."
   'What sholde I mo ensamples herof sayn,
Sith that so many han hemselven slain   1420
Wel rather than they wolde defouled be?
I wol conclude that it is bet for me
To sleen myself than ben defouled thus.
I wol be trewe unto Arveragus,

1393 **arace** tear away   1394 **selve** same   1400 **birafte** deprived
1402 **skipte** jumped   1404 **dide** should do **vileinye** dishonour
1406 **oppressed** raped   1407 **Of** by   1408 **name** reputation
1411 **Gawle** Gaul   1417 **at the leeste way** at least   1419 **What** why
1422 **bet** better

1425   Or rather sle myself in som manere,
        As dide Democionis doghter deere,
        Bicause that she wolde nat defouled be.
        O Cedasus, it is ful greet pitee
        To reden how thy doghtren deide, allas,
1430   That slowe hemselven for swich maner cas.
        As greet a pitee was it, or wel moore,
        The Theban maiden that for Nichanore
        Hirselven slow, right for swich manere wo.
        Another Theban maiden dide right so,
1435   For oon of Macedoine hadde hire oppressed;
        She with hir deeth hir maidenhed redressed.
        What shal I seyn of Nicerates wif,
        That for swich cas birafte hirself hir lif?
        How trewe eek was to Alcibiades
1440   His love, that rather for to dien chees,
        Than for to suffre his body unburied be?
        Lo, which a wif was Alceste!' quod she.
        'What seyth Omer of goode Penolopee?
        Al Grece knoweth of hir chastitee.
1445   Pardee, of Laodomia is writen thus,
        That whan at Troye was slain Protheselaus,
        No lenger wolde she live after his day.
        The same of noble Porcia telle I may:
        Withoute Brutus koude she nat live,
1450   To whom she hadde al hool hir herte yeve.
        The parfit wifhod of Arthemesye
        Honoured is thurgh al the Barbarye.
        O Teuta queene, thy wifly chastitee
        To alle wives may a mirour bee!
1455   The same thing I seye of Bilyea,
        Of Rodogone, and eek Valeria.'
            Thus pleined Dorigene a day or tweye,
        Purposinge evere that she wolde deye.

1430 **slowe** slew **for swich maner cas** because of a situation of this sort
1436 **redressed** restored   1441 **suffre** allow   1442 **which a** what a
1450 **hool** wholly **yeve** given   1457 **pleined** lamented

But nathelees, upon the thridde night,
Hoom cam Arveragus, this worthy knight,   1460
And asked hire why that she weep so soore;
And she gan wepen, ever lenger the moore.
     'Allas,' quod she, 'that evere was I born!
Thus have I seid,' quod she, 'thus have I sworn' –
And tolde him al, as ye han herd bifore;   1465
It nedeth nat reherce it yow namoore.
     This housbond, with glad cheere, in frendly
          wise,
Answerde and seide as I shal yow devise:
'Is ther oght ellis, Dorigen, but this?'
'Nay, nay,' quod she, 'God help me so as wys,   1470
This is to muche, and it were Goddes wille!'
     'Ye, wif,' quod he, 'lat slepen that is stille.
It may be wel, paraunter, yet today.
Ye shul youre trouthe holden, by my fay!
For, God so wysly have mercy upon me,   1475
I hadde wel levere ystiked for to be,
For verray love which that I to yow have,
But if ye sholde youre trouthe kepe and save.
Trouthe is the hyeste thing that man may kepe.'
– But with that word he brast anon to wepe,   1480
And seide, 'I yow forbede, up peine of deeth,
That nevere, whil thee lasteth lif ne breeth,
To no wight tel thow of this aventure.
As I may best, I wol my wo endure;
Ne make no contenance of hevinesse,   1485
That folk of yow may demen harm or gesse.'

1461 weep wept   1466 reherce repeat   1467 cheere expression
1468 devise tell   1469 oght ellis anything else   1470 as wys as surely
1471 and even if   1472 lat slepen that is stille let what is quiet, sleep (n.)
1473 paraunter perchance yet today even now
1474 youre trouthe holden keep your word   1476 I would rather be run
through with a sword   1477 verray true   1478 But if ye sholde than that
you should not   1480 brast . . . to wepe burst into tears
1483 aventure occurrence   1485 And do not show any sorrow
1486 demen believe gesse suspect

And forth he cleped a squier and a maide;
'Goth forth anon with Dorigen,' he saide,
'And bringeth hire to swich a place anon.'
1490   They take hire leve, and on hir wey they gon,
But they ne wiste why she thider wente;
He nolde to no wight tellen his entente.

Paraventure an heep of yow, ywys,
Wol holden him a lewed man in this,
1495   That he wol putte his wif in jupartye.
Herkneth the tale er ye upon hire crye;
She may have bettre fortune than yow semeth;
And whan that ye han herd the tale, demeth.

This squier, which that highte Aurelius,
1500   On Dorigen that was so amorus,
Of aventure happed hir to meete,
Amidde the toun, right in the quikkest strete,
As she was boun to goon the wey forth right
Toward the gardin theras she had hight.

1505   And he was to the gardinward also,
For wel he spied whan she wolde go
Out of hir hous to any maner place.
But thus they mette, of aventure or grace,
And he salueth hire with glad entente,
1510   And asked of hire whiderward she wente.
And she answerde, half as she were mad,
'Unto the gardin, as min housbond bad,
My trouthe for to holde, allas, allas!'
Aurelius gan wondren on this cas,
1515   And in his herte hadde greet compassioun
Of hire and of hir lamentacioun,

1487 **cleped** called   1492 He did not want to tell anyone of his intention
1493 **heep** multitude   1494 **lewed** stupid   1495 **in jupartye** at risk
1496 **upon hire crye** condemn her   1497 **yow semeth** it seems to you
1498 **demeth** judge   1501 **Of aventure** by chance   1502 **quikkest** busiest
1503 **boun to** about to **forth right** directly   1504 **hight** promised
1505 **to the gardinward** on the way to the garden
1508 **of aventure or grace** by chance or good fortune
1510 **whiderward** whither, where   1514 **on this cas** at this situation

And of Arveragus, the worthy knight,
That bad hir holden al that she had hight,
So looth him was his wif sholde breke hir
    trouthe.
And in his herte he caughte of this greet routhe,   1520
Consideringe the beste on every side,
That fro his lust yet were him levere abide
Than doon so heigh a cherlissh wrecchednesse
Agains franchise and alle gentillesse.
For which in fewe wordes seide he thus: 1525
   'Madame, seyth to youre lord Arveragus,
That sith I se his grete gentillesse
To yow, and eek I se wel youre distresse,
That him were levere han shame – and that were
    routhe –
Than ye to me sholde breke thus youre trouthe,   1530
I have wel levere evere to suffre wo
Than I departe the love bitwix yow two.
I yow relesse, madame, into youre hond
Quit every serement and every bond
That ye han maad to me as heerbiforn,   1535
Sith thilke time which that ye were born.
My trouthe I plighte, I shal yow nevere repreve
Of no biheeste; and here I take my leve
As of the treweste and the beste wif
That evere yet I knew in al my lif.'   1540
– But every wif be war of hir biheste;
On Dorigene remembreth, at the leste!
Thus kan a squier doon a gentil dede
As wel as kan a knight, withouten drede.

1519 **So looth him was** so hateful was it to him that   1520 **routhe** pity
1522 That he would prefer to abstain from his desire
1523 **cherlissh** churlish   1524 **franchise** generosity **gentillesse** nobility
1529 That he would rather be shamed – and that would be a pity
1531 **I have wel levere** I much prefer   1532 **departe** separate
1534 **Quit** paid, fulfilled **serement** oath   1537–8 **plighte** pledge
repreve Of reproach for

1545   She thonketh him upon hir knees al bare,
          And hom unto hir housbond is she fare,
          And tolde him al, as ye han herd me said.
          And be ye siker, he was so wel apaid
          That it were inpossible me to write.
1550   What sholde I lenger of this cas endite?
          Arveragus and Dorigene his wif
          In soverein blisse leden forth hir lif.
          Nevere eft ne was ther angre hem bitwene;
          He cherisseth hire as thogh she were a queene,
1555   And she was to him trewe for everemoore.
          Of thise two folk ye gete of me namoore.

              Aurelius, that his cost hath al forlorn,
          Curseth the time that evere he was born.
          'Allas,' quod he, 'allas, that I bihighte
1560   Of pured gold a thousand pound of wighte
          Unto this philosophre! How shal I do?
          I se namoore but that I am fordo!
          Min heritage moot I nedes selle,
          And been a beggere – heere may I nat dwelle,
1565   And shamen al my kinrede in this place –
          But I of him may gete bettre grace.
          But nathelees, I wol of him assaye
          At certein dayes, yeer by yeer, to paye,
          And thonke him of his grete curteisye.
1570   My trouthe wol I kepe; I wol nat lie.'
              With herte soor he gooth unto his cofre,
          And broghte gold unto this philosophre,
          The value of five hundred pound, I gesse,
          And him bisecheth, of his gentillesse,
1575   To graunte him dayes of the remenant;
          And seide, 'Maister, I dar wel make avant

1546 **is she fare** she went   1548 **siker** sure **wel apaid** pleased
1550 **What** why **endite** write   1557 **forlorn** wasted   1560 **pured** refined,
pure **wighte** weight   1562 I cannot see that I am anything but ruined
1563 **nedes** of necessity   1566 **But** unless   1571 **soor** aching
cofre money-chest   1574 **of his gentillesse** out of kindness
1575 **graunte him dayes of** allow him time for   1576 **make avant** boast

I failled nevere of my trouthe as yit.
For sikerly, my dette shal be quit
Towardes yow, however that I fare,
To goon abegged in my kirtel bare.   1580
But wolde ye vouchesauf, upon seuretee,
Two yeer or thre for to respiten me,
Thanne were I wel, for ellis moot I selle
Min heritage; ther is namoore to telle.'

   This philosophre sobrely answerde,   1585
And seide thus, whan he thise wordes herde:
'Have I nat holden covenant unto thee?'
'Yis, certes, wel and trewely,' quod he.
'Hastow nat had thy lady as thee liketh?'
'No, no,' quod he, and sorwefully he siketh.   1590
'What was the cause? Tel me if thow kan.'
   Aurelius his tale anon bigan,
And tolde him al, as ye han herd bifore;
It nedeth nat to yow reherce it moore.
He seide, 'Arveragus, of gentillesse,   1595
Hadde levere die in sorwe and in distresse,
Than that his wif were of hir trouthe fals.'
The sorwe of Dorigen he tolde him als,
How looth hir was to ben a wikked wif,
And that she levere had lost that day hir lif,   1600
And that hir trouthe she swoor thurgh
            innocence;
She nevere erst hadde herd speke of apparence.
'That made me han of hire so greet pitee,
And right as frely as he sente hir me,
As frely sente I hire to him again.   1605
This al and som; ther is namoore to sayn.'

1578 **quit** paid   1580 Even if I were to go begging in nothing but my tunic
1581 **wolde ye vouchesauf** if you would grant **seuretee** security
1582 **respiten** grant a respite to   1583 **were I wel** I would be in a good
position   1587 **holden covenant** kept the agreement   1594 **reherce** repeat
1598 **als** also   1599 **looth hir was** reluctant she was
1602 **apparence** illusion   1606 **This al and som** this is the long and the
short of it

This philosophre answerde, 'Leeve brother,
Everich of yow dide gentilly til oother.
Thow art a squier, and he is a knight;
1610   But God forbede, for his blisful might,
But if a clerk koude doon a gentil dede
As wel as any of yow, it is no drede!
Sire, I relesse thee thy thousand pound,
As thow right now were crope out of the ground,
1615   Ne nevere er now ne haddest knowen me.
For sire, I wol nat take a peny of thee
For al my craft, ne noght for my travaille.
Thow hast ypayed wel for my vitaille;
It is inogh, and farewel, have good day!'
1620   And took his hors, and forth he goth his way.
           Lordinges, this questioun than wol I aske now:
Which was the mooste free, as thinketh yow?
Now telleth me, er that ye ferther wende!
I kan namoore; my tale is at an ende.

Heere is ended the Frankeleins Tale.

1608 **dide gentilly til oother** acted nobly towards the other   1614 As if you
had just arrived on earth (*lit.* crept out of the ground)   1622 **free** generous

THE PHYSICIAN'S TALE

Ther was, as telleth Titus Livius,
A knight that called was Virginius,
Fulfild of honour and of worthinesse,
And strong of freendes, and of greet richesse.
  This knight a doghter hadde by his wif;   5
No children hadde he mo in al his lif.
Fair was this maide in excellent beautee
Aboven every wight that man may see;
For Nature hath with soverein diligence
Yformed hire in so greet excellence   10
As thogh she wolde seyn: 'Lo, I, Nature,
Thus kan I forme and peinte a creature
Whan that me list! Who kan me countrefete?
Pygmalion noght, thogh he ay forge and bete,
Or grave or peinte, for I dar wel seyn   15
Apelles, Zanzis, sholde werche in vein
Outher to grave, or peinte, or forge, or bete,
If they presumed me to countrefete.
For he that is the formere principal
Hath maked me his vicaire-general   20
To forme and peinten erthely creaturis
Right as me list, and ech thing in my cure is
Under the moone that may wane and waxe,
And for my werk right nothing wol I axe;

---

3 **Fulfild of** filled with   4 **strong of** well provided with   8 **wight** creature
9 **soverein** supreme   13 When it pleases me. Who can imitate me
14 **bete** hammer   15 **grave** engrave   17 **Outher** either
19 **formere** creator   20 **vicaire-general** deputy (n.)   22 **cure** control
24 **axe** ask

25   My lord and I been ful of oon acord.
        I made hire to the worship of my lord;
        So do I alle mine othere creatures,
        What colour that they han, or what figures.'
        – Thus semeth me that Nature wolde seye.

30   This maide of age twelf yeer was and tweye,
        In which that Nature hadde swich delit;
        For right as she kan peinte a lilye whit
        And reed a rose, right with swich peinture
        She peinted hath this noble creature,

35   Er she were born, upon hire limes free,
        Wheras by right swiche colours sholde be.
        And Phebus dyed hath hir tresses grete
        Lik to the stremes of his burned hete.
        And if that excellent was hir beautee,

40   A thousand fold moore vertuous was she.
        In hir ne lakked no condicioun
        That is to preise as by discrecioun.
        As wel in goost as body chaast was she,
        For which she floured in virginitee

45   With alle humilitee and abstinence,
        With alle attemperance and pacience,
        With mesure eek of bering and array.
        Discreet she was in answering alway,
        Thogh she were wis as Pallas, dar I seyn.

50   Hir facound eek ful wommanly and plein;
        No countrefeted termes hadde she
        To seme wis, but after hir degree
        She spak, and alle hir wordes, moore and lesse,
        Sowninge in vertu and in gentillesse.

---

25 **been ful of oon acord** are completely in harmony   26 **worship** honour
33 **peinture** colouring   35 **limes free** beautiful limbs
38 **burned hete** burnished heat   42 **to preise** to be praised
discrecioun discernment   43 **goost** spirit   46 **attemperance** moderation
47 **mesure** restraint   **bering** behaviour   50 **facound** eloquence
plein unadorned   51 **countrefeted** affected   52 **after hir degree** according to
her position in society   54 **Sowninge in** conducing to

Shamefast she was, in maidens shamefastnesse;   55
Constant in herte, and evere in bisinesse,
To drive hire out of idel slogardye.
Bacus hadde of hir mouth right no maistrye;
For win and youthe dooth Venus encresse,
As men in fir wol casten oille or gresse.   60
And of hir owene vertu, unconstreined,
She hath ful ofte time sik hir feined,
For that she wolde fleen the compaignye
Where likly was to treten of folye,
As is at festes, revels, and at daunces   65
That been occasions of daliaunces.
Swiche thinges maken children for to be
To soone ripe and boold, as men may se,
Which is ful perilous and hath ben yoore;
For al to soone may they lerne loore   70
Of boldnesse, whan she woxen is a wif.

  And ye maistresses, in youre olde lif,
That lordes doghtres han in governaunce –
Ne taketh of my wordes no displesaunce –
Thenketh that ye been set in governinges   75
Of lordes doghtres oonly for two thinges:
Outher for ye han kept youre honestee,
Or elles ye han falle in freletee,
And knowen wel inow the olde daunce,
And han forsaken fully swich meschaunce   80
For everemo; therfore, for Cristes sake,
To teche hem vertu looke that ye ne slake.

---

55 **Shamefast** modest   56 **in bisinesse** active   58 Bacchus had absolutely no
control over her mouth   59 **dooth . . . encresse** causes to increase
60 **gresse** fat   61 **unconstreined** unconstrained   62 **sik hir feined** pretended
to be sick   64 **treten of folye** engage in foolish behaviour
66 **occasions of** opportunities for **daliaunces** flirtations   69 **yoore** for a long
time   70 **loore** practice   71 **woxen is** has become   72 **olde lif** old age
73 **han in governaunce** have in your care
74 **Ne taketh . . . no displesaunce** do not be displeased
75 **governinges** authority   77 **honestee** chastity   78 **freletee** frailty
79 **wel inow** very well **the olde daunce** all the old tricks   82 **slake** tire

A theef of venisoun that hath forlaft
His likerousnesse and al his olde craft
85   Kan kepe a forest best of any man.
Now kepeth wel, for if ye wole ye kan.
Looke wel that ye unto no vice assente,
Lest ye be dampned for youre wikke entente;
For whoso dooth, a traitour is, certein.
90   And taketh kepe of that that I shal seyn:
Of alle tresoun, soverein pestilence
Is whan a wight bitrayseth innocence.

Ye fadres, and ye modres eek also,
Thogh ye han children be it oon or mo,
95   Youre is the charge of al hir surveaunce,
Whil that they been under youre governaunce.
Beth war, if by ensample of youre livinge,
Or by youre necligence in chastisinge,
That they perisse; for I dar wel seye,
100   If that they doon, ye shul it deere abeye.
Under a shepherde softe and necligent
The wolf hath many a sheep and lamb to-rent.
Suffiseth oon ensample now as heere,
For I moot turne again to my matere.

105   This maide of which I wol this tale expresse
So kepte hirself, hir neded no maistresse.
For in hir living maidens mighten rede,
As in a book, every good word or dede
That longeth to a maiden vertuous,
110   She was so prudent and so bountevous.
For which the fame out sprong on every side
Bothe of hir beautee and hir bountee wide,

83 **forlaft** abandoned   84 **likerousnesse** unlicensed behaviour
86 **kepeth wel** keep guard   90 **taketh kepe** take note
91 **soverein pestilence** the greatest evil   92 **bitrayseth** betrays
95 **Youre** yours **charge** responsibility **surveaunce** surveillance
97 **Beth war** take care   99 **perisse** perish   100 **abeye** pay for
102 **to-rent** torn in pieces   103 **ensample** example
106 **kepte hirself** governed herself   109 **longeth to** befits
110 **bountevous** virtuous   111 **out sprong** spread   112 **bountee** goodness

That thurgh that land they preised hire echone
That loved vertu, save envye allone,
That sory is of oother mennes wele,   115
And glad is of his sorwe and his unheele –
The Doctour maketh this discripcioun.

This maide upon a day wente in the toun
Toward a temple, with hir moder deere,
As is of yonge maidens the manere.   120
Now was ther thanne a justice in that toun
That governour was of that regioun;
And so bifel, this juge hise eyen caste
Upon this maide, avisinge him ful faste,
As she cam forby ther this juge stood.   125
Anoon his herte chaunged and his mood,
So was he caught with beautee of this maide.
And to himself ful prively he saide:
'This maide shal be min, for any man!'

Anon the feend into his herte ran,   130
And taughte him sodeinly that he by slighte
The maiden to his purpos winne mighte.
For certes, by no force ne by no meede
Him thoughte he was nat able for to speede,
For she was strong of freendes, and eek she   135
Confermed was in swich soverein bountee,
That wel he wiste he mighte hire nevere winne
As for to make hir with hir body sinne.
For which, by greet deliberacioun,
He sente after a cherl was in the toun,   140
Which that he knew for subtil and for bold.
This juge unto this cherl his tale hath told

115 Which is sorry at other men's prosperity   116 unheele misfortune
118 upon a day one day   120 manere custom
124 avisinge him ful faste pondering deeply   125 forby ther past the place
where   128 prively secretly   129 for in spite of   130 feend devil
131 slighte cunning   133 meede bribery   134 speede be successful
135 strong of well provided with   136 Confermed securely established
137 wiste knew   140 was who was   141 for subtil to be cunning

In secree wise, and made him to ensure
He sholde telle it to no creature,
145   And if he dide, he sholde lese his heed.
Whan that assented was this cursed reed,
Glad was this juge and maked him gret cheere,
And yaf him yiftes preciouse and deere.
      Whan shapen was al hir conspiracye
150   Fro point to point, how that his lecherye
Parfourned sholde been ful subtilly –
As ye shul heere it after openly –
Hoom goth the cherl, that highte Claudius.
This false juge, that highte Apius –
155   So was his name, for this is no fable,
But knowen for historial thing notable;
The sentence of it sooth is, out of doute –
This false juge gooth now faste aboute
To hasten his delit al that he may.
160   And so bifel, soone after, on a day,
This false juge, as telleth us the storye,
As he was wont, sat in his consistorye,
And yaf his domes upon sondry cas.
This false cherl cam forth a ful gret pas
165   And seide, 'Lord, if that it be youre wille,
As dooth me right upon this pitous bille,
In which I pleine upon Virginius.
And if that he wol seyn it is nat thus,
I wol it preve, and finde good witnesse
170   That sooth is that my bille wol expresse.'

143 **secree wise** secretly **ensure** give assurance   145 **lese** lose
146 **assented** agreed **reed** plan   147 **maked him gret cheere** made much of
him   150 **Fro point to point** in every detail   151 **Parfourned** put into effect
ful subtilly very cunningly   153 **highte** was called
156 **historial thing notable** a well-known historical fact
157 **sentence** substance **sooth** true   158 **gooth . . . faste aboute** is earnestly
intent on   159 **hasten** hurry on   162 **consistorye** law-court
163 **domes** judgements   164 **a ful gret pas** quickly
166 **As dooth me right** give me justice **bille** petition (n.)
167 **pleine upon** make a complaint against   170 **sooth** true

The juge answerde: 'Of this in his absence
I may nat yeve diffinitif sentence.
Lat do him calle, and I wol gladly heere;
Thow shalt have al right, and no wrong heere.'

Virginius cam, to wite the juges wille,   175
And right anon was rad this cursed bille.
The sentence of it was as ye shul heere:
'To yow, my lord sire Apius so deere,
Sheweth youre povre servant Claudius
How that a knight, called Virginius,   180
Agains the lawe, again al equitee,
Holdeth expres again the wil of me
My servant, which that is my thral by right,
Which fro min hous was stole upon a night
Whil that she was ful yong; this wol I preve   185
By witnesse, lord, so that it nat yow greve.
She nis his doghter nat, whatso he seye.
Wherfore to yow, my lord the juge, I preye,
Yeld me my thral, if that it be youre wille!'
Lo, this was al the sentence of his bille.   190

Virginius gan upon the cherl biholde;
But hastily, er he his tale tolde,
And wolde have preved it as sholde a knight,
And eek by witnessinge of many a wight,
That it was fals that seide his adversarye,   195
This cursed juge wolde nothing tarye,
Ne here a word moore of Virginius,
But yaf his juggement and seide thus:
'I deme anon this cherl his servant have.
Thow shalt no lenger in thin hous hir save;   200

172 **diffinitif** conclusive   173 **Lat do him calle** have him summoned
174 **al right** full justice   175 **wite** learn   176 **rad** read out
177 **sentence** content   179 **Sheweth** declares   182 **expres again** directly
opposed to   183 **thral** bondswoman, serf   184 **stole** stolen
186 **so that** provided that   **greve** displease   189 **Yeld** give back
199 **deme** adjudge, rule   200 **save** keep

Go bring hire forth, and put hire in oure warde.
The cherl shal have his thral; this I awarde.'
   And whan this worthy knight Virginius,
Thurgh sentence of this justice Apius,
205   Moste by force his deere doghter yeven
Unto the juge, in lecherye to liven,
He gooth him hoom, and sette him in his halle,
And leet anoon his deere doghter calle;
And with a face deed as asshen colde
210   Upon hir humble face he gan biholde,
With fadres pitee stikinge thurgh his herte,
Al wolde he from his purpos nat converte.
   'Doghter,' quod he, 'Virginia, by thy name,
Ther been two weyes, outher deeth or shame,
215   That thow most suffre – allas, that I was bore!
For nevere thow deservedest wherfore
To dien with a sword or with a knif.
O deere doghter, endere of my lif,
Which I have fostred up with swich plesaunce
220   That thow were nevere out of my remembraunce,
O doghter, which that art my laste wo,
And in my lif my laste joye also,
O gemme of chastitee, in pacience
Tak thow thy deeth, for this is my sentence.
225   For love, and nat for hate, thow most be deed;
My pitous hand moot smiten of thin heed.
Allas, that evere Apius thee say!
Thus hath he falsly juged thee today' –
And tolde hire al the cas, as ye bifore
230   Han herd; nat nedeth for to telle it moore.
   'O mercy, deere fader!' quod this maide,
And with that word she bothe hir armes laide

---

201 **warde** guardianship   202 **awarde** determine   207 **sette him** seated
himself   208 **leet ... calle** had called   209 **asshen** ashes
211 **stikinge** piercing   212 **converte** swerve   215 **bore** born
216 **wherfore** on any account   218 **endere** ender (one who ends)
224 **sentence** decision   226 **smiten of** cut off   227 **say** saw
229 **al the cas** the whole event

Aboute his nekke, as she was wont to do.
The teeris borste out of hir eyen two,
And seide, 'Goode fader, shal I die?   235
Is ther no grace? Is ther no remedye?'
'No, certes, deere doghter min,' quod he.
     'Thanne yif me leiser, fader min,' quod she,
'My deeth for to compleine a litel space.
For, pardee, Jepte yaf his doghter grace   240
For to compleine, er he hir slow, allas!
And God it woot, nothing was hir trespas
But for she ran hir fader first to see,
To welcome him with greet solempnitee.'
And with that word she fil aswowne anon.   245
And after, whan hir swowning is agon,
She riseth up, and to hir fader saide,
'Blessed be God that I shal die a maide!
Yif me my deeth, er that I have a shame.
Dooth with youre child youre wil, a Goddes   250
     name!'
     And with that word she preyed him ful ofte
That with his swerd he wolde smite softe;
And with that word aswowne doun she fil.
Hir fader, with ful sorweful herte and wil,
Hir heed of smoot, and by the top it hente,   255
And to the juge he gan it to presente,
As he yet sat in doom in consistorye.
And whan the juge it saw, as seyth the storye,
He bad to take him and anhange him faste.
But right anon a thousand peple in thraste   260
To save the knight, for routhe and for pitee,
For knowen was the false iniquitee.

---

234 **borste** burst   238 **leiser** time   239 **compleine a litel space** lament a
little while   241 **slow** slew   242 **trespas** offence
244 **solempnitee** celebration   245 **aswowne** in a swoon   246 **agon** over
252 **softe** gently   255 **hente** seized   257 **yet** still **doom** judgement
260 **in thraste** thrust their way in

The peple anon had suspect in this thing,
By manere of the cherles chalanging,
265 That it was by th'assent of Apius;
They wisten wel that he was lecherus.
For which unto this Apius they gon
And caste him in a prisoun right anon,
Theras he slow himself; and Claudius,
270 That servant was unto this Apius,
Was demed for to hange upon a tree,
But that Virginius, of his pitee,
So preide for him that he was exiled;
And elles, certes, he hadde been bigiled.
275 The remenant were anhanged, moore and lesse,
That were consentant of this cursednesse.
   Heere may men seen how sinne hath his merite!
Beth war, for no man woot whom God wol smite
In no degree, ne in which manere wise;
280 The worm of conscience may agrise
Of wikked lif, thogh it so privee be
That no man woot therof but God and he.
For be he lewed man or ellis lered,
He noot how soone that he shal been afered.
285 Therfore I rede yow this conseil take:
Forsaketh sinne, er sinne yow forsake.

Heere endeth the Physiciens Tale.

263 **suspect** suspicion   264 **chalanging** false accusation   266 **wisten** knew
267 **For which** therefore   269 **Theras** where   271 **demed** sentenced
273 **So preide** made such entreaties   274 **hadde been bigiled** would have
been undone   275 **moore and lesse** great and small
276 **consentant of** accessory to   279 **degree** social rank
280–81 **worm** pangs (*lit.* serpent) **agrise Of** revolt from **privee** secret
282 **but** except   283 **lewed** uneducated **lered** educated   284 **noot** does not
know   285 **rede** advise **conseil** counsel

THE PHYSICIAN –
PARDONER LINK

The wordes of the Hoost to the
Physicien and the Pardoner.

Oure Hooste gan to swere as he were wood;
'Harrow!' quod he, 'by nailes and by blood!
This was a fals cherl and a fals justise!
As shameful deeth as herte may devise   290
Come to thise juges and hir advocatz!
Algate this sely maide is slain, allas!
Allas, to deere boghte she beautee!
Wherfore I seye alday that men may se
That yiftes of Fortune and of Nature   295
Been cause of deeth to many a creature.
Of bothe yiftes that I speke of now   299
Men han ful ofte moore for harm than prow.   300
    'But trewely, min owene maister deere,
This is a pitous tale for to heere!
But nathelees, passe over is no fors.
I pray to God so save thy gentil cors,
And eek thine urinals and thy jurdones,   305
Thin ipocras and eek thy galiones,
And every boiste ful of thy letuarye –
God blesse hem, and oure Lady Seinte Marye!

287 **as he were wood** as if he was mad   290 **devise** imagine
292 **Algate** nevertheless **sely** innocent   293 Alas, she paid too high a price
for beauty   294 **alday** constantly   300 **prow** benefit
303 **passe over is no fors** it does no harm to move on   304 **cors** person
305 **urinals . . . jurdones** glass vessels used by physicians (n.)
306 **ipocras** cordials **galiones** medicines (n.)   307 **boiste** box
letuarye medicine

So mote I theen, thow art a propre man,
310   And lik a prelat, by Seint Ronian!
Seide I nat wel? I kan nat speke in terme;
But wel I woot thow doost min herte to erme,
That I almoost have caught a cardinacle.
By *corpus* bones, but I have triacle,
315   Or elles a draghte of moiste and corny ale,
Or but I heere anon a mirye tale,
Min herte is lost for pitee of this maide!
Thow *beel ami*, thow Pardoner,' he saide,
'Tel us som mirthe, or japes, right anon.'
320   'It shal be doon,' quod he, 'by Seint Ronion.
But first,' quod he, 'heere at this ale-stake,
I wol bothe drinke and eten of a cake.'
But right anon thise gentils gonne to crye:
'Nay, lat him telle us of no ribaudye!
325   Tel us som moral thing, that we may leere
Som wit, and thanne wol we gladly heere.'
'I graunte, iwys,' quod he, 'but I moot thinke
Upon som honeste thing whil that I drinke.'

309 **theen** prosper   310 **prelat** prelate   311 **terme** jargon, technical
language   312 **erme** grieve   313 **cardinacle** see n.
314 **By *corpus* bones** by God's bones (n.)   **triacle** medicinal potion
315 **corny** tasting strongly of malt   318 ***beel ami*** dear friend
319 **japes** jokes   321 **ale-stake** inn-sign (g.)   324 **ribaudye** obscenity
325 **leere** learn   326 **wit** wisdom   328 **honeste** proper

THE PARDONER'S
PROLOGUE

*Heere folweth the Prologe of
the Pardoners Tale.*

*Radix malorum est Cupiditas.
Ad Thimotheum, sexto.*

'Lordinges,' quod he, 'in chirches whan I preche,
I peine me to han an hautein speche,   330
And ringe it out as round as gooth a belle,
For I kan al by rote that I telle.
My theme is alwey oon, and evere was:
"*Radix malorum est cupiditas.*"
   'First I pronounce whennes that I come,   335
And thanne my bulles shewe I, alle and some.
Oure lige lordes seel on my patente,
That shewe I first, my body to warente,
That no man be so boold, ne preest ne clerk,
Me to destourbe of Cristes holy werk,   340
And after that thanne telle I forth my tales.
Bulles of popes and of cardinales,
Of patriarkes and bisshopes I shewe,
And in Latin I speke a wordes fewe,

---

330 **peine me** make an effort **hautein** loud   331 **round** loudly
332 **kan al** know everything   333 **theme** text **oon** the same   334 Avarice is
the root of all evil   335 **pronounce** announce **whennes** whence
336 **bulles** papal edicts **alle and some** one and all   337 The bishop's seal on
my ecclesiastical licence   338 **warente** safeguard
340 **destourbe of** hinder from   343 **patriarkes** patriarchs, high-ranking
bishops

345 To saffron with my predicacioun,
     And for to stire hem to devocioun.
     Thanne shewe I forth my longe cristal stones,
     Ycrammed ful of cloutes and of bones;
     Relikes been they, as wenen they echon.
350 Thanne have I in latoun a shulder-bon,
     Which that was of an holy Jewes sheep.
     "Goode men," I seye, "tak of my wordes keep:
     If that this boon be wasshe in any welle,
     If cow, or calf, or sheep, or oxe swelle
355 That any worm hath ete, or worm ystonge,
     Taak water of that welle and wassh his tonge,
     And it is hool anoon; and forthermoor,
     Of pokkes and of scabbe and every soor
     Shal every sheep be hool that of this welle
360 Drinketh a draughte. Taak kepe eek what I telle:
     If that the goodman that the bestes oweth
     Wol every wike, er that the cok him croweth,
     Fastinge, drinken of this welle a draughte,
     As thilke holy Jew oure eldres taughte,
365 Hise bestes and his stoor shal multiplye.
         ' "And, sires, also it heeleth jalousye;
     For thogh a man be falle in jalous rage,
     Lat maken with this water his potage,
     And nevere shal he moore his wif mistriste,
370 Thogh he the soothe of hir defaute wiste,
     Al hadde she taken preestes two or thre.
         ' "Heere is a mitein eek, that ye may se;

345 **saffron** season with saffron, add spice to **predicacioun** preaching
346 **stire** incite   348 **Ycrammed** crammed **cloutes** rags
349 **wenen** believe   350 **latoun** brass **shulder-bon** shoulder-bone
352 **tak of my wordes keep** pay attention to my words   355 **worm** snake
ystonge stung   358 **pokkes** pustules **scabbe** scab (a disease affecting sheep)
soor disease   360 **Taak kepe** pay attention to   361 **goodman** householder
oweth owns   362 **wike** week   365 **stoor** livestock
368 **Lat maken . . . his potage** have his soup made   369 **mistriste** mistrust
370 **defaute** sin   372 **mitein** mitten, glove

He that his hand wol putte in this mitain,
He shal have multiplying of his grain
Whan he hath sowen, be it whete or otes,   375
So that he offre pens, or ellis grotes.
   ' "Goode men and wommen, o thing warne I
      yow:
If any wight be in this chirche now
That hath doon sinne horrible, that he
Dar nat for shame of it yshriven be,   380
Or any womman, be she yong or old,
That hath ymaad hir housbond cokewold,
Swich folk shal have no power ne no grace
To offren to my relikes in this place.
And whoso findeth him out of swich blame,   385
He wol come up and offre, a Goddes name,
And I assoille him, by th'auctoritee
Which that by bulle ygraunted was to me."
   'By this gaude have I wonne, yeer by yeer,
An hundred mark sith I was pardoner.   390
I stonde lik a clerk in my pulpet,
And whan the lewed peple is doun set,
I preche so as ye han herd bifore,
And telle an hundred false japes more.
Thanne peine I me to strecche forth the nekke,   395
And est and west upon the peple I bekke,
As dooth a dowve sitting on a berne.
Mine handes and my tonge goon so yerne
That it is joye to se my bisinesse.
Of avarice and of swich cursednesse   400
Is al my preching, for to make hem free
To yeve hir pens, and namely unto me.

---

376 **So that** provided that **grotes** groats (g.)   377 **o** one
380 **yshriven** confessed   382 **cokewold** cuckold   386 **a** in
387 **assoille** absolve   389 **gaude** trick   390 **mark** sum of money equivalent
to £$\frac{2}{3}$ 392 **lewed** lay **is doun set** have sat down   394 **japes** tricks
395 **peine I me** I exert myself   396 **est and west** in all directions **bekke** nod
397 **dowve** dove **berne** barn   398 **yerne** busily   401 **free** generous

For min entente is nat but for to winne,
And nothing for correccioun of sinne.

405   I rekke nevere, whan that they been beried,
Thogh that hir soules goon a-blakeberied!
For certes, many a predicacioun
Comth ofte time of ivel entencioun:
Som for plesance of folk and flaterye,

410   To been avanced by ypocrisye,
And som for veine glorye, and som for hate.
For whan I dar noon oother weyes debate,
Thanne wol I stinge him with my tonge smerte
In preching, so that he shal nat asterte

415   To been defamed falsly, if that he
Hath trespased to my bretheren or to me.
For thogh I telle noght his propre name,
Men shal wel knowe that it is the same,
By signes and by othere circumstances.

420   Thus quite I folk that doon us displesances;
Thus spitte I out my venim under hewe
Of holinesse, to seme holy and trewe.
     'But shortly min entente I wol devise:
I preche of nothing but for coveitise.

425   Therfore my theme is yet, and evere was:
"*Radix malorum est cupiditas.*"
Thus kan I preche again that same vice
Which that I use, and that is avarice.

---

403 **entente** aim   405 **rekke nevere** do not care at all **beried** buried
406 **goon a-blakeberied** go astray, go to perdition (*lit.* go picking
blackberries)   409 **for plesance of** in order to please
410 **been avanced** win promotion   412 **noon oother weyes** in no other way
debate quarrel   413 **smerte** sharply   414 **asterte** escape
415 **defamed** slandered   416 **trespased** done offence   420 In this way I pay
back people who offend the likes of me   421 **hewe** appearance
423 **devise** describe   424 **coveitise** covetousness   427 **again** against

But though myself be gilty in that sinne,
Yet kan I maken oother folk to twinne   430
From avarice, and soore to repente.
But that is nat my principal entente;
I preche nothing but for coveitise.
Of this matere it oghte inow suffise.
        'Thanne telle I hem ensamples many oon   435
Of olde stories longe time agoon.
For lewed peple loven tales olde;
Swiche thinges kan they wel reporte and holde.
What, trowe ye, that whiles I may preche,
And winne gold and silver for I teche,   440
That I wol live in poverte wilfully?
Nay, nay, I thoghte it nevere, trewely!
For I wol preche and begge in sondry landes.
I wol nat do no labour with mine handes,
Ne make baskettes and live therby,   445
Bicause I wol nat beggen idelly;
I wol noon of the apostles countrefete.
I wol have moneye, wolle, chese, and whete,
Al were it yeven of the povereste page
Or of the povereste widwe in a village,   450
Al sholde hir children sterve for famine.
Nay, I wol drinke licour of the vine,
And have a joly wenche in every toun!
        'But herkneth, lordinges, in conclusioun:
Youre liking is that I shal telle a tale.   455
Now have I dronke a draghte of corny ale,
By God, I hope I shal yow telle a thing
That shal by resoun been at youre liking!

430–31 **twinne From** forsake, renounce **soore** bitterly
435 **ensamples** illustrative anecdotes   437 **lewed** uneducated
439 **trowe ye** do you think   440 **for** because   441 **wilfully** voluntarily
446 **idelly** unprofitably   447 **countrefete** imitate   449 Even if it were given
by the poorest peasant   451 **sterve** die   455 **liking** pleasure
456 **corny** tasting strongly of malt   458 **by resoun** with reason
at youre liking to your liking

For thogh myself be a ful vicious man,
460   A moral tale yet I yow telle kan,
Which I am wont to preche for to winne.
Now holde youre pees; my tale I wol biginne.'

THE PARDONER'S TALE

Heere biginneth the Pardoners Tale.

In Flaundres whilom was a compaignye
Of yonge folk that haunteden folye,
465   As riot, hasard, stewes, and tavernes,
Whereas with harpes, lutes, and giternes,
They daunce and pleyen at dees bothe day and
        night,
And ete also and drinke over hir might,
Thurgh which they doon the devel sacrifise
470   Withinne that develes temple in cursed wise
By superfluitee abhominable.
Hir othes been so grete and so dampnable
That it is grisly for to heere hem swere;
Oure blissed Lordes body they to-tere –
475   Hem thoughte that Jewes rente him noght
        inough –
And ech of hem at otheres sinne lough.
And right anon thanne comen tombesteres,
Fetis and smale, and yonge frutesteres,

---

461 **wont** accustomed

463 **whilom** once   464 **haunteden folye** indulged in dissipation
465 **hasard** gambling **stewes** brothels   466 **giternes** gitterns (lute-like
instruments)   467 **dees** dice   468 **over hir might** more than their capacity
472 **othes** oaths **dampnable** worthy of damnation   473 **grisly** horrible
474 **to-tere** tear to pieces   475 **rente** tore   476 **lough** laughed
477 **tombesteres** female tumblers, acrobats   478 **Fetis** elegant
smale slender **frutesteres** female fruit-sellers

Singeres with harpes, baudes, wafereres,
Whiche been the verray develes officeres,   480
To kindle and blowe the fir of lecherye,
That is annexed unto glotonye.
The holy writ take I to my witnesse
That luxurye is in win and dronkenesse.
  Lo, how that dronken Loth unkindely   485
Lay by his doghtres two, unwitingly;
So dronke he was, he niste what he wroghte.
Herodes, whoso wel the stories soghte,
Whan he of win was replet at his feste,
Right at his owene table he yaf his heste   490
To sleen the Baptist John, ful giltelees.
Senec seyth a good word, doutelees:
He seyth, he kan no difference finde
Bitwix a man that is out of his minde
And a man which that is dronkelewe,   495
But that woodnesse, yfallen in a shrewe,
Persevereth lenger than dooth dronkenesse.
O glotonye, ful of cursednesse!
O cause first of oure confusioun!
O original of oure dampnacioun,   500
Til Crist hadde boght us with his blood again!
Lo, how deere, shortly for to sayn,
Aboght was thilke cursed vileinye;
Corrupt was al this world for glotonye.
  Adam oure fader, and his wif also,   505
Fro Paradis, to labour and to wo,
Were driven for that vice, it is no drede.
For whil that Adam fasted, as I rede,

---

479 **wafereres** wafer-sellers   484 **luxurye** lechery
485 **unkindely** unnaturally   486 **unwitingly** unknowingly   487 **niste** did
not know   488 **soghte** were to examine   489 **replet** filled
490 **heste** command   491 **sleen** slay   495 **dronkelewe** a drunkard
496 **woodnesse** madness   **yfallen in** occurring in   **shrewe** villain
497 **Persevereth** lasts   499 **confusioun** ruin   500 **original** cause
503 **Aboght** paid for   **vileinye** wickedness   507 **it is no drede** there is no
doubt

He was in Paradis, and whan that he
510 Eet of the fruit defended on the tree,
Anon he was out cast to wo and peine.
O glotonye, on thee wel oghte us pleine!
O, wiste a man how manye maladies
Folwen of excesse and of glotonyes,
515 He wolde been the moore mesurable
Of his diete, sitting at his table.
Allas, the shorte throte, the tendre mouth
Maketh that est and west and north and south,
In erthe, in eir, in water, men to-swinke,
520 To gete a glotoun deintee mete and drinke!
Of this matere, O Paul, wel kanstow trete:
'Mete unto wombe, and wombe eek unto mete,
Shal God destroyen bothe,' as Paulus seyth.
Allas, a foul thing is it, by my feith,
525 To seye this word, and fouler is the dede,
Whan man so drinketh of the white and rede
That of his throte he maketh his privee
Thurgh thilke cursed superfluitee.
     Th'Apostle weping seyth ful pitously:
530 'Ther walken manye of whiche yow toold have I –
I seye it now, weping with pitous vois –
That they been enemys of Cristes crois,
Of whiche the ende is deth; wombe is hir God.'
O wombe, O bely, O stinking cod,
535 Fulfilled of donge and of corrupcioun,
At either ende of thee foul is the soun!
How greet labour and cost is thee to finde!

---

510 **Eet** ate   **defended** forbidden   512 **pleine** complain   513 **wiste a man** if
a man knew   515 **mesurable** moderate   517 **shorte throte** short stretch of
the gullet   519 **to-swinke** labour away   520 **glotoun** glutton
deintee mete delicious food   522 **wombe** stomach   526 **rede** red (wine)
527 **privee** latrine (n.)   534 **cod** bag, belly   535 **donge** dung
536 **soun** sound   537 **finde** provide for

Thise cokes, how they stampe and streine and
    grinde,
And turnen substaunce into accident,
To fulfille al thy likerous talent.   540
Out of the harde bones knokke they
The mary, for they caste noght awey
That may go thurgh the golet softe and soote.
Of spicerye of leef, and bark, and roote
Shal been his sauce ymaked by delit,   545
To make him yet a newer appetit.
But certes, he that haunteth swiche delices
Is deed, whil that he liveth in tho vices.

   A lecherous thing is win, and dronkenesse
Is ful of striving and of wrecchednesse.   550
O dronke man, disfigured is thy face,
Sour is thy breeth, foul artow to embrace!
And thurgh thy dronke nose semeth the soun
As thogh thou seidest ay 'Sampsoun, Sampsoun'.
– And yet, God woot, Sampsoun drank nevere   555
    no win.
Thou fallest as it were a stiked swin;
Thy tonge is lost, and al thin honest cure,
For dronkenesse is verray sepulture
Of mannes wit and his discrecioun.
In whom that drinke hath dominacioun,   560
He kan no conseil kepe, it is no drede.
Now kepe yow fro the white and fro the rede,
And namely fro the white win of Lepe
That is to selle in Fisshstrete or in Chepe!
This win of Spaigne crepeth subtilly   565
In othere wines growinge faste by,

538 **cokes** cooks **stampe** pound   539 see n.   540 **likerous talent** gluttonous
desire   542 **mary** marrow **noght** nothing   543 **golet** gullet **soote** sweetly
545 **by delit** delightfully   547 **haunteth** indulges in **delices** pleasures
550 **striving** strife   554 **ay** continually   556 **stiked swin** stuck pig
557 **honest cure** desire for decency   558 **sepulture** grave
561 **conseil** secret   564 **to selle** for sale

Of which ther riseth swich fumositee
That whan a man hath dronken draghtes thre,
And weneth that he be at hoom in Chepe,
He is in Spaigne, right at the toune of Lepe –
Nat at the Rochel, ne at Burdeux toun –
And thanne wol he seyn 'Sampsoun, Sampsoun'.
  But herkneth, lordinges, o word I yow preye,
That alle the soverein actes, dar I seye,
Of victories in the Olde Testament,
Thurgh verray God that is omnipotent,
Were doon in abstinence and in prayere.
Looketh the Bible, and ther ye may it leere.
  Looke, Attila, the grete conquerour,
Deide in his sleep, with shame and dishonour,
Bleding at his nose in dronkenesse;
A capitain sholde live in sobrenesse!
And over al this, aviseth yow right wel,
What was comaunded unto Lamuel –
Nat Samuel, but Lamuel seye I –
Redeth the Bible, and find it expresly,
Of win-yeving to hem that han justise.
Namoore of this, for it may wel suffise.
  And now that I have spoken of glotonye,
Now wol I yow defenden hasardrye.
Hasard is verray moder of lesinges,
And of deceite and cursed forsweringes,
Blaspheme of Crist, manslaughtre, and wast also
Of catel and of time, and forthermo,
It is repreve and contrarye of honour
For to ben holde a commune hasardour,

567 **fumositee** vapour 569 **weneth** thinks 574 **soverein** outstanding
578 **leere** learn 583 **aviseth yow** consider 586 **expresly** explicitly
587 **Of win-yeving** about giving wine **justise** jurisdiction
590 **defenden** forbid **hasardrye** gambling 591 **lesinges** lies
592 **forsweringes** perjuries 593 **Blaspheme** blasphemy **wast** waste
594 **catel** property 595 It is a disgrace and dishonour 596 To be regarded as a common gambler

And evere the hyer he is of estaat,
The moore is he yholden desolat.
If that a prince useth hasardrye,
In alle governaunce and policye   600
He is, as by commune opinioun,
Yholde the lasse in reputacioun.

    Stilbon, that was a wis embassadour,
Was sent to Corinthe in ful gret honour
Fro Lacedomie, to make hire alliaunce.   605
And whan he cam, him happede par chaunce
That alle the gretteste that were of that lond
Pleyinge atte hasard he hem fond.
For which, as soone as it mighte be,
He stal him hoom again to his contree,   610
And seide, 'Ther wol I nat lese my name,
N'I wol nat take on me so greet defame
Yow for t'allye unto none hasardours.
Sendeth othere wise embassadours;
For, by my trouthe, me were levere die   615
Than I yow sholde to hasardours allye.
For ye that been so glorious in honours
Shal nat allyen yow with hasardours
As by my wil, ne as by my tretee.'
This wise philosophre, thus seide he.   620

    Looke eek, that to the king Demetrius,
The king of Parthes, as the book seyth us,
Sente him a paire of dees of gold in scorn,
For he hadde used hasard therbiforn;
For which he heeld his glorye or his renoun   625
At no value or reputacioun.
Lordes may finden oothere manere pley
Honeste inow to drive the day awey.

---

598 **yholden desolat** socially shunned   600 **policye** administration
602 **Yholde** considered   606 **happede** it befell   **par chaunce** by chance
610 **stal him** stole, went unobtrusively   612 **N'I wol nat** nor will I
defame dishonour   615 **me were levere** I would prefer
619 **tretee** negotiation   624 **therbiforn** previously   627 **pley** amusement
628 **Honeste** seemly

      Now wol I speke of oothes false and grete

630   A word or two, as olde bokes trete.

      Greet swering is a thing abhominable,

      And fals swering is yet moore reprevable.

      The heighe God forbad swering at al;

      Witnesse on Mathew, but in special

635   Of swering seyth the holy Jeremie:

      'Thow shalt swere sooth thine othes and nat lie,

      And swere in doom, and eek in rightwisnesse.'

      But idel swering is a cursednesse.

      Bihoold and se, that in the firste table

640   Of heighe Goddes hestes honurable,

      How that the seconde heste of him is this:

      'Take nat my name in idel or amis.'

      Lo, rather he forbedeth swich swering

      Than homicide, or many a cursed thing!

645   I seye that as by ordre thus it standeth;

      This knowen that hise hestes understandeth,

      How that the seconde heste of God is that.

      And forther over I wol thee telle al plat

      That vengeance shal nat parten from his hous

650   That of hise othes is to outrageous.

      'By Goddes precious herte, and by his nailes,

      And by the blood of Crist that is in Hailes,

      Sevene is my chaunce, and thin is cink and treye!

      By Goddes armes, if thow falsly pleye,

655   This daggere shal thurghout thin herte go!'

      This fruit cometh of the bicched bones two:

      Forswering, ire, falsnesse, homicide.

      Now, for the love of Crist that for us dide,

---

632 **reprevable** reprehensible   633 **at al** completely
637 **swere in doom** take an oath in court   638 **idel** frivolous
639 **table** tablet (n.)   640 **hestes** commandments   642 **in idel** in vain
643 **rather** earlier (in the list) **forbedeth** forbids   646 **that** those who
648 **forther over** besides **plat** bluntly   650 **outrageous** unrestrained
653 **chaunce** number thrown at dice **cink** five **treye** three
656 **bicched bones** cursed bones, i.e. dice   658 **dide** died

Lete youre othes, bothe grete and smale.
But sires, now wol I telle forth my tale.   660
   Thise riotoures thre of which I telle,
Longe erst er prime rong of any belle,
Were set hem in a taverne to drinke.
And as they sat, they herde a belle clinke
Biforn a cors was caried to his grave.   665
That oon of hem gan callen to his knave:
'Go bet,' quod he, 'and axe redily
What cors is this, that passeth heer forby;
And looke that thow reporte his name wel.'
   'Sire,' quod this boy, 'it nedeth never a del;   670
It was me told er ye cam heer two houres.
He was, pardee, an old felawe of youres,
And sodeinly he was yslain tonight,
Fordronke, as he sat on his bench upright.
Ther cam a privee theef men clepeth Deeth,   675
That in this contree al the peple sleeth,
And with his spere he smoot his herte atwo,
And wente his wey withouten wordes mo.
He hath a thousand slain this pestilence.
And maister, er ye come in his presence,   680
Me thinketh that it were necessarye
For to be war of swich an adversarye.
Beth redy for to meete him everemoore –
Thus taughte me my dame; I sey namoore.'
   'By Seinte Marye!' seide this taverner,   685
'The child seyth sooth, for he hath slain this yer,

659 **Lete** leave off   660 **telle forth** proceed to tell
661 **riotoures** profligates   662 **erst er** before **prime** 9 a.m. (g.) **rong** was
rung   663 **Were set hem** were seated   664 **clinke** ring   665 **cors** corpse
666 **knave** servant   667 **Go bet** go quickly   668 **heer forby** past this place
670 **it nedeth never a del** it is not necessary   674 **Fordronke** blind drunk
675 **privee** sly **clepeth** call   677 **smoot** struck   679 **pestilence** plague
681 **were** would be   683 **everemoore** always   684 **dame** mother

Henne over a mile, withinne a greet village,
Bothe man and womman, child, and hine, and
      page.
I trowe his habitacioun be there.
690 To been avised greet wisdom it were,
Er that he dide a man a dishonour.'
   'Ye, Goddes armes,' quod this riotour,
'Is it swich peril with him for to meete?
I shal him seke by wey and eek by strete,
695 I make avow to Goddes digne bones!
Herkneth, felawes, we thre been al ones:
Lat ech of us holde up his hand til oother,
And ech of us bicomen otheres brother,
And we wol sleen this false traitour Deeth!
700 He shal be slain, he that so manye sleeth,
By Goddes dignitee, er it be night!'
   Togidres han thise thre hir trouthes plight,
To live and dien ech of hem for oother,
As thogh he were his owene ybore brother.
705 And up they stirte, al dronken in this rage,
And forth they goon towardes that village
Of which the taverner hadde spoke biforn.
And many a grisly ooth thanne han they sworn,
And Cristes blessed body they to-rente;
710 Deeth shal be deed, if that they may him hente!
   Whan they han goon nat fully half a mile,
Right as they wolde han treden over a stile,
An old man and a povre with hem mette.
This olde man ful mekely hem grette,
715 And seide thus: 'Now lordes, God yow se!'
   The proudeste of thise riotoures thre

---

687 **Henne** from here   688 **hine** farm labourer **page** peasant
690 **been avised** take care   694 **by wey and eek by strete** everywhere
695 **digne** noble   697 **til** to   702 **Togidres** together
hir trouthes plight pledged their word   704 **ybore** born   705 **stirte** leaped
709 **to-rente** tore in pieces   710 **hente** lay hold of   713 **povre** poor
714 **grette** (= *gretede*) greeted   715 **God yow se** may God protect you

Answerde again, 'What, carl, with sory grace!
Why artow al forwrapped save thy face?
Why livestow so longe in so greet age?'
   This olde man gan looke in his visage,   720
And seide thus: 'For I ne kan nat finde
A man, thogh that I walked into Inde,
Neither in citee ne in no village,
That wolde chaunge his youthe for min age.
And therfore moot I han min age stille,   725
As longe time as it is Goddes wille,
Ne deeth, allas, ne wol nat han my lif!
Thus walke I, lik a restelees caitif,
And on the ground, which is my modres gate,
I knokke with my staf, bothe erly and late,   730
And seye, "Leeve moder, leet me in!
Lo, how I vanisshe, flessh and blood and skin!
Allas, whan shul my bones been at reste?
Moder, with yow wolde I chaunge my cheste
That in my chaumbre longe time hath be,   735
Ye, for an heire clowte to wrappe me!"
– But yet to me she wol nat do that grace,
For which ful pale and welked is my face.
   'But sires, to yow it is no curteisye
To speken to an old man vileinye,   740
But he trespase in word or elles in dede.
In holy writ ye may yourself wel rede:
"Agains an old man, hoor upon his heed,
Ye sholde arise"; wherfore I yeve yow reed,
Ne dooth unto an old man noon harm now,   745
Namoore than that ye wolde men dide to yow

717 **carl** knave **with sory grace** bad luck to you 718 **forwrapped** wrapped
up 722 **Inde** India 725 **moot I han** I must keep 728 **caitif** wretch
731 **Leeve** dear 732 **vanisshe** waste away 736 **heire clowte** hair-cloth
738 **welked** withered 740 **vileinye** discourtesy 741 **But he trespase** unless
he does wrong 743 **Agains** in the presence of 744 **reed** advice
746 **wolde** would wish

In age, if that ye so longe abide.
And God be with yow, wher ye go or ride!
I moot go thider as I have to go.'

750   'Nay, olde cherl, by God, thow shalt nat so!'
Seide this oother hasardour anon.
'Thow partest nat so lightly, by Seint John!
Thow spak right now of thilke traitour Deeth,
That in this contree alle oure freendes sleeth;

755   Have here my trouthe, as thow art his espye.
Telle wher he is, or thow shalt it abye,
By God and by the holy sacrament!
For soothly thow art oon of his assent
To sleen us yonge folk, thow false theef!'

760   'Now, sires,' quod he, 'if that yow be so leef
To finde deeth, turn up this croked wey,
For in that grove I lafte him, by my fey,
Under a tree, and ther he wol abide;
Nat for youre boost he wol him nothing hide.

765   Se ye that ook? Right ther ye shal him finde.
God save yow, that boghte again mankinde,
And yow amende!' – thus seide this olde man.
And everich of thise riotoures ran
Til they came to that tree, and ther they founde

770   Of florins fine of gold ycoined rounde
Wel ny an eighte busshels, as hem thoughte.
No lenger thanne after Deeth they soughte,
But ech of hem so glad was of that sighte,
For that the florins been so faire and brighte,

775   That doun they sette hem by this precious hoord.
        The worste of hem he spak the firste word:

---

747 **abide** last   748 **wher** wherever   752 **partest** depart **lightly** easily
755 **espye** spy   756 **abye** pay for   758 **of his assent** in league with him
760 **yow be so leef** it is so desirable to you   762 **fey** faith
764 **nothing** not at all   765 **ook** oak-tree   766 **boghte again** redeemed
768 **everich** each   771 **Wel ny** very nearly **an eighte busshels** the quantity of
eight bushels   775 **sette hem** sat **hoord** hoard

'Bretheren,' quod he, 'taak kepe what I seye;
My wit is greet, thogh that I bourde and pleye.
This tresor hath Fortune unto us yeven,
In mirthe and jolitee oure lif to liven;   780
And lightly as it comth, so wol we spende.
Ey, Goddes precious dignitee, who wende
Today that we sholde han so fair a grace?
But mighte this gold be caried fro this place
Hoom to min hous – or ellis unto youres –   785
For wel ye woot that al this gold is oures –
Thanne were we in heigh felicitee.
But trewely by daye it may nat be.
Men wolde seyn that we were theves stronge,
And for oure owene tresor doon us honge.   790
This tresor moste ycaried be by nighte,
As wisely and as slyly as it mighte.
Wherfore I rede that cut among us alle
Be drawe, and lat se wher the cut wol falle;
And he that hath the cut with herte blithe   795
Shal renne to the toune, and that ful swithe,
And bringe us breed and win ful prively.
And two of us shul kepen subtilly
This tresor wel, and, if he wol nat tarye,
Whan it is night we wol this tresor carye   800
By oon assent wheras us thinketh best.'
    That oon of hem the cut broghte in his fest,
And bad hem drawe, and looke wher it wol falle;
And it fil on the yongeste of hem alle,
And forth toward the toun he wente anon.   805
And also soone as that he was agon,

777 **taak kepe** pay attention to   778 **wit** understanding **bourde** joke
781 **lightly** easily   782 **wende** would have thought   783 **grace** piece of
good luck   787 **were** would be   789 **stronge** out-and-out
790 **doon us honge** have us hanged   792 **wisely** cunningly   793 **cut** short
straw   796 **swithe** quickly   797 **prively** secretly   798 **subtilly** cunningly
801 By common agreement wherever seems best to us   802 **fest** fist
804 **fil** fell

That oon of hem spak thus unto that oother:
'Thou knowest wel thow art my sworne brother;
Thy profit wol I telle thee anon.
810   Thow woost wel that oure felawe is agon,
And heere is gold, and that ful greet plentee,
That shal departed been among us thre.
But nathelees, if I kan shape it so
That it departed were among us two,
815   Hadde I nat doon a freendes torn to thee?'
          That oother answerde, 'I noot how that may be.
He woot wel that the gold is with us tweye;
What shal we doon? What shal we to him seye?'
      'Shal it be conseil?' seide the firste shrewe,
820   'And I shal tellen in a wordes fewe
What we shul doon, and bringe it wel aboute.'
'I graunte,' quod that oother, 'out of doute,
That by my trouthe I wol thee nat biwreye.'
          'Now,' quod the firste, 'thow woost wel we be
                  tweye,
825   And two of us shul strenger be than oon.
Looke whan that he is set, that right anoon
Aris as though thow woldest with him pleye;
And I shal rive him thurgh the sides tweye
Whil that thow strogelest with him as in game,
830   And with thy daggere looke thow do the same.
And thanne shal al this gold departed be,
My deere freend, bitwixe me and thee.
Thanne may we bothe oure lustes al fulfille,
And pleye at dees right at oure owene wille.'
835   And thus acorded been thise shrewes tweye
To sleen the thridde, as ye han herd me seye.

---

810 **woost** know   812 **departed** divided   813 **shape it** bring it about
815 Would I not have done you a good turn   816 **noot** do not know
819 **be conseil** be a secret **shrewe** villain   823 **biwreye** betray
824 **tweye** two   826 **set** seated   828 **rive** stab   829 **strogelest** struggle
833 **lustes** desires

This yongeste, which that wente to the toun,
Ful ofte in herte he rolleth up and doun
The beautee of thise florins newe and brighte.
'O Lord,' quod he, 'if so were that I mighte   840
Have al this tresor to myself allone,
Ther is no man that liveth under the trone
Of God that sholde live so mirye as I!'
And atte laste the feend, oure enemy,
Putte in his thoght that he sholde poison beye,   845
With which he mighte sleen his felawes tweye,
For-why the feend foond him in swich livinge
That he hadde leve him to sorwe bringe.
For this was outrely his ful entente:
To sleen hem bothe, and nevere to repente.   850
And forth he goth – no lenger wolde he tarye –
Into the toun unto a pothecarye,
And preyed him that he him wolde selle
Som poisoun, that he mighte his rattes quelle,
And eek ther was a polcat in his hawe,   855
That, as he seide, his capouns hadde yslawe,
And fain he wolde wreke him, if he mighte,
On vermin that destroyed him by nighte.
     The pothecarye answerde, 'And thow shalt
          have
A thing that, also God my soule save,   860
In al this world ther is no creature
That ete or dronke hath of this confiture
Nat but the montaunce of a corn of whete,
That he ne shal his lif anoon forlete.

---

838 He often turns over in his mind   842 **trone** throne   844 **feend** devil
847 **For-why** because   848 **leve** permission   849 **outrely** wholly
entente intention   852 **pothecarye** pharmacist, druggist   853 **preyed** asked
854 **quelle** kill   855 **hawe** yard   856 **capouns** chickens **yslawe** killed
857 **fain** gladly **wreke him** take vengeance   858 **destroyed** were ruining
860 **also** as   862 **confiture** concoction   863 **montaunce** quantity
corn of whete grain of wheat   864 **forlete** lose

865   Ye, sterve he shal, and that in lasse while
      Than thow wolt goon a paas nat but a mile,
      The poisoun is so strong and violent.'
          This cursed man hath in his hond yhent
      This poisoun in a box, and sith he ran
870   Into the nexte strete unto a man,
      And borwed of him large botels thre,
      And in the two his poison poured he;
      The thridde he kepte clene for his drinke,
      For al the night he shoop him for to swinke
875   In carying of the gold out of that place.
      And whan this riotour, with sory grace,
      Hadde filled with win hise grete botels thre,
      To hise felawes again repaireth he.
          What nedeth it to sermone of it moore?
880   For right as they hadde cast his deeth bifore,
      Right so they han him slain, and that anon.
      And whan that this was doon, thus spak that oon:
      'Now lat us sitte and drinke, and make us merye,
      And afterward we wol his body berye.'
885   And with that word it happed him *par cas*
      To take the botel ther the poisoun was,
      And drank, and yaf his felawe drinke also,
      For which anon they storven bothe two.
          But certes, I suppose that Avicen
890   Wroot nevere in no canon, n'in no fen,
      Mo wonder signes of empoisoning
      Than hadde thise wrecches two, er hir ending.
      Thus ended been thise homicides two,
      And eek the false empoisonere also.

865 sterve die   866 a paas at walking-pace   868 yhent taken
869 sith afterwards   874 shoop him planned   swinke labour
878 repaireth returns   879 sermone speak   880 cast plotted
882 that oon one of them   884 berye bury   885 par cas by chance
886 ther where   888 storven died   889–90 see n.
893 homicides murderers

O cursed sinne of alle cursednesse!   895
O traitours homicide, O wikkednesse!
O glotonye, luxurye, and hasardrye!
Thou blasphemour of Crist with vileinye,
And othes grete, of usage and of pride!
Allas, mankinde, how may it bitide   900
That to thy Creatour, which that thee wroghte,
And with his precious herte-blood the boghte,
Thow art so fals and so unkinde, allas?
    Now goode men, God foryeve yow youre
        trespas,
And ware yow fro the sinne of avarice!   905
Min holy pardoun may yow alle warice,
So that ye offre nobles or sterlinges,
Or elles silver broches, spones, ringes.
Boweth youre heed under this holy bulle.
Com up, ye wives, offreth of youre wolle;   910
Youre name I entre here in my rolle anon.
Into the blisse of hevene shul ye gon;
I yow assoille by min heigh power –
Yow that wol offre – as clene and eek as cler
As ye were born. – And lo, sires, thus I preche.   915
And Jesu Crist, that is oure soules leche,
So graunte yow his pardoun to receive,
For that is best; I wol yow nat deceive.
    'But, sires, o word forgat I in my tale:
I have relikes and pardon in my male   920
As faire as any man in Engelond,
Whiche were me yeven by the Popes hond.
If any of yow wol, of devocioun,
Offren and han min absolucioun,

897 **luxurye** lechery   898 **with vileinye** shamefully   899 **of usage** from
habit   901 **wroghte** created   902 **boghte** redeemed
903 **unkinde** ungrateful   904 **trespas** wrong-doing
905 **ware yow fro** guard against   906 **warice** save   907 **So that** provided
that   **nobles** gold coins (g.)   **sterlinges** silver pennies   908 **spones** spoons
910 **of youre wolle** some of your wool   913 **assoille** absolve
914 **clene** innocent   **cler** pure   916 **leche** healer   920 **male** bag

925 Com forth anon, and kneleth here adoun,
And mekely receiveth my pardoun;
Or ellis taketh pardoun as ye wende,
Al newe and fressh at every miles ende –
So that ye offren, alwey newe and newe,
930 Nobles or pens whiche that been goode and trewe.
It is an honour to everich that is heer
That ye mowe have a suffisant pardoner
T'assoille yow in contree as ye ride,
For aventures whiche that may bitide.
935 Paraventure ther may falle oon or two
Doun of his hors, and breke his nekke atwo.
Looke, which a seuretee is it to yow alle
That I am in youre felaweship yfalle,
That may assoille yow, bothe moore and lasse,
940 Whan that the soule shal fro the body passe.
I rede that oure Hooste shal biginne,
For he is moost envoluped in sinne.
Com forth, sire Hoost, and offre first anon,
And thow shalt kisse the relikes everychon,
945 Ye, for a grote! Unbokele anon thy purs.'
        'Nay, nay,' quod he, 'thanne have I Cristes curs!
Lat be!' quod he, 'It shal nat be, so thee'ch!
Thow woldest make me kisse thin olde breech,
And swere it were a relik of a seint,
950 Thogh it were with thy fundement depeint.
But, by the crois which that Seint Eleine fond,
I wolde I hadde thy coilons in my hond

925 **anon** at once   927 **wende** go   929 **alwey newe and newe** again and
again   931 **everich** each one   932 **mowe** may   **suffisant** competent
934 **For aventures** in case of accidents   935 **Paraventure** perhaps
936 **atwo** in two   937 **which a seuretee** what a safeguard
941 **rede** advise   942 **envoluped** steeped   945 **grote** groat (g.)
946 **have I** may I have   947 **so thee'ch** as I prosper   948 **breech** breeches
950 **fundement** arse, anus   **depeint** stained   951 **fond** found
952 **coilons** testicles, balls

In stede of relikes or of seintuarye!
Lat kutte hem of; I wol thee helpe hem carye.
They shul be shrined in an hogges toord!'   955
    This Pardoner answerde nat a word;
So wrooth he was, no word ne wolde he seye.
    'Now,' quod oure Hoost, 'I wol no lenger pleye
With thee, ne with noon oother angry man.'
But right anon the worthy Knight bigan,   960
Whan that he saugh that al the peple lough,
'Namoore of this, for it is right inough!
Sire Pardoner, be glad and murye of cheere,
And ye, sire Hoost, that been to me so deere,
I pray yow that ye kisse the Pardoner.   965
And Pardoner, I pray thee, drawe thee neer,
And as we diden, lat us laughe and pleye.'
Anon they kiste, and riden forth hir weye.

Heere is ended the Pardoners Tale.

953 **seintuarye** reliquary   954 **Lat kutte hem of** have them cut off
955 **shrined** enshrined **hogges toord** pig's turd   957 **wrooth** angry
958 **pleye** joke   961 **lough** laughed   963 **murye of cheere** in a cheerful
mood   966 **drawe thee neer** come near   968 **riden** rode

THE SHIPMAN'S TALE

Heere biginneth the Shipmannes Tale.

A marchant whilom dwelled at Seint-Denis,
That riche was, for which men helde him wis.
A wif he hadde, of excellent beautee,
And compaignable and revelous was she –
5   Which is a thing that causeth moore dispence
Than worth is al the cheere and reverence
That men hem doon at festes and at daunces.
Swiche salutacions and contenaunces
Passen as dooth a shadwe upon the wal.
10   But wo is him that payen moot for al!
The sely housbonde, algate he moot paye;
He moot us clothe, and he moot us arraye,
Al for his owene worship, richely,
In which array we dauncen jolily.
15   And if that he noght may, paraventure,
Or ellis list no swich dispence endure,
But thinketh it is wasted and ylost,
Thanne moot another payen for oure cost,
Or lene us gold, and that is perilous.
20   This noble marchant heeld a worthy hous,
For which he hadde alday so greet repair,
For his largesse, and for his wif was fair,
That wonder is; but herkneth to my tale!
Amonges alle hise gestes, grete and smale,

1 **whilom** in former times   4 **compaignable** sociable **revelous** fond of
amusement   5 **dispence** expense   6 **cheere** attentive behaviour
reverence respect   8 **contenaunces** gestures   9 **shadwe** shadow
11 **sely** poor **algate** always   12 **arraye** adorn   13 **worship** credit
14 **jolily** gaily   15 **noght may** cannot **paraventure** perhaps   16 Or else is
not willing to bear such expense   19 **lene** lend   21 **alday** always
repair crowd of visitors   22 **largesse** generosity   24 **gestes** guests

Ther was a monk, a fair man and a bold –   25
I trowe a thritty winter he was old –
That evere in oon was drawing to that place.
This yonge monk, that was so fair of face,
Aqueinted was so with the goode man,
Sith that hir firste knoweliche bigan,   30
That in his hous as famulier was he
As it is possible any freend to be.
    And for as muchel as this goode man,
And eek this monk of which that I bigan,
Were bothe two yborn in o village,   35
The monk him claimeth as for cosinage,
And he again; he seyth nat ones nay,
But was as glad therof as fowel of day,
For to his herte it was a gret plesaunce.
Thus been they knit with eterne alliaunce,   40
And ech of hem gan oother for t'assure
Of bretherhede whil that hir lif may dure.
    Free was daun John, and manly of dispence
As in that hous, and ful of diligence
To doon plesaunce, and also greet costage.   45
He nat forgat to yeve the leeste page
In al that hous, but after hir degree;
He yaf the lord, and sith al his meinee,
Whan that he com, som manere honeste thing.
For which they were as glad of his coming   50
As fowel is fain whan that the sonne up riseth.
Namoore of this as now, for it suffiseth.
    But so bifel, this marchant on a day
Shoop him to make redy his array

---

26 **a thritty winter** about thirty years   27 **evere in oon** constantly
29 **goode man** master of the house   30 **hir . . . knoweliche** their
acquaintance   35 **o** one   36 **cosinage** kinship   38 **fowel** bird **of day** at
daybreak (n.)   39 **plesaunce** pleasure   42 **dure** last   43 **Free** generous
manly of dispence liberal in expenditure   45 **To give pleasure and to spend
a lot of money   46 **leeste page** lowliest servant   47 **after** according to
48 **sith** afterwards **meinee** household   49 **honeste** decent, suitable
51 **fain** glad   54 **Shoop him** was preparing **array** effects

55   Toward the toun of Brugges for to fare,
        To byen there a porcioun of ware;
        For which he hath to Paris sent anon
        A messager, and preyed hath daun John
        That he sholde come to Seint-Denis and pleye
60   With him and with his wif a day or tweye,
        Er he to Brugges wente, in alle wise.
            This noble monk of which I yow devise
        Hath of his abbot, as him list, licence,
        Bicause he was a man of heigh prudence
65   And eek an officer, out for to ride,
        To seen hir graunges and hir bernes wide;
        And unto Seint-Denis he comth anon.
        Who was so welcome as my lord daun John,
        Oure deere cosin, ful of curteisye?
70   With him broghte he a jubbe of malvesye,
        And eek another, ful of fin vernage,
        And volatil, as ay was his usage.
        And thus I lete hem ete and drinke and pleye,
        This marchant and this monk, a day or tweye.
75   The thridde day this marchant up ariseth,
        And on his nedes sadly him aviseth,
        And up into his countour-hous goth he,
        To rekene with himself, wel may be,
        Of thilke yeer how that it with him stood,
80   And how that he despended hadde his good,
        And if that he encressed were or noon.
        Hise bookes and hise bagges many oon

55 **fare** go   56 **ware** merchandise   59 **pleye** amuse himself
61 **in alle wise** at all costs   62 **devise** tell   63 **as him list** as he pleases
65 **officer** see n.   66 **hir graunges** their monastic farms (n.)   **bernes** barns
70 **jubbe** jar   **malvesye** Malmsey wine   71 **vernage** white Italian wine
72 **volatil** wild-fowl   **ay** always   **usage** custom   73 **lete** leave   76 And
seriously takes stock of his business affairs
77 **countour-hous** counting-house   79 **thilke** that same
81 **encressed were** was worth more

He leyth biforn him on his counting-bord.
Ful riche was his tresor and his hord,
For which ful faste his countour-dore he shette;   85
And eek he nolde that no man sholde him lette
Of his acountes for the mene-time.
And thus he sit til it was passed prime.

   Daun John was risen in the morwe also,
And in the gardin walketh to and fro,   90
And hath his thinges seid ful curteisly.

   This goode wif cam walking prively
Into the gardin ther he walketh softe,
And him salueth, as she hath doon ofte.
A maide child cam in hir compaignye,   95
Which as hir list she may governe and gye,
For yet under the yerde was the maide.
'O deere cosin min, daun John,' she saide,
'What eileth yow, so rathe for to rise?'

   'Nece,' quod he, 'it oghte inow suffise   100
Five houres for to slepe upon a night,
But it were for an old apalled wight,
As been thise wedded men, that lie and dare,
As in a forme sit a wery hare
Were al forstraught with houndes grete and   105
       smale.
But deere nece, why be ye so pale?
I trowe, certes, that oure goode man
Hath yow laboured sith the night bigan,
That yow were nede to resten hastily.'
And with that word he lough ful mirily,   110

---

83 **counting-bord** table used for keeping accounts (n.)   86 **nolde** did not
want **lette** hinder   88 **sit** (= *sitteth*) sits **prime** 9 a.m. (g.)
91 **thinges** devotions   93 **ther** where **softe** peacefully   94 **salueth** greets
95 **maide** girl   96 Whom she can control and rule as she pleases
97 **under the yerde** in tutelage   99 **eileth** ails **rathe** early   102 Except for
an old enfeebled creature   103 **dare** cower   104 **forme** form, lair of a hare
105 **Were** who was **forstraught with** tormented by
107 **oure goode man** the master of the house   108 **laboured** kept you busy
110 **lough** laughed

And of his owene thoght he wex al reed.
   This faire wif gan for to shake hir heed,
And seide thus: 'Ye, God woot al!' quod she.
'Nay, cosin min, it stant nat so with me!
115 For, by that God that yaf me soule and lif,
In al the reawme of France is ther no wif
That lasse lust hath to that sory pley;
For I may singe "allas!" and "weilawey
That I was born!"; but to no wight', quod she,
120 'Dar I nat telle how that it stant with me.
Wherfore I thinke out of this lande to wende,
Or elles of myself to make an ende,
So ful am I of drede and eek of care.'
   This monk bigan upon this wif to stare,
125 And seide, 'Allas, my nece, God forbede
That ye for any sorwe or any drede
Fordo youreself; but telleth me youre grief.
Paraventure I may in youre meschief
Conseille or helpe, and therfore telleth me
130 Al youre anoy, for it shal been secree.
For on my portehors I make an oth,
That nevere in my lif, for lief ne loth,
Ne shal I of no conseil yow biwreye.'
   'The same again to yow', quod she, 'I seye.
135 By God and by this portehors I swere,
Thogh men me wolde al into peces tere,
Ne shal I nevere, for to gon to helle,
Biwreye a word of thing that ye me telle,
Nat for no cosinage ne alliance,
140 But verraily for love and affiance.'

111 **wex** became   114 **it stant nat so** such is not the case
116 **reawme** realm   117 **lust** pleasure **pley** game (in sexual sense)
121 **wende** go   123 **care** sorrow   127 **Fordo** destroy
128 **meschief** affliction   130 **anoy** trouble   131 **portehors** breviary (n.)
132 **for lief ne loth** for fear nor favour (*lit*. for friend nor foe)
133 **conseil** secret **biwreye** betray   135–40 see n.   137 **for to gon** even
were I to go   139 **cosinage** kinship   140 **affiance** trust

Thus been they sworn, and herupon they kiste,
And ech of hem tolde oother what hem liste.
    'Cosin,' quod she, 'if that I hadde a space –
As I have noon, and namely in this place –
Thanne wolde I telle a legende of my lif,   145
What I have suffred sith I was a wif
With min housbonde, al be he youre cosin.'
    'Nay,' quod this monk, 'by God and Seint
        Martin,
He is namore cosin unto me
Than is this leef that hangeth on the tree!   150
I clepe him so, by Seint Denis of Fraunce,
To have the moore cause of aqueintaunce
Of yow, which I have loved specially
Aboven alle wommen, sikerly;
This swere I yow on my professioun.   155
Telleth youre grief, lest that he come adoun,
And hasteth yow, and goth youre wey anon.'
    'My deere love,' quod she, 'O my daun John,
Ful lief were me this conseil for to hide,
But out it moot; I may namoore abide.   160
Min housbonde is to me the worste man
That evere was sith that the world bigan!
But sith I am a wif, it sit nat me
To tellen no wight of oure privetee,
Neither abedde, ne in noon oother place.   165
God shilde I sholde it tellen, for his grace!
A wif ne shal nat seyn of hir housbonde
But al honour, as I kan understonde.
Save unto yow thus muche I tellen shal:
As help me God, he is noght worth at al   170

141 **herupon** on this point   142 **what hem liste** what they pleased
143 **a space** time   147 **al be he** although he is   151 **clepe** call
154 **sikerly** assuredly   155 **professioun** monastic vows
159 **Ful lief were me** I should very much like   160 **abide** hold off
163 **sit nat** does not befit   164 **privetee** private affairs   166 **shilde** forbid
for his grace by His grace

In no degree the value of a flye.
But yet me greveth moost his nigardye!
And wel ye woot, that wommen naturelly
Desiren thinges sixe, as wel as I:
175   They wolde that hir housbondes sholde be
Hardy, and wise, and riche, and therto free,
And buxom unto his wif, and fressh abedde.
But by that ilke Lord that for us bledde,
For his honour, myself for to arraye,
180   A Sonday next I moste nedes paye
An hundred frankes, or ellis am I lorn.
Yet were me levere that I were unborn
Than me were doon a sclaundre or vileinye.
And if min housbonde eek it mighte espye,
185   I nere but lost; and therfore I yow preye,
Lene me this somme, or ellis moot I deye.
Daun John, I seye, lene me thise hundred frankes;
Pardee, I wol noght faille yow my thankes,
If that yow list to doon that I yow praye.
190   For at a certein day I wol yow paye,
And doon to yow what plesaunce and servise
That I may doon, right as yow list devise.
And but I do, God take on me vengeance
As foul as evere hadde Geneloun of France!'
195   This gentil monk answerde in this manere:
'Now trewely, min owene lady deere,
I have', quod he, 'on yow so greet a routhe
That I yow swere and plighte yow my trouthe
That, whan youre housbond is to Flaundres fare,
200   I wol delivere yow out of this care,

---

172 **greveth** vexes **nigardye** meanness   173 **woot** know   176 **Hardy** brave
therto free also generous   177 **buxom** obedient **abedde** in bed
179 **arraye** clothe   180 **A** on   181 **frankes** francs (n.)
182 **were me levere** I would rather   185 **I nere but lost** I would be ruined
188 **faille yow my thankes** be lacking in gratitude to you
191 **what plesaunce** whatever pleasure   192 **right as yow list devise** just as it
pleases you to direct   193 **but I do** if I do not   195 **gentil** noble
197 **routhe** compassion   199 **fare** gone   200 **care** distress

For I wol bringe yow an hundred frankes.'
And with that word he caughte hire by the
    flankes,
And hire embraceth harde, and kiste hire ofte.
'Goth now youre wey,' quod he, al stille and
    softe,
'And lat us dine as soone as that ye may,   205
For by my chilindre it is prime of day.
Goth now, and beth as trewe as I shal be.'
   'Now, elles God forbede, sire,' quod she;
And forth she goth, as jolif as a pie,
And bad the cokes that they sholde hem hie,   210
So that men mighte dine, and that anon.
Up to hir housbonde is this wif ygon,
And knokketh at his countour boldely.
   '*Qui la?*' quod he. 'Peter, it am I!'
Quod she; 'What, sire, how longe wol ye faste?   215
How longe time wol ye rekene and caste
Youre sommes, and youre bokes and youre
    thinges?
The devel have part on alle swiche rekeninges!
Ye have inogh, pardee, of Goddes sonde;
Com doun today, and lat youre bagges stonde.   220
Ne be ye nat ashamed that daun John
Shal fastinge al this day elenge gon?
What, lat us heere a masse, and go we dine.'
   'Wif,' quod this man, 'litel kanstow devine
The curious bisinesse that we have;   225
For of us chapmen, also God me save,
And by that lord that clepid is Seint Ive,
Scarsly amonges twelve tweye shul thrive

---

206 **chilindre** portable sun-dial (n.)   209 **jolif** frisky **pie** magpie
210 **hem hie** hurry   213 **countour** counting-house   216 **caste** calculate
217 **thinges** business affairs   218 **have part on** take
219 **Goddes sonde** what God has sent   222 **elenge** miserable
223 **go we** let us go   224 **devine** guess   225 **curious bisinesse** complicated
business   226 **chapmen** merchants   228 **thrive** prosper

Continuelly, lasting unto oure age.
230   We may wel make cheere and good visage,
And drive forth the world as it may be,
And kepen oure estat in privetee
Til we be dede, or elles that we pleye
A pilgrimage, or goon out of the weye,
235   And therfore have I gret necessitee
Upon this queinte world t'avise me.
For everemo we mote stonde in drede
Of hap and Fortune in oure chapmanhede.
       'To Flaundres wol I go tomorwe at day,
240   And come again as soone as evere I may.
For which, my deere wif, I thee biseke,
As be to every wight buxom and meke,
And for to kepe oure good be curious,
And honestly governe wel oure hous.
245   Thow hast inow, in every manere wise,
That to a thrifty houshold may suffise.
Thee lakketh noon array ne no vitaille;
Of silver in thy purs shaltow nat faille.'
And with that word his countour-dore he shette,
250   And doun he goth; no lenger wolde he lette.
But hastily a masse was ther seid,
And spedily the tables were yleid,
And to the diner faste they hem spedde;
And richely this monk the chapman fedde.
255   At after-diner, daun John sobrely
This chapman took apart, and prively

229 **age** old age   230–31 We may well look cheerful and put up a good
front, and take life as it comes   232 **estat** (financial) condition
in privetee secret   233–4 **pleye** A pilgrimage see n.
234 **goon out of the weye** retire from the public eye   236 **queinte** strange
t'avise me to reflect   237 **mote** must   238 **hap** chance **chapmanhede** trade
241 **biseke** beseech   242 **buxom** submissive   243 **good** property
curious careful   244 **honestly** properly   246 **thrifty** respectable
247 **array** household fittings **vitaille** provisions   248 **faille** run out of
249 **shette** shut   250 **lette** delay   253 **hem spedde** hastened

He seide him thus: 'Cosin, it standeth so
That wel I se to Brugges wol ye go.
God and Seint Austin spede yow and gide!
I pray yow, cosin, wisely that ye ride;   260
Governeth yow also of youre diete
Atemprely, and namely in this hete.
Bitwix us two nedeth no strange fare.
Farwel, cosin, God shilde yow fro care!
And if that any thing, by day or night,   265
If it lie in my power and my might,
That ye me wol comande in any wise,
It shal be doon, right as ye wol devise!
    'O thing, er that ye goon, if it may be,
I wolde preye yow for to lene me   270
An hundred frankes, for a wike or tweye,
For certein bestes that I moste beye,
To store with a place that is oures –
God help me so, I wolde it were youres!
I shal nat faille, surely, of my day,   275
Nat for a thousand frankes, a mile-way.
But lat this thing be secree, I yow preye,
For yet tonight thise bestes moot I beye.
And fare now wel, min owene cosin deere;
Graunt merci of youre cost and of youre cheere.'   280
    This noble marchant gentilly anon
Answerde and seide, 'O cosin min, daun John,
Now sikerly this is a smal requeste!
My gold is youres whan that it yow leste,

---

259 **spede** prosper **gide** guide   261 **Governeth yow ... of** regulate
262 **Atemprely** moderately   263 **strange fare** formal behaviour
264 **shilde** protect **care** misfortune   268 **wol devise** wish to prescribe
270 **preye** ask   271 **wike** week   272 **beye** buy   273 **store** stock
275 **faille ... of** fail to keep   276 **a mile-way** by twenty minutes (the time
taken to walk a mile)   280 *Graunt merci* of thank you for
cheere hospitality   281 **gentilly** courteously   283 **sikerly** certainly
284 **yow leste** pleases you

285   And nat oonly my gold but my chaffare;
       Take what yow list, God shilde that ye spare!
          'But o thing is, ye knowe it wel inow
       Of chapmen, that hir moneye is hir plow.
       We may creaunce whil we have a name,
290   But goldlees for to been, it is no game.
       Pay it again whan it lith in youre ese;
       After my might ful fain wolde I yow plese.'
          Thise hundred frankes he fette forth anon,
       And prively he took hem to daun John.
295   No wight in al this world wiste of this lone,
       Saving this marchant and daun John allone.
       They drinke, and speke, and rome a while and
                  pleye,
       Til that daun John rideth to his abbeye.
          The morwe cam, and forth this marchant rideth
300   To Flaundres-ward; his prentis wel him gideth
       Til he cam into Brugges murily.
       Now goth this marchant faste and bisily
       Aboute his nede, and byeth and creaunceth.
       He neither pleyeth at the dees ne daunceth,
305   But as a marchant, shortly for to telle,
       He let his lif; and ther I lete him dwelle.
          The Sonday next this marchant was agon,
       To Seint-Denis ycomen is daun John,
       With crowne and berd al fressh and newe yshave.
310   In al the hous ther nas so litel a knave,
       Ne no wight elles, that he nas ful fain
       That my lord daun John was come again.

---

285 **chaffare** merchandise   286 **spare** hold back   288 **plow** plough
289 **creaunce** obtain credit **name** (good) reputation   290 But it is no joke to
be without gold   291 Repay it when it is within your means (to do so)
292 **After my might** according to my ability   293 **fette** fetched
294 **took** gave   295 **lone** loan   296 **Saving** except   297 **rome** stroll about
300 **To Flaundres-ward** towards Flanders   302 **faste** energetically
303 **nede** business   304 **dees** dice   306 **let** (= *ledeth*) leads
309 **crowne** tonsure **yshave** shaved   310 **knave** servant   311 Nor anyone
else who was not very glad

And shortly to the point right for to gon,
This faire wif acorded with daun John
That for thise hundred frankes he sholde al night   315
Have hire in hise armes bolt-upright.
And this acord parfourned was in dede;
In mirthe al night a bisy lif they lede
Til it was day, that daun John wente his way,
And bad the meinee 'fare wel; have good day!'   320
– For noon of hem, ne no wight in the toun,
Hath of daun John right no suspecioun.
And forth he rideth hoom to his abbeye,
Or where him list; namoore of him I seye.

This marchant, whan that ended was the faire,   325
To Seint-Denis he gan for to repaire;
And with his wif he maketh feste and cheere,
And telleth hire that chaffare is so deere
That nedes moste he make a chevissaunce,
For he was bounde in a reconissaunce   330
To paye twenty thousand sheeld anon;
For which this marchant is to Paris gon
To borwe of certeine freendes that he hadde
A certein frankes, and somme with him he ladde.
And whan that he was come into the toun,   335
For greet chiertee and greet affeccioun
Unto daun John he first goth him to pleye –
Nat for to axe or borwe of him moneye,
But for to wite and seen of his welfare,
And for to tellen him of his chaffare,   340

---

314 **acorded** agreed   316 **bolt-upright** flat on her back
317 **parfourned** put into effect   318 **mirthe** pleasure
320 **bad the meinee 'fare wel'** said goodbye to the household
324 **where him list** wherever he pleased   326 **gan for to repaire** returned
327 **maketh feste and cheere** relaxes, enjoys himself
329 **make a chevissaunce** raise a loan   330 **reconissaunce** recognizance (n.)
331 **sheeld** Flemish *écus* (n.)   334 **A certein** a certain quantity of
ladde carried   336 **chiertee** love   337 **pleye** amuse himself   339 **wite** learn
340 **chaffare** trade

As freendes doon whan they been met ifeere.
Daun John him maketh feste and murye cheere,
And he him tolde again ful specially
How he hadde wel yboght and graciously,
345   Thanked be God, al hool his marchandise;
Save that he moste, in alle maner wise,
Maken a chevissance as for his beste,
And thanne he sholde been in joye and reste.
        Daun John answerde: 'Certes, I am fain
350   That ye in heele ar comen hom again.
And if that I were riche, as have I blisse,
Of twenty thousand sheeld sholde ye nat misse,
For ye so kindely, this oother day,
Lente me gold; and as I kan and may
355   I thanke yow, by God and by Seint Jame!
But nathelees, I took unto oure dame,
Youre wif at hom, the same gold again
Upon youre bench; she woot it wel, certain,
By certein tokenes that I kan yow telle.
360   Now, by youre leve, I may no lenger dwelle;
Oure abbot wol out of this toun anon,
And in his compaignye moot I gon.
Grete wel oure dame, min owene nece swete,
And fare wel, deere cosin, til we meete!'
365   This marchant, which that was ful war and wis,
Creanced hath, and paid eek in Paris
To certein Lumbards, redy in hir hond,
The somme of gold, and gat of hem his bond.

341 **ifeere** together   342 **him maketh feste and murye cheere** makes much of
him   343 **ful specially** in detail   344 **graciously** successfully
345 **al hool** all of   346 Except that he absolutely had to
347 **as for his beste** in his best interests   350 **in heele** safe and sound
352 **Of . . . misse** lack   353 **For** because   356 **took** gave **oure dame** the
lady of the house   358 **woot** knows   360 **dwelle** stay
361 **wol out of** intends to leave   365 **war** prudent
366 **Creanced** borrowed money   367 **redy in hir hond** in ready money
368 **gat of hem** obtained from them

And hoom he gooth, murye as a papinjay,
For wel he knew he stood in swich array   370
That nedes moste he winne in that viage
A thousand frankes above al his costage.

His wif ful redy mette him atte gate,
As she was wont of old usage, algate,
And al that night in mirthe they bisette,   375
For he was riche, and cleerly out of dette.
Whan it was day, this marchant gan embrace
His wif al newe, and kiste hire on hir face,
And up he goth and maketh it ful tough.
     'Namoore!' quod she, 'by God, ye have   380
          inough!'
And wantownely again with him she pleyde,
Til, atte laste, thus this marchant seide:
'By God,' quod he, 'I am a litel wroth
With yow, my wif, althogh it be me looth;
And woot ye why? By God, as that I gesse,   385
That ye han maad a manere straungenesse
Bitwixen me and my cosin daun John.
Ye sholde han warned me er I had gon
That he yow hadde an hundred frankes payed
By redy tokene, and heeld him ivele apaied   390
For that I to him spak of chevissaunce –
Me semed so, as by his contenaunce.
But nathelees, by God, oure hevene king,
I thoghte nat to axe of him nothing.
I prey thee, wif, ne do namoore so;   395
Tel me alwey, er that I fro thee go,

---

369 **papinjay** parrot   370 **array** state   371 **viage** deal
372 **costage** expenditure   374 **usage** custom   375 **mirthe** pleasure
bisette spent   376 **cleerly** completely   378 **al newe** all over again
379 **maketh it . . . tough** makes a performance of it   381 **wantownely** sexily,
provocatively **again** in return **pleyde** fooled around   383 **wroth** angry
384 **althogh it be me looth** though I am reluctant to be so
386 **manere straungenesse** kind of estrangement
390 **heeld him ivele apaied** was not very pleased

If any dettour hath in min absence
Ypayed thee, lest thurgh thy necligence
I mighte him axe a thing that he hath payed.'

400 This wif was nat afered nor affrayed,
But boldely she seide, and that anon:
'Marye, I deffye the false monk, daun John!
I kepe nat of his tokenes never a del!
He took me certein gold, this woot I wel –

405 What, ivel thedam on his monkes snowte! –
For, God it woot, I wende, withouten doute,
That he hadde yeve it me bicause of yow,
To doon therwith min honour and my prow,
For cosinage, and eek for bele cheere

410 That he hath had ful ofte times heere.
But sith I se I stonde in this disjoint,
I wol answere yow shortly to the point.
Ye han mo slakker dettours than am I,
For I wol paye yow wel and redily

415 Fro day to day; and if so be I faille,
I am youre wif, score it upon my taille,
And I shal paye as soone as evere I may.
For, by my trouthe, I have on min array,
And nat on wast, bistowed every del.

420 And for I have bistowed it so wel
For youre honour, for Goddes sake, I seye,
As be nat wrooth, but lat us laughe and pleye.
Ye shal my joly body have to wedde;
By God, I wol noght paye yow but abedde!

425 Forgive it me, min owene spouse deere;
Turne hiderward, and maketh bettre cheere.'

---

400 **afered** frightened   402 **deffye** scorn   403 I don't care a bit about his
tokens   405 **ivel thedam** bad luck   406 **wende** thought   408 **prow** benefit
409 **cosinage** kinship **bele cheere** hospitality   411 **disjoint** difficulty
413 **slakker** tardier, slower to pay   415 **faille** fall short
416 **taille** tally (n.)   419 **nat on wast** not on extravagances
422 **As be nat wrooth** do not be cross   423 You shall have my fine person
as security   426 **maketh bettre cheere** cheer up

This marchaunt saugh ther was no remedye,
And for to chide it nere but folye,
Sith that the thing may nat amended be.
'Now, wif,' he seide, 'and I foryeve it thee;   430
But by thy lif, ne be namoore so large.
Keep bet oure good; this yeve I thee in charge.'
Thus endeth my tale, and God us sende
Tailling inough unto oure lives ende! Amen.

Heere endeth the Shipmannes Tale.

THE SHIPMAN –
PRIORESS LINK

*Bihoold the murye wordes of the
Hoost to the Shipman and
to the Lady Prioresse.*

'Wel seid, by *corpus dominus*!' quod oure Hoost.   435
'Now longe moote thou saille by the coost,
Sire gentil maister, gentil mariner!
God yeve the monk a thousand last quade yeer!
A ha, felawes, beth ware of swich a jape!
The monk putte in the mannes hood an ape,   440
And in his wives eek, by Seint Austin;
Draweth no monkes moore unto youre in.

428 And that it would only be foolish to scold   431 **large** extravagant
432 **bet** better **good** wealth **yeve . . . in charge** order
434 **Tailling inough** plenty of tallying (with a pun on 'tailing' and perhaps 'tale-ing')

435 *corpus dominus* God's body (n.)   438 **a thousand last quade yeer** a wagon load of misery (*lit.* a thousand cartloads of bad years)
439 **jape** trick   440 I.e. the monk made a monkey out of the man
442 **in** house

'But now passe over, and lat us seke aboute
Who shal now telle first of al this route
445   Another tale' – and with that word he saide,
As curteisly as it hadde been a maide:
'My lady Prioresse, by youre leve,
So that I wiste I sholde yow nat greve,
I wolde demen that ye tellen sholde
450   A tale next, if so were that ye wolde.
Now wol ye vouchesauf, my lady deere?'
'Gladly,' quod she, and seide as ye shal heere.

THE PRIORESS'S PROLOGUE

The Prologe of the Prioresses Tale.

Domine dominus noster.

'O Lord, oure Lord, thy name how merveillous
Is in this large world ysprad!' quod she,
455   'For nat oonly thy laude precious
Parfourned is by men of dignitee,
But by the mouth of children thy bountee
Parfourned is; for on the brest soukinge
Somtime shewen they thin heryinge.

443 **passe over** move on **seke aboute** find out   444 **route** company
446 **as it hadde been** as if he were **maide** girl   448 **So that** provided that
greve displease   449 **demen** judge   450 **wolde** were willing
451 **vouchesauf** agree

454 **ysprad** spread   455 **laude** praise   456 **Parfourned** celebrated
457 **bountee** worth   458 **soukinge** sucking   459 **heryinge** praise

Wherfore in laude, as I best kan or may,   460
Of thee, and of the white lilye flour
Which that the bar, and is a maide alway,
To telle a storye I wol do my labour –
Nat that I may encressen hir honour,
For she hirself is honour and the roote   465
Of bountee, next hir sone, and soules boote.

O moder maide, o maide moder free!
O bussh unbrent, brenninge in Moises sighte,
That ravisedest doun fro the deitee,
Thurgh thin humblesse, the Goost that in   470
     th'alighte,
Of whos vertu, whan he thin herte lighte,
Conceived was the Fadres Sapience,
Help me to telle it in thy reverence!

Lady, thy bountee, thy magnificence,
Thy vertu, and thy grete humilitee,   475
Ther may no tonge expresse in no science.
For somtime, lady, er men praye to thee,
Thow goost biforn, of thy benignitee,
And getest us the light of thy prayere
To giden us unto thy sone so deere.   480

My konning is so waik, o blisful queene,
For to declare thy grete worthinesse,
That I ne may the weighte nat sustene,

462 the thee a maide alway still a virgin   466 boote salvation
468 unbrent unburned brenninge burning   469 ravisedest ravished
deitee deity   470 Goost (Holy) Ghost in th'alighte descended into you
471 Of whos vertu by whose power lighte illuminated
472 Sapience Wisdom (n.)   473 in thy reverence in honour of you
476 science branch of learning   479 getest obtain for
481 konning ability waik weak blisful blessed

But as a child of twelf-month old or lesse,
485   That kan unnethes any word expresse,
Right so fare I; and therfore I yow preye,
Gideth my song that I shal of yow seye.'

THE PRIORESS'S TALE

Heere biginneth the Prioresses Tale.

Ther was in Asie, in a greet citee,
Amonges Cristen folk, a Jewerye,
490   Sustened by a lord of that contree,
For foule usure and lucre of vileinye,
Hateful to Crist and to his compaignye.
And thurgh this strete men mighte ride or wende,
For it was free and open at either ende.

495   A litel scole of Cristen folk ther stood
Doun at the ferther ende, in which ther were
Children an heep, ycomen of Cristen blood,
That lerned in that scole, yeer by yere,
Swich manere doctrine as men used there –
500   This is to seyn, to singen and to rede,
As smale children doon in hir childhede.

---

485 **unnethes** with difficulty   487 **Gideth** guide **of yow** about you

489 **Jewerye** ghetto, Jewish quarter   490 **Sustened** maintained
491 **lucre of vileinye** shameful profit   492 **compaignye** followers
493 **wende** walk   495 **scole** school   497 **an heep** many
499 **Swich manere doctrine** such kind of teaching

Among thise children was a widwes sone,
A litel clergeoun, seven yeer of age,
That day by day to scole was his wone.
And eek also, wheras he say th'image   505
Of Cristes moder, hadde he in usage,
As him was taught, to knele adoun and seye
His *Ave Marie*, as he goth by the weye.

Thus hath this widwe hir litel sone ytaught
Oure blisful lady, Cristes moder deere,   510
To worshipe ay; and he forgat it naught,
For sely child wol alwey soone lere.
But ay whan I remembre on this matere,
Seint Nicholas stant evere in my presence,
For he so yong to Crist dide reverence.   515

This litel child, his litel book lerninge,
As he sat in the scole at his primer,
He *Alma redemptoris* herde singe,
As children lerned hir antiphoner;
And as he dorste, he drow him ner and ner,   520
And herkned ay the wordes and the note,
Til he the firste vers koude al by rote.

Noght wiste he what this Latin was to seye,
For he so yong and tendre was of age;
But on a day his felawe gan he preye   525
T'expounden him this song in his langage,

---

503 **clergeoun** schoolboy   504 **was his wone** was accustomed (to go)
505 **say** saw   506 **hadde he in usage** he was accustomed
512 **sely** innocent   **soone lere** learn quickly   513 **ay** always
514 **stant** (= *standeth*) stands   515 **For** because
to Crist dide reverence honoured Christ   517 **primer** Book of Hours, used
as an elementary reading book (n.)   519 **antiphoner** see n.
520 **ner and ner** nearer and nearer   522 **vers** line **koude** knew
523 **was to seye** meant   525 **gan he preye** he asked

Or telle him why this song was in usage.
This preide he him to construe and declare,
Ful often time, upon his knowes bare.

530   His felawe, which that elder was than he,
Answerde him thus: 'This song, I have herd seye,
Was maked of oure blisful Lady free,
Hire to salue, and eek hire for to preye
To been oure help and socour whan we deye.
535   I kan namoore expounde in this matere;
I lerne song; I kan but smal gramere.'

'And is this song maked in reverence
Of Cristes moder?' seide this innocent.
'Now, certes, I wol do my diligence
540   To konne it al er Cristemasse is went,
Thogh that I for my primer shal be shent,
And shal be beten thries in an houre,
I wol it konne, Oure Lady for t'honoure.'

His felawe taughte him homward prively,
545   Fro day to day, til he koude it by rote,
And thanne he song it wel and boldely,
Fro word to word, acording with the note.
Twies a day it passed thurgh his throte,
To scoleward and homward whan he wente;
550   On Cristes moder set was his entente.

As I have seid, thurghout the Juerye,
This litel child, as he cam to and fro,
Ful murily than wolde he singe and crye
'O *alma redemptoris*' everemo.

528 **construe** explain   529 **knowes** knees   532 **of** about **free** gracious
536 I am learning to sing the liturgy; I know very little Latin grammar (n.)
539 **do my diligence** do my utmost   540 **konne** learn **is went** has passed
541 **shent** punished   544 **homward** on the way home   546 **song** sang
549 **To scoleward** to school   550 He was completely devoted to Christ's
mother   551 **Juerye** Jewish quarter   553 **murily** sweetly

The swetnesse hath his herte perced so   555
Of Cristes moder that, to hire to preye,
He kan nat stinte of singing by the weye.

Oure firste foo, the serpent Sathanas,
That hath in Jewes herte his waspes nest,
Up swal and seide, 'O Hebraik peple, allas!   560
Is this to yow a thing that is honest,
That swich a boy shal walken as him lest
In youre despit, and singe of swich sentence,
Which is agains youre lawes reverence?'

Fro thennesforth the Jewes han conspired   565
This innocent out of this world to chace.
An homicide therto han they yhired,
That in an aleye hadde a privee place,
And as the child gan forby for to pace,
This cursed Jew him hente, and heeld him faste,   570
And kitte his throte, and in a pit him caste.

I seye, that in a wardrobe they him threwe,
Wheras thise Jewes purgen hir entraille.
O cursed folk of Herodes al newe,
What may youre ivel entente yow availle?   575
Mordre wol out, certein, it wol nat faille,
And namely ther th'onour of God shal sprede;
The blood out cryeth on youre cursed dede.

557 **stinte of** cease from   558 **foo** enemy **Sathanas** Satan, the devil
560 **swal** swelled **Hebraik** Hebraic   561 **honest** creditable
562 **as him lest** as it pleases him   563 **In youre despit** in contempt of you
sentence subject   565 **thennesforth** thenceforth   566 **chace** drive
567 **homicide** murderer   569 **gan forby for to pace** passed by
570 **hente** seized **faste** tightly   571 **kitte** cut   572 **wardrobe** latrine
573 **hir entraille** their bowels   576 **Mordre** murder **wol out** will become
known

O martyr, souded to virginitee,
580 Now maystow singen, folwing evere in oon
The white Lamb celestial – quod she –
Of which the grete evangelist, Seint John,
In Pathmos wroot, which seyth that they that gon
Biforn this lamb, and singe a song al newe,
585 That nevere, flesshly, wommen they ne knewe.

This povre widwe awaiteth al that night
After hir litel child, but he cam noght.
For which, as soone as it was dayes light,
With face pale of drede and bisy thoght,
590 She hath at scole and elleswhere him soght;
Til finally she gan so fer espye
That he last seyn was in the Jewerye.

With modres pitee in hir brest enclosed,
She goth, as she were half out of hir minde,
595 To every place wher she hath supposed
By liklihede hir litel child to finde;
And evere on Cristes moder meke and kinde
She cride, and at the laste thus she wroghte:
Among the cursed Jewes she him soghte.

600 She fraineth and she preyeth pitously
To every Jew that dwelte in thilke place,
To telle hire if hir child wente oght forby.
They seide 'nay'; but Jesu, of his grace,
Yaf in hir thoght, inwith a litel space,
605 That in that place after hir sone she cride,
Wher he was casten in a pit biside.

---

579 **souded to** bonded with   580 **evere in oon** constantly
585 **flesshly** carnally   586–7 **awaiteth . . . After** waits for
589 **bisy thoght** frantic anxiety   591 **gan so fer espye** discovered this much
596 **liklihede** probability   598 **wroghte** acted   600 **fraineth** inquires
602 **wente oght forby** passed by at all   604 **Yaf** put **inwith** within
605 **after** for

O grete God, that parfournest thy laude
By mouth of innocentz, lo here thy might!
This gemme of chastitee, this emeraude,
And eek of martyrdom the ruby bright,   610
Ther he with throte ykorven lay upright,
He *Alma redemptoris* gan to singe
So loude that al the place gan to ringe.

The Cristen folk that thurgh the strete wente
In coomen for to wondre upon this thing,   615
And hastily they for the provost sente.
He cam anon withouten tarying,
And herieth Crist, that is of hevene king,
And eek his moder, honour of mankinde,
And after that the Jewes leet he binde.   620

This child with pitous lamentacioun
Up taken was, singinge his song alway;
And with honour of greet processioun
They caryen him unto the nexte abbay.
His moder swowning by his beere lay;   625
Unnethe mighte the peple that was there
This newe Rachel bringen fro his beere.

With torment and with shameful deth echon
This provost dooth the Jewes for to sterve
That of this mordre wiste, and that anon.   630
He nolde no swich cursednesse observe.
Ivel shal have that ivel wol deserve;
Therfore with wilde hors he dide hem drawe,
And after that he heng hem by the lawe.

---

609 **emeraude** emerald   611 **Ther** where   **ykorven** cut   **upright** on his back
615 **coomen** came   616 **provost** chief magistrate (n.)   618 **herieth** praises
620 **leet he binde** he had bound   625 **swowning** in a swoon   **beere** bier
626 **Unnethe** with difficulty   628 **torment** torture
629 **dooth . . . for to sterve** puts to death   631 He would not sanction such
wickedness   633 **with . . . hors . . . dide hem drawe** had them dragged
behind a horse   634 **heng** hanged

635 Upon his beere ay lith this innocent,
Biforn the chief auter, whil the masse laste,
And after that the abbot with his covent
Han sped hem for to buryen him ful faste.
And whan they holy water on him caste,
640 Yet spak this child, whan spreind was holy water,
And song 'O *alma redemptoris mater*'.

This abbot, which that was an holy man,
As monkes ben – or elles oghten be –
This yonge child to conjure he bigan,
645 And seide, 'O deere child, I halsen thee,
In vertu of the Holy Trinitee,
Tel me what is thy cause for to singe,
Sith that thy throte is kit, to my seminge?'

'My throte is kit unto my nekke-boon,'
650 Seide this child, 'and, as by wey of kinde,
I sholde have died – ye, longe time agoon.
But Jesu Crist, as ye in bokes finde,
Wol that his glorye laste and be in minde;
And for the worship of his moder deere,
655 Yet may I singe "O *alma*" loude and clere.

'This welle of mercy, Cristes moder swete,
I loved alwey, as after my konninge;
And whan that I my lif sholde forlete,
To me she cam, and bad me for to singe
660 This antheme verraily in my deyinge,
As ye han herd; and whan that I had songe,
Me thoughte she leide a grein upon my tonge.

635 **ay** all the time   636 **auter** altar   637 **covent** monks
638 **Han sped hem** made haste   640 **spreind** sprinkled
644 **conjure** beseech   645 **halsen** entreat   648 Since your throat is cut, as it
appears to me   650 **as by wey of kinde** according to nature
653 **Wol** wishes **laste** should last   654 **worship** honour
656 **welle** fountain   657 **as after my konninge** according to my ability
658 **sholde forlete** was about to lose   660 **antheme** antiphon (n.)
in my deyinge as I died   662 **grein** seed

'Wherfore I singe, and singe moot, certein,
In honour of that blisful maiden free,
Til fro my tonge of-taken is the grein.   665
And after that, thus seide she to me:
"My litel child, now wol I fecche thee
Whan that the grein is fro thy tonge ytake.
Be nat agast; I wol thee nat forsake."'

This holy monk – this abbot, him mene I –   670
His tonge out caughte, and took awey the grein,
And he yaf up the goost ful softely.
And whan this abbot hadde this wonder seyn,
His salte teeris trikled doun as rein,
And gruf he fil al plat upon the grounde,   675
And stille he lay, as he had been ybounde.

The covent eek lay on the pavement
Wepinge, and herien Cristes moder deere.
And after that they rise, and forth been went,
And toke awey this martyr from his beere.   680
And in a tombe of marbilstones cleere
Enclosen they his litel body swete.
Ther he is now, God leve us for to meete!

O yonge Hugh of Lincoln, slain also
With cursed Jewes, as it is notable,   685
For it is but a litel while ago,
Preye eek for us, we sinful folk unstable,
That of his mercy God so merciable
On us his grete mercy multiplye,
For reverence of his moder Marye. Amen.   690

Heere is ended the Prioresses Tale.

663 **moot** must   664 **free** gracious   665 **of-taken** taken away
669 **agast** afraid   672 **softely** calmly   674 **trikled** trickled **as rein** like rain
675 **gruf** face down **plat** flat   676 **as** as if   678 **herien** praise
679 **been went** went   681 **marbilstones cleere** gleaming marble slabs
685 **With** by **notable** well known

THE PRIORESS –
SIR THOPAS LINK

Bihoold the murye wordes of
the Hoost to Chaucer.

Whan seid was al this miracle, every man
As sobre was that wonder was to se;
Til that oure Hoost to japen tho bigan,
And thanne at erst he looked upon me,
695　　And seide thus: 'What man artow?' quod he.
'Thow lookest as thow woldest finde an hare,
For evere upon the ground I se thee stare.

'Approche neer, and looke up mirily!
Now war yow, sires, and lat this man have place!
700　　He in the wast is shape as wel as I;
This were a popet in an arm t'enbrace
For any womman smal and fair of face!
He semeth elvissh by his contenaunce,
For unto no wight dooth he daliaunce.

705　　'Sey now somwhat, sin oother folk han said;
Telle us a tale of mirthe, and that anon!'
'Hoost,' quod I, 'ne beth nat ivele apaid,
For oother tale, certes, kan I noon,
But of a rym I lerned longe agoon.'
710　　'Ye, that is good,' quod he, 'now shul we heere
Som deintee thing, me thinketh by his cheere.'

691 **seid** told　693 **japen** joke　**tho** then　694 **at erst** for the first time
696 **woldest** would like to　699 **war yow** look out　700 **wast** waist
shape formed　701 This would be a dainty little person to embrace in one's
arms　702 **smal** slender　703 **elvissh** otherworldly　704 For he does not
chat with anybody　705 **said** said their piece　707 **ivele apaid** displeased
711 **deintee** delightful　**cheere** appearance

SIR THOPAS

Heere biginneth Chaucers
Tale of Thopas.

Listeth, lordes, in good entent,
And I wol telle verrayment
  Of mirthe and of solas,
Al of a knight was fair and gent   715
In bataille and in tornament;
  His name was Sire Thopas.

Yborn he was in fer contree,
In Flaundres, al biyonde the see,
  At Popering in the place.   720
His fader was a man ful free,
And lord he was of that contree,
  As it was Goddes grace.

Sire Thopas wax a doghty swain;
Whit was his face as paindemain,   725
  Hise lippes rede as rose.
His rode is lik scarlet in grain,
And I yow telle in good certein
  He hadde a semely nose.

His heer, his berd, was lik safroun,   730
That to his girdel raughte adoun;
  His shoon of cordewane.

712 **Listeth** listen   713 **verrayment** truly   714 **solas** fun   715 **gent** noble
721 **free** noble   724 **wax** became   **doghty swain** brave youth
725 **paindemain** white bread   727 **rode** complexion
scarlet in grain fast-dyed scarlet cloth (n.)   730 **safroun** saffron
731 **raughte** reached   732 His shoes were of Cordovan leather

Of Brugges were his hosen broun;
His robe was of siklatoun,
   That coste many a jane.

735

He koude hunte at wilde deer,
And ride an hauking for river
   With grey goshauk on honde.
Therto he was a good archeer;
Of wrastling was ther noon his peer,
   Ther any ram shal stonde.

740

Ful many a maide bright in bour,
They moorne for him *par amour*,
   Whan hem were bet to slepe.
But he was chaast and no lechour,
And swete as is the brambel-flour
   That bereth the rede hepe.

745

And so bifel, upon a day,
For sothe as I yow telle may,
   Sire Thopas wolde out ride.
He worth upon his steede gray,
And in his hand a launcegay,
   A long swerd by his side.

750

He priketh thurgh a fair forest,
Therinne is many a wilde best –
   Ye, bothe bukke and hare.

755

733 **hosen** hose   734 **siklatoun** rich silken fabric   735 **jane** a small Genoese
coin (g.)   737 **an hauking for river** hawking for waterfowl
739 **Therto** also   741 **Ther** where **stonde** be on view (as a prize)
742 **bour** chamber   743 **moorne** yearn *par amour* with passion
744 When it would be better for them to sleep   746 **brambel-flour** dog-rose
747 **rede hepe** red hip   748 **upon a day** one day   751 **worth upon** mounts
752 **launcegay** light lance   754 **priketh** rides   756 **bukke** male deer

And as he priketh north and est,
I telle it yow, him hadde almest
   Bitidde a sory care.

There springen herbes grete and smale,   760
The licoris and the cetewale,
   And many a clowe-gilofre,
And notemuge, to putte in ale,
Wheither it be moiste or stale,
   Or for to leye in cofre.   765

The briddes singe, it is no nay,
The sparhauk and the popinjay,
   That joye it was to here.
The thrustelcok made eek hire lay;
The wodedowve upon the spray,   770
She sang ful loude and clere.

Sire Thopas fil in love-longinge,
Al whan he herde the thrustel singe,
   And priked as he were wood.
His faire steede in his prikinge   775
So swatte that men mighte him wringe;
   His sides were al blood.

Sire Thopas eek so wery was
For priking on the softe gras,
   So fiers was his corage,   780

758 **almest** almost   759 **Bitidde** befallen **sory care** painful misfortune
761 Liquorice and zedoary (a spice)   762 **clowe-gilofre** clove
763 **notemuge** nutmeg   764 **moiste** fresh   765 **cofre** chest
766 **it is no nay** it cannot be denied   767 The sparrowhawk and the parrot
769 **thrustelcok** male song-thrush **lay** song   770 **wodedowve** wood-pigeon
spray twig   773 **thrustel** thrush   774 And galloped as if he were mad
776 **swatte** sweated **wringe** wring out   780 **corage** spirit

That doun he leide him in the plas
To make his steede som solas,
   And yaf him good forage.

'O Seinte Marye, *benedicite*!
785   What eileth this love at me
     To binde me so soore?
Me dremed al this night, pardee,
An elf-queene shal my lemman be,
   And slepe under my goore.

790   'An elf-queene wol I love, iwys,
For in this world no womman is
    Worthy to be my make,
       In towne.
Al othere wommen I forsake,
795   And to an elf-queene I me take,
    By dale and eek by downe.'

Into his sadel he clamb anoon,
And priketh over stile and stoon,
   An elf-queene for t'espye;
800   Til he so longe hath riden and goon
That he foond in a privee woon
    The contree of Fairye
      So wilde.
For in that contree was ther noon
805   That to him dorste ride or goon,
    Neither wif ne childe.

782 **make . . . som solas** give some relief to 783 **forage** fodder (n.)
785 What does this love have against me 788 **lemman** mistress
789 **goore** gown (n.) 790 **iwys** assuredly 792 **make** mate
793 Among men 796 **downe** hill 797 **clamb** climbed
799 **t'espye** to search out 801 **privee woon** secret place

Til that ther cam a greet geaunt;
His name was Sire Olifaunt,
   A perilous man of dede.
He seide, 'Child, by Termagaunt,   810
But if thow prike out of min haunt,
   Anon I sle thy steede
         With mace.
Heere is the Queene of Faierye,
With harpe and pipe and symphonye,   815
   Dwelling in this place.'

The child seide: 'Also mote I thee,
Tomorwe wol I meete thee,
   Whan I have min armoure.
And yet I hope, *par ma fay*,   820
That thow shalt with this launcegay
   Abyen it ful soure.
         Thy mawe
Shal I percen, if I may,
Er it be fully prime of day,   825
   For here shaltow be slawe.'

Sire Thopas drow abak ful faste;
This geant at him stones caste,
   Out of a fel staf-slinge.
But faire escapeth Child Thopas,   830
And al it was thurgh Goddes gras,
   And thurgh his fair beringe.

---

810 **Child** young knight (n.)   811 **But if** unless **haunt** territory
812 **sle** slay   815 **symphonye** hurdy-gurdy (n.)   817 **Also mote I thee** as I
may prosper   820 *par ma fay* on my word   822 Pay for it bitterly
823 **mawe** belly   826 **slawe** slain   829 **fel** deadly **staf-slinge** sling whose
strings are attached to the end of a staff   831 **gras** grace
832 **beringe** behaviour

[*The Second Fit*]

Yet listeth, lordes, to my tale;
Murier than the nightingale,
835   For now I wol yow rowne
How Sire Thopas, with sides smale,
Priking over hill and dale
      Is come again to towne.

His murye men comanded he
840   To make him bothe game and glee,
      For nedes moste he fighte
With a geaunt with hevedes thre,
For paramour and jolitee
      Of oon that shoon ful brighte.

845   'Do come', he seide, 'my minestrales,
And gestours for to tellen tales,
      Anon in min arminge,
Of romances that been reales,
Of popes and of cardinales,
850   And eek of love-likinge.'

They fette him first the swete win,
And mede eek in a maselin,
      And real spicerye
Of gingebred that was ful fin,
855   And licoris, and eek comin,
      With sugre that is trie.

---

833 **listeth** listen   834 **Murier** sweeter   835 **rowne** tell (*lit.* whisper)
836 **sides smale** a slim waist   839 **murye men** followers   840 To provide
him with entertainment   842 **hevedes** heads   843 **paramour** love
jolitee passion   845 **Do come** summon   846 **gestours** story-tellers
848 **reales** regal (n.)   850 **love-likinge** romantic love   852 **mede** mead
maselin maple drinking-bowl   853 **real** regal   854 **gingebred** preserved
ginger   855 **comin** cumin   856 **trie** fine

He dide next his white leere
Of clooth of lake, fin and cleere,
   A breech, and eek a sherte;
And next his sherte an aketoun,   860
And over that an haubergeoun,
   For percing of his herte.

And over that a fin hauberk
Was al ywroght of Jewes werk,
   Ful strong it was of plate.   865
And over that his cote-armour,
As whit as is a lilye-flour,
   In which he wol debate.

His sheeld was al of gold so reed,
And therinne was a bores heed,   870
   A charbocle biside.
And there he swoor on ale and breed
How that the geaunt shal be deed,
   Bitide what bitide!

Hise jambeux were of quirboily,   875
His swerdes shethe of ivory,
   His helm of latoun bright;
His sadel was of rewel-bon,
His bridel as the sonne shon,
   Or as the moone-light.   880

857 **leere** flesh   858 **clooth of lake** fine linen **cleere** beautiful
860 **aketoun** padded jacket worn under the armour
861 **haubergeoun** mail-coat   862 **For** to prevent   863 **hauberk** set of plate-armour   866 **cote-armour** tunic bearing heraldic device   868 **debate** fight
870 **bores** boar's   871 **charbocle** carbuncle   874 Come what may
875 **jambeux** pieces of leg-armour **quirboily** hardened leather (n.)
876 **shethe** sheath   877 **latoun** brass (n.)   878 **rewel-bon** ivory

His spere was of fin cypres,
That bodeth werre and nothing pes,
   The heed ful sharp ygrounde.
His steede was al dappel gray;
885   It gooth an ambel in the way,
   Ful softely and rounde,
      In londe.
Lo, lordes mine, here is a fit!
If ye wole any moore of it,
890   To telle it wol I fonde.

[*The Third Fit*]

Now holde youre mouth, *par charitee*,
Bothe knight and lady free,
   And herkneth to my spelle,
Of bataille and of chivalry,
895   And of ladies love-drury
   Anon I wol yow telle.

Men speken of romances of pris,
Of Horn Child and of Ipotis,
   Of Beves and Sire Gy,
900   Of Sire Libeux and Pleindamour –
But Sire Thopas, he bereth the flour
   Of real chivalry!

His goode steede al he bistrood,
And forth upon his wey he glood,
905   As sparcle out of the bronde.

882 Which bodes war and not peace   885 **gooth an ambel** goes at an easy
walking pace   886 Very slowly and easily   888 **fit** part of a poem, section
889 **wole** want   890 **fonde** try   891 *par charitee* for charity
893 **spelle** tale   895 **love-drury** wooing   897 **of pris** excellent
901 **bereth the flour** is the best   902 **real chivalry** kingly knights
903 **bistrood** mounted   904 **glood** went   905 **sparcle** spark **bronde** torch

Upon his creest he bar a tour,
And therinne stiked a lilye-flour;
   God shilde his cors fro shonde!

And for he was a knight auntrous,
He nolde slepen in noon hous,   910
   But liggen in his hoode.
His brighte helm was his wonger,
And by him baiteth his destrer,
   Of herbes fine and goode.

Himself drank water of the well,   915
As dide the knight Sire Percivell,
   So worly under wede.
Til on a day –

THE THOPAS –
MELIBEE LINK

*Here the Hoost stinteth
Chaucer of his Tale of Thopas.*

'Namoore of this, for Goddes dignitee!'
Quod oure Hooste, 'for thow makest me   920
So wery of thy verray lewednesse
That, also wysly God my soule blesse,
Mine eris aken of thy drasty speche!
Now swich a rym the devel I biteche!

---

907 **stiked** was stuck   908 May God keep his body from disgrace
909 **knight auntrous** knight-errant, knight wandering in search of
exploits (n.)   911 **liggen** lie   912 **wonger** pillow   913 **baiteth** feeds
destrer war-horse   917 So worthy under his garments (n.)

921 **wery** weary **lewednesse** stupidity   922 **wysly** surely
923 **eris aken of** ears ache from **drasty** crude   924 **biteche** consign to

925 This may wel be rym dogerel,' quod he.
         'Why so?' quod I, 'Why wiltow lette me
     Moore of my tale than another man? –
     Sin that it is the beste rym I kan.'
         'By God,' quod he, 'for pleinly, at o word,
930 Thy drasty ryming is nat worth a tord!
     Thow doost noght ellis but despendest time.
     Sire, at o word, thow shalt no lenger ryme.
     Lat se wher thow kanst tellen aught in geste,
     Or telle in prose somwhat at the leeste,
935 In which ther be som mirthe or som doctrine.'
         'Gladly,' quod I, 'by Goddes swete pine!
     I wol yow telle a litel thing in prose,
     That oghte liken yow, as I suppose,
     Or elles, certes, ye be to daungerous.
940 It is a moral tale vertuous,
     Al be it toold somtime in sondry wise
     Of sondry folk, as I shal yow devise.
     As thus: ye woot, that every evaungelist
     That telleth us the peine of Jesu Crist
945 Ne seyth nat alle thing as his felawe dooth;
     But nathelees hir sentence is al sooth,
     And alle acorden as in hir sentence,
     Al be ther in hir telling difference.
     For somme of hem seyn moore, and somme seyn
              lesse,
950 Whan they his pitous passioun expresse –
     I mene of Mark, Mathew, Luk, and John –
     But doutelees, hir sentence is al oon.
         'Therfore, lordinges alle, I yow biseche,
     If that ye thinke I varye as in my speche –

---

925 **rym dogerel** doggerel rhyme   926 **lette** hinder   928 **kan** know
929 **at o word** in a word   930 **tord** turd   931 **despendest** waste
933 **aught** anything **geste** ?alliterative verse (n.)   935 **doctrine** edification
936 **pine** suffering   938 **liken** please   939 **to daungerous** too choosy
941 Although it is sometimes told in different ways   942 **Of** by
946 **sentence** substance, meaning   947 **acorden** agree

As thus: thogh that I telle somwhat moore   955
Of proverbes than ye han herd bifore
Comprehended in this litel tretis heere,
To enforcen with th'effect of my matere –
And thogh I nat the same wordes seye
As ye han herd, yet to yow alle I preye   960
Blameth me nat; for, as in my sentence,
Shullen ye nowher finden difference
Fro the sentence of this tretis lite
After the which this mirye tale I write.
And therfore, herkneth what that I shal seye,   965
And lat me tellen al my tale, I preye.'

THE TALE OF MELIBEE

Heere biginneth Chaucers Tale of Melibee.

A yong man called Melibeus, mighty and riche, bigat upon his
wif, that called was Prudence, a doghter which that called was
Sophie. | Upon a day, bifel that he for his desport is went into
the feeldes him to pleye. | His wif and eek his doghter hath he
laft inwith his hous, of which the dores weren faste yshette. |
Thre of his olde foos han it espied, and setten laddres to the
walles of his hous and by windowes ben entred, [970] | and
betten his wif and wounded his doghter with five mortal
woundes in five sondry places | – this is to seyn, in hir feet, in
hir handes, in hir eris, in hir nose, and in hir mouth – and leften
hire for deed and wenten awey. |

957 **Comprehended** included **tretis** treatise   958 **enforcen** strengthen
962 **Shullen** shall   964 **After** according to **mirye** entertaining

967 **bigat** engendered   968 **desport** amusement **is went** went
969 **yshette** shut   971 **betten** beat

Whan Melibeus retourned was into his hous and seigh al this meschief, he lik a mad man rentinge his clothes gan to wepe and crye. | Prudence, his wif, as ferforth as she dorste, bisoughte him of his weping for to stinte, | but nat-forthy he gan to crye and wepen, evere lenger the moore. [975] | This noble wif Prudence remembred hire upon the sentence of Ovide, in his book that cleped is the *Remedye of Love*, whereas he seyth, | 'He is a fool that destourbeth the moder to wepe in the deth of hir child til she have wept hir fille as for a certein time, | and thanne shal man doon his diligence with amiable wordes hire to reconforte, and preye hire of hir wepyng for to stinte.' | For which resoun this noble wif Prudence suffred hir housbonde for to wepe and crye as for a certein space, | and whan she say hir time she seide him in this wise: 'Allas, my lord,' quod she, 'why make ye youreself for to be lik a fool? [980] | For sothe, it aperteneth nat to a wis man to maken swich a sorwe. | Youre doghter, with the grace of God, shal warisshe and escape. | And al were it so that she right now were deed, ye ne oghte nat as for hir deth yourself to destroye. | Senek seyth: "The wise man shal nat take to greet disconfort for the deth of his children, | but certes he sholde suffren it in pacience, as wel as he abideth the deth of his owene propre persone."' [985] |

This Melibeus answerde anon and seide: 'What man', quod he, 'sholde of his weping stinte that hath so greet a cause for to wepe? | Jesu Crist, oure Lord, himself wepte for the deth of Lazarus his freend.' | Prudence answerde: 'Certes, wel I woot attempree weping is nothing defended to him that sorweful is, amonges folk in sorwe, but it is rather graunted him to wepe. | The apostle Poul unto the Romains writeth: "Man shal rejoise with hem that maken joye, and wepen with swich folk as wepen." | But though attempree weping be graunted, outrageous weping, certes, is defended. [990] | Mesure of weping sholde

973 **seigh** saw **rentinge** tearing   974 **as ferforth as** as far as **stinte** cease
975 **nat-forthy** nevertheless   976 **sentence** saying **cleped** called
978 **doon his diligence** do his best **reconforte** console   979 **suffred** allowed
980 **say** saw   981 **aperteneth nat** is not fitting for   982 **warisshe** recover
985 **abideth** endures   988 **attempree** moderate **defended** forbidden
990 **outrageous** excessive   991 **Mesure of** moderation in

be considered, after the loore that techeth us Senek. | "Whan that thy frend is deed," quod he, "lat nat thine eyen to moiste ben of teeris ne to muche drye; althogh the teeris come to thine eyen, lat hem nat falle. | And whan thow hast forgoon thy freend, do diligence to geten another freend; and this is moore wisdom than for to wepe for thy freend which that thou hast lorn, for therinne is no boote." | And therfore, if ye governe yow by sapience, put awey sorwe out of youre herte. | Remembre yow that Jesus Sirak seyth: "A man that is joyous and glad in herte, it him conserveth florisshinge in his age, but soothly, sorweful herte maketh his bones drye." [995] | He seyth eek thus, that sorwe in herte sleeth ful many a man. | Salomon seyth, that right as moththes in the shepes flees anoyeth to the clothes, and the smale wormes to the tree, right so anoyeth sorwe to the herte. | Wherfore us oghte as wel in the deth of oure children as in the losse of oure goodes temporels have pacience. | Remembre yow upon the pacient Job, whan he hadde lost his children and his temporel substance, and in his body endured and received ful many a grevous tribulacion, yet seide he thus: | "Oure Lord hath yeven it me, oure Lord hath biraft it me; right as oure Lord hath wold, right so it is doon. Yblessed be the name of oure Lord!"' [1000] |

To thise forseide thinges answerde Melibeus unto his wif Prudence: 'Alle thy wordes', quod he, 'been sothe and therto profitable, but trewely min herte is troubled with this sorwe so grevously that I noot what to doone.' | 'Lat calle', quod Prudence, 'thy trewe freendes alle and thy linage whiche that ben wise; telleth youre cas, and herkneth what they seye in conseillinge, and yow governe after hire sentence. | Salomon seyth: "Werk alle thy thinges by conseil, and thow shalt nevere repente."' |

Thanne, by the conseil of his wif Prudence, this Melibeus leet

993 **forgoon** lost **do diligence** endeavour **boote** benefit
994 **sapience** wisdom   996 **sleeth** slays   997 **flees** fleece **anoyeth to** harm
999 **temporel substance** worldly goods   1000 **biraft** taken away from
wold willed   1001 **sothe** true **therto** also   1002 **Lat calle** summon
linage kindred **cas** situation **yow governe after** be guided by
1003 **Werk** do **conseil** taking counsel

callen a greet congregacioun of folk, | as sirurgiens, phisiciens, olde folk and yonge, and somme of hise olde enemys, reconsiled, as by hir semblaunt, to his love and into his grace. [1005] | And therwithal ther coomen somme of hise neighebores, that diden him reverence moore for drede than for love, as it happeth ofte. | Ther coomen also ful many subtile flatereres, and wise advocatz lerned in the lawe. | And whan this folk togidre assembled weren, this Melibeus in sorweful wise shewed hem his cas. | And by the manere of his speche it semed that in herte he baar a cruel ire, redy to doon vengeaunce upon his foos, and sodeinly desired that the werre sholde biginne, | but nathelees yet axed he hir conseil upon this matere. [1010] |

A sirurgien, by licence and assent of swiche as weren wise, up roos, and unto Melibeus seide as ye may heere: | 'Sire,' quod he, 'as to us sirurgiens aperteneth that we do to every wight the beste that we kan whereas we be withholden, and to oure pacientz that we do no damage. | Wherfore it happeth many time and ofte, that whan twey men han everich wounded oother, o same sirurgien heeleth hem bothe. | Wherfore unto oure art it is nat pertinent to norice werre, ne parties to supporte. | But certes, as to the warisshinge of youre doghter, al be it so that she perilously be wounded, we shullen do so ententif bisinesse fro day to night that with the grace of God she shal be hool and sound as soone as is possible.' [1015] | Almoost right in the same wise the phisiciens answerden, save that they seiden a fewe woordes moore: | that right as maladies ben cured by hir contraries, right so shal men warisshe werre by vengeaunce. |

Hise neighebores, ful of envye, hise feined freendes that

1005 **sirurgiens** surgeons **hir semblaunt** their appearance
1006 **coomen** came   1009 **baar** bore   1011 **licence** permission
1012 **aperteneth** it is fitting **withholden** retained, employed
1013 **twey** two **everich** each **o** one   1014 **pertinent** appropriate
norice foment   1015 **warisshinge** healing **do so ententif bisinesse** make such an earnest effort   1017 **hir contraries** their opposites **warisshe** cure
1018 **feined** pretended

semeden reconsiled, and hise flaterers | maden semblant of weping, and empeired and agregged muchel of this matere, in preisinge gretly Melibe of might, of power, of richesse, and of freendes, despisinge the power of hise adversaries, | and seiden outrely that he anon sholde wreke him on hise foos and biginne werre. [1020] |

Up roos thanne an advocat that was wis, by leve and by conseil of othere that weren wise, and seide: | 'Lordinges, the nede for the which we been assembled in this place is a ful hevy thing and an heigh matere, | bicause of the wrong and of the wikkednesse that hath be doon, and eek by resoun of the grete damages that in time cominge been possible to fallen for the same cause, | and eek by resoun of the grete richesse and power of the parties bothe; | for the whiche resouns it were a ful greet peril to erren in this matere. [1025] | Wherfore, Melibeus, this is oure sentence: we conseille yow aboven alle thing that right anon thow do thy diligence in kepinge of thy propre persone in swich a wise that thow ne wante noon espye ne wacche, thy body for to save. | And after that, we conseille that in thin hous thow sette suffisant garnisoun so that they may as wel thy body as thin hous defende. | But certes, for to moeve werre, ne sodeinly for to doon vengeaunce, we may nat deme in so litel time that it were profitable. | Wherfore we axen leiser and espace to have deliberacioun in this cas to deme, | for the commune proverbe seyth thus: "He that soone demeth, soone shal repente." [1030] | And eek men seyn that thilke juge is wis that soone understondeth a matere, and juggeth by leiser. | For al be it so that al tarying be anoyful, algates it is nat to repreve in yeving of juggement ne in vengeance-taking, whan it is suffisant and resonable, | and that shewed oure Lord Jesu Crist

---

1019 **semblant** semblance **empeired** made worse
agregged muchel of exaggerated   1020 **outrely** emphatically
wreke him take vengeance   1022 **nede** business
1023 **by resoun of** because of   1026 **do thy diligence** do your best
propre own **wacche** guard **save** protect   1027 **garnisoun** garrison
1028 **moeve werre** instigate war **deme** believe **were profitable** would be
advantageous   1029 **espace** opportunity   1030 **soone** quickly
1031 **by leiser** at leisure   1032 **anoyful** irritating **to repreve** to be blamed

by ensample. For whan that the womman that was taken in avoutrye was broght in his presence to knowen what sholde be doon with hir persone, albeit that he wiste wel himself what that he wolde answere, yet ne wolde he nat answere sodeinly, but he wolde have deliberacioun, and in the ground he wroot twies. | And by thise causes we axen deliberacioun, and we shul thanne by the grace of God conseille thee thing that shal be profitable.' | Up stirten thanne the yonge folk atones, and the mooste partie of that compaignye han scorned this olde wise man, and bigonnen to make noise, and seiden that [1035] | right so as whil that iren is hoot, men sholde smite, right so sholde men wreken hir wronges whil that they been fresshe and newe; and with loud vois they criden 'Werre, werre!' |

Up roos tho oon of thise olde wise, and with his hand made contenaunce that men sholde holden hem stille and yeven him audience. | 'Lordinges,' quod he, 'ther is ful many a man that cryeth "Werre, werre!" that woot ful litel what werre amounteth. | Werre at his biginning hath so greet an entring and so large, that every wight may entre whan him liketh and lightly finde werre. | But certes, what ende that shal therof bifalle, it is nat light to knowe. [1040] | For soothly, whan that werre is ones bigonne, ther is ful many a child unborn of his moder that shal sterve yong bicause of thilke werre, or elles live in sorwe and die in wrecchednesse. | And therfore, er that any werre be bigonne, men moste have gret conseil and gret deliberacioun.' | And whan this olde man wende to enforcen his tale by resons, wel neigh alle atones bigonne they to rise for to breken his tale, and beden him ful ofte hise wordes for to abregge, | for soothly, he that precheth to hem that listen nat heren hise wordes, his sarmon hem anoyeth. | For Jesus Sirak seyth that musik in weping is anoyous thing; this is to seyn, as

---

1033 **avoutrye** adultery **wiste** knew **wroot** wrote **twies** twice
1035 **stirten** sprang **the mooste partie** the largest part   1036 **iren** iron
wreken avenge   1037 **contenaunce** sign **stille** quiet **audience** a hearing
1038 **amounteth** means   1039 **lightly** easily   1041 **sterve** die
1043 **wende** thought **breken** put a stop to **tale** words **beden** ordered
abregge cut short   1044 **sarmon** sermon   1045 **anoyous** irritating

much availleth to speken biforn folk to whiche his speche anoyeth, as it is to singe biforn him that wepeth. [1045] | And whan this wise man say that him wanted audience, al shamefast he sette him doun again. | For Salomon seyth: 'Theras thow ne mayst have non audience, enforce thee nat to speke.' | 'I se wel', quod this wise man, 'that the commune proverbe is sooth, that good conseil wanteth whan it is moost nede.' | Yet hadde this Melibeus in his conseil many folk that prively in his ere conseilled him certein thing, and conseilled him the contrarye in general audience. |

Whan Melibeus hadde herd that the gretteste partie of his conseil were acorded that he sholde make werre, anon he consented to hir conseiling, and fully affermed hir sentence. [1050] | Thanne dame Prudence, whan that she say how that hir housbonde shoop him for to wreke him on his foos and to biginne werre, she in ful humble wise, whan she say hir time, seide to him thise wordes: | 'My lord,' quod she, 'I yow biseche as hertely as I dar and kan, ne haste yow nat to faste, and, for alle gerdons, as yif me audience. | For Piers Alfonce seyth: "Whoso that dooth to thee outher good or harm, haste thee nat to quiten it, for in this wise thy freend wol abide, and thin enemy shal the lenger live in drede." | The proverbe seyth, "He hasteth wel that wisely kan abide", and "In wikked haste is no profite." ' |

This Melibe answerde unto his wif Prudence: 'I purpose nat', quod he, 'to werken by thy conseil, for many causes and resons; for certes, every wight wolde holde me thanne a fool [1055] | – this is to seyn, if I for thy conseilling wolde chaunge thinges that ben ordeined and affermed by so manye wise. | Secoundely, I seye that alle wommen ben wikke, and noon good of hem alle, for "Of a thousand men", seyth Salomon, "I foond o good man, but certes, of alle wommen, good womman foond

1046 **say** saw **him wanted** he lacked   1047 **enforce thee nat** do not try
1048 **wanteth** is lacking   1049 **in general audience** publicly
1050 **acorded** agreed   1051 **say** saw **shoop him** planned
1052 **for alle gerdons** as you hope to prosper   1053 **quiten it** pay it back
1054 **abide** wait   1057 **wikke** wicked **foond** found **o** one

I nevere." | And also, certes, if I governed me by thy conseil, it
sholde seme that I hadde yeve to thee over me the maistrye, and
Goddes forbode that it so were! | For Jesus Sirak seyth that if
the wif have maistrye, she is contrarious to hir housbonde. |
And Salomon seyth: "Nevere in thy lif to thy wif, ne to thy
child, ne to thy freend, ne yeve no power over thyself, for bettre
it were that thy children axen of thy persone thinges that hem
nedeth, than thow see thyself in the handes of thy children."
[1060] | And also, if I wolde werke by thy conseilling, certes,
my conseil moste somtime be secree til it were time that it moste
be knowe, and this ne may nat be. |

<*For it is written, that women's talkativeness can hide noth-
ing except what they are ignorant of.* | *Later, the Philosopher
says that women overcome men with evil counsel; and for these
reasons I should not follow your advice.'*> |

Whanne dame Prudence ful debonairly and with gret pacience hadde herd al that hir housbonde liked for to seye, thanne
axed she of him licence for to speke, and seide in this wise: |
'My lord,' quod she, 'as to youre firste reson, certes it may
lightly been answered; for I seye that it is no folye to chaunge
conseil whan the thing is chaunged, or elles whan the thing
semeth ootherweyes than it was biforn. [1065] | And moore-
over, I seye that though ye han sworn and bihight to perfourne
youre emprise, and nathelees ye weive to perfourne thilke same
emprise by juste cause, men sholde nat seyn therfore that ye
were a liere ne forsworn. | For the book seyth that the wise man
maketh no lesing whan he turneth his corage to the bettre. |
And al be it so that youre emprise be establissed and ordeined
by gret multitude of folk, yet thar ye nat accomplice thilke
ordinaunce but yow like; | for the trouthe of thinges and the
profit ben rather founde in fewe folk that ben wise and ful of
reson, than by gret multitude of folk ther every man cryeth and

1058 **maistrye** control **Goddes forbode** God forbid
1061 **moste be knowe** ought to be known   1064 **debonairly** meekly
1065 **ootherweyes** otherwise   1066 **bihight** promised **perfourne** perform
emprise enterprise **weive** abandon **liere** liar   1067 **lesing** lie
corage inclination   1068 **thar ye nat** you need not **but yow like** unless it
pleases you

clatereth what that him liketh. Soothly swich multitude is nat honeste. |

'And as to the seconde resoun, whereas ye seyn that alle wommen ben wikke, save youre grace, certes ye despise alle wommen in this wise, and "He that al despiseth, al displeseth", as seyth the book. [1070] | And Senec seyth that "Whoso wole have sapience shal no man dispreise, but he shal gladly teche the science that he kan withoute presumpcion or pride, | and swiche thinges as he noght ne kan, he shal nat ben ashamed to lerne hem, and enquere of lasse folk than himself." | And, sire, that ther hath been ful many a good womman may lightly be preved. | For certes, sire, oure Lord Jesu Crist wolde nevere han descended to be born of a womman if alle wommen hadde ben wikke; | and after that, for the grete bountee that is in wommen, oure Lord Jesu Crist, whan he was risen fro deeth to lif, appered rather to a womman than to his apostles. [1075] | And though that Salomon seyth that he ne foond nevere womman good, it folweth nat therfore that alle wommen ben wikke; | for though that he ne foond no good womman, certes, many another man hath founde many a womman ful good and trewe. | Or elles, paraventure, the entente of Salomon was this: that, as in soverein bountee he foond no womman | – this is to seyn, that ther is no wight that hath soverein bountee save God allone, as he himself recordeth in his Evaungelie. | For ther nis no creature so good that him ne wanteth somwhat of the perfeccioun of God that is his makere. [1080] |

'Youre thridde reson is this: ye seyn that if ye governe yow by my conseil, it sholde seme that ye hadde yeve me the maistrye and the lordshipe over youre persone. | Sire, save youre grace, it is nat so, for if so were that no man sholde be conseiled but oonly of hem that hadde lordshipe and maistrye of his persone, men wolde nat ben conseilled so ofte. | For soothly, thilke man

---

1069 **clatereth** jabbers **honeste** respectable   1070 **save youre grace** with respect   1071 **science** knowledge **kan** knows   1073 **preved** proved
1075 **bountee** virtue   1078 **paraventure** perhaps
soverein bountee unqualified goodness   1079 **Evaungelie** Gospel
1080 **him ne wanteth** he does not lack

that axeth conseil of a purpos, yet hath he free chois wheither he wole werke by that conseil or noon. |

'And as to youre ferthe reson, ther ye seyn that the janglerye of wommen kan hide thinges that they woot nat (as who seyth, that a womman kan nat hide that she woot) | – sire, thise wordes been understonde of wommen that ben jangleresses and wikked; [1085] | of whiche wommen men seyn that thre thinges driven a man out of his hous: that is to seyn, smoke, dropping of rein, and wikked wives. | And of swiche wommen seyth Salomon that it were bettre dwelle in desert than with a woman that is riotous. | And sire, by youre leve, that am nat I, | for ye han ful ofte assayed my grete silence and my grete pacience, and eek how wel that I kan hide and hele thinges that men oghte secreely to hide. |

'And soothly, as to youre fifthe reson, whereas ye seyn that in wikked conseil wommen venquisse men, God woot, thilke reson stant heere in no stede. [1090] | For understond now ye axen conseil to do wikkednesse; | and if ye wole werke wikkednesse, and youre wif restreineth thilke wikked purpos, and overcometh yow by reson and by good conseil, | certes, youre wif oghte rather to be preised than yblamed. | Thus sholde ye understonde the philosophre that seyth: "In wikked conseil wommen venquissen hir housbondes." |

'And theras ye blamen alle wommen and hir resons, I shal shewe by manye ensamples that many a womman hath ben ful good, and yet ben, and hir conseils holsom and profitable. [1095] | Eke som men han seid that the conseiling of wommen is outher to deere or elles to litel of pris. | But al be it so that ful many a womman is badde, and hir conseil vile and noght worth, yet han men founde ful many a good womman, and ful discrete and wise in conseilinge. | Lo, Jacob, by conseil of his

1083 **werke by** act in accordance with   1084 **janglerye** talkativeness
woot nat do not know   1085 **jangleresses** gossips
1087 **riotous** quarrelsome   1089 **assayed** put to the test **hele** conceal
1090 **venquisse** vanquish **stant . . . in no stede** is of no avail
1095 **yet ben** still are **holsom** sound   1096 **outher** either **to litel of pris** of too little value

moder Rebekka wan the benisoun of Isaak his fader and the
lordshipe over alle his bretheren; | Judith by hir good conseil
delivered the citee of Bethulie, in which she dwelled, out of the
handes of Olofernus, that hadde it biseged and wolde it al
destroye; | Abigail delivered Nabal hir housbonde fro David
the king, that wolde han slain him, and apaised the ire of the
king by hir wit and by hir good conseilling; [1100] | Hester by
hir good conseil enhaunced gretly the peple of God in the regne
of Assuerus the king; | and the same bountee in good conseilling
of many a good womman may men telle. | And mooreover,
whan oure Lord hadde creat Adam oure forme-fader, he seide
in this wise: | "It is nat good to be a man allone; make we to
him an help semblable to himself." | Heere may ye se, that if that
wommen were nat goode, and hir conseil good and profitable,
[1105] | oure Lord God of hevene wolde neither han wroght
hem ne called hem help of man, but rather confusioun of man. |
And ther seide oones a clerk in two vers: "What is bettre than
gold? Jaspre. What is bettre than jaspre? Wisdom. | And what
is bettre than wisdom? Womman. And what is bettre than a
good womman? Nothing." | And, sire, by manye othere resons
may ye seen that manye wommen ben goode, and hir conseil
good and profitable. | And therfore, sire, if ye wol truste to my
conseil, I shal restore yow youre doghter hool and sound,
[1110] | and eek I wol do to yow so muche that ye shul have
honour in this cause.' |

Whan Melibe hadde herd the wordes of his wif Prudence, he
seide thus: | 'I se wel that the word of Salomon is sooth. He
seyth that wordes that ben spoken discretly by ordinaunce beth
honycombes, for they yeve swetnesse to the soule and holsom-
nesse to the body. | And, wif, bicause of thy swete wordes, and
eek for I have assayed and preved thy grete sapience and thy grete
trouthe, I wol governe me by thy conseil in alle thing.' |

1098 benisoun blessing   1100 apaised appeased wit cleverness
1101 enhaunced advanced   1103 forme-fader first father, progenitor
1104 help helper semblable to like   1106 wroght created
1107 Jaspre jasper (a precious stone)   1113 by ordinaunce in due order
1114 governe me be ruled

'Now, sire,' quod dame Prudence, 'and sin ye vouchesauf to
been governed by my conseil, I wol enforme yow how ye shal
governe youreself in chesinge of youre conseillours. [1115] | Ye
shal first in alle youre werkes mekely biseken to the heighe God
that he wol be youre conseillour, | and shapeth yow to swich
entente that he yeve yow conseil and confort, as taughte Thobie
his sone: | "At alle times thow shalt blesse God, and praye him
to dresse thy weyes, and looke that alle thy conseils ben in him
for everemoore." | Seint Jame eek seyth: "If any of yow have
nede of sapience, axe it of God." | And afterward thanne shal
ye take conseil in youreself, and examine wel youre thoghtes of
swiche thinges as yow thinketh that is best for youre profit.
[1120] | And thanne shal ye drive fro youre herte thre thinges
that been contrariouse to good conseil: | that is to seyn, ire,
coveitise, and hastinesse. |

'First, he that axeth conseil of himself, certes he moste ben
withouten ire, for many causes. | The firste is this: he that hath
greet ire and wrathe in himself, he weneth alwey that he may
do thing that he may nat do. | And secoundly, he that is irous
and wroth, he ne may nat wel deme; [1125] | and he that may
nat wel deme, may nat wel conseille. | The thridde is this: that
he that is irous and wroth, as seyth Senek, ne may nat speke
but blameful thinges, | and with hise viciouse wordes he stireth
oother folk to angre and to ire. | And eek, sire, ye moste drive
coveitise out of youre herte; | for the Apostle seyth that coveitise
is the roote of alle harmes. [1130] | And trust wel that a coveit-
ous man ne kan nat deme ne thinke but oonly to fulfille the
ende of his coveitise; | and certes that ne may nevere been
acompliced, for evere the moore habundaunce that he hath of
richesse, the moore he desireth. | And, sire, ye moste also drive
out of youre herte hastifnesse; for certes, | ye may nat deme for
the best by a sodein thought that falleth in youre herte, but ye
moste avise yow on it ful ofte. | For as ye herde herebiforn, the

1115 **vouchesauf** grant **chesinge** choosing   1116 **biseken to** entreat
1117 **shapeth yow** dispose yourself **entente** state of mind
1118 **dresse** guide   1120 **take conseil** deliberate   1124 **weneth** believes
1125 **irous** angry **deme** judge   1134 **falleth in** strays into **avise yow** reflect

commune proverbe is this, that he that soone demeth, soone repenteth. [1135] | Sire, ye ne be nat alwey in like disposicioun, | for certes, somthing that somtime semeth to yow that it is good for to do, another time it semeth to yow the contrarye. |

'Whan ye han taken conseil in youreself, and han demed by good deliberacioun swich thing as yow semeth best, | thanne rede I yow that ye kepe it secree. | Biwrey nat youre conseil to no persone but if so be that ye wenen sikerly that thurgh youre biwreying youre condicioun shal be to yow the moore profitable. [1140] | For Jesus Sirak seyth: "Neither to thy foo ne to thy freend discovere nat thy secree ne thy folye, | for they wol yeve yow audience and loking and supportacioun in thy presence, and scorne thee in thin absence." | Another clerk seyth that scarsly shaltow finden any persone that may kepe conseil secrely. | The book seyth: "Whil that thow kepest thy conseil in thin herte, thow kepest it in thy prison; | and whan thow biwreyest thy conseil to any wight, he holdeth thee in his snare." [1145] | And therfore, yow is bettre to hide youre conseil in youre herte than preye him to whom ye han biwreyed youre conseil that he wol kepen it cloos and stille. | For Seneca seyth: "If so be that thou ne mayst nat thin owene conseil hide, how darstow preyen any oother wight thy conseil secrely to kepe?" | But nathelees, if thow wene sikerly that thy biwreying of thy conseil to a persone wol make thy condicioun to stonden in the bettre plit, thanne shaltow telle him thy conseil in this wise: | first, thow shalt make no semblant wheither thee were levere pees or werre, or this or that, ne shewe him nat thy wille and thin entente. | For trust wel, that comunely thise conseillours ben flatereres, [1150] | namely the conseillours of grete lordes, | for they enforcen hem alwey rather to speke plesante wordes, enclininge to the lordes lust, than wordes that

1139 **rede** advise   1140 **Biwrey** reveal   **but if so be that** unless
wenen believe   **sikerly** for a certainty   1142 **loking** favourable looks
supportacioun support   1143 **kepe conseil secrely** keep a secret discreetly
1146 **cloos** concealed   **stille** quiet   1148 **plit** condition
1149 **make no semblant** not allow it to be apparent   **thee were levere** you
prefer   **entente** intention   1152 **enforcen hem** try   **lust** wish

ben trewe or profitable. | And therfore men seyn that the riche
man hath selde good conseil but if he have it of himself. |

'And after that, thow shalt considere thy freendes and thine
enemys. | And as touchinge thy freendes, thow shalt considere
whiche of hem been moost feithful and moost wise, and eldest
and most approved in conseilling, [1155] | and of hem shaltow
axe thy conseil, as the cas requireth. | I seye, that first ye shul
clepe to youre conseil youre freendes that ben trewe. | For
Salomon seyth that right as the herte of a man deliteth in savour
that is soote, right so the conseil of trewe freendes yeveth
swetnesse to the soule. | He seyth also, ther may nothing be
likned to the trewe freend; | for certes, gold ne silver ben nat so
muche worth as the goode wil of a trewe freend. [1160] | And
eek he seyth that a trewe freend is a strong defense; whoso that
it findeth, certes he findeth a gret tresor. | Thanne shul ye eek
considere if that youre trewe freendes been discrete and wise,
for the book seyth: "Axe alwey thy conseil of hem that been
wise." | And by this same reson shul ye clepen to youre conseil,
of youre freendes that ben of age, swiche as han seighen and ben
expert in manye thinges, and ben approved in conseillinges; | for
the book seyth that in olde men is the sapience, and in longe
time the prudence. | And Tullius seyth that grete thinges ne ben
nat ay acompliced by strengthe ne by delivernesse of body, but
by good conseil, by auctoritee of persones, and by science; the
whiche thre thinges ne been nat fieble by age but certes they
enforcen and encressen day by day. [1165] | And thanne shal
ye kepe this for a general reule: first shal ye clepe to youre conseil
a fewe of youre freendes that ben especiale. | For Salomon seyth:
"Manye freendes have thow, but among a thousand chees thee
oon to be thy conseillour." | For al be it so that thow first ne
telle thy conseil but to a fewe, thow mayst afterward telle it to
mo folk if it be nede. | But looke alwey that thy conseillours
have thilke thre condicions that I have seid bifore: that is to

1153 **selde** seldom   1157 **clepe** summon   1158 **soote** sweet
1163 **seighen** seen   **expert** experienced   1165 **delivernesse** agility
fieble by age weak with age   **enforcen** grow stronger
1166 **especiale** intimate   1168 **mo** more

seye, that they be trewe, wise, and of old experience. | And werk nat alwey in every nede by o conseillour allone; for somtime bihoveth it to be conseiled by manye. [1170] | For Salomon seyth: "Salvacion of thinges is wheras ther ben manye conseillours." |

'Now sith that I have told yow of which folk ye sholde be conseilled, now wol I teche yow which conseil ye oghte eschue. | First, ye shul eschue the conseilling of fooles; for Salomon seyth: "Take no conseil of a fool, for he ne kan nat conseille but after his owene lust and his affeccioun." | The book seyth that the propretee of a fool is this: he troweth lightly harm of every wight and lightly troweth alle bountee in himself. | Thow shalt eek eschue the conseilling of alle flaterers, swiche as enforcen hem rather to preise youre persone by flaterye than for to telle yow the soothfastnesse of thinges. [1175] | Wherfore Tullius seyth, among alle the pestilences that been in frendshipe the gretteste is flaterye; and therfore is it moore nede that thow eschue and drede flaterers than any oother peple. | The book seyth thow shalt rather drede and flee fro the swete wordes of flateringe preiseres than fro the egre wordes of thy freend that seyth thee thy sothes. | Salomon seyth that the wordes of a flaterere is a snare to cacchen innocentz. | He seyth also that he that speketh to his freend wordes of swetnesse and of plesaunce setteth a net biforn his feet to cacchen him. | And therfore seyth Tullius: "Encline nat thine eres to flatereres, ne take no conseil of wordes of flaterye." [1180] | And Caton seyth: "Avise thee wel, and eschue wordes of swetnesse and of plesaunce." | And eek thow shalt eschue the conseilling of thine olde enemys that been reconsiled. | The book seyth that no wight retourneth saufly into the grace of his olde enemy. | And Isope seyth: "Ne trust nat to hem to whiche thow hast had somtime werre or enmitee, ne telle hem nat thy conseil." | And Seneca telleth the cause why: "It may nat be", seyth he, "that whereas greet fir

1172 **eschue** avoid   1173 **lust** desire   1174 **troweth** believes
1175 **soothfastnesse** truth   1177 **egre** sharp
1180 **Encline nat thine eres to** do not lend an ear to
1181 **Avise thee** reflect   1183 **grace** favour

hath longe time endured, that ther ne dwelleth som vapour of warmnesse." [1185] | And therfore seyth Salomon: "In thin olde foo trust nevere; | for sikerly, though thin enemy be reconsiled, and maketh thee cheere of humilitee and louteth to thee with his heed, ne trust him nevere. | For certes he maketh thilke feined humilitee moore for his profit than for any love of thy persone, bicause that he demeth to have victorye over thy persone by swich feined contenance, the which victorye he mighte nat have by strif or werre." | And Peter Alfonce seyth: "Make no felaweshipe with thine olde enemys, for if thow do hem bountee, they wol perverten it into wikkednesse." | And eek thow most eschue the conseilling of hem that ben thy servantz and beren thee greet reverence, for paraventure they doon it moore for drede than for love. [1190] | And therfore seyth a philosophre in this wise: "Ther is no wight parfitly trewe to him that he to soore dredeth." | And Tullius seyth: "Ther nis no might so gret of any emperour that longe may endure, but if he have moore love of the peple than drede." | Thow shalt also eschue the conseilling of folk that ben dronkelewe, for they ne kan no conseil hide. | For Salomon seyth: "Ther is no privetee theras regneth dronkenesse." | Ye shal also han in suspect the conseilling of swich folk as conseille yow a thing prively and conseille yow the contrarye openly. [1195] | For Cassiodorie seyth that it is a manere sleighte to hindre, whan he sheweth to doon a thing openly and werketh prively the contrarye. | Thow shalt also have in suspect the conseilling of wikked folk, for the book seyth: "The conseilling of wikked folk is alwey ful of fraude." | And David seyth: "Blisful is that man that hath nat folwed the conseiling of shrewes." | Thow shalt also eschue the conseilling of yong folk, for hir conseil is nat ripe. |

'Now, sire, sith I have shewed yow of which folk ye shul take youre conseil, and of which folk ye shul folwe the conseil,

1187 **sikerly** certainly **maketh thee cheere of humilitee** puts on a humble expression **louteth** bows   1188 **demeth** thinks **contenance** behaviour
1189 **Make no felaweshipe with** do not keep company with
bountee kindness   1191 **to soore** too deeply   1193 **dronkelewe** drunkards
1194 **privetee** secrecy   1196 **sleighte** cunning **sheweth** seems
1198 **shrewes** villains   1199 **ripe** mature

[1200] | now wol I teche yow how ye shul examine youre conseil, after the doctrine of Tullius. | In the examininge thanne of youre conseillour, ye shul considere manye thinges. | Alderfirst, thow shalt considere that in thilke thing that thow purposest, and upon what thing thow wolt have conseil, that verray trouthe be seid and conserved (this is to seyn, telle trewely thy tale), | for he that seyth fals may nat wel be conseiled in that cas of which he lieth. | And after this, thow shalt considere the thinges that acorden to that thow purposest for to do by thy conseillours, if resoun acorde therto, [1205] | and eek if thy might may atteine therto, and if the moore part and the bettre part of thy conseillours acorde therto or no. | Thanne shaltow considere what thing shal folwe of that conseilling, as hate, pees, werre, grace, profit, or damage, and many othere thinges. | And in alle thise thinges thow shalt chese the beste, and weive alle othere thinges. | Thanne shaltow considere of what roote is engendred the matere of thy conseil, and what fruit it may conceive and engendre. | Thow shalt eek considere alle thise causes fro whennes they ben sprongen. [1210] | And whan ye have examined youre conseil as I have seid, and which partie is the bettre and moore profitable, and han approved it by manye wise folk and olde, | thanne shaltow considere if thou mayst parforme it and maken of it a good ende. | For resoun wol nat that any man sholde biginne a thing but if he mighte parforme it as him oghte, | ne no wight sholde take upon him so hevy a charge that he mighte nat bere it. | For the proverbe seyth: "He that to muche embraceth, distreineth litel." [1215] | And Caton seyth: "Assay to do swich thing as thow hast power to doon, lest that the charge oppresse thee so soore that thee bihoveth to weive thing that thow hast bigonne." | And if so be that thow be in doute wheither thow mayst parfourne a thing or noon, chees rather to suffre than biginne. | And Peter Alfonce seyth: "If

1205 **acorden to** are in harmony with   1206 **atteine therto** achieve it
moore greater   1207 **as** such as   1208 **weive** reject
1210 **ben sprongen** have sprung   1215 **distreineth** retains
1216 **Assay** attempt   **charge** burden   **weive** abandon   1217 **suffre** forbear

thow hast might to doon a thing of which thow most repente,
it is bettre 'nay' than 'ye'." | This is to seyn, that thee is bettre
to holde thy tonge stille than for to speke. | Thanne may ye
understonde by strenger resons that if thow hast power to
parforme a werk of which thow shalt repente, thanne is it bettre
that thow suffre than biginne. [1220] | Wel seyn they, that
defenden every wight to assaye a thing of which he is in doute
wheither he may parforme it or no. | And after, whan ye have
examined youre conseil as I have seid biforn, and knowen wel
that ye may parforme youre emprise, conferme it thanne sadly
til it be at an ende. |

'Now is it resoun and time that I shewe yow whanne and
wherfore that ye may chaunge youre conseil withoute youre
repreve. | Soothly, a man may chaungen his purpos and his
conseil if the cause cesseth, or whan a newe cas bitideth; | for
the lawe seyth that upon thinges that newely bitideth, bihoveth
newe conseil. [1225] | And Seneca seyth: "If thy conseil is come
to the eris of thin enemy, chaunge thy conseil." | Thow mayst
also chaunge thy conseil if so be that thou finde that by errour,
or by oother cause, harm or damage may bitide. | Also if
thy conseil be dishoneste, or ellis cometh of dishoneste cause,
chaunge thy conseil, | for the lawes seyn that alle bihestes that
ben dishoneste ben of no value; | and eek if it so be that it be
inpossible, or may nat goodly be parformed or kept. [1230] |
And take this for a general reule, that every conseil that is
affermed so strongly that it may nat be chaunged for no con-
dicioun that may bitide, I seye that thilke conseil is wikked.' |

This Melibeus, whanne he hadde herd the doctrine of his wif
dame Prudence, answerde in this wise: | 'Dame,' quod he, 'as
yet into this time ye han wel and covenably taught me as
in general how I shal governe me in the chesinge and in the
withholding of my conseillours. | But now wolde I fain that ye

1218 **most** may   1221 **defenden** forbid   1222 **conferme** prosecute, follow
through **sadly** steadfastly   1223 **repreve** reproach   1224 **cas** situation
1225 **bihoveth** is necessary   1228 **dishoneste** dishonourable
1229 **bihestes** promises   1230 **goodly** well   1233 **covenably** suitably
withholding retention

wolde condescende in especial, | and telle me how liketh yow,
or what semeth yow, by oure conseillours that we han chosen
in oure present nede.' [1235] |

'My lord,' quod she, 'I biseke yow in al humblesse that ye
wol nat wilfully replye again my resons, ne distempre youre
herte, thogh I speke thing that yow displese, | for God woot
that as in min entente I speke it for youre beste, for youre
honour, and for youre profite eke. | And soothly I hope that
youre benignitee wol taken it in pacience. | Trusteth me wel,'
quod she, 'that youre conseil as in this cas ne sholde nat, as to
speke proprely, be called a conseilling, but a mocioun or a
moeving of folye, | in which conseil ye han erred in many a
sondry wise. [1240] |

'First and forward, ye han erred in the assembling of youre
conseillours, | for ye sholde first have cleped a fewe folk to
youre conseil, and after ye mighte han shewed it to mo folk, if
it hadde be nede. | But certes, ye han sodeinly cleped to youre
conseil a gret multitude of peple, ful chargeant and ful anoyous
for to heere. | Also ye han erred for thereas ye sholde oonly han
cleped to youre conseil youre trewe frendes olde and wise, | ye
han ycleped straunge folk, yong folk, false flatereres, and
enemys reconsiled, and folk that doon yow reverence withouten
love. [1245] | And eek also ye have erred for ye han broght
with yow to youre conseil ire, coveitise, and hastifnesse, | the
whiche thre thinges ben contrariouse to every conseil honeste
and profitable; | the whiche thre thinges ye han nat anientissed
or destroyed hem, neither in youreself ne in youre conseillours,
as ye oghte. | Ye han erred also for ye han shewed to youre
conseillours youre talent and youre affeccioun to make werre
anon and for to do vengeance. | They han espied by youre
wordes to what thing ye ben enclined. [1250] | And therfore
han they rather conseilled yow to youre talent than to youre

1234 **condescende in especial** get down to detail   1236 **replye again** object
to **distempre** upset   1239 **mocioun** impulse   1241 **First and forward** first
of all   1243 **chargeant** burdensome   **anoyous** troublesome
1244 **thereas** whereas   1245 **doon yow reverence** show you respect
1248 **anientissed** eradicated   1249 **talent** inclination   **affeccioun** desire

profit. | Ye han erred also for it semeth that yow suffiseth to han ben conseilled by thise conseillours oonly and with litel avis, | whereas in so gret and so heigh a nede it hadde ben necessarye mo conseillours and moore deliberacioun to parforme youre emprise. | Ye han erred also for ye ne han nat examined youre conseil in the forseide manere, ne in due manere, as the cas requireth. | Ye han erred also for ye han maked no divisioun bitwixe youre conseillours – this is to seyn, bitwixe youre trewe freendes and youre feined conseillours – [1255] | ne ye ne have nat knowe the wil of youre trewe freendes olde and wise, | but ye han cast alle hir wordes in an hochepot, and enclined youre herte to the moore part and to the gretter nombre, and there ben ye condescended. | And sith ye woot wel that men shal alwey finde a gretter nombre of fooles than of wise men, | and therfore the conseils that ben at congregacions and multitudes of folk, theras men take moore reward to the nombre than to the sapience of persones, | ye se wel that in swiche conseillinges fooles han the maistrye.' [1260] |

Melibeus answerde again and seide: 'I graunte wel that I have erred, | but theras thow hast toold me heerbiforn that he nis nat to blame that chaungeth his conseillours in certein cas and for certeine juste causes, | I am al redy to chaunge my conseillours right as thow wolt devise. | The proverbe seyth that for to do sinne is mannissh, but certes, for to persevere longe in sinne is werk of the devel.' |

To this sentence answerde anon dame Prudence, and seide: [1265] | 'Examineth', quod she, 'youre conseil, and lat us se the whiche of hem han spoken moost resonably and taught yow best conseil. | And forasmuche as that the examinacioun is necessarye, lat us biginne at the sirurgiens and at the phisiciens, that first speeken in this matere. | I sey yow, that the sirurgiens and phisiciens han seid yow in youre conseil discretly, as hem oghte, | and in hir speche seiden ful wisely that to the office of

---

1252 **yow suffiseth** it is satisfactory to you **avis** deliberation
1253 **hadde ben** would have been **emprise** enterprise
1257 **hochepot** hotch-potch **moore** greater **ben ye condescended** have you settled   1260 **han the maistrye** dominate   1264 **mannissh** human

hem aperteneth to doon to every wight honour and profit, and
no wight to anoye, | and after hir craft to doon gret diligence
unto the cure of hem whiche that they han in hir governaunce.
[1270] | And, sire, right as they han answered wisely and
discreetly, | right so rede I that they be heighly and sovereinly
gerdoned for hir noble speche, | and eek for they shullen do the
moore ententif bisinesse in the curacioun of thy doghter deere. |
For al be it so that they ben youre freendes, therfore shal ye nat
suffren that they serve yow for noght, | but ye oghte the rather
gerdone hem and shewe hem youre largesse. [1275] | And as
touchinge the proposicioun which that the phisiciens encresc-
eden in this cas – this is to seyn, | that in maladies that oon
contrarye is warisshed by another contrarye – | I wolde fain
knowe how ye understande thilke text, and what is youre
sentence.' |

'Certes,' quod Melibeus, 'I understonde it in this wise: | that
right as they han doon me a contrarye, right so sholde I doon
hem another; [1280] | for right as they han venged hem on me
and doon me wrong, right so shal I venge me upon hem and
doon hem wrong, | and thanne have I cured oon contrarye by
another.' |

'Lo, lo!' quod dame Prudence, 'how lightly is every man
enclined to his owene desir and to his owene plesaunce! |
Certes,' quod she, 'the wordes of the phisiciens ne sholde nat
han ben understonden in that wise; | for certes, wikkednesse is
nat contrarye to wikkednesse, ne vengeance to vengeance, ne
wrong to wrong, but they ben semblable. [1285] | And ther-
fore o vengeance is nat warisshed by another vengeance, ne o
wrong by another wrong, | but everich of hem encresceth and
aggreggeth oother. | But certes, the wordes of the phisiciens

1269 **aperteneth** it appertains **anoye** harm   1270 **after hir craft** according
to their skill **doon gret diligence** take great pains   1272 **rede** advise
sovereinly gerdoned handsomely rewarded   1273 **ententif bisinesse** earnest
diligence **curacioun** cure   1274 **suffren** allow   1276 **encresceden** advanced
1277 **warisshed** cured   1278 **thilke text** that precept **sentence** opinion
1280 **a contrarye** an injury   1283 **plesaunce** pleasure
1284 **understonden** understood   1285 **semblable** alike   1287 **everich** each
aggreggeth aggravates

sholde ben understonde in this wise: | for good and wikked-
nesse ben two contraries, and pees and werre, vengeance and
suffrance, discord and acord, and many othere thinges. | But
certes, wikkednesse shal be warisshed by goodnesse, discord by
acord, werre by pees, and so forth of othere thinges; [1290] |
and herto acordeth Seint Poul the apostle in many places. | He
seyth: "Ne yeldeth noght harm for harm, ne wikked speche for
wikked speche, | but do wel to him that dooth to thee harm,
and blesse him that seyth to thee harm"; | and in manye othere
places he amonesteth pees and acord. |

'But now wol I speke to yow of the conseil which that was
yeven to yow by the men of lawe and the wise folk, [1295] |
that seiden alle by oon acord (as ye han herd bifore) | that over
alle thinges ye shal do youre diligence to kepe youre persone
and to warnestore youre hous; | and seiden also that in this cas
ye oghten for to werke ful avisely and with greet deliberacioun. |
And, sire, as to the firste point, that toucheth to the keping of
youre persone, | ye shul understonde that he that hath werre shal
everemoore devoutly and mekely preyen, biforn alle thinges,
[1300] | that Jesus Crist of his mercy wol han him in his
proteccioun and ben his soverein helping at his nede. | For
certes, in this world ther is no wight that may be conseilled ne
kept suffisantly withoute the keping of oure Lord Jesu Crist. |
To this sentence acordeth the prophete David, that seyth: | "If
God ne kepe the citee, in idel waketh he that it kepeth." | Now
sire, thanne shul ye committe the keping of youre persone to
youre trewe freendes that been approved and yknowe, [1305] |
and of hem shul ye axen help youre persone for to kepe. For
Catoun seyth: "If thou hast nede of help, axe it of thy freendes, |
for ther nis noon so good a phisicien as thy trewe freend." |
And after this thanne shul ye kepe yow fro alle straunge folk

---

1289 **suffrance** forbearance   1291 **herto acordeth** agrees with this
1292 **yeldeth** give back   1294 **amonesteth** recommends   **acord** harmony
1296 **by oon acord** unanimously   1297 **over** above   **do youre diligence** do
your best   **kepe** protect   **warnestore** fortify   1298 **avisely** with forethought
1299 **toucheth to** relates to   1301 **soverein** greatest
1304 **in idel waketh** watches in vain

and fro lieres, and have alwey in suspect hir compaignye. | For
Piers Alfonce seyth: "Ne taak no compaignye by the weye of a
straunge man, but if so be that thow have knowe him of a
lenger time. | And if so be that he falle into thy compaignye
paraventure, withouten thin assent, [1310] | enquere thanne as
subtilly as thow mayst of his conversacioun and of his lif bifore,
and feine thy wey: sey that thow wolt go thider as thow wolt
nat go. | And if he bereth a spere, hoold thee on the right side,
and if he bere a swerd, hoold thee on the left side." | And after
this, thanne shal ye kepe yow wisely from al swich manere
peple as I have seid bifore, and hem and hir conseil eschewe. |
And after this, than shal ye kepe yow in swich manere | that,
for any presumpcioun of youre strengthe that ye ne despise nat
ne accompte nat the might of youre adversarye so lite that ye
lete the keping of youre persone for youre presumpcioun,
[1315] | for every wis man dredeth his enemy. | And Salomon
seyth: "Weleful is he that of alle hath drede, | for certes, he that
thurgh the hardinesse of his herte, and thurgh the hardinesse of
himself, hath to gret presumpcioun, him shal ivel bitide." |
Thanne shal ye everemo countrewaite emboissementz and alle
espiaille, | for Senek seyth that the wise man that dredeth harmes
escheweth harmes, [1320] | ne he ne falleth into perils that
perils escheweth. | And al be it so that it seme that thow art in
siker place, yet shaltow alwey do thy diligence in kepinge of
thy persone; | this is to seyn, ne be nat necligent to kepe thy
persone, nat oonly fro thy grettest enemys, but fro thy leeste
enemy. | Senek seyth: "A man that is well avised, he dredeth his
leste enemy." | Ovide seyth that the litel wesele wol slee the
grete bole and the wilde hert. [1325] | And the book seyth: "A

1308 have . . . in suspect be suspicious of   1309 but if so be unless
1310 paraventure by chance   1311 conversacioun conduct
feine thy wey conceal where you are going   1312 hoold thee keep
1313 eschewe shun   1315 accompte consider lite little lete abandon
keping protection   1317 Weleful fortunate   1318 hardinesse boldness
1319 everemo countrewaite continually guard against
emboissementz ambushes espiaille spying   1322 siker safe
1324 well avised wise   1325 wesele weasel bole bull

litel thorn may prikke a king ful soore, and an hound wol holde
the wilde boor." | But nathelees, I sey nat thow shalt be so
coward that thow doute ther wheras is no drede. | The book
seyth that som folk have gret lust to deceive, but yet they dreden
hem to be deceived. | Yet shaltow drede to been empoisoned,
and kepe the from the compaignye of scorneres; | for the book
seyth: "With scorneres make no compaignye, but flee hire
wordes as venim." [1330] |

'Now as to the seconde point, whereas youre wise conseill-
lours conseilled yow to warnestore youre hous with gret
diligence, | I wolde fain knowe how that ye understonde thilke
wordes, and what is youre sentence.' |

Melibeus answerde and seide, 'Certes, I understonde it in this
wise: that I shal warnestore min hous with toures, swiche as
han castelles and othere manere edifices, and armure, and
artelries, | by whiche thinges I may my persone and min hous
so kepen and defenden that mine enemys shul been in drede
min hous for to approche.' |

To this sentence answerde anon Prudence: 'Warnestoring',
quod she, 'of heighe toures and of grete edifices aperteneth
somtime to pride; [1335] | and eek men make heighe toures,
and grete edifices with grete costages and with gret travaille,
and whan that they been accompliced, yet be they nat worth a
stree but if they been defended by trewe freendes that been olde
and wise. | And understonde wel, that the gretteste and the
strongeste garnisoun that a riche man may have, as wel to
kepen his persone as his goodes, is | that he be biloved with his
subgetz and with his neighebores. | For thus seyth Tullius, that
ther is a manere garnesoun that no man may venquisse ne
discomfite, and that is | a lord to be biloved of his citezeins and
of his peple. [1340] |

'Now sire, as to the thridde point, whereas youre olde and

1326 **holde** bring to bay   1327 **doute** fear   1328 **lust** desire
1329 **kepe the** abstain from   1330 **make no compaignye** do not associate
1333 **artelries** ballistic engines   1335 **aperteneth . . . to** is connected with
1336 **costages** expense **stree** straw   1337 **garnisoun** defence
1339 **discomfite** defeat

wise conseillours seiden that yow ne oghte nat sodeinly ne
hastily proceden in this nede, | but that yow oghte purveyen
and apparailen yow in this cas with greet diligence and greet
deliberacioun, | trewely I trowe that they seiden right wisely
and right sooth. | For Tullius seyth: "In every nede, er thow
biginne it, apparaile thee with greet diligence." | Thanne seye I
that in vengeance-takinge, in werre, in bataille, and in warnesto-
ringe, [1345] | er thow biginne, I rede that thow apparaile thee
therto, and do it with greet deliberacioun. | For Tullius seyth
that longe apparailinge biforn the bataille maketh short
victorye. | And Cassidorus seyth the garnesoun is strenger whan
it is longe time avised. |

'But now lat us speken of the conseil that was acorded by
youre neighebores, swiche as doon yow reverence withouten
love, | youre olde enemys reconsiled, youre flaterers, [1350] |
that conseileden yow certeine thinges prively, and openly con-
seileden yow the contrarye, | the yonge folk also that con-
seileden yow to venge yow and make werre anoon. | And certes,
sire, as I have seid biforn, ye han greetly erred to han cleped
swich maner folk to youre conseil, | whiche conseillours been
inow repreved by the resons aforeseid. | But nathelees, lat us
now descende to the special. Ye shuln first proceden after the
doctrine of Tullius. [1355] | Certes, the trouthe of this matere
or of this conseil nedeth nat diligently enquere, | for it is wel
wist whiche they been that han doon to yow this trespas and
vileinye, | and how manye trespassours, and in what manere
they han to yow doon al this wrong and al this vileinye. | And
after this, thanne shul ye examine the seconde condicioun which
that the same Tullius addeth in this matere, | for Tullius put a
thing which that he clepeth "consentinge". This is to seyn,
[1360] | who been they, and whiche been they, and how manye,

1342 **purveyen and apparailen yow** make provision and prepare yourself
1348 **avised** thought about   1349 **acorded** agreed
1354 **inow repreved** sufficiently reproved   1355 **descende to the special** get
down to detail   **after the doctrine** according to the advice
1357 **trespas** offence **vileinye** injury   1358 **trespassours** offenders
1360 **put** (= *putteth*) puts

that consenten to thy conseil in thy wilfulnesse to do hastif vengeance. | And lat us considere also who been they, and how manye been they, and whiche been they, that consenteden to youre adversaries. | And certes, as to the firste point, it is wel knowen whiche folk been they that consenteden to youre hastif wilfulnesse, | for trewely, alle tho that conseileden yow to maken sodein werre ne been nat youre freendes. | Lat us now considere whiche been they that ye holde so greetly youre freendes as to youre persone; [1365] | for al be it so that ye be mighty and riche, certes ye ne been but allone, | for certes, ye ne han no child but a doghter, | ne ye ne han bretheren, ne cosins germains, ne noon oother ny kinrede | wherfore that youre enemys for drede sholde stinte to plede with yow or destroye youre persone. | Ye knowen also that youre richesses moten be dispended in diverse parties, [1370] | and whan that every wight hath his part, they ne wollen take but litel reward to venge thy deeth. | But thine enemys been thre, and they han manye children, bretheren, cosins, and oother ny kinrede. | And though so were that thow haddest slain of hem two or thre, yet dwellen ther inowe to wreken hir deeth and to sle thy persone. | And though so be that youre kinrede be moore siker and stede-fast than the kin of youre adversarye, | yet nathelees youre kinrede nis but a fer kinrede; they been but litel sib to yow, [1375] | and the kin of youre enemys been ny sib to hem. And certes, as in that, hir condicioun is bet than youres. | Thanne lat us considere also if the conseilling of hem that conseileden yow to taken sodein vengeance, wheither it acorde to resoun; | and certes, ye knowe wel, nay. | For as by right and resoun, ther may no man taken vengeance on no wight but the juge, that hath the jurisdiccioun of it, | whan it is ygraunted him

---

1361 **wilfulnesse** determination   1368 **cosins germains** first cousins
ny kinrede near relations   1369 **wherfore** on whose account
stinte to plede with yow abandon a law-suit against you   1370 **moten** must
dispended distributed   1371 **take but litel reward** have little concern
1373 **so were** it were the case   1374 **siker** trusty   1375 **fer** distant
litel sib distantly related   1377 **acorde to** is compatible with

to take thilke vengeance, hastily or attemprely, as the lawe
requireth. [1380] | And yet moreover of thilke word that Tullius
clepeth consentinge: | thow shalt considere if thy might and thy
power may consente and suffise to thy wilfulnesse and to thy
conseillours; | and certes, thow mayst wel seyn that nay. | For
sikerly, as for to speke proprely, we may do nothing but oonly
swich thing as we may do rightfully; | and certes, rightfully ne
mowe ye take no vengeance as of youre propre auctoritee.
[1385] | Thanne mowe ye seen that youre power ne consenteth
nat ne acordeth nat with youre wilfulnesse. |

'Lat us now examine the thridde point, that Tullius clepeth
"consequent". | Thow shalt understande that the vengeance
that thow purposest for to take is the consequent; | and therof
folweth another vengeance, peril, and werre, and othere dam-
ages withoute nombre of whiche we be nat waar as at this
time. |

'And as touchinge the ferthe point, that Tullius clepeth
"engendringe", [1390] | thow shalt considere that this wrong
which that is doon to thee is engendred of the hate of thine
enemys, | and of the vengeance-takinge upon that wolde
engendre another vengeance, and muchel sorwe and wastinge
of richesses, as I seide. |

'Now sire, as to the point that Tullius clepeth "causes",
which that is the laste point: | thow shalt understonde that the
wrong that thow hast received hath certeine causes, | whiche
that clerkes clepen *oriens* and *efficiens*, and *causa longinqua*,
and *causa propinqua* – this is to seyn, the fer cause and the ny
cause. [1395] | The fer cause is almighty God that is cause of
alle thinges. | The neer cause is thy thre enemys. | The cause
accidental was hate. | The cause material been the five woundes
of thy doghter. | The cause formal is the manere of hir werkinge,
that broghten laddres and clomben in at thy windowes. [1400] |

1380 **attemprely** with restraint   1382 **consente** be consistent with
suffise to be adequate for   1387 **consequent** consequence
1389 **waar** aware   1395 **fer cause** remote cause   **ny cause** immediate cause
1398 **accidental** contingent (n.)   1400 **cause formal** see n.   **werkinge** action
clomben climbed

The cause final was for to sle thy doghter; it letted nat inasmuche as in hem was. | But for to speke of the fer cause, as to what ende they shul come, or what shal finally bitide of hem in this cas, ne kan I nat deme but by conjectinge and by supposinge; | for we shuln suppose that they shul come to a wikked ende, | bicause that the book of Decrees seyth: "Selden or with greet peine been causes ybroght to good ende whan they been baddely bigonne." |

'Now sire, if men wolde axe me why that God suffred men to do yow this vileinye, certes I kan nat wel answere as for no soothfastnesse. [1405] | For the Apostle seyth that the sciences and the jugementz of oure Lord God almighty been ful depe; | ther may no man comprehende ne serchen hem suffisantly. | Nathelees, by certeine presumpcions and conjectinges I holde and bileve | that God, which that is ful of justice and of rightwisnesse, hath suffred this bitide by juste cause resonable. |

'Thy name is Melibe; this is to seyn, a man that drinketh hony. [1410] | Thow hast ydronke so muchel hony of swete temporel richesses and delices and honours of this world | that thow art dronken, and hast forgeten Jesu Crist thy creatour. | Thow ne hast nat doon to him swich honour and reverence as thee oghte, | ne thow ne hast nat wel ytaken kepe to the wordes of Ovide, that seyth: | "Under the hony of the goodes of the body is hid the venim that sleeth the soule." [1415] | And Salomon seyth: "If thow hast founden hony, ete of it that suffiseth, | for if thow ete of it out of mesure, thow shalt spewe and be needy and poore." | And paraventure Crist hath thee in despit, and hath turned awey fro thee his face and his eris of misericorde; | and also he hath suffred that thow hast been punisshed in the manere that thow hast ytrespased. | Thow hast

---

1401 **it letted nat inasmuche as in hem was** there was no holding back on their part   1402 **deme** judge   **conjectinge** conjecture
supposinge supposition   1405 **suffred** allowed   **as for no soothfastnesse** in truth   1406 **depe** mysterious   1407 **serchen** explore   **suffisantly** adequately
1414 **ytaken kepe** paid attention   1415 **sleeth** slays   1416 **that** what
1417 **out of mesure** immoderately   1418 **hath . . . in despit** despises
eris ears   **misericorde** mercy

doon sinne again oure Lord Crist; [1420] | for certes, the thre
enemys of mankinde – that is to seyn, the flessh, the feend, and
the world – I thow hast suffred hem entre into thin herte wilfully
by the windowes of thy body, | and hast nat defended thyself
suffisantly agains hir assautes and hir temptacions, so that they
han wounded thy soule in five places I – this is to seyn, the dedly
sinnes that been entred into thin herte by thy five wittes. | And
in the same manere oure Lord Crist hath wold and suffred that
thy thre enemys been entred into thin hous by the windowes,
[1425] | and han ywounded thy doghter in the forseide
manere.' |

'Certes,' quod Melibee, 'I se wel that ye enforce yow muchel
by wordes to overcome me in swich manere that I shal nat
venge me of mine enemys, | shewinge me the perils and the
iveles that mighte falle of this vengeance. | But whoso wolde
considere in alle vengeances the perils and iveles that mighte
sewe of vengeance-takinge, | a man wolde nevere take ven-
geance, and that were harm, [1430] | for by the vengeance-
takinge been the wikked men disserved fro the goode men, |
and they that han wil to do wikkednesse restreine hir wikked
purpos whan they seen the punisshinge and chastisinge of
trespassours.' |

<And to this dame Prudence replied: 'Certainly,' she said, 'I
grant that from vengeance come many evil things and many
good things. | But vengeance does not belong to anyone other
than judges, and those who have jurisdiction over wrong-
doers.> | And yet seye I moore, that right as a singuler persone
sinneth in takinge vengeance of another man, [1435] | right so
sinneth the juge if he do no vengeance of hem that it han
disserved. | For Senek seyth thus: "That maister", he seyth, "is
good that preveth shrewes." | And as Cassidore seyth: "A man
dredeth to do outrages whan he woot and knoweth that

1424 **five wittes** five senses   1425 **wold** willed   1427 **enforce yow** try
1429 **sewe of** follow from   1430 **were harm** would be a pity
1431 **dissevered** separated   1432 **trespassours** offenders
1435 **singuler persone** private individual   1437 **preveth** finds out
1438 **do outrages** commit crimes

it displeseth to the juges and the sovereins." | And another seyth:
"The juge that dredeth to do right maketh men shrewes." | And
Seint Poule th'apostle seyth in his Epistle, whan he writeth unto
the Romains, that the juges beren nat the spere withouten cause,
[1440] | but they beren it to punisshe the shrewes and misdoers,
and for to defende the goode men. | If ye wol thanne take
vengeance of youre enemys, ye shul retourne or have youre
recours to the juge that hath the jurisdiccioun upon hem, | and
he shal punisshe hem as the lawe axeth and requireth.' |

'A,' quod Melibe, 'this vengeance liketh me nothing. | I
bithenke me now and take hede, how Fortune hath norisshed
me fro my childhode, and hath holpen me to passe many a
strong paas. [1445] | Now wol I assayen hire, trowinge, with
Goddes help, that she shal helpe me my shame for to venge.' |

'Certes,' quod Prudence, 'if ye wol werke by my conseil, ye
shul nat assaye Fortune by no wey, | ne ye shul nat lene or bowe
unto hire, after the word of Senek: | "for thinges that been folily
doon and that been in hope of Fortune shullen nevere come to
good ende." | And, as the same Senek seyth: "The moore cleer
and the moore shininge that Fortune is, the moore brotil and
the sonner broke she is." [1450] | Trusteth nat in hire, for she
nis nat stedefast ne stable, | for whan thow trowest to be moost
seur or siker of hir help, she wol faile thee and deceive thee. |
And whereas ye seyn that Fortune hath norisshed yow fro youre
childhode, | I seye that in so muchel shal ye the lasse truste in hire
and in hir wit; | for Senek seyth: "What man that is norisshed by
Fortune, she maketh him to greet a fool." [1455] | Now thanne,
sin ye desire and axe vengeance, and the vengeance that is doon
after the lawe and bifore the juge ne liketh yow nat, | and the
vengeance that is doon in hope of Fortune is perilous and
uncertein, | thanne have ye noon oother remedye but for to

1444 **liketh me nothing** does not please me at all
1445 **bithenke me** recollect   **passe many a strong paas** get out of many a tight
corner   1447 **assaye** make trial of   1448 **lene** bend
1449 **folily** foolishly   1450 **cleer** bright   **brotil** brittle   1452 **seur** sure
siker certain   1454 **in so muchel** to that extent

have youre recours unto the soverein juge that vengeth alle vileinyes and wronges, | and he shal venge yow, after that himself witnesseth, whereas he seyth: | "Leveth the vengeance to me, and I shal do it." ' [1460] |

Melibe answerde, 'If I ne venge me nat of the vileinye that men han doon to me, | I somne or warne hem that han doon to me that vileinye, and alle othere, to do me another vileinye; | for it is writen: "If thow take no vengeance of an old vileinye, thow somnest thine adversaries to do thee a newe vileinye." | And also, for my suffrance men wolden do me so muchel vileinye that I mighte neither bere it ne sustene, | and so sholde I been put and holden over lowe; [1465] | for men seyn: "In muchel suffringe shul manye thinges falle unto thee whiche thow shalt nat mowe suffre." ' |

'Certes,' quod Prudence, 'I graunte yow that over-muchel suffraunce is nat good, | but yet ne folweth it nat therof that every persone to whom men doon vileinye take of it vengeance, | for that aperteneth and longeth al oonly to the juges, for they shul venge the vileinyes and injuries. | And therfore tho two auctoritees that ye han seid above been oonly understonden in the juges, [1470] | for whan they suffren over muchel the wronges and vileinyes to be doon withouten punisshinge, | they somne nat a man al oonly for to do newe wronges, but they comanden it. | Also a wis man seyth that the juge that correcteth nat the sinnere comandeth and biddeth him do sinne; | and the juges and sovereins mighten in hir land so muchel suffre of the shrewes and misdoers | that they sholden, by swich suffrance, by proces of time wexen of swich power and might that they sholden putte out the juges and the sovereins from hir places, [1475] | and atte laste maken hem lese hir lordshipes. |

'But lat us now putte that ye have leve to venge yow: | I seye ye be nat of might and power as now to venge yow, | for if ye

---

1458 **soverein juge** supreme judge (i.e. God) **vileinyes** injuries
1462 **somne** encourage **warne** invite 1464 **suffrance** forbearance
1465 **holden over lowe** kept too low 1466 **mowe** be able to
1469 **longeth** belongs 1472 **al oonly** only 1475 **wexen** grow
1476 **lese** lose 1477 **putte** suppose

wol maken comparisoun unto the might of youre adversaries,
ye shul finde in manye thinges that I have shewed yow er this
that hir condicioun is bettre than youres; | and therfore seye I
that it is good as now that ye suffre and be pacient. [1480] |
Forthermoore, ye knowen wel that, after the commune sawe,
it is a woodnesse a man to strive with a strenger or a moore
mighty man than he is himself, | and for to strive with a man
of evene strengthe – that is to seyn, with as strong a man as he
is – it is peril, | and for to strive with a weiker man, it is
folye. | And therfore sholde a man flee strivinge as muchel as
he mighte, | for Salomon seyth: "It is a greet worship to a man
to kepen him fro noise and strif." [1485] | And if it so bifalle
or happe that a man of gretter might and strengthe than thow
art do thee grevaunce, | studye and bisye thee rather to stille
the same grevaunce than for to venge thee. | For Senek seyth
that he putteth him in greet peril that striveth with a gretter
man than he is himself. | And Catoun seyth: "If a man of hyer
estaat or degree, or moore mighty than thow, do thee anoy or
grevaunce, suffre him, | for he that ones hath greved thee may
another time releve thee and helpe." [1490] | Yet sette I cas
ye have bothe might and licence for to venge yow | – I seye,
that ther be ful manye thinges that shul restreine yow of
vengeance-takinge, | and make yow for to encline to suffre,
and for to han pacience in the wronges that han been doon to
yow. |

'First and foreward, if ye wole considere the defautes that
been in youre owene persone, | for whiche defautes God hath
suffred yow have this tribulacioun, as I have seid yow heerbi-
forn. [1495] | For the poete seyth that we oghten paciently
taken the tribulaciouns that comen to us, whan that we thinken
and consideren that we han disserved to have hem. | And Seint
Gregorye seyth that whan a man considereth wel the nombre

1481 **sawe** saying **woodnesse** madness   1483 **weiker** weaker
1484 **flee** avoid   1485 **worship** source of credit **noise** quarrelling
1486 **grevaunce** injury   1487 **studye** take pains **stille** appease
1491 **sette I cas** I put the case   1492 **of** from   1495 **defautes** faults

of his defautes and of his sinnes, | the peines and the tribu-
laciouns that he suffreth semen the lesse unto him; | and in as
muche as him thinketh his sinnes moore hevy and grevous, | in
so muche semeth his peine the lighter and the esier unto him.
[1500] | Also ye owen to encline and bowe youre herte to take
the pacience of oure Lord Jesu Crist, as seyth Seint Peter in his
Epistles. | "Jesu Crist", he seyth, "hath suffred for us and yeven
ensample to every man to folwe and sewe him; | for he dide
nevere sinne, ne nevere cam ther a vileins word out of his
mouth. | Whan men cursed him, he cursed hem noght, and
whan men betten him, he manaced hem noght." | Also the
grete pacience which seintes that been in Paradis han had, in
tribulaciouns that they han ysuffred withouten hir desert or
gilt, [1505] | oghte muchel stire yow to pacience. |

'Forthermoore ye sholde enforce yow to have pacience | con-
sideringe that the tribulaciouns of this world but litel while
endure, and soone passed been and goon; | and the joye that a
man seketh to have by pacience in tribulaciouns is pardurable,
after that the Apostle seyth in his Epistle: | "The joye of God",
he seyth, "is pardurable" – that is to seyn, everelastinge. [1510] |
Also troweth and bileveth stedefastly that he nis nat wel ynorisshed ne wel ytaught that kan nat have pacience or wol nat
receive pacience. | For Salomon seyth that the doctrine and the
wit of a man is knowen by pacience. | And in another place he
seyth that he that is pacient governeth him by greet prudence. |
And the same Salomon seyth: "The angry and wrathful man
maketh noises, and the pacient man attempreth hem and
stilleth." | He seyth also: "It is moore worth to be pacient than
for to be right strong, [1515] | and he that may have the
lordshipe of his owene herte is moore to preise than he that by
his force or strengthe taketh grete citees." | And therfore seyth

---

1501 owen ought encline bow   1503 vileins surly   1504 betten beat
1507 enforce yow try   1509 pardurable permanent after that according to
that which   1511 troweth trust wel ynorisshed well brought up
1512 doctrine wisdom wit understanding   1514 attempreth restrains
1516 to preise to be praised

Seint Jame in his Epistle that pacience is a greet vertu of perfeccioun.' |

'Certes,' quod Melibe, 'I graunte yow, dame Prudence, that pacience is a greet vertu of perfeccioun, | but every man may nat have the perfeccioun that ye seken, | ne I nam nat of the nombre of right parfite men, [1520] | for min herte may nevere be in pees unto the time it be venged. | And al be it so that it was greet peril to mine enemys to do me a vileinye in takinge vengeance upon me, | yet token they noon hede of the peril, but fulfilleden hir wikked wil and hir corage. | And therfore me thinketh men oghten nat repreve me, though I putte me in a litel peril for to venge me, | and though I do a greet excesse; that is to seyn, that I venge oon outrage by another.' [1525] |

'A,' quod dame Prudence, 'ye seyn youre wil, and as yow liketh, | but in no caas of the world a man sholde nat doon outrage ne excesse for to vengen him, | for Cassidore seyth that as ivele dooth he that vengeth him by outrage as he that dooth the outrage. | And therfore ye shul venge yow after the ordre of right – that is to seyn, by the lawe – and nat by excesse ne by outrage. | And also, if ye wol venge yow of the outrage of youre adversaries in oother manere than right comandeth, ye sinnen. [1530] | And therfore seyth Senek that a man shal nevere venge shrewednesse by shrewednesse. | And if ye seye that right axeth a man to defende violence by violence, and fightinge by fightinge, | certes, ye seye sooth whan the defense is doon anon withouten intervalle, or withouten taryinge or delay, | for to defenden him, and nat for to vengen him. | And it bihoveth that a man putte swich attemperance in his defense [1535] | that men have no cause ne matere to repreven him that defendeth him of excesse and outrage, for ellis were it again resoun. | Pardee, ye knowe wel that ye maken no defense as now for to defende yow, but for to venge yow, | and so seweth it that ye

---

1523 **corage** inclination   1524 **repreve** to blame   1525 **outrage** crime
1531 **shrewednesse** wickedness   1532 **defende** ward off
1533 **anon** immediately   1535 **putte swich attemperance** practise such moderation   1536 **repreven ... of** blame for   1538 **seweth** follows

han no wil to do youre dede attemprely; | and therfore me
thinketh that pacience is good, for Salomon seyth that he that
is nat pacient shal have greet harm.' |

'Certes,' quod Melibe, 'I graunte yow that whan a man is
inpacient and wrooth of that that toucheth him nat, and that
aperteneth nat unto him, though it harme him, it is no wonder.
[1540] | For the lawe seyth that he is coupable that entremetteth
him or medleth with swich thing as aperteneth nat unto him. |
And Salomon seyth that he that entremeteth him of the noise
or strif of another man is lik to him that taketh an hound by
the eris; | for right as he that taketh a straunge hound by the
eris is outherwhile biten with the hound, | right in the same
wise is it resoun that he have harm that by his inpacience
medleth him of the noise of another man whereas it aperteneth
nat unto him. | But ye knowe wel that this dede – that is to
seyn, my grief and my disese – toucheth me right ny, [1545] |
and therfore, though I be wrooth and inpacient, it is no
mervaille. | And, savinge youre grace, I kan nat se that it mighte
greetly harme me though I tooke vengeaunce, | for I am richere
and moore mighty than mine enemys been, | and wel knowen
ye that by moneye and by havinge grete possessions been alle
the thinges of this world governed. | And Salomon seyth that
alle thinges obeyen to moneye.' [1550] |

Whanne Prudence hadde herd hir housbonde avanten him of
his richesse and of his moneye, dispreisinge the power of hise
adversaries, she spak and seide in this wise: | 'Certes, deere sire,
I graunte yow that ye been riche and mighty, | and that the
richesses been goode to hem that han wel ygeten hem and
that wel konne usen hem; | for right as the body of a man
may nat live withoute the soule, namoore may it live withoute
temporel goodes, | and by richesses may a man gete him grete

1540 **wrooth of** angry at **toucheth him nat** does not affect him
1541 **coupable** blameworthy **entremetteth him** interferes
1542 **noise** quarrel   1543 **outherwhile biten with** sometimes bitten by
1544 **medleth him of** interferes with   1545 **grief** injury **ny** nearly
1546 **no mervaille** no wonder   1551 **avanten him** boast
1553 **ygeten** acquired   1554 **temporel** worldly

freendes. [1555] | And therfore seyth Pamphilles: "If a net-
herdes doghter", he seyth, "be riche, she may chese of a thou-
sand men which she wol take to hir housbonde, | for of a
thousand men oon wol nat forsaken hire ne refusen hire." |
And this Pamphilles seyth also: "If thow be right happy – that
is to seyn, if thow be right riche – thow shalt finde a greet
nombre of felawes and freendes; | and if thy fortune chaunge,
that thow wexe poore, farewel, freendshipe and felaweshipe! |
– for thow shalt be allone withouten any compaignye, but if it
be the compaignye of poore folk." [1560] | And yet seyth this
Pamphilles mooreover that they that been thralle and bonde of
linage shuln be maad worthy and noble by the richesses. |
And right so as by richesses ther comen manye goodes, right
so by poverte come ther manye harmes and iveles, | for
greet poverte constreineth a man to do manye iveles. | And
therfore clepeth Cassidore poverte the moder of ruine | (that is
to seyn, the moder of overthrowinge or fallinge doun). [1565] |
And therfore seyth Piers Alfonce: "Oon of the gretteste ad-
versitees of this world is | whan a free man by kinde or of
burthe is constreined by poverte to eten the almesse of his
enemy." | And the same seyth Innocent, in oon of hise bookes;
he seyth that sorweful and mishappy is the condicioun of a
poore beggere, | for if he axe nat his mete, he dieth for hunger, |
and if he axe, he dieth for shame, and algates necessitee constrei-
neth him to axe. [1570] | And therfore seyth Salomon that
bettre is to die than for to have swich poverte. | And as the
same Salomon seyth: "Bettre it is to die of bitter deeth than for
to liven in swich wise." | By thise resons that I have seid unto
yow, and by manye othere resons that I koude seye, | I graunte
yow that richesses been goode to hem that geten hem wel and
to hem that wel usen tho richesses. | And therfore wol I shewe
yow how ye shul have yow and how ye shul bere yow in

1556 **net-herdes** cowherd's **chese** choose   1557 **oon wol nat** not one will
1558 **happy** fortunate   1559 **wexe** become   1561 **thralle** enslaved
bonde of linage born in bondage   1564 **ruine** toppling   1567 **by kinde** by
nature **burthe** birth **eten the almesse** live on the charity
1568 **mishappy** unfortunate   1570 **algates** nevertheless
1575 **have yow** behave **bere yow** conduct yourself

gaderinge of richesses, and in what manere ye shul usen hem.
[1575] |

'First, ye shul geten hem withouten greet desir, by good leiser,
sokingly, and nat over hastily; | for a man that is to desiringe
to gete richesses abandoneth him first to thefte and to alle
othere iveles. | And therfore seyth Salomon: "He that hasteth
him to bisily to wexe riche shal be noon innocent." | He seyth
also that the richesse that hastily cometh to a man soone and
lightly gooth and passeth from a man, | but that richesse that
cometh litel and litel wexeth alwey and multiplieth. [1580] |
And, sire, ye shullen gete richesses by youre wit and by youre
travaille unto youre profit, | and that withouten wrong or harm-
doinge to any oother persone. | For the lawe seyth that ther
maketh no man himself riche if he do harm to another wight. |
This is to seyn, that nature defendeth and forbedeth by right
that no man make himself riche unto the harm of another
persone. | And Tullius seyth that no sorwe, ne no drede of
deeth, ne nothing that may falle unto a man, [1585] | is so
muchel ageins nature as a man to encresse his owene profit to
the harm of another man. | And thogh the grete men and
the mighty men geten richesses moore lightly than thow, | yet
shaltow nat be idel ne slow to do thy profit, for thow shalt in alle
wise flee idelnesse. | For Salomon seyth that idelnesse techeth a
man to do manye iveles. | And the same Salomon seyth that he
that travaileth and bisieth him to tilien his lond shal ete breed,
[1590] | but he that is idel and casteth him to no bisinesse ne
occupacioun shal falle into poverte and die for hunger. | And
he that is idel and slow kan nevere finde covenable time for to
do his profit. | For ther is a versifiour seyth, that the idel man
excuseth him in winter bicause of the grete coold, and in somer
by encheson of the grete hete. | For thise causes seyth Catoun:
"Waketh and enclineth yow nat over muchel for to slepe, for

1576 **sokingly** gradually, slowly   1577 **desiringe** eager
abandoneth him devotes himself   1579 **lightly** easily
1580 **wexeth** increases   1584 **defendeth** forbids   1585 **falle unto** happen
to   1590 **tilien** till   1591 **casteth him to no bisinesse** applies himself to no
labour   1592 **covenable** suitable   1593 **versifiour** poet
by encheson of because of

over-muchel reste norissheth and causeth manye vices." | And therfore seyth Seint Jerome: "Dooth somme goode dedes, that the devel which is oure enemy ne finde yow nat unocupied." [1595] | For the devel ne taketh nat lightly unto his werkinge swiche as he findeth ocupied in goode werkes. | Thanne thus, in getinge richesses ye mosten flee idelnesse. |

'And afterward ye shul use the richesses whiche ye have geten, by youre wit and by youre travaille, | in swich a manere that men holde yow nat to scars, ne to sparinge, ne to fool-large – that is to seyn, over-large a spendere. | For right as men blamen an avaricious man bicause of his scarsitee and chincherye, [1600] | in the same wise is he to blame that spendeth over largely. | And therfore seyth Catoun: "Use", he seyth, "thy richesses that thow hast ygeten | in swich a manere that men have no matere ne cause to calle thee neither wrecche ne chinche; | for it is greet shame to a man to have a poore herte and a riche purs." | He seyth also: "The goodes that thow hast ygeten, use hem by mesure – that is to seyn, spende hem mesurably; [1605] | for they that folily wasten and despenden the goodes that they han, | whan they han namoore propre of hir owene, they shapen hem to take the goodes of another man. | I seye thanne that ye shul flee avarice, | usinge youre richesses in swich manere that men seye nat that youre richesses been yburied, | but that ye have hem in youre might and in youre weldinge. [1610] | For a wis man repreveth the avaricious man, and seyth thus in two vers: | "Wherto and why burieth a man his goodes by his grete avarice, and knoweth wel that nedes moste he die? | For deeth is the ende of every man as in this present lif." | And for what cause or encheson joineth he him or knitteth he him so faste unto his goodes | that alle hise wittes mowen nat disseveren him or departen him from hise

1596 **werkinge** work   1599 **scars** parsimonious   **sparinge** frugal
fool-large spendthrift   **over-large** too generous   1600 **scarsitee** parsimony
chincherye miserliness   1603 **chinche** niggard   1605 **by mesure** in
moderation   1607 **propre** property   **shapen hem** take steps   1608 **flee** shun
1610 **weldinge** control   1614 **encheson** reason
1615 **departen** separate

goodes, [1615] | and knoweth wel – or oghte knowe – that
whan he is deed he shal nothing bere with him out of this
world? | And therfore seyth Seint Austin that the avaricious
man is likned unto helle, | that the moore it swolweth, the
moore desir it hath to swolwe and devoure. | And as wel as ye
wolde eschewe to be called an avaricious man or chinche, | as
wel sholde ye kepe yow and governe yow in swich a wise that
men calle yow nat fool-large. [1620] | Therfore seyth Tullius:
"The goodes", he seyth, "of thin hous sholde nat been hid ne
kept so cloos but that they mighte been opned by pitee and
debonairetee" | (that is to seyn, to yeve hem part that han greet
nede) | "ne thy goodes sholden nat be so open to be every
mannes goodes." |

'Afterward, in getinge of youre richesses and in usinge hem,
ye shul alwey have thre thinges in youre herte: | that is to seyn,
oure Lord God, conscience, and good name. [1625] | First, ye
shul have God in youre herte, | and for no richesse ye shullen
do nothing which may in any manere displese God, that is
youre creatour and makere. | For after the word of Salomon:
"It is bettre to have a litel good with the love of God, | than to
have muchel good and tresor, and lese the love of his Lord
God." | And the prophete seyth that bettre it is to been a good
man and have litel good and tresor, [1630] | than to be holden
a shrewe and have grete richesses. | And yet seye I ferthermoore
that ye sholden alwey doon youre bisinesse to gete yow
richesses, | so that ye gete hem with good conscience. | And
th'Apostle seyth that ther nis thing in this world of which we
sholden have so greet joye as whan oure conscience bereth us
good witnesse. | And the wise man seyth: "The substance of a
man is ful good whan sinne is nat in mannes conscience."
[1635] | Afterward, in getinge of youre richesses and in usinge
of hem, | yow moste have greet bisinesse and greet diligence

1618 **swolweth** swallows   1620 **kepe yow** behave
1621 **debonairetee** kindness   1625 **name** reputation
1630 **the prophete** David   1631 **holden** considered
1632 **doon youre bisinesse** make an effort   1633 **so that** provided that
1634 **th'Apostle** Paul   1635 **substance** wealth

that youre goode name be alwey kept and conserved. | For
Salomon seyth that bettre it is and moore it availeth a man to
have a good name than for to have grete richesses. | And therfore
he seyth in another place: "Do greet diligence", seyth Salomon,
"in keping of thy freend and of thy goode name, | for it shal
lenger abide with thee than any tresor, be it nevere so precious."
[1640] | And certes he sholde nat be called a gentil man that
after God and good conscience, alle thinges left, ne dooth
his diligence and bisinesse to kepen his goode name. | And
Cassidore seyth that it is signe of a gentil herte whan a man
loveth and desireth to have a good name. | And therfore seyth
Seint Austin that ther been two thinges that arn necessarye and
nedefulle, | and that is good conscience and good loos | – that
is to seyn, good conscience to thin owene persone inward, and
good loos for thy neighebore outward. [1645] | And he that
trusteth him so muchel in his goode conscience | that he
dispiseth, and setteth at noght his goode name or loos, and
rekketh noght thogh he kepe nat his goode name, nis but a
cruel cherl. |

'Sire, now have I shewed yow how ye shul do in getinge
richesses and how ye shullen usen hem, | and I se wel that for
the trust that ye han in youre richesses ye wol moeve werre and
bataille. | I conseille yow that ye biginne no werre in trust of
youre richesses, for they ne suffisen noght werres to main-
tene. [1650] | And therfore seyth a philosophre: "That man
that desireth and wole algates han werre shal nevere have
suffisaunce, | for the richer that he is, the gretter despenses
moste he make, if he wol have worshipe and victorye." | And
Salomon seyth that the gretter richesses that a man hath, the
mo despendours he hath. | And, deere sire, al be it so that for
youre richesses ye mowe have muchel folk, | yet bihoveth it nat,
ne it is nat good, to biginne werre whereas ye mowe in oother

---

1640 **abide** remain   1641 **gentil** noble   **alle thinges left** disregarding
everything else   1644 **loos** reputation   1647 **rekketh noght thogh** does not
care whether **nis but** is nothing but   1649 **moeve** stir up
1650 **they ne suffisen noght werres to maintene** they are not adequate to
support war   1651 **algates** always   **suffisaunce** a sufficiency
1653 **mo despendours** more people to spend them   1655 **mowe** may

manere have pees unto youre worship and profit. [1655] | For
the victorye of batailles that been in this world lith nat in greet
nombre or multitude of peple, ne in the vertu of man, | but it
lith in the wil and in the hand of oure Lord God almighty. |
And therfore Judas Machabeus, which was Goddes knight, |
whan he sholde fighte agein his adversarye that hadde a gretter
nombre and a gretter multitude of folk and strenger than was
the peple of Machabee, | yet he reconforted his litel compaignye,
and seide right in this wise: [1660] | "Als lightly", quod he,
"may oure Lord God almighty yeve victorye to fewe folk as to
manye folk; | for the victorye of a bataile cometh nat by the
grete nombre of peple | but it cometh from oure Lord God of
hevene." | And, deere sire, for as muchel is ther is no man
certein if he be worthy that God yeve him victorye or naught,
after that Salomon seyth, | therfore every man sholde greetly
drede werres to biginne. [1665] | And bicause that in batailles
fallen manye perils, | and happeth outherwhile that as soone is
the grete man slain as the litel man, | and as it is ywriten in the
seconde book of Kinges: "The dedes of batailles been aventur-
ouse and nothing certeine, | for as lightly is oon hurt with a
spere as another"; | and for ther is greet peril in werre, therfore
sholde a man flee and eschewe werre in as muchel as a man
may goodly. [1670] | For Salomon seyth: "He that loveth peril
shal falle in peril." ' |

After that dame Prudence hadde spoken in this manere, Mel-
ibe answerde and seide: | 'I se wel, dame Prudence, that by
youre faire wordes, and by youre resons that ye han shewed
me, that the werre liketh yow nothing, | but I have nat yet herd
youre conseil, how I shal do in this nede.' |

'Certes,' quod she, 'I conseile yow that ye acorde with youre
adversaries and that ye have pees with hem. [1675] | For Seint
Jame seyth in hise Epistles that by concord and pees the smale

1656 **lith** lies   1659 **sholde fighte agein** was to fight against
1660 **reconforted** encouraged   1667 **outherwhile** sometimes
1668 **aventurouse** risky   1670 **in as muchel as a man may goodly** as far as
he possibly can   1673 **liketh yow nothing** does not please you at all
1674 **conseil** advice   **nede** exigency   1675 **acorde** be reconciled

richesses wexen grete, | and by debaat and discord the grete
richesses fallen doun. | And ye knowen wel that oon of the
gretteste and moost soverein thing that is in this world is unitee
and pees. | And therfore seide oure Lord Jesu Crist to hise
apostles in this wise: | "Wel happy and blessed been they that
loven and purchacen pees, for they been called children of
God."' [1680] |

'A,' quod Melibe, 'now se I wel that ye loven nat min honour
ne my worshipe! | Ye knowen wel that mine adversaries han
bigonnen this debaat and brige by hire outrage, | and ye se wel
that they ne requeren ne preyen me nat of pees, ne they asken
nat to be reconsiled; | wol ye thanne that I go and meke me and
obeye me to hem and crye hem mercy? | For sothe, that were
nat my worship! [1685] | For right as men seyn that over-greet
hoomlinesse engendreth dispisinge, so fareth it by to greet humi-
litee or mekenesse.' |

Thanne bigan dame Prudence to maken semblant of wrathe
and seide: | 'Certes, sire, sauf youre grace, I love youre honour
and youre profit as I do min owene, and evere have doon; | ne
ye ne noon oother syen nevere the contrarye. | And yet if I
hadde seid that ye sholde han purchaced the pees and the
reconsiliacioun, I ne hadde nat muchel mistaken me, ne seid
amis. [1690] | For the wise man seyth: "The dissensioun bigin-
neth by another man, and the reconsiling biginneth by thyself." |
And the prophete seyth: "Flee shrewednesse and do goodnesse; |
seke pees and folwe it, as muchel as in thee is." | Yet seye I nat
that ye shul rather pursue to youre adversaries for pees than
they shuln to yow, | for I knowe wel that ye been so hard-herted
that ye wol do nothing for me. [1695] | And Salomon seyth

1676 wexen grow   1677 debaat strife   1680 purchacen bring about
1681 worshipe honour   1682 brige strife
1683 ne requeren ne preyen me nat of do not ask or beg me for
1684 meke me humble myself
1686 hoomlinesse engendreth dispisinge familiarity breeds contempt
1687 semblant a show   1688 sauf youre grace with respect
1689 syen saw   1690 ne hadde nat muchel mistaken me would not greatly
have erred   1692 shrewednesse wickedness   1694 pursue sue shuln shall

that he that hath over-hard an herte, atte laste he shal mishappe and mistide.' |

Whanne Melibe hadde herd dame Prudence make semblant of wrathe, he seide in this wise: | 'Dame, I pray yow that ye be nat displesed of thinges that I seye, | for ye knowe wel that I am angry and wrooth – and that is no wonder – | and they that been wrothe witen nat wel what they doon, ne what they seyn. [1700] | Therfore the prophete seyth that troubled eyen han no cleer sighte. | But seyeth and conseileth me as yow liketh, for I am redy to do right as ye wol desire. | And if ye repreve me of my folye, I am the moore holden to love yow and to preise yow. | For Salomon seyth that he that repreveth him that dooth folye, | he shal finde gretter grace than he that deceiveth him by swete wordes.' [1705] |

Thanne seide dame Prudence: 'I make no semblant of wrathe ne of angir but for youre grete profit. | For Salomon seyth: "He is moore worth that repreveth or chideth a fool for his folye, shewinge him semblant of wrathe, | than he that supporteth him and preiseth him in his misdoinge, and laugheth at his folye." | And this same Salomon seyth afterward that by the sorweful visage of a man (that is to seyn, by the sory and hevy contenaunce of a man) | the fool correcteth and amendeth himself.' [1710] |

Thanne seide Melibe: 'I shal nat konne answere to so manye resons as ye putten to me and shewen. | Seyeth shortly youre wil and youre conseil, and I am al redy to fulfille and parfourne it.' |

Thanne dame Prudence discovered al hir wil to him and seide: | 'I conseille yow', quod she, 'aboven alle thinges that ye make pees bitwene God and yow, | and beth reconsiled unto him and to his grace, [1715] | for as I have seid yow heerbiforn, God hath suffred yow to have this tribulacioun and disese for youre sinnes. | And if ye do as I seye yow, God wol sende youre

1696 **mishappe** be unfortunate   **mistide** have bad luck   1700 **witen** know
1703 **repreve me of** reprove me for   **holden** obliged   1711 **konne** be able to
1713 **discovered** revealed   1716 **disese** suffering

adversaries unto yow, | and maken hem falle at youre feet, redy to do youre wil and youre comandementz. | For Salomon seyth: "Whan the condicioun of man is plesaunt and likinge to God, | he chaungeth the hertes of the mannes adversaries and constreineth hem to biseken him of pees and of grace." [1720] | And I prey yow, lat me speke with youre adversaries in privee place, | for they shal nat knowe that it be of youre wil or youre assent; | and thanne, whan I knowe hir wil and hir entente, I may conseille yow the moore seurly.' |

'Dame,' quod Melibe, 'dooth youre wil and youre likinge, | for I putte me hoolly in youre disposicioun and ordinaunce.' [1725] |

Thanne dame Prudence, whan she say the goode wil of hir housbonde, she delibered and took avis in hirself, | thinkinge how she mighte bringe this nede unto a good conclusioun and to a good ende. | And whan she saugh hir time, she sente for thise adversaries to come unto hire into a privee place, | and shewed wisely unto hem the grete goodes that comen of pees, | and the grete harmes and perils that been in werre, [1730] | and seide to hem in a goodly manere how that hem oughten have greet repentaunce | of the injurye and wrong that they hadden doon to Melibe hir lord, and to hire, and to hir doghter. |

And whan they herden the goodliche wordes of dame Prudence, | they weren so surprised and ravisshed, and hadden so greet joye of hire, that wonder was to telle. | 'A, lady,' quod they, 'ye han shewed unto us the blessinge of swetnesse, after the sawe of David the prophete; [1735] | for the reconsilinge which we been nat worthy to have in no manere, | but we oghten requeren it with greet contricioun and humilitee, | ye, of youre grete goodnesse, have presented unto us. | Now se we wel that the science and the konninge of Salomon is ful trewe, |

1719 **likinge** pleasing   1720 **biseken him of** entreat him for
1722 **of . . . youre assent** with your consent   1725 **disposicioun** power
ordinaunce control   1726 **say** saw **delibered** deliberated **took avis** took
thought   1731 **goodly** courteous   1734 **ravisshed** enraptured
1735 **after the sawe** according to the saying   1737 **requeren** to request
1739 **science** knowledge **konninge** wisdom

for he seyth that swete wordes multiplien and encressen
freendes, and maken shrewes to be debonaire and meke.
[1740] | Certes,' quod they, 'we putten oure dede and al oure
matere and cause al hoolly in youre goode wil, | and been redy
to obeye to the speche and comandement of my lord Melibe. |
And therfore, deere and benigne lady, we preyen yow and
biseken yow, as mekely as we konne and mowen, | that it like
unto youre grete goodnesse to fulfille in dede youre goodliche
wordes; | for we consideren and knowelichen that we han
offended and greved my lord Melibe out of mesure, [1745] | so
ferforth that we been nat of power to maken his amendes. |
And therfore we oblige and binde us and oure freendes for to
do al his wil and his comandementz. | But paraventure he hath
swich hevinesse and swich wrathe to usward bicause of oure
offense | that he wole enjoine us swich a peine as we mowe nat
bere ne sustene; | and therfore, noble lady, we biseke to youre
wommanly pitee [1750] | to taken swich avisement in this nede
that we ne oure freendes be nat desherited ne destroyed thurgh
oure folye.' |

'Certes,' quod Prudence, 'it is an hard thing and right
perilous | that a man putte him al outrely in the arbitracioun
and juggement and in the might and power of hise enemys. |
For Salomon seyth: "Leeveth me, and yeveth credence to that I
shal seyn: I seye," quod he, "ye peple, folk, and governours of
holy chirche, | to thy sone, to thy wif, to thy freend, ne to thy
brother, [1755] | ne yeve thow nevere might ne maistrye of thy
body whil thow livest." | Now sithen he defendeth that man
sholde nat yeve to his brother ne to his freend the might of his
body, | by a strenger resoun he defendeth and forbedeth a man

1740 **shrewes** villains **debonaire** gentle   1743 **konne and mowen** are able
1744 **like unto** may please **youre grete goodnesse** your excellency
1745 **knowelichen** acknowledge **greved** angered   1746 **so ferforth** to such
an extent   1747 **oblige** bind   1748 **paraventure** perhaps
hevinesse resentment **to usward** towards us   1749 **enjoine** impose on
peine punishment   1751 **avisement** thought **desherited** dispossessed
1753 **putte him al outrely** should place himself entirely
1754 **Leeveth** believe   1756 **might ne maistrye** power or control
1757 **sithen** since **defendeth** forbids

to yeve himself to his enemy. | And nathelees, I conseille yow
that ye mistruste nat my lord, | for I woot wel and knowe
verraily that he is debonaire and meke, large, curteis, [1760] |
and nothing desirous ne coveitous of good ne richesse, | for ther
nis nothing in this world that he desireth, save oonly worship
and honour. | Forthermoore I knowe wel and am right seur
that he shal nothing do in this nede withouten my conseil, | and
I shal so werken in this cause that, by the grace of oure Lord
God, ye shul be reconsiled unto us.' |

Thanne seiden they with o vois: 'Worshipful lady, we putten
us and oure goodes al fully in youre wil and disposicioun,
[1765] | and been redy to come, what day that it like unto
youre noblesse to limite us or assigne us, | for to maken oure
obligacioun and boond as strong as it liketh unto youre
goodnesse, | that we mowe fulfille the wil of yow and of my
lord Melibe.' |

Whanne dame Prudence hadde herd the answeres of thise
men, she bad hem go again prively, | and she retourned to hir
lord Melibe and tolde him how she fand hise adversaries ful
repentant, [1770] | knowelechinge ful lowely hir sinnes and
trespas, and how they weren redy to suffren al peine, | requer-
inge and preyinge him of mercy and pitee. |

Thanne seide Melibe: 'He is wel worthy to have pardoun
and foryifnesse of his sinne that excuseth nat his sinne | but
knowelecheth it and repenteth him, axinge indulgence. | For
Senek seyth: "There is the remissioun and foryifnesse, whereas
the confessioun is; [1775] | for confessioun is neighebore to
innocence." | And he seyth in another place: "He is worthy to
have remissioun and foryifnesse that hath shame of his sinne
and knowelecheth it." And therfore I assente and conferme me

1760 **debonaire** gentle **large** generous   1761 **nothing** not at all
1765 **disposicioun** power   1766 **youre noblesse** your excellency
limite appoint   1767 **obligacioun** pledge   1769 **go again** return
1771 **knowelechinge** acknowledging **lowely** humbly **trespas** offence
1772 **requeringe** requesting **of** for   1774 **indulgence** mercy
1777 **conferme me** resolve

to have pees; | but it is good that we do it nat withouten
th'assent and wil of oure freendes.' |

Thanne was Prudence right glad and joyeful, and seide: |
'Certes, sire,' quod she, 'ye han wel and goodly answerd,
[1780] | for right as by the conseil, assent, and help of youre
frendes ye han ben stired to venge yow and make werre, | right
so withouten hire conseil shul ye nat acorde yow ne have pees
with youre adversaries. | For the lawe seyth: "Ther nis nothing
so good by wey of kinde as a thing to be unbounde by him that
it was ybounde." ' |

And thanne dame Prudence, withouten delay or taryinge,
sente anon hir messages for hir kin and for hire olde freendes
which that were trewe and wise, | and tolde hem by ordre in
the presence of Melibe al this matere as it is above expressed
and declared, [1785] | and preyde hem that they wolde yeven
hire avis and conseil what best were to do in this nede. | And
whan Melibees freendes hadde taken hire avis and deliber-
acioun of the forseide matere, | and hadden examined it by
greet bisinesse and greet diligence, | they yave ful conseil for to
have pees and reste, | and that Melibe sholde receive with good
herte hise adversaries to foryifnesse and mercy. [1790] | And
whanne dame Prudence hadde herd the assent of hir lord Melibe
and the conseil of his freendes | acorde with hire wil and hire
entencioun, | she was wonderly glad in hire herte, and seide: |
'Ther is an old proverbe', quod she, 'seyth that the goodnesse
that thow mayst do this day, do it, | and abide nat ne delaye it
nat til tomorwe. [1795] | And therfore I conseille that ye sende
youre messages, swiche as been discrete and wise, | unto youre
adversaries, tellinge hem on youre bihalve | that if they wol
trete of pees and of acord, | that they shape hem withouten
delay or taryinge to come unto us.' | – Which thing parfourned
was in dede. [1800] | And whanne thise trespassours and

1780 **goodly** excellently   1782 **acorde yow** be reconciled
1783 **kinde** nature   1784 **messages** messengers   1788 **bisinesse** diligence
1795 **abide** wait   1798 **trete of** negotiate   1799 **shape hem** prepare
1801 **trespassours** offenders

repentinge folk of hire folies – that is to seyn, the adversaries
of Melibe – I hadden herd what thise messagers seiden unto
hem, I they weren right glad and joyeful, and answereden ful
mekely and benignely, I yeldinge graces and thankinges to hire
lord Melibe and to al his compaignye, I and shopen hem withouten delay to go with the messagers and obeye to the comandement of hire lord Melibe. [1805] I And right anon they tooken
hire wey to the court of Melibe, I and tooken with hem somme
of hir trewe freendes, to make feith for hem and for to been
hire borwes. I

And whan they were come to the presence of Melibe, he seide
hem thise wordes: I 'It standeth thus,' quod Melibe, 'and sooth
it is, that ye, I causelees and withouten skile and resoun, [1810] I
han doon grete injuries and wronges to me, and to my wif
Prudence, and to my doghter also, I for ye han entred into min
hous by violence, I and have doon swich outrage that alle men
knowen wel that ye have deserved the deeth. I And therfore wol
I knowe and wite of yow I wheither ye wol putte the punisshinge
and the chastisinge and the vengeance of this outrage in the wil
of me, and of my wif Prudence, or ye wol nat.' [1815] I

Thanne the wiseste of hem thre answerde for hem alle and
seide: I 'Sire,' quod he, 'we knowen wel that we been unworthy
to comen unto the court of so greet a lord and so worthy as ye
been, I for we han so gretly mistaken us, and han offended and
agilt in swich a wise agein youre heye lordshipe I that trewely
we han deserved the deeth. I But yet, for the grete goodnesse
and debonairetee that al the world witnesseth of youre persone,
[1820] I we submitten us to the excellence and benignitee of
youre gracious lordshipe, I and ben redy to obeye to alle youre
comandementz, I bisekinge yow that of youre merciable pitee
ye wol considere oure grete repentaunce and lowe sub-
missioun, I and graunten us foryevenesse of oure outrageous

1804 **yeldinge graces and thankinges** giving thanks
1805 **shopen hem** prepared   1807 **feith** pledge   **borwes** guarantors
1810 **skile** reason   1813 **outrage** crime   1814 **wite of yow** learn from you
1818 **mistaken us** done wrong   **agilt** transgressed
1820 **debonairetee** graciousness   1823 **bisekinge** beseeching

trespas and offense. | For wel we knowen that youre liberal
grace and mercy strecchen hem ferther into goodnesse than
doon oure outrageouse giltes and trespas into wikkednesse,
[1825] | albeit that cursedly and dampnablely we han agilt agein
youre heye lordshipe.' |

Thanne Melibee took hem up fro the ground ful benignely, |
and received hire obligaciouns and hir bondes by hir othes upon
hir plegges and borwes, | and assigned hem a certein day to
retourne unto his court | for to accepte and receive the sentence
and jugement that Melibe wolde comande to be doon on hem
by the causes aforeseid; [1830] | whiche thinges ordeined, every
man retourned to his hous. |

And whan that dame Prudence saugh hir time, she freined
and axed hir lord Melibe | what vengeance he thoughte to taken
of hise adversaries. | To which Melibe answerde and seide:
'Certes,' quod he, 'I thinke and purpose me fully | to disherite
hem of al that evere they han, and for to putte hem in exil for
evere.' [1835] |

'Certes,' quod dame Prudence, 'this were a cruel sentence,
and muchel agein resoun, | for ye been riche inow and han no
nede of oother mennes good, | and ye mighten lightly in this
wise gete yow a coveitous name, | which is a vicious thing, and
oghte been eschewed of every good man. | For after the sawe
of the word of th'Apostle, "Coveitise is roote of alle harmes."
[1840] | And therfore it were bettre for yow to lese so muchel
good of youre owene than for to take of hire good in this
manere; | for bettre it is to lese good with worshipe, than it is
to winne good with vileinye and shame. | And every man oghte
to do his diligence and his bisinesse to geten him a good name; |
and yet shal he nat oonly bisye him in kepinge of his goode
name, | but he shal also enforcen him alwey to do somthing by
which he may renovelle his goode name. [1845] | For it is writen

---

1825 **strecchen hem** stretch   1826 **dampnablely** damnably
1828 **obligaciouns** pledges **plegges** sureties   1832 **freined** asked
1840 **after the sawe** according to the saying   1845 **enforcen him** try
renovelle renew

that the olde goode loos or good name of a man is soone goon and passed, whan it is nat newed ne renovelled. | And as touchinge that ye seyn ye wol exile youre adversaries, | that thinketh me muchel again resoun and out of mesure, | considered the power that they han yeven yow upon hemself. | And it is writen that he is worthy to lesen his privilege that misuseth the might and the power that is yeven him. [1850] | And I sette cas ye mighte enjoine hem that peine by right and by lawe | – which I trowe ye mowe nat do – | I seye ye mighte nat putte it to execucioun paraventure; | and thanne were it likly to retourne to the werre, as it was biforn. | And therfore, if ye wole that men do yow obeisance, ye moste deme moore curteisly [1855] | – this is to seyn, ye moste yeve moore esy sentences and jugementz. | For it is writen that he that moost curteisly commandeth, to him men moste obeyen. | And therfor I prey yow that in this necessitee and in this nede ye caste yow to overcome youre herte. | For Senek seyth that he that overcometh his herte, overcometh twies. | And Tullius seyth: "Ther is nothing so commendable in a greet lord [1860] | as whan he is debonaire and meke, and appeiseth him lightly." | And I prey yow that ye wole forbere now to do vengeance, | in swich a manere that youre goode name may be kept and conserved, | and that men may have cause and matere to preise yow of pitee and of mercy, | and that ye have no cause to repente yow of thing that ye doon. [1865] | For Senek seyth: "He overcometh in an ivel manere that repenteth him of his victorye." | Wherfore I prey yow, lat mercy be in youre herte, | to th'effect and entente that God almighty have mercy on yow in his Laste Jugement. | For Seint Jame seyth in his Epistle: "Jugement withoute mercy shal be doon to him that hath no mercy of another wight." ' |

Whanne Melibe hadde herd the grete skiles and resons of

1846 **loos** reputation **newed** renewed   1848 **out of mesure** immoderate
1851 **enjoine** impose on **peine** punishment   1852 **trowe** believe
1853 **putte it to execucioun** carry it into effect   1855 **obeisance** obedience
deme order   1858 **caste yow** decide   1861 **debonaire** gentle
appeiseth him lightly quickly grows calm   1864 **matere** cause **of** for
1868 **to th'effect and entente that** in order that

dame Prudence, and hir wise informaciouns and techinges, [1870] | his herte gan encline to the wil of his wif, consideringe hir trewe entente, | and conformed him anon, and assented fully to werken after hir conseil, | and thonked God, of whom procedeth al vertu and al goodnesse, that him sente a wif of so greet discrecioun. |

And whan the day came that hise adversaries sholde appieren in his presence, | he spak to hem ful goodly and seide in this wise: [1875] | 'Al be it so that of youre pride and hye presumpcioun and folye, and of youre necligence and unkonninge, | ye have misborn yow and trespased unto me, | yet for as muche as I se and biholde youre grete humilitee, | and that ye been sory and repentant of youre giltes, | it constreineth me to do yow grace and mercy. [1880] | Wherfore I receive yow to my grace, | and foryeve yow outrely alle the offenses, injuries, and wronges that ye have doon agein me and mine, | to this effect and to this ende, that God of his endelees mercy | wole at the time of oure dyinge foryeven us oure giltes that we han trespassed to him in this wrecched world. | For douteless, if we be sory and repentant of the sinnes and giltes whiche we han trespased in the sighte of oure Lord God, [1885] | he is so free and so merciable | that he wole foryeven us oure giltes, | and bringen us to the blisse that nevere hath ende.' Amen.

Heere is ended Chaucers Tale of Melibee and of Dame Prudence.

1870 **informaciouns** advice   1871 **gan encline** bowed
1872 **conformed him** acquiesced   1875 **goodly** kindly
1876 **unkonninge** stupidity   1877 **misborn yow** behaved wickedly
trespased done wrong   1882 **outrely** completely   1886 **free** generous

THE MONK'S PROLOGUE

The murye wordes of the
Hoost to the Monk.

	Whan ended was my tale of Melibee
1890	And of Prudence and hire benignitee,

Whan ended was my tale of Melibee
1890 And of Prudence and hire benignitee,
Oure Hooste seide, 'As I am feithful man,
And by that precious *corpus Madrian*,
I hadde levere than a barel ale
That Goodelief my wif hadde herd this tale!
1895 For she nis nothing of swich pacience
As was this Melibeus wif Prudence.
By Goddes bones, whan I bete my knaves,
She bringeth me the grete clobbed staves,
And cryeth, "Slee the dogges everychon,
1900 And breke hem bothe bak and every bon!"
    'And if that any neighebore of mine
Wol nat in chirche to my wif encline,
Or be so hardy to hire to trespace,
Whan she comth hoom she raumpeth in my face,
1905 And cryeth, "False coward, wrek thy wif!
By *corpus* bones, I wol have thy knif,
And thow shalt have my distaf and go spinne!"
Fro day to night right thus she wol biginne.
"Allas!" she seyth, "that evere I was shape
1910 To wedde a milksop, or a coward ape

1891 **feithful man** true Christian   1892 *corpus Madrian* see n.
1893 **hadde levere** would rather   1895 **nothing** not at all
1897 **knaves** servants   1898 **clobbed staves** knobbed staffs
1902 **encline** bow   1903 **be so hardy** is so bold as   **trespace** do offence
1904 **raumpeth** rages   1905 **wrek** avenge   1906 *corpus* **bones** God's
bones (n.)   1909 **shape** destined   1910 **coward ape** cowardly fool

That wol been overlad with every wight!
Thow darst nat stonden by thy wives right!"
   'This is my lif, but if that I wol fighte,
And out at dore anon I moot me dighte,
Or elles I am but lost, but if that I   1915
Be lik a wilde leoun foolhardy.
I woot wel she wol do me sle som day
Som neighebore, and thanne go my way,
For I am perilous with knif in honde,
Albeit that I dar nat hire withstonde,   1920
For she is big in armes, by my feith;
That shal he finde that hire misdooth or seyth!
– But lat us passe awey fro this matere.
   'My lord the Monk,' quod he, 'be mirye of
      cheere,
For ye shul telle a tale, trewely.   1925
Lo, Rouchestre stant heer faste by!
Rid forth, min owene lord, brek nat oure game.
But, by my trouthe, I knowe nat youre name;
Wher shal I calle yow my lord daun John,
Or daun Thomas, or elles daun Albon?   1930
Of what hous be ye, by youre fader kin?
I vow to God, thow hast a ful fair skin!
It is a gentil pasture ther thow goost;
Thou art nat lik a penaunt or a goost.
Upon my feith, thou art som officer,   1935
Som worthy sextein, or som celerer.
For by my fader soule, as to my doom,
Thou art a maister whan thou art at hom –

1911 **overlad with** browbeaten by   1913 **but if that** unless
1914 **moot me dighte** must go   1917 **do me sle** make me kill
1921 **big** strong   1922 **hire misdooth or seyth** does wrong to her or insults
her   1923 **passe awey fro** pass on from   1926 **stant** (= *standeth*) stands
1927 **brek nat** do not interrupt   1929 **Wher shal I** shall I
1934 **penaunt** penitent **goost** ghost   1936 **sextein** sacristan (g.)
celerer cellarer (monk in charge of provisions in a monastery)
1937 **as to my doom** in my opinion

No povre cloisterer, ne no novis,
1940   But a governour, wily and wis,
And therwithal, of brawnes and of bones,
A wel-faringe persone for the nones.
I pray to God yeve him confusioun
That first thee broghte unto religioun!
1945   Thou woldest han been a tredefoul aright;
Haddestow as greet a leve as thow hast might
To parfourne al thy lust in engendrure,
Thow haddest bigeten many a creature.
Allas, why werestow so wid a cope?
1950   God yeve me sorwe but, and I were a pope,
Nat oonly thow, but every mighty man,
Thogh he were shore ful hye upon his pan,
Sholde have a wif, for al the world is lorn!
Religioun hath take up al the corn
1955   Of treding, and we borel men been shrimpes.
Of feble trees ther comen wrecched impes;
This maketh that oure heires beth so sklendre
And feble that they may nat wel engendre.
This maketh that oure wives wole assaye
1960   Religious folk, for ye mowe bettre paye
Of Venus paiementz than may we.
God woot, no lussheburghes payen ye!
But be nat wrooth, my lord, thogh that I pleye;
Ful ofte in game a sooth I have herd seye.'

1939 **povre** poor **novis** novice   1940 **governour** official, person of
importance   1941 **brawnes** muscles   1942 **wel-faringe** good-looking
1945 **tredefoul** hen-shagger, stud   1946 **leve** licence   1947 **lust** desire
engendrure procreation   1948 **haddest** would have   1949 **werestow** do you
wear **cope** monastic cowl   1950 **and** if   1952 **shore** shorn **pan** head
1953 **lorn** ruined   1954–5 I.e the religious orders have cornered the market
in sex   1955 **borel men** laymen   1956 **impes** shoots   1957 **maketh** brings
it about **sklendre** thin   1959 **wole assaye** want to make trial of
1961 **Venus paiementz** the wages of Venus (i.e. sex)
1962 **lussheburghes** coins of poor quality (n.)   1963 **pleye** joke

This worthy Monk took al in pacience,   1965
And seide, 'I wol doon al my diligence,
As fer as sowneth into honestee,
To telle yow a tale, or two or three.
And if yow list to herkne hiderward,
I wol yow seyn the lif of Seint Edward –   1970
Or ellis, first, tragedies wol I telle,
Of whiche I have an hundred in my celle.
"Tragedye" is to seyn a certein storye,
As olde bokes maken us memorye,
Of him that stood in greet prosperitee,   1975
And is yfallen out of heigh degree
Into miserye, and endeth wrecchedly.
And they ben versified comunly
Of sixe feet, whiche men clepe *"exametron"*;
In prose eek been endited many oon,   1980
And eek in metre, in many a sondry wise.
Lo, this declaring oghte inogh suffise.
    'Now herkneth, if yow liketh for to heere!
But first I yow biseke in this matere,
Though I by ordre telle nat thise thinges,   1985
Be it of popes, emperours, or kinges,
After hir ages, as men writen finde,
But telle hem som bifore, and som bihinde,
As it now comth unto my remembraunce,
Have me excused of min ignoraunce.'   1990

1966 **doon al my diligence** do my best   1967 As far as is consistent with
decency   1970 **seyn** tell   1974 **maken us memorye** remind us
1976 **degree** social position   1979 **sixe feet** see n.   *exametron* hexameter
1980 **endited** written   1982 **declaring** explanation   1984 **biseke** beseech
1987 **After hir ages** according to their chronological positions
1988 **bifore** first   **bihinde** afterwards

THE MONK'S TALE

Heere biginneth the Monkes Tale
De casibus virorum illustrium.

I wol biwaille, in manere of tragedye,
The harm of hem that stoode in heigh degree,
And fillen so that ther nas no remedye
To bringe hem out of hire adversitee.
1995   For certein, whan that Fortune list to flee,
Ther may no man the cours of hire withholde.
Lat no man truste on blind prosperitee!
Be war by thise ensamples trewe and olde.

Lucifer

At Lucifer, thogh he an aungel were,
2000   And nat a man, at him wol I biginne;
For thogh Fortune may noon aungel dere,
From heigh degree yet fel he, for his sinne,
Doun into helle, whereas he yet is inne.
O Lucifer, brightest of aungels alle,
2005   Now artow Sathanas, that mayst nat twinne
Out of miserye in which that thou art falle.

Adam

Lo, Adam, in the feeld of Damissene
With Goddes owene finger wroght was he,
And nat bigeten of mannes sperme unclene,

1990 *De casibus virorum illustrium* On the Fall of Famous Men
1993 **fillen** fell   1995 **list** wishes   1998 **ensamples** exemplary anecdotes
2001 **dere** harm   2005 **Sathanas** Satan, the devil **twinne** escape
2008 **wroght** created

And welte al Paradis, saving o tree.   2010
Hadde nevere worldly man so heigh degree
As Adam, til he for misgovernaunce
Was drive out of his hye prosperitee
To labour, and to helle, and to meschaunce.

Sampson

Lo, Sampson, which that was anunciat   2015
By th'aungel, longe er his nativitee,
And was to God almighty consecrat,
And stood in noblesse whil he mighte se,
Was nevere swich another as was he,
To speke of strengthe, and therwith hardinesse.   2020
But to his wives tolde he his secree,
Thurgh which he slow himself for wrecchednesse.

Sampson, this noble almighty champioun,
Withouten wepne save hise hondes tweye
He slow and al to-rente the leoun,   2025
Toward his wedding walkinge by the weye.
His false wif koude him so plese and preye
Til she his conseil knew; and she untrewe
Unto his foos his conseil gan biwreye,
And him forsook, and took another newe.   2030

Thre hundred foxes took Sampson for ire,
And alle hir tailes he togidre bond,
And sette the foxes tailes alle on fire,
For he on every tail had knit a brond;

2010 **welte** (= *weldede*) governed **saving** except **o** one
2012 **misgovernaunce** sin   2014 **meschaunce** misfortune
2015 **anunciat** announced   2016 **nativitee** birth
2017 **consecrat** consecrated   2020 **hardinesse** bravery   2021 **secree** secret
2022 **slow** killed   2024 **wepne** weapons   2025 **to-rente** tore to pieces
2027 **preye** beg   2028 **conseil** secret **untrewe** treacherously
2029 **gan biwreye** betrayed   2034 **knit a brond** tied a firebrand

2035 And they brende alle the cornes in that lond,
      And alle hire oliveris, and vines eke.
      A thousand men he slow eek with his hond,
      And hadde no wepne but an asses cheke.

      Whan they were slain, so thursted him that he
2040 Was wel ny lorn, for which he gan to preye
      That God wolde on his peine have som pitee
      And sende him drinke, or elles moste he deye.
      And of this asses cheke that was dreye,
      Out of a wang-tooth, sprang anon a welle,
2045 Of which he drank inogh, shortly to seye.
      Thus heelp him God, as *Iudicum* kan telle.

      By verray force, at Gazan on a night,
      Maugree Philistiens of that citee,
      The gates of the toun he hath up plight,
2050 And on his bak ycaried hem hath he
      Hye on an hill, wheras men mighte hem se.
      O noble almighty Sampsoun, leef and deere,
      Had thow nat toold to wommen thy secree,
      In al this world ne hadde been thy peere!

2055 This Sampsoun nevere ciser drank ne win,
      Ne on his heed cam rasour noon ne shere,
      By precept of the messager divin,
      For alle hise strengthes in hise heres were.
      And fully twenty winter, yeer by yere,
2060 He hadde of Israel the governaunce.
      But soone shal he wepe many a teere,
      For wommen shul him bringen to meschaunce.

2035 **cornes** corn-crops   2036 **oliveris** olive-trees   2038 **cheke** jawbone
2039 **so thursted him** he was so thirsty   2040 **ny lorn** near dead
2041 **peine** suffering   2044 **wang-tooth** molar tooth **welle** water-spring
2045 **inogh** plentifully   2046 **heelp** helped   2049 **up plight** pulled up
2052 **leef** beloved   2055 **ciser** cider   2056 **rasour** razor **shere** scissors
2060 He ruled over Israel

Unto his lemman Dalida he tolde
That in his heeris al his strengthe lay,
And falsly to his foomen she him solde;   2065
And slepinge in hir barm, upon a day,
She made to clippe or shere his heer away,
And made his foomen al this craft espyen.
And whan that they him fond in this array,
They bounde him faste and putten out his   2070
    eyen.

But er his heer was clipped or yshave,
Ther was no bond with which men mighte him
    binde.
But now is he in prisoun in a cave,
Whereas they made him at the querne grinde.
O noble Sampsoun, strengest of mankinde,   2075
O whilom juge, in glorye and in richesse!
Now maystow wepen with thine eyen blinde,
Sith thow fro wele art falle in wrecchednesse.

The ende of this caitif was as I shal seye:
His foomen made a feste upon a day,   2080
And made him as hire fool bifore hem pleye;
And this was in a temple of greet array.
But atte laste, he made a foul affray,
For he two pilers shook and made hem falle;
And doun fil temple and al, and there it lay,   2085
And slow himself, and eek his foomen alle.

2063 **lemman** mistress   2065 **foomen** enemies
2066 **barm** lap   2067 She caused his hair to be clipped or shorn off
2068 **craft** trick **espyen** watch   2069 **array** state   2070 **faste** tightly
2074 **querne** mill   2076 **whilom** former   2078 **wele** prosperity
art falle in have fallen into   2079 **caitif** captive   2082 **array** splendour
2083 **foul affray** terrible commotion   2084 **pilers** pillars

This is to seyn, the princes everychon,
And eek thre thousand bodies, were ther slain
With falling of the grete temple of stoon.
2090   Of Sampson now wol I namoore sayn.
Beth war by this ensample old and plain
That no men telle hir conseil til hir wives,
Of swich thing as they wolde han secree fain,
If that it touche hir limes or hir lives.

Hercules

2095   Of Hercules, the soverein conquerour,
Singen his werkes laude and heigh renoun,
For in his time of strengthe he was the flour.
He slow and rafte the skin fro the leoun;
He of Centauros leide the boost adoun;
2100   He Arpies slow, the cruel briddes felle;
He golden apples rafte of the dragoun;
He drow out Cerberus, the hound, of helle.

He slow the cruel tyrant Busirus,
And made his hors to frete him, flessh and bon;
2105   He slow the firy serpent venimus;
Of Achilois two hornes he brak oon,
And he slow Cakus in a cave of stoon;
He slow the geant Antheus the stronge;
He slow the grisly boor, and that anoon,
2110   And bar the hevene on his nekke longe.

2091 **Beth war** take warning   2092 **til** to
2093 **wolde han secree fain** would gladly keep secret
2094 **touche** concerns **limes** limbs   2096 **laude** praise   2098 **rafte** took
2099 **leide the boost adoun** destroyed the pride   2100 **briddes felle** fierce
birds   2102 **of** from   2104 **frete** devour   2106 **brak** broke
2109 **grisly** terrible **anoon** without delay

Was nevere wight, sith that this world bigan,
That slow so manye monstres as dide he.
Thurghout this wide world his name ran,
What for his strengthe and for his heigh bountee,
And every reawme wente he for to se;   2115
He was so strong that no man mighte him lette.
At bothe the worldes endes, seyth Trophee,
In stede of boundes he a piler sette.

A lemman hadde this noble champioun
That highte Dianira, fressh as May;   2120
And, as thise clerkes maken mencioun,
She hath him sent a sherte, fressh and gay.
Allas! this sherte – allas and weilaway! –
Envenimed was so subtilly withalle
That, er that he hadde wered it half a day,   2125
It made his flessh al from his bones falle.

But nathelees, somme clerkes hire excusen,
By oon that highte Nessus, that it maked.
Be as be may, I wol hire noght accusen;
But on his bak this sherte he wered al naked   2130
Til that his flessh was for the venim blaked.
And whan he say noon oother remedye,
In hote coles he hath himselven raked,
For with no venim deigned him to die.

Thus starf this worthy mighty Hercules.   2135
Lo, who may truste on Fortune any throwe?
For him that folweth al this world of prees,
Er he be war, is ofte yleid ful lowe.

2111 **wight** a person   2114 **bountee** prowess   2115 **reawme** realm
2116 **lette** prevent   2118 **boundes** boundary marks   2120 **highte** was
called   2124 **Envenimed** poisoned   2129 **Be as be may** however it may be
2131 **blaked** blackened   2134 Because he scorned to die from any poison
2135 **starf** died   2136 **throwe** space of time   2137 **of prees** dangerous
2138 **be war** is aware

Ful wis is he that kan himselven knowe!
2140   Beth war, for whan that Fortune list to glose,
Thanne waiteth she hir man to overthrowe
By swich a wey as he wolde leest suppose.

Nabugodonosor

The mighty trone, the precious tresor,
The glorious ceptre, and royal majestee
2145   That hadde the king Nabugodonosor
With tonge unnethe may discrived be.
He twies wan Jerusalem the citee;
The vessel of the temple he with him ladde.
At Babiloigne was his soverein see,
2150   In which his glorye and his delit he hadde.

The faireste children of the blood royal
Of Israel he leet do gelde anon,
And maked ech of hem to been his thral.
Amonges othere Daniel was oon,
2155   That was the wiseste child of everychoon;
For he the dremes of the king expowned,
Wheras in Chaldeye clerk ne was ther noon
That wiste to what fin his dremes sowned.

This proude king leet make a statue of gold,
2160   Sixty cubites long and sevene in brede,
To which image bothe yonge and old
Comanded he to loute, and have in drede,

2140 **list to glose** wants to beguile   2141 **waiteth** watches for a chance
2146 **unnethe** hardly   2148 **ladde** carried   2149 His chief residence was at
Babylon   2152 **leet do gelde** had castrated   2153 **thral** slave
2154 **othere** others   2156 **expowned** interpreted   2157 **Wheras** although
Chaldeye Chaldea, Babylonia   2158 **fin** outcome   **sowned** tended
2159 **leet make** had made   2160 **cubites** cubits (a measure of length, about
eighteen inches)   **brede** breadth   2162 **loute** bow   **have in drede** venerate

Or in a fourneis, ful of flambes rede,
He shal be brend that wolde noght obeye.
But nevere wolde assente to that dede   2165
Daniel, ne hise yonge felawes tweye.

This king of kinges proud was and elat.
He wende that God that sit in magestee
Ne mighte him nat bireve of his estat.
But sodeinly he loste his dignitee,   2170
And lik a beest him semed for to be,
And eet hey as an oxe, and lay theroute.
In rein with wilde beestes walked he,
Til certein time was ycome aboute.

And lik an egles fetheres wax hise heres;   2175
Hise nailes lik a briddes clawes weere,
Til God relessed him a certein yeres,
And yaf him wit; and thanne with many a teere
He thanked God, and evere his lif in feere
Was he to doon amis or moore trespace;   2180
And til that time he leid was on his beere,
He knew that God was ful of might and grace.

Balthasar

His sone, which that highte Balthasar,
That heeld the regne after his fader day,
He by his fader koude noght be war,   2185
For proud he was of herte and of array,

2163 **fourneis** furnace **flambes** flames   2164 **brend** burned
2167 **elat** haughty   2168 **wende** believed   2169 **bireve** deprive
2170 **dignitee** rank   2172 **hey** grass **theroute** out of doors
2175 **wax** grew **heres** hair   2177 **relessed** released **a certein** a certain
number of   2178 **wit** (human) intelligence   2179 **evere his lif** all his life
2180 **trespace** transgress   2181 **beere** bier   2184 **regne** kingdom
2185 **be war** take warning   2186 **array** finery

And eek an idolastre was he ay.
His hye estat assured him in pride;
But Fortune caste him doun, and ther he lay,
2190   And sodeinly his regne gan divide.

A feste he made unto hise lordes alle
Upon a time, and made hem blithe be,
And thanne hise officeres gan he calle:
'Gooth bringeth forth the vesseles', quod he,
2195   'Whiche that my fader in his prosperitee
Out of the temple of Jerusalem birafte,
And to oure hye goddes thanke we
Of honour that oure eldres with us lafte.'

His wif, hise lordes, and hise concubines
2200   Ay dronken, whil hire appetites laste,
Out of thise noble vessels sondry wines.
And on a wal this king hise eyen caste,
And say an hand, armlees, that wroot ful faste,
For feere of which he quook and siked soore.
2205   This hand that Balthasar so soore agaste
Wroot *Mane techel phares*, and namoore.

In al that land magicien was noon
That koude expounde what this lettre mente.
But Daniel expowned it anoon
2210   And seide, 'King, God to thy fader lente
Glorye and honour, regne, tresor, rente;
And he was proud, and nothing God ne dradde,
And therfore God greet wreche upon him sente,
And him birefte the regne that he hadde.

2187 **idolastre** idolater   2188 **assured him** made him confident
2194 **Gooth bringeth forth** go and bring out   2196 **birafte** took away
2198 **Of** for   **with us lafte** bequeathed to us   2200 **Ay dronken** drank
continually   **laste** (= *lastede*) lasted   2203 **say** saw   **armlees** without an arm
2204 **quook** trembled   **siked soore** sighed deeply   2205 **agaste** frightened
2211 **rente** revenue   2212 **nothing God ne dradde** did not fear God at all
2213 **wreche** vengeance   2214 **him birefte** took away from him

'He was out cast of mannes compaignye;   2215
With asses was his habitacioun,
And eet hey as a beest, in weet and drye,
Til that he knew, by grace and by resoun,
That God of hevene hath dominacioun
Over every regne and every creature.   2220
And thanne hadde God of him compassioun,
And him restored his regne and his figure.

'Eek thow that art his sone art proud also,
And knowest alle thise thinges verraily,
And art rebel to God and art his fo.   2225
Thow drank eek of his vessels boldely –
Thy wif eke, and thy wenches, sinfully
Dronke of the same vessels sondry winis –
And heriest false goddes cursedly;
Therfore to thee yshapen ful greet pine is.   2230

'This hand was sent fro God, that on the wal
Wroot "*Mane techel phares*", truste me.
Thy regne is doon; thou weyest noght at al.
Divided is thy regne, and it shal be
To Medes and to Perses yeven,' quod he.   2235
And thilke same night this king was slawe,
And Darius occupieth his degree,
Thogh he therto hadde neither right ne lawe.

Lordinges, ensample heerby may ye take
How that in lordshipe is no sikernesse.   2240
For whan Fortune wol a man forsake,
She bereth awey his regne and his richesse

2217 **eet** ate   2218 **knew** acknowledged   2222 **figure** (human) shape
2228 **Dronke** drank   2229 **heriest** worship   2230 **yshapen** ordained
pine punishment   2233 **weyest noght at al** are of no weight
2236 **slawe** slain   2237 **degree** position   2240 **sikernesse** security

And eke hise freendes, bothe moore and lesse.
For what man that hath freendes thurgh Fortune,
2245   Mishap wol make hem enemys, I gesse;
This proverbe is ful sooth and ful commune.

Cenobia

Cenobia, of Palimerye queene,
As writen Persiens of hir noblesse,
So worthy was in armes and so keene
2250   That no wight passed hire in hardinesse,
Ne in linage, ne oother gentilesse.
Of kinges blood of Perce is she descended.
I sey nat that she hadde moost fairnesse,
But of hir shap she mighte nat been amended.

2255   From hire childhede, I finde that she fledde
Office of wommen, and to wode she wente,
And many a wilde hertes blood she shedde
With arwes brode that she to hem sente;
She was so swift that she anoon hem hente.
2260   And whan that she was elder, she wolde kille
Leons, leopardes, and beres, al to-rente,
And in hir armes welde hem at hir wille.

She dorste wilde beestes dennes seke,
And rennen in the montaines al the night,
2265   And slepe under the bussh; and she koude eke
Wrastlen by verray force and verray might

2243 **moore and lesse** great and small   2244 **what** whatever
2245 **Mishap** misfortune   2246 **sooth** true **commune** widely known
2249 **keene** brave   2250 **hardinesse** courage   2251 **linage** lineage
gentilesse mark of nobility   2254 **of hir shap** with respect to her figure
amended surpassed   2256 **Office of wommen** female employments
2258 **brode** broad   2259 **hente** seized   2261 **to-rente** torn to pieces
2262 **welde** deal with   2265 **under the bussh** in the woods
2266 **verray might** main strength

With any yong man, were he never so wight;
Ther mighte nothing in hir armes stonde.
She kepte hir maidenhede from every wight;
To no man deigned hire for to be bonde.   2270

But atte laste, hir freendes han hire maried
To Odenake, a prince of that contree,
Al were it so that she hem longe taried.
And ye shul understande how that he
Hadde swiche fantasies as hadde she.   2275
But nathelees, whan they were knit in-feere,
They lived in joye and in felicitee,
For ech of hem hadde oother lief and deere.

Save o thing: that she wolde nevere assente
By no wey that he sholde by hire lie   2280
But ones, for it was hir plein entente
To have a child, the world to multiplye.
And also soone as that she mighte espye
That she was nat with childe with that dede,
Thanne wolde she suffre him doon his fantasye   2285
Eftsoone, and noght but ones, out of drede.

And if she were with childe at thilke cast,
Namoore sholde he pleyen thilke game
Til fully fourty wikes weren past;
Thanne wolde she ones suffre him do the same.   2290

2267 **wight** strong   2269 **kepte** protected   2270 She scorned to be bound
to any man   2273 **taried** kept waiting   2275 **swiche fantasies** the same
kind of inclinations   2276 **knit in-feere** joined together   2278 **lief** beloved
2281 **plein entente** whole purpose   2283 **espye** observe
2285 **doon his fantasye** fulfil his desire   2286 A second time, and only once,
without doubt   2287 **at thilke cast** on that occasion
2288 **game** game of love   2290 **suffre** allow

Al were this Odenake wilde or tame,
He gat namoore of hire, for thus she seide:
It was to wives lecherye and shame
In oother cas if that men with hem pleyde.

2295 Two sones by this Odenake hadde she,
The whiche she kepte in vertu and lettrure.
But now unto oure tale turne we:
I seye, so worshipful a creature,
And wis therwith, and large with mesure,
2300 So penible in the werre, and curteis eke,
Ne moore laboure mighte in werre endure,
Was noon, thogh al this world men sholde seke.

Hir riche array ne mighte nat be told,
As wel in vessel as in hire clothing;
2305 She was al clad in perree and in gold.
And eek she lafte noght, for noon hunting,
To have of sondry tonges ful knowing,
Whan that she leiser hadde; and for to entende
To lerne bookes was al hir liking,
2310 How she in vertu mighte hir lif despende.

And shortly of this storye for to trete,
So doughty was hire housbonde and eek she,
That they conquered manye regnes grete
In th'Orient, with many a fair citee
2315 Appertenant unto the magestee
Of Rome, and with strong hond held hem ful faste.
Ne nevere mighte hir foomen doon hem flee
Ay whil that Odenakes dayes laste.

2294 **oother cas** other circumstances **pleyde** had enjoyment
2296 **lettrure** learning   2298 **worshipful** honourable
2299 **large with mesure** generous in moderation   2300 **penible** strenuous
2305 **perree** jewellery   2306 **lafte noght** did not neglect
2308–9 **entende** To devote herself to **liking** pleasure   2312 **doughty** brave
2314 **th'Orient** the East   2315 **Appertenant** belonging   2316 **hem** them
2317 **hir foomen** their enemies

Hir batailles, whoso list hem for to rede,
Again Sapor the king and othere mo,   2320
And how that al this proces fil in dede,
Why she conquered, and what title had therto,
And after, of hire meschief and hire wo,
How that she was biseged and ytake –
Lat him unto my maister Petrak go,   2325
That writ inow of this, I undertake.

Whan Odenake was deed, she mightily
The regnes heeld, and with hire propre hond
Agains hir foos she faught so cruelly
That ther nas king ne prince in al that lond   2330
That he nas glad, if he that grace fond
That she ne wolde upon his lond werreye.
With hire they maden alliance by bond
To been in pees, and lete hire ride and pleye.

The emperour of Rome, Claudius,   2335
Ne him biforn, the Romain Galien,
Ne dorsten nevere been so corageus,
Ne noon Ermin, ne noon Egipcien,
Ne Surryen, ne noon Arabien,
Withinne the feelde that dorste with hire fighte,   2340
Lest that she wolde hem with hir handes slen,
Or with hire meinee putten hem to flighte.

In kinges habit wente hire sones two,
As heires of hir fadres regnes alle,
And Hermanno and Thimalao   2345
Hir names were, as Persiens hem calle.

2320 **Again** against   2324 **ytake** captured   2326 **writ** (= *writeth*) writes
2327 **mightily** vigorously   2328 **propre** own   2331 **that grace fond** had the
good luck   2332 **werreye** make war   2337 **corageus** courageous
2338 **Ermin** Armenian   2339 **Surryen** Syrian   2341 **slen** slay
2342 **meinee** army

But ay Fortune hath in hire hony galle:
This mighty queene may no while endure.
Fortune out of hir regne made hire falle
2350   To wrecchednesse and to misaventure.

Aurelian, whan that the governaunce
Of Rome cam into hise handes tweye,
He shoop upon this queene to doon vengeance,
And with his legions he took his weye
2355   Toward Cenobie; and shortly for to seye,
He made hire flee, and atte laste hire hente,
And fettred hire, and eek hire children tweye,
And wan the land, and hoom to Rome he wente.

Amonges othere thinges that he wan,
2360   Hir chaar, that was with gold wroght and perree,
This grete Romain, this Aurelian,
Hath with him lad, for that men sholde it see.
Biforen his triumphe walketh she,
With gilte cheines on hire nekke hanginge;
2365   Crowned was she, as after hire degree,
And ful of perree charged hir clothinge.

Allas, Fortune! she that whilom was
Dredeful to kinges and to emperoures,
Now gaureth al the peple on hire, allas!
2370   And she that helmed was in starke stoures,
And wan by force townes stronge and toures,
Shal on hire heed now were a vitremite;
And she that bar the ceptre ful of floures
Shal bere a distaf, hire costes for to quite.

2347 see n.   2348 **may no while endure** may not last for long
2353 **shoop** determined   2356 **hente** seized   2357 **fettred** put in fetters
2358 **wan** conquered   2360 **chaar** chariot **perree** jewels   2362 **lad** led
2366 **charged** weighed down   2369 **gaureth** stare   2370 **helmed** helmeted
starke stoures fierce battles   2372 **vitremite** ?a woman's cap (n.)
2374 **hire costes for to quite** to pay for her keep

De Petro Rege Ispannie

O noble, o worthy Petro, glorye of Spaine,   2375
Whom Fortune heeld so heighe in magestee,
Wel oghten men thy pitous deeth complaine!
Out of thy land thy brother made thee flee;
And after, at a sege, by subtiltee
Thow were bitraysed and lad unto his tente,   2380
Whereas he with his owene hand slow thee,
Succedinge in thy regne and in thy rente.

The feeld of snow, with th'egle of blak therinne,
Caught with the limerod coloured as the glede,
He brew this cursednesse and al this sinne!   2385
The wikked nest was werkere of this nede –
Noght Charles Oliver, that took ay hede
Of trouthe and honour, but of Armorike
Geniloun Oliver, corrupt for mede,
Broghte this worthy king in swich a brike.   2390

De Petro Rege de Cipro

O worthy Petro, king of Cipre, also,
That Alisaundre wan by heigh maistrye,
Ful many an hethen wroghtestow ful wo,
Of which thine owene liges hadde envye,
And for nothing but for thy chivalrye   2395
They in thy bed han slain thee by the morwe.
Thus kan Fortune hire wheel governe and gye,
And out of joye bringe men to sorwe.

2379 **subtiltee** cunning   2380 **bitraysed** betrayed   2382 **rente** revenue
2383 **feeld** ground   2384 **limerod** twig smeared with birdlime (to trap
birds) **glede** live coal   2385 **brew** brewed   **cursednesse** wickedness
2386 **wikked nest** see n. **nede** disaster   2387–8 **took ay hede Of** was always
concerned for   2389 **corrupt for mede** corrupted by bribery
2390 **brike** plight   2393 **wroghtestow ful wo** you brought much affliction
on   2394 **liges** subjects   2397 **gye** guide

De Barnabo de Lumbardia

Of Melan grete Barnabo Viscounte,
2400   God of delit, and scourge of Lumbardye,
Why sholde I noght thin infortune acounte,
Sith in estat thow clombe were so hye?
Thy brother sone, that was thy double allye,
For he thy nevew was and sone-in-lawe,
2405   Withinne his prisoun made thee to die.
But why, ne how, noot I that thou were slawe.

De Hugelino Comite de Pize

Of the Erl Hugelin of Pize the langour
Ther may no tonge telle for pitee.
But litel out of Pize stant a tour,
2410   In which tour in prisoun put was he,
And with him been hise litel children thre;
The eldest scarsly five yeer was of age.
Allas, Fortune! It was greet crueltee
Swiche briddes for to putte in swich a cage!

2415   Dampned was he to die in that prisoun,
For Roger, which that bisshop was of Pize,
Hadde on him maad a fals suggestioun,
Thurgh which the peple gan upon him rise,
And putten him to prisoun in swich wise
2420   As ye han herd; and mete and drinke he hadde
So smal, that wel unnethe it may suffise,
And therwithal it was ful povre and badde.

2400 **delit** pleasure   2401 **infortune** misfortune   **acounte** tell of
2402 **estat** rank   **clombe were** had climbed   2406 **noot I** I do not know
2407 **langour** suffering   2415 **Dampned** condemned
2417 **suggestioun** charge   2418 **gan upon him rise** rose against him
2421 **unnethe** hardly

And on a day, bifel that in that hour
Whan that his mete wont was to be broght,
The gailer shette the dores of the tour.   2425
He herde it wel, but he spak right noght,
And in his herte anon ther fil a thoght
That they for hunger wolde doon him dien.
'Allas!' quod he, 'allas, that I was wroght!'
Therwith the teeris fillen from hise eyen.   2430

His yonge sone, that thre yeer was of age,
Unto him seide, 'Fader, why do ye wepe?
Whanne wol the gailer bringen oure potage?
Is ther no morsel breed that ye do kepe?
I am so hungry that I may nat slepe.   2435
Now wolde God that I mighte slepen evere!
Thanne sholde noght hunger in my wombe crepe;
Ther is nothing, but breed, that me were levere.'

Thus day by day this child bigan to crye,
Til in his fadres barm adoun it lay,   2440
And seide, 'Farewel, fader, I moot die!'
And kiste his fader, and deide the same day.
And whan the woful fader deed it say,
For wo hise armes two he gan to bite,
And seide, 'Allas, Fortune, and weilaway!   2445
Thy false wheel my wo al may I wite.'

Hise children wende that it for hunger was
That he hise armes gnow, and nat for wo,
And seiden, 'Fader, do nat so, allas,
But rather ete the flessh upon us two.   2450

2424 **mete** food **wont was** was accustomed   2425 **shette** shut
2428 **doon him dien** cause him to die   2430 **fillen** fell   2433 **potage** soup
2434 **morsel breed** mouthful of bread   2438 **me were levere** would be more
agreeable to me   2440 **barm** lap   2443 **say** saw   2446 **wite** blame for
2447 **wende** thought   2448 **gnow** gnawed

Oure flessh thow yaf us, taak oure flessh us fro,
And ete inow.' – Right thus they to him seide.
And after that, withinne a day or two,
They leide hem in his lappe adoun and deide.

2455   Himself, despeired, eek for hunger starf.
Thus ended is this mighty Erl of Pize!
From heigh estat Fortune awey him carf.
Of this tragedye it oghte inogh suffise;
Whoso wol heere it in a lenger wise,
2460   Redeth the grete poete of Itaille
That highte Dant, for he kan al devise
Fro point to point; nat o word wol he faille.

Nero

Althogh that Nero were as vicius
As any feend that lith ful lowe adoun,
2465   Yet he, as telleth us Swetonius,
This wide world hadde in subjeccioun,
Bothe Est and West, South and Septemtrioun.
Of rubies, saphires, and of perles white
Were alle hise clothes brouded up and doun,
2470   For he in gemmes greetly gan delite.

Moore delicat, moore pompous of array,
Moore proud was nevere emperour than he.
That ilke clooth that he hadde wered o day,
After that time he nolde it nevere see.

2452 **ete inow** eat your fill   2455 **starf** died   2457 **carf** cut
2461 **devise** describe   2462 **faille** lack   2464 **feend** devil **lith** lies
2467 **Septemtrioun** North   2469 **brouded** embroidered   2471 More
voluptuous, more splendid in finery   2473 The garment that he had worn
for one day

Nettes of gold threed hadde he greet plentee,   2475
To fisshe in Tibre whan him liste pleye.
Hise lustes were al lawe in his decree,
For Fortune as his freend him wolde obeye.

He Rome brende for his delicacye.
The senatours he slow upon a day,   2480
To heere how that men wolde wepe and crye,
And slow his brother, and by his suster lay.
His moder made he in pitous array,
For he hire wombe slitte, to biholde
Where he conceived was; so weilaway,   2485
That he so litel of his moder tolde!

No teere out of hise eyen for that sighte
Ne cam, but seide, 'A fair womman was she!'
Greet wonder is how that he koude or mighte
Be domesman of hire dede beautee.   2490
The win to bringen him comanded he,
And drank anoon; noon oother wo he made.
Whan might is joined unto crueltee,
Allas, to depe wol the venim wade!

In youthe a maister hadde this emperour,   2495
To teche him letterure and curteisye,
For of moralitee he was the flour
As in his time, but if bookes lie.
And whil this maister hadde of him maistrye,
He maked him so konning and so souple   2500
That longe time it was er tyrannye
Or any vice dorste in him uncouple.

2476 **Tibre** (the river) Tiber   **him liste pleye** he wanted to amuse himself
2477 **lustes** desires   2479 **brende** burned **delicacye** pleasure
2483 **array** state   2486 **of ... tolde** esteemed   2490 **domesman** judge
2492 **noon oother wo he made** he expressed no other sorrow
2494 **wade** go   2495 **maister** teacher   2496 **letterure** literacy
2498 **but if** unless   2500 **konning** wise **souple** docile
2502 **uncouple** unleash itself

This Seneca, of which that I devise,
Bicause Nero hadde of him swich drede,
2505 For he fro vices wolde him ay chastise,
Discretly, as by word and nat by dede –
'Sire,' wolde he seyn, 'an emperour moot nede
Be vertuous and hate tyrannye' –
For which he in a bath made him to blede
2510 On bothe hise armes, til he moste die.

This Nero hadde eek of acustumance
In youthe agains his maister for to rise,
Which afterward him thoughte a greet grevance;
Therefore he made him dien in this wise.
2515 But nathelees this Seneca the wise
Chees in a bath to die in this manere,
Rather than han another tormentise.
And thus hath Nero slain his maister deere.

Now fil it so, that Fortune liste no lenger
2520 The hye pride of Nero to cherice,
For though that he was strong, yet was she strenger.
She thoghte thus: 'By God, I am to nice
To sette a man that is fulfild of vice
In heigh degree, and emperour him calle!
2525 By God, out of his sete I wol him trice;
Whan he leest weneth, sonnest shal he falle.'

The peple roos upon him on a night
For his defaute, and whan he it espied,
Out of his dores anon he hath him dight
2530 Allone, and there he wende han been allied

2504 **drede** fear   2507 **nede** necessarily
2511 **hadde ... of acustumance** was in the habit of   2512 **agains** in the
presence of   2513 **grevance** grievance   2516 **Chees** chose
2517 **tormentise** method of execution   2520 **cherice** foster
2522 **nice** foolish   2525 **sete** seat **trice** pluck   2526 **weneth** expects
2528 **defaute** wickedness   2529 **hath him dight** went   2530 **there** where
wende han been allied thought he had friends

He knokked faste, and ay the moore he cried,
The fastere shette they the dores alle.
Tho wiste he wel he hadde himself misgyed,
And wente his wey; no lenger dorste he calle.

The peple cried and rombled up and doun,   2535
That with his eris herde he how they seide:
'Where is this false tyraunt, this Neroun?'
For fere almoost out of his wit he breide,
And to hise goddes pitously he preyde
For socour, but it mighte noght bitide.   2540
For drede of this, him thoughte that he deide,
And ran into a gardin, him to hide.

And in this gardin foond he cherles tweye,
That seten by a fir, greet and reed,
And to thise cherles two he gan to preye   2545
To sleen him, and to girden of his heed,
That to his body, whan that he were deed,
Were no despit ydoon for his defame.
Himself he slow; he koude no bettre reed,
Of which Fortune lough, and hadde a game.   2550

De Oloferno

Was nevere capitain under a king
That regnes mo putte in subjeccioun,
Ne strenger was in feeld of alle thing
As in his time, ne gretter of renoun,

2531 **faste** hard   2533 **misgyed** misled   2534 **calle** shout
2535 **rombled** made a rumbling noise   2538 He almost lost his mind for
fear   2540 **mighte noght bitide** was impossible   2543 **foond** found
2546 **girden of** cut off   2548 **despit** insult   **for his defame** to disgrace him
2549 **koude no bettre reed** knew no better remedy   2550 **Of** at
hadde a game amused herself   2552 **regnes mo** more kingdoms

2555   Ne moore pompous in heigh presumpcioun
        Than Oloferne, which Fortune ay kiste
        So likerously, and ladde him up and doun,
        Til that his heed was of er that he wiste.

        Nat oonly that this world hadde him in awe
2560   For lesinge of richesse or libertee,
        But he made every man reneye his lawe.
        Nabugodonosor was god, seide he;
        Noon oother god sholde adoured be.
        Agains his heste no wight dorste trespace,
2565   Save in Bethulia, a strong citee,
        Where Eliachim a preest was of that place.

        But tak kepe of the deeth of Oloferne:
        Amidde his hoost he dronke lay a-night,
        Withinne his tente, large as is a berne;
2570   And yet, for al his pompe and al his might,
        Judith, a womman, as he lay upright
        Slepinge, his heed of smoot, and from his tente
        Ful prively she stal from every wight,
        And with his heed unto hir toun she wente.

                De Rege Antiocho illustri

2575   What nedeth it of King Anthiochus
        To telle his hye royal magestee,
        His hye pride, hise werkes venimus?
        For swich another was ther noon as he.

2555 **pompous** vainglorious   2556 **which** whom **ay** always
2557 **likerously** amorously   2558 **of** off **er that he wiste** before he knew
2560 **For lesinge** for fear of losing   2561 **reneye his lawe** abjure his religion
2564 **trespace** transgress   2567 **tak kepe** take note   2569 **berne** barn
2571 **upright** on his back   2572 **of smoot** struck off   2573 **stal** stole away

Rede which that he was in Machabee,
And rede the proude wordes that he seide,   2580
And why he fil fro heigh prosperitee,
And in an hill how wrecchedly he deide.

Fortune him hadde enhaunced so in pride
That verraily he wende he mighte attaine
Unto the sterres upon every side,   2585
And in balance weyen ech montaine,
And alle the floodes of the see restraine.
And Goddes peple hadde he moost in hate;
Hem wolde he sleen in torment and in paine,
Weninge that God ne mighte his pride abate.   2590

And for that Nichanore and Thimothee
Of Jewes weren venquisshed mightily,
Unto the Jewes swich an hate hadde he
That he bad greithe his chaar ful hastily,
And swoor and seide ful despitously   2595
Unto Jerusalem he wolde eftsoone,
To wreke his ire on it ful cruelly –
But of his purpos he was let ful soone.

God for his manace him so soore smoot
With invisible wounde ay incurable,   2600
That in hise guttes carf it so and boot
That hise peines weren inportable.

2579 **which that** what   2582 **in** on   2583 **enhaunced** elevated
2584 **attaine** reach   2586 **balance** pair of scales   2590 **Weninge** believing
abate destroy   2591 **for that** because   2592 **Of** by
2594 **greithe his chaar** his chariot be prepared   2595 **despitously** angrily
2596 **wolde eftsoone** would go without delay   2597 **wreke his ire** vent his
anger   2598 **of . . . let** hindered in   2599 **manace** threat **soore** severely
2601 **carf** cut **boot** gnawed   2602 **inportable** unendurable

And certeinly the wreche was resonable,
For many a mannes guttes dide he peine.
2605   But from his purpos cursed and dampnable,
For al his smert, he wolde him nat restreine,

But bad anon apparaillen his hoost.
And sodeinly, er he was of it war,
God daunted al his pride and al his boost;
2610   For he so soore fil out of his char
That it hise limes and his skin totar,
So that he neither mighte go ne ride,
But in a chaier men aboute him bar,
Al forbrused, bothe bak and side.

2615   The wreche of God him smoot so cruelly
That thurgh his body wikked wormes crepte,
And therwithal he stank so horribly
That noon of al his meinee that him kepte,
Wheither so he wook or ellis slepte,
2620   Ne mighte noght the stink of him endure.
In this meschief he wailed and eek wepte,
And knew God lord of every creature.

To al his hoost, and to himself also,
Ful wlatsom was the stink of his careine;
2625   No man ne mighte him bere to ne fro.
And in this stink and this horrible peine
He starf ful wrecchedly, in a monteine.
Thus hath this robbour and this homicide,
That many a man made to wepe and pleine,
2630   Swich gerdon as bilongeth unto pride.

2603 **wreche** vengeance   2606 **smert** pain   2607 **apparaillen his hoost** his
army be got ready   2608 **war** aware   2610 **soore** severely   **char** chariot
2611 **totar** tore to pieces   2612 **go** walk   2613 **chaier** sedan chair
2614 **forbrused** severely bruised   2618 **meinee** household   **kepte** looked
after   2619 **Wheither so** whether   2622 **knew** acknowledged
2624 **wlatsom** loathsome   **careine** gangrenous flesh   2627 **starf** died   **in** on
2628 **homicide** murderer   2630 **gerdon** reward

De Alexandro

The storye of Alisaundre is so commune
That every wight that hath discrecioun
Hath herd somwhat or al of his fortune.
This wide world, as in conclusioun,
He wan by strengthe, or for his hye renoun   2635
They weren glad for pees unto him sende.
The pride of man and beest he leide adoun
Whereso he cam, unto the worldes ende.

Comparisoun mighte nevere yet ben maked
Bitwixe him and another conquerour;   2640
For al this world for drede of him hath quaked.
He was of knighthod and of fredom flour;
Fortune him made the heir of hire honour.
Save win and wommen, nothing mighte aswage
His hye entente in armes and labour,   2645
So was he ful of leonin corage.

What pris were it to him, thogh I yow tolde
Of Darius, and an hundred thousand mo,
Of kinges, princes, dukes, erles bolde,
Whiche he conquered, and broghte hem into wo?   2650
I seye, as fer as man may ride or go,
The world was his; what sholde I moore devise?
For thogh I write or tolde yow everemo
Of his knighthode, it mighte nat suffise.

2632 **hath discrecioun** has reached the age of adult reasoning
2635 **wan** conquered   2636 **sende** to send   2637 **leide adoun** destroyed
2642 **fredom** magnanimity **flour** peak, pinnacle   2644 **aswage** subdue
2645 **hye entente** high purpose   2646 **leonin** lion-like   2647 **pris** praise
2652 **what sholde I moore devise** why should I say more   2653 **write** were
to write

2655   Twelf yeer he regned, as seyth Machabee;
         Philippes sone of Macidoine he was,
         That first was king in Grece the contree.
         O worthy, gentil Alisandre, allas,
         That evere sholde fallen swich a cas!
2660   Empoisoned of thin owene folk thou weere.
         Thy *sis* Fortune hath turned into *aas*,
         And yet for thee ne weep she nevere a teere.

         Who shal me yeven teeris to compleine
         The deeth of gentilesse and of franchise,
2665   That al the world welded in his demeine,
         And yet him thoughte it mighte nat suffise,
         So ful was his corage of heigh emprise?
         Allas, who shal me helpe to endite
         False Fortune, and poison to despise?
2670   – The whiche two of al this wo I wite.

De Julio Cesare

         By wisdom, manhede, and by greet labour,
         From humble bed to royal magestee
         Up roos he Julius the conquerour,
         That wan al th'Occident by land and see,
2675   By strengthe of hond, or elles by tretee,
         And unto Rome made hem tributarye;
         And sith of Rome the emperour was he,
         Til that Fortune weex his adversarye.

2656 **Philippes sone of Macidoine** son of Philip of Macedon
2661 *sis* six (highest possible throw in dice)   *aas* one (lowest possible throw in dice; hence an emblem of bad luck)   2662 **weep** wept
2663 **compleine** bewail   2664 **franchise** magnanimity
2665 **demeine** control   2667 **corage** spirit   **emprise** adventurousness
2668 **endite** indict   2670 **of . . . wite** blame for   2674 **th'Occident** the West   2675 **tretee** negotiation   2678 **weex** became

O mighty Cesar, that in Thessalye
Again Pompeus, fader thin in lawe,   2680
That of th'Orient hadde al the chivalrye
As fer as that the day biginneth dawe,
Thow thurgh thy knighthod hast hem take and
        slawe,
Save fewe folk that with Pompeus fledde,
Thurgh which thow puttest al th'Orient in awe;   2685
Thanke Fortune, that so wel thee spedde!

But now a litel while I wol biwaille
This Pompeus, this noble governour
Of Rome, which that fleigh at this bataille.
I seye, oon of hise men, a fals traitour,   2690
His heed of smoot, to winnen him favour
Of Julius, and him the heed he broghte.
Allas, Pompeye, of th'Orient conquerour,
That Fortune unto swich a fin thee broghte!

To Rome again repaireth Julius   2695
With his triumphe, lauriat ful hye.
But on a time, Brutus Cassius,
That evere hadde of his hye estat envye,
Ful prively hath maad conspiracye
Agains this Julius in subtil wise,   2700
And caste the place in which he sholde die
With boidekins, as I shal yow devise.

2680 **Again** against **fader thin in lawe** your father-in-law
2682 **biginneth dawe** dawns   2683 **knighthod** prowess **slawe** slain
2686 **spedde** prospered   2689 **fleigh** ran away   2691 **of smoot** struck off
him himself   2694 **fin** end   2695 **repaireth** returns   2696 **lauriat** crowned
with laurel **hye** exalted   2697 **on a time** one day   2698 **estat** social
position   2699 **prively** secretly   2701 **caste** determined on
2702 **boidekins** daggers **devise** tell

This Julius to the Capitolie wente
Upon a day, as he was wont to goon,
2705   And in the Capitolie anon him hente
This false Brutus and hise othere foon,
And stiked him with boidekins anoon
With many a wounde, and thus they lete him lie.
But nevere gronte he at no strook but oon,
2710   Or elles at two, but if his storye lie.

So manly was this Julius of herte,
And so wel lovede estatly honestee,
That thogh hise deedly woundes soore smerte,
His mantel over his hipes casteth he,
2715   For no man sholde seen his privetee.
And as he lay of-dying in a traunce,
And wiste verraily that deed was he,
Of honestee yet hadde he remembraunce.

Lucan, to thee this storye I recomende,
2720   And to Swetoun, and to Valerius also,
That of this storye writen word and ende,
How that to thise grete conquerours two
Fortune was first freend, and sitthe foo.
No man ne truste upon hire favour longe,
2725   But have hire in await for everemo;
Witnesse on alle thise conqueroures stronge.

2705 **hente** seized   2706 **foon** foes   2707 **stiked** stabbed
2709 **gronte** groaned   2712 **estatly honestee** a dignified decorum
2713 **soore smerte** hurt severely   2715 **For** in order that **privetee** private
parts   2716 **of-dying** dying   2721 **word and ende** from beginning to end
2723 **sitthe** afterwards   2724 **No man ne truste** let no one trust   2725 But
watch her suspiciously all the time

Cresus

This riche Cresus, whilom king of Lyde,
Of which Cresus Cirus soore him dradde,
Yet was he caught amiddes al his pride,
And to be brent men to the fir him ladde;   2730
But swich a rein doun fro the welkne shadde
That slow the fir, and made him to escape.
But to be war no grace yet he hadde,
Til Fortune on the galwes made him gape.

Whanne he escaped was, he kan nat stente   2735
For to biginne a newe werre again.
He wende wel, for that Fortune him sente
Swich hap that he escaped thurgh the rain,
That of his foos he mighte nat be slain;
And eek a swevene upon a night he mette,   2740
Of which he was so proud and eek so fain
That in vengeance he al his herte sette.

Upon a tree he was, as that him thoughte,
Ther Juppiter him wessh, bothe bak and side,
And Phebus eek a fair towaille him broughte   2745
To drye him with, and therfore wax his pride.
And to his doghter, that stood him biside,
Which that he knew in heigh sentence habounde,
He bad hire telle him what it signifide,
And she his dreem bigan right thus expounde: 2750

2727 **whilom** formerly   2728 **him dradde** was afraid   2730 **brent** burned
2731 **welkne** sky **shadde** fell   2732 **slow** extinguished   2733 But he still
did not have the good fortune to be on his guard   2734 **galwes** gallows
2735 **stente** forbear from   2737 **wende** believed   2738 **hap** luck
2740 **swevene** dream **mette** dreamed   2743 **him thoughte** it seemed to him
2744 **wessh** washed   2745 **towaille** towel   2746 **wax** increased
2748 **heigh sentence** great wisdom

'The tree', quod she, 'the galwes is to mene,
And Juppiter bitokneth snow and rein,
And Phebus, with his towaille so clene,
Tho been the sonnes stremes for to seyn.
2755   Thou shalt anhanged be, fader, certein.
Rein shal thee wasshe, and sonne shal thee drye.'
Thus warned him ful plat and eke ful plein
His doghter, which that called was Phanye.

Anhanged was Cresus, the proude king;
2760   His royal trone mighte him nat availle.
Tragedies noon oother manere thing
Ne kan in singing crye ne biwaille
But that Fortune alwey wole assaille
With unwar strook the regnes that been proude;
2765   For whan men trusteth hire, thanne wol she faille,
And covere hire brighte face with a clowde.

Heere stinteth the Knight the
Monk of his Tale.

THE NUN'S PRIEST'S PROLOGUE

The Prologe of the Nonnes Preestes Tale.

'Ho!' quod the Knight, 'good sire, namoore of this!
That ye han seid is right inow, iwys,
And muchel moore, for litel hevinesse
2770   Is right inow to muche folk, I gesse.

2754 **stremes** rays   2755 **anhanged** hanged   2757 **plat** bluntly
2758 **Phanye** Phania   2764 **unwar strook** an unexpected stroke
2765 **faille** let them down

2768 **That** what   **iwys** for certain   2769 **hevinesse** sorrow

I seye for me, it is a greet disese
Wheras men han been in greet welthe and ese,
To heeren of hir sodein fal, allas!
And the contrarye is joye and greet solas,
As whan a man hath been in povre estaat,   2775
And climbeth up and wexeth fortunat,
And there abideth in prosperitee.
Swich thing is gladsom, as it thinketh me,
And of swich thing were goodly for to telle.'
    'Ye,' quod oure Hooste, 'by Seint Poules belle,   2780
Ye seye right sooth! This Monk, he clappeth
            loude;
He spak how Fortune covered with a cloude
I noot nat what, and also of a tragedye –
Right now ye herde; and, pardee, no remedye
It is for to biwaille ne compleine   2785
That that is doon, and als it is a peine,
As ye han seid, to heere of hevinesse.
    'Sire Monk, namoore of this, so God yow blesse!
Youre tale anoyeth al this compaignye.
Swich talking is nat worth a boterflye,   2790
For therinne is ther no desport ne game.
Wherfore, sire Monk, daun Piers by youre name,
I prey yow hertely, telle us somwhat elles;
For sikerly, nere clinking of youre belles,
That on youre bridel hange on every side,   2795
By hevene king, that for us alle dide,
I sholde er this have fallen doun for sleep,
Althogh the slough hadde nevere ben so deep.
Thanne hadde youre tale al be toold in vein!
For certeinly, as that thise clerkes seyn,   2800

2771 **disese** distress   2774 **solas** pleasure   2776 **wexeth fortunat** becomes
prosperous   2778 **gladsom** cheerful   2781 **clappeth loude** talks loudly
2783 **noot nat** do not know   2785 **compleine** lament   2786 **als** also
2789 **anoyeth** irritates   2791 **desport** amusement   2794 **nere clinking** were
it not for the jingling   2796 **dide** died   2798 **slough** mire
2799 **hadde . . . be** would have been

Whereas a man may have noon audience,
Noght helpeth it to tellen his sentence.
And wel I woot, the substaunce is in me,
If any thing shal wel reported be.
2805   Sire, sey somwhat of hunting, I yow preye.'
'Nay,' quod this Monk, 'I have no lust to pleye.
Now lat another telle, as I have toold.'
   Thanne spak oure Hoost with rude speche and
      boold,
And seide unto the Nonnes Preest anon:
2810   'Com neer, thow Preest; com hider, thow Sire
      John!
Telle us swich thing as may oure hertes glade.
Be blithe, though thow ride upon a jade!
What though thin hors be bothe foul and lene?
If he wol serve thee, rekke nat a bene!
2815   Looke that thin herte be murye everemo.'
   'Yis, sire,' quod he, 'yis, Hoost, so mote I go,
But I be murye, iwys, I wol be blamed.'
And right anon his tale he hath attamed.
And thus he seide unto us everychon,
2820   This sweete Preest, this goodly man, Sire John.

2801 **audience** hearing   2802 **Noght helpeth it** it's no use
2803 **substaunce** capacity   2805 **somwhat of** something about
2806 **lust** desire   2808 **rude** rough   2811 **glade** gladden   2812 **jade** hack
2813 **foul** wretched   2814 **rekke nat a bene** do not give a bean
2815 **Looke** see   2817 **But I be** if I am not   2818 **attamed** begun

THE NUN'S PRIEST'S TALE

*Heere biginneth the Nonnes
Preestes Tale of the cok and hen,
Chauntecleer and Pertelote.*

A povre widwe, somdel stape in age,
Was whilom dwellinge in a narwe cotage,
Biside a grove, stonding in a dale.
This widwe of which I telle yow my tale,
Sin thilke day that she was last a wif,   2825
In pacience ladde a ful simple lif,
For litel was hire catel and hire rente.
By housbondrye, of swich as God hire sente,
She foond hireself, and eek hire doghtren two.
Thre large sowes hadde she and namo,   2830
Thre kyn, and eek a sheep that highte Malle.
Ful sooty was hire bour and eek hire halle,
In which she eet ful many a sklendre meel.
Of poinaunt sauce hir neded never a deel;
No deintee morsel passed thurgh hir throte.   2835
Hir diete was acordant to hir cote.
Repleccioun ne made hire nevere sik;
Attempree diete was al hir physik,
And excercise, and hertes suffisaunce.
The goute lette hire nothing for to daunce,   2840
N'apoplexye shente nat hir heed.
No win ne drank she, neither whit ne reed.

2821 **stape** advanced   2822 **whilom** once **narwe** cramped
2827 **catel** property **rente** income   2829 **foond** supported
2831 **kyn** cows   2832 **bour** bedroom   2833 **sklendre** scanty
2834 **poinaunt** pungent **never a deel** not a bit   2835 **deintee** delicious
2836 **cote** cottage   2837 **Repleccioun** surfeit   2838 **Attempree** moderate
physik medicine   2839 **suffisaunce** contentment   2840 Gout did not
prevent her from dancing   2841 **shente nat** did not injure

Hir bord was served moost with whit and blak –
Milk and broun breed, in which she foond no lak,
2845   Seind bacoun, and somtime an ey or tweye,
For she was, as it were, a maner deye.
    A yeerd she hadde, enclosed al aboute
With stikkes, and a drye dich withoute,
In which she hadde a cok heet Chauntecleer.
2850   In al the land, of crowing nas his peer;
His vois was murier than the mirye orgon
On masse-dayes that in the chirche gon.
Wel sikerer was his crowing in his logge
Than is a clokke or an abbey orlogge.
2855   By nature he knew ech ascencioun
Of th'equinoxial in thilke toun;
For whan degrees fiftene were ascended,
Thanne krew he, that it mighte nat ben amended.
His comb was redder than the fin coral,
2860   And batailled as it were a castel wal.
His bile was blak, and as the jeet it shoon;
Lik asure were hise legges and his toon;
Hise nailes whitter than the lilye flour,
And lik the burned gold was his colour.
2865   This gentil cok hadde in his governaunce
Sevene hennes, for to doon al his plesaunce,
Whiche were hise sustres and his paramours,
And wonder like to him, as of colours;
Of whiche the faireste hewed on hire throte
2870   Was cleped faire damoisele Pertelote.

2844 **foond no lak** found no fault   2845 **Seind** grilled **ey** egg
2846 **a maner deye** a kind of dairywoman   2847 **yeerd** enclosure
2848 **stikkes** palings   2849 **heet** who was called   2850 **nas his peer** there
was none equal to him   2851 **murier** sweeter-sounding **orgon** organ (n.)
2853 **sikerer** more reliable **logge** coop   2854 **orlogge** clock
2856 **equinoxial** celestial equator (n.)   2858 **amended** improved on
2860 **batailled** crenellated   2861 **bile** bill **jeet** jet   2862 **asure** lapis lazuli
toon toes   2864 **burned** shining   2865 **governaunce** care
2866 **plesaunce** pleasure   2867 **paramours** mistresses
2868 **wonder** wonderfully   2869 **hewed** coloured   2870 **damoisele** lady

Curteis she was, discreet, and debonaire,
And compaignable, and bar hirself so faire
Sin thilke day that she was seven night oold,
That trewely she hath the herte in hoold
Of Chauntecleer, loken in every lith.   2875
He loved hire so that wel was him therwith.
But swich a joye was it to here hem singe,
Whan that the brighte sonne gan to springe,
In swete acord, 'My leef is faren in londe'.
– For thilke time, as I have understonde,   2880
Beestes and briddes kouden speke and singe.

    And so bifel, that in a daweninge,
As Chauntecleer among hise wives alle
Sat on his perche, that was in the halle,
And next him sat this faire Pertelote,   2885
This Chauntecleer gan gronen in his throte,
As man that in his dreem is drecched soore.
And whan that Pertelote thus herde him rore,
She was agast, and seide, 'Herte deere,
What eileth yow, to grone in this manere?   2890
Ye ben a verray slepere! fy, for shame!'

    And he answerde and seide thus: 'Madame,
I prey yow that ye take it nat agrief.
By God, me mette I was in swich meschief
Right now, that yet min herte is soore afright!   2895
Now God', quod he, 'my swevene recche aright,
And kepe my body out of foul prisoun!
Me mette how that I romed up and doun

2871 **debonaire** gentle   2872 And an entertaining companion, and behaved
so elegantly   2874 **hath . . . in hoold** possesses   2875 **loken** locked
lith limb   2876 **therwith** for that reason   2878 **gan to springe** rose
2879 In sweet harmony, 'My love has gone away'   2882 **in a daweninge** one
day at dawn   2886 **gan gronen** groaned   2887 **drecched soore** deeply
troubled   2889 **agast** afraid   2893 **agrief** amiss   2894 **me mette** I
dreamed **meschief** affliction   2895 **afright** frightened
2896 **God . . . my swevene recche aright** may God interpret my dream for the
good

Withinne oure yeerd, whereas I say a beest
2900 Was lik an hound, and wolde han maad areest
Upon my body, and han had me deed.
His colour was bitwixe yelow and reed,
And tipped was his tail and bothe hise eris
With blak, unlik the remenaunt of hise heris.
2905 His snowte smal, with glowing eyen tweye.
– Yet of his look for fere almoost I deye!
This caused me my groning, doutelees.'
        'Avoy!' quod she, 'fy on yow, hertelees!
Allas!' quod she, 'for, by that God above,
2910 Now han ye lost min herte and al my love!
I kan nat love a coward, by my feith!
For certes, whatso any womman seyth,
We alle desiren, if it mighte be,
To han housbondes hardy, wise, and fre,
2915 And secree, and no nigard, ne no fool,
Ne him that is agast of every tool,
Ne noon avauntour, by that God above!
How dorste ye seyn for shame unto youre love
That any thing mighte make yow aferd?
2920 Have ye no mannes herte, and han a berd?
Allas, and konne ye ben agast of swevenis?
Nothing, God woot, but vanitee in swevene is.
Swevenes engendren of replexions,
And ofte of fume, and of complexions,
2925 Whan humours ben to habundant in a wight.
Certes, this dreem which ye han met to-night

2899 **say** saw   2900–2901 **maad areest Upon** seized   2904 **remenaunt** rest
2906 **Yet** still   2908 **Avoy** shame **hertelees** cowardly
2912 **whatso** whatever   2914 **hardy** brave **fre** generous
2915 **secree** discreet **nigard** miser   2916 **tool** weapon
2917 **avauntour** boaster   2919 **aferd** afraid   2921 Alas! And are you
capable of being frightened by dreams   2923 **engendren of** arise from
replexions surfeits of food   2924 **fume** bodily 'exhalation'
complexions mixtures of humours (n.)   2925 **humours** bodily fluids (n.)

Comth of the grete superfluitee
Of youre rede colera, pardee,
Which causeth folk to dreden in hir dremes
Of arwes, and of fir with rede lemes,   2930
Of rede bestes, that they wol hem bite,
Of contek, and of whelpes grete and lite
– Right as the humour of malencolye
Causeth ful many a man in sleep to crye
For fere of blake beres, or boles blake,   2935
Or elles blake develes wol hem take.
Of othere humours koude I telle also,
That werken many a man in sleep ful wo,
But I wol passe as lightly as I kan.

'Lo, Catoun, which that was so wis a man,   2940
Seide he nat thus, "Ne do no fors of dremes"?
Now, sire,' quod she, 'whan we fle fro the bemes,
For Goddes love, as taak som laxatif!
Up peril of my soule and of my lif,
I conseille yow the beste, I wol nat lie,   2945
That bothe of colere and of malencolye
Ye purge yow; and for ye shal nat tarye,
Thogh in this toun is noon apothecarye,
I shal myself to herbes techen yow
That shul ben for youre heele and for youre   2950
    prow.
And in oure yerd tho herbes shal I finde,
The whiche han of hire propretee by kinde
To purge yow binethe and eek above.
Foryet nat this, for Goddes owene love!
Ye ben ful colerik of complexioun;   2955
Ware the sonne in his ascensioun

2928 **rede colera** red choler   2930 **arwes** arrows **lemes** flames
2932 **contek** warfare **whelpes** dogs   2935 **boles** bulls
2938 **werken ... ful wo** do harm to   2941 **Ne do no fors of** attach no
importance to   2944 **Up** upon   2945 **conseille** advise   2949 **techen** direct
2950 **heele** health **prow** benefit   2951 **tho** those   2952 **by kinde** by nature
2953 I.e. both laxative and emetic   2955 **colerik** dominated by the humour
of choler **complexioun** temperament   2956 **Ware** take care that

Ne finde yow nat replet of humours hote!
And if it do, I dar wel leye a grote
That ye shul have a fevere terciane,

2960   Or an agu that may be youre bane.
A day or two ye shul have digestives
Of wormes, er ye take youre laxatives,
Of lauriol, centaure, and fumetere,
Or elles of ellebor that groweth there,

2965   Of katapuce, or of gaitris beryis,
Of herbe yve growing in oure yerd, ther merye is.
Pekke hem up right as they growe and ete hem in!
By mirye, housbonde, for youre fader kin!
Dredeth no dreem – I kan sey yow namoore.'

2970   'Madame,' quod he, '*graunt merci* of youre
                loore!
But nathelees, as touching daun Catoun,
That hath of wisdom swich a gret renoun,
Though that he bad no dremes for to drede,
By God! men may in olde bokes rede

2975   Of many a man moore of auctoritee
Than evere Catoun was, so mote I thee,
That al the revers seyn of his sentence,
And han wel founden by experience
That dremes ben significaciouns

2980   As wel of joye as tribulaciouns
That folk enduren in this lif present.
Ther nedeth make of this noon argument;

2957 **replet of** filled with   2958 **leye a grote** bet a groat (g.)
2959 **terciane** tertian (reaching a climax every third day)   2960 **agu** fever
be youre bane be the death of you   2961 **digestives** digestive medicines
2963 **lauriol** spurge laurel **centaure** centaury **fumetere** fumitory
2964 **ellebor** hellebore   2965 **katapuce** caper spurge
gaitris beryis ?buckthorn berries (n.)   2966 **herbe yve** buck's-horn
plantain (n.) **merye** pleasant   2968 **fader kin** father's kindred
2970 *graunt merci* **of your loore** thank you for your advice
2975 **moore of auctoritee** of greater authority   2976 **so mote I thee** as I may
prosper   2977 **revers** contrary   2979 **significaciouns** signs

The verray preeve sheweth it in dede.
   'Oon of the gretteste auctor that men rede
Seyth thus: that whilom two felawes wente   2985
On pilgrimage, in a ful good entente;
And happed so, they coomen in a toun
Whereas ther was swich congregacioun
Of peple, and eek so streit of herbergage,
That they ne founde as muche as o cotage   2990
In which they bothe mighte ylogged be.
Wherfore they mosten of necessitee,
As for that night, departen compaignye;
And ech of hem gooth to his hostelrye,
And took his logging as it wolde falle.   2995
That oon of hem was logged in a stalle,
Fer in a yeerd, with oxen of the plow;
That oother man was logged wel inow,
As was his aventure, or his fortune,
That us governeth alle as in commune.   3000
   'And so bifel that, longe er it were day,
This man mette in his bed, theras he lay,
How that his felawe gan upon him calle,
And seide, "Allas! – for in an oxes stalle
This night I shal be mordred ther I lie!   3005
Now help me, deere brother, or I die!
In alle haste com to me," he saide.
This man out of his sleep for feere abraide;
But whan that he was wakned of his sleep,
He turned him, and took of this no keep.   3010
Him thoughte his dreem nas but a vanitee.
Thus twies in his sleping dremed he,

2983 **preeve** experience   2984 **auctor** writers
2989 **streit of herbergage** short of accommodation   2990 **o** one
2991 **ylogged** lodged   2992 **mosten** had to   2993 **departen** part
2995 And took his lodging as chance determined   2996 **That oon** one
2997 **Fer** a long way off   2999 **aventure** chance   3000 **as in commune** on
an equal footing   3002 **mette** dreamed   3008 **abraide** woke suddenly
3010 He turned over and paid no attention to this   3011 **vanitee** foolishness

And atte thridde time yet his felawe
Cam, as him thoughte, and seide, "I am now slawe.
3015 Bihoold my blody woundes depe and wide!
Aris up erly in the morwe-tide,
And at the west gate of the toun", quod he,
"A carte ful of donge ther shaltow se,
In which my body is hid ful prively.
3020 Do thilke carte aresten boldely.
My gold caused my mordre, sooth to seyn."
– And tolde him every point how he was slain,
With a ful pitous face, pale of hewe.
And truste wel, his dreem he fond ful trewe;
3025 For on the morwe, as soone as it was day,
To his felawes in he took the way.
And whan that he cam to this oxes stalle,
After his felawe he bigan to calle.
        'The hostiler answerede him anon,
3030 And seide, "Sire, youre felawe is agon.
As soone as day, he wente out of the toun."
        'This man gan fallen in suspecioun,
Remembringe on hise dremes that he mette;
And forth he gooth – no lenger wolde he lette –
3035 Unto the west gate of the toun, and fond
A dong carte, as it were to donge lond,
That was arrayed in that same wise
As ye han herd the dede man devise.
And with an hardy herte he gan to crye
3040 Vengeaunce and justice of this felonye:
"My felawe mordred is this same night,
And in this carte he lith gaping upright!
I crye out on the ministres", quod he,
"That sholden kepe and reulen this citee!

3014 **slawe** slain   3016 **morwe-tide** morning   3018 **donge** dung
3020 Have that cart stopped without delay   3022 **point** detail
3023 **hewe** complexion   3026 **in** lodgings   3028 **After** for
3029 **hostiler** inn-keeper   3030 **is agon** has left   3034 **lette** delay
3036 **donge** spread dung on   3039 **hardy** bold   3042 **upright** on his back
3043 **on** against   3044 **kepe** govern

Harrow! allas! Heere lith my felawe slain!"   3045
What sholde I moore unto this tale sayn?
The peple out sterte and caste the cart to grounde,
And in the middel of the dong they founde
The dede man, that mordred was al newe.
  'O blisful God, that art so just and trewe,   3050
Lo how that thow biwreyest mordre alway!
Mordre wol out, that se we day by day.
Mordre is so wlatsom and abhominable
To God, that is so just and resonable,
That he ne wol nat suffre it heled be,   3055
Though it abide a yeer, or two, or thre.
Mordre wol out; this my conclusioun.
And right anon, ministres of that toun
Han hent the cartere and so soore him pined,
And eek the hostiler so soore engined,   3060
That they biknewe hir wikkednesse anon,
And were anhanged by the nekke-bon.
  'Heere may men seen that dremes ben to drede.
And certes, in the same book I rede,
Right in the nexte chapitre after this   3065
– I gabbe nat, so have I joye or blis –
Two men that wolde han passed over see,
For certein cause, into a fer contree,
If that the wind ne hadde ben contrarye,
That made hem in a citee for to tarye,   3070
That stood ful mirye upon an haven-side.
But on a day, again the even-tide,
The wind gan chaunge, and blew right as hem
          leste.
Jolif and glad they wenten unto reste,

3047 **out sterte** rushed out   3049 **al newe** recently   3051 **biwreyest** reveal
3052 **wol out** will become known   3053 **wlatsom** loathsome
3055 **heled be** to be concealed   3059 **hent** seized   **pined** tortured
3060 **engined** tortured   3061 **biknewe** confessed   3062 **anhanged** hanged
3063 **to drede** to be feared   3066 **gabbe nat** do not lie   3071 That stood
very pleasantly by the side of a harbour   3072 **again the even-tide** towards
evening   3074 **Jolif** cheerful

3075   And casten hem ful erly for to saille.
            'But herkneth: to that o man fil a greet mervaille.
        That oon of hem, in sleping as he lay,
        Him mette a wonder dreem again the day.
        Him thoughte a man stood by his beddes side,
3080   And him comanded that he sholde abide,
        And seide him thus: "If thou tomorwe wende,
        Thow shalt be dreint; my tale is at an ende."
            'He wook, and tolde his felawe what he mette,
        And preyde him his viage for to lette;
3085   As for that day, he preyde him to abide.
        His felawe, that lay by his beddes side,
        Gan for to laughe, and scorned him ful faste.
        "No dreem", quod he, "may so min herte agaste
        That I wol lette for to do my thinges!
3090   I sette nat a straw by thy dreminges,
        For swevenes ben but vanitees and japes.
        Men dreme alday of owles or of apes,
        And eek of many a maze therwithal.
        Men dreme of thing that nevere was ne shal.
3095   But sith I see that thou wolt here abide,
        And thus forslewthen wilfully thy tide,
        God woot, it reweth me; and have good day!"
        – And thus he took his leve and wente his way.
        But er that he hadde half his cours yseiled,
3100   Noot I nat why, ne what meschaunce it eiled,
        But casuelly the shippes botme rente,
        And ship and man under the water wente,
        In sighte of othere shippes it biside,
        That with hem seiled at the same tide.

3075 **casten hem** decided   3076 **that o man** one man   3078 Towards day
he dreamed a wonderful dream   3082 **dreint** drowned
3084 **viage** journey **lette** postpone   3088 **agaste** frighten   3089 That I will
put off carrying out my business affairs   3091 **japes** delusions
3093 **maze** delusion   3094 **shal** shall be   3096 **forslewthen** idle away
tide time   3097 **it reweth me** I am sorry   3099 **yseiled** sailed
3100 **Noot I nat** I don't know   3101 **casuelly** by chance **botme** bottom

'And therfore, faire Pertelote so deere,   3105
By swiche ensamples olde maystow leere
That no man sholde been to recchelees
Of dremes, for I sey thee, doutelees,
That many a dreem ful soore is for to drede.

'Lo, in the lif of Seint Kenelm I rede,   3110
That was Kenulphus sone, the noble king
Of Mercenrike, how Kenelm mette a thing.
A lite er he was mordred, on a day,
His mordre in his avisioun he say.
His norice him expowned everydel   3115
His swevene, and bad him for to kepe him wel
For traisoun; but he nas but sevene yeer old,
And therfore litel tale hath he ytold
Of any dreem, so holy was his herte.
By God, I hadde levere than my sherte   3120
That ye hadde rad his legende as have I!

'Dame Pertelote, I sey yow trewely,
Macrobeus, that writ th'avisioun
In Affrike of the worthy Cipioun,
Affermeth dremes, and seyth that they ben   3125
Warninge of thinges that men after sen.
And forthermoore, I pray yow, looketh wel
In th'Olde Testament, of Daniel,
If he heeld dremes any vanitee.
Rede eek of Joseph, and there shul ye see   3130
Wher dremes be somtime – I sey nat alle –
Warninge of thinges that shul after falle.
Looke, of Egypte the king, daun Pharao,
His bakere and his butiller also,

3106 leere learn   3107–8 recchelees Of careless about
3109 soore seriously   3113 A lite er a little before   3114 avisioun dream
3115 expowned interpreted   3116 kepe him guard himself
3117 For against   3118 And therefore he took little account   3120–21 By
God, I would give my shirt for you to have read his legend, as I have
3123 writ (= writeth) writes   3129 Whether he considered dreams
foolishness   3131 Wher whether

3135 Wher they ne felte noon effect in dremes!
Whoso wol seken actes of sondry remes
May rede of dremes many a wonder thing.
'Lo, Cresus, which that was of Lyde king,
Mette he nat that he sat upon a tree,
3140 Which signified he sholde anhanged be?
Lo heere, Andromacha, Ectores wif,
That day that Ector sholde lese his lif,
She dremed on the same night biforn
How that the lif of Ector sholde be lorn
3145 If thilke day he wente into bataille.
She warned him, but it mighte nat availle;
He wente for to fighte nathelees,
But he was slain anon of Achilles.
But thilke tale is al to long to telle,
3150 And eek it is ny day; I may nat dwelle.
Shortly I seye, as for conclusioun,
That I shal han of this avisioun
Adversitee; and I seye forthermoor
That I ne telle of laxatives no stoor,
3155 For they been venimes, I woot it wel.
I hem deffye; I love hem never a del!
'Now lat us speke of mirthe, and stinte al this.
Madame Pertelote, so have I blis,
Of o thing God hath sent me large grace,
3160 For whan I se the beautee of youre face,
Ye ben so scarlet-reed aboute youre eyen,
It maketh al my drede for to dien.
For al so siker as *In principio*,
Mulier est hominis confusio.

3135 **effect** consequence   3136 **remes** realms   3138 **Lyde** Lydia
3142 **sholde lese** was to lose   3144 **lorn** lost   3148 **anon** immediately
3150 **dwelle** linger   3154 **telle of ... no stoor** set no store by
3155 **venimes** poisons   3156 **deffye** reject   **never a del** not at all
3157 **stinte** leave off   3159 **large grace** great good fortune   3162 It causes
all my fear to vanish   3163 **siker** sure   3164 see n.

– Madame, the sentence of this Latin is: 3165
"Womman is mannes joye and al his blis."
For whan I feele a-night your softe side
– Al be it that I may nat on yow ride,
For that oure perche is maad so narwe, allas! –
I am so ful of joye and of solas,   3170
That I deffye bothe swevene and dreem.'
    And with that word, he fley doun fro the beem,
For it was day, and eke hise hennes alle,
And with a chuk he gan hem for to calle,
For he hadde founde a corn lay in the yerd.   3175
Real he was, he was namoore aferd;
He fethered Pertelote twenty time,
And trad hire eke as ofte, er it was prime.
He looketh as it were a grim leoun,
And on hise toos he rometh up and doun;   3180
Him deined nat to sette his foot to grounde.
He chukketh whan he hath a corn yfounde,
And to him rennen thanne his wives alle.
Thus real, as a prince is in his halle,
Leve I this Chauntecleer in his pasture,   3185
And after wol I telle his aventure.
    Whan that the monthe in which the world
            bigan,
That highte March, whan God first maked man,
Was complet, and ypassed were also,
Sin March was gon, thritty dayes and two,   3190
Bifel that Chauntecler, in al his pride,
Hise sevene wives walking him biside,
Caste up hise eyen to the brighte sonne,
That in the signe of Taurus hadde yronne

3165 **sentence** meaning   3168 **ride** mount (sexual sense)
3170 **solas** pleasure   3172 **fley** flew   3175 **corn** grain of wheat
3176 **Real** regal **aferd** afraid   3177 **fethered** covered with outstretched
wing-feathers (while copulating)   3178 **trad** mounted (in a sexual sense)
prime 9 a.m. (g.)   3180 **rometh** strolls   3182 **chukketh** clucks
3185 **in his pasture** feeding   3186 **his aventure** what happened to him
3188 **highte** is called   3194 **yronne** run

3195   Twenty degrees and oon, and somwhat moore,
        And knew by kinde, and by noon oother loore,
        That it was prime, and krew with blisful stevene.
        'The sonne', he seide, 'is clomben up on hevene
        Fourty degrees and oon, and moore, iwys.
3200   Madame Pertelote, my worldes blis,
        Herkneth thise blisful briddes how they singe,
        And se the fresshe floures how they springe!
        Ful is min herte of revel and solas!'
            But sodeinly him fil a sorweful cas;
3205   For evere the latter ende of joye is wo.
        God woot that worldly joye is soone ago;
        And if a rethor koude faire endite
        He in a cronicle saufly mighte it write
        As for a soverein notabilitee.
3210   Now every wis man, lat him herkne me;
        This storye is also trewe, I undertake,
        As is the book of Launcelot de Lake,
        That wommen holde in ful gret reverence.
        Now wol I torne again to my sentence.
3215   A col-fox, ful of sly iniquitee,
        That in the grove hadde woned yeres three,
        By heigh imaginacioun forncast,
        The same night thurghout the hegges brast
        Into the yerd ther Chauntecleer the faire
3220   Was wont, and eek hise wives, to repaire;
        And in a bed of wortes stille he lay
        Til it was passed undren of the day,

3196 **kinde** nature **loore** teaching   3197 **stevene** voice
3198 **is clomben** has climbed   3200 **worldes blis** worldly happiness
3204 **fil** befell   3207 **rethor** rhetorician **faire endite** write well
3209 **notabilitee** notable fact   3211 **also** as   3214 **sentence** subject
3215 **col-fox** fox with black feet, ears and tail   3216 **woned** lived
3217 **imaginacioun forncast** premeditated scheming (n.)   3218 **brast** broke
3219 **ther** where   3220 **repaire** resort   3221 **wortes** greens
3222 **undren** mid-morning (g.)

Waitinge his time on Chauntecleer to falle,
As gladly doon thise homicides alle
That in await liggen to mordre men.   3225
    O false mordrour, lurkinge in thy den!
O newe Scariot, newe Geniloun!
False dissimulour, O Greek Sinoun,
That broghtest Troye al outrely to sorwe!
O Chauntecleer, acursed be that morwe   3230
That thow into the yerd flaugh fro the bemes!
Thow were ful wel ywarned by thy dremes
That thilke day was perilous to thee.
– But what that God forwoot moot nedes be,
After the opinioun of certein clerkis.   3235
Witnesse on him that any parfit clerk is,
That in scole is greet altercacioun
In this matere, and greet disputisoun,
And hath ben of an hundred thousand men.
But I ne kan nat bulte it to the bren   3240
As kan the holy doctour Augustin,
Or Boece, or the bisshop Bradwardin
– Wheither that Goddes worthy forewiting
Streineth me nedely for to doon a thing
– 'Nedely' clepe I simple necessitee –   3245
Or ellis if fre chois be graunted me
To do that same thing, or do it noght,
Though God forwoot it er that I was wroght,
Or if his witing streineth never a del
But by necessitee condicionel.   3250

3223 **Waitinge** watching for   3224 **gladly** customarily
homicides murderers   3225 **in await liggen** lie in ambush
3226 **mordrour** murderer   3228 **dissimulour** dissembler
3229 **al outrely** utterly   3231 **flaugh** flew   3234 **forwoot** has
foreknowledge of   3235 **After** according to   3237 **altercacioun** wrangling
3240 **bulte it to the bren** sift out the valid arguments
3243 **forewiting** foreknowledge   3244 **Streineth** constrains
nedely necessarily   3245 **simple necessitee** see n.   3248 **wroght** created
3249 **witing** knowledge   3250 **But** except   **necessitee condicionel** see n.

I wol nat han to do of swich matere;
My tale is of a cok, as ye may heere,
That took his conseil of his wif, with sorwe,
To walken in the yerd upon that morwe
3255   That he hadde met the dreem that I yow tolde.
Wommens conseils ben ful ofte colde;
Wommanes conseil broghte us first to wo,
And made Adam fro Paradis to go,
Theras he was ful mirye and wel at ese.
3260   But for I noot to whom it mighte displese
If I conseil of wommen wolde blame,
Passe over, for I seide it in my game.
Rede auctours, where they trete of swich matere,
And what they seyn of wommen ye may heere.
3265   Thise been the cokkes wordes, and nat mine;
I kan noon harm of no womman devine.

         Faire in the sond, to bathe hire mirily,
Lith Pertelote, and alle hir sustres by,
Again the sonne, and Chauntecleer so free
3270   Song mirier than the mermaide in the see
(For Phisiologus seyth sikerly
How that they singen wel and mirily).
And so bifel, that as he caste his eye,
Among the wortes, on a boterflye,
3275   He was war of this fox that lay ful lowe.
Nothing ne liste him thanne for to crowe,
But cride anon, 'Cok! cok!', and up he sterte,
As man that was affrayed in his herte;
For naturelly a beest desireth flee
3280   Fro his contrarye, if he may it see,

3251 of with   3253 conseil advice with sorwe more's the pity
3255 met dreamed   3256 colde fatal   3262 in my game in jest
3266 devine imagine   3267 sond sand   3268 Lith lies
3269 Again the sonne in the sun free noble   3270 mirier more sweetly
3271 sikerly for a certainty   3276 Nothing ne liste him he had no desire at
all   3277 sterte sprang   3280 contrarye enemy

Though he nevere erst hadde seyn it with his eye.
   This Chauntecleer, whan he gan him espye,
He wolde han fled, but that the fox anon
Seide, 'Gentil sire, allas, wher wol ye gon?
Be ye affrayd of me that am youre freend?   3285
Now, certes, I were worse than a feend
If I to yow wolde harm or vileinye!
I am nat come youre conseil for t'espye;
But trewely, the cause of my cominge
Was oonly for to herkne how that ye singe.   3290
For trewely, ye han as mirye a stevene
As any aungel hath that is in hevene.
Therwith ye han in musik moore feelinge
Than hadde Boece, or any that kan singe.
My lord youre fader – God his soule blesse! –   3295
And eek youre moder, of hire gentillesse,
Han in min hous yben, to my greet ese.
And certes, sire, ful fain wolde I yow plese.
   'But for men speke of singinge, I wol seye
– So mote I brouke wel mine eyen tweye –   3300
Save yow, I herde nevere man so singe
As dide youre fader in the morweninge.
Certes, it was of herte, al that he song!
And for to make his vois the moore strong,
He wolde so peine him that with bothe hise eyen   3305
He moste winke, so loude he wolde cryen,
And stonden on his tiptoon therwithal,
And strecche forth his nekke long and smal;
And eek he was of swich discrecioun
That ther nas no man in no regioun   3310

3281 **erst** before   3282 **gan him espye** caught sight of him
3287 **wolde** were to wish   3288 **youre conseil for t'espye** to spy on your
private affairs   3291 **stevene** voice   3293 **feelinge** skill
3296 **gentillesse** kindness   3299 **for men speke of singinge** since singing has
been mentioned   3300 As I live (*lit.* as I may have the use of my two eyes)
3303 **of herte** from the heart   3305 **so peine him** make such an effort
3306 **moste winke** had to shut   3307 **tiptoon** tiptoes   3308 **smal** thin

That him in song or wisdom mighte passe.
I have wel rad, in Daun Burnel the Asse,
Among his vers, how that ther was a cok,
That, for a preestes sone yaf him a knok
3315 Upon his leg, whil he was yong and nice,
He made him for to lese his benefice.
But certein, ther nis no comparisoun
Bitwix the wisdom and discrecioun
Of youre fader, and of his subtiltee!
3320 Now singeth, sire, for seinte charitee;
Lat se, konne ye youre fader countrefete!'
      This Chauntecleer hise winges gan to bete,
As man that koude his traisoun nat espye,
So was he ravisshed with his flaterye.
3325   Allas, ye lordes, many a fals flatour
Is in youre courtes, and many a losengeour,
That plesen yow wel moore, by my feith,
Than he that soothfastnesse unto yow seyth!
Redeth Ecclesiaste of flaterye;
3330 Beth war, ye lordes, of hir trecherye.
      This Chauntecleer stood hye upon his toos,
Strecchinge his nekke, and heeld hise eyen cloos,
And gan to crowe loude for the nones.
And daun Russell the fox stirte up atones,
3335 And by the gargat hente Chauntecleer,
And on his bak toward the wode him beer,
For yet ne was ther no man that him sewed.
      O destinee, that mayst nat been eschewed!
Allas, that Chauntecler fleigh fro the bemes!
3340 Allas, his wif ne roghte nat of dremes!
– And on a Friday fil al this meschaunce.
      O Venus, that art goddesse of plesaunce,

3315 **nice** foolish   3316 **benefice** ecclesiastical living
3320 **seinte charitee** holy charity's sake   3321 **countrefete** imitate
3323 **espye** detect   3325 **flatour** flatterer   3326 **losengeour** sycophant
3332 **cloos** shut   3334 **stirte** sprang **atones** at once   3335 **gargat** throat
hente seized   3337 **sewed** pursued   3338 **eschewed** evaded
3339 **fleigh** flew   3340 **ne roghte nat** did not take any notice

Sin that thy servant was this Chauntecleer,
And in thy service dide al his power,
Moore for delit than world to multiplye, 3345
Why woldestow suffre him on thy day to die?

O Gaufred, deere maister soverain,
That, whan thy worthy king Richard was slain
With shot, compleinedest his deth so soore,
Why nadde I now thy sentence and thy loore, 3350
The Friday for to chide, as diden ye?
– For on a Friday, soothly, slain was he.
Thanne wolde I shewe yow how that I koude
      pleine
For Chauntecleres drede, and for his peine.

Certes, swich cry ne lamentacioun 3355
Was nevere of ladies maad whan Ilioun
Was wonne, and Pirrus with his streite swerd,
Whan he hadde hent King Priam by the berd
And slain him, as seyth us *Eneydos*,
As maden alle the hennes in the clos 3360
Whan they hadde seyn of Chauntecleer the sighte.
But sovereinly dame Pertelote shrighte,
Ful louder than dide Hasdrubales wif,
Whan that hire housbonde hadde ylost his lif,
And that the Romains hadden brend Cartage; 3365
She was so ful of torment and of rage
That wilfully into the fir she sterte,
And brende hirselven with a stedefast herte.

O woful hennes, right so criden ye
As, whan that Nero brende the citee 3370
Of Rome, criden senatoures wives,
For that hir housbondes losten alle hire lives;

3343 Sin that since   3346 suffre allow   3347 soverain supreme
3349 shot an arrow   soore bitterly   3350 sentence wisdom loore skill
3353 pleine lament   3354 peine suffering   3357 streite swerd drawn
sword   3360 clos yard   3361 seyn seen   3362 sovereinly pre-eminently
shrighte shrieked   3365 brend burned   3367 wilfully voluntarily
sterte leaped

Withouten gilt this Nero hath hem slain.
Now wol I turne to my tale again.
3375   The sely widwe, and eek hire doghtres two,
Herden thise hennes crye and maken wo,
And out at dores stirten they anon,
And syen the fox toward the grove gon,
And bar upon his bak the cok away,
3380   And criden, 'Out! Harrow!' and 'Weilaway!
Ha, ha, the fox!' – and after him they ran,
And eek with staves many another man.
Ran Colle oure dogge, and Talbot, and Gerland,
And Malkin with a distaf in hire hand;
3385   Ran cow and calf, and eek the verray hogges,
So fered for the berking of the dogges,
And showtinge of the men and wommen eek,
They ronne so, hem thoughte hir herte breek.
They yelleden as fendes doon in helle;
3390   The dokes criden as men wolde hem quelle;
The gees for feere flowen over the trees;
Out of the hive cam the swarm of bees.
So hidous was the noise – a, *benedicitee!* –
Certes, he Jakke Straw and his meinee
3395   Ne made nevere shoutes half so shrille,
Whan that they wolden any Fleming kille,
As thilke day was maad upon the fox.
Of bras they broghten bemes, and of box,
Of horn, of boon, in whiche they blewe and powped,
3400   And therwithal they skriked and they howped;
It semed as that hevene sholde falle!
Now, goode men, I prey yow, herkneth alle:
Lo, how Fortune turneth sodeinly

3375 **sely** poor   3377 **stirten** rushed   3378 **syen** saw
3380 **Weilaway** alas   3382 **staves** staffs   3386 **fered for** frightened by
berking barking   3388 They ran so hard they thought their hearts would
break   3390 **as** as if **quelle** kill   3391 **flowen** flew
3394 **meinee** followers   3398 **bemes** trumpets **box** box-wood
3399 **powped** tooted   3400 **skriked** shrieked **howped** whooped

The hope and pride eek of hire enemy!
This cok, that lay upon the foxes bak,   3405
In al his drede unto the fox he spak
And seide, 'Sire, if that I were as ye,
Yit sholde I seyn, as wis God helpe me,
"Turneth again, ye proude cherles alle!
A verray pestilence upon yow falle!   3410
Now I am come unto this wodes side,
Maugree youre heed, the cok shal here abide.
I wol him ete, in feith, and that anon!"'
    The fox answerde, 'In feith, it shal be don!'
– And as he spak that word, al sodeinly   3415
This cok brak from his mouth deliverly,
And hye upon a tree he fley anon.
And whan the fox say that the cok was gon,
'Allas!' quod he, 'O Chauntecleer, allas!
I have to yow', quod he, 'ydoon trespas,   3420
Inasmuche as I maked yow aferd,
Whan I yow hente and broghte out of the yerd.
But sire, I dide it in no wikke entente;
Com doun, and I shal telle yow what I mente.
I shal seye sooth to yow, God help me so!'   3425
    'Nay, thanne', quod he, 'I shrewe us bothe two!
And first I shrewe myself, bothe blood and bones,
If thow bigile me any ofter than ones!
Thou shalt namoore, thurgh thy flaterye,
Do me to singe and winken with min eye;   3430
For he that winketh whan he sholde see,
Al wilfully, God lat him nevere thee!'
    'Nay,' quod the fox, 'but God yeve him
           meschaunce
That is so undiscreet of governaunce

3408 Yit then   3410 pestilence plague   3412 Maugree youre heed in spite
of all you can do   abide remain   3416 deliverly nimbly   3417 fley flew
3418 say saw   3420 trespas wrong   3423 entente intention
3426 shrewe curse   3430 Do me to singe cause me to sing
3432 thee prosper   3434 governaunce behaviour

3435   That jangleth whan he sholde holde his pees!'
     Lo, swich it is for to be recchelees,
     And necligent, and truste on flaterye!
      But ye that holden this tale a folye,
     As of a fox, or of a cok and hen,
3440   Taketh the moralitee, goode men.
     For Seint Paul seyth that al that writen is,
     To oure doctrine it is ywrite, iwys.
     Taketh the fruit, and lat the chaf be stille.
     Now, goode God, if that it be thy wille
3445   (As seyth my lord), so make us alle goode men,
     And bringe us to thy heighe blisse! Amen.

Heere is ended the Nonnes Preestes Tale.

THE EPILOGUE TO THE
NUN'S PRIEST'S TALE

     'Sire Nonnes Preest,' oure Hooste seide anoon,
     'Iblissed be thy breche, and every stoon!
     This was a murye tale of Chauntecleer.
3450   *But, by my trouthe, if thou were seculer,*
     Thou woldest ben a tredefoul aright;
     For if thou have corage as thou hast might,
     The were nede of hennes, as I wene,
     Ya, mo than sevene times seventene!
3455   *Se, whiche braunes hath this gentil preest,*
     So gret a nekke, and swich a large breest!

3435 **jangleth** chatters   3436 **recchelees** careless   3443 **chaf** chaff

3448 **breche** breeches   **stoon** ball, testicle   3451 **tredefoul** hen-shagger, stud
3453 **The were nede** you would need   3455 **braunes** muscles

He loketh as a sparhauke with hise eyen;
Him nedeth nat his colour for to dyghen
With brasile, ne with grein of Portingale.
Now, sire, faire falle yow for youre tale!'   3460
And after that he, with ful merye chere,
Seide unto another, as ye shuln heere.

3457 **sparhauke** sparrow-hawk   3458 **dyghen** dye   3459 **brasile** dye made
from brazilwood **grein of Portingale** scarlet dye from Portugal
3460 **faire falle yow** blessings on you

THE SECOND NUN'S
PROLOGUE

The Prologe of the Seconde Nonnes Tale.

The ministre and the norice unto vices,
Which that men clepe in Englissh idelnesse,
That porter of the gate is of delices,
To eschue, and by hir contrarye hire oppresse
5   – That is to seyn, by leveful bisinesse –
Wel oghten we to doon al oure entente,
Lest that the feend thurgh idelnesse us hente.

For he, that with his thousand cordes slye
Continuelly us waiteth to biclappe,
10   Whan he may man in idelnesse espye,
He kan so lightly cacche him in his trappe,
Til that a man be hent right by the lappe,
He nis nat war the feend hath him in honde!
Wel oghte us werche, and idelnesse withstonde.

15   And thogh men dradden nevere for to die,
Yet seen men wel by resoun, doutelees,
That idelnesse is roten slogardye,
Of which ther nevere comth no good n'encrees,

---

1 **ministre** servant **norice** nurse   2 **clepe** call   3 **delices** pleasures   4 To avoid, and to oppress by means of her (Idleness's) opposite
5 **leveful bisinesse** legitimate activity   6 **doon al oure entente** take great pains   7 **feend** devil **hente** lay hold of   8 **slye** subtle   9 **waiteth** lies in wait **biclappe** trap suddenly   11 **lightly** easily   12 **lappe** sleeve
13 **hath him in honde** has control of him   14 **oghte us** we ought **withstonde** resist   15 **dradden nevere** were not to be at all afraid

And seen that slouthe hir holdeth in a lees
Oonly to slepe, and for to ete and drinke,   20
And to devouren al that othere swinke.

And for to putte us from swich idelnesse
That cause is of so greet confusioun,
I have here doon my feithful bisinesse,
After the legende in translacioun   25
Right of thy glorious lif and passioun –
Thow with thy gerland wroght of rose and lilye,
Thee mene I, maide and martyr, Seinte Cecilye.

And thow, that flour of virgines art alle,
Of whom that Bernard list so wel to write,   30
To thee at my biginning first I calle;
Thow confort of us wrecches, do m'endite
Thy maidens deeth, that wan thurgh hir merite
The eternal lif, and of the feend victorye,
As man may after reden in hir storye.   35

Thow maide and moder, doghter of thy sone,
Thow welle of mercy, sinful soules cure,
In whom that God for bountee chees to wone,
Thow humble, and heigh over every creature,
Thow nobledest so ferforth oure nature   40
That no desdein the Makere hadde of kinde
His sone in blood and flessh to clothe and winde.

19 **hir holdeth in a lees** confines herself   21 **othere swinke** others produce by
labour   23 **so** such   24 **doon my feithful bisinesse** made an honest effort
25 **After** according to   **legende** saint's life   26 **passioun** martyrdom
27 **wroght** made   30 **list** likes   32 **do m'endite** enable me to write
37 **welle** fount   38 **chees** chose   **wone** dwell   40 **nobledest** ennobled
so ferforth to such an extent   41 **Makere . . . of kinde** Creator of nature

Withinne the cloistre blisful of thy sidis
Took mannes shap the eternal love and pees,
45   That of the trine compas lord and gide is,
Whom erthe, and see, and hevene, out of relees,
Ay herien, and thow, virgine wemmelees,
Bar of thy body, and dweltest maiden pure,
The creatour of every creature.

50   Assembled is in thee magnificence
With mercy, goodnesse, and with swich pitee
That thow, that art the sonne of excellence,
Nat oonly helpest hem that prayen thee,
But ofte time, of thy benignitee,
55   Ful frely, er that men thin help biseche,
Thow goost biforn, and art hir lives leche.

Now help, thow meke and blisful faire maide,
Me, flemed wrecche, in this desert of galle!
Think on the womman Cananee, that saide
60   That whelpes eten somme of the crommes alle
That from hir lordes table been yfalle.
And though that I, unworthy sone of Eve,
Be sinful, yet accepte my bileve.

And, for that feith is deed withouten werkis,
65   So for to werken yif me wit and space
That I be quit from thennes that moost derk is.
O thow, that art so fair and ful of grace,

43 **blisful** blessed **sidis** sides (of the body)   45 **the trine compas** the three
'worlds' (heaven, earth and sea)   46 **out of relees** without ceasing
47 **herien** worship **wemmelees** undefiled   48 **dweltest** remained
54 **benignitee** graciousness   55 **frely** generously   56 **leche** healer
58 **flemed** exiled **galle** bitterness   59 **Cananee** Canaanite
60 **whelpes** dogs **crommes** crumbs   61 **been yfalle** have fallen
63 **bileve** faith   65 **wit and space** ability and opportunity
66 **I be quit** I may be free   **from thennes** from the place

Be min advocate in that heighe place
Theras withouten ende is songe 'Osanne',
Thow, Cristes moder, doghter deere of Anne.   70

And of thy light my soule in prison lighte,
That troubled is by the contagioun
Of my body, and also by the wighte
Of erthely lust and fals affeccioun.
O havene of refut, O savacioun   75
Of hem that been in sorwe and in distresse,
Now help, for to my werk I wol me dresse.

Yet praye ich yow that reden that I write,
Foryeve me that I do no diligence
This ilke storye subtilly t'endite;   80
For bothe have I, the wordes and sentence,
Of him that at the seintes reverence
The storye wroot, and folwen hir legende,
And pray yow that ye wol my werk amende.

First wolde I yow the name of Seint Cecilye   85
Expowne, as men may in hir storye se.
It is to seye in Englissh 'hevenes lilye',
For pure chastnesse of virginitee;
Or, for she whitnesse hadde of honestee,
And grene of conscience, and of good fame   90
The swote savour, 'lilye' was hir name.

Or Cecile is to seye 'the wey to blinde',
For she ensample was by good techinge.
Or ellis Cecile, as I writen finde,
Is joined by a manere conjoininge   95

69 **Theras** where **Osanne** Hosanna   71 **lighte** illuminate
73 **wighte** weight   74 **lust** pleasure   75 **refut** refuge   77 **me dresse** turn
79 **do no diligence** take no pains   80 **subtilly** artfully   81 **sentence** content
82 From him who, in honour of the saint   85 **wolde I** I would like
86 **Expowne** explain   89 **honestee** purity   91 **swote savour** sweet smell
95 **conjoininge** conjunction

Of 'hevene' and 'lia'; and here in figuringe
The hevene is set for thoght of holinesse,
And 'lia' for hir lasting bisinesse.

Cecile may eek be seid in this manere:
'Wantinge of blindnesse', for hir grete light
Of sapience, and for hir thewes clere.
Or elles, lo, this maidenes name bright
Of 'hevene' and 'leos' comth, for which by right
Men mighte hire wel 'the hevene of peple' calle,
Ensample of goode and wise werkes alle.

For 'leos' 'peple' in Englissh is to seye,
And right as men may in the hevene see
The sonne and moone and sterres every weye,
Right so men goostly in this maiden free
Sayen of feith the magnanimitee,
And eek the cleernesse hool of sapience,
And sondry werkes brighte of excellence.

And right so as thise philosophres write
That hevene is swift and round and eek brenninge,
Right so was faire Cecilye the white
Ful swift and bisy evere in good werkinge,
And round and hool in good perseveringe,
And brenning evere in charite ful brighte.
Now have I yow declared what she highte.

---

96 **in figuringe** symbolically   98 **lasting bisinesse** constant activity
100 **Wantinge** lack   101 **sapience** wisdom **thewes clere** pure morals
108 **every weye** in every direction   109 **goostly** spiritually **free** gracious
110 **Sayen** saw **magnanimitee** lofty-mindedness   114 **brenninge** burning
117 **perseveringe** perseverance   119 **declared** explained **highte** was called

THE SECOND NUN'S TALE

Heere biginneth the Seconde Nonnes
Tale of the lif of Seinte Cecile.

This maiden bright Cecile, as hir lif seyth,   120
Was come of Romains, and of noble kinde;
And from hir cradel up fostred in the feith
Of Crist, and bar his gospel in hir minde.
She nevere cessed, as I writen finde,
Of hir prayere, and God to love and drede,   125
Biseking him to kepe hir maidenhede.

And whan this maiden sholde unto a man
Ywedded be, that was ful yong of age,
Which that ycleped was Valerian,
And day was comen of hir mariage,   130
She, ful devout and humble in hir corage,
Under hir robe of gold that sat ful faire,
Hadde next hir flessh yclad hire in an haire.

And whil the organs maden melodye,
To God allone in herte thus song she: 135
'O lord, my soule and eek my body gye
Unwemmed, lest that I confounded be!'
And for his love that deide upon a tree,
Every seconde and thridde day she faste,
Ay bidding in hir orisons ful faste.   140

121 **kinde** family   125 **drede** reverence   126 **kepe hir maidenhede** preserve
her virginity   131 **corage** heart   132 **sat ful faire** sat very well on her
133 **yclad hire** clothed herself   **haire** hair-shirt   134 **organs** organ (n.)
136 **gye** keep   137 **Unwemmed** undefiled   **confounded** led into perdition
139 **faste** (= *fastede*) fasted   140 **bidding in hir orisons** saying her prayers
faste earnestly

The night cam, and to bedde moste she gon
With hire housbonde, as ofte is the manere;
And prively to him she seide anon:
'O swete and wel biloved spouse deere,
145   Ther is a conseil, and ye wolde it heere,
Which that right fain I wolde unto yow seye,
So that ye swere ye shul it nat biwreye.'

Valerian gan faste unto hir swere
That for no cas, ne thing that mighte be,
150   He sholde neveremo biwreyen here.
And thanne at erst to him thus seide she:
'I have an aungel which that loveth me,
That with gret love, wherso I wake or slepe,
Is redy ay my body for to kepe.

155   'And if that he may feelen, out of drede,
That ye me touche or love in vileinye,
He right anon wol sleen yow with the dede,
And in youre youthe thus ye shullen die.
And if that ye in clene love me gye,
160   He wol yow love as me, for youre clennesse,
And shewen yow his joye and his brightnesse.'

Valerian, corrected as God wolde,
Answerde again: 'If I shal trusten thee,
Lat me that aungel seen, and him biholde,
165   And if that it a verray aungel be,

141 **moste** had to   143 **prively** privately   145 **conseil** secret **and if**
146 **fain** gladly   147 **So that** provided that **biwreye** reveal
148 **faste** solemnly   149 **for no cas** under no circumstances
150 **neveremo** never   151 **at erst** first   153 **wherso** whether
154 **my body for to kepe** to protect my person   155 **out of drede** without
doubt   156 **in vileinye** in a shameful way   157 **sleen** kill **with the dede** in
the act   159 **clene** chaste   162 **corrected** disciplined

Thanne wol I doon as thow hast prayed me.
And if thow love another man, for sothe,
Right with this swerd than wol I sle yow bothe.'

Cecile answerde anon-right in this wise:
'If that yow list, the aungel shal ye se,   170
So that ye trowe on Crist and yow baptise.
Goth forth to Via Apia,' quod she,
'That fro this toun ne stant but miles thre,
And to the povre folkes that ther dwelle
Sey hem right thus, as that I shal yow telle.   175

'Telle hem that I, Cecile, yow to hem sente,
To shewen yow the goode Urban the olde,
For secree nedes, and for good entente.
And whan that ye Seint Urban han biholde,
Telle him the wordes whiche I to yow tolde.   180
And whan that he hath purged yow fro sinne,
Thanne shal ye seen that aungel er ye twinne.'

Valerian is to the place ygon,
And right as him was taught by his lerninge,
He foond this holy olde Urban anon,   185
Among the seintes buriels lotinge.
And he anon, withouten taryinge,
Dide his message; and whan that he it tolde,
Urban for joye hise handes gan up holde.

The teeris from hise eyen leet he falle.   190
'Almighty lord, O Jesu Crist,' quod he,
'Sowere of chaast conseil, hierde of us alle,
The fruit of thilke seed of chastitee

168 **sle** kill   169 **anon-right** at once   170 **yow list** it pleases you
171 **So that** provided that   **trowe on** believe in   173 **stant** (= *standeth*) is
located   174 **povre** poor   178 **nedes** business **entente** purpose
182 **twinne** depart   186 **buriels** tombs (see n. to SN 172)   **lotinge** lurking
192 **conseil** intention   **hierde** shepherd

That thow hast sowe in Cecile, taak to thee!
195   Lo, lik a bisy bee, withouten gile,
Thee serveth ay thin owene thral Cecile!

'For thilke spouse that she took but now
Ful lik a fiers leoun, she sendeth heere
As meke as evere was any lamb, to yow.'
200   And with that word anon ther gan appeere
An old man, clad in white clothes cleere,
That hadde a book with lettre of gold in honde,
And gan bifore Valerian to stonde.

Valerian as deed fil doun for drede
205   Whan he him say, and he up hente him tho,
And on his book right thus he gan to rede:
'O lord, o feith, o God withoute mo;
O Cristendom, and fader of alle also,
Aboven alle and overal everywhere.'
210   Thise wordes al with gold ywriten were.

Whan this was rad, thanne seide this olde man:
'Levestow this thing or no? – Sey ye or nay!'
'I leve al this thing,' quod Valerian,
'For sother thing than this, I dar wel say,
215   Under the hevene no wight thinke may.'
Tho vanisshed this olde man – he niste where –
And Pope Urban him cristnede right there.

Valerian goth hoom and fint Cecilye
Withinne his chambre with an aungel stonde.
220   This aungel hadde of roses and of lilye
Corones two, the whiche he bar in honde.

196 **thral** servant   201 **cleere** shining   205 **say** saw   **up hente** raised up
207 **O** one   **withoute mo** alone   208 **Cristendom** baptism   211 **rad** read
out   212 **Levestow** (= *levest thow*) do you believe   214 **sother** truer
215 **no wight** no one   **may** can   216 **Tho** then   **niste** did not know
218 **fint** (= *findeth*) finds   221 **Corones** crowns   **bar** carried

And first to Cecile, as I understonde,
He yaf that oon, and after gan he take
That oother to Valerian, hir make.

'With body clene, and with unwemmed thoght,   225
Kepeth ay wel thise corones,' quod he.
'Fro Paradis to yow have I hem broght;
Ne neveremo ne shal they roten be,
Ne lese hir swote savour, trusteth me,
Ne nevere wight shal seen hem with his eye   230
But he be chaast and hate vileinye.

'And thow, Valerian, for thow so soone
Assentedest to good conseil also,
Sey what thee list, and thow shalt han thy boone.'
'I have a brother,' quod Valerian tho,   235
'That in this world I love no man so.
I pray yow that my brother may han grace
To knowe the trouthe, as I do in this place.'

The aungel seide, 'God liketh thy requeste,
And bothe, with the palm of martyrdom,   240
Ye shullen come unto his blisful feste.'
And with that word Tiburce his brother coom,
And whan that he the savour undernoom
Which that the roses and the lilies caste,
Withinne his herte he gan to wondre faste,   245

And seide, 'I wondre, this time of the yere,
Whennes that swote savour cometh so
Of roses and lilies that I smelle heer!
For thogh I hadde hem in mine handes two,

250   The savour mighte in me no depper go.
       The swete smel that in min herte I finde
       Hath chaunged me al in another kinde.'

       Valerian seide, 'Two corones han we,
       Snow white and rose reed, that shinen clere,
255   Whiche that thine eyen han no might to se;
       And as thow smellest hem thurgh my prayere,
       So shaltow seen hem, leve brother deere,
       If it so be thow wolt, withouten slouthe,
       Bileve aright, and knowen verray trouthe.'

260   Tiburce answerde, 'Seistow this to me
       In soothnesse, or in dreem I herkne this?'
       'In dremes', quod Valerian, 'han we be
       Unto this time, brother min, iwys,
       And now at erst in trouthe oure dwelling is.'
265   'How wostow this?' quod Tiburce, 'in what wise?'
       Quod Valerian, 'That shal I thee devise.

       'The aungel of God hath me the trouthe ytaught,
       Which thow shalt seen, if that thow wolt reneye
       The idoles and be clene, and elles naught.'
270   – And of the miracle of thise corones tweye
       Seint Ambrose in his Preface list to seye;
       Solempnely this noble doctour deere
       Commendeth it, and seyth in this manere:

       'The palm of martyrdom for to receive,
275   Seinte Cecile, fulfild of Goddes yifte,
       The world and eek hir chambre gan she weive.
       Witnesse Tiburces and Valerians shrifte,

252 kinde nature   257 leve beloved   259 knowen acknowledge
261 soothnesse truth   264 at erst for the first time
265 wostow (= *wost thow*) do you know   266 devise tell
268 reneye renounce   269 clene pure   271 Preface see n.
276 chambre marriage-chamber **gan . . . weive** gave up
277 shrifte profession of faith

To whiche God of his bountee wolde shifte
Corones two of floures wel smellinge,
And made his aungel hem the corones bringe.   280

'The maide hath broght thise men to blisse above;
The world hath wist what it is worth, certein,
Devocioun of chastitee to love.'
Tho shewed him Cecile al open and plein
That alle idoles nis but a thing in vein,   285
For they been dombe, and therto they been deve,
And charged him hise idoles for to leve.

'Whoso that troweth nat this, a beest he is,'
Quod tho Tiburce, 'if that I shal nat lie.'
And she gan kisse his brest that herde this,   290
And was ful glad he koude trouthe espye.
'This day I take thee for min allye,'
Seide this blisful faire maide deere,
And after that she seide as ye may heere:

'Lo, right so as the love of Crist', quod she,   295
'Made me thy brotheres wif, right in that wise
Anon for min allye heere take I thee,
Sin that thow wolt thine idoles despise.
Go with thy brother now, and thee baptise,
And make thee clene, so that thow mowe biholde   300
The aungeles face, of which thy brother tolde.'

Tiburce answerde and seide, 'Brother deere,
First tel me whider I shal, and to what man.'
'To whom?' quod he, 'Com forth with right good
        cheere;

278 **bountee** goodness **shifte** assign   282 **wist** learned   286 **dombe** dumb
deve deaf   287 **leve** renounce   291 **espye** discern   292 **allye** kinsman
300 **mowe** may   303 **whider I shal** where I shall go
304 **with right good cheere** cheerfully

305   I wol thee lede unto the Pope Urban.'
        'Til Urban, brother min Valerian?'
        Quod tho Tiburce, 'Woltow me thider lede?
        Me thinketh that it were a wonder dede!

        'Ne menestow nat Urban,' quod he tho,
310   'That is so ofte dampned to be deed,
        And woneth in halkes alwey to and fro,
        And dar nat ones putte forth his heed?
        Men sholde him brennen in a fir so reed
        If he were founde, or that men mighte him spye,
315   And we also, to bere him compaignye!

        'And whil we seken thilke divinitee
        That is yhid in hevene prively,
        Algate ybrend in this world shul we be.'
        To whom Cecile answerde boldely:
320   'Men mighten dreden wel and skilfully
        This lif to lese, min owene deere brother,
        If this were living oonly, and noon oother.

        'But ther is bettre lif in oother place,
        That nevere shal be lost, ne drede thee noght,
325   Which Goddes Sone us tolde thurgh his grace.
        That Fadres Sone hath alle thinges wroght,
        And al that wroght is, with a skilful thoght
        The Goost that fro the Fader gan procede
        Hath souled hem, withouten any drede.

306 **Til** to   308 It seems to me that that would be an amazing thing to do
310 **dampned** condemned   311 And lives in hiding-places, always here and
there   312 **putte forth his heed** show himself   313 **brennen** burn
318 **Algate** entirely **ybrend** burned   320 **skilfully** reasonably
322 **living oonly** the only life   324 **ne drede thee noght** do not doubt
326 **wroght** created   327 **skilful** rational   329 **souled** endowed with a soul

'By word and by miracle, he Goddes Sone,   330
Whan he was in this world, declared heere
That ther was oother lif ther men may wone.'
To whom answerde Tiburce, 'O suster deere,
Ne seidestow right now in this manere,
Ther nis but o God, lord in sothfastnesse?   335
And now of thre how maystow bere witnesse?'

'That shal I telle,' quod she, 'er I go.
Right as a man hath sapiences thre –
Memorye, engin, and intellect also –
So in o beinge of divinitee   340
Thre persones may ther right wel be.'
Tho gan she him ful bisily to preche
Of Cristes come, and of his peines teche,

And manye pointes of his passioun –
How Goddes Sone in this world was withholde   345
To doon mankinde plein remissioun,
That was ybounde in sinne and cares colde –
Al this thing she unto Tiburce tolde.
And after this, Tiburce, in good entente,
With Valerian to Pope Urban he wente,   350

That thanked God, and with glad herte and light
He cristned him, and made him in that place
Parfit in his lerninge, Goddes knight.
And after this, Tiburce gat swich grace
That every day he say, in time and space,   355
The aungel of God; and every maner boone
That he God axed, it was sped ful soone.

332 **ther** where **wone** exist   338 **sapiences** kinds of intelligence
339 **engin** imagination (n.)   342 **bisily** earnestly   343 **come** coming
345 **withholde** kept in bondage   346 **doon . . . remissioun** win pardon for
347 **cares colde** suffering   353 **Parfit** perfect   355 **say** saw
in time and space in due time   356 **boone** request   357 **sped** accomplished

It were ful harde by ordre for to seyn
How many wondres Jesus for hem wroghte.
360 But at the laste, to tellen short and plein,
The sergeantz of the toun of Rome hem soghte,
And hem biforn Almache, the prefect, broghte,
Which hem opposed, and knew al hir entente,
And to the image of Juppiter hem sente,

365 And seide, 'Whoso wol nat sacrifise,
Swap of his heed! This is my sentence heer.'
Anon thise martyrs that I yow devise,
Oon Maximus, that was an officer
Of the prefectes, and his corniculer,
370 Hem hente, and whan he forth the seintes ladde,
Himself he weep for pitee that he hadde.

Whan Maximus hadde herd the seintes loore,
He gat him of the tormentoures leve,
And ladde hem to his hous withoute moore;
375 And with hir preching, er that it were eve,
They gonnen fro the tormentours to reve,
And fro Maxime, and fro his folk echone,
The false feith, to trowe in God allone.

Cecile cam, whan it was woxen night,
380 With preestes that hem cristned alle ifeere;
And afterward, whan day was woxen light,
Cecile hem seide, with a ful stedefast cheere:
'Now, Cristes owene knightes, leve and deere,
Cast al awey the werkes of derknesse,
385 And armeth yow in armure of brightnesse.

361 sergeantz city officers   363 opposed interrogated   366 Swap of strike
off   367 yow devise tell you about   369 corniculer assistant (n.)
370 hente took ladde led   371 weep wept   372 loore teaching
373 tormentoures executioners leve permission
376 gonnen . . . to reve took away   379 was woxen had become
380 ifeere together   383 leve beloved   385 armeth yow arm yourselves

'Ye han, for sothe, ydoon a greet bataille.
Youre cours is doon; youre feith han ye conserved.
Goth to the corone of lif that may nat faille!
The rightful juge which that ye han served
Shal yeve it yow, as ye han it deserved.'   390
And whan this thing was seid as I devise,
Men ledde hem forth to doon the sacrifise.

But whan they weren to the place broght,
To tellen shortly the conclusioun,
They nolde encense ne sacrifise right noght,   395
But on hir knees they setten hem adoun
With humble herte and sad devocioun,
And losten bothe hir hevedes in the place;
Hir soules wenten to the king of grace.

This Maximus, that say this thing bitide,   400
With pitous teeris tolde it anon-right
That he hir soules saugh to hevene glide
With aungeles ful of cleernesse and of light;
And with his word converted many a wight,
For which Almachius dide him so bete   405
With whippe of leed, til he his lif gan lete.

Cecile him took and buried him anon
By Tiburce and Valerian softely,
Withinne hir burying-place under the stoon.
And after this Almachius hastily   410
Bad hise ministres fecchen openly
Cecile, so that she mighte in his presence
Doon sacrifise, and Juppiter encense.

---

386 **ydoon** performed   394 **conclusioun** outcome
395 **nolde encense** would not burn incense   397 **sad** steadfast
398 **hevedes** heads   **in the place** on the spot   400 **say** saw   **bitide** happen
403 **cleernesse** radiance   404 **wight** person   405 **dide him . . . bete** had him
beaten   406 **whippe of leed** whip with leaden balls attached to the thongs
gan lete lost   408 **softely** tenderly

But they, converted at hir wise loore,
415   Wepten ful sore and yaven ful credence
Unto hir word, and criden moore and moore,
'Crist, Goddes sone, withouten difference
Is verray God – this is al oure sentence –
That hath so good a servant him to serve!
420   This with o vois we trowen, thogh we sterve.'

Almachius, that herde of this doinge,
Bad fecchen Cecile, that he mighte hir se;
And alderfirst, lo, this was his axinge:
'What maner womman artow?' tho quod he.
425   'I am a gentil womman born,' quod she.
'I axe thee,' quod he, 'thogh it thee greve,
Of thy religioun, and of thy bileve.'

'Ye han bigonne youre question folily,'
Quod she, 'that wolden two answeres conclude
430   In o demande; ye axed lewedly.'
Almache answerde unto that similitude:
'Of whennes comth thin answering so rude?'
'Of whennes?' quod she, whan that she was freined,
'Of conscience and of good feith unfeined.'

435   Almachius seide, 'Ne takestow noon hede
Of my power?' And she answerde him this:
'Youre might', quod she, 'ful litel is to drede,
For every mortal mannes power nis
But lik a bladdre ful of wind, iwys,

---

414 **at** by   415 **yaven** gave   417 **withouten difference** i.e. between God the
Father and God the Son   418 **sentence** opinion
420 **with o vois** unanimously **trowen** believe **sterve** were to die
421 **doinge** occurrence   423 **alderfirst** first of all **axinge** question
426 **greve** may displease   428 **han bigonne** have begun **folily** foolishly
429 **conclude** include   430 **lewedly** stupidly   431 **similitude** description
433 **freined** asked   434 **Of** from **unfeined** sincere   437 **to drede** to be
feared   438–9 **nis But** is only

For with a nedles point, whan it is blowe,   440
May al the boost of it be leid ful lowe.'

'Ful wrongfully bigonne thow,' quod he,
'And yet in wrong is thy perseveraunce!
Wostow nat how oure mighty princes free
Han thus comanded, and maad ordinaunce   445
That every Cristen wight shal han penaunce,
But if that he his Cristendom withseye,
And goon al quit, if he wol it reneye?'

'Youre princes erren, as youre nobleye dooth,'
Quod tho Cecile, 'and with a wood sentence   450
Ye make us gilty, and it is nat sooth;
For ye, that knowen wel oure innocence,
Forasmuche as we doon a reverence
To Crist, and for we bere a Cristen name,
Ye putte on us a crime, and eek a blame.   455

'But we, that knowen thilke name so
For vertuous, we may it nat withseye.'
Almache answerde, 'Chees oon of thise two:
Do sacrifice, or Cristendom reneye,
That thow mowe now escapen by that weye.'   460
At which the holy blisful faire maide
Gan for to laughe, and to the juge she saide:

'O juge, confus in thy nicetee!
Wiltow that I reneye innocence
To maken me a wikked wight?' quod she.   465
'Lo, he dissimuleth heere in audience!

---

440 **blowe** inflated   441 **leid ful lowe** destroyed   443 **yet** still
perseveraunce continuation   444 **free** noble   446 **han penaunce** be
punished   447 **But if** unless   **withseye** deny   448 **quit** free
449 **nobleye** nobles   450 **wood sentence** mad judgement   454 **for** because
457 **For** as   463 **confus** confused   **nicetee** folly
466 **dissimuleth** dissembles   **audience** court hearing

He spareth and woodeth in his advertence.'
To whom Almachius: 'Unsely wrecche,
Ne wostow nat how fer my might may strecche?

470   'Han noght oure mighty princes to me yeven,
Ye, bothe power and auctoritee
To maken folk to dien or to liven?
Why spekestow so proudly thanne to me?'
'I speke noght but stedefastly,' quod she,
475   'Nat proudly; for I seye, as for my side,
We haten dedly thilke vice of pride.

'And if thow drede nat a sooth to here,
Thanne wol I shewe al openly, by right,
That thow hast maad a ful greet lesing here.
480   Thow seyst thy princes han thee yeven might
Bothe for to sleen and for to quike a wight.
Thow that ne mayst but oonly lif bireve,
Thow hast noon oother power ne no leve.

'But thow mayst seyn thy princes han thee maked
485   Ministre of deeth; for if thow speke of mo
Thow liest, for thy power is ful naked.'
'Do wey thy boldnesse,' seide Almachius tho,
'And sacrifice to oure goddes, er thow go.
I recche nat what wrong that thow me profre,
490   For I kan suffre it as a philosophre;

'But thilke wronges may I nat endure
That thow spekest of oure goddes here,' quod he.
Cecile answerde, 'O nice creature,
Thow seidest no word, sin thow spak to me,

467 He restrains himself (outwardly) and mentally rages (n.)
468 **Unsely** miserable   475 **side** part   476 **dedly** to the death
479 **maad a ... lesing** told a lie   481 **quike** bring to life   482 **bireve** take
away   483 **leve** permission   486 **naked** weak   487 **Do wey** stop
489 **recche** care **profre** offer   490 **suffre** endure   493 **nice** foolish

That I ne knew therwith thy nicetee,   495
And that thow were, in every maner wise,
A lewed officer and a vein justise.

'Ther lakketh nothing to thine outter eyen
That thow n'art blind; for thing that we seen alle
That it is stoon – that men may wel espyen –   500
That ilke stoon a god thow wolt it calle.
I rede thee, lat thin hand upon it falle,
And taste it wel, and stoon thow shalt it finde,
Sin that thow seest nat with thine eyen blinde.

'It is a shame that the peple shal   505
So scornen thee, and laughe at thy folye,
For comuly men woot it wel overal
That mighty God is in hise hevenes hye,
And thise images, wel thow mayst espye,
To thee ne to hemself mowe noght profite,   510
For in effect they be nat worth a mite.'

Thise wordes, and swiche othere, seide she;
And he weex wrooth, and bad men sholde hir lede
Hoom til hir hous, 'and in hir hous', quod he,
'Brenne hire right in a bath of flambes rede.'   515
And as he bad, right so was doon the dede,
For in a bath they gonne hire faste shetten
And night and day greet fir they under betten.

The longe night, and eek a day also,
For al the fir, and eek the bathes hete,   520
She sat al coold, and feelede no wo;

495 That I did not recognize your foolishness by it   497 **lewed** ignorant
vein justise worthless judge   498–9 Your outer eyes have all the
characteristics of blindness   502 **rede** advise   503 **taste** feel
507 **woot** know **overal** everywhere   510 **profite** do good
513 **weex wrooth** grew angry   516 **bad** ordered
517 **gonne ... shetten** shut up   518 **under** underneath **betten** kindled
520 **For al** in spite of   521 **wo** pain

It made hir nat a drope for to swete.
But in that bath hir lif she moste lete,
For he Almachius, with a ful wikke entente,
525   To sleen hire in the bath his sonde sente.

Thre strokes in the nekke he smoot hire tho,
The tormentour; but for no maner chaunce
He mighte noght smite al hir nekke atwo.
And for ther was that time an ordinaunce
530   That no man sholde doon man swich penaunce
The ferthe strook to smiten, softe or soore,
This tormentour ne dorste do namoore,

But half deed, with hir nekke ycorven there,
He lefte hir lie, and on his wey he went.
535   The Cristen folk whiche that aboute hire were
With shetes han the blood ful faire yhent.
Thre dayes lived she in this torment,
And nevere cessed hem the feith to teche
That she hadde fostred; hem she gan to preche,

540   And hem she yaf hir moebles and hir thing,
And to the Pope Urban bitook hem tho,
And seide, 'I axed this of hevene king,
To han respit thre dayes and namo,
To recommende to yow, er that I go,
545   Thise soules, lo, and that I mighte do werche
Here of min hous perpetuelly a cherche.'

---

523 **lete** lose   525 **sonde** messenger   526 **smoot** struck
527 **tormentour** executioner **for no maner chaunce** under no circumstances
530 **penaunce** punishment   531 **ferthe** fourth **softe or soore** gently or hard
532 **ne dorste** did not dare   533 **ycorven** cut   536 **shetes** sheets
yhent taken up   539 **fostred** taught   540 **moebles** movable property
thing possessions   541 **bitook** entrusted   544 **recommende** commend
545 **do werche** have made   546 **cherche** church

Seint Urban, with hise deknes, prively
The body fette, and buried it by nighte,
Among hise othere seintes honestly.
Hir hous the chirche of Seinte Cecilye highte;   550
Seint Urban halwed it, as he wel mighte;
In which, into this day, in noble wise,
Men doon to Crist and to his seinte servise.

Heere is ended the Seconde Nonnes Tale.

THE CANON'S YEOMAN'S PROLOGUE

*The Prologe of the Chanouns
Yemannes Tale.*

Whan ended was the lif of Seinte Cecile,
Er we hadde riden fully five mile,   555
At Boghtoun under Blee us gan atake
A man that clothed was in clothes blake,
And undernethe he hadde a whit surplis.
His hakeney, that was al pomely gris,
So swatte that it wonder was to see;   560
It semed as he hadde priked miles three.
The hors eek that his yeman rood upon
So swatte that unnethe mighte it gon.
Aboute the peitrel stood the foom ful hye;
He was of foom al flekked as a pie.   565

547 **deknes** deacons   548 **fette** fetched   551 **halwed** consecrated

556 **gan atake** overtook   558 **surplis** surplice (n.)   559 **hakeney** horse
pomely gris dappled grey   560 **swatte** sweated   561 **priked** galloped
563 **unnethe** with difficulty   564 **peitrel** straps going from the saddle round
the horse's chest **foom** sweat   565 **pie** magpie

A male tweyfolde on his croper lay;
It semed that he caried lite array.
Al light for somer rood this worthy man.
And in min herte to wondren I bigan
570 What that he was, til that I understood
How that his cloke was sowed to his hood;
For which, whan I hadde longe avised me,
I demed him som chanoun for to be.
His hat heeng at his bak doun by a laas,
575 For he hadde riden moore than trot or paas;
He hadde ay priked lik as he were wood.
A clote-leef he hadde under his hood,
For swoot, and for to kepe his heed from heete.
But it was joye for to seen him swete!
580 His forheed dropped as a stillatorye
Were ful of plantaine and of paritorye.
And whan that he was come, he gan to crye,
'God save', quod he, 'this joly compaignye!
Faste have I priked', quod he, 'for youre sake,
585 Bicause that I wolde yow atake,
To riden in this mirye compaignye.'
His yeman eek was ful of curteisye,
And seide, 'Sires, now in the morwe-tide,
Out of youre hostelrye I saugh yow ride,
590 And warned heer my lord and soverain,
Which that to riden with yow is ful fain
For his desport; he loveth daliaunce.'
     'Freend, for thy warning God yeve thee good
          chaunce!'

566 **male tweyfolde** double bag **croper** crupper (strap attached to rear of
saddle)   567 **array** gear   572 **avised me** reflected   573 **chanoun** canon
574 **heeng** hung **laas** cord   575 **moore than trot or paas** faster than a trot
or a walk   576 **lik as** as if **wood** mad   577 **clote-leef** burdock leaf
578 **swoot** sweat   580 **stillatorye** still, vessel used in distillation
581 **Were** which was **paritorye** pellitory (a herb)   583 **joly** lively
588 **morwe-tide** morning   590 **warned** told **soverain** superior
591 **fain** eager   592 **desport** amusement **daliaunce** sociable conversation
593 **good chaunce** good luck

Thanne seide oure Hoost, '– for, certein, it wolde
    seme
Thy lord were wis, and so I may wel deme.   595
He is ful jocunde also, dar I leye!
Can he oght telle a mirye tale or tweye,
With which he glade may this compaignye?'
    'Who, sire, my lord? ye, ye, withouten lie!
He kan of mirthe, and eek of jolitee,   600
Nat but inogh; also, sire, trusteth me,
And ye him knewe as wel as do I,
Ye wolde wondre how wel and craftily
He koude werke, and that in sondry wise.
He hath take on him many a greet emprise,   605
Which were ful hard for any that is heere
To bringe aboute, but they of him it leere.
As hoomly as he rit amonges yow,
If ye him knewe, it wolde be for youre prow.
Ye wolde nat forgoon his aqueintaunce   610
For muchel good, I dar leye in balaunce
Al that I have in my possessioun!
He is a man of heigh discrecioun;
I warne yow wel, he is a passing man.'
    'Wel,' quod oure Hoost, 'I pray thee, tel me   615
    than,
Is he a clerk, or noon? Telle what he is.'
'Nay, he is gretter than a clerk, iwys,'
Seide this Yeman, 'and in wordes fewe,
Hoost, of his craft somwhat I wol yow shewe.
    'I seye, my lord kan swich subtilitee –   620
But al his craft ye may nat wite at me –

595 **deme** believe   596 **jocunde** entertaining   **leye** bet   597 **oght** at all
598 **glade may** may entertain   601 **Nat but inogh** quite enough
602 **And if**   605 **emprise** enterprise   606 **were** would be   607 **but** unless
leere learn   608 **rit** (= *rideth*) rides   609 **prow** benefit   610 **forgoon** lose
611 **leye in balaunce** wager   614 **warne** tell   **passing** excellent
620 **kan** knows   **subtilitee** skill   621 **wite at** learn from

And somwhat helpe I yet to his wirking –
That al this ground on which we been riding,
Til that we come to Caunterbury toun,
625   He koude al clene turne it up-so-doun,
And pave it al of silver and of gold.'
        And whan this Yeman hadde this tale ytold
Unto oure Hoost, he seide, '*Benedicitee!*
This thing is wonder merveillous to me –
630   Sin that thy lord is of so heigh prudence,
Bicause of which men sholde him reverence –
That of his worship rekketh he so lite.
His oversloppe nis nat worth a mite,
As in effect, to him, so moot I go!
635   It is al baudy, and to-tore also.
Why is thy lord so sluttissh, I thee preye?
– And is of power bettre cloth to beye,
If that his dede acorde with thy speche.
Telle me that, and that I thee biseche!'
640   'Why?' quod this Yeman, 'wherto axe ye me?
God help me so, for he shal nevere thee!
– But I wol nat avowe that I seye,
And therfore kepe it secree, I yow preye –
He is to wis, in feith, as I bileve.
645   That that is overdoon, it wol nat preve
Aright, as clerkes seyn; it is a vice.
Wherfore in that I holde him lewed and nice;
For whan a man hath over-greet a wit,
Ful ofte him happeth to misusen it.
650   So dooth my lord, and that me greveth soore.
God it amende! I kan seye yow namoore.'

622 And yet I help his work to some extent   625 **clene** completely
632 **worship** good repute **rekketh** cares   633 **oversloppe** cassock
634 **As in effect** in fact   635 **baudy** dirty **to-tore** torn
636 **sluttissh** slovenly   637 **beye** buy   638 **acorde with** agrees with
641 **thee** prosper   642 **avowe** acknowledge   645–6 **overdoon** carried to
excess **preve Aright** turn out well   647 **lewed** stupid **nice** foolish
648 **over-greet a wit** too much intelligence

'Therof no fors, good Yeman,' quod oure
   Hoost;
'Sin of the konning of thy lord thow woost,
Telle how he dooth, I pray thee hertely,
Sin that he is so crafty and so sly. 655
Where dwelle ye, if it to telle be?'
'In the suburbes of a toun,' quod he,
'Lurkinge in hernes and in lanes blinde,
Whereas thise robbours and thise theves by kinde
Holden hir privee fereful residence, 660
As they that dar nat shewen hir presence.
So faren we, if I shal seye the sothe.'
   'Now,' quod oure Hoost, 'yet lat me talke to the.
Why artow so discoloured of thy face?'
'Peter!' quod he, 'God yeve it harde grace, 665
I am so used in the fir to blowe
That it hath chaunged my colour, I trowe.
I am nat wont in no mirour to prye,
But swinke soore, and lerne multiplye.
We blondren evere, and pouren in the fir, 670
And for al that, we faille of oure desir,
For evere we lakken oure conclusioun.
To muchel folk we doon illusioun,
And borwe gold – be it a pound or two,
Or ten, or twelve, or manye sommes mo – 675
And make hem wenen, at the leeste weye,
That of a pound we koude make tweye.
Yet is it fals; but ay we han good hope
It for to doon, and after it we grope,

652 **no fors** no matter   653 **konning** skill **woost** know   655 **sly** cunning
656 **if it to telle be** if it can be told   658 **hernes** out-of-the-way places
blinde dark   659 **Whereas** where **by kinde** customarily   660 **privee** secret
665 **harde grace** ill luck   666 **used** accustomed   668 **wont** accustomed
prye gaze   669 **swinke soore** labour hard **multiplye** practise alchemy (n.)
670 **blondren** act in the dark **pouren in** gaze into   671 **faille of** fail to
achieve   672 **conclusioun** successful result   673 **doon illusioun** deceive
676 **wenen** believe   679 **after it we grope** we search for it

680   But that science is so fer us biforn
           We mowen nat, althogh we hadde it sworn,
           It overtake; it slit awey so faste.
           It wol us maken beggers atte laste.'
               Whil this Yeman was thus in his talking,
685   This Chanoun drough him neer, and herde al thing
           Which that this Yeman spak; for suspecioun
           Of mennes speche evere hadde this Chanoun.
           For Catoun seyth, that he that gilty is
           Demeth al thing be spoke of him, iwys.
690   That was the cause he gan so ny him drawe
           To his Yeman, to herknen al his sawe.
           And thus he seide unto his Yeman tho:
           'Hoold thow thy pees, and speke no wordes mo!
           For if thow do, thow shalt it deere abye.
695   Thow sclaundrest me heere in this compaignye,
           And eek discoverest that thow sholdest hide.'
           'Ye,' quod oure Hoost, 'telle on, whatso bitide!
           Of al his threting rekke nat a mite.'
           'In feith,' quod he, 'namoore I do but lite.'
700   And whan this Chanoun saw it wolde nat bee,
           But his Yeman wolde telle his privetee,
           He fledde awey, for verray sorwe and shame.
           'A,' quod the Yeman, 'heere shal arise game!
           Al that I kan, anon now wol I telle,
705   Sin he is goon – the foule feend him quelle!
           For nevere heerafter wol I with him mete
           For peny ne for pound, I yow bihete.
           He that me broghte first unto that game,
           Er that he die, sorwe have he, and shame!

---

680 **so fer us biforn** so far ahead of us   682 **slit** (= *slideth*) **awey** slips away
685 **drough him** drew   689 Thinks that everything is being spoken about
him, for sure   691 **sawe** speech   694 **abye** pay for   696 **that** that which
697 **whatso bitide** whatever happens   698 **threting** threatening
rekke nat a mite don't care a farthing   701 **privetee** secrets   703 **game** fun
704 **kan** know   705 **quelle** kill   707 **bihete** promise

For it is ernest to me, by my feith.   710
That feele I wel, whatso any man seyth.
And yet, for al my smerte, and al my grief,
For al my sorwe, labour, and meschief,
I koude nevere leve it in no wise.
Now wolde God my wit mighte suffise   715
To tellen al that longeth to that art!
But nathelees, yow wol I tellen part;
Sin that my lord is gon, I wol nat spare.
Swich thing as that I knowe, I wol declare.'

Heere endeth the Prologe of the
Chanouns Yemannes Tale.

THE CANON'S
YEOMAN'S TALE

Heere biginneth the
Chanouns Yeman his Tale.

With this Chanoun I dwelt have seven yeer,   720
And of his science am I nevere the neer.
Al that I hadde, I have ylost therby,
And, God woot, so hath many mo than I!
Ther I was wont to be right fressh and gay
Of clothing, and of oother good array,   725
Now may I were an hose upon min heed;
And wher my colour was bothe fressh and reed,

711 **whatso** whatever   712 **smerte** pain   713 **meschief** misfortune
716 **longeth** belongs   718 **spare** hold back

721 **neer** nearer   724 **Ther** whereas   725 **array** accoutrements
726 **were an hose** see n.

Now is it wan and of a leden hewe.
Whoso it useth, soore shal he rewe!
730 And of my swink yet blered is min eye.
Lo, which avantage is to multiplye!
That slidinge science hath me maad so bare
That I have no good, wher that evere I fare.
And yet I am endetted so therby,
735 Of gold that I have borwed, trewely,
That whil I live I shal it quite nevere.
Lat every man be war by me for evere!
What maner man that casteth him therto,
If he continue, I holde his thrift ydo.
740 So helpe me God, therby shal he nat winne,
But empte his purs, and make his wittes thinne.
And whan he, thurgh his madnesse and folye,
Hath lost his owene good thurgh jupartye,
Thanne he exciteth oother folk therto,
745 To lese hir good, as he himself hath do.
For unto shrewes joye it is and ese
To have hir felawes in peine and disese.
– Thus was I ones lerned of a clerk.
Of that no charge; I wol speke of oure werk.
750   Whan we been thereas we shul excercise
Oure elvisshe craft, we semen wonder wise;
Oure termes been so clergial and so queinte.
I blowe the fir til that min herte feinte.
What sholde I tellen ech proporcioun
755 Of thinges whiche that we werche upon?

728 **wan** livid **leden** leaden   729 **soore** bitterly **rewe** regret
730 **swink** labour   731 **which** what an **multiplye** see n. to CY 669
732 **slidinge** slippery   733 **fare** go   734 **endetted** in debt
736 **quite** repay   737 **be war by** take warning from
738 **casteth him therto** applies himself to it   739 **thrift ydo** prosperity done
for   741 **make his wittes thinne** wear out his brains   743 **jupartye** taking
risks   745 **lese hir good** lose their wealth   746 **shrewes** villains
747 **disese** hardship   749 **no charge** no matter   750 ff. see n. for technical
terms in lines 750–853 **thereas** where   751 **elvisshe** magical
752 **clergial** learned **queinte** esoteric   753 **feinte** becomes exhausted

– As on five or sixe ounces, may wel be,
Of silver, or som oother quantitee –
And bisye me to telle yow the names
Of orpiment, brent bones, iren squames,
That into poudre grounden been ful smal;   760
And in an erthen pot how put is al,
And salt yput in, and also papeer,
Biforn thise poudres that I speke of heer,
And wel ycovered with a lampe of glas;
And of muche oother thing which that ther was;   765
And of the pot and glasses enluting,
That of the eir mighte passe out nothing;
And of the esy fir, and smerte also,
Which that was maad, and of the care and wo
That we hadde in oure matires subliming,   770
And in amalgaming and calcening
Of quiksilver, yclept mercurye crude?
For alle oure sleightes we kan nat conclude.
Oure orpiment and sublimed mercurye,
Oure grounden litarge eek, on the porfurye;   775
Of ech of thise of ounces a certein –
Noght helpeth us; oure labour is in vein!
Ne eek oure spirites ascencioun,
Ne oure matires that lien al fix adoun
Mowe in oure werking nothing us availle,   780
For lost is al oure labour and travaille.
And al the cost, a twenty devel weye,
Is lost also, which we upon it leye.

758 **bisye me** exert myself   759 **orpiment** trisulphide of arsenic
brent burned **iren squames** iron flakes   760 **smal** fine   762 **papeer** pepper
764 **lampe** lamp-shaped vessel   766 **enluting** process of sealing with clay
768 **esy fir** slow fire **smerte** hot   769 **care** trouble
770 **subliming** sublimation   771 **amalgaming** blending
calcening calcination   772 **yclept** called   773 **sleightes** tricks
conclude succeed   774 **sublimed** sublimated   775 **litarge** lead monoxide
porfurye porphyry slab   776 **certein** a certain quantity   778 **spirites** see n.
ascencioun vaporization   779 **fix** stable, not volatile
782 **a twenty devel weye** in the devil's name

Ther is also ful many another thing
785   That is unto oure craft apertening,
Though I by ordre hem nat reherce kan,
Bicause that I am a lewed man.
Yet wol I telle hem as they come to minde,
Thogh I ne kan nat sette hem in hir kinde:
790   – As bole armoniak, vertgrees, boras,
And sondry vessels maad of erthe and glas,
Oure urinals, and oure descensories,
Violes, crosletz, and sublimatories,
Cucurbites and alembikes eek,
795   And othere swiche, deere inogh a leek –
Nat nedeth it for to reherce hem alle –
Watres rubifying, and boles galle,
Arsenik, sal armoniak, and brimstoon;
And herbes koude I telle eek many oon
800   – As egremoine, valerian, and lunarye,
And othere swiche, if that me liste tarye.
Oure lampes brenning, bothe night and day,
To bringe aboute oure purpos, if we may;
Oure fourneis eek of calcinacioun,
805   And of watres albificacioun;
Unslekked lim, chalk, and gleire of an ey,
Poudres diverse, asshes, donge, pisse, and cley,

---

785 **apertening** belonging   786 **reherce** repeat   787 **lewed** uneducated
789 **sette hem in hir kinde** classify them according to their nature
790 **bole armoniak** Armenian bole (a red clay) **vertgrees** verdigris
boras borax   792 **descensories** retorts for distillation by condensation
793 **Violes** phials **crosletz** crucibles **sublimatories** vessels used for
sublimation   794 **Cucurbites** gourd-shaped vessels used for distillation
alembikes still-heads   795 **deere inogh a leek** not worth a leek
797 **rubifying** reddening **boles** bull's   798 **Arsenik** arsenic compounds
sal armoniak ammonium chloride **brimstoon** sulphur (see n. to CY
820–24)   800 **egremoine** agrimony **lunarye** ?moonwort   801 **me liste** it
pleased me   802 **lampes** vessels   804 **fourneis** furnace
805 **albificacioun** whitening   806 **Unslekked lim** unslaked lime
gleire of an ey white of an egg   807 **donge** dung

Cered poketz, sal peter, vitriole,
And divers fires maad of wode and cole;
Sal tartre, alkali, and sal preparat,   810
And combust matires and coagulat;
Cley maad with hors or mannes heer, and oile
Of tartre, alum glas, berm, wort, argoile,
Resalgar, and oure matires embibing;
And eek of oure matires encorporing,   815
And of oure silver citrinacioun,
Oure cementing and fermentacioun,
Oure ingottes, testes, and many mo.
    I wol yow telle, as was me taught, also,
The foure spirites and the bodies sevene,   820
By ordre, as ofte I herde my lord hem nevene:
The firste spirit quiksilver called is;
The seconde, orpiment; the thridde, iwys,
Sal armoniak, and the ferthe brimstoon.
The bodies sevene eek, lo, hem heer anoon: 825
Sol gold is, and Luna silver we threpe;
Mars, iren, Mercurye quiksilver we clepe;
Saturnus, leed, and Juppiter is tin,
And Venus coper, by my fader kin.
    This cursed craft whoso wol excercise,   830
He shal no good han that him may suffise,
For al the good he spendeth theraboute
He lese shal; therof have I no doute.
Whoso that listeth outen his folye,
Lat him com forth and lerne multiplye.   835

---

808 **Cered poketz** waxed bags **sal peter** saltpetre   809 **cole** charcoal
810 **Sal tartre** salt of tartar, potassium carbonate **alkali** an alkaline
substance obtained from the calcined ashes of plants **sal preparat** prepared
salt   811 **combust** burnt **coagulat** coagulated   813 **alum glas** potash alum
berm yeast **wort** unfermented beer **argoile** crude potassium bitartrate
814 **Resalgar** realgar, disulphide of arsenic **embibing** moistening
815 **encorporing** process of forming a compound   816 **citrinacioun** the
process of turning metal yellow   817 **cementing** process for testing metal
818 **testes** vessels used in assaying gold or silver   820 **spirites** see n.
821 **nevene** name   826 **Sol** the sun **Luna** the moon **threpe** call
832 **theraboute** on it   833 **lese** lose   834 **outen** display

And every man that oght hath in his cofre,
Lat him appere and wexe a philosophre,
Ascaunce that craft is so light to lere!
Nay, nay, God woot, al be he monk or frere,
840   Preest or chanoun, or any oother wight,
Though he sitte at his book bothe day and night
In lerning of this elvissh nice loore,
Al is in vein – and pardee, muchel moore
To lerne a lewed man this subtiltee!
845   Fy! Spek nat therof, for it wol nat be.
And konne he letterure, or konne he noon,
As in effect, he shal finde it al oon;
For bothe two, by my savacioun,
Concluden in multiplicacioun
850   Ilike wel, whan they han al ydo –
This is to seyn, they faillen bothe two.
      Yet forgat I to maken rehersaille
Of watres corosif, and of limaille,
And of bodies mollificacioun,
855   And also of hir induracioun,
Oilles, abluciouns, and metal fusible –
To tellen al wolde passen any bible
That owher is; wherfore, as for the beste,
Of alle thise names now wol I me reste.
860   For, as I trowe, I have yow told inowe
To reise a feend, al looke he nevere so rowe.
      A, nay, lat be! The philosophres stoon,
Elixir clept, we sechen faste echoon,

837–8 see n.   839 **al be he** whether he is   842 **nice** silly   844 **lewed** lay
subtiltee lore   846 And whether he is literate or not
849 **multiplicacioun** art of alchemy   850 **Ilike** equally
852 **maken rehersaille** enumerate   853 **corosif** corrosive **limaille** metal
filings   854 **mollificacioun** softening   855 **induracioun** hardening
856 **abluciouns** cleansing processes (n.) **fusible** fusible, susceptible of being
melted   857 **bible** book, treatise   858 **owher** anywhere
861 **reise** summon up **rowe** rough, savage   863 **Elixir** see n.
sechen faste seek diligently

For hadde we him thanne were we siker inow.
But unto God of hevene I make avow,   865
For al oure craft, whan we han al ydo,
And al oure sleighte, he wol nat come us to.
He hath ymaad us spenden muchel good,
For sorwe of which almoost we wexen wood,
But that good hope crepeth in oure herte,   870
Supposinge evere, thogh we soore smerte,
To be releved by him afterward.
Swich supposing and hope is sharp and hard;
I warne yow wel, it is to seken evere.
That futur temps hath maad men to dissevere,   875
In trust therof, from al that evere they hadde;
Yet of that art they kan nat wexen sadde,
For unto hem it is a bittre swete.
So semeth it – for nadde they but a shete,
Which that they mighte wrappe hem in a-night,   880
And a brat to walken in by daylight,
They wolde hem selle, and spenden on this craft.
They kan nat stinte til nothing be laft.
And everemoore, wher that evere they goon,
Men may hem knowe by smel of brimstoon.   885
For al the world they stinken as a goot!
Hir savour is so rammissh and so hoot
That though a man a mile from hem be,
The savour wol infecte him, trusteth me.
Lo, thus, by smelling, and threedbare array,   890
If that men liste, this folk they knowe may.
And if a man wol aske hem prively
Why they been clothed so unthriftily,

864 **him** it **siker inow** quite sure   867 **sleighte** ingenuity **he** it
869 **wexen wood** go mad   871 **soore smerte** suffer severely
873 **supposing** assumption   874 **to seken evere** always to be sought for
875 **temps** time **dissevere** part   877 **sadde** satiated   881 **brat** cloak of
coarse cloth   883 **stinte** leave off   887 **rammissh** rank   889 **savour** smell
892 **prively** privately   893 **unthriftily** shabbily

They right anon wol rownen in his ere,
895   And seyn that if that they espied were
Men wolde hem slee, bicause of hir science.
Lo, thus this folk bitrayen innocence!
   Passe over this; I go my tale unto.
Er that the pot be on the fir ydo,
900   Of metals with a certein quantitee
My lord hem trempreth, and no man but he –
Now he is goon, I dar sey boldely –
For, as men seyn, he kan doon craftily
(Algate, I woot wel he hath swich a name),
905   And yet ful ofte he renneth in a blame.
And wite ye how? Ful ofte it happeth so,
The pot to-breketh, and farewel, al is go!
Thise metals been of so greet violence,
Oure walles mowe nat make hem resistence,
910   But if they weren wroght of lim and stoon.
They percen so, and thurgh the wal they goon,
And somme of hem sinken into the ground –
Thus han we lost bitimes many a pound –
And somme ar scatered al the floor aboute,
915   Somme lepe into the roof. Withouten doute,
Though that the feend noght in oure sighte him
       shewe,
I trowe he with us be, that ilke shrewe!
In helle, wher that he lord is and sire,
Nis ther moore wo, ne moore rancour ne ire,
920   Whan that oure pot is broke, as I have said;
Every man chit and halt him ivele apaid.
   Somme seide it was long on the fir making;
Somme seide nay, it was on the blowing;

---

894 **rownen** whisper   895 **espied** detected   896 **slee** kill   899 **ydo** placed
901 **trempreth** blends   904 **Algate** at any rate **name** reputation
905 **renneth in** incurs   906 **wite ye** do you know   907 **to-breketh** breaks in
pieces   909 **mowe** may   910 **But if** unless   911 **percen** pierce
913 **bitimes** straightway   917 **shrewe** rascal   921 Everyone grumbles and
considers himself discontent   922 **long on** on account of

Thanne was I fered, for that was min office.
'Straw!' quod the thridde, 'ye been lewed and   925
        nice!
It was nat tempred as it oghte be!'
'Nay,' quod the ferthe, 'stinte, and herkne me.
Bicause oure fir ne was nat maad of beech,
That is the cause, and oother noon, so thee'ch!'
I kan nat telle wheron it was long,   930
But wel I woot greet strif is us among.
'What!' quod my lord, 'ther is namoore to doone.
Of thise perils I wol be war eftsoone.
I am right siker that the pot was crased.
Be as be may, be ye nothing amased;   935
As usage is, lat swepe the floor as swithe.
Plukke up youre hertes, and beeth glad and blithe!'
    The mullok on an heep ysweped was,
And on the floor ycast a canevas,
And al this mullok in a sive ythrowe,   940
And sifted and ypiked many a throwe.
'Pardee,' quod oon, 'somwhat of oure metal
Yet is ther heere, thogh that we han nat al.
And thogh this thing mishapped have as now,
Another time it may be wel inow.   945
Us moste putte oure good in aventure!
A marchant, pardee, may nat ay endure,
Trusteth me wel, in his prosperitee.
Somtime his good is drowned in the see,
And somtime comth it sauf unto the londe.'   950
'Pees!' quod my lord, 'the nexte time I shal fonde

---

924 **fered** afraid   925 **lewed** stupid **nice** foolish   929 **so thee'ch** as I may
prosper   930 **wheron it was long** what it was on account of
933 **war eftsoone** wiser next time   934 **right siker** very sure **crased** cracked
935 However it may be, do not be dismayed at all
936 **as swithe** without delay   937 **Plukke** pluck   938 **mullok** rubbish
ysweped swept   939 **ycast** thrown **canevas** piece of canvas   940 **sive** sieve
ythrowe thrown   941 **ypiked** picked over **many a throwe** many times
946 We have to put our wealth at risk   950 **sauf** safe   951 **fonde** try

To bringe oure craft al in another plite,
And but I do, sires, lat me han the wite!
Ther was defaute in somwhat, wel I woot.'
955 Another seide the fir was over-hoot –
But, be it hoot or coold, I dar seye this,
That we concluden everemoore amis.
We faille of that which that we wolden have,
And in oure madnesse everemoore we rave.
960 And whan we been togidres everychon,
Every man semeth a Salomon;
But al thing which that shineth as the gold
Ne is nat gold, as that I have herd told,
Ne every appul that is fair at eye
965 Ne is nat good, whatso men clappe or crye.
Right so, lo, fareth it amonges us:
He that semeth the wisest, by Jesus,
Is moost fool whan it cometh to the preef,
And he that semeth trewest is a theef.
970 That shul ye knowe, er that I fro yow wende,
By that I of my tale have maad an ende.

[Part Two]

Ther is a chanoun of religioun
Amonges us wolde infecte al a toun,
Thogh it as greet were as was Ninivee,
975 Rome, Alisaundre, Troye, and othere three.
His sleightes and his infinite falsnesse
Ther koude no man writen, as I gesse,
Though that he live mighte a thousand yeer.
In al this world of falshede nis his peer,

952 **plite** condition 953 **wite** blame 955 **over-hoot** too hot 957 That we
always end badly 962 **as** like 964 **at eye** to the eye 965 **clappe** jabber
968 **preef** test 971 **By that** by the time that 974 **greet** large
Ninivee Nineveh 975 **Alisaundre** Alexandria 979 **falshede** deceitfulness
nis his peer there is none equal to him

For in hise termes so he wol him winde, 980
And speke hise wordes in so sly a kinde,
Whan he commune shal with any wight,
That he wol make him doten anon-right,
But it a feend be, as himselven is.
Ful many a man hath he bigiled er this, 985
And wol, if that he live may a while.
And yet men ride and goon ful many a mile
Him for to seke, and have his aqueintaunce,
Noght knowinge of his false governaunce.
And if yow list to yeve me audience, 990
I wol it tellen here in youre presence.

But, worshipful chanones religious,
Ne demeth nat that I desclaundre youre hous,
Althogh that my tale of a chanoun be.
Of every ordre som shrewe is, pardee! 995
And God forbede that al a compaignye
Sholde rewe o singuler mannes folye.
To sclaundre yow is nothing min entente,
But to correcten that is mis I mente.
This tale was nat oonly told for yow, 1000
But eek for othere mo. Ye woot wel how
That among Cristes apostelles twelve
Ther nas no traitour but Judas himselve;
Thanne why sholde al the remenant have a blame
That giltlees were? By yow I seye the same – 1005
Save oonly this, if ye wol herkne me:
If any Judas in youre covent be,
Remeveth him bitimes, I yow rede,
If shame or los may causen any drede.

980 termes jargon   981 sly wily   983 doten become a fool
984 But it a feend be unless it is a fiend   989 governaunce behaviour
990 audience a hearing   993 desclaundre slander   995 shrewe rascal
997 rewe do penance for   o singuler one individual   998 nothing not at all
999 that is mis what is wrong   1001 othere mo others
1005 By concerning   1006 herkne listen to   1007 covent (religious) house
1008 Remove him promptly, I advise you

1010   And beth nothing displesed, I yow preye,
        But in this cas herketh what I shal seye.
            In London was a preest annueleer,
        That therinne hadde ydwelled many a yeer,
        Which was so plesaunt and so servisable
1015   Unto the wif wheras he was at table,
        That she wolde suffre him nothing for to paye
        For bord ne clothing, wente he nevere so gaye;
        And spending-silver hadde he right inow.
        Therof no fors; I wol procede as now,
1020   And telle forth my tale of the chanoun
        That broghte this preest to confusioun.
            This false chanoun cam upon a day
        Unto this preestes chambre wher he lay,
        Biseching him to lene him a certein
1025   Of gold, and he wolde quite it him agein.
        'Lene me a marke,' quod he, 'but dayes three,
        And at my day I wol it quiten thee.
        And if so be that thow me finde fals,
        Another day do hange me by the hals!'
1030   This preest him took a marke, and that as swithe,
        And this chanoun him thanked ofte sithe,
        And took his leve and wente forth his weye,
        And at the thridde day broghte his moneye,
        And to the preest he took his gold again,
1035   Wherof this preest was wonder glad and fain.

1010 **nothing** not at all   1012 **preest annueleer** priest who is retained to
celebrate memorial masses for the dead   1014 **plesaunt** agreeable
servisable attentive   1015 **at table** at board   1016 **suffre** allow
1017 **wente he nevere so gaye** however finely dressed he was
1018 **spending-silver** pocket money   **right inow** in plenty   1019 **no fors** no
matter   1024 **lene** lend   **a certein** a certain quantity
1025 **quite . . . agein** pay back   1026 **marke** sum of money equivalent to £$\frac{2}{3}$
but only   1029 **do hange me** have me hanged   **hals** neck
1030 **took** gave   **as swithe** at once   1031 **ofte sithe** many times
1035 **Wherof** at which   **fain** pleased

'Certes,' quod he, 'nothing anoyeth me
To lene a man a noble, or two, or thre,
Or what thing were in my possessioun,
Whan he so trewe is of condicioun
That in no wise he breke wol his day.   1040
To swich a man I kan nevere seye nay.'
'What,' quod this chanoun, 'sholde I be untrewe?
Nay, that were thing yfallen al of newe!
Trouthe is a thing that I wol evere kepe
Unto that day in which that I shal crepe   1045
Into my grave, and ellis God forbede!
Bileveth this as siker as the Crede!
God thanke I, and in good time be it said,
That ther was nevere man yet ivele apaid
For gold ne silver that he to me lente,   1050
Ne nevere falshede in min herte I mente.
And sire,' quod he, 'now of my privetee,
Sin ye so goodlich han been unto me,
And kithed to me so greet gentillesse,
Somwhat to quite with youre kindenesse   1055
I wol yow shewe: if that yow list to lere,
I wol yow teche pleinly the manere
How I kan werken in philosophye.
Taketh good heed; ye shul wel seen at eye
That I wol doon a maistrye er I go.'   1060
'Ye?' quod the preest, 'Ye, sire, and wol ye so?
Marye! therof I pray yow hertely.'
'At youre comandement, sire, trewely,'

1036 **nothing anoyeth me** it is no trouble to me   1037 **noble** gold coin (g.)
1040 **breke . . . his day** fail to pay punctually
1043 **thing yfallen** occurrence **al of newe** for the first time
1046 **ellis God forbede** God forbid that it should be otherwise
1047 **siker** surely **Crede** Creed   1048 **in good time** at a propitious
moment (n.)   1049 **ivele apaid** dissatisfied   1052 **privetee** private affairs
1053 **goodlich** kind   1054 And shown me such great kindness
1055 **quite with** repay   1056 **yow list to lere** it pleases you to learn
1058 **philosophye** alchemy   1059 **seen at eye** see with (your own) eyes
1060 **maistrye** tour de force   1061 **Ye** yes

Quod the chanoun, 'and ellis God forbede!'
1065   Loo, how this theef koude his servise bede!
Ful sooth it is that swich profred servise
Stinketh, as witnessen thise olde wise;
And that ful soone I wol it verifye
In this chanoun, roote of al trecherye,
1070   That everemoore delit hath and gladnesse –
Swiche feendly thoghtes in his herte impresse –
How Cristes peple he may to meschief bringe.
God kepe us from his false dissimulinge!
     Noght wiste this preest with whom that he delte,
1075   Ne of his harm cominge he nothing felte.
O sely preest, o sely innocent!
With coveitise anon thow shalt be blent.
O gracelees, ful blind is thy conceit!
Nothing ne artow war of the deceit
1080   Which that this fox yshapen hath for thee.
Hise wily wrenches thow ne mayst nat flee;
Wherfore, to go to the conclusioun
That refereth to thy confusioun,
Unhappy man, anon I wol me hie
1085   To tellen thin unwit and thy folye,
And eek the falsnesse of that oother wrecche,
As ferforth as my konning may strecche.
     This chanoun was my lord, ye wolden wene?
Sire Hoost, in feith, and by the hevenes queene,
1090   It was another chanoun, and nat he,
That kan an hundred fold moore subtiltee.

1065 **bede** offer   1066 **profred** volunteered   1068 **verifye** prove true
1071 **impresse** are fixed   1072 **meschief** misfortune
1073 **dissimulinge** dissembling   1074 **Noght wiste** did not know **delte** was
dealing   1076 **sely** simple   1077 **blent** blinded   1078 **gracelees** unwary
conceit mind, understanding   1080 **yshapen** planned
1081 **wrenches** tricks **flee** escape   1083 **refereth to** concerns
confusioun destruction   1084 **Unhappy** unfortunate **me hie** hasten
1085 **unwit** stupidity   1087 **konning** ability   1088 **wene** think
1091 **kan** knows

He hath bitrayed folkes many time;
Of his falsnesse it dulleth me to rime.
Evere whan that I speke of his falshede,
For shame of him my chekes wexen rede   1095
– Algates they biginnen for to glowe,
For reednesse have I noon, right wel I knowe,
In my visage, for fumes diverse
Of metals, which ye han herd me reherce,
Consumed and wasted han my reednesse.   1100
Now tak heed of this chanons cursednesse!
　　'Sire,' quod he to the preest, 'lat youre man
　　　　goon
For quiksilver, that we it hadde anoon;
And lat him bringen ounces two or three;
And whan he comth, as faste shul ye see   1105
A wonder thing, which ye sey nevere er this.'
'Sire,' quod the preest, 'it shal be doon, iwys.'
He bad his servant fecchen him this thing,
And he al redy was at his bidding,
And wente him forth, and cam anon again   1110
With this quiksilver, shortly for to sayn,
And took thise ounces thre to the chanoun;
And he hem leide faire and wel adoun,
And bad the servant coles for to bringe,
That he anon mighte go to his werkinge.   1115
　　The coles right anon weren yfet,
And this chanoun took out a crosselet
Of his bosom, and shewed it to the preest.
'This instrument', quod he, 'which that thow
　　　　seest,
Taak in thin honde, and put thyself therinne   1120
Of this quiksilver an ounce, and heer biginne,

1093 **dulleth** distresses   1096 **Algates** at any rate   1097 **reednesse** redness
1098 **fumes** vapours   1099 **reherce** list   1103 **quiksilver** mercury
anoon without delay   1105 **as faste** immediately   1106 **sey** saw
1110 **anon again** straight back   1112 **took** gave   1113 **faire** carefully
1114 **coles** coals   1116 **yfet** fetched   1117 **crosselet** crucible

In name of Crist, to wexe a philosofre.
Ther been ful fewe to whiche I wolde profre
To shewen hem thus muche of my science,
1125   For ye shul seen heer, by experience,
That this quiksilver I wol mortifye
Right in youre sighte anon, withouten lie,
And make it as good silver and as fin
As ther is any in youre purs, or min,
1130   Or elleswher, and make it malliable –
And elles holdeth me fals and unable
Amonges folk for evere to appeere!
I have a poudre heer, that coste me deere,
Shal make al good, for it is cause of al
1135   My konning, which that I yow shewen shal.
Voideth youre man, and lat him be theroute,
And shette the dore whiles we been aboute
Oure privetee, that no man us espye
Whils that we werke in this philosophye.'
1140   Al as he bad fulfilled was in dede:
This ilke servant anon-right out yede,
And his maister shette the dore anon,
And to hir labour spedily they gon.
This preest, at this cursed chanons bidding,
1145   Upon the fir anon sette this thing,
And blew the fir, and bisied him ful faste.
And this chanoun into the crosselet caste
A poudre – noot I wherof that it was
Ymaad, outher of chalk, outher of glas,
1150   Or somwhat elles was nat worth a flye,
To blinde with this preest – and bad him hie

1122 **philosofre** alchemist   1126 **mortifye** harden (see n. to CY 1431–40)
1131 And otherwise consider me false and unfit   1134 **Shal** which shall
1136 **Voideth** send away **theroute** outside   1137 **shette** shut
1138 **privetee** secret business   1141 **yede** went   1148 **wherof** of what
1149 **outher . . . outher** either . . . or   1150 **was** which was
1151 **hie** make haste

The coles for to couchen al above
The crosselet, 'for, in tokening I thee love,'
Quod this chanoun, 'thine owene handes two
Shul werche al thing which shal here be do.'   1155
  'Graunt merci,' quod the preest, and was ful
        glad,
And couched coles as the chanoun bad.
And whil he bisy was, this feendly wrecche,
This false chanoun – the foule feend him fecche! –
Out of his bosom took a bechen cole,   1160
In which ful subtilly was maad an hole,
And therinne put was of silver limaille
An ounce, and stopped was, withouten faille,
This hole with wex, to kepe the limaille in.
And understondeth that this false gin   1165
Was nat maad ther, but it was maad bifore;
And othere thinges I shal tellen moore
Herafterward, which that he with him broghte.
Er he cam ther, him to bigile he thoghte;
And so he dide, er that they wente atwinne.   1170
Til he had terved him koude he nat blinne.
It dulleth me whan that I of him speke;
On his falshede fain wolde I me wreke
If I wiste how, but he is here and ther;
He is so variaunt, he abit nowher.   1175
  But taketh heed now, sires, for Goddes love:
He took his cole, of which I spak above,
And in his hand he baar it prively,
And whils the preest couched bisily

1152 **couchen** lay   1153 **in tokening I thee love** as a token that I love you
1155 **do** done   1156 *Graunt merci* thank you   1158 **feendly** fiendish
1160 **bechen cole** piece of charcoal made from beech-wood
1161 **subtilly** cunningly   1162 **limaille** filings   1163 **withouten faille** truly
1165 **gin** contrivance   1169 **bigile** deceive   **thoghte** intended
1170 **wente atwinne** separated   1171 **terved** fleeced   **blinne** cease
1172 **dulleth** vexes   1173 **me wreke** avenge myself   1175 He is so
changeable that he doesn't settle anywhere   1178 **baar** carried
prively secretly

1180   The coles, as I tolde yow er this,
      This chanoun seide, 'Freend, ye doon amis.
      This is nat couched as it oghte be.
      But soone I shal amenden it,' quod he.
      'Now lat me medle therwith but a while,
1185   For of yow have I pitee, by Seint Gile!
      Ye been right hoot – I se wel how ye swete.
      Have here a clooth, and wipe awey the wete.'
      And whils that the preest wiped his face,
      This chanoun took his cole, with sory grace!
1190   And leide it above, upon the middeward
      Of the crosselet, and blew wel afterward,
      Til that the coles gonne faste brenne.
        'Now yeve us drinke,' quod the chanoun thenne,
      'As swithe al shal be wel, I undertake.
1195   Sitte we doun, and lat us mirye make.'
      And whan that this chanounes bechen cole
      Was brent, al the lemaille out of the hole
      Into the crosselet fil anon adoun
      – And so it moste nedes, by resoun,
1200   Sin it so evene above it couched was.
      But therof wiste the preest nothing, allas!
      He demed alle the coles iliche good,
      For of that sleighte he nothing understood.
      And whan this alkamistre saugh his time,
1205   'Ris up,' quod he, 'sire preest, and stondeth by me,
      And for I woot wel ingot have ye noon,
      Goth walketh forth, and bring us a chalk-stoon,
      For I wol make it of the same shap
      That is an ingot, if I may han hap.

1184 **therwith** with it **but a while** only for a short space of time
1187 **wete** moisture   1189 **with sory grace** bad luck to him
1190 **middeward** middle   1192 **gonne faste brenne** were burning vigorously
1194 **As swithe** in a trice   1199 **nedes** of necessity
1200 **evene above** exactly above   1202 **iliche** equally   1203 **sleighte** trick
1204 **alkamistre** alchemist   1207 Go out and bring back a piece of chalk
1209 **han hap** have good fortune

And bringeth eek with yow a bolle or a panne   1210
Ful of water, and ye shul se wel thanne
How that oure bisinesse shal thrive and preve.
And yet, for ye shul han no misbileve
Ne wrong conceite of me in youre absence,
I ne wol nat been out of youre presence,   1215
But go with yow and come with yow agein.'
The chambre-dore, shortly for to seyn,
They opened and shette, and wente hir weye,
And forth with hem they carieden the keye,
And come again withouten any delay.   1220
What sholde I taryen al the longe day?
He took the chalk, and shoop it in the wise
Of an ingot, as I shal yow devise.

    I seye, he took out of his owene sleve
A teine of silver – ivele moot he cheve! –   1225
Which that ne was nat but an ounce of weighte.
And taak heed now of his cursed sleighte:
He shoop his ingot in lengthe and eek in brede
Of this teine, withouten any drede,
So slyly that the preest it nat espide,   1230
And in his sleve again he gan it hide,
And fro the fir he took up his matere,
And in th'ingot putte it with mirye cheere,
And in the water-vessel he it caste
Whan that him liste; and bad the preest as faste,   1235
'Look what ther is – put in thin hand and grope!
Thow finde shalt ther silver, as I hope.'
What, devel of helle, sholde it elles be?
Shaving of silver silver is, pardee!

1210 **bolle** bowl   1212 **thrive** prosper **preve** succeed   1213 **for** so that
misbileve mistrust   1214 **conceite** notion   1221 **What** why
1222 **shoop** formed **wise** fashion   1223 **devise** tell   1225 **teine** rod
ivele moot he cheve bad luck to him   1228 **brede** breadth
1229 **drede** doubt   1230 **nat espide** did not notice   1233 **mirye cheere** a
cheerful expression   1235 When it pleased him, and immediately ordered
the priest

1240   He putte his hand in and took up a teine
        Of silver fin, and glad in every veine
        Was this preest, whan he sey it was so.
        'Goddes blessing, and his modres also,
        And alle halwes, have ye, sire chanoun!'
1245   Seide this preest, 'and I hir malisoun,
        But – and ye vouchesauf to techen me
        This noble craft and this subtilitee –
        I wol be youre, in al that evere I may.'
            Quod the chanoun, 'Yet wol I make assay
1250   The seconde time, that ye may taken hede
        And been expert of this, and in youre nede
        Another day assaye in min absence
        This discipline and this crafty science.
        Lat take another ounce', quod he tho,
1255   'Of quiksilver, withouten wordes mo,
        And do therwith as ye han doon er this
        With that oother, which that now silver is.'
            This preest him bisieth in al that he kan
        To doon as this chanoun, this cursed man,
1260   Comaunded him, and faste he blew the fir
        For to come to th'effect of his desir.
        And this chanoun, right in the mene-while,
        Al redy was the preest eft to bigile;
        And for a countenance in his hande he bar
1265   An holwe stikke – taak keep and be war! –
        In the ende of which an ounce, and namoore,
        Of silver limaille put was, as bifore
        Was in his cole, and stopped with wex weel,
        For to kepe in his limaille every deel.

1242 **sey** saw   1244 **halwes** saints   1245 **hir malisoun** their curse
1246–8 **But . . . I wol be youre** if I am not yours **and ye vouchesauf** if you
agree   1249 **assay** trial   1251 **expert of** trained in   1253 **discipline** craft
crafty learned   1260 **faste** vigorously   1263 **eft** a second time
1264 **for a countenance** as a pretence   1265 **holwe** hollow **taak keep** take
note   1268 **weel** well   1269 **every deel** every bit

And whil this preest was in his bisinesse,   1270
This chanoun with his stikke gan him dresse
To him anon, and his poudre caste in,
As he dide er – the devel out of his skin
Him terve, I pray to God, for his falshede!
For he was evere fals in thoght and dede –   1275
And with his stikke, above the crosselet,
That was ordeined with that false get,
He stired the coles til relente gan
The wex again the fir, as every man,
But it a fool be, woot wel it moot nede,   1280
And al that in the stikke was out yede,
And in the crosselet hastilich it fel.

    Now, gode sires, what wol ye bet than wel?
Whan that this preest thus was bigiled agein,
Supposinge noght but trouthe, sooth to seyn,   1285
He was so glad that I kan nat expresse
In no manere his mirthe and his gladnesse;
And to the chanoun he profred eftsone
Body and good. 'Ye,' quod the chanoun sone,
'Thogh povre I be, crafty thow shalt me finde,   1290
I warne thee; yet is ther moore bihinde.
Is ther any coper herinne?' seide he.
'Ye,' quod the preest, 'sire, I trowe wel ther be.'
'– Elles go bye us som, and that as swithe!
Now, goode sire, go forth thy wey, and hie the.'   1295
    He wente his wey, and with the coper cam,
And this chanoun it in hise handes nam,

1270 **in his bisinesse** occupied   1271 **gan him dresse** went   1273 **er** before
1274 **terve** flay   1277 **ordeined** prepared **get** contrivance
1278 **relente** melt   1279 **again the fir** under the effect of the fire
1280 Unless he is a fool, knows well that it necessarily must
1281 **yede** came   1283 **what wol ye bet than wel** what more do you want
1288 **profred** offered **eftsone** again   1289 **good** wealth **sone** straightway
1290 **crafty** skilful   1291 **warne** tell **bihinde** to follow   1292 **herinne** in
the house   1294 **bye** buy **as swithe** without delay   1295 **hie the** make
haste   1297 **nam** took

And of that coper weyed out but an ounce.
   Al to simple is my tonge to pronounce,
1300   As ministre of my wit, the doublenesse
Of this chanoun, roote of al cursednesse!
He semed freendly to hem that knewe him noght,
But he was feendly, bothe in werke and thoght.
It werieth me to telle of his falsnesse,
1305   And nathelees, yet wol I it expresse,
To th'entente that men may be war therby,
And for noon oother cause, trewely.
   He putte the ounce of coper in the crosselet,
And on the fir as swithe he hath it set,
1310   And caste in poudre, and made the preest to blowe,
And in his werking for to stoupe lowe,
As he dide er – and al nas but a jape;
Right as him liste, the preest he made his ape!
And afterward, in th'ingot he it caste,
1315   And in the panne putte it at the laste
Of water, and in he putte his owene hond,
And in his sleve (as ye biforenhond
Herde me telle) he hadde a silver teine.
He slyly took it out, this cursed heine,
1320   Unwiting this preest of his false craft,
And in the pannes botme he hath it laft,
And in the water rumbled to and fro,
And wonder prively took up also
The coper teine, noght knowing this preest,
1325   And hidde it, and him hente by the breest,
And to him spak, and thus seide in his game:
'Stoupeth adoun – by God, ye be to blame! –

1299 **pronounce** tell   1300 **wit** understanding **doublenesse** duplicity
1303 **feendly** fiendish   1304 **werieth** wearies   1306 **To th'entente that** in
order that   1309 **as swithe** at once   1311 **stoupe** stoop   1312 **jape** trick
1313 **made his ape** duped   1318 **teine** rod   1319 **heine** rogue
1320 **Unwiting** not knowing   1321 **laft** left   1322 **rumbled** made a
rumbling noise   1323 **wonder prively** very secretly   1325 **hente** seized
1326 **in his game** jocularly

Helpeth me now, as I dide yow whil-er.
Putte in youre hand, and looketh what is ther.'
    This preest took up this silver teine anon;   1330
And thanne seide the chanoun, 'Lat us gon
With thise thre teines, which that we han wroght,
To som goldsmith, and wite if they been oght.
For, by my feith, I nolde, for min hood,
But if that they were silver fin and good,   1335
And that as swithe preved it shal be.'
    Unto the goldsmith with thise teines thre
They wente, and putte thise teines in assay
To fir and hamer; mighte no man seye nay,
But that they weren as hem oghte be.   1340
    This sotted preest, who was gladder than he?
Was nevere brid gladder again the day,
Ne nightingale in the sesoun of May
Was nevere noon that liste bet to singe,
Ne lady lustier in carolinge,   1345
Or for to speke of love and wommanhede,
Ne knight in armes to doon an hardy dede,
To stonde in grace of his lady deere,
Than hadde this preest this sory craft to leere!
And to the chanoun thus he spak and seide: 1350
'For love of God, that for us alle deide,
And as I may deserve it unto yow,
What shal this receit coste? Telleth now!'
    'By oure lady,' quod this chanoun, 'it is dere,
I warne yow wel; for save I and a frere,   1355
In Engelond ther kan no man it make.'
'No fors,' quod he, 'now, sire, for Goddes sake,

1328 **whil-er** a while before   1333 **wite** find out **oght** worth anything
1334 **nolde** would not wish **for min hood** by my hood
1338 **putte ... in assay** tested   1339 **seye nay** deny   1341 **sotted** stupid
1345 **lustier** more eager **carolinge** singing in a round-dance
1347 **hardy** brave   1348 **grace** favour   1349 **sory** wretched **leere** learn
1352 **unto** from   1353 **receit** formula   1355 **save** except **frere** friar
1357 **No fors** no matter

What shal I paye? Telleth me, I preye.'
'Iwys,' quod he, 'it is ful deere, I seye.
1360   Sire, at o word, if that thee list it have,
Ye shul paye fourty pound, so God me save!
And nere the freendshipe that ye dide er this
To me, ye sholde paye moore, iwys.'
        This preest the somme of fourty pound anon
1365   Of nobles fette, and took hem everychon
To this chanoun for this ilke receit.
Al his werking nas but fraude and deceit.
        'Sire preest,' he seide, 'I kepe han no loos
Of my craft, for I wolde it kept were cloos;
1370   And, as ye love me, kepeth it secree,
For, and men knewen al my soutiltee,
By God, they wolden han so greet envye
To me, bicause of my philosophye,
I sholde be deed; ther were noon oother weye.'
1375   'God it forbede!' quod the preest, 'What sey ye?
Yet hadde I levere spenden al the good
Which that I have, and elles wexe I wood,
Than that ye sholden falle in swich mescheef.'
'For youre good wil, sire, have ye right good preef!'
1380   Quod the chanoun, 'and farewel, *grant merci*!'
He wente his wey, and nevere the preest him sy
After that day; and whan that this preest sholde
Maken assay, at swich time as he wolde,
Of this receit, farewel! – it wolde nat be.
1385   Lo, thus bijaped and bigiled was he!
Thus maketh he his introduccioun
To bringe folk to hir destruccioun.

1360 **at o word** in a word   **thee list** it pleases you   1362 **nere** were it not for
1364 **somme** sum   1365 **fette** fetched   **took** gave
1368–9 **kepe han no loos Of** do not wish to have any fame because of
cloos secret   1371 **and if** **soutiltee** skill   1374 **were** would be
1376 **hadde I levere** I would rather   1377 **wexe I wood** may I go mad
1378 **mescheef** misfortune   1379 **good preef** success   1381 **sy** saw
1383 **wolde** wished   1385 **bijaped** tricked
1386 **introduccioun** preparation

Considereth, sires, how that in ech estaat,
Bitwixe men and gold ther is debaat,
So ferforth that unnethes is ther noon.   1390
This multiplying blent so many oon
That, in good feith, I trowe that it be
The cause grettest of swich scarsetee.
Philosophres speken so mistily
In this craft, that men kan nat come therby,   1395
For any wit that men han nowadayes.
They mowe wel chiteren as doon thise jayes,
And in hire termes sette hir lust and peine,
But to hir purpos shul they nevere atteine.
A man may lightly lerne, if he have aught,   1400
To multiplye, and bringe his good to naught.

Lo, swich a lucre is in this lusty game:
A mannes mirthe it wol turne unto grame,
And empten also grete and hevy purses,
And maken folk for to purchasen curses   1405
Of hem that han hir good therto ylent.
O fy, for shame! – they that han been brent,
Allas, kan they nat flee the fires hete?
Ye that it use, I rede ye it lete,
Lest ye lese al; for bet than nevere is late.   1410
Nevere to thrive were to long a date;
Thogh ye prolle ay, ye shul it nevere finde.
Ye been as boold as is Bayard the blinde,

1388 **estaat** rank of society   1389 **debaat** strife   1390 **So ferforth** to such
an extent **unnethes** hardly   1391 **blent** (= *blendeth*) blinds
1393 **scarsetee** scarcity   1394 **mistily** figuratively   1395 **come therby** grasp
it   1396 **wit** cleverness   1397 **chiteren** jabber   1398 And revel in their
jargon and take trouble over it   1400 **lightly** easily **aught** anything
1401 **good** wealth   1402 **lucre** profit **lusty** pleasant   1403 **grame** sorrow
1404 **empten** empty   1405 **purchasen** obtain   1406 **Of** from
1407 **brent** burned   1409 I advise you who practise it to abandon it
1410 **lese** lose **bet than nevere is late** better late than never
1411 **date** time   1412 **prolle ay** search for ever

That blondreth forth, and peril casteth noon.
1415 He is as boold to renne again a stoon
As for to goon bisides in the weye.
So faren ye that multiplye, I seye.
If that youre eyen kan nat seen aright,
Looke that youre minde lakke noght his sight;
1420 For thogh ye looken nevere so brode and stare,
Ye shul nothing winne on that chaffare,
But wasten al that ye may rape and renne.
Withdrawe the fir, lest it to faste brenne;
Medleth namoore with that art, I mene,
1425 For if ye doon, youre thrift is goon ful clene.
And right as swithe I wol yow tellen here
What philosophres seyn in this matere.

   Lo, thus seyth Arnold of the Newe Toun
   – As his *Rosarye* maketh mencioun –
1430 He seyth right thus, withouten any lie:
'Ther may no man mercurye mortifye
But it be with his brother knowleching.'
How be that he which that first seide this thing
Of philosophres fader was, Hermes;
1435 He seyth how that the dragon, doutelees,
Ne dieth nat but if that he be slain
With his brother, and that is for to sayn,
By the dragon, mercurye, and noon oother
He understood, and brimstoon by his brother,
1440 That out of Sol and Luna were ydrawe.
'And therfor,' seide he – tak heed to my sawe –

1414 **blondreth** blunders **casteth** perceives   1415 **renne** run
1416 **bisides** aside   1420 **brode** with eyes wide open
1421 **on that chaffare** in that trade   1422 **rape and renne** seize and make off
with   1423 **to faste** too vigorously   1425 **thrift** prosperity
ful clene completely   1426 **right as swithe** right away
1428 **Newe Toun** Villanova (n.)   1431 **mortifye** harden (n.)   1432 Unless
it is with his brother's co-operation   1433 **How be that** although
1435 **dragon** mercury (n.)   1439 **brimstoon** sulphur   1440 **Sol** sun (gold)
Luna moon (silver) (n.)   1441 **sawe** saying

'Lat no man bisy him this art for to seche,
But if that he th'entencioun and speche
Of philosophres understonde kan.
And if he do, he is a lewed man;   1445
For this science and this konning', quod he,
'Is of the secree of secretes, pardee.'
    Also ther was a disciple of Plato
That on a time seide his maister to
– As his book *Senior* wol bere witnesse –   1450
And this was his demande, in soothfastnesse:
'Tel me the name of the privee stoon.'
And Plato answerde unto him anoon:
'Take the stoon that Titanos men name –'
'Which is that?' quod he; 'Magnasia is the   1455
        same,'
Seide Plato. 'Ye, sire? and is it thus?
This is *ignotum per ignocius*!
What is Magnasia, good sire, I yow preye?'
'It is a water that is maad, I seye,
Of elementes foure,' quod Plato.   1460
'Telle me the roote, good sire,' quod he tho,
'Of that water, if it be youre wille.'
'Nay, nay,' quod Plato, 'certein, that I nille!
The philosophres sworn were everychoon
That they sholde discovere it unto noon,   1465
Ne in no book it write in no manere,
For unto Crist it is so leef and deere
That he wol nat that it discovered be,
But wher it liketh to his deitee
Men for t'enspire, and eek for to defende   1470
Whom that him liketh; lo, this is the ende!'

1442 **bisy him** exert himself   1445 **lewed** stupid   1446 **konning** skill
1447 **secree** secret   1451 **soothfastnesse** truth   1452 **privee** secret
1457 ***ignotum per ignocius*** see n.   1461 **tho** then   1463 **nille** will not
1465 **discovere** reveal   1467 **leef** precious   1469 **liketh** pleases
his deitee him   1470 **enspire** enlighten   **defende** prohibit

Thanne conclude I thus, sith that God of
    hevene
Ne wol nat that the philosophres nevene
How that a man shal come unto this stoon,
1475   I rede, as for the beste, lat it goon!
For whoso maketh God his adversarye,
As for to werken anything in contrarye
Of his wil, certes, nevere shal he thrive,
Thogh that he multiplye terme of his live.
1480   And ther a point; for ended is my tale.
God sende every trewe man boote of his bale!

Heere is ended the Chanouns
Yemannes Tale.

1473 **nevene** speak of   1475 **rede** advise **lat it goon** let it pass
1477 **anything** at all   1478 **thrive** succeed   1480 **point** full stop
1481 **boote of his bale** remedy for his tribulations

THE MANCIPLE'S
PROLOGUE

Woot ye nat where ther stant a litel toun
Which that ycleped is Bobbe-up-and-doun,
Under the Blee, in Caunterbury weye?
Ther gan oure Hooste for to jape and pleye,
And seide, 'Sires, what! Dun is in the mire!   5
Is ther no man, for preyere ne for hire,
That wol awake oure felawe al bihinde?
A theef might him ful lightly robbe and binde.
Se how he nappeth! Se how, for cokkes bones,
That he wol falle from his hors atones!   10
Is that a Cook of Londoun, with meschaunce?
Do him com forth; he knoweth his penaunce,
For he shal telle a tale, by my fey,
Althogh it be nat worth a botel hey.
Awake, thow Cook!' quod he, 'God yeve thee   15
    sorwe!
What eileth thee to slepe by the morwe?
Hastow had fleen al night? Or artow dronke?
Or hastow with som quene al night yswonke,
So that thow mayst nat holden up thin heed?'
    This Cook, that was ful pale and nothing reed,   20

---

1 **Woot** know **stant** (= *standeth*) stands   2 **ycleped** called   4 **jape** joke
5 **Dun is in the mire** see n.   6 **hire** money (n.)   7 **al bihinde** at the rear
9 **nappeth** sleeps **cokkes bones** a euphemistic substitution for 'Goddes
bones'   10 **atones** any minute   11 **with meschaunce** curse him
12 **Do him com forth** make him come forward   14 **botel hey** bundle of hay
16 **by the morwe** in the morning   17 **fleen** fleas   18 **quene** trollop
yswonke laboured   20 **nothing** not at all

Seide to oure Hoost, 'So God my soule blesse,
As ther is falle on me swich hevinesse –
Noot I nat why – that me were levere slepe
Than the beste galoun win in Chepe.'

25   'Wel,' quod the Maunciple, 'if it may doon ese
To thee, sire Cook, and to no wight displese
Which that here rideth in this compaignye,
And that oure Hoost wol, of his curteisye,
I wol as now excuse thee of thy tale.

30   For in good feith, thy visage is ful pale.
Thine eyen daswen eek, as that me thinketh,
And wel I woot thy breeth ful soure stinketh;
That sheweth wel thow art nat wel disposed.
Of me, certein, thow shalt nat been yglosed!

35   Se how he ganeth, lo, this dronken wight,
As thogh he wolde swolwe us anon-right.
Hoold cloos thy mouth, man, by thy fader kin!
The devel of helle sette his foot therin!
Thy cursed breeth infecte wol us alle.

40   Fy, stinking swin, fy! Foule moot thee falle!
A, taketh hede, sires, of this lusty man!
Now, swete sire, wol ye justen atte fan?
Therto me thinketh ye been wel yshape!
I trowe that ye dronken han win-ape,

45   And that is whan men pleyen with a straw.'
            And with this speche the Cook wax wrooth and
                    wraw
And on the Manciple he gan nodde faste
For lakke of speche, and doun the hors him caste,

---

22 **hevinesse** drowsiness   23 **Noot I nat** I do not know **me were levere** I
would rather   24 **galoun win** gallon of wine   31 **daswen** grow dim
33 **wel disposed** in good health   34 **yglosed** flattered   35 **ganeth** yawns
wight creature   36 **swolwe** swallow   40 **Foule moot thee falle** I hope you
come to a bad end   41 **lusty** gallant   42 **justen atte fan** joust at the
quintain (n.)   43 **yshape** prepared   44 **dronken han win-ape** have drunk
yourself stupid   46 **wax wrooth and wraw** grew angry
47 **on . . . gan nodde** shook his head at **faste** vigorously   48 **caste** threw

Wheras he lay til that men up him took.
This was a fair chivachee of a cook! 50
Allas, he nadde yholde him by his ladel!
And, er that he again were in his sadel,
Ther was gret showving, bothe to and fro,
To lifte him up, and muchel care and wo,
So unweldy was this sory palled goost. 55
And to the Manciple thanne spak oure Hoost:
    'Bicause drinke hath dominacioun
Upon this man, by my savacioun,
I trowe he lewedly wolde telle his tale.
For, were it win or old or moisty ale 60
That he hath dronke, he speketh in his nose,
And fneseth faste, and eek he hath the pose.
He hath also to do moore than inow
To kepe him and his capul out of the slow;
And if he falle from his capul eftsoone, 65
Thanne shal we alle have inow to doone
In liftinge up his hevy dronken cors.
Telle on thy tale; of him make I no fors.
– But yet, Manciple, in feith, thow art to nice
Thus openly repreve him of his vice. 70
Another day he wole, paraventure,
Reclaime thee, and bringe thee to lure.
I mene, he speke wole of smale thinges,
As for to pinchen at thy rekeninges,
That were nat honeste, if it cam to preef.' 75
    'No,' quod the Manciple, 'that were a gret
        mescheef!

49 **Wheras** where   50 **chivachee** feat of horsemanship   52 **were** was
53 **showving** shoving   54 **care and wo** trouble and distress   55 **So** helpless
was this wretched feeble soul   59 **lewedly** incompetently   60 **moisty** new
62 **fneseth** wheezes **the pose** a cold in the head   63 **inow** enough
64 **capul** horse **slow** mire   65 **eftsoone** a second time
66 **inow to doone** our hands full   67 **cors** body   68 **make I no fors** I do not
care about   69 **to nice** too foolish   70 **repreve him of** reprove him for
72 **Reclaime thee** cut short your flight **lure** see n.   73 **smale** trivial
74–5 Such as finding fault with your accounts, which would not be to your
credit, if it came to the crunch   76 **mescheef** misfortune

So mighte he lightly bringe me in the snare.
Yet hadde I levere payen for the mare
Which he rit on, than he sholde with me strive.
80   I wol nat wrathe him, also mote I thrive!
That that I spak, I seide it in my bourde.
And wite ye what? I have here in a gourde
A draghte of win, ye, of a ripe grape,
And right anon ye shul seen a good jape.
85   This Cook shal drinke therof, if that I may;
Up peine of deeth, he wol nat seye me nay.'
      And certeinly, to tellen as it was,
Of this vessel the Cook drank faste – allas!
What neded it? He drank inow biforn!
90   And whan he hadde pouped in this horn,
To the Manciple he took the gourde again;
And of that drinke the Cook was wonder fain,
And thanked him, in swich wise as he koude.
      Thanne gan oure Hoost to laughen wonder loude,
95   And seide, 'I se wel, it is necessarye,
Where that we goon, good drinke we with us carye,
For that wol turne rancour and disese
T'acord and love, and many a wrong appese.
      'O Bacus, yblessed be thy name,
100   That so kanst turnen ernest into game!
Worship and thank be to thy deitee!
Of that matere ye gete namoore of me;
Telle on thy tale, Manciple, I the preye.'
      'Wel, sire,' quod he, 'now herkneth what I seye.'

---

77 **lightly** easily   79 **rit** (= *rideth*) rides   80 **wrathe** anger
also mote I thrive as I may prosper   81 **in my bourde** jokingly
82 **gourde** flask   88 **faste** heartily   90 **pouped** tooted
91 **took . . . again** gave back   92 **fain** glad   94 **wonder** wonderfully
96 **Where that** wherever   97 **disese** vexation   98 **appese** appease
99 **Bacus** Bacchus, god of wine   101 **Worship** honour   **thy deitee** you
103 **I the preye** I beg you

THE MANCIPLE'S TALE

Heere biginneth the Maunciples
Tale of the crowe.

Whan Phebus dwelled here in this erthe adoun,   105
As olde bookes maken mencioun,
He was the mooste lusty bachiler
In al this world, and eek the beste archer.
He slow Phitoun, the serpent, as he lay
Slepinge again the sonne upon a day.   110
And many another noble worthy dede
He with his bowe wroghte, as men may rede.
    Pleyen he koude on every minstralcye,
And singen that it was a melodye
To heren of his clere vois the soun.   115
Certes, the king of Thebes, Amphioun,
That with his singing walled that citee
Koude nevere singen half so wel as he.
Therto he was the semelieste man
That is, or was, sith that the world bigan.   120
What nedeth it hise fetures to discrive?
– For in this world was noon so fair on live.
He was therwith fulfild of gentillesse,
Of honour, and of parfit worthinesse.
    This Phebus, that was flour of bachelrye   125
As wel in fredom as in chivalrye,

---

105 **Phebus** Phoebus Apollo, god of the sun
107 **mooste lusty bachiler** most gallant knight   110 **again the sonne** in the
sun   112 **wroghte** performed   113 **minstralcye** musical instruments
114 **that** so that   119 **Therto** in addition **semelieste** most handsome
121 **fetures** features **discrive** describe   122 **on live** alive
123 **therwith** besides   124 **parfit worthinesse** perfect nobility
125 **bachelrye** knighthood   126 **fredom** magnanimity

For his desport – in signe eek of victorye
Of Phitoun, so as telleth us the storye –
Was wont to beren in his hand a bowe.

130   Now hadde this Phebus in his hous a crowe,
Which in a cage he fostred many a day,
And taughte it speke, as men teche a jay.
Whit was this crowe as is a snow-whit swan,
And countrefete the speche of every man

135   He koude, whan he sholde telle a tale.
Therwith in al this world no nightingale
Ne koude by an hondred thousand deel
Singen so wonder mirily and weel.

        Now hadde this Phebus in his hous a wif,
140   Which that he lovede moore than his lif,
And night and day dide evere his diligence
Hire for to plese, and doon hire reverence;
Save oonly, if the sothe that I shal sayn,
Jalous he was, and wolde han kept hire fain,

145   For him were looth bijaped for to be.
And so is every wight in swich degree;
But al in idel, for it availleth noght.
A good wif, that is clene of werk and thoght,
Sholde nat be kept in noon await, certain;

150   And trewely, the labour is in vain
To kepe a shrewe, for it wol nat be.
This holde I for a verray nicetee,
To spille labour for to kepe wives.
– Thus writen olde clerkes in hir lives.

127 **desport** recreation   132 **speke** to speak   134 **countrefete** imitate
137 **by an hondred thousand deel** a hundred thousandth part
138 **mirily** sweetly   141 **dide evere his diligence** always endeavoured
142 **doon hire reverence** show her respect   143 **sothe** truth
144 **wolde han kept hire fain** would gladly have kept her confined   145 For
he was unwilling to be deceived   146 **swich degree** such a position
147 **in idel** in vain   148 **clene of** pure in   149 **kept in . . . await** watched
suspiciously   151 **shrewe** bad woman   152 **verray nicetee** true folly
153 **spille** waste   154 **writen** wrote **in hir lives** while they were alive

But now to purpos, as I first bigan: 155
This worthy Phebus dooth al that he kan
To plesen hire, weninge for swich plesaunce,
And for his manhode and his governaunce,
That no man sholde han put him from hire grace.
But, God it woot, ther may no man embrace   160
As to destreine a thing which that nature
Hath naturelly set in a creature.

　Take any brid, and put it in a cage,
And do al thin entente and thy corage
To fostre it tendrely with mete and drinke,   165
Of alle deintees that thow kanst bithinke,
And kepe it also clenly as thow may,
Although his cage of gold be never so gay,
Yet hath this brid by twenty thousand fold
Levere in a forest, that is rude and cold,   170
Goon ete wormes and swich wrecchednesse.
For evere this brid wol doon his bisinesse
To eschape out of his cage, if he may;
His libertee this brid desireth ay.

　Lat take a cat, and fostre him wel with milk   175
And tendre flessh, and make his couche of silk,
And lat him seen a mous go by the wal –
Anon he weiveth milk and flessh and al,
And every deintee that is in that hous,
Swich appetit hath he to ete a mous!   180
Lo, heere hath lust his dominacioun,
And appetit flemeth discrecioun.

157 **weninge** believing **plesaunce** attentiveness 158 **manhode** courtesy
governaunce behaviour 159 **grace** favour 160 **embrace** bring it about
161 **destreine** restrain 164 And give your whole mind and attention
166 **bithinke** imagine 167 **clenly** neatly 168 **gay** fine
170 **Levere** rather 171 **wrecchednesse** vile things
172 **doon his bisinesse** do his best 175 **Lat take** suppose one were to take
178 **weiveth** abandons 181 **lust** desire 182 **flemeth** banishes
discrecioun judgement

A she-wolf hath also a vileins kinde:
The lewedeste wolf that she may finde,
185 Or leest of reputacioun, that wol she take,
In time whan hir lust to han a make.
      Alle thise ensamples speke I by thise men
That ben untrewe, and nothing by wommen.
For men han evere a likerous appetit
190 On lower thing to parforme hir delit
Than on hire wives, be they never so faire,
Ne never so trewe, ne so debonaire.
Flessh is so newefangel – with meschaunce! –
That we ne konne in nothing han plesaunce
195 That sowneth into vertu any while.
      This Phebus, which that thoghte upon no gile,
Deceived was, for al his jolitee,
For under him another hadde she,
A man of litel reputacioun,
200 Nat worth to Phebus in comparisoun.
The moore harm is, it happeth ofte so,
Of which ther cometh muchel harm and wo.
      And so bifel, whan Phebus was absent,
His wif anon hath for hir lemman sent.
205 Hir lemman? Certes, this is a knavissh speche!
Foryeveth it me, and that I yow biseche.
      The wise Plato seyth, as ye may rede,
The word moot nede acorde with the dede.
If men shal telle proprely a thing,
210 The word moot cosin be to the werking.

---

183 **vileins kinde** base nature   184 **lewedeste** coarsest   186 **hir lust** she
wants **make** mate   187 **by** concerning   188 **nothing** not at all
189 **likerous** lecherous   190 **parforme hir delit** take their pleasure
192 **debonaire** meek   193 **newefangel** fond of novelty
with meschaunce curse it   194 **konne** can   195 **sowneth into** is consistent
with   197 **jolitee** handsomeness   198 **under him** behind his back
201 **moore** greater   204 **lemman** lover   205 **knavissh speche** vulgar
expression   208 **moot nede acorde with** must necessarily match   210 The
word must be akin to the action

I am a boistous man, right thus seye I:
Ther nis no difference, trewely,
Bitwix a wif that is of heigh degree,
If of hir body dishoneste she be,
And a povre wenche, oother than this –   215
If it so be they werke bothe amis –
But that the gentile, in estat above,
She shal be cleped his lady, as in love,
And for that oother is a povre womman,
She shal be cleped his wenche or his lemman.   220
And God it woot, min owene deere brother,
Men leyn that oon as lowe as lith that oother.
     Right so, bitwix a titlelees tyraunt
And an outlawe or a theef erraunt,
The same I seye: ther is no difference.   225
To Alisandre told was this sentence,
That for the tyraunt is of gretter might,
By force of meinee for to sleen dounright,
And brennen hous and hoom, and make al plain,
Lo, therfore is he cleped a capitain;   230
And for the outlawe hath but smal meinee,
And may nat doon so gret an harm as he,
Ne bringe a contree to so gret meschief,
Men clepen him an outlawe or a theef.
But for I am a man noght textuel,   235
I wol noght telle of textes never a del;
I wol go to my tale, as I bigan.
     Whan Phebus wif hadde sent for hire lemman,
Anon they wroghten al hire lust volage.
The white crowe, that heng ay in the cage   240

211 **boistous** straightforward   213 **degree** rank   214 **dishoneste** unchaste
215 **povre** poor   217 **gentile** high-born lady   218 **cleped** called
223 **titlelees** having no title, usurping   224 **theef erraunt** bandit
226 **sentence** saying   227 **for** because   228 **meinee** troops   **dounright** out of
hand   229 **make al plain** level everything   231 **but** only
233 **meschief** affliction   235 **textuel** learned   236 **never a del** not a bit
239 **wroghten** performed   **lust volage** wanton pleasure   240 **ay** all the time

Biheld hir werk, and seide never a word.
And whan that hoom was come Phebus the lord,
This crowe sang, 'Cokkow! Cokkow! Cokkow!'
　　'What, brid?' quod Phebus, 'what song
　　　　singestow?
245　Ne were thow wont so mirily to singe
That to min herte it was a rejoisinge
To here thy vois? Allas, what song is this?'
'By God!' quod he, 'I singe nat amis!
Phebus,' quod he, 'for al thy worthinesse,
250　For al thy beautee and thy gentillesse,
For al thy song and al thy minstralcye,
For al thy waiting, blered is thin eye
With oon of litel reputacioun,
Nat worth to thee, as in comparisoun,
255　The montaunce of a gnat, so moot I thrive!
For on thy bed thy wif I sey him swive.'
　　What wol ye moore? The crowe anon him tolde,
By sadde toknes and by wordes bolde,
How that his wif hadde doon hire lecherye,
260　Him to gret shame and to gret vileinye,
And tolde him ofte he sey it with hise eyen.
　　This Phebus gan aweyward for to wryen,
And thoghte his sorweful herte brast atwo;
His bowe he bente, and sette therinne a flo,
265　And in his ire his wif thanne hath he slain –
This is th'effect; ther nis namoore to sayn.
For sorwe of which, he brak his minstralcye,
Bothe harpe and lute and giterne and sawtrye;

245 **mirily** sweetly　　248 **amis** wrongly　　249 **for** in spite of
251 **minstralcye** musical ability　　252 **waiting** watching
blered is thin eye you have been hoodwinked　　255 **montaunce** value
so moot I thrive as I may prosper　　256 **sey** saw　**swive** fuck
258 **sadde toknes** reliable signs　　260 To his great shame and dishonour
262 **gan aweyward for to wryen** turned away　　263 **brast atwo** would break
in two　　264 **flo** arrow　　266 **th'effect** all there is to say
267 **minstralcye** musical instruments　　268 **giterne** gittern (g.)
sawtrye psaltery (g.)

And eek he brak hise arwes and his bowe.
And after that thus spak he to the crowe: 270
   'Traitour,' quod he, 'with tonge of scorpioun,
Thow hast me broght to my confusioun!
Allas, that I was wroght! Why nere I ded?
O deere wif, o gemme of lustihed,
That were to me so sad and eek so trewe,   275
Now listow deed, with face pale of hewe,
Ful giltelees – that dorste I swere, iwys!
O rakel hand, to doon so foule amis!
O trouble wit! O ire recchelees,
That unavised smitest giltelees!   280
O wantrust, ful of fals suspecioun!
Where was thy wit and thy discrecioun?
O, every man be war of rakelnesse!
Ne trowe nothing withouten strong witnesse.
Smit nat to soone, er that ye witen why,   285
And beth avised wel and sobrely,
Er ye doon any execucioun
Upon youre ire for suspecioun.
Allas, a thousand folk hath rakel ire
Fully fordoon, and broght hem in the mire!   290
Allas, for sorwe I wol myselven sle!'
   And to the crowe, 'O false theef!' seide he,
'I wol thee quite anon thy false tale.
Thow songe whilom lik a nightingale;
Now shaltow, false theef, thy song forgon,   295
And eek thy white fetheres everychon,
Ne nevere in al thy lif ne shaltow speke.
Thus shal men on a traitour been awreke!

272 **confusioun** ruin   273 **nere I** should I not be   274 **lustihed** delight
275 **sad** constant   276 **listow** you lie   277 **dorste I** I dare   278 **rakel** rash
279 **trouble wit** disturbed mind   **recchelees** heedless
280 **unavised** thoughtlessly   281 **wantrust** mistrust   282 **wit** reason
discrecioun judgement   283 **rakelnesse** rashness   285 **witen** know
286 **beth avised** take thought   290 **fordoon** destroyed   293 **thee quite** pay
you back for   294 **whilom** formerly   295 **forgon** lose
298 **awreke** avenged

Thow and thy ofspring evere shul be blake,
300   Ne nevere swete noise shul ye make,
But evere crye again tempest and rain,
In tokeninge that thurgh thee my wif is slain.'
And to the crowe he stirte, and that anon,
And pulled hise white fetheres everychon,
305   And made him blak, and rafte him al his song,
And eek his speche, and out at dore him slong
Unto the devel, which I him bitake.
And for this cas ben alle crowes blake.

Lordinges, by this ensample I yow preye,
310   Beth war, and taketh kepe what that ye seye:
Ne telleth nevere no man in youre lif
How that another man hath dight his wif.
He wol yow haten mortally, certein.
Daun Salomon, as wise clerkes seyn,
315   Techeth a man to kepen his tonge wel –
But, as I seide, I am nat textuel –
But nathelees, thus taughte me my dame:
'My sone, thenk on the crowe, a Goddes name!
My sone, keep wel thy tonge, and kepe thy freend.
320   A wikked tonge is worse than a feend;
My sone, from a feend men may hem blesse!
My sone, God, of his endelees goodnesse,
Walled a tonge with teeth and lippes eke,
For man sholde him avise what he speeke.
325   My sone, ful ofte for to muche speche
Hath many a man ben spilt, as clerkes teche,
But for litel speche, avisely,
Is no man shent, to speke generally.

---

301 **again** at the approach of   302 **In tokeninge** as a sign
303 **stirte** sprang **anon** without delay   304 **pulled** plucked out
305 **rafte** took away   306 **slong** slung   307 **bitake** consign to
308 **for this cas** because of this incident   310 **Beth war** take note
taketh kepe be careful   312 **dight** had it off with   320 **feend** devil
321 **hem blesse** guard themselves   324 **him avise** consider **speeke** says
326 **spilt** ruined   327 **avisely** with forethought   328 **shent** destroyed

My sone, thy tonge sholdestow restreine
At alle times, but whan thow doost thy peine   330
To speke of God in honour and preyere.
The firste vertu, sone, if thow wolt leere,
Is to restreine and kepe wel thy tonge;
Thus lernen children whan that they ben yonge.
My sone, of muchel speking ivele avised,   335
Ther lasse speking hadde inow suffised,
Comth muchel harm; thus was me told and taught.
In muchel speche sinne wanteth naught.
Wostow wherof a rakel tonge serveth?
Right as a swerd forkutteth and forkerveth   340
An arm atwo, my deere sone, right so
A tonge kutteth frendship al atwo.
A janglere is to God abhominable.
Rede Salomon, so wis and honurable;
Rede David in his Psalmes; rede Senekke.   345
My sone, spek noght, but with thin heed thow
       bekke.
Dissimule as thow were deef, if that thow heere
A janglere speke of perilous matere.
The Fleming seyth – and lerne it if thee leste –
That litel jangling causeth muchel reste.   350
My sone, if thow no wikked word hast seid,
Thee thar nat drede for to be biwreid;
But he that hath misseid, I dar wel sayn,
He may by no wey clepe his word again.
Thing that is seid, is seid, and forth it gooth,   355
Thogh him repente, or be him leef or looth.

330 **but** except **doost thy peine** endeavour   332 **leere** learn
335 **ivele avised** ill-considered   336 Where less speech would have been
quite sufficient   338 **wanteth naught** is not lacking   339 Do you know
what a rash tongue is good for   340 **forkutteth** cuts **forkerveth** slices
343 **janglere** gossip   346 **bekke** nod   347 **Dissimule as** pretend
349 **if thee leste** if it please you   350 **jangling** chattering   352 You need not
fear to be betrayed   353 **misseid** said something wrong
354 **clepe . . . again** call back   356 **be him leef or looth** whether he likes it or
not

He is his thral to whom that he hath said
A tale of which he is now ivel apaid.
My sone, be war, and be noon auctour newe
360   Of tidinges, wheither they been false or trewe.
Wherso thow come, amonges hye or lowe,
Kepe wel thy tonge, and think upon the crowe.'

Heere is ended the Maunciples
Tale of the crowe.

358 **ivel apaid** sorry   359 **auctour newe** originator   361 **Wherso** wherever

THE PARSON'S PROLOGUE

*Heere folweth the Prologe of
the Persouns Tale.*

By that the Maunciple hadde his tale al ended,
The sonne fro the south line was descended
So lowe that he nas nat, to my sighte,
Degrees nine and twenty as in highte.
Foure of the clokke it was, so as I gesse,   5
For ellevene foot, or litel moore or lesse,
My shadwe was at thilke time as there,
Of swiche feet as my lengthe parted were
In sixe feet equal of proporcioun.
Therwith the mones exaltacioun –   10
I mene Libra – alwey gan ascende,
As we were entring at a thropes ende.
    For which oure Hoost, as he was wont to gye,
As in this cas, oure joly compaignye,
Seide in this wise: 'Lordinges everychon,   15
Now lakketh us no tales mo than oon.
Fulfild is my sentence and my decree;
I trowe that we han herd of ech degree.
Almoost fulfild is al min ordinaunce.
I pray to God, so yeve him right good chaunce   20
That telleth this tale to us lustily!
    'Sire preest,' quod he, '– artow a vicary

1 **By that** by the time that   2 **the south line** meridian (n.)   7 **as there** in that
place   8 **lengthe** height   10 see n.   12 **thropes** of a village   13 **gye** govern
14 **joly** gay   18 **of ech degree** from each social rank   19 **ordinaunce** plan
20 **good chaunce** good luck   21 **lustily** entertainingly
22 **vicary** vicar (n.)

Or arte a person? Sey sooth, by thy fey! –
Be what thow be, ne breke thow nat oure pley,
25   For every man save thow hath toold his tale.
Unbokele, and shewe us what is in thy male,
For, trewely, me thinketh by thy cheere
Thou sholdest knitte up wel a greet matere.
Telle us a fable anon, for cokkes bones!'
30   This Persoun answerde al atones:
'Thou getest fable noon ytoold for me.
For Paul, that writeth unto Thimothe,
Repreveth hem that weiven soothfastnesse
And tellen fables and swich wrecchednesse.
35   Why sholde I sowen draf out of my fest,
Whan I may sowen whete, if that me lest?
For which I seye, if that yow list to heere
Moralitee and vertuous matere,
And thanne that ye wol yeve me audience,
40   I wole ful fain, at Cristes reverence,
Do yow plesaunce leefful, as I kan.
But trusteth wel, I am a southren man;
I kan nat geste "rum, ram, ruf" by lettre,
Ne, God woot, rym holde I but litel bettre.
45   And therfore, if yow lest – I wol nat glose –
I wol yow telle a mirye tale in prose,
To knitte up al this feste and make an ende.
And Jesu, for his grace, wit me sende
To shewe yow the wey, in this viage,
50   Of thilke parfit glorious pilgrimage

---

23 **person** parson   24 Whatever you are, do not put a stop to our fun
26 **Unbokele** unbuckle **male** bag (of stories)   27 **cheere** appearance
29 **cokkes bones** a euphemistic substitution for 'Goddes bones'   31 **for** by
33 **weiven soothfastnesse** reject truth   35 **draf** chaff **fest** fist
36 **if that me lest** if it pleases me   39 **that** if (n.) **audience** a hearing
40 **fain** gladly **at Cristes reverence** in honour of Christ   41 **leefful** lawful
42 **southren** southern   43 **geste** recite alliterative verse   45 **glose** use fine
words   47 **feste** entertainment   48 **wit** intellectual capacity

That highte Jerusalem celestial.
And if ye vouchesauf, anon I shal
Biginne upon my tale, for which I preye
Telle youre avis; I kan no bettre seye.
  'But nathelees, this meditacioun   55
I putte it ay under correccioun
Of clerkes, for I am nat textuel.
I take but the sentence, trusteth wel.
Therfore I make protestacioun
That I wol stonde to correccioun.'   60
  Upon this word we han assented soone;
For, as us semed, it was for to doone
To enden in som vertuous sentence,
And for to yeve him space and audience.
And bede oure Hoost he sholde to him seye   65
That alle we to telle his tale him preye.
  Oure Hoost hadde the wordes for us alle:
'Sire preest,' quod he, 'now faire yow bifalle!
Sey what yow list, and we wol gladly heere.'   [73]
And with that word he seide in this manere: [74] 70
'Telleth', quod he, 'youre meditacioun,   [69]
But hasteth yow, the sonne wole adoun.   [70]
Beth fructuous, and that in litel space,   [71]
And to do wel God sende yow his grace.'   [72]

---

52 **vouchesauf** agree 54 **avis** opinion 57 **textuel** learned
58 **sentence** content 61 **word** speech 62 **for to doone** a fit thing to do
64 **space** time 68 **faire yow bifalle** good luck to you
69 **what yow list** what pleases you 73 **fructuous** fruitful, edifying

THE PARSON'S TALE

Heere biginneth the Persouns Tale.

Ier. 6°. State super vias et videte et interrogate de viis antiquis que sit via bona et ambulate in ea et invenietis refrigerium animabus vestris etc.

Oure swete lord God of hevene, that no man wole perisse, but wole that we comen alle to the knoweleche of him and to the blisful lif that is perdurable, [75] | amonesteth us by the prophete Jeremye that seyth in this wise: | 'Stondeth upon the weyes, and seeth and axeth of olde pathes (that is to seyn, of olde sentences) which is the goode wey, | and walketh in that wey, and ye shal finde refresshinge for youre soules, etc.' | Manye been the weyes espirituels that leden folk to oure lord Jesu Crist and to the regne of glorye; | of whiche weyes, ther is a ful noble wey and a ful covenable, which may nat faile to man ne to womman that thurgh sinne hath misgoon fro the righte wey of Jerusalem celestial, [80] | and this wey is cleped penitence, of which man sholde gladly herknen and enquere with al his herte | to wite what is penitence, and whennes it is cleped penitence, and in how manye maneres been the accions or werkinges of penitence, | and how manye spices ther ben of penitence, and whiche thinges apertenen and bihoven to penitence and whiche thinges destourben penitence. |

Seint Ambrose seyth that penitence is the pleininge of man for the gilt that he hath doon, and namoore to do any thing for

Rubric *Ier. 6°* Jeremiah 6 (n.)   75 **wole perisse** will perish **wole that** wishes that **perdurable** everlasting   76 **amonesteth** admonishes
77 **sentences** teachings   80 **covenable** suitable   81 **cleped** called
82 **wite** know **whennes** why **accions** performances   83 **spices** sorts
apertenen belong **bihoven to** are fitting for   84 **pleininge** bewailing

which him oghte to pleine. | And som doctour seyth, 'Penitence is the waimentinge of man that sorweth for his sinne and pineth himself for he hath misdoon.' [85] | Penitence, with certeine circumstances, is verray repentance of a man that halt himself in sorwe and oother peine for hise giltes; | and for he shal be verray penitent, he shal first biwailen the sinnes that he hath doon, and stedefastly purposen in his herte to have shrift of mouthe and to doon satisfaccioun, | and nevere to doon thing for which him oghte moore to biwaile or to compleine, and to continue in goode werkes, or elles his repentance may nat availle. | For, as seyth Seint Isidre, 'he is a japere and a gabbere and no verray repentant, that eftsoone dooth thing for which him oghte repente.' | Wepinge and nat for to stinte to do sinne may nat availe. [90] | But nathelees, men shal hope that at every time that man falleth, be it never so ofte, that he may arise thurgh penitence, if he have grace, but certeinly it is greet doute; | for, as seyth Seint Gregorye, unnethe ariseth he out of his sinne that is charged with the charge of ivel usage. | And therfore repentant folk, that stinte for to sinne, and forlete sinne er that sinne forlete hem, Holy Chirche halt hem siker of hire savacion. | And he that sinneth and verraily repenteth him in his laste, Holy Chirche yet hopeth his savacioun, by the grete mercy of oure lord Jesu Crist, for his repentaunce; but taak the siker wey. |

And now, sith I have declared yow what thing is penitence, now shul ye understonde that ther been three accions of penitence. [95] | The firste is that if a man be baptised after that he hath sinned, | Seint Augustin seyth, but he be penitent for his olde sinful lif, he may nat biginne the newe clene lif. | For, certes, if he be baptised withouten penitence of his olde gilt, he receiveth the mark of baptesme, but nat the grace, ne the

85 **som** a certain **waimentinge** lamentation **pineth** tortures   86 **verray** true
87 **shrift** confession   89 **japere** trifler **gabbere** idle talker **eftsoone** again
90 **stinte** cease   92 **unnethe** with difficulty **charged** weighed down
93 **forlete** renounce **siker** sure   94 **in his laste** at his death   97 **but** unless
clene pure

remissioun of hise sinnes, til he have repentance verray. |
Another defaute is this: that men doon deedly sinne after that
they han received baptesme. | The thridde defaute is that men
fallen in venial sinnes after hir baptesme fro day to day. [100] |
Therof seyth Seint Augustin that penitence of goode and humble
folk is the penitence of every day. |

The spices of penaunce been three: that oon of hem is
solempne, another is commune, and the thridde is privee. |
Thilke penaunce that is solempne is in two maneres, as to be
put out of Holy Chirche in Lente for slaughtre of children and
swich maner thing. | Another is whan a man hath sinned openly,
of which sinne the fame is openly spoken in the contree, and
thanne Holy Chirche by jugement destreineth him for to do
open penaunce. | Commune penaunce is that preestes enjoinen
men communly in certein cas, as for to goon, paraventure,
naked in pilgrimage or barefoot. [105] | Privee penaunce is
thilke that men doon alday for privee sinnes, of whiche we
shrive us prively and receive privee penance. |

Now shaltow understande what is bihovely and necessarye
to verray parfit penitence, and this stant on three thinges: |
contricioun of herte, confessioun of mouth, and satisfaccioun. |
For which seyth Seint John Crisostomus: 'Penitence destreineth
a man to accepte benignely every peyne that him is enjoined,
with contricioun of herte and shrift of mouth, with satis-
faccioun, and in wirkinge of alle manere humilitee.' | And this
is fruitful penitence again three thinges in which we wrathe
oure lord Jesu Crist [110] | – this is to seyn, by delit in thinkinge,
by recchelesnesse in spekinge, and by wikked sinful wirkinge. |
And agains thise wikkede giltes is penitence, that may be likned
unto a tree. |

The roote of this tree is contricioun, that hideth him in the
herte of him that is verray repentant right as the roote of a tree
hideth him in the erthe. | Of the roote of contricioun springeth
a stalke that bereth braunches and leves of confessioun

102 **solempne** ritual **commune** public **privee** private 104 **fame** report
destreineth constrains 106 **shrive us** confess 109 **benignely** patiently
110 **again** for **wrathe** anger 111 **recchelesnesse** carelessness

and fruit of satisfaccioun. | For which Crist seyth in his gospel, 'Dooth digne fruit of penitence'; for by this fruit may men knowe this tree, and nat by the roote that is hid in the herte of man, ne by the braunches ne the leves of confessioun. [115] | And therfore oure lord Jesu Crist seyth thus: 'By the fruit of hem shul ye knowe hem.' | Of this roote eek springeth a seed of grace, the which seed is moder of sikernesse, and this seed is egre and hoot. | The grace of this seed springeth of God, thurgh remembrance on the day of dome and on the peines of helle. | Of this matere seyth Salomon that in the drede of God man forleteth his sinne. | The heete of this seed is the love of God and the desiring of the joye perdurable. [120] | This heete draweth the herte of man to God and dooth him hate his sinne; | for soothly, ther is nothing that savoureth so wel to a child as the milk of his norice, ne nothing is to him moore abhominable than thilke milk whan it is medled with oother mete. | Right so, the sinful man that loveth his sinne, him semeth that it is to him moost swete of any thing, | but fro that time that he loveth sadly oure lord Jesu Crist, and desireth the lif perdurable, ther nis to him nothing moore abhominable. | For soothly, the lawe of God is the love of God; for which David the prophete seyth, 'I have loved thy lawe, and hated wikkednesse and hate.' He that loveth God kepeth his lawe and his word. [125] | This tree saugh the prophete Daniel in spirit upon the avisioun of Nabugodonosor, whan he conseiled him to do penitence. | Penance is the tree of lif to hem that it receiven, and he that holdeth him in verray penitence is blessed, after the sentence of Salomon. |

In this penitence or contricioun man shal understonde foure thinges: that is to seyn, what is contricioun, and whiche ben the causes that moeven a man to contricioun, and how he sholde be contrit, and what contricioun availeth to the soule. | Thanne is it thus, that contricioun is the verray sorwe that a man receiveth in his herte for his sinnes, with sad purpos to

---

115 **digne** worthy   117 **sikernesse** security **egre** pungent
118 **dome** judgement   121 **dooth him** causes him to   122 **norice** nurse
124 **sadly** steadfastly   127 **after** according to   129 **sad** steadfast

shrive him and to do penance, and neveremoore to do sinne. |
And this sorwe shal been in this manere, as seyth Seint Bernard:
'It shal been hevy, and grevous, and ful sharp and poinaunt in
herte.' [130] | First, for man hath agilt his lord and his creatour,
and moore sharp and poinaunt for he hath agilt his fader
celestial, | and yet moore sharp and poinaunt, for he hath
wrathed and agilt him that boghte him, that with his precious
blood hath delivered us fro the bondes of sinne, and fro the
crueltee of the devel, and fro the peines of helle. |

The causes that oghte moeve a man to contricioun been sixe.
First, a man shal remembre him of hise sinnes | (but looke he
that thilke remembraunce ne be to him no delit by no wey, but
gret shame and sorwe for his gilt); for Job seyth sinful men doon
werkes worthy of confusioun. | And therfore seyth Ezechie, 'I
wol remembre me alle the yeres of my lif in bitternesse of min
herte.' [135] | And God seyth in the Apocalips: 'Remembre yow
fro whennes that ye ben falle', for biforn that time that ye
sinned, ye were the children of God, and limes of the regne
of God. | But for youre sinne ye ben woxen thral, and foul,
and membres of the feend, hate of aungels, sclaundre of Holy
Chirche, and foode of the false serpent, perpetuel matere of the
fir of helle; | and yet moore foul and abhominable, for ye
trespassen so ofte time as dooth the hound that retourneth to
ete his spewing. | And yet be ye fouler, for youre longe con-
tinuinge in sinne and youre sinful usage, for which ye been
roten in youre sinne, as a beest in his donge. | – Swiche manere
of thoughtes maken a man to have shame of his sinne and no
delit, as God seyth by the prophete Ezechiel: [140] | 'Ye shal
remembre yow of youre weyes and they shuln displese yow.'
Soothly, sinnes been the weyes that leden folk to helle. |

The seconde cause that oghte make a man to have desdein of
sinne is this: that, as seyth Seint Peter, 'whoso that dooth sinne
is thral of sinne', and sinne put a man in greet thraldam. |

---

130 **poinaunt** piercing   131 **agilt** offended against
136 **Apocalips** Apocalypse, Book of Revelation **limes** members
137 **ben woxen** have become **thral** enslaved **hate** object of hatred
138 **spewing** vomit   139 **continuinge** continuance

And therfore seyth the prophete Ezechiel: 'I wente sorweful in desdain of myself.' Certes, wel oghte a man have desdain of sinne, and withdrawe him fro that thraldom and vileinye. | And lo, what seyth Seneca in this matere? He seyth thus: 'Though I wiste that neither God ne man ne sholde nevere knowe it, yet wolde I have desdain for to do sinne.' | And the same Seneca also seyth, 'I am born to gretter thinges than to be thral to my body, or than for to maken of my body a thral.' [145] | Ne a fouler thral may no man ne womman make of his body than for to yeve his body to sinne. | Al were it the fouleste cherl or the fouleste womman that liveth, and leest of value, yet is he thanne moore foul and moore in servitute. | Evere fro the hyer degree that man falleth, the moore is he thral, and moore to God and to the world vil and abhominable. | O goode God, wel oghte man have desdain of sinne, sith that thurgh sinne, ther he was free now is he maked bonde. | And therfore seyth Seint Augustin: 'If thow hast desdain of thy servant if he agilte or sinne, have thow thanne desdain that thou thyself sholdest do sinne.' [150] | Take reward of thy value, that thou ne be to foul to thyself. | Allas, wel oghten they thanne have desdain to ben servantz and thralles to sinne, and soore ben ashamed of hemself, | that God of his endelees goodnesse hath set hem in heigh estat or yeven hem wit, strengthe of body, heele, beautee, prosperitee, | and boghte hem fro the deeth with his herte-blood, that they so unkindely, agains his gentilesse, quiten him so vileinsly, to slaughtre of hir owene soules! | O goode God, ye wommen that been of so greet beautee, remembreth yow of the proverbe of Salomon! He seyth: [155] | 'Likneth a fair womman that is a fool of hire body lik to a ring of gold that were in the groin of a sowe.' | For right as a sowe wroteth in everich ordure, so wroteth she hire beautee in stakinge ordure of sinne. |

The thridde cause that oghte moeve a man to contricioun is drede of the day of dome and of the horrible peines of helle. |

---

144 **Though I wiste** even if I knew   151 **Take reward of** have regard to
152 **soore** bitterly   153 **heele** health   154 **unkindely** ungratefully
vileinsly vilely   156 **Likneth** compare   **groin** snout   157 **wroteth** grubs
about

For, as Seint Jerome seyth, 'at every time that me remembreth
of the day of dome I quake; | for whan I ete, or drinke, or
whatso that I do, evere semeth me that the trompe sowneth in
min ere: [160] | "Riseth ye up that ben dede, and cometh to the
jugement!" ' | O goode God, muchel oghte a man to drede swich
a jugement, 'theras we shullen ben alle', as seyth Seint Poul,
'biforn the sete of oure lord Jesu Crist,' | whereas he shal make
a general congregacioun, whereas no man may ben absent | –
for certes there availeth noon essoine ne excusacioun – | and
nat oonly that oure defautes shullen be juged, but eek that alle
oure werkes shullen openly be knowe. [165] | And, as seyth
Seint Bernard, 'ther ne shal no pledinge availle ne no sleighte;
we shullen yeve rekeninge of everich idel word.' | There shul
we han a juge that may nat ben deceived ne corrupt; and why?
For, certes, alle oure thoghtes ben discovered as to him, ne for
preyere ne for mede he shal nat ben corrupt. | And therfore
seyth Salomon, 'the wrathe of God ne wol nat spare no wight,
for preyere ne for yifte,' and therfore at the day of dome, ther
nis noon hope to escape. | Wherfore, as seyth Seint Anselme,
'ful gret angwissh shullen the sinful folk have at that time. |
Ther shal the stierne and wrothe juge sitte above, and under
him the horrible pit of helle open to destroyen him that moot
biknowen hise sinnes, whiche sinnes openly ben shewed biforn
God and biforn every creature; [170] | and on the left side, mo
develes than herte may bithinke, for to harye and drawe the
sinful soules to the peine of helle. | And withinne the hertes of
folk shal be the bitinge conscience, and withoute-forth shal be
the world al brenninge. | Whider shal thanne the wrecched
sinful man flee to hide him? Certes, he may nat hide him; he
moste come forth and shewe him.' | For certes, as seyth Seint
Jerome, 'the erthe shal caste him out of him, and the see also,
and the eir also, that shal be ful of thonderclappes and
lightninges.' | Now soothly, whoso wel remembreth him of

162 **sete** throne   164 **essoine** excuse for non-appearance in court at the
appointed time   166 **sleighte** cunning   167 **corrupt** corrupted
mede bribery   170 **moot biknowen** must confess   171 **harye** drag
172 **withoute-forth** outside

thise thinges, I gesse that his sinne shal nat turne him into delit
but to gret sorwe, for drede of the peine of helle. [175] | And
therfore seyth Job to God, 'Suffre, lord, that I may a while
biwaile and wepe, er I go withoute returninge to the dirke lond
covered with the derknesse of deeth, | to the lond of misese and
of derknesse, whereas is the shadwe of deeth, whereas ther is
noon ordre or ordinaunce, but grisly drede that evere shal
laste.' | Lo, here may ye seen that Job preyde respit a while, to
biwepe and waile his trespas; for soothly, o day of respit is
bettre than al the tresor of this world. | And forasmuche as a
man may acquite himself biforn God by penitence in this world,
and nat by tresor, therfore sholde he preye to God to yeve him
respit a while to biwepe and biwailen his trespas. | For certes,
al the sorwe that a man mighte make fro the biginning of the
world nis but a litel thing at regard of the sorwe of helle. [180] |
The cause why that Job clepeth helle 'the lond of derknesse': |
understondeth that he clepeth it lond or erthe for it is stable
and nevere shal faille; dirk, for he that is in helle hath defaute
of light material | – for certes, the derke light that shal come
out of the fir that evere shal brenne, shal turne him al to peine
that is in helle, for it sheweth him to the horrible develes that
him tormenten; | 'covered with the derknesse of deeth' – that is
to seyn, that he that is in helle shal have defaute of the sighte
of God, for certes, the sighte of God is the lif perdurable. | 'The
derknesse of deeth' ben the sinnes that the wrecched man hath
doon, whiche that destourben him to see the face of God, right
as a derk clowde bitwixe us and the sonne. [185] | 'Lond of
miseise', bicause that ther ben three maneres of defautes, agains
three thinges that folk of this world han in this present lif: that
is to seyn, honours, delices, and richesses. | Agains honour,
have they in helle shame and confusioun; | for wel ye woot that
men clepen honour the reverence that man doth to man, but in
helle is noon honour ne reverence, for certes, namoore reverence

---

177 **misese** suffering   178 **o** one   179 **acquite himself** make amends
180 **at regard of** in comparison with   182 **defaute** lack
185 **destourben him to see** prevent him from seeing   186 **miseise** misery
187 **confusioun** disgrace

shal be doon there to a king than to a knave. | For which God
seyth by the prophete Jeremye: 'Thilke folk that me despisen
shulle ben in despit.' | Honour is eek cleped greet lordshipe;
ther shal no wight serven oother, but of harm and torment.
Honour is eek cleped greet dignitee and heighnesse, but in helle
shullen they ben al fortroden of develes. [190] | As God seyth,
'the horrible develes shulle goon and comen upon the hevedes
of dampned folk', and this is forasmuche as the hyer that they
were in this present lif, the moore shulle they ben abated and
defouled in helle. | Agains the richesse of this world shul they
han miseise of poverte, and this poverte shal be in foure
thinges: | in defaute of tresor, of which that David seyth, 'The
riche folk, that embraceden and oneden al hire herte to tresor
of this world, shulle slepe in the slepinge of deeth, and nothing
ne shal they finden in hire handes of al hire tresor.' | And
mooreover the miseise of helle shal ben in defaute of mete and
drinke. | For God seyth thus by Moises: 'They shul ben wasted
with hunger, and the briddes of helle shul devouren hem with
bitter deeth, and the galle of the dragon shal ben hire drinke,
and the venim of the dragon hire morsels.' [195] | And forther
over, hire miseise shal ben in defaute of clothing, for they shulle
be naked in body as of clothing, save the fir in which they
brenne and othere filthes, | and naked shul they ben of soule,
as of alle manere vertues, which that is the clothing of soule.
Where ben thannne the gaye robes and the softe shetes and the
smale shertes? | Loo, what seyth God of hem by the prophete
Isaie, that 'under hem shul ben strawed motthes and hire cover-
tures shulle ben of wormes of helle'. | And forther over hire
miseise shal ben in defaute of frendes, for he is nat povere that
hath goode frendes; but there is no freend, | for neither God ne
no creature shal ben freend to hem, and everich of hem shal
haten oother with deedly hate. [200] | The sones and the
doghtren shullen rebellen agains fader and moder, and kinrede

188 **knave** commoner   190 **heighnesse** high rank **fortroden of** trampled by
191 **hevedes** heads **abated** degraded   193 **oneden** united
196 **forther over** in addition   197 **smale** fine-spun   198 **strawed** strewn
covertures coverlets

agains kinrede, and chiden and despisen everich of hem oother
bothe day and night, as God seyth by the prophete Michias. |
And the lovinge children that whilom loveden so flesshly everich
oother, wolden everich of hem eten oother if they mighte; | for
how sholde they loven hem togidre in the peine of helle, whan
they hateden everich of hem oother in the prosperitee of this
lif? | For truste wel, hire flesshly love was deedly hate, as seyth
the prophete David: 'Whoso that loveth wikkednesse, he hateth
his soule,' | and whoso hateth his owene soule, certes, he may
love noon oother wight in no manere. [205] | And therfore, in
helle is no solas ne no frendshipe, but evere the moore flesshly
kinredes that ben in helle, the moore cursinges, the moore
chidinges, and the moore deedly hate ther is among hem. | And
forther over, they shul have defaute of alle manere delices; for
certes, delices ben after the appetites of the five wittes, as sighte,
heringe, smellinge, savoringe, and touchinge, | but in helle hir
sighte shal be ful of derknesse and of smoke, and therfore ful
of teeres, and hire heringe ful of waimentinge and of grintinge
of teeth, as seyth Jesu Crist. | Hir nosethirles shul be ful of
stinkinge stink, and as seyth Isaie the prophete, 'hire savoringe
shal be ful of bitter galle,' | and touchinge of al hir body
ycovered with 'fir that nevere shal quenche, and with wormes
that nevere shul dien', as God seyth by the mouth of Isaie.
[210] | And forasmuche as they shul nat wene that they may
dien for peine, and by hire deeth fle fro peine, that may they
understonde in the word of Job, that seyth 'theras is the shadwe
of deth'. | Certes, a shadwe hath the liknesse of the thing of
which it is shadwe, but shadwe is nat the same thing of which
it is shadwe. | Right so fareth the peine of helle: it is lik deeth
for the horrible angwissh. And why? – for it peineth hem evere
as thogh men sholde die anon, but certes, they shal nat die. |
For, as seyth Seint Gregorye, 'to wrecche kaitives shal be deeth

---

201 everich each   202 whilom formerly flesshly in the flesh
206 solas comfort   207 delices luxuries after according to
savoringe tasting   208 grintinge gnashing   209 nosethirles nostrils
211 wene believe   213 peineth tortures   214 wrecche kaitives miserable
wretches

withoute deeth, and ende withouten ende, and defaute withoute failinge, | for hire deeth shal alwey liven, and hir ende shal everemo biginne, and hir defaute shal nat faile.' [215] | And therfore seyth Seint John the evaungelist: 'They shullen folwe deeth, and they shul nat finde him, and they shul desiren to die, and deeth shal fle fro hem.' | And eek Job seyth that in helle is noon ordre of rewle. | And al be it so that God hath creat alle thinges in right ordre, and nothing withouten ordre, but alle thinges ben ordeined and nombred, yet nathelees, they that ben dampned ben nothing in ordre, ne holden noon ordre, | for the erthe ne shal bere hem no fruit. | For as the prophete David seyth, God shal destroye the fruit of the erthe as fro hem, ne water ne shal yeve hem no moisture, ne the eir no refresshing, ne fir no light. [220] | For, as seyth Seint Basilie, 'the brenninge of the fir of this world shal God yeven in helle to hem that ben dampned, | but the light and the cleernesse shal be yeven in hevene to hise children', right as the goode man yeveth flessh to hise children and bones to hise houndes. | And for they shullen have noon hope to escape, seyth Seint Job atte laste that 'ther shal horrour and grisly drede dwelle withouten ende.' | Horrour is alwey drede of harm that is to come, and this drede shal evere dwelle in the hertes of hem that ben dampned, and therfore han they lorn al hire hope, for sevene causes. | First, for God, that is hir juge, shal be withoute mercy to hem, ne they may nat plese him ne noon of hise halwes, ne they ne may yeve nothing for hire raunson; [225] | ne they have no vois to speke to him, ne they may nat fle fro peine, ne they have no goodnesse in hem that they may shewe to delivere hem fro peine. | And therfore seyth Salomon: 'The wikked man dieth, and whan he is deed, he shal have noon hope to escape fro peine.' | Whoso thanne wolde wel understonde thise peines, and bithinke him wel that he hath deserved thilke peines for his sinnes, certes, he sholde have moore talent to siken and to wepe than for to singen and to pleye. | For, as that seyth Salomon:

217 **rewle** rule   218 **creat** created   **nombred** numbered   224 **lorn** lost
225 **halwes** saints   228 **bithinke him** recollect   **talent** desire

'Whoso that hadde the science to knowe the peines that ben
establised and ordeined for sinne, he wolde make sorwe.' |
'Thilke science', as seyth Seint Augustin, 'maketh a man to
waimente in his herte.' [230] |

The fourthe point that oghte make a man have contricioun
is the sorweful remembrance of the good that he hath left to
doon here in erthe, and eek the good that he hath lorn. | Soothly,
the goode werkes that he hath lost, either they ben the goode
werkes that he wroghte er he fil into deedly sinne, or elles the
goode werkes that he wroghte whil he lay in sinne. | Soothly,
the goode werkes that he dide biforn that he fil in sinne ben al
mortefied and astoned and dulled by the ofte sinning. | The
othere goode werkes, that he wroghte whil he lay in dedly sinne,
thei ben outrely dede as to the lif perdurable in hevene. | Thanne
thilke goode werkes that ben mortefied by ofte sinning – whiche
goode werkes he dide while he was in charitee – ne mowe nevere
quiken again withouten verray penitence. [235] | And therof
seyth God by the mouth of Ezechiel, that 'if the rightful man
returne again from his rightwisnesse and werke wikkednesse,
shal he lyve?' | Nay, for 'alle the goode werkes that he hath
wroght ne shulle nevere ben in remembraunce, for he shal die
in his sinne.' | And upon thilke chapitre seyth Seint Gregorye
thus: that 'we shul understonde this principally, | that whan we
doon dedly sinne it is for noght thanne to reherce or drawen
into memorye the goode werkes that we han wroght biforn.' |
For certes, in the werkinge of the dedly sinne, ther is no trust
to no good werk that we han doon biforn (that is to seyn, as
for to have therby the lif perdurable in hevene). [240] | But
nathelees, the goode werkes quiken again and comen again,
and helpen and availlen to have the lif perdurable in hevene,
whan we han contricioun. | But soothly, the goode werkes
that men doon whil they been in dedly sinne, forasmuche as
they were doon in dedly sinne, they may nevere quike again. |
For certes, thing that nevere hadde lif may nevere quiken.

---

229 **science** knowledge 230 **waimente** lament, wail
233 **mortefied** deprived of life **astoned** rendered lifeless 235 **in charitee** in a
state of grace **quiken** come to life 239 **reherce** enumerate

And natheles, al be it that they ne availle noght to han the lif
perdurable, yet availlen they to abregge of the peine of helle, or
elles to gete temporal richesse, | or elles that God wole the
rather enlumine and lightne the herte of the sinful man to have
repentance. | And eek they availen for to usen a man to doon
goode werkes, that the feend have the lasse power of his soule.
[245] | And thus the curteis lord Jesu Crist ne wole that no good
werk be lost, for in somwhat it shal availle. | But forasmuche as
the goode werkes that men doon whil they ben in good lif ben
al mortified by sinne folwinge, and eek sith that alle the goode
werkes that men doon whil they ben in dedly sinne ben outrely
dede as for to have the lif perdurable, | wel may that man that
no good werk ne dooth singe thilke newe Frenshe song, '*J'ay
tout perdu mon temps et mon labour*'. | For certes, sinne
bireveth a man bothe goodnesse of nature and eek the good-
nesse of grace. | For soothly, the grace of the Holy Goost fareth
lik fir, that may nat ben idel; for fir faileth anon as it forleteth
his werkinge, and right so grace faileth anon as it forleteth his
werkinge. [250] | Thanne leseth the sinful man the goodnesse
of glorye, that oonly is bihight to goode men that labouren and
werken. | Wel may he be sory thanne, that oweth al his lif to
God, as longe as he hath lived, and eek as longe as he shal live,
that no goodnesse ne hath to paye with his dette to God to
whom he oweth al his lif. | For truste wel, he shal yeve acountes,
as seyth Seint Bernard, of alle the goodes that han ben yeven
him in this present lif, and how he hath hem despended, | in so
muche that ther shal nat perisse an heer of his heed, ne a
moment of an houre ne shal nat perisse of his time, that he ne
shal yeve of it a rekeninge. |

The fifthe thing that oghte moeve a man to contricioun is
remembrance of the passion that oure lord Jesu Crist suffred
for oure sinnes. [255] | For, as seyth Seint Bernard: 'Whil that

---

243 **abregge** shorten   244 **enlumine and lightne** illuminate and enlighten
245 **usen** accustom   246 **ne wole** does not wish
248 *J'ay tout perdu ... labour* I have completely wasted my time and my
effort   250 **fareth** acts **forleteth** leaves off   251 **bihight** promised
254 **moment** (in medieval reckoning) the fortieth or fiftieth part of an hour
rekeninge account

I live I shal have remembrance of the travailes that oure lord
Jesu Crist suffred in prechinge, | his werinesse in travailinge,
hise temptacions whan he fasted, hise longe wakinges whan he
preyde, hise teeres whan that he weep for pitee of good peple, |
the wo, and the shame, and the filthe that men seiden to him,
of the foule spitting that men spitte in his face, of the buffettes
that men yave him, of the foule mowes and of the repreves that
men to him seiden, | of the nailes with whiche he was nailed to
the crois, and of al the remenant of his passioun that he suffred
for my sinnes, and nothing for his gilt.' | And ye shal under-
stonde that in mannes sinne is every manere of ordre or ordi-
naunce turned up-so-doun. [260] | For it is sooth that God, and
reson, and sensualitee, and the body of man ben so ordeined,
that everich of thise foure thinges sholde have lordshipe over
that oother, | as thus: God sholde have lordshipe over resoun,
and resoun over sensualitee, and sensualitee over the body of
man. | But soothly, whan man sinneth, al this ordre or ordinance
is turned up-so-doun. | And therfore, thanne, forasmuche as
the reson of man ne wol nat be subget ne obeisaunt to God,
that is his lord by right, therfore leseth it the lordshipe that it
sholde have over sensualitee, and eek over the body of man. |
And why? – for sensualitee rebelleth thanne agains resoun, and
by that way leseth reson the lordshipe over sensualitee and over
the body. [265] | For right as reson is rebel to God, right so is
bothe sensualitee rebel to reson and the body also. | And certes,
this desordinaunce, and this rebellioun, oure lord Jesu Crist
aboghte upon his precious body ful deere, and herkneth in
which wise. | Forasmuche thanne as reson is rebel to God,
therfore is man worthy to have sorwe and to be deed. | This
suffred oure lord Jesu Crist for man, after that he hadde be
bitraysed of his disciple, and destreined and bounde so that the
blood brast out at every nail of hise handes, as seyth Seint
Augustin. | And forther over, forasmuchel as reson of man ne

257 **wakinges** vigils   258 **mowes** grimaces **repreves** insults
259 **nothing** not at all   264 **obeisaunt** obedient
267 **desordinaunce** flouting of order **aboghte** paid for
269 **bitraysed** betrayed **destreined** tied up **brast** burst

wol nat daunte sensualitee whan it may, therfore is man worthy
to have shame, and this suffred oure lord Jesu Crist for man
whan they spette in his visage. [270] | And forther over, foras-
muche thanne as the caitif body of man is rebel bothe to resoun
and to sensualitee, therfore is it worthy the deeth, | and this
suffred oure lord Jesu Crist for man upon the crois, whereas
ther was no part of his body free withoute gret peine and bitter
passioun. | And al this suffred Jesu Crist, that nevere forfeted.
'To muchel am I peined for the thinges that I nevere deserved,
and to muche defouled for shendshipe that man is worthy to
have.' | And therfore may the sinful man wel seye, as seyth Seint
Bernard, 'Acursed be the bitternesse of my sinne, for which ther
moste be suffred so muche bitternesse!' | For certes, after the
diverse disordinaunces of oure wikkednesses was the passioun
of Jesu Crist ordeined in diverse thinges, [275] | as thus: certes,
sinful mannes soule is bitraysed of the devel by coveitise of
temporel prosperitee, and scorned by deceite whan he cheseth
flesshly delices, and yet is it tormented by inpacience of adversitee, and bispet by servage and subjeccioun of sinne, and atte
laste it is slain finally. | For this disordinaunce of sinful man
was Jesu Crist first bitraysed, and after that was he bounde,
that cam for to unbinde us of sinne and peine; | thanne was he
biscorned, that oonly sholde ben honoured in alle thinges and
of alle thinges; | thanne was his visage, that oghte be desired to
be seyn of alle mankinde, in which visage angels desiren to
looke, vileinsly bispet; | thanne was he scourged, that nothing
hadde agilt, and finally thanne was he crucified and slain. [280] |
Thanne was acompliced the word of Isaie: 'He was wounded
for oure misdedes and defouled for oure felonies.' | Now sith
that Jesu Crist took upon himself the peine of alle oure wikkednesses, muchel oghte sinful man wepe and biwaile that for hise
sinnes Goddes sone of hevene sholde al this peine endure. |

270 **daunte** subdue   271 **caitif** wretched   273 **forfeted** sinned
shendshipe disgrace   275 **disordinaunces** violations of order
276 **bispet** spat upon   278 **biscorned** scoffed at   279 **seyn** seen
vileinsly shamefully   280 **nothing hadde agilt** had done no wrong

The sixte thing that oghte moeve a man to contricioun is the hope of three thinges: that is to seyn, foryevenesse of sinne, and the yifte of grace wel for to do, and the glorye of hevene, with which God shal gerdone man for hise goode dedes. | And forasmuche as Jesu Crist yeveth us thise yiftes of his largesse and of his soverein bountee, therfore is he cleped *Jesus Nazarenus rex Judeorum.* | 'Jesus' is to seyn 'saveour' or 'savacioun', on whom men shal hope to have foryifnesse of sinnes, which that is propardly savacioun of sinnes. [285] | And therfore seide the aungel to Joseph, 'thow shalt clepe his name Jesus, that shal save his peple of hire sinnes.' | And heerof seyth Seint Peter, 'ther is noon oother name under hevene that is yeve to any man by which a man may be saved, but oonly Jesus.' | '*Nazarenus*' is as muche for to seye as 'florisshinge', in which a man shal hope that he that yeveth him remissioun of sinnes shal yeve him eek grace wel to do, for in the flour is hope of fruit in time cominge, and in foryifnesse of sinnes hope of grace wel to do. | 'I was atte dore of thin herte,' seyth Jesus, 'and cleped for to entre. He that openeth to me shal have foryifnesse of sinne. | I wol entre into him by my grace, and soupe with him' (by the goode werkes that he shal doon, whiche werkes been the foode of God), 'and he shal soupe with me' (by the grete joye that I shal yeve him). [290] | Thus shal man hope that for hise werkes of penaunce God shal yeve him his regne, as he biheteth him in the gospel. |

Now shal man understonde in which manere shal ben his contricioun. I seye, that it shal ben universal and total; this is to seyn, a man shal be verray repentaunt for alle hise sinnes that he hath doon in delit of his thoght, for delit is ful perilous. | For ther ben two manere of consentinges: that oon of hem is cleped consentinge of affeccion, whan a man is moeved to do sinne and deliteth him longe for to thinke on that sinne. | And his reson aperceyveth wel that it is sinne agains the lawe of

283 **gerdone** reward   284 **soverein bountee** supreme generosity
287 **yeve** given   290 **soupe** eat supper   291 **regne** kingdom
biheteth promises

God, and yet his resoun refreineth nat his foul delit or talent, though he se wel apertly that it is agains the reverence of God. Although his resoun ne consente nat to doon that sinne in dede, | yet seyn somme doctours that swich delit that dwelleth longe, it is ful perilous, al be it never so lite. [295] | And also a man sholde sorwe namely for al that evere he hath desired again the lawe of God with parfit consentinge of his resoun, for therof is no doute that it is dedly sinne in consentinge. | For certes, ther is no dedly sinne that it nas first in mannes thoght, and after that in his delit, and so forth into consentinge and into dede. | Wherfore I seye that many men ne repenten hem nevere of swiche thoghtes and delites, ne nevere shriven hem of it, but oonly of the dede of grete sinnes outward. | Wherfore I seye that swiche wikked delites and wikked thoghtes ben subtile bigileres of hem that shullen ben dampned. | Mooreover man oghte to sorwe for hise wikkede wordes as wel as hise wikkede dedes; for certes, the repentaunce of a singuler sinne, and nat repente of alle hise othere sinnes, or elles repente him of alle hise othere sinnes, and nat of a singuler sinne, may nat availe. [300] | For certes, God almighty is al good, and therfore he foryeveth al, or elles right noght. | And herof seyth Seint Augustin: | 'I woot certeinly that God is enemy to everich sinnere'; and how thanne, he that observeth o sinne, shal he have foryevenesse of the remenant of hise othere sinnes? Nay! | And forther over, contricioun sholde be wonder sorweful and anguissous, and therfore yeveth him God pleinly his mercy. And therfore, whan my soule was anguissous withinne me, I hadde remembraunce of God, that my prayere mighte come to him. | Forther over, contricioun moste be continuel, and that man have stedefast purpos to shrive him, and for to amende him of his lif. [305] | For soothly, whil contricioun lasteth, man may evere have hope of foryevenesse, and of this cometh hate of sinne, that destroyeth sinne bothe in himself and eek in

---

294 **refreineth** restrains **talent** desire **apertly** plainly   295 **dwelleth** lasts
al be it never so lite however little it is   296 **again** against
298 **shriven hem** are confessed   299 **bigileres** deceivers
304 **anguissous** anxious **pleinly** fully   305 **amende him of** correct

oother folk at his power. | For which seyth David: 'Ye that loven God, hateth wikkednesse.' For trusteth wel, to love God is for to love that he loveth, and hate that he hateth. |

The laste thing that man shal understonde in contricioun is this: wherof availeth contricioun. I seye that som time contricioun delivereth man fro sinne, | of which that David seyth, 'I seye', quod David (that is to seyn, I purposed fermely) 'to shrive me, and thow, lord, relessedest my sinne.' | And right so as contricioun availeth nat withouten sad purpos of shrifte, if man have oportunitee, right so litel worth is shrifte or satisfaccioun withouten contricioun. [310] | And mooreover, contricion destroyeth the prisoun of helle, and maketh waik and feble alle the strengthes of the develes, and restoreth the yiftes of the Holy Goost and of alle goode vertues. | And it clenseth the soule of sinne, and delivereth the soule fro the peine of helle, and fro the compaignye of the devel, and fro the servage of sinne, and restoreth it to alle goodes espirituels, and to the compaignye and communioun of Holy Chirche. | And forther over, it maketh him that whilom was sone of ire to be sone of grace. And alle thise thinges ben preved by holy writ. | And therfore, he that wolde sette his entente to thise thinges, he were ful wis, for soothly he ne sholde nat thanne in al his lif have corage to sinne, but yeve his body and al his herte to the service of Jesu Crist, and therof doon him hommage. | For soothly, oure swete lord Jesu Crist hath spared us so debonairly in oure folies, that if he ne hadde pitee of mannes soule, a sory song we mighten alle singe. [315] |

[*The Second Part of Penitence: Confession*]

The seconde partie of penitence is confessioun, that is signe of contricioun. | Now shul ye understonde what is confessioun,

306 **at his power** to the best of his ability   308 **wherof availeth** of what benefit is   309 **relessedest** forgave   310 **sad** firm   311 **waik** weak
312 **servage** bondage   **goodes** benefits   314 **sette his entente to** set his heart on   **were** would be   **corage** inclination   **therof** with them
315 **debonairly** gently   316 **partie** part

and wheither it oghte nedes be doon or noon, and whiche thinges ben convenable to verray confessioun. |

First shaltow understonde that confession is verray shewinge of sinnes to the preest. | This is to seyn, 'verray', for he moste confesse him of alle the condiciouns that bilongen to his sinne, as ferforth as he kan. | Al moot be seid, and nothing excused, ne hid, ne forwrapped, and nat avaunte him of hise goode werkes. [320] | And forther over, it is necessarye to understonde whennes that sinnes springen, and how they encressen, and whiche they ben. |

Of the springinge of sinnes seyth Seint Paul in this wise: that 'right as by a man sinne entred first into this world, and thurgh that sinne deth, right so thilke deth entred into alle men that sinneden.' | And this man was Adam, by whom sinne entred into this world whan he brak the comaundementz of God. | And therfore, he that first was so mighty that he sholde nat have died, bicam swich oon that he moste nedes die, wheither he wolde or noon, and al his progenye in this world, that in thilke man sinneden. | Looke that in th'estat of innocence, whan Adam and Eve naked weren in Paradis, and nothing ne hadden shame of hir nakednesse, [325] | how that the serpent, that was moost wily of alle othere bestes that God hadde maked, seide to the womman, 'Why comaunded God to yow ye sholde nat eten of every tree in Paradis?' | The womman answerde: 'Of the fruit', quod she, 'of the trees in Paradis we feden us, but soothly, of the fruit of the tree that is in the middel of Paradis, God forbad us for to ete, ne nat touche it, lest paraventure we sholde dien.' | The serpent seide to the womman, 'Nay, nay, ye shul nat dien of deth; for sothe, God woot that what day that ye eten therof, youre eyen shulle opene and ye shul ben as goddes, knowinge good and harm.' | The womman thanne saugh that the tree was good to feding, and fair to the eyen, and delitable to sighte. She took of the fruit of the tree and eet it, and yaf to

317 **convenable** appropriate   319 **condiciouns** circumstances
320 **moot** must   **forwrapped** covered up   **avaunte him** boast
321 **whennes** whence   322 **springinge** origin   325 **nothing** not at all
329 **eet** ate

hire housbonde, and he eet, and anon the eyen of hem bothe opnede. | And whan that they knewe that they were naked, they sowed of figge-leves a maner of breches to hiden hire membres. [330] | Here may ye seen that dedly sinne hath, first, suggestioun of the feend, as sheweth heere by the naddre, and afterward, the delit of the flessh, as sheweth heere by Eve, and after that, the consentinge of resoun, as sheweth heere by Adam. | For truste wel, though so were that the feend tempted Eve (that is to seyn, the flessh), and the flessh hadde delit in the beautee of the fruit deffended, yet certes, til that reson (that is to seyn, Adam) consented to the eting of the fruit, yet stood he in the estaat of innocence. | Of thilke Adam toke we thilke sinne original, for of him flesshly descended be we alle, and engendred of vile and corrupt matere. | And whan the soule is put in oure body, right anoon is contract original sinne; and that that was erst but oonly peine of concupiscence is afterward bothe peine and sinne. | And therfore be we alle born sones of wratthe and of dampnacioun perdurable, if it nere baptesme that we receiven, which binimeth us the culpe; but for sothe the peine dwelleth with us as to temptacioun (which peine highte concupiscence). [335] | And this concupiscence, whan it is wrongfully disposed or ordeined in man, it maketh him coveite, by coveitise of flessh, flesshly sinne, by sighte of hise eyen as to erthely thinges, and eek coveitise of heynesse by pride of herte. |

Now, as to speke of the firste coveitise, that is concupiscence, after the lawe of oure membres, that weren lawefulliche ymaked and by rightful jugement of God, | I seye, forasmuche as man is nat obeisaunt to God, that is his lord, therfore is the flessh to him desobeisaunt thurgh concupiscence, which that is cleped norissinge of sinne and occasioun of sinne. | Therfore al the while that a man hath in him the peine of concupiscence, it is impossible but he be tempted som time, and moeved in his

---

330 **membres** genitals   331 **by** as regards   **naddre** adder
332 **deffended** forbidden   334 **contract** incurred   **erst** before
335 **perdurable** everlasting   **if it nere** were it not for   **binimeth** takes away
from   **culpe** guilt   336 **heynesse** high rank   337 **after** according to
338 **desobeisaunt** disobedient   **norissinge** nourishing

flessh to sinne, | and this thing may nat faile as longe as he liveth. It may wel wexe feble and faile by vertu of baptesme, and by the grace of God thurgh penitence, [340] | but fully ne shal it nevere quenche, that he ne shal som time be moeved in himself, but if he were al refreided by siknesse, or by malefice of sorcerye, or colde drinkes. | For lo, what seyth Seint Paul: 'The flessh coveiteth again the spirit, and the spirit again the flessh; they ben so contrarye, and so striven, that a man may nat alwey do as he wolde.' | The same Seint Paul, after his grete penaunce in water and in londe – in water by night and by day in gret peril and in gret peine; in londe, in famine and thurst, in coold and clothlees, and ones stoned almoost to the deth | – yet seide he: 'Allas, I kaitif man, who shal delivere me fro the prison of my kaitif body?' | And Seint Jerom, whan he longe time hadde woned in desert, whereas he ne hadde no compaig-nye but of wilde bestes, whereas he ne hadde no mete but herbes, and water to his drinke, ne no bed but the naked erthe, for which his flessh was blak as an Ethiopen for hete, and ney destroyed for cold [345] | – yet seide he that the brenninge of lecherye boiled in al his body. | Wherfore I woot wel sikerly that they ben deceived that seyn that they ne be nat tempted in hir body. | Witnesse on Seint Jame the apostel, that seyth that every wight is tempted in his owene concupiscence; that is to seyn, that everich of us hath matere and occasioun to be tempted of the norissinge of sinne that is in his body. | And therfore seyth Seint John the evaungelist: 'If that we seyn that we be withoute sinne, we deceive us selve, and trouthe is nat in us.' |

Now shal ye understonde in what manere that sinne wexeth and encresceth in man. The firste thing is thilke norissinge of sinne of which I spak biforn, thilke flesshly concupiscence. [350] | And after that comth the subjeccioun of the devel – this

---

341 **quenche** be quenched **refreided** cooled **malefice** witchcraft
342 **again** against   343 **penaunce** suffering **clothlees** without clothes
344 **kaitif** wretched   345 **woned** lived **ney** almost   347 **sikerly** assuredly
348 **everich** each   350 **wexeth** grows

is to seyn, the develes bely, with which he bloweth in man the
fir of flesshly concupiscence. | And after that, a man bithinketh
him wheither he wol doon, or no, thilke thing to which he is
tempted. | And thanne, if that a man withstonde and waive the
firste entisinge of his flessh and of the feend, thanne is it no
sinne; and if so be that he do nat so, thanne feeleth he anoon a
flawmbe of delit. | And thanne is it good to be war and kepe
him wel, or elles he wole falle anon into consentinge of sinne,
and thanne wol he do it, if he may have time and place. | And
of this matere seyth Moises by the devel in this manere: 'The
feend seyth, "I wol chace and pursue the man by wikked suggestioun, and I wol hente him by moevinge or stiringe of sinne,
and I wol departe my prise or my preye by deliberacioun, and
my lust shal ben acompliced in delit. I wol drawe my swerd in
consentinge" [355] | (for certes, right as a swerd departeth a
thing in two peces, right so consentinge departeth God fro man)
"and thanne wol I sle him with min hand in dede of sinne" –
thus seyth the feend.' | For certes, thanne is a man al deed in
soule. And thus is sinne acompliced by temptacioun, by delit,
and by consentinge, and thanne is the sinne cleped actuel. |

   For sothe, sinne is in two maneres: outher it is venial or dedly
sinne. Soothly, whan man loveth any creature moore than Jesu
Crist oure creatour, thanne is it dedly sinne, and venial sinne is
it if man love Jesu Crist lasse than him oghte. | For sothe, the
dede of this venial sinne is ful perilous, for it amenuseth the
love that men sholde han to God moore and moore. | And
therfore if a man charge himself with manye swiche venial
sinnes, certes, but if so be that he som time descharge him of
hem by shrifte, they mowe ful lightly amenuse in him al the
love that he hath to Jesu Crist. [360] | And in this wise skippeth

351 **bely** bellows   352 **bithinketh him** considers   353 **waive** reject
flawmbe flame **delit** pleasure   354 **kepe him** guard himself
355 **by** concerning **chace** harass **hente** catch **departe** single out **prise** booty
lust desire   356 **departeth** divides **dede** the act   357 **actuel** committed by
one's own act (as opposed to original sin)   358 **outher** either
359 **amenuseth** diminishes   360 **charge** burden **but if so be** unless
descharge him rid himself **lightly** easily   361 **skippeth** passes

venial into dedly sinne; for certes, the moore that a man
chargeth his soule with venial sinnes, the moore is he enclined
to falle into dedly sinne. | And therfore lat us nat be necligent
to deschargen us of venial sinnes, for the proverbe seyth that
manye smale maken a greet. | And herkne this ensample: a greet
wawe of the see comth somtime with so greet a violence that it
drencheth the ship. And the same harm doon somtime the smale
dropes of water, that entren thurgh a litel crevace into the
thurrok and in the botme of the ship, if men be so necligent
that they ne descharge hem nat bitime. | And therfore, althogh
ther be a difference bitwixe thise two causes of drenchinge,
algates the ship is dreint. | Right so fareth it somtime of dedly
sinne and of anoyouse veniale sinnes, whan they multiplye in a
man so gretly that thilke worldly thing that he loveth, thurgh
which he sinneth venially, is as gret in his herte as the love of
God, or moore. [365] | And therfore, the love of every thing
that is nat biset in God, ne doon principally for Goddes sake,
althogh that a man love it lasse than God, yet is it venial sinne, |
and dedly sinne whan the love of any thing weyeth in the herte
of man as muche as the love of God, or moore. | 'Dedly sinne',
as seyth Seint Augustin, 'is whan a man turneth his herte fro
God, which that is verray soverein bountee that may nat
chaunge, and yeveth his herte to thing that may chaunge and
flitte.' | And certes, that is every thing save God of hevene. For
sooth is, that if a man yeve his love, the which that he oweth al
to God with al his herte, unto a creature, certes, as muche of
his love as he yeveth to thilke creature, so muche he bireveth
fro God. | And therfore dooth he sinne, for he that is dettour
to God ne yeldeth nat to God al his dette – that is to seyn, al
the love of his herte. [370] |

Now sith man understondeth generally which is venial sinne,
thanne is it covenable to tellen specially of sinnes whiche that

363 **wawe** wave **drencheth** sinks **crevace** crack **thurrok** bilge
364 **dreint** sunk   365 **anoyouse** harmful   366 **biset** fixed
367 **weyeth . . . as muche** is of as much weight   368 **flitte** vary
369 **bireveth** takes away   371 **sith** since **covenable** appropriate

many a man, peraventure, ne demeth hem nat sinnes, and ne
shriveth him nat of the same thinges, and yet nathelees they
been sinnes | soothly, as thise clerkes writen. This is to seyn, that
at every time that man eteth or drinketh moore than suffiseth to
the sustenaunce of his body, in certein he dooth sinne. | And
eek whan he speketh moore than nedeth, it is sinne; eek whan
he herkneth nat benignly the compleinte of the povere; | eek
whan he is in heele of body, and wol nat faste whan oother
folk fasten, withouten cause resonable; eek whan he slepeth
moore than nedeth; or whan he comth by thilke encheson to
late to chirche, or to othere werkes of charite; | eek whan he
useth his wif withoute soverein desir of engendrure, to the
honour of God, or for the entente to yelde to his wif the dette
of his body; [375] | eek whan he wol nat visite the sike and the
prisoner, if he may; eek if he love wif, or child, or oother
worldly thing, moore than reson requireth; eek if he flatere or
blandise moore than him oghte for any necessitee; | eke if he
amenuse or withdrawe the almesse of the povre; eke if he
apparaileth his mete moore deliciously than nede is, or ete to
hastily by likerousnesse; | eek if he tale vanitees at chirche, or
at Goddes service, or that he be a talkere of idel wordes of folye
or of vileinye, for he shal yelde acounte of it at the day of
dome; | eek whan he biheteth or assureth to do thinges that he
may nat parfourne; eek whan that he by lightnesse or folye
misseyeth or scorneth his neighebore; | eek whan he hath any
wikked suspecioun of thing ther he ne woot of it no
soothfastnesse. [380] | Thise thinges, and mo withoute nombre,
ben sinnes, as seyth Seint Augustin. |

Now shal men understonde that, al be it so that noon erthely

---

372 **suffiseth to** is sufficient for   373 **benignly** graciously   374 **heele** health
by thilke encheson for the same reason   375 **useth** has sexual intercourse
with **soverein** supreme **engendrure** procreation **entente** purpose
376 **blandise** blandish   377 **almesse** alms **apparaileth his mete** prepares his
food **deliciously** sumptuously **likerousnesse** gluttony   378 **tale vanitees** tells
idle tales **of vileinye** shameful   379 **biheteth** promises
lightnesse frivolousness **misseyeth** speaks ill of   380 **ther** when
soothfastnesse truth

man may eschewe alle venial sinnes, yet may he refreine him by the brenninge love that he hath to oure lord Jesu Crist, and by preyeres, and confessioun, and othere goode werkes, so that it shal but litel greve. | For, as seyth Seint Augustin, 'if a man love God in swich manere that al that evere he dooth is in the love of God or for the love of God – verraily, for he brenneth in the love of God, | looke how muche that a drope of water that falleth in a furneis ful of fir anoyeth or greveth, so muche anoyeth a venial sinne unto a man that is parfit in the love of Jesu Crist.' | Men may also refreine venial sinne by receivinge worthily of the precious body of Jesu Crist, [385] | by receivinge eek of holy water, by almes-dede, by general confession of *Confiteor* at masse and at complin, and by blessinge of bisshopes and of preestes, and by othere goode werkes. |

[On the Seven Deadly Sins and their Offspring, with Circumstances and Types]

[On Pride]

Now is it bihovely thing to telle whiche ben deedly sinnes; that is to seyn, chieftaines of sinnes. Alle they renne in o lees, but in diverse maneres. Now ben they cleped chieftaines, forasmuche as they ben chief and spring of alle othere sinnes. | Of the roote of thise sevene sinnes thanne is pride the general roote of alle harmes, for of this roote springen certein braunches, as ire, envye, accidie or slewthe, avarice (or coveitise, to commune understondinge), glotonye, and lecherye. | And everich of thise chief sinnes hath hise braunches and hise twigges, as shal be declared in hire chapitres folwinge. |

And thogh so be that no man kan outrely telle the nombre of the twigges, and of the harmes that comen of pride, yet wol

382 **eschewe** avoid **refreine him** restrain himself **greve** harm
384 **anoyeth** harms   386 **almes-dede** alms-giving **Confiteor** see n.
complin compline (g.)   387 **bihovely** necessary **chieftaines** leaders
renne in o lees run on one leash **spring** source   388 **accidie** laziness
slewthe sloth   390 **outrely** completely

I shewe a partie of hem, as ye shul understonde. [390] | Ther is inobedience, avauntinge, ypocrisye, despit, arrogance, impudence, swellinge of herte, insolence, elacioun, inpacience, strif, contumacye, presumpcioun, irreverence, pertinacye, veineglorye, and many another twig that I kan nat declare. | Inobedient is he that desobeyeth, for despit, to the comandementz of God, and to hise sovereins, and to his goostly fader. | Avantour is he that bosteth of the harm or of the bountee that he hath doon. | Ypocrite is he that hideth to shewe him swich as he is, and sheweth him swich as he noght is. | Despitous is he that hath desdein of his neighebore – that is to seyn, of his evene Cristen – or hath despit to doon that him oghte to do. [395] | Arrogant is he that thinketh that he hath thilke bountees in him that he hath nat, or weneth that he sholde have hem by hise desertes, or elles he demeth that he be that he nis nat. | Impudent is he that for his pride hath no shame of hise sinnes. | Swellinge of herte is whan a man rejoiseth him of harm that he hath doon. | Insolent is he that despiseth in his jugement alle oothere folk as to regard of his value, and of his konninge, and of his spekinge, and of his beringe. | Elacioun is whan he ne may neither suffre to have maister ne felawe. [400] | Inpacient is he that wol nat ben ytaught ne undernome of his vice, and by strif werreyeth trouthe witingly, and deffendeth his folye. | Contumax is he that thurgh his indignacioun is agains everich auctoritee or power of hem that ben hise sovereins. | Presumpcioun is whan a man undertaketh an emprise that him oghte nat do, or elles that he may nat do, and that is called surquidye. Irreverence is whan men do nat honour theras hem oghte to doon, and waiten

391 **inobedience** disobedience **avauntinge** boastfulness **despit** disdain
elacioun self-esteem **contumacye** rebelliousness **pertinacye** obstinacy
392 **for despit** out of spite **goostly** spiritual   393 **bountee** good
395 **Despitous** contemptuous **evene Cristen** fellow Christians
396 **demeth** believes   399 **as to regard of** with reference to
konninge intelligence **beringe** behaviour   400 **Elacioun** arrogance
suffre endure   401 **undernome of** reproved for **werreyeth** attacks
witingly knowingly   402 **Contumax** contumacious **indignacioun** arrogance
403 **emprise** enterprise **surquidye** over-ambition **theras** where
waiten expect

to be reverenced. | Pertinacye is whan a man deffendeth his folye and trusteth to muche to his owene wit. | Veineglorye is for to have pompe and delit in his temporel heynesse, and glorifye him in worldly estaat. [405] | Janglinge is whan a man speketh to muche biforn folk, and clappeth as a mille, and taketh no kepe what he seyth. |

And yet is ther a privee spice of pride that waiteth first to be salewed er he wole salewe, al be he lasse worthy than that oother is, paraventure; and eek he waiteth or desireth to sitte, or elles to goon above him in the weye, or kisse pax, or ben encensed, or goon to offringe biforn his neighebore, | and swiche semblable thinges, agains his duetee, paraventure, but that he hath his herte and his entente in swich a proud desir to be magnified and honoured biforn the peple. |

Now ben ther two maneres of pride: that oon of hem is withinne the herte of man, and that oother is withoute. | Of whiche, soothly, thise forseide thinges, and mo than I have seid, apertenen to pride that is in the herte of man, and that othere speces of pride ben withoute. [410] | But natheles, that oon of thise speces of pride is signe of that oother, right as the gaye levesel atte taverne is signe of the win that is in the celer. | And this is in manye thinges, as in speche and contenaunce, and in outrageous array of clothing. | For certes, if ther ne hadde be no sinne in clothing, Crist wolde nat so soone have noted and spoken of the clothing of thilke riche man in the gospel. | And, as seyth Seint Gregorye, that 'precious clothing is cowpable for the derthe of it, and for his softenesse, and for his straungenesse and degisynesse, and for the superfluitee or for the inordinat scantnesse of it.' | Allas, may man nat seen as in oure dayes the

---

405 **temporel heynesse** worldly rank   406 **Janglinge** chattering
clappeth as a mille clacks like a mill   407 **waiteth** expects **salewed** greeted
pax pax-board (n.) **encensed** censed **offringe** the Offertory
408 **semblable** similar **agains his duetee** contrary to what is due to him
411 **levesel** bunch of leaves (used as a tavern sign)
412 **contenaunce** behaviour **outrageous** extravagant
414 **cowpable** blameworthy **derthe** costliness **his** its **straungenesse** rarity
degisynesse elaborateness **inordinat** excessive

sinful costlewe array of clothinge, and namely in to muche
superfluitee or elles in to desordinat scantnesse? [415] |

   As to the firste sinne, that is in superfluitee of clothinge,
which that maketh it so deere, to harm of the peple | – nat oonly
the cost of embrawdinge, the degise endentinge or barringe,
owndinge, palinge, windinge or bendinge, and semblable wast
of clooth in vanitee, | but ther is also costlewe furringe in hire
gownes; so muche pownsoninge of chisel to maken holes, so
muche dagginge of sheris; | forth with the superfluitee in lengthe
of the forseide gownes trailinge in the dong and in the mire, on
horse and eek on foote, as wel of man as of womman, that
al thilke trailinge is verraily as in effect wasted, consumed,
thredbare, and roten with donge, rather than it is yeven to the
povere, to gret damage of the forseide povere folk, | and that
in sondry wise. This is to seyn, that the moore that clooth is
wasted, the moore moot it coste to the peple for the scarsnesse.
[420] | And forther over, if so be that they wolde yeve swich
pownsoned and dagged clothinge to the povere folk, it is nat
convenient to were for hir estaat, ne suffisant to beete hire
necessitee, to kepe hem fro the distemperance of the firmament. |
Upon that oother side, to speke of the horrible disordinat
scantnesse of clothing, as ben thise kutted sloppes or hanselins,
that thurgh hire shortnesse ne covere nat the shameful membres
of man, to wikked entente. | Allas, somme of hem shewen the
shap and the boce of hire horrible swollen membres, that semeth
lik the maladye of hirnia, in the wrappinge of hire hoses, | and
eek the buttokes of hem, that faren as it were the hindre part

415 **costlewe** expensive **to desordinat** excessive
417 **embrawdinge** embroidering **degise** fancy **endentinge** indentation
barringe ornamenting with stripes **owndinge** ornamenting with waved lines
palinge decoration with vertical stripes **windinge** twining (with thread or
silk) **bendinge** decorating with stripes   418 **pownsoninge** punching
chisel pointed blade **dagginge** ornamenting clothing with pointed edges
sheris scissors   419 **forth with** together with   421 **convenient** suitable
estaat rank **beete** relieve **distemperance** inclemency
422 **disordinat** inordinate **kutted** shortened **sloppes** loose tunics
hanselins very short jackets   423 **boce** bulge **hirnia** hernia **wrappinge** folds
424 **hindre part** rear

of a she-ape in the fulle of the moone. | And mooreover the wrecched swollen membres that they shewe thurgh degisinge, in departinge of hire hoses in whit and reed, semeth that half hire shameful privee membres weren flayn. [425] | And if so be that they departen hire hoses in othere colours, as is whit and blew, or whit and blak, or blak and reed, and so forth, | thanne semeth it as by variaunce of colour that half the partie of hire privee membres ben corrupt by the fir of Seint Antony, or by cancre, or oother swich meschaunce. | Of the hindre part of hire buttokes it is ful horrible for to see, for certes, in that partie of hire body theras they purgen hire stinkinge ordure, | that foule partie shewe they to the peple proudly, in despit of honestetee, which honestetee that Jesu Crist and hise frendes observede to shewen in hir live. | Now, as of the outrageous array of wommen, God woot that thogh the visages of somme of hem seme ful chaast and debonaire, yet notifye they in hire array of atir likerousnesse and pride. [430] | I sey nat that honestetee in clothinge of man or woman is uncovenable, but certes, the superfluitee or desordinat scantitee of clothinge is reprevable. | Also, the sinne of aornement or of apparaille is in thinges that apertenen to ridinge, as in to manye delicat horses that ben holden for delit, that ben so faire, fatte, and costlewe, | and also many a vicious knave that is sustened bicause of hem, in to curious harneis, as in sadeles, in crouperes, peitrels, and bridles covered with precious clothing and riche barres and plates of gold and of silver. | For which God seyth by Zakarye the prophete: 'I wol confounde the rideres of swiche horses.' | Thise folk taken litel reward of the ridinge of Goddes sone of hevene, and of his harneis, whan he rood upon the asse, and ne hadde

425 **degisinge** fancy clothing **departinge** dividing **flayn** flayed
427 **corrupt** infected **fir of Seint Antony** skin disease (e.g. erysipelas)
cancre spreading ulcer   429 **in despit of honestetee** in contempt of decency
430 **debonaire** meek **atir** fine clothing **likerousnesse** lecherousness
431 **honestetee** beauty **uncovenable** unfitting **scantitee** scantiness
reprevable blameworthy   432 **aornement** adornment **apertenen to** are
connected with **delicat** fine   433 **to curious** over-elaborate
crouperes cruppers **peitrels** breast-plates   435 **taken litel reward of** have
little concern for

noon oother harneis but the povere clothes of hise disciples; ne
we ne rede nat that evere he rood on oother beest. [435] | I
speke this for the sinne of superfluitee, and nat for resonable
honestetee, whan reson it requireth. |

And forther over, certes, pride is gretly notified in holdinge
of greet meinee, whan they been of litel profit or of right no
profit, | and namely whan that meinee is felonous and dam-
ageous to the peple by hardinesse of hey lordshipe or by wey
of offices. | For certes, swiche lordes sellen thanne hir lordship
to the devel of helle, whan they sustenen the wikkednesse of
hire meinee; | or elles whan thise folk of lowe degree, as thilke
that holden hostelries, sustenen the thefte of hire hostilers, and
that is in many manere of deceites. [440] | Thilke manere of
folk ben the flies that folwen the hony, or elles the houndes that
folwen the careine. Swich forseide folk stranglen spiritually hire
lordshipes. | For which thus seyth David the prophete: 'Wikked
deth mote come upon thilke lordshipes, and God yeve that
they mote descende into helle al doun, for in hire houses been
iniquitees and shrewednesses, and nat God of hevene.' | And
certes, but if they doon amendement, right as God yaf his
benisoun to Laban by the service of Jacob, and to Pharao by
the service of Joseph, right so God wol yeve his malisoun to
swiche lordshipes as sustenen the wikkednesse of hire ser-
vauntz, but they come to amendement. | Pride of the table
appeereth eek ful ofte, for certes, riche men ben cleped to festes,
and povere folk ben put awey and rebuked. | Also in excesse of
diverse metes and drinkes, and namely swiche manere bake-
metes and dissh-metes, brenninge of wilde fir, and peinted and
castelled with papir, and semblable wast, so that it is abusioun
for to thinke. [445] | And eek in to gret preciousnesse of vessel,

437 **notified** made known **meinee** retinue   438 **felonous** cruel
damageous harmful **hardinesse** arrogance   439 **sustenen** support
441 **careine** carrion   442 **God yeve** may God grant
443 **benisoun** blessing **malisoun** curse **but** unless   444 **cleped** invited
rebuked repelled   445 **bake-metes** pies **dissh-metes** food cooked in dishes
wilde fir artificial flames **castelled with papir** decorated with paper
towers (n.) **abusioun** perversion

and curiositee of minstralcye, by whiche a man is stired the
moore to delices of luxurye. I If so be that he sette his herte the
lasse upon oure lord Jesu Crist, certein, it is a sinne, and
certeinly the delices mighte ben so grete in this cas that man
mighte lightly fallen by hem into dedly sinne. I The especes
that sourden of pride, soothly, whan they sourden of malice,
imagined, avised, and forncast, or elles of usage, ben dedly
sinnes, it is no doute. I And whan they sourden by freletee,
unavised, sodeinly, and sodeinly withdrawe agein, al be they
grevouse sinnes, I gesse that they ne be nat dedly. I

Now mighte men axe wherof that pride sourdeth and springeth; and I seye, somtime it springeth of the goodes of nature,
and somtime of the goodes of fortune, and somtime of the
goodes of grace. [450] I Certes, the goodes of nature stonden
outher in goodes of body or goodes of soule. I Certes, goodes
of body been heele of body, strengthe, delivernesse, beautee,
gentrice, franchise. I Goodes of nature of the soule ben good
wit, sharp understondinge, subtil engin, vertu naturel, good
memorye. I Goodes of fortune ben richesses, hey degrees of
lordshipes, preisinges of the peple. I Goodes of grace ben
science, power to suffre spiritual travaille, benignitee, vertuous
contemplacioun, withstondinge of temptacioun, and semblable
thinges. [455] I Of whiche forseide goodes, certes, it is a ful gret
folye a man to priden him in any of hem alle. I Now, as for to
speke of goodes of nature, God woot, that somtime we han
hem in nature as muche to oure damage as to oure profit. I As
for to speke of heele of body, certes, it passeth ful lightly, and
eek it is ful ofte enchesoun of the siknesse of oure soule; for,
God woot, the flessh is a ful greet enemy to the soule, and

446 **curiositee** elaborateness **delices of luxurye** self-indulgent pleasures
448 **especes** species **sourden of** arise from
imagined, avised, and forncast plotted, planned, and premeditated
of usage from habit   449 **freletee** frailty **unavised** without premeditation
451 **stonden . . . in** consist in   452 **delivernesse** agility **gentrice** nobility of
birth **franchise** being free-born   453 **wit** intelligence **engin** inventiveness
vertu naturel natural ability   454 **preisinges** praises
455 **science** knowledge   458 **heele** health **enchesoun** cause

therfore, the moore that the body is hool, the moore be we in peril to falle. | Eke for to pride him in his strengthe of body, it is an heigh folye, for certes, the flessh coveiteth again the spirit, and ay the moore strong that the flessh is, the sorier may the soule be. | And over al this, strengthe of body and worldly hardinesse causeth ful ofte many a man to peril and meschaunce. [460] | Eke for to pride him of his gentrye is ful gret folye, for ofte time the gentrye of the body binimeth the gentrye of the soule, and eek we ben alle of o fader and of o moder, and alle we ben of o nature, roten and corrupt, bothe riche and povre. | For sothe, o manere gentrye is for to preise: that apparailleth mannes corage with vertues and moralitees, and maketh him Cristes child; | for truste wel, that over what man that sinne hath maistrye, he is a verray cherl to sinne. |

Now ben ther general signes of gentilesse, as eschewinge of vice and ribaudye, and servage of sinne in word, in werk, and contenaunce, | and usinge vertu, curteisye, and clennesse, and to be liberal – that is to seyn, large by mesure, for thilke that passeth mesure is folye and sinne. [465] | Another is to remembre him of bounte that he of oother folk hath received. | Another is to be benigne to hise goode subgetz. Wherfore seyth Senek, 'Ther is nothing moore covenable to a man of heigh estaat than debonairetee and pitee. | And therfore thise flies that men clepe bees, whan they maken hire king, they chesen oon that hath no prikke wherwith he may stinge.' | Another is, a man to have a noble herte and a diligent to attaine to hye vertuouse thinges. | Now certes, a man to pride him in the goodes of grace is eek an outrageous folye, for thilke yiftes of grace that sholde have turned him to goodnesse and to medicine turneth him to venim and to confusioun, as seyth Seint Gregorye. [470] | Certes also,

459 **coveiteth** desires **again** against **sorier** more wretched
460 **hardinesse** boldness   461 **gentrye** nobility **binimeth** takes away
462 **apparailleth** furnishes **corage** heart   463 **cherl** bondsman
464 **eschewinge** avoidance **servage** bondage **contenaunce** behaviour
465 **large by mesure** generous in moderation   467 **covenable** fit
debonairetee kindness   468 **flies** insects   470 **goodes** blessings
turned him to goodnesse been beneficial to him

whoso prideth him in the goodes of fortune, he is a ful gret fool, for somtime is a man a gret lord by the morwe that is a kaitif and a wrecche er it be night. | And somtime the richesse of a man is cause of his deeth; somtime the delices of a man ben cause of the grevous maladye thurgh which he dieth. | Certes, the commendacioun of the peple is somtime ful fals, and ful brotel for to triste; this day they preise, tomorwe they blame. | God woot, desir to have commendacioun eek of the peple hath caused deth to many a bisy man. |

[The Remedy Against the Sin of Pride]

Now, sith that so is that ye han understonde what is pride, and whiche ben the speces of it, and whennes pride sourdeth and springeth, [475] | now shul ye understonde which is the remedye agains pride, and that is humilitee or mekenesse. | That is a vertu thurgh which a man hath verray knoweleche of himself and holdeth of himself no pris ne deintee as in regard of hise desertes, consideringe evere his freletee. | Now ben ther three maneres of humilitee: as, humilitee in herte; another, humilitee in his mouth; the thridde, in hise werkes. | The humilitee in herte is in foure maneres: that oon is whan a man holdeth himself as naught worth biforn God of hevene; another is whan he ne despiseth noon oother man; | the thridde is whan he rekketh nat though men holde him noght worth; the ferthe is whan he nis nat sory of his humiliacioun. [480] | Also the humilitee of mouth is in foure thinges: in atempree speche, and in humblesse of speche, and whan he biknoweth with his owene mouth that he is swich as him thinketh that he is in his herte; another is whan he preiseth the bountee of another man and nothing therof amenuseth. | Humilitee eek in werkes is in foure

471 **kaitif** captive   473 **brotel** brittle
477 **holdeth of himself no pris ne deintee** sets no store or value by himself
as in regard of with respect to   479 **naught worth** worth nothing
480 **rekketh nat** does not care   481 **atempree** moderate
biknoweth acknowledges **bountee** virtue **amenuseth** diminishes

maneres: the firste is whan he putteth othere men biforn him; the seconde is to chese the loweste place overal; the thridde is gladly to assente to good conseil; | the ferthe is to stonde gladly to the award of his soverein, or of him that is in hyer degree. Certein, this is a greet werk of humilitee. |

[On Envy]

After pride wol I speke of the foule sinne of envye, which that is, as by the word of the philosophre, 'sorwe of othere mennes prosperitee', and after the word of Seint Augustin, it is 'sorwe of othere mennes wele, and joye of othere mennes harm'. | This foule sinne is platly agains the Holy Goost. Al be it so that every sinne is agains the Holy Goost, yet nathelees, forasmuche as bountee aperteneth proprely to the Holy Goost, and envye cometh proprely of malice, therfore is it proprely agains the bountee of the Holy Goost. [485] | Now hath malice two speces, that is to seyn, hardnesse of herte in wikkednesse, or elles the flessh of man is so blind that he considereth nat that he is in sinne, or rekketh nat that he is in sinne, which is the hardnesse of the devel. | That oother spece of malice is whan that a man werreyeth trouthe, whan he woot that it is trouthe, and eek whan he werreyeth the grace that God hath yeve to his neighe-bore, and al this is by envye. | Certes, thanne is envye the worste sinne that is, for soothly, alle othere sinnes ben som time oonly agains o special vertu, | but certes, envye is agains alle vertues and agains alle goodnesses, for it is sory of alle the bountees of his neighebore, and in this manere it is divers from alle othere sinnes. | For wel unnethe is ther any sinne that it ne hath som delit in itself, save oonly envye, that evere hath in itself angwissh and sorwe. [490] | The speces of envye ben thise: ther is first sorwe of othere mennes goodnesse and of hir

---

482 **chese** choose **conseil** advice   483 **stonde . . . to** submit to
award judgement   484 **wele** prosperity   485 **platly** directly
487 **werreyeth** attacks **grace** good fortune **yeve** given
489 **bountees** virtues **divers** different   490 **wel unnethe** hardly

prosperitee; and prosperitee is kindely matere of joye; thanne
is envye a sinne agains kinde. | The seconde spece of envye is
joye of oother mannes harm, and that is proprely lik to the
devel, that evere rejoiseth him of mannes harm. | Of thise
two speces comth bakbitinge, and this sinne of bakbitinge or
detraccion hath certeine speces, as thus: som man preiseth his
neighebore by a wikked entente, | for he maketh alwey a wikked
knotte atte laste ende – alwey he maketh a 'but' at the laste ende,
that is digne of moore blame than worth is al the preisinge. | The
seconde spece is that if a man be good, and dooth or seyth a
thing to good entente, the bakbitere wol turne al thilke good-
nesse up-so-doun to his shrewed entente. [495] | The thridde is
to amenuse the bountee of his neighebore. | The ferthe spece of
bakbitinge is this, that if men speke goodnesse of a man, thanne
wol the bakbitere seyn 'parfey, swich a man is yet bet than he',
in dispreisinge of him that men preise. | The fifte spece is this,
for to consente gladly and herkne gladly to the harm that men
speke of oother folk. This sinne is ful greet, and ay encreseth
after the wikked entente of the bakbitere. | After bakbitinge
cometh grucchinge or murmuracioun, and somtime it springeth
of inpacience agains God, and somtime agains man. | Agains God
is it whan a man gruccheth again the pine of helle, or agains poverte or los of catel, or again rein or tempest, or elles gruccheth
that shrewes han prosperitee, or elles for that goode men han
adversitee. [500] | And alle thise thinges sholde men suffre
paciently, for they comen by the rightful jugement and ordi-
naunce of God. | Somtime cometh grucching of avarice, as Judas
grucched agains the Magdeleine whan she enointe the heved of
oure lord Jesu Crist with hire precious oinement. | This manere
murmure is swich as whan man gruccheth of goodnesse that him-
self dooth, or that oother folk doon of hire owene catel. | Som-

491 **kindely** natural **kinde** nature   493 **bakbitinge** slander
494 **digne** worthy   495 **shrewed entente** wicked purpose   498 **fifte** fifth
ay continually **after** in proportion to   499 **grucchinge** grumbling
murmuracioun murmuring   500 **pine** suffering **catel** property
shrewes wicked people   501 **ordinaunce** decree   502 **enointe** anointed
heved head   503 **murmure** grumbling **of hire owene catel** with their own
property

time comth murmure of pride, as whan Simon the Pharisee grucched again the Magdeleine whan she approched to Jesu Crist and weep at his feet for hire sinnes. | And somtime it sourdeth of envye, whan men discoveren a mannes harm that was privee, or bereth him on hond thing that is fals. [505] | Murmure eek is ofte amonges servauntz that grucchen whan hire sovereins bidden hem to doon leveful thinges, | and forasmuche as they dar nat openly withseye the comaundementz of hire soverins, yet wol they seyn harm and grucche and murmure prively, for verray despit | – whiche wordes men clepe the develes *Pater Noster* (though so be that the devel ne hadde nevere *Pater Noster*, but that lewed folk yeven it swich a name). | Somtime it comth of ire or privee hate that norisseth rancour in herte, as afterward I shal declare. | Thanne comth eek bitternesse of herte, thurgh which bitternesse every good dede of his neighebore semeth to him bitter and unsavory. [510] | Thanne comth discord, that unbindeth alle manere of frendshipe. Thanne comth scorninge of his neighebore, al do he never so wel. | Thanne comth accusinge, as whan man seketh occasioun to anoyen his neighebore, which that is lik the craft of the devel that waiteth bothe night and day to accusen us alle. | Thanne comth malignitee, thurgh which a man anoyeth his neighebore prively, if he may; | and if he nat may, algate his wikked wil ne shal nat wante, as for to brennen his hous prively, or empoisone or sleen hise bestes, and semblable thinges. |

[*The Remedy Against the Sin of Envy*]

Now wol I speken of the remedye agains this foule sinne of envye. First is the love of God principal, and lovinge of his neighebore as himself, for soothly, that oon ne may nat ben withoute that oother. [515] | And truste wel, that in the name of thy neighebore thow shalt understonde the name of thy

504 **weep** wept   505 **bereth him on hond** accuses him of
506 **leveful** lawful   507 **verray despit** pure resentment
508 **lewed folk** uneducated people   511 **al do he never so wel** however well
he does   512 **waiteth** lies in wait   514 **wante** be lacking

brother, for certes, alle we have o fader flesshly and o moder, that is to seyn Adam and Eve, and eek o fader spirituel, that is God of hevene. | Thy neighebore artow holden for to love and wilne him alle goodnesse, and therfore seyth God, 'love thy neighebore as thyself' – that is to seyn, to savacion bothe of lif and of soule. | And mooreover thow shalt love him in word and in benigne amonestinge and chastisinge, and conforte him in hise anoyes, and preye for him with al thin herte. | And in dede thow shalt love him in swich wise that thow shalt doon to him in charitee as thow woldest that it were doon to thin owene persone. | And therfore thow ne shalt doon him no damage in wikked word, ne harm in his body, ne in his catel, ne in his soule by entising of wikked ensample. [520] | Thow shalt nat desiren his wif, ne none of hise thinges. Understoond eek, that in the name of neighebore is comprehended his enemy. | Certes, man shal love his enemy by the comandement of God, and soothly thy freend shaltow love in God. | I seye, thin enemy shaltow love for Goddes sake, by his comandement, for if it were resoun that man sholde hate his enemy, for sothe God nolde nat receiven us to his love, that ben hise enemys. | Agains three manere of wronges that his enemy dooth to him he shal doon three thinges, as thus: | agains hate and rancour of herte, he shal love him in herte; agains chiding and wikked wordes, he shal preye for his enemy; agains the wikked dede of his enemy, he shal doon him bountee. [525] | For Crist seyth, 'Loveth youre enemys, and preyeth for hem that speke yow harm, and eek for hem that yow chacen and pursuen, and dooth bountee to hem that yow haten.' Loo, thus comaundeth us oure lord Jesu Crist to do to oure enemys. | For soothly, nature driveth us to loven oure frendes, and parfey, oure enemys han moore nede to love than oure frendes, and they that moore nede have, certes to hem shal men doon goodnesse. | And certes, in thilke dede have we remembraunce of the love of Jesu Crist, that deide for hise enemys. | And inasmuche as thilke love is

---

517 **wilne** wish   518 **amonestinge** admonishment **anoyes** troubles
520 **catel** property   525 **bountee** good   526 **chacen** afflict
pursuen persecute

the moore grevous to perfourne, so muche is the moore gret the merite. And therfore the lovinge of oure enemy hath confounded the venim of the devel; | for right as the devel is disconfited by humilitee, right so is he wounded to the deeth by love of oure enemy. [530] | Certes, thanne is love the medicine that casteth out the venim of envye fro mannes herte. | The speces of this paas shullen be moore largely declared in hire chapitres folwinge. |

[On Wrath]

After envye wol I discriven the sinne of ire; for soothly, whoso hath envye upon his neighebore, anon he wole comunly finde him a matere of wratthe, in word or in dede, agains him to whom he hath envye. | And as wel comth ire of pride as of envye, for soothly, he that is proud or envious is lightly wrooth. | This sinne of ire, after the discriving of Seint Augustin, is wikked wil to ben avenged by word or by dede. [535] | Ire, after the philosophre, is the fervent blood of man, yquiked in his herte, thurgh which he wole harm to him that he hateth. | For certes, the herte of man, by eschawfinge and moevinge of his blood, wexeth so trouble that he is out of alle jugement of resoun. |

But ye shal understonde that ire is in two maneres: that oon of hem is good, and that oother is wikked. | The goode ire is by jalousye of goodnesse, thurgh which a man is wrooth with wikkednesse and agains wikkednesse; and therfore seyth a wis man that ire is bet than pley. | This ire is with debonairetee, and it is wrooth withoute bitternesse – nat wrooth agains the man, but wrooth with the misdede of the man, as seyth the prophete David: 'Irascimini et nolite peccare.' [540] | Now, understondeth that wikked ire is in two maneres: that is to

529 **grevous** difficult **perfourne** put into action **confounded** destroyed
530 **disconfited** defeated 532 **paas** see n. **largely** fully
533 **finde him a matere of** find a reason for 534 **lightly** easily
wrooth angry 536 **fervent** hot **yquiked** kindled 537 **eschawfinge** heating
moevinge agitation **trouble** disturbed 539 **jalousye of** zeal for
540 **debonairetee** mildness *Irascimini et nolite peccare* Be ye angry, and sin not

seyn, sodein ire or hastif ire, withoute avisement and con-
sentinge of reson. | The mening and the sens of this is that the
reson of a man ne consente nat to thilke sodein ire, and thanne
is it venial. | Another ire is ful wikked, that comth of felonye of
herte, avised and cast biforn, with wikked wil to do vengeaunce,
and therto his resoun consenteth, and soothly, this is deedly
sinne. | This ire is so displesant to God that it troubleth his
hous, and chaceth the Holy Goost out of mannes soule, and
wasteth and destroyeth the liknesse of God – that is to seyn,
the vertu that is in mannes soule – | and put in him the liknesse
of the devel, and binimeth the man fro God, that is his rightful
lord. [545] | This ire is a ful gret plesaunce to the devel, for it
is the develes forneis, that is eschawfed with the fir of helle. |
For certes, right so as fir is moore mighty to destroye erthely
thinges than any oother element, right so ire is mighty to
destroye alle spirituel thinges. | Looke how that fir of smale
gleedes that ben almoost dede under asshen wolen quike again
whan they ben touched with brimstoon, right so ire wole
everemo quike again whan it is touched by the pride that is
covered in mannes herte. | For certes, fir ne may nat come out
of nothing but if it were first in the same thing naturelly, as fir
is drawen out of flintes with steel. | And right so as pride is ofte
time matere of ire, right so is rancour norice and kepere of ire.
[550] | Ther is a manere tree, as seyth Seint Isidre, that whan
men maken fir of thilke tree and covere the coles of it with
asshen, soothly, the fir of it wol lasten al a yeer or moore. | And
right so fareth it of rancour: whan it is ones conceived in the
hertes of som men, certein, it wol lasten, paraventure, from oon
Estre day unto another Estre day, and moore. | But certes, thilke
man is ful fer fro the mercy of God al thilke while. | In this for-
seide develes fourneis ther forgen thre shrewes: pride, that ay

541 **avisement** reflection   543 **avised** deliberate   **cast biforn** premeditated
544 **wasteth** destroys   545 **put** (= *putteth*) puts   **binimeth** takes away
546 **forneis** furnace   **eschawfed** heated   548 **gleedes** embers   **quike** kindle
brimstoon sulphur   **everemo** always   549 **but if** unless   550 **matere** cause
norice nurse   **kepere** guardian   551 **a manere tree** a kind of tree
552 **Estre day** Easter Sunday   554 **shrewes** villains

bloweth and encreseth the fir by chidinge and wikked wordes; |
thanne stant envye and holdeth the hoote iren upon the herte
of man with a peire of longe toonges of long rancour; [555] |
and thanne stant the sinne of contumelye, or strif and cheeste,
and batereth and forgeth by vileins reprevinges. |

Certes, this cursed sinne anoyeth bothe to the man himself
and eek to his neighebore. For soothly, almoost al the harm
that any man dooth to his neighebore comth of wratthe. | For
certes, outrageous wratthe dooth al that evere the devel him
comaundeth, for he ne spareth neither Crist ne his swete
moder. | And in his outrageous anger and ire, allas, allas, ful
many oon at that time feleth in his herte ful wikkedly bothe of
Crist and eek of alle hise halwes. | Is nat this a cursed vice? Yis,
certes. Allas, it binimeth from man his wit, and his resoun, and
al his debonaire lif espirituel that sholde kepen his soule. [560] |
Certes, it binimeth eek Goddes due lordshipe, and that is
mannes soule and the love of his neighebores. It striveth eek
alday again trouthe; it reveth him the quiete of his herte and
subverteth his soule. |

Of ire comen thise stinkinge engendrures: first, hate, that is
oold wratthe; discord, thurgh which a man forsaketh his olde
freend that he hath loved ful longe; | and thanne cometh werre,
and every manere of wrong that man dooth to his neighebore
in body or in catel. | Of this cursed sinne of ire cometh eek
manslaughtre. And understonde wel, that homicide, that is
manslaughtre, is in diverse wise: som manere of homicide is
spirituel, and som is bodily. | Spirituel manslaughtre is in sixe
thinges: first, by hate; as seyth Seint John, 'he that hateth his
brother is homicide.' [565] | Homicide is eek by bakbitinge, of
whiche bakbiteres seyth Salomon that they han two swerdes
with whiche they sleen hire neighebores; for soothly, as wikke
is to binime him his good name as his lif. | Homicide is eek in

---

555 **toonges** tongs   556 **cheeste** quarreling   **reprevinges** reproaches
557 **anoyeth . . . to** harms   558 **outrageous** excessive
559 **of Crist** towards Christ   **halwes** saints   560 **debonaire** humble
561 **alday** continually   **reveth him** deprives him of   564 **in diverse wise** in
different ways   565 **homicide** a murderer

yevinge of wikked conseil by fraude, as for to yeven conseil
to areisen wrongful custumes and taillages | (of whiche seyth
Salomon: 'Leoun roringe, and bere hongry, ben like to the cruel
lordshipes'), in witholdinge or abregginge of the shepe, or the
hire, or of the wages of servauntz, or elles in usure, or in
withdrawinge of the almesse of povere folk. | For which the
wise man seyth, 'Fedeth him that almoost dieth for honger.'
For soothly, but if thow fede him, thow sleest him; and alle
thise ben dedly sinnes. | Bodily manslaughtre is whan thow
sleest him with thy tonge in oother manere, as whan thow
comandest to sleen a man, or elles yevest him conseil to sleen a
man. [570] | Manslaughtre in dede is in foure maneres: that
oon is by lawe, right as a justice dampneth him that is coupable
to the deeth; but lat the justice be war that he do it rightfully,
and that he do it nat for delit to spille blood, but for kepinge
of rightwisnesse. | Another homicide is doon for necessitee, as
whan a man sleeth another in his defendaunt, and that he
ne may noon ootherwise escape from his owene deeth. | But
certeinly, if he may escape withouten slaughtre of his adversarye
and sleeth him, he dooth sinne, and he shal bere penance as for
deedly sinne. | Eek, if a man by caas or aventure shete an arwe
or caste a stoon with which he sleeth a man, he is homicide. |
Eek, if a womman by necligence overlieth hire child in hir
sleping, it is homicide and deedly sinne. [575] | Eek, whan man
destourbeth concepcioun of a child, and maketh a womman
outher bareine by drinkinge of venemouse herbes thurgh whiche
she may nat conceive, or sleeth a child by drinkes wilfully, or
elles putteth certeine material thinges in hire secree places to
slee the child, | or elles dooth unkindely sinne by which man or
womman shedeth hire nature in manere or in place theras

567 conseil advice areisen levy custumes customary services taillages taxes
568 abregginge reduction shepe wages   571 justice judge
dampneth condemns coupable guilty kepinge preservation
572 in his defendaunt in self-defence   574 caas or aventure chance or
accident shete shoots   575 overlieth lies on   576 outher either
secree places private parts   577 unkindely unnatural
shedeth hire nature emit their seminal fluid

a child may nat be conceived, or elles if a womman have con-
ceived, and hurt hirself and sleeth the child, yet is it homicide. |
What seye we eek of wommen that mordren hir children for
drede of worldly shame? Certes, an horrible homicide. | Homi-
cide is eek if a man approcheth to a womman by desir of
lecherye thurgh which the child is perissed, or elles smiteth a
womman witingly thurgh which she leseth hir child. Alle thise
been homicides and horrible dedly sinnes. |

Yet comen ther of ire manye mo sinnes, as wel in word as in
thoght and in dede; as he that arretteth upon God or blameth
God of thing of which he is himself gilty, or despiseth God and
alle hise halwes, as doon thise cursede hasardours in diverse
contrees. [580] | This cursede sinne doon they whan they felen
in hir herte ful wikkedly of God and of hise halwes. | Also,
whan they treten unreverently the sacrement of the auter, thilke
sinne is so greet that unnethe may it ben releessed but that the
mercy of God passeth alle hise werkes; it is so greet, and he so
benigne. | Thanne comth of ire attry anger; whan a man is
sharply amonested in his shrifte to forleten his sinne, | thanne
wole he be angry, and answeren hokerly and angrily, and
deffenden or excusen his sinne by unstedefastnesse of his flessh;
or elles he dide it for to holde compaignye with hise felawes; or
elles, he seyth, the feend enticed him; | or elles he dide it for his
youthe; or elles his compleccioun is so corageous that he may
nat forbere; or elles it is his destinee, as he seyth, unto a certein
age; or elles, he seyth, it cometh him of gentillesse of hise
auncestres, and semblable thinges. [585] | Alle this manere of
folk so wrappen hem in hir sinnes that they ne wol nat delivere
hemself. For soothly, no wight that excuseth him wilfully of his
sinne may nat been delivered of his sinne til that he mekely
biknoweth his sinne. | After this thanne cometh swering, that

579 **approcheth to** assembles with (sexually) **is perissed** perishes
leseth loses   580 **arretteth upon** attributes to **hasardours** gamblers
582 **unreverently** irreverently **auter** altar **releessed** forgiven
583 **attry** venomous **amonested** admonished **forleten** renounce
584 **hokerly** scornfully **unstedefastnesse** frailty
585 **compleccioun** temperament (g.) **corageous** spirited, ardent
586 **delivere** release **biknoweth** confesses

is expres again the comandement of God, and this bifalleth ofte
of anger and of ire. | God seyth: 'Thow shalt nat take the name
of thy lord God in vein or in idel.' Also, oure lord Jesu Crist
seyth by the word of Seint Mathew: | 'Ne wol ye nat swere in
alle manere; neither by hevene, for it is Goddes trone; ne by
erthe, for it is the bench of his feet; ne by Jerusalem, for it is
the citee of a greet king; ne by thin heed, for thow mayst nat
make an heer whit ne blak; | but seyeth by youre word "ye, ye"
and "nay, nay", and what that is moore, it is of ivel' – thus
seyth Crist. [590] | For Cristes sake, ne swereth nat so sinfully
in dismembringe of Crist, by soule, herte, bones, and body.
For certes, it semeth that ye thinke that the cursede Jewes ne
dismembred nat inough the preciouse persone of Crist, but ye
dismembre him moore. | And if so be that the lawe compelle
yow to swere, thanne rule yow after the lawe of God in youre
swering; as seyth Jeremye, *quarto capitulo*, thow shalt kepe
thre condicions: thou shalt swere 'in trouthe, in doom, and in
rightwisnesse'. | This is to seyn, thow shalt swere sooth, for
every lesinge is agains Crist, for Crist is verray trouthe. And
thinke wel this, that 'every greet swerere nat compelled lawe-
fully to swere, the wounde shal nat departe from his hous' whil
he useth swich unleveful swering. | Thow shalt sweren eek in
doom, whan thow art constreined by thy domesman to wit-
nessen the trouthe. | Eek thow shalt nat swere for envye, ne for
favour, ne for mede, but for rightwisnesse, for declaracioun of
it to the worship of God and helping of thine evene Cristene.
[595] | And therfore, every man that taketh Goddes name in
idel, or falsly swereth with his mouth, or elles taketh on him
the name of Crist, to be called a Cristene man, and liveth agains
Cristes livinge and his techinge, alle they taken Goddes name
in idel. | Looke, eek, what seyth Seint Peter, *Actuum quarto*:
'*non est aliud nomen sub celo,*' *etc.* 'Ther nis noon oother
name', seyth Seint Peter, 'under hevene yeven to men, in which

---

589 **in alle manere** in any way   592 **rule yow after** be guided by
quarto capitulo chapter 4   **swere . . . in doom** take an oath in court
593 **unleveful** unlawful   594 **domesman** judge   595 **mede** reward
worship honour   597 *Actuum quarto* Acts 4

they mowe be saved' – that is to seyn, but the name of Jesu Crist. | Take kepe eek how precious is the name of Jesu Crist; as seyth Seint Paul, *ad Philipenses secundo*, *'in nomine Jesu, etc.*,' that 'in the name of Jesu every knee, of hevenely creatures or erthely or of helle, sholden bowe', for it is so heigh and so worshipful that the cursede feend in helle sholde tremblen to heren it ynempned. | Thanne semeth it that men that sweren so horribly by his blessed name, that they despise it moore boldely than dide the cursede Jewes, or elles the devel, that trembleth whan he hereth his name. | Now certes, sith that swering, but if it be lawefully doon, is so heighly deffended, muche worse is forswering falsly and yet nedelees. [600] | What seye we eek of hem that deliten hem in swering, and holden it a gentrye or a manly dede to swere grete othes? And what of hem that of verray usage ne cesse nat to swere grete othes, al be the cause nat worth a straw? Certes, this is horrible sinne. | Sweringe sodeinly withoute avisement is eek a sinne. | But lat us go now to thilke horrible swering of adjuracioun and conjuracioun, as doon thise false enchauntours or nigromanciens in bacins ful of water, or in a bright swerd, in a cercle, or in a fir, or in a shulder-boon of a sheep. | I kan nat seye but that they doon cursedly and dampnably, agains Crist and al the feith of Holy Chirche. | What seye we of hem that bileeven in divinailes, as by flight or by noise of briddes, or of beestes, or by sort, by geomancye, by dremes, by chirkinge of dores or crakkinge of houses, by gnawinge of rattes and swich manere wrecched-nesse? [605] | Certes, al this thing is deffended by God and by Holy Chirche, for which they been acursed, til they come to amendement, that on swich filthe setten hire bileve. | Charmes for woundes or maladye of men or of bestes, if they taken any

---

598 **Take kepe** take note *ad Philipenses secundo* Philippians 2
heigh exalted **worshipful** honourable **ynempned** named
600 **heighly** solemnly **deffended** forbidden **forswering** perjury
601 **deliten hem** take pleasure **gentrye** mark of breeding
602 **avisement** reflection 603 **adjuracioun** exorcism
conjuracioun conjuration, the invocation of spirits
nigromanciens necromancers 605 **divinailes** divination **sort** casting of lots
geomancye geomancy (n.) **chirkinge** creaking **crakkinge** creaking

effect, it may be, paraventure, that God suffreth it for folk sholden yeve the moore feith and reverence to his name. |

Now wol I speken of lesinges, which generally is fals significacioun of word, in entente to deceiven his evene Cristene. | Som lesinge is of which ther comth noon avantage to no wight, and som lesinge turneth to the ese and profit of o man, and to disese and damage of another man. | Another lesinge is for to saven his lif, or his catel. Another lesinge comth of delit for to lie, in which delit they wol forge a long tale and peinten it with alle circumstaunces, where al the ground of the tale is fals. [610] | Som lesinge comth for he wole sustene his word; and som lesinge comth of reccheleesnesse withouten avisement, and semblable thinges. | Lat us now touche the vice of flateringe, which ne comth nat gladly but for drede or for coveitise. | Flaterye is generally wrongful preisinge. Flatereres ben the develes norices, that norissen hise children with milk of losengerye. | For sothe Salomon seyth that flaterye is wors than detraccioun; for som time detraccioun maketh an hautein man be the moore humble for he dredeth detraccion, but certes, flaterye maketh a man to enhauncen his herte and his contenaunce. | Flatereres ben the develes enchauntours, for they make a man to wene of himself be lik that he nis nat lik. [615] | They ben lik to Judas, that bitraysed a man to sellen him to his enemy, that is to the devel. | Flatereres ben the develes chapelleins, that singen evere '*Placebo*'. | I rekene flaterye in the vices of ire, for ofte time if o man be wrooth with another thanne wole he flatere som wight to sustene him in his querele. | Speke we now of swich cursinge as comth of irous herte. Malisoun generally may be seid every maner power of harm. Swich

607 **suffreth** allows **for** in order that   608 **lesinges** lies
significacioun meaning **evene Cristene** fellow Christians
610 **catel** property **peinten** embellish **with alle circumstaunces** with full
details   611 **sustene** back up   612 **gladly** customarily
613 **losengerye** flattery   614 **hautein** proud
enhauncen his herte and his contenaunce become overbearing
615 **wene of himself be** think himself to be   617 *Placebo* I shall please (n.)
618 **sustene** support **querele** quarrel   619 **Malisoun** cursing

cursinge bireveth man fro the regne of God, as seyth Seint Paul. |
And ofte time swich cursinge wrongfully retorneth again to him
that curseth, as a brid that retorneth again to his owene nest.
[620] | And over alle thing men oghten eschewe to cursen hire
children, and yeven to the devel hire engendrure, as ferforth as
in hem is; certes, it is greet peril and greet sinne. |

Lat us thanne speken of chidinge and reproche, whiche ben
ful grete woundes in mannes herte, for they unsowen the semes
of frendshipe in mannes herte. | For certes, unnethes may a man
pleinly ben accorded with him that hath him openly reviled and
repreved and disclaundred. This is a ful grisly sinne, as Crist
seyth in the gospel. | And taak kepe now, that he that repreveth
his neighebore, outher he repreveth him by som harm of peine
that he hath on his body, as 'mesel', 'croked harlot', or by som
sinne that he dooth. | Now if he repreve him by harm of peine,
thanne turneth the repreve to Jesu Crist, for peine is sent by the
rightwis sonde of God and by his suffrance, be it meselrye or
maime or maladye. [625] | And if he repreve him uncharitably
of sinne, as 'thow holour', 'thow dronkelewe harlot', and so
forth, thanne aperteneth that to the rejoisinge of the devel, that
evere hath joye that men doon sinne. | And certes, chidinge may
nat come but out of a vileins herte, for after the habundance of
the herte speketh the mouth ful ofte. | And ye shul understonde
that, looke, by any wey, whan any man shal chastise another,
that he be war from chidinge or reprevinge, for trewely, but he
be war, he may ful lightly quiken the fir of angre and of wratthe,
which that he sholde quenche, and paraventure sleeth him
which that he mighte chastise with benignitee. | For, as seyth
Salomon, 'the amiable tonge is the tree of lif' (that is to seyn,
of lif espirituel), and soothly, a deslavee tonge sleeth the

bireveth . . . fro deprives of   621 over above   eschewe refrain from
as ferforth as far   622 unsowen unsew   623 unnethes with difficulty
pleinly ben accorded be fully reconciled   disclaundred slandered
624 mesel leper   harlot rogue   625 rightwis sonde just dispensation
suffrance permission   meselrye leprosy   maime maiming   626 holour lecher
dronkelewe drunken   627 vileins wicked   628 by any wey at all costs
reprevinge taunting   quiken kindle   629 deslavee unbridled

spirites of him that repreveth and eek of him that is repreved. |
Loo, what seyth Seint Augustin: 'Ther is nothing so lik the
develes child as he that ofte chideth.' Seint Paul seyth eek: 'The
servant of God bihoveth nat to chide.' [630] | And how that
chidinge be a vileins thing bitwixe alle manere folk, yet is it
certes moost uncovenable bitwixe a man and his wif, for there
is nevere reste. And therfore seyth Salomon: 'An hous that is
uncovered and droppinge, and a chidinge wif, ben like.' | A
man that is in a droppinge hous in manye places, though he
eschewe the droppinge in o place, it droppeth on him in another
place. So fareth it by a chidinge wif: but she chide him in o
place, she wol chide him in another. | And therfore 'bettre is a
morsel of breed with joye than an hous ful of delices with
chidinge', seyth Salomon. | Seint Paul seyth, 'O ye wommen, be
ye subgetes to youre housbondes, as bihoveth in God, and ye
men, loveth youre wives' (*Ad Colossenses tertio*). | Afterward
speke we of scorninge, which is a wikked sinne, and namely
whan he scorneth a man for hise goode werkes. [635] | For
certes, swiche scorneres faren lik the foule tode, that may nat
endure to smelle the soote savour of the vine whanne it
florissheth. | Thise scorneres ben parting-felawes with the devel,
for they han joye whan the devel winneth, and sorwe whan he
leseth. | They ben adversaries of Jesu Crist, for they haten that
he loveth – that is to seyn, savacioun of soule. | Speke we now
of wikked conseil, for he that wikked conseil yeveth is a traitour, for he deceiveth him that trusteth in him, *ut Achitofel ad
Absolonem*. But nathelees, yet is his wikked conseil first again
himself. | For, as seyth the wise man, 'every fals livinge hath
this propretee in himself, that he that wole anoye another man,
he anoyeth first himself.' [640] | And men shul understonde
that man shal nat taken his conseil of fals folk, ne of angry folk,

630 **bihoveth nat** it is not fitting for   631 **how that** although
uncovenable unfitting   634 *Ad Colossenses tertio* Colossians 3
636 **tode** toad   637 **parting-felawes** partners
639 *ut Achitofel ad Absolonem* as Achitofel (did) to Absalon (n.)
again himself to his own disadvantage   640 **livinge** way of life
anoye harm

or grevous folk, ne of folk that loven specially to muchel hir owene profit, ne to muche worldly folk, namely in conseilinge of soules. |

Now comth the sinne of hem that sowen and maken discord amonges folk, which is a sinne that Crist hateth outrely; and no wonder is, for he deide for to make concord. | And moore shame do they to Crist than dide they that him crucifiede; for God loveth bettre that frendshipe be amonges folk than he dide his owene body, the which that he yaf for unitee. Therfore ben they likned to the devel, that evere is aboute to maken discord. | Now comth the sinne of double tonge, swiche as speken faire biforn folk and wikkedly bihinde; or elles they maken semblant as though they speke of good entencioun, or elles in game and pley, and yet they speke of wikked entente. | Now comth biwreying of conseil, thurgh which a man is defamed; certes, unnethe may he restore the damage. [645] | Now comth manace, that is an open folye; for he that ofte manaceth, he threteth moore than he may perfourne ful ofte time. | Now cometh idel wordes; that is, withouten profit of him that speketh tho wordes, and eek of him that herkneth tho wordes. Or elles, idel wordes ben tho that ben nedelees, or withouten entente of naturel profit. | And al be it that idel wordes ben som time venial sinne, yet sholde men douten hem, for we shul yeve rekeninge of hem bifore God. | Now comth jangling, that may nat ben withoute sinne. And, as seyth Salomon, it is a signe of apert folye. | And therfore a philosophre seide, whan men axed him how that men sholde plese the peple, and he answerde, 'Do manye goode werkes, and spek fewe jangles.' [650] | After this comth the sinne of japeres, that ben the develes apes, for they maken folk to laughen at hire japerye as folk doon at the gawdes of an ape. Swiche japes deffendeth Seint Paul. | Looke

641 **grevous** hostile **specially** in particular   642 **outrely** utterly
643 **is aboute to maken** is intent on making   644 **maken semblant** pretend
645 **biwreying** disclosure **conseil** secrets **unnethe** with difficulty
restore repair   646 **threteth** threatens   647 **idel** frivolous **naturel** normal
649 **jangling** gossiping **apert** open   651 **japeres** buffoons
japerye buffoonery **gawdes** tricks

how that vertuouse wordes and holy conforten hem that
travaillen in the servise of Crist, right so conforten the vileins
wordes and knakkes of japeris hem that travaillen in the service
of the devel. |

Thise ben the sinnes that comen of the tonge, that comen of
ire, and of othere sinnes mo. |

[*The Remedy Against the Sin of Wrath*]

The remedye agains ire is a vertu that men clepen mansuetude,
that is debonairetee, and eek another vertu that men callen
pacience or suffraunce. |

Debonairetee withdraweth and refreineth the stiringes and
the moevinges of mannes corage in his herte, in swich manere
that they ne skippe nat out by angre ne by ire. [655] | Suffrance
suffreth swetely alle the anoyaunces and the wronges that men
doon to man outward. | Seint Jerome seyth thus of debonairetee,
that 'it dooth noon harm to no wight ne seyth, ne for noon
harm that men doon or seyn he ne eschawfeth nat agains his
resoun.' | This vertu som time comth of nature, for, as seyth
the philosophre, 'a man is a quik thing, by nature debonaire'
and tretable to goodnesse, but whan debonairetee is enformed
of grace thanne is it the moore worth. | Pacience, that is another
remedye agains ire, is a vertu that suffreth swetely every mannes
goodnesse, and is nat wrooth for noon harm that is doon to
him. | The philosophre seyth that pacience is thilke vertu that
suffreth debonairely alle the outrages of adversitee and every
wikked word. [660] | This vertu maketh a man lik to God, and
maketh him Goddes owene deere child, as seyth Crist. This
vertu disconfiteth thin enemy; and therfore seyth the wise man,
'If thow wolt venquisse thin enemy, lerne to suffre.' |

652 **conforten** encourage **travaillen** labour **vileins** shameful **knakkes** tricks
654 **mansuetude** meekness **debonairetee** gentleness **suffraunce** forbearance
655 **refreineth** curbs **moevinges** impulses **corage** inclination
657 **eschawfeth nat** does not become inflamed   658 **quik** living
tretable inclinable **enformed of** perfected by   660 **outrages** injuries
661 **disconfiteth** defeats **venquisse** conquer

And thow shalt understonde that man suffreth foure manere of grevances in outward thinges, agains the whiche foure he moot have foure manere of paciences. | The firste grevance is of wikkede wordes; thilke suffrede Jesu Crist withouten grucching, ful paciently, whan the Jewes despised and repreved him ful ofte. | Suffre thow therfore paciently, for the wise man seyth, 'If thow strive with a fool, though the fool be wrooth or though he laughe, algate thow shalt have no reste.' | That oother grevance outward is to have damage of thy catel. Theragains suffred Crist ful paciently whan he was despoiled of al that he hadde in this lif, and that nas but hise clothes. [665] | The thridde grevance is a man to have harm in his body; that suffred Crist ful paciently in al his passioun. | The fourthe grevance is in outrageous labour in werkes. Wherfore I seye that folk that maken hir servantz to travaillen to grevously, or out of time, as on haly dayes, soothly they do greet sinne. | Heeragains suffred Crist ful paciently, and taughte us pacience, whan he baar upon his blissed shulder the crois upon which he sholde suffren despitous deth. |

Heer may men lerne to be pacient, for certes, noght oonly Cristen men ben pacient for love of Jesu Crist and for gerdoun of the blisful lif that is pardurable, but certes, the olde paiens that nevere were Cristene commendeden and useden the vertu of pacience. | A philosophre, upon a time, wolde have beten his disciple for his grete trespas, for which he was greetly amoeved, and broghte a yerde to scoure with the child; [670] | and whan this child saugh the yerde, he seide to his maister, 'What thenke ye do?' 'I wol bete thee', quod the maister, 'for thy correccioun.' | 'For sothe,' quod the child, 'ye oghten first correcte youreself, that han lost al youre pacience for the gilt of a child.' | 'For sothe,' quod the maister, al wepinge, 'thow seyst sooth!

662 **grevances** injuries   663 **repreved** taunted   664 **algate** in either case
665 **catel** property **nas but** was only   667 **outrageous** excessive
travaillen labour **haly dayes** holy days   668 **Heeragains** in response to this
despitous cruel   669 **gerdoun** reward **pardurable** everlasting
670 **trespas** offence **amoeved** incensed **yerde** rod **scoure** beat

Have thow the yerde, my deere sone, and correcte me for min inpacience.' |

Of pacience comth obedience, thurgh which a man is obedient to Crist, and to alle hem to whiche he oghte to ben obedient in Crist. | And understond wel, that obedience is parfit whan that a man dooth gladly and hastily, with good herte, entierly al that he sholde do. [675] | Obedience generally is to parfourne the doctrine of God and of his sovereins, to whiche him oghte to ben obeisaunt in alle rightwisnesse. |

[*On Sloth*]

After the sinnes of envye and of ire, now wol I speken of the sinne of accidie; for envye blindeth the herte of a man, and ire troubleth a man, and accidie maketh him hevy, thoghtful, and wrawe. | Envye and ire maken bitternesse in herte, which bitternesse is moder of accidie, and binimeth him the love of alle goodnesse. Thanne is accidie the angwissh of troubled herte. And Seint Augustin seyth, 'It is anoy of goodnesse and joye of harm.' | Certes, this is a dampnable sinne, for it dooth wrong to Jesu Crist, inasmuche as it binimeth the service that men oghte doon to Crist with alle diligence, as seyth Salomon. | But accidie dooth no swich diligence; he dooth alle thing with anoy, and with wrawnesse, slaknesse, and excusacioun, and with idelnesse and unlust, for which the book seyth, 'Acursed be he that dooth the service of God necligently.' [680] | Thanne is accidie enemy to everich estaat of man, for certes, the estaat of man is in thre maneres. | Outher it is th'estaat of innocence, as was th'estaat of Adam biforn that he fil into sinne, in which estaat he was holden to wirche as in heryinge and adowringe of God. | Another estaat is the estaat of sinful men, in which

676 **parfourne the doctrine** practise the teaching   677 **accidie** sloth
troubleth disturbs **thoghtful** moody **wrawe** peevish
678 **binimeth him** takes away from him **anoy of** vexation at
680 **anoy** irritation **wrawnesse** peevishness **unlust** slothfulness
682 **holden** obliged **heryinge** praise **adowringe** worship

estaat men ben holden to laboure in preyinge to God for amendement of hire sinnes, and that he wole graunte hem to arisen out of hir sinnes. | Another estaat is th'estaat of grace, in which estaat he is holden to werkes of penitence. And certes, to alle thise thinges is accidie enemy and contrarye, for he loveth no bisinesse at al. | Now certes, this foule sinne accidie is eek a ful greet enemy to the liflode of the body, for it ne hath no purveaunce again temporel necessitee, for it forsleweth and forsluggeth and destroyeth alle goodes temporels by reccheleesnesse. [685] | The fourthe thing is that accidie is lik to hem that ben in the peine of helle, bicause of hir slouthe and of hir hevinesse, for they that ben dampned ben so bounde that they ne may neither wel do ne wel thinke. | Of accidie comth first that a man is anoyed and encombred for to doon any goodnesse, and maketh that God hath abhominacioun of swich accidie, as seyth Seint John. |

Now comth slouthe, that wol nat suffre noon hardnesse ne no penaunce, for soothly slouthe is so tendre and so delicat, as seyth Salomon, that he wol nat suffre noon hardnesse ne penaunce, and therfore he shendeth al that he dooth. | Agains this roten-herted sinne of accidie and slouthe sholde men excercise hemself to doon goode werkes and manly, and vertuously cacchen corage wel to doon, thinkinge that oure lord Jesu Crist quiteth every good dede, be it never so lite. | Usage of labour is a greet thing, for it maketh, as seyth Seint Bernard, the laborer to have stronge armes and harde sinwes; and slouthe maketh hem feble and tendre. [690] | Thanne comth drede to biginne to werke any goode werkes; for certes, he that is enclined to sinne, him thinketh it is so greet an emprise for to undertake to doon werkes of goodnesse, | and

684 **bisinesse** activity   685 **liflode** sustenance **purveaunce** provision
temporel worldly **forsleweth** is sluggish about **forsluggeth** neglects
686 **hevinesse** sluggishness **bounde** constrained   687 **is anoyed** is reluctant
encombred hindered   688 **hardnesse** hardship **penaunce** distress
delicat sensitive **shendeth** ruins   689 **cacchen corage** get the courage
quiteth repays   690 **Usage** the exercise **sinwes** sinews
691 **emprise** enterprise

casteth in his herte that the circumstaunces of goodnesse ben so grevouse, and so chargeaunt for to suffre, that he dar nat undertake to do werkes of goodnesse, as seyth Seint Gregorye. |

Now comth wanhope, that is despeir of the mercy of God, that comth somtime of to muche outrageous sorwe, and somtime of to muche drede, imagininge that he hath doon so muche sinne that it wol nat availlen him though he wolde repenten him and forsake sinne, | thurgh which despeir or drede he abaundoneth al his herte to every maner sinne, as seyth Seint Augustin. | Which dampnable sinne, if that it continue unto his ende, it is cleped sinning in the Holy Goost. [695] | This horrible sinne is so perilous that he that is despeired, ther nis no felonye ne no sinne that he douteth for to do, as shewed wel by Judas. | Certes, aboven alle sinnes thanne is this sinne moost displesant to Crist and moost adversarye. | Soothly, he that despeireth him is lik the coward champioun recreant that seyth 'creant' withoute nede. Allas, allas, nedelees is he recreant, and nedelees despeired! | Certes, the mercy of God is evere redy to the penitent, and is aboven alle hise werkes. | Allas, kan a man nat bithinke him on the gospel of Seint Luc, 15, whereas Crist seyth that 'as wel shal ther be joye in hevene upon a sinful man that dooth penitence than upon ninety and nine rightful men that neden no penitence'? [700] | Looke forther in the same gospel, the joye and the feeste of the goode man that hadde lost his sone, whan his sone with repentaunce was retourned to his fader. | Kan they nat remembren hem eek that, as seyth Seint Luc, 23, how that the theef that was hanged biside Jesu Crist seide, 'Lord, remembre of me, whan thow comest into thy regne'? | 'For sothe,' seide Crist, 'I seye to thee, today shaltow been with me in Paradis.' | Certes, ther is noon so horrible sinne of man that it ne may in his lif be destroyed by penitence, thurgh vertu of the passion and of the deeth of Crist. | Allas,

692 **casteth** reflects **circumstaunces** conditions **chargeaunt** burdensome
693 **wanhope** despair **outrageous** unrestrained **wolde** were willing
695 **in** against 696 **douteth** fears 698 **recreant** faint-hearted
seyth 'creant' surrenders 700 **bithinke him on** recollect
702 **regne** kingdom

what nedeth man thanne to ben despeired, sith that his mercy so redy is and large? Axe and have! [705] | Thanne cometh sompnolence, that is sloggy slombringe, which maketh a man be hevy and dul in body and in soule, and this sinne comth of slouthe. | And certes, the time that, by wey of resoun, men sholde nat slepe, that is by the morwe, but if ther were cause resonable. | For soothly, the morwe-tide is moost covenable a man to seye hise preyeres, and for to thinken on God, and for to honoure God and to yeven almesse to the povre that first cometh in the name of Crist. | Lo, what seyth Salomon: 'Whoso wol by the morwe awaken and seke me, he shal finde.' | Thanne cometh necligence, or reccheleesnesse, that rekketh of nothing. And how that ignoraunce be moder of alle harm, certes, necligence is the norice. [710] | Necligence ne doth no fors, whan he shal doon a thing, wheither he do it wel or baddely. | Of the remedye of thise two sinnes, as seyth the wise man, that 'he that dredeth God, he spareth nat to doon that him oghte doon.' | And he that loveth God, he wol doon diligence to plese God by hise werkes, and abaundone himself with al his might wel for to doon. |

Thanne comth idelnesse, that is the yate of alle harmes. An idel man is lik to a place that hath no walles: the develes may entre on every side, or sheten at him at discovert by temptacion on every side. | This idelnesse is the thurrok of alle wikked and vileins thoughtes, and of alle jangles, trufles, and of alle ordure. [715] | Certes, the hevene is yeven to hem that wol labouren, and nat to idel folk. Eek David seyth, that 'they ne been nat in the labour of men, ne they shul nat been whipped with men' – that is to seyn, in purgatorye. | Certes, thanne semeth it they shul be tormented with the devel in helle, but if they doon

---

705 **large** generous   706 **sompnolence** somnolence
sloggy slombringe sluggish slumber   707 **by wey of resoun** according to reason   708 **morwe-tide** morning   **covenable** suitable   **almesse** alms
710 **rekketh of** cares about   **how that** although   711 **ne doth no fors** does not care   713 **doon diligence** do his utmost   **abaundone** devote
714 **yate** gate   **sheten** shoot   **at discovert** in an exposed position
715 **thurrok** bilge   **jangles** idle chatter   **trufles** yarns

penitence. | Thanne comth the sinne that men clepen *tarditas*, as whan a man is to laterede or taryinge er he wole turne to God; and certes that is a greet folye. He is lik to him that falleth in the dich and wol nat arise. | And this vice comth of a fals hope, that he thinketh that he shal live longe; but that hope failleth ful ofte. | Thanne comth lachesse; that is he that whan he biginneth any good werk, anon he shal forleten it, and stinten, as doon they that han any wight to governe, and ne taken of him namoore kepe, anon as they finden any contrarye or any anoy. [720] | Thise ben the newe sheepherdes that leten hir sheep witingly go renne to the wolf that is in the breres, or do no fors of hir owene governaunce. | Of this comth poverte and destruccioun, bothe of spirituel and temporel thinges. Thanne comth a manere cooldnesse that freseth al the herte of a man. | Thanne comth undevocioun, thurgh which a man is so blent, as seyth Seint Bernard, and hath swich langour in soule, that he may neither rede ne singe in holy chirche, ne heere ne thinke of no devocioun, ne travaille with hise handes in no good werk that it nis to him unsavory and al apalled. | Thanne wexeth he slough and slombry, and soone wol be wrooth, and soone is enclined to hate and to envye. | Thanne comth the sinne of worldly sorwe, swich as is cleped *tristicia*, that sleeth man, as seyth Seint Paul. [725] | For certes, swich sorwe werketh to the deeth of the soule and of the body also, for therof comth that a man is anoyed of his owene lif; | wherfore swich sorwe shorteth ful ofte the lif of man, er that his time be come by wey of kinde. |

718 *tarditas* tardiness **laterede** dilatory   720 **lachesse** laziness
forleten abandon **stinten** leave off **governe** control
ne taken of him namoore kepe are no longer concerned about him
contrarye difficulty **anoy** hardship   721 **witingly** knowingly **breres** briars
governaunce control   722 **freseth** freezes   723 **undevocioun** lack of
devotion **blent** blinded **apalled** lack-lustre   724 **slough** slow
slombry sleepy   725 *tristicia* sadness   726 **anoyed of** irritated by
727 **by wey of kinde** in the course of nature

[*The Remedy Against the Sin of Sloth*]

Agains this horrible sinne of accidie and the branches of the same, ther is a vertu that is called *fortitudo* or strengthe; that is an affeccioun thurgh which a man despiseth anoyouse thinges. | This vertu is so mighty and so vigorous that it dar withstonde mightily, and wisely kepen himself fro perils that ben wikked, and wrastle again the assautes of the devel. | For it enhaunceth and enforceth the soule, right as accidie abateth it and maketh it feble. For this *fortitudo* may endure by long-suffraunce the travailles that ben covenable. [730] |

This vertu hath manye speces, and the firste is cleped magnanimitee; that is to seyn, greet corage, for certes, ther bihoveth greet corage agains accidie, lest that it ne swolwe the soule by the sinne of sorwe, or destroye it by wanhope. | This vertu maketh folk to undertake harde thinges and grevouse thinges, by hir owene wil, wisely and resonably; | and forasmuchel as the devel fighteth agains a man moore by queintise and by sleighte than by strengthe, therfore a man shal withstonden him by wit and by resoun and by discrecioun. | Thanne arn ther the vertues of feith and hope in God and in hise seintes, to acheve and acomplice the goode werkes in the whiche he purposeth fermely to continue. | Thanne comth seuretee or sikernesse, and that is whan a man ne douteth no travaille in time cominge of the goode werkes that a man hath bigonne. [735] | Thanne comth magnificence; that is to seyn, whan a man dooth and perfourneth grete werkes of goodnesse that he hath bigonne. And that is the ende why that men sholde do goode werkes, for in the acomplissinge of grete goode werkes lith the grete gerdoun. | Thanne is ther constaunce, that is,

---

728 **affeccioun** movement of the spirit   730 **enhaunceth** elevates **enforceth** fortifies **abateth** weakens **long-suffraunce** long-suffering **travailles** labours   731 **magnanimitee** fortitude **corage** spirit **bihoveth** is necessary **swolwe** swallow   733 **queintise** cunning **sleighte** trickery 735 **seuretee** confidence **sikernesse** security **ne douteth** does not fear 736 **magnificence** stout-heartedness **gerdoun** reward

stablenesse of corage, and this sholde ben in herte by stedefast
feith, and in mouth, and in beringe, and in cheere, and in dede. |
Eke ther ben mo speciale remedies agains accidie, in diverse
werkes, and in consideracioun of the peines of helle and of the
joyes of hevene, and in trust of the grace of the Holy Goost,
that wole yeve him might to perfourne his goode entente. |

[On Avarice]

After accidie wol I speke of avarice and of coveitise, of which
sinne seyth Seint Paul that 'the roote of alle harmes is coveitise'
(*Ad Thimotheum sexto*). | For soothly, whan the herte of a man
is confounded in itself and troubled, and that the soule hath
lost the confort of God, thanne seketh he an idel solas of
worldly thinges. [740] |

  Avarice, after the descripcion of Seint Augustin, is a likerous-
nesse in herte to have erthely thinges. | Som oother folk seyn
that avarice is for to purchacen manye erthely thinges and
nothing yeve to hem that han nede. | And understond that
avarice ne stant nat oonly in lond ne catel, but somtime in
science, and in glorye, and in every manere of outrageous thing
is avarice and coveitise. | And the difference bitwixe avarice
and coveitise is this: coveitise is for to coveite swiche thinges as
thow hast nat, and avarice is for to withholde and kepe swiche
thinges as thow hast, withoute rightful nede. | Soothly, this
avarice is a sinne that is ful dampnable, for al holy writ curseth
it and speketh agains that vice, for it dooth wrong to Jesu Crist,
[745] | for it bireveth him the love that men to him owen, and
turneth it bakward agains alle resoun, | and maketh that the
avaricious man hath moore hope in his catel than in Jesu Crist,
and dooth moore observance in kepinge of his tresor than he

737 **stablenesse** steadfastness **beringe** behaviour **cheere** demeanour
739 *Ad Thimotheum sexto* (1) Timothy 6   740 **confounded** perplexed
idel solas vain comfort   741 **likerousnesse** greed   742 **purchacen** acquire
743 **ne stant nat** does not consist in **catel** property **science** learning
outrageous superfluous   744 **withholde** retain
747 **dooth moore observance** takes greater care

dooth to the servise of Jesu Crist. | And therfore seyth Seint Paul,
ad Ephesios quinto, that an avaricious man is the thraldom
of idolatrye. | What difference is bitwixe an idolastre and an
avaricious man, but that an idolastre peraventure ne hath but
o mawmet or two, and the avaricious man hath manye? For
certes, every florin in his cofre is his mawmet. | And certes, the
sinne of mawmettrie is the firste thing that God deffended in
the ten comaundementz, as bereth witnesse in *Exodi capitulo
vicesimo*: [750] | 'Thow shalt have no false goddes bifore me,
ne thow shalt make to thee no grave thing.' Thus is an avar-
icious man, that loveth his tresor biforn God, an idolastre |
thurgh this cursed sinne of avarice.

Of coveitise comen thise harde lordshipes, thurgh whiche
men ben distreined by tailages, custumes, and cariages, moore
than hire duetee or resoun is, and eek taken they of hire bonde-
men amercimentz, whiche mighten moore resonably ben cleped
extorcions than amercimentz. | Of whiche amercimentz and
raunsoninge of bonde-men somme lordes stiwardes seyn that it
is rightful, forasmuche as a cherl hath no temporel thinge that
it ne is his lordes, as they seyn. | But certes, thise lordshipes
doon wrong that bireven hire bonde-folk thinges that they
nevere yave hem. *Augustinus de civitate libro nono*: | 'Sooth is,
that the condicioun of thraldom and the firste cause of thraldom
is for sinne (*Genesis nono*). [755] | Thus may ye seen that the
gilt disserveth thraldom, but nat nature.' | Wherfor thise lordes
ne sholde nat muche glorifyen hem in hir lordshipes, sith that
by naturel condicioun they ben nat lordes over thralles, but
that thraldom comth first by the desert of sinne. | And forther
over, theras the lawe seyth that temporel goodes of bonde-folk

---

748 *ad Ephesios quinto* Ephesians 5   749 **idolastre** idolater **mawmet** idol
750 **mawmettrie** idolatry *Exodi capitulo vicesimo* Exodus 20
751 **grave thing** graven object   752 **distreined** oppressed **tailages** forced
levies **custumes** customary services **cariages** taxes (g.)
than hire duetee or resoun is than they owe or than is reasonable
amercimentz fines   753 **raunsoninge of** exacting payment from
bonde-men serfs   754 **bireven** take away from
Augustinus de civitate libro nono Augustine, *City of God*, Book IX (n.)
755 *Genesis nono* Genesis 9

ben the goodes of hir lordshipes, ye, that is for to understonde the goodes of the emperour, to deffenden hem in hir right, but nat for to robben hem ne reven hem. | And therfore seyth Seneca, 'Thy prudence sholde live benignely with thy thralles.' | Thilke that thow clepest thy thralles ben Goddes peple, for humble folk ben Cristes freendes; they ben contubernial with the Lord. [760] | Think eek that of swich seed as cherles springeth, of swich seed springen lordes. As wel may the cherl be saved as the lord. | The same deeth that taketh the cherl, swich deeth taketh the lord. Wherfore I rede, do right so with thy cherl as thow woldest that thy lord dide with thee, if thow were in his plit. | Every sinful man is a cherl to sinne. I rede thee, certes, that thow, lord, werke in swich wise with thy cherles that they rather love thee than drede. | I woot wel ther is degree above degree, as reson is, and skile is that men do hir devoir theras it is due, but certes, extorcions and despit of youre underlinges is dampnable. | And forther over, understond wel that conquerours or tyrauntz maken ful ofte thralles of hem that ben born of as royal blood as ben they that hem conqueren. [765] | This name of thraldom was nevere erst kouth til that Noe seide that his sone Canaan sholde be thral to hise bretheren for his sinne. |

What seye we thanne of hem that pilen and doon extorcions to Holy Chirche? Certes, the swerd that men yeven first to a knight whan he is newe dubbed signifieth that he sholde deffenden Holy Chirche, and nat robben it ne pilen it, and whoso dooth is traitour to Crist. | And as seyth Seint Augustin, 'They ben the develes wolves that stranglen the sheep of Jesu Crist,' and doon worse than wolves. | For soothly, whan the wolf hath ful his wombe, he stinteth to strangle sheep, but soothly the pilours and destroyours of goodes of Holy Chirche ne do nat so, for they ne stinte nevere to pile. |

Now as I have seid, sith so is that sinne was first cause of

758 **reven** plunder   760 **contubernial** familiar   762 **rede** advise
plit situation   764 **degree** rank   **skile is** it is reasonable   **devoir** duty
despit humiliation   766 **kouth** known   767 **pilen** plunder
769 **wombe** stomach   **stinteth** ceases

thraldom, thanne is it thus, that thilke time that al this world
was in sinne, thanne was al this world in thraldom and subjecci-
oun. [770] | But certes, sith the time of grace cam, God ordeined
that som folk sholde be moore heigh in estaat and in degree,
and som folk moore lough, and that everich sholde be served
in his estaat. | And therfore in somme contrees ther they byen
thralles, whan they han turned hem to the feith they maken
hire thralles free out of thraldom. And therfore, certes, the lord
oweth to his man that the man oweth to his lord. | The Pope
calleth himself servant of the servauntz of God; but forasmuche
as the estaat of Holy Chirche ne mighte nat han be, ne the
commune profit mighte nat han be kept, ne pees and reste in
erthe, but if God hadde ordeined that som men hadde hyer
degree and som men lower, | therfore was sovereintee ordeined,
to kepe and maintene and deffenden hire underlinges or hire
subgetz in resoun, as ferforth as it lith in hire power, and nat
to destroyen hem ne confounde. | Wherfore I seye that thilke
lordes that ben lik wolves that devouren the possessiouns or
the catel of povre folk wrongfully, withouten mercy or mesure,
[775] | they shul receiven by the same mesure that they han
mesured to povre folk the mercy of Jesu Crist, but if it be
amended. | Now comth deceite bitwixe marchaunt and mar-
chaunt. And thow shalt understonde that marchandise is in
manye maneres: that oon is bodily, and that oother is goostly;
that oon is honeste and leveful, and that oother is deshoneste
and unleveful. | Of thilke bodily marchandise that is leveful and
honeste is this: that thereas God hath ordeined that a regne or
a contree is suffisaunt to himself, thanne is it honeste and leveful
that of habundaunce of this contree that men helpe another
contree that is moore nedy. | And therfore ther moote ben
marchantz to bringen fro that o contree to that oother hire

771 **lough** low   **served in his estaat** treated according to his rank
772 **byen** buy   773 **but if** if . . . not   774 **as ferforth as** as far as   **lith** lies
confounde harass   775 **mesure** moderation   776 **mesured** measured out
but if unless   777 **marchandise** trade   **goostly** spiritual   **honeste** honourable
leveful lawful   **deshoneste** dishonourable
778 **suffisaunt to himself** self-sufficient

marchandises. | That oother marchandise, that men haunten
with fraude and trecherye and deceite, with lesinges and false
othes, is cursed and dampnable. [780] | Espirituel marchandise
is proprely simonye; that is, ententif desir to byen thing espirituel – that is, thing that aperteneth to the seintuarye of God and
to cure of the soule. | This desir, if so be that a man do his
diligence to perfournen it, al be it that his desir ne take noon
effect, yet is it to him a deedly sinne, and if he be ordred he is
irreguler. | Certes, simonye is cleped of Simon Magus, that
wolde han boght for temporel catel the yifte that God hadde
yeven by the Holy Goost to Seint Peter and to the apostles. |
And therfore understond that bothe he that selleth and he that
beyeth thinges espirituels ben cleped simonials, be it by catel,
be it by procuringe or by flesshly preyere of hise freendes –
flesshly freendes or spirituel freendes. | 'Flesshly' in two man-
eres: as by kinrede, or othere freendes. Soothly, if they praye
for him that is nat worthy and able, it is simonye if he take the
benefice; and if he be worthy and able, ther nis noon. [785] |
That oother manere is whan a man or womman preyen for folk
to avauncen hem oonly for wikked flesshly affeccioun that they
han unto the persone, and that is foul simonye. | But certes, in
service, for which men yeven thinges espirituels unto hir servantz, it moot ben understonde that the service moot ben honeste, and elles nat; and eek that it be withouten bargaininge,
and that the persone be able. | For, as seyth Seint Damasie: 'Alle
the sinnes of the world at regard of this sinne arn as thing of
noght,' for it is the gretteste sinne that may be, after the sinne
of Lucifer and Antecrist. | For by this sinne God forleseth the
chirche, and the soule that he boghte with his precious blood,
by hem that yeven chirches to hem that ben nat digne. | For
they putten in theves, that stelen the soules of Jesu Crist and

779 **marchandises** goods   781 **simonye** see g. **ententif** earnest
seintuarye sanctuary, church **cure** care   782 **do his diligence** does his best
ordred in religious orders **irreguler** see n.   783 **cleped of** named after
temporel catel worldly wealth   784 **simonials** simoniacs
procuringe solicitation   786 **avauncen** promote   787 **honeste** honourable
bargaininge making deals   788 **at regard of** in comparison with
789 **forleseth** loses utterly **digne** worthy

destroyen his patrimoine. [790] | By swiche undigne preestes
and curates han lewed men the lasse reverence of the sacramentz
of Holy Chirche, and swiche yeveres of chirches putten out the
children of Crist, and putten into the chirche the develes owene
sone. | They sellen the soules, that lambes sholde kepen, to the
wolf that strangleth hem, and therfore shul they nevere han
part of the pasture of lambes – that is, the blisse of hevene. |
Now comth hasardrye with hise apurtenaunces, as tables and
rafles, of which comth deceite, false othes, chidinges, and alle
ravines, blaspheminge and reneyinge of God, and hate of hise
neighebores, wast of goodes, misspendinge of time, and som-
time manslaughtre. | Certes, hasardours ne mowe nat ben with-
outen greet sinne whiles they haunte that craft. | Of avarice
comen eek lesinges, thefte, fals witnesse and false othes. And
ye shul understonde that thise ben grete sinnes, and expres
again the comaundementz of God, as I have seid. [795] | Fals
witnesse is in word, and eek in dede. In word, as for to bireve
thy neighebores goode name by thy fals witnessing, or bireven
him his catel or his heritage by thy fals witnessing, whan thow
for ire, or for mede, or for envye berest fals witnesse, or accusest
him or excusest him by thy fals witnesse, or elles excusest thyself
falsly. | Ware, yow questemongeres and notaries! Certes, for
fals witnessing was Susanna in ful greet sorwe and peine, and
many another mo. | The sinne of thefte is eek expres agains
Goddes heste, and that in two maneres, corporel or spirituel: |
corporel, as for to take thy neighebores catel again his wil, be
it by force or by sleighte, be it by met or by mesure; | by steling
eek of false enditementz upon him, and in borwinge of thy
neighebores catel in entente nevere to payen it again, and

790 **patrimoine** patrimony   791 **lewed** lay **yeveres of chirches** patrons of
churches   792 **han part of** have a share in   793 **hasardrye** gambling
as tables such as backgammon **rafles** a game of chance, played with three
dice **chidinges** quarrels **ravines** thefts **reneyinge** denial   794 **haunte** indulge
in   795 **lesinges** lies   796 **bireve** take away **mede** bribery
797 **questemongeres** jurymen   799 **sleighte** trickery **by met or by mesure** by
(false) measuring   800 **enditementz** indictments

semblable thinges. [800] | Espirituel thefte is sacrilege, that is
to seyn, hurtinge of holy thinges or of thinges sacred to Crist,
in two maneres: by reson of the holy place, as chirches or
chirche-hawes, | – for which every vileins sinne that men doon
in swich places may be cleped sacrilege, or every violence in the
semblable places – also they that withdrawen falsly the rightes
that longen to Holy Chirche. | And pleinly and generally, sacri-
lege is to reven holy thing fro holy place, or unholy thing out
of holy place, or holy thing out of unholy place. |

[The Remedy Against the Sin of Avarice]

Now shul ye understonde that the relevinge of avarice is misericorde and pitee, largely taken. And men mighten axe why
that misericorde and pitee is relevinge of avarice. | Certes, the
avaricious man sheweth no pitee ne misericorde to the nedeful
man, for he deliteth him in the kepinge of his tresor, and nat in
the rescowinge ne relevinge of his evene Cristene. And therfore
speke I first of misericorde. [805] | Thanne is misericorde, as
seyth the philosophre, a vertu by which the corage of a man is
stired by the misese of him that is misesed. | Upon which
misericorde folweth pitee, in parfourninge of charitable werkes
of misericorde. | And certes, thise thinges moeven a man to
misericorde of Jesu Crist, that he yaf himself for oure gilt,
and suffred deeth for misericorde, and forgaf us oure originale
sinnes, | and therby relessed us fro the peines of helle, and
amenused the peines of purgatorye by penitence, and yeveth
grace wel to do, and atte laste the blisse of hevene. | The speces
of misericorde ben as for to lene, and for to yeve, and to
foryeven and relesse, and for to han pitee in herte and compassioun of the meschief of his evene Cristene, and eek to
chastise, theras nede is. [810] | Another manere of remedye

---

801 **chirche-hawes** churchyards   802 **vileins** shameful   803 **reven** take
away   804 **relevinge of** remedy for   **largely taken** broadly understood
misericorde mercy   805 **rescowinge** rescuing   **evene Cristene** fellow
Christians   806 **corage** heart   **misese** distress   809 **amenused** reduced
810 **lene** lend

agains avarice is resonable largesse; but soothly, here bihoveth
the consideracioun of the grace of Jesu Crist, and of hise temporel goodes, and eek of the goodes perdurables that Crist yaf to
us; | and to han remembrance of the deeth that he shal receive,
he noot whanne, where, ne how; and eek that he shal forgoon
al that he hath, save oonly that he hath despended in goode
werkes. | But forasmuche as som folk ben unmesurable, men
oghten eschue fool-largesse, that men clepen wast. | Certes, he
that is fool-large ne yeveth nat his catel, but he leseth his
catel. Soothly, what thing that he yeveth for veine glorye, as to
minestrals and to folk for to beren his renoun in the world, he
hath sinne therof and noon almesse. | Certes, he leseth foule his
good that ne seketh with the yifte of his good nothing but sinne.
[815] | He is lik to an hors that seketh rather to drinken drovy
or trouble water than for to drinken water of the clere welle. |
And forasmuchel as they yeven theras they sholde nat yeven, to
hem aperteneth thilke malisoun that Crist shal yeven at the day
of dome to hem that shullen ben dampned. |

[On Gluttony]

After avarice comth glotonye, which is expres eek again the
comandement of God. Glotonye is unmesurable appetit to ete
or to drinke, or elles to doon inogh to the unmesurable appetit
and desordeinee coveitise to eten or to drinke. |

This sinne corrumped al this world, as is wel shewed in the
sinne of Adam and of Eve. Looke eek, what seyth Seint Paul
of glotonye: | 'Manye', seyth Seint Paul, 'goon, of whiche I
have ofte seid to yow, and now I seye it wepinge, that ben the
enemys of the crois of Crist, of whiche the ende is deeth, and
of whiche hire wombe is hire god, and hire glorye in confusioun
of hem that so savouren erthely things.' [820] | He that is

usaunt to this sinne of glotonye, he ne may no sinne withstonde; he moot ben in servage of alle vices, for it is the develes hoord, ther he hideth him and resteth. | This sinne hath manye speces. The firste is dronkenesse, that is the horrible sepulture of mannes resoun, and therfore whan a man is dronken he hath lost his resoun, and this is deedly sinne. | But soothly, whan that a man is nat wont to strong drinke, and paraventure ne knoweth nat the strengthe of the drinke, or hath feblesse in his heed, or hath travailled, thurgh which he drinketh the moore, al be he sodeinly caught with drinke, it is no deedly sinne, but venial. | The seconde spece of glotonye is that the spirit of a man wexeth al trouble, for dronkenesse bireveth him the discrecioun of his wit. | The thridde spece of glotonye is whan a man devoureth his mete and hath no rightful manere of etinge. [825] | The ferthe is whan thurgh the grete habundaunce of his mete the humours in his body ben destempred. | The fifthe is foryetelnesse by to muchel drinkinge, for which som time a man foryeteth er the morwe what he dide at even, or on the night biforn. | In oother manere ben distinct the speces of glotonye, after Seint Gregorye. The firste is for to ete biforn time to ete. The seconde is whan a man gete him to delicat mete or drinke. | The thridde is whan men taken to muche over mesure. The fourthe is curiositee, with greet entente to maken and apparaillen his mete. The fifthe is for to eten to gredily. | Thise ben the five fingres of the develes hand, by whiche he draweth folk to sinne. [830] |

[The Remedy Against the Sin of Gluttony]

Agains glotonye is the remedye abstinence, as seyth Galien; but that holde I nat meritorye if he do it oonly for the hele of his

821 usaunt to given to servage of bondage to hoord store
822 sepulture burial   823 wont accustomed travailled been labouring
824 wexeth al trouble becomes confused   825 mete food
826 humours bodily fluids (g.) destempred unbalanced
827 foryetelnesse forgetfulness   828 gete him procures for himself
delicat rich   829 curiositee elaborateness apparaillen prepare
831 meritorye meritorious hele health

body. Seint Augustin wole that abstinence be doon for vertu, and with pacience. | 'Abstinence', he seyth, 'is litel worth, but if a man have good wil therto, and but it be enforced by pacience and by charitee, and that men doon it for Goddes sake and in hope to have the blisse of hevene.' | The felawes of abstinence ben attemperaunce, that holdeth the mene in alle thinges; eek shame, that eschueth alle deshonestee; suffisance, that seketh no riche metes ne drinkes, ne dooth no fors of to outrageous apparaillinge of mete; | mesure also, that restreineth by resoun the deslavee appetit of etinge; sobrenesse also, that restreineth the outrage of drinke; | sparinge also, that restreineth the delicat ese to sitte longe at his mete and softely, wherfore som folk stonden of hir owene wil, to eten at the lasse leiser. [835] |

[On Lechery]

After glotonye thanne comth lecherye, for thise two sinnes ben so ny cosins that ofte time they wol nat departe. | God woot, this sinne is ful displesaunt thing to God, for he seide himself 'Do no lecherye', and therfore he putte grete peines agains this sinne in the olde lawe. | If womman thral were taken in this sinne, she sholde be beten with staves to the deeth; and if she were a gentil womman she sholde be slain with stones, and if she were a bisshopes doghter she sholde been brent, by Goddes comandement. | Further over, by the sinne of lecherye God dreinte al the world at the diluge. And after that he brente five citees with thonder-leit, and sank hem into helle. |

Now lat us speke thanne of thilke stinkinge sinne of lecherye that men clepe avowtrye of wedded folk; that is to seyn, if that oon of hem be wedded, or elles bothe. [840] | Seint John seyth that avowtiers shullen ben in helle, in a stank brenninge of fir

832 **enforced** strengthened   833 **attemperaunce** temperance   **the mene** the golden mean   **eschueth** shuns   **deshonestee** dishonour   **suffisance** sufficiency   **dooth no fors of** does not bother about   834 **deslavee** unbridled   **outrage** excess   835 **sparinge** abstemiousness   836 **ny cosins** close relations   **departe** separate   837 **peines** punishments   838 **staves** sticks   839 **dreinte** drowned   **diluge** flood   **thonder-leit** lightning   840 **avowtrye** adultery   841 **stank** lake

and of brimston – in fir for lecherye, in brimston for the stink of hire ordure. | Certes, the brekinge of this sacrement is an horrible thing; it was maked of God himself in Paradis, and confermed by Jesu Crist, as witnesseth Seint Mathew in the gospel: 'A man shal lete fader and moder and taken him to his wif, and they shullen be two in o flessh.' | This sacrement bitokneth the knittinge togidre of Crist and of Holy Chirche. | And nat oonly that God forbad avowtrye in dede, but eek he comanded that thow sholdest nat coveite thy neighebores wif. | 'In this heste', seyth Seint Augustin, 'is forboden alle manere coveitise to doon lecherye.' Lo, what seyth Seint Mathew in the gospel, that 'whoso seeth a womman to coveitise of his lust, he hath doon lecherye with hire in his herte.' [845] | Here may ye seen that nat oonly the dede of this sinne is forboden, but eek the desir to doon that sinne. | This cursed sinne anoyeth grevousliche hem that it haunten, and first, to hire soule, for he obligeth it to sinne and to peine of deeth that is perdurable. | Unto the body anoyeth it grevously also, for it dreyeth him, and wasteth him, and shent him, and of his blood he maketh sacrifice to the feend of helle; it wasteth eek his catel and his substaunce. | And certes, if it be a foul thing a man to waste his catel on wommen, yet is it a fouler thing whan that for swich ordure wommen dispenden upon men hir catel and sub-staunce. | This sinne, as seyth the prophete, bireveth man and womman hir goode fame and al hir honour, and it is ful plesaunt to the devel, for therby winneth he the mooste partie of this world. [850] | And right as a marchant deliteth him moost in chaffare that he hath moost avantage of, right so deliteth the feend in this ordure. |

This is that oother hand of the devel, with five fingres to cacche the peple to his vileinye. | The firste finger is the

---

842 **lete** leave **taken him to** devote himself to   843 **bitokneth** signifies
845 **heste** commandment **alle manere** every kind of   847 **anoyeth** is
harmful to **haunten** indulge in **obligeth** binds **perdurable** everlasting
848 **dreyeth** dries up **shent** (= *shendeth*) destroys   849 **dispenden** spend
851 **deliteth him moost** takes most pleasure **chaffare** trade **avantage** profit
852 **cacche** incite **vileinye** wickedness

fool lookinge of the fool womman and of the fool man, that
sleeth right as the basilicok sleeth folk by the venim of his
sighte, for the coveitise of eyen folweth the coveitise of the
herte. | The seconde finger is the vileins touchinge, in wikkede
manere; and therfore seyth Salomon that 'whoso toucheth and
handleth a womman, he fareth lik him that handleth the scorpioun that stingeth and sodeinly sleeth thurgh his enveniminge' –
as whoso toucheth warm pich, it shent his fingres. | The thridde
is foule wordes, that fareth lik fir that right anon brenneth the
herte. [855] | The ferthe finger is the kissinge, and trewely, he
were a greet fool that wolde kisse the mouth of a brenninge
ovene or of a fourneis, | and moore fooles ben they that kissen
in vileinye, for that mouth is the mouth of helle; and namely,
thise olde dotardes holours, yet wol they kisse, though they
may nat do, and smatre hem. | Certes, they ben lik to houndes,
for an hound whan he comth by the roser or by othere busshes,
thogh he may nat pisse, yet wole he heve up his leg and make
a contenaunce to pisse. | And for that many man weneth that
he may nat sinne for no likerousnesse that he doth with his wif,
certes, that opinion is fals. God woot, a man may sleen himself
with his owene knif, and make himselven dronken of his owene
tonne. | Certes, be it wif, be it child, or any worldly thing that
he loveth biforn God, it is his mawmet, and he is an idolastre.
[860] | Man sholde loven his wif by discrecioun, paciently and
atemprely, and thanne is she as thogh it were his suster. |
The fifthe finger of the develes hand is the stinkinge dede of
leccherye. | Certes, the five fingres of glotonye the feend put in
the wombe of a man, and with hise five fingres of lecherye he
gripeth him by the reines, for to throwen him into the fourneis
of helle, | theras they shul han the fir and the wormes that evere
shul lasten, and wepinge and wailinge, sharp hunger and thurst,

---

853 **fool** lecherous **basilicok** basilisk (n.)   854 **pich** pitch **shent** injures
856 **fourneis** furnace   857 **holours** lechers **do** perform the act
smatre beslobber   858 **roser** rose-bush **make a contenaunce** make as if
859 **likerousnesse** lechery   861 **by discrecioun** in moderation
atemprely moderately   863 **wombe** stomach **gripeth** grasps **reines** loins

grimnesse of develes that shullen al totrede hem withouten respit and withouten ende. | Of leccherye, as I seide, sourden diverse speces, as fornicacioun, that is bitwixe man and womman that ben nat maried; and this is deedly sinne and agains nature. [865] | Al that is enemy and destruccioun to nature is agains nature. | Parfay, the resoun of a man telleth eek him wel that it is deedly sinne, forasmuche as God forbad leccherye. And Seint Paul yeveth hem the regne that nis dewe to no wight but to hem that doon deedly sinne. | Another sinne of leccherye is to bireve a maiden of hir maidenhede, for he that so dooth, certes, he casteth a maiden out of the hyeste degree that is in this present lif, | and bireveth hire thilke precious fruit that the book clepeth 'the hundred fruit'. (I ne kan seye it noon oother weyes in Englissh, but in Latin it highte *centesimus fructus*.) | Certes, he that so dooth is cause of manye damages and vileinyes, mo than any man kan rekene, right as he somtime is cause of alle damages that beestes don in the feeld that breketh the hegge or the closure, thurgh which he destroyeth that may nat ben restored. [870] | For certes, namoore may maidenhede be restored than an arm that is smiten fro the body may retourne again to wexe. | She may have mercy, this woot I wel, if she do penitence but nevere shal it be that she nas corrupt. | And al be it so that I have spoken somwhat of avowtrye, it is good to shewen mo perils that longen to avowtrye, for to eschue that foule sinne. | Avowtrye in Latin is for to seyn 'approchinge of oother mannes bed', thurgh which tho that whilom weren o flessh abawndone hir bodies to othere persones. | Of this sinne, as seyth the wise man, folwen manye harmes: first, brekinge of feith, and certes, in feith is the keye of Cristendom, [875] | and whan that feith is broken and lorn, soothly, Cristendom stant vein and withouten fruit. | This sinne is eek a thefte, for thefte generally is for to reve a wight his thing agains his wille. |

---

864 **grimnesse** horribleness **totrede** trample down   867 **regne** kingdom
dewe due   868 **bireve** deprive **maidenhede** virginity
870 **vileinyes** wickednesses **closure** fence   871 **wexe** grow
873 **longen** belong   874 **tho that** those who **whilom** formerly
876 **lorn** destroyed **stant vein** is worthless   877 **reve** take away from

Certes, this is the fouleste thefte that may be, whan a womman
steleth hir body from hir housbonde and yeveth it to hire holour
to defoulen hire, and steleth hir soule fro Crist and yeveth it to
the devel. | This is a fouler thefte than for to breke a chirche
and stele the chalice, for thise avowtiers breken the temple of
God spiritually and stelen the vessel of grace, that is the body
and the soule, for which Crist shal destroyen hem, as seyth
Seint Paul. | Soothly, of this thefte douted gretly Joseph, whan
that his lordes wif preyed him of vileinye, whan he seide, 'Lo,
my lady, how my lord hath take to me under my warde al that
he hath in this world, ne nothing of hise thinges is out of my
power but oonly ye that ben his wif. [880] | And how sholde I
thanne do this wikkednesse and sinne so horrible, agains God
and agains my lord? – God it forbede.' Allas, al to litel is swich
trouthe now yfounde! | The thridde harm is the filthe thurgh
which they breken the comandement of God and defoulen the
auctour of matrimoine, that is Crist. | For certes, insomuche as
the sacrement of mariage is so noble and so digne, so muche is
it gretter sinne for to breken it, for God made mariage in
Paradis, in the estaat of innocence, to multiplye mankinde to
the service of God. | And therfore is the brekinge therof moore
grevous, of which brekinge comen false heires ofte time, that
wrongfully occupien folkes heritages, and therfore wol Crist
putte hem out of the regne of hevene that is heritage to goode
folk. | Of this brekinge comth eek ofte time that folk unwar
wedden or sinnen with hire owene kinrede, and namely thilke
harlotes that haunten bordels of thise fool wommen, that mowe
be likned to a commune gonge whereas men purgen hire ordure.
[885] | What seye we eek of putours, that liven by the horrible
sinne of puterye, and constreine wommen to yelden to hem a
certein rente of hire bodily puterye – ye, somtime of his owene
wif or his child, as doon thise bawdes? Certes, thise ben cursed

878 **holour** lover   880 **douted** was afraid   **preyed him of vileinye** asked him
to do wrong   **take** given   **warde** guardianship   882 **matrimoine** matrimony
883 **digne** worthy   885 **unwar** unwittingly   **harlotes** lechers
bordels brothels   **fool wommen** prostitutes   **gonge** latrine   **purgen** evacuate
886 **putours** pimps   **puterye** prostitution   **bawdes** procurers

sinnes! | Understond eek that avowtrye is set gladly in the Ten Comandementz bitwixe thefte and manslaughtre for it is the gretteste thefte that may be, for it is thefte of body and of soule. | And it is lik to homicide for it kerveth atwo and breketh atwo hem that first were maked o flessh, and therfore by the olde lawe of God they sholde be slain. | But nathelees, by the lawe of Jesu Crist, that is lawe of pitee, whan he seide to the womman that was founden in avowtrye and sholde han ben slain with stones after the wil of the Jewes, as was hir lawe, 'Go,' quod Jesu Crist, 'and have namoore wil to sinne', or, 'wille namoore to do sinne.' | Soothly, the vengeaunce of avowtrye is awarded to the peines of helle, but if so be that it be destourbed by penitence. [890] | Yet ben ther mo speces of this cursed sinne, as whan that oon of hem is religious, or elles bothe, or of folk that ben entred into ordre, as subdekne, or dekne, or preest, or hospitaliers, and evere the hyer that he is in ordre the gretter is the sinne. | The thinges that gretly agreggen hire sinne is the brekinge of hire avow of chastitee whan they received the ordre. | And forther over, sooth is that holy ordre is chief of al the tresorye of God and his especial signe and mark of chastitee to shewe that they ben joined to chastitee, which that is the moost precious lif that is. | And thise ordred folk ben specially titled to God and of the special meignee of God, for which, whan they doon deedly sinne they ben the special traitours of God and of his peple, for they liven of the peple to preye for the peple, and whil they ben swiche traitours, hir preyeres availlen nat to the peple. | Preestes ben aungeles as by the dignitee of hir misterye, but, for sothe, Seint Paul seyth that Sathanas transformeth him in an aungel of light. [895] | Soothly, the preest that haunteth deedly sinne, he may be likned to the aungel of derknesse transformed in the aungel of light: he

887 **gladly** customarily   888 **kerveth atwo** cuts in two   889 **hir** their
891 **religious** in a religious order   **entred into ordre** in orders
subdekne subdeacon **dekne** deacon **hospitaliers** Knights Hospitallers (n.)
892 **agreggen** increase   894 **ordred folk** people in orders   **titled** dedicated
meignee company **liven of** live off   895 **misterye** ministry **Sathanas** Satan,
the devil   896 **haunteth** indulges in

semeth aungel of light, but for sothe, he is aungel of derknesse. |
Swiche preestes ben the sones of Helie, as sheweth in the book
of Kinges that they weren the sones of Belial – that is the devel. |
'Belial' is to seyn 'withouten juge', and so faren they: hem
thinketh they ben free and han no juge, namoore than hath a
free bole, that taketh which cow that him liketh in the town. |
So faren they by women; for right as a free bole is inough for
al a toun, right so is a wikked preest corrupcioun inough for al
a parisshe, or for al a contree. | Thise preestes, as seyth the
book, ne konne nat the misterye of preesthode to the peple, ne
God ne knowe they nat; they ne helde hem nat apaid, as seyth
the book, of soden flessh that was to hem offred, but they tooke
by force the flessh that is rawe. [900] | Certes, so thise shrewes
ne holden hem nat apaied of roosted flessh and sode flessh, with
which the peple feden hem in greet reverence, but they wole
have raw flessh of folkes wives and hir doghtres. | And certes,
thise wommen that consenten to hire harlotrye doon greet
wrong to Crist, and to Holy Chirche and alle halwes, and to
alle soules, for they bireven alle thise him that sholde worshipe
Crist and Holy Chirche, and preye for Cristene soules. | And
therfore han swiche preestes, and hire lemmanes eek that consenten to hir leccherye, the malisoun of al the court Cristien, til
they come to amendement. |

The thridde spece of avowtrye is somtime bitwixe a man and
his wif, and that is whan they take no reward in hire assemblinge
but oonly to hire flesshly delit, as seyth Seint Jerome, | and ne
rekken of nothing but that they ben assembled; bicause that
they ben maried, al is good inough, as thinketh to hem, [905] |
but in swich folk hath the devel power, as seide the aungel
Raphael to Thobie, for in hire assemblinge they putten Jesu
Crist out of hire herte, and yeven hemself to alle ordure. | The

---

897 Helie Eli sheweth appears   898 juge see n. free bole see n.
liketh pleases   899 faren ... by act towards   900 ne konne nat are
incapable of apaid satisfied soden boiled   901 shrewes rascals
902 harlotrye lechery halwes saints   903 lemmanes mistresses
malisoun curse court Cristien ecclesiastical court   904 reward regard
905 ne rekken of do not care about   906 Thobie Tobias

fourthe spece is the assemblee of hem that ben of hire kinrede, or of hem that ben of oon affinitee, or elles with hem with whiche hir fadres or hir kinrede han deled in the sinne of lecherye. This sinne maketh hem lik to houndes, that taken no kepe to kinrede. | And certes, parentele is in two maneres, outher goostly or flesshly. Goostly, as for to delen with hise godsibbes; | for right so as he that engendreth a child is his flesshly fader, right so is his godfader his fader espirituel. For which a womman may in no lasse sinne assemblen with hire godsib than with hire owene flesshly brother. | The fifthe spece is thilke abhominable sinne of which that no man unnethe oghte speke ne write; nathelees, it is openly reherced in holy writ. [910] | This cursednesse doon men and wommen in diverse entente, and in diverse manere. But though that holy writ speke of horrible sinne, certes, holy writ may nat ben defouled, namoore than the sonne that shineth on the mixne. | Another sinne aperteineth to leccherye, that comth in slepinge, and this sinne cometh ofte to hem that ben maidenes, and eek to hem that ben corrupt. And this sinne men clepen polucioun, that comth in foure maneres: | somtime of langwissinge of body, for the humours ben to ranke and habundaunt in the body of man; somtime of infermetee, for the feblesse of the vertu retentif, as phisik maketh mencion; somtime for surfeet of mete and drinke; | and somtime of vileins thoghtes that ben enclosed in mannes minde whan he gooth to slepe, which may nat ben withoute sinne, for which men moste kepen hem wisely, or elles may men sinnen ful grevously. |

---

907 **affinitee** group of people related by marriage (n.)   **deled** participated
taken no kepe pay no attention   908 **parentele** kinship   **goostly** spiritual
delen have sexual intercourse   **godsibbes** relations by baptism (g.)
911 **mixne** dunghill   912 **maidenes** virgins   **corrupt** sexually experienced
913 **langwissinge** infirmity   **humours** bodily fluids (g.)   **ranke** luxuriant
vertu retentif natural faculty to retain bodily effluents   **phisik** medical science
surfeet surfeit   914 **vileins** shameful   **kepen hem** control themselves

[*The Remedy Against the Sin of Lechery*]

Now comth the remedye agains leccherye, and that is generally
chastitee and continence, that restreineth alle the desordeinee
moevinges that comen of flesshly talentes. [915] | And evere the
gretter merite shal he han that moost restreineth the wikkede
eschawfinges of the ardour of this sinne, and this is in two
maneres: that is to seyn, chastitee in mariage, and chastitee of
widwehode. | Now shaltow understonde that matrimoine is
leefful assemblinge of man and of womman, that receiven by
vertu of the sacrement the boond thurgh which they may nat
be departed in al hir lif; that is to seyn, whil that they liven
bothe. | This, as seyth the book, is a ful greet sacrement. God
maked it, as I have seid, in Paradis, and wolde himself be born
in mariage; | and for to halwen mariage he was at a weddinge
whereas he turned water into win, which was the firste miracle
that he wroghte in erthe biforn hise disciples. | Trewe effect of
mariage clenseth fornicacioun, and replenisseth Holy Chirche
of good linage, for that is the ende of mariage, and it chaungeth
deedly sinne into venial sinne bitwixe hem that ben ywedded,
and maketh the hertes al oon of hem that ben ywedded, as wel
as the bodies. [920] | This is verray mariage, that was establissed
by God er that sinne bigan, whan naturel lawe was in his right
point in Paradis, and it was ordeined that o man sholde have
but o womman, and o womman but o man, as seyth Seint
Augustin, by manye resouns. | First, for mariage is figured
bitwixe Crist and Holy Chirche; and that oother is for a man
is heved of a womman, algate by ordinaunce it sholde be so. |
For if a womman hadde mo men than oon, thanne sholde she
have mo hevedes than oon, and that were an horrible thing
biforn God; and eek a womman ne mighte nat plese to many

915 **desordeinee moevinges** inordinate impulses **talentes** desires
916 **eschawfinges** inflammations **widwehode** widowhood
917 **leefful** lawful **departed** separated   918 **wolde** wished
919 **halwen** sanctify   921 **point** state   **o** one   922 **figured** symbolized
heved head   **algate** at any rate   **by ordinaunce** according to the principle of
order

folk at ones. And also ther ne sholde nevere be pees ne reste amonges hem, for everich wolde axen his owene thing. | And forther over, no man ne sholde knowe his owene engendrure, ne who sholde have his heritage, and the womman sholde ben the lasse biloved fro the time that she were conjoint to many men. |

Now comth how that a man sholde bere him with his wif, and namely in two thinges: that is to seyn, in suffraunce and reverence, as shewed Crist whan he made first womman. [925] | For he ne made hire nat of the heved of Adam, for she sholde nat claime to greet lordshipe; | for theras the womman hath the maistrye, she maketh to much desray. Ther neden none ensamples of this; the experience of day by day oghte suffise. | Also, certes, God ne made nat womman of the foot of Adam, for she ne sholde nat ben holden to lowe, for she kan nat paciently suffre; but God made womman of the rib of Adam, for womman sholde be felawe unto man. | Man sholde bere him to his wif in feith, in trouthe, and in love, as seyth Seint Paul, that a man sholde loven his wif as Crist loved Holy Chirche, that loved it so wel that he deide for it; so sholde a man for his wif, if it were nede. |

Now, how that a womman sholde be subget to hire housbonde, that telleth Seint Peter. First, in obedience. [930] | And eek, as seyth the decree, a womman that is wif, as longe as she is a wif, she hath noon auctoritee to swere ne bere witnesse withoute leve of hir housbonde that is hire lord; algate, he sholde be so by resoun. | She sholde eek serven him in alle honestee, and ben attempree of hir array. I woot wel that they sholde setten hire entente to plesen hir housbondes, but nat by hire queintise of array. | Seint Jerome seyth that 'wives that ben apparailled in silk and in precious purpre ne mowe nat clothen hem in Jesu Crist.' Loke what seyth Seint John eek in this

---

924 **engendrure** offspring **conjoint to** united with   925 **bere him** behave
suffraunce forbearance   927 **the maistrye** the upper hand **desray** trouble
928 **holden** kept   931 **decree** canon law (n.) **leve** permission
932 **attempree** restrained **array** clothing **setten hire entente to** take care to
queintise elaboration   933 **purpre** purple

matere. | Seint Gregorye eek seyth that 'no wight seketh precious array but oonly for veine glorye, to ben honoured the moore biforn the peple.' | It is a greet folye a womman to have a fair array outward, and in hirself be foul inward. [935] | A wif sholde eek be mesurable in lookinge, and in beringe, and in lawghinge, and discreet in alle hire wordes and hire dedes; | and aboven alle worldly thing she sholde loven hire housbonde with al hire herte, and to him be trewe of hir body. | So sholde an housbonde eek be to his wif, for sith that al the body is the housbondes, so sholde hire herte ben, or elles ther is bitwixe hem two as in that no perfit mariage. |

Thanne shal men understonde that for thre thinges a man and his wif flesshly mowen assemble. The firste is in entente of engendrure of children to the service of God, for certes, that is the cause final of matrimoine. | Another cause is to yelden everich of hem to oother the dette of hire bodies, for neither of hem hath power of his owene body. The thridde is for to eschewe leccherye and vileinye. The ferthe is for sothe deedly sinne. [940] | As to the firste, it is meritorye; the seconde also, for, as seyth the decree, that she hath merite of chastitee that yeldeth to hire housbonde the dette of hir body – ye, though it be again hir likinge and the lust of hire herte. | The thridde manere is venial sinne – and trewely, scarsly may ther any of thise be withoute venial sinne, for the corrupcioun and for the delit. | The fourthe manere is for to understonde if they assemble oonly for amorous love and for noon of the forseide causes, but for to accomplice thilke brenninge delit, they rekke nevere how ofte. Soothly, it is deedly sinne; and yet, with sorwe, somme folk wol peinen hem moore to doon than to hire appetit suffiseth. |

The seconde manere of chastitee is for to ben a clene widewe, and eschue the embracinges of man and desiren the embracinge of Jesu Crist. | Thise ben tho that han ben wives and han

---

936 **mesurable** restrained **beringe** behaviour   938 **perfit** perfect
939 **engendrure** procreation   940 **eschewe** avoid   941 **merite of** credit for
lust wish   943 **rekke nevere** do not care

forgoon hire housbondes, and eek wommen that han doon leccherye and ben releved by Penitence. [945] | And certes, if that a wif koude kepen hire al chaast by licence of hir housbonde, so that she yeve nevere noon occasion that he agilte, it were to hire a greet merite. | Thise manere wommen that observen chastitee moste be clene in herte as wel as in body and in thought, and mesurable in clothinge and in contenaunce, and been abstinent in etinge and drinkinge, in spekinge, and in dede; they been the vessel or the boiste of the blissed Magdalene, that fulfilleth Holy Chirche of good odour. | The thridde manere of chastitee is virginitee, and it bihoveth that she be holy in herte and clene of body; thanne is she spouse to Jesu Crist, and she is the lif of aungels. | She is the preisinge of this world, and she is as thise martyrs in egalitee; she hath in hire that tonge may nat telle ne herte thinke. | Virginitee baar oure lord Jesu Crist, and virgine was himselve. [950] |

Another remedye agains leccherye is specially to withdrawen swiche thinges as yeve occasion to thilke vileinye, as ese, etinge, and drinkinge; for certes, whan the pot boileth strongly the beste remedye is to withdrawe the fir. | Slepinge longe in greet quiete is eek a greet norice to leccherye. | Another remedye agains leccherye is that a man or a womman eschue the compaignye of hem by whiche he douteth to be tempted, for al be it so that the dede is withstonden, yet is ther greet temptacioun. | Soothly, a whit wal, although it ne brenne noght fully by stikinge of a candele, yet is the wal blak of the leit. | Ful ofte time I rede that no man truste in his owene perfeccioun, but he be stronger than Sampsoun, and holier than David, and wiser than Salomon. [955] |

Now after that I have declared yow, as I kan, the sevene deedly sinnes, and somme of hire braunches and hire remedies, soothly, if I koude, I wolde telle yow the Ten Comandementz; |

945 **forgoon** lost **releved** rescued   946 **agilte** should do wrong
947 **contenaunce** behaviour **boiste** jar   948 **bihoveth** is necessary
949 **preisinge** glory **as . . . in egalitee** on a par with   951 **ese** comfort
954 **stikinge** fastening **leit** flame   955 **but he be** unless he is

but so heigh a doctrine I lete to divines. Nathelees, I hope to God they ben touched in this tretice, everich of hem alle. |

[*The Second Part of Penitence: continued*]

Now, forasmuche as the seconde partie of Penitence stant in confessioun of mouth, as I bigan in the firste chapitre, I seye, Seint Augustin seyth: | 'Sinne is every word, and every dede, and al that men coveiten again the lawe of Jesu Crist.' And this is for to sinne, in herte, in mouth, and in dede, by thy fyve wittes, that ben sighte, heringe, smellinge, tastinge or savouringe, and feelinge. | Now is it good to understonde the circumstaunces that agreggeth muchel every sinne. [960] | Thow shalt considere what thow art that doost the sinne, wheither thow be male or female, yong or old, gentil or thral, free or servant, hool or sik, wedded or sengle, ordred or unordred, wis or fool, clerk or seculer; | if she be of thy kinrede, bodily or goostly, or noon; if any of thy kinrede have sinned with hire or noon; and manye mo thinges. | Another circumstaunce is this: wheither it be doon in fornicacioun or in avowtrye or noon; incest or noon, maiden or noon, in manere of homicide or noon, horrible grete sinnes or smale, and how longe thow hast continued in sinne. | The thridde circumstaunce is the place ther thow hast do sinne, wheither in oother mennes hous, or in thin owene, in feeld, or in chirche or in chirche-hawe, in chirche dedicat or noon. | For if the chirche be halwed, and man or womman spille his kinde inwith that place by wey of sinne or by wikked temptacioun, the chirche is entredited; [965] | and the preest that dide swich a vileinye, to terme of al his lif he sholde namoore singe masse, and if he dide, he sholde doon deedly sinne at every time that

957 **heigh** lofty **lete** leave **divines** theologians   958 **stant in** consists in
959 **coveiten** desire   960 **agreggeth** increase
961 **gentil or thral** nobly-born or a serf **ordred** in religious orders
963 **maiden** virgin **in manere of** in the nature of
964 **chirche-hawe** churchyard **dedicat** consecrated
965 **halwed** consecrated **spille his kinde** emits seminal fluid
entredited interdicted   966 **to terme of al his lif** for the rest of his life

he so songe masse. | The ferthe circumstaunce is by whiche
mediatours or by whiche messagers, as for enticement or for
consentement to bere compaignye with felaweshipe; for many
a wrecche for to bere compaignye wole go to the devel of helle. |
For they that eggen or consenten to the sinne ben parteners of
the sinne and of the dampnacioun of the sinnere. | The fifthe
circumstaunce is how manye times that he hath sinned, if it be
in his minde, and how ofte that he hath falle. | For he that ofte
falleth in sinne, he despiseth the mercy of God, and encreseth
his sinne, and is unkinde to Crist; and he wexeth the moore
feble to withstonde sinne, and sinneth the moore lightly, [970] |
and the latter ariseth, and is the moore eschew for to shriven
him, and namely to him that is his confessour. | For which that
folk, whan they falle again in hir olde folies, outher they forleten
hir olde confessours al outrely, or elles they departen hir shrift
in diverse places. But soothly, swich departed shrift deserveth
no mercy of God of hise sinnes. | The sixte circumstaunce is
why that a man sinneth, as by whiche temptacioun, and if
himself procure thilke temptacioun, or by the excitinge of
oother folk; or if he sinne with a womman by force, or by hire
owene assent, | or if the womman, maugree hir heed, hath ben
afforced or noon (this shal she telle); for coveitise or for poverte,
and if it was hire procuringe or noon, and swich manere
harneis. | The seventhe circumstaunce is in what manere he
hath doon his sinne, or how that she hath suffred that folk han
doon to hire. [975] | And the same shal the man telle, pleinly,
with alle circumstaunces, and wheither he hath sinned with
comune bordel-wommen or noon; | or doon his sinne in holy
times or noon, in fasting-times or noon, or biforn his shrifte,

---

967 **consentement** consent   968 **eggen** incite   **parteners** accomplices
970 **unkinde** ungrateful   **wexeth** becomes   971 **latter** later   **eschew** loath
shriven him be confessed   972 **forleten** abandon   **al outrely** completely
departen divide   **shrift** confession   973 **excitinge** urging
974 **maugree hir heed** in spite of all she could do   **afforced** forced
harneis details   975 **suffred** allowed   976 **with alle circumstaunces** with
full details   **bordel-wommen** prostitutes

or after his latter shrifte, | and hath peraventure broken ther-
fore his penance enjoined; by whos help and whos conseil, by
sorcerye or craft; al moste be toold. |

Alle thise thinges, after that they ben grete or smale,
engreggen the conscience of man. And eek the preest, that is
thy juge, may the bettre ben avised of his juggement in yevinge
of thy penaunce, and that is after thy contricioun. | For
understond wel, that after time that a man hath defouled his
baptesme by sinne, if he wole come to savacioun ther is noon
oother wey but by penitence and shrifte and satisfaccioun,
[980] | and namely by the two, if ther be a confessour to which
he may shriven him, and the thridde, if he have lif to perfournen
it. | Thanne shal man looke and considere that if he wole
maken a trewe and a profitable confessioun ther moste be foure
condiciouns: | first, it moot ben in sorweful bitternesse of herte,
as seide the king Ezechie to God: 'I wol remembre me alle the
yeres of my lif in bitternesse of min herte.' | This condicioun of
bitternesse hath five signes. The first is that confessioun moste
be shamefast, nat for to covere ne hide his sinne, for he hath
agilt his God and defouled his soule. | And therof seyth Seint
Augustin, 'The herte travailleth for shame of his sinne,' and for
he hath greet shamefastnesse, he is digne to have greet mercy
of God. [985] | Swich was the confessioun of the publican, that
wolde nat heven up hise eyen to hevene for he hadde offended
God of hevene, for which shamefastnesse he hadde anon the
mercy of God. | And therof seyth Seint Augustin that swich
shamefast folk ben next foryevenesse and remissioun. | Another
signe is humilitee in confessioun, of which seyth Seint Peter:
'Humbleth yow under the might of God.' The hond of God is
mighty in confessioun, for therby God foryeveth thee thy sinnes,
for he allone hath the power. | And this humilitee shal ben in
herte and in signe outward, for right as he hath humilitee to

977 **latter** more recent   978 **conseil** advice   979 **after that** according as
engreggen burden **ben avised of** reflect on   984 **agilt** offended against
985 **therof** about this **travailleth** suffers   986 **publican** tax-collector
heven lift   987 **next** nearest to

God in his herte, right so sholde he humble his body outward
to the preest, that sit in Goddes place. | For which, in no manere
– sith that Crist is soverein, and the preest meene and mediatour
bitwixe Crist and the sinnere, and the sinnere is the laste, by
wey of resoun [990] | – thanne sholde nat the sinnere sitte as
hye as his confessour, but knele biforn him or at his feet, but if
maladye destourbe it. For he shal nat taken kepe who sit there,
but in whos place that he sitteth. | A man that hath trespased
to a lord, and comth for to axe mercy and maken his accord,
and set him doun anon by the lord, men wolde holden him
outrageous, and nat worthy so soone for to have remissioun ne
mercy. | The thridde signe is that thy shrift sholde be ful of
teeris, if man may, and if man may nat wepe with hise bodily
eyen, lat him wepe in herte. | Swich was the confession of Seint
Peter, for after that he hadde forsake Jesu Crist, he wente out
and weep ful bitterly. | The fourthe signe is that he ne lette nat
for shame to shewen his confessioun. [995] | Swich was the
confessioun of the Magdalene, that ne spared for no shame of
hem that weren atte feste for to go to oure lord Jesu Crist and
biknowe to him hire sinnes. | The fifthe signe is that a man or
a womman be obeisant to receiven the penaunce that him is
enjoined for hise sinnes, for certes, Jesu Crist for the giltes of o
man was obedient to the deeth. |

The seconde condicioun of verray confession is that it be
hastily doon; for certes, if a man hadde a deedly wounde, evere
the lenger that he taried to warisshe himself, the moore wolde
it corrupte and haste him to his deeth, and eek the wounde
wolde be the wors for to hele. | And right so fareth sinne that
longe time is in a man unshewed. | Certes, a man oghte hastily
shewen hise sinnes for manye causes, as for drede of deeth, that
cometh ofte sodeinly, and no certein what time it shal be, ne in
what place; and eek the drecchinge of o sinne draweth in

---

990 **meene** intermediary   991 **but if maladye destourbe it** unless sickness
prevents it **taken kepe** pay any attention to **sit** (= *sitteth*) sits
992 **trespased** done wrong **maken his accord** be reconciled
outrageous impudent   995 **ne lette nat** should not delay
996 **biknowe** confess   998 **warisshe** cure   999 **unshewed** undisclosed
1000 **certein** certainty **drecchinge** continuance

another; [1000] | and eek the lenger that he tarieth, the ferther
he is fro Crist. And if he abide to his laste day, scarsly may he
shriven him or remembre him of hise sinnes or repenten him,
for the grevous maladye of his deeth. | And forasmuche as he
ne hath nat in his lif herkned Jesu Crist whanne he hath spoken,
he shal crye to Jesu Crist at his laste day, and scarsly wol he
herkne him. | And understond that this condicioun moste han
foure thinges. Thy shrift moste be purveyed bifore and avised,
for wikked haste dooth no profit; and that a man konne shrive
him of hise sinnes, be it of pride, or of envye, and so forth, with
the speces and circumstances; | and that he have comprehended
in his minde the nombre and the greetnesse of hise sinnes, and
how longe that he hath lein in sinne; | and eek that he be contrit
of hise sinnes, and in stedefast purpos, by the grace of God,
nevere eft to falle in sinne; and eek that he drede and countrewaite himself that he fle the occasiouns of sinne to whiche he is
enclined. [1005] | Also, thow shalt shrive thee of alle thy sinnes
to o man, and nat a parcel to o man and a parcel to another –
that is to understonde, in entente to departe thy confessioun as
for shame or drede, for it nis but stranglinge of thy soule. | For
certes, Jesu Crist is entierly al good; in him nis noon imperfecc-
ioun, and therefore, outher he foryeveth al parfitly, or never a
deel. | I seye nat that if thow be assigned to the penitauncer
for certein sinne that thow art bounde to shewen him al the
remenaunt of thy sinnes of whiche thow hast be shriven of thy
curaat, but if it like to thee of thin humilitee; this is no
departinge of shrifte. | Ne I seye nat, theras I speke of divisioun
of confessioun, that if thow have licence for to shrive thee to a
discreet and an honeste preest where thee liketh and by licence
of thy curaat, that thow ne mayst wel shrive thee to him of alle
thy sinnes; | but lat no blotte be bihinde, lat no sinne ben
untoold, as fer as thow hast remembraunce. [1010] | And whan

1003 **purveyed** prepared **avised** thought about   1005 **drede** fear
countrewaite guard **fle** avoid   1006 **parcel** part **departe** divide
1007 **never a deel** not at all   1008 **penitauncer** assigner of penance
curaat parish priest **but if it like to thee** unless it pleases you
1010 **bihinde** left behind

thow shalt be shriven to thy curaat, telle him eek alle the sinnes
that thow hast doon sin thow were last yshriven; this is no
wikked entente of divisioun of shrifte. |

Also, the verray shrifte axeth certeine condiciouns. First, that
thow shrive thee by thy free wil, noght constreined, ne for
shame of folk, ne for maladye, ne swiche thinges; for it is resoun
that he that trespaseth by his free wil, that by his free wil he
confesse his trespas, | and that noon oother man telle his sinne,
but he himself. Ne he shal nat naite ne denye his sinne, ne
wratthe him again the preest for his amonestinge to leve sinne. |
The seconde condicioun is that thy shrift be laweful; that is to
seyn, that thow that shrivest thee, and eek the preest that hereth
thy confessioun, ben verraily in the feith of Holy Chirche, | and
that a man ne be nat despeired of the mercy of Jesu Crist, as
Caim or Judas. [1015] | And eek a man moot accusen himself
of his owene trespas, and nat another, but he shal blame and
witen himself and his owene malice of his sinne, and noon
oother. | But nathelees, if that another man be occasioun or
enticere of his sinne, or the estaat of a persone be swich thurgh
which his sinne is agregged, or elles that he may nat pleinly
shriven him but he telle the persone with which he hath sinned,
thanne may he telle it, | so that his entente ne be nat to bakbite
the persone but oonly to declaren his confessioun. | Thow ne
shalt nat eek make no lesinges in thy confessioun, for humilitee – paraventure, to seyn that thow hast doon sinnes of whiche
that thow were nevere gilty. | For Seint Augustin seyth, 'if
thow, bicause of thin humilitee, makest lesinges on thyself,
thogh thow ne were nat in sinne biforn, yet artow thanne
in sinne thurgh thy lesinges.' [1020] | Thow most eek shewe
thy sinne by thin owene propre mouth, but thow be woxe
dombe, and nat by no lettre, for thow that hast doon the
sinne, thou shalt have the shame therfore. | Thow shalt nat eek

1013 **naite** deny **wratthe him** become angry **amonestinge** admonishment
leve abandon   1015 **as Caim** such as Cain   1016 **witen** blame
1017 **estaat** social position **agregged** increased **pleinly** completely
1019 **lesinges** lies   1021 **be woxe** have become

peinte thy confessioun by faire subtile wordes, to covere the
moore thy sinne, for thanne bigilestow thyself, and nat the
preest. Thow most tellen it pleinly, be it nevere so foul ne so
horrible. | Thow shalt eek shrive thee to a preest that is discreet
to conseille thee, and eek thow shalt nat shrive thee for veine
glorye, ne for ypocrisye, ne for no cause but oonly for the doute
of Jesu Crist and the heele of thy soule. | Thow shalt nat eek
renne to the preest sodeinly to tellen him lightly thy sinne, as
whoso telleth a jape or a tale, but avisely, and with greet
devocioun. | And generally, shrive thee ofte. If thow ofte falle,
ofte thow arise by confessioun. [1025] | And though thow
shrive thee ofter than ones of sinne of which thow hast be
shriven, it is the moore merite. And as seyth Seint Augustin,
thow shalt have the moore lightly relessing and grace of God,
bothe of sinne and of peine. | And certes, ones a yeere, atte
leeste wey, it is laweful for to ben housled; for certes, ones a
yeere alle thinges renovellen. |

Now have I toold yow of verray confessioun, that is the
seconde partie of penitence. |

[The Third Part of Penitence: Satisfaction]

The thridde partie of penitence is satisfaccioun, and that stant
moost generally in almesse and in bodily peine. | Now ben ther
thre manere of almesses: contricioun of herte, where a man
offreth himself to God; another is to han pitee of defaute of
hise neighebores; and the thridde is in yevinge of good conseil
and comfort, goostly and bodily, where men han nede, and
namely in sustenaunce of mannes foode. [1030] | And tak kepe
that a man hath nede of thise thinges generally: he hath nede

1022 **peinte** embellish **bigilestow** you deceive   1023 **conseille** counsel
doute fear **heele** health   1024 **lightly** frivolously **avisely** with
forethought   1026 **lightly** easily **relessing** forgiveness
1027 **ben housled** receive the Eucharist **renovellen** are renewed
1029 **stant . . . in** consists in **almesse** alms-giving **peine** suffering
1030 **defaute** lack **goostly** spiritual

of foode; he hath nede of clothing and herberwe; he hath nede
of charitable conseil and visitinge in prisone and in maladye,
and sepulture of his dede body. | And if thow mayst nat visite
the nedeful with thy persone, visite him by thy message and by
thy yiftes. | Thise ben general almesses or werkes of charitee, of
hem that han temporel richesses or discrecioun in conseilinge.
Of thise werkes shaltow heren at the day of doome. | Thise
almesses shaltow doon of thine owene propre thinges, and
hastily, and prively, if thow mayst; | but nathelees, if thow
mayst nat doon it prively, thow shalt nat forbere to doon
almesse, though men seen it, so that it be nat doon for thank
of the world but oonly for thank of Jesu Crist. [1035] | For, as
witnesseth Seint Mathew, *capitulo quinto*, 'A citee may nat ben
hid that is set on a montaine, ne men lighte nat a lanterne and
put it under a busshel, but men sette it on a candelstikke to
yeve light to the men in the hous. | Right so shal youre light
lighten bifore men, that they may seen youre goode werkes and
glorifye youre fader that is in hevene.' |

Now as to speken of bodily peine, it stant in preyeres, in
wakinges, in fastinges, in vertuouse techinges of orisons. | And
ye shul understonde that orisouns or preyeres is for to seyn a
pitous wil of herte that redresseth it in God, and expresseth it
by word outward, to remoeven harmes, and to han thinges
espirituel and durable, and somtime temporel thinges, of
whiche orisouns, certes, in the orison of the *Pater noster* hath
Jesu Crist enclosed moost thinges. | Certes, it is privileged of
thre thinges in his dignitee, for which it is moore digne than
any oother preyere, for that Jesu Crist himself maked it; [1040] |
and it is short, for it sholde be koud the moore lightly, and for
to withholden it the moore esily in herte, and helpen himself
the ofter with the orisoun; | and for a man sholde be the lasse
wery to seyen it, and for a man may nat excusen him to lerne

1031 **herberwe** shelter **maladye** sickness **sepulture** burial
1034 **hastily** without delay **prively** secretly   1035 **forbere** refrain from
thank praise   1037 **lighten** shine   1038 **orisons** prayers
1039 **pitous** devout **redresseth it in** directs itself to   1040 **digne** worthy
1041 **koud** learned **lightly** easily **withholden** keep

it, it is so short and so esy; and for it comprehendeth in itself
alle goode preyeres. | The exposicioun of this holy preyere, that
is so excellent and digne, I bitake to thise maistres of theologye,
save thus muchel wol I seyn, that whan thow prayest that God
sholde foryeve thee thy giltes as thow foryevest hem that agilten
to thee, be ful wel war that thow ne be nat out of charitee. |
This holy orisoun amenuseth eek venial sinne, and therfore it
aperteneth specially to penitence. | This preyere moste be trewe-
ly seid, and in verray feith, and that men preye to God ordinatly, and discreetly, and devoutly; and alwey a man shal putten
his wil to be subget to the wille of God. [1045] | This orisoun
moste eek ben seid with greet humblesse and ful pure, honestly,
and nat to the anoyaunce of any man or womman. It moste eek
ben continued with the werkes of charitee. | It availeth eek
again the vices of the soule, for, as seyth Seint Jerome, 'by
fastinge ben saved the vices of the flessh, and by preyere the
vices of the soule.' | After this, thow shalt understonde that
bodily peine stant in wakinge, for Jesu Crist seyth, 'Waketh and
preyeth, that ye ne entre in wikked temptacioun.' |

  Ye shul understanden also that fastinge stant in thre thinges:
in forberinge of bodily mete and drinke, and in forberinge of
worldly jolitee, and in forberinge of deedly sinne. This is to
seyn that a man shal kepen him fro deedly sinne with al his
might. | And thow shalt understanden eek that God ordeined
fastinge, and to fastinge apertenen foure thinges: [1050] | large-
nesse to povre folk; gladnesse of herte espirituel; nat to ben
angry ne anoyed ne grucche for he fasteth, and also resonable
houre for to ete by mesure – that is for to seyn, a man shal nat
ete in untime, ne sitte the lenger at his table to ete for he fasteth. |

1043 bitake consign agilten do wrong   1044 amenuseth reduces
aperteneth is fitting   1045 ordinatly methodically
1046 honestly reverently ben continued with be accompanied by
1048 wakinge vigil Waketh watch   1049 forberinge of abstinence from
jolitee pleasure   1050 apertenen are connected
1051 largenesse liberality grucche grumble by mesure in moderation
in untime at an improper time

Thanne shaltow understonde that bodily peine stant in discipline, or techinge, by word, or by writinge, or in ensample; also
in weringe of heires, or of stamin, or of haubergeons on hire
naked flessh, for Cristes sake, and swiche manere penaunces. |
But war thee wel that swiche manere penaunces on thy flessh
ne make thee nat bitter or angry or anoyed of thyself, for bettre
is to caste awey thin heire than for to caste awey the swetenesse
of Jesu Crist. | And therfore seyth Seint Paul: 'Clothe yow, as
they that ben chosen of God, in herte of misericorde, debonairetee, suffraunce, and swich manere of clothinge,' of whiche
Jesu Crist is moore apaied than of heires, or haubergeouns, or
hauberkes. | Thanne is discipline eek in knokkinge of thy brest,
in scourginge with yerdes, in knelinges, in tribulaciouns,
[1055] | in suffringe paciently wronges that ben doon to thee,
and eek in pacient suffraunce of maladies, or lesinge of worldly
catel, or of wif, or of child, or othere freendes. |

Thanne shaltow understonde whiche thinges destourben
penaunce, and this is in foure maneres: that is, drede, shame,
hope, and wanhope, that is desperacioun. | And for to speke
first of drede, for which he weneth that he may suffre no
penaunce: | theragains is remedye for to thinke that bodily
penaunce is but short and litel at regard of the peine of helle
that is so cruel, and so long that it lasteth withouten ende. |
Now, again the shame that a man hath to shriven him – and
namely thise ypocrites that wolden ben holden so parfite that
they han no nede to shriven hem – [1060] | agains that shame
sholde a man thinke that, by wey of resoun, that he that hath
nat ben shamed to doon foule thinges, certes, him oghte nat
ben ashamed to do faire thinges, and that is confessiouns. | A
man sholde eek thinke that God seeth and woot alle hise

1052 **discipline** teaching (n.) **heires** hair-shirts **stamin** coarse worsted cloth
haubergeons mail-coats   1053 **anoyed of** irritated with
1054 **debonairetee** gentleness **suffraunce** forbearance **apaied** pleased
hauberkes mail-coats   1055 **discipline** mortification of the flesh **yerdes** rods
1056 **suffraunce** endurance **lesinge** loss **catel** possessions
1057 **destourben** hinder **wanhope** despair   1059 **theragains** against that
at regard of in comparison with   1060 **again** with regard to
1061 **by wey of** according to

thoghtes and alle hise werkes; to him may no thing ben hid ne covered. | Men sholden eek remembren hem of the shame that is to come at the day of doome to hem that ben nat penitent and shriven in this present lif. | For alle the creatures in hevene, in erthe, and in helle, shullen seen apertly al that they hiden in this world. | Now, for to speken of the hope of hem that ben necligent and slowe to shriven hem, that stant in two maneres. [1065] | That oon is that he hopeth for to live longe, and for to purchacen muche richesse for his delit, and thanne he wol shriven him; and as he seyth, him semeth thanne timely inough to come to shrifte. | Another is of surquidrye that he hath in Cristes mercy. | Agains the firste vice, he shal thinke that oure lif is in no sikernesse, and eek that alle the richesses in this world ben in aventure, and passen as a shadwe on the wal. | And as seyth Seint Gregorye, that it aperteneth to the grete rightwisnesse of God that nevere shal the peine stinte of hem that nevere wolde withdrawen hem fro sinne, hir thankes, but ay continue in sinne. For thilke perpetuel wil to do sinne shul they han perpetuel peine. | Wanhope is in two maneres: the firste wanhope is in the mercy of Crist; that oother is that they thinken that they ne mighte nat longe persevere in goodnesse. [1070] | The firste wanhope comth of that he demeth that he hath sinned so greetly, and so ofte, and so longe lein in sinne, that he shal nat be saved. | Certes, agains that cursed wanhope sholde he thinke that the passion of Jesu Crist is moore strong for to unbinde than sinne is strong for to binde. | Agains the seconde wanhope he shal thinke that as ofte as he falleth, he may arise again by penitence, and though he nevere so longe have lein in sinne, the mercy of Crist is alwey redy to receiven him to mercy. | Agains the wanhope that he demeth that he sholde nat longe persevere in goodnesse, he shal thinke that the feblesse of the devel may nothing doon but if men wol suffren him; | and eek he shal han strengthe of the help of God, and of

1064 **apertly** openly   1066 **purchacen** acquire **timely** soon
1067 **surquidrye** over-confidence   1068 **sikernesse** security
ben in aventure are at risk   1069 **hir thankes** voluntarily **peine** punishment
1070 **that oother** the second   1071 **demeth** believes   1074 **suffren** allow

al Holy Chirche, and of the proteccioun of aungels, if him list.
[1075] |

Thanne shal men understonde what is the fruit of penaunce.
And after the word of Jesu Crist, it is the endelees blisse of
hevene, | ther joye hath no contrarioustee of wo ne grevaunce;
ther alle harmes ben passed of this present lif; theras is the
sikernesse fro the peine of helle; theras is the blisful compaignye
that rejoisen hem everemo, everich of otheres joye; | theras the
body of man, that whilom was foul and derk, is moore cleer
than the sonne; theras the body that whilom was sik, freele,
and feble, and mortal, is inmortal, and so strong, and so hool,
that ther may no thing apeiren it; | theras ne is neither hunger,
thurst, ne coold, but every soule replenissed with the sighte of
the parfit knowinge of God. | This blisful regne may men pur-
chace by poverte espirituel, and the glorye by lowenesse, the
plentee of joye by hunger and thurst, and the reste by travaille,
and the lif by deeth and mortificacioun of sinne. [1080] |

CHAUCER'S RETRACTIONS

Here taketh the makere of this book his leve.

Now preye I to hem alle that herkne this litel tretis or rede, that
if ther be anything in it that liketh hem, that therof they thanken
oure lord Jesu Crist, of whom procedeth al wit and al
goodnesse. | And if ther be anything that displese hem, I preye
hem also that they arrette it to the defaute of min unkonninge,
and nat to my wil, that wolde ful fain have seid bettre if I hadde

1075 **if him list** (= *listeth*) if it pleases him   1077 **contrarioustee** contrary
grevaunce sorrow **sikernesse** security   1078 **freele** frail **apeiren** harm
1079 **replenissed** filled **knowinge** knowledge   1080 **regne** kingdom
purchace obtain **lowenesse** humility

1081 **tretis** treatise **liketh** pleases **therof** for it   1082 **arrette it to** blame it
on **unkonninge** lack of skill

had konninge. | For oure book seyth, 'Al that is writen, is writen for oure doctrine,' and that is min entente. | Wherfore I biseke yow mekely, for the mercy of God, that ye preye for me, that Crist have mercy on me and foryeve me my giltes; | and namely of my translacions and enditinges of worldly vanitees, the whiche I revoke in my retracciouns: [1085] | as is The Book of Troilus, The Book also of Fame, The Book of the xxv Ladies, The Book of the Duchesse, The Book of Seint Valentines day of the Parlement of Briddes, The Tales of Caunterbury, thilke that sownen into sinne, | The Book of the Leoun, and many another book, if they were in my remembrance, and many a song and many a leccherous lay, that Crist for his grete mercy foryeve me the sinne. | But of the translacioun of Boece de Consolacione, and othere bookes of legendes of seintes, and omelies, and moralitee and devocioun, | that thanke I oure lord Jesu Crist and his blisful moder, and alle the seintes of hevene, | bisekinge hem that they from hennesforth unto my lives ende sende me grace to biwaile my giltes, and to studye to the savacioun of my soule, and graunte me grace of verray penitence, confessioun, and satisfaccioun to doon in this present lif, [1090] | thurgh the benigne grace of him that is king of kinges and preest over alle preestes, that boughte us with the precious blood of his herte, | so that I may ben oon of hem at the day of doome that shulle be saved. *Qui cum patre etc.*

Heere is ended the book of the Tales of
Caunterbury compiled by Geffrey Chaucer,
of whos soule Jesu Crist have mercy. Amen.

1085 **enditinges** compositions   1086 **sownen into** conduce to
1088 **omelies** homilies   1089 **blisful** blessed   1090 **studye to** take thought
for   1092 **day of doome** Day of Judgement   *Qui cum patre etc.* who with
the Father (and the Holy Spirit lives and reigns as God for ever and ever.
Amen)

Abbreviated References

Alan of Lille, *De Planctu Naturae* ed. Nikolaus M. Häring (Spoleto, 1978).

— *The Plaint of Nature*, tr. James J. Sheridan (Toronto, 1980).

Albertano of Brescia, *Liber consolationis et consilii* ed. Thor Sundby, Chaucer Society (London, 1873).

Albertano of Brescia, *De amore dei Albertani moralissimi opus de loquendi ac tacendi modo, necnon et de quamplurimis notatum dignissimis* . . . (Coni [Cuneo], 1507) (*De amore et dilectione dei et proximi*, ff. 25r–62v).

Albertano of Brescia, *Liber de doctrina dicendi et tacendi* ed. and (Italian) tr. Paola Navone (Florence, 1998).

Anel Geoffrey Chaucer, *Anelida and Arcite*.

AnM Annuale Mediaevale.

Apocryphal NT The Apocryphal New Testament, ed. Montague Rhodes James (Oxford, 1924).

Archiv Archiv für das Studium der neueren Sprachen und Literaturen.

Astrol Geoffrey Chaucer, *A Treatise on the Astrolabe*.

AV The Holy Bible (Authorized King James Version).

Avianus *Fabulae*, in *Minor Latin Poets*, ed. J. Wight Duff and Arnold M. Duff (Cambridge, MA, and London, 1934; rev. edn 1935), pp. 669–749.

Bächtold-Stäubli E. Hoffmann-Krayer and Hanns Bächtold-Stäubli, eds., *Handwörterbuch des deutschen Aberglaubens*, 10 vols. (Berlin, 1927–42).

Barron, 'England and the Low Countries' Caroline Barron, 'Introduction: England and the Low Countries 1327–1477', in *England and the Low Countries in the Late Middle Ages*, ed. Caroline Barron and Nigel Saul (Stroud, 1995), pp. 1–28.

Bartholomaeus Anglicus, *On the Properties of Things* *On the Properties of Things: John Trevisa's Translation of Bartholomaeus*

Anglicus De Proprietatibus Rerum, ed. M. C. Seymour et al., 3 vols. (Oxford, 1975–88).

Baugh Albert C. Baugh, ed., *Chaucer's Major Poetry* (New York, 1963).

BD Geoffrey Chaucer, *The Book of the Duchess*.

Bennett J. A. W. Bennett, *Chaucer at Oxford and at Cambridge* (Oxford, 1974).

Benson and Andersson Larry D. Benson and Theodore M. Andersson, eds., *The Literary Context of Chaucer's Fabliaux: Texts and Translations* (Indianapolis and New York, 1971).

Bernard of Clairvaux, *Opera Sancti Bernardi Opera*, ed. J. Leclercq, C. H. Talbot and H. M. Rochais, 8 vols. (Rome, 1957–77).

Bernard Silvestris, *Cosmographia* ed. Peter Dronke (Leiden, 1978).
— tr. Winthrop Wetherbee (New York and London, 1973).

Blair Claude Blair, *European Armour circa 1066 to circa 1700* (London, 1958).

Boccaccio, *Opere* Giovanni Boccaccio, *Tutte le Opere*, ed. Vittore Branca, 12 vols. (Milan, 1964–98): *Filocolo* in vol. I (1967), *Filostrato* and *Teseida* in vol. II (1964), *Decameron* in vol. IV (1976), *De casibus illustrium virorum* in vol. IX (1983), *De mulieribus claris* in vol. X (1967).
— *Filocolo*, tr. D. Cheney and T. G. Bergin (New York and London, 1985).
— *The Book of Theseus*, tr. Bernadette Marie McCoy (New York, 1974).
— *The Decameron*, tr. G. H. McWilliam (Harmondsworth, 1972).
— *Concerning Famous Women*, tr. G. A. Guarino (London, 1964).

Boece Geoffrey Chaucer, *Boece* (*Liber Boecii de Consolacione Philosophie*).

Bowden Muriel Bowden, *A Commentary on the General Prologue to the Canterbury Tales*, 2nd edn (New York and London, 1967).

Boyde, *Dante Philomythes* Patrick Boyde, *Dante Philomythes and Philosopher: Man in the Cosmos* (Cambridge, 1981).

Bracton on the Laws and Customs of England ed. George E. Woodbine, tr. Samuel E. Thorne, 4 vols. (Cambridge, MA, 1968–77).

CA see Gower, *CA*.

Carlin, *Medieval Southwark* Martha Carlin, *Medieval Southwark* (London, 1996).

Carter, *Rape* John Marshall Carter, *Rape in Medieval England: An Historical and Sociological Study* (Lanham, MD, 1985).

CCCM Corpus Christianorum Continuatio Medievalis.

CCSL Corpus Christianorum Series Latina.

ChauR *Chaucer Review*.

Corpus Iuris Canonici ed. E. Friedberg, 2nd edn, 2 vols. (Leipzig, 1879–81; repr. 1959).

CSEL Corpus Scriptorum Ecclesiasticorum Latinorum.

CT Geoffrey Chaucer, *Canterbury Tales*.

Curry Walter Clyde Curry, *Chaucer and the Mediaeval Sciences*, rev. edn (London, 1960).

Daniell, *Death and Burial* Christopher Daniell, *Death and Burial in Medieval England 1066–1550* (London and New York, 1997).

Dante, *Convivio* Opere Minori II.1, ed. Cesare Vasoli and Domenico de Robertis (Milan and Naples, 1995).

— *The Banquet*, tr. Christopher Ryan (Stanford, CA, 1989).

Dante, *Inferno/Purgatorio/Paradiso* Dante Alighieri, *The Divine Comedy*, ed. and tr. Charles S. Singleton, 6 vols. (Princeton, NJ, 1970–75; corr. printing 1977).

Decameron see Boccaccio, *Opere*.

Deschamps, *Miroir de Mariage* Eustache Deschamps, *Le Miroir de Mariage*, in *Oeuvres Complètes*, vol. IX, ed. G. Raynaud, Société des Anciens Textes Français (Paris, 1894).

Dissuasio Valerii 'Dissuasio Valerii ad Ruffinum philosophum ne uxorem ducat', Walter Map, *De Nugis Curialium: Courtiers' Trifles*, ed. and tr. M. R. James, rev. C. N. L. Brooke and R. A. B. Mynors (Oxford, 1983; repr. with bibliographical note 1994), Dist. IV, c.3 (pp. 288–313).

Distichs of Cato Disticha Catonis, in *Minor Latin Poets*, ed. J. Wight Duff and Arnold M. Duff (Cambridge, MA, and London, 1934; rev. edn 1935), pp. 585–621.

Donaldson, *Chaucer's Poetry* E. T. Donaldson, ed., *Chaucer's Poetry: An Anthology for the Modern Reader*, 2nd edn (New York, 1975).

Douai-Rheims *The Holy Bible. Douay-Rheims Version* (Baltimore, MD, 1899).

Eade J. C. Eade, *The Forgotten Sky. A Guide to Astrology in English Literature* (Oxford, 1984).

EETS e.s./o.s. Early English Text Society extra series/original series.

Eisner, *Kalendarium* The Kalendarium of Nicholas of Lynn, ed. Sigmund Eisner, tr. Gary Mac Eoin and Sigmund Eisner (London, 1980).

El Ellesmere (San Marino, CA, Huntington Library, MS EL 26 C 9).

ELH ELH: A Journal of English Literary History.

Ellesmere Essays The Ellesmere Chaucer: Essays in Interpretation, ed. Martin Stevens and Daniel Woodward (San Marino, CA, 1995).

Elliott Ralph W. V. Elliott, *Chaucer's English* (London, 1974).

ELN English Language Notes.

Farmer, *Dictionary of Saints* David Hugh Farmer, *The Oxford Dictionary of Saints* (Oxford, 1978).

Filocolo see Boccaccio, *Opere.*

Gawain Sir Gawain and the Green Knight, ed. J. A. Burrow (Harmondsworth, 1972).

Geoffrey of Vinsauf, *Poetria Nova Les arts poétiques du XIIe et du XIIIe siècle,* ed. Edmond Faral (Paris, 1962), pp. 194–262.

— *Poetria Nova of Geoffrey of Vinsauf,* tr. Margaret F. Nims (Toronto, 1967).

Golden Legend Jacobus de Voragine, *The Golden Legend,* tr. William Granger Ryan, 2 vols. (Princeton, NJ, 1993).

Gower, *CA Confessio Amantis,* in *The English Works of John Gower,* ed. G. C. Macaulay, 2 vols., EETS e.s. 81–2 (London, 1900–1901).

Grant, *Source Book* Edward Grant, ed., *A Source Book in Medieval Science* (Cambridge, MA, 1974).

Grierson, *Coins* Philip Grierson, *The Coins of Medieval Europe* (London, 1991).

Grimm, *Astronomical Lore* Florence M. Grimm, *Astronomical Lore in Chaucer* (Lincoln, NE, 1919; repr. New York, 1970).

Guido delle Colonne [de Columnis], *History of the Destruction of Troy Historia Destructionis Troiae,* ed. Nathaniel Edward Griffin (Cambridge, MA, 1936).

— *Historia Destructionis Troiae,* tr. Mary Elizabeth Meek (Bloomington, IN, 1974).

Habig, *St Francis* Marion Habig, ed., *St Francis of Assisi: Writings and Early Biographies,* 3rd edn (Chicago, 1973).

Hanna, *Pursuing History* Ralph Hanna III, *Pursuing History: Middle English Manuscripts and their Texts* (Stanford, CA, 1996).

Hanna and Lawler, *Jankyn's Book Jankyn's Book of Wykked Wyves,* ed. Ralph Hanna III and Traugott Lawler, vol. I (Athens, GA, and London, 1997).

Harvey, *Living and Dying* Barbara Harvey, *Living and Dying in England 1100–1540: The Monastic Experience* (Oxford, 1993).

Hassell James Woodrow Hassell, Jr, *Middle French Proverbs, Sentences and Proverbial Phrases* (Toronto, 1982).

Havely, *Chaucer's Boccaccio* N. R. Havely, *Chaucer's Boccaccio* (Cambridge, 1980).

Hervieux, *Les fabulistes latins* Léopold Hervieux, ed., *Les fabulistes latins,* 5 vols. (Paris, 1893–99; vols. 1–2 in a second edition).

HF Geoffrey Chaucer, *The House of Fame.*

Hg Hengwrt (Aberystwyth, National Library of Wales, MS Peniarth 392D).

Hodges, *Chaucer and Costume* Laura F. Hodges, *Chaucer and Costume: The Secular Pilgrims in the General Prologue* (Cambridge, 2000).

Hornsby Joseph Allen Hornsby, *Chaucer and the Law* (Norman, OK, 1988).

Hudson, *Wycliffite Writings* *Selections from English Wycliffite Writings*, ed. Anne Hudson (Cambridge, 1978).

Hyland, *Horse* Ann Hyland, *The Horse in the Middle Ages* (Stroud, Glos., 1999).

Innocent III, *De Miseria* Lotario dei Segni (Pope Innocent III), *De Miseria Condicionis Humane*, ed. and tr. Robert E. Lewis (Athens, GA, 1978; London, 1980).

Jean de Meun, *Testament* *Le Testament Maistre Jehan de Meun: Un caso letterario*, ed. Silvia Buzzetti Gallarati (Alessandria, 1989).

Jehan le Fèvre *Les Lamentations de Matheolus et le Livre de Leesce de Jehan le Fèvre, de Ressons*, ed. A. G. Van Hamel, 2 vols. (Paris, 1893–1905).

JEGP *Journal of English and Germanic Philology.*

Jerome, *Against Jov.* Jerome, *Against Jovinian. Adversus Jovinianum*, *PL* 23, cols. 211–338.

— tr. W. H. Fremantle, *A Select Library of Nicene and Post-Nicene Fathers of the Christian Church*, ed. Henry Wace and Philip Schaff, vol. VI (New York, 1893; repr. Grand Rapids, MI, 1979), pp. 346–416.

Jerome Biblical Commentary *The Jerome Biblical Commentary*, ed. Raymond E. Brown, Joseph A. Fitzmyer and Roland E. Murphy, 2 vols. in 1 (London, 1968).

John of Salisbury, *Policraticus* *Ioannis Saresberiensis episcopi Carnotensis Policratici: sive, De nugis curialium et vestigiis philosophorum libri VIII*, ed. C. C. J. Webb, 2 vols. (Oxford, 1909).

— Books I–IV, ed. K. S. B. Keats-Rohan, CCCM 108 (Turnhout, 1993).

— tr. Joseph B. Pike, *Frivolities of Courtiers and Footprints of Philosophers* [Books I–III, and selections from Books VII and VIII] (New York, 1972).

— tr. John Dickinson, *The Statesman's Book of John of Salisbury* [Books IV–VI, and selections from Books VII and VIII] (New York, 1963).

Justinian, *Codex* *Corpus Juris Civilis*, 3 vols. (Dublin and Zürich, 1968–70), vol. II: *Codex*, ed. Paul Krüger.

Justinian, *Digest* The Digest of Justinian, Latin text ed. Theodor Mommsen with the aid of Paul Krüger, English translation ed. Alan Watson, 4 vols. (Philadelphia, PA, 1985).

Justinian, *Novellae* Corpus Juris Civilis, 3 vols. (Dublin and Zürich, 1968–70), vol. III: *Novellae*, ed. Rudolph Schöll and Wilhelm Kroll.

Kane George Kane, 'John M. Manly (1865–1940) and Edith Rickert (1871–1938)', in *Editing Chaucer: The Great Tradition*, ed. Paul G. Ruggiers (Norman, OK, 1984), pp. 207–29.

Kellogg, *Chaucer, Langland* Alfred L. Kellogg, *Chaucer, Langland, Arthur: Essays in Middle English Literature* (New Brunswick, NJ, 1972).

Kelly, *Love and Marriage* Henry Ansgar Kelly, *Love and Marriage in the Age of Chaucer* (Ithaca, NY, 1975).

Kolve and Olson Geoffrey Chaucer, *The Canterbury Tales: Nine Tales and the General Prologue*, ed. V. A. Kolve and Glending Olson (New York and London, 1989).

LGW Geoffrey Chaucer, *The Legend of Good Women*.

Life-Records *Chaucer Life-Records*, ed. Martin M. Crow and Clair C. Olson (Oxford, 1966).

Li Fet des Romains Li Fet des Romains. Compilé ensemble de Saluste et de Suetoine et de Lucan, ed. L.-F. Flutre and K. Sneyders de Vogel, 2 vols. (Paris and Groningen, 1935–8).

Lobel, ed., *The City of London* Mary D. Lobel, ed., *The City of London from Prehistoric Times to c. 1520 (The British Atlas of Historic Towns*, vol. III) (Oxford, 1989; corr. repr. 1991).

Machaut, Guillaume, *La Prise d'Alexandrie* ed. L. de Mas Latrie (Geneva, 1877).

Macrobius, *Commentary on the Dream of Scipio*
— *Commentarii in Somnium Scipionis*, ed. J. Willis (Berlin, 1970).
— *Commentary on the Dream of Scipio*, tr. William Harris Stahl (New York and London, 1952).

MÆ Medium Ævum.

Magoun Francis P. Magoun, Jr, *A Chaucer Gazetteer* (Stockholm, 1961).

Manly, *New Light* John Matthews Manly, *Some New Light on Chaucer* (London, 1926).

Manly and Rickert John M. Manly and Edith Rickert, eds., *The Text of the Canterbury Tales Studied on the Basis of All Known Manuscripts*, 8 vols. (Chicago and London, 1940).

Mann, *Estates Satire* Jill Mann, *Chaucer and Medieval Estates Satire* (Cambridge, 1973).

Mann, *Feminizing Chaucer* Jill Mann, *Feminizing Chaucer* (Cambridge, 2002).

Mann, 'Parents and Children' Jill Mann, 'Parents and Children in the "Canterbury Tales"', in *Literature in Fourteenth-Century England*, ed. Piero Boitani and Anna Torti (Tübingen and Cambridge, 1983), pp. 165–83.

Mann, 'Chance and Destiny' Jill Mann, 'Chance and Destiny in *Troilus and Criseyde* and the *Knight's Tale*', in *The Cambridge Companion to Chaucer*, ed. Piero Boitani and Jill Mann, 2nd edn (Cambridge, 2003), pp. 93–111.

Marie de France, *Fables* *The Fables of Marie de France*, tr. Mary Lou Martin, with Karl Warnke's edition of the French text (Birmingham, AL, 1984).

Martin of Braga *Martini Episcopi Bracarensis Opera Omnia*, ed. Claude W. Barlow (New Haven, CT, 1950).

Matheolus, *Lamentations* see Jehan le Fèvre.

MED *Middle English Dictionary*, ed. H. Kurath, S. M. Kuhn and Robert E. Lewis (Ann Arbor, MI, 1954–2001).

MedHum *Medievalia et Humanistica*.

Miller Robert P. Miller, ed., *Chaucer: Sources and Backgrounds* (New York, 1977).

MLN *Modern Language Notes*.

MLR *Modern Language Review*.

MP *Modern Philology*.

Mustanoja Tauno F. Mustanoja, *A Middle English Syntax*, Part I (Helsinki, 1960).

New Grove Dictionary *The New Grove Dictionary of Music and Musicians*, ed. Stanley Sadie, 2nd edn (New York, 2001).

Nicholas of Lynn see Eisner.

NM *Neuphilologische Mitteilungen*.

North, *Chaucer's Universe* J. D. North, *Chaucer's Universe* (Oxford, 1988).

***Novellino*, ed. Consoli** *The Novellino or One Hundred Ancient Tales*, ed. and tr. Joseph P. Consoli (New York and London, 1997).

NQ *Notes and Queries*.

OED *The Oxford English Dictionary . . . edited by James A. H. Murray, Henry Bradley, W. A. Craigie, and C. T. Onions*, 16 vols. (Oxford, 1933); 2nd edn prepared by J. A. Simpson and E. S. C. Weiner, 20 vols. (Oxford, 1989).

Oxford Companion to Classical Literature *The Oxford Companion to Classical Literature*, ed. M. C. Howatson, 2nd edn (Oxford, 1989).

Oxford Dictionary of the Christian Church The Oxford Dictionary of the Christian Church, ed. F. L. Cross, 3rd edn ed. E. A. Livingstone (Oxford, 1997).

Oxford Dictionary of English Proverbs[3] Oxford Dictionary of English Proverbs, 3rd edn, rev. F. P. Wilson (Oxford, 1970).

Page, *Voices and Instruments* Christopher Page, *Voices and Instruments of the Middle Ages* (London, 1987).

Pamphilus Pamphilus: *Prolegomena zum Pamphilus (de amore) und kritische Textausgabe*, ed. Franz G. Becker, (Ratingen, Kastellaun and Düsseldorf, 1972).

— tr. Alison Goddard Elliott, *Seven Medieval Latin Comedies* (New York and London, 1984), pp. 1–25.

Patch, *Goddess Fortuna* Howard R. Patch, *The Goddess Fortuna in Medieval Literature* (Cambridge, MA, 1927; repr. London, 1967).

PBA Proceedings of the British Academy.

Pearsall, *Life* Derek Pearsall, *The Life of Geoffrey Chaucer: A Critical Biography* (Oxford, 1992).

Petrarch, *Opere latine* Francesco Petrarca, *Opere latine*, ed. Antonietta Bufano, 2 vols. (Turin, 1975).

Petrus Alfonsi, *Disciplina Clericalis* ed. Alfons Hilka and Werner Söderhjelm (Heidelberg, 1911).

— *The Scholar's Guide*, tr. Joseph Ramon Jones and John Esten Keller (Toronto, 1969).

— *The Disciplina Clericalis of Petrus Alfonsi*, tr. and ed. Eberhard Hermes; English tr. by P. R. Quarrie (London, 1977).

PF Geoffrey Chaucer, *The Parliament of Fowls.*

PL Patrologiae Cursus Completus Series Latina, ed. J.-P. Migne, 221 vols. (Paris, 1844–55).

PMLA Publications of the Modern Language Association of America.

Pollock and Maitland Frederick Pollock and Frederic William Maitland, *The History of English Law Before the Time of Edward I*, 2nd edn, 2 vols. (Cambridge, 1968).

Poubelle, *Body and Surgery* Marie-Christine Poubelle, *The Body and Surgery in the Middle Ages*, tr. Rosemary Morris (Cambridge, 1990).

PPl William Langland, *The Vision of Piers Plowman: A Complete Edition of the B-Text*, ed. A. V. C. Schmidt, 2nd edn (London, 1995).

PPl C Piers Plowman by William Langland: An Edition of the C-Text, ed. Derek Pearsall (London, 1978).

PQ Philological Quarterly.

Pratt, CT Robert A. Pratt, ed., *The Tales of Canterbury, Complete* (Boston, 1974).

Publilius Syrus *Minor Latin Poets*, ed. J. Wight Duff and Arnold M. Duff (Cambridge, MA, and London, 1934; rev. edn 1935), pp. 3–111.

Rawcliffe, *Medicine* Carole Rawcliffe, *Medicine and Society in Later Medieval England* (Stroud, Glos., 1995).

Renart le Contrefait, **ed. Raynaud and Lemaître** *Renart le Contrefait*, ed. Gaston Raynaud and Henri Lemaître, 2 vols. (Paris, 1914).

RES Review of English Studies.

Rewriting Chaucer, ed. Prendergast and Kline *Rewriting Chaucer: Culture, Authority, and the Idea of the Authentic Text 1400–1602*, ed. Thomas A. Prendergast and Barbara Kline (Columbus, OH, 1999).

Riley, *Memorials* Henry Thomas Riley, ed., *Memorials of London and London Life in the XIIIth, XIVth, and XVth Centuries* (London, 1868).

Riverside The Riverside Chaucer, ed. Larry D. Benson (Boston, 1987).

Riverside CT Geoffrey Chaucer. The Canterbury Tales Complete, ed. Larry D. Benson (Boston, 2000).

Robertson, *Chaucer's London* D. W. Robertson, Jr, *Chaucer's London* (New York, 1968).

Robinson *The Works of Geoffrey Chaucer*, ed. F. N. Robinson, 2nd edn (Boston, 1957).

RomR Romanic Review.

Rowland, *Blind Beasts* Beryl Rowland, *Blind Beasts: Chaucer's Animal World* (Kent, OH, 1971).

RPh Romance Philology.

RR Guillaume de Lorris and Jean de Meun, *Romance of the Rose*, ed. Félix Lecoy, CFMA, 3 vols. (Paris, 1966–70).

— *The Romance of the Rose*, tr. Frances Horgan (Oxford, 1994).

Russell, *Intervention* P. E. Russell, *The English Intervention in Spain and Portugal in the Time of Edward III and Richard II* (Oxford, 1955).

SA Sources and Analogues of Chaucer's Canterbury Tales, ed. W. F. Bryan and Germaine Dempster (Chicago, 1941; repr. New York, 1958).

SA² *Sources and Analogues of the Canterbury Tales*, ed. Robert M. Correale and Mary Hamel, 2 vols. (Cambridge, 2002–5). No page references are given for vol. 2 because it was not published when this edition of CT went to press.

SAC Studies in the Age of Chaucer.

Salzer, *Sinnbilder* Anselm Salzer, *Die Sinnbilder und Beiworte*

Mariens in der deutschen Literatur und lateinischen Hymnenpoesie des Mittelalters (Linz, 1886–94; repr. Darmstadt, 1967).

Saul, *Richard II* Nigel Saul, *Richard II* (New Haven, CT, 1997).

Singer Samuel Singer, *Sprichwörter des Mittelalters*, 3 vols. (Bern, 1944–7).

Skeat *The Complete Works of Geoffrey Chaucer*, ed. Walter W. Skeat, 7 vols., 2nd edn (Oxford 1899; repr. 1972).

Song of Roland La Chanson de Roland, ed. F. Whitehead (Oxford, 1965).

— *The Song of Roland*, tr. Glyn Burgess (Harmondsworth, 1990).

South English Legendary The South English Legendary, ed. Charlotte d'Evelyn and Anna J. Mill, 3 vols., EETS o.s. 235–6, 244 (London, 1956–9; repr. 1967–9).

SP Studies in Philology.

Sumption, *Pilgrimage* Jonathan Sumption, *Pilgrimage: An Image of Mediaeval Religion* (London, 1975).

Tatlock, *Development and Chronology* John S. P. Tatlock, *The Development and Chronology of Chaucer's Works* (London, 1907; repr. Gloucester, MA, 1963).

TC Geoffrey Chaucer, *Troilus and Criseyde*, ed. Barry Windeatt (London, 2003).

Teseida see Boccaccio, *Opere.*

Tilley Morris Palmer Tilley, *A Dictionary of the Proverbs in England in the Sixteenth and Seventeenth Centuries* (Ann Arbor, MI, 1950).

Vincent of Beauvais, *Speculum Historiale Bibliotheca Mundi. Vincentii Burgundi ... Speculum Quadruplex*, vol. IV (Douai, 1624; repr. Graz, 1965).

Walter of Châtillon, *Alexandreis Galteri de Castellione Alexandreis*, ed. Marvin L. Colker (Padua, 1978).

— *The Alexandreis*, tr. R. Telfryn Pritchard (Toronto, 1986).

Walther Hans Walther, *Proverbia Sententiaeque Latinitatis Medii Aevi*, 5 vols. (Göttingen, 1963–7).

Whiting B. J. Whiting, with the collaboration of Helen Westcott Whiting, *Proverbs, Sentences, and Proverbial Phrases From English Writings Mainly Before 1500* (London and Cambridge, MA, 1968).

Wise, *Influence of Statius* Boyd Ashby Wise, *The Influence of Statius upon Chaucer* (Baltimore, MD, 1911; repr. New York, 1967).

Wood Chauncey Wood, *Chaucer and the Country of the Stars: Poetic Uses of Astrological Imagery* (Princeton, NJ, 1970).

Zijlstra-Zweens H. M. Zijlstra-Zweens, *Of his array telle I no lenger tale: Aspects of Costume, Arms and Armour in Western Europe* (Amsterdam, 1988).

Notes

These Notes provide some guidance towards critical interpretation of the *Canterbury Tales*, but are not intended as a full literary-critical commentary, or as a summary of current critical opinion. Their primary aims are to explain places in the text that a modern reader will find hard to understand, to indicate the most important literary sources and traditions on which Chaucer drew, and to indicate some of the more interesting textual questions. As far as possible within the inevitable space restrictions, they aim to contain relevant information within themselves, rather than simply referring the reader to sources where it may be found.

References in the Notes to works of Chaucer other than the *Canterbury Tales* are to *The Riverside Chaucer*, general editor L. D. Benson (Boston, 1987; Oxford, 1988). *Troilus and Criseyde* may also be consulted in the Penguin Classics edition by Barry Windeatt (London, 2003). Abbreviated References are used in the Notes for works that are cited in connection with two or more different tales. Works cited more than once within the notes *on the same tale* (and accompanying prologue/epilogue) are cited in full on their first occurrence, and thereafter in abbreviated form. Classical authors are cited from editions in the Loeb Classical Library; in such cases, details of editors, place and date of publication are not supplied (with the exception of works included in the *Minor Latin Poets* volume, which may be traced through the Abbreviated References list). The same is true for patristic and medieval Latin authors whose works are cited from the series Corpus Christianorum Series Latina (CCSL), Corpus Christianorum Continuatio Medievalis (CCCM) or Corpus Scriptorum Ecclesiasticorum Latinorum (CSEL). Biblical references are to the Latin Vulgate Bible (which includes the apocryphal books omitted from the King James Authorized Version of 1611); however, I follow the Authorized Version in referring to 1–2 Samuel, followed by 1–2 Kings, rather than 1–4 Kings, and use its more familiar spellings for the books of the Bible. English translations are generally taken from the Douai-Rheims version of the Vulgate, though they have occasionally been adjusted for the sake of greater clarity or to bring out correspondences with the relevant passage in Chaucer. In textual notes, an asterisk against the headword (lemma) before the square bracket means that an emendation of the El/Hg text is supported by readings in other manuscripts. The abbreviations for grammatical forms are those used in the Glossary. Other abbreviations used are:

AN Anglo-Norman
AV The Holy Bible (Authorized King James Version)
BL British Library
ME Middle English
MS, MSS manuscript, manuscripts
OF Old French

GENERAL PROLOGUE

The portraits that make up the General Prologue are so vivid that scholars were long convinced that Chaucer was here drawing not on literary sources but on contemporary life. In this belief, J. M. Manly attempted to identify real-life models for the Host and several of the pilgrims (see nn. to GP 326, 410; Co 4336, 4358), and claimed that Chaucer's audience would probably have recognized more. Only with the Host, however, is the evidence for a real-life model strong, and it is now generally recognized that the General Prologue is structured on the model of the literary genre known as estates satire, in which the various classes of society are reviewed in turn (Mann, *Estates Satire*). The list of social classes included in the General Prologue is longer and more varied than is often the case, but the details of the pilgrims' appearance and behaviour are largely those associated with their estate or profession. Their portraits conjure up the everyday realities of their professional or working lives. Unlike the writers of estates satire, however, Chaucer refrains for the most part from moral criticism, and also withholds the information on which such criticism might be based. His own responses to the pilgrims, as narrator and their fictional companion, are based on a general criterion of sociability. The complex responses to each pilgrim which are constructed and manipulated by the pilgrim-narrator, often by adopting their own point of view on the world, animate the estates stereotypes and create the impression that they are three-dimensional figures (ibid., pp. 190–202).

1–14 The description of spring in these lines closely resembles a
      passage in Book IV of Guido delle Colonne's *History of the
      Destruction of Troy* (ed. Griffin, pp. 34–5), a work on which
      Chaucer drew for his *Troilus and Criseyde*:

> It was the time when the aging sun in its oblique circle of the zodiac
> had already entered into the sign of Aries, in which the equal length
> of nights and days is celebrated in the equinox of spring; when the
> weather begins to entice eager mortals into the pleasant air; when
> the ice has melted, and the breezes [*zephiri*] ripple the flowing
> streams; when the springs gush forth in fragile bubbles; when moist-
> ures exhaled from the bosom of the earth are raised up to the tops
> of the trees and branches, for which reason the seeds sprout, the
> crops grow, and the meadows bloom, embellished with flowers of
> various colors; when the trees on every side are decked with renewed
> leaves; when earth is adorned with grass, and the birds sing and
> twitter in music of sweet harmony. Then almost the middle of the
> month of April had passed . . .   (tr. Meek, pp. 33–4)

In Guido, however, spring is the prelude to war rather than
pilgrimage.

2   *droghte of March*: The often expressed view that Chaucer is here
      basing himself on literary convention rather than actual weather
      conditions in England has been convincingly contested by J. A.
      Hart, *Texas Studies in Literature and Language*, 4 (1963), 525–
      9, and A. S. Daley, *ChauR*, 4 (1970), 171–9.

7   *the yonge sonne*: The sun is 'young' because it has just passed
      the spring equinox, which is the beginning of the solar year.

8   *the Ram*: The zodiacal sign of Aries (Latin for 'ram'). (On the
      zodiac, see n. to Mch 2222–4.) The sun passes through Aries
      from 12 March to 11 April; the opening reference to April
      shows that 'his halve cours' cannot mean 'half his course'
      (which would place the date around the end of March), but
      must mean that the sun has completed the half of its course
      that fell in April (North, *Chaucer's Universe*, p. 132). This sup-
      position is confirmed by ML 5–6, which gives the date as 18
      April.

> And how would you know when [the Ram was half-way through
> Aries]? You might have in the church or town hall a zodiac sun-dial,
> such as can be seen on the wall of the Royal Observatory at

> Greenwich. Then the shadow of the sun at midday would tell you
> where the sun was in the zodiac . . .
>
>   (S. J. Tester, *A History of Western Astrology*
>   (Woodbridge, 1987), p. 127)

For an argument that the constellation of Aries, whose position
in the sky no longer coincided with the zodiacal sign, is meant
here, see S. Eisner, *ChauR*, 28 (1994), 330–43.

13   *palmeres*: The name originally denotes a pilgrim who had
returned from the Holy Land and carried a palm-branch as a
sign of this.

16–17 The 'martyr' is St Thomas Becket, Archbishop of Canterbury,
who was murdered in his own cathedral in 1170 and canonized
three years later. His shrine at Canterbury was one of the most
important pilgrimage resorts in the Middle Ages, and was made
resplendent by the priceless treasures offered to the saint. See
H. Loxton, *Pilgrimage to Canterbury* (Newton Abbot, 1978).

20   The Tabard Inn stood in the High Street of the borough of
Southwark, which lies across London Bridge on the south bank
of the Thames, conveniently placed for the main route to Canterbury (now the Old Kent Road). The Inn no longer exists, but the
site on which it stood is the present-day Talbot Yard. It is number
119 on the map at p. 34 of Carlin, *Medieval Southwark*.

24   The number of pilgrims described in GP, excluding Chaucer
himself, is not twenty-nine but twenty-seven; if the 'preestes thre'
of GP 164 are included, the number rises to thirty. Numbers
were usually represented in the manuscripts by Roman numerals
rather than words, and so could more easily be misread.

43   *A KNIGHT*: For a detailed analysis of the Knight's portrait, see
T. Jones, *Chaucer's Knight: The Portrait of a Medieval Mercenary* (London, 1980); his view that Chaucer's praise is ironical,
and that the Knight is in fact a callous and brutal mercenary, has
not, however, found general acceptance. For a refutation, see
J. H. Pratt, *ChauR*, 22 (1987), 8–27; for a reassessment, see
M. Keen, in *Armies, Chivalry and Warfare in Medieval Britain
and France*, ed. M. Strickland (Stamford, 1998), pp. 1–12.

47   *his lordes werre*: The lord in question has been variously interpreted as God, the king or the Knight's feudal overlord. The
latter is the most probable, since knights belonged to the lower
orders of the aristocracy, providing armed service for greater
lords in return for their landed holdings. This means that the
claim often made by critics, that Chaucer begins his series of

pilgrims at the top of the social scale, does not hold good; see further n. to GP 744.

51 ff. The list of the Knight's campaigns covers too long a time-span to be a realistic account of one person's career; it is rather a traditional literary device for indicating the scope and magnitude of a knight's achievements (Mann, *Estates Satire*, pp. 110–13). Some of the places mentioned by Chaucer (Alexandria, Prussia, Lithuania, Russia) also appear in other lists of this sort. Useful maps may be found in Jones, *Chaucer's Knight*, pp. 50, 60, 68, and N. Housley, *The Later Crusades, 1274–1580* (Oxford, 1992).

Most, though not all, of the campaigns in which the Knight has fought are of a religious character, directed against the heathen on the boundaries of Christian Europe in Spain, North Africa, the Baltic and the Near East; see the detailed discussion by J. M. Manly, *Transactions and Proceedings of the American Philological Association*, 38 (1907), 89–107, and A. S. Cook, *Transactions of the Connecticut Academy of Arts and Sciences*, 20 (1916), 165–240. Although not as popular (or as lucrative) as fighting in France, participation in crusading campaigns was by no means uncommon among fourteenth-century English knights; see M. Keen, in *English Court Culture in the Later Middle Ages*, ed. V. J. Scattergood and J. W. Sherborne (London, 1983), pp. 45–61 (repr. in Keen, *Nobles, Knights, and Men-at-Arms in the Middle Ages* (London and Rio Grande, 1996), pp. 101–19), for the involvement of numerous English knights in crusading activities in these areas, and Thomas J. Hatton, *ChauR*, 3 (1968), 77–87, for crusading propaganda in the last decades of the fourteenth century.

Alisaundre: The rich city of Alexandria fell in 1365 to the forces of Peter of Lusignan, king of Cyprus, but after a week of plunder the victors abandoned it, being unable to garrison it (Housley, *The Later Crusades*, pp. 40–43). Its capture was the subject of a long, celebratory poem (*La Prise d'Alexandrie*) by Chaucer's French contemporary Guillaume de Machaut. Cf. Mk 2391–2.

52 *hadde the bord bigonne*: To 'begin the board' is to sit at the head of the table, in the place of highest honour. Since Prussia is specified, A. S. Cook suggested that the reference is to the 'table of honour' held by the Teutonic Knights (*JEGP*, 14 (1915), 375–88); see following notes.

53–4 *Pruce . . . Lettow*: The crusading Order of the Teutonic Knights (largely Germans) campaigned against the heathen in Prussia and Lithuania, on the southern side of the Baltic Sea. The fourteenth century saw an intensification of their activities, which were supported by foreign volunteers, including Englishmen. See E. Christiansen, *The Northern Crusades: The Baltic and the Catholic Frontier 1100–1525* (London, 1980), esp. pp. 132–70.

reised: The word reflects the German name 'Reisen' (journeys), which was given to the campaigns of the Teutonic knights (see Housley, *The Later Crusades*, pp. 339–41).

Ruce: Russia, although a Christian country, adhered to the Orthodox rather than the Catholic sect, and this allowed hostilities against the Russians to be construed as crusades against schismatics. In 1378, Pope Urban VI granted indulgences to those who aided a 'crusade' against the Russians, but nothing much came of this. W. Urban suggests therefore that 'Ruce' refers not to Russia, but to Rossenia, which lay between Livonia and Prussia, and was visited by most of the English crusading expeditions (*ChauR*, 18 (1984), 347–53; cf. Cook, *JEGP*, 14 (1915), 385).

56–7 *Gernade ... Algezir*: Algeciras, in the Moorish kingdom of Granada, was besieged by the king of Spain from 1342 to 1344. For the presence of English knights at the siege, see Russell, *Intervention*, pp. 7–8.

Belmarye: Usually taken to be the Moorish kingdom in North Africa (roughly corresponding with present-day Morocco) ruled by the Ben-Marin or Marinids (see C. E. Bosworth, *The New Islamic Dynasties: A Chronological and Genealogical Manual*, 2nd edn (New York, 1996), pp. 41–2).

58 *Lyeys ... Satalye*: King Peter of Cyprus besieged the castle of Lyeys in Lesser Armenia (modern Ayash) and destroyed its town in 1367. 'Satalye' is the modern town of Antalya in southern Turkey; it was taken by Peter of Cyprus in 1361.

60 *armee*: This is the reading of both El and Hg. The case against the alternative reading *aryue* is argued by S. M. Kuhn, *Medieval Studies Conference Aachen 1983*, ed. W.-D. Bald and H. Weinstock (Frankfurt, 1984), pp. 85–102.

62–3 *Tramissene*: Tlemcen, in Algeria, a Marinid stronghold from 1337 onwards (J. M. Abun-Nasir, *A History of the Maghrib*, 2nd edn (Cambridge, 1975), p. 128. The words 'in listes' show that the type of combat referred to is the duel, in which two combatants faced each other alone; death was a common result of such combats, and is not, as Jones suggests (pp. 81–6), evidence of the Knight's 'homicidal character' (G. A. Lester, *Neophilologus*, 66 (1982), 460–68).

65 *Palatye*: Probably to be identified with modern Balat on the west coast of Turkey. The Emir of Palatye formed a temporary alliance with King Peter of Cyprus in 1365.

73–6 The sobriety of the Knight's attire and equipment conforms to the ascetic ideal of knighthood outlined by St Bernard in the twelfth century (Mann, *Estates Satire*, pp. 108–9).

gipoun: A padded, close-fitting tunic, reaching to the thigh, worn under the habergeoun, a coat of protective chain-mail, to prevent chafing (Zijlstra-Zweens, pp. 20, 24). On top of the chain-mail habergeoun a knight wore plate-armour, and over that a surcoat or 'coat-armour' bearing the coat-of-arms which identified him (ibid; cf. Kn 1016, Th 857–68 and nn.). The term gipoun is generally used for this surcoat by modern scholars (Blair, p. 75), and was also occasionally so used in medieval sources (see n. to Kn 2119–20); this confused terminology appears to have misled Jones (*Chaucer's Knight*, pp. 125–35) into thinking that the Knight's gipoun was the outer surcoat, and arguing that the marks on it from the hauberk show that the Knight has dispensed with plate-armour, in the manner of the fourteenth-century English mercenaries. It is difficult, however, to see how the gipoun could show on its outer surface the marks from a habergeoun worn beneath it. The more natural interpretation is that rust or oil from the metal habergeoun has marked the fustian gipoun worn *underneath* it. Medieval terminology for clothing is notoriously both imprecise and fluctuating, and the terms 'gipoun', 'aketoun', 'pourpoint', and 'gambeson' all refer to forms of this protective tunic (Zijlstra-Zweens, p. 68 and n. 110; Hodges, *Chaucer and Costume*, pp. 42–9, 52).

79 *SQUIER*: The term denotes an aspirant to knighthood, usually but not necessarily a young man; the expense of equipping oneself with a knight's arms led to a growing reluctance to assume knighthood in the later Middle Ages. Chaucer himself was a squire of the king's household from the late 1360s on (Pearsall, *Life*, pp. 47–9), but acquired this title by service rather than by birth (see P. Strohm, *Social Chaucer* (Cambridge, MA, 1989), pp. 8–13).

85–6 *chivachye ... Picardye*: Chaucer himself apparently took part in a campaign in Artois and Picardy in 1369 (*Life-Records*, pp. 31–2), which was part of the long sequence of conflicts between England and France known as the Hundred Years War.

Since Tatlock (*Development and Chronology*, pp. 147–8), it has been accepted that the reference here is to the 'crusading' campaign led by Henry Despenser, bishop of Norwich, in support of the citizens of Ghent in 1383 (Saul, *Richard II*, pp. 102–7). A. Gaylord has argued that the sorry hypocrisies of this 'crusade', so-called because it was directed against subjects of the king of France, who supported the anti-Pope Clement VII, were intended by Chaucer to tarnish the Squire's glamorous image (*Papers of the Michigan Academy of Science, Arts and Letters*, 45 (1960), 341–61). But the Despenser campaign does not quite fit the Squire's 'chivachye' geographically, since the fighting took place in Flanders, and there was only a brief sortie to Picardy, with a portion of the English force, in August 1383, in the course of which, Tatlock points out, Despenser 'must have passed through Artois going each way'. (Cf. Gaylord, p. 351.)

However, another campaign that Chaucer might plausibly be referring to here is the 'chevauchée' led by Thomas of Woodstock, earl of Buckingham, in 1380. The expedition aimed to bring support to the duke of Brittany, but it landed at Calais and rode south and then westwards across France, passing by Saint-Omer, Arras, Cléry on the Somme, Rheims and Troyes (see Saul, *Richard II*, pp. 52–3, and for a map, *Atlas of Medieval Europe*, ed. A. Mackay with D. Ditchburn (London and New York, 1997), p. 158). Although this expedition never entered into a full-scale engagement with the French army (thanks to the prudence of the French king), Froissart's *Chronicles* describe numerous small skirmishes and individual combats in which young squires and knights sought to win glory and ransom money (*Chroniques*, ed. G. Raynaud, vol. IX (Paris, 1894), pp. 236–89, and vol. X (Paris, 1899), pp. 1–44; cf. esp. IX, pp. 272–9, describing a French squire challenging any English gentleman to fight for love of his lady, and GP 88). The word 'chivachye' seems better suited to this great sweep through Artois and Picardy, beginning in the historical territory of the county of Flanders, than to the relatively restricted expedition led by Despenser.

93 The Squire is wearing a houppelande, a new type of gown in the late fourteenth century, which instead of following the body closely, like his father's gipoun, has ample folds caught in at the waist by a belt, and instead of tight-fitting sleeves, has sleeves which are funnel-shaped, widening at the wrist in an exaggerated manner. The houppelande could be full length, or very short, as

the Squire's is (C. W. Cunnington and P. Cunnington, *Handbook of English Mediaeval Costume* (London, 1952), p. 82).

94–6 The Squire's accomplishments (including the flute-playing mentioned at GP 91) are those in which young men of his class were traditionally trained (N. Orme, *ChauR*, 16 (1981), 38–59, at pp. 44–5), and also correspond to the activities enjoined on the aspiring lover by the God of Love in the *Romance of the Rose* (2183–98, tr. Horgan, p. 34). Drawing is not otherwise attested as a gentlemanly skill at this date, but the *MED* does not support Orme's suggestion (ibid.) that 'purtreye' means 'describe in speech or writing'.

100 Carving at table was a Squire's household duty (cf. Sum 2243–4; Mch 1772–3), and considered a courtly accomplishment: 'every man that wille come to knighthode him behoveth to lerne | in his yongthe to kerve at the table | to serve to arme | and to adoube a knight' (William Caxton's translation of *The Book of the Ordre of Chyvalry*, ed. A. T. P. Byles, EETS o.s. 168 (London, 1926), p. 21; cf. Miller, p. 183).

101 *YEMAN*: The word 'yeoman' could denote 'either a freeholder of some substance or a household official of some status' (J. C. Holt, *Robin Hood* (London, 1982), p. 120); the Yeoman's relation to the Knight makes clear that the latter sense is relevant here. In military terms, yeomen were foot-soldiers (see Kn 2509, 2728), and thus ranked below the mounted knights and squires; in household service, a yeoman also ranked below a squire. Chaucer was a yeoman of the king's chamber before becoming a squire (see Pearsall, *Life*, p. 48, and cf. n. to GP 79).

he: That is, the Knight. The modesty of the Knight's retinue is in line with the general sobriety of his appearance and equipment.

103 Green clothing was traditionally favoured by foresters and hunters (Hodges, *Chaucer and Costume*, pp. 152–5).

104 *pecok arwes*: Peacock feathers on arrows are praised by contemporary writers (Bowden, p. 87; Hodges, *Chaucer and Costume*, pp. 140–41; see also G. A. Test, *American Notes and Queries*, 2 (1964), 67–8). Robert Hardy, author of *Longbow* (New York, 1977), a practising archer and keeper of peacocks, confirms that the bronze pinion feathers (not the showy tail feathers) of the male bird are the best for use in arrows. They are 'bright' in comparison with the duller pinions of other birds, such as goose or crow, and 'kene' because they have a close texture and cut with a good, sharp edge.

105–7 *Under his belt*: That is, he did not let his arrows rattle loose in a back or side quiver. Their feathers did not 'droupe', as they might have done if the glue and binding which attached them to the arrow was not kept in good order, so that the fletching came partly unstuck.

115 Medals bearing the image of St Christopher were superstitiously supposed, in the Middle Ages as nowadays, to offer protection against accidents and danger. I have been unable to find evidence for the assertion in older editions of *CT* that St Christopher was the patron saint of foresters. However, the account of his martyrdom relates that when four hundred archers tried to shoot him, the arrows hovered in mid-air and one of them turned back on his persecutor (*Golden Legend*, II, 14). Perhaps this made him a good protector against stray arrows.

117 *A forster was he*: The forests of medieval England were subject to special laws which safeguarded game for the king's hunting; these laws were enforced by officers called foresters (W. B. McColly, *ChauR*, 20 (1985), 14–27). Bow and arrows were the characteristic accoutrements of the foresters, who were the only persons allowed to carry them in the forest (R. Grant, *The Royal Forests of England* (Stroud, Glos., 1991), pp. 112–24, esp. pp. 117, 121). The text does not make clear whether the Yeoman's role as forester is related to his role as the Knight's servant.

120 *by Seinte Loy*: St Eligius (Eloi in French) was the patron saint of goldsmiths, and therefore a saint who might appeal to one who, like the Prioress, was fond of jewellery (J. L. Lowes, *RomR*, 5 (1914), 368–85). He also had several female disciples (A. S. Haskell, *Essays on Chaucer's Saints* (The Hague and Paris, 1976), pp. 32–3).

123 'Chanting the service has always demanded a nasal quality to avoid strain on the vocal chords' (Bowden, p. 102); however, some medieval writers deplored singing 'from the nose' as 'womanish' (H. A. Kelly, *ChauR*, 31 (1996), 115–32, at pp. 127–8).

124–6 The Norman Conquest established French as the language of the upper classes; by the fourteenth century, English was reasserting itself, but French still had the prestige of courtly speech. That the Prioress spoke Anglo-Norman, rather than Parisian French, is not in itself ridiculous (see W. Rothwell, *MLR*, 80 (1985), 39–54, and *ChauR*, 36 (2001), 184–207), but Chaucer's reference to the 'scole of Stratford-atte-Bowe' does suggest that this is one of the contemporary jokes about 'English

French' (I. Short, *RPh*, 33 (1980), 467–79). Stratford-at-Bow in East London was the site of a Benedictine nunnery (St Leonard's Bromley); see M. P. Hamilton, in *Philologica: The Malone Anniversary Studies*, ed. T. A. Kirby and H. B. Woolf (Baltimore, MD, 1949), pp. 179–90, and D. Knowles and R. N. Hadcock, *Medieval Religious Houses, England and Wales* (London, 1971), p. 266.

127–36 The description of the Prioress's table-manners is closely modelled on the rules for female deportment outlined by the Old Woman (La Vieille) in the *Romance of the Rose* (13378–402, tr. Horgan, pp. 206–7).

159 The rosary was used to facilitate counting during the recitation of 150 *Ave Marias*. The large green beads were probably not, as Skeat claimed, intended to mark the recitation of a *Pater noster* after every tenth *Ave*, since this custom was not practised until after Chaucer's time (B. Boyd, *Modern Language Quarterly*, 11 (1950), 404–16), but simply made counting easier.

162 *Amor vincit omnia*: 'Love conquers all'. The saying originates in Vergil (*Eclogues* X.69), and is quoted in *RR* (21302, tr. Horgan, pp. 328–9); in both cases the reference is to human, secular love, rather than the divine love appropriate to a nun, but the ambiguity in the phrase allows a convenient vagueness in the Prioress's case about which kind of love is in question.

164 *chapeleine*: A prioress or abbess had a nun appointed as her chaplain, to act as her secretary and assist her at church services (F. J. Furnivall, *Anglia*, 4 (1881), 238–40).
preestes thre: Since we hear no more of two of these three priests, it has been suggested that Chaucer left this line incomplete, and the reference to the priests was supplied by a scribe (cf. n. to GP 24). However, the second half-line appears in all manuscripts, and thus has a strong claim to be original. A female companion would have been a necessity for a travelling nun, and there is nothing historically implausible about her being attended by as many as three priests in addition. For a full discussion of the arguments on each side, see M. Andrew, ed., *A Variorum Edition of the Works of Geoffrey Chaucer: The General Prologue*, 2 vols. (Norman, OK, and London, 1993), I, 173–6.

165 *A MONK*: Strict moralists would have said that neither the Monk nor the Prioress should have been on the pilgrimage at all, since claustration was an essential feature of the monastic life to which they had committed themselves (see G. Constable, *Studia Gratiana*, 19 (1976), 123–46), but it was not unusual for monks

and nuns to be given permission to travel outside the cloister for various purposes (see F. H. Ridley, *The Prioress and the Critics* (Berkeley, CA, 1965), p. 19, and H. A. Kelly, *ChauR*, 31 (1996), 115–32, at pp. 119–21). See also following n.

166 *outridere*: For a full discussion of this term, see H. E. Ussery, *Tulane Studies in English*, 17 (1969), 1–30, at pp. 13–26. Benedictine monasteries drew their income from landed property, and the administration of their estates frequently required the monks to ride out on business (see Harvey, *Living and Dying*, p. 1). See also n. to Mil 3668, Sh 65–6 and n.

172 *kepere of the celle*: Monasteries frequently had subordinate cells dependent on them, of varying size; the head of such a cell was often a likely candidate for promotion to an abbacy at the mother house or elsewhere (Ussery, *Tulane Studies in English*, 17 (1969), 1–30).

  Riverside punctuates with a full stop at the end of this line, so as to link it with GP 171. I agree with Robinson's punctuation in taking it as introducing GP 173.

173 The Rule of St Benedict of Nursia (*c.* 480–*c.* 550) laid down the principles and structure of monastic life. St Maurus, Benedict's disciple, did not himself compose a monastic rule, and his linking with his master here must be explained by the legend that credits him with introducing the Benedictine Rule into France (see D. Knowles, *The Religious Orders in England*, vol. II (Cambridge, 1961), pp. 365–6). The names of the two saints are linked in a similar manner by Gower (Mann, *Estates Satire*, pp. 28–9).

177–8 The text Chaucer has in mind may be Augustine's comment on Nimrod, the 'mighty hunter before the Lord' (Genesis 10:9; *City of God* XVI.4), or it may be Gratian's *Decretum* (quoting ps. Jerome's comment on Esau); see O. F. Emerson, *MP*, 1 (1903), 105–10. Despite numerous prohibitions against the sport, members of the monastic orders, and especially heads of religious houses, often engaged in hunting (N. Orme, in *Chaucer's England: Literature in Historical Context*, ed. B. Hanawalt (Minneapolis, 1992), pp. 133–53, esp. p. 135).

180 The comparison is proverbial; see Mann, *Estates Satire*, pp. 29–31.

187 *Austin*: The C-fragment of the ME translation of the *Romance of the Rose* (but not the French original) similarly cites St Augustine (of Hippo) as urging manual labour on the religious orders (6583–98). The reference is most probably to Augustine's *De opere monachorum* (CSEL 41, pp. 529–96; extracts trans-

lated in G. G. Coulton, *Life in the Middle Ages*, vol. IV (Cambridge, 1930), pp. 32–9).

206 *fat swan*: The Benedictine Rule forbade monks to eat the flesh of quadrupeds. Whether or not St Benedict intended to allow the consumption of two-legged fowl, this is how his Rule was generally interpreted throughout the Middle Ages (see Harvey, *Living and Dying*, pp. 38–41).

207 *as broun as is a berye*: A proverbial comparison. See Whiting B259–259a, and cf. Co 4368 and *Wynnere and Wastoure* 91, ed. S. Trigg, EETS o.s. 297 (Oxford, 1990).

209 *limitour*: In contrast to monks, who lived off the income from the monastery's lands, and who were normally confined to the monastic enclosure, friars lived off the proceeds of their begging and travelled around to solicit and collect donations, also preaching and hearing confessions. In the fourteenth century, each convent of friars was assigned by its order a specific territory within whose limits certain of its members, called 'limitours', were permitted to beg on behalf of the convent. See A. Williams, *SP*, 57 (1960), 463–78.

210 *ordres foure*: The four orders of friars were the Franciscans or Minorites, Dominicans or Jacobites, Carmelites and Augustinians.

218 As GP 223–32 suggest, considerable profits could be made from hearing confessions, since the penitent might make a charitable donation by way of reparation (and if dying, might leave the convent a bequest). Parish priests thus viewed with indignant disapproval the practice of confessing to a friar rather than to themselves, and there was considerable friction between the two groups (see Mann, *Estates Satire*, pp. 47–50). The conflict was to some extent controlled by a papal bull of 1300 which stipulated that friars must be licensed to hear confessions (usually within the 'limitation' of their convent) by the bishop or archbishop of their diocese (Williams, *SP*, 57 (1960), 470–73). The licence would give the friar no more power than that of a priest or curate – that is, he could not grant absolution in certain types of case which were reserved for the bishop – unless the bishop also granted him a penitential commission; Huberd's boast that he has more power than a curate implies that he lays claim to such a commission (ibid., pp. 475–7).

224 *pitaunce*: This term applied both to additional dishes of food served at meals in religious houses and to the donation or bequest that paid for such dishes (see *MED*, s.v.).

233–4 Friars could take advantage of their peripatetic life to act as pedlars; see Mann, *Estates Satire*, pp. 42–3, for contemporary references to the practice.

236–7 *rote*: The *rota* was a 'triangular zither with strings on both sides of the soundbox' (see Page, *Voices and Instruments*, p. 123, with a picture). According to his biographer Thomas of Celano, St Francis used to sing God's praises while going through the motions of fiddle-playing with a stick over his left arm (Habig, *St Francis*, 'Second Life', ch. 90, p. 467). The so-called 'Legend of Perugia' relates that he taught his followers to sing in praise of God after preaching a sermon, and to announce themselves to the audience as 'jongleurs of God' (ibid., p. 1022; also in *The Writings of Leo, Rufino and Angelo, Companions of St Francis*, ed. and tr. R. B. Brooke (Oxford, corr. edn 1990), pp. 166–7). Chaucer's Friar is more like a worldly 'jongleur' (minstrel/entertainer) than a spiritual one (see Mann, *Estates Satire*, p. 45).

252a–b These two lines are absent from El but present in Hg; it is difficult to see who could have written them except Chaucer, and they may have been accidentally omitted (see Kane, p. 227). Donaldson suggests that repetition (in his hous/in his haunt) prompted eyeskip (*Medieval Studies in Honor of Lillian Herlands Hornstein*, ed. J. B. Bessinger, Jr, and R. R. Raymo (New York, 1976), pp. 99–110, at p. 104). Williams (*SP*, 57 (1960), 477–8) points out that it was not usual for friars to pay for their begging rights, and suggests Chaucer may have cancelled the lines on finding that he had misunderstood the system on which begging territories were assigned.

254 *In principio*: 'In the beginning'. These are the opening words of St John's Gospel, the first fourteen verses of which were recited as a devotional text, which friars used as a blessing on entering a house.

256 This proverbial expression (cf. Fri 1451, and see Mann, *Estates Satire*, p. 46) seems to mean that the Friar's gains 'on the side' were worth more than his regular income from donations. The suggestion that 'rente' here is equivalent to the 'ferme' in line 252a (i.e., an outgoing payment made by the Friar) is implausible, since Chaucer generally uses 'rente' to mean 'income'. The same phrase is used in the *Romance of the Rose* (11536, tr. Horgan, p. 178) by the hypocrite False-Seeming, an important influence on Chaucer's portrait of the Friar; see Mann, *Estates Satire*, p. 49.

258 A 'love-day' was a meeting for the private settlement of a dispute,

whether it had previously been taken to court or not. False-Seeming also arbitrates in quarrels ('je faz pes'; *RR* 11650, tr. Horgan, p. 180). As arbitrator, the Friar would have the opportunity to curry favour with the rich and powerful, and also to take bribes; see J. W. Bennett, *Speculum*, 33 (1958), 351–70.

261 *maister*: That is, one who had been awarded a master's degree at a university. The friars seem to have prided themselves on their learning, and the title 'master' is repeatedly and pointedly applied to them throughout *CT*; see Fri 1300, 1337, Sum 1781, 1800, 1836, 2184–8 (and n.), and cf. Langland's reference to friars as 'maistres', *PPl* Prol.62. See Mann, *Estates Satire*, p. 39.

263 *presse*: *Riverside*'s note glosses this as 'casting mold' (referring to the bell rather than the semicope), but the *MED* does not attest this sense of the word.

271 *mottelee*: See Hodges, *Chaucer and Costume*, pp. 86–9.

272 *Flaundrissh bevere hat*: The Merchant has evidently purchased his hat while travelling on business. Trading relations between England and Flanders were very close in the fourteenth century, despite sporadic bans on imports or exports imposed by rulers for political reasons. See Barron, 'England and the Low Countries', pp. 1–7, and, for more detailed treatment, V. Harding in the same volume, pp. 153–68.

276–7 Middleburgh was an important port on the coast of Flanders, situated close to the marketing and banking centre of Bruges in Flanders; from 1384 to 1388 it was the staple (authorized export centre) for English wool. The harbour afforded by the estuary of the river Orwell lay directly across the Channel from it on the coast of Suffolk, not far from Ipswich, which was also a wool-trading town. See the map facing p. 1 of Barron, 'England and the Low Countries'. The Merchant would have been concerned that this important trade route was kept free from molestation by pirates and raiders (T. A. Knott, *PQ*, 1 (1922), 1–16). Chaucer's work as Controller of Customs brought him into direct contact with the wool trade (*Life-Records*, pp. 148–270).

278 *sheeldes*: According to K. S. Cahn, *SAC*, 2 (1980), 81–119, at p. 85, this is not a reference to the French *écu*, but a nominal unit of exchange used in Flanders, and the Merchant is manipulating currency exchange as a way of borrowing money. However, Peter Spufford (personal communication) disagrees with this suggestion, not least because the money of account used in Flanders would be the Flemish *groot*. The simplest explanation of this line is that it refers to the Flemish *écu* (see n. to Sh 330–33); if the

Merchant is an exporter of (say) wool, as his concern with the trade route to the wool staple suggests, he will have been paid for his wool with *écus*, and over time will have amassed considerable amounts of this currency in Flanders; rather than shipping the money home in cash form (a risky enterprise), he makes a paper agreement to 'sell' (i.e., exchange) these *écus* to a Flemish merchant who imports goods into England and has a corresponding surplus of pounds sterling which he needs converting into his local currency. As today, the art of this transaction is to execute it at a time when the exchange rate is favourable.

286 *logik*: The study of Aristotelian philosophy formed a major part of the medieval university curriculum (see G. Leff, *Paris and Oxford Universities in the Thirteenth and Fourteenth Centuries* (New York, 1968), pp. 119–46). For an assessment of Chaucer's knowledge of Oxford and Cambridge, the two medieval English universities, see Bennett.

291–2 The Clerk has not been lucky enough to acquire a post as priest of a parish ('benefice'), but he has not taken the route followed by many more worldly clerics who sought employment on the administrative staff of the king or a great lord (cf. *PPl* Prol.92–9). See Mann, *Estates Satire*, pp. 82–3.

294 Books were very costly items in the fourteenth century, so that twenty books would constitute an impressive collection.

296 *sautrye*: A stringed instrument similar to a zither (see Page, *Voices and Instruments*, pp. 113, 122–3). Nicholas in the Miller's Tale (3213, 3305) is one of the more worldly clerks who are fond of such musical instruments.

297–8 Chaucer punningly refers to the mythical 'philosopher's stone', which alchemists believed would turn base metals into gold; although a philosopher, the Clerk has no benefits from this magical stone.

301–2 Medieval university students were usually funded by their relatives; in return they were expected to pray for them (Mann, *Estates Satire*, pp. 81–2).

309 Serjeants at Law were a select group of barristers practising in the king's courts; they had the exclusive right to plead cases in the Court of Common Pleas, the principal court in England. They were persons of high status in fourteenth-century England. See J. H. Baker, *The Order of Serjeants at Law* (London, 1984), pp. 3–107.

310 The 'Parvis' is a name given to a part of St Paul's Cathedral where lawyers customarily consulted with their clients; 'it may

have meant the colonnaded north aisle as well as the yard' (Baker, *Serjeants at Law*, p. 103).

314 The assizes were county courts which were held at regular intervals for the hearing of civil cases; the itinerant justices who presided over them were appointed for fixed periods by royal commission (W. S. Holdsworth, *A History of English Law*, 7th edn, 17 vols. (London, 1956–72), I, 275–85).

315 *patente*: The word means 'open', and is applied to public documents which were left open for general inspection, with the seal appended from the bottom, instead of being folded over and closed with the seal, as was the case with documents of a private and individual nature. The 'patente' here is a letter of appointment from the king.

    plein commissioun: 'Full authority'; that is, there were no restrictions on the kind of cases the Serjeant was authorized to deal with.

317 Baker (*Serjeants at Law*, pp. 25–6) explains this line as meaning that the Serjeant 'was retained permanently by many clients for annuities of money and robes'.

319 *fee simple*: The holding of landed property could be subject to an entail which would oblige the holder to bequeath it to a designated heir and would also prevent him from selling it or otherwise disposing of it as he wished. The Serjeant manages to gain unrestricted rights over all the property he purchases.

324 *King William*: William the Conqueror (1066–87). Under the Norman kings, English law was extensively remodelled and transformed (see Pollock and Maitland, I, 79–110). This is why the Conquest is treated as synonymous with the beginning of legal records, but Chaucer's claim for the Serjeant's knowledge is obvious hyperbole.

326 *pinche at*: Manly suggested that this might be a punning allusion to Thomas Pinchbek, a serjeant of law contemporary with Chaucer (*New Light*, pp. 151–7); for Chaucer's contacts with Pinchbek and other lawyers, see W. F. Bolton, *MP*, 84 (1987), 401–7. However, the phrase 'pinche at' seems to have been part of Chaucer's normal lexicon (cf. Mcp 74 and Chaucer's 'Fortune' 57), and its use here may simply be coincidental.

328 The Serjeant's 'medlee coote' seems to be an early example of the striped, parti-coloured robe which had become the usual dress of serjeants of law by the fifteenth century (Hodges, *Chaucer and Costume*, pp. 112–21, and Baker, *Serjeants at Law*, pp. 73–7). For some contemporary pictures of serjeants wearing this robe,

see W. N. Hargreaves-Mawdsley, *A History of Legal Dress in Europe until the End of the Eighteenth Century* (Oxford, 1963), Frontispiece and Plates 11–12, and Hodges, *Chaucer and Costume*, Colour Plate III. It is surprising that Chaucer does not mention the white coif which was the most distinctive part of a serjeant's dress; it is clearly shown in the Ellesmere miniature depicting the Serjeant.

331 *FRANKELEIN*: Etymologically, the term 'franklin' meant 'a man of free birth' (as opposed to a serf). The infrequent appearance of the term in historical records makes it difficult to define the exact social status it denoted in fourteenth-century England; H. Specht (*Chaucer's Franklin in the Canterbury Tales* (Copenhagen, 1981)) argued that Chaucer's Franklin was a member of the gentry, whereas N. Saul (*MÆ*, 52 (1983), 10–26) sees him as a *parvenu*. For a summary of contributions to the dispute, see E. Mauer Sembler, ch. 12 in *Chaucer's Pilgrims. An Historical Guide to the Pilgrims in the Canterbury Tales*, ed. L. C. Lambdin and R. T. Lambdin (Westport, CT, and London, 1996). However, Saul does not disagree with R. H. Hilton's comment that 'the description of [the Franklin's] social and political role, as well as of his way of life, puts him firmly among the county gentry' (*The English Peasantry in the Later Middle Ages* (Oxford, 1975), p. 25). The various offices that he has held carried high status in county society (Saul, pp. 16–20). Cf. n. to GP 360.

333 *complexioun*: According to medieval medical theory, the human body was an amalgamation of four 'humours' or bodily fluids: blood (hot and moist), phlegm (cold and moist), choler (hot and dry); melancholy (cold and dry). The preponderance of one or other of these humours determined a person's 'complexioun' and thus their physical and personal characteristics. See Grant, *Source Book*, pp. 701–2, 705, 717–19, and Rawcliffe, *Medicine*, pp. 33–7. The Franklin's 'complexioun' is sanguine – that is, dominated by blood; this would give him a ruddy colouring and a cheerful and generous disposition.

334 *sop in win*: A piece of bread dipped in wine was a normal medieval breakfast; cf. Mch 1843.

336–8 *Epicurus*: A Greek philosopher who held pleasure to be the highest good, and who was therefore associated in the popular mind with sensual indulgence, although he himself defined 'pleasure' rather as an untroubled and independent mental serenity, to be achieved by withdrawal from the world.

353 *table dormaunt*: Medieval dining tables were usually trestle

tables, which were taken down after the meal in order to clear space in the hall for other activities. The Franklin has a table with a fixed frame, always ready for a meal.

355 *sessions*: That is, legal sessions, over which the Franklin will have presided as justice of the peace (see Holdsworth, *History of English Law*, I, 285–98), or possibly as lord of the manor (cf. Sum 2162).

356–9 *knight of the shire*: A Member of Parliament, elected by the county court (R. C. Palmer, *The County Courts of Medieval England 1150–1350* (Princeton, NJ, 1982), pp. 293–4). The offices of sheriff (see Palmer, ch. 2), justice of the peace and knight of the shire were posts frequently and routinely held by the class of country gentry to which the Franklin belonged (Specht, *Chaucer's Franklin*, pp. 124–34). Chaucer himself was both justice of the peace (in Kent, 1385–9), and knight of the shire (for Kent, in 1386); see *Life-Records*, pp. 348–63 and 364–9, and also M. Galway, *MLR*, 36 (1941), 1–36.

countour: *MED* lists this quotation under sense 1a, 'An accountant; esp. an official who oversees the collecting and auditing of taxes for a shire, a kingdom, etc.' See C. Johnson, *The English Government at Work, 1327–1336*, vol. II, ed. W. A. Morris and J. R. Strayer (Cambridge, MA, 1947), pp. 201–7. However, the word also denoted 'A pleader in court, a lawyer' (*MED* 1c; cf. P. Brand, *The Origins of the English Legal Profession* (Oxford, 1992), p. 94), and N. Saul (*MÆ*, 52 (1983), p. 19) thinks that the Franklin may have been a pleader in a county court (see R. C. Palmer, *English Historical Review*, 91 (1976), 776–801). If so, that might explain why he rides in company with the Serjeant of Law.

357–8 *anlaas . . . gipser*: Funerary effigies of medieval men show that this combination of a short sword and a purse hanging from one's belt was conventional (Hodges, *Chaucer and Costume*, Plates 10–12; Saul, *MÆ*, 52 (1983), p. 20).

360 *vavasour*: A term applied to landowners who 'held a recognized though modest place at the bottom of the feudal aristocratic hierarchy' (R. J. Pearcy, *ChauR*, 8 (1973), 33–59, at p. 33). In romance literature the vavassor is associated with generous hospitality and old-world values (ibid.). See also P. R. Coss, *Social Relations and Ideas: Essays in Honour of R. H. Hilton*, ed. T. H. Aston and others (Cambridge, 1983), pp. 109–50.

363 *liveree*: Each fraternity (see next n.) had a distinctive livery, consisting of hood and gown, which was worn at the annual

feast of the guild's patron saint and on other special occasions (G. Unwin, *The Gilds and Companies of London*, 4th edn (London, 1963), pp. 123, 189–92).

364 *fraternitee*: Since the Guildsmen all belong to different trades, it is not easy to identify the fraternity to which they belong with a craft guild, and it has been proposed that it was one of the parish fraternities which provided financial support to their members in times of illness or poverty while they were alive, and paid for their funerals and the singing of masses for their souls when they were dead (see A. Fullerton, *MLN*, 61 (1946), 515–23, and T. J. Garbáty, *JEGP*, 59 (1960), 691–709). However, this leaves unexplained the Guildsmen's hopes of becoming aldermen (GP 372), since 'the Aldermancy of later fourteenth century London was the preserve of a rich and influential oligarchy whose members were drawn from a few gilds at most, and none of the gilds Chaucer refers to provided aldermen during the period' (P. Goodall, *MÆ*, 50 (1981), 284–92, at p. 284). J. W. McCutchan therefore proposed that they were members of the Drapers' Fraternity, a politically active and influential guild which admitted members of other crafts (*PMLA*, 74 (1959), 313–17), while B. J. Harwood (*RES*, n.s. 39 (1988), 413–17) – more plausibly – suggested that the Guildsmen are *honorary* members of a craft guild, such as the tailors' fraternity of St John the Baptist, which admitted to such honorary membership tradesmen from the lesser companies, and afforded them contact with the members of the greater companies from which the aldermanic class was drawn. For more recent research on the Tailors, see M. Davies, 'The Tailors of London and their Guild *c.* 1300–1500', Oxford DPhil dissertation (1994). Another possibility mentioned by Caroline Barron (personal communication) is that the Guildsmen were not Londoners at all; if they lived in a provincial town, they would have had a much greater chance of becoming aldermen. Cf. J. Simpson, in *England in the Fourteenth Century*, ed. N. Rogers (Stamford, 1993), pp. 109–27, at p. 116, n. 15.

372 London was divided into 24 wards (25 after 1394), each governed by an elected alderman (Robertson, *Chaucer's London*, pp. 69–71).

377 *vigilies*: This is probably a reference to the vigil or wake which took place in church the night before a funeral mass. Members of fraternities were expected to join the funeral procession from the house of the deceased to the church, wearing their liveries, and to attend the vigil service. See Riley, *Memorials*, pp. 232,

463, and Unwin, *Gilds*, pp. 53, 101, 118. It is unlikely, however, that the processions were so grand that women's gowns were carried for them, and this may be a joke on Chaucer's part.

390 *as he kouthe*: This seems to be a joke against the poor riding ability of sailors.

397 Bordeaux, which at this period was still an English possession (being part of the territory that Eleanor of Aquitaine brought as dowry on her marriage to Henry II of England), conducted a flourishing export trade in wine with England and Flanders.

404 Hull (on the east coast of England) and Cartagena (on the south-east coast of Spain) are obviously chosen for the sake of hyperbole rather than as precise indications of the scope of the Shipman's travels (elsewhere in Chaucer, 'Cartage' means Carthage, but see K. Malone, *MLN*, 45 (1930), 229–30).

408 *Gootland*: Probably not Jutland, but Gotland, an island off the Swedish coast; see Magoun, pp. 80–81. *Finistere*: Cape Finis-terre, a prominent headland in Galicia (north-west Spain); see Magoun, pp. 72–3. The general meaning of the line is 'from North to South'.

410 A Dartmouth ship called the *Maudelayne* is to be found in four-teenth-century records; Manly suggested that one of its masters, Peter Risshenden, was the model for Chaucer's Shipman (*New Light*, pp. 169–81).

414 The four 'humours' of the body (see n. to GP 333) were thought to be affected by stellar and planetary influences; a physician therefore had to take care to administer his remedies at a time when their effects would not be negated by adverse stellar con-junctions. See Curry, pp. 13–19, and Poubelle, *Body and Surgery* (tr. Morris), pp. 78–9.

416 *houres*: The periods between sunrise and sunset, and between sunset and sunrise, were each divided into twelve 'inequal hours' (so called because their exact length would obviously vary according to the time of year) or 'hours of the planets', in each of which the influence of a particular planet was thought to be predominant. See North, *Chaucer's Universe*, p. 78. Again, the Doctor must administer his treatment under the influence of a benign rather than a malevolent planet.

417–18 *ascendent*: The ascendant is the zodiacal sign which at any given moment is rising on the eastern horizon at the point where it intersects with the ecliptic (see n. to Mch 2222–4); the planets were each assigned 'mansions' or 'domiciles' in the various signs of the zodiac, and the planet whose mansion was the sign in the ascendant at any time would then exercise greater influence (see North, *Chaucer's Universe*, pp. 195–6). The 'images' were metal talismans engraved at this astrologically important moment, and thus, in theory, became impregnated with the powers of the beneficent planetary influence, so that they acted as charms. The Doctor must calculate the times when the right ascendant will ensure that the images are imbued with favourable influences. Advice on all these astrologico-medical matters is given at the end of the *Calendar* of Nicholas of Lynn (Eisner, *Kalendarium*, pp. 208–22), which Chaucer says he consulted in writing his *Treatise on the Astrolabe*. See also Curry, pp. 20–26.

420–21 See n. to GP 333. Illness was thought to be the result of an imbalance between the four humours of the body; the physician would treat this imbalance by administering substances with the opposite elemental qualities to act as a corrective. See Rawcliffe, *Medicine*, pp. 34–6.

425–8 *apothecaries*: Other medieval writers comment on the collusion between doctors and apothecaries, which is more to their benefit than the patient's (Mann, *Estates Satire*, pp. 95–6).

429–34 Similar lists of medical authorities are found elsewhere in medieval literature; see Mann, *Estates Satire*, pp. 92–3. Chaucer aims at impressiveness rather than verisimilitude. The name of Aesculapius, the legendary founder of Greek medicine who was worshipped as a god in the ancient world, was attached to numerous medical treatises in the Middle Ages. The other persons mentioned

include all the eminent authorities of medicine . . . Dioscorides, who wrote on the materia medica, flourished AD *c.* 50. Rufus of Ephesus lived in the second century; Hippocrates is well known. Haly, probably the Persian Hali ibn el Abbas (d. 994), was a physician of the Eastern Caliphate; Galen, of course, the famous authority of the second century. Serapion was probably an Arab of the eleventh or twelfth century, author of the *Liber de Medicamentis Simplicibus*; Rhazes of Baghdad lived in the ninth or tenth century. Both Avicenna and Averroes were well known philosophers as well as physicians of the eleventh and twelfth centur[y] respectively. The name of Johannes Damascenus was attached to the writings of two ninth century medical authorities, Yuhanna ibn Masawaih and the elder Serapion. Constantinus Afer, a monk from Carthage [cf. Mch 1810–11 and n.] . . . came to Salerno in the eleventh century, bringing Arabian learning with him, whereas the last three are all British practitioners who wrote medical compendiums of great influence. The Scot, Bernard Gordon, was professor of medicine at Montpellier *c*. 1300. Gilbertus Anglicus lived in the latter part of the thirteenth century, and John of Gaddesden, whom Chaucer undoubtedly knew personally, taught at Merton College, Oxford, and died 1361. It is an impressive list . . .

(T. J. Garbáty, *Medical History*, 7 (1963), 348–58, at p. 350)

438 Most physicians in Chaucer's time were clerics; the Doctor very probably either was a priest or aimed at becoming one; see Ussery, *Chaucer's Physician*, pp. 29–30. Yet so far from being devout, doctors were usually thought of as a godless class; see Curry, pp. 30–31.

442 *pestilence*: Bubonic plague (the Black Death) raged through England in 1348; sporadic outbreaks of pestilence (not necessarily bubonic plague) occurred for the rest of the century (J. F. D. Shrewsbury, *A History of Bubonic Plague in the British Isles* (Cambridge, 1970), pp. 126–41).

443 Liquid gold was held to be medically efficacious. Chaucer ironically ascribes the Doctor's love of gold to his professional dedication.

445 *biside BATHE*: Manly (*New Light*, pp. 231–3) argued that this was a precise reference to the parish of St Michael's *juxta Bathon*, outside the town walls, where weaving (see GP 447) was an important activity. But Chaucer may simply mean 'near Bath' in general.

446 For the cause of the Wife's deafness, see WB 668, 788–96.

448 *Ypres . . . Gaunt*: Ypres and Ghent are towns in Flanders, the centre of the medieval cloth trade; the Wife is thus 'better than the best'.

450 At the Offertory of the Mass, the congregation went up to the altar in order of rank to lay their offerings on it. Pars 407 mentions eagerness to take precedence on such an occasion as an example of the sin of Pride; see also Mann, *Estates Satire*, pp. 122–3. For historical evidence of quarrels over precedence in church, see E. Duffy, *The Stripping of the Altars: Traditional Religion in England 1400–1580* (New Haven, CT, 1992), pp. 126–7.

454 For medieval complaints about women's fondness for exaggerated headgear, see Mann, *Estates Satire*, p. 124.

456 Scarlet was a very fine and costly woollen fabric, usually (but not inevitably) dyed red in colour (Hodges, *Chaucer and Costume*, pp. 173–6).

460 *chirche-dore*: Marriage was not generally accepted as a sacrament until the twelfth century; what gave it validity was not the priest's blessing but the public vows uttered by the couple in front of witnesses. The ceremony therefore took place not inside the church but outside the church door, throughout the Middle Ages (J. Goody, *The Development of the Family and Marriage in Europe* (Cambridge, 1983), pp. 146–51).

463–6 The places visited by the Wife include the major pilgrimage-centres of the Middle Ages: Jerusalem (for visits to the scenes of Christ's life and other biblical events); Rome (for its churches and holy relics); Santiago de Compostela in Galicia, north-west Spain (for the shrine containing the body of St James); Cologne (for the shrines of the three Magi, and of St Ursula and the 11,000 virgins). Boulogne possessed a shrine containing a miraculous image of the Virgin, which had arrived in a rudderless boat. For women's fondness for going on pilgrimage, cf. WB 557, and see Mann, *Estates Satire*, pp. 123–4.

475 *remedies of love*: That is, the kind of 'know-how' in prosecuting or terminating a love-affair which is taught by Ovid in his *Art of Love* and *Remedies of Love*.

476 *olde daunce*: The Old Woman (La Vieille) in the *Romance of the Rose*, who is one of the literary progenitors of the Wife of Bath, also knows all about the 'old dance' ('la vielle dance') of love (3908j, tr. Horgan, p. 60). She also boasts of the 'compaignie' that flocked around her in her days of youth and beauty (12745–51, tr. Horgan, p. 197; cf. GP 461).

478 For a comparison of the Parson's portrait with the historical evidence for the late-medieval English priesthood, see R. N. Swanson, *SAC*, 13 (1991), 41–80.

486 Parishioners were obliged to pay tithes (one-tenth of their income) to their parish priest; the penalty of non-payment was excommunication, which a grasping priest would be quick to impose.

497–8 Matthew 5:19.

500 The same question is to be found in the (early 13th c.) *Roman de carité*, ed. A. G. Van Hamel (Paris, 1885): 'Se ors enrunge, queus ert fers?' (LXII.10). For other examples of this image applied to priestly corruption, see J. Fleming, *NQ*, 209 (1964), 167, and cf. G. L. Kittredge, *MLN*, 12 (1897), 113–15.

504 This image too is paralleled in the *Roman de carité* (LXXI.9–11), and also in Gower's *Vox Clamantis* (*The Complete Works of John Gower: The Latin Works*, ed. G. C. Macaulay (Oxford,

1902; repr. 1968), III.1063), but in slightly less vivid form (the priest is 'dirtied' rather than 'shiten').

507–11 See n. to Pars 22. Langland complains that after the country population (and thus tithes) had been depleted by the Black Death, parish priests hired curates to look after their parishes and flocked to London to take on the more lucrative and less onerous office of chantry priest (*PPl* Prol.83–6). Historical evidence suggests, however, that this complaint was not well founded (see H. A. Kelly, *ChauR*, 28 (1993), 5–22, at pp. 12–13). The function of a chantry chapel was to provide regular Masses for the soul of the person who had founded and endowed it, or the souls of the members of a religious fraternity which maintained it for that purpose.

Seinte Poules: St Paul's Cathedral contained many chantries of this sort (see G. H. Cook, *Medieval Chantries and Chantry Chapels* (rev. edn, London, 1963), esp. pp. 139–46).

512–14 The imagery of the shepherd, wolf and hireling ('mercenarye') is biblical; see John 10:11–13.

540 The Plowman is most probably a peasant who owned his own plough and cultivated his own land (typically fifteen acres or more), rather than a landless labourer working for wages. He would thus pay greater tithes (see n. to GP 486) on his corn crop (the result of his 'propre swink'), and lesser tithes on the increase of his livestock ('catel'), such as lambs, calves, milk, eggs, and so on. See R. N. Swanson, *Church and Society in Late Medieval England* (Oxford, 1989), pp. 210–15.

541 A tabard was a sleeveless overgarment, made of two rectangular pieces of cloth joined together at the shoulders. It was worn 'primarily by members of the lower classes or by monks' (*MED* s.v. 1a; see also Hodges, *Chaucer and Costume*, pp. 219–21).

548 For the ram as prize in a wrestling match, see Th 740–41, and J. Strutt, *The Sports and Pastimes of the People of England*, ed. W. Hone (London, 1876), p. 146.

562 *tollen*: The owner of a mill (normally the lord of the manor) claimed a toll of the grain ground at it (in addition to payment); in the late fourteenth century, it would not have been unusual for the miller himself to have bought the freedom of the mill, so that the toll would belong to him (Bennett, p. 91). This Miller manages to take three times his due.

563 'And yet' implies a contrast between lines 562 and 563, and since the first line is about stealing, the second is probably introducing an ironic reference to honesty by way of a reference to the proverb

'An honest miller hath a golden thumb', although it is recorded only after the medieval period (Tilley M953). A miller used his thumb in testing samples of grain; presumably the miller's thumb is 'golden' because his rewards depend on using it with skill. Chaucer ironically implies that his Miller's thumb is 'golden' because he has managed to grow rich by dishonest practices.

567 *MAUNCIPLE*: A manciple was an official something like a steward, charged with buying provisions for the members of a corporate community such as a university college or (as in this case) one of the Inns of Court where lawyers were trained (the Inner Temple, Middle Temple, Gray's Inn and Lincoln's Inn). Chaucer's Manciple is connected with one of the two Temples; for the history of their names and foundation, see Bowden, pp. 256–7.

579 Lawyers, like clerks, might find lucrative employment with a lord, overseeing the running of his estates.

587 *REVE*: A reeve was a manorial official whose duty was to oversee the work of the manor and to keep the accounts. Hence he had on the one hand to keep an eye on the efficient running of the manor and the behaviour of the other peasants, and on the other to make sure that his own efficiency and honesty could not be impugned by the auditor of his accounts.

colerik: Choler was one of the four 'complexiouns' of the body (see n. to GP 333). The Reeve's thinness and implied irascibility (GP 605) fit the traditional picture of the choleric man, but he lacks other features of the type (Mann, *Estates Satire*, p. 163).

603 The bailiff was usually the manorial overseer appointed by the lord, and thus superior in station to the reeve, who was a serf in charge of his fellows. But 'bailiff' was also a term more generally used of various manorial servants, and this may be why Chaucer lumps the bailiff with 'hierdes' and 'hines'.

620 *Baldeswelle*: The present-day Bawdeswell in northern Norfolk. Norfolk people seem to have been generally thought of as crafty, treacherous and avaricious (Mann, *Estates Satire*, p. 166; A. J. Fletcher, *MÆ*, 52 (1983), 100–103; *William Langland. Piers Plowman: The Z Version*, ed. A. G. Rigg and C. Brewer (Toronto, 1983), pp. 16–17). However, they were also traditionally portrayed as numbskulls, which does not fit the Reeve (C. Lindahl, *Earnest Games: Folkloric Patterns in the Canterbury Tales* (Bloomington, IN, 1987), pp. 136–9).

621 *Tukked . . . as is a frere*: See Sum 1737 and n.

622 The Reeve perhaps rides at the rear of the procession in order to

be as far away as possible from the Miller, who rides at the front (566). As manorial officials, reeves and millers were likely to have conflicting interests (F. Tupper, *JEGP*, 14 (1915), 265–70, at pp. 267–8), and these two pilgrims certainly fall into a quarrel at a later point in the journey (Rv 3864–5, 3913–20, 4318–24).

623 *SOMNOUR*: A summoner was a minor official attached to the ecclesiastical court of a bishop or archdeacon, which dealt with various religious or moral offences (a sample list may be found at Fri 1304–14). His duty was to summon offenders and witnesses to appear before the court, and to act as an usher while it was in session (L. A. Haselmayer, *Speculum*, 12 (1937), 43–57).

624 In medieval illustrations, seraphim have their faces coloured red, while cherubim are coloured blue; Chaucer seems to have confused the two orders of angels.

625–35 Curry (pp. 37–47) diagnosed the Summoner's skin disease in medieval medical terms as *gutta rosacea* (which gives him his red face and pimples), which has developed into *alopicia*, considered in the Middle Ages to be a type of leprosy, and has turned his pimples into 'knobbes', thinned his hair and swollen his eyelids. His liking for strong wine, garlic, onions and leeks, and for lechery, would have both caused and aggravated his condition (see T. J. Garbáty, *Medical History*, 7 (1963), 348–58). The medicaments listed by Chaucer (GP 629–31) are recommended by medical authorities for treating this complaint.

637–8 These two lines are omitted in Hg, clearly as a result of eyeskip between 636 and 638.

638 *no word but Latin*: Gower (*Mirour de l'Omme* 8149–52; *The Complete Works of John Gower: The French Works*, ed. G. C. Macaulay (Oxford, 1899)) comments that drunkenness has magical effects: it makes laymen talk Latin and French, while at the same time causing the clergy to forget what Latin they know. See also Mann, *Estates Satire*, p. 143.

650 The ecclesiastical court dealt with sexual offences (fornication, adultery, etc.); the Summoner can be bribed to excuse an offender from appearing before the court.

652 'Pulle a finch' means literally 'to pluck a finch'; *MED* (s.v. finch) glosses the phrase 'to do something with cunning, to pull a clever trick', but gives no other example besides this one. The context suggests a sexual innuendo, but the evidence adduced by G. L. Kittredge in support of this interpretation is slight (*MP*, 7 (1910), 475–7).

655 *curs*: That is, excommunication, the punishment that would be

imposed by the ecclesiastical court over which the archdeacon presided (see n. to Fri 1302).

662 *significavit*: The first word of the writ authorizing imprisonment of someone who had been excommunicated by the ecclesiastical court and had not made reparation (usually by paying a fine) within forty days.

669 *PARDONER*: The doctrine of pardons developed by the medieval papacy depended on the idea of a 'treasury of merit' consisting of the virtuous deeds of Christ and the saints, which could be drawn on by ordinary Christians who gave alms as a sign of repentance. The system inevitably dwindled into a simple cash transaction, in which pardons remitting part or the whole of the purgatorial punishment due after death were bought from pardoners, who carried them through Europe drumming up custom. For a detailed study of the activities of pardoners in medieval England, see A. L. Kellogg and L. A. Haselmayer, in Kellogg, *Chaucer, Langland*, pp. 212–44.

670 *Rouncival*: The Hospital of our Lady of Roncesvalles was a house of Augustinian canons situated at one end of the pass of Roncevaux through the Pyrenees (made famous by the death of Roland), which lay on the major pilgrimage-route to Compostela (see n. to GP 463–6). It had a dependent house, St Mary Roncevall, at Charing Cross in London, which specialized in the selling of pardons, and was accused of improper practice in 1379 (Bowden, pp. 284–6).

685 *vernicle*: According to legend, St Veronica wiped the sweat from Christ's face as he was carrying his cross to Calvary, and the image of his face was imprinted on the cloth, which was identified with one preserved at Rome. The 'vernicle' is a pilgrim badge bearing an image of Christ's face as it appears on the cloth; it is a sign that the Pardoner has made the pilgrimage to Rome (Sumption, *Pilgrimage*, pp. 222, 249–56).

686 lay*] *om*. El Hg. Manly and Rickert (III, 425) and *Riverside* (Textual Notes, p. 1122) attempt to defend the omission, reading the line as 'headless', with stress on the second syllable of 'walet'. But a headless line necessarily begins with a strong stress, and 'His' hardly announces itself as such.

691 Critics have differed on whether this line merely means that the Pardoner was effeminate, or whether it means he was a eunuch ('gelding') or a homosexual ('mare'); in the latter case the comment that the Summoner bears him a 'stif burdoun' (673) may be taken as a punning indication ('burdoun' meaning 'staff' as

well as 'accompaniment') that the two men have a sexual relationship. The Pardoner's reference to his projected marriage (WB 166) and his claim to have a girl in every town (Pard 453) indicate that publicly at least he is heterosexual, but Chaucer's comment here certainly calls his masculinity into question in one way or another. See M. E. McAlpine, *PMLA*, 95 (1980), 8–22, and for a discussion of different views, R. S. Sturges, *Chaucer's Pardoner and Gender Theory: Bodies of Discourse* (Basingstoke, 2000), ch. 2.

692 *fro Berwik into Ware*: Probably Berwick-upon-Tweed, situated on the border of England and Scotland, and Ware (Herts), to the north of London. The phrase is thus roughly equivalent to 'the whole length of England'. See Magoun, pp. 31–2, and Whiting B260.

694–700 On the use of relics by pardoners, see Kellogg and Haselmayer, in Kellogg, *Chaucer, Langland*, p. 215 and n. 51; they conclude, however, that the fraudulent use of relics was quite successfully prevented by the Church. S. Wenzel (*SAC*, 11 (1989), 37–41) compares a passage in the early fourteenth-century preachers' handbook, *Fasciculus Morum*, which describes a pardoner passing off animal bones as holy relics; he also provides other evidence of medieval pardoners carrying relics (whether with honest or dishonest intent). For literary satire of false relics, see Mann, *Estates Satire*, pp. 150–52. The archdeceiver in this vein is Boccaccio's Fra Cipolla (*Decameron* VI.10), who claims to have a feather of the Angel Gabriel (in fact from a parrot), and when two jokers substitute some coals for it, promptly asserts that they come from the fire that roasted St Lawrence.

719 Records from around 1550 show the Bell Inn as situated on the opposite side of Southwark High Street from the Tabard, and a little further south. See Carlin, *Medieval Southwark*, number 44 on the map at p. 34.

741–2 The source for this idea is Plato's *Timaeus* (29B), which was widely known in the Middle Ages in the Latin version of Calcidius. Chaucer's wording suggests, however, that his more immediate source was Boethius's *Consolation of Philosophy*, which in his own translation reads as follows: 'sith thow hast lernyd by the sentence of Plato that nedes the wordis moot be cosynes to the thinges of whiche thei speken' (*Boece* III pr.12.205–7). Chaucer cites the same maxim at Mcp 207–10.

744 It is often assumed that Chaucer begins 'correctly' at the top of

the social order, and that his apology for abandoning the order of social ranking refers to the latter part of the Prologue. However, a medieval sense of proper social order, as represented not only by literary works cataloguing the different social 'estates', but also by such sources as the scale for the graduated poll tax of 1379, would have allotted first place to the clerical figures (Monk, Friar, Parson), and second place to the laity (Knight, Squire, etc.), with the women occupying the last place in each series (Prioress and Second Nun at the end of the first, and the Wife of Bath at the end of the second). See Mann, *Estates Satire*, pp. 5–6, p. 215, n. 18.

747 *oure HOOST*: On the likely identity of the Host, see n. to Co 4358.

752 *marchal in an halle*: That is, he had enough social expertise to be capable of acting as a master of ceremonies in 'high society'.

754 *Chepe*: Cheapside was the main trading area of London. See n. to Co 4377.

772 Langland draws a vivid picture of pilgrims flocking to Santiago and Rome 'with many wise tales' (*PPl* Prol.48). Doubtless there were many opportunities for anecdotes and stories en route, but the idea of telling a tale audible to a mounted company of thirty belongs to fiction rather than reality, as anyone who has tried to conduct conversations on horseback will appreciate.

792–4 If each pilgrim told four tales, and we assume that Chaucer intended the total number of pilgrims to be thirty (see n. to GP 24), this would make a total of 120 tales in all. It has been suggested that Chaucer aimed to outdo the hundred tales of Boccaccio's *Decameron*. However, the Parson's Prologue implies that each pilgrim is to make a single contribution only: the Parson is said to be the only pilgrim who has not told 'his tale' (Pars 25). At what stage Chaucer changed his mind, and whether the change took the form of contraction of a grandiose project, or expansion of an originally more modest plan (in which case the General Prologue would have been composed *after* most of the tales), is not clear.

819–20 Wine was drunk as a bed-time drink (cf. *TC* III.674), but it was also drunk to seal the making of a bargain (*Gawain* 1112; see also Hornsby, pp. 82–3), and this may be what Chaucer has in mind here.

826 *the watering of Seint Thomas*: A brook where horses could be watered, about two miles out of London on the Kent Road (Carlin, *Medieval Southwark*, p. 25).

844 *aventure ... sort ... cas*: Compare the role of 'aventure' in bringing the pilgrims together (GP 25). For an examination of the Boethian notions of the relationship between chance and destiny which permeate Chaucer's work, see Mann, 'Chance and Destiny'.

THE KNIGHT'S TALE

The principal source for the Knight's Tale is the *Teseida* of Boccaccio, an epic poem in twelve Books (*Opere*, ed. Branca, vol. II; tr. McCoy). Text and translation of those portions of the *Teseida* that are reproduced in the Knight's Tale, with summary of intervening passages, are to be found in *SA²* II, which also contains detailed tables of correspondence between the two works. Translated passages of the *Teseida* with linking summaries are also included in Havely, *Chaucer's Boccaccio*, pp. 103–52. Chaucer not only drastically condensed the *Teseida* but also altered it in significant ways. He removed many of the cause-and-effect connections in Boccaccio's plot so as to give 'aventure' or chance a much greater role in the story (see Mann, 'Chance and Destiny', pp. 106–9); he turned Boccaccio's decorative references to astrology and to the pagan gods into a coherent cosmological framework for the action; he added passages of Boethian questioning and reflection which probe the meaning of the story's events; and he made subtle but telling adjustments to the roles played by Palamon, Arcite, Emily and Theseus. For a detailed analysis of the relation between the two works, see P. Boitani, *Chaucer and Boccaccio* (Oxford, 1977).

Rubric *Iamque domos ...*: The lines are from the *Thebaid* of Statius (XII.519–20), a Latin epic of the first century AD, which recounts the strife in Thebes following on Oedipus's self-blinding and cursing of the sons born of his incestuous marriage. For Theseus's place in the story of Thebes, see n. to Kn 932. Boccaccio drew on the *Thebaid* in writing his *Teseida*, and it was also directly known to Chaucer (see Wise, *Influence of Statius*). The Latin quotation stands before the Knight's Tale in El, Hg and many other manuscripts, and its presence is highly likely to be due to Chaucer himself. A fuller version of it appears in Chaucer's *Anelida and Arcite*, the narrative of which likewise begins with Theseus's triumphal return.

866–7 The identification of 'Femenye', the land of the Amazons, with Scythia is ultimately based on the quotation from Statius cited above (Magoun, p. 140), and adopted by Boccaccio, *Teseida* I.6.

884 Neither Boccaccio nor Statius mentions a tempest at Theseus's return (Wise, *Influence of Statius*, pp. 47–9).

892 At this point Hg has a heading, '*Incipit narracio*' ('The story begins'), which is not in El. The two manuscripts differ on the internal divisions of the tale: Hg marks only one break, after line 1880, whereas El marks breaks after lines 1354, 1880 and 2482. I have followed El.

925 The changeability of Fortune was frequently represented in classical and medieval art and literature by the image of a wheel, which never stops turning; see Patch, *Goddess Fortuna*, ch. 5. Cf. *Boece* II pr.2.51–4: 'I torne the whirlynge wheel with the turnynge sercle; I am glad to chaungen the loweste to the heyeste, and the heyeste to the loweste.'

932 Capaneus was one of the so-called Seven Against Thebes, who attacked the city with Oedipus's son Polynices when his brother Eteocles broke his agreement to share its rule with him. In the ensuing battle Eteocles, Polynices and all except one of his six companions were slain. The story is told at length in Statius's *Thebaid* (see Headnote), which concludes with the account of the widows' subsequent appeal to Theseus to give their husbands burial, and Theseus's revenge on Creon.

938–47 Creon had seized power in Thebes after the death of Eteocles and Polynices. Boccaccio explains in a gloss to his poem that Creon's refusal of burial to those who had attacked the city was an act of revenge for their failure to bury his son, who had been killed in the fighting and had fallen outside the city walls.

975 Following the *Teseida* (I.3), Chaucer gives Mars the cognomen 'the rede' at Kn 1747 and 1969; the colour of blood suits the god of war, and is also the colour of the planet Mars.

980 The Minotaur was a monstrous creature, half man, half bull, to which the Athenians were compelled by Minos, king of Crete, to offer a regular tribute of young men and women, chosen by lot. The lot eventually fell on Theseus, but he slew the Minotaur, and with the help of Minos's daughter Ariadne escaped from the labyrinth in which it was kept. The story is told by Chaucer in *LGW*, where Theseus is presented as a heartless deceiver rather than the wise and 'pitous' hero of the Knight's Tale. Boccaccio, in contrast, conceives the action of the *Teseida* as taking place *before* the Minotaur episode (VI.46).

1016 The 'cote-armure' is a light surcoat worn over plate-armour, bearing a heraldic device by which the wearer could be identified (see nn. to GP 73–6 and Th 857–68). See also n. to Kn 1129–40.

1024 *raunsoun*: As the account of the Hundred Years War in Froissart's *Chronicles* makes clear, combatants in war could expect large profits from ransoming their captives; Theseus's refusal to take ransom (which is not mentioned by Boccaccio) is thus to be taken as a sign of his unmercenary character.

1057 The 'dongeoun' of a medieval castle was not an underground chamber, but the keep-tower, which was a 'castle within a castle', as it were, and thus a suitable place to hold prisoners. Palamon and Arcite are lodged on an upper storey of the keep (see Kn 1065).

1087–8 Saturn is here represented not as a god, but as a planet, whose influence on human affairs is malevolent. See further n. to Kn 2454 ff.

1129–40 Palamon's reproach implies that he and Arcite are 'brothers in arms' (as also indicated at Kn 1012 by their wearing the same heraldic device in battle). Brotherhood-in-arms was a legally enforceable bond entered into by two knights, ratified by a solemn oath or exchange of documents, which obliged them to treat each other's interests as their own (see M. Keen, *Nobles, Knights, and Men-at-Arms in the Middle Ages* (London and Rio Grande, 1996), pp. 43–62).

1164 In Boethius's *Consolation of Philosophy*, which Chaucer translated, this dictum is a comment on Orpheus's failure to obey the instruction not to look behind him at his wife Eurydice as he led her out of hell (*Boece* III m.12.52–3). It was also proverbial (Whiting L579).

1177–80 There is no exact parallel to this story in the surviving medieval fable-collections, but its narrative pattern (excessive desire leading to total loss) is characteristic of the form.

1191–1200 The story that Theseus followed Pirithous into hell after his death is found in the *Romance of the Rose* (8119–24, tr. Horgan, p. 125), but there Jean de Meun seems to be garbling the more usual legend that the two heroes went to hell together with the aim of carrying off Proserpina as a wife for Pirithous.

1252 on Fortune*] Hg and El both read 'of Fortune', but in the Boethian scheme of things 'purveiaunce' belongs to God alone, not to Fortune (*Boece* IV pr.6); it is likely therefore that Fortune is a separate object of complaint.

1260 witen nat what thing*] witen nat what El; woot nat what thing that Hg. The El/Hg versions are both unmetrical; the two metrical alternatives are 'witen nat what thing' and 'witen nat what that', and the ugly threefold repetition of '-at' makes the latter unlikely. The most likely explanation is that 'thing' dropped out in El, and 'that' was added in Hg.

Arcite's statement is later ironically verified by his own case when he prays for victory in the tournament and this leads indirectly to his death.

1261   *dronke . . . as a mous*: Proverbial; see Whiting M731, and cf. WB 246.

1262–74   Arcite's speech here echoes Boethius's *Consolation of Philosophy*, which uses the comparison with the drunkard who cannot find his way home to describe the condition of human beings, 'exiled' on earth and unable to find the true way to the heavenly home to which they are drawn by natural instinct (*Boece* III pr.2.82–8). They 'seken fast after felicitee', but mistakenly imagine it is to be found in such incomplete and transitory earthly goods as riches, honour, power, fame and pleasure, whereas perfect happiness is to be found only in God, the supreme and eternal good. Ironically, Arcite's identification of Emily as the sole source of his 'wele' would, from Boethius's point of view, be equally mistaken.

1302   The comparison with the box-tree also appears at *LGW* 866, and may be proverbial.

1313–14   This question is central to Boethius's *Consolation of Philosophy*, written when he was disgraced and imprisoned. Lamenting his undeserved misfortunes, he questions God's 'governaunce' of the world, which inflicts misery on the innocent and allows the guilty to prosper (*Boece* I m.5). He also complains that divine foresight deprives humankind of free will (*Boece* V pr.3). In the course of the work, Lady Philosophy patiently shows him that these complaints are mistaken. Chaucer develops Boethius's lament one stage further, having Palamon complain that the gods treat men like beasts and yet still require them to live by moral principles.

1329   Juno's hostility to Thebes, which is a constant theme of Boccaccio's *Teseida*, was caused by Jupiter's adultery with the Theban women Semele and Alcmena.

1348   Questions of this sort ('demaundes d'amour') were popular in medieval literature, whether as the subject of debate-poems or as a response to narrative situations; Book IV of Boccaccio's *Filocolo* contains stories specifically designed to generate them. Cf. Fkl 1621–2.

1374 *hereos*: The word is a confusion of Greek *eros*, 'love', with
      Latin *heros*, 'hero' and *herus*, 'lord'. Medieval physicians defined
      lovesickness, or 'amor hereos', as a disease, whose symptoms
      accord with those ascribed to Arcite at Kn 1361–71. If un-
      corrected, it was thought to lead to mania, caused by an excess
      of the humour of melancholy (see n. to GP 333). See J. L. Lowes,
      MP, 11 (1914), 491–546, and M. F. Wack, *Lovesickness in the
      Middle Ages: The Viaticum and its Commentaries* (Philadelphia,
      PA, 1990).

1376 Biforn, in his celle*] Biforn his owene celle El; Biforn his celle
      Hg. Neither El's nor Hg's version offers good sense or metre; the
      omission of 'in' may have been caused by failure to grasp the
      medical data, and El's addition of 'owene' is a characteristic
      example of scribal over-explicitness.

      Medieval 'faculty psychology' conceived of the brain as divided
      into three cells, controlling the imagination, judgement and
      memory. The 'imaginative' cell, situated at the front ('Biforen'),
      was the seat of 'fantasye'; it turned the information transmitted
      by the five bodily senses into images, which were then passed on
      to the 'estimative' or judging faculty to assess (as familiar or
      unfamiliar, threatening or harmless, good or bad, etc.), and were
      finally stored in the memory, the rearmost cell. (See Bartholo-
      maeus Anglicus, *On the Properties of Things* V.3, and E. R.
      Harvey, *The Inward Wits. Psychological Theory in the Middle
      Ages and the Renaissance* (London, 1975), pp. 10, 17, 38, 44–5,
      52–3). The 'fantasye' also has the power to produce images
      independent of sense-impressions. Arcite's 'mania', his fixation
      on the single image of Emily, blocks off all other images and thus
      leads to an imbalance of his cerebral functions generally.

1385 Mercury is the messenger of the gods in pagan mythology; his
      intervention in the narrative is original with Chaucer.

1387 *slepy yerde*: Mercury's staff, the caduceus, is 'sleepy' because
      he used it to put to sleep the hundred-eyed Argus, whom Juno
      had set to guard Io, object of Jupiter's love.

1391–2 Mercury's words are accurate but ambiguous, as is the way
      of oracular prophecies. Arcite's woes will indeed be ended, but
      by his death, not by a happy life with Emily. Among his other
      characteristics, Mercury was the god of deceit.

1418–41 Arcite's rapid promotion seems to represent an idealized,
      not a realistic, version of medieval court life (R. F. Green, *ELN*,
      18.4 (1981), 251–7).

1428 Chaucer took the name Philostrate from Boccaccio, whose

Filostrato was the source of *Troilus and Criseyde*. Boccaccio interpreted the name (erroneously) as meaning 'prostrated by love'; this interpretation makes it a suitable pseudonym for Arcite.

1462–3 May 3 is also the date specified for Chauntecleer's encounter with the fox at NP 3187–90; the reason for the choice is not clear in either case.

1522 For other examples of the proverb, see Whiting F127 and Singer, I, 72, and II, 44.

1524 Another proverb; see Whiting M210.

1529 *roundel*: Rondeau, a short poem using only two rhymes, with the opening line used as a refrain in the middle and at the end (for an example, see *PF* 680–92). Cf. n. to Fkl 948.

1533 For other examples of the bucket-image to express the rise and fall of Fortune, see Patch, *Goddess Fortuna*, pp. 53–4.

1534–5 Whiting (F621) lists this as proverbial, but has no other medieval examples.

1539 Proverbial; see Whiting F622, and Alexander Neckam, *De naturis rerum* I.7 (ed. T. Wright (London, 1863; repr. Nendeln, 1967)).

1546 Cadmus founded the city of Thebes with the warriors who sprang up from the ground where he had sown the teeth of a dragon he had slain. Amphion built the city's walls through the power of his music; see nn. to Mch 1716 and Mcp 116–18.

1606 *love is free*: Proverbial; see Whiting L516, and cf. Fkl 767, echoing *RR* 9411–12 (tr. Horgan, p. 144).

1625–6 Proverbial; see Whiting L495. Cf. Ovid, *Art of Love* III.564: 'non bene cum sociis regna Venusque manent' ('kingdoms and love do not take well to being shared').

1663–9 Chaucer derived this notion of the relation between providence and destiny from Boethius's *Consolation of Philosophy* (*Boece* IV pr.6): God's providence, existing in a timeless present, beholds the pattern of events in a single eternal moment, while destiny executes this pattern in the temporal sequence of past, present and future. Strictly speaking, therefore, God's providence does not foresee ('sein biforn') the future, but simply sees it. The pattern of 'destinal ordenaunce' is 'strong' in that it sometimes thwarts the patterns projected by human will or expectation; nevertheless, in Boethius's view, it is the result of a spontaneous confluence of events, each of which can be individually the result of human will. Thus, the sequence of chances ('aventures') that brings Palamon and Arcite together in the grove is sealed into a destinal pattern by the equally chance arrival of Theseus, which gives events a development unenvisaged by any of the participants. For fuller discussion, see Mann, 'Chance and Destiny', pp. 106–7.

1697   *Under the sonne*: Possibly 'towards the sun', but this phrase occurs in ballads as a set expression meaning simply 'everywhere, on all sides' (R. M. Smith, *MLN*, 51 (1936), 318).

1712–13   Theseus is angry that Palamon and Arcite are fighting privately, and so flouting the regulations governing battle in judicial combat. For a set of such rules, drawn up by Thomas of Woodstock, duke of Gloucester and uncle of Richard II, to whom the rules are dedicated, see *Monumenta Juridica: The Black Book of the Admiralty*, ed. T. Twiss, 4 vols. (London, 1871–6; repr. 1965), I, 300–329. For historical instances of judicial combat, see G. Neilson, *Trial by Combat* (Glasgow, 1890), esp. pp. 147–93.

1748   Royal women often played the role of intercessors in medieval life as well as literature; for examples and discussion, see P. Strohm, *Hochon's Arrow* (Princeton, NJ, 1992), ch. 5. Queen Philippa played the role of mediator when Edward III pardoned the rebellious citizens of Calais, as did Queen Anne when Richard II was reconciled with the citizens of London in 1392. The chronicler Henry Knighton likewise attributed Richard's issuing of a general pardon in 1382, after the uprising led by John Ball, to the Queen's solicitations. Doubtless this regal yielding to feminine pleas was often a graceful fiction which dramatized a previous decision on the king's part; but Queen Anne's dramatic intervention on behalf of John of Northampton, when he had angered King Richard by a tactless remark, seems to have been quite spontaneous (Saul, *Richard II*, pp. 132–3), and when Anne pleaded on her knees before the earl of Arundel for the life of Sir Simon Burley in 1388, she was unsuccessful (ibid., p. 194), so that not all instances of female intercession can have been staged.

1761   This maxim is repeated several times in Chaucer's poetry: see ML 660, Mch 1986, Sq 479 and *LGW* F 503 (G 491).

1821–5   *Riverside* places a full stop at the end of line 1824, but it makes more sense to take 'And' in line 1821 as meaning 'If', and the whole of 1821–5 as one sentence, as in *Riverside CT*.

1850 ff.   The style of combat ordained by Theseus is an odd mixture of the duel (in which two knights engaged in a battle that could well result in death for one) and the tourney (in which a large number of knights engaged in jousting, with sporting rather than hostile intentions). As put into effect, however, the tournament conforms with fourteenth-century rules and practices (see G. A. Lester, *Neophilologus*, 66 (1982), 460–68).

1885 *theatre*: On jousting as a theatrical spectacle, with the knights often adopting the role of characters in a fictional drama, see G. Wickham, *Early English Stages 1300 to 1600*, vol. I (London, 1963), ch. 2.

1887–92 Lists were usually temporary structures made of wood, and square in outline. Thomas of Woodstock's chivalric rules (see n. to Kn 1712–13) specify that they should be sixty paces long and forty paces wide (*Black Book of the Admiralty*, I, 307). The lists described by Chaucer, who is here following Boccaccio, are not only unusually splendid but also impossibly large. Thomas of Woodstock (ibid. I, 307, 309) also specifies that there shall be two gates, one in the west and one in the east, through which the combatants are to enter, as at Kn 2581 and 2585.

1906 gate*] om. El Hg. A great deal of scribal variation and confusion at this point suggests that the omission occurred at a very early stage, and that some scribes tried to mend matters. Those manuscripts which have 'gate' place it before 'westward', but this is not so satisfactory metrically, and since their scribes are probably emending a corrupt text, there is no reason against placing it more felicitously.

1936 *mount of Citheroun*: Chaucer, like Boccaccio (*Teseida* VII.43) and other medieval authors (e.g., *RR* 15631–40), confused the island of Cythera, celebrated for worship of Venus, with Mount Cithaeron, home of Bacchus and the Muses.

1940–41 Idleness is the keeper of the gate to the garden of love in the *Romance of the Rose* (cf. SN 2–3 and n.); inside the garden the dreamer finds the fountain in which Narcissus saw his own reflection and fell in love with it.

1942–6 Venus's power over Solomon was demonstrated by the number of his wives (see WB 35–6 and n.). Hercules fell in love with Iole, and died when his wife Deianira caused him to put on a poisoned shirt, in the mistaken belief that it had the magic power to restore his affection for her; cf. Mk 2119–34 and n. Medea could not prevent her lover Jason from abandoning her, nor could Circe retain Ulysses on her island for more than a year, despite the fact that both women were skilled in magic (cf. *RR* 14374–8, tr. Horgan, p. 222). Turnus, the betrothed of Lavinia, was supplanted and killed by Aeneas. Croesus is not known as a victim of love (see Mk 2727–66); he is cited here as a conventional example of wealth, which, like wisdom (Solomon), strength (Hercules), magic (Medea, Circe) and bravery (Turnus), is powerless against love.

1945   Turnus*] of Turnus El Hg. The 'of' seems to be a scribal repetition of the construction in the preceding line. It does not make sense, since Turnus did not enchant anyone (as did Medea and Circe), nor was he enchanted.

1955–62 Chaucer's description of Venus (and of Mars and Diana) is more easily visualized as a painting than as a 'statue'. Venus is represented as floating in the waves because, according to legend, she was born from the sea after Jupiter castrated his father Saturn and threw his genitals into the ocean (RR 5505–12, tr. Horgan, p. 85). The roses and the doves are her traditional attributes; the 'citole' (a kind of lute) is more unusual, but representations of the planetary Venus sometimes show her playing a stringed instrument (M. Twycross, The Medieval Anadyomene (Oxford, 1972), pp. 50–70; on the citole, see Page, Voices and Instruments, p. 147). Boccaccio's description of Venus (Teseida VII.64–6) takes a quite different form; Chaucer incorporated it into PF (260–79).

1967 ff. The description of the temple (though not of Mars himself) is largely taken from Teseida VII.29–37, but Chaucer makes the pictures of death and disaster both more numerous and more detailed.

1972–4 Boccaccio explains in a gloss to the Teseida that the temple of Mars is in Thrace (in northern Greece) because cold climates produce men of sanguine complexion, who are naturally warlike.

1995–2028 Since medieval manuscripts do not regularly use capital letters to signal personifications, it is sometimes difficult to tell whether an abstract noun in this passage should be regarded as a fully-fledged personification or not.

2031–2 Julius Caesar was murdered in the Roman senate at the height of his powers (cf. Mk 2695–2718); the Emperor Nero committed suicide during a rebellion against him (cf. Mk 2527–50); Mark Antony committed suicide after losing the sea-battle of Actium (cf. LGW 651–62). R. H. Nicholson's suggestion (ELN, 25.3 (1988), 16–22) that 'Antonius' refers rather to the emperor Antonius Bassianus, better known as Caracalla, is unconvincing.

2045   Puella . . . Rubeus: These are names given to two figures in geomancy, a means of casting horoscopes without actually consulting the heavens. Random dots are jotted down, then counted; according to whether they are odd or even in number, either one or two dots are entered in the geomantic figure. Repeating this procedure two or three times produces a pattern made up of four rows of either one or two dots, and this pattern is identified with an astrological equivalent. A treatise contemporary with Chaucer identified Rubeus as Mars direct (beneficent), and Puella as Mars retrograde (maleficent) (*Canterbury Tales*, ed. J. M. Manly [London, n.d.], pp. 553–4).

2051 ff. Boccaccio does not describe the temple of Diana in detail (*Teseida* VII.72); Chaucer invents a description to match the two preceding ones.

2056–61 *Calistopee*: Boccaccio's gloss to *Teseida* VII.50 relates how Callisto was expelled from Diana's band of virgin nymphs because she had become pregnant by Jupiter. It was Jupiter's jealous wife Juno, not Diana, who transformed her into a bear, and Jupiter eventually further transformed her into the constellation known as the Great Bear. Her son Arcas was turned into the Lesser Bear, in which is situated the Pole Star.

2062 *Dane*: Daphne, a nymph who aspired to emulate Diana's perpetual virginity, was turned into a laurel-tree by her father, the river-god Peneus, to save her from being raped by the god Apollo.

2065 *Attheon*: Actaeon unexpectedly came upon Diana and her nymphs bathing while he was out hunting; Diana transformed him into a stag and he was torn to pieces by his own hounds.

2070–71 *Atthalante . . . Meleagree*: Diana sent a monstrous boar to ravage the country of Calydon because its king, Oeneus, had neglected her worship; the boar was killed by the king's son Meleager, with the help of the maiden Atalanta. Cf. *TC* V.1464–78.

2081–2 See n. to Kn 2297–9.

2085 *Lucina*: A name applied to Diana and Juno in their role as goddesses of childbirth.

2119–20 Since Chaucer here seems to be working from the inside out, naming first the haubergeoun or coat of chain-mail, and then the plate-armour which was buckled on over it, it seems probable that the 'light gipoun' is a tight-fitting surcoat (elsewhere called 'cote-armure'; see Kn 1016, Th 857–68 and nn.), worn over the plate-armour. The term 'gipoun' was sometimes used for this outer garment as well as for the heavier padded gipoun worn under the chain-mail (see *MED*, s.v. jupon, and n. to GP 73–6).

2129 ff. *Lygurge*: Lycurgus appears in the *Teseida* (VI.14), but the

details of his description here are original with Chaucer; Curry
argued that they corresponded to the features ascribed in medieval astrological tracts to someone born under the influence of
Saturn (pp. 134–7). See also North, *Chaucer's Universe*,
pp. 407–8, and n. to Kn 2156 ff.

king of Trace: Boccaccio's Lycurgus comes from Nemea;
Chaucer seems to have confused him with Lycurgus of Thrace,
mentioned in Statius's *Thebaid* (IV.386, VII.180).

2141 The bear's claws have been gilded, as was customary with
animal pelts worn as cloaks. Cf. *Teseida* VI.22.

2156 ff. The figure of Emetreus, and the details of his description, are
original with Chaucer. Curry argued that he is a Martian type,
opposed to the Saturnalian influence represented by Lycurgus
(pp. 131–4); D. Brooks and A. Fowler (*MÆ*, 39 (1970), 123–
46, at pp. 131–3) claim the influence of the Sun as well as Mars.
But the explicit comparison with Mars at Kn 2159 raises the
question of why there is no matching 'clue' to an astrological
significance in the case of Lycurgus; perhaps Chaucer simply
wanted the visual contrast between the dark, shaggy figure of
Lycurgus and the golden, sparkling appearance of Emetreus.

2202 chaunten best] dauncen best El; daunse best Hg. The El/Hg
reading repeats 'best daunsinge' in the previous line and is an
obvious error. The error seems to have occurred at a very early
stage; some scribes try to repair it by substituting 'carolle' or
'pley', but 'chaunten' is closer to 'daunsen' graphically and thus
a more likely basis for the misreading (see Manly and Rickert
III, 433).

2217 *hir hour*: On the 'hours of the planets', see n. to GP 416. The
first hour after sunrise was assigned to the planet whose day it
was (the Moon for Monday, Mars for Tuesday, Mercury for
Wednesday, and so on) and the succeeding hours in the day were
assigned to the other planets in order of their distance from the
earth in the medieval cosmological scheme, working from the
outside in – viz.: Saturn, Jupiter, Mars, Sun, Venus, Mercury,
Moon. Working through the list in regular order brings one, as
if by magic, to the 'correct' planet to preside over the first hour
of the succeeding day (thus if one starts with the Moon on
Monday, the order of succession quite naturally brings Mars into
position at the first hour on Tuesday). Cf. *Astrol*, II.12. Since the
first hour after sunrise on Monday belongs to the Moon, Venus's
hour will be two hours before sunrise (the intervening one being
Mercury's), and Palamon carefully chooses this as the time when

the goddess is likely to be favourable to human prayers (or, to put it astrologically, when the planet's influence may be turned to human ends). Similarly, Emily goes to the temple of Diana, goddess of the Moon, immediately after sunrise, in the hour of the Moon (Kn 2271–4), and Arcite goes to the temple of Mars in the 'nexte houre of Mars folwinge this' (Kn 2367) – that is, three hours later, when the intervening hours of Saturn and Jupiter have passed.

2224 *Adoon*: The beautiful youth Adonis, beloved of Venus, was killed by a wild boar while hunting.

2245–6 Both *Riverside* and Donaldson (*Chaucer's Poetry*, p. 78) interpret line 2245 as meaning 'I do not care if/whether it is better . . .', but such a use of *but* to mean 'whether' has no parallel in *MED*. Chaucer regularly follows 'recche' with the infinitive (Kn 1398, Cl 1090, Mch 1994), which suggests that 'but it may be bettre be' should be taken as a parenthesis: 'I don't care – if it can't be any better – whether I have victory . . .' This is the interpretation followed in J. H. Fisher, ed., *The Complete Poetry and Prose of Geoffrey Chaucer*, 2nd edn (New York, 1989).

2271 *The thridde hour inequal*: See nn. to GP 416 and Kn 2217. In calling the Moon's hour the third hour after that of Venus (when Palamon had gone to her temple), Chaucer is counting inclusively; the sequence of hours is Venus, Mercury, Moon.

2281 *Smokinge the temple*: Presumably, with incense. The elliptical phrase is generally explained as a misreading of the Boccaccian original, 'Fu mondo il tempio' ('the temple was clean') as 'Fumando il tempio' ('the temple [was] smoking').

2294 *Stace of Thebes*: The *Thebaid* of Statius (see n. to Rubric of KnT) is named here because it is a suitably antique authority on pagan ritual (see, in particular, IV.443–72), but the more directly relevant source is Boccaccio's detailed description of the rites followed by Emily at *Teseida* VII.71–6.

2297–9 The goddess Hecate was credited with a threefold existence as Luna (the Moon) in the heavens, Diana on earth, and Proserpina, wife of the god Pluto, in hell (cf. Kn 2313). This is explained in Boccaccio's gloss to *Teseida* VII.77.

2303 See n. to Kn 2065.

2367 See n. to Kn 2217.

2385–90 Vulcan, god of fire and of metal-forging, trapped his wife Venus and her lover Mars in a net which fell over them as they were making love.

2421 *The prayere stint*: 'Stint' is not a past tense but a past participle.

For this type of absolute nominative construction, which imitates the Latin ablative absolute, see Mustanoja, pp. 114–16. Chaucer's use of it seems to have been influenced by his Italian sources.

2437 A proverbial comparison. See Whiting F561, and cf. Sh 38, 51.

2442 Jupiter's action here accords with the nature of his planetary influence, which was benevolent, bringing peace and concord.

2443 In the *Teseida*, Saturn does not appear, and it is Venus herself who devises the means by which she can get her own way (IX.3–5). Saturn is represented as old not only because he is the father of Jupiter, but also because his Greek name, Kronos, was interpreted as 'time' (Greek *chronos*). He is 'cold' because he is associated with the complexion of melancholy (cold and dry); see n. to GP 333. See R. Klibansky and F. Saxl, *Saturn and Melancholy* (London, 1964).

2448 Cf. Mel 1164, quoting Job 12:12.

2449 Proverbial; see Whiting O29.

2453 Venus was daughter of Jupiter, as Chaucer knew (Kn 2222), and thus Saturn's granddaughter; Saturn uses the term 'doghter' in the general sense of 'female descendant'.

2454 ff. In the cosmological system accepted in the Middle Ages, Saturn's was the outermost of the planetary spheres (see n. to Kn 2217). His course is therefore wider than that of the other planets (2454), and exerts power on the planets beneath it (2455). His planetary influence was conceived as malevolent, resulting in disasters of the kind listed at Kn 2456–69 (see North, *Chaucer's Universe*, pp. 410–11).

2462 *the signe of the Leoun*: The zodiacal sign of Leo. For sources that Chaucer might have had in mind in saying that Saturn's malevolent influence was increased in this sign, see North, *Chaucer's Universe*, p. 410.

2466 On the death of Samson, see n. to ML 201.

2475 Venus's 'complexioun' (see n. to GP 333) is sanguine (hot and moist), whereas Mars's is choleric (hot and dry).

2491 ff. The details of the tournament – the procession to the lists, the careful seating arrangements, the use of spears and then of swords (2549–50), and the pause allowed for refreshments (2621–2) – match those of the tournament held by Richard II at Smithfield in 1390, as described by Froissart (S. Robertson, *JEGP*, 14 (1915), 238–40). As Clerk of the King's Works, Chaucer was involved in the construction of the lists for this tournament (*Life-Records*, pp. 456, 472). If, however, the

Knight's Tale is substantially the same as the story 'of Palamon and Arcite | Of Thebes' which is included in the list of Chaucer's writings in the Prologue to *LGW* (F 420–21, G 408–9), the earliest version of which is usually dated 1386–8, then it predates the Smithfield tournament; for an argument that Chaucer revised KnT in 1390, see J. Parr, *PMLA*, 60 (1945), 307–24.

2581 For the simultaneous entry by the west and east gates, see n. to Kn 1887–92.

2598 *Do now your devoir*: The same phrase is prescribed for the initiation of judicial combat in Thomas of Woodstock's chivalric rules (*Black Book of the Admiralty*, I, 323).

2639 For omission of *Riverside*'s comma at the end of this line, see E. Brown, *ChauR*, 21 (1986), 133–41.

2655–6 Line 2655 is found in El and Hg (as well as other MSS), but omitted in a large group of MSS, which make line 2656 the first line of the couplet, and follow it with a new line: 'Ne non shal lenger to his felawe gon'. Kane (p. 227) argues that this version is more likely to be authentic than the one found in El/Hg.

2681–2 These lines are not in El or Hg; they are here taken from Oxford, Corpus Christi College, MS 198. Manly and Rickert (III, 434) suggest that if they were in O^1(the presumed archetype of all surviving MSS), they were marked for omission, probably because they 'badly break the connection between 2680 and 2683'. Kane (p. 227) points out that the loss is more probably due to eyeskip from one 'And she' to the next (obscured in Manly and Rickert by their adoption of the El reading 'And was' in 2683). Hanna's suggestion (*Pursuing History*, p. 307, n. 20) that the lines were suppressed by a scribe, 'because impolite', probably over-estimates the gallantry of scribes. Chaucer himself may have suppressed the lines because they appeared misogynistic, but that need not mean that he intended them as such; they are a humorous reminder of the human, and conventionally feminine, propensity to change, which has tragic consequences in *TC*, but which in this tale takes on a positive form in the openness to 'pitee' shown by Theseus and Emily (see Mann, *Feminizing Chaucer*, pp. 18–25, 132–44).

2689 E. T. Donaldson (*Middle English Studies Presented to Norman Davis*, ed. D. Gray and E. G. Stanley (Oxford, 1983), pp. 65–7), noting that the sense 'crown [of the head]' for 'pomel' is not found elsewhere in ME (see *OED* 4a, *MED* 2c), suggests that the word has its ordinary meaning 'saddle-bow', and that the line means 'Arcite impaled himself (or: Arcite's horse impaled him) on his saddle-bow'. Donaldson is, however, unable to suggest a meaning for the phrase 'of his heed' that would fit this interpretation, and *Riverside*, which glosses 'pomel' as Donaldson does, does not supply a gloss for the following phrase.

2743–56 Medieval medicine conceived of the human body as regulated by three physiological forces, the *virtus naturalis* (natural power), *virtus spiritualis* or *vitalis* (spiritual power), and the *virtus animalis* (animating power). The *virtus naturalis* apprehends the presence of substances harmful to itself, which the *virtus animalis* then acts to expel by coughing. In Arcite's case, the clotted blood resulting from his internal bleeding obstructs this process of expulsion, and neither emetics nor laxatives are of any assistance; the corrupted blood remains in the body and poisons him (see Curry, pp. 139–45).

2779–82 These lines are omitted in Hg, but the echo of line 2779 in Mil 3204 is strong evidence for their being authorial rather than scribal. The phrase 'Allone withouten any compaignye' also appears at Mel 1560.

2832 See n. to ML 198.

2843–6 In the *Teseida*, these lines introduce Theseus's concluding speech (XII.6); Egeus is represented as ineffectually trying to console Palamon and the Athenians with stories of life's mutability (XI.10–12).

2892 that were grete and white*] grete and white El Hg. The El/Hg line is obviously defective metrically, and the defect is shared by a large number of MSS. Two, however, make good the deficiency with 'that weren', which may reflect the original reading, or be a good scribal guess.

2919–66 This passage is an extended example of the rhetorical device known as *occupatio*, in which the writer describes something while protesting that he is *not* going to describe it.

2921–3 Such catalogues of trees are a medieval poetic convention; see P. Boitani, *Reading Mediaeval Studies*, 2 (1976), 28–44, and cf. *PF* 176–82.

2987 ff. The First Mover, which, itself unmoved, is the source of motion in the planetary spheres, is an Aristotelian concept (*Physics* VIII.6.259b, *Metaphysics* XII.7.1072b); Christian philosophy naturally identified the First Mover with God, as did Boethius ('thow that duellest thiselve ay stedefast and stable, and yevest alle othere thynges to ben meved': *Boece* III m.9.5–7). By referring to the First Mover, Chaucer enlarges the poem's perspective beyond the spheres of the planets, which seemed in the planetary debate to be controlling earthly events, to focus on the ultimate cause which governs the planets themselves. When Theseus identifies the First Mover as Jupiter (3035), therefore, it is not in his role as planet (which is not as powerful as Saturn's), but in his mythological role as supreme deity, the pagan equivalent of the Christian God. The only cosmological basis for this identification known to me is Macrobius's statement that 'to cosmogonists Jupiter is the soul of the World' (*Commentary on the Dream of Scipio*, tr. Stahl, p. 158).

The core of Theseus's speech is taken from the *Teseida*; cf. Kn 3017-34 and *Teseida* XII.7-10, Kn 3041-56 and *Teseida* XII.11-14. Chaucer has, however, created a Boethian framework for Teseo's reflections on the inevitability of death and the advantages of dying before age has destroyed one's fame: for the notion that the cosmos is bound together by love, which reconciles the discord between the four elements of fire, air, earth and water, see *Boece* II m.8; for the notion that to recognize imperfection in the nature of things implies a pre-existing concept of perfection, and that just as a part implies the whole from which it is taken, so all imperfect, corruptible things must derive from this perfection, see III pr.10; for the notion that God's eternal providence ('purveiaunce') realizes itself in time as an 'ordinaunce' giving events an ordered pattern, and controlling growth and decay, see IV pr.6; and for the notion that this 'ordinaunce' governs all changes in the natural world and brings them back to their beginning – that is, God – see IV m.6.

3028 nedes*] nedeth El Hg. The error was introduced at an early stage, and was presumably due to a scribe mistaking 'nedes' as a Northern form of the 3rd pers pres indic, and consciously or unconsciously substituting the Southern form (Manly and Rickert III, 438).

3041-2 The phrase echoes *Teseida* XII.11.1-2, but is also a well-known proverb (see Whiting V43 and Hassell V79). Chaucer uses it elsewhere in his works (Sq 593, *TC* IV.1586); it expresses the flexible response to disaster and difficulty which characterizes his idea of patience (cf. Fkl 773-86).

THE MILLER'S PROLOGUE

3115 Cf. Pars 26. The phrase seems to have become proverbial in connection with tale-telling after Chaucer; see *MED* mal(e *n* (2) 1c.

3124 *in Pilates vois*: In stentorian tones. The medieval mystery plays represented biblical 'villains', such as Pilate and Herod, as blustering tyrants.

3155–6 These lines are in El (and other MSS) but absent from Hg (and other MSS). Since they are a reversal of the Solomonic dictum that in a thousand women one will not find a single good one, which is a focus for debate elsewhere in *CT* (Mch 2247–8, 2277–90, Mel 1057, 1076–80), they are likely to be original.

3159 *for the oxen in my plough*: This sounds proverbial, but is not recorded in Whiting, and *MED* gives no other examples.

THE MILLER'S TALE

The two main narrative motifs of the Miller's Tale, the 'misdirected kiss' and the story of Noah's flood, can be paralleled in numerous other tales, but most of them post-date Chaucer, and none can be confidently identified as his source (see the analogues assembled in *SA*, and in Benson and Andersson). Only in Chaucer's version is it the woman, rather than one of her lovers, who sticks her behind out of the window to be kissed. Chaucer's version is also highly unusual in the vividness of its descriptions and its detailed presentation of provincial life. In its interest in sexual intrigue and trickery, the Miller's Tale resembles the medieval French tales known as fabliaux, but they are much briefer (typically 200–300 lines only), and their narrative style is very much sparser than the one Chaucer adopts for this tale. The long descriptions of Nicholas, Alison and Absalon, the account of Noah's Flood, and the details of Oxford life, are narrative embellishments not normally found in fabliaux.

3192 *astrologye*: The medieval term included astronomy. Nicholas's interest in the heavens is characteristic of fourteenth-century Oxford, where Merton College was in the forefront of scientific studies.

3202 *lik a maiden meke for to see*: Medieval clerks were supposed to be maidenly in demeanour (see n. to Cl 2), but in Nicholas's case the maidenliness is purely superficial.

3204 This line repeats, in a very different context, Kn 2779. Its use at Mel 1560 suggests that it is a proverbial phrase.

3208 *Almageste*: The *Almagest* of the Greek astronomer Ptolemy (2nd c. AD) was 'the basic text for all mathematical and astronomical study' (Bennett, p. 80). It was known to the Middle Ages in a Latin translation by Gerard of Cremona. A modern English translation of the Greek original by R. C. Taliaferro is included in Vol. 16 of the *Great Books of the Western World* (Chicago, 1952).

3209 *astrelabye*: An astrolabe is a metal disc bearing a map of the heavens, overlaid with various moving parts which can be used to calculate the relative positions of the various astral bodies at any particular time. Chaucer himself translated a treatise explaining its use. For a photograph of a late medieval astrolabe, see Wood, frontispiece, and for a detailed diagram of its parts and explanation of its function, see North, *Chaucer's Universe*, pp. 40–42.

3210 *augrim-stones*: 'Augrim' is the ME form of 'algorism', a medieval term for arithmetic. Because Roman numerals made written calculations cumbersome and difficult, it was customary to use instead stones or counters laid out on a board (known as an abacus) in columns representing units, tens, hundreds, thousands, and so on. Later, the stones were inscribed with arabic numerals indicating their value, thereby reducing the number of stones it was necessary to use (thus a stone marked 2 would be worth 20 when placed in the tens column). For a detailed description of the way such calculations were carried out, see F. A. Yeldham, *The Story of Reckoning in the Middle Ages* (London, 1926), pp. 36–45. It was far from usual for a poor scholar to possess such aids to study; the Fellows of Merton had only three astrolabes and one set of augrim-stones between them (Bennett, p. 33).

3212 A 'presse' was a wooden cupboard, which was fitted with shelves for linen or pegs on which to hang clothes (H. C. R. Edwards, *The Shorter Dictionary of English Furniture* (London, 1964), s.vv. Cupboards, Presses and Wardrobes). Medieval furniture terminology was very imprecise, and it is impossible to tell whether the press was full height, with the red cloth hung in front as a kind of dust-sheet, or a lower cupboard, fitted with solid doors, with the cloth laid over the top of it.

3213–15 *sautrye*: A stringed instrument similar to a zither (see n. to GP 296). Since the strings were of metal, this instrument made a great deal of noise, so that it is not surprising that the chamber 'rang'.

3216 *Angelus ad virginem*: 'The angel to the Virgin [said]'; these are the first words of a highly popular medieval song on the Annunciation; text and music have been edited by J. Stevens in

Medieval Studies for J. A. W. Bennett: Aetatis Suae LXX, ed.
P. L. Heyworth (Oxford, 1981), pp. 297–328.

3217 *the kinges note*: None of the various attempts to identify this
piece of music has won general acceptance.

3220 See n. to GP 301–2.

3227 *Catoun*: Chaucer means the *Distichs of Cato (Disticha Catonis)*,
a collection of two-line proverbs, which was the first in a group
of texts (collectively known as the 'Liber Catonianus'), which
were widely used as a first reader for young students of Latin
(see P. M. Clogan, *MedHum*, n.s. 11 (1982), 199–209, and for
Chaucer's use of 'Cato' in *CT*, see R. Hazelton, *Speculum*, 35
(1960), 357–80). The carpenter's 'wit' is so 'rude' that he has
not reached this elementary stage of education. However, the
maxim cited here is not to be found in 'Cato', but in another
Latin school-text of the same type, the *Facetus* 'Cum utilius',
in which maxim 37 reads: 'Duc tibi prole parem morumque vigore
venustam, | Si cum pace velis vitam deducere iustam' ('Take a
wife who is your peer in birth and beautified by moral excellence
if you want to lead a righteous life in peace'); see A. Brusendorff,
Studies in English Philology . . . in Honor of Frederick Klaeber,
ed. K. Malone and M. B. Rudd (Minneapolis, 1929), pp. 320–
39, at pp. 337–8). For a translation of the *Facetus*, see R. E.
Pepin, *An English Translation of Auctores Octo* (Lewiston, NY,
1995), pp. 41–54.

3233 ff. The long and detailed portraits of Alison and Absolon (3314
ff.) correspond in general form to the rhetorical figure called
descriptio or *effictio*, which anatomized a character's personal
appearance from head to toe; however, the model examples given
in medieval handbooks of rhetoric do not include the particu-
larized details of clothing or the vivid similes that characterize
these descriptions. For examples, see Geoffrey of Vinsauf, *Poetria
Nova*, 563–621, tr. Nims, pp. 36–8, and Matthew of Vendôme,
Ars Versificatoria I.50–58, tr. R. R. Parr (Milwaukee, WI, 1981),
pp. 29–39.

3274 *Oseneye*: Osney abbey (a large and wealthy house of Augustinian canons) lay on the west side of Oxford, just across the river
Thames; it is later made clear (3664–8) that Alison's carpenter
husband is regularly employed by the abbey, where 'there would
always be jobs for a carpenter, including the building or repair
of houses on the abbey's city properties' (Bennett, p. 55).

3276 *queinte*: L. D. Benson (*SAC Proceedings*, 1 (1984), 23–47) has
argued that the word 'queinte' is not (as is often assumed) the

usual word for the female genitalia, which in ME was spelled
'cunte' (*OED* Supplement), but rather a euphemistic substitute
which uses the same opening and closing sounds (as, for example,
'shoot' for 'shit'). For a sceptical response to this argument, see
J. V. Fleming, *Classical Imitation and Interpretation in Chaucer's
Troilus* (Lincoln, NE, and London, 1990), ch. 1. However, there
is no disagreement about what the word *denotes* in this line;
Benson's argument concerns the difference of register between
the use of a euphemism and the use of a 'four-letter word'.
Fleming is mainly concerned with the possibility of a pun on the
past participle 'queynt' ('quenched') at *TC* V.543, and does not
directly address the question of register in the Miller's Tale.

3285 quod she*] quod ich El Hg. Manly and Rickert try to defend
this reading by arguing that 'quod ich' is part of Alison's speech
(III, 440), but as Kane points out, 'quod' is only used as a frame
for direct speech, not as meaning 'I have (already) said' (p. 219).

3286 *I wol crye "out, harrow!"*: In order to accuse a man of rape, a
woman had to have cried out in protest (raised the 'hue and cry')
at the time of the deed. See *Bracton on the Laws and Customs
of England*, II, 415, and Carter, *Rape*, pp. 24, 94, 110, 142.

3291 *Seint Thomas of Kent*: The cult of St Thomas Becket was
popular in Oxford (Bennett, p. 15), but one reason for his frequent invocation in this tale is that his name offers a convenient
rhyme with 'Nicholas' (3425/6, 3461/2).

3312 A parish clerk assisted the priest in the performance of the
liturgy, and was paid with fees and seasonal offerings in kind
(Bennett, pp. 43, 45).

3314–15 Absolon takes after his biblical namesake, the son of King
David, who was renowned for his beauty, and especially for his
luxuriant hair (2 Samuel 14:25–6).

3318–19 The leather uppers of Absolon's shoes were elaborately cut
into a latticed pattern resembling the tracery in the windows of
St Paul's Cathedral. For a picture of such a shoe, see F. W.
Fairholt, *Costume in England: A History of Dress to the End of
the Eighteenth Century*, 3rd edn, 2 vols. (London, 1885), II, 65.
Absolon's red hose, showing through the holes, would make the
pattern especially striking.

3322 *pointes*: Laces or ties, with pointed tags on the end, were often
used instead of buttons in the Middle Ages to attach one part of
clothing to another (for example, hose to shirt, or sleeves to a
jacket). These pointed tags could become a decorative feature
(see Fairholt, *Costume*, II, 330–31).

3326 Being a parish clerk was only a part-time occupation, and not well paid, so Absolon also acts as a barber-surgeon, shaving beards and letting blood, which was a regular practice in the Middle Ages. 'Everyone, healthy or sick, clergyman or layman, had himself purged and bled regularly each year, at the boisterous time of spring and autumn when the humours are particularly disturbed', in order to get rid of 'overactive humours and super-fluities of every kind' (Poubelle, *Body and Surgery*, tr. Morris, p. 176; see also Rawcliffe, *Medicine*, pp. 133–4 on barber-surgeons).

3227 Absolon uses his clerical knowledge of Latin to draw up legal documents for a fee.

3328–9 It is not clear what the special style of Oxford dancing might have been, nor whether this reference to it involves mockery. Bennett (p. 48) notes that Morris dancing has a long tradition in the Oxford area.

3331–3 A ribible was a two-stringed bowed instrument, played in the lap (Page, *Voices and Instruments*, p. 145); a gittern was similar to a lute, but smaller (ibid., p. 147).

3358 *MED* gives no other examples of the term 'shot-windowe' besides Mil 3358 and 3695, but the story makes clear that it must be a casement window which is placed low enough on the wall (3677, 3696) for Alison's behind to be at the same height as Absolon's head when she later plays her trick on him. The carpenter's 'bour' or bedroom may be over a cellar or shop (see Bennnett, p. 28, for two possible diagrams), and so raised above street level while still being 'lowe' in relation to the upper storey of the house.

3384 *Herodes*: Absolon acts the part of Herod in a play performed on the upper storey of a pageant wagon in the street. The medieval mystery-cycles portray Herod as a bombastic tyrant, so the part would allow Absolon to impress the audience by 'hamming it up'. Bennett (p. 49) notes that Oxford had enough trade guilds to have mounted a full-scale play cycle, but no record of any such thing survives.

3392–3 Proverbial; see Whiting S395.

3449 The Oxford carpenter appropriately invokes St Frideswide, patron saint of the city. In Chaucer's time, a priory of Augus-tinian canons dedicated to her stood on the site of the present-day college of Christ Church.

3451 *astromye*: Not (as is sometimes suggested) an instance of the carpenter's mangling of a learned word, but a genuine variant form of 'astronomye' (see J. F. Huntsman, *MP*, 73 (1976), 276–9).

3457 The story of the star-gazing philosopher goes back to antiquity, and was well known in the Middle Ages; it is found, for example, in a letter of Peter Damian (*PL* 145, col. 615; 11th c.), and is no. 38 in the late thirteenth/early fourteenth-century Italian story-collection known as the *Novellino*, or *One Hundred Ancient Tales* (ed. Consoli, pp. 60–61).

3480–86 The context makes clear that the 'night-spel' is a charm recited at each side of the house and on the threshold as protection against evil spirits at night. The 'White Paternoster' ('Our Father') is the name of a charm, recorded in varying versions from the sixteenth to the nineteenth century, which performed the same function, and which, like the carpenter's 'night-spel', is largely composed of garbled religious phrases. The word 'verye' is otherwise unknown, and may well be intentional nonsense on Chaucer's part.

Seinte Benedight: St Benedict of Nursia (d. *c.* 550), author of the Rule which was the foundation of medieval monastic life. 'Benedict medals' engraved with protective charms were popular in the seventeenth century, and quite possibly in the Middle Ages also.

Seinte Petres soster: St Peter's sister is an unrecorded figure, although the Bible mentions his mother-in-law (Matthew 8:14), and the early Roman martyr Petronilla was supposed to be his daughter. One of the versions of the 'White Paternoster' begins 'White Pater-noster, Saint Peter's brother' (W. J. Thoms, *Folk-Lore Record*, 1 (1878), 153), and a charm quoted by Robert Grosseteste (13th c.) runs 'Grene pater noster | Petris leue soster' (S. Wenzel, *NQ*, 215 (1970), 449–50). Ignorant garbling of the Latin liturgy and saints' names was a frequent source of comedy in medieval literature.

3512 *harwed helle*: The apocryphal gospel of Nicodemus (?5th c.) relates that between the Crucifixion on Good Friday and the Resurrection on Easter Sunday, Christ descended into hell and forced the devils to release the souls of Adam and other Old Testament figures (*Apocryphal NT*, pp. 94–146). The Harrowing of Hell was a very popular motif in medieval art and literature.

3515 The phases of the moon played an important role in popular astrology, with each day of the monthly cycle being considered favourable or unfavourable to specific conditions or activities (illness, travel, buying or selling, etc.). See the ME poem on this subject, edited by W. Farnham, *SP*, 20 (1923), 70–82.

3530 Nicholas is quoting Ecclesiasticus (32:24), a biblical book which is no longer accepted as canonical. (An English translation of the Vulgate's Latin text is included in the Douai-Rheims Bible.) Ecclesiasticus is one of the 'Wisdom books' of the Bible, which were associated with the name of Solomon. This verse passed into proverbial usage in English (Whiting C470), and is also quoted at Mch 1485–6 and Mel 1003.

3539–40 The recalcitrance of Noah's wife is not mentioned in the Bible, but was a regular feature of medieval drama. In three of the four surviving mystery-cycles (York, Towneley, Chester), Mrs Noah is a quarrelsome termagant who stubbornly resists her husband's commands or entreaties to come on board the Ark.

3571 The gable is the triangular upper part of an end wall under a pitched roof; the wall must have been of wattle and daub, which could easily be broken through with an axe. Being at rafter level, the improvised boats would then sail out on the water above the roof of the one-storey stable adjoining the end wall of the house.

3598 Proverbial; see Whiting W399.

3645 *corfew-time*: The time of day (8 or 9 p.m.) announced by ringing of a bell, when fires in houses are to be covered (French *couvre-feu*, 'cover fire') or put out, and inhabitants must leave public places.

3655 Lauds was the second of the eight liturgical Offices (Matins, Lauds, Prime, Terce, Sext, None, Vespers, Compline) which were celebrated during the course of the day by the members of the regular clergy (monks, friars and canons); it was sung at daybreak. See *Oxford Dictionary of the Christian Church*, s.vv. Lauds, and Office, Divine.

3659–60 The scene of Absolon's recreation is probably Osney Mead, a large piece of meadowland to the west of Osney.

3668 *graunge*: Medieval religious houses were supported by the income from the landed estates they owned, which could be at some distance from the monastery or abbey (see n. to GP 166). The grange was a monastic farm, which served as an administrative centre for such an estate and a storehouse for its produce; see C. Platt, *The Monastic Grange in Medieval England* (London, 1969). This particular estate must also have had woodland which supplied the abbey with timber.

3698–9 Absolon borrows the language of the Song of Solomon (honey 4:11, cinnamon 14:14). For suggestions as to further allusions of this sort in Absolon's speech and the rest of the tale, see R. E. Kaske, *SP*, 59 (1962), 479–500.

3709 *com pa me*: Some manuscripts read 'ba' instead of 'pa', suggesting that the latter is simply a variant spelling of the former, which means 'kiss' (cf. WB 433). The phrase sounds like 'a bit of some popular song' (Elliott, p. 239).

3721–2 These lines are omitted in Hg and other MSS. For a defence of their authenticity, see Kane, p. 225.

3742 *A berd, a berd*: Since Nicholas has no way of knowing Absolon's reaction to Alison's pubic hair (3737–8), A. C. Baugh suggested that his mocking comment alludes to the expression 'to make (someone's) beard', meaning 'to outwit someone' (*MED* 4a; cf. Rv 4096, WB 361). J. D. Burnley argues, however, that 'the centrality of the narrative events' here displaces psychological realism – that is, the characters are assumed to possess the same knowledge as the reader (*Chaucer and the Craft of Fiction*, ed. L. A. Arrathoon (Rochester, NY, 1986), pp. 195–218, at p. 202).

3759 Proverbial; see Whiting C223.

3762 Blacksmiths often worked at night, so that they could carry out repairs while instruments were not being used (Bennett, p. 41). A fourteenth-century alliterative poem ('Swarte smekid smithes smatered with smoke') complains that the noise they create makes it impossible to get any sleep (*Medieval English Lyrics 1200–1400*, ed. T. G. Duncan (Harmondsworth, 1995), pp. 178–9).

3770 *viritoot*: The word is of doubtful etymology and meaning; for the suggestion that it means a whip-top, see J. L. Singman, *ELN*, 31.2 (1993), 1–9.

3771 *Seinte Note*: Possibly a garbled form of St Neot (9th c.), but if so, it is not clear why Gervase swears by him; his cult is associated with Cornwall and Huntingdonshire rather than Oxford.

3806 The fart is not just a gratuitous obscenity, but a deliberate answer to Absolon's 'speak'. Classical and medieval grammarians defined speech (*vox*) in two ways: (1) in its physical aspect as 'broken air' (see *Grammatici Latini*, ed. H. Keil, 7 vols. (Leipzig, 1857–80), II, 5 (Priscian), and IV, 367 (Donatus), and cf. *HF* 765–8: 'Soun ys noght but eyr ybroken; | And every speche that ys spoken, | . . . | In his substaunce ys but air'); (2) in its intellectual aspect as 'a sound which signifies according to a convention'. Nicholas's fart represents the purely physical element of speech, divorced from signification; it answers Absolon's flowery verbiage with no more than 'hot air'.

3821–22 *he fond neither to selle . . .*: This seems to mean that nothing impeded his headlong descent; a parallel in a French fabliau shows it to have been an idiomatic expression used to describe a plummeting fall; see *Aloul*, 591–2, printed in *Nouveau Recueil Complet des Fabliaux*, vol. III, ed. W. Noomen and N. van den Boogaard (Assen, 1986).

THE REEVE'S PROLOGUE

3868 The Reeve compares himself to a horse, which changes its diet from fresh grass in summer to hay in winter; the 'summer-time' of his own life is now over.

3871–3 *openers*: The medlar is eaten when the flesh turns brown and begins to rot, two or three weeks after it has been picked.

3890–95 The passage of time is compared to the flow of wine from a barrel. The barrel was customarily laid on its side, and a tap-hole made in its base, close to the lower part of the rim, or 'chine', formed by the ends of the barrel-staves protruding beyond its flat base. The Reeve compares the moment of birth to the pulling out of the 'tappe', the tapered stick used to plug the tap-hole; the wine then runs out freely until in old age there is nothing left but the drips trickling down onto the 'chine' below the tap-hole (A. H. MacLaine, *MÆ*, 31 (1962), 129–31).

3904 Cobblers were traditionally selected as examples of those wishing to meddle in other trades (cf. the proverb 'the cobbler should stick to his last', which goes back to Roman times). Phaedrus (*Fables* I.14) tells a story of a cobbler dabbling in medicine, who was exposed as a charlatan by the king of his city.

3906–7 *Depeford . . . Grenewich*: Deptford is about five miles from Southwark, the starting-point of the pilgrimage; Greenwich is just beyond it. It has been plausibly suggested that Chaucer lived there in the late 1380s (M. Galway, *MLR*, 36 (1941), 1–36, at pp. 16–17), which would give a joking point to the Host's reference to the 'many rogues' who live there.

3912 The Reeve is referring to a principle of natural law, as defined in Isidore, *Etymologies* V.iv.2, and quoted in Gratian's *Decretum* I.i.7 (*Corpus Iuris Canonici*, I, col. 2): 'violentiae per vim repulsio' ('the repelling of violence by force').

3919–20 The Reeve is quoting the Bible (Matthew 7:3). The substitution of 'a straw' for the biblical 'mote' appears to have been a regular variant of the saying in English proverbial usage; see Whiting M710.

THE REEVE'S TALE

The narrative of the Reeve's Tale closely resembles a French fabliau
(see Headnote to MilT) called 'The Miller and the Two Clerks' ('Le
meunier et les deux clers'); this and other versions of the story are
printed and translated in Benson and Andersson (see also *SA*, pp. 124–
47). In the French tale, the clerks do not realize they have been cheated
of their corn until after their sexual adventures with the miller's wife
and daughter, whereas in Chaucer the sexual adventures are under-
taken in a spirit of revenge.

   As the Miller's Tale is set in Oxford, so the Reeve's Tale is set
in Cambridge, and university students play a major role in both.
Competitiveness between town and gown is expressed not only in
sexual rivalry but in the carpenter's suspicion of book-learning and
complacent pride in his own plain common sense in the Miller's Tale
(3451–61), and in the miller's ridicule of the clerks' skill in philosophy
in the Reeve's Tale (4122–6; cf. 4049–56).

3921 *Trompingtoun . . . Cantebrigge*: The village of Trumpington is
         now continuous with the outskirts of the city of Cambridge, but
         in the fourteenth century was separated from it by open country
         (see map in Bennett, p. 86). At Trumpington the river Rhee
         becomes the Cam, and is reinforced by a brook called the Bourn.
         No trace of a mill remains, but its former existence is witnessed
         in the name 'the Old Mills', formerly given to the spot in the
         river now known as Byron's Pool (ibid., p. 111).

3933 Sheffield was famous for its steel.

3942–3 The wife's pride in her noble origins conveniently ignores the
         fact that she must be illegitimate, since medieval priests were not
         permitted to marry.

3949 *yemanrye*: See n. to GP 101.

3964 The comparison is proverbial; see Whiting D268.

3973–6 These lines resemble in form the rhetorical *descriptio* (see n. to
         Mil 3233 ff.), but their content does not answer to the unqualified
         beauty or ugliness which is conventional in the figure. Although
         the grey eyes and fair hair of the miller's daughter accord with
         the medieval image of a romantic heroine, her snub nose and
         sturdy physique do not.

3990 *Soler Halle*: There was no such Cambridge college, although
         there were two buildings in Oxford which bore this name. A
         solar was an upper room with windows allowing access to sun-
         light; halls were frequently named after a prominent architectural

feature of this sort (e.g., Oriel Hall, Garrett Hostel). The likeliest model for Chaucer's 'greet collegge' is the King's Hall, the largest and most important foundation in Cambridge at the time, as Merton College was in Oxford (A. B. Cobban, *The King's Hall Within the University of Cambridge in the Later Middle Ages* (Cambridge, 1969), p. 45).

3991 The wheat was ground for bread, the malt for beer; colleges brewed their own beer as well as baking their own bread (Bennett, p. 6). There were mills in Cambridge itself, but the river Cam was too small and flowed too slowly to keep them turning at a rate sufficient to keep up with demand (ibid., p. 107), so that the manciple of 'Soler Hall' is plausibly represented as sending the college's grain to the mill at Trumpington.

3993 *maunciple*: See n. to GP 567. The officer who ran the college household at King's Hall (see n. to Rv 3990) was at this period called a 'butler' (*pincerna*), rather than a 'manciple' (*manicipulus*), which was in general an Oxford rather than a Cambridge title (Cobban, *King's Hall*, p. 165, n. 5; Bennett, pp. 103–4). Similarly, 'warden' (3999) was a more usual title for the head of a college in Oxford than in Cambridge, although the head of the King's Hall was referred to indiscriminately as 'wardein' (*custos*) or 'master' (*magister*) (Cobban, p. 75, n. 5). Either Chaucer's information about Cambridge college life was less than perfect, or he was deliberately using inaccurate terminology to avoid identification of his fictional 'Soler Hall' with a real college.

4014 Strother is a frequent place-name in the North (now found only north of the Tees: Bennett, p. 101), but the village ('toun') that Chaucer had in mind (if any) cannot be identified with certainty.

4015 It is misleading to say, as Bennett does (pp. 99–100), that the King's Hall had a specially high number of students from the North; the passage of Cobban (*King's Hall*, pp. 157–61) that he cites actually points out that the King's Hall had *no* particular regional bias (unlike other colleges), and had virtually no scholars from Durham and Northumberland, the area suggested by dialect and other indications as the home of the two scholars (see nn. to Rv 4014, 4022 ff. and 4127).

4022 ff. True to their origins (4015), the two clerks speak in a distinctive northern dialect. This appears to be the first example in English literature of the imitation of dialectal speech, and Chaucer carries it out with striking accuracy and verve. The main differences from Chaucer's Southern speech, as they are identified by J. R. R. Tolkien in an important article (*Transactions of the*

Philological Society (1934), 1–70), are the following (where both forms are given, the Northern one comes first):

1. Sounds

    a for *o*: *na, nan, swa, ham, ga, fra, banes, (at) anes, alswa, wat, ra, bathe, twa, wha, a* [for *o* in *a point*, 4181], *saule, awen*
    ald for *old*: *tald, halden*
    ang for *ong*: *sang, lang, wrang*
    k for *ch*: *whilk*

2. Grammatical forms

    (e)s for *(e)th* in 3 sg pres: e.g., *has, boes, gas, wagges, falles, findes, bringes, tides, sayes*
    es for *e(n)* in 3 pl pres: *fares, werkes*
    past participles: Northern forms have no *y-* prefix (optional in Southern speech), and retain the *-n* ending in participles of strong verbs (which may be dropped in Southern speech): e.g., *stoln, shapen*

3. Forms of the verb 'to be'

    is for *am* (1st sg pres); *is* for *art* (2 sg pres); *ar* for *be(n)* (1–3 pl pres)

4. Forms of the pronoun: *thair* for *hire*

5. Other distinctively Northern forms

    sal for *shal*; *taa* for *take*; *boes* for *bihoves*; *pit* for *put*; *sek* for *sak* [in *draf-sek*]; *gif* for *if*
    To these examples may be added the loss of the weak inflexion on adjectives; see the note on 'This lang night' in Rv 4175.
    Tolkien also cites as Northern the 'inflexionless' forms of the 2 sg past, 'nad thow' (4087), 'herd thow' (4170), but the loss of the *-est* ending in such inverted phrases is found elsewhere in Chaucer (e.g., Mk 2053).

6. Vocabulary

    fonne, heithen (for *henne*), *hething, hope* (in the sense 'think, expect', rather than 'wish for'), *howgat, il(le), imel, slik* (for *swich*), *swain* (in the sense 'servant'), *til* (for *to*, before a consonant).

These are only the most clearcut examples; other words which may contribute to the idiosyncratic flavour of the clerks' speech are discussed by Tolkien, pp. 31–45.

My text of the relevant passages does not incorporate as many northernisms as the one Tolkien prints in his article, since I have restricted myself to those recorded in either El or Hg or both (with the exception of 'howgat' at 4042, which, as Tolkien pointed out (pp. 21–2), would have been very easily corrupted into El/Hg's 'how þat'); Tolkien not only included all northernisms found in any of the manuscript transcripts available to him (on the grounds that a scribe was unlikely to have invented them), but also 'normalized' the text by extending single instances of Northern features to all other possible cases, even when no manuscript offered support for this. Tolkien probably went too far; on the other hand, N. F. Blake's view (*Lore and Language*, 3 (1979), 1–8) that many of the northernisms in El and other manuscripts are due to the enthusiastic initiative of their scribes (or that of an 'editorial committee') is unconvincing and inadequately documented. According to C. Elliott, *NQ*, 209 (1964), 167–70, Hg has more distinctively Northern forms than El. Blake has also argued that the El/Hg reading 'By god hert(e)' at 4087, and the El reading 'By god sale' at 4187 are examples of a 'Northern uninflected genitive' and so should be adopted in the text (*NQ*, 222 (1977), 400–401), but the inflected form 'Goddes' fits the metre better in both cases. For discussion of other manuscript spellings which might be an attempt to represent Northern forms, see S. C. P. Horobin, *NQ*, 245 (2000), 16–18.

Thorough as the imitation of Northern speech is, some southernisms persist (and are attested as correct readings by rhyme), and the northernisms seem to fade away somewhat at the end of the tale (see n. to Rv 4237).

4026–7 The two sayings in these lines sound proverbial but are not recorded elsewhere in medieval English literature.

4036–43 The hopper is the cone-shaped funnel through which the grain is directed into the 'eye' of the millstone; it shakes from side to side ('wagges til and fra') to stimulate the movement of the grain. Having passed through the millstones, the ground flour falls into a sack beneath. The clerks set themselves to watch the beginning and end of this process, so that the miller can steal neither from the grain going into the hopper, nor from the flour coming through the millstones.

4055 The reference is to a fable, surviving in several different forms, in which a horse or mule persuades another animal that a desired piece of information is written on its hoof; when the other animal bends down to read it, the horse kicks it in the head. Of the surviving versions that Chaucer might have known, that in *Renart le Contrefait* is the only one that tells the story of a wolf and mare, but its moral ('Or voi ge bien tout an apert | Que clergie bien sa saison pert'; 'Now I see clearly that learning is a

waste of time': ed. Raynaud and Lemaître, p. 243) is not so close
to Chaucer's as that which closes the story of the fox and the ass
included in Odo of Cheriton's fables: 'Qui clerici probantur
periciores, non sunt in opere cauciores' ('Those who are the most
learned clerks are not the most prudent in action': Hervieux, *Les
fabulistes latins*, IV, 365–6), or the story of wolf and mule in the
Novellino (no. 94, ed. Consoli, pp. 118–19): 'Ongni uomo kessa
lettera non è savio' ('not every man who knows his letters is
wise'); see P. F. Baum, *MLN*, 37 (1922), 350–53.

4065 The fenland of modern Cambridgeshire has been largely drained
and cultivated as arable land, flat and open in appearance. In the
fourteenth century, before large-scale draining, it would have
been more like a watery meadow, offering excellent pasture. 'At
least as early as the twelfth century, the grazing of animals had
become one of the most important fenland occupations' (H. C.
Darby, *The Medieval Fenland* (Cambridge, 1940; repr. Newton
Abbot, 1974), p. 66). The local villagers held common grazing
rights on the fens; the 'wilde mares' will not have been truly wild,
but animals turned out for summer pasture. Bennett (p. 113)
points out that a piece of land still known as Lingay Fen adjoined
the (putative) site of Trumpington Mill.

4101 *Jossa, warderere!*: These calls for controlling horses (cf. modern
English 'Whoa!') are obscure in origin and meaning, and are not
otherwise recorded in ME.

4117 Although Trumpington was only three miles from Cambridge,
the clerks could not return home because the town gates would
have been closed at nightfall, as was customary in the Middle
Ages; 'no one travelled after sunset' (Bennett, p. 109). In addition,
the gate of their college would have been locked.

4123–4 The miller is mocking the philosophical sophistry practised
in the university schools, which could provide verbal 'proofs' of
apparently absurd or impossible propositions. Gerald of Wales
(1146–1223) tells a story of a student returning home from Paris
who 'proved' that six eggs were in fact twelve; his father then
ate the six and left him with the hypothetical remainder (S.
Wenzel, *SP*, 73 (1976), 138–61, at p. 144).

4127 *Cutberd*: John's appeal to Cuthbert, the most famous saint of
the North, is in keeping with his Northern origins. Cuthbert
(7th c.) was bishop of Lindisfarne; his remains are the treasured
possession of Durham Cathedral.

4129–30 The proverb is not otherwise recorded in medieval English
literature.

4134 Proverbial; see Whiting H89 and Singer, I, 115, and cf. WB 415 and n.

4175 This lang night Hg] This lange night El. The El reading represents Chaucer's normal use of an -e ending on weak adjectives, but this usage had disappeared in the North of England; the Hg reading thus better fits Alein's Northern dialect (J. J. Smith, *Studies in Middle English Linguistics*, ed. J. Fisiak (Berlin, 1997), pp. 557–8). Compare Alein's 'thin awen clerk' at line 4239 with Malin's 'thin owene mele' at line 4245.

4181–2 Since the y- prefix in past participles was not used in Nothern dialect, Hg's 'agreved' is more likely than El's 'ygreved'; see Smith (as cited in the preceding n.).

   Two manuscripts of *CT* give a Latin version of this maxim in the margin: 'Qui in uno gravatur in alio debet relevari' (Manly and Rickert III, 492).

4210 A variant of the more familiar proverbs 'Nothing venture, nothing win' (cf. Whiting N146 and *TC* II.807–8), and 'Fortune favours the brave' (cf. Whiting F519 and *TC* IV.600–602).

4236–7 Alein's farewell to Malin is a low-life version of the *aubade*, the conventional lament of romantic lovers at the parting enforced on them by dawn; cf. *TC* III.1415–70.

4237 The Northern character of Alein's speech begins to fade rather noticeably at this point. The following forms are 'incorrect': *no* (for *na*), *everemo* (for *everema*), *wherso* (for *whersa*), *go* (for *ga*). This tendency continues in Alein's subsequent speeches, which contain the following southernisms: *crepen* (for *crepe*), *misgon* (for *misgan*; attested as original by the rhyme with *anon*, which is not part of Alein's speech and so cannot be emended to Northern *anan*), *maketh* (for *makes*), *go* (for *ga*), *woot* (for *wat*), *misgo* (as before, with the additional, incorrect, loss of final -*n*), *also* (for *alswa*), *lith* (for *lis*). Some (but not all) of these could be eliminated by emendation, but in view of the sporadic occurrence of southernisms earlier (e.g., *slepest* for *slepes* at 4169, *hem* for *thaim* at 4171) it is probable that Chaucer was less interested in perfect accuracy than in the general impression of Northern speech.

4264 St James was one of Christ's disciples, and the first to be martyred for his faith. According to a ninth-century legend, his relics are preserved in Santiago de Compostela in Spain (see n. to GP 463–6).

4286 The Priory of St Andrew at Bromholm in Norfolk claimed possession of a fragment of the Cross, which reportedly worked miracles and was an object of pilgrimage (F. Wormald, *Journal of the Warburg Institute*, 1 (1937–8), 31–45). It is mentioned by Langland at *PPl* V.227.

4287 Christ's last words on the cross, 'Pater, in manus tuas commendo spiritum meum' ('Father, into thy hands I commend my spirit': Luke 23:46), were used to invoke divine protection when going to sleep, or on the point of death. The wife melodramatically implies that she is threatened with loss of life and limb.

4300 This is somewhat inconsistent, in view of the wife's assumption that her husband is in bed with her and that the two combatants are Alein and John (4288, 4291); it should not, in that case, matter which of them she hits. But Chaucer seems to have worried less about the inconsistency than about providing a reason why her blow is *not* aimed at Alein.

4320 Proverbial; see Whiting E185.

4321 Proverbial; see Whiting G491.

THE COOK'S PROLOGUE

4331 Ecclesiasticus 11:31: 'Bring not every man into thy house: for many are the snares of the deceitful.' On this apocryphal book of the Bible, and its association with Solomon, see n. to Mil 3530.

4336 'Hogge' is a nickname for Roger, and a Roger Knight de Ware of London, Cook, appears in historical records, so that Chaucer may have had a real person in mind (Bowden, pp. 187–8).

4346 The Cook has drained off the gravy to prolong the pasty's 'shelf-life'.

4347 A 'Jack of Dover' seems to have been some kind of pie, which the Cook is accused of reheating day after day until it is sold.

4357 'A true joke is a bad joke' (because it is too hurtful). Proverbial; see Whiting P257. J. Grauls and J. F. Vanderheijden (*Revue belge de philologie et d'histoire*, 13 (1934), 745–9) say there is nothing Flemish about the proverb except the word 'quaad' (modern Dutch 'kwaad'), which means 'bad'. There were large numbers of Flemish merchants and craftsmen living in London in Chaucer's day (A. R. Myers, *London in the Age of Chaucer* (Norman, OK, 1972), pp. 145–6). Edward III's queen, Philippa of Hainault, came from the Low Countries; Chaucer's wife, also called Philippa, served as a lady of her household and probably was herself Flemish (see Pearsall, *Life*, pp. 35–8, 49–50).

4358 *Herry Bailly*: A Harry Bailly of Southwark who was an inn-keeper appears in late fourteenth-century historical records (Manly, *New Light*, pp. 77–81); whether his inn was the Tabard is not known.

THE COOK'S TALE

The source of the Cook's Tale (if it had one) is unidentifiable; the tale breaks off unfinished, and there is no way of knowing how it would have turned out. Some possibilities are discussed by V. A. Kolve, *Chaucer and the Imagery of Narrative: The First Five Canterbury Tales* (Stanford, CA, 1984), pp. 275–9). Later on, in the Manciple's Prologue, the Cook is called upon to tell a tale as if he had not already made a contribution, suggesting that Chaucer meant to cancel the Cook's Tale (though it is also possible that he was working on it when he died).

4365–6 Apprentices practised their trade under a master, who was a member of the trade guild, and in whose house the apprentice would normally live (Robertson, *Chaucer's London*, p. 79). The victualling guilds of London were especially powerful in the late fourteenth century.

4368 The comparison is proverbial; cf. GP 207 and n.

4377 *Chepe*: Cheapside, a busy London street with many shops, formed the central part of the street running between Newgate, on the west side of the city, and Aldgate, on the east (see Lobel, ed., *The City of London*, Map 3). It was frequently the scene of festive processions (see Robertson, *Chaucer's London*, pp. 75–7).

4402 Because of the thickness of the city walls, there was ample room for accommodation above and to the sides of the city gates; in the case of Newgate and Ludgate this living-space was used as a prison (see Robertson, *Chaucer's London*, p. 23).

4406–7 Proverbial; see Whiting A167.

4415 The idea is proverbial; see Whiting M69 and T73.

4422 The scribe of Hg, having originally left part of a leaf free so as to be able to continue the Cook's Tale if more of the text became available, later wrote in the left-hand margin 'Of this cokes tale maked Chaucer na moore'. This suggests that he was given reliable information that Chaucer had left the tale incomplete (rather than that the final part of it was lost).

THE MAN OF LAW'S PROLOGUE

1–4 Measuring the time by the length of shadows or the height of the sun in the sky was a normal practice in Chaucer's time; Nicholas of Lynn's *Calendar* (see n. to GP 417–18) made the task easier by including tables showing shadow lengths, and the angular distance of the sun above the celestial equator, according to the day of the year and the time of day (during daylight hours). The figures Chaucer gives here correspond exactly with those Nicholas of Lynn gives for 10 a.m. on 18 April (and are unusual in that both are round numbers). In contrast, the information given in lines 2–3 is inaccurate: the 'artificial day' (the time between sunrise and sunset) would on 18 April have lasted 14 hours 26 minutes, a quarter of which is 3 hours 36½ minutes, whereas the period from sunrise to 10 a.m. on that day would have been far longer (5 hours 13 minutes), even when 'half an houre and moore' is added on. It is unlikely that Chaucer would have expected his readers to recognize that he was making fun of the Host's ignorance (Eisner, *Kalendarium*, p. 30), and more probable that he himself simply made a mistake (see North, *Chaucer's Universe*, pp. 124–5). On different methods of telling the time, see L. Mooney, *SAC*, 15 (1993), 91–109.

20–24 These lines resemble *RR* 361–74 (tr. Horgan, p. 8); a comparison of passing time with flowing water is also found in Ovid, *Art of Love* III.62–4, and *Metamorphoses* XV.179–85.

25–8 *Senec*: The first of Seneca's *Moral Epistles* warns against wasting time, and contrasts the loss of material possessions, which can be replaced, with the loss of time, which cannot (I.3). Cf. also Gower, *CA* IV.1485–7.

30 *Malkin*: A typical name for a lower-class woman (cf. NP 3384, and see A. J. Fletcher, *ELN*, 24.2 (1986), 15–20). The irrecoverability of lost virginity was proverbial; cf. Gower, *CA* V.5647–8, 6208–11.

33 The imposing Serjeant at Law of the General Prologue (see n. to GP 309) has here become a common-or-garden Man of Law. It is not clear that Chaucer intended anything specific by making the change.

41 *Biheste is dette*: 'A promise is an obligation.' Proverbial; see Whiting B214.

43–5 The reference to 'oure text' in line 45 suggests that Chaucer has a specific source in mind, which is probably the *Digest* of Justinian, II.ii, rubric (I, 42).

53–5 The work referred to is Ovid's *Heroides*, a collection of fictional letters written by unhappy women to the male lovers who have, for the most part, abandoned or betrayed them. The last six (XVI–XXI) are letters of courtship exchanged between three pairs of lovers: Paris/Helen, Leander/Hero, Acontius/Cydippe. See further nn. to ML 61–85.

57 Chaucer had retold the story of King Ceyx and his wife Alcyone in the first section of the *Book of the Duchess* (62–230); his source was Ovid's *Metamorphoses* (XI.410–748). Ceyx was drowned on a sea-voyage, leaving Alcyone uncertain of his fate; in answer to her prayer Juno sent Morpheus to her in the shape of the drowned Ceyx to tell her of his death. In Chaucer's version Alcyone then dies of grief; in Ovid's, she and Ceyx are changed into sea-birds.

61 ff. The reference is to Chaucer's *Legend of Good Women*, a collection of stories about women who were 'martyred' by the cruelty of the male lovers who abandoned or betrayed them. The list of the *Legend*'s contents given here suggests that the work as we have it may be seriously incomplete, since it refers to eight more legends (those of Deianira, Hermione, Hero, Helen, Briseida, Laodamia, Penelope and Alcestis) than are included in the version we have (conversely, however, this version includes the stories of Cleopatra and Philomela, who are not mentioned here). Chaucer's Retractions of his profane writings at the end of *CT*, which refer to the *Legend* as 'The Book of the xxv Ladies', support the notion that part of the work has been lost (see n. to Retr 1086).

Fifteen of the lovers mentioned by the Man of Law are included in Ovid's *Heroides* (Dido, Phyllis, Deianira, Hermione, Ariadne, Hypsipyle, Leander, Hero, Helen, Briseida, Laodamia, Medea, Hypermnestra, Penelope, Canace).

62–3 *Lucresse*: Chaucer's source for the story of the Roman matron Lucretia in *LGW* (1680–1885) is Ovid's *Fasti* (II.685–852). Having been raped by Tarquin, king of Rome, Lucretia committed suicide; popular indignation at the crime led to Tarquin's banishment. Cf. Fkl 1405–8.

Babilan Tesbee: Thisbe, a maiden of Babylon, could communicate with her lover Piramus only through a crack in the wall between their houses. When they arranged to meet outside the city and run away together, Piramus found Thisbe's blood-stained cloak at their rendezvous, and believing that she had been killed by a lion, committed suicide; finding his dead body, Thisbe followed suit. Chaucer's source for this story in *LGW* (706–923) was Ovid's *Metamorphoses* (IV.55–166). Cf. Mch 2128–31.

64 *Dido . . . Enee*: Chaucer's account, in *LGW* 924–1367, of Dido's abandonment by Aeneas and subsequent suicide draws on both Vergil (*Aeneid*, Book IV) and Ovid (*Heroides* VII).

65 *Phillis . . . Demophon*: Phyllis (*LGW* 2394–2561; cf. *Heroides* II) hanged herself when her lover Demophoon failed to return by the date he had promised.

66 *Dianire . . . Hermion*: On Deianira, wife of Hercules, see n. to Kn 1942–6. Hermione (*Heroides* VIII), the betrothed of Orestes, was married against her will to Pyrrhus, son of Achilles, after the fall of Troy.

67 *Adriane . . . Isiphilee*: Ariadne (*LGW* 1886–2227, *Heroides* X) helped Theseus to slay the Minotaur and escape from Crete in return for a promise of marriage, but was abandoned by Theseus on the island of Naxos, the 'bareine ile' of line 68 (cf. *Heroides* X.59–62). Hypsipyle (*LGW* 1368–1579; cf. *Heroides* VI) was abandoned by her husband Jason in favour of Medea.

69 *Leandre . . . Erro*: Leander, a youth of Abydos, was the secret lover of Hero of Sestos, and would swim across the Hellespont at night to her tower (*Heroides* XVIII–XIX). One stormy night he was drowned, and when Hero found his body cast up on the shore, she threw herself into the sea.

70 *Eleine*: Helen, wife of Menelaus, king of Lacedaemon, was abducted by Paris, son of King Priam of Troy; the result was the siege and fall of Troy. *Heroides* XVI–XVII represent Paris's first declaration of his love, and Helen's ambivalent response, but make no mention of her weeping. Chaucer seems to have in mind Guido delle Colonne's *History of the Destruction of Troy*: although Helen there acquiesces in her own abduction, when brought to Troy she is 'tormented with great anguish' by the loss of her family and native land, and is drowned in continual tears until Paris consoles her (Book VII, ed. Griffin, p. 76; tr. Meek, p. 75).

71 *Brixseide*: The Trojan girl Briseis was given as a captive to the Greek hero Achilles, but taken away from him by Agamemnon, leader of the Greeks, when he was obliged to give up his own captive Chryseis. Achilles' wrath at this injury, and consequent refusal to fight for the Greeks against Troy, is the subject of Homer's *Iliad*. *Heroides* III is an impassioned plea from Briseis to Achilles, complaining at his delay in reclaiming her from Agamemnon.

Ladomia: Laodamia (*Heroides* XIII) was wife of Protesilaus, the first Greek leader to be killed by the Trojans, according to the prophecy that this fate would befall the first Greek warrior to set foot on the Trojan shore. The gods later granted Laodamia's plea that he be restored to life for three hours, and when he died a second time, she committed suicide in order to be with him. Cf. Fkl 1445–7.

72–4 Medea (*LGW* 1580–1679; *Heroides* XII) by her magic arts helped Jason win the Golden Fleece, in return for which he made her his wife, but eventually abandoned her to marry the daughter of Creon, king of Corinth. Medea's murder of her two children by Jason is not mentioned in *Heroides* XII, and is only obliquely referred to in *LGW* (1574) as a fate wished on Medea by her abandoned predecessor Hypsipyle. The statement that the children were hanged by the neck is without parallel elsewhere; in *RR* (13229) she is said to have strangled them.

75 *Ypermystra*: Hypermnestra (*LGW* 2562–2723; *Heroides* XIV) was the youngest of the fifty daughters of Danaus, whose brother Aegyptus insisted that they be married to his fifty sons. Danaus gave each of his daughters a knife, and ordered them to kill their husbands on the wedding night, but Hypermnestra disobeyed and helped her husband Lynceus to escape. Chaucer's version of the story in *LGW* says nothing of the marriages between the other forty-nine sisters and brothers, and reverses the names of the fathers.

Penolopee: Penelope (*Heroides* I) was the wife of Ulysses, one of the Greek leaders at the siege of Troy, and remained faithful to him, despite being importuned by numerous suitors, throughout his twenty-year absence. Cf. Fkl 1443.

Alceste: Alcestis, wife of King Admetus, volunteered to save her husband's life by dying in his stead when the Fates agreed to spare him if his father, mother or wife were willing to take his place. She was brought back from the Underworld by Hercules. In the Prologue to *LGW*, she appears as the God of Love's queenly consort, and intercedes with the God of Love on Chaucer's behalf. Cf. Fkl 1442.

77–85 *Canacee*: The incestuous love between Canace, daughter of King Aeolus, and her brother Macareus became known when she gave birth to their son; her father had the child exposed on a mountain-side and ordered Canace to kill herself (*Heroides* XI). In the Prologue to *LGW*, Chaucer includes her, without any sign of distaste, in the list of faithful women lovers in the *Balade* sung in Alcestis's honour (F 265, G 219).

Tyro Appollonius: Apollonius, prince of Tyre, was a suitor for the hand of the daughter of Antiochus, king of Antioch; he successfully decoded the riddle that Antiochus required her suitors to solve, on pain of death, but found to his horror that its answer revealed an incestuous relationship between father and daughter. The Apollonius story was extremely widespread in the Middle Ages and Renaissance; see E. Archibald, *Apollonius of Tyre: Medieval and Renaissance Themes and Variations* (Cambridge, 1991).

Gower tells both the story of Canace (with striking sympathy for the incestuous pair) and the story of Apollonius in *CA* (III.143–336, VIII.271–2008), and it may be that Chaucer is here teasing his friend Gower by having the Man of Law express disgust for such 'cursed stories'. However, Chaucer expresses a similar reluctance to rehearse a 'foule storye' when embarking on the tale of Tereus's rape of Philomela in *LGW* (2228–43), so these lines may reflect genuine feeling. Gower's story says nothing about Antiochus throwing his daughter 'upon the pavement'; Chaucer may have remembered a Latin version of the story (see J. H. Fisher, *John Gower: Moral Philosopher and Friend of Chaucer* (London, 1965), p. 370, n. 18).

Some narrative analogues of the Man of Law's Tale begin with the heroine's flight from threatened incest (see E. Archibald, *ChauR*, 20 (1986), 259–72); Chaucer may thus be signalling his refusal to tell the story in this form.

92   *Pierides*: The Muses are so called because according to legend they were born at the foot of Mount Olympia in Pieria. They are here confused with the nine daughters of Pierus, who foolishly challenged the Muses to a singing contest and were changed into magpies when they lost (*Metamorphoses* V.294–678). The Man of Law fears that his own tale will be as inferior to Chaucer's as the song of Pierus's daughters was to that of the Muses.

93   *Methamorphosios*: The ending of this word represents the Greek genitive singular, and is a common medieval error for the genitive plural in the full form of Ovid's title: *Metamorphoseon Libri Quindecim* ('15 Books of Metamorphoses'). See E. F. Shannon, *Chaucer and the Roman Poets* (Cambridge, MA, 1929), pp. 307–12.

96   *I speke in prose*: Despite this claim, the Man of Law's tale is in the verse-form known as rhyme royal (stanzas of seven five-stress lines, rhyming ababbcc). This line may thus indicate that Chaucer had originally assigned another tale to the Man of Law – most

likely the Tale of Melibee, whose ultimate source was the *Liber consolationis et consilii*, written by a lawyer, Albertano of Brescia (see Headnote to Mel).

99–121 These lines are based on a section (I.14) of the *De Miseria Condicionis Humane* of Pope Innocent III (written in 1195), a moralizing work in fairly simple Latin which was very widely read in the Middle Ages and beyond (see the edition and translation by R. E. Lewis (London, 1980), pp. 3–5). This is almost certainly the work of Pope Innocent's which Chaucer is said to have translated in the Prologue to *LGW* (G 414–15). It is drawn on at several other points in ML (see nn. to ML 421–7, 771–7, 925–31 and 1135–8); marginal Latin glosses in many *CT* MSS, including Hg and El, make the borrowings clear by quoting the relevant passages of Innocent's work (for details of these glosses, see Manly and Rickert III, 492–6).

Although Chaucer here follows Pope Innocent's words quite closely, his picture of the constraints of poverty culminates in a very different conclusion: whereas Innocent concludes that riches bring moral dangers, and people should be estimated according to their virtue rather than their wealth, Chaucer blithely ignores moral questions and expresses admiration for the life of wealthy merchants. The worldly-wise attitude of these stanzas is nearer to the reflections on poverty and riches in Mel 1551–74, which quote the same section of the *De Miseria* (see 1568–70 and n.), but Dame Prudence does not have the strain of flippancy which makes itself heard here. In contrast, Chaucer's later quotations of Innocent's work in this tale preserve and even heighten the solemnity of tone.

This whole section (99–133) is connected with the preceding part of MLPr by the Man of Law's protestation that he is 'of tales desolat' (131), and with the following Tale by the use of the rhyme royal stanza, but its content is not obviously relevant to either. Perhaps the picture of poverty's grumbling discontent was intended as a thematic contrast to the tale of patience in adversity which follows, since 'grucchyng' is an opposite of patience (see Introduction, p. xxxiii).

114 Ecclesiasticus 40:29; also quoted at Mel 1571.

115 Proverbs 14:20.

118 Proverbs 15:15.

120–21 Proverbs 19:7; cf. Whiting P295 and Mel 1559.

124 *ambes as*: In the game of dice, the lowest possible score, hence an emblem of bad luck.

125　*sis cink*: The highest possible throw with two dice, with the exception of two sixes.

THE MAN OF LAW'S TALE

Parallels to the narrative motifs of the Man of Law's Tale (the voyage in a rudderless boat, the wicked mother-in-law) can be found in a wide range of medieval romances and tales (see M. Schlauch, *Chaucer's Constance and Accused Queens* (New York, 1927), and J. R. Reinhard, 'Setting Adrift in Medieval Law and Literature', *PMLA*, 56 (1941), 33–68), but it is generally agreed that Chaucer's direct source was a section of the AN prose chronicle by the fourteenth-century Dominican friar Nicholas Trevet. Trevet's *Chronicle* was composed for Mary, daughter of Edward I, who was a nun at Amesbury, and who might have felt a special interest in the story of the high-born and devout heroine Constance. Chaucer may also have been influenced by the version of the Constance story included in Gower's *Confessio Amantis* (II.587–1612); see P. Nicholson, *ChauR*, 26 (1991), 153–74.

Like Trevet's, Chaucer's telling of the tale is closer to hagiography than to romance; Chaucer, however, omits many of Trevet's circumstantial details, and increases the intellectual weightiness of the tale by setting it in a cosmological framework, and by weaving into it passages – some original, some drawn from other writers (Innocent III, Bernard Silvestris, Boethius) – which make the action a basis for reflection on the human condition and the justice or injustice of divine providence. He also gives the tale much greater solemnity and dignity of style through the constant use of apostrophes, exclamations and rhetorical questions, and by the frequent use of biblical and classical allusions. The rhyme royal stanza (see n. to ML 96) adds to this solemn effect. At the same time, he increases the pathos of the tale by vivid representations of Constance's sufferings and by appeals to the audience's pity.

Trevet's *Chronicle* is unedited, but the section containing the Constance story was printed, with facing English translation, in *Originals and Analogues of Some of Chaucer's Canterbury Tales*, ed. F. J. Furnivall, E. Brock and W. A. Clouston (London, [1888]); a freshly edited text and parallel English translation by R. M. Correale are included in *SA²* II, together with Gower's Constance story and relevant excerpts from Innocent III. Correale has analysed all the manuscripts of Trevet's work in order to determine which best represents the text of Chaucer's source (*ChauR*, 25 (1991), 238–65), in preparation for a new edition in the Chaucer Library series. For a full account of Chaucer's handling of his source material, see E. A. Block, *PMLA*, 68 (1953), 572–616, and the article by Nicholson cited above.

134 In Chaucer's day, Syria was a non-Christian country, having passed into Arab hands in the seventh century. However, at the date that the events of the Constance story supposedly took place (see n. to ML 1121–2), Syria was part of the Roman Empire, of which Christianity was the official religion; the story is therefore founded on a major anachronism. Trevet and Gower are geographically vaguer, locating the Sultan in 'Saracenland' and 'Barbary' respectively, but Trevet's statement that the Sultan promised free Christian access to Jerusalem and the Holy Land in return for Constance's hand shows that he too is thinking of circumstances appropriate to a date after the Arab conquest of the Middle East.

190–203 A Latin marginal gloss which appears in most *CT* manuscripts (including Hg and El) identifies the source of these stanzas as a passage in the *Cosmographia* of Bernard Silvestris (fl. 1130–60) on the future destinies foretold in the stars: '[There are] the sceptre of Phoroneus, the conflict between the brothers at Thebes, the flames of Phaethon, Deucalion's flood. In the stars are . . . the splendour of Priam, the daring of Turnus, the wisdom of Ulysses, and the strength of Hercules' (ed. Dronke, *Megacosmos* III.39–44; tr. Wetherbee, p. 76). But whereas the stars foretell a varied range of attributes and events in Bernard, in Chaucer they record only death.

198 *Ector*: Hector, eldest son of Priam, king of Troy, was the chief defender of the Trojans against the Greeks; his death at the hands of Achilles, the leading warrior on the Greek side, marks the end of Homer's *Iliad*. Although the *Iliad* was not read in Greek during the Middle Ages, its narrative events were known through a number of Latin versions; see C. D. Benson, *The History of Troy in Middle English Literature* (Woodbridge, 1980).

Achilles' death is not related in the *Iliad*; Chaucer could have read an account of how he was lured by his love of the Trojan girl Polyxena to the Trojan temple of Apollo, and there ambushed and slain by Paris, in Guido delle Colonne's *History of the Destruction of Troy* (XXVII), or in Benoît de Sainte-Maure's *Roman de Troie*, lines 21838–2334 (ed. L. Constans, 6 vols. (Paris, 1904–12)).

199 *Pompey, Julius*: Pompey and Julius Caesar were for a long time

political collaborators at Rome, but their growing differences eventually led to the outbreak of civil war (49 BC), in which Pompey was defeated, and later treacherously murdered in Egypt. Caesar then assumed supreme powers, but was murdered in the Roman senate (44 BC) by a group of conspirators who claimed to be acting in defence of the republic (cf. Mk 2671–2726 and n.).

200 *The strif of Thebes*: The sons of Oedipus, Eteocles and Polynices, were supposed to rule Thebes in alternation, but war broke out between them, and they eventually killed each other in single combat. The story of their strife is related in Statius's *Thebaid*, a work which Chaucer knew well; see n. to Rubric of KnT, and Wise, *Influence of Statius*. For the death of the hero Hercules, see n. to Kn 1942–6.

201 The biblical hero Samson, although blind, killed both himself and his enemies the Philistines by pulling down the pillars supporting a house in which they were making merry (Judges 16:23–31). The death of Turnus at the hands of Aeneas, his rival for the hand of Lavinia, is related at the end of Vergil's *Aeneid*. Socrates, the Greek philosopher (5th c. BC), was accused of corrupting the youth of Athens, and sentenced to die by drinking hemlock.

224 The prophet Mohammed (AD 570?–632), founder of the Islamic religion. At the time most of this story supposedly takes place (see n. to ML 1121–2), he was either not yet born or still a child.

286–7 Submission to her husband was one of the punishments imposed on Eve, and thus on all womankind, after the Fall: 'thou shalt be under thy husband's power, and he shall have dominion over thee' (Genesis 3:16).

288 *Pirrus*: Pyrrhus, son of Achilles, was among the Greek warriors smuggled into Troy in the Wooden Horse; the *Aeneid* (II.469–88) describes how he broke through the doors of Priam's palace, and the shrieks and wails of those within. Cf. NP 3355–9, where the same comparison is used of the hens bewailing Chauntecleer's capture by the fox.

289 Or Ilion brende, at Thebes*] Or Ilion brende Thebes El; Or Ylion brent hadde Thebes Hg. Confusion seems to have been caused by the assumption that 'Ilion' is a personal name and the subject of 'brende' ('brent hadde' takes this assumption one stage further). Only two manuscripts read 'at' before 'Thebes' but the parallel constructions in lines 288 and 290 suggest that this is the correct reading.

Ilion: Ilium was the Greek name of Troy; like other medieval writers, Chaucer used it to designate the inner citadel of Troy. The burning of Troy is mentioned numerous times in Aeneas's account of the fall of the city (*Aeneid* II.309 ff.).

Thebes: The grief of the survivors over the dead at the end of the war of the Seven Against Thebes is described in Book XII of Statius's *Thebaid*; cf. n. to Kn 932.

290–91 The great Carthaginian general Hannibal (*c.* 247–183 BC) was an implacable enemy of Rome; his three great victories against the Roman army were at the river Trebbia, at Lake Trasimeno and at Cannae.

295–301 A marginal Latin gloss in Hg, El, and many other MSS quotes the Latin translation of Ptolemy's *Almagest* (I.8; see n. to Mil 3208):

> there are two different primary motions in the heavens. One is that by which everything moves uniformly from east to west, above the spheres, et cetera. There is a second motion which moves the sphere of the moving stars [i.e., the planets] in opposition to the first motion – that is, from west to east around two other poles, et cetera.

Cf. E. Flügel, *Anglia*, 18 (1896), 133–40. Medieval cosmology, following Ptolemy, pictured the universe with the Earth at the centre, surrounded by the seven spheres of the planets, an eighth sphere carrying the fixed stars, and an outer sphere known as the Primum Mobile or 'First Moving' sphere. The existence of the Primum Mobile was hypothesized as a way of accounting for the observed phenomenon known as the precession of the equinoxes; that is, the minute annual shift eastward (1° in 100 years, by medieval calculations) of the stellar constellations in relation to the point where the sun's annual path (the ecliptic) crosses the celestial equator at the spring equinox. It was supposed that the *natural* movement of the first eight spheres (travelling at different speeds) was from west to east around the poles of the ecliptic, but that the Primum Mobile travelled from east to west around the equatorial poles, and its greater size and power carried the inner spheres with it; the apparent motions of the heavenly bodies as seen from the earth are a product of the two motions combined. For a helpfully clear and concise explanation of the medieval cosmological scheme, and its relation to the motions of the heavenly bodies as we now understand them, see Boyde, *Dante Philomythes*, pp. 143–56.

The double motion of the cosmic framework was often given a moral or intellectual interpretation by medieval writers, but it was usually seen in positive terms: Alan of Lille, for example, saw it as an analogue to the necessary domination of reason over the senses (*De Planctu Naturae* pr. 3.52–65 (ed. Häring, pp. 826–7; tr. Sheridan, pp. 119–20). Although even so prosaic a work as Sacrobosco's treatise 'On the Sphere' uses terms such as 'rapit' ('hurls') of the Primum Mobile and 'nitentibus' ('striving against') of the other spheres, which might have yielded the sense of violence implicit in Chaucer's 'crowdest' and 'hurlest' (J. C. Eade, *SAC*, 4 (1982), 53–85, at pp. 78–9), his stanza is still highly unusual in seeing the operation of the Primum Mobile as 'cruel'. It is also strictly speaking inaccurate, in that the Primum Mobile's motion does not affect the positions of the planets in relation to each other. The passage is best interpreted as poetic imagery rather than as scientific explanation; see Mann, 'Parents and Children', pp. 169–71.

302–8 Despite the technical terminology of this stanza, its account of the position of the heavens at Constance's departure, and the reasons why it blighted her marriage, is highly unspecific (Eade, as cited in previous note, pp. 76–82). The 'ascendant' is the sign of the zodiac appearing on the eastern horizon (at the point where it intersects the ecliptic) at any given moment; the 'lord of the ascendant' is the planet whose power was thought to be increased by that sign (see *Astrol* II.4). The sign referred to here is 'tortuous' – that is, it is one of the six that rise obliquely to the horizon (see *Astrol* II.28). Astrologers divided the celestial sphere into twelve segments known as 'houses' (to be distinguished from the houses of the planets, which are signs of the zodiac that increase the power of the particular planet to which they are assigned). The houses were numbered counterclockwise from the eastern horizon, and were of three types: angles (houses 1, 4, 7 and 10), succedents (2, 5, 8 and 11) and cadents (3, 6, 9 and 12; see Wood, pp. 221–2, 304–5). The last of these houses, which lay immediately above the eastern horizon, was called *carcer* or 'prison', and this is probably what is meant by the 'derkest hous'. The planet who is lord of the ascendant has fallen from one of the 'angles' into the twelfth house, *carcer*, with disastrous effects. As Eade points out (p. 80), this means that the lord of the ascendant cannot be identified with Mars, invoked in line 305, since he is a maleficent planet, and his loss of influence would therefore have beneficial results (cf. *Astrol* II.4.30–40); all that can be said is that Mars is somehow exerting baneful influence. The word 'atazir' is a technical term referring to a procedure for checking the directions in which good and evil influences fell (North, *Chaucer's Universe*, pp. 225–8).

For an interpretation of this scientific terminology in terms of its function in relation to the narrative motifs of the Man of Law's Tale, see Mann, 'Parents and Children', pp. 171–3.

309–14 A Latin gloss in the margin of many manuscripts (including Hg and El) at this point reads: 'All are agreed that elections are weak unless in the case of the rich, for they (although their elections are weakened) have a root (that is, their nativity) which strengthens every weak planet in its course, et cetera.' This is the opening of a Latin translation of the treatise *On Elections* by the ninth-century Jewish writer Zahel Benbriz (on whose works see F. J. Carmody, *Arabic Astronomical and Astrological Sciences in Latin Translation: A Critical Bibliography* (Berkeley, CA, 1956), pp. 40–41). An 'election' is the choice of a favourable time for undertaking an enterprise; the 'roote ... of a burthe' is the position of the heavenly bodies at the time of one's birth, which would exercise influence one way or another over later astrological configurations. Only the rich would be able to afford to pay experts to make the calculations necessary to determine their 'root', and so to make reasonably reliable elections.

In his *Treatise on the Astrolabe* (II.4), Chaucer mentions nativities and elections as part of judicial astrology (the attempt to determine planetary influence on human affairs), which he rejects as pagan rites, in which 'my spirit hath no feith'; in MLT, however, as elsewhere in his work, he makes poetic use of the concept of astrological influence as appropriate to the pagan world of his narrative.

325 The reference to 'sacrifices' shows Chaucer's vagueness about Islamic practices, which do not include anything of the sort. Medieval writers in general tended to collapse Islam and classical paganism into one (heathen figures swear indiscriminately by Mohammed, Jupiter and Apollo), and it is probably the religious rites of ancient Rome that Chaucer has in mind here.

330–40 The Sultaness's stirring affirmation of her faith has no parallel in Trevet or in Gower.

359 *Semirame*: Semiramis, legendary queen of the Assyrians, assumed rule over the empire after her husband's death. Since her son was only a boy, she disguised herself in masculine clothes and took on his identity, leading the armies in his place and extending the

empire through conquest. A famous anecdote relates that when news was brought to her, as her maids were plaiting her hair, that Babylon had rebelled against her, she straightway sallied forth with one side of her hair still unplaited, and brought the city under her subjection. Her manly vigour is emphasized by Boccaccio, *De mulieribus claris* (*Concerning Famous Women*, tr. Guarino), ch. 2; Chaucer thus compares her to the Sultaness, in whom feminine qualities are likewise suppressed.

360 Chaucer may have had in mind the medieval tradition that the serpent who brought about the Fall of Eve had a woman's face (cf. *PPl* XVIII.336–9). He may also have been thinking of the enmity between the serpent and the woman decreed by God as a result of the Fall (Genesis 3:15; cf. Revelation 12:4–17), an allusion which would give this line a paradoxical character.

361 'And I saw an angel come down from heaven, having the key of the bottomless pit, and a great chain in his hand. And he laid hold on the dragon the old serpent, which is the devil and Satan, and bound him for a thousand years' (Revelation 20:1–2). See also 2 Peter 2:4, Jude 1:6, and the gospel of Nicodemus (*Apocryphal NT*, pp. 134–5).

365–6 *envious*: According to St Augustine (*Enchiridion* IX.29, CCSL 46, p. 65), God created mankind to replace the tenth order of angels who fell from heaven with Satan (cf. *South English Legendary* II, 'St Michael', lines 210–14; Dante, *Convivio* II.5.12; and Gower, *CA* VIII.21–36); Satan's implacable hatred for mankind was thus motivated by envy for man, who was destined to inherit the glory he had lost. This idea is commonplace in patristic thought; in addition to the references given by T. Fry, *SP*, 48 (1951), 527–70, at p. 540, n. 43, see Augustine, *Enarrationes in Psalmos* CXXXIX.8 (CCSL 40, p. 2017), and Cassian, *Collationes* VIII.9–10 (CSEL 13, pp. 225–7). For occurrences of the idea in ME, see *The N-Town Plays*, ed. S. Spector, 2 vols. (Oxford, 1991), Play 2, 235–42, and *Wisdom* 325–8, in *The Macro Plays*, ed. M. Eccles (Oxford, 1969).

400–401 The *Pharsalia* of Lucan (AD 39–65), which recounts the civil war between Julius Caesar and Pompey, refers only briefly to Caesar's triumph as something that *might* have been glorious had he not fought against a fellow-Roman (III.73–9). J. L. Lowes (see Robinson's note to ML 400) suggested that Chaucer might have been thinking of the French prose version of Lucan by Jehan de Tuim (13th c.); the general form of a Roman triumph is described early in this work, and it concludes with a brief account of Caesar's triumph after the death of Pompey and his election as emperor of Rome (*Li Hystore de Julius Cesar*, ed. F. Settegast (Halle, 1881), pp. 8–10, 244–5). An even more likely possibility is that Chaucer was thinking of the French prose history *Li Fet des Romains* (*c.* 1213–14), a compilation of Lucan, Suetonius and Sallust, which survives in around 50 manuscripts (as opposed to only four for Jehan de Tuim's work). This work too gives a brief general account of a triumph (I.9[2]), but more relevant is that it reproduces Suetonius's account of the five triumphs, four of them in the space of a single month, that Caesar held on his return to Rome at the end of the civil war (IV.1[1]). Cf. n. to Mk 2671–2726. The compiler, who frequently names his sources, does not, however, make clear that Lucan's narrative had ended shortly before this point and he is now relying on Suetonius; Chaucer might therefore have gained the impression that the source was still Lucan.

421–7 As a Latin gloss in El and Hg (and other MSS) makes clear, this rhetorical interpolation is based on a section (I.21) of the *De Miseria Condicionis Humane* of Pope Innocent III (see n. to ML 99–121). Innocent's section incorporates a number of biblical quotations, which are also identifiable in Chaucer; thus line 424 echoes Proverbs 14:13 (cf. NP 3205), and lines 426–7 echo Ecclesiasticus 11:27. Line 422 echoes the wording of Chaucer's *Boece* II pr.4.118–19.

451–62 The wording of this prayer echoes the last verse of a famous Latin hymn ('Pange, lingua, gloriosi proelium certaminis') of Venantius Fortunatus (6th c.), which was sung during the last two weeks of Lent, on Good Friday, and at the feast of the Invention of the Cross: 'You alone [i.e., the Cross] were worthy to bear the treasure of the world, and, like a sailor, to provide a harbour for the shipwrecked world, you who were anointed with the holy blood of the Lamb, poured from his body' (*Opera Poetica*, ed. F. Leo (Berlin, 1881), II.ii). The nautical metaphor in these lines harmonizes with the narrative imagery of MLT.

464–5 *See of Grece*: The eastern Mediterranean. Constance's boat takes her westward from Syria all the way across the Mediterranean and through the straits of Gibraltar ('the Straite of Marrok'). She must then sail up the west coast of Spain and France, eastward through the Channel, and up the east coast of England, to arrive, finally, in Northumberland (508).

473–5 For the biblical story of Daniel in the lions' den, see Daniel 6:16–24.

477–83 Cf. Romans 11:33, also echoed at Mel 1406–7.

486–7 Chaucer is slightly misremembering the biblical story of Jonah: the whale did not cast Jonah up at Nineveh, but simply 'upon the dry land' (Jonah 2:11). God then commanded him for the second time to go to Nineveh and denounce the wickedness of its people, which he did.

489–90 When Moses was leading the Israelites out of Egypt, the waters of the Red Sea parted to allow them to pass through, but returned to drown the pursuing Egyptians (Exodus 14:21–31).

491–4 The command to the four angels holding the four winds of the earth to 'Hurt not the earth, nor the sea, nor the trees' is given by a fifth angel in Revelation 7:1–3; Chaucer may also have had in mind Christ's stilling of the tempest in Mark 4:39.

500–501 St Mary of Egypt (?5th c.) was a penitent prostitute who lived a hermit's life in the desert for 37 years, eating only weeds (*Golden Legend*, I, 227–9). Her legend was very popular in the Middle Ages.

502–3 Christ's miraculous feeding of 5,000 people with five loaves and two fishes is described in all four Gospels (Matthew 14:14–21, Mark 6:34–44, Luke 9:13–17, John 6:1–14).

519 Trevet's Constance is proficient in languages, and she therefore speaks to the constable in 'Saxon'. In changing his source and having Constance speak 'a kind of corrupt Latin', Chaucer is perhaps aiming at historical authenticity, but he may also have wished to emphasize the isolation which is characteristic of his heroine's situation throughout the tale.

534–46 *payens*: Chaucer's account of Britain is a more accurate representation of the situation in the sixth century than his account of Syria. After the fall of the Roman Empire, Britain was invaded by heathen Saxons, who drove the Christian Britains westwards into Wales.

578 *Alla*: Trevet here incorporates into his fictional narrative a historical king, Aelle of Deira (roughly equivalent to modern Yorkshire, not Northumberland), who reigned 560–88.

617 Cf. Cl 537–8 and n.

634 Christ's binding of Satan is the conclusion of his Harrowing of Hell, as described in the apocryphal gospel of Nicodemus (*Apocryphal NT*, pp. 185–6).

639–40 *Susanne*: The story of Susanna, who was falsely accused of adultery by two elders when she refused their sexual advances, and was saved from death by the prophet Daniel, is told in an appendix to Daniel (ch. 13) included in the Vulgate version of the Bible.

641 Mary's mother is named as Anna in the apocryphal gospel known as the Book of James (*Apocryphal NT*, pp. 38–49).

659 In both Trevet and Gower, Alla is not present when Constance is accused; he arrives only after she has been miraculously exculpated and so has no role in her preservation.

666 *A Briton book . . . Evangiles*: Chaucer's narrative does not make clear why a copy of the Gospels was so readily to hand in a pagan country, nor why a pagan knight should be required to swear on this Christian book. Trevet, who generally tries to disguise the overall implausibility of the narrative with circumstantial detail, explains that the book was present in the bedroom because Constance and Hermengild had been using it in their devotions; he had earlier related that the knight who accuses Constance had been baptized along with the rest of the constable's household, thus making it natural for him to swear on the Gospels.

701–2 The wheat/chaff metaphor is conventional; see Whiting C428, and cf. NP 3443 and n., Pars 35–6 and *LGW* G 312, 529.

710 Chaucer is probably punning on the word 'patience', since Latin *patientia* is a technical term for the female role in sexual intercourse (J. N. Adams, *The Latin Sexual Vocabulary* (London, 1982), pp. 189–90; see also Mann, *Feminizing Chaucer*, p. 126).

771–7 This stanza is another of the borrowings in this tale from Innocent III's *De Miseria* (II.19); see n. to ML 99–121.

784 Dante asserts that an evil person 'is dead though he appears to be alive . . . Someone might ask: how can he be dead yet walking around? My reply is: he is dead as a man, but he continues to live as a beast' (*Convivio* IV.7, tr. Ryan, pp. 138–9; cf. *Inferno* XXXIII.122–47). In Trevet, Domild's forged letters accuse Constance of being an evil spirit in the form of a woman (*Originals and Analogues*, p. 26).

813–16 The constable echoes Boethius's questioning of God's justice at the opening of the *Consolation of Philosophy*:

> O thou governour, governynge alle thynges by certein ende, whi refusestow oonly to governe the werkes of men by duwe manere? Why suffrestow that slydynge Fortune turneth so grete enterchaungynges of thynges? So that anoyous peyne, that scholde duweliche punysche felons, punyssheth innocentz; and folk of

> wikkide maneres sitten in heie chayeres; and anoyinge folk treden,
> and that unrightfully, on the nekkes of holi men . . .
>
> *(Boece* I m.5.31–40)

Boethius's image of mankind 'turmented in this see of fortune'
(54) finds concrete realization in the narrative of MLT.

845–7 Patristic writers interpreted Simeon's prophecy to Mary that
'a sword shall pierce through thy own soul also' (Luke 2:35) as
referring to her grief at the Crucifixion; medieval writers suggested that, although she gave birth painlessly, the pain she
suffered at the Crucifixion equalled the pangs of childbirth (K.
Lochrie, *Margery Kempe and the Translations of the Flesh* (Philadelphia, PA, 1991), pp. 178–81).

852 *haven of refut . . . sterre of day*: The phrase 'haven of refut' is
also used at SN 75, and in Chaucer's translation of Deguileville's
prayer to the Virgin (*An ABC*, line 14, translating 'de salu porte',
Pèlerinage de la vie humaine, ed. J. J. Stürzinger, London, n.d.,
line 10,907). 'Harbour' (*portus*) and 'morning star' (*stella
matutina*) are traditional appellations of the Virgin; see Salzer,
Sinnbilder, pp. 401, 528–31.

921–2 In Trevet, Constance manages to throw the would-be rapist
overboard by a trick, rather than by main force; in Gower, she
likewise tricks him but he is thrown overboard by divine agency.

925–31 This stanza is another of the borrowings in this tale from
Innocent III's *De Miseria* (II.21); see n. to ML 99–121.

934–6 *Golias*: The slaying of the Philistine giant Goliath by the boy
David is related in 1 Samuel 17:4–51.

939–42 The book of Judith in the Vulgate version of the Bible relates
how the Assyrian captain Holofernes was decapitated by the
Israelite widow Judith in order to save her people. See also Mk
2551–74 and n., and cf. Mch 1366–8.

947 *Septe*: The name of a ridge of seven peaks, called 'the seven
brothers' (*Septem fratres*) in former Spanish Morocco, opposite
Gibraltar ('Jubaltare'). Constance's journey now takes her back
over the course she had travelled earlier (see n. to ML 464–5),
through the Straits of Gibraltar into the Mediterranean and
towards Rome.

1086–92 Trevet and Gower both state that Maurice was sent as
messenger to the Emperor, but since in Trevet he is explicitly
said to be in his eighteenth year, the objection Chaucer makes
here is groundless. Is this too an instance of Chaucer mildly
teasing Gower? (cf. n. to ML 77–85).

1088–91 *so nice . . . Sente*: A modern reader would expect 'that he' before 'sente', but omission of the subject pronoun is more usual in ME than in modern English.

1121–2 These lines constitute a fragile link with real historical events, since there was a Roman Emperor called Maurice in the late sixth century (AD 582–602). However, he was not the son of a Saxon king, but was born to a Roman family in Cappadocia, and his claim to the imperial succession was not based on his descent from the Emperor's daughter, but on his marriage to Constantia, the daughter of the Emperor Tiberius Constantinus. Furthermore, neither Maurice nor his predecessor ruled from Rome, since the site of imperial government had been transferred to Constantinople (present-day Istanbul) two centuries earlier. As noted above (n. to ML 134), it was only after Maurice's death that Syria passed into Muslim hands, so that in his (and *a fortiori*, his mother's) day, it would have been part of the Roman Empire and an officially Christian country.

1126–7 Maurice's life does not appear in the *Gesta Romanorum*, nor in any other identifiable 'olde Romain gestes', so this statement must be taken as no more than a vague gesture towards historiography in general. As R. A. Pratt pointed out (*Studies in Language, Literature and Culture of the Middle Ages*, ed. E. B. Atwood and A. A. Hill (Austin, TX, 1969), pp. 303–4), the running title of the last part of Trevet's *Chronicle* is 'les gestes des aposteles, emperours, et rois'; however, the section covering Maurice's reign is mostly devoted to the history of the Church, and includes almost no account of his own activities (see, for example, London, BL, MS Arundel 56, ff. 51v–52r).

1132–4 A marginal gloss in Hg, El and many other MSS quotes Ecclesiasticus 18:26 and Job 21:12 (with an 'etc' that implies inclusion of 21:13 also); both texts speak of sudden changes in human fortunes.

1135–8 These lines are based on a passage of Innocent III's *De Miseria* (I.20; see n. to ML 99–121), but the lines that precede and follow them in ML give them a haunting melancholy which is quite different from Innocent's preacherly tone.

THE MAN OF LAW'S EPILOGUE

1163–90 This link is not found in either El or Hg, but appears in 35 other MSS; the text here is based on Oxford, Corpus Christi College, MS 198. It is possible that it is a spurious link created by a particularly clever scribe, but its length and complexity are greater than this purely functional purpose would require, and its subject-matter includes the characteristically Chaucerian theme of 'glosinge' (see J. Mann, *PBA*, 76 (1990), 203–23, and Introduction, pp. xxxv–xxxvi). A further difficulty is created by variation in the identification of the next tale-teller in line 1179: 28 MSS read 'Squier', six read 'Sommonour/Sompnour' and one (late) MS reads 'Shipman'; in each case, the appropriate tale follows. However, both the Squire and the Summoner are firmly identified as tale-tellers elsewhere (see Sq 1–8 and Sum 1665–1708), and are the less likely to have been introduced here. The uncertain identification has been linked with the Man of Law's statement that he will speak in prose (see n. to ML 96), and the indication that the teller of the Shipman's Tale is a woman (see n. to Sh 12), and interpreted as evidence of changes in Chaucer's assignment of tales to tellers. Since the Wife of Bath's Prologue follows the Man of Law's Tale in El and other manuscripts, and the robust tone of the Man of Law's Epilogue fits the Wife of Bath's voice, it has been suggested that she was the pilgrim originally mentioned here, and that the Shipman's tale was originally told by the Wife and followed the Man of Law's Tale, while Melibee was assigned to the Man of Law (see R. F. Jones, *JEGP*, 24 (1925), 512–47; R. A. Pratt, *PMLA*, 66 (1951), 1141–67; W. W. Lawrence, *Speculum*, 33 (1958), 56–68). Supposedly, Chaucer then gave the Man of Law the tale of Constance, reassigned Melibee to himself, gave the Wife a new Prologue and Tale, and transferred her previous tale to the Shipman. However, this does not explain why a hypothetical reading 'Wife of Bath' should have been erased in line 1179, since the link would still have been a perfectly good introduction to the Wife of Bath's Prologue.

An alternative theory is that line 1179 originally read 'Shipman', and that the Epilogue was cancelled when Chaucer decided to move the position of the Shipman's Tale, possibly to break up the concentration of fabliaux in the early part of *CT*; at an even earlier stage he might have transferred the Shipman's Tale from the Wife of Bath to the Shipman, possibly in order to achieve a contrast between the Wife's comic persona and the serious nature of the tale she tells.

The Epilogue is here set in italics, as most probably an authentic piece of Chaucerian writing, but one that he had discarded from *CT* as his plans evolved (see E. T. Donaldson, in *Medieval*

Literature and Folklore Studies: Essays in Honor of Francis Lee Utley, ed. J. Mandel and B. A. Rosenberg (New Brunswick, NJ, 1970), pp. 193–204, 363–7, at p. 202).

1173 *Loller*: The Lollards were members of a religious movement associated with John Wyclif, whose views concerning the Eucharist, the authority of the clergy and other religious matters were condemned as heretical in 1382. See *English Historical Documents, Vol. IV: 1327–1485*, ed. A. R. Myers (London, 1969), pp. 844–8, and Hudson, *Wycliffite Writings*. Disapproval of swearing was not, however, confined to Lollards (cf. Pard 631–59); the Host is simply interpreting any direct expression of moral reproof as a sign of religious fanaticism. Since Lollards disapproved of pilgrimages, it would have been unlikely that one of their number would be found among the Canterbury pilgrims. Chaucer himself had friends at court who were Lollard sympathizers (J. A. Tuck, *SAC Proceedings*, 1 (1984), 149–61), and would therefore have been well acquainted with their views.

Anti-Lollard sentiments gained the ascendancy in the last years of the fourteenth century, culminating in 1401 in the bill *De haeretico comburendo*, which imposed death by burning as a punishment for heresy (see A. Hudson, *The Premature Reformation: Wycliffite Texts and Lollard History* (Oxford, 1988), p. 15). Thus it is possible that the reference to Lollardy was the reason why the Epilogue was prudently omitted from some manuscripts (see preceding n.)

1180 'Glosinge' was the practice of interpreting Scripture, and was often regarded with suspicion because it allowed for the imposition of meanings which suited the interpreter's interests. Friars, whose association with the universities made them particularly adept in textual exegesis, were often associated with specious 'glosinge'; SumT provides an excellent example of one such friar (see Introduction, pp. xxxv–xxxvi). Again, the accusation is an unfair representation of Lollards, who preferred a literal interpretation of the biblical text.

1183 The reference is to Matthew 13:24–30, the parable of the man who sowed tares in his enemy's wheat-field. Traditionally this parable was interpreted as a reference to the presence of heretics among the faithful; since the Latin word for 'tares' is *lolium*, it was specially appropriate to Lollards. See P. F. Braude, in *No Graven Images: Studies in Art and the Hebrew Bible*, ed. J. Gutmann (New York, 1971), pp. 559–99, esp. p. 560.

1189 *phislyas*: A nonce-word, which may be due to scribal corruption of an unrecoverable original, or may represent the (presumably) uneducated speaker's garbled reproduction of a learned term (see R. C. Goffin, *MLR*, 18 (1923), 335–6, for a suggestion).

THE WIFE OF BATH'S PROLOGUE

The Wife of Bath's Prologue is the first in a series of contributions (comprising also her tale, and the tales of the Clerk, Merchant, Squire and Franklin) traditionally known as the 'Marriage Group', since G. L. Kittredge argued that it initiates a debate on whether the man or the woman should have the upper hand in marriage, a debate which is satisfactorily resolved by the 'mutual love and forbearance' between Dorigen and Arveragus in the Franklin's Tale; see Kittredge, *MP*, 9 (1912), 435–67; repr. in E. Wagenknecht, *Chaucer: Essays in Criticism* (Oxford, 1959). Kittredge was, however, unable to explain the intrusion of the Friar's Tale and Summoner's Tale into this group as anything other than a 'comic interlude'. For an argument that the theme running through these tales is not marriage but patience, together with its opposites, 'maistrye', 'ire' and 'glosinge', see J. Mann, *PBA*, 76 (1990), 203–23; the tales of the Friar and Summoner form a natural part of the group as tales of 'ire' and 'glosinge', and also as tales which result from the 'ire' between the Friar and the Summoner. This view also enables links to be established between those tales and others which treat these themes outside the context of marital relations.

The autobiographical mode of the Wife of Bath's Prologue has a forerunner in the reminiscences of La Vieille (the Old Woman), who is set to guard Bel Acueil (Fair Welcome), representative of the lady's good will to the Lover, in the *Romance of the Rose* (12731–918, tr. Horgan, pp. 197–9). Like the Wife, La Vieille knows the 'old dance' of love from experience (GP 476; cf. *RR* 3908j), and also like her, she relishes the memory of her youthful frivolity and regrets the advance of age (see n. to WB 469–75). But whereas La Vieille goes on to catalogue the treachery of men, and to instruct Bel Acueil in the arts by which they may be deluded in turn (12971–14426), the Wife cheerfully engages in direct attacks on men, whether intellectual or personal.

The first part of the Wife's Prologue is devoted to a vigorous discussion of the legitimacy of marrying more than once, and on the relative merits of marriage and virginity. Her invisible antagonist in this argument is St Jerome (*c.* 350–420), who wrote a polemical treatise refuting the view of his contemporary Jovinian that sexual abstinence was in no way superior to wedded life in the sight of God. Later in the Prologue (674–5) we are told that Jerome's treatise formed part of the collection owned by the Wife's fifth husband. Jerome's *Against Jovinian* has been translated in its entirety by W. H. Fremantle (see Abbreviated References); excerpts from Fremantle's translation which are particularly relevant to the Wife of Bath's Prologue are reprinted in Miller, pp. 417–36. In the following notes, references are given to the Book and section numbers of the Latin version of Jerome's text in *PL* 23, cols. 211–338, to which both translations are keyed. The Wife's argument sometimes repeats points made by Jovinian, but sometimes appropriates Jerome's own points and turns them against him (see nn. to WB 99–101 and 143–4). In general, her method of using biblical texts in a way that suits her interests is very similar to Jerome's own style of interpretation (and her arguments cannot therefore be disqualified on methodological grounds), although distinguished from it by its playful and comic tone; a similar playfulness with textual 'authorities' characterizes the tradition of comic-satiric Latin verse known as 'Goliardic' poetry; see J. Mann, in *Writers and their Background: Geoffrey Chaucer*, ed. D. Brewer (London, 1974; repr. Cambridge, 1990), pp. 172–83.

Jerome's *Against Jovinian* also plays an important role in the second part of the Wife's Prologue (224–450), her account of how she bullied her three old husbands. In order to press home the advantages of chastity, Jerome had quoted extensively from a 'golden book' (*Liber aureolus*) written by a pagan called Theophrastus (otherwise unknown), who vividly described the disadvantages of married life. This portion of Jerome's treatise became a staple element in medieval antifeminist writings (see nn. to WB 235–45 and 248–302). The Wife of Bath's sample of the tirades she inflicted on her husbands draws heavily on this Theophrastan model and its later reflexes in medieval literature.

In the last part of her Prologue, the Wife tells of her marriage to her fifth husband Jankin, a clerk, who tormented her by reading aloud from his 'book of wicked wives', a collection of antifeminist material containing, along with other items, the texts of Jerome and Theophrastus already mentioned, and Walter Map's *Dissuasio Valerii ad Rufinum* (see nn. to WB 671–80). For an edition and translation of the *Dissuasio*, Theophrastus, and relevant passages of Jerome, together with a full discussion of the manuscript tradition in which these texts were linked, see Hanna and Lawler, *Jankyn's Book*. Useful selections from the antifeminist tradition are also anthologized in *SA*² II, in Miller (pp. 397–473) and in *Woman Defamed and Woman*

Defended: An Anthology of Medieval Texts, ed. A. Blamires, with
K. Pratt and C. W. Marx (Oxford, 1992).

1-2   La Vieille likewise claims that experience, not theoretical instruc-
       tion, has made her sufficiently knowledgeable about love to give
       lectures on the subject (*RR* 12771–90, tr. Horgan, p. 197).
       For a similar contrast between experience and authority, see Kn
       3000–3001.

4   Twelve was the legal age of consent to marriage for girls.

6   *at chirche-dore*: See n. to GP 460.

7   There were no legal restraints on the number of times a widow
       could remarry in fourteenth-century England (see J. A. Brundage,
       in *Wife and Widow in Medieval England*, ed. S. Sheridan Walker
       (Ann Arbor, MI, 1993), pp. 17–31), and the Wife's defensiveness
       on this point is therefore unnecessary. But St Jerome, like St Paul,
       had argued that celibacy was preferable to remarriage (*Against
       Jov.* I.14–15), and he must therefore be taken as the butt of her
       arguments.

10-13 At a marriage feast in 'Cana of Galilee', Christ performed his
       first miracle by turning water into wine (John 2:1–11). Jerome
       develops the argument that 'by going once to a marriage, [Christ]
       taught that men should marry only once' (*Against Jov.* I.40).

14-19 For Christ's encounter with a Samaritan woman at Jacob's
       well, see John 4:5–30; the words quoted by the Wife are Christ's
       response to the woman's statement 'I have no husband'. Jerome
       misquotes the exchange in using it as an argument against marry-
       ing more than once: 'it is better to know a single husband, though
       he be a second or third, than to have many paramours . . . At all
       events this is so if the Samaritan woman in John's Gospel who
       said she had her sixth husband was reproved by the Lord because
       he was not her husband. For where there are more husbands
       than one the proper idea of a husband, who is a single person, is
       destroyed' (*Against Jov.* I.14).

26   On 'glosinge', see n. to ML 1180.

28   Jovinian had likewise quoted God's command 'Increase and mul-
       tiply, and fill the earth' (Genesis 1:28) in support of marriage
       (Jerome, *Against Jov.* I.5); Jerome's response to this text is, 'while
       we honour marriage, we prefer virginity' (I.3), and 'marriage
       replenishes the earth, virginity fills Paradise' (I.16).

30-31 The Wife is quoting Christ's words at Matthew 19:5 ('For this
       cause shall a man leave father and mother, and shall cleave to
       his wife', quoted by St Paul at Ephesians 5:31), a text also invoked

by Jovinian (Jerome, *Against Jov.* I.5; for Jerome's comments, see I.16).

32–3 Jerome states 'I do not condemn second, nor third, nor, pardon the expression, eighth marriages (*octogamos*)', but qualifies this by quoting 1 Corinthians 6:12: 'All things are lawful . . . but all things are not expedient' (*Against Jov.* I.15).

35–6 *Salomon*: At 1 Kings 11:3, Solomon is said to have had 700 wives and 300 concubines, which earns him the title of 'lechour' at Mch 2298. Solomon is cited as an example in support of marriage by Jovinian (Jerome, *Against Jov.* I.5; cf. Jerome's comments at I.24).

44a–f These lines are not in El or Hg, and are found in only seventeen witnesses (fourteen MSS and three early printed editions). The text here is based on Cambridge, University Library, MS Dd.4.24. Manly and Rickert (II, 191–4; III, 454–5) suggest that, along with other lines in WBPr which are found in El (and a limited number of other MSS) but not in Hg (575–84, 609–12, 619–26, 717–20), they were 'later insertions by Chaucer himself in a single MS', whence they were borrowed by others. They reject the (nevertheless plausible) suggestion that their absence elsewhere may (except in the case of lines 717–20) be attributed to bowdlerization (by Chaucer or someone else) by pointing out that lines 613–18, which are of a similar nature to 609–12 and 619–26, are generally allowed to stand in the manuscripts (II, 191). Hanna (*Pursuing History*, p. 153) accounts for the absence of these passages in Hg by the supposition that it represents an earlier version of the text, while El represents a later version incorporating revisions (although it is also theoretically possible that the passages survived in El because they were imperfectly marked for cancellation in the exemplar). E. Solopova's analysis of the manuscript transmission of these passages leads to the same conclusion (*The Canterbury Tales Project Occasional Papers*, ed. N. Blake and P. Robinson, vol. II (London, 1997), pp. 133–42). Their length and relative complexity make it unlikely that they were added by a misogynistic scribe, as argued by B. Kennedy (*ChauR*, 30 (1996), 343–58; see also her article in *Rewriting Chaucer*, ed. Prendergast and Kline, pp. 203–33).

Lines 44a–f are the weakest, and the least certainly Chaucerian, of the added passages, but the concept of 'scoleying' (a word that gave trouble to the scribes, and therefore speaks against scribal composition) fits the Wife's tendency to mimic clerical language and techniques, and argues for the authenticity of these lines. For a parallel to this representation of women's lore as the equivalent of a unversity education, see *RR* 13469–86, tr. Horgan, p. 208. The idea expressed in lines 44c–e is repeated at Mch 1427–8.

49–50 'The Apostle' is St Paul, whose first Epistle to the Corinthians answers their enquiries about the acceptability of marrying. Paul's clearly expressed preference is for virginity or chastity, but he acknowledges that marriage is not sinful and is a safeguard against fornication, which is. He is therefore appealed to both by Jerome, for whom he is 'the bravest of generals' leading the attack on Jovinian (*Against Jov.* I.6), and by Jovinian, who quotes the passage here borrowed by the Wife: 'A woman is bound by the law as long as her husband liveth; but if her husband die, she is at liberty. Let her marry whom she will, only in the Lord' (1 Corinthians 7:39; cf. *Against Jov.* I.5).

51–2 The Wife is quoting St Paul accurately, but in each case is leaving aside a prefatory remark which indicates that marriage is a second-best option: 'I say to the unmarried, and to the widows: It is good for them if they so continue, even as I. But if they do not contain themselves, let them marry. For it is better to marry than to burn' (1 Corinthians 7:8–9; discussed by Jerome, *Against Jov.* I.7, 9); 'Art thou loosed from a wife? seek not a wife. But if thou take a wife, thou hast not sinned. And if a virgin marry, she hath not sinned' (1 Corinthians 7:27–8; discussed by Jerome, *Against Jov.* I.13).

54–8 *Lameth*: According to Jerome, Jovinian had also cited the multiple wives of Old Testament figures, including Lamech, Abraham, and Jacob, as evidence of God's approval of marriage (*Against Jov.* I.5; see further I.14, 19). Lamech's two wives are mentioned in Genesis 4:19–23 (cf. Sq 550–51 and *Anel* 150–53). Because Abraham's wife Sarah was childless, she urged him to take her maid Hagar as a second wife (11:29–30; 16); after Sarah's death, he took a third wife, Keturah (25:1). Jacob had four wives: Leah, Rachel, and their maids Bilhah and Zilpah (29:15–30:24).

64–5 'Now concerning virgins, I have no commandment of the Lord; but I give counsel, as having obtained mercy of the Lord, to be faithful' (1 Corinthians 7:25). Jerome launches a violent attack on Jovinian's use of this text as a 'battering-ram' to shake 'the walls of virginity' (*Against Jov.* I.12).

71–2 The Wife borrows this point from Jovinian, as quoted by St Jerome: 'If the Lord had commanded virginity He would have seemed to condemn marriage, and to do away with the seed-plot of mankind, of which virginity itself is a growth' (*Against Jov.* I.12). In the *Romance of the Rose*, Nature's priest Genius argues along similar lines (19553–98, tr. Horgan, p. 302).

75–6 The image of the race, with virginity as prize, is borrowed from St Jerome (who borrowed it from St Paul, 1 Corinthians 9:24): 'The Master of the Christian race offers the reward, invites candidates to the course, holds in His Hand the prize of virginity, points to the fountain of purity, and cries aloud "If any man thirst, let him come unto me and drink"' (*Against Jov.* I.12). The Wife refuses to let her competitive instincts be aroused.

Cacche whoso may: Proverbial (see Whiting C112).

80–90 The Wife is quoting St Paul's words, but reversing the thrust of what he says:

> It is good for a man not to touch a woman [cf. line 87]. But for fear of fornication, let every man have his own wife, and let every woman have her own husband [cf. lines 83–4]. Let the husband render the debt to his wife, and the wife also in like manner to the husband . . . But I speak this by indulgence, not by commandment. For I would that all men were even as myself [cf. lines 80–82].
>
> (1 Corinthians 7:1–7)

For Jerome's use of this passage in support of virginity, see *Against Jov.* I.7–9.

89 Proverbial; see Whiting F182. The stimulus for the analogy may be Jerome's comment on the same verse of Paul (1 Corinthians 7:1): 'As then he who touches fire is instantly burned, so by the mere touch the peculiar nature of man and woman is perceived' (*Against Jov.* I.7).

99–101 'We know that in a great house, there are not only vessels of gold and silver, but also of wood and earthenware' (Jerome, *Against Jov.* I.3; cf. I.40. Jerome borrows the image from 2 Timothy 2:20). Jerome is allowing marriage its own worthiness, but stressing the superior values of virginity; the Wife appropriates his metaphor and slants it in the opposite direction.

103–4 The Wife is again quoting St Paul: 'but every one hath his proper gift from God; one after this manner, and another after that' (1 Corinthians 7:7), but in context St Paul's comment has a rather different slant (see n. to WB 80–90).

107–12 A rich young man who asked Jesus what he should do to have eternal life was told, 'If thou wilt be perfect, go sell what thou hast, and give to the poor, and thou shalt have treasure in heaven: and come follow me' (Matthew 19:21); the incident is cited by St Jerome when he is explaining that the apostles did not impose sexual abstinence on gentile believers because not everyone is capable of perfection (*Against Jov.* I.34).

115–18 Jerome represents Jovinian as posing the same question: 'Why then, you will say, were the organs of generation created, and why were we so fashioned by the all-wise creator, that we burn for one another, and long for natural intercourse?' (*Against Jov.* I.36).

117 wright*] wight El Hg. The emendation to 'wright' was proposed by E. T. Donaldson, *Speaking of Chaucer* (London, 1970), pp. 119–30; the El/Hg reading is defended by R. F. Green, *NQ*, 241 (1996), 259–61.

129–30 *dette*: The idea that sexual intercourse was a 'debt' (*debitum*) which each marital partner might claim of the other goes back to St Paul (1 Corinthians 7:3–4), and was widely accepted in the Middle Ages as one of the few legitimizations of sexual activity (cf. Pars 375, 940).

139 Jerome cites Christ as the supreme instance of the principle that the possession of sexual members carries no obligation to use them in sexual activity (*Against Jov.* I.36).

143–4 Jerome had sought to recommend virginity by comparing it to wheat-bread, marriage to barley-bread and fornication to dung; it is better to eat barley-bread than dung, but that does not mean that wheat-bread is not better than barley-bread (*Against Jov.* I.7). The Wife omits the third element of the comparison, and makes the difference between the breads a mere matter of taste.

145–6 The Wife wittily links the barley-bread image used by St Jerome with the 'five barley loaves' used by Christ in the feeding of the five thousand (see n. to ML 502–3). It is not Mark but John (6:9) who specifies that they are barley loaves.

147–8 'Let every man remain in the calling to which he has been called' (1 Corinthians 7:20, quoted by Jerome, *Against Jov.* I.11).

149–53 On the marriage 'debt', see n. to WB 129–30.

155 'He who has a wife is regarded as a debtor, and is said to be uncircumcised, to be the servant of his wife, and like bad servants to be *bound*' (Jerome, *Against Jov.* I.12).

158–61 'The wife hath not power of her own body, but the husband. And in like manner the husband also hath not power of his own body, but the wife' (1 Corinthians 7:4); cf. *Against Jov.* I.7.

165 In accordance with St Paul's directive (1 Timothy 2:12: 'But I

suffer not a woman to teach'), women were forbidden to preach in the Middle Ages.

167   Previous editors have taken 'What' to mean 'Why', but for 'what' as an interjection, cf. WB 311.

170   The reference is to the idea that Jupiter had in his cellar two casks, one full of good, and one full of evil, from which Fortune dispensed sweet or bitter drinks to mankind (*Boece* II pr.2.72–6; *RR* 6783–6804, tr. Horgan, p. 104).

180–83   *Ptholome*: On Ptolemy's *Almagest*, see n. to Mil 3208. The maxim quoted by the Wife is not part of the *Almagest* proper, but is one of a series of moral apophthegms (pithy maxims) in the preface to Gerard of Cremona's Latin translation of the work; these sayings were quoted and attributed to Ptolemy (although not specifically to the *Almagest*) in the *De vita et moribus philosophorum* of Walter Burley (1275–c. 1343), which was used as a school-text (ed. H. Knust (Tübingen, 1886), cap. CXXI). Chaucer's translation is closer to Burley's text ('Qui per alios non corrigitur per ipsum alii corrigentur'; 'He who does not learn from the mistakes of others will become an example from whose mistakes others will learn') than to Gerard's (at least as the latter appears in London, BL, MS Burney 275, and in the 1515 edn printed in Venice), which reads 'non corrigentur' ('will not learn'); see K. Young, *SP*, 34 (1937), 1–7. Chaucer may have taken both text and attribution from Burley, or he may have known a manuscript of Gerard's translation which had the text in the form quoted by Burley. Both versions of the maxim are reflected in the English proverbial tradition, alongside other proverbs on the instructive nature of other people's mistakes (Whiting A118, M170).

198–9   On the marriage 'debt', see n. to WB 129–30. In Deschamps, *Miroir de Mariage* (1576–84), the intending husband is similarly warned that he will find himself unable to pay the marital debt, but this is because of his wife's sexual voracity rather than his own old age.

204   That is, the Wife's husbands had settled property on her as her dower, the gift made by husband to wife at the time of marriage at the church door. The husband kept control of this property while he was alive, but on his death it passed to the wife, and according to English common law she retained it even if she remarried (C. S. Margulies, *Mediaeval Studies*, 24 (1962), 210–16).

217–18   *bacon ... at Donmowe*: At Little Dunmow in Essex, a side of bacon was offered annually to any married couple who had lived together a year and a day without quarrelling. Cf. *PPl* IX.170–72.

227–8 These lines echo *RR* 18106–7: '[women] swear and lie more boldly than any man' (tr. Horgan, p. 279).

232 *cow*: The chough is a talking bird; the allusion is to a widespread story-type in which such a bird tells a husband that it has witnessed his wife's adultery. Chaucer's Manciple's Tale is a story of this sort; for its Ovidian source, see Headnote. Cf. also the story of The Merchant and his Magpie in *The Seven Sages of Rome*, printed from one of the ME versions of this work in *SA*, pp. 716–19.

235–45 These lines are modelled on the sample of female nagging given by Theophrastus in his arguments against marriage, as quoted by St Jerome (*Against Jov.* I.47; for a translation, see Miller, pp. 412–14). See further Headnote. The Theophrastan passage was also reproduced in a number of medieval antifeminist texts, including John of Salisbury, *Policraticus* VIII.11; Pope Innocent III's *De Miseria* I.16; the *Lamentations* of Matheolus, 1107–14 (tr. Jehan le Fèvre, II.1452–9); Deschamps, *Miroir de Mariage*, 1594–1611.

246 *as dronken as a mous*: Proverbial; see Whiting M731, and cf. Kn 1261.

248–302 All these complaints against women are taken from Theophrastus, as quoted by St Jerome (*Against Jov.* I.48; see Miller, pp. 412–14). Cf. Mcp 148–54 and n. Most of them are repeated in John of Salisbury's *Policraticus* (VIII.11), in the speech of the jealous Husband in the *Romance of the Rose* (8531–74, 8631–56, tr. Horgan, pp. 131–3), and in Deschamps, *Miroir de Mariage* (1538–75, 1625–48, 1734–77). The Wife turns the table by using these conventional attacks on women as the weapon with which she attacks her husbands; see Mann, *Feminizing Chaucer*, pp. 60–64.

257–62 The Wife gives examples of what makes women attractive to men; the corresponding passage in Theophrastus (Jerome, *Against Jov.* I.47) gives examples of what makes men attractive to women, but the conclusion (all women are seduced) is the same in each case.

269–70 This sounds proverbial, but no earlier instance is recorded; see Whiting G382.

278–80 Proverbial (Whiting T187, and cf. Mel 1086); also quoted (for example) in Innocent III, *De Miseria* I.16, and the *Lamenta-*

tions of Matheolus, 682–5 (tr. Jehan le Fèvre, II.68–76). The ultimate source is Proverbs 27:15 (which, however, omits the smoke), quoted by St Jerome, *Against Jov.* I.26.

303–5 A marginal Latin gloss ('Et procurator calamistratus et cetera') in El and two other MSS makes clear that Jankin corresponds to the 'curled darling who manages [the wife's] affairs', and who is her clandestine lover, mentioned in Theophrastus's antifeminist diatribe (Jerome, *Against Jov.* I.47).

312 On St James, see n. to Rv 4264.

323–7 As with the Wife's earlier reference to the *Almagest* (see n. to WB 180–83), the proverb is taken from the preface to Gerard of Cremona's Latin translation of the work, possibly mediated through Walter Burley's *De Vita et Moribus Philosophorum* (ed. Knust, cap. CXXI).

332 *queinte*: See n. to Mil 3276.

333–4 Proverbial; see Whiting C24. The immediate source is probably *RR* 7379–82, where the proverb is likewise applied to sex ('it is the candle in the lantern, and if you gave its light to a thousand people, you would not find its flame smaller'; tr. Horgan, pp. 113–14). But the quasi-magical 'inexhaustibility' of light is also used to express more serious concepts; see *BD* 961–5, and Dante, *Purgatorio* XV.67–75, where it serves to explain why the souls in heaven do not suffer any diminution in bliss from an increase in the number sharing it.

342–5 The reference is to 1 Timothy 2:9, quoted by Jerome, *Against Jov.* I.27.

348–56 The comparison of woman and cat derives from Matheolus's *Lamentations*, 1939–44 (tr. Jehan le Fèvre, II.3071–80), and also appears in Deschamps, *Miroir de Mariage*, 3214–15.

358 Jealous of her husband Jupiter's love for Io, Juno turned her into a heifer, and set Argus, who had a hundred eyes, to keep guard over her; Mercury put Argus to sleep by touching his eyes with his staff, and then cut off his head (Ovid, *Metamorphoses* I.622–723). La Vieille likewise asserts that even Argus's eyes are not adequate to keep watch on a woman (*RR* 14351–64, tr. Horgan, pp. 221–2). Cf. Mch 2111–13.

362–7 'By three things the earth is disturbed, and the fourth it cannot bear: By a slave when he reigns; by a fool when he is filled with food; By an odious woman when she is married: and by a bondwoman when she is heir to her mistress' (Proverbs 30:21–3, quoted by Jerome, *Against Jov.* I.28).

371–5 'There are three things that never are satisfied, and the fourth never saith: It is enough. Hell, and the mouth of the womb, and the earth which is not satisfied with water: and the fire never saith: It is enough' (Proverbs 30:15–16, quoted by Jerome, *Against Jov.* I.28, with 'amor mulieris' ('a woman's love') in place of 'the mouth of the womb').

376-7 The saying is taken from Jerome, *Against Jov.* I.28 (who is giving an antifeminist form to Proverbs 25:20): 'Like a worm in wood, so a wicked woman destroyeth her husband.'

386 Proverbial, as *Anel* 157 shows, but otherwise recorded only after Chaucer (Whiting H530).

389 The first recorded use of this proverb in English; see Whiting M558.

393-4 For parallels to the Wife browbeating her husbands by accusing them of having mistresses, see Matheolus 686-7, 1045-6 (tr. Jehan le Fèvre, II.77–9, 1080–84).

401-2 The Latin proverb which the Wife is translating ('Fallere, flere, nere | Statuit deus in muliere') is entered as a marginal gloss to this line in a number of MSS.

415 Proverbial; see Whiting H89 and Singer, I, 115; cf. Rv 4134. For its use in a sexual context, see *RR* 7488–94, tr. Horgan, p. 115. The lure was a device made of feathers attached to a long string, from which hawks were fed during their early training, so that they would later return to the falconer's hand when he twirled it in the air, in expectation of food.

435 *MED* glosses 'spiced conscience' as 'an overly scrupulous or fastidious conscience', as at GP 526, but the context, and the modifying 'swete' ('sweetly'), suggest that it here means a mild or benign disposition, as proposed by K. A. Rockwell (*NQ*, 202 (1957), 84).

436 *Jobes pacience*: The biblical book of Job recounts Job's patient endurance of the evils which the devil, with God's permission, inflicted on him. Cf. Cl 932–8. Job's patience would have been enjoined on the Wife to counteract the anger which was in the Middle Ages considered a typically female characteristic (Mann, *Estates Satire*, p. 123); for patience as a remedy against 'ire', see Pars 654.

447-50 Cf. *RR* 13090–92: 'You alone will have the rose, fair sir, and no one else will ever have a share. May God fail me if I divide it!' (tr. Horgan, p. 202).

460-62 A marginal gloss in El gives the source of this anecdote as Valerius Maximus's *Memorable Doings and Sayings* VI.iii.9; in some manuscripts the husband is called Egnatus Mecennius, not

Metellius. However, as the wording of the El gloss indicates, this anecdote (and the further two from Valerius quoted at WB 643–6 and 647–9) may have reached Chaucer via the *Communiloquium* of John of Wales (late 13th c.), a vast compendium of quotations from classical and medieval authors (R. A. Pratt, *Speculum*, 41 (1966), 619–42, at p. 621).

464–8 The idea that drinking leads to sexual arousal is found in Ovid's *Art of Love* (I.229–44), and was commonplace in the Middle Ages. (Cf., for example, Phys 58–60, Pard 480–87, Pars 836, 951.) The anecdote from Valerius referred to in the preceding note is cited in the *Communiloquium* of John of Wales in the context of some quotations from St Jerome's letters which offer a fairly close parallel to these lines (see Pratt, *Speculum*, 41 (1966), 621). See also Jerome, *Against Jov.* II.7: 'The eating of flesh, and drinking of wine, and fulness of stomach, is the seed-plot of lust.'

466 Proverbial, though this is the first recorded use in English (Whiting M753, Tilley T395).

469–75 The Wife echoes La Vieille in *RR*: 'now I must sigh and weep when I gaze at my ravaged face, with its inevitable wrinkles, and remember how my beauty made the young men skip ... And yet, by God, the memory of my heyday still gives me pleasure, and when I think back to the gay life that my heart so desires, my thoughts are filled with delight and my limbs with new vigour. The thought and the recollection of it rejuvenates my whole body; it does me all the good in the world to remember everything that happened, for I have at least had my fun, however I may have been deceived' (12735–9, 12902–12, tr. Horgan, pp. 197, 199).

477–8 Perhaps proverbial, but no other instances are recorded (Whiting F229).

483 *Seint Joce*: St Judoc, a seventh-century Breton saint whose English cult was centred on Winchester. His usual emblem was a pilgrim's staff. Chaucer's reason for choosing him here was probably that his name makes a convenient rhyme with 'croce', as Chaucer could have noticed in the *Testament* of Jean de Meun, lines 461–4).

487 Proverbial; see Whiting G443.

489–90 In the *Lamentations* of Matheolus, God answers a typical husband's complaints by explaining that he has designed marriage as another, but more cruel, version of purgatory; if the husband endures its torments patiently, he will go straight to heaven when he dies (3024–38; tr. Jehan le Fèvre, III.1675–1720). Cf. Mch 1668–73.

492 The expression is proverbial (Whiting S266), but its use in a marital context goes back to a story told by Jerome, *Against Jov.* I.48: 'We read of a certain Roman noble who, when his friends found fault with him for having divorced a wife, beautiful, chaste, and rich, put out his foot and said to them, "And the shoe before you looks new and elegant, yet no one but myself knows where it pinches."' Cf. Mch 1553. See also *Dissuasio Valerii*, pp. 302–3, and John of Salisbury, *Policraticus* V.10.

496 *roode-beem*: A beam running across the entrance to the choir in a church, on which a crucifix was usually placed. Although frequently prohibited by ecclesiastical authorities, burial in church was a regular practice throughout the Middle Ages; it was a privilege generally enjoyed by the wealthier members of the community, although not exclusively reserved to them. The nearer to the altar, the more prestigious was the burial-place. See Daniell, *Death and Burial*, pp. 95, 96–9.

498–9 A marginal gloss in El refers to the *Alexandreis* of Walter of Châtillon, a twelfth-century Latin epic which enjoyed wide circulation as a school-text, and which describes how Darius, king of the Persians, was killed in battle against his long-time enemy Alexander the Great. The splendid tomb of marble, gold and silver, elaborately carved, which was made for Darius by the craftsman Apelles, is described in Book VII (not VI, as El has it) of the *Alexandreis*, lines 379–430. Cf. Phys 16.

505–14 The favourite lover of La Vieille (*RR* 14446–77, tr. Horgan, p. 223) likewise beat her black and blue, but managed to appease her by his performance in bed.

515–19 The idea of wanting something the more because it is forbidden goes back to a much-quoted line of Ovid ('nitimur in vetitum semper cupimusque negata'; *Amores* III.iv.17), but there it is applied to men desiring the wives of jealous husbands. Its application to women is proverbial (see Whiting W549 and Singer, II, 174).

521–3 La Vieille similarly explains that a woman 'will be held more dear because she was dearly bought', since 'we have nothing but scorn for the things we get for nothing' (*RR* 13671–4, tr. Horgan, p. 211).

527 *Oxenford*: R. A. Pratt has shown that a number of medieval commentaries on the *Dissuasio Valerii* (see n. to WB 671) can

be connected with Oxford, and concludes that the antifeminist tradition flourished there (*AnM*, 3 (1962), 5–27).

551–9 La Vieille advises that women should take care to be seen and admired by going out to church, on visits, journeys, to weddings, games, feasts and round dances (*RR* 13487–98, tr. Horgan, p. 208). Cf. Matheolus's *Lamentations* 988–9 (tr. Jehan le Fèvre, II.947–51).

556 *vigilies*: The Wife may be referring to the vigils before funerals (see n. to GP 377), which were sometimes the source of unseemly merry-making (see Riley, *Memorials*, p. 463, n. 2), or (more probably) to the vigils before important saints' days, which were the occasion of great festivities. For the Midsummer festivities surrounding the vigils before the feasts of John the Baptist and the Beheading of St Paul (24 and 29 June), see J. Stow, *A Survey of London, Reprinted from the Text of 1603*, ed. C. L. Kingsford, 2 vols. (Oxford, 1908), I, 101–3.

processions: Processions, both secular and religious, were a regular feature of urban life in the Middle Ages, and were occasions of festive splendour (see, for example, Robertson, *Chaucer's London*, pp. 75–7, 136–7, 172, 213–14, 217).

572–4 Proverbial, though this is the only recorded instance in Whiting (M739). See Singer I, 103–4, and II, 89, for many continental European examples. La Vieille applies the proverb to the same end as the Wife (*RR* 13120–22, tr. Horgan, p. 202).

575–84 These lines are not in Hg (see n. to WB 44a–f). The text is based on El.

576 *My dame*: This may be a reference to the Wife's mother, since antifeminist writings often accused mothers of teaching their daughters how to deceive men (see *RR* 9290–9320, tr. Horgan, p. 143).

581 The notion that blood signifies gold is found in a work on dreams by Arnold of Villanova (see n. to CY 1428–9); see Curry, pp. 212–13.

587–92 It was a commonplace charge in medieval antifeminist literature that women's tears at their husband's funeral were feigned, and that they were already looking for their next husband, even among the mourners (cf. 596–9); see, for example, the *Lamentations* of Matheolus 862–5 (tr. Jehan le Fèvre, II.597–601, 847–52) and Deschamps, *Miroir de Mariage*, 1971–7. The idea goes back as far as Ovid (*Art of Love* III.431–2).

604 *preente of Seinte Venus seel*: Curry cites two – unfortunately,

post-medieval – writers who state that when Venus is the dominant star in a nativity, she imprints a birthmark on a (variously identified) part of the body (pp. 106–7).

608 The Latin word *quoniam* (meaning 'since') is used as a euphemism for the female genitals in the *Lamentations* of Matheolus (1237, 1369; also in Jehan le Fèvre's translation, II.1749).

609–13 Lines 609–12 are not in Hg (see n. to WB 44a–f); the text is based on El. This passage gives only a sketchy indication of the Wife's horoscope (North, *Chaucer's Universe*, pp. 291–2). At the time of her birth, the zodiacal sign of Taurus was in the ascendant (i.e., rising on the eastern horizon at the point where it intersects with the ecliptic), and the planet Mars was in this sign. Taurus is a 'domicile' of Venus (that is, a sign ruled by her influence), and this would make her powerful in the nativity, but we are not given any specific information about her position or its relation to Mars, and are thus unable to analyse in detail what the Wife says about the different contributions of the two planets. A marginal gloss in El quotes one of Almansor's *Aphorisms*: 'When malign [planetary] influences are in anyone's ascendant, he will suffer a foul mark on the face' (no. 14; printed in *Astrologia Aphoristica*, Ulm, 1641, p. 66), followed by one of the *Aphorisms* of Hermes Trismegistus: 'In the nativities of women, when any of the houses [domiciles] of Venus is in the ascendant and Mars is in them, or vice versa, the woman will be unchaste. Likewise if she has Capricorn in the ascendant' (no. 25; ibid., p. 21). See also E. S. Laird, *ELN*, 28.1 (1990), 16.

The Wife's astrological determinism would not have been generally accepted in the Middle Ages; planetary influence was held merely to create inclinations, which could be curbed by the exercise of free will (Wood, pp. 37–43).

619–26 These lines are not in Hg (see n. to WB 44a–f). The text is based on El.

Martes mark: See the passage from Almansor quoted in n. to 609–12.

630–31 Jankin was already entitled to control of his wife's property during their marriage, but it appears that the Wife gives him outright ownership of it by means of a 'fine' or legal deed to which she would have given her consent in court (see Margulies, cited in n. to WB 204).

643–6 A marginal gloss in El gives a reference to Valerius Maximus's *Memorable Doings and Sayings* VI.iii.10, where the story is told of Sulpicius, not Simplicius, Gallus. See also n. to WB 460–62.

647–9 This is also a story told by Valerius Maximus (VI.iii.12) of
P. Sempronius Sophus. See also n. to WB 460–62.

someres game: In fourteenth-century England, this term referred
to the traditional festivities held on Midsummer Day (24 June,
the feast of the Nativity of John the Baptist), which involved the
crowning of a young man and girl as 'summer king' and 'summer
queen' to preside over the day's entertainments. See R. E. Parker,
Studies in Honor of John C. Hodges and Alwin Thaler (Knox-
ville, 1961), pp. 19–26, and S. Billington, *Midsummer: A Cultural Sub-Text from Chrétien de Troyes to Jean Michel*
(Turnhout, 2000), pp. 22–3. Though these amusements were
doubtless innocent enough, they were viewed with hostility by
puritanical clerics.

651–3 *Ecclesiaste*: The biblical book of Ecclesiasticus (see n. to Mil
3530) contains many maxims concerning the dangers of women
and the need to control them; the one quoted here is in 25:34.

655–8 These lines sound proverbial, but the other instances given by
Whiting (H618) are later than Chaucer.

662–3 The Friend advises the Lover in *RR*: 'Women do not like to
be corrected . . . every woman, however foolish, knows through
her own natural judgement that in absolutely everything she
does, good or bad, wrong or right, everything you like, she is
always acting as she ought, and so she hates anyone who corrects
her' (9933–56, tr. Horgan, pp. 152–3).

671 *Valerie and Theofraste*: 'Valerie' most probably refers not to
Valerius Maximus, although he supplied the anecdotes in 460–
62 and 643–9, but to the *Dissuasio Valerii* (*Dissuasion of Valerius to Rufinus*), an argument against marrying which shows the
influence of Jerome's *Against Jovinian*. Chaucer may have
thought that its author was Valerius Maximus, as some medieval
manuscripts ascribed it to him (Hanna and Lawler, *Jankyn's
Book*, I, 61), but the twelfth-century writer Walter Map claimed
authorship of this piece when incorporating it into his *De Nugis
Curialium* (pp. 288–313). The *Dissuasio* had an independent
manuscript circulation, and often travelled in company with
Jerome and/or Theophrastus (see below). An edition and translation are provided in *Jankyn's Book*; substantial portions are also
translated in Miller, pp. 437–46.

'Theofraste' refers to the large section of Theophrastus's dissuasion against marriage quoted by St Jerome (see Headnote); it
too circulated independently in MSS (C. B. Schmitt, *Viator*, 2
(1971), 251–70, at p. 267).

Jankin's antifeminist book resembles a number of surviving medieval manuscripts: Hanna and Lawler have identified sixteen which combine Map's *Dissuasio* with Theophrastus, eight which combine Theophrastus with antifeminist selections from Jerome, and eleven which have all three texts (*Jankyn's Book*, I, 6).

673–5 Jerome spent much of his life in Rome, but was not a cardinal; the tradition that says he was goes back to a sixth-century *Life* (*PL* 22, cols. 202, 204), and in medieval art he was often represented with a cardinal's hat (*SA*, pp. 488–9, n. 5). For Jerome's treatise *Against Jovinian*, see Headnote.

676 *Tertulan*: Tertullian was an early Church Father (*c.* 155–*c.* 220), of pronounced ascetic tendencies. Among his many works, the most likely candidates for inclusion in Jankin's collection are his treatise 'On the Dress of Women', a diatribe against female adornments, and three treatises inveighing against second marriages: 'To His Wife', 'Exhortation to Chastity' and 'Monogamy'.

677 *Crisippus*: Chrysippus was a Greek Stoic philosopher, whose works were not available in Latin translation in the Middle Ages, and so could not have been known to Chaucer; nor do they have anything to do with women or marriage. Jerome quotes him as saying 'jokingly' that a wise man should marry (*Against Jov.* I.48), but this is hardly enough to link him with antifeminist writing. Horace refers to him as a moralist (*Epistles* I.ii.4), in a passage which seems to have supplied Chaucer with the name of the fictitious author 'Lollius' whom he claims as his source for *TC*.

Trotula: Trotula di Ruggiero was an eleventh-century woman physician; two works on gynaecology and a work on female cosmetics are attributed to her in manuscripts. See Rawcliffe, *Medicine*, pp. 176–7, and M. H. Green, *SAC*, 14 (1992), 53–88. It is not immediately obvious why she should appear in a list of antifeminist writings; for an attempted explanation, see L. Y. Baird-Lange, *SAC*, *Proceedings*, 1 (1984), 245–56.

Helowis: Heloise was successively the pupil, lover and wife of the renowned twelfth-century scholar Peter Abelard. She was reluctant to marry him because it would block his road to promotion in the Church, and in his autobiography he recounts how she tried to dissuade him, drawing on Theophrastus's arguments against marriage, as quoted by St Jerome (*Historia Calamitatum*, tr. B. Radice in *The Letters of Abelard and Heloise* (Harmondsworth, 1974), pp. 70–74). After their marriage, her uncle Fulbert mistakenly thought Abelard was trying to get rid of Heloise, and had him castrated; in a letter to Abelard written some years later, Heloise blames herself as the cause of this calamity, and compares herself with women notorious in antifeminist literature for having been the downfall of men, such as Eve, Delilah and Solomon's wives (ibid., p. 131). See further Mann, *Feminizing Chaucer*, pp. 41–5. Heloise's arguments against marriage would also have been known to Chaucer through the speech of the Jealous Husband in *RR* (8729–8802, tr. Horgan, p. 135).

678 After Abelard's castration, Heloise became a nun in the convent of Argenteuil near Paris, of which she eventually became prioress. Later, she and her community were expelled from the monastery, and removed to the abbey of the Paraclete in the district of Troyes.

679 *Parables of Salomon*: The biblical book of Proverbs (the Latin word *parabolae* denotes both proverbs and exemplary stories), which was attributed to Solomon. It contains many misogynistic sayings (see, for example, nn. to WB 278–80, 362–7, 371–5, 778–9, 784–5).

680 *Ovides Art*: Ovid's *Art of Love* instructs men in how to seduce women, and takes up a generally cynical attitude towards the female sex.

688–91 Medieval clerks who wished to advance in the Church were bound to a life of celibacy; antifeminist literature played a role in persuading them of the wisdom of this choice. Cf. Cl 935.

692 The reference is to a widespread beast fable, in which a man and a lion argue over which of them is the stronger. To support his case, the man shows the lion a sculpture or painting of a man overpowering a lion; the lion asks, 'And who made the sculpture/ painting?' – to which the answer is, of course, a man. The version of this story included in the fables of Avianus (fl. AD *c.* 400?) probably had the widest circulation, but there the work of art is a sculpted tombstone (fable XXIV). A painting rather than a sculpture appears in the Latin prose collection of beast fables known as the *Romulus* and its derivatives, direct and indirect; see Hervieux, *Les fabulistes latins*, II, 231, 544–5, 623. The marginal Latin gloss in El, 'Quis pinxit leonem?', suggests a Latin source, and so makes less likely Pratt's suggestion (*CT*, p. 269) that Chaucer took the tale directly from Marie de France's *Fables* (no. 37). However, the phrase is not exactly matched in the Latin translation of Marie's collection, which has 'A quo facta est pictura hec, ab homine vel a leone?' (Hervieux, II, 263); closer is

the *Romulus Nilantii* (Marie's source) 'Quis hanc ymaginem pinxit?' (Hervieux, II, 545).

701–5 A marginal gloss in El quotes a passage of Almansor's *Aphorisms* (no. 2, pp. 64–5, in the 1641 Ulm edition; see n. to WB 609–12), which explains that the 'exaltation' of any planet is the sign of the zodiac in which its influence is at its height, and that of a contrary planet at its lowest. Venus, which signifies 'song, gaieties, and whatever is pleasing to the body', and Mercury, which signifies 'knowledge and philosophy', are contraries of this sort; thus, when Venus has her exaltation in Pisces, Mercury's influence is at its lowest, and when Mercury has his exaltation in Virgo, Venus suffers a 'fall' or 'dejection' (Eisner, *Kalendarium*, p. 180).

715 *Eva*: Eve's role in the Fall of man (Genesis 3) is mentioned as indicative of female disobedience in the *Dissuasio Valerii* (pp. 292–3), and was made a subject of reproach to women throughout the Middle Ages.

717–20 These lines are not in Hg. The text is based on El.

721–3 The Israelite Samson was betrayed by his mistress Delilah, who cut off the hair which was the miraculous source of his strength, so that his enemies the Philistines were able to overpower and blind him (Judges 16; cf. Mk 2015–94).

725–6 *Dianire*: For the details of how Deianira unwittingly caused the death of Hercules, see n. to Kn 1942–6, and cf. Mk 2119–35. His story is included as an example of the banefulness of women in the *Dissuasio Valerii*, pp. 304–7, and he is similarly linked with Samson in *RR* (9153–76, tr. Horgan, p. 141).

727–32 The story is told by Jerome, *Against Jov.* I.48 (though Xanthippe there douses Socrates with dirty water rather than urine).

732 Proverbial (though this is the earliest recorded instance); see Whiting T267.

733–6 *Phasipha*: Pasiphae, wife of King Minos of Crete, had sex with a bull, and gave birth to the Minotaur, half man, half bull. She is cited, along with Clytemnestra and Eriphyle (see following notes), as an example of the banefulness of women, by Jerome, *Against Jov.* I.48; the passage is quoted as a marginal gloss in El.

737–9 *Clitermystra*: Clytemnestra and her lover Aegisthus killed her husband Agamemnon on his return home from the Trojan war; see also preceding n.

740–46 *Amphiorax ... Eriphilem*: The seer Amphiaraus was reluctant to join the expedition of the Seven Against Thebes (see n. to Kn 932) because he foresaw its failure and his own death; according to the mythographer Hyginus (*Fabulae*, ed. H. I. Rose, Leiden, n.d., LXXIII), he hid himself, but his hiding-place was betrayed by his wife Eriphyle, who had been bribed by her brother Adrastus with a splendid golden necklace he had made. Chaucer may have taken this version of the story from Boccaccio's *De casibus virorum illustrium* (I.18), where it appears in the context of an antifeminist diatribe (Boccaccio, *Opere*, ed. Branca, IX, 97). In the more usual version, Eriphyle persuades her husband to go to Thebes, having been bribed by Polynices with the magnificent necklace of Harmonia, made by Vulcan, which had passed into the possession of Argia, Polynices' wife (Statius, *Thebaid* II.265–305, IV.187–213). Jerome mentions Eriphyle's treachery in *Against Jov.* I.48; see n. to WB 733–6.

ouche: Boccaccio says that Eriphyle was bribed with a necklace ('monile'). Statius also uses the word 'monile' for the jewelled ornament given to Harmonia by Vulcan (*Thebaid* II.266), but Chaucer refers to it as a 'broche' in *The Complaint of Mars* (245). Both *broche* and *ouche* could be used for a wide range of jewelled artifacts (see *MED* s.vv. broche and nouche), and Chaucer probably had in mind a pendant or amulet worn as a neck ornament.

747–56 *Livia . . . Lucye*: These stories of Livia and Lucilia are taken from the *Dissuasio Valerii*, pp. 304–5.

757–64 The story is told in the *Dissuasio Valerii*, pp. 302–3; the name Latumius seems to be Chaucer's substitution for Pacuvius.

775–7 Ecclesiasticus 25:23. Cf. Proverbs 21:19, quoted at Mel 1087.

778–9 'It is better to sit in a corner of the housetop, than in a house shared with a brawling woman' (Proverbs 21:9, 25:24, quoted by Jerome, *Against Jov.* I.28).

782–3 This saying of Herodotus is quoted by Jerome, *Against Jov.* I.48.

784–5 A translation of Proverbs 11:22; the Latin is quoted as a marginal gloss in El.

794 *as dooth a wood leoun*: A proverbial expression; see Sum 2152 and Whiting L326–7.

801 The Wife has already transferred her property to Jankin (see WB 630–31 and n.); the assumption here is presumably that if he murdered her he would enjoy sole possession of it. Since dower usually reverted to the husband's family after the widow's death, the implication must be that there are no surviving children from

the Wife's previous marriages or other collateral heirs with a
superior claim on the property.

813–14 These lines do not go so far as to say that Jankin restores the
gift of property that the Wife had earlier made him, but he allows
her day-to-day control of it, and of the income it produced,
which was legally the right of the husband (see nn. to WB 204,
630–31).

835–6 Proverbial; see Whiting F336.

838 paas] pees El Hg. The word 'pees' does not fit well into this
sequence. Manly and Rickert (III, 460) mention the suggestion
of J. Koch that it should be emended to 'pace' (v), meaning 'go'.
More likely is 'paas', which like 'amble' and 'trot' is a specific
term for a horse's gait (according to Hyland, Horse, p. 28, it
resembles the trot in that it is two-time, but instead of each
diagonal pair moving together, each lateral pair moves at the
same time). Cf. CY 575, and see *MED* s.v. pas(e), *n* (1), 2a,
though the word is not recorded elsewhere as a verb at this date.

847 *Sidingborne*: This reference to Sittingbourne, a town about 40
miles from London and 17 miles from Canterbury, has been the
source of great confusion in Chaucer scholarship, since at a very
much later point in *CT* (Mk 1926) the pilgrims are clearly said
to be at Rochester, which is some ten miles nearer to London. In
response to the supposed contradiction, Henry Bradshaw suggested emending the Ellesmere order of *CT* by moving the entire
block of tales from the Shipman's Tale to the Nun's Priest's Tale
forwards, so that it followed the Man of Law's Tale (and thus
confirmed the reading 'Shipman' at ML 1179); this change (the
so-called 'Bradshaw shift') restores the place-names to their correct geographical position. (For a more recent defence of the
'Bradshaw shift', see G. R. Keiser, *ChauR*, 12 (1978), 191–201.)
Scholars have generally defended the Ellesmere tale-order on the
grounds that the unfinished nature of *CT* at Chaucer's death
meant that he had not yet had opportunity to eliminate inconsist-
encies of this sort (for a particularly eloquent argument along
these lines, see E. T. Donaldson, in *Medieval Literature and
Folklore Studies: Essays in Honor of Francis Lee Utley*, ed.
J. Mandel and B. A. Rosenberg (New Brunswick, NJ, 1970),
pp. 193–204, 363–7). However, an even more important consideration is that the Summoner does not say that the pilgrims
are at Sittingbourne, but that he will tell two or three tales about
friars *before they reach Sittingbourne* – which precisely means
that they are some way off it, and that the Summoner mentions

it simply as a place further down the road, not the next one they will reach (see S. B. Greenfield, *MLR*, 48 (1953), 51–2, and H. Cooper, in *The Ellesmere Chaucer: Essays in Interpretation*, ed. M. Stevens and D. Woodward (San Marino, CA, 1995), pp. 245–61, at p. 255). The supposed geographical contradiction does not, therefore, exist; it is simply a product of inattentive reading of the text. This line thus gives no cause to quarrel with the Ellesmere order or to attribute it to anyone other than Chaucer.

THE WIFE OF BATH'S TALE

The two main motifs of the Wife of Bath's Tale – the task of finding out what women most desire, and the enforced marriage to an ugly old woman who is then magically transformed into a beautiful young one – are paralleled in Gower's tale of Florent (*CA* I.1396–1861), in a fifteenth-century romance (*The Wedding of Sir Gawain and Dame Ragnell*), and in a ballad of uncertain date (*The Marriage of Sir Gawain*). These analogues are printed in *SA*, pp. 223–68, and *SA²* II; for a full study of similar story-types, see S. Eisner, *A Tale of Wonder* (Wexford, 1957). But only in Chaucer's version is the knight's imposed task a punishment for rape. The nature of the choice presented to the knight by the ugly old lady after their marriage also differs. In Gower and the *Wedding*, the lady has already been transformed by the knight's reciprocation of her embrace when she asks him whether he will have her fair by day or by night (rather than ugly and faithful, or beautiful and possibly unchaste). (The fragmentary nature of the ballad leaves the exact process of the transformation unclear, but the choice offered is as in the other analogues.) As in Chaucer, the knight leaves the choice to his wife, and is rewarded by having her young and beautiful all the time. The ugly lady's long speech on 'gentilesse' and poverty is Chaucer's addition to the story.

857–9 *king Arthour*: Although adopted as a national hero by the English, Arthur was king of the Britons (the original Celtic inhabitants of Britain, represented in the Middle Ages by the Welsh and the Cornish), whom he allegedly defended against the invading Romans. Medieval writers often credited Breton story-tellers, the continental cousins of the insular Britons, with spreading tales of Arthur and the Round Table.

876 Like monks and canons, friars were obliged to recite daily, at fixed times of the day and night, the eight liturgical offices which made up the Canonical Hours: Matins, Lauds, Prime, Terce,

Sext, None, Vespers and Compline. The obligation was in force not only when they were in their convent but also when they were travelling outside it. Matins (which was strictly speaking a night office) and Lauds were often sung together in the early morning. Cf. n. to Mil 3655.

880–81 According to legend, an incubus was an evil spirit which had sexual intercourse with women in their sleep. D. Yamamoto (*ChauR*, 28 (1994), 275–7) has shown that there is no evidence to support F. N. Robinson's statement that the incubus always made a woman pregnant (in supposed contrast to the friar), but she does not entirely succeed in making a case that the incubus is contrasted with the friar because it brought other kinds of disaster. The claim that the friars had expelled the incubi is made in earnest in a fourteenth-century collection of exempla; see P. Mroczkowski, *Kwartalnik Neofilologiczny*, 8 (1961), 191–2.

887–8 Such casual rapes of country girls are a regular feature of the medieval French lyric genre known as the *pastourelle*, which usually shows the girl's struggles giving way to pleased acquiescence; see K. Gravdal, *Ravishing Maidens: Writing Rape in Medieval French Literature and Law* (Philadelphia, PA, 1991), pp. 104–21, and (on WBT's relation to this tradition) Mann, *Feminizing Chaucer*, p. 71.

893 The legal punishment for rape was technically blinding and castration or hanging, but it was seldom enforced in the fourteenth century; offenders were usually fined or imprisoned. See *Bracton on the Laws and Customs of England*, II, 414–15, and Carter, *Rape*, pp. 119–37.

894 On the intercessory role conventionally played by fourteenth-century English queens, see n. to Kn 1748.

909 A year and a day was the period frequently specified as a time-limit for the fulfilment of certain actions in English law (Pollock and Maitland, II, 102).

950 Proverbial; see Whiting W534. Cf. Mel 1062 and *RR* 19190 (tr. Horgan, p. 296).

951 ff. *Mida*: Ovid tells the story of Midas in *Metamorphoses* XI.174–93, but there it is the slave who cuts his hair who reveals the secret, not his wife.

1109 ff. The idea that nobility derives from virtue rather than high birth or riches was a commonplace idea in the Middle Ages; see G. M. Vogt, *JEGP*, 24 (1925), 102–24. Chaucer's short poem 'Gentilesse' is devoted to this theme. As WB 1125–7 make clear, Chaucer here draws on Dante (see following notes), and will also have known *RR* 18577–866 (tr. Horgan, pp. 287–8). Cf. Pars 462–3.

1116 the gretteste gentil man*] In El, 'gentil man' is added by another hand after 'grettest', but this is the generally attested reading; Hg's 'the gentileste man' is shared with only one other manuscript.

1119–24 Cf. *RR* 18589–604, tr. Horgan, p. 287.

1125–6 The nature of true *gentilezza* is the theme of Book IV of Dante's *Convivio*; see esp. the introductory canzone and chs. 3, 7, 10, 14–16.

1128–30 'Rarely does human worth rise through the branches, and this He wills who gives it, in order that it may be asked of Him' (Dante, *Purgatorio* VII.121–3); the origin of nobility in divine grace is also expounded in *Convivio* IV.20–21.

1139–49 Boethius draws a similar contrast between the natural properties of fire and the adventitious properties of worldly honour; *Boece* III pr.4.64–77. Cf. also Servius's *Commentary on the Aeneid*, ed. G. Thilo and H. Hagen, 2 vols. (Leipzig, 1881–4), II, 101.15–21.

1140 *Kaukasous*: The Caucasus, an Asian mountain range stretching from the Black Sea to the Caspian.

1165–7 *Valerius . . . Tullius Hostillius*: According to legend, Tullus Hostilius rose from humble origins to become the third king of Rome; see Valerius Maximus, *Memorable Doings and Sayings* III.iv.1–3. As with preceding quotations from Valerius (see n. to WB 460–62), the intermediate source may well be the *Communiloquium* of John of Wales (see Pratt, *Speculum*, 41 (1966), 624).

1168 *Senek*: See Seneca, *Moral Epistles* XLIV, which asserts that 'the soul alone makes us noble, and it may rise above Fortune out of any state of life', and *On Benefits* III.28, which argues that 'no one is more noble than another, except he who has a mind which is more upright and more inclined to virtuous conduct'.
Boece: See *Boece* III pr.6.32–51 and m.6.

1177–1200 The quotations from 2 Corinthians, Seneca, Gregory, Juvenal and Secundus the Philosopher cited in the following notes to these lines, as well as the quotation from Revelation 3:17 in the El gloss to line 1186, had already been brought together in the discussion of poverty in John of Wales's *Communiloquium* (III.iv.2), which may well have been Chaucer's immediate source; see n. to WB 460–62, and Pratt, *Speculum*, 41 (1966), 625–7.

1178–9 Cf. 2 Corinthians 8:9. In Chaucer's day, the poverty of Christ was a highly controversial subject, bordering on heresy, since it

was appealed to as a basis for trenchant criticism of the established possessions and substantial income of monks and the secular clergy.

1183–4 As a gloss in El makes clear, the quotation is from Seneca's
Moral Epistles II.5; lines 1185–90 paraphrase the rest of the
Senecan passage.

1187–90 A marginal Latin gloss in El quotes Gregory the Great's
Homilies on Ezekiel II (VI.16; CCSL 142, p. 307): 'he who feels
the lack of what he does not have is poor, but he who neither
possesses nor wishes to possess anything is rich', followed by the
opening words of Revelation 3:17: 'You say: "I am rich [and
made wealthy and have need of nothing", and you do not know
that you are wretched, and miserable, and poor, and blind, and
naked].' The idea that the covetous man is always poor is a
medieval commonplace; see Mel 1131–2 and n.

1192–4 'The empty-handed traveller will sing in the presence of the
robber': Juvenal, *Satires* X.22 (quoted in a marginal gloss in El).
The saying was also proverbial; see Whiting M266.

1195–1200 El's marginal Latin gloss identifies the source of these
lines in an apophthegm of Secundus the Philosopher (2nd c. AD,
Syriac author of a Greek collection of *Sententiae*, translated into
Latin *c.* 1180 by William of St-Denis), which is quoted by Vincent
of Beauvais, *Speculum Historiale* X.71 (IX.71 in several early
editions), and also by John of Wales (see n. to WB 1177–1200):
'Poverty is a hateful good [line 1195], the mother of good health,
the remover of cares [line 1196], the restorer of wisdom [line
1197], possession without trouble [line 1200].' A fuller version
is quoted and expounded at *PPl* XIV.275–319; this passage also
incorporates the quotation from Juvenal used by Chaucer at WB
1193–4.

It is obvious from the Latin original ('curarum remocio') that
'bringere out of bisinesse' in line 1196 does not mean 'one that
brings out, encourages, industry', as glossed in *Riverside*, and
similarly in other editions of *CT*, but a *remover* of 'bisinesse' in
the pejorative sense of 'trouble, cares' (the error is corrected in
Riverside CT).

THE FRIAR'S PROLOGUE

1280–81 The hostility between the Friar and the Summoner is a
specific instance of the general antagonism between the mendicant orders and the secular clergy, who were in competition both

for spiritual authority over the laity, and for the financial benefits which resulted from it (in the form of charitable payments made as an act of penance, bequests and other gifts).

1283–4 Medieval society was regulated not only by civil law, administered by secular rulers and their agents, but also by canon law, which embodied the decrees issued by popes and other ecclesiastical authorities, and was administered by clerical courts. A summoner was an official attached to the court presided over by the archdeacon; his job was to summon defendants and witnesses, and to act as an usher when the court was in session (see nn. to GP 623 and Fri 1302, 1303–20). For a general account of ecclesiastical law and court procedures, see J. A. Brundage, *Medieval Canon Law* (London and New York, 1995).

1285 Hostility to summoners did on occasion lead to physical violence against them; see T. Hahn and R. W. Kaeuper, *SAC*, 5 (1983), 67–101, esp. pp. 85–6.

1300 *maister*: On the Host's use of this title, see nn. to GP 261 and Sum 2184–8.

THE FRIAR'S TALE

Anecdotes involving companionship with the devil, and a distinction between curses which are mere verbal formulae and curses that come from the heart, are to be found in medieval collections of Latin exempla (brief stories with a moralizing point), as well as in vernacular verse narrative. For texts and translations, see *SA*² I, 87–99; one of these stories is also included in Benson and Andersson, pp. 362–5. P. Nicholson (*ELN*, 17.2 (1979), 93–8) has drawn attention to an analogue in a sermon-anecdote summarized by G. R. Owst, *Literature and Pulpit in Medieval England*, 2nd edn (Oxford, 1961), pp. 162–3. In these analogues, the devil's companion is not a summoner, but a representative of some equally unpopular class (a peasant, a lawyer, and so on). Similarly, the insincere curses may be directed at a pig or cow, or even a child, rather than at horses, and the heartfelt curse may be issued by all the inhabitants of a village, rather than a poor woman. Only in Chaucer's version is the devil's companion so unperturbed by discovering his identity that he questions him at length about hell and demonic activities. The opening description of the archdeacon's court, and further details of the summoner's extortions, also mark out Chaucer's tale by embedding a simple joke at the expense of an unpopular social class in a context of social satire.

1302   *erchedekene*: An archdeacon ranked immediately below a
bishop in the ecclesiastical hierarchy, and assisted the bishop in
enforcing Christian discipline in the diocese. He presided over
local courts, known as rural chapters, giving summary judgements on issues not sufficiently important to be taken to the
bishop's court. 'Much of the business of the lower courts involved enforcement of the church's disciplinary rules concerning
sexual misbehaviour, drunkenness, marital disputes, infractions
of the church's prohibition of work on Sundays and feast days,
and the like. The archdeacon's courts touched matters of personal
conduct and morality in particularly intimate ways and lay
people often resented this intrusion into their daily lives and
domestic relationships' (Brundage, *Medieval Canon Law*,
p. 122). Since the archdeacon was both prosecutor and judge,
the opportunities offered to him and his officers for bribery and
extortion were considerable, and it appears that they were fully
exploited.

1303–20   This account of the typical offences dealt with by the
archdeacon's court, and of the corrupt practices that accompanied its workings, tallies well with the historical evidence; see
the article by Hahn and Kaeuper cited in n. to Fri 1285.

1307–8   *testamentz ... contractes*: That is, disputes over wills and
marriage contracts.
   lakke of sacramentz: Failure to participate in the sacraments of
the Church, such as baptism, confession and the Eucharist. (The
Fourth Lateran Council of 1215 had decreed that all Christians
should be confessed and take the Eucharist at least once a year;
cf. Pars 1027.)

1309   *usure ... simonye*: Usury, the lending of money at interest, was
prohibited by the Church. Simony was the term applied to the
practice of buying and selling ecclesiastical offices or promotions
for money; it took its name from Simon Magus, who tried to
buy the power of bestowing the Holy Ghost from the apostle
Peter (Acts 8:9–24).

1314   Beating was a usual punishment for offenders, but fines were
imposed in addition.

1330   The mendicant orders were under the direct authority of the
pope, and thus exempt from the jurisdiction of the bishop
(A. Williams, *AnM*, 1 (1960), 22–95, at pp. 86–7).

1332–3   *the stives*: The 'Stews' was the name given to the string of
licensed brothels in the Bankside area of Southwark, just across
the river from the City of London; this area lay within the liberty

of the bishop of Winchester (Carlin, *Medieval Southwark*, p. 211). The stews were thus outside the jurisdiction of the mayor and sheriffs of London, and subject instead to the manorial court of the bishop, acting in his capacity as territorial lord. This court would have dealt with any sexual offences that affected public order, but prostitution also came under the purview of the ecclesiastical courts; see the article on the regulation of brothels in late medieval England by R. M. Karras, *Signs: Journal of Women in Culture and Society*, 14 (1988–9), 399–433, at pp. 406, 410–11. It is not immediately clear, therefore, why the Summoner represents himself (that is, an official of the ecclesiastical courts) as having no power over the prostitutes of the stews. Karras suggests that it may be that the bishop, who profited financially from the Southwark stews, declined to punish the women who worked there (*Common Women: Prostitution and Sexuality in Medieval England* (New York, 1996), p. 152, n. 62); unfortunately, records of his ecclesiastical court do not survive, so this possibility cannot be explored further. H. A. Kelly suggests that the Summoner simply means that the authority of the archidiaconal court (which he represents) is overridden by the bishop's authority (*ChauR*, 31 (1996), 115–32, at pp. 125–6).

1337 *maister*: See nn. to GP 261 and Sum 2184–8.

1350 Judas carried the common purse of Christ's twelve disciples, and stole from it (John 12:6).

1356 The title 'Sir' was used of priests as well as knights, and since the rural chapter was especially interested in priests who had mistresses, they may be intended here.

1369 *dogge for the bowe*: For other proverbial expressions involving this phrase, see Mch 2014 and Whiting D303.

1380 *yeman*: See n. to GP 101, and, on the bow and arrows, n. to GP 117. The green clothing is appropriate both for a forester, and for the devil, who appears as a hunter dressed in green in Germanic folklore (Bächtold-Stäubli, II, cols. 1182–3).

1392–4 *bailly*: The term 'bailiff' denoted both 'an agent of a lord, responsible to the lord or his seneschal for the management of a manor' (*MED* 3), and 'a minor officer of justice' (*MED* 4); the devil supposes from the summoner's reference to his 'lord' in lines 1390–91 that he is a bailiff in the first sense, and the summoner does not disabuse him of this idea, although it is the latter sense that is applicable.

1408 *wariangle*: A local name for a shrike, also known as butcherbirds from their habit of impaling the insects they catch for food on a thorn, to form a 'larder'. It was believed in the Middle Ages that the thorn became poisonous as a result (T. P. Harrison, *NQ*, 199 (1954), 189).

1413 The devil was traditionally associated with the north; see the words attributed to Lucifer at Isaiah 14:13: 'I will sit in the mountain of the covenant, in the sides of the north.' Further evidence of this association is given by Pearsall in his note to *PPl* C I.110.

1436 *to hevy or to hoot*: Proverbial; see Whiting H316.

1443 *Seint Jame*: On St James see n. to Rv 4264.

1475 The devil is quoting the Bible: 'All things have their season' (Ecclesiastes 3:1); the saying was also proverbial (Whiting T88). Cf. Cl 6, Mch 1972.

1491 The biblical book of Job relates how Satan persuaded God to allow him to inflict a series of disasters on Job in order to test his uprightness and faith.

1502 St Dunstan, archbishop of Canterbury 960–88, was said by his earliest hagiographer to have overcome the devil in various manifestations, notably that of a bear (see *Memorials of St Dunstan*, ed. W. Stubbs, Rolls series (London, 1874; repr. 1965), pp. 13–14, 26–8).

1503 The power of the apostle Paul over demons is described in Acts 19:11–16. The *Golden Legend* of Jacobus de Voragine (*c.* 1230–98), a highly popular collection of saints' lives, relates similar stories of the apostles Andrew, Thomas, Peter, James the Greater, Bartholomew, and Simon and Jude; ME versions of these stories are included in the thirteenth-century *South English Legendary*.

1510 *Phitonissa*: *Pythonissa* is a Latin word meaning 'sorceress', and is used in the Latin Vulgate Bible at 1 Chronicles 10:13 of the Witch of Endor, who raised up for King Saul the spirit of the dead prophet Samuel (1 Samuel 28:7–25). The idea that this apparition was the work of the devil was often put forward in the Middle Ages (see, for example, John of Salisbury, *Policraticus* II.27).

1518 University teachers gave their lectures from a chair, with their students seated on the floor around them.

1519–20 *Virgile . . . Dant*: Vergil described Aeneas's visit to Hell, to seek out his father's spirit, in Book VI of the *Aeneid*; Dante's *Divine Comedy* begins with an account of his journey through Hell, under Vergil's guidance.

1564 *Seinte Loy*: According to legend, St Eligius (French Eloi) cut off a horse's leg, replaced the shoe and then miraculously reunited it with the body. For this reason he was the patron saint of blacksmiths, carters, grooms, saddlers, and all whose work linked them with horses. See also n. to GP 120.

1583 The summoner implies that some sexual misbehaviour is taking place. Friars in particular had the reputation of being 'ladies' men'; see GP 217, 234, and Mann, *Estates Satire*, pp. 42–3. The Friar who is telling the tale characterizes the summoner as animated by the same dislike of friars as the pilgrim Summoner.

1595–6 The libel (*libellus*) was the written petition necessary to initiate proceedings in a canon law court. It named the plaintiff, defendant and judge, and described the grounds for the lawsuit alleged by the plaintiff, and the remedy sought (Brundage, *Medieval Canon Law*, pp. 3, 130). Both plaintiff and defendant were represented in court by a 'procuratour' or proctor, a legal representative who argued the case on behalf of his client, and could do so in the client's absence (ibid., pp. 137–8).

1604 For sample prices of everyday commodities in late fourteenth-century London, see Robertson, *Chaucer's London*, pp. 92–5. In 1388, two large loaves of bread could be bought for 1 penny.

1613 *Seinte Anne*: See n. to ML 641.

1654 'Watch and pray' is a biblical expression; see Mark 13:33, 14:38, and cf. Colossians 4:2.

1657–60 The quotation fuses Psalm 9B (AV 10):8–9, 'He [the wicked man] sitteth in ambush . . . that he may kill the innocent . . . he lieth in wait in secret like a lion in his den', and 1 Peter 5:8–9, 'be sober, be vigilant; because your adversary the devil roams about like a roaring lion, seeking whom he may devour. Resist him, steadfast in the faith.' A marginal gloss in El quotes the beginning of Psalm 9B:8.

1661 Cf. 1 Corinthians 10:13.

THE SUMMONER'S PROLOGUE

1675–1706 The story about the friars hidden in the devil's tail may be a parody of medieval legends in which a monk or friar, vouchsafed a vision of heaven, laments that he sees none of his own order there; he is then shown a multitude of them beneath the Virgin Mary's mantle, as a sign of her special favour to them (see J. V. Fleming, *ChauR*, 2 (1967), 95–107).

THE SUMMONER'S TALE

The Summoner's Tale has a close analogue in a thirteenth-century French fabliau called 'The Tale of the Priest's Bladder' ('Li dis de le vescie a prestre'), in which a pious priest, when on his deathbed, is urged by two Jacobin friars to revoke some of the charitable bequests he has already made, so that he may give something to their order. The priest promises to give them a precious jewel, which turns out to be his bladder (see *SA*, pp. 275–86; *SA*² II; Benson and Andersson, pp. 344–59). Chaucer expands the early part of this story into a comic portrait of a hypocritical and greedy friar, drawing on the conventional criticisms of the mendicant orders in contemporary satire and polemic (see following notes). The friar's long sermon on Ire is Chaucer's own addition to the story, as is the concluding puzzle of how to divide the fart into twelve (see n. to Sum 2253–77 for possible sources of this feature). These additions are linked by a thematic interest in the status of the word, which also accounts for the choice of the fart as the burlesque legacy (see n. to Sum 2149); this interest in words, and what gives them validity, provides thematic continuity with the Friar's Tale.

1710 Holderness, a district to the east of the city of Hull in south-east Yorkshire, was in the fourteenth century the site of a rural deanery (*The Victoria History of the County of York*, vol. III, ed. W. Page (1913; repr. Folkestone and London, 1974), p. 85). The plain of Holderness 'formerly contained many meres and marshes, but they are now drained by countless streams and dikes' (*A History of the County of York East Riding*, vol. V, ed. K. J. Allinson (Oxford, 1984), p. 1). Chaucer may have known of it through Sir Peter Bukton of Holderness, if he is the person to whom Chaucer's 'Envoy to Bukton' is addressed (E. P. Kuhl, *PMLA*, 38 (1923), 115–32). Chaucer may also have known the archdeacon of Holderness, Walter Skirlawe (ibid., pp. 123–4).

1712 *To preche*: Friars had to obtain a licence to preach from the bishop (see A. Williams, *SP*, 57 (1960), 471, 477). They were successful and popular preachers, drawing large audiences; see H. G. Pfander, *The Popular Sermon of the Medieval Friar in England* (New York, 1937), and D. L. d'Avray, *The Preaching of the Friars* (Oxford, 1985).

1717 *trentals*: A series of thirty requiem masses, which were supposed to give the soul of the departed a quicker and easier passage through Purgatory, or even to release it from Hell. According to legend, they were instituted by Pope Gregory after his dead mother appeared to him in a vision and begged him to save her from hell's torments by this means (see the ME poem 'Saint Gregory's Trental', ed. F. J. Furnivall, in *Political, Religious and Love Poems*, EETS o.s. 15, 2nd edn (London, 1903; repr. 1965), pp. 114–22). Trentals would be paid for by the relatives of the dead, or else by a bequest made by the dead person her/himself. The friar is anxious that the money should go to his order rather than to chantry priests (see n. to GP 507–11).

1722 *possessioners*: The term was applied to monks and parish priests, whose main source of income was landed estates, which provided a regular and reasonably predictable annual yield. Friars, in contrast, lived on the fruits of their daily begging, modelling themselves (at least in theory) on the poverty of Christ and his early disciples.

1726 The thirty requiem masses that made up a trental were, according to the St Gregory legend (see n. to Sum 1717), meant to be sung three at a time on each of the ten major feasts in the Church year; however, they could also be performed on a single occasion (*English Gilds*, ed. L. Toulmin Smith, EETS o.s. 40 (London, 1870), p. 8).

1734 *qui cum patre*: Part of the formula used to conclude prayers and sermons ('[Christ] who with the Father [and the Holy Spirit livest and reignest for ever and ever]').

1737 *scrippe and tipped staf*: According to the original Rule of his order, the friar should not have been carrying either. St Francis was inspired to dedicate himself to a life of evangelical poverty when he heard a reading of the biblical passage (Luke 10:1–12) which describes how Christ sent out 72 (AV 70) disciples to preach the word, and he adopted Christ's instructions to these disciples as a model to be emulated by his followers. Sending out the disciples two by two, Christ commanded them: 'Do not carry a bag, nor a staff, nor shoes, and salute no man by the way. Into whatsoever house you enter, first say: Peace be to this house . . . And in the same house, remain, eating and drinking such things as they have: for the labourer is worthy of his hire' (4–7). See P. R. Szittya, *The Antifraternal Tradition in Medieval Literature* (Princeton, NJ, 1986), pp. 41–54, 239–46, for a discussion of the role played by this text in the founding of the mendicant orders, and medieval criticisms of the friars for attempting to arrogate to themselves the apostolic mission. See also nn. to Sum 1770, 1973. *ytukked hye*: That is, with his tunic pulled up high over his belt so that it would not impede movement or get dirty.

1740 *His felawe*: Modelling themselves on the 72 disciples whom
      Christ sent out to preach (Luke 10:1), friars travelled about in
      pairs; see preceding n., and W. A. Hinnebusch, *The Early English
      Friars Preachers* (Rome, 1951), p. 285.

1741-2 *peire of tables*: Paper was in fairly general use in the four-
      teenth century, but writing of an informal or temporary nature
      was still often set down on small wax-coated tablets, using the
      pointed end of a metal stylus. Once the writing was no longer
      needed, or had been transferred to a more permanent form, the
      wax was smoothed over with the broad-bladed end of the stylus
      so that it could be reused. The friar's tables are a hinged pair
      which would fold together and so protect the writing; their frame
      is of ivory (see E. M. Thompson, *An Introduction to Greek and
      Latin Palaeography* (Oxford, 1912), pp. 14–18, 37, 39).

1755 *hir hostes man*: That is, servant of the innkeeper at the inn
      where the friars are lodging.

1770 *Deus hic!*: 'May God be in this place!' The more usual greeting
      of a friar would be 'Pax huic domui' ('Peace be to this house');
      see n. to Sum 1737.

1794 *lettre sleeth*: The friar is quoting 2 Corinthians 3:6: 'the letter
      kills, but the spirit gives life' (the Latin original of the first half
      of this quotation is given as a marginal gloss in El). This text was
      often invoked to justify the practice of interpreting the Bible
      metaphorically rather than literally, if its literal sense was at odds
      with Christian doctrine, or simply if it could thus be made to fit
      an argument one wanted to make.

1803-4 It would be normal for the friar to give the wife the 'kiss of
      peace', but he clearly enjoys the experience rather more than
      he should. For contemporary comments on the abuse of the
      clerical kiss, see Kellogg, *Chaucer, Langland*, pp. 273–5.

1816-18 *Riverside* places the syntactic break after 'shrift' rather than
      at the end of 1817, but it makes little sense for the friar to boast
      of his expertise in preaching as proof that he is better than the
      priests who are incompetent to hear confessions. On the friars'
      eagerness that confessions should be made to them, rather than
      to the parish priest, see n. to GP 218.

1820 The friar is echoing the words used by Christ when he called
      the fishermen Peter and Andrew to be his disciples: 'Follow me,
      and I shall make you fishers of men' (Matthew 4:19; cf. Luke
      5:10).

1825 *pissemire*: The name derives from the urinous smell of an
      anthill. I can find no parallels to this conception of an ant as

characteristically angry (prompted by the seething appearance of an ant-hill?). The ant is more usually an emblem of industry (Proverbs 6:6; cf. John Lydgate, *Pilgrimage of the Life of Man*, ed. F. J. Furnivall, EETS e.s. 77–8, 92, lines 10101–98).

1827–31 The wife is making sure that the friar knows that she is getting no sexual satisfaction from her husband; the implication is that the friar might be able to supply what is lacking. Cf. the wife of ShT, who similarly claims an inactive sexual life (114–23), although we see later that this is far from true (375–81).

1832 The friar's use of French betokens a certain pretentiousness; see n. to GP 124–6.

1862 Friars were obliged to travel about in pairs, so that each could act as chaperone to the other (see n. to Sum 1740), but after fifty years' service they earned the right to travel alone.

1866 *Te deum*: The first words of a Latin song of praise which formed part of the service of Matins ('We praise thee, O God, we acknowledge thee to be the lord'); it was also used as a song of thanksgiving (J. S. P. Tatlock, *MLN*, 29 (1914), 144).

1877 *Lazar ... Dives*: See Luke 16:19–31 for the story of the rich man Dives (Latin *dives*, 'rich'), who feasted daily, but after his death was tormented in Hell, and the beggar Lazarus, who lay starving at his gate, but after his death was carried by the angels into Abraham's bosom (i.e., Heaven). This story, and the following instances involving Moses, Elijah and Aaron, are similarly cited in support of fasting in Jerome, *Against Jov.* II.15, 17 (see Headnote to WBPr).

1880 A marginal Latin gloss in El quotes Jerome, *Against Jov.* II.6: 'It is better to fatten the soul than the body.'

1881–2 *as seyth th'Apostle*: The reference is to 1 Timothy 6:8: 'having food and clothing, let us be content with these', which in the Vulgate reads 'Habentes autem alimenta, et quibus tegamur, his contenti simus'. A marginal gloss in El ('Victum et vestitum hiis contenti sumus') reproduces a form of this verse which is closer to that in Jerome, *Against Jov.* II.11: 'Habentes victum, et vestitum, his contenti simus', indicating that Jerome is again Chaucer's source here. This biblical text is quoted in the first Rule of the Franciscan order (*Die Opuscula des hl. Franziskus von Assisi*, ed. K. Esser (Rome, 1976), p. 385).

1885–90 *Moises*: Moses received two sets of commandments for the people of Israel from God on the top of Mount Sinai. The first set were written by 'the finger of God' on two tablets of stone (Exodus 31:18; 32:15–16), which Moses later broke in anger at

the Israelites' idolatry (32:19); the second, received after Moses
had fasted forty days and nights, were written down by Moses
himself (34:28, but cf. 34:1). Chaucer seems to be paraphrasing
St Jerome (*Against Jov.* II.15): 'Moses with empty stomach
received the law written with the finger of God.'

1890–93 *Elie . . . Mount Oreb*: The prophet Elijah fasted forty days
and nights before God spoke to him in 'a whistling of a gentle
air' on Mount Horeb (1 Kings 19:8–12).

1894–1901 'Aaron and the other priests when about to enter the
temple, refrained from all intoxicating drink for fear they should
die' (Jerome, *Against Jov.* II.15). Aaron, brother of Moses, and
his sons were the priests of the people of Israel; God's prohibition
against their drinking before entering the tabernacle is to be
found at Leviticus 10:9.

1915–17 This connection between fasting and chastity derives from
Jerome, *Against Jov.* II.15:

> Adam received a command in paradise to abstain from one tree
> though he might eat the other fruit. The blessedness of paradise
> could not be consecrated without abstinence from food. So long as
> he fasted, he remained in paradise; he ate, and was cast out; he was
> no sooner cast out than he married a wife. While he fasted in
> paradise he continued a virgin: when he filled himself with food in
> the earth, he bound himself with the tie of marriage.

Part of this passage is quoted as a marginal gloss in El at Pard
508–11 (see n.). Cf. also Pars 819.

1919–23 'Blessed are the poor in spirit' is a quotation from Christ's
Sermon on the Mount (Matthew 5:3); 'glosing' has to be
stretched to the limit to make it apply to friars, since they were
first founded some 1200 years later.

1929 *Jovinian*: The opponent attacked by Jerome in his *Against
Jovinian* (see Headnote to WBPr) for his view that marriage was
no less meritorious than celibacy, and eating and drinking no
less meritorious than fasting. Jerome vividly pictures Jovinian's
well-fed appearance:

> . . . Jovinianus speaking with swelling cheeks and nicely balancing
> his inflated utterances . . . For although he boasts of being a monk,
> he has exchanged his dirty tunic, bare feet, common bread, and
> drink of water, for a snowy dress, sleek skin, honey-wine and dainty
> dishes . . . Is it not clear that he prefers his belly to Christ, and

> thinks his ruddy complexion worth the kingdom of heaven? ...
> that handsome monk so fat and sleek, and of bright appearance ...
>
> (*Against Jov.* I.40)

A similar description appears in II.21.

1933-4 The Latin quotation is the opening of Psalm 44 (AV 45): 'My heart has brought forth [a good utterance]'. Since the literal meaning of *eructavit* is 'has belched', the recitation of the Psalm is here represented as an apt comment on the digestive processes of these gluttonous clerics.

1937 The reference is to James 1:22: 'But be ye doers of the word, and not hearers only.'

1938-9 The friars' prayers are supposed to rise as high in the air as a hovering bird of prey.

1943 *Seint Ive*: It is not clear whether this is a reference to St Ivo of Chartres or St Ives of Huntingdonshire.

1944 *oure brother*: That is, a member of a lay confraternity associated with the friar's convent. In return for charitable donations, the members of the confraternity would enjoy the convent's prayers, both when alive and after death. Such confraternities flourished in late medieval England (see Fleming, *ChauR*, 2 (1967), 101-2).

1967 The similarity between 'ferthing' and 'farting' makes it possible that the friar's words here suggest to the sick man the manner in which he later takes his revenge.

1968 A marginal gloss in El gives this dictum in Latin form: 'Omnis virtus unita forcior est seipsa dispersa'; previously unidentified, this is a variant version of proposition XVI in the *Liber de causis*: 'Omnis virtus unita plus est infinita quam virtus multiplicata' (*Le Liber de Causis*, ed. A. Pattin, *Tijdschrift voor Filosofie*, 28 (1966), 90-203, at p. 171; tr. D. J. Brand, *The Book of Causes*, 2nd edn (Milwaukee, 1984), p. 33). The *Liber* was well known in the Middle Ages, and this axiom also appears, for example, in a collection of philosophical quotations falsely attributed to Bede (*PL* 90, col. 1032C).

1973 The friar is quoting Luke 10:7 (copied as a marginal gloss in El), from Christ's words to the disciples whom he sent out to preach his gospel; see n. to Sum 1737.

1980 *Thomas lif of Inde*: According to legend, St Thomas, the disciple who at first doubted Christ's resurrection (John 20:24-30), spent the latter part of his life in India, where he converted many to Christianity (see the Acts of Thomas, *Apocryphal NT*, pp. 364-438, and Jacobus de Voragine, *Golden Legend*, I, 29-35). Commanded by the king to build him a palace, Thomas spent the money given him for the purpose on the needy, thus constructing 'mansions in Heaven' rather than on earth. The information about church building seems to come from the life of Thomas in the *South English Legendary* (II, 571–86), which mentions that 'Churchen he rerde menyon. & preostes he sette there' (line 175; cf. 149, 233–4).

1989–91 The wise man is Solomon, putative author of the apocryphal book of Ecclesiasticus, from which the quotation is taken: 'Be not as a lion in your house, causing your servants to scatter and oppressing those who are under you' (4:35). The Latin original is quoted as a marginal gloss in El.

1993 *hire*: Many manuscripts read 'ire' for 'hire' (her) in this line, a reading which is adopted by *Riverside* and assumed to be correct by Manly and Rickert (III, 467) and by Kane (p. 216), though for different reasons (he points out that the two words were 'as good as identical phonetically', and suspects a pun). Manly and Rickert observe that it is unlikely that the friar intends to call the wife a serpent. But that is just what he does at lines 2001–3, and it is difficult to read lines 1993–4 as a description of anger. That 'hire' is the correct reading, and 'ire' an easier variation, influenced by the frequency of the word's occurrence in this section of the tale, is strongly suggested by the continuity of these lines with the serpent image in 2001–3, the parallelism between lines 1993 and 1996, and the application of the 'snake in the grass' warning to women in *RR* (see next n.). Nature's priest Genius's quotation of the biblical warning (Micah 7:5), 'Guard the gates of your mouth against her who sleeps in your bosom' (*RR* 16664–5, tr. Horgan, p. 257), only a little later on in the same speech, may also have influenced the wording of this line.

1994–5 Vergil's warning against 'the snake in the grass' (*Eclogues* III.93) had achieved proverbial status (Whiting S153; cf. Sq 512). It is applied to women at *RR* 16556–86 (tr. Horgan, p. 256).

2001–3 No serpent is 'so venomous when his tail is trampled under-foot ... as is a woman when she finds her lover with his new sweetheart. She breathes fire and flames in all directions and is prepared to lose both her body and her soul' (*RR* 9770–76, tr. Horgan, p. 150). These lines are modelled on Ovid, *Art of Love* II.376–8. Cf. Ecclesiasticus 25:22–3: 'There is no head worse than the head of a serpent: And there is no anger above the anger of a woman' (quoted at *RR* 16300–303, tr. Horgan, p. 252).

2005 The Seven Deadly Sins were Pride, Envy, Wrath, Sloth, Avarice, Gluttony and Lechery. For the history of the formulation and development of this concept, see M. W. Bloomfield, *The Seven Deadly Sins* (State College, MI, 1952). Pars 387–957 offers an example of a highly elaborate analysis of the vices and virtues based on this structure.

2008 *viker or persoun*: For the difference between a vicar and a parson, see n. to Pars 22.

2010 That is, Ire carries out the actions which are prompted by Pride. Cf. Pars 534: 'And as wel comth ire of pride as of envye, for soothly, he that is proud or envious is lightly wrooth.'

2017–42 *As seyth Senek*: The story comes from Seneca's *On Anger* I.18. This and the following two stories of Cambises and Cyrus are also included in John of Wales's *Communiloquium* (I.iv.4, I.iii.11; see n. to WB 460–62), which may have been Chaucer's immediate source (R. A. Pratt, *Speculum*, 41 (1966), 619–42, at pp. 627–31). The Senecan versions of the three anecdotes are given in *SA*, pp. 286–7.

2043–73 This story is told in Seneca's *On Anger* III.14; see also preceding n.

2075 *Placebo*: A Latin word meaning 'I shall please', 'sung' because it is the first word in a verse of the Psalms (114:9; AV 116:9 follows a different Latin wording), used as an antiphon in the Office for the Dead. Cf. Pars 617: 'Flatereres ben the develes chapelleins, that singen evere "*Placebo*".' Placebo is also the name of the flatterer in MchT (1476). Friars were notorious as flatterers in the Middle Ages; see Mann, *Estates Satire*, pp. 37–8.

2079–84 The story of how Cyrus the Great, emperor of Persia (see n. to Mk 2728), dispersed the river Gindes into a multitude of channels so that it dried up, is told in Seneca's *On Anger* III.21. See also n. to Sum 2017–42.

       Gisen: The river Gindes, a tributary of the Tigris.

2085–8 *he that . . . teche kan*: Solomon; the lines quoted are Proverbs 22:24–5.

2090 The comparison was proverbial; see Whiting S645.

2093–5 See nn. to GP 218 and Sum 2195.

2094 *Seint Simoun*: St Simon was one of Christ's disciples (Mark 3:18).

2097–8 *Riverside* takes 'seyth he' to be outside of Thomas's speech, but the shift to the present tense jars, and it makes more sense to take it as a reference to what the curate has told Thomas. Cf. Pars 1008, where the Christian is given leave to repeat confession 'if it like to thee of thin humilitee'.

2099–2105 Friars' convents were often very large and splendid
buildings, and friars were much criticized for this (see Mann,
Estates Satire, p. 232, n. 139).

fundement: The word here means 'foundation', but its secondary
meaning 'anus' (cf. Pard 950) again strikes a chord with the sick
man's intentions (cf. n. to Sum 1967).

2108 St Francis refused to allow friars of his order to have books,
but the Dominicans, who were devoted to study and learning,
were 'assiduous bibliophiles' (J. V. Fleming, *JEGP*, 65 (1966),
688–700, at p. 697). To Chaucer, the friar's willingness to sell
books is evidently a bad sign.

2113 The simile is borrowed from Cicero, *On Friendship* XIII.47:
'Those who deprive life of friendship seem to take away from
the world the sun, since the immortal gods have given us nothing
better or more delightful.' The axiom is quoted in John of Wales's
Communiloquium (see n. to WB 460–62) II.vii.3 (Pratt, *Speculum*, 41 (1966), 631).

2116–17 This may be a reference to the Carmelite Friars, who,
although not founded until the early thirteenth century, traced
their origins back to Elijah, who destroyed the prophets of Baal
on Mount Carmel (1 Kings 18:19–40), and his disciple Elisha.
See R. A. Koch, *Speculum*, 34 (1959), 547–60, and A. Williams,
MP, 54 (1956), 117–20, and cf. *Pierce the Ploughman's Crede*
(?late 14th c.), lines 382–3, ed. H. Barr, *The Piers Plowman
Tradition* (London, 1993). Or it may refer to the medieval
controversy over mendicant poverty, since the friars justified
their commitment to poverty and mendicancy by references to
Elijah and Elisha. St Bonaventure cited the story of Elijah being
fed by ravens, and asking for bread and water from the widow
of Zarephath (1 Kings 17:6–16); see his *Apologia pauperum*
XII.24, *Opera Omnia*, vol. VIII (Quaracchi, 1898), p. 324. The
Carmelite friar Richard of Maidstone also appealed to the story
of Elijah and the widow of Zarephath to justify begging, and
used the story of Elisha leaving his ploughing to follow Elijah
(1 Kings 19:19–21) to justify mendicant poverty; (*Protectorium
pauperis*, ed. A. Williams, *Carmelus*, 5 (1958), 132–80, at
pp. 174–5). Such claims are contemptuously dismissed in a Lollard sermon (Hudson, *Wycliffite Writings*, pp. 93–4).

2126–8 *youre brother*: See n. to Sum 1944.

2149 The fart corresponds to the grammarians' definition of the word
as 'broken air' (see n. to Mil 3806), and is thus an apposite
riposte to the friar's sermon on anger, which to Thomas is just

so much 'hot air', devoid of signification. This view of the sermon on anger is reinforced by the fact that it makes the person to whom it is addressed furiously angry (2121–3), and what is more, the preacher himself becomes frenzied with rage after receiving the fart (2152, 2158–61, 2166–9). See further Mann, *PBA*, 76 (1990), 203–23.

2152 *as dooth a wood leoun*: A proverbial expression; see WB 794 and Whiting L326–7.

2158–69 The first Franciscan Rule explicitly forbade friars to give way to anger ('Et non irascantur, quia *omnis, qui irascitur fratri suo, reus erit iudicio* [Luke 5:22]'; cap. XI, ed. Esser (see n. to Sum 1881–2), p. 387).

2184–8 On the friars' liking for the title 'master' (which this particular friar has accepted without protest on several occasions; see lines 1781, 1800, 1836), see n. to GP 261. St Francis had urged humility on his followers by quoting Christ's denunciation of the Scribes and Pharisees (Matthew 23:6–12):

> And they love the highest places at feasts, and the best seats in synagogues, and greetings in the market-place [cf. Sum 2188], and to be called 'Rabbi' by men. But you [Christ's disciples] are not to be called 'Rabbi' ... nor be called 'master', for you have one Master, Christ. Whoever is greater among you, shall be your servant, for he who exalts himself, will be humbled, and he who humbles himself, will be exalted.

Medieval satirists delighted in turning this passage against the friars, casting them in the role of the Scribes and Pharisees; see Szittya, *Antifraternal Tradition*, pp. 201–7. The friar of SumT is clearly aware of the traditional satire against his kind and attempts to deflect it.

2195 Friars could be given a licence by the bishop to hear the confessions of named individuals (A. Williams, *AnM*, 1 (1960), 22–95, at p. 38); obvious advantages were likely to accrue to them if these individuals were persons of wealth and social standing (see n. to GP 218).

2196 *salt of th'erthe*: The lord is flattering the friar by applying to him the phrase that Christ used of his disciples: 'You are the salt of the earth' (Matthew 5:13). Implicitly he is also reminding him of how Christ goes on: 'But if the salt lose its savour, wherewith shall it be salted?'

2222 *ars-metrik*: It is tempting to suppose a pun on 'arse', but Chaucer

seems to have spelled this word 'ers', as is attested by rhyme at
Mil 3734 and 3755.

2231 *inpossible*: Perhaps a reference to the scholastic *impossibile*, a
proposition which violates common sense (e.g., 'The Trojan war
is still in progress', or 'a man's foot is greater than the world'),
but which is defended by ingenious arguments. Disputations over
impossibilia were used in medieval universities to train students
in combating false arguments (see R. J. Pearcy, *NQ*, 212 (1967),
322–3).

2244 On the squire's duty to carve the meat, see n. to GP 100 and cf.
Mch 1773.

2253–77 The scenario envisaged by the squire has a striking resemblance to some late medieval pictures of the Coming of the Holy
Spirit to Christ's twelve disciples at Pentecost: the disciples are
depicted as sitting in a circle, with the tongues of flame that
manifest the power of the Holy Spirit descending on them represented by twelve lines radiating from a central point; to the
casual eye, this segmented circle resembles a wheel with twelve
spokes (see A. Levitan, *University of Toronto Quarterly*, 40
(1971), 236–46). In the parodic version of SumT, the 'mighty
wind' which signalled the arrival of the Holy Ghost (Acts 2:1–
4) is replaced by the very earthly fart, and the 'gift of tongues'
which the Spirit bestowed on the disciples has been transposed
into a bodily flatus (see n. to Sum 2149). R. F. Green has drawn
attention to a late fifteenth-century French riddle which poses
the problem of dividing a fart in twelve and solves it in the same
way as SumT (*ELN*, 24.2 (1987), 24–7), and has suggested that
a similar riddle may have been Chaucer's source for the idea.
Even if this were the case, it would not rule out the Pentecostal
parody, which gives the riddle added meaning in the context of
Chaucer's tale. For another possible iconographical parallel, see
V. A. Kolve, in *The Centre and its Compass: Studies in Medieval
Literature in Honor of Professor John Leyerle*, ed. R. A. Taylor
and others (Kalamazoo, MI, 1993), pp. 265–96, and for a
thorough review of the Pentecostal associations of the end of
SumT, see G. Olson, *SAC*, 21 (1999), 209–45.

2258–9 Twelve is 'the number normally required to maintain conven-
tual life by the monastic and mendicant orders' (Williams, *AnM*,
1 (1960), p. 78, n. 8). In accordance with the mendicant imitation
of the apostolic life (see n. to Sum 1737), St Francis had twelve
chosen companions (*The Little Flowers of St Francis*, tr. R.
Brown, ch. 1, in Habig, *St Francis*, pp. 1301–2).

2289 *Euclide . . . Ptholomee*: Euclid and Ptolemy are mentioned as famous Greek mathematicians.

THE CLERK'S PROLOGUE

2   A 'maidenly simplicity' was considered the fitting demeanour for clerks (see Mann, *Estates Satire*, pp. 76 and 243, n. 112). Cf. n. to Mil 3202.

5   *som sophime*: A large part of the training of an Oxford clerk was devoted to disputation on questions of logic, termed *sophismata* or sophisms (J. A. Weisheipl, *Mediaeval Studies*, 26 (1964), 143–85, at pp. 177–81).

6   Ecclesiastes 3:1; cf. Fri 1475 and n., Mch 1972.

10–11   Proverbial; see W. W. Skeat, *Early English Proverbs* (Oxford, 1910), no. 275.

12   On the preaching of the medieval friars, see n. to Sum 1712.

16–18   Medieval rhetoric distinguished three levels of style – high, medium and low – to be adopted according to the genre in which one was writing and the audience one was addressing. The art of letter-writing, known as the *ars dictaminis*, was a special branch of rhetoric with entire treatises devoted to it. See J. J. Murphy, *Rhetoric in the Middle Ages* (Berkeley, CA, 1974), pp. 19, 59, and (on letter-writing) ch. 5. The more elevated the style, the greater the amount of stylistic ornamentation used. The different types of ornamentation were known as 'colours', and were subdivided into figures of words and figures of thought (Geoffrey of Vinsauf, *Poetria Nova*, 1094–1588, tr. Nims, pp. 56–72).

27   *Padwe*: Petrarch (see next n.) acquired the use of a house in Padua when he became a canon of the cathedral in 1349, and spent much time there; from 1368 to his death in 1374 Padua and nearby Arquà were his principal places of residence. Scholars have speculated on the possibility that Chaucer might have met Petrarch on his first trip to Italy in 1373, but there is no hard evidence for this, and the probabilities are against it (*Life-Records*, p. 40). The most likely reason for the Clerk's presence in northern Italy is that he had gone, like so many others of his kind, to study law in Bologna.

31   *Fraunceis Petrak*: Francis Petrarch (1304–74), the famous Italian writer and humanist. His family name, which was adopted from his father's first name, was often spelled Petracco or (in Latin) Petrachus.

laureat: In imperial Rome, the winner of a quinquennial poetry

contest was crowned with a garland of oak leaves (not laurel).
In imitation of this ancient practice, some pre-eminent poets in
fourteenth-century Italy were offered a laurel crown; Petrarch
was awarded this honour at a splendid ceremony on the Roman
Capitol, on 8 April 1341 (E. H. Wilkins, *Life of Petrarch*
(Chicago, 1961), pp. 24–9).

34–5 *Linian*: Giovanni da Lignano (*c.* 1310–83) was a professor of
canon law at Bologna, known for his writings on law, ethics,
theology and astronomy. His involvement in the Great Schism
in defence of Pope Urban VI gave him an international reputation. See A. S. Cook, *RomR*, 8 (1917), 353–82, and J. P.
McCall, *Speculum*, 40 (1965), 484–9.

41–55 Petrarch's proem is not much longer than the Clerk's résumé
of it; it reads: 'In the chain of the Apennines, in the west of Italy,
stands Mount Viso, a very lofty mountain, whose summit towers
above the clouds and rises into the bright upper air. It is a
mountain notable in its own nature, but most notable as the
source of the Po, which rises from a small spring upon the
mountain's side, bends slightly toward the east, and presently,
swollen with abundant tributaries, becomes, though its down-
ward course has been but brief, not only one of the greatest
streams but, as Vergil called it, the king of rivers. Through Liguria
its raging waters cut their way, and then, bounding Aemilia and
Flaminia and Venetia, it empties at last into the Adriatic sea,
through many mighty mouths' (Miller, p. 140). Since this description of the course of the Po is omitted in the French translations
of Petrarch's Griselda story (see Headnote below), Chaucer's
reference to it is a sign that he had read the Latin original.

44 *Pemond . . . Saluces*: Saluzzo, a town in Piedmont, a region in
the north of Italy, the historic seat of a line of marquesses.

45 *Appenin*: The Appennines, a range of mountains forming the
spine of Italy. Their northernmost section borders the south of
the Lombard plain which forms the Po basin, and merges into
the Alps in the west.

46 *Lumbardye*: Lombardy, a region in the far north of Italy, to the
east of Piedmont. Its principal city is Milan.

47 *Mount Vesulus*: Monte Viso or Monviso, the highest of the
Italian Alps (3841 m), lies directly west of Saluzzo. As lines 48–9
state, it is the source of the river Po, the largest river in Italy, and
the dominating feature of north Italian geography.

48–51 *the Poo . . . Ferare . . . Venise*: The general course of the Po is
eastwards; rising in Piedmont, it flows through Lombardy and

Emilia-Romagna ('Emeleward'), where Ferrara is situated, and finally enters the Adriatic sea just south of Venice.

THE CLERK'S TALE

As the Clerk's Prologue makes clear, Chaucer's source for the story of Griselda was the Latin prose tale written by Francis Petrarch (see n. to Cl 31). Quotations from the Latin original are copied into the margins of El at equivalent points in the story. Petrarch's own source was Boccaccio's *Decameron*, where the tale of Griselda is the last in the whole collection (X.10). (It is not impossible that Chaucer knew the *Decameron* also, but there is no direct evidence for this; see, however, n. to Cl 1163–1212). Petrarch's version forms the bulk of a letter to Boccaccio, and is prefaced by an explanation of how he came to rewrite the tale in Latin (*Epistolae Seniles* XVII.3, ed. A. Bufano, *Opere latine di Francesco Petrarca* (Turin, 1975), II, 1312–39). Petrarch's Latin was the basis of two fourteenth-century prose translations, one by Philippe de Mézières (later incorporated into *Le Ménagier de Paris*, a handbook written by a French *bourgeois* for his young wife), and one anonymous; verbal echoes show that Chaucer used the latter alongside the Latin original. Petrarch's letter and the anonymous French version are printed with facing English translation in *SA*[2] I, 108–29, 140–67. An English translation of Petrarch's letter is printed in Miller, pp. 136–52, and also in Kolve and Olson, pp. 378–91, where it is accompanied by English translations of Boccaccio's tale, and a short excerpt from *Le Ménagier de Paris* giving the Parisian husband's comments on the story.

Petrarch's most important change to Boccaccio's story was to give it a religious interpretation (see n. to Cl 1142–60); Chaucer takes this over and intensifies the religious resonances of the tale, using the rhyme royal stanza (see n. to ML 96) he reserves for religious tales. At the same time he increases its human immediacy by encouraging critical responses to Walter's conduct, and by expanding Griselda's speeches so as to elicit emotional sympathy for her situation and emphasize its pathos (see E. Salter, *Chaucer: The Knight's Tale and the Clerk's Tale* (London, 1962), pp. 50–59, and R. Kirkpatrick's comparison of Boccaccio, Petrarch and Chaucer in *Chaucer and the Italian Trecento*, ed. P. Boitani (Cambridge, 1983), pp. 231–48, esp. pp. 240–43). This emphasis on Griselda's suffering gives the religious meaning of the tale an extra dimension: if Walter images the apparently arbitrary cruelty of God the Father, who must be loved and trusted even when he takes away one's children, Griselda on her side images the patient suffering of God the Son, enduring the arbitrary cruelty of mankind with an unstinted love (see Mann, *Feminizing Chaucer*, pp. 120–28). The enigma of these two conflicting images, each of which represents both the divine and the human, gives Chaucer's version a depth and complexity of meaning not shared by the other versions.

128 *thin*: This use of the second person singular is inconsistent with the spokesman's general use of the respectful plural 'ye', which befits Walter's superior rank, but, as Kane notes, usage in this respect was 'far from systematic in Chaucer's time' (p. 218).

155–8 The view that goodness comes from God, rather than from noble birth, echoes the old lady's speech in WBT, esp. lines 1117–18, 1128–32, 1162–4. For Boccaccio, the Griselda story shows 'that celestial spirits may sometimes descend even into the houses of the poor, whilst there are those in royal palaces who would be better employed in royal palaces as swineherds than as rulers of men' (*Decameron* X.10, tr. McWilliam, p. 824). Cf. Cl 206–7 and n.

206–7 Petrarch's original reads: 'heavenly grace, which sometimes lights on even the poorest dwellings' (*SA*[2] I, 114). In introducing the 'litel oxes stalle', Chaucer creates a reminiscence of the Nativity (which was traditionally depicted in medieval art with the ox and ass mentioned in Isaiah 1:3 present in the stable), and gives Griselda a Christ-like aura; see also Cl 291 and 398.

291 *oxes stalle*: Not in Petrarch. See preceding n.

365 *This is inogh*: Repeated at line 1051 when Walter brings Griselda's trials to an end. Petrarch's Walter likewise uses the word *satis* ('enough') in both instances. For a discussion of the significance of the repetition, and the use of 'inogh' as a key-word in this tale, see J. Mann, *SAC*, 5 (1983), 17–48, esp. pp. 31–45.

398 *oxe-stalle*: Not in Petrarch. See n. to Cl 206–7.

413 The same expression is used at ML 532 and *TC* I.1078.

428–41 Medieval women among the landowning classes often played an active role in administration and government; see R. G. Archer, in *Woman is a Worthy Wight: Women in English Society c. 1200–1500*, ed. P. J. P. Goldberg (Stroud, Glos., 1992), pp. 149–81.

429 hoomlinesse*] humblenesse El Hg. The French source supports the reading 'hoomlinesse' (Manly and Rickert III, 470).

455–62 These comments on Walter's behaviour are Chaucer's own addition to the story.

508 *ye*: Both El and Hg read 'thee', but follow it with 'vel [= 'or'] ye'. Grammatically, 'thee' is more correct as an accusative form, but it does not fit Griselda's usual care in using the respectful 'ye' form to her husband. The El/Hg scribe may be registering unease with the switch to the familiar form, or (conversely) unease with 'ye' in the accusative position, so that either of these readings may be regarded as the *durior lectio* (a reading which is 'harder' and therefore more likely to be original, since a scribe is likely to substitute a more familiar word or form).

537–8 Cf. Isaiah 53:7 (a passage interpreted as a prophecy of Christ's Passion): 'He was sacrificed because he himself wished it, and he did not open his mouth. He shall be led as a sheep to the slaughter, and shall be dumb as a lamb before his shearer, and he shall not open his mouth.'

554–67 These lines are Chaucer's own addition to the story; they both increase the pathos of Griselda's situation, and deepen the religious significance of the tale by invoking the image of divine suffering in the Crucifixion (see Mann, 'Parents and Children', pp. 180–83).

589–90 *Boloigne . . . Panik*: Bologna lies well to the east of Saluzzo; 'Panik' is probably the castle of Panico, some 18–20 miles south of Bologna (R. B. Pearsall, *MLN*, 67 (1952), 529–31).

617–18 The children of upper-class families were often suckled by a wet-nurse of lower social class.

621–3 This comment is Chaucer's own addition to the story.

696–700 This appeal to women to pass judgement on Walter is Chaucer's own addition to the story.

736 Twelve was the legal age of consent to marriage for girls; cf. WB 4.

739–42 Divorce in the medieval period, though not common, was less rare among the upper classes, who often wished to make a new marriage for dynastic or property reasons, than among their inferiors. It was accomplished by a papal dispensation which annulled the marriage on such grounds as impotence, bigamy, non-consummation or consanguinity (i.e., bride and groom were related to each other within the proscribed degrees of kinship). Dispensations were not normally given on the grounds that a marriage was unpopular with a ruler's subjects. See R. H. Helmholz, *Marriage Litigation in Medieval England* (Cambridge, 1974), ch. 3.

807 *dowere*: Here, the dowry which the bride brought to her husband at her marriage (as opposed to the dower, the property which

the husband settled on her at marriage to support her after his death).

810-12   Walter here mimics the role of Philosophy in Boethius's *Consolation of Philosophy* (see n. to Kn 1313-14), who teaches Boethius to accept with patient resignation the vicissitudes of Fortune, the evil as well as the good. The grim irony of these lines is that Walter *is* the 'strook of Fortune or of aventure' which he counsels Griselda to endure with patience.

852-61   These lines, which heighten the pathos of Griselda's situation, are Chaucer's own addition.

867-8   *youre*: El and Hg have 'my' where other manuscripts have 'youre' in both these lines; 'youre' much better fits the humble tenor of Griselda's speech, and 'my' looks like a variation to an easier reading.

871-2   Griselda's words echo Job's patient response to the news that his wealth has been lost and his children killed: 'Naked came I out of my mother's womb, and naked shall I return thither: the Lord gave, and the Lord hath taken away: as it hath pleased the Lord so is it done: blessed be the name of the Lord' (Job 1:21). Cf. also the words which Philosophy imagines Fortune speaking to Boethius (*Boece* II pr.2.15-27), in response to his laments over his misfortunes:

> Whan that nature brought the foorth out of thi modir wombe, I resceyved the nakid and nedy of alle thynges, and I norissched the with my richesses, and was redy and ententyf thurwe my favour to sustene the – and that maketh the now inpacient ayens me; and I envyrounde the with al the habundaunce and schynynge of alle goodes that ben in my ryght. Now it liketh me to withdrawe myn hand. Thow hast had grace as he that hath used of foreyne goodes; thow hast no ryght to pleyne the, as though thou haddest outrely forlorn alle thy thynges.

Griselda shows the patience that Philosophy is trying to encourage in Boethius.

880-82   These lines are Chaucer's addition. The expression 'naked as a worm' is conventional; see Whiting W673 and *RR* 443.

916   *she moore of age*: *Riverside* (like many manuscripts) omits 'she' (which admittedly cumbers the metre somewhat). The El/Hg reading is supported by the French version of the Griselda story, which refers both to Griselda's having grown and to the deterioration of the garment ('la couvry a grant mesaise, car la

femme estoit devenue grande et embarnie et la povre robe enru-
diee et empiree'; *SA²* I, 161). Petrarch mentions the garment's
roughness and age ('tunicam eius hispidam et attritam senio . . .
seminudam antiqua veste coperuit'; *SA²* I, 127), but not the
difficulty in getting it to cover Griselda's body, nor her change
in size.

927–38 These lines are Chaucer's own addition.

932 On Job as an exemplary type of patience, see n. to WB 436.

935 On the traditional antagonism between women and clerks, see
WB 688–710, and nn. to WB 527, 688–91. Chaucer thus creates
an irony here by having his Clerk speak favourably of women.

1047 For this and similar proverbial comparisons (e.g., 'steadfast as
a wall',) see Whiting W11, 13–15.

1142–60 These lines follow Petrarch closely; this religious interpretation is his original contribution to the Griselda story.

1148 *heigh style*: Petrarch's tale is not written in a particularly elevated style. At the corresponding point of his story he says that
he has written it 'in a different style' ('stilo . . . alio'; see *SA²* I,
129, and *Opere latine*, ed. Bufano, II, 1336) from Boccaccio, by
which he probably just means that he has told it differently. The
manuscript Chaucer had in front of him seems to have read 'stilo
. . . alto' ('high style'), as is confirmed by the fact that this is the
reading of the marginal quotation of Petrarch in El and Hg at
this point (see G. L. Hendrickson, *MP*, 4 (1906), 179–92, at
pp. 189–91).

1153–4 'Let no man, when he is tempted, say that he is tempted by
God. For God is not a tempter of the wicked, and he tempteth
no man' (James 1:13).

1163–1212 With these stanzas Chaucer leaves his Petrarchan source
and shifts to a note of flippancy which interestingly parallels
Boccaccio's shift from seriousness to flippancy at the end of his
Griselda story. After making the serious observation quoted in
the n. to Cl 155–6, he concludes:

Who else but Griselda could have endured so cheerfully the cruel
and unheard of trials that Gualtieri [Walter] imposed upon her
without shedding a tear? For perhaps it would have served him
right if he had chanced upon a wife, who, being driven from the
house in her shift, had found some other man to shake her skin-coat
for her, earning herself a fine new dress in the process.

(*Decameron* X.10, tr. McWilliam, p. 824)

The shift in mood is marked by a shift in verse-form: the Envoy (lines 1177–1212) is written in six-line stanzas rhyming ababcb, with the same rhymes repeated in each stanza, in place of the seven-line stanzas of rhyme royal used for the tale.

1188 Chichevache was the name of a mythical cow who fed on patient wives and was in consequence always thin and hungry, while her companion Bicorne, who fed on patient husbands, was always fat (A. Jubinal, *Mystères inédits du quinzième siècle*, vol. I (Paris, 1837), pp. 248, 389–91; John Lydgate, *The Minor Poems*, ed. H. N. MacCracken, vol. II (1934; repr. London, 1961), EETS o.s. 192, pp. 433–8).

1189 *Ekko*: The nymph Echo had incurred the enmity of the goddess Juno, who deprived her of the power of saying anything other than repeating the last words spoken to her (Ovid, *Metamorphoses* III.359–401).

1200 *clappeth as a mille*: Proverbial; see Pars 406 and Whiting C276 and M557.

1211 *as light as leef on linde*: Proverbial; see Whiting L139.

1212a–g The so-called 'Host's stanza' is not found in a large number of *CT* MSS (although it appears in both El and Hg), and it raises problems of several kinds. First, it returns to the seven-line rhyme royal of ClT, and is thus metrically discontinuous with the six-line stanzas of the preceding Envoy. Second, it interrupts the verbal link between line 1212 ('care, and wepe, and wringe, and waille') and the first line of MchPr ('Weping and wailing, care and oother sorwe'). Third, its content suggests scribal padding or patching: lines 1212c–d are very close to Mk 1893–4, and may have been borrowed from there, while lines 1212e–g are so vacuous as to be virtually meaningless. The first two of these points might suggest that the link belonged to an early stage in the writing of *CT*, and was discarded later; combined with the third, however, they suggest that the stanza is not by Chaucer, and was a scribal attempt to provide a tidy ending for ClT (possibly in separate circulation). In view of its doubtful authenticity, it is set in italics.

THE MERCHANT'S PROLOGUE

The Merchant's Prologue is absent from Hg, evidently as a result of the piecemeal order in which the scribe was receiving the material to be copied (see the *Facsimile and Transcription of the Hengwrt Manuscript*, ed. P. G. Ruggiers (Norman, OK, 1979), pp. xxvi–xxxiii).

This meant that the Merchant's Tale had already been copied after the Squire's Tale (with a leaf left blank to accommodate a link, if one were to arrive), and the scribe was then obliged to adapt the Sq–Fkl link by substituting 'Marchant' for 'Frankeleyn'. The text of the Prologue printed here is based on El.

1230 *Seint Thomas of Inde*: See n. to Sum 1980. Presumably it is for the sake of rhyme that St Thomas is invoked here.

THE MERCHANT'S TALE

The Merchant's Tale draws on much of the same antifeminist material as the Wife of Bath's Prologue (see Headnote). The advice given to January by his friends Justinus and Placebo on his belated decision to get married has obvious affiliations to the literary form known as the 'dissuasion against marriage' (*dissuasio de non ducenda uxore*). For an accessible account of the dissuasion tradition, see K. M. Wilson and E. M. Makowski, *Wikked Wyves and the Woes of Marriage: Misogamous Literature from Juvenal to Chaucer* (Albany, NY, 1990). Juvenal's sixth Satire, and the long passage of Theophrastus quoted by Jerome (see Headnote to WBPr), formed models for the genre, which were imitated by medieval writers from Walter Map's *Dissuasion of Valerius to Rufinus* (see n. to WB 671) in the twelfth century, to Deschamps, *Miroir de Mariage* in the fourteenth (see Miller, pp. 411–14, 438–46, and Mann, *Feminizing Chaucer*, pp. 40–47). Chaucer's own *Envoy to Bukton* is an example of the type. Less obviously, the enthusiastic encomium on marriage with which the tale opens also derives from this tradition; the dissuasion disguises itself as *per*suasion, given an ironic inflection by the context, so that the selfish expectations men have of marriage, and the knowledge that they are doomed to be disappointed, coexist within the same discourse (Mann, *Feminizing Chaucer*, pp. 47–52).

The old man married to a young wife is a familiar situation in the comic tales known as fabliaux (see Headnote to MilT), and the story of the blind husband cuckolded by his wife making love in a fruit-tree above his head has many parallels (see *SA*, pp. 341–56, and *SA*[2] II). In some stories, his sight is restored when he himself prays to God; in others, it is because God and St Peter observe the scene and the latter asks God to work the miracle. Only in Chaucer are Pluto and Proserpina the invisible spectators of the adultery; this change enables him to enrich his theme with another picture of a marital relationship that shows male aggression answered by female shrewishness (Mann,

Feminizing Chaucer, pp. 52–4). In all versions, the wife exculpates herself by claiming that her motive was to restore her husband's sight; thus taking her place with other fabliau wives who manage to persuade their husbands to disbelieve the evidence of their own eyes (see n. to Mch 2272–5).

1245–6 *Lumbardye ... Pavie*: Pavia, in the region of Lombardy in northern Italy, was a wealthy city in the fourteenth century. Lombard merchants were active in international trade and finance, and there were numbers of them resident in medieval London, whom Chaucer may have known.

1251 Some critics have thought that this line implies that the speaker is a cleric, and is therefore an indication that the tale was originally assigned to someone other than the Merchant; however, others have pointed out that it could quite well be spoken by a layman commenting sardonically on the folly of his own kind.

1294–1310 *Theofraste*: Theophrastus's arguments against marriage, including the points quoted here, are known only through their incorporation into Jerome's treatise *Against Jovinian* (I.47); see further Headnote to WBPr.

1305–6 The second half of line 1305, and line 1306, were originally left blank in Hg (presumably because the exemplar was illegible), and completed by a later hand with a unique and obviously spurious variant: 'she wole destroye I Thy good substance and thy body annoye'.

1310 The confident 'herke me' in this line throws into relief the difficulty of deciding who is to be identified as the speaker of this introductory passage. Its exuberant enthusiasm for women and marriage sorts oddly with the gloomy bitterness on these subjects exhibited by the Merchant in his Prologue. Although much of it can be read as sarcasm, and thus would fit the Merchant, it incorporates materials used elsewhere in *CT* in serious praise of women (see following notes). It might be taken as a quasi-dramatic representation of January's naive delusions, were it not that a more knowing attitude occasionally reveals itself (see lines 1316–18, 1378). For discussion of the problem, see D. R. Benson, *ChauR*, 14 (1979), 48–60, and for an attempt to resolve it, see Mann, *Feminizing Chaucer*, pp. 47–52.

1311–14 A Latin gloss in El and Hg quotes Albertano of Brescia, *De amore dei* (f. 40r): 'A wife should be loved because she is a gift of God. Jesus, son of Sirach [says that] "a house and riches are given by one's parents, but a good and prudent wife is truly from the Lord"' (the biblical quotation is actually from Proverbs 19:14). On this and other borrowings in MchT from the *De amore dei*, see E. Koeppel, *Archiv*, 86 (1891), 40–46.

1315 'To pass like a shadow' is a proverbial expression (see Whiting S185); 'upon the wal' is Chaucer's characteristic addition to it (see Sh 9, Pars 1068).

1325–35 These lines allude to Genesis 2:18, 21–4: 'And the Lord God said, "It is not good for man to be alone: let us make him a helpmeet like unto himself" ... So the Lord God put Adam to sleep, and when he had fallen asleep, he took one of his ribs, and replaced it with flesh. And the Lord God made the rib which he had taken from Adam into a woman, and led her to Adam. And Adam said, "This now is bone of my bones and flesh of my flesh" ... wherefore a man shall leave his father and mother and shall cleave to his wife, and they shall be two in one flesh.' A Latin gloss in El and Hg quotes the résumé of this biblical passage in Albertano of Brescia's *De amore dei*, f. 39v.

1341 The claim that something exceeds human powers of description is a rhetorical convention in medieval literature, known as the 'inexpressibility topos' (E. R. Curtius, *European Literature and the Latin Middle Ages*, tr. W. R. Trask (New York, 1953), p. 159).

1345 This line echoes Walter's proposal to Griselda at Cl 355.

1358–61 These lines are omitted in El, obviously by eyeskip between the end of line 1357 and the end of line 1361.

1362–74 The biblical heroines Rebecca, Judith, Abigail and Esther are also cited as examples of the 'good conseil' of women in Mel (1098–1101), whose ultimate source is the *Liber consolationis et consilii* (*Book of Consolation and Counsel*) of Albertano of Brescia (see Headnote to Mel); portions of this passage in the *Liber consolationis* (ed. Sundby, p. 17.7–17) are reproduced as marginal glosses in El and Hg. This makes it highly unlikely that these lines are to be read ironically (as they sometimes are), as *ipso facto* examples of the trickery or wiliness of women.

Rebekke: Jacob's mother Rebecca tied the skins of goat-kids on his hands and neck, so that his blind father Isaac was deceived into thinking he was his hairier brother Esau, and gave Jacob his elder brother's inheritance (Genesis 27:1–29).

Judith ... Olofernus: On Judith and Holofernes, see nn. to ML 939–42 and Mk 2551–74.

Abigail ... Nabal: Abigail appeased the anger of King David

against her husband Nabal; after Nabal's death, David took her
as his wife (1 Samuel 25).

Ester ... Mardochee ... Assuere: The biblical book of Esther
relates how Esther, wife of Ahasuerus, king of the Persians, saved
her people the Jews when they were threatened with destruction
by the king's councillor Haman; Mordecai, Esther's cousin and
adopted father, was then promoted in Haman's place.

1375–6 *Senek*: A Latin gloss in El and Hg likewise attributes to
Seneca the maxim 'As nothing is [superior] to a meek wife, so
nothing is worse than a quarrelsome woman'; in fact the quotation is taken from the story of Alcestis in Fulgentius's *Myth-
ologies* (I.22), and the immediate source is probably Albertano
of Brescia's *Liber consolationis et consilii*, ed. Sundby, p. 18.14–
18 (see n. to Mch 1362–74).

1377 *Caton*: On 'Cato', see n. to Mil 3227, and on Chaucer's use of
this well-known text, see R. Hazelton, *Speculum*, 35 (1960),
357–80. The proverb quoted is 'See that you endure your wife's
tongue, if she is thrifty' (*Distichs of Cato* III.23); it is also quoted
in Albertano of Brescia's *Liber consolationis* as part of the
defence of women which includes the passages used in Mch
1362–74 and 1375–6 (see nn.). The Latin original appears as a
marginal gloss in El and Hg.

1379 Probably an allusion to the passage of Albertano's *Liber consolationis* which immediately follows the quotations from 'Cato'
and Petrus Alfonsi referred to in the preceding and following
notes: 'a good woman, by acting well and obeying her husband,
wins him over to the extent that ... she seems to rule him' (ed.
Sundby, p. 19.6–9).

1380 A Latin gloss in El reads 'A good wife is a good and faithful
keeper of the household.' The maxim originates in Petrus
Alfonsi's *Disciplina clericalis* (Exemplum XIV, p. 22.4–5), and
is quoted both in Albertano of Brescia's *De amore dei* (f. 40v)
and in his *Liber consolationis* (ed. Sundby, p. 19.5–6), in the
section which includes the passages used in Mch 1362–74,
1375–6 and 1377 (see nn.).

1381–2 These lines are based on Ecclesiasticus 36:27: 'Where there
is no hedge, the property is despoiled, and where there is no wife,
a man will lament his poverty.' Chaucer's 'sike man' shows that
the intermediate source was Albertano's *De amore dei* (f. 40r),
where *eger* ('sick') is given as an alternative reading to the Bible's
egens ('poor').

1384–8 This compilation of verses from Paul's Epistle to the Ephesians (quoted as a marginal gloss in El and Hg) is borrowed from Albertano of Brescia's *De amore dei* (ff. 39v–40r), where it follows the quotation of Genesis used in Mch 1325–35 (see n.): 'The Apostle Paul to the Ephesians: Love your wives as Christ loved his church et cetera [Ephesians 5:25] . . . Thus the Apostle: Husbands ought to love their wives like their own bodies, for he who loves his wife loves himself. No one ever hated his own flesh, but nourishes and cherishes it [5:28–9] . . . And later: Let everyone love his wife as himself [5:33].'

1416–26 Albertano of Brescia similarly advises marrying a young girl rather than a widow (*De amore dei*, f. 40r).

1418–20 Proverbial; this is the first recorded example in English (see Whiting F236).

1424 *Wades boot*: Thomas Speght's edition of Chaucer (1598) refers to the story of Wade 'and his bote called Guingelot, as also his strange exploits in the same', but does not recount it, on the grounds that it was 'long and fabulous'. This decision was unfortunate, since no English version of the tale survives; for evidence of its nature provided by stories about Wade in Norse, German and Anglo-Latin, as well as brief allusions to it in English sources, see K. P. Wentersdorf, *JEGP*, 65 (1966), 274–86. Speght's characterization of the story, taken together with Chaucer's other reference to it at *TC* III.614, suggests that what the term means in this line is 'romancing' or 'spinning a line'.

1425 *broken harm*: F. G. Cassidy (*MLN*, 58 (1943), 23–7) suggests that 'broken' is not the past participle of 'break' but an infinitive of the verb 'brook', meaning 'to make use of, avail oneself of'. See *MED* s.v. brouken 2b.

1427–8 The Wife of Bath expresses a similar idea at WB 44c–e.

1448–52 The procreation of children, the avoidance of lechery and the payment of the marital 'debt' are the three reasons for sexual intercourse sanctioned in Pars 939–40; for a discussion of the views of medieval churchmen on the subject, see Kelly, *Love and Marriage*, pp. 245–63.

1452 For the idea that sexual intercourse is a 'debt' owed by one marital partner to the other, see n. to WB 129–30.

1476 *Placebo*: A Latin word meaning 'I shall please'. The name reflects Placebo's character as a yes-man. See also n. to Sum 2075.

1485–6 A quotation of Ecclesiasticus 32:24; see further n. to Mil 3530.

1524–5 The maxim is not from Seneca, but from the brief proverbs that preface the *Distichs of Cato*: 'Take care to whom you give' (17). The maxim is used as a warning against marriage in the *Dissuasio Valerii*: 'Friend, it is heathen wisdom to say: "Take heed to whom thou givest": it is Christian ethics to say "Take heed to whom thou givest thyself"' (pp. 294–5).

1532–6 This is a variation on the traditional complaint that whereas other goods can be tried out before purchase, a wife's character-istics can only be fully known after marriage; see WB 285–92, which is based on Jerome, *Against Jov.* I.47.

1537–9 Albertano of Brescia similarly insists that no wife is perfect, quoting the verse of Ecclesiastes to this effect which is used later in MchT by Pluto (*De amore dei*, f. 40v; cf. n. to Mch 2247–8).

1582–7 After falling in love with Criseyde, Troilus likewise makes 'a mirour of his mynde' in which he contemplates her image (*TC* I.365–6).

1598 The blindness of love, represented visually by the figure of the blind Cupid, was proverbial (see Whiting C634, and cf. Kn 1965, *HF* 137–8, *TC* III.1808).

1601–4 The details of May's beauty, and the language in which it is described, fit the conventional pattern of a rhetorical *descriptio* (see n. to Mil 3233 ff., and cf. the description of Criseyde at *TC* III.1247–50).

1640–41 Cf. Pars 388 and n.

1662 That is, 'before you are buried' (W. B. Ewald III, *ELN*, 15.4 (1978), 267–8).

1668–73 For the idea that the pains of marriage may replace the torments of purgatory, see n. to WB 489–90.

1685 This reference to the Wife of Bath by a character within the Merchant's story disrupts verisimilitude, and has been seen as a careless slip which Chaucer would have erased on revision. But it is not fundamentally different from the blurring of the boundaries between the fictional and the real worlds that occurs when the Man of Law cites Chaucer as a famous story-teller, or indeed when Chaucer includes himself as a character in *CT*.

1697–8 That is, January designated part of his property as May's dower, which would pass to her on his death; cf. nn. to WB 204, 801.

1703 The priest comes out of the church in order to perform the ceremony publicly at the church door; see n. to GP 460, and cf. WB 6.

1704 *Sarra ... Rebekke*: Sarah was wife of Abraham, Rebecca of Isaac (see n. to Mch 1362–74). The reference here is to the prayer in the marriage service that the wife may be 'wise as Rebecca, long-lived and faithful as Sara' (Miller, p. 381).

1716 In classical myth, Orpheus was a famous harpist whose music exerted such a powerful effect on the hearers that not only wild animals but also trees and rocks were drawn to him by the sound; see *Boece* III m.12; J. B. Friedman, *Orpheus in the Middle Ages* (Cambridge, MA, 1970). According to legend, Amphion, ruler of Thebes, built the walls of the city by playing music of such charm that the rocks moved of their own accord from the mountain-side (Statius, *Thebaid* I.9–10, VIII.232–3, X.873–7; Ovid, *Metamorphoses* VI.177–9; Horace, *Art of Poetry* 394–6. Cf. nn. to Kn 1546 and Mcp 116–18. Martianus Capella (see n. to Mch 1732) has Orpheus and Amphion play beautiful music at the marriage of Philology and Mercury (tr. Stahl, pp. 351–2).

1719 Joab was a commander of King David's army; for his trumpet-blowing, see 2 Samuel 2:28, 18:16, 20:22. He is also linked with Thiodamas at *HF* 1245–6.

1720 Thiodamas, a member of the expedition of the Seven Against Thebes (see n. to Kn 932), became the priestly augur of the attacking army after the death of Amphiaraus (Statius, *Thebaid* VIII.270–93). Statius does not represent him as blowing a trumpet, but trumpets sounded on the occasion of an assault on Thebes following a successful attack on the Theban encampment outside the walls, which Thiodamas had inspired (X.552–3).

1722–3 It seems that two participants in the wedding festivities were dressed as the classical gods Bacchus and Venus, representing wine and love respectively. Chaucer speaks as if the deities themselves were rendering the occasion auspicious by their presence.

1727 Venus's torch is a metaphor for sexual passion in the *Romance of the Rose* (3406–8, tr. Horgan, p. 52); the lady's final yielding to her lover is achieved when Venus uses her torch to set fire to the castle that represents her body (20755–66, 21221–32, tr. Horgan, pp. 320, 327).

1730 *Imeneus*: Hymen was the god of marriage in classical mythology.

1732 *Marcian*: Martianus Capella, a fifth-century Latin poet, was the author of a long allegorical work entitled *The Marriage of Philology and Mercury*, which was widely used as an educational text in the Middle Ages. The bulk of the work is an outline of the Seven Liberal Arts, which are metaphorically 'deified' by the marriage of Philology to the god. For a translation, see W. H. Stahl, *Martianus Capella and the Seven Liberal Arts*, 2 vols. (New York and London, 1971).

1734-5 Martianus describes the songs sung by each of the Nine Muses in turn in honour of the marriage between Philology and Mercury (II.117–26, tr. Stahl, pp. 40–45).

1736-9 Another example of an 'inexpressibility topos' (see n. to Mch 1341).

1744-5 On Esther and King Ahasuerus, see n. to Mch 1362–74. In order to save her people, Esther approached the king without being summoned, an action punishable by death unless the king held out his golden sceptre; her humble and timorous appearance as she did so is described in an apocryphal chapter (15) of the book of Esther.

1754 *Paris . . . Eleine*: The passionate love between Paris, prince of Troy, and Helen, wife of Menelaus, king of Lacedaemon, was the cause of the siege of Troy; cf. ML 70 and n.

1763 When Jupiter made love to Alcmena, he caused the night to be extended to twice (or three times, in some sources) its normal length; January wishes to have even greater scope for the satisfaction of his sexual appetite.

1773 On the squire's duty to carve his master's meat, see n. to GP 100 and cf. Sum 2244.

1784 *famulier foo*: Chaucer may have borrowed the phrase from Innocent III, who calls lechery a 'familiar enemy' ('Familiaris inimicus') because it lives not outside but within the person (*De Miseria* II.22), or from Boethius, who warns of the danger of 'a famylier enemy' (*Boece* III pr.5.70).

1786 This proverbial simile (Whiting A42) refers to the well-known fable in which a man warms a frozen snake in his bosom and takes it into his home, only to find that when revived it spreads poison everywhere (Hervieux, *Les fabulistes latins*, II, 199, 320).

1810-11 Constantinus Africanus was an eleventh-century medical authority whose books were for the most part translations of Arabic works (cf. GP 433); late in life he became a monk at Monte Cassino in southern Italy. His treatise *De Coitu* describes the biological treatments for sexual disorders, and concludes with a number of recipes for aphrodisiacs (M. Bassan, *Mediaeval Studies*, 24 (1962), 127–40); for an English translation by P. Delany, see *ChauR*, 4 (1970), 55–65.

1817 Wine was drunk as a bed-time drink; cf. GP 819–20 and *TC* III.674.

1818 *as stille as stoon*: The comparison is proverbial; see Whiting S772, and cf. Sq 171.

1819 The blessing of the marital bed and bedroom often formed part of the ceremonial rites of medieval marriage; see Miller, pp. 383–4.

1839–41 January has got this saying upside down, as can be seen from Pars 859. The analogy appears in Friar Lorens of Orléans's *Somme le Roi*, and the popularity of this work gave it wide currency as a warning against indulgence in lechery within marriage. See Whiting M154 and P. J. C. Field, *NQ*, 215 (1970), 84–6.

1843 A piece of bread dipped in wine was a normal medieval breakfast; cf. GP 334.

1885–7 *Taur . . . Cancre*: Taurus and Cancer are signs of the zodiac (see n. to Mch 2222–4). The moon's course passes through the zodiac approximately once every month; at noon on the day of January's marriage it was 2° into the sign of Taurus, and then passed through the remaining 28° of the sign and the whole 30° of the following sign of Gemini before entering the first degree of Cancer – that is, 59° in all. To cover this distance within four days, as Mch 1893 implies, the moon would have to be travelling faster than her average rate of motion, which is around 13° a day (Eade, pp. 133–4).

1926 True to Italian custom, January takes a siesta after the midday meal.

1951 That is, to the latrine or privy.

1967–81 Chaucer here ironically suggests a number of grandiose explanations for May's favourable response to the handsome young Damian, which needs no further explanation at all; the cosmic machinery of chance, destiny and planetary influence which plays a serious role in KnT (see Mann, 'Chance and Destiny', and cf. n. to Kn 1663–9) is here rendered comically superfluous.

1972 The maxim comes from the biblical book of Ecclesiastes (3:1); see further Fri 1475 and n., Cl 6.

1986 See n. to Kn 1761.

2014 *dogge for the bowe*: Proverbial; see Whiting D303 and cf. Fri 1369.

2021–2 At GP 336–8, this belief is attributed to the Greek philosopher Epicurus (see n.).

2029 January's walled garden evokes the 'garden enclosed' of the Song of Solomon (see n. to Mch 2138–48), which was interpreted in medieval biblical exegesis as a metaphor for the Virgin Mary's conception of Jesus without violation of her sexual intactness, and was thus a familiar motif in religious iconography. The walled garden also, however, appeared in secular contexts; see next n.

2032 The *Romance of the Rose* opens with a description of a surpassingly beautiful walled garden, in which the dreamer falls in love with the rosebud which represents his lady.

2034–5 In classical mythology, Priapus was the god of fruitfulness, and images of him were often placed in gardens. The story of the god's unbridled sexual desire for a nymph, and its humiliating exposure, which Chaucer alludes to in *PF* 253–6, is also relevant to January's uses for his garden, and the later development of the story.

2038–9 In Roman mythology, Pluto was the god who ruled over hell; he abducted Proserpina, daughter of Ceres, goddess of crops and fertility, as she gathered flowers in the fields of Enna, and although Ceres rescued her, she was obliged to return to the Underworld for six months every year because she had eaten six pomegranate seeds while there. The identification of Pluto and Proserpina with the King and Queen of 'Fairye' is unusual; Chaucer may have borrowed the idea from the ME romance *Sir Orfeo*, a reworking of the Orpheus myth in which the role played by Pluto in the classical story is played by a fairy king who presides over a Celtic otherworld rather than the pagan hell (ed. J. A. Burrow and T. Turville-Petre, *A Book of Middle English*, 2nd edn (Oxford, 1996), pp. 112–31). *Sir Orfeo* is contained in the large composite manuscript known as the Auchinleck MS, which Chaucer probably knew (L. H. Loomis, *SP*, 38 (1941), 14–33).

2048 On sex as a marital 'debt' see WB 129–30 and n.

2057–9 The comparison of Fortune to a scorpion is traditional; see Patch, *Goddess Fortuna*, p. 52, and cf. *BD* 636–41.

2080 The turtle-dove's fidelity to its mate was legendary; see *PF* 578–88 and Whiting T542.

2111–13 For the blinding of Argus, see n. to WB 358.

2115 *Passe over is an ese*: The expression is proverbial; see Whiting P44.

2125–7 love*] he El Hg. The quotation from Ovid confirms that 'love' is the correct reading; 'What is it that Love does not notice?' is his comment on Piramus and Thisbe's discovery of the crack in the wall between their parents' houses, through which they communicated (*Metamorphoses* IV.68).

2128–30 For the story of Piramus and Thisbe, see n. to ML 62–3.

2133 All manuscripts read 'Juil', but the mention of the zodiacal sign of Gemini in Mch 2222 led Manly and Rickert (III, 477) to conclude that this is an error for 'Juin'. *Riverside* adopts this reading, and also changes 'er' in this line to 'of', giving a date 'on or shortly before June 8'. Neither emendation seems necessary; if the sun is in Gemini but not far off crossing into Cancer, the date is early to mid-June (see n. to Mch 2222–4), and thus 'before the month of July' (cf. North, *Chaucer's Universe*, p. 447). The 'dayes eighte' (2132) are counted not from the beginning of June, but from the time when Damian copied the key; 'eighte dayes' is a conventional phrase meaning 'a week' (*MED* s.v. eighte 4), and is here used to indicate the shortness of the period rather than a precise date.

2138–48 January's 'olde lewed wordes' (2149) are a tissue of reminiscences of the biblical Song of Solomon, a passionate love-song uttered by two main speakers (man and woman). The erotic content was rendered acceptable to the Middle Ages by allegorical interpretations which explained it as an image of the love between Christ and his church (as, for example, in Jerome, *Against Jov.* I.30–31); January's lyrical invitation to May restores its literal meaning. The biblical verses alluded to are as follows (Song of Solomon 2:10–11, 12, 14; 4:1, 7, 9, 10, 12):

> See, my beloved says to me, Rise up, make haste, my love, my dove, my fair one, and come. For now the winter is past, the rain is over and gone [cf. lines 2138–40] ... the voice of the turtle-dove is heard in our land [cf. line 2139] ... My dove [cf. line 2139] ... thou hast doves' eyes [cf. line 2141] ... Thou art all fair, my love, and there is no spot in thee [cf. line 2146] ... Thou hast wounded my heart, my sister, my spouse [cf. line 2145] ... thy breasts are fairer than wine [cf. line 2142] ... A garden enclosed is my sister, my spouse [cf. line 2143].

2172–3 January has already settled part of his property on May as her dower (see n. to Mch 1697–8); he is now proposing to bequeath her the entirety of his estate.

2220 Phoebus is a Latin name for Apollo, god of the sun in classical mythology, and is here used as a synonym for the sun.

2222–4 The zodiac is an imaginary band round the earth lying on either side of the ecliptic, the sun's annual path through the heavens as it rises (in summer) or falls (in winter) in the sky. This band of the heavens is divided into 12 segments, each measuring

30°, and each named after a different sign of the zodiac. In the course of the year, each of these signs in turn serves as a background against which the sun rises and sets each day. In Chaucer's time, the sun rose and set in the sign of Gemini from 13 May to 12 June; it then passed into the sign of Cancer, in which its annual course reached its highest point in the sky at the summer solstice (21 June). This point represents the sun's greatest 'declinacion' or angular distance from the celestial equator, the imaginary band circling the earth at the level of the terrestrial equator (see Boyde, *Dante Philomythes*, pp. 144–9). The time specified thus seems to be the second week in June. The planet Jupiter has its 'exaltation' or greatest influence in the sign of Cancer (see n. to WB 701–5), and this influence would be of a benevolent character.

2229–33 Line 2230 was originally left blank in Hg; a later hand filled it with 'Whos answere hath doon many a man pine' (rhyming with 'Proserpine'). El has a different but equally spurious line, added in different ink: 'Ech after oother, right as a line'. Manly and Rickert (III, 477–8) plausibly suggest that the scribe of O¹ (the presumed archetype of all surviving MSS) erroneously copied 'Proserpina' at the end of line 2230 (an error preserved in many manuscripts), and that scribal attempts to recover the original reading led to worse corruption. What must be the correct version of Mch 2230 is found in only two manuscripts.

On Pluto's abduction of Proserpina, see n. to Mch 2038–9. The fifth-century Roman poet Claudian wrote a Latin poem on the subject called 'The Rape of Proserpina' (*De Raptu Proserpinae*), which vividly describes the terror and lamentations of the helpless girl as she is carried off, hair streaming in the wind, in Pluto's gloomy chariot (II.247–72). The work was widely known, since it formed part of the collection of school-texts (known as the 'Liber Catonianus') traditionally used in the Middle Ages as an initial reading programme for those learning Latin (see n. to Mil 3227). On Chaucer's knowledge of Claudian, see R. A. Pratt, *Speculum*, 22 (1947), 419–29. For the conflation of the concepts of rape and abduction in medieval thought, see C. Saunders, *Rape and Ravishment in the Literature of Medieval England* (Cambridge, 2001), esp. p. 20.

Ethna: Proserpina's abduction took place in a flowery meadow near Enna in the island of Sicily. Mount Etna is the most prominent geographical feature of Sicily, and is frequently mentioned in Claudian's poem.

2235 Turf benches, made by laying pieces of turf on a supporting
       base of earth or wood, were a popular form of seating in medieval
       gardens (see T. McLean, *Medieval English Gardens* (London,
       1981), p. 104, and cf. *LGW* F 203–5).

2240 tales] *om.* El Hg. The line as it stands is obviously defective in
       sense; a few manuscripts supply 'stories' or 'histories', but it is
       more likely that 'tales' was omitted through homeoarchy with
       'thousand' and 'telle'.

2242 *Salomon*: Solomon, son of David, king of Israel, when offered
       a gift by God, asked for wisdom, and was granted riches and
       honour in addition (2 Chronicles 1:7–12).

2247–8 Pluto is quoting the biblical book of Ecclesiastes, which was
       attributed to Solomon: 'One man among a thousand have I
       found, [but] a woman among them all I have not found' (7:29;
       AV 7:28). The text is also quoted by Melibee as a reason for
       rejecting the advice of his wife Prudence (Mel 1057).

2249 On Solomon's misogyny, see n. to WB 679.

2250 *filius Sirak*: The apocryphal book of Ecclesiasticus (see n. to
       Mil 3530) is attributed to one Jesus, son of Sirach; it contains
       numerous misogynist maxims (see, for example, 9:1–13, 26:5–
       15, 42:9–14). Cf. WB 651–3 and n.

2265 The father of Proserpina's mother Ceres was Saturn, father of
       the gods, and, as planet, wielder of great power (see n. to Kn
       2454 ff.).

2272–5 The women in medieval fabliaux (see Headnote to MilT)
       often manage to persuade their husbands to disbelieve the evi-
       dence of their own eyes when they have seen their wives with
       their lovers. In addition to the analogues to MchT referred to in
       the Headnote, see, for example, Marie de France, *Fables*, nos.
       44–5, and Boccaccio, *Decameron* VII.9 (a tale involving a pear-
       tree), which is based on the early medieval Latin poem *Lydia*.
       Nature's priest Genius in the *Romance of the Rose* also claims
       that, if only Venus had been able to cover up her nakedness
       before being found by her husband Vulcan with her lover Mars,
       she would easily have managed to make him believe the adultery
       had never happened: 'Even if he had actually seen it, she would
       have told him that his sight was dim and disturbed' (18079–99,
       tr. Horgan, p. 279).

2277–90 Proserpina's arguments here are also used by Prudence
       against her husband Melibee (Mel 1076–80).

2290 Proserpina is referring to Christ's words to a man who had
       addressed him as 'Good master': 'Why callest thou me good?

None is good but one, that is God' (Mark 10:18; cf. Matthew
19:17 and Luke 18:19).

2293–2302 The building of the temple in Jerusalem by Solomon is
described in 1 Kings, chs. 5–7. He had, however, many wives of
different faiths, and in his old age they persuaded him to worship
their gods and build shrines to them, for which God decreed that
the kingdom should be lost to his son after his death (1 Kings
11:1–13).

lechour: On Solomon's lechery, see n. to WB 35–6.

2307 The reference is not precise enough to make it clear which
passage of the Solomonic books of the Bible is here referred to;
women are represented as quarrelsome shrews in Proverbs 19:13,
21:9, 19, 25:24, 27:15, and Ecclesiasticus 25:27, 26:9.

2315 The romance convention that a king cannot go back on his
word once it has been pledged plays a crucial role in *Sir Orfeo*
(ed. Burrow and Turville-Petre, *Book of Middle English*, lines
449–71; cf. n. to Mch 2038–9).

2335–7 *plit*: It appears from this that May is pregnant, and pretends
to be subject to one of the cravings for particular food that
women in this condition often experience.

THE MERCHANT'S EPILOGUE/
THE SQUIRE'S PROLOGUE

Mch 2419–40/Sq 1–8 Editors have conventionally divided these lines
into the 'Merchant's Epilogue' and the 'Introduction to the Squire's
Tale', with a break at line 2440. However, they form a continuous
unit in all the manuscripts in which they occur (though in Hg, 'Frankelein' is substituted for 'Squier' in line 2441, to cope with the fact that
the Franklin's Tale had already been copied after the Merchant's Tale
when the link reached the scribe). In El, the heading 'The Prologe of
the Squieres Tale' is placed before line 2419. For the sake of conformity
with the current practice of line-numbering in *CT*, this transitional
passage has been divided between Sq and Mch, and the El heading
has been omitted.

2422 *bisy as bees*: A proverbial comparison; see Whiting B165, and
cf. SN 195.

2426 *trewe as . . . steel*: Also a proverbial comparison; see Whiting
S709.

2435–7 Since there are only three women among the Canterbury
pilgrims, and it seems unlikely that the Prioress or the Second

Nun would indulge in tell-tale gossip of this sort, it appears that the Host is making a fairly obvious reference to the Wife of Bath.

THE SQUIRE'S TALE

There is no single source or analogue which provides a close parallel to the narrative of this fragmentary tale, or which makes it possible to conjecture how it would have ended; rather, it appears to be an assemblage of motifs, most of which are taken from the world of oriental legend or romance (see *SA*[2] I, 169–209, and nn. to Sq 115–28, 132–6).

The core of the narrative, at least in the form we have it, or what Chaucer calls the 'knotte' of the tale (401, 407), is Canacee's encounter with the female falcon lamenting the infidelity of her lover. The theme of betrayal is of major importance in Chaucer's works (see Mann, *Feminizing Chaucer*, ch. 1), and this episode draws on a passage of Boethius (*Boece* III m.2) on the ineradicability of natural instinct (see n. to Sq 607–20), which Chaucer also paraphrases in the Manciple's Tale (163–74). In both cases, natural instinct in men is said to take the form of 'newfangelnesse' (610; cf. Mcp 187–95), the changeability which takes a tragic shape in the act of betrayal, but which in benign form manifests itself as the 'pitee' that characterizes the 'gentil herte' of Canacee, as of Theseus in the Knight's Tale (see n. to Sq 479–83). So, although this tale is unfinished, it is possible to recognize in it some central Chaucerian themes and significant links with some of the other tales.

9 *Sarray*: 'Sarai ... the imperial capital of the Golden Horde in Russia during the fourteenth century, was a flourishing metropolis and international trade center which attracted merchants and statesmen from all over the world' (C. Jordan, *ChauR*, 22 (1987), 128–40). The Golden Horde was the name given to the thirteenth-century Mongol invaders, led by Genghis Khan, who came down from the Mongolian steppes and conquered China, eventually establishing an empire that stretched from Persia to Korea.

 Tartarye: A loose geographical term, here referring to the western Mongol empire in the steppes of southern Russia (Magoun, p. 151). For knowledge of this region in medieval Europe, and the travellers' tales that gave it its romantic associations in Chaucer's day, see D. Bethurum, ed., *Chaucer. The Squire's Tale*

(Oxford, 1965), pp. vii–xvii, and M. Cornelia, *Dalhousie Review*, 57 (1977), 81–9.

10   *werreyed Russie*: For the constant struggles between Russia and the Mongols, see C. J. Halperin, *Russia and the Golden Horde* (Bloomington, IN, 1985).

12   Since 'Khan' was the title given to Mongol rulers, it has been suggested that 'Cambiuskan' is a westernized version of Ghengis Khan (see n. to Sq 9). However, it was only after his death that the Mongols overran Russia, where Sarai was situated (C. McEvedy, *The Penguin Atlas of Medieval History* (Harmondsworth, 1961), pp. 74–7).

29–33   Elpheta is the name of a star (α Coronae Borealis), and because of this, some scholars have attempted to read SqT as an astrological allegory (North, *Chaucer's Universe*, pp. 263–88; D. Metlitzki, *The Matter of Araby in Medieval England* (New Haven, CT, 1977), pp. 77–80), but since Algarsif, Cambalo and Canacee are not star names, it seems probable that Chaucer chose all of them for their exotic sound rather than for an occult meaning. Canace is the name of one of Ovid's heroines (see n. to ML 77–8), but the tale told of her incestuous relationship with her brother has no point of contact with SqT as it stands.

47–51   According to the Roman calendar, the Ides of March fall on the 15th of the month. On this date, the sun has travelled 3° into the zodiacal sign of Aries (see nn. to GP 8 and Mch 2222–4), which is a domicile or 'mansion' of Mars – that is, one of the two signs over which this planet exerts special influence. In addition, each sign of the zodiac is subdivided into three equal parts of ten degrees each, known as faces, and each face is governed by one of the planets; the first face of Aries is governed by Mars, who is thus doubly influential at this point. The sun is near its 'exaltation' or position of greatest influence (see n. to WB 701–5), which occurs at 19° in Aries (Eisner, *Kalendarium*, pp. 180–81; North, *Chaucer's Universe*, p. 265).

colerik hote signe: The signs of the zodiac were each characterized in terms of the four 'humours' which were held to determine the nature of the cosmos as well as of the human body (see n. to GP 333); Aries has the characteristics of choler (hot and dry); see *The Kalender of Shepherdes*, ed. H. O. Sommer, 3 vols. in 1 (London, 1892), III, 100, and North, *Chaucer's Universe*, p. 197.

64   *a someres day*: Specified because the 'artificial' day (the time between sunrise and sunset) is longer in summer than in winter.

80–81 The ME romance *Sir Gawain and the Green Knight* likewise begins with a strange knight riding into the king's hall during a feast, and the mention of 'Gawain, with his olde curteisye' (95) makes it tempting to suppose that Chaucer had it in mind here, but there are numerous parallels in other romances (see B. J. Whiting, *Mediaeval Studies*, 9 (1947), 189–234, at p. 232). It also happened in real life; for example, at the coronation feasts of the English kings, it was customary for the king's champion to ride into the hall to defend, if necessary, his claim to the crown against all comers; see the *Anonimalle Chronicle*, ed. V. H. Galbraith (Manchester, 1970), p. 115 (Richard II), and Froissart, *Chronicles*, tr. G. Brereton (Harmondsworth, 1968), p. 466 (Henry IV).

95 For exhaustive documentation of Gawain's reputation for courtesy in medieval Arthurian romance, see Whiting, *Mediaeval Studies*, 9 (1947), 189–234, esp. pp. 215–30. It is referred to in *RR* 18668–9 (tr. Horgan, p. 288).

96 The magical events which take place in Arthurian romances must have led Chaucer to associate them with the fairy world (cf. WBT 857–61), although they are actually set in Britain.

103–4 Rhetorical treatises regularly prescribed that voice, expression and gesture should match the subject-matter of a speech; see, for example, Horace, *Ars poetica* 99–118; *Ad C. Herennium* III.15; Geoffrey of Vinsauf, *Poetria Nova* 2031–65 (tr. Nims, pp. 90–91). See further B. Rowland, *SAC*, 4 (1982), 33–51.

110 *of Arabe and of Inde*: R. Pratt (*CT*, p. 375, n.) 'identifies *Arabe and Inde* with Mameluke Egypt, that is, Egypt and the Arab countries of the Near East, or India Minor, as it was called . . . It is, of course, unproved whether or not, whatever title Chaucer used, he had a precise idea of the geography' (D. C. Baker, ed., *A Variorum Edition of the Works of Geoffrey Chaucer: The Squire's Tale* (Norman, OK, 1990), p. 152, n.; see further *SA²* I, 173).

115–28 A flying horse which is operated by turning various pins plays an important part in two long romances in medieval French: the *Roman de Cléomadès* of Adenès li Rois (see the excerpts in *SA*, pp. 364–74), and the *Méliacin* of Girard of Amiens (see the excerpts in *SA²* I, 176–80). In both cases, the horse is one of a number of amazing gifts presented by strangers arriving at a king's feast.

131 *seel*: *MED* (sel(e *n* (3) 4b) glosses this as 'a seal having some function in magic' (see also Skeat's note on this line).

bond: *MED* classifies this quotation under 5a, 'A force that dominates, controls, compels, constrains, or restrains . . .' *Riverside* explains it as 'the controlling force of the practitioner's knowledge', unless 'used in a more technical sense (elsewhere unattested)'; this seems to extend sense 5a further than is natural, and the immediate meaning is still not clear. The proximity of 'bond' to 'seel' suggests rather that it is used here in the sense of 'legal document' (see *MED* 4), but the precise meaning of the whole line remains elusive.

132–6 A similar magic mirror appears in the legends concerning Prester John, the mythical Christian ruler of a remote land in Asia (*SA*, pp. 357–63, and *SA*² I, 187). See also n. to Sq 231.

146–52 The magical ability to communicate with birds and/or animals is a recurrent feature of romance narratives and popular tales in both East and West. For a collection of examples, see the section on 'The Language of Animals', pp. 348–71 in W. A. Clouston, *Notes on the Magical Elements in Chaucer's Squire's Tale, and Analogues*, printed in *John Lane's Continuation of Chaucer's Squire's Tale*, ed. F. J. Furnivall (London, 1888–90). See also n. to Sq 247–51.

164–5 See n. to Sq 236–40.

171 The comparison is proverbial; see Whiting S772, and cf. Mch 1818.

193–5 *Lumbardye . . . Poileis*: Lombardy (N. Italy) and Apulia (S. Italy) 'had produced quality horses for centuries'; see Hyland, *Horse*, p. 27.

203 An English version of the Latin proverb 'Quot homines, tot sententiae' ('There are as many opinions as men'); see Walther 26216 and Whiting H230.

207 *Pegasee*: The winged horse Pegasus sprang from the blood of Medusa when the Greek hero Perseus struck off her head. He was later caught by Bellerophon, who tried to ascend to heaven on his back, but fell to earth; Pegasus, however, continued his ascent and took up a place among the stars.

209–10 The Greek Sinon, posing as a renegade, deceived the Trojans into believing that the Greek army had sailed for home, leaving behind a huge wooden horse as an appeasement to Pallas Athene for the theft of the sacred image known as the Palladium. The Trojans then broke down their city walls in order to drag the horse inside, and at night Sinon let out the body of armed Greeks concealed within its belly, who set about the destruction of Troy (*Aeneid* II.57–267).

217–19 For the elaborate theatrical illusions produced as entertainments at medieval feasts, see nn. to Fkl 1142–51 and 1189–
1201.

228–35 Alocen (Latin, Alhazen) is the Arab Ibn al-Haithan (c. 965–
1039), author of an influential treatise on optics. Vitulon (Latin
Vitello) is the thirteenth-century Pole Witelo, who wrote a treatise on perspectives which drew on Alhazen's work. Aristotle
may be mentioned because of his explanations of rainbows in
Meteorologica III.2–4, or because he is cited, along with Alhazen,
in a discussion of optics, rainbows and mirrors in *RR* 18000–30
(tr. Horgan, p. 278). For translated extracts from medieval works
discussing mirrors and angles of reflection, see Grant, *Source
Book*, pp. 410–35.

231 In the Middle Ages, the Roman poet Vergil enjoyed an entirely
mythical reputation as a magician and inventor, and he was said
to have made a magic mirror, placed on a tower, which revealed
approaching enemies (see D. Comparetti, *Vergil in the Middle
Ages*, tr. E. F. M. Benecke (Hamden, CT, 1966), pp. 303–5).
This mirror is mentioned in *Cléomadès* (*SA²* I, 188), and also in
Gower, *CA* V.2031–2224); the legend seems to have been well
known. Cf. *SA²* I, 186–95.

236–40 *Thelophus*: The Greek hero Achilles wounded and healed
Telephus, king of Mysia, with the same magic spear; see Ovid,
Metamorphoses XII.112, XIII.171–2; *Tristia* V.ii.15; *Remedies
of Love* 44–8. Further references in *SA²* I, 200–201.

247–51 According to legend, Moses got rid of his Ethiopian wife
Tarbis by making two rings set with magic stones, one of which
induced memory and the other forgetfulness, and giving the latter
to his wife. This story is found in Peter Comestor's *Historia
Scholastica*, *PL* 198, col. 1144, repeated verbatim by Vincent of
Beauvais, *Speculum Historiale*, II.ii (p. 48). It also appears in
Nicholas Trevet's *Chronicle* (R. M. Correale, *ChauR*, 25 (1991),
238–65, at pp. 260–61), and in Gower, *CA* IV.647. See *SA²* I,
196–200.

The idea that Solomon could speak with animals arose from a
misinterpretation of 1 Kings 4:33, which represents him as speaking *about* animals.

254 Skeat's note to this passage explains that 'Glass contains two
principal ingredients, sand and some kind of alkali'. Ferns were
burned to supply the latter until long after Chaucer's time (F. de
Tollenaere, *English Studies*, 31 (1950), 97–9). Chaucer may have
learned of the making of glass from ashes of ferns in *RR* (16066–

75, tr. Horgan, p. 249). The whole process is described in the technical treatise *On the Colours and Arts of the Romans* written by Eraclius, ed. Mrs Merrifield, *Original Treatise . . . on the Arts of Painting*, vol. I (London, 1849), pp. 212–13.

263–5 *angle meridional*: This is the tenth of the twelve 'houses' into which astrologers divided the heavens, and which were numbered counterclockwise round the earth from a starting-point on the eastern horizon (see n. to ML 302–8). The meridian is a notional line which passes from north to south through the zenith (the point immediately over an observer's head), and it is crossed by the sun at midday (Grimm, *Astronomical Lore*, p. 81). Hence, the time is just after noon. The zodiac, as part of the sphere of fixed stars, rotates daily round the earth; since the sun is rising in Aries, this sign moves with him round the sky, and when it is passing through the meridian, Leo is, in Chaucer's latitude, rising on the eastern horizon. Aldiran was the name given to a star in the constellation Leo (North, *Chaucer's Universe*, pp. 268–70).

272 Those born under the influence of a planet partook of its qualities and were known as its 'children'; see J. Seznec, *The Survival of the Pagan Gods*, tr. B. F. Sessions (New York, 1953), pp. 70–76.

273 The zodiacal sign of Pisces (the Fishes) is Venus's 'exaltation' (the sign in which she exerts greatest influence); see Eisner, *Kalendarium*, p. 180, North, *Chaucer's Universe*, p. 268, and n. to WB 701–5.

287 Lancelot is mentioned as the prime representative of Arthurian chivalry (cf. Sq 95–7) rather than as someone notable for narrative skill.

306 See n. to Sq 209–10. According to Vergil, the Trojan horse was made of wood (*Aeneid* II.16), but according to Guido delle Colonne, Bk XXX (ed. Griffin, p. 230; tr. Meek, p. 221), who is followed by Gower (*CA* I.1131), it was made of brass.

352 According to *The Kalender of Shepherdes* (ed. Sommer, III, 117), the 'humour' of blood (see n. to GP 333) was dominant from midnight until 6 a.m.

376–7 The syntax in these two lines is strangely back to front; what is meant is clearly, 'Her governess, being one of these old women who like to be held wise, answered . . .'

385 *the yonge sonne*: See n. to GP 7.

386 *the Ram*: On 16 March, the sun was at 4° 35' in Aries (Eisner, *Kalendarium*, p. 77; see n. to Sq 47–51); Eade (pp. 143–4) argues

that lines 386–7 also imply that the sun was only 4° above the horizon when Canacee went out.

428–9 Since the Latin *peregrinus* means 'traveller, pilgrim', the notion that the bird was 'from a foreign land' seems to derive from a fanciful interpretation of its name.

479–83 The affinity between 'pitee' and the 'gentil herte' is demonstrated in Theseus (Kn 1761), King Alla (ML 660) and Alcestis (*LGW* F 503, G 491), as well as Canacee. It appears in parodic form in Chaucer's comment on May's receptiveness to Damian (Mch 1986).

485–7 Chaucer sees pity, like patience, as a fundamentally female quality; the phrase 'wommanly pitee' is frequent in his works (see Kn 3083, and cf. Mann, *Feminizing Chaucer*, pp. 32–4, 134–6).

491 That is, great men can learn from the example of their inferiors. A very common medieval proverb in various languages; for its English version, see Whiting W211. The idea is that beating a puppy in front of a lion will subdue the lion, who does not realize that his own strength is great enough to resist.

511 *in grein*: The term is used of colours that are fast dyed (cf. Th 727, NP 3459). There is a pun on the literal meaning of 'colours' and its metaphorical sense, 'false appearances'; cf. *Boece* I m.5.44–5.

537 This proverb is recorded only in Chaucer; see Whiting W259, and cf. *LGW* F 464–5 and *Anel* 105.

543 Biblical exegesis of Job 4:11 interpreted the tiger as a type of the hypocrite (M. Storm, *ELN*, 14.3 (1977), 172–4).

548 On Paris's seduction of Helen, wife of Menelaus, see n. to ML 70. On Jason's treachery to his lover Medea, see n. to ML 72–4.

550–51 On Lamech and his two wives, see n. to WB 54–8.

562–71 This picture of male 'obeisaunce' leading to a reciprocal female 'obeisaunce' and thus to a fusion of two wills into one is characteristic of Chaucer's pictures of happiness in love; see *TC* III.477–83, 1690; WB 1236–56; Fkl 738–90. Cf. Mann, *Feminizing Chaucer*, pp. 51, 74, 84–6, 88–90.

593 *made vertu of necessitee*: The phrase is proverbial, and one that was important to Chaucer; see n. to Kn 3041–2.

602–3 The first recorded use of this proverb; see Whiting S639.

605–6 *Riverside* follows Hg's paragraph mark and makes a syntactic break at the end of line 605, but it makes little sense to take line 606 with what follows.

607–20 The 'text' referred to here is Boethius's *Consolation of*

Philosophy, which describes the power of Nature through a series
of examples illustrating the irrepressibility of natural instinct.

> And the janglynge brid that syngeth on the heghe braunches (that
> is to seyn, in the wode), and after is enclosed in a streyte cage,
> althoughe that the pleyinge bysynes of men yeveth [hym] honyed
> drynkes and large metes with swete studye, yit natheles yif thilke
> bryd skippynge out of hir streyte cage seith the agreables schadwes
> of the wodes, sche defouleth with hir feet hir metes ischad, and
> seketh mornynge oonly the wode, and twytereth desyrynge the
> wode with hir swete voys . . . Alle thynges seken ayen to hir propre
> cours, and alle thynges rejoysen hem of hir retornynge ayen to hir
> nature.   (*Boece* III m.2.21–31, 39–42)

Chaucer's addition to this passage is to identify the nature of
men as 'newfangelnesse', the appetite for novelty. In Boethius,
the caged bird is offered as an instructive example to the human
reader; in SqT, it is another bird who quotes this instructive
example, and it is given human implications through the anthro-
pomorphism with which the falcon and her mate are represented.
As A. David suggests (*SAC, Proceedings*, 1 (1984), 105–15, at
pp. 112–13), Chaucer may also have been consciously inverting
Jean de Meun's use of Boethius's caged bird passage in the speech
of the Old Woman, where it is applied to *women's* ineradicable
desire for sexual freedom (*RR* 13911–36, tr. Horgan, p. 215).
Cf. Mcp 163–74 and n.

644 Alternative spellings such as 'velewet' confirm that 'veluettes' is
to be pronounced with four syllables (see *MED* s.v. velvet).

645 The refrain of Chaucer's poem 'Against Women Unconstant',
which reproaches a mistress for her 'newefangelnesse', runs 'In
stede of blew, thus may ye were al grene'. Criseyde's offer to
send Troilus a blue ring in token of her fidelity likewise implies
that blue symbolizes constancy (*TC* III.885).

648 The 'tidif' (a bird whose identity is uncertain) is said to be guilty
of infidelity to its mate at *LGW* F 154. It is not clear why tercels
and owls should be considered unfaithful.

649–50 All manuscripts have these lines in the reverse order, but this
makes little sense, and *Riverside* is induced to omit 'And', and
make a syntactic break at the end of line 648 to mend matters.
It is simpler to assume that the lines were reversed in the archetype (as Sq 509–10 are in Hg).

654–5 If this indication of the later development of the story had been fulfilled, SqT would have been the only instance in Chaucer's works of betrayal healed by repentance and reconciliation. Was SqT left unfinished because this task proved too difficult?

661–70 In the absence of any close analogue to SqT (see Headnote), it is impossible to flesh out this skeletal account of the subsequent narrative. If related at the same leisurely pace as the story so far, the narrative here outlined would have been extremely lengthy; perhaps that is another reason why Chaucer abandoned it.

668–9 Since Cambalo is Canacee's brother (see Sq 28–33), these lines have been taken to mean that the tale would have turned into a story of brother-sister incest, comparable to Ovid's story of Canace and Macareus (see n. to ML 77–85). However, in the romance *Cléomadès*, which provides a distant analogue to SqT, the hero defends his sister against an unwelcome marriage, and it may be that something similar is alluded to here.

671–2 With the approach of summer, the sun (Apollo) rises higher in the sky each day; it is now rising and setting in one of the two zodiacal signs which are 'mansions' or 'domiciles' of Mercury (see n. to Sq 47–51) – probably Gemini, which the sun enters on 13 May, rather than Virgo, which it enters in August (North, *Chaucer's Universe*, pp. 195, 282–3).

THE SQUIRE–FRANKLIN LINK

673–4 The Franklin's words imply that the Squire has finished his tale, and do not support the suggestion sometimes made that he is interrupting the young man in mid-stream.

693 The Franklin's concern over his son's lack of 'gentillesse' has often been seen as a sign of 'middle-class' aspirations to the values of a higher social stratum, but it can equally (or more plausibly) be seen as the traditional lament of a member of the country gentry that the younger generation is 'going to the dogs'. On the Franklin's social status, see nn. to GP 331 and 360.

THE FRANKLIN'S TALE

Chaucer's most probable source for the Franklin's Tale is Boccaccio's *Filocolo* (Book IV, Question 4), where a similar story is one of a number told to illustrate 'questions of love' (see n. to Fkl 1621–2); an almost identical version appears in the *Decameron* (X.5). Both versions are printed with facing English translation in *SA*[2] I, 220–44. English translations of the *Filocolo* story are also included in Miller, pp. 122–35, Kolve and Olson, pp. 393–403, and (excerpts only) Havely, *Chaucer's Boccaccio*, pp. 153–61. Chaucer made a number of significant changes to the narrative: he gave it a setting in Brittany and claimed it was a Breton lay (see n. to Fkl 709–15); he added a long prefatory section concerning the love between Dorigen and Arveragus and its basis in patience; he added Dorigen's lament over the threatening black rocks, and changed the nature of the impossible task which must be performed by her would-be lover from the creation of a spring garden in winter to the removal of these rocks from the coast of Brittany; finally, he changed the nature of the magic through which this impossible task is accomplished, so that instead of a sorcerer concocting a 'witch's brew' from exotic ingredients collected during an aerial ride in a chariot drawn by dragons, the magician is a clerk from the University of Orleans using astronomical tables and scientific calculations (see nn. to Fkl 1273–9, 1280–90). In Chaucer's hands, the tale is not merely material for a playful intellectual exercise, but an exploration of patience in action, worked out in a successive chain of generous acts, which bring about a final harmony (see Mann, *Feminizing Chaucer*, pp. 88–95).

709–15 No lays in the Breton language survive (if, indeed, they ever existed); the AN poet Marie de France (late 12th c.) is the first writer to speak of the form and to claim to reproduce some of its material in her verse narratives. Chaucer most probably became acquainted with the genre through the two ME romances in the Auchinleck MS which call themselves Breton lays, *Lai le Freine* and *Sir Orfeo* (L. H. Loomis, *SP*, 38 (1941), 14–33). From the prologue to *Le Freine* he could have gleaned all the information about Breton lays that appears in these lines: they belong to 'olden days'; they have a musical accompaniment; they are about 'aventures' (see *SA²* I, 218).

The story of the Franklin's Tale is nowhere else presented as a Breton lay, and Chaucer seems to have taken it from Boccaccio (see Headnote). His reasons for associating it with the Breton lay may have been (first) that the development of the plot turns on 'aventure' (1501, 1508), and (second) that the Breton lay characteristically endorses a surrender of the self to 'aventure' which resembles the responses of Arveragus, Dorigen and Aurelius to the events that challenge them (see Mann, 'Chaucerian Themes and Style in the Franklin's Tale', *The New Pelican Guide to English Literature*, ed. B. Ford, vol. I (Harmondsworth, 1982), pp. 144–51).

716–19   The Franklin's protestation of his lack of rhetorical skill is itself a conventional rhetorical formula, known as the 'modesty-topos' (E. R. Curtius, *European Literature and the Latin Middle Ages*, tr. W. R. Trask (New York, 1953), pp. 83–5).

721   *mount of Parnaso*: Mount Parnassus was reputed to be the home of the Muses, the goddesses of poetry and song. This line echoes the Prologue to the *Satires* written by the Roman poet Persius (AD 34–62), who similarly claims a lack of poetic skill: 'I never washed my lips in the horse's spring [Hippocrene, struck from the ground by the hoof of the winged horse Pegasus], nor did I ever dream on twin-peaked Parnassus, that I should suddenly come forth as a poet.'

722   *Scithero*: The Roman writer Marcus Tullius Cicero (106–43 BC) was the author of two rhetorical treatises which were influential in the Middle Ages (*De inventione* and *Topica*), and the putative author of the even more influential *Rhetorica ad Herennium* (J. J. Murphy, *Rhetoric in the Middle Ages* (Berkeley, CA, 1974), pp. 8–21).

723, 726   On rhetorical 'colours', see n. to Cl 16–18.

729   *Armorik . . . Britaine*: Armorica is an ancient name for Brittany or 'Little Britain', which was sometimes used to distinguish it from Great Britain (cf. Fkl 810, and see J. S. P. Tatlock, *The Scene of the Franklin's Tale Visited* (London, 1914), pp. 17–18).

764–6   The ultimate source of this idea is probably Ovid's comment on the levelling effects of love on Jupiter, king of the gods, 'Love and majesty do not go together well, nor dwell in the same place' (*Metamorphoses* II.846–7), but Chaucer is closer to *RR* 9409–12, where Friend advises the lover that 'love must die when lovers assume authority. Love cannot last or survive except in hearts that are free and at liberty' (tr. Horgan, p. 144). For the surrender of 'maistrye' as fundamental to Chaucer's ideas of happiness in love, see Mann, *Feminizing Chaucer*, ch. 3.

773–8   'Patience conquers' ('patientia vincit') was an extremely well-known proverb; see Whiting P61 and Walther 16974, 20833f and 24454, and cf. Pars 661 and n., and *TC* IV.1584. It is an idea of central importance in Chaucer's works (see Mann, *Feminizing Chaucer*, pp. 89–94, 125–8), and is exemplified in the narrative of MLT and ClT as well as FklT.

801   Penmark*] Pedmark El Hg. J. S. P. Tatlock plausibly identified this as the Pointe de Penmarch, 'the southern cape of the most southerly of the three parallel peninsulas in which Brittany ends to the west' (*Scene of the Franklin's Tale*, p. 2). But Tatlock's

attempt to justify the spelling 'Pedmark' is unconvincing; Penmark unquestionably better represents the Breton place-name, and there is no reason why it should have undergone phonetic change in English. 'Pedmark' is probably a simple scri-bal error.

808 *Kairrud*: This is recognizably a Breton name, meaning 'red vil-lage' or 'red town', though it is more likely to have been spelled Kaerruz (in Breton) or Carru (in French). There are some villages with this name (or similar) in modern Brittany, but none that is close enough to the sea to fit FklT (Tatlock, *Scene of the Franklin's Tale*, pp. 10–16).

Arveragus: The name seems to have been borrowed by Chaucer from Geoffrey of Monmouth's *History of the Kings of Britain* IV.12–16 (tr. L. Thorpe (Harmondsworth, 1966), pp. 119–23), where it belongs to the younger son of Cymbeline, king of Britain. It thus fits the setting of FklT in Celtic antiquity.

810 See n. to Fkl 729.

815 *Dorigene*: For similar (though not identical) Breton names, see Tatlock, *Scene of the Franklin's Tale*, pp. 37–41.

829–31 In the tale from *Filocolo* which is Chaucer's source (see Headnote), the image of dripping water wearing away a stone is applied to the possibility that the lover may, by persevering in his attentions, succeed in winning the wife's favour (SA^2 I, 220). The source of the dictum is Ovid, *Ex Ponto* IV.x.5; it is also proverbial (see Walther 5599a and Singer, I, 23). Chaucer gives an unusual turn to the notion by linking it to the process of engraving.

859 The rocks off the cape of Penmarch (see n. to Fkl 801) are indeed 'grisly', and particularly dangerous to ships; however, the shore-line is flat, and does not correspond to the picture given here of a bank 'an heigh' (849) from which Dorigen looks down at them (Tatlock, *Scene of the Franklin's Tale*, pp. 4–9).

865–72 Dorigen's questioning of God's providence echoes Boethius's complaints about divine justice in the *Consolation of Philosophy* (*Boece* I m.5), and is a characteristically Chaucerian addition to the tale (cf. Kn 1262–74, 1313–14, and nn., and ML 813–17 and n.).

880 Dorigen is referring to God's creation of man in his own image (Genesis 1:27) – anachronistically, since the story is supposed to be set in pagan antiquity.

906–17 A beautiful spring garden is a traditional setting for courtly enjoyments and for love (cf. *PF* 172–210, and Mch 2028–37);

the *locus classicus* for this tradition is the opening of the *Romance of the Rose*, but these lines have some echoes of Machaut's *Dit dou Vergier* (*Oeuvres*, ed. E. Hoepffner, vol. I (Paris, 1908), lines 37–67).

938 The name Aurelius is, like Arveragus (see n. to Fkl 808), apparently borrowed from Geoffrey of Monmouth's *History of the Kings of Britain*, where it is the name of a British king (VIII.1–14, tr. Thorpe, pp. 186–200).

942 For the expression 'to drink without cup', meaning 'to suffer intensely', see Whiting C628.

948 *compleintes*: Poetic love-laments. Chaucer's shorter poems include several laments of this sort.

   roundels, virelayes: The rondeau and the virelai were two of the three fixed lyric forms which dominated French song and poetry in the fourteenth and fifteenth centuries (the other being the ballade). Their usual subject-matter was love. The most common form of the rondeau in the fourteenth century was an eight-line strophe which began and ended with a two-line refrain, and also included the first line of the refrain as the fourth line of the strophe. (Cf. n. to Kn 1529.) The virelai has a more complex form: its basic musical structure is AbbaA, where the letters indicate the musical segments and the capital indicates the repetition of refrain text (*New Grove Dictionary*, s.vv. Rondeau, Virelai).

950 In Greek mythology, the Furies (Erinyes) are 'spirits of punishment avenging without pity wrongs done to kindred and especially murder within the family' (*Oxford Companion to Classical Literature*, p. 231). Dante (*Inferno* IX.45–51) represents them as tearing their breasts, beating themselves with their hands and wailing loudly; cf. Sq 448, Fkl 1101 and *TC* IV.22–4.

951–2 *Ekko ... Narcisus*: Juno deprived Echo of the power of independent speech, so that she could only echo the words spoken by another (cf. Cl 1189 and n.); she fell in love with Narcissus and was rejected by him, after which she wasted away from grief and was reduced to a mere voice (Ovid, *Metamorphoses* III.359–401).

999–1006 In numerous manuscripts, lines 1001–6 are placed before lines 999–1000, while one manuscript omits 1001–6 altogether. Manly and Rickert (IV, 485–6) conclude from this that lines 1001–6 were inserted in the margin in a draft version of the tale, and incorporated into the text at the wrong point by early scribes. Repositioning 1001–6 would obviate the tautologous effect of

1006–7, but create a new awkwardness with line 999, which makes best sense as a response to the proposed removal of the rocks (lines 995–8), rather than to the blunt rejection of lines 1002–5. I have therefore thought it best to let the El/Hg order stand. It remains likely that 1001–6 were a marginal addition (to strengthen the force of Dorigen's rejection and thus leave no doubt of her fidelity to Arveragus?).

1017–18 B. S. Harrison (SP, 32 (1935), 55–61) points out that these lines are an example of the rhetorical figure *expolitio*, when 'an assertion is made and then explained in the next line by repeating the thought in other words' (p. 58). Cf. Geoffrey of Vinsauf, *Poetria Nova* 1244–51, tr. Nims, p. 61.

1031–5 *Appollo . . . declinacioun*: The sun's declination is its angular distance from the celestial equator (cf. n. to Mch 2222–4), which changes as it rises to the Tropic of Cancer in summer and falls to the Tropic of Capricorn in winter (cf. n. to Fkl 1246–9). This annual motion of the sun brings about the changes in the seasons and so governs the growth and decay of vegetation. The sun thus plays as important a role in medieval cosmology as in the modern heliocentric model of the universe. Cf. Bernard Silvestris, *Cosmographia* II.5 (tr. Wetherbee, p. 102):

> Among the Usiarchs and genii of the heavens, whom eternal wisdom has appointed to adorn and govern the universe, the sun is pre-eminent in brilliance, foremost in power, supreme in majesty; it is the mind of the universe, the spark of perception in creatures, source of the power of the heavenly bodies and eye of the universe, and interpenetrates all creation with an immensity of both radiance and warmth.

1045–6 Lucina is an alternative name for Diana, goddess of the moon, and sister of Apollo, god of the sun. She is here called goddess of the sea because of the moon's effect on the tides.

1057–64 *opposicioun*: A term used to denote an angular relation of 180° to the sun; when the moon is in opposition to the sun, it is full, and at this time particularly high tides were thought to occur (North, *Chaucer's Universe*, pp. 425–6). Aurelius prays that when the sun and moon are next in opposition, while the sun is in the zodiacal sign of Leo, the moon should slow her course so that for two whole years it matches the sun's; she will thus remain full and the tides will remain high and cover the rocks during the whole period. The reason why Aurelius specifies Leo is probably that this is the 'house' of the sun – that is, the sign in which the sun's influence is at its strongest (Grimm, *Astronomical Lore*, p. 42, n. 1).

1070 *spring flood*: Tides are especially high at the spring equinox.

1074–5 Aurelius is here referring to Diana's role as Proserpina, wife of Pluto, king of the classical Underworld (see n. to Kn 2297–9).

1077 *Delphos*: Delphi, a small town on the side of Mount Parnassus, was the site of a famous oracle of Apollo. Cf. *TC* IV.1411.

1082 The brother, who is later to play an important role in alleviating Aurelius's predicament, is Chaucer's own addition to the story.

1110–12 Pamphilus is the hero of a twelfth-century Latin verse drama, which relates his wooing of the beautiful Galathea; his opening words are 'I am wounded', and he goes on to describe the sufferings he endures from the hidden wound of love (*Seven Medieval Latin Comedies*, tr. A. G. Elliott (New York, 1984), pp. 1–25). This text was extremely well known in the Middle Ages, since it was used as a school-text for young boys learning to read Latin.

1118–28 *at Orliens in Fraunce*: The university of Orleans had an international reputation as a law-school from the thirteenth century on (H. Rashdall, *The Universities of Europe in the Middle Ages*, 2nd edn rev. by F. M. Powicke and A. B. Emden, vol. II (Oxford, 1936), pp. 139–51). For evidence that it also had a reputation for astrological and magical studies, see J. F. Royster, *SP*, 23 (1926), 380–84.

1130 *mansiouns*: Astrologers divided the moon's course during the lunar month into twenty-eight parts, known as the mansions or stations of the moon; they were used to forecast natural phenomena and to determine favourable or unfavourable times for specific types of human activity (cf. J. C. Eade, *SAC*, 4 (1982), 53–85, at pp. 66–7).

1131–4 This jocular dismissal of heathen practices may be compared with Chaucer's rejection of astrology in the *Treatise on the Astrolabe* (II.4.57–9): 'these ben observaunces of judicial matere and rytes of payens, in whiche my spirit [ne] hath no feith' (the comment is not in Chaucer's source). Though Chaucer may not have believed in astrology, he found its narrative possibilities useful.

1142–51 The entertainments at medieval feasts often included dramatic effects of the kind described here, with wooden castles or ships, large enough to hold numbers of men, brought into the hall and moved around by means of concealed wheels. See L. H.

Loomis, in *Medieval English Drama: Essays Critical and Contextual*, ed. J. Taylor and A. H. Nelson (Chicago, 1972), pp. 98–115, repr. from *Speculum*, 33 (1958), 242–55; G. Wickham, *Early English Stages 1300 to 1660*, vol. I (London, 1959), pp. 212–25; M. F. Braswell, *Mosaic*, 18 (1985), 101–10. The flowers and grape-vine were presumably made to 'grow' by some mechanical device.

1174 *in Latin*: Latin was the common language of the educated class in the Middle Ages, and was used in speech as well as writing.

1189–1201 The magician here produces even more elaborate versions of the theatrical illusions created by medieval 'tregetoures' (1141); see n. to Fkl 1142–51.

1222 *from Gerounde to the mouth of Saine*: That is, from the Gironde, an estuary at the juncture of the Garonne and the Dordogne rivers in south-west France, to the Seine estuary in northern France. The meaning of the phrase is thus 'along the whole French coast, from the south to the north'.

1244 *Decembre*: In the *Filocolo* story which was Chaucer's source (see Headnote), the winter season is essential to the plot, since the lover's 'impossible task' is to create a spring garden in winter. Chaucer retains the wintry setting even though narrative logic no longer requires it, thus giving a bleak, sterile feel to the proposed adulterous liaison (whereas in the spring-time setting mentioned in Fkl 906–17 it might have seemed a more romantic prospect).

1245 *Phebus*: See n. to Mch 2220.

1246–9 *hote declinacioun*: The highest point of the sun's annual path through the heavens, which it reaches at the summer solstice (see nn. to Mch 2222–4 and Fkl 1031–5); it reaches its lowest point in the skies around 21 December, while in the zodiacal sign of Capricorn (Grimm, *Astronomical Lore*, p. 35).

1252–4 The two-faced (and hence 'double-bearded') Janus was the Roman god of beginnings and endings, and thus presided over the turn of the year, lending his name to the month of January. Medieval representations of the months of the year in carvings and manuscript illuminations often represent January as a two-faced man sitting feasting (R. Tuve, *Seasons and Months: Studies in a Tradition of Middle English Poetry* (Paris, 1933; repr. Cambridge, 1974), pp. 123–4).

1273–9 The technical language in these lines relates to methods by which planetary positions can be determined. The clerk makes his calculations by using a set of astronomical tables drawn up in Toledo – either those produced around 1272 under the direction of Alfonso X, king of Castile (for translated extracts, see Grant, *Source Book*, pp. 465–87), or the earlier Toledan tables drawn up by the astronomer Arzachel. In either case, these tables, having been calculated for the latitude of Toledo, would have been 'Ful wel corrected' to fit the location in which they were to be used. Copies of the Alfonsine Tables corrected to the meridian of Oxford were produced by astronomers at Merton College, Oxford, and were in general use in the second half of the fourteenth century (R. T. Gunther, *Early Science in Oxford*, vol. II (Oxford, 1923), pp. 44–7). The tables give figures for rates of planetary motion for larger blocks of years (e.g., thousands, hundreds and twenties), and also for individual years below the smallest unit of the block groupings (in the above case, one to nineteen); the block groupings are known as 'collect years' and the individual years as 'expanse years' (cf. *Astrol* II.44). Figures would also be given for the 'root', the year chosen as the starting-point for the calculations (often the Incarnation). Starting from this root, the astronomer would add on the figures supplied by the tables for the number of years necessary to bring him to the date he was interested in, and thus fix a planet's position at that date.

The tables are, however, based on the fiction that the heavenly bodies move at even rates, and thus yield a 'mean' rather than a true position for a planet (similar to the modern convention of Mean Time); cf. *Astrol* II.44–5. In order to determine the true position, the astronomer must perform further calculations, involving the planet's 'equation of centre', its 'equation of argument' and the 'proportionals' needed to convert the equation of argument from mean to true (Eade, *SAC*, 4 (1982), 60–62; E. S. Laird, *ELN*, 25.3 (1988), 23–6).

1280–90 These lines describe calculations by which the clerk determines which of the moon's twenty-eight 'mansions' she is currently occupying (see n. to Fkl 1130). The starting-point is what is known as 'the first point of Aries' ('thilke fixe Aries'), which is the place where the ecliptic (the sun's annual path through the skies as it rises and falls from the Tropic of Cancer to the Tropic of Capricorn) crosses the celestial equator at the spring equinox. This point is a basis from which the positions of heavenly bodies are measured (the measurement being known as their 'celestial longitude'). It was conceived as located in the ninth of the heavenly spheres, the Primum Mobile (see n. to ML 295–301).

A gloss in El makes clear that Alnath is a name given to the first mansion of the moon (and not, as commentators since Skeat have supposed, a star). The clerk fixes the position of this mansion by calculating the amount of precession (see n. to ML 295–301) undergone by the eighth sphere (the sphere of the fixed stars), which will have had the effect of increasing the mansion's celestial longitude. When the clerk has fixed the position of the first mansion, he can determine the other twenty-seven 'by proporci-oun'. He then determines the sign of the zodiac in which the moon is currently rising, and in which of the subdivisions of the sign known as 'faces' and 'terms' it is situated. Once the position of the moon is thus fixed, he knows in which of its 'mansions' it is located, and can calculate the date at which it will reach a mansion appropriate to his enterprise (Eade, SAC, 4 (1982), 63–7). Eade comments that 'what we are told of the clerk's efforts is enough for us to reconstruct what he was doing, enough to show that the procedures were grindingly laborious, but such, too, as had no power whatever to effect the magical results he obtained' (p. 67). Aside from the simple fact that the moon has a general effect on the tides, it is not possible to see how the processes described have anything to do with the removal of the rocks, which is vaguely ascribed to 'othere observaunces' (1291); rather, the spate of technical terminology operates its own 'illu-sioun' on the reader and gives the impression that a process of 'natural magic' has indeed been carrried out.

1367–1456 Dorigen's long list of examples of women who preferred death to sexual defilement is taken from Jerome, *Against Jov.* I.41–6; quotations below are taken from Fremantle's translation (see Abbreviated References). For a text and translation of this portion of Jerome, see Hanna and Lawler, *Jankyn's Book*, I, 160–75; for comparison with Dorigen's lament, see I, 75–80. Hanna and Lawler's text is reproduced, with facing English trans-lation by R. R. Edwards, in *SA²* I, 256–65. Jerome is thus, paradoxically, the source both of the antifeminist material incor-porated into WBPr (see Headnote), and of these examples of heroic female virtue (cf. *LGW* G 281–304). Dorigen's long soli-loquy establishes beyond doubt that she sees the fulfilment of her promise to Aurelius as equivalent to rape, and thus demonstrates that it did not indicate any secret inclinations in his favour. For other narrative functions of the soliloquy, see Mann, *Feminizing Chaucer*, pp. 91–2.

Not all of what Jerome says about these women agrees with

other sources, and in a number of cases nothing more is known of them; see Hanna and Lawler's notes, I, 231–44. Jerome presents his examples in two groups:

1. Virgins (I.41). This group includes (in the order in which they appear in FklT) the anecdotes concerning the thirty tyrants and Phidon's daughters (Fkl 1368–78); the attempted rape of fifty Lacedaemonian virgins by the men of Messene (Fkl 1379–85); Aristoclides, tyrant of Orchomenos, and the virgin of Stymphalus (Fkl 1387–94); the seven virgins of Miletus who killed themselves to avoid being raped by marauding Gauls (Fkl 1409–11); the daughter of Demotion, chief of the Areopagites, who killed herself on hearing of the death of her betrothed, Leosthenes (Fkl 1426–7); the daughters of Scedasus, who killed each other after they had been raped by two strangers to whom they had given hospitality (Fkl 1428–30); Nicanor, conqueror of Thebes, and the Theban maiden who committed suicide rather than yield herself to him (Fkl 1431–3); a second Theban maiden, 'deflowered by a Macedonian foe', who killed both her ravisher and herself (Fkl 1434–6).

2. Wives and widows (I.43–6). This group includes the wife of the Carthaginian leader Hasdrubal (Fkl 1399–1404; cf. NP 3363–8 and n.); Lucretia (Fkl 1405–8); the wife of Abradatas (Fkl 1414–18), a Persian king of Susa, who committed suicide on her husband's body when he was killed fighting against the Egyptians (Xenophon, *Cyropaedia* VII.iii.14); the wife of Niceratus, who killed herself 'rather than subject herself to the lust of the thirty tyrants whom Lysander had set over conquered Athens' (Fkl 1437–8); the concubine of the Athenian Alcibiades, friend of Socrates, who disobeyed the command that his body should be left unburied after he had been killed by the Spartan conquerors of Athens (Fkl 1439–41); Alcestis (Fkl 1442); Penelope (Fkl 1443); Laodamia, wife of Protesilaus (Fkl 1445–7); Portia, wife of Brutus, one of the assassins of Julius Caesar (Fkl 1448–50); Artemisia, queen of Caria (352–350 BC) and wife of Mausolus, who built for her husband 'a tomb so great that even to the present day all costly sepulchres are called after his name, *mausoleums*' (Fkl 1451–2); Teuta, who became queen of the Illyrians on the death of her husband Agron (231 BC), and 'owed her long sway over brave warriors, and her frequent victories over Rome, to her marvellous chastity' (Fkl 1453–4); Bilia, wife of the Roman Duilius, who when reproached by her husband with failing to tell him that his breath smelled, replied that she had thought all

men had foul breath (Fkl 1455); Rhodogue, daughter of Darius, king of Persia, who 'after the death of her husband, put to death the nurse who was trying to persuade her to marry again' (Fkl 1456); Valeria, a Roman of the Messala family, who refused to marry again after her husband's death (Fkl 1456).

1379–85 The context for this attempted rape, Jerome explains, was that so 'close a friendship long existed between Sparta [Lacedaemonia] and Messene that for the furtherance of certain religious rites they even exchanged virgins' (*Against Jov.* I.41).

1405–8 *Lucresse*: For the story of Lucretia, see n. to ML 62–3.

1442 For the story of Alcestis, who offered to die in place of her husband, see n. to ML 75.

1443 *Penolopee*: For Penelope's faithfulness to her husband Ulysses, see n. to ML 75.

Omer: Chaucer will have known Homeric stories such as this one only through Latin intermediaries; see n. to ML 198.

1445–7 *Laodomia . . . Protheselaus*: For the story of Laodamia and her husband Protesilaus, see n. to ML 71.

1472 A variant of the proverb 'let sleeping dogs lie'; see Whiting H569 and Singer, I, 54, and cf. *TC* III.764.

1501 In the *Filocolo* story, the wife, accompanied by attendants, goes to the lover's house to fulfil her promise. Chaucer, in contrast, stresses the role of 'aventure' in their meeting (cf. line 1508), in accordance with his interest in the role of chance in human affairs (see nn. to GP 844 and Kn 1663–9, and, for a fuller discussion, Mann, 'Chance and Destiny').

1533–6 R. Blanner-Hassett (*Speculum*, 28 (1953), 791–800) points out that the legalistic language here used by Aurelius echoes that used by Cecily Champain in relation to her 'raptus' (*Life-Records*, p. 343).

1541–4 The punctuation in *Riverside*, in line with the demarcations suggested by the paraphs in El and Hg, places the end of Aurelius's speech at line 1544, but it does not seem plausible that he would be guilty either of boasting of his own 'gentil dede' or of delivering the finger-wagging admonition to wives.

1614 *crope out of the ground*: Compare the parallel expressions, all meaning 'as if he had just arrived on earth', cited by A. Putter, *MÆ*, 70 (2001), 191–203, at nn. 35–6.

1621–2 In Boccaccio's *Filocolo* (see Headnote), posing this question is the main point of the story, since it appears in a collection of tales designed to serve as a basis of courtly debate among the listeners (see *SA*² I, 213–14). Such 'demandes d'amour' were popular in medieval literature; see Kn 1347–8 (and n.), WB 904–5. In *Filocolo*, the question is finally answered by the conclusion that the husband is the most generous, since the sacrifice of honour is greater than the sacrifice of money (by the magician) or of sexual pleasure (by the lover).

THE PHYSICIAN'S TALE

The original source for the story of Virginia is, as Chaucer indicates in the first line of the tale, Livy's history of Rome (*Ab urbe condita* III.44–58). Although some details suggest that Chaucer may have consulted Livy directly (*SA*, pp. 398–407), the narrative outline of the Physician's Tale is closer to the much briefer version of the story in the *Romance of the Rose* (5559–5628, tr. Horgan, pp. 86–7). The story was also told by Gower (*CA* VII.5131–5306) and Boccaccio (*De mulieribus claris*, *Opere*, ed. Branca, vol. X, ch. 56), but the Physician's Tale appears to be quite independent of these versions. For Livy, the story illustrates the defence of Roman liberty against the tyrannical *decemviri*, who were overthrown as a result of Apius's attempted violation of Virginia, just as the rape of Lucretia had led to the expulsion of the Roman king Tarquin and the extirpation of the monarchy. Boccaccio and Gower are likewise interested in the political and social implications of the tale and its moral lessons for judges, rulers and people. In *RR*, the specific historical and local setting of the story is discarded, and it becomes a brief exemplum illustrating the abuse of power by wicked judges. Chaucer similarly discards reference to Rome and its history, and shows little interest in the specific political or social implications of the tale (see S. Delany, *SAC*, 3 (1981), 47–60). For him, this is primarily a tale of pathos, with its emotional centre in the 'piteous' exchange between father and daughter before he kills her (213–50), which is his own addition to the story (see also n. to Phys 226). Another addition is the long introductory passage on Virginia's physical and moral perfections (5–117), which likewise gives the tale an exemplary rather than a historical character. Finally, Chaucer gives the tale a religious dimension by adding Virginia's reference to the biblical story of Jephthah's daughter, which was interpreted as a prefiguration of Christ's sacrifice of his own flesh for mankind (see n. to Phys 240). The story resembles the Man of Law's Tale in expressing human subjection to greater powers in terms of the contrasting images of thrall and child (see Mann, *Feminizing Chaucer*, p. 113; 'Parents and Children', p. 176).

1   *Titus Livius*: See Headnote.

14   The story of the sculptor Pygmalion is told in Ovid, *Metamorphoses* X.243–97, to which a marginal gloss in El and Hg refers. Pygmalion carved the statue of a woman of such beauty that he fell in love with it; Venus answered his wishes by bringing it to life.

16   The craftsman Apelles was famous for the marvellous tomb he made for the emperor Darius; a marginal gloss in El and Hg refers to the description of this tomb in the *Alexandreis* of Walter of Châtillon (cf. WB 498–9 and n.). The marginal gloss also cites Cicero for information on 'Zanzis', better known as Zeuxis, a Greek painter; the reference is probably to *De inventione* II.i.1–3, where Cicero tells a story about Zeuxis painting a picture of Helen, as an example of perfect female beauty, by assembling the five most beautiful women he could find and combining their best features, 'because in no single case has Nature made anything perfect and finished in every part'. Cicero also mentions Zeuxis in conjunction with Apelles in *De oratore* III.vii.26. Almost certainly, however, Chaucer's immediate source was *RR* 16135–80 (tr. Horgan, p. 250), where Pygmalion, Apelles and Zeuxis are listed as examples of great sculptors and painters who would nevertheless be unequal to the task of depicting the beauty of the goddess Nature; only God could do it. Here it is Nature herself who outdoes the human craftsmen in making a beautiful woman.

20   *vicaire-general*: The idea that Nature is God's deputy comes from Alan of Lille, *De Planctu Naturae*, pr. 3.128–39, pr. 4.224–8, pr. 8.187–8 (ed. Häring, pp. 829, 840, 871; tr. Sheridan, pp. 124, 146, 206). It is reproduced by Jean de Meun in *RR* (16751–4, 19475–96, tr. Horgan, pp. 259, 301). Cf. *PF* 379–81. On the development of this conception from classical literature onwards, see G. D. Economou, *The Goddess Natura in Medieval Literature* (Cambridge, MA, 1972).

23   *Under the moone*: In the cosmological scheme which the Middle Ages inherited from Aristotle, the sublunary world is composed of the four elements (air, earth, fire, water), whose constant counteracting force causes physical bodies to decay and be regenerated ('wane and waxe'). Above the moon is the realm of pure aether, which is not subject to natural corruption. See Macrobius, *Commentary on the Dream of Scipio* I.xi.6 and xxi.33–4 (tr. Stahl, pp. 131, 180–81), and Bartholomaeus Anglicus, *On the Properties of Things* VIII.5.

37   *Phebus*: See n. to Mch 2220.

41–69 This description of Virginia's virtues has some close parallels in the treatise of St Ambrose *On Virgins* (*De virginibus*); see *SA*, pp. 407–8.

49 Pallas is a name for Athene, the Greek goddess of wisdom.

58–60 Bacchus is the god of wine, Venus the goddess of love. The idea that wine-drinking inflames sexual desire was commonplace; see n. to WB 464–8 for some examples.

79 For this notion that elderly women are expert in 'the olde daunce' of love, see n. to GP 476.

83–5 The idea that a former poacher makes the best gamekeeper is still proverbial; see Whiting T76; *Oxford Dictionary of English Proverbs*³, p. 592, s.v. Old poacher.

101–2 This is a gentler version of the proverb 'Under a weak shepherd, the wolf shits wool'; see Whiting S241–2, Walther 30541–2, Singer, I, 48, and cf. *PPl* C IX.264–6.

107–9 Cf. 2 Corinthians 3:2–3.

114–17 'The Doctour' is St Augustine, as a Latin gloss in El and Hg makes clear. Augustine defines envy as hatred of someone else's good fortune (*Enarrationes in Psalmos* CIV.17 (CCSL 40, p. 1545, line 18); *Sermo* CCCLIII.1 (*PL* 39, col. 1561); *De Genesi ad litteram* XI.14 (*PL* 34, col. 436)). The extension of this definition to include rejoicing at another's misfortune was traditional; see C. A. Owen, Jr, *MLN*, 71 (1956), 84–7, at p. 86, and cf. Pars 484 and n.

119 Chaucer is the only writer to mention Virginia's mother at this point, and it is notable that she plays no role in the further events of the story.

135 Foremost among these 'freendes', in Livy's account (and in Boccaccio's), is Virginia's betrothed, Icilius, who makes valiant attempts to defend her against the false legal claim instigated by Apius. (Icilius is mentioned by Gower but plays no part in the events of the tale.) Chaucer omits him altogether (as does the *Romance of the Rose*), and thus makes Virginia's commitment to her virginity more absolute.

162 A consistory was more usually the name for an ecclesiastical court, administering canon law (see n. to Fri 1283–4), but the term was also applied to secular tribunals (see *MED*, s.v. consistorie).

166 A bill was a legal document petitioning for the remedy of an injustice (Hornsby, pp. 155–7).

183 *thral:* In Livy's story, Claudius claims that Virginia is his slave, born in his house (*Ab urbe condita* III.44). Except for his opening

reference to Livy, Chaucer leaves the time and place of his story
vague (as does the *Romance of the Rose*), while introducing
details which have the effect of assimilating it to his own culture
– e.g., calling Virginius a knight (Phys 2, and passim), and having
Virginia refer to a biblical story (Phys 240), and to a single (and
apparently Judeo-Christian) God (Phys 248–50). In this context,
Claudius would be claiming that she is a serf, bound to service
as a member of his household.

211 The line recalls Simeon's prophecy of Mary's grief at the Crucifixion (as it was interpreted): 'a sword shall pierce through thy
own soul also' (Luke 2:35). Seen in the context of the religious
typology that permeates this tale (see n. to Phys 240, and Mann,
Feminizing Chaucer, p. 112), Virginius's grief unites Mary's suffering with the pity of the divine Father sacrificing his Son. Cf.
ML 845–7 and n.

225 Cf. *RR* 5605–7: 'in love rather than in hate he instantly cut
off the head of his beautiful daughter Virginia' (tr. Horgan,
p. 86).

226 In Livy's account, Virginius kills his daughter by taking her to
the shops near the shrine of Cloacina, seizing a butcher's knife
and stabbing her to the heart (*Ab urbe condita* III.48); Gower
and Boccaccio follow Livy in this. In the *Romance of the Rose*,
as in Chaucer, Virginius cuts off her head. Beheading was a
characteristic manner of dispatching virgin martyrs (cf. SNT),
and this mode of death thus accords with Virginia's saint-like
quality. In none of the other versions is Virginia given any say in
her own death; only in Chaucer does her father tell her what he
proposes to do, and receive her acquiescence in it. In Livy and
Gower, Virginia's chastity seems to be important to her male
relatives for the sake of their own honour, rather than in relation
to her own personal integrity (see the speech of Icilius in Livy,
III.45, and of Virginius in Gower, *CA* VII.5247–52). Chaucer is
the only writer to give us Virginia's point of view.

240 *Jepte*: A Latin gloss in El and Hg refers to the biblical source of
the story of Jephthah, Judges 11. As leader of the Israelite army,
which was fighting against the Ammonites, Jephthah vowed that
if God gave him victory, he would sacrifice to him whatever first
came out of his house to meet him on his return (11:30–31).
This turned out to be his daughter. Like Virginia, she acquiesced
in her own death, but asked for two months' grace to go to the
mountains with her companions and lament her virginity before
he fulfilled his vow. (11:36–40). For medieval poetic develop-

ments of the lament of Jephthah's daughter, see the essay by P. Dronke and M. Alexiou, reprinted in P. Dronke, *Intellectuals and Poets in Medieval Europe* (Rome, 1992), pp. 345–88.

Although medieval writers often condemned Jephthah's rashness in making his vow and stubbornness in carrying it out (see Dante, *Paradiso* V.65–72, and R. L. Hoffman, *ChauR*, 2 (1967), 20–31, at pp. 25–6), St Paul lists him among the Old Testament figures notable for their faith (Hebrews 11:32), and (perhaps as a result) the story was also often interpreted as a prefiguration of Christ's sacrifice of his own flesh to save mankind (see Hoffman, p. 29). In this respect the story resembles Abraham's (unfulfilled) sacrifice of his son Isaac (also cited by St Paul in Hebrews 11), to which the Jephthah story is compared in Peter Abelard's poetic *Planctus* ('lament') for Jephthah's daughter (Dronke and Alexiou, p. 381).

250 Cf. Christ's prayer to God before his crucifixion: 'Father, if you are willing, remove this cup from me: nevertheless, not my will, but thine, be done' (Luke 22:42; cf. Matthew 26:39, 42).

275–6 There has been no previous mention of others involved in Apius's deception, and their appearance here comes as something of a surprise, nor is it immediately clear why they should receive worse punishment than Claudius. The corresponding passage of the *Romance of the Rose* (5627–8, tr. Horgan, p. 87) makes clear that they were the witnesses called to support Claudius's claim, whose role is implied in Phys 169.

286 Proverbial; see Whiting S335, and cf. Pars 93.

THE PHYSICIAN–PARDONER LINK

295 The gifts of Nature are one's bodily and mental properties; the gifts of Fortune are external goods, such as wealth, honours, comforts, and so on. See Patch, *Goddess Fortuna*, pp. 65–6, 75–6, and cf. Pars 450 and n.

296 At this point, *Riverside* and some other modern editions print the following couplet as lines 297–8: 'Hire beautee was hire deth, I dar wel sayn. | Allas, so pitously as she was slayn!' These lines are not in El or Hg; they appear in a number of manuscripts along with a series of other variant readings in the link which appear to represent scribal rewriting (though the motive for it is unclear). See Manly and Rickert IV, 490–92 (where, however, it is assumed that the variant version is an early draft by Chaucer); *Riverside*, p. 1130; Hanna, *Pursuing History*, p. 151.

966 NOTES TO THE PARDONER'S PROLOGUE

305 The inspection of a patient's urine played a central role in diagnosis in medieval medicine, and doctors were often depicted holding glass urinals (see Grant, *Source Book*, pp. 748–52; Rawcliffe, *Medicine*, pp. 46–52, and accompanying illustrations).

306 *galiones*: The ME word *galien* is a form of Galen, the name of the great medical authority (see n. to GP 429–34); it was used to refer to various medical preparations (see *MED* s.v. Galien). Apparently by analogy with 'ipocras', a drink of wine and spices whose name recalls another great medical authority, Hippocrates, it here appears to denote a medical drink. See Elliott, p. 308.

310 *Seint Ronian*: The Host probably means St Ronan. There were several saints of this name; see Farmer, *Dictionary of Saints*, s.v.

313 *cardinacle*: A nonce-word. The Host seems to have confused 'cardiacle', meaning 'palpitations', with 'cardinal'.

314 *By corpus bones*: Another of the Host's confused oaths, half Latin (*corpus Domini*, 'the Lord's body') and half English ('Christ's bones', 'God's bones'). He uses it again at Mk 1906.

320 The Pardoner picks up the saint's name by which the Host has just sworn, and mangles it still further (see Pard 310 and n.).

THE PARDONER'S PROLOGUE

Like the Wife of Bath and the Canon's Yeoman, the Pardoner prefaces his tale with a long account of his life. As a paradoxically honest confession of trickery and deception, the Pardoner's Prologue resembles the self-description of False Seeming (Faus Semblant) in the *Romance of the Rose* (10973–11950, tr. Horgan, pp. 169–84; see also *SA*[2] I, 270–77, and Kolve and Olson, pp. 410–15), but the content of his confession seems to have been largely Chaucer's own invention (see, however, n. to Pard 377–8).

Rubric *Radix malorum* ... : 1 Timothy 6:10. Cf. Mel 1130, 1840 and Pars 739.

329 *preche*: Strictly speaking, pardoners were permitted only to expound the nature of their pardons, and not to preach, but such restrictions were frequently ignored. See A. Kellogg and L. A. Haselmayer, in Kellogg, *Chaucer, Langland*, pp. 212–44.

336–7 Papal documents were known as bulls because of the leaden seal (Latin *bulla*) which authenticated them. The Pardoner also displays a document from the bishop ('Oure lige lord'), authorizing him to collect money in return for the absolution offered by his pardons. (Cf. *PPl* Prol.68–73.) It is a 'patente' – that is, a document left open (Latin *patens*) for all to read, with the seal hanging from the bottom, as opposed to private documents ('letters close') which were folded up and sealed shut so that they could be read only by the person to whom they were addressed (see *OED* s.v. Patent).

347–51 On the Pardoner's false relics, see n. to GP 694–700.

350–51 In his note on this line, Skeat suggested that the 'holy Jew' was Jacob, who used stripped tree-branches to make his sheep increase in number (Genesis 30); however, if the Pardoner was referring to Jacob there seems to be no reason why he should not have said so. Relics of Old Testament figures were revered along with Christian ones (L. J. Henkin, *MLN*, 55 (1940), 254–9, at p. 258), but this does not, of course, apply to their sheep. The connection seems to be with the use of a sheep's shoulder-bone in magic; see Pars 603 and n.

377–88 For parallels in medieval literature to this effective means of ensuring that everyone will be keen to make an offering, see *SA*, pp. 411–14, and A. C. Friend, *JEGP*, 53 (1954), 383–8, at p. 384.

390 The mark was not a coin but a unit of account, which had different values in different parts of Europe. In England and Scotland, it was equal to 13s 4d ($£\frac{2}{3}$). See P. Spufford, *Money and its Use in Medieval Europe* (Cambridge, 1988), p. 223.

407–8 Cf. *RR* 5083–8: 'An evil intention may well produce a good sermon, which, although worth nothing to the preacher, may bring salvation to others who learn a good lesson from it while he is so filled with vainglory' (tr. Horgan, p. 78).

429–32 Compare the passage from *RR* quoted in the preceding note.

444–7 The Pardoner refuses to imitate the apostles by earning his living through manual labour instead of begging. The apostle he seems to have particularly in mind is St Paul, whose injunction to 'work with your own hands . . . that you want nothing of any other man's' (1 Thessalonians 4:11) is cited by False Seeming in his discussion of the ethics of begging (*RR* 11357–8, tr. Horgan, p. 175; see Headnote to PardPr). According to Langland (*PPl* XV.290), St Paul put his preaching into practice by making baskets for a living, although according to the Bible (Acts 18:3) he was a tent-maker.

A. Williams (*Mediaeval Studies in Honor of Urban Tigner*

Holmes, Jr., ed. J. Mahoney and J. E. Keller (Chapel Hill, NC, 1965), pp. 197–207, at pp. 204–5) and J. V. Fleming (*Christianity and Literature*, 28.4 (1979), 19–26, at p. 22) compare a passage from St Jerome (*PL* 29, col. 61), in which he vituperates against those who criticize him for not earning his bread by manual labour, such as basket-weaving, rather than working on the Bible; this text was cited in defence of mendicant poverty by (e.g.) St Bonaventure and Richard of Maidstone. Jerome does not, however, mention the apostles, and he is *rejecting* manual labour, not recommending 'ascetic industry', as Fleming implies. Chaucer's lines may be intended to set the Pardoner in a parodic relation to the debate over mendicant poverty: he rejects unprofitable begging and 'wilful poverty', not for the sake of earning his bread by labour, but for the sake of earning a rich living from his preaching.

THE PARDONER'S TALE

The Pardoner's Tale is presented as a sermon, in which the story functions as an exemplum illustrating the main theme of avarice. It does not conform to the strict organization characteristic of scholastic sermons, and is probably to be taken only as a general approximation to the more colourful type of preaching addressed to popular audiences, in which exempla would figure largely (see A. J. Fletcher, *SAC*, 11 (1989), 15–35). To reinforce the impression of a sermon style, Chaucer makes heavy use of rhetorical elaborations, for which (as elsewhere in *CT*: see Headnotes to MLT and WBPr) he draws on Jerome, *Against Jovinian*, and Innocent III, *De Miseria Condicionis Humane*.

The narrative core of the tale, the story of the three young men who find a heap of gold and treacherously slay each other in an attempt to reduce the number of shares in it, was a widespread tale in the Middle Ages, in oriental as well as western versions (*SA*² I, 279–81, 287–313). In a number of these versions, the young men are told about the gold by a hermit who identifies it with death (see n. to Pard 760–65). In Chaucer's version, the hermit is replaced by a sinister Old Man, who is not fleeing but seeking death as a relief from his ills (see n. to Pard 728–38). Chaucer makes this notion of 'seeking death' the central motif of his story by adding the preface in which the three 'riotoures' swear to seek out Death and slay him. This linguistic transformation from abstract noun to personified concretion climaxes in a grim parody of biblical paradox as they declare that 'death shall be dead' (see

n. to Pard 710). These shifts and paradoxes highlight the autonomous powers of language, and so link the central narrative with the Pardoner's virtuoso display of rhetoric and its powers. The sombre mood of the tale is increased by its setting in the context of plague, where death is a universal presence (see n. to Pard 679).

463 *Flaundres*: In Chaucer's day, Flanders was a wealthy country with a thriving urban culture. It was easily accessible by sea from south-east England, with which it had many trading and cultural contacts. See D. Wallace, *SAC*, 19 (1997), 63–91. Chaucer probably chose it as the setting for PardT because of the reputation for heavy drinking enjoyed by its inhabitants, but it plays no specific role in the rest of the story.

470 For the tavern as the devil's temple, see the ME parallels quoted in *SA*, p. 438. The sins against which the Pardoner preaches – gluttony, gambling and blasphemous oath-swearing – were conventionally associated with the tavern; see F. Tupper, *JEGP*, 13 (1914), 553–65, and R. F. Yeager, *SP*, 81 (1984), 42–55.

474–5 The notion that swearing by God's blood, nails, bones, etc. re-enacts Christ's torture and crucifixion has a parallel in a story told by the thirteenth-century Dominican friar Thomas of Cantimpré (*Liber de apibus*, ed. Georges Colveneere, 3rd edn (Douai, 1627), II.xlix.10; translated in Kolve and Olson, p. 417), in which a man leaving a tavern where young revellers were blaspheming and swearing found a wounded and bleeding stranger lying in the street. The stranger claimed that his wounds had been inflicted by the men in the tavern, but when they were brought out to protest their innocence, they found that the stranger had disappeared. They realized that he was Christ, and his wounds had been caused by their oaths. See also Pars 591.

483–588 This long tirade against gluttony draws at several points on Jerome's treatise *Against Jovinian*, Book II, and Innocent III's *De Miseria* II.17–20; relevant passages are printed with translation in *SA*² I, 282–7. See further following notes.

483–4 A marginal gloss in El and Hg quotes Ephesians 5:18: 'be not drunk with wine, wherein is luxury', which is also quoted (with slightly different wording) in Innocent III, *De Miseria* II.19.

485 *Loth*: Lot's two daughters made him drunk and had sex with him in order to conceive children by him and carry on the family line; see Genesis 19:30–38. This story, like the succeeding one of Herod (488–91), is referred to in Innocent III's denunciation

of gluttony: 'Gluttony ... beheaded the Baptist' (II.18), 'Drunkenness ... committed incest' (II.20, tr. Lewis).

488–91   *Herodes*: The biblical stories of Herod's slaying of John the Baptist (Matthew 14:1–12, Mark 6:17–28) mention that Herod's rash vow to give Herodias's daughter whatever she asked was made at his birthday feast, but they do not say that he was drunk at the time. See, however, the quotation from Innocent III in the preceding note.

492–7   *Senec*: Seneca makes this comparison between drunkenness and insanity in his *Moral Epistles*, LXXXIII.18.

508–11   A marginal gloss in El (defective in Hg) identifies the source of these lines as Jerome, *Against Jov.* II.15: 'So long as Adam fasted, he remained in paradise; he ate, and was cast out, and straightway took a wife.' Cf. Sum 1915–17 and n., Pars 819. See also Innocent III, *De Miseria* II.18: 'Gluttony closed paradise' (tr. Lewis).

513–16   Cf. Ecclesiasticus 37:32–4: 'Be not greedy in any feasting, and pour not out thyself upon any meat: For in many meats there will be sickness, and greediness will turn to choler. By surfeiting many have perished: but he that is temperate, shall prolong life.' These verses are quoted by Innocent III, *De Miseria* II.17.

517–20   Cf. Jerome, *Against Jov.* II.8: 'On account of the brief pleasure of the throat, lands and seas are scoured.' Cf. also Innocent III, *De Miseria* II.17: 'the fruits of the trees are not sufficient for gluttons, nor the varieties of vegetables, nor the roots of plants, nor the fish of the sea, nor the beasts of the earth, nor the birds of the sky ... Yet the pleasure of gluttony is so brief that as to the size of the place it is scarcely four inches, as to length of time scarcely as many moments' (tr. Lewis).

521–3   A marginal gloss in El and Hg quotes 1 Corinthians 6:13: 'Meat for the belly, and the belly for the meats; but God shall destroy both it and them.' Quoted by Jerome, *Against Jov.* II.6, and Innocent III, *De Miseria* II.17.

527–8   That is, the glutton vomits up what he has consumed, instead of evacuating it in the normal way. Chaucer may be thinking of Jerome's reference to the use of emetics by gluttons, *Against Jov.* II.10, or he may be referring to involuntary vomiting as a result of excess.

530–33   A marginal gloss in El and Hg gives the source of this quotation as Philippians (3:18–19). It is also quoted at Pars 820.

534–6   Cf. Innocent III, *De Miseria* II.18: 'Gluttony demands a costly tribute, but it returns the smallest value, because the more delicate the foods are, the more stinking the excrements are. What goes in vilely comes out vilely, expelling a horrible wind above and below, and emitting an abominable sound' (tr. Lewis).

538–40 Cf. Innocent III, *De Miseria* II.17, on the skill of cooks: 'One grinds and strains, another mixes and prepares, turns substance into accident, changes nature into art, so that satiety turns into hunger, squeamishness recovers an appetite; to stimulate gluttony, not to sustain nature; not to fill a need, but to satisfy a desire' (tr. Lewis). The terms 'substance' and 'accident' are borrowed from Aristotelian philosophy; the 'accidents' of any physical body are its particular characteristics, such as colour, size, shape, material, and so on, while its 'substance' is that in which all these characteristics inhere. The joke here suggests that in the hands of the cooks, the substance of the food is changed into such different forms that it disappears. The terms were used in the latter part of the Middle Ages to explain the transformation of the bread and wine of the Eucharist into Christ's body and blood: it was said that the 'substance' of the Eucharistic elements changed, while the 'accidents' of bread and wine remained intact. The fourteenth-century Oxford theologian John Wyclif rejected this theory as philosophically untenable, and was followed in this by the Lollards; their view was denounced as heretical (see Hudson, *Wycliffite Writings*, pp. 18, 142–3). At the time that PardT was written, therefore, these terms were suggestive of controversy, whether or not Chaucer intended them to have that connotation here (see P. Strohm, *SAC*, 17 (1995), 23–42). It is possible that they form part of the vein of religious parody in the tale; cf. n. to Pard 710, and see D. Lawton, *Blasphemy* (New York, 1993), pp. 100–102.

547–8 A marginal gloss in El and Hg quotes 1 Timothy 5:6: 'Who lives in pleasures is dead while living' (the subject is grammatically masculine in the gloss, although feminine in the Bible).

549–50 A marginal gloss in El and Hg quotes Proverbs 20:1: 'Wine is a luxurious thing, and drunkenness riotous', which is also quoted in the sections on gluttony in Jerome, *Against Jov.* (II.10) and Innocent III, *De Miseria* (II.19). For wine as a source of 'fights and brawls, disputes and quarrels', see Innocent III, *De Miseria* II.19 (tr. Lewis).

551–2 Cf. Innocent III, *De Miseria* II.19: 'What is more unsightly than a drunkard, in whose mouth is a stench . . . whose face is transformed?' (tr. Lewis).

555   *Sampsoun*: Samson was a Nazirite; the Nazirites were 'a body of
      Israelites specially consecrated to the service of God who were
      under vows to abstain from eating or drinking the produce of
      the vine, to let their hair grow, and to avoid defilement with a
      dead body' (*Oxford Dictionary of the Christian Church*, s.v.).
      See Numbers 6:3 and Judges 13:5–7.

558–9 The phrase 'sepulchre of reason' is applied to drunkenness in
      Walter of Châtillon's *Alexandreis* (ed. Colker, I.171–2): 'Imperat
      et suadet rationis uile sepulcrum | Ebrietas.' Cf. Pars 822 and n.
      It seems to have been a well-known tag; see Alan of Lille, *Senten-
      tiae* 34 (*PL* 210, col. 249): 'Quid est gula, nisi luxuriae sem-
      inarium, rationis sepulcrum?' The idea is commonplace: see
      Jerome, *Against Jov.* II.12: 'Nothing is so destructive to the
      mind as a full belly', and Innocent III, *De Miseria* II.19 (of the
      drunkard): '[his] reason is taken away' (tr. Lewis). Innocent goes
      on to quote Hosea 4:11: 'Fornication, and wine, and drunkenness
      take away the understanding.'

560–61 Proverbs 31:4; see n. to Pard 583–7. The quotation ap-
      pears in Innocent III, *De Miseria* II.19. Cf. MLT 771–7 and Mel
      1194.

563   Lepe is the name of a town near Huelva in south-west Spain.
      White wines are still produced in the region (Condado de
      Huelva); see H. Duijker, *The Wine Atlas of Spain and Traveller's
      Guide* (London, 1992), pp. 206–9.

564   *Fisshstrete . . . Chepe*: Chaucer may be referring to Newe Fissh-
      strete (now Fish Street Hill), which ran northwards from London
      Bridge, and Estchepe (now Eastcheap), which intersected it at
      right-angles and ran parallel to the river; both were near the
      wharves of Billingsgate. Or (more likely?) he meant Olde
      Fisshstrete, which formed part of Knightrider Street, and ran
      along the northern boundary of the area known as the Vintry,
      which was the centre of the London wine trade. In this case,
      'Chepe' would more probably mean Cheapside (see n. to Co
      4377), to the north of Olde Fisshstrete. See the Gazetteer and
      Map 3 in Lobel, ed., *The City of London*, and C. Barron's
      comments on the London wine trade, ibid., p. 54. The latter set
      of options seems more likely in that Chaucer's father was a
      vintner and lived in the Vintry, where Chaucer probably spent
      his childhood (*Life-Records*, pp. 1–12).

571   *Rochel . . . Burdeux*: French wines from La Rochelle and Bor-
      deaux were imported into London in Chaucer's day (Barron in
      Lobel, ed., *The City of London*, p. 54).

574–8 Examples of Old Testament victories that were won through fasting are given by Jerome, *Against Jov.* II.15.

579–81 Attila, king of the Huns, died on his wedding night from a nose-bleed, which was the result of heavy drinking (E. A. Thompson, *A History of Attila and the Huns* (Oxford, 1948), p. 149).

583–7 Proverbs 31:4: 'Give not to kings, O Lamuel, give not wine to kings: because there is no secret where drunkenness reigneth'; the second half of the quotation (which is not in the AV) is reproduced in Pard 560–61. The first few words of this verse are quoted as a marginal gloss in El and Hg.

591–4 A marginal gloss in El and Hg quotes from the chapter on gambling in John of Salisbury's *Policraticus* (I.5): 'Dicing is the mother of lies and perjuries.' There are further parallels to Chaucer's lines in the rest of the chapter: 'Gambling . . . is prodigal as the result of her lust for others' possessions . . . it seems the more ruinous in that nothing is less profitable than to expend much labour on that by which one profits little . . . It arms men for strife' (tr. Pike, pp. 27–8). Cf. Pars 793.

603–20 *Stilbon*: The story is taken from the chapter on gambling in the *Policraticus* of John of Salisbury (I.5; see *SA*, p. 438), but the name of the ambassador who was sent from Corinth to Sparta (both cities in the Greek Peloponnese) is Chilo, not Stilbo. Stilbon is a Greek name for the planet Mercury, and also the name of a Greek philosopher mentioned by Seneca (*Moral Epistles* IX.18–19; *On Firmness* (*Moral Essays* II) 5). Chaucer may have confused the names in his memory.

Lacedomie: Lacedaemon is the ancient Greek name for Sparta.

621–6 This story immediately follows the story of Chilo (see preceding n.) in John of Salisbury's *Policraticus* I.5.

Parthes: the people of Parthia, in northern Persia (Magoun, p. 123).

631–2 Cf. Pars 600.

633–4 A marginal gloss in El and Hg underscores this reference to Matthew 5:34, where Christ forbids any kind of oath.

635–7 See Jeremiah 4:2: 'And thou shalt swear: [As the Lord liveth,] in truth, and in judgment, and in justice.' A marginal gloss in El and Hg gives the Latin version of these words (without the bracketed phrase). Cf. Pars 592.

639 *the firste table*: The Ten Commandments given to Moses by God were written on two stone 'tables' or tablets (Exodus 31:18, 34:28–9; see n. to Sum 1885–90). The medieval exegetical tradition interpreted these two tablets in the light of Mark 12:29–31,

where Christ collapses these commandments into two: love of
God and love of one's neighbour. The first tablet was thus supposed to have held the first three commandments, setting out
man's duty to God, and the second to have held the remaining
seven, setting out man's duty to his neighbour. See, for example,
The Lay Folks' Catechism, ed. T. F. Simmons and H. E. Nolloth,
EETS o.s. 118 (London, 1901), p. 30, and *Dives and Pauper*, ed.
P. H. Barnum, vol. I, Part 1, EETS o.s. 275 (London, 1976),
p. 298.

641–2 For the Ten Commandments in their most generally used
form, see Deuteronomy 5:6–21. In Protestant reckoning, the
commandment 'Thou shalt not take the name of the Lord thy
God in vain' is the third commandment, but medieval reckoning
counted the first two (against worshipping other gods, and
against worshipping graven images) as one; see *The Lay Folks'
Catechism*, p. 36, and *Dives and Pauper* I.1, pp. 81 and 221
(both as cited in the preceding note). To compensate, the last
commandment is split into two by distinguishing between covetousness of immovable and movable goods.

649–50 Cf. Ecclesiasticus 23:12, 14: 'A man that sweareth much,
shall be filled with iniquity, and a scourge shall not depart from
his house ... And if he swear in vain, he shall not be justified:
for his house shall be filled with retribution.'

652 Hailes Abbey in Gloucestershire possessed a phial allegedly containing the blood of Christ (L. Butler and C. Given-Wilson,
Medieval Monasteries of Great Britain (London, 1979), p. 258);
it could be seen only by those who had pure consciences – a ruse
worthy of the Pardoner (see the ME poem printed in *Altenglische
Legenden*, ed. C. Horstmann (Heilbronn, 1881), pp. 275–81).

653 Skeat (see his notes to MLT 124, Pard 653) interprets this line
in terms of the rules of the game of hazard, in which only one
player throws the dice; before making his throw, the caster calls
one of the numbers five, six, seven, eight or nine. This number is
called his 'main'. If he calls a seven and then throws seven or
eleven, he wins; if he throws two ones, two-one or two sixes, he
loses. If he throws any other number, it is called his 'chance'. He
continues to throw until either the main reappears and he loses
or the chance reappears and he wins. It is not clear, however,
exactly which of the many medieval dice-games is in question
here (the references to 'hasard' at Pard 465, 591, 608 seem to
mean simply dicing in general), and there is no mention of a
main. Probably, therefore, 'chaunce' means no more than 'throw'

(for examples of this meaning, and discussion of Skeat's proposal, see F. Semrau, *Würfel und Würfelspiel im alten Frankreich* (Halle a/S., 1910), pp. 52–6).

662   Prime is the third in the series of eight liturgical Offices sung daily by the regular clergy (see n. to Mil 3655), and the first of the so-called 'Little Hours' (the others being Terce, Sext and None). The 'riotoures', who are clearly not early risers, must have been up all night.

664   For the custom of ringing a handbell before a corpse on its way to burial, see Daniell, *Death and Burial*, pp. 44–5.

679   Chaucer darkens the mood of his tale by setting it against the background of the Black Death. See n. to GP 442. Some contemporary reactions to the plague are quoted and related to PardT by P. G. Beidler, *ChauR*, 16 (1982), 257–69.

696–7   For another example of sworn brotherhood which ends disastrously, see Fri 1404–5.

709   Cf. Pard 474–5 and n.

710   The oath sworn by the three men is a bizarre echo of God's words in Hosea (13:14): 'O death, I will be thy death'; these words were taken to be a prophecy of the Crucifixion (cf. *PPl* XVIII.35). The literalism of the revellers thus leads them to a parodic restatement of this divine paradox, which is part of PardT's exploration of the levels on which language makes contact with reality (see Introduction, pp. xl–xli).

728–38   These lines are based on a passage in the first elegy of the sixth-century Latin poet Maximian; lamenting his own old age and loss of his powers, he paints a vivid picture of a typical old man, shrunken and wrinkled, striking the earth with his cane as he pleads:

> Take me, my mother, pity the sufferings of your child. I seek to rest my tired limbs in your bosom. Children shudder at me; I have lost the appearance I once had. Why do you allow your offspring to become loathsome? I have nothing to do with the living; I have used up the gift of life. Return my lifeless limbs to their native soil, I beg. What profit is there in dragging wretches through varied tortures? It's not the sign of a motherly heart to allow this.
>
> (ed. R. Webster, *The Elegies of Maximianus* (Princeton, NJ, 1900), I.227–34; my translation)

A complete English translation can be found in L. R. Lind, *Gabriele Zerbi, Gerontocomia: On the Care of the Aged, and*

Maximianus, Elegies on Old Age and Love (Philadelphia, PA, 1988). Lengthy excerpts, with facing translation, are printed in *SA²* I, 312–19. Maximian's *Elegies* were well known, since they formed part of the group of texts known as the 'Liber Catonianus' which were used in the Middle Ages as an elementary reader for those learning Latin (see n. to Mil 3227). The influence of Maximian is perceptible in two ME lyrics on the subject of old age; see G. R. Coffman, *Speculum*, 9 (1934), 249–77, at p. 270.

743–4 A marginal gloss in El and Hg quotes the source in Leviticus 19:32: 'Rise up before the hoary head, and honour the person of the aged man.'

760–65 In some analogues to PardT, the story begins with the finding of the gold by a hermit, who immediately runs away, and when asked by the three companions what he is fleeing from, replies 'Death'. For text and translation, see *SA²* I, 286–9, 290–93.

770 *florins*: The florin was a Florentine gold coin, which circulated throughout medieval Europe and was imitated in other currencies. Since PardT is set in Flanders, Chaucer may be referring to the Flemish florin rather than to the English florin, which was minted only from January to August of 1344, or he may be using the term simply to mean 'gold coins' in general (D. C. Baker, *Speculum*, 36 (1961), 282–7; Grierson, *Coins*, pp. 110, 220).

781 Proverbial; see Whiting C384.

889–91 Avicenna, the important Arabic philosopher (980–1037), wrote a *Book of the Canon of Medicine* which treats of poisons in Book IV, Fen 6.
fen: Arabic 'fann', a division of a science; the term is used for the chapters of Avicenna's *Canon*.

922 For the role of the papacy in authorizing pardons, see n. to GP 669.

946–50 R. F. Green has suggested that the Host's words allude to a medieval comic tale (found in numerous versions) in which a gullible husband is persuaded that his wife's lover's breeches are a saint's relic, and is made to show his reverence by kissing them (*SAC*, 15 (1993), 131–45).

951 *crois . . . Seint Eleine*: The finding of the Holy Cross at Jerusalem by St Helena, mother of the Emperor Constantine, is related in the *Golden Legend* (I, no. 68).

952–3 This equation of testicles and relics may derive from the *Romance of the Rose*, where the Lover reproves Reason for using the word 'testicles' ('coilles') instead of a euphemism, and she defends herself: 'if you object ... that the words are ugly and base, I tell you before God who hears me that if, when I gave things the names that you dare find fault with and condemn, I had called testicles relics and relics testicles, then you who thus attack and reproach me would tell me instead that relics was an ugly, base word' (7076–85, tr. Horgan, p. 108).

THE SHIPMAN'S TALE

The narrative outline of the Shipman's Tale belongs to a story-type known as 'The Lover's Gift Regained' (*SA*, pp. 439–46); a story of this sort appears in Boccaccio's *Decameron* (VIII.1), and even though there is no direct evidence that Chaucer knew it (cf. Headnote to ClT), it is at least a close enough analogue to furnish a useful comparison. Text and translation are given in *SA*² II, along with a slightly less close parallel from the *Decameron* (VIII.2); both stories are readily available in McWilliam's translation of the *Decameron*). Boccaccio's brief narrative contains little beyond the mechanics of the plot; the Shipman's Tale, in contrast, is enriched with a vivid picture of life in a merchant's household, and also greatly expands the account of the way in which the wife and her lover come to a mutual agreement. The dialogue in which the wife agrees to have sex with the monk Dom John, while he agrees to pay her one hundred francs for the privilege, without any of this being explicitly stated, is a masterpiece of verbal disguise (98–208). In Boccaccio's version, the lover – not a monk but a German soldier – who is genuinely in love with the wife, is rudely awakened to her true nature by her demand for money, and takes his revenge by tricking her out of the payment. In the Shipman's Tale, neither the monk nor the wife is in any doubt as to the self-interested nature of their relationship, and instead of being left as the humiliated dupe of the lover's trick at the end of the tale, the wife takes the trickery a stage further by claiming that she has already spent the amount given her by the monk on her own 'array', which will enhance her husband's status, and asking him to take payment in the form of the marriage 'debt' – that is, in sex (see n. to WB 129–30). The situation thus achieves equilibrium through reciprocal deception, in a kind of comic parody of the equilibrium achieved through patience and generosity in the Franklin's Tale. The façade of deception is never disrupted, as befits the household of a merchant whose creditworthy status depends on keeping up appearances (12–13, 230–34, 418–21).

1   Saint-Denis, a town eight miles north of Paris, was famous for
     its abbey, rebuilt in splendid style in the twelfth century by Abbot
     Suger; it became the burial-place of French kings. It was also a
     good place for a merchant to live, since the fairs of Champagne
     were an international centre of commerce, credit, and currency
     exchange; one of these fairs was located at neighbouring Lendit
     (see *Dictionary of the Middle Ages*, ed. J. R. Strayer, 13 vols.
     (New York, 1982–9), s.v. Fairs of Champagne).

9   On this proverbial expression, see n. to Mch 1315.

12   The use of 'us' in this line implies that the speaker is a woman;
     this has led scholars to suggest that ShT was originally assigned
     to the Wife of Bath, and re-allocated to the Shipman as Chaucer's
     plans for CT developed (see n. to ML 1163–90).

38   *as glad . . . as fowel of day*: A proverbial comparison. See Whiting
     F561, and cf. Kn 2437 and Sh 51.

51   See preceding n.

55   Bruges (Dutch Brugge) was one of the great weaving towns of
     medieval Flanders and an important trading and banking centre;
     from about 1350 to 1450 it was 'the commercial capital of
     Europe' (Barron, 'England and the Low Countries', pp. 2–11).
     A great trading fair was held there every year in April–May; see
     J. A. van Houtte, *Essays on Medieval and Early Modern Econ-
     omy and Society* (Leuven, 1977), pp. 81–108, esp. pp. 88–9.

65–6 On monastic granges, see n. to Mil 3668. The monk acts as
     an administrative officer overseeing the landed estates which
     provided the monastery with its income (see n. to GP 166).

83   *counting-bord*: Medieval merchants made their calculations with
     jettons or counters placed on a table marked with squares, each
     vertical column representing a different monetary value. For a
     full account of the methods of calculations, with illustrations of
     counting-tables, see F. P. Barnard, *The Casting-Counter and the
     Counting-Board* (Oxford, 1916).

114–23 In view of the sexual energy displayed by the merchant on
     his return from Paris (375–81), the wife's insinuation that she is
     sexually deprived seems to be simply a way of indicating to the
     monk that she is open to advances from other quarters. Cf. Sum
     1827–31 and n.

131   The monk is carrying his breviary because it contained the texts
     of the eight liturgical 'Hours' which he (like other religious) was
     obliged to recite at fixed hours daily; see n. to Mil 3655.

135–40 'I swear . . . never to betray a word of what you tell me –
     [swearing this] not because of the bonds of loyalty obtaining

between kindred, but out of personal affection and trust.' The syntactic relation between lines 139–40 and what precedes them has the looseness characteristic of speech, but it is not so problematic as to warrant R. F. Green's suggestion that lines 139–40 should be repunctuated so as to form part of the narrator's following comments (*ChauR*, 26 (1991), 95–7).

148 St Martin (*c.* 316–97) began life as a Roman soldier, but left the army to become a monk and, later, bishop of Tours (*Golden Legend*, II, 292–300).

151 St Denis (d. *c.* 250), bishop of Paris, is the patron saint of France. The abbey of Saint-Denis (see n. to Sh 1) was built over his tomb.

171 Proverbial; see Whiting F345.

172 Since the narrator has already told us of the merchant's 'largesse' (22), the wife's claim that he is niggardly seems to be a blatant falsehood, which is not meant to convince the monk, but rather to provide a façade behind which their tacit negotiations can be conducted (cf. n. to Sh 114–23).

174 For a similar list of desirable qualities in a husband, see NP 2912–17.

181 The franc was a French gold coin, introduced in the fourteenth century, worth about 37–9 English pennies (Grierson, *Coins*, pp. 142–3; P. Spufford, *Handbook of Medieval Exchange* (London, 1986), p. 191); 100 francs was therefore equivalent to £15–£16 sterling, a considerable sum. Chaucer's annual income in 1389 has been estimated at £36 10s (Pearsall, *Life*, p. 210).

194 *Geneloun*: Ganelon, stepfather of Roland, the hero of the *Song of Roland*, betrayed his stepson by nominating him as leader of the rearguard army in the Emperor Charlemagne's withdrawal from Spain, and arranging for it to be ambushed and destroyed by the pagan king Marsile (557–616). As punishment for his treachery, he was torn apart by four horses (3962–74). Cf. Mk 2389 and NP 3227.

204 *al stille and softe*: In *Riverside*, these words are included in the monk's speech. The punctuation adopted here is suggested by J. Mandel, *PQ*, 70 (1991), 99–102.

206 *chilindre*: This portable sun-dial took the form of an upright cylinder with a conical top (North, *Chaucer's Universe*, pp. 111–13).

214 *Qui la**] Who ther El; Who ther Hg ('ys' is inserted over a caret mark). Both El and Hg read 'qui la' in the margin; Manly and Rickert conjecture that in Chaucer's original 'qui la' stood in the text, with 'Who ther' as a marginal gloss, and that this was read

by later scribes as an intended substitution (IV, 497). This seems the likeliest explanation, despite N. Blake's arguments in favour of 'Who ther' as the textual reading and 'Qui la' as the marginal gloss (*New Perspectives in Chaucer Criticism*, ed. D. M. Rose (Norman, OK, 1981), pp. 223–40, at pp. 228–32). If 'Who ther' was the original reading, there would have been no point in supplying a French gloss.

221–3 Fasting before the Eucharist became a common practice from the fourth century onwards. These lines also imply that the merchant, like many pious laymen in the fourteenth century, kept a resident chaplain to celebrate mass in his house; even if the monk were in priestly orders (as some but not all monks were), he would have been prohibited from administering the sacraments to the laity without special permission (H. A. Kelly, *ChauR*, 28 (1993), 5–22, at p. 9).

227 *Seint Ive*: See n. to Sum 1943.

228 tweye*] ten El x. Hg. The use of Roman numerals makes the confusion of 'x' and 'ii' easier, especially after the preceding 'xii', and the merchant's gloomy tone would suggest that the rate of success that causes him such concern is two out of twelve rather than ten out of twelve. The *CT* scribes also freely substituted their own figures: twelve out of twenty, twelve out of ten hundred, two out of twenty. It is possible, however, that 'ten out of twelve' is correct, and that Chaucer is making fun of the professional pessimism exhibited by merchants, even in the face of success.

230–34 This passage has given difficulties. M. Copland (*MÆ*, 35 (1966), 11–28, at p. 19) takes 'pleye a pilgrimage' to be a euphemism for 'die'. It seems more likely that the merchant mentions pilgrimage because pilgrims customarily settled their debts and made a will before setting out, leaving their property in the protection of the Church (cf. *PPl* VI.83–5, and see Sumption, *Pilgrimage*, pp. 168–9). The merchant thus thinks of death and pilgrimage alike as signalling the end of his worldly activity.

259 *Seint Austin*: St Augustine (354–430), bishop of Hippo, was one of the early Church Fathers.

300 On medieval apprentices, see n. to Co 4365–6.

309 Monks, like other clergymen in the Middle Ages, were clean-shaven, and monastic life prescribed regular shaving and renewal of their tonsures (Harvey, *Living and Dying*, pp. 132–3).

330–34 The merchant has bought (unspecified) goods at the fair in Bruges, and has bound himself by a 'reconissaunce' (a written pledge of repayment) to pay 20,000 shields for them. K. S. Cahn (*SAC*, 2 (1980), 81–119, at pp. 116–17) claims that the shield was not a real coin but a notional monetary unit used in foreign exchange (see, however, n. to GP 278). But since the merchant has made his purchase in Bruges, the obvious interpretation of this passage is that the 'sheelde' is the Flemish *écu* (in Dutch, *schild*), a gold coin issued by Louis of Mâle, count of Flanders (1346–84), in imitation of the French coin of the same name (see O. Elsen, *Revue belge de numismatique et de sigillographie*, 141 (1995), 37–183, at pp. 84–7, 141–2, and the statistical tables on pp. 172, 180). Since the merchant is French, he is to pay for the shields in French francs. He already has most of the sum required, but since the goods were dearer than he anticipated (328), he has to borrow more from friends in Paris (James Murray and Peter Spufford, personal communications).

355 On St James, see n. to Rv 4264.

359 In medieval law, a man who delivered goods to another was advised to take and leave a token as proof of delivery (M. F. Braswell, *ChauR*, 22 (1988), 295–304, at p. 301).

366–8 By repaying the loan, the merchant redeems the bond or 'reconissaunce' that he had given as security for the shields. G. Joseph (*ChauR*, 17 (1983), 341–57, at p. 348) suggests that the merchant makes his repayment to the Paris branch of the Lombard bank that lent him the 20,000 shields in Bruges (see n. to Sh 330–34). All the major Italian banking companies had permanent branches at Bruges.

Lumbards: On the Lombards, see R. de Roover, *Money, Banking and Credit in Mediaeval Bruges* (Cambridge, MA, 1948), pp. 99–108; the term was, however, used as a virtual synonym for 'Italian'. Money-lending was common, despite the fact that, strictly speaking, it was forbidden by the Church.

416 The wife is punning on 'taille' ('tally', a scored wooden stick kept by a creditor as a record of sums owing) and 'tail' (in the sense 'arse', 'genitals'); for the latter, see *MED* tail *n*, 1b (c).

THE SHIPMAN–PRIORESS LINK

435 *corpus dominus*: The correct form would be 'corpus domini', 'the Lord's body'. As an uneducated layman, the Host has only an imperfect grasp of Latin. For other examples of the Host's garbled oaths, see Pard 310, 314, Mk 1892, 1906, and nn.

441 *Seint Austin*: On St Augustine, see n. to Sh 259.

THE PRIORESS'S PROLOGUE

Rubric *Domine dominus noster*: 'O Lord, our Lord'. These are the opening words of Psalm 8; see next n.

453–9 These lines echo verses 2–3 (AV 1–2) of Psalm 8: 'O Lord our Lord, how admirable is thy name in the whole earth! For thy magnificence is elevated above the heavens. Out of the mouth of infants and of sucklings thou hast perfected praise . . .' These verses were used (in reverse order) as the Introit of the Mass of the Holy Innocents (M. P. Hamilton, in *Chaucer: Modern Essays in Criticism*, ed. E. Wagenknecht (New York, 1959), pp. 88–97, at p. 90).

468 The allusion is to the bush, burning but not consumed by fire, out of which God's voice spoke to Moses (Exodus 3:1–6). In Christian tradition, the burning bush was interpreted as a prefiguration of the virgin birth (Salzer, *Sinnbilder*, pp. 12–14).

472 *Fadres Sapience*: That is, Christ. Medieval theologians assigned particular qualities to the three persons of the Trinity. God the Father was identified as Power, God the Son as Wisdom, and God the Holy Ghost as Love. See, for example, *PPl* XVI.30, 36, and Julian of Norwich, *Shewings*, ed. G. R. Crampton (Kalamazoo, MI, 1994), ch. 58, 2408–11. The inscription on the gate to Dante's Hell proclaims it to have been made by 'The Divine Power . . . | The Supreme Wisdom, and the Primal Love' (*Inferno* III.5–6).

474–80 This stanza echoes lines 50–56 of SNPr, which are themselves based on Dante, *Paradiso* XXXIII.16–21.

THE PRIORESS'S TALE

The Prioress's Tale belongs to the literary genre known as Miracles of the Virgin, brief narratives recounting the miraculous assistance granted by the Virgin Mary to her devotees or suppliants (who may be sinners, criminals or Jews, as well as devout Christians). Collections of such stories 'took Europe by storm in the twelfth and thirteenth centuries, reached their fullest extension in the fourteenth and fifteenth centuries, and survived as a living literature here and there till the seventeenth century' (R. W. Southern, *Mediaeval and Renaissance Studies*, 4 (1958), 176–216, at p. 178). For some ME examples, see B. Boyd, ed., *The Middle English Miracles of the Virgin* (San Marino, CA, 1964). As in the tales of the Man of Law, Clerk and Second Nun, the solemn tone of the Prioress's Tale is sustained by the use of rhyme royal (see n. to ML 96), which is continued into the following link.

The story of the boy murdered by Jews for singing a song in praise of Mary survives in many different versions; most of them were printed and discussed by C. Brown in *A Study of the Miracle of Our Lady Told by Chaucer's Prioress* (London, 1910). His findings were reproduced, incorporating some supplementary material, in *SA*, pp. 447–66, followed by texts or summaries of the tales which offer the closest resemblances to Chaucer's version (Brown's Group C). The texts in Brown's Group C, along with some newly identified analogues, are reproduced with parallel translations in *SA*[2] II. See also M. H. Statler, *PMLA*, 65 (1950), 896–910. Two of these tales are included in Kolve and Olson, pp. 418–27. Broadly speaking, the other tales (Brown's Groups A and B) differ from the story told by Chaucer in the following respects: (1) the murdered boy is buried by the Jews (rather than being thrown into a latrine), but having been discovered by his singing, he is dug up alive and unharmed; (2) the Jews are not punished for their crime, since they are so impressed by the boy's miraculous resurrection that they are converted and baptized; (3) the song in praise of Mary which is sung by the boy is not 'Alma redemptoris' but 'Gaude Maria' or another Marian chant. 'Gaude Maria' ends with the line 'Erubescat Iudaeus infelix, qui dicit Christum Joseph semine esse natum' ('Let the cursed Jew blush, who says that Christ was born of the seed of Joseph'), which several of these versions represent as having provoked the Jews to the murder.

As far as one can tell in the absence of a clearly identifiable direct source, Chaucer himself seems to have been responsible for setting the Prioress's Tale in Asia (see n. to Pri 488), and also for making the boy as young as seven, thus increasing the pathos of the tale and foregrounding Mary's role, not only as miracle-worker, but as heavenly mother, as is evident especially in her final words of maternal comfort (667–9). Chaucer also gave the tale greater solemnity and wider significance by weaving into it allusions to Herod's Slaughter of the Innocents and to the liturgy of their feast; see Hamilton (cited in n. to Pri 453–9), and also nn. to Pri 453–9, 574, 578, 580–85 and 627. For the Proper (the elements that changed according to the liturgical occasion) of the Mass for this feast, see *The Sarum Missal*, ed. J. W. Legg (Oxford, 1916; repr. 1969), pp. 32–3.

The anti-Semitism implicit in the tale, and explicit in lines 559, 574–8, has given difficulties in modern times, and attempts have been made to exculpate Chaucer by attributing its disturbing combination of tenderness and cruelty to the Prioress, from whom Chaucer is supposed to be ironically distancing himself (see F. H. Ridley, *The Prioress and the Critics* (Berkeley, CA, 1965), pp. 1–4, for a summary of such attempts, and for a more recent argument along these lines, see R. Rex, *Modern Language Quarterly*, 45 (1984), 107–22). But, as R. W. Frank, Jr, has pointed out (*The Wisdom of Poetry: Essays in Early English Literature in Honor of Morton W. Bloomfield*, ed. L. D. Benson and S. Wenzel (Kalamazoo, MI, 1982), pp. 177–88, 290–97), anti-Semitism is pervasive in Miracles of the Virgin, and there is no reason to credit Chaucer with greater sensitivity than his contemporaries in this matter; the pathos of Christian martyrdom required villainous persecutors, and also required that a difference of faith should motivate their persecutions. The complete absence of Jews in fourteenth-century England, following their expulsion by Edward I in 1290, did not prevent them from playing an important role in the emotional and symbolic configurations of medieval Christian literature. The best route to understanding the Prioress's Tale is probably through comparison with – in the first instance – the Man of Law's Tale, which shares its combination of violence and pathos. In both tales, Satan is portrayed as exerting his influence in the world by making specific social groups (the Jews in the Prioress's Tale, women in the Man of Law's Tale, 365–71) into instruments of his will. The Prioress's Tale also shares with the Man of Law's Tale an emphasis on Mary as an exemplar of suffering and compassionate motherhood; both tales can be linked with those of the Clerk and Physician as being especially concerned with the relation between parents and children as a model for the relation between humankind and God (see Mann, 'Parents and Children'). Throughout these tales there runs an implicit contrast between the cruel father and the tender mother, which focuses the question of the relation between suffering and love. In the Prioress's Tale this takes the form of the problematic relation between the tenderness represented by Mary and the boy's mother on the one hand, and on the other, the cruelty inflicted by and on the Jews, both of which (from a medieval Christian point of view) form part of the divinely dictated plan of salvation history. It is not the Prioress but the Christian Church, and ultimately God, who authorizes the attitude to the Jews expressed in Pri 574–8. While this interpretation of the tale as an exploration of suffering and love does not defend it against the charge of contributing to the reinforcement of anti-Semitic stereotypes, and so to the perpetuation of the cruelty it deplores, it perhaps makes it possible to see the particular interest that Chaucer might have had in this story.

488 *Asie*: PriT is the only version of this story to set the action in
     Asia, and Chaucer's motive in choosing this remote setting is not
     obvious. Many versions of the tale do not specify its location,
     but those that do, place it in England (where its action must be
     assumed to pre-date the expulsion of the Jews in 1290, and in
     one instance is said to have been its cause), in Italy (Pisa), Spain
     (Toledo) or France (Le Puy, Paris, Carcassonne or the region of
     Albi).

489 *Jewerye*: 'Throughout history, religious and social solidarity,
     reinforced by Gentile aversion, brought about a tendency for the
     Jews to foregather in one street or quarter of each town. This
     received a powerful impetus when the Third Lateran Council
     [1179] forbade Christians to live in the immediate propinquity
     of the infidel, so as to avoid any possibility of being contaminated
     by his disbelief. The Jewish quarter was thus universally familiar.
     In England it was called the *Jewry*', C. Roth, *A Short History of
     the Jewish People*, rev. edn (London, 1969), p. 216.

491 *usure*: The Church forbade Christians to practise usury (the
     lending of money at interest), but a monetary economy could
     hardly function without it. Since Jews were largely debarred from
     other kinds of commercial activity, they increasingly took on the
     role of bankers or money-lenders in medieval society (Roth,
     History of the Jewish People, pp. 204–8).

494 The Jewish quarter in medieval towns was usually surrounded
     by a wall, with a gate at each end, guarded by Christian gate-
     keepers. After nightfall Jews were not allowed outside the ghetto
     nor Christians within it (Roth, *History of the Jewish People*,
     p. 298). Chaucer seems to imagine the Jewish quarter here as a
     single street without any enclosure.

500 *to singen and to rede*: The elementary education that Chaucer
     describes here is that which obtained in fourteenth-century Eng-
     land. Children began their education around the age of seven, and
     after mastering the alphabet would immediately begin learning to
     recognize and pronounce Latin words. 'Little attention at the
     beginning stage was given to meaning and grammar. Word recog-
     nition and pronunciation were sufficient and were taught in two
     ways. One way was through plainchant, by which the student
     learned the pronunciation of the words that occurred in the
     liturgical texts of the church, the hymns, and the Psalter. The
     other way was through reading a primer containing religious and
     devotional texts, such as the Creed, the Lord's Prayer, the *Ave
     Maria*, and simple prayers' (W. J. Courtenay, *Schools and*

Scholars in Fourteenth-Century England (Princeton, NJ, 1987), pp. 16–17; see also n. to Pri 517). This education prepared students to become choristers or to enter minor orders, as well as serving as a basis for those going on to more advanced study of Latin grammar and syntax which would qualify them for the higher orders of the clergy (ibid., p. 17). See also J. A. Hoeppner Moran, *The Growth of English Schooling 1340–1548* (Princeton, NJ, 1985), ch. 2.

503 The boy's extreme youth is an individual touch of Chaucer's; see Headnote.

505–6 The implication is that images of the Virgin were placed in niches on the outside of buildings or in wayside shrines, as in Catholic countries today.

508 The Ave Maria is a simple prayer based on the words used by the Angel Gabriel to Mary at the Annunciation (Luke 1:28): 'Ave Maria gratia plena, dominus tecum. Benedicta tu in mulieribus et benedictus fructus uteris tui' ('Hail Mary, full of grace, the Lord is with thee. Blessed art thou among women, and blessed is the fruit of thy womb'). It was one of the first prayers learned by children (see n. to Pri 517).

512 Proverbial; see Whiting C219.

514–15 St Nicholas was a fourth-century bishop of Myra (in south-western Turkey). Little else is known about his life, but the popularity of his cult ensured the proliferation of legends about him. The reference here is probably to the story that, as a suckling infant, he took the breast only on Wednesdays and Fridays, and fasted on the other days of the week (*Golden Legend*, I, 21).

517 *primer*: The ME term for a Book of Hours, which was a collection of liturgical texts designed as a devotional manual for lay people. Its core constituents were the Little Office (or Hours) of the Virgin (composed of selected biblical texts to be recited daily at each of the eight 'canonical' hours, in parallel to the Hours recited by members of the regular clergy; see n. to Mil 3655), the seven Penitential Psalms and the Office of the Dead. Other devotional texts (such as the fifteen Gradual Psalms, the Litany of the Saints and the Commendation of Souls) were added to this core. See C. Wordsworth and H. Littlehales, *The Old Service-Books of the English Church* (London, 1904), pp. 248–54, and C. de Hamel, *The Bible as Book: The Manuscript Tradition*, ed. J. L. Sharpe III and K. van Kampen (London, 1998), pp. 137–43. The Book of Hours 'was known by heart by nearly every person of any education whatsoever in late medieval Europe. It

was the text from which children first learned to read ... and then recited every subsequent day of their lives' (de Hamel, pp. 138–9). Most primers of this sort were in Latin, but a number of English primers also survive (Wordsworth and Littlehales, p. 249); for an example, see *The Prymer or Lay Folks Prayer Book*, ed. H. Littlehales, EETS o.s. 105, 109 (London, 1895–7).

Based on this model, there were also elementary reading books designed specifically for children, beginning with an alphabet, and containing basic prayers such as the Pater Noster and Ave Maria, and other elements of the faith such as the Creed and the Ten Commandments. See Courtenay, quoted in n. to Pri 500, and N. Orme, *English Schools in the Middle Ages* (London, 1973), p. 62. A manuscript of this type, written in French and Latin, is reproduced in G. A. Plimpton, *The Education of Chaucer Illustrated from the Schoolbooks in Use in his Time* (London, 1935), Plates XIII.1–39. It includes both the Ave Maria (see Pri 508) and 'Alma redemptoris' (see Pri 518).

518 *Alma redemptoris*: The first words of one of the four major Marian antiphons (Latin songs in praise of Mary), written in hexameter verse. For texts and translations of all four, see M. Britt, *The Hymns of the Breviary and Missal* (London, 1922), pp. 86–9. The full text of 'Alma redemptoris' is as follows:

> Alma redemptoris mater quae pervia caeli
> Porta manes et stella maris, succurre cadenti
> Surgere qui curat populo, tu quae genuisti
> Natura mirante tuum sanctum genitorem,
> Virgo prius ac posterius, Gabrielis ab ore
> Sumens illud Ave, peccatorum miserere.

('Gentle mother of the Redeemer, ever-open door of heaven and star of the sea, succour your fallen people who long to arise – you who gave birth, to Nature's wonderment, to your own holy Father, a virgin both before and afterwards, receiving that "Ave" from Gabriel's mouth – be merciful to sinners.')

For a ME version of this antiphon, see *SA*, p. 469. The tune of the antiphon has been reconstructed from medieval sources by A. Davidson, *Substance and Manner: Studies in Music and the Other Arts* (St Paul, MN, 1977), pp. 21–9, 92–5 (reproduced in B. Boyd, ed., *A Variorum Edition of the Works of Geoffrey Chaucer: The Prioress's Tale* (Norman, OK, 1987), p. 16). The term 'antiphon' usually denotes a short text sung (rather like a refrain) between the verses of a psalm, but the Marian antiphons are pieces of liturgical chant quite separate from psalmody (see W. Apel, *Gregorian Chant* (London, 1958), p. 189, and *New Grove Dictionary*, s.v. Antiphon). According to Davidson, M. P. Hamilton was wrong to conjecture, on the basis of later practice, that 'Alma redemptoris' was sung, as it is now, in the Mass from Advent to Candlemas (p. 97, n. 15), but it was so frequently used at Vespers and other services of the English rite as to be 'ubiquitous in liturgical practice' (Davidson, p. 27).

519 *antiphoner*: A book containing a collection of antiphons, or pieces of sacred chant (see preceding n.). For a facsimile of a thirteenth-century antiphoner (Cambridge, University Library, MS Mm.2.9) containing the words and music of 'Alma redemptoris', see W. H. Frere, *Antiphonale Sarisburiense: A Reproduction in Facsimile from Early Manuscripts* (London, 1901–24), V, 529. Since the words and music in antiphoners were written in large separate letters, they were 'especially suitable for children to study' (N. Orme, *ChauR*, 16 (1981), 38–59, at p. 48).

536 That is, the older boy is learning to pronounce Latin by memorizing the words and music of liturgical texts, songs and the Psalter; Latin grammar and syntax would be taught, if at all, at a later stage (see n. to Pri 500).

540 Since the Feast of the Innocents takes place on 28 December, the Christmas season is an appropriate time for the action of this tale.

541 Instead of memorizing the items in his primer (see n. to Pri 517), the little boy intends to devote himself to learning the antiphon. This combination of naughtiness and sanctity resembles Virginia's avoidance of parties by pretending to be sick (Phys 61–6); sanctity in both these children is a kind of natural instinct rather than a willed conformity to rules.

564 youre*] oure El Hg. The reading 'oure' could be defended on the grounds that Satan is speaking through the mouth of one of the Jews, who is stirring up his fellows, but in that case one would expect 'us' and 'oure' to be used in lines 561 and 563 respectively.

574 Herod, king of the Jews, ordered the slaughter of all male children under two years old in Bethlehem and the surrounding region because he had been told by the wise men of the appearance of a star heralding the birth of a child born to be king of the Jews (Matthew 2:13–18). These verses of Matthew formed the Gospel

reading at the Feast of the Innocents (Hamilton, p. 91). For other references to the Slaughter of the Innocents in this tale, see Headnote.

576 Proverbial; see Whiting M806, and cf. NPT 3052, 3057.

578 Cf. Genesis 4:10, where the blood of the murdered Abel is said to cry out from the ground. The responsories in the first and second nocturns of Matins for the Feast of the Innocents (see Headnote) incorporate verses from Psalm 78 (AV 79) (3, 10) and Revelation 6 (9–11), which supplicate God for vengeance on blood that has been shed, and the fifth lesson is a passage from a sermon of St John Chrysostom, which links the blood of Abel crying to heaven with the Innocents ('They speak with blood, because they cannot do so with their tongue. They sing with their suffering, because they never knew speech ... since the blood of Abel cries to heaven, let the souls of these murdered ones also cry out to God from the altar'). See H. A. Kelly, *MedHum*, n.s. 19 (1992), 133–46, at p. 144; *Breviarium ad usum insignis ecclesiae Sarum*, ed. F. Procter and C. Wordsworth, 3 vols. (Cambridge, 1879–86), I, ccxxxi–ccxxxvii.

580–85 These lines refer to Revelation 14:1–5, which describes a vision of the Lamb who is Christ, accompanied by 144,000 virgins, 'who were not defiled with women', singing a 'new song'. (A marginal Latin gloss in Hg quotes Jerome's citation of this passage in *Adv. Jov.* I.40.) Revelation 14:1–5 was the first Lesson at the Feast of the Innocents (Hamilton, pp. 91–2); see Headnote. *the grete evangelist ... In Pathmos*: The author of Revelation gives his name as John (1:4, 9; 22:8); he also indicates that he wrote the book on Patmos, an island in the Aegean off the coast of present-day Turkey (1:9). In medieval tradition this John was identified with the author of the fourth Gospel, but this has been disputed by modern biblical scholars (see *Jerome Biblical Commentary*, II, 64:10–13).

585 *flesshly*: An interlinear gloss 'carnaliter' in El/Hg shows that this is an adverb rather than an adjective.

607–8 Like the opening of PriPr (see n. to Pri 453–9), these lines echo Psalm 8:2–3.

616 *provost*: This term was used of a variety of officials, both religious and secular, but here it seems to be used as on the Continent to denote the chief magistrate of a town (*MED* a). Boyd suggests that this provost is 'a secular official with some kind of judicial authority over the Jews corresponding to that of a sheriff, a royal appointee under English law through whom the king normally

dealt with the Jews in borrowing and repaying money' (*Variorum: Prioress's Tale*, p. 22).

627 The historical Rachel was the mother of Joseph (Genesis 30:22–4) and Benjamin (Genesis 35:16–18), but she did not suffer bereavement. The reference here is to a prophecy of Jeremiah (31:15) in which her name is used to typify Jewish motherhood: 'A voice was heard on high of lamentation, of mourning, and weeping, of Rachel weeping for her children, and refusing to be comforted for them, because they are not.' The Gospel of Matthew quotes this prophecy (rather freely), seeing its fulfilment in Herod's slaughter of the Innocents (2:18). Matthew's verse (which is partially quoted in a marginal Latin gloss in Hg) was used as the *Communio* of the Mass of the Innocents (Hamilton, p. 91); see Headnote.

632 The principle enunciated in this maxim underlies the Old Testament law of 'an eye for an eye, a tooth for a tooth', for which Christ substituted the rule of turning the other cheek (see Exodus 21:23–4, Matthew 5:38–9). The idea here is that the Jews are punished according to the principle of their own law.

633–4 In Chaucer's day, those convicted of treason (which included a range of particularly heinous crimes) were subjected to 'an aggravated form of capital punishment': men were drawn behind carts to the gallows and then hanged (B. A. Hanawalt, *Crime and Conflict in English Communities 1300–1348* (Cambridge, MA, 1979), p. 44).

660 *antheme*: The anglicized form of the word antiphon (see n. to Pri 519).

676 been*] lein El Hg. Manly and Rickert claim that 'lein' 'was not the reading of O¹', on the grounds that it is absent in other manuscripts belonging to the same group as Hg, El and several related manuscripts (IV, 498–9). G. Dempster justifiably calls this judgement 'puzzling' (*PMLA*, 61 (1946), 379–415, at p. 412, n. 193). But 'been' may still be preferred to 'lein' on the grounds that the latter repeats 'lay' in a stylistically clumsy way.

684–5 *yonge Hugh of Lincoln*: Under the year 1255, the thirteenth-century chronicler Matthew Paris relates that in the city of Lincoln, an eight-year-old boy named Hugh was ritually murdered by Jews, in a grotesque re-enactment of Christ's crucifixion, and his body was thrown into a well. As in PriT, the distraught mother of the boy sought for him and eventually discovered his body (*Chronica Majora*, ed. H. R. Luard, vol. V (London, 1880; repr. 1964), pp. 516–19; *Matthew Paris's English History*, tr.

J. A. Giles, vol. III (London, 1854), pp. 138–41). Nineteen Jews
were executed for this alleged crime. For an analysis of the
historical documents and an attempted reconstruction of the
circumstances giving rise to the accusation, see J. Jacobs, *Jewish
Ideals and Other Essays* (London, 1896), pp. 192–224. The
initial stimulus to such tales of ritual child-murder seems to have
been the story of William of Norwich, allegedly crucified by
Jews in 1144 (*SA*, pp. 455–6). For a recent analysis, see J. M.
McCulloh, *Speculum*, 72 (1997), 698–740.

Although a feast in honour of Hugh was celebrated in the
diocese of Lincoln, he was never officially canonized. Chaucer's
wife Philippa was admitted to the fraternity of Lincoln cathedral
on 19 February 1386 (*Life-Records*, pp. 91–3), and it may have
been through this connection that Chaucer learned of the story.
King Richard II and Queen Anne were likewise enrolled in the
cathedral confraternity on 26 March 1387, and S. Ferris has
argued that the Prioress's Tale was written to be recited on this
occasion (*ChauR*, 15 (1981), 295–321).

THE PRIORESS–SIR THOPAS LINK

700–704   Apparently the Host means that Chaucer has an ample
waist-line. His description of Chaucer's appearance can be compared with near-contemporary portraits of the poet. Beginning
with the miniature in El (which depicts each pilgrim-teller at the
beginning of his or her tale), there is a tradition of Chaucer
portraiture 'remarkable both for the early date at which it became
established and for the exceptional attention that is paid to life-
likeness of representation' (Pearsall, *Life*, p. 285; see pp. 285–
305 for a full discussion of Chaucer portraits and reproductions
of the most important of them). The precise visual effect indicated
by 'elvissh' is not clear.

SIR THOPAS

The first of the two tales that Chaucer tells is a parody of ME popular
romances. He imitates their narrative motifs, metre, rhyme and characteristic vocabulary. Examples of the kind of romance that he had in
mind are given in lines 897–900 (see n., with details of editions).
Three of those named are found together in the Auchinleck MS, a
large literary miscellany which was put together in the second quarter
of the fourteenth century; Loomis suggests that Chaucer might have

known this very manuscript; see L. H. Loomis, pp. 111–28 in *Essays and Studies in Honor of Carleton Brown*, ed. P. W. L[ong] (New York, 1940). Loomis demonstrates numerous detailed parallels between the phraseology of the tail-rhyme version of *Guy of Warwick*, uniquely preserved in the Auchinleck MS, and Chaucer's parody (ibid.). Many other parallels, culled from a wide range of romances, were presented by Loomis in *SA*, pp. 486–559; see also *SA²*II. They illustrate not only the conventional phraseology of the romances, but also the conventional nature of their narrative components. The arming of the hero, the combat with a giant, the encounter with an elf-queen, are examples of the traditional elements that Chaucer incorporates into Thopas, while stretching the episodic structure of the typical romance to the point of total incoherence.

Chaucer imitates the vocabulary of popular romance by introducing words and expressions not found elsewhere in his works: *listeth* (see 712, 833, and n. to Th 712–13), *spray* (770), *downe* (796), *murye men* (839), *dappel gray* (884), *love-drury* (895), *auntrous* (909), *worly* (917 and n.). On the high proportion of 'nonce words' in Thopas, see W. Scheps, *NM*, 80 (1979), 69–77. A small group of words in Thopas are shared with the Miller's Tale, where they seem to represent low-life attempts at romance phraseology: *gent* (715, Mil 3234), *rode* (727, Mil 3317), *love-longinge* (772, Mil 3349); cf. E. T. Donaldson, *Speaking of Chaucer* (London, 1970), pp. 16–29. *Lemman* (788), which Chaucer uses frequently in the Miller's Tale (3278, 3280, 3700, 3705, 3719, 3726) and the Reeve's Tale (4240, 4247), and calls a 'knavissh' word in the Manciple's Tale (204–5), may give the same effect. Chaucer also allows himself licences with rhyme which depart from his normal practice, such as identical rhyme (*contree* at 718 and 722, *goon* at 800 and 805), and the suppression of final *-e* on words which normally carry it, so that they can rhyme with words that lack it (*entent* at 712, *plas* instead of *place* at 781, *gras* instead of *grace* at 831, *chivalry* at 902, *well* at 915). Occasionally the reverse occurs: *childe* at 806 has an *-e* that it would not normally carry. Finally, Chaucer pads out his verse with the aid of the kind of line-fillers characteristic of romance, whose only function is to provide a rhyme: e.g., *verrayment* (713), *in the place* (720), *in good certein* (728), *it is no nay* (766), *In towne* (793), *By dale and eek by downe* (796), *In londe* (887).

It is the verse-form, however, which is the greatest contributor to the comic effect of Thopas. It is written in a version of the stanza-form known as tail-rhyme. The most usual form of stanza has 'twelve lines divided into four groups of three, each group containing, as a rule, a

couplet with four accents [stresses] to the line, and a concluding line,
a "tail", with three accents' (A. McI. Trounce, *MÆ*, 1 (1932), 87–
108, at p. 87; for a full survey of ME tail-rhyme romances, see also
the subsequent articles by the same author in *MÆ*, 1 (1932), 168–82,
MÆ, 2 (1933), 34–57, 189–98, and *MÆ*, 3 (1934), 30–50). The
stanza-form adopted in Thopas has only six lines, rhyming aabaab or
aabccb. A similar stanza-form (in which, however, the third and sixth
lines have only two stresses) is used in lines 1–474 of *Bevis of Hampton*
in the Auchinleck MS. Other tail-rhyme romances in Auchinleck
include *The King of Tars*, *Amis and Amiloun*, *Roland and Vernagu*,
and *Horn Child*; see pp. xix–xxiv in the Introduction by D. Pearsall
and I. C. Cunningham to the facsimile edition, *The Auchinleck Manuscript, National Library of Scotland Advocates' MS.19.2.1* (London,
1977).

The stanza-form in Thopas is sometimes longer and the rhyme-
scheme more complicated (e.g., 797–826, 881–90); in such cases a
'bob' of two syllables is introduced to rhyme with one of the three-
stress lines. A number of MSS (including El and Hg) draw attention
to the verse-form by bracketing the four-stress lines so as to indicate
the links created by rhyme, and writing the three-stress lines in a
separate column to the right of them, bracketed in the same way. The
bob, if there is one, is placed in yet another column to the right of
the second one (see J. Tschann, *ChauR*, 20 (1985), 1–13). Chaucer
brilliantly orchestrates the apparently meaningless variations in line-
length, and the prominence given to the rhymes by the brevity of the
lines, to create the comic bathos of Thopas. Commenting on the
'extraordinary variety' of the rhyme-schemes in the five stanzas containing a bob, E. G. Stanley says that 'No writer of Middle English
stanzaic verse shows such versatile technical mastery as Chaucer does
in the Prologue and Tale of *Sir Thopas* – to demonstrate his incompetence' (*NM*, 73 (1972), 417–26, at p. 426).

712–13 The appeal for the audience's attention, and the introduction
of the hero with the promise 'I wol [yow] telle', are characteristic
of the minstrel poetry that Chaucer is parodying (see *SA*,
pp. 496–503 for numerous examples). J. A. Burrow points out
that Chaucer's usual word for 'listen' is 'hark/hearken', and he
does not use 'list' anywhere else in his work; he suggests that the
word (and its alliterative pairing with 'lordes/lordinges') is part
of Chaucer's imitation of romance diction (*Essays on Medieval
Literature* (Oxford, 1984), pp. 60–78, at pp. 66–9).

717 *Sire Thopas*: Chaucer does not use the title 'Sir' of any other

knight in his works, but it occurs twelve times in Th; it is used eight times of Thopas himself, once of the giant (Th 808), and three times of other knights (Th 899–900, 916). Burrow suggests that the collocation '*sir + knight's name*' 'is to be numbered among those non-U expressions which Chaucer confines to burlesque contexts' (*Essays on Medieval Literature*, p. 70).

719–20 *Flaundres ... Popering*: Poperinge is a town in Flanders, noted for its cloth. The name is doubtless chosen for its comic sound, but there may also be an allusion to 'the poor reputation that the Flemish had for chivalric and military prowess' (V. J. Scattergood, in *Court and Poet*, ed. G. S. Burgess (Liverpool, 1981), pp. 287–96, at p. 293). The burlesque French parody that J. A. Burrow compares with Th (*Yearbook of English Studies*, 14 (1984), 44–55) likewise makes fun of Flemish chivalry.

724–35 The terms in which Sir Thopas is described have often been seen as more appropriate for women and children than for a male hero (*SA*, p. 504, and see n. to 725–7 in *Riverside*). But the beauty of the young hero Horn is praised in very similar terms: 'He was bright so the glas, | He was whit so the flur, | Rose red was his colour' (14–16; see *SA*, p. 505). The AN *Romance of Horn* is even more insistent on the hero's dazzling beauty: 'His hair is long and blonde, like no one else's; his eyes are large, bright, soft and smiling, for looking at women; his nose and mouth well-shaped, for bestowing sweet kisses; his face is open and his expression laughing, his hands white and his arms long, for embracing women; his body shapely and slim, quite flawless; straight legs, fine feet, in well-chosen hose' (ed. M. K. Pope, vol. I (Oxford, 1955), lines 1255–61; tr. J. Weiss in *The Birth of Romance: An Anthology* (London, 1992), pp. 29–30). Though such descriptions are seriously meant, Chaucer may well be implying effeminacy in Sir Thopas by offering his good looks as evidence of his being 'a doghty swain'.

727 *scarlet in grain*: See nn. to GP 456 and Sq 511.

733 On Bruges as a weaving and commercial centre, see n. to Sh 55. L. H. Loomis points out that cloth from Bruges is less exotic than the stuffs from India or Tars which are more usual in romance (*SA*, p. 504, n. 4).

736–41 Skill in hunting and hawking was established as an essential part of the hero's accomplishments by the Tristram romances; for parallels in ME romance, see *SA*, pp. 508–10. According to N. Orme (*ChauR*, 16 (1981), 38–59, at p. 44), there is nothing incongruous in a knight practising wrestling and archery; along with hunting and hawking, these formed part of a gentleman's training in leisure pursuits. Perhaps, however, Thopas's entry into 'plebeian wrestling competitions' is an object of ridicule (p. 57, n. 10). Cf. GP 548 and n.

742–7 Women similarly sigh in vain for Guy of Warwick (*SA*, pp. 516–17). The AN *Romance of Horn* continually emphasizes the devastating effect that Horn's charms have on women (ed. Pope, lines 446–7, 476–9; tr. Weiss, *The Birth of Romance*, p. 11). However, Horn refuses to 'do shame of his body' (lines 385–6), which presumably means that like Thopas he is 'no lechour'.

747 *That bereth the rede hepe*: This piece of redundant information is typical of many lines in ME romance which exist only to supply a rhyme.

760 ff. Catalogue lists – of flowers, birds, spices, food and drink, musical instruments – are frequently used in medieval romance and lyric, to provide an impression of luxuriant profusion; for examples, see *SA*, pp. 550–55.

772–3 Cf. *Guy of Warwick*, lines 4519–20 (*SA*, p. 518): 'So michel he herd tho foules sing, | That him thought he was in gret longyng.' The singing of birds (including the 'throstyll cokke' and 'wodewale') is the prelude for Thomas of Erceldoune's romance with his fairy mistress (see n. to Th 788).

783 *forage*: This usually means 'dry food, hay' (cf. Rv 3868). It would be typical of Sir Thopas's absurd behaviour to feed a horse on hay in the midst of a grassy meadow.

788 In Thomas Chestre's *Sir Launfal* and in *Thomas of Erceldoune* (which may, however, post-date Th), the hero has a romance with a fairy mistress (see *SA*, pp. 521–6), but in the first instance it is the fairy mistress who makes the first advances, and in the second Thomas at least sees the lady before falling in love with her. Thopas's decision to fall in love with an elf-queen seems ridiculous in that it occurs in the total absence of any such personage in the narrative at this point.

789 *goore*: Strictly speaking, 'a triangular strip of cloth, hence by synecdoche a skirt or apron' (Donaldson, *Speaking of Chaucer*, p. 23). Phrases such as 'geynest under gore', 'glad under gore' form part of the descriptions of beautiful ladies in the Harley lyrics (ibid.); in transferring it to a male hero, Chaucer seems to mock the emptiness of the phrase.

793 *In towne*: This is the first example of a bob-line in Th (see Headnote). Stanley's comparative survey of bob-lines in ME

literature shows that they are more common in lyric and drama than in romance (*NM*, 73 (1972), 422–5).

794–5   Compare the fairy lady's promise to Sir Launfal (lines 316–18; see *SA*, p. 522): 'Yf thou wylt truly to me take | And alle wemen for me forsake, | Ryche I wyll make thee.'

805   This line is missing in El and Hg, but its authenticity is guaranteed by the stanza-form.

808   *Sire Olifaunt*: 'Sir Elephant'. Combats with giants are frequent in ME romances (see *SA*, pp. 530–41). Guy of Warwick fights with a giant named Sir Amoraunt (*SA*, p. 534); as Burrow comments (see n. in *Riverside*), both names conveniently rhyme with 'geaunt' and 'Termagaunt' (see next n).

810   *Child*: A title used in romances or ballads for young knights or aspirants to knighthood. Chaucer uses it only in Th (cf. lines 817, 830, 898).
Termagaunt: The name of a fictional Saracen deity, conventionally invoked by pagans in ME literature. (The other 'gods' invoked by Saracens are Apollo and Mahomet, making up a parodic pagan Trinity.) Chaucer's serious depiction of Muslims in MLT does not include these conventional oaths, and presumably he found them absurd.

812   Slaying an opponent's horse was regarded in romances as an unknightly act, which is committed by the giant opponents of Guy of Warwick and Libeaus Desconus (*SA*, pp. 536, 538).

815   *symphonye*: 'During the Gothic period, *symphonia* and its vernacular offsprings was a general name for hurdy-gurdies' (Page, *Voices and Instruments*, p. 150). Thomas of Erceldoune's fairy mistress welcomes him with 'alle manere of mynstralcye', but a hurdy-gurdy is not among the instruments mentioned (*SA*, p. 526).

828–9   The David-and-Goliath story here seems to have got itself reversed, with the giant deploying the sling that in the biblical account belongs to the giant-killer (*SA*, p. 531).

833–5   These lines imitate the opening of *Bevis of Hampton*: 'Lordinges, herkneth to my tale! | Is merier than the nightingale, | That y schel singe; | Of a knight ich wile yow rowne...' (see *SA*, p. 498). The appeal for the audience's attention signals a fresh beginning in the narrative (cf. Th 712 and n. and Th 891), and numerous manuscripts of *CT* (including El and Hg) indicate by the use of paragraph markings or large capital letters that a section-break occurs at this point (see Burrow, *Essays on Medieval Literature*, pp. 60–65). On the use of the term 'fit' for a section-break, see Th 888 and n. Burrow points out that the three fits diminish consistently in number of stanzas, the first fit having eighteen stanzas, the second nine and the third four and a half, giving the impression that the whole poem is dwindling away to nothing.

836 *sides smale*: A slender middle is appropriate to masculine as well as feminine beauty in the fourteenth century (cf. *Gawain*, line 144), but its sudden mention at this point is irrelevant to the matter in hand. Once again rhyme rather than reason dictates the content of the narrative.

839 *murye men*: In the fourteenth century, as today, this phrase suggested tales of Robin Hood and the greenwood. See *Gamelyn*, line 774 (*Middle English Metrical Romances*, ed. W. H. French and C. B. Hale, 2 vols. (1930; repr. New York, 1964), vol. I), and the *Gest of Robyn Hode* (*The English and Scottish Popular Ballads*, ed. F. J. Child, 5 vols. (1884–98; repr. New York, 1965), vol. III, no. 117), stanzas 205, 281, 316, 340, 382.

842 There is no other example of a many-headed giant in the ME romances. 'Chaucer's failure to mention the extra heads earlier may reflect either upon the narrator's competence or upon the hero's veracity' (Burrow, n. in *Riverside*).

848 *reales*: The final -s on the adjective is an imitation of French practice.

849 Medieval romance miscellanies often included didactic or religious materials, but the idea of romances about popes and cardinals is a comic absurdity, again probably conjured up by the need to find a rhyme for 'reales'.

851–6 On such lists in medieval romance, see n. to Th 760 ff.

857–68 The arming of the hero is a conventional narrative motif in medieval romance (see D. Brewer, *Tradition and Innovation in Chaucer* (London, 1982), pp. 142–60, 170–73, and *SA*, pp. 526–30). Sir Thopas wears the layers of clothing and armour usual for a fourteenth-century knight (see n. to GP 73–6): first, a linen shirt and drawers, next, an 'aketoun' or tunic (the equivalent of the Knight's 'gipoun'), then a chain-mail 'haubergeoun', and finally plate-armour ('hauberk') and an outer tunic bearing his heraldic device ('cote-armour'). Cf. Burrow, *Yearbook of English Studies*, 14 (1984), 53.

867 The comparison is proverbial; see Whiting L285.

869–70 Libeaus Desconus has a gold shield with three boars' heads depicted on it (lines 1567–9; *SA*, p. 530, where 'The' should read 'Thre'); Sir Degaré's father also carries an azure shield with three boars' heads on it, painted with gold (*Middle English Metrical Romances*, ed. French and Hale, vol. I, lines 996–8).

872 Heroic vows to slay an opponent are frequent in medieval romances (see *SA*, pp. 541–4, for examples), but they are usually sworn on a festive dish such as a swan, heron or peacock, rather than homely bread and ale (ibid., p. 542, n. 4).

875 *quirboily*: Hardened leather or 'cuir-bouilli' was frequently used for pieces of armour for arms or legs; it could be moulded into almost any shape, and also painted or embossed (Zijlstra-Zweens, p. 23).

877 *latoun*: Latten, a brass-like alloy, was used for armour (see Blair, pp. 41, 66, 171).

888 The word 'fit', meaning a section of a poem, is of Germanic origin (*OED* s.v. fit, fytte sb¹). In English, it is associated with popular romances and alliterative verse. This is the only instance where Chaucer applies it to his own verse, doubtless in mocking imitation of minstrel poetry.

897–900 For comparable roll-calls of knightly names, designed to create a heroic atmosphere, see *SA*, pp. 556–9.

Horn Child: The reference is either to the ME romance *King Horn* (ed. in *Four Romances of England*, ed. R. B. Herzman, G. Drake and E. Salisbury (Kalamazoo, MI, 1999)), in which Horn is often called 'Horn child', or to the tail-rhyme version which is preserved (incompletely) only in the Auchinleck MS (see Headnote), where it is titled 'Horn Childe and Maiden Rimnild' (printed in the Appendix to J. Hall's edition of *King Horn* (Oxford, 1901), pp. 179–92). The lengthy romances relating the exploits of the English heroes Bevis of Hampton (ed. in *Four Romances of England*) and Guy of Warwick (ed. J. Zupitza, EETS e.s. 42, 49, 59, 3 vols. in 1 (London, 1883; repr. 1966)) are also contained in the Auchinleck MS (and elsewhere); both were highly popular.

Libeux: The knight known as Libeaus Desconus ('The Fair Unknown'), the hero of a tail-rhyme romance of the same name (ed. M. Mills, EETS o.s. 261 (London, 1969)). For fuller descriptions of the above romances, see *A Manual of the Writings in Middle English*, vol. I, ed. J. B. Severs (New Haven, CT, 1967).

No romance with a hero named Pleindamour ('full of love') is known. Ipotis is an odd man out here; he is the hero of a didactic verse tale which relates how he instructed the emperor Hadrian in the Christian faith. The work is found alongside romances in London, BL, MS Cotton Caligula A.ii, and edited by C. Horstmann, *Altenglische Legenden* (Heilbronn, 1881), pp. 341–8.

909 *knight auntrous*: 'No word in the romances more compactly suggests fantastic knight-errantry than does *auntrous*' (Loomis, *SA*, p. 547). For numerous examples of its use in ME popular romances, see *SA*, pp. 547–9. Chaucer uses the word only here.

915–16 These lines parody the opening of the tail-rhyme romance *Sir Perceval of Galles* (lines 5–7): 'His righte name was Percyvell, | He was ffosterde in the felle, | He drank water of the welle' (*Middle English Metrical Romances*, ed. French and Hale, vol. II).

917 *worly under wede*: 'Alliterative phrases of the fair-under-garment type ('lovely under linen', 'seemly under sark', 'comely under kell', etc.) are among the most overworked clichés of Middle English poetry' (Burrow, *Essays on Medieval Literature*, p. 75). Burrow defends 'worly', the reading found in both El and Hg (and two other manuscripts), against the alternatives 'worthy', 'worthly' and 'worthily'; although a rare word, 'worly' occurs in contexts that show it to belong 'to that general stock of well-worn native poetic words and forms which Chaucer picks over elsewhere in *Sir Thopas*' (ibid., p. 78).

918 The rhyme gives a clue to the way this line will end: 'it so bifel' (cf. Th 748, where the two conventional components are reversed). See Burrow, *Essays on Medieval Literature*, p. 74. The final irony of Th is that the reader's mental completion of the line serves only to defeat the expectation of action (at last!) which is raised by the opening 'Til on a day'.

THE THOPAS–MELIBEE LINK

933 'Geste' (from OF *geste*, Latin *gesta*, 'deeds') usually refers to tales of heroic deeds (see P. Strohm, *Speculum*, 46 (1971), 348–59, at pp. 353–4, and cf. ML 1126, WB 642, *LGW* G 87, etc.). Here, it seems to refer to a literary form that is neither rhymed verse nor prose. At Pars 43 (see n.) the Parson uses the verb 'geste' while evidently referring to alliterative verse, and this type of verse may also be referred to here, but there is no other evidence of this meaning for the word.

955–7 For an assessment of the accuracy of this claim, see Headnote to Mel.

THE TALE OF MELIBEE

The ultimate source of Melibee is a Latin prose treatise called *The Book of Consolation and Counsel* (*Liber consolationis et consilii*), written by Albertano of Brescia, a thirteenth-century Italian judge; it was one of three treatises which Albertano wrote and presented to each of his three sons. (For Chaucer's use of *On the Love of God* (*De amore dei*), see nn. to MchT, and for his use of the *Book of Speaking and Keeping Silent* (*Liber de doctrina dicendi et tacendi*), see nn. to McpT.) A French version, which drastically abridges and changes the Latin original, was composed sometime after 1336 by Renaud de Louens, a Dominican friar, and it is on this version that Chaucer's translation is based. The Latin text was edited by Thor Sundby, Chaucer Society (London, 1873); it is also available on the following website: http//:freespace.virgin.net/angus.graham/Albertano.htm. The French version is printed in *SA²* I, 331–408, interlarded with English translations of the portions of the Latin text not represented in the French; unfortunately, these translations of the Latin text are wildly inaccurate. Chaucer's Melibee generally follows Renaud's version closely. Some changes that he made towards the end of Melibee bring it into line with other examples in *CT* of the desirability of male submission to women (see Mel 1750, 1871–2 and nn.). The subject-matter of Melibee might also have had a special relevance to the members of Richard II's court, which was sharply divided between those who favoured aggressive pursuit of war with France, and those (including the king himself) who favoured diplomatic methods. See Saul, *Richard II*, pp. 204–34, and G. Stillwell, *Speculum*, 19 (1944), 433–44.

Melibee belongs to the body of ancient and medieval writings known collectively as 'wisdom literature', intended largely but not exclusively for the young, which aims to furnish the memory with a store of anecdotes and wise sayings, to be drawn on as a practical guide in appropriate circumstances. Hence it is densely packed with proverbs, maxims and apophthegms, many of which are taken from other examples of wisdom literature, such as the Solomonic books of the Bible: Wisdom, Proverbs, Ecclesiastes, and the book known as Ecclesiasticus or Jesus Sirach (included in the Vulgate Bible, but not the AV), which was likewise attributed to Solomon. Also part of this tradition are the late antique *Distichs of Cato* (see n. to Mil 3227), and the proverb-collection excerpted from the mimes of Publilius Syrus, both of which enjoyed a wide circulation in the Middle Ages (for editions of both, see the Abbreviated References). Albertano also quotes sayings garnered from the Stoic tradition, represented by the *Moral Epistles* and other writings by (or attributed to) Seneca, and the *De officiis* (*On Duties*) and other writings of Cicero, which he will probably have taken from medieval florilegia rather than directly from the texts themselves. The textual transmission of Publilius is a good example of the growth and proliferation of such florilegia (see the Introduction to the Loeb edition, pp. 7–8); some manuscripts incorporate proverbs from the pseudo-Senecan *De moribus*, and entitle the collection as a whole *Senecae sententiae* or *Senecae proverbia* ('Proverbs of Seneca'). This explains why Albertano frequently misattributes to Seneca sayings which are actually from Publilius or the *De moribus* (see nn. below). I cite the *De moribus* from the edition by E. Woelfflin, *Publilii Syri Sententiae* (Leipzig, 1869), pp. 136–52, where the proverbs are individually numbered, rather than the text in *PL* 72, cols. 29–32, where they are grouped into six sections (and where the text is attributed to Martin of Braga; however, see Barlow, pp. 285–6, as cited in n. to Mel 1071). Other maxims are drawn from the *Disciplina Clericalis* (*The Scholar's Guide*) of Petrus Alfonsi (1062–*c*. 1140), a converted Spanish Jew; in this work, proverbial sayings are interspersed with instructive anecdotes.

In the Prologue to Melibee, Chaucer claims to have increased the number of proverbs it contains, but comparison with the French text reveals only three possible instances of this sort (see nn. to Mel 1054 and 1325–6), and even here we cannot be certain that the proverbs were not additions already present in the manuscript of the French text that he was using. His claim may therefore be simply a way of drawing attention to the heavily proverbial nature of his source, and beyond this, to the importance of proverbs, and the communal experience they embody, within his own poetry (see Introduction, pp. xxiii–xxv).

967 *Melibeus*: Meliboeus is the name of one of the shepherds in Vergil's first Eclogue, but Albertano's choice of it was probably influenced by an epigram by Godfrey of Winchester (1050?–1107), which he quotes in the *Liber consolationis* (ed. Sundby, p. 53): 'Consilio juvenum fidis, Melibee; ruinam | Expectare potes, dum sine consilio es.' ('You trust in young men's counsel, Melibeus; you may expect disaster, since you are devoid of counsel.' For the original, see *Anglo-Latin Satirical Poets and Epigrammatists of the Twelfth Century*, ed. T. Wright, Rolls series, vol. II (London, 1872), p. 127, CLIV.)

Sophie: The daughter's name appears in neither the Latin original nor the French version of *Melibeus*, and seems to have been Chaucer's own addition (*SA²* I, 332, n.). 'Sophia' means 'wisdom' in Greek, and may have been intended to evoke Melibee's own wisdom, which for most of the tale is in need of healing (see Z. Thundy, *NM*, 77 (1976), 582–98, at p. 596).

968 *into the feeldes*: This detail is added by Chaucer (but see *SA²* I, 332, n.).

976 The reference is to Ovid, *Remedies of Love* 127–30.

980 *whan she say hir time*: Here and at Mel 1728, Chaucer is translating his French source (cf. *SA²* I, 332:2.1), but he later adds a similar phrase at two separate points where there is no warrant for it in the French (see Mel 1051, 1832, and cf. *SA²* I, 337:2.45, and 404:49.58). This stress on Prudence's ability to await the right moment to act accords with the passage on patience in Fkl 785–6: 'After the time moste be temperaunce | To every wight that kan on governaunce.'

984–5 *Senek*: Seneca, *Moral Epistles* LXXIV.30.

987 John 11:33–5.

989 Romans 12:15.

992 Seneca, *Moral Epistles* LXIII.1.

993 Seneca, *Moral Epistles* LXIII.11.

995 *Jesus Sirak*: Jesus, son of Sirach, is the author of the book of Ecclesiasticus (see Headnote), but this quotation is from Proverbs 17:22. The error was taken over by Chaucer from his source.

996 Ecclesiasticus 30:25.

997 Proverbs 25:20 (Vulgate; not in the AV version): 'As a moth doth by a garment, and a worm by the wood: so the sadness of a man consumeth the heart.'

999–1000 Job 1:21. The first part of this verse is echoed by Griselda at Cl 871–2.

1003 Ecclesiasticus 32:24. Also quoted at Mil 3530 (see n.) and Mch 1485–6.

1008–10 Melibee's indication of the kind of counsel he would like to receive resembles January's behaviour in MchT (1399–1468). Cf. Mann, *Feminizing Chaucer*, pp. 45–6.

1017 Proverbial; see Whiting C414 and Walther 35738b.

1030 Proverbial; see Publilius Syrus 32; cf. 293. Also quoted at Mel 1135.

1031 Although this is claimed as a popular saying in Albertano's Latin original ('dici enim vulgo consuevit'; ed. Sundby, p. 9), it is not recorded in Walther's *Proverbia*, and Mel 1031 is the only example given in Whiting J75.

1032 Cf. Whiting T44: 'In long tarying is noys.'

1033 John 8:3–11.

1036 Proverbial in Chaucer's day as now: see Whiting I60, Hassell F51, and cf. *TC* II.1276.

1039 For another (later) example of this saying, see Whiting W41.

1045 Ecclesiasticus 22:6: 'A tale out of time is like music in mourning.'

1047 Ecclesiasticus 32:6: 'Where there is no hearing, pour not out words.' Cf. NP 2801–2.

1048 A proverb found in the collection of Publilius Syrus (see Headnote), 653; see also Whiting C458.

1051 *whan she say hir time*: Chaucer's addition. See n. to Mel 980.

1053 *Piers Alfonce*: On Petrus Alfonsi, see Headnote. The reference is to *Disciplina Clericalis*, 'De rege bono et malo', p. 37.24–5 (tr. Jones and Keller, p. 93).

1054 This sentence seems to be Chaucer's own addition (see *SA²* I, 338:2.46 and n.). For the proverbs, see Whiting H171, H166. For the first, cf. *TC* I.956 and (more distantly) IV.1567–8, and for the second, cf. Pars 1003.

1057 Ecclesiastes 7:29 (AV 7:28). This text also forms a subject of dispute between Pluto and Proserpina in MchT (2247–8); see n. to Mel 1076–80.

1059 Ecclesiasticus 25:30. Cf. Pars 927.

1060 This quotation from Ecclesiasticus (33:20–22) is also used by Prudence later on (Mel 1754–6).

1062–3 The passage within brackets is a translation of the conclusion of Melibee's speech as it appears in Chaucer's French source (see *SA²* I, 338:3.5–6). Although no *CT* manuscript has anything corresponding to these lines, their omission is unlikely to have been intentional on Chaucer's part, since Prudence's reply refers to the points they make (see Mel 1084–94). For that reason, modern editors have usually supplied the French original or a translation of it, and included it within the line-numbering of Mel.

The first quotation is from Seneca the Elder (*Controversiae* II.v.12); cf. Whiting W534, W485 and WB 950 and n. The second quotation is from Publilius Syrus, 365.

1065 Seneca, *On Benefits* IV.xxxviii.2.

1067 Unidentified.

1069 See the *Novellae* of Justinian, Collatio II tit.5 (*Corpus Juris*

Civilis, III, 93): 'multudo enim numerosa nihil habet honesti' ('a numerous multitude has nothing reputable about it').

1070 *He that al despiseth, al displeseth*: Untraced.

1071 The work quoted is the *Formula honestae vitae*, which is erroneously attributed to Seneca by Albertano of Brescia both at this point and elsewhere in the Latin original of Mel; it is actually by the sixth-century bishop Martin of Braga (see *Martini Episcopi Bracarensis Opera Omnia*, ed. C. W. Barlow (New Haven, CT, 1950), pp. 236–50; the passage quoted here is at 4.67–71).

1075 The first appearance of the risen Christ was to Mary Magdalene; see Mark 16:9–11, John 20:14–18, and cf. Matthew 28:9–10.

1076–80 Prudence's arguments here are also used by Proserpina in MchT (2277–90). For the reference to the Gospel in 1079, see n. to Mch 2290.

1084 See n. to Mel 1062–3.

1086 For this misogynist commonplace, see n. to WB 278–80.

1087 Proverbs 21:19; cf. Ecclesiasticus 25:23, quoted at WB 775–7.

1094 The French source and Latin original go on to say that women sometimes restrain men when they want to follow evil counsel (see *SA*² I, 340); this is omitted in Chaucer.

1098–1102 These biblical examples of women's counsel are repeated at Mch 1362–74 (see n.).

1104 Genesis 2:18. Cf. Mch 1325–9.

1106 Cf. NP 3164 and n.

1107 *two vers*: A later gloss in Hg supplies the 'two lines' (a hexameter followed by a pentameter – that is, an elegiac distich) which are the Latin original of this saying: 'Auro quid melius? Jaspis. Quid jaspide? Sensus. | Sensu quid? Mulier. Quid muliere? Nichil.' The verses were well known; see Hervieux, *Les fabulistes latins*, V, 622, and Walther 24980.

1113 Proverbs 16:24.

1117–18 *Thobie*: The quotation is from the book of Tobias (4:20), which is included in the Vulgate though not in the AV; it forms part of the advice given to Tobias by his father Tobit, which is a small-scale example of wisdom literature (see Headnote).

1119 James 1:5.

1121–2 See n. to Mel 1246.

1125 Cf. *Distichs of Cato* II.4.

1127 The source is not Seneca but Publilius Syrus, 319.

1130 1 Timothy 6:10 (quoted again at Mel 1840). It is on this text that the Pardoner preaches all his sermons (Pard 333–4); cf. Pars 739.

1131–2 This is Renaud de Louens's addition. The idea that the covetous man is always poor is a classical and medieval commonplace: see, for example, Juvenal, *Satires* XIV.139; *Boece* II m.2 and pr.5.114–21, III pr.3; Alan of Lille, *The Complaint of Nature*, m.7 (tr. Sheridan, p. 182); Innocent III, *De Miseria* II.6, 'Of the Insatiable Desire of Covetous Men' (quoting Ecclesiasticus 14:9, Ecclesiastes 5:9 and Proverbs 30:15); *RR* 18531–8 (tr. Horgan, p. 286).

1135 Publilius Syrus, 32. Also quoted at Mel 1030 (see n.).

1141–2 Ecclesiasticus 19:8–9.

1143 Unidentified in Latin sources. Sundby's edition of Albertano's *Liber consolationis* cites a parallel in Plutarch (p. 40, n.)

1144–5 Petrus Alfonsi, *Disciplina Clericalis*, 'De consilio', p. 6.35–7 (tr. Jones and Keller, p. 42).

1147 Not from Seneca, but from the ps.-Senecan *De moribus* (see Headnote), 16.

1158 Proverbs 27:9.

1159–60 Ecclesiasticus 6:15.

1161 Ecclesiasticus 6:14.

1162 Part of the advice given to Tobias by his father (Tobias 4:19; see n. to Mel 1117–18). Cf. Proverbs 22:17.

1164 The French source of Mel attributes this saying to Job, and the Latin original enables it to be identified as Job 12:12. Cf. Kn 2448.

1165 *Tullius*: Marcus Tullius Cicero, *On Old Age* VI.17.

1167 Ecclesiasticus 6:6.

1171 Proverbs 11:14.

1173 Ecclesiasticus 8:20.

1174 Cicero, *Tusculan Disputations* III.xxx.73.

1176 Cicero, *On Friendship* XXV.91.

1177 Martin of Braga, *Formula honestae vitae*, ed. Barlow, 4.45–6.

1178 Not from the Bible, but found in a tenth-century florilegium which survives in a Munich manuscript (Bayerische Staatsbibliothek, clm 6292, ff. 84r–91r); it is there attributed to Zeno. This proverb-collection was erroneously identified by E. Woelfflin as a fragment of a work by the mysterious 'Caecilius Balbus' cited in John of Salisbury's *Policraticus* (III.14). I cite Woelfflin's edition, *Caecilii Balbi De Nugis Philosophorum Quae Supersunt* (Basle, 1855), p. 27 (XXIV.1). For a demolition of Woelfflin's attribution to Caecilius, see A. Reifferscheid, *Rheinisches Museum*, n.s. 16 (1861), 1–26.

1179 Proverbs 29:5.

1180 Cicero, *On Duties* I.xxvi.91.

1181 *Distichs of Cato* III.4.

1183 Publilius Syrus, 106.

1184 *Isope*: *Riverside* glosses this as 'the Latin version of Aesop's Fables', but fails to specify which of the many different Latin versions circulating in the Middle Ages might be relevant here. For Chaucer, 'Aesop' would most probably have meant the version of the *Romulus* in elegiac verse (*The Fables of 'Walter of England'*, ed. A. E. Wright (Toronto, 1997); Hervieux, *Les fabulistes latins*, II, 316–51). Albertano is, however, referring to the *Novus Aesopus* by a twelfth/thirteenth-century writer named Baldo, which, despite its title, does not derive from the Aesopic tradition at all, but is a collection of stories drawn from the oriental work known as *Kalila and Dimna* or the *Pantchatantra*. The lines quoted at this point in the Latin original of Mel (cap. XX, ed. Sundby, p. 49) are leonine hexameters: 'Ne confidatis secreta nec hijs detegatis, | Cum quibus egistis pugnae discrimina tristis'('Do not confide your secrets or reveal them to those with whom you have had bitter altercation'). These are the concluding lines of Baldo's fable XI, the fable of the owls and the ravens (*Beiträge zur lateinischen Erzählungsliteratur des Mittelalters*, ed. A. Hilka (Berlin, 1928), p. 30). They are twice quoted (and attributed to 'Ysopus') in the Latin prose version of *Kalila and Dimna* by Raymond of Beziers (Hervieux, *Les fabulistes latins*, V, 473, 727).

1185 Not from Seneca, but from Publilius Syrus, 434.

1186–8 The first part of the quotation is Ecclesiasticus 12:10–11; cf. Whiting E100, F364, F367, C467. The second part, as quoted in the Latin source of Mel, has a parallel in the Munich florilegium (see n. to Mel 1178), ed. Woelfflin, p. 25 (XV.15–16): '[Nunquam fidelem tibi, quem ex amico inimicum habueris: et si in gratiam reverti quaesierit,] ne credas illi: captatus enim utilitate, non amica revertitur voluntate, ut fingendo decipiat, quem non potuit persequendo' ('The friend who has become your enemy will never be faithful to you, and if he tries to come back into your favour, do not trust him; for he returns out of self-interest, not out of friendly feeling, so that he may deceive you by pretence, when he could not do it by opposing you').

1189 *Peter Alfonce*: Petrus Alfonsi, *Disciplina Clericalis*, 'De consilio', p. 6.37–8 (tr. Jones and Keller, p. 42).

1191 Unidentified.

1192 The Latin original quotes Cicero, *On Duties* II.vii.23, which is rather loosely rendered by the French translation.

1194 Proverbs 31:4 (Vulgate; not in the AV version): 'there is no secret where drunkenness reigneth'. Cf. ML 776–7 and Pard 560–61.

1196 *Cassiodorie*: Cassiodorus (6th c.), *Variae* X.18 (CCSL 96, p. 400).

1197 The Latin original of Mel quotes Publilius Syrus, 395 ('The wicked man never proposes a good plan to himself'), but the French version is closer to Proverbs 12:5.

1198 Psalm 1:1.

1199 Both Latin and French versions of Mel here quote Ecclesiastes 10:16: 'Woe to thee, O land, when thy king is a child, and when the princes eat in the morning.' J. S. P. Tatlock supposed that Chaucer omitted the quotation in deference to the young Richard II, who was ten years old when he came to the throne in 1377 (*Development and Chronology*, p. 192).

1200 One would expect the second clause here to contrast with the first, rather than repeat it, and this expectation is met in the French source, where Prudence claims to have shown whose counsel is to be followed and whose is to be avoided ('eschever et fuir'; SA^2 I, 360). J. B. Severs suggests that Chaucer's 'folwe' arose from a confusion between 'fuir' and 'suir' (*SA* p. 582).

1201–10 *the doctrine of Tullius*: The line of thought is paralleled in Cicero, *On Duties* II.v.18.

1215 Proverbial; see Whiting M774 and Hassell E23.

1216 *Distichs of Cato* III.14.

1218 Petrus Alfonsi, *Disciplina Clericalis*, 'De mendacio', p. 11.17–18 (tr. Jones and Keller, p. 49).

1219 Cf. Whiting T366 and *PF* 514–16. Injunctions to keep silent as much as possible are characteristic of wisdom literature; see, for example, *Disciplina clericalis*, 'De silentio', p. 8:9–14 (tr. Jones and Keller, p. 44) and Mcp 314–62. Cf. *RR* 7007–13 (tr. Horgan, p. 107).

1221 This echoes Cicero, *On Duties* I.ix.30, though Cicero is talking about doubt as to whether an action is right or not, rather than doubt about the ability to carry it through.

1223 conseil*] conseillours El Hg. The sense of the passage requires 'conseil', and the French source of Mel confirms this reading (Manly and Rickert IV, 503; cf. SA^2 I, 364).

1225 Cf. Walther 3180.

1226 Not identified in Seneca.

1229 *the lawes seyn*: In the Latin original of Mel, these statements are supported by a quotation of Cicero, *On Duties* I.x.32, but the reference to the laws suggests that Renaud de Louens is alluding to the *Digest* of Justinian, XLV.i.26–7 (IV, 653).

1231 In the Latin original of Mel, this is identifiable as a quotation of Publilius Syrus, 403.

1246 Cf. the Munich florilegium (see n. to Mel 1178), ed. Woelfflin, p. 29 (XXVIII.5): 'Duo maxime contraria esse consilio, festinationem et iram' ('Two things are especially inimical to forming plans, haste and anger').

1257 *cast . . . in an hochepot*: This vivid phrase is Chaucer's addition (cf. *SA²* I, 366).

1264 See Walther 11267b.

1269 Cf. Gregory IX, *Decretals* I.xxxviii.3 (*Corpus Iuris Canonici*, II, col. 211), where it is said of priests, not physicians.

1283 Cf. Whiting M75, M121.

1288–90 In fact the physicians had made clear that their interpretation of the 'remedy by contrasts' was the one put forward by Melibeus; see Mel 1016–17. For an attempt to explain the contradiction, see *SA²* I, 355, n.

1292 The beginning of this quotation reflects 1 Peter 3:9, but its conclusion echoes Christ's words at Matthew 5:44; cf. Romans 12:17, 1 Thessalonians 5:15, 1 Corinthians 4:12.

1304 Psalm 126:1 (AV 127:1).

1306–7 *Distichs of Cato* IV.13.

1309–12 Petrus Alfonsi, *Disciplina Clericalis*, 'De societate ignota', p. 27.34–8 (tr. Jones and Keller, p. 76).

1317–18 Proverbs 28:14.

1320 Not from Seneca, but from Publilius Syrus, 666. (Albertano also quotes 594, which is another formulation of the same idea.)

1321 Publilius Syrus, 425 (Albertano has the variant reading 'ruinam' instead of 'rimam').

1324 Also from Publilius Syrus, 294.

1325–6 Ovid, *Remedies of Love* 421–2: 'A viper kills a bull with a little bite; a boar is often caught by a dog of no great size.' Skeat (V, 214) suggested that Chaucer's 'wesele' was the result of a confusion between French *vivre* ('viper') and Latin *viverra* ('ferret'). Chaucer interpolates into the Ovidian quotation the reference to the wild hart and the saying about the king being pricked by a little thorn; neither is in his French source or its Latin original (*SA²* I, 369:32.13 and n.).

1328 Seneca, *Moral Epistles* III.3.

1330 The same quotation appears in Albertano's *Liber de doctrina dicendi et tacendi* III.39, but its source has not been traced.

1335–6 aperteneth ... grete edifices*] *om*. El Hg. The omission is evidently due to eyeskip; it is shared with many other manuscripts.

1339–40 Not from Cicero, but from Seneca, *On Mercy* I.xix.6.

1344 Cicero, *On Duties* I.xxi.73.

1347 Not from Cicero. Cf. Publilius Syrus, 148.

1348 Cassiodorus, *Variae* I.17 (CCSL 96, p. 26).

1355 Cf. n. to Mel 1201–10.

1364 *ne been nat youre freendes*: Not in the French source.

1380 Cf. Justinian, *Digest* II.ii (I, 40–42).

1395 The Latin terms used here are not contained in Chaucer's French source nor (with the exception of 'efficiens') in its Latin original (*SA*² I, 376).

1398–1401 The terminology here is indebted to Aristotle's distinction of four types of cause (*Physics* II.iii, vii; *Metaphysics* I.iii), which became commonplace in scholastic thought. In the case of a statue, for example, the *material cause* is the matter from which it is made, the *formal cause* is its conformity with the characteristics of a statue, the *efficient cause* (here called the 'cause accidental') is the source of the activity that produces it, and the *final cause* is the end for which it is produced.

1404 *the book of Decrees*: Gratian's *Decretum*. For the passage cited, see II.i.i.25 (*Corpus Iuris Canonici*, I, col. 369).

1406 The Latin original of Mel refers explicitly to 1 Corinthians 4:5; however, the wording of the French version (which Chaucer, as usual, follows) reflects Romans 11:33. Cf. ML 479–83.

1410 The Latin etymology here proposed for Melibee's name is *mel bibens*, 'drinking honey'.

1415 Ovid, *Amores* I.viii.104. For a definition of the 'goodes of the body', see Pars 452.

1416–17 Proverbs 25:16.
     and be needy and poore: Chaucer's addition.

1421 On the world, the flesh, and the devil as the three enemies of the spiritual health of humankind, see D. R. Howard, *The Three Temptations* (Princeton, NJ, 1966), pp. 61–3.

1422 *windowes of thy body*: Medieval writings often metaphorically represented the human body as a building, emphasizing the need to keep it closed against the assaults of temptation. See R. D. Cornelius, *The Figurative Castle* (Bryn Mawr, 1930), ch. 3.

1433–4   The change of speaker apparent in what follows shows
that something has dropped out here, and this is confirmed by
comparison with the French source. The omission was evidently
caused by eyeskip as a result of the repetition of 'malfaitteurs' in
the French source (see Manly and Rickert IV, 504). Since one of
the manuscripts of the French source has exactly such an omission, Severs concluded that the error was in the manuscript used
by Chaucer, and that he failed to notice or remedy it (*SA*, p. 593).
Odd though this seems, it would be too much of a coincidence
to suppose scribal error at exactly the same point in Chaucer's
text as in his source. A translation of the appropriate portion of
the French text is supplied in brackets.

1437   The Latin original of Mel quotes the ps.-Senecan *De moribus*
(see Headnote), 114: 'bonis nocet, qui malis parcit' ('he who
spares the wicked harms the good'); the French version renders
this accurately, but Chaucer's version does not. Robinson suggests that the manuscript he was using was corrupt.

1438   Cassiodorus, *Variae* I.4 (CCSL 96, p. 14).

1439   Publilius Syrus, 580.

1440–41   Romans 13:4 (with 'sword', not 'spear').

1449   Not from Seneca, but from Publilius Syrus, 361.

1450   Also from Publilius Syrus, 219.

1451–2   Cf. *TC* IV.2–3.

1455   Not from Seneca, but from Publilius Syrus, 203.

1460   Romans 12:19.

1463   Publilius Syrus, 715.

1466   Publilius Syrus, 535.

1473   Cf. the Munich proverb-collection (see n. to Mel 1178), ed.
Woelfflin, p. 33 (XLI.4): 'Qui non corripit peccantem, peccare
imperat.'

1481–3   Seneca, *On Wrath* II.xxxiv.1.

1485   Proverbs 20:3.

1488   Not from Seneca, but from Publilius Syrus, 531.

1489–90   *Distichs of Cato* IV.39.

1496   The poet is not identified in either the Latin original or the
French source of Mel, and the thought is too commonplace to
be easily traced to a single source.

1497–1500   Unidentified in Gregory's works.

1502–4   1 Peter 2:21–3.

1510   The French source of Mel identifies the 'epistle' as 2 Corinthians;
the reference seems to be to 4:17, which contrasts the brevity of
earthly tribulation with the eternity of glory that it merits.

1512 Proverbs 19:11 (Vulgate; the AV text differs): 'the learning of a man is known by patience'.

1513 Proverbs 14:29.

1514 Proverbs 15:18.

1515–16 Proverbs 16:32.

1517 Alluding to James 1:4.

1519–20 Cf. WB 111–12.

1525 Cf. Rv 3912 and n.

1528 Cassiodorus, *Variae* I.30 (CCSL 96, p. 37).

1531 Not from Seneca, but from the ps.-Senecan *De moribus* (see Headnote), 139.

1532–4 Justinian, *Digest* IX.ii.45 (4) (I, 291), and *Codex* VIII.4.1 (*Corpus Juris Civilis*, II, 332).

1539 An allusion to Proverbs 19:19.

1541 Justinian, *Digest* L.xvii.36 (IV, 959).

1542 Proverbs 26:17.

1550 Ecclesiastes 10:19. Cf. Whiting M633.

1556–7 *Pamphilles*: *Pamphilus* 53–4 (see n. to Fkl 1110–12 on this work). Excerpts from *Pamphilus* appeared in numerous medieval florilegia; see *Florilegium Gallicum*, ed. J. Hamacher (Bern, 1975), pp. 36, 63–78, 85.

1558–60 Not from *Pamphilus*. The wording of the quotation in the French source does not reflect either of the two texts quoted by the Latin original at this point (*SA²* I, 387), and is closer to Ovid, *Tristia* I.ix.5–6. A version of Ovid's lines became proverbial in the Middle Ages; see Innocent III, *De Miseria* I.14.14–15 (and n.), and Walther 4165: 'Cum fueris felix, multos numerabis amicos. | Tempora si fuerint nubila, solus eris' ('When you are happy, you will count many friends. If times are dark, you will be alone'). Cf. Whiting R108 and ML 120. In 1559–60, Chaucer expands on the word 'alone' by using his favourite phrase 'allone withouten any compaignye' (also used at Kn 2779, Mil 3204).

1561 Mistakenly attributed to *Pamphilus* by Chaucer's French source; the corresponding quotation in the Latin original is a pair of Latin hexameters: 'Glorificant gaze privatos nobilitate | Paupertasque domum premit altam nobilitate', quoted and attributed to a 'versificator' in Petrus Alfonsi, *Disciplina clericalis*, p. 10.22–3 (tr. Jones and Keller, p. 48). The couplet also seems to have circulated as a proverb, see Walther 10342.

1564–5 The Latin original of Mel has 'mater criminum' ('mother of crimes'; ed. Sundby, p. 99.4), which the French version accurately renders as 'mere de crimes' (*SA²* I, 388). Possibly the manuscript

used by Chaucer was corrupt at this point. 'Falling down' is the
root meaning of 'ruin' (from Latin *ruere*, 'to fall down').

1566–7 Petrus Alfonsi, *Disciplina Clericalis*, 'De consilio', pp. 6.40–
7.2 (tr. Jones and Keller, p. 42). Chaucer's manuscript of the
French source must have read 'mengier' ('eten'), as do some
surviving manuscripts, but the Latin original shows that this is a
scribal error for 'mendier' or 'demander' ('beg'), readings preserved in other manuscripts (*SA*² I, 388, corrected against
Sundby).

1568–70 Innocent III, *De Miseria* I.14.4–6; this passage is also the
basis of ML 99–105 (see n.).

1571 Ecclesiasticus 40:29. Cf. ML 114.

1572 Cf. Ecclesiasticus 30:17.

1576 sokingly*] sekingly El Hg. The unusual word 'sokingly', 'gradually', was apparently not understood by the El/Hg scribe. Its
authenticity is supported by the French source, which has 'attem-
prement' ('moderately'; *SA*² I, 390).

1576–1647 This long section on the acquisition of riches is Renaud
de Louens's addition to Albertano's original, and is not fully
integrated into the main line of Prudence's argument (see 1648–
50). In compiling it, Renaud used quotations from another work
by Albertano, *De amore et dilectione dei* (*SA*, p. 563), prompted
by a cross-reference to this work at the relevant point in the *Liber
consolationis* (ed. Sundby, p. 102.1–4).

1578 Proverbs 28:20.

1579–80 Proverbs 13:11.

1583 Source unknown.

1585–6 Cicero, *On Duties* III.v.21.

1589 Ecclesiasticus 33:29; cf. SN 1–14.

1590–91 Proverbs 28:19.

1593 The versifier is unidentified, but the first half of this saying
reflects Proverbs 20:4.

1594 *Distichs of Cato* I.2.

1595 The French source attributes this saying to Innocent, but some
manuscripts have 'Jerome' (*SA*² I, 391). It has not been traced in
either author. Cf. SN 6–7.

1602–4 This is a very free rendering of the *Distichs of Cato* IV.16.

1605 *Distichs of Cato* III.21.

1612–13 Unidentified. Cf. Kn 3034.

1617 Not identified in St Augustine. Cf. Proverbs 27:20, and Innocent
III, *De Miseria* III.6.8–9.

1621–3 Cicero, *On Duties* II.xv.55.

1628–9 Proverbs 15:16.

1630–31 Psalm 36:16 (AV 37:16).

1634 2 Corinthians 1:12.

1635 Ecclesiasticus 13:30.

1638 Proverbs 22:1.

1639 The biblical text has 'name' only, not 'friend': 'Take care of a good name: for this shall continue with thee, more than a thousand treasures precious and great' (Ecclesiasticus 41:15). Manly and Rickert (IV, 506) trace the error to the variant reading 'amy', which is attested in one manuscript of Chaucer's French source.

1642 Cassiodorus, *Variae* I.4 (CCSL 96, p. 15). Chaucer's 'gentil' goes back to Albertano's substitution of 'ingenui' for 'indigni' in this passage; see Robinson's note.

1643–5 Augustine, *Sermo* CCCLV.1 (*PL* 39, cols. 1568–9).

1647 dispiseth*] displeseth El Hg. The El/Hg reading is shared by most manuscripts, but does not make good sense. 'Dispiseth' better renders the reading of the French source, which is 'neglige' ('neglects').

1651–2 Unidentified.

1653 Ecclesiastes 5:10 (AV 5:11).

1658–63 Judas Maccabeus (d. 161 BC) led the revolt of the Jews against the king of Syria; his exploits are recounted in the apocryphal biblical books of Maccabees. In the Middle Ages he was revered as one of the martial heroes known as the Nine Worthies (three Jewish, three pagan and three Christian).

1663 cometh*] come El Hg. El/Hg interpret 'but' as concessive rather than adversative, and therefore use the subjunctive. The biblical source (1 Maccabees 3:18–19) supports the indicative ('For the success of war is not in the multitude of the army, but strength cometh from heaven').

1664 Apparently an allusion to Ecclesiastes 9:1 (in the Vulgate version; the AV text differs): 'and yet man knoweth not whether he be worthy of love, or hatred'.

1667 Cf. Kn 3030, and Whiting D101, K49.

1668 See the Vulgate text of II Kings (II Samuel in the AV) 11:25 (the AV text differs), which in the Douai-Rheims translation reads: 'various is the event of war: and sometimes one, sometimes another is consumed by the sword'.

1671 Ecclesiasticus 3:27.

1676–7 All manuscripts attribute this quotation to St James, but it is in fact from Seneca (*Moral Epistles* XCIV.46). One manuscript of the French source reads 'Saint Jacques' instead of 'Senecques' and the manuscript used by Chaucer must have contained the same error (*SA²* I, 396).

1680 Matthew 5:9.

1686 Proverbial; see Whiting H426.

1691 From the ps.-Senecan *De moribus* (see Headnote), 49.

1692–3 Psalm 33:15 (AV 34:14).

1696 Proverbs 28:14.

1701 Chaucer has 'prophete' instead of the French *philosophe*. The quotation has not been traced.

1704–5 Proverbs 28:23.

1707–8, 1709–10 Apparently a free rendering of Ecclesiastes 7:4, 6–7 (AV 7:3, 5–6): 'Anger is better than laughter: because by the sadness of the countenance the mind of the offender is corrected ... It is better to be rebuked by a wise man, than to be deceived by the flattery of fools. For as the crackling of thorns burning under a pot, so is the laughter of a fool ...'

1719–20 Proverbs 16:7.

1728 *whan she saugh hir time*: Chaucer is here translating his French source, but on his introduction of this phrase elsewhere in Mel, see n. to Mel 980.

1735 Psalm 20:4 (AV 21:3): 'You have outstripped him with sweet blessings; you have set a crown of precious stones on his head.'

1740 Ecclesiasticus 6:5.

1750 The reference to Prudence's 'wommanly pitee' is Chaucer's own addition (cf. *SA²* I, 401), and serves to harmonize Mel with other representations of this womanly quality in *CT* and his other works (cf. Kn 3083, Sq 479–87).

1754–6 Ecclesiasticus 33:19–20. Partially quoted at Mel 1060.

1775–6 Not from Seneca, but from the ps.-Senecan *De moribus* (see Headnote), 94.

1777 Publilius Syrus, 537. Hg lacks the main clause of this quotation ('He is worthy ... foryifnesse'), leaving two half-lines blank for its later insertion; El lacks the quotation entirely. Other manuscripts have similar lacunae or attempts at correction; only one (Cambridge, Fitzwilliam Museum, MS McClean 181) fills Hg's gap intelligibly and in a way that accurately renders the French source ('Celui est presque innocent qui ...'), and its reading is adopted here. Other manuscripts repair the defect by supplying similar main clauses after 'knowelecheth it'.

1783 Justinian, *Digest* L.xvii.35 (IV, 959).

1794–5 For this proverb, see Whiting T348.

1816–25 Chaucer expands and alters this speech of submission in comparison with the French source; in particular, lines 1825–6 appear to be entirely his own addition (*SA*² I, 403–4).

1832 *whan that dame Prudence saugh hir time*: Chaucer's addition. See n. to Mel 980.

1840 1 Timothy 6:10, quoted at Mel 1130 (see n.).

1842 Publilius Syrus, 527.

1846 Publilius Syrus, 333.

1850 From the *Decretals* of Pope Gregory IX, III.xxxi.18 (*Corpus Iuris Canonici*, II, col. 576).

1857 Seneca, *On Mercy* I.xxiv.1.

1859 Not from Seneca, but from Publilius Syrus, 77.

1860–61 Cicero, *On Duties* I.xxv.88.

1866 Not from Seneca, but from Publilius Syrus, 407.

1869 James 2:13.

1871–2 Chaucer adds these two lines emphasizing Melibee's submission to his wife's will (cf. *SA*² I, 407), thus aligning Mel with the male surrenders of 'maistrye' found in WBPr, WBT and FklT (see Mann, *Feminizing Chaucer*, pp. 97–8).

1885–8 This final sentence is Chaucer's own addition to his source (cf. *SA*² I, 408). Cf. John 1:9.

THE MONK'S PROLOGUE

1892 *corpus Madrian*: 'The body of [St] Madrian'. No saint of this name is known, and this seems to be yet another of the Host's garbled oaths (see Pard 310, 314, Sh 435, Mk 1906, and nn.)

1906 *corpus bones*: See n. to Pard 314.

1926 *Rouchestre*: On the problems that have been caused by this reference to Rochester, a town about 30 miles from London, see n. to WB 847.

1928–30 Though the Monk does not reply to this question about his name, the Host later (NP 2792) confidently addresses him as 'daun Piers'.

1956 Cf. Whiting T465.

1962 *lussheburghes*: A name given to coins which imitated English sterling in appearance but were of poorer quality. The name reflects the fact that most such imitations originated in Luxembourg. See Grierson, *Coins*, p. 157.

1970 *Seint Edward*: Probably Edward the Confessor, king of England 1042–66 (rather than Edward the Martyr, king of England 975–8). His reputation for holiness began during his life, and was confirmed by miracles both during his life and after his death; he was canonized in 1161 (Farmer, *Dictionary of Saints*). There were numerous lives of Edward the Confessor in Latin, French and ME (for full details, see *The Middle English Verse Life of Edward the Confessor*, ed. G. E. Moore (Philadelphia, PA, 1942), pp. iii–vi, xxxiii–lii, lvii–lxii, 72–3). Richard II had a particular reverence for this royal saint, and in the Wilton Diptych Edward and Edmund of East Anglia (king and martyr) are shown, together with John the Baptist, presenting Richard to the Madonna and child (see S. Mitchell, pp. 115–24 in *The Regal Image of Richard II and the Wilton Diptych*, ed. D. Gordon, L. Monnas and C. Elam (London, 1997), pp. 115–24). There may also be a secondary allusion to Edward II, Richard's great-grandfather, whose canonization Richard tried to secure (see A. W. Astell, *SAC*, 22 (2000), 399–405).

1973 This definition of tragedy agrees with Chaucer's translation of a gloss on Boethius (*Boece* II pr.2.70–72): '*Tragedye is to seyn a dite of a prosperite for a tyme, that endeth in wrecchidnesse.*' The gloss appears to be have been borrowed from Nicholas Trevet's commentary on Boethius (see *Chaucer's Boece and the Medieval Tradition of Boethius*, ed. A. J. Minnis (Cambridge, 1993), pp. 107–8). Cf. Mk 1991–4, 2761–4.

1978–81 Like most people in the Middle Ages, Chaucer did not conceive of tragedy as a primarily dramatic form; instead he describes tragedies as verse or prose narratives. The hexameter, a line divided into six metrical units known as 'feet', is the usual verse form of Latin epic, such as Vergil's *Aeneid* (which Dante's Vergil refers to as a 'high tragedy' at *Inferno* XX.113). For discussion of other works in hexameters that Chaucer might have thought of as tragedies, see H. A. Kelly, *Chaucerian Tragedy* (Cambridge, 1997), pp. 61–2. As for tragedies in prose, Kelly suggests (p. 61) that Chaucer might have been thinking of Boccaccio's *De casibus* (see Headnote, below) and Guido delle Colonne's *History of the Destruction of Troy*. The other metres that seem to be implied in line 1981 may include elegiac couplets (a hexameter followed by a pentameter). The stanza-form that Chaucer uses for MkT (eight lines rhyming ababbcbc) is one he employs for some of his shorter lyric poems, including his ballade 'Fortune'; it is not found elsewhere in *CT*.

1985–90 These lines cannot be used to determine the correct placing of the 'Modern Instances' (see n. to Mk 2375–2462), since their occurrence in the middle of MkT is by no means the only violation of chronological order in the tale. Whereas Boccaccio's *De casibus* has a 'determinedly chronological order', Chaucer 'is fairly chronological up through Zenobia, though unlike Boccaccio he places Samson before Hercules. But then he moved from Zenobia's third-century Christian era back to the first with Nero, and then back to the sixth century before Christ with Holofernes, a general of Nabuchodonosor. He ended in the same century with Croesus, following upon Antiochus, Alexander, and Julius Caesar, who date from the second, third, and first centuries before Christ, respectively' (Kelly, *Chaucerian Tragedy*, pp. 67–8).

THE MONK'S TALE

The Monk's Tale is an example of the medieval literary genre known as the Fall of Princes; in some manuscripts (including El) it bears the title *De casibus virorum illustrium* (*On the Fall of Famous Men*). As this title suggests, Chaucer's general model was probably Boccaccio's *De casibus virorum illustrium*, a Latin prose work in nine books (Boccaccio, *Opere*, ed. Branca, vol. IX; selections are translated by L. B. Hall as *The Fates of Illustrious Men* (New York, 1965)). Stories of this sort were intended to act as a warning of the fickleness of Fortune, and were considered especially appropriate for those in positions of power; see R. F. Green, *Poets and Princepleasers: Literature and the English Court in the Late Middle Ages* (Toronto, 1980), pp. 143–9. It may be, therefore, that Chaucer originally composed this tale-collection as an independent work, intending to dedicate it to an aristocratic patron (e.g., the young Richard II), and later incorporated it into *CT*, but there is no hard evidence for this. D. Wallace has also suggested that the Modern Instances in particular (see n. to Mk 2375–2462) might have been intended as a curb to Richard II's tyrannical tendencies in later life (*Chaucerian Polity: Absolutist Lineages and Associational Forms in England and Italy* (Stanford, CA, 1997), p. 331).

As Kelly has pointed out (*Chaucerian Tragedy*, p. 11), Boccaccio nowhere calls the *De casibus* a tragedy, whereas Chaucer lays great stress on this definition of the genre of the Monk's Tale (see Mk 1973–82, 1991–4, 2761–4). 'Chaucer seems to have been the first major author of postclassical times who considered himself to be a composer of tragedies' (Kelly, p. 39) – not only the Monk's Tale, but also *Troilus and Criseyde* (see V.1786). Chaucer's definition of tragedy seems to have been derived mainly from Boethius's *Consolation of Philosophy* and its accompanying glosses (see n. to Mk 1973 and Kelly,

Chaucerian Tragedy, pp. 50–65). His repeated emphasis on Fortune's responsibility for the tragic downfall of the heroes and heroines whose stories he summarizes is also reminiscent of Boethius's urgent questioning of the role of Fortune in human affairs. But as L. Scanlon has pointed out (*Narrative, Authority and Power: The Medieval Exemplum and the Chaucerian Tradition* (Cambridge, 1994), p. 221), the Monk's Tale, unlike the Knight's Tale, bears no trace of the complex framework of Boethian philosophy; instead, Chaucer presents Fortune 'as Boethius argued she appears most immediately to the philosophically unsophisticated' – that is, as a malevolent personal agent, rather than as a simple name given to the workings of chance.

If Boccaccio's *De casibus* was Chaucer's general model, it is not the primary source for the individual stories that he includes in the Monk's Tale; they are eclectically drawn from classical legend and history, the *Romance of the Rose*, Dante, the Bible and (it would appear) oral reports of contemporary events (see *SA²* I, 409–47; the Boccaccian elements in the compilation are usefully summarized by P. Boitani, *MÆ*, 45 (1976), 50–69, at pp. 50–54). For his biblical stories, Chaucer seems also to have drawn on the tradition represented in medieval biblical histories such as the *Historia Scholastica* of Peter Comestor and the *Bible historiale* of Guyart Desmoulins (see D. R. Johnson, *PMLA*, 66 (1951), 827–43), and possibly on the *Speculum historiale* of Vincent of Beauvais (P. Aiken, *Speculum*, 17 (1942), 56–68).

1999 Lucifer ('light-bearer') is the name of the morning star. It was applied to Satan in his character as fallen angel because Isaiah 14:12 ('How art thou fallen from heaven, O Lucifer, who didst rise in the morning') was interpreted as a reference to his fall.

2007–14 This stanza was originally omitted in Hg (as in some other manuscripts), the most likely cause being eyeskip to the 'Lo' of the following stanza (see Manly and Rickert II, 406, and Hanna, *Pursuing History*, p. 151); it was added in the margin by a later (15th-c.) hand.

2007 *feeld of Damissene*: Tradition had it that Adam was created in a field which was later the site of the city of Damascus; the detail is found in biblical histories (see Aiken, *Speculum*, 17 (1942), 57, and Johnson, *PMLA*, 66 (1951), 829 and n. 8) and also in Boccaccio's *De casibus* (*SA*, p. 625).

2009 Cf. Innocent III, *De Miseria* I.1: 'Man is formed . . . from the filthiest sperm' ('de spurcissimo spermate'), and I.3: 'But perhaps you will reply that Adam himself was made from the slime of the earth but that you were created from human seed. On the contrary, he was made from earth, but virgin; you were created from seed, but unclean.' A similar phrase ('de immundo semine') is used by Vincent of Beauvais in his *Speculum historiale* (Aiken, *Speculum*, 17 (1942), 57).

2014 Adam was condemned to win his bread by labour as a punishment for eating the apple (Genesis 3:17–19).

2015 The story of Samson is retold in Boccaccio's *De casibus virorum illustrium* I.17 (see Headnote), but Chaucer's reference to the book of Judges at Mk 2046 suggests he is drawing directly on the Bible. For the announcement of Samson's birth by an angel, see Judges 13:2–21.

2023–30 The events recounted in this stanza appear in Judges 14. Samson married a woman of the Philistines (the enemies of Israel); on his way to visit her, he killed a lion, and when returning, he found a swarm of bees and honey inside the lion's carcase. At his wedding feast, he made this occurrence the subject of a riddle, which he posed to his wife's people for a wager: 'Out of the eater came forth meat, and out of the strong came forth sweetness' (14:14). His wife pleaded with him to tell her the answer, and then revealed it to her people, thus losing Samson the wager. In anger, he killed thirty of the Philistines and returned home; his wife was given to another.

2031–46 The events of these two stanzas are narrated in Judges 15. Angry that his wife had been given to another man, Samson tied together 300 foxes by their tails, with firebrands between them, and sent them into the Philistines' crops, vineyards and olive-groves. The Philistines burned the wife and her father and went to attack Samson and the Israelites. Samson was delivered to them in cords, but he broke his bonds, seized the jawbone of an ass and slew a thousand of his enemies. When the slaughter was over, he was thirsty, but in answer to his prayer, God made water spring miraculously from the ass's jawbone and he revived.

2046 *Iudicum*: 'Liber Judicum', the Latin name of the biblical book of Judges. On the citation of titles in the genitive case, see n. to ML 93.

2047–54 Samson's enemies planned to attack him while he was spending the night with a prostitute in the city of Gaza, but he rose at midnight and left the city, carrying off with him its gates, barred as they were, which he took to the top of a hill (Judges 16:1–3).

2055–8 See n. to Pard 555.

2059–60 These lines echo Judges 15:20 and 16:31.

2063–70 *Dalida*: Delilah, see n. to WB 721–3.

2068 *this craft*: So El Hg. Other manuscripts read 'his craft', and this
reading is adopted by *Riverside*. But this makes the line overlap
in meaning with line 2065, and it makes better sense to take 'this
craft' as referring to Delilah's trickery, observed by the Philistines
lying in wait to seize Samson once his strength was gone (see
Judges 16:20–21, and cf. 16:12).

2079–90 On the death of Samson, see n. to ML 201.

2091–4 The moral echoes Jean de Meun's comment on the story of
Samson and Delilah at *RR* 16661–70, tr. Horgan, p. 257.

2095–2110 This list of the deeds performed by the Greek hero
Hercules is drawn from Boethius's *Consolation of Philosophy*
(*Boece* IV m.7.28–62); the twelve feats referred to do not exactly
correspond to the traditional list of Twelve Labours imposed
on Hercules by King Eurystheus (see following notes). Chaucer
probably also knew Ovid, *Metamorphoses* IX.181–98, in which
the dying Hercules recalls his exploits (repr. and tr. in *SA²* I,
417–21).

2098 The slaying of the Nemaean lion was the first of the twelve
Labours of Hercules; he afterwards wore its skin.

2099 *Centauros*: During his pursuit of the Erymanthian Boar, Hercules was offered hospitality by the centaur Pholus. Other centaurs, inflamed by the smell of wine, besieged Pholus's cave;
Hercules defended himself by shooting poisoned arrows at them,
but in doing so he accidentally killed both Pholus and his old
friend Chiron.

2100 *Arpies*: The Harpies were monstrous birds with the faces of
young women, who spoiled or carried off food when diners
approached it (see *Aeneid* III.225). Chaucer seems to have confused them with the Stymphalian birds, eaters of human flesh,
whom Hercules shot with arrows (his sixth labour).

2101 The eleventh labour of Hercules was to fetch the golden apples
entrusted by Hera (Juno) to the women known as the Hesperides;
the tree on Mount Atlas on which the apples grew was guarded
by the dragon Ladon. According to one version of the story,
Hercules killed the dragon and seized the apples himself; according to another, he persuaded Atlas to fetch the apples, and held
up the weight of heaven in his place while he was gone. On his
return, Atlas refused to resume his burden, and had to be tricked
into doing so.

2102 *Riverside* punctuates 'Cerberus, the hound of helle', but this
leaves 'drow out' rather meaningless. It is better to take 'of helle'

with 'drow out' ('he brought/dragged the dog Cerberus out from hell'), as the myth confirms: Hercules obtained permission from Pluto, king of the Underworld, to carry Cerberus to the upper world, provided he could do so without force of arms. Hercules succeeded in this feat (his twelfth labour), and then took Cerberus back to the lower world.

2103 The eighth labour of Hercules was to capture the mares of the Thracian king Diomedes, which were fed on human flesh; Hercules killed Diomedes and fed his body to his mares. Diomedes is here confused with Busiris, a king of Egypt who sacrificed to Zeus all strangers who came to his land, and who was likewise killed by Hercules. Chaucer's translation of Boethius's *Consolation* had correctly distinguished between these two tyrants (see *Boece* II pr.6.67–70 and IV m.7.37–41), so that his error here is hard to understand. For a discussion of possible sources for the confusion, see R. L. Hoffman, *Ovid and the Canterbury Tales* (London, 1966), pp. 186–9.

2105 The Hydra was a monster with nine heads, of which the middle one was immortal; every time one head was cut off, two new ones grew in its place. Hercules killed it (his second labour) by burning away its heads and burying the immortal one under a rock. The Hydra was not 'firy'; W. C. McDermott suggested that Chaucer's mistake arose from a misreading of *Aeneid* VI.287–8 (*Classica et Mediaevalia*, 23 (1962), 216–17).

2106 *Achilois*: Achelous was a river-god, who fought Hercules for the hand of Deianira. In the course of the battle, Achelous took the form of a snake and then a bull, but Hercules overcame him and deprived him of one of his horns, which, according to Ovid (*Metamorphoses* IX.85–8), was turned into the horn of plenty.

2107 *Cakus*: According to Vergil (*Aeneid* VIII.190–302), the giant Cacus stole some of the oxen of Geryon from Hercules (their capture was his tenth labour), and dragged them into his cave. Hercules fought with Cacus inside the cave, slew him, and retrieved the oxen.

2108 *Antheus*: The giant Antaeus was the son of Poseidon and Gaia (Earth); he was invincible so long as his body remained in contact with the earth, his mother. Hercules fought with him while in search of the golden apples of the Hesperides (see n. to Mk 2101); realizing the source of his strength, he lifted him off the ground and crushed him to death.

2109 The capture of the Erymanthian Boar was the fourth labour of

Hercules; he wore it out by chasing it through deep snow, and then trapped it in a net. Since he had been ordered to bring it back alive to King Eurystheus, he did not in fact kill the boar.

2110 See n. to Mk 2101.

2117 *Trophee*: No writer of this name is known. A marginal gloss in both El and Hg (as well as other manuscripts) reads 'Ille vates C(h)aldeor*um* Trophaeus' ('Trophaeus, prophet of the Chaldaeans'), but F. Tupper (*MLN*, 31 (1916), 11–14) plausibly suggested that this conflates two originally separate glosses, adjacent to each other on the inner margins of the page; the first will have been a simple author reference, reading 'Trophaeus', and the second, referring to Daniel, who appears in the following section on Nebuchadnezzar, 'vates Chaldeorum' (cf. Mk 2157). Skeat suggested in the notes to his edition of Chaucer (II, liv–lvi; V, 233) that 'Trophee' referred to Guido delle Colonne, since the Latin *trophaeum* can (he alleged) refer to a column or pillar; this suggestion was accepted by Tupper (ibid.), and by O. F. Emerson (*MLN*, 31 (1916), 142–6). However, *trophaeum* properly means 'monument' and only contextually refers to a pillar, so that such an allusion is unlikely to have been understood. G. L. Kittredge proposed that the name arose from blurred recollection of a passage in the Latin *Epistle of Alexander to Aristotle*, referring to 'Herculis Liberique trophaea' ('the pillars of Hercules and Bacchus'); see *Putnam Anniversary Volume* (New York, 1909; repr. Cambridge, MA, 1976), pp. 545–66. Pratt objected that if 'trophaea' is here interpreted as a proper name, there is no word for pillars (*Studies in Honor of Ullman*, ed. L. B. Lawler, D. M. Robathan and W. C. Korfmacher (St Louis, MO, 1960), pp. 118–25, at p. 119); V. DiMarco has attempted to answer this objection by suggesting another passage of the *Epistle* as the source of the error (*Names*, 34 (1986), 275–83).

The obscurity of 'Trophee' is further increased by the fact that Lydgate (*Fall of Princes* I.283–7) declares it to be the title of the book (in 'Lumbard tunge') that Chaucer used as his source for *Troilus and Criseyde*.

2118 According to a medieval tradition, Hercules is said to have marked the limits of his travels by erecting two pillars on either side of the Straits of Gibraltar and another pair at the limits of the oriental world; see Kittredge, *Putnam Anniversary Volume*, pp. 545–57. Pratt (*Studies in Honor of Ullman*, pp. 119–21) cites examples of this tradition in the Latin commentaries on the *Dissuasio Valerii* of Walter Map (see n. to WB 671).

2119–34 *Dianira*: Deianira was jealous of Hercules' love for Iole; she was deceived by the dying centaur Nessus into thinking that the shirt dipped in his blood would restore her husband's affections (cf. n. to Kn 1942–6). Nessus was killed by Hercules for attempting to rape Deianira as he carried her across a river, and devised this method of taking his revenge. The blood of Nessus was infected by the poison on Hercules' arrows; when, therefore, Hercules put on the shirt, the poison was reactivated by the warmth of his body. Unable to remove the shirt without tearing off chunks of his flesh, he lit a funeral pyre on Mount Oeta and burned himself alive. (His father Jove took pity on him and immortalized him.) The story is recounted by Ovid, *Metamorphoses* IX.101–272; see *SA*[2] I, 417–21.

2136 Proverbial; see Whiting F546.

2139 Proverbial; see Whiting K100.

2145 *Nabugodonosor*: The ultimate source for this story of Nebuchadnezzar, king of Babylon (*c.* 605–562 BC), is the biblical book of Daniel, chs. 1–4. On the blend of history and fiction in Daniel, see *Jerome Biblical Commentary*, I, 446–7. Chaucer's version differs from the biblical account in some details (see following notes), suggesting that he may have had an intermediate source.

2147–8 The two sieges of Jerusalem by Nebuchadnezzar are recounted in 2 Kings 24–5 and 2 Chronicles 36; the first was against King Jehoiachin in 597 BC, and the second against King Zedekiah in 588–587 BC (*Jerome Biblical Commentary*, I, 208, 449). On both occasions, he is said to have carried off gold and silver vessels from the temple in Jerusalem, and also to have brought back Israelite captives.

2151–2 The Bible reports that Daniel and his companions were in the charge of the chief eunuch (Daniel 1:9–16), but does not say that they were themselves castrated; this detail goes back to Joesphus' history of the Jews, and is found in the *Historia scholastica* of Peter Comestor (Daniel, cap. 1) and the *Bible historiale* of Guyart Desmoulins (see Johnson, *PMLA*, 66 (1951), 833–5).

2155–8 On Daniel's skill in dream-lore, see n. to NP 3128.

2159–66 According to the book of Daniel (3:1), Nebuchadnezzar's image was six cubits broad, not seven. His command that it should be worshipped was disobeyed by three Jews called Shadrach, Meshach and Abednego, who were thrown into a fiery furnace but miraculously survived unharmed (Daniel 3). Despite what is said in lines 2165–6, Daniel was not one of the three.

For suggestions as to the source of the error, see Aiken, *Speculum*, 17 (1942), 60, and Johnson, *PMLA*, 66 (1951), 836.

2173 *Riverside* punctuates so as to make a break after 'In rein', but there seems no reason to link the phrase with 2172 rather than 2173.

2183 *Balthasar*: The historical Belshazzar was not the son of Nebuchadnezzar, but of Nabonidus, the last king of Babylon (556–539 BC); see *Jerome Biblical Commentary*, I, 447, 453–4. The source for the story of Belshazzar's feast is ch. 5 of the book of Daniel.

2194 *Gooth bringeth*: *Riverside* takes these to be two parallel imperatives and separates them with a comma, but the verb 'go' frequently loses its full semantic force in imperative constructions and functions as a quasi-auxiliary, while 'the other verb, carrying the main verbal function, has been given the same form as the auxiliary, obviously for clarity and emphasis' (Mustanoja, p. 476), rather than taking the form of the infinitive.

2206 *Mane techel phares*: Interpreted as follows in the (Douai-Rheims) Bible: 'Mane: God hath numbered thy kingdom and hath finished it. Thecel: thou art weighed in the balance, and art found wanting. Phares: thy kingdom is divided, and is given to the Medes and Persians' (Daniel 5:26–8).

2234–8 Darius, king of the Medes, to whom Belshazzar's kingdom passes in Daniel 5 (31), is not a historical personage; according to history, Belshazzar fell in battle against the Persians, and his father's kingdom passed to Cyrus, the Persian emperor (*Jerome Biblical Commentary*, I, 447, 454).

2244–5 An echo of Boethius's *Consolation of Philosophy* (*Boece* III pr.5.66–8), and also proverbial; see Whiting A56, F667.

2247 *Cenobia ... Palimerye*: Zenobia was the queen of Palmyra in Syria, in the third century AD. Her story is included in Boccaccio's *De casibus virorum illustrium* (see Headnote), but only the final stanza of Chaucer's version draws on this source. The remainder of his narrative closely follows the fuller account of her life in Boccaccio's *De mulieribus claris*, *Opere*, ed. Branca, vol. X, ch. 98; for the Latin text and a translation, see *SA*^{2} I, 422–7 (also tr. Guarino, pp. 226–30). For a modern account of her reign, see R. Stoneman, *Palmyra and its Empire. Zenobia's Revolt Against Rome* (Ann Arbor, MI, 1992).

2248 No Persian writings about Zenobia have been identified; Chaucer may have misread Boccaccio's 'priscis testantibus literis' ('as ancient writings witness') as 'persis testantibus literis' ('as Persian writings witness'). See H. Lüdeke, *Festschrift zum 75. Geburtstag von Theodor Spira*, ed. H. Viebrock and W. Erzgräber (Heidelberg, 1961), pp. 98–9, and cf. Mk 2252 and n.

2252 *Perce*: Persia; but according to Boccaccio (*De mulieribus claris*, ch. 98), Zenobia was descended from the Ptolemies, rulers of Egypt.

2272 *Odenake*: See n. to Mk 2327.

2289 wikes*] dayes El Hg. Only two manuscripts read 'wikes', but since what is required by the context is something equivalent to the length of pregnancy, 'wikes' makes much better sense. Boccaccio's *De mulieribus claris*, which Chaucer is here following closely, confirms this reading.

2307–8 Boccaccio specifies the languages that Zenobia knew as Egyptian, Greek, Latin and Syrian.

2311–16 According to Boccaccio, Zenobia conquered 'all the Eastern Empire which belonged to the Romans' (*De mulieribus claris*, ch. 98; tr. Guarino, p. 227. Cf. *SA*² I, 425).

2320 *Sapor*: Shopus I, king of Persia, AD *c.* 240–72, had occupied much of Mesopotamia, but was driven out by Zenobia.

2325 *Petrak*: It is unclear why Chaucer should mention Petrarch here, since his source is Boccaccio; for a hypothesis, see P. Boitani, *MÆ*, 45 (1976), 69, n. 35. He never in fact mentions Boccaccio, despite using his writings as sources on a number of occasions, and this may therefore be a deliberate obfuscation.

2327 'Odaenathus was condemned and killed together with his son Herodes by his cousin Maeonius. Some authors say Maeonius acted through envy. Others believe that Zenobia had consented to Herodes' death because she had often condemned his softness and so that her sons Herennianus and Timolaus [Mk 2345], whom she had borne to Odaenathus, might succeed to the kingdom' (Boccaccio, *De mulieribus claris*, ch. 98; tr. Guarino, p. 227. Cf. *SA*² I, 425).

2335–7 *Claudius ... Galien*: The emperors Claudius Gothicus (AD 268–70) and Gallienus (AD 253–68). Chaucer is again echoing Boccaccio in saying that neither of them dared oppose Zenobia.

2345 *Hermanno ... Thimalao*: See n. to Mk 2327.

2347 The contrast between honey and gall is proverbial; see Whiting G12, H433.

2351 *Aurelian*: The Roman emperor Aurelianus (AD 270–75) defeated Zenobia in 272.

2367–74   These lines echo the conclusion of the Zenobia story in
Boccaccio's *De casibus virorum illustrium* (VIII.6):

> She who just lately was fearful to Persian and Syrian kings is now
> spurned by commoners! She who just lately was admired by
> emperors is now pitied by plebeians! She who just lately, with
> helmet on head [*galeata*], was wont to harangue the troops, now
> wears a veil [*velata*] and is forced to listen to women's chit-chat!
> She who, just lately, bore the sceptre as ruler of the Orient, now
> subject to Rome, carries a distaff like other women!
>
> (For the Latin text, see *SA*, p. 633.)

2372   *vitremite*: This word, which is spelled in a wide variety of ways
in manuscripts of *CT* (see *MED*, s.v.), is not found elsewhere in
ME, and its etymology and meaning are uncertain. T. Atkinson
Jenkins suggested that the two elements of the word derive,
through OF, from Latin *vitta* ('headband') and *mitra* ('headdress'); see *Mélanges de linguistique et de littérature offerts à M.
Alfred Jeanroy* (Paris, 1928), pp. 141–7. *Riverside* and the *MED*
opt for an alternative explanation offered by R. Pratt, in an
unpublished note, that the first element might represent ME *vitry*,
from OF *vitré*, and refer to a kind of light canvas made at
Vitré in Brittany, while the second element represents OF *mite*,
'headdress' (see *Riverside* n. to this line); however, neither of
these meanings for the OF words is attested in *Tobler-
Lommatzsch Altfranzösisches Wörterbuch* (Wiesbaden, 1925–),
nor does 'vitry' appear in the *MED*. Since 'vitremite' clearly
contrasts with 'helmed' (2370), paralleling Boccaccio's contrast
between 'galeata' and 'velata' (see preceding n.), it must refer to
some kind of feminine headgear.

2375–2462   The placing of these lines, containing the stories of Pedro
of Spain, Peter of Cyprus, Bernabò Visconti, and Ugolino of Pisa
(the so-called 'Modern Instances') constitutes a major textual
problem in the Monk's Tale. In both El and Hg (and in thirteen
other manuscripts), they appear at the end of the tale, following
the story of Croesus. But in a majority of manuscripts (29) they
appear in the order adopted here, after the story of Zenobia; for
details, see Manly and Rickert II, 406–9, IV, 511–12, and D. K.
Fry, *JEGP*, 71 (1972), 355–68, esp. pp. 361–2. The Modern
Instances may be a later addition, especially if the Monk's Tale
was an earlier, independent work which was later incorporated
into *CT* (see Headnote). The stanza on Bernabò Visconti must

have been written after his death in December 1385, and the group hangs together as a whole by virtue of the fact that the central figures belong to the thirteenth–fourteenth centuries, rather than to classical antiquity or biblical times. General uncertainty in the manuscripts as to the placing of the Modern Instances (two manuscripts have part or all of this sequence in *both* places) suggests that Chaucer changed his mind, although R. Hanna (*Riverside* Textual Notes, p. 1132) points out that the passage may have been on loose sheets inserted into the archetype diversely by different scribes.

In Fry's view, the placing of the Modern Instances at the end of the Monk's Tale represents Chaucer's final intentions. The reason for preferring medial placing is that in the Nun's Priest's Prologue (2782–3), the Host echoes line 2766 (and also, probably, 2761) as if he has just been listening to the story of Croesus. The Host's allusion belongs to the passage of the Nun's Priest's Prologue which is lacking in a number of manuscripts (including Hg), and which may be a later addition by Chaucer (see n. to NP 2771–90). Since the Host's speech certainly reads like authentic Chaucer, and I can see no reason why it should have been cancelled later, I have assumed that Chaucer's latest discernible intention was to place the story of Croesus last.

If the Modern Instances were originally added at the end of the Monk's Tale, Chaucer may have changed his mind about their placing because he thought it inappropriate that the Knight's interruption should appear to have been provoked by the story of Ugolino, which achieves a genuine pathos that sets it well above the general level of the other stories. However, he may have wished to place this tale more centrally as a way of sustaining interest through the tale as a whole.

2375–90 *Petro ... of Spaine*: Pedro I, king of Castile and León (known as Peter the Cruel), was murdered on 23 March 1369, by his illegitimate half-brother, Don Enrique of Trastamare, with the assistance of Bertrand du Guesclin, Oliver de Mauny and others (see Pearsall, *Life*, pp. 51–3, and Russell, *Intervention*, pp. 147–8). Chaucer's account does not follow any written source, and he probably learned of the murder by word of mouth, since there were close links between Pedro's family and the English court. The Black Prince fought on Pedro's behalf against Enrique in 1367, and it is likely that Pedro attended Richard II's baptism in Bordeaux in the same year (Saul, *Richard II*, pp. 10, 12). In 1371 John of Gaunt married Pedro's daughter Constance

(Costanza), assuming the title of king of Castile and León through her claim (Saul, *Richard II*, p. 96). Chaucer's wife Philippa apparently served in Constance's household from 1372 onwards (Pearsall, *Life*, pp. 97, 141–2). Chaucer himself travelled to Spain in 1366 (the year that Enrique laid claim to Pedro's throne), and may have been on an unofficial diplomatic mission connected with the threat to Pedro (*Life-Records*, pp. 64–5; for further bibliography see p. 65, n. 2). H. Savage suggested that the details of Pedro's betrayal and death were given to Chaucer either by his wife (who would have got them from Constance of Castile), or by Don Fernando de Castro, one of Pedro's followers, who was with him on the fatal night, and who came to England in 1375 (*Speculum*, 24 (1949), 357–75, at pp. 372–3).

2378 Many manuscripts have an alternative version of this line: 'Thy bastard brother made the to flee' (Manly and Rickert II, 406–7). Manly and Rickert (IV, 511) suggest that the change was made when Enrique's grandson married Catalina, daughter of Constance of Castile and John of Gaunt, in 1388 (see Russell, *Intervention*, pp. 506, 508–10).

2383–4 These are the arms of Bertrand du Guesclin (a silver shield with a black two-headed eagle, and a red stick); see A. Brusendorff, *The Chaucer Tradition* (Oxford, 1925), p. 489. Savage speculates that Chaucer may have seen them with his own eyes since Bertrand visited England in 1354 and again in 1361 (*Speculum*, 24 (1949), 373–5). Bertrand (*c.* 1320–80), a Breton by birth, was one of the most famous knights of the fourteenth century. He distinguished himself in the Hundred Years War, and in 1370 was made constable of France. For an account of his colourful career, see F. Gies, *The Knight in History* (London, 1986), ch. 7. After his death, his exploits were celebrated in a long verse chronicle (*Chronique de Bertrand du Guesclin par Cuvelier*, ed. E. Charrière, 2 vols. (Paris, 1839)). His role in bringing about Pedro's death, as related by the fourteenth-century Spanish historian Pero Lopez de Ayala, shows a distinctly unchivalric side of his character (see Savage, pp. 365–7).

2386 *wikked nest*: Chaucer is punning on Oliver de Mauny's name (Mauny = OF *mau nid*, 'evil nest').

2387–90 Oliver was one of Charlemagne's Twelve Peers, and the faithful friend of Charlemagne's nephew Roland; their heroic death in battle at Roncesvalles is narrated in the *Song of Roland*. For Roland's betrayal by his stepfather Ganelon, see n. to Sh 194. Chaucer's point is that despite his name, Oliver de

Mauny behaved more like Ganelon than like Roland's friend Oliver.

2388   *Armorike*: Brittany (the home of Oliver de Mauny).

2391–3   *Petro ... Cipre ... Alisaundre*: Peter of Lusignan, king of Cyprus, won international renown for his crusading campaigns, the most spectacular of which was the capture of Alexandria in 1365. Chaucer's Knight is said to have participated in this and other military exploits led by Peter (see nn. to GP 51, 58, 65). In 1363, Peter visited England in an attempt to persuade King Edward III to join his crusading endeavours, but Edward offered only financial support. Whether or not Chaucer was present at any of the lavish entertainments provided for the royal visitor, he would surely have heard of them (see the translation of Froissart's account of the visit in Bowden, pp. 59–60).

2394–8   Peter of Lusignan was killed by three of his own knights on 17 January 1369. If Chaucer had a source other than oral report, it was probably the account in Machaut's poem *La Prise d'Alexandrie* (lines 8631–8769), as H. Braddy suggested (*Geoffrey Chaucer: Literary and Historical Studies* (Port Washington, NY, 1971), p. 29). Cypriot chroniclers differ from Machaut in their identification of the guilty parties, and other details (see L. de Mas Latrie, *Bibliothèque de l'école des chartes*, 37 (1876), 445–70, at pp. 458–63); Chaucer's account is, however, so abbreviated that its content can hardly be said to be 'at variance with historical fact' (*SA*, p. 637, citing Braddy), except in the reason given for the murder. Contemporary sources indicate that it was Peter's arbitrary and high-handed rule, rather than envy of his chivalry, that led to his death (P. Edbury, *Journal of Medieval History*, 6 (1980), 219–33).

2397   On Fortune's wheel, see n. to Kn 925.

2399–2406   *Melan ... Barnabo Viscounte ... Lumbardye*: The tyrannical cruelty of Bernabò Visconti, duke of Milan (in Lombardy), was a legend in his own lifetime (see D. Wallace, *Chaucerian Polity*, pp. 319–26). On 6 May 1385 he was seized and imprisoned by Gian Galeazzo Visconti, his nephew and son-in-law, and was dead by the end of the year. His fall from power was recorded 'by almost every chronicler in Italy, by chroniclers in England and France, by *canterini*, sonneteers, *novellatori*, by Visconti and Florentine propagandists [and] religious moralists' (ibid., p. 326). Bernabò had strong connections with the English court: his niece, Violanta, married Lionel, duke of Clarence (in whose household, as well as his wife's, Chaucer served as a young

man); in 1378–9, Bernabò's daughter Caterina was considered
as a possible bride for Richard II (Saul, *Richard II*, p. 84).
Chaucer had also met him personally: in 1374, he was sent by
Richard II on a diplomatic mission to Bernabò and the English
condottiere Sir John Hawkwood, who had married another of
Bernabò's many daughters (*Life-Records*, p. 54; Pearsall, *Life*,
pp. 107–9). Another daughter married Peter of Lusignan's son
and successor, also called Peter (G. L. Kittredge, *The Date of
Chaucer's 'Troilus' and Other Chaucer Matters* (London, 1909),
p. 50).

2407 *Hugelin of Pize*: As Chaucer's reference to Dante at Mk 2460–
61 makes clear, his source for this story was *Inferno* XXXIII
(text and Singleton's translation repr. in *SA²* I, 429–32), where
Ugolino della Gherardesca, Count of Pisa, is discovered among
the traitors in the ninth circle of Hell. Ugolino

> was born *ca.* 1220 and belonged to a noble and traditionally Ghibel-
> line family that controlled vast territories in the Pisan Maremma
> and in Sardinia. In 1275, he conspired with the Guelph leader
> Giovanni Visconti to seize control of Pisa, traditionally a Ghibelline
> city, but when the plot was discovered he was banished and his
> property was confiscated. He returned to Pisa the following year
> and in a short time again acquired great power and prestige. After
> the defeat of Pisa in the battle of Meloria (1284), a defeat which
> some accounts accuse him of contriving, he was made *podestà*
> [mayor] of Pisa, and the next year entered into the negotiations
> referred to by his opponents as the 'tradimento de le castella'
> ('betrayal of the castles' . . .). For this supposed treachery he was
> put in prison, where he died of starvation in 1289.
>
>   (Singleton, *Inferno*, *Commentary*, p. 606)

The agent of Ugolino's downfall was the archbishop of Pisa,
Ruggieri degli Ubaldini ('Roger . . . bisshop . . . of Pize'), who
was of the Ghibelline party (supporters of the emperor), with
whom Ugolino, despite having shifted his allegiance to the
Guelphs (supporters of the pope), entered into a conspiracy
aimed at destroying the political influence of Ugolino's grandson,
Nino Visconti. Once Nino was out of the way, the archbishop
incited the people against Ugolino by accusing him of treachery
in having ceded some Pisan castles to Lucca and to Florence.
Together with two of his sons and two of his grandsons, Ugolino
was shut up in a tower and starved to death (see Singleton,

Inferno, *Commentary*, pp. 607–11, for further details). In Chaucer, Ugolino's treachery exists only at the level of Ruggieri's 'fals suggestioun', and he becomes as innocent a victim as his children.

According to contemporary legend, Ugolino's hunger drove him to eat the flesh of his dead children. Dante perhaps refers to this in Ugolino's ambiguous last words: 'for two days I called them after they were dead. Then fasting did more than grief had done' ('Poscia, più che'l dolor, poté'l digiuno'). Singleton rejects this interpretation (*Inferno*, *Commentary*, p. 617), but for a contrary view, see J. Freccero, *Dante: The Poetics of Conversion* (Cambridge, MA, 1986), pp. 152–66, esp. p. 159. The idea of cannibalism is suggested, not only by the children's offer of their own flesh to their father (*Inferno* XXXIII.61–3), but also by the fact that in Hell Ugolino gnaws continually on the skull of his enemy Ruggieri. Whether or not Chaucer knew of this legend, he omits any suggestion that Ugolino actually ate his children. He preserves, however, the children's offer of their own flesh as food for their father, which, with its echo of Job (see n. to Mk 2451–2), forms part of a network of Christological and biblical resonances in Dante's canto. In Chaucer, these religious resonances link the Ugolino story with other explorations in *CT* of parent/child relationships as models of divine/human relationships (see Mann, 'Parents and Children', esp. pp. 166–7).

For a detailed comparison of *Inferno* XXXIII with Chaucer's version of the Ugolino story, see P. Boitani, *The Tragic and the Sublime in Medieval Literature* (Cambridge, 1989), pp. 20–55.

2411   In Dante's version of the story, there are four children, not three. Chaucer was perhaps influenced by *Inferno* XXXIII.71: 'I saw the three fall, one by one' ('vid'io cascar li tre ad uno ad uno'), which follows on from an account of the first death.

2412   Dante does not give the ages of the children, although like Chaucer, he represents them as infants (in real life they were considerably older; see Singleton, *Inferno*, *Commentary*, nn. to XXXIII.38, 50, 68, 89). Chaucer's stress on their extreme youth (see also Mk 2431) increases the pathos of his narrative (cf. Pri 503 and n.).

2416–18   Dante does not give any details of the manner in which Ruggieri betrayed Ugolino, and it has been suggested that Chaucer derived this information from the chronicle of Giovanni Villani or other Italian chronicles (see P. Toynbee, *NQ*, 8th series, 11 (1897), 205–6, and St C. Baddeley, *NQ*, 8th series, 11

(1897), 369–70; the relevant section of Villani's chronicle is printed and translated in Singleton, *Inferno, Commentary*, pp. 607–9). It is also possible that Chaucer might have acquired his knowledge from oral sources during his time in Italy. Significantly, Chaucer represents Ruggieri's accusation as 'fals'; his Hugelin is not, like Dante's, a traitor, but a victim of Fortune.

2430 Dante's Ugolino specifically says that he did not weep when he heard the door being nailed up, because he 'turned to stone within' (*Inferno* XXXIII.49).

2434 The child's request for bread recalls the Lord's Prayer ('Our Father . . . give us this day our daily bread', Matthew 6:11), and the Sermon on the Mount ('Or what man is there among you, of whom if his son shall ask bread, will he give him a stone?', Matthew 7:9). Hugelin's torture is that he is unable to respond to this elemental appeal to a father's obligation to his child.

2451–2 The children's words echo Job 1:21: 'the Lord gave, and the Lord hath taken away'. Ironically, this is Job's response to news of the death of his children (see Mann, 'Parents and Children', pp. 166–7). Cf. Mel 999–1000. Griselda also echoes Job's patient response; see Cl 871–2 and n.

2463–2550 The story of Nero is included in Boccaccio's *De casibus*, but Chaucer's account is almost entirely derived from the *Romance of the Rose* (6153–6220, 6383–6458, tr. Horgan, pp. 94–5, 98–9), where it forms part of Reason's warnings to the Lover against the fickleness of Fortune. As Jean de Meun himself makes clear, his account derives (whether directly or indirectly) from the *Lives of the Caesars* by Suetonius (see next n.), but it also includes details drawn from medieval legends about Nero. For a discussion of Jean's sources, see E. Langlois, *Origines et sources du Roman de la Rose* (Paris, 1891), pp. 127–31. As Chaucer would have recognized, Jean de Meun was also influenced by Boethius, *Consolation of Philosophy*, where Nero is presented as a victim of Fortune:

> We han wel knowen how many grete harmes and destrucciouns weren idoon by the emperour Nero. He leet brennen the cite of Rome, and made sleen the senatours; and he cruel whilom sloughe his brothir, and he was maked moyst with the blood of his modir (that is to seyn, he leet sleen and slitten the body of his modir to seen wher he was conceyved); and he lookede on every halve uppon hir cold deed body, ne no teer ne wette his face, but he was so hardherted that he myghte ben domesman or juge of hir dede

beaute. And natheles yit governed this Nero by septre alle the peples
that Phebus, the sonne, may seen, comynge fro his uttreste arysynge
til he hide his bemes undir the wawes. (*That is to seyn he governede
al the peples by ceptre imperial that the sonne goth aboute from est
to west.*) And eek this Nero governyde by ceptre alle the peples that
ben undir the colde sterres that highten the septemtryones. (*This is
to seyn he governede alle the peples that ben under the partye of
the north.*) And eek Nero governede alle the peples that the vyolent
wynd Nothus scorklith, and baketh the brennynge sandes by his
drye heete (*that is to seyn, al the peples in the south*). But yit ne
myghte nat al his heie power torne the woodnesse of this wikkid
Nero? Allas! It is grevous fortune as ofte as wikkid sweerd is joyned
to cruel venym (*that is to seyn, venymows cruelte to lordschipe*).

> (*Boece* II m.6; the passages in brackets are not part of
> Boethius's text but translations of medieval glosses.)

The explanation that Nero killed his mother because he wanted
to see where he was conceived (Mk 2484–5) was probably
derived from Jean de Meun's translation of Boethius (*Chaucer's
Boece and the Medieval Tradition of Boethius*, ed. Minnis,
pp. 118–19).

2465   *Swetonius*: Suetonius's *Lives of the Caesars* were known to
Petrarch and Boccaccio, and enjoyed great popularity among
Italian humanists from the late fourteenth century onwards. They
were also popular in northern Europe, and were translated into
French in 1381 (*Texts and Transmission*, ed. L. D. Reynolds
(Oxford, 1983), pp. 403–4). Since, however, there is no hard
evidence elsewhere in Chaucer's works that he had direct knowledge of Suetonius, it is likely that he is simply echoing the
reference to Suetonius at the corresponding point in *RR* (6425–
9): 'And according to the old book entitled *The Twelve Caesars*,
where we find the account of his [Nero's] death as Suetonius
wrote it down . . .' (tr. Horgan, p. 98).

2467   South] North El Hg. Since 'Septemtrioun' means 'North' the
El/Hg reading makes no sense. 'South' is obviously required (cf.
RR 6218–19, tr. Horgan, p. 95, and the quotation from Boethius
in n. to Mk 2463–2550), although no manuscript has it; they
either read 'North' or omit the word altogether. Manly and
Rickert (IV, 512) plausibly suggest that 'North' was a marginal
gloss for 'Septemtrioun' and may have been misinterpreted as a
marginal correction of 'South'.

2473–6   These details of Nero's extravagance are to be found in

Suetonius (VI.30) but not in *RR*. Since Chaucer is unlikely to have used Suetonius directly (see n. to Mk 2465), he probably took them from some intermediate source, such as Boccaccio's *De casibus* (VII.3; see *SA*, p. 640), or Vincent of Beauvais's *Speculum historiale* (VIII.7; see Aiken, *Speculum*, 17 (1942), 60–61).

2482 The *Romance of the Rose* says that Nero lay with his mother as well as his sister, and also with men (6177–9, tr. Horgan, p. 95); Chaucer omits these details.

2495–2502 Both Suetonius (*Lives of the Caesars* VI.10) and Jean de Meun (*RR* 6437–48, tr. Horgan, p. 99) stress that Nero began his reign well, but neither of them attributes this to Seneca's influence.

2503–14 Jean de Meun's account of Nero's motives for putting Seneca to death corresponds to the second of these two stanzas (*RR* 6199–6215, tr. Horgan, p. 95); he seems to have invented this reason himself (Langlois, *Origines et sources*, p. 130). Aiken has suggested that the first stanza is based on Vincent of Beauvais's *Speculum historiale* (VIII.9; see *Speculum*, 17 (1942), 62), which says of Nero 'sometimes, on seeing Seneca and calling to mind the blows which he had given him from boyhood, he shuddered'; this is not, however, a very close parallel to Chaucer's picture of Seneca chastising Nero 'Discretly, as by word and nat by dede', and warning him against tyranny. Chaucer's admiration for the wisdom of Seneca, which is evident elsewhere in *CT* (see, e.g., ML 25, WB 1168, Sum 2018, Mch 1523, Pard 492, Mel passim, Mcp 345), perhaps led him to expand the account of his attempts to restrain Nero's tryanny (cf. also *LGW* F 373–80).

2509–10 Suetonius makes only the briefest reference to Seneca's suicide (*Lives of the Caesars* VI.35), as does Boethius (*Boece* III pr.5). Jean de Meun, however, devotes more attention to it than to any of Nero's other crimes (see *RR* 6181–6215, tr. Horgan, p. 95), and Chaucer gives it even greater prominence.

2527–50 Chaucer's account of Nero's death follows Jean de Meun's fairly closely (see *RR* 6389–6424, tr. Horgan, p. 98), but the 'fir, greet and reed' (2544) and the two churls sitting by it seem to be his own addition; in *RR*, two of Nero's servants enter the garden with him.

2551–74 *Oloferno*: The source for the story of Holofernes is the biblical book of Judith, which is included in the Latin Vulgate (but not in the Authorized Version). Holofernes, chief captain of the Assyrian army, led it against the Israelites at a place called

Bethulia, and besieged the inhabitants with the aim of starving them into surrender. Judith, an Israelite widow, went out at night with her maid to the Assyrian camp, won her way into Holofernes's good favour, and cut off his head as he lay in a drunken sleep after a feast (Judith chs. 7–13). Cf. ML 939–42 and n., and Mch 1366–8.

2562 *Nabugodonosor*: This is not Nebuchadnezzar, the historical king of Babylon who captured Jerusalem and who is the subject of Mk 2143–82; the author of Judith has given his name to an unhistorical Assyrian king who is said to have reigned in Nineveh (impossibly, since it was destroyed by the Babylonian Nebuchadnezzar's father). See Judith 1:5, and cf. *Jerome Bible Commentary*, I, 625. For Holofernes's proclamation, see Judith 6:2–4.

2565 *Bethulia*: 'No city by this name is known. It is, quite plainly, a fictitious city'(*Jerome Biblical Commentary*, I, 625).

2566 A Latin gloss in El and Hg quotes Judith 4:6: 'Et fecerunt filii Israel secundum quod constituerat eis sacerdos domini Eliachym' ('And the children of Israel did as the priest of the Lord Eliachim had directed them'). Eliachim commanded the Israelites to make defences on the mountain-tops against the Assyrians, after Nebuchadnezzar had ordered Holofernes to destroy the worship of all gods other than himself.

2575–2630 *Anthiochus*: For the story of Antiochus IV, king of Syria from 175 to 163 BC, Chaucer is following 2 Maccabees, ch. 9. (The two books of Maccabees are part of the Latin Vulgate Bible, but not the Authorized Version.)

2586–7 These lines paraphrase 2 Maccabees 9:8.

2591 *Nichanore . . . Thimothee*: Nicanor and Timotheus were leaders of the Syrian army, against which the Jews, inspired by Judas Maccabeus, won a great victory (2 Maccabees 8, 9:1–3).

2603–4 This comment is borrowed from 2 Maccabees 9:6.

2616 Cf. 2 Maccabees 9:9.

2631–70 *Alisaundre*: As Chaucer himself says, the story of Alexander was extremely well known in the Middle Ages. Son of Philip II, king of Macedon, Alexander succeeded his father in 336 BC, at the age of twenty. He was renowned for his military conquests, which included the defeat of Darius, king of Persia. The earliest accounts of his death attribute it to a fever, following a drinking-party, but the story that he was poisoned is almost as old, and became the accepted one in the Middle Ages (see *Alexander the Great in the Middle Ages. Ten Studies on the Last Days of Alexander in Literary and Historical Writing*, ed. W. J. Aerts,

J. M. M. Hermans and E. Visser (Nijmegen, 1978), esp. pp. 2–9). The major biographical source was the *Life of Alexander* by Quintus Curtius (1st c. AD), on which was based the Latin epic *Alexandreis* of Walter of Châtillon (1184 x 1187), which enjoyed great popularity (see G. Cary, *The Medieval Alexander* (Cambridge, 1956), pp. 16–17, and cf. n. to WB 498–9). The rather general information that Chaucer gives here makes it impossible to single out any particular source (see Cary, p. 252, and *SA*, p. 641), but it may be noted that virtually all the details given here (except for the manner of Alexander's death and his penchant for wine and women) are to be found in the brief account at the opening of 1 Maccabees (1:1–8); see n. to Mk 2655.

2644   For Alexander's (medieval) reputation for drinking and womanizing, see Cary, *The Medieval Alexander*, pp. 99–100.

2648   *Darius*: Darius III, the last king of Persia (*c.* 380–330 BC), not to be confused with the unhistorical Darius mentioned at Mk 2237. His vast army was defeated by Alexander in 333 BC.

2655   Alexander's reign is said to have lasted twelve years in 1 Maccabees 1:8, following a brief account of his conquests and death (the cause of which is not specified). He died in June 323 BC, after a reign of twelve years and eight months.

2671–2726   For a discussion of the difficulties involved in identifying a single source for this account of Julius Caesar, see *SA*, pp. 652–4. In lines 2719–21, Chaucer himself seems to point to Lucan (AD 39–65), author of the *Pharsalia* (*De bello civili*), a Latin epic concerning the civil war between Julius Caesar and Pompey; to Suetonius (AD *c.* 70–150), whose *Lives of the Caesars* begins with Julius; and to Valerius Maximus, whose *Memorable Doings and Sayings* includes numerous anecdotes and details concerning him. However, it is doubtful whether Chaucer knew Suetonius first-hand (see n. to Mk 2465), and his reference to Lucan in connection with a triumph of Caesar which Lucan quite explicitly does *not* describe (see n. to ML 400–401) suggests that he did not know Lucan either. As noted in connection with ML 400–401, J. L. Lowes suggested that Chaucer was drawing on the French translation of Lucan by Jehan le Tuim. Chaucer's coupling of Lucan and Suetonius here makes it even more likely that he was using the French conflation of these two authors (and also Sallust) known as *Li Fet des Romains*; for discussion and further bibliography, see G. M. Spiegel, *Romancing the Past* (Berkeley, CA, 1993), pp. 118–82). This work strings together the *Pharsalia*, Suetonius's *Lives*, and Sallust's *Catiline Con-*

spiracy, with liberal use of commentaries and other sources, to make a full-scale biography of Julius Caesar. The authors of the Latin sources are frequently named throughout. Written around 1213–14, this work is preserved in 59 MSS, and exercised wide influence on vernacular literature. For the details that Chaucer might have taken from this work, see nn. to Mk 2680, 2690–92, 2695–6, 2709–15.

2672 So far from being of humble birth, Julius Caesar was a member of the *gens Julia*, a patrician family that traced its origins back to Julus, son of Aeneas, the founder of Rome. However, Suetonius's *Life* lacks its introductory paragraphs in all surviving manuscripts, so it furnishes no information on Caesar's birth. (*Li Fet des Romains*, however, does include an account of his noble lineage; see I.8, p. 15, and III.15, p. 616.) The myth that he was the son of a baker seems to have been a peculiarly English tradition; it is found in Lydgate, Hoccleve and the historian Ranulph Higden. For documentation, and a hypothesis as to the source of the legend, see M. S. Waller, *Indiana Social Studies Quarterly*, 31 (1978), 46–55.

2677 Caesar was in fact never made emperor of Rome; this was an honour enjoyed by his adopted son Augustus and his successors.

2679–86 Gnaius Pompeius (Pompey the Great) was a successful Roman general and statesman. His finest military achievement was his defeat of Mithridates, king of Pontus, who was Rome's great enemy in the east. Through this campaign, Pompey 'established an eastern frontier for Rome that lasted – with few changes – for 500 years' (*Oxford Companion to Classical Literature*, s.v. Pompey). Pompey and Caesar were initially allies; together with Marcus Crassus, they formed the so-called 'first triumvirate', which effectively ruled Rome. Eventually, however, Pompey tried to exclude Caesar from power, and civil war broke out between them. In a battle on the plain of Pharsalus in Thessaly, in 48 BC, Pompey was decisively defeated. Cf. ML 199 and n.

2680 Pompey was not Caesar's father-in-law, but his son-in-law, since he married his daughter Julia. The mistake seems to have arisen from Suetonius's statement that Caesar married Pompeia, daughter of Quintus Pompeius Rufus (*Lives of the Caesars* I.vi.2; see also *Li Fet des Romains* I.5 [2]); medieval writers apparently confused this Pompeius with Gnaius Pompeius, the triumvir (see preceding n.). See Ranulph Higden, *Polychronicon* III.41, ed. J. R. Lumby, vol. IV (London, 1872), pp. 188, 192, and the ME translation by John Trevisa, ibid., pp. 189, 193. The error may have been reinforced by Suetonius's statement that Caesar later asked for the hand of Pompey's daughter (I.xxvii.1; *Li Fet des Romains* II.23 [8]).

2690–92 After his defeat at the battle of Pharsalus, Pompey fled to Egypt, where he was murdered at the instigation of the Egyptian king Ptolemy. One of the assassins, Septimius, had formerly been a Roman soldier (Lucan, *Pharsalia* VIII.595–610). Chaucer's comment on this act of disloyalty is close to that in *Li Fet des Romains* III.13 [20], lines 8–9: 'Cil qui devoit estre huem Pompee, osoit metre espee ou chief son seignor' ('He who ought to be Pompey's man dared to set his sword to his master's head'). Pompey's head was cut off and sent to Ptolemy (Lucan, *Pharsalia* VIII.679–91; *Li Fet des Romains* III.13 [22]). Later, when Caesar arrived in Egypt, one of Ptolemy's servants took him the head, hoping (in vain) to win favour by doing so (Lucan, *Pharsalia* IX.1010–1108; *Li Fet des Romains* III.15 [5–9]).

2695–6 At the end of the civil war, Caesar celebrated his earlier victories with five triumphs, four of them held in a single month (Suetonius, *Lives of the Caesars* I.37; *Li Fet des Romains* IV.1 [1]). See further ML 400–401 and n.

2697 The two major conspirators, Brutus and Cassius, are here conflated into a single person. Though not common, the error is found in other medieval sources (see H. T. Silverstein, *MLN*, 47 (1932), 148–50), and probably arose simply from the scribal omission of an 'et' joining the two names in a Latin source.

2703 *Capitolie*: According to Suetonius (*Lives of the Caesars* I.80; cf. *Li Fet des Romains* IV.3 [1]), the meeting of the Senate at which Caesar was killed was held in the Hall of Pompey, not the Capitol.

2709–15 The ultimate source of this account of Caesar's death is Suetonius (*Lives of the Caesars* I.82):

> When he [Julius Caesar] saw that he was beset on every side by drawn daggers, he muffled his head in his robe, and at the same time drew down its fold to his feet with his left hand, in order to fall more decently, with the lower part of his body also covered. And in this wise he was stabbed with three and twenty wounds, uttering not a word, but merely a groan at the first stroke . . .

The passage is translated in *Li Fet des Romains* IV.3 [4]. Valerius Maximus relates the anecdote about Caesar's care to keep his body covered, as an example of modesty (*verecundia*), but he does not include the detail that Caesar groaned only once, so he cannot have been Chaucer's only source (*Memorable Doings and Sayings* IV.v.6).

2727–66 *Cresus ... of Lyde*: Chaucer's source for the story of Croesus, king of Lydia from 560 to 546 BC, is the *Romance of the Rose* (6459–6592, tr. Horgan, pp. 99–101), where it is related immediately after the story of Nero as another example of the fickleness of Fortune (see n. to Mk 2463–2550).

2728 *Cirus*: Cyrus the Great, founder of the Persian empire, conquered Sardis, the Lydian capital, in 547 BC, and took Croesus prisoner. He is not mentioned in *RR*, but he appears in the context of the story about the miraculous shower of rain in Boethius, *Consolation of Philosophy* (*Boece* II pr.2.58–63).

THE NUN'S PRIEST'S PROLOGUE

2767 Seven manuscripts attribute this interruption to the Host rather than to the Knight. Four of them have the short form of the Prologue and three the long form (see next n. and Manly and Rickert II, 410–11, IV, 513). G. Dempster suggested that the shorter version, with the Host as interrupter, was original, and was revised by Chaucer to avoid repetition of the Host's role as interrupter of Mel (*PMLA*, 68 (1953), 1142–59, at pp. 1147, 1151–2); this view was accepted by Manly and Rickert (II, 412), and, more recently, by D. K. Fry (*JEGP*, 71 (1972), 355–68, at pp. 361–3), but R. Hanna (*Riverside* Textual Notes, p. 1132) rejects the connection between the short form and the 'erroneous' reading 'Hoste'.

2771–90 These lines are found in El and thirty-two other witnesses, but are lacking in fourteen witnesses, including Hg (Manly and Rickert IV, 513). In the Hg version, line 2791 reads 'Youre tales doon us no desport ne game'. It is difficult to see any reason that would have caused this passage to drop out, which makes it at least likely that it represents a revision of the Prologue by Chaucer. (See n. to Mk 2375–2462.) For a summary of the scholarly discussions of the problem, see D. Pearsall, ed., *A Variorum Edition of the Works of Geoffrey Chaucer: The Nun's Priest's Tale* (Norman, OK, 1984), pp. 85–7.

2780 The present-day cathedral of St Paul's was built by Sir Christopher Wren; its medieval predecessor, which was destroyed in the Great Fire of 1666, was 'one of the most magnificent Gothic buildings in Christendom' (*The City of London*, ed. Lobel, p. 49).

The great bell of St Paul's was used to summon assemblies of citizens.

2782–3   Cf. Mk 2766 and 2761, and see n. to Mk 2375–2462.

2801–2   The Host is quoting Ecclesiasticus 32:6. Cf. Mel 1047.

2809   *Nonnes Preest*: See n. to GP 164.

THE NUN'S PRIEST'S TALE

The Nun's Priest's Tale is often referred to as a beast fable, but it is not found in the classic Aesopic collections, and its stylistic affiliations are rather with beast epic, a genre first fully developed in the twelfth-century Latin poem *Ysengrimus*, whose central figures are the wily fox Reinardus and the victim of his tricks, the wolf Ysengrimus. The *Ysengrimus* includes the story of how the fox, having tricked the cock, was himself outwitted by him (see the edition with facing translation by J. Mann (Leiden, 1986), IV.811–V.316). This story is not found in the oldest surviving collection of Aesopic fables, which was composed by the Latin writer Phaedrus in the first century AD; it was probably developed from the Phaedran fable of the fox and the crow (which likewise has the fox flatter the bird, and includes the 'mouth-opening trick'). Different versions (not always with the same animals, and not always including both halves of the trick) appear in independent poems and in fable-collections from the eighth century onwards. (The accounts of this literary tradition given by E. P. Dargan, *MP*, 4 (1906), 38–65, and by K. O. Petersen, *On the Sources of the Nonne Prestes Tale* (Boston, 1898; repr. New York, 1966), are based on outdated scholarship.) R. A. Pratt (*Speculum*, 47 (1972), 422–44, 646–68) argued that Chaucer's immediate source for the fable section of his tale was the late twelfth/early thirteenth-century French collection of Marie de France (*Fables*, no. 60), but the verbal parallels Pratt cites are not utterly convincing (pp. 442–3), and Pratt himself acknowledges that 'the over-all design of Chaucer's narrative' (p. 444) derives from Branch II of the *Roman de Renart* (for the French text and an English translation, see *SA*² I, 456–75; also tr. in Kolve and Olson, pp. 429–33), which borrowed the cock-and-fox story from the *Ysengrimus*. Pierre de St Cloud, the author of Branch II, added to the story the account of Chauntecleer's premonitory dream of the fox's attack, the argument between Chauntecleer and his wife Pinte over the significance of dreams, and a vivid description of the farm on which Chauntecleer and his hens live – all of which differentiate the narrative of the Nun's Priest's Tale from the fable version.

It is style rather than content, however, that constitutes the crucial link between Chaucer's tale and the beast epic tradition. Whereas beast fable is characteristically succinct to the point of baldness (in the words of La Fontaine, 'brevity is the soul of fable'), and aims to provide a simple, exemplary action that can be summarized by an instructive moral, beast epic gives the moralizing to the animals themselves, and allows them to develop it to the point where the narrative is buried under the weight of extravagant rhetoric. Beast epic aims at comedy rather than moral wisdom. Although Chaucer did not know the *Ysengrimus*, he certainly knew the Anglo-Latin beast epic entitled the *Mirror for Fools* (*Speculum Stultorum*), to which his fox refers (see n. to NP 3312–16), and in which these characteristics are amply demonstrated (see J. Mann, *ChauR*, 9 (1975), 262–82). Pratt's description of the Nun's Priest's Tale as 'overwhelmed with digressions' (p. 425) also applies to the *Mirror for Fools*. The comic blurring of the human and the animal which is found in the tale (as in the references to the cock's beard or shirt, or the beauty of Pertelote's red eyes) is also characteristic of epic rather than fable (cf. Pratt, pp. 658–60). As generally in the *Roman de Renart*, the animals are presented not just as humans but as aristocrats, beside whose splendour the life of their peasant owners pales into insignificance (Pratt, p. 658). Chauntecleer's warning dream forms part of the mock-heroic scenario, since it is modelled on the dreams which conventionally foretold impending disaster to the heroes of the French *chansons de geste* (see Pratt, pp. 662–3, and H. Braet, *Le moyen âge*, 3–4 (1971), 405–16). But in Chaucer's tale, the roles of the cock and the hen in the argument over dreams are reversed: in the *Renart*, it is the cock who makes light of his dream and the hen who insists that it foretells disaster. Chaucer may have made the change independently for his own purposes, or he may, as Pratt claimed (see the article cited above, pp. 429–33), have been influenced in this by the early fourteenth-century satirical poem *Renart le Contrefait* (ed. Raynaud and Lemaître; excerpts and translation in *SA*² I, 474–87). The effect of the change is to sever any meaningful connection between the intellectual superstructure of the debate on dreams and the subsequent action of the tale (since Chauntecleer ignores the import of his own argument); the same could be said of the narrator's elaborate attempts to interpret the cock's seizure by the fox in the light of theories of destiny and free will, the evil effects of women's counsel, or the tragic events of classical history – all of which are Chaucer's own additions. As in the Latin beast epic, the comedy plays around the ease with which human beings (especially poets) can summon up appropriate rhetoric for every occasion, without ever managing to integrate it meaningfully with action. When events change, it is simply time to switch clichés to match.

2832   The living area of the widow's 'narwe' cottage is rather grandly designated a hall; the bedroom ('bour'), which she presumably shared with her two daughters, may have been no more than an open upper room, reached by a ladder (see Pearsall, *Variorum: Nun's Priest's Tale*, p. 142). The whole cottage will have been sooty because it was heated by an open fire on a central hearth, without a chimney. The widow's hens (and quite possibly her other animals also) are brought into the cottage at night to keep them safe (see NP 2884).

2849   The animals in beast fable are characteristically nameless; it is in the beast epic tradition that they are given names, which are often carried over from one work to another. 'Chantecler' ('sing-beautifully') is the name given to the cock in Branch II of the *Roman de Renart* (see Headnote).

2851   *orgon*: As the following verb ('gon') shows, the word is plural, probably because it derives from the Latin neuter plural *organa* (see *OED* s.v. organ[1], 2b). At SN 134, the form 'organs' is unequivocally plural, though only one organ is in question.

       Medieval organs were worked by bellows, and existed in various sizes, the smallest being portable instruments that could sit on the player's lap. The church-organ referred to here will have been larger, but still probably of modest size. See C. Clutton and A. Niland, *The British Organ* (London, 1963), ch. 2, esp. pp. 46–7, and J. Perrot, *The Organ from its Invention in the Hellenistic Period to the End of the Thirteenth Century*, tr. N. Deane (London, 1971), ch. 14.

2854   Mechanical, weight-driven clocks were invented in the late thirteenth century and were still relatively rare in Chaucer's day. They were found only in important buildings such as cathedrals, abbeys or royal residences. The earliest examples were located inside at ground level; later on they were placed in a tower and later still the clock-face appeared on the outside wall. See C. F. Beeson, *English Church Clocks 1280–1850* (London, 1971), ch. 1. The earliest types rang a bell every hour (the word 'clock' is cognate with the French *cloche*, bell); the later type, with a face or dial, was known as an 'horologe'. By Chaucer's time, however, the two terms seem to have been interchangeable (see L. Mooney, *SAC*, 15 (1993), 91–109, at pp. 101–9).

2855   knew*] krew El Hg. Kane (p. 218) defends the quasi-transitive use of 'krew' as a 'harder reading' (on which see n. to Cl 508), but as Pearsall points out, 'know by nature' is a more idiomatic collocation than 'crow by nature' (*Variorum: Nun's Priest's Tale*, p. 149).

2855–8 *equinoxial*: The equinoctial is the celestial equator, an imaginary line projected on to the celestial sphere on the plane of the terrestrial equator. The equinoctial circles the earth from east to west with the daily rotation of the celestial sphere; Chauntecleer recognizes instinctively each degree of its ascension above the horizon (whereas a human astrologer would have to use an astrolabe to work out its movement from the changing position of the heavenly bodies). Since the complete circle of its revolution comprises 360°, the equinoctial will pass through 15° in each of the 24 hours of the day. The cock, that is, crows every hour, on the hour.

2870 See n. to NP 2849 on the naming of animals in beast literature. The hen in Branch II of the *Roman de Renart* is called Pinte, not Pertelote; Chaucer may have changed it for the sake of finding easier rhymes.

2874–6 The romantic love between Chauntecleer and Pertelote is Chaucer's addition to the narrative; see Pratt, *Speculum*, 47 (1972), 657–8.

2879 This is the first line of a song found in Trinity College, Cambridge, MS 599 (R.3.19), which is printed in R. H. Robbins, *Secular Lyrics of the XIVth and XVth Centuries*, 2nd edn (Oxford, 1955), p. 152:

> My lefe is faren in a lond.
> Allas, why is she so?
> And I am so sore bound
> I may nat com her to.
> She hath my hert in hold
> Where ever she ride or go,
> With trew love a thousand fold!

The fifth line is echoed in NP 2874.

2884 See n. to NP 2832.

2912–17 For these husbandly qualities, cf. Sh 173–7.

2923 ff. On the medieval medical theory of the bodily 'humours', see n. to GP 333. Curry (pp. 222–3) cites numerous examples of medical authorities explaining dreams of red things as caused by an excess of red choler, and of black things as caused by an excess of black choler, or melancholia. P. Aiken cites passages of a similar tenor in Vincent of Beauvais's *Speculum naturale* and *Speculum doctrinale* (*Speculum*, 10 (1935), 281–7, at pp. 281–2). Robert Holcot, in his commentary on Wisdom (see n. to NP 2984 ff.), also discusses the effects of an imbalance of the humours on dreaming (R. A. Pratt, *Speculum*, 52 (1977), 538–70, at pp. 543–5).

2940–41 'Cato' is the pseudonymous author of the *Distichs of Cato* (cf. n. to Mil 3227), a Latin proverb-collection which contains the maxim 'Somnia ne cures [nam mens humana quod optat, | dum vigilans sperat, per somnium cernit id ipsum]' ('Pay no attention to dreams [for what the human mind wishes and hopes for when awake, that it sees in sleep]'; II.31). With a slightly different ending, it also circulated as a Latin proverb: 'Somnia ne cures, nam fallunt plurima plures' ('Pay no attention to dreams, since many of them deceive many people'); see Walther 30027, and cf. 30026.

2963–6 With the exception of 'gaitris beryis' (see below), all these herbs are recommended as purgatives in the *Speculum doctrinale* and *Speculum naturale* of Vincent of Beauvais (Aiken, *Speculum*, 10 (1935), 281–7, at pp. 283–4). See further Curry, pp. 225–6, and the notes in Pearsall, *Variorum: Nun's Priest's Tale*, pp. 170–73.
gaitris beryis: Apart from this line, the only examples of the word 'gaitris' cited by the *MED* are place-names. In later usage, 'gaiter' is associated with the dogwood, but its berries have no medicinal properties (Pearsall, ibid., p. 172). Skeat (V, 252) suggested that the word represents 'gayt-tre' ('goat-tree'), and refers to the buck-thorn, which is given similar names in Swedish dialects (see *MED*), and whose berries are a purgative.
herbe yve: Not the plant commonly known as ground ivy (*Nepeta glechoma*), but, according to *MED*, either buck's horn plantain (*Plantago coronopus*) or the European ground pine (*Ajuga chamaepitys*). The name derives from OF *herbe yve* (see the *Anglo-Norman Dictionary*, ed. L. W. Stone and W. Rothwell (London, 1977–), s.v. herbe).

2984 ff. This story, and the one that follows (3067–3104) are pre-sented as a pair (but in the reverse order) by Cicero, *De divina-tione* I.27. Some manuscripts (though not El or Hg) have a marginal gloss identifying the 'auctor' of line 2984 as 'Tullius' (Manly and Rickert III, 520). Cicero's brief narratives were para-phrased by Valerius Maximus in his *Memorable Doings and Sayings* (I.7.ext.10, and I.7.ext.3; both excerpts printed in *SA*, pp. 662–3), but again, so far from the second story following the first 'Right in the nexte chapitre' (3065), they are in reverse order, and also separated by several other anecdotes about dreams. The two stories are related in Chaucer's order, and separated by only one sentence, in Giraldus Cambrensis's *Expugnatio Hibernica* (*Opera*, vol. V, ed. J. F. Dimock (London, 1867), pp. 294–5); Giraldus took them from Valerius, but the first story is retold in abbreviated form. The first story is loosely paraphrased by Albertus Magnus in *De somno et vigilia* III.10 (mid-13th c.), where it is incorrectly attributed to Book II of Cicero's *De natura deorum* ('Tullius in secundo de natura deorum'); see *Opera omnia*, ed. P. Jammy (Lyons, 1651), V, 100. Finally, Valerius's versions of both stories are quoted almost verbatim by the fourteenth-century Dominican friar Robert Holcot in his celebrated commentary on the book of Wisdom; here they are in the same order as in NPT but widely separated, the first appearing in *lectio* 103 and the second in *lectio* 202 (text and translation in *SA*² I, 486–9; on Chaucer's probable familiarity with Holcot's work, see p. 450). Chaucer may also have known Valerius Maximus directly (but see Pratt's contrary opinion, quoted in n. to WB 460–62). Pratt's detailed analysis of all these versions concludes that Chaucer's narratives have unique points of resemblance with each of them except for Giraldus, so that it is impossible to identify a single source with confidence (*Speculum*, 52 (1977), 538–70, esp. pp. 548–63).

3013 Only in Chaucer and Albertus Magnus are there three dreams; Cicero and Valerius Maximus have only one warning dream, not two, before the murder takes place (see Pratt, *Speculum*, 52 (1977), 551).

3052, 3057 *Mordre wol out*: Proverbial. See Pri 576 and n.

3076 This is a metrically dense line, but can be read as follows: 'But hérkneth: to that ó man fíl a gréet merváille.'

3110 Kenelm was the son of Coenwulf ('Kenulphus'), a ninth-century king of Mercia ('Mercenrike'); having succeeded his father at the age of seven, he was murdered at the instigation of his elder sister, who wanted the crown for herself. His life and posthumous miracles are related in an eleventh-century legend, which includes the story of his premonitory dream (see *Three Eleventh-Century Anglo-Latin Saints' Lives*, ed. and tr. R. C. Love (Oxford, 1996), pp. 56–9). Kenelm's legend was well known in medieval England; it was included in several Latin chronicles (Love, pp. cxxxvi–cxxxviii) and also in the *South English Legendary* (I, 279–91), though Coenwulf is there said to be king of 'the March of Wales' rather than Mercia.

3123–4 *th'avisioun ... Cipioun*: The *Dream of Scipio* was actually written by Cicero (it forms Book VI of his *De republica*), but it was known in the Middle Ages only as quoted in the lengthy commentary by Macrobius (fl. AD *c.* 400); see the edition of Macrobius's *Commentary* by J. Willis, with the text of the *Dream* on pp. 155–63, and the translation by W. H. Stahl, with the *Dream* on pp. 69–77. The *Dream* relates that the Roman consul Scipio Africanus the Younger dreamed that his dead grandfather, Scipio Africanus the Elder, conqueror of Carthage, led him up through the stars to the Milky Way, explained the nature of the planetary system, foretold his future glory and potential dangers, and discoursed to him of his public duties. Macrobius's commentary on this text begins with an analysis of different types of dreams, and the importance to be attached to each (I.3).

In Affrike: The opening of the *Dream* explains that Scipio was visiting Masinissa, king of Numidia, when he had his vision.

3128 The Old Testament prophet Daniel had understanding in 'all visions and dreams' (Daniel 1:17). He won the favour of Nebuchadnezzar, king of Babylon, by interpreting his dream of a colossal statue made out of gold, silver, brass, iron and clay as a symbol of Nebuchadnezzar's kingdom and its increasingly inferior successors (ch. 2). He also interpreted Nebuchadnezzar's dream of the felling of a mighty tree as a sign of the king's downfall (ch. 4). Chs. 7–12 of the book of Daniel describe a series of apocalyptic visions granted to Daniel. Cf. Mk 2155–8, Pars 126.

3130 Joseph dreamed two dreams which foretold his future dominion over his parents and brothers (Genesis 37:5–10).

3133–4 Joseph interpreted two dreams of the Egyptian Pharaoh as prophesying seven years of plenty followed by seven years of famine (Genesis 41:1–36). He also correctly interpreted the dream of Pharaoh's imprisoned butler as a sign of his restoration to favour, and the dream of Pharaoh's baker as a sign of his impending execution (Genesis 40:5–23).

3138 *Cresus*: On Croesus and his dream, see Mk 2740–60, and n. to Mk 2727–66.

3141–8 *Andromacha ... Ector*: The tradition that Andromache had a premonitory dream the night before her husband Hector was killed in battle, and vainly tried to dissuade him from going out to fight the next day, is not Homeric, but is found in the Latin prose history of the fall of Troy allegedly by 'Dares the Phrygian' (6th c. AD), and became widespread in medieval literature (for references, see Pratt, *Speculum*, 47 (1972), 648, and J. Mann, in *The European Tragedy of Troilus*, ed. P. Boitani (Cambridge, 1989), p. 237, n. 57). Pratt points out (pp. 649–50) that this story is used by the hen Pinte in *Renart le Contrefait* (see Headnote) to persuade her husband Chantecler of the value of women's counsel; since, however, Pinte is discounting the importance of dreams, she fails to notice that the story contradicts her position. In giving the exemplum to Chauntecleer, Chaucer creates an opposite kind of paradox: the story supports the cock's case about dreams, but might equally be used to imply that he should listen to his wife's advice.

3163 *In principio*: 'In the beginning . . .' These are the opening words of the book of Genesis, and also of St John's Gospel. The allusion is probably to the latter; Chauntecleer is asserting that what he says is 'gospel truth' (cf. *MED* s.v. gospel 4).

3164–6 The Latin means 'woman is the confusion of man'; it forms part of a misogynist definition of woman which enjoyed wide circulation (for manuscript examples, see C. Brown, *MLN*, 35 (1920), 479–82). 'Quid est mulier? Hominis confusio, insaturabilis bestia, continua solicitudo, indesinens pugna, viri continentis naufragium, humanum mancipium' ('What is woman? The confusion of man, an insatiable beast, a continual trouble, ceaseless strife, the downfall of a continent man, human bondage'). Cf. Mel 1106. It is not clear whether Chauntecleer's obvious mistranslation is to be attributed to his condescending deception of Pertelote, or to his own ignorance; for attempts to explain it, see Pearsall, *Variorum: Nun's Priest's Tale*, p. 201. Whatever it implies about the cock, the unmediated yoking of condemnation and adulation makes evident the contradictory stereotyping of women and the male oscillation from one view to the other, as convenience dictates (see Mann, *Feminizing Chaucer*, pp. 148–9).

3187–8 The belief that God created the world at the spring equinox was widespread in Chaucer's time (North, *Chaucer's Universe*, p. 119).

3190 was gon] bigan El Hg. All manuscripts read 'bigan', but this yields a date in early April, which does not square with the position of the sun in Taurus indicated in lines 3194–5; the implication is that the 32 days mentioned in line 3190 follow the *end* of March, fixing the date as 3 May (also a significant date at Kn 1462–3 and *TC* II.56). The emendation 'was gon' is made in *Riverside* (see Textual Notes, p. 1132).

3193–9 The calendar of Nicholas of Lynn, which Chaucer consulted when writing his *Treatise on the Astrolabe*, confirms that the details given here of the sun's position in the zodiac, and its height in the heavens at 9 o'clock ('prime'), are correct for 3/4 May. See Eisner, *Kalendarium*, pp. 31–2, and North, *Chaucer's Universe*, pp. 119–21.

3205 Three manuscripts (but not El or Hg) have a marginal gloss attributing this sentiment to Solomon; cf. Proverbs 14:13, 'Laughter shall be mingled with grief, and woe is the end of rejoicing.' Cf. ML 424 and n.

3212 The reference is to the long French prose romance (13th c.) entitled *Lancelot* (ed. A. Micha, 9 vols. (Paris and Geneva, 1978–83); tr. S. N. Rosenberg and C. W. Carroll, *Lancelot-Grail. The Old French Arthurian Vulgate and Post-Vulgate in Translation*, ed. N. J. Lacy, vol. III (New York and London, 1993)). This is the work that Dante's Paolo and Francesca were reading when they fell in love (*Inferno* V.127–38).

3217 N. Davis (*MÆ*, 40 (1971), 75–80, at p. 79) compares the use of 'forncast', meaning 'planned or arranged beforehand, premeditated', at Pars 448 and *TC* III.521, and cites examples of similar combinations with 'imagine' or 'imaginacioun' to show that the phrase means something like 'malice aforethought'. (The same conclusion was reached independently by K. P. Wentersdorf, *Studia neophilologica*, 52 (1980), 31–4.) The phrase thus refers to the fox's treacherous scheming rather than to divine foreknowledge or to Chauntecleer's dream.

3227 *Scariot . . . Geniloun*: Judas Iscariot was the betrayer of Christ (Matthew 26, Mark 14, Luke 22, John 13, 18). On Ganelon, the famous traitor of the *Song of Roland*, see n. to Sh 194 and cf. Mk 2389.

3228 *Sinoun*: On the Greek Sinon, who tricked the Trojans into taking the Trojan horse into their city, see n. to Sq 209–10.

3234–44 Chaucer (in the persona of the Nun's Priest) here comically assumes a helpless incompetence on the subject of the relationship between destiny and free will, of which he elsewhere shows a deep understanding (see Mann, 'Chance and Destiny', and cf. Kn 1663–9 and n.). The major influence on Chaucer's thinking on this question was Boethius, whose *Consolation of Philosophy* Chaucer had translated; for Boethius's attempt to resolve the apparent conflict between God's knowledge of things to come and the freedom of the human will by distinguishing between time and eternity, see next n. Chaucer also invokes St Augustine (AD 354–430), whose treatise 'On Grace and Free Will' (tr. P. Holmes, *A Select Library of the Nicene and Post-Nicene Fathers of the Christian Church*, ed. P. Schaff, vol. V (New York, 1887; repr. Grand Rapids, MI, 1971), pp. 443–65) was directed against the followers of the contemporary heretic Pelagius, who emphasized the role of free will, rather than divine grace, as the means to salvation (see also Augustine, *City of God* V.8–11). Thomas Bradwardine (*c.* 1290–1349) was an Oxford theologian who was for a short period archbishop of Canterbury. His long treatise *De causa dei* was written to combat the views of those contemporary theologians whom he called 'the new Pelagians'. 'Bradwardine's reply was to reassert God's grace to the exclusion of all merit ... the whole world became, in effect, nothing more than the extension of God's will, with no part of it capable of acting but by His immutable decree' (G. Leff, *Bradwardine and the Pelagians* (Cambridge, 1957), p. 15). Bradwardine was employed as chaplain and confessor to Edward III, and accompanied the young king on his Crécy campaign (ibid., pp. 2–3), so that 'some of Chaucer's senior colleagues at court may well have been able to remember him' (R. F. Green, *A Crisis of Truth* (Philadelphia, PA, 1999), p. 357).

3245–50 This distinction between simple necessity and conditional necessity derives from Boethius, *Consolation of Philosophy* V pr.6. Simple necessity inheres in the nature of things (the examples given are that all men are mortal, or that the sun rises), whereas conditional necessity inheres in a reciprocally defining relationship between the knower and the known (thus, *if* one knows that a man is walking, then of necessity he must be walking – otherwise the knowledge is not knowledge). Since God knows all things, whether past, present or future, in his eternally present moment, his knowledge of a contingent event at any of these times means that it is bound by conditional necessity. But that does not destroy the free will of the human agent to determine her/his course of action, since he/she is not acting in an eternal present but in linear time. This sort of necessity, therefore, exists when things are seen from the perspective of divine knowledge, but not when they are considered in themselves.

3256 This is a proverbial saying, which is originally found in Old Norse; Singer suggests that it was brought to England by the Vikings (I, 22). It is included in the mid-twelfth-century work known as the *Proverbs of Alfred* (see Whiting R66) (Pearsall, *Variorum: Nun's Priest's Tale*, p. 221). A Latin version is listed in Walther 3181: 'Consilium rere fore frigens in muliere' ('Believe that a woman's counsel is cold').

3258 See Genesis 3.

3260–66 Chaucer is mimicking, and in all likelihood ridiculing, the conventional apologies to women made by numerous medieval writers (including Chaucer himself) after having made slighting remarks about them or portrayed them in an unflattering light; for other examples, see J. Mann, *Apologies to Women* (Cambridge, 1991). Whereas other writers evade responsibility for their remarks by attributing them to previous authors, whose opinion they claim to be merely reporting, Chaucer (in the persona of the Nun's Priest) nonsensically claims to be reporting the words of the cock, who has said nothing for the last fifty lines.

3270–72 'Physiologus' ('the Naturalist') is the name given to the putative author of the Latin (originally Greek) bestiary, which exists in several versions. As well as real animals and birds, the bestiaries include a number of fabulous creatures (centaurs, griffins, etc.), among which are the sirens, the deceptive song-stresses of the sea, who lure sailors to their deaths with their sweet music. The sirens were originally supposed to have a lower body in the shape of a bird, but over time they were also credited with the fish-tail of the mermaid. See F. McCulloch, *Mediaeval Latin and French Bestiaries*, rev. edn (Chapel Hill, NC, 1962), pp. 166–9, and S. de Rachewiltz, *De Sirenibus: An Inquiry into Sirens from Homer to Shakespeare* (New York, 1987), pp. 86–120; for an illustration of this hybrid creature, based on a medieval manuscript, see T. H. White, *The Bestiary: A Book of Beasts* (New York, 1954), p. 135.

3279–81 Although not noted in any Chaucer edition to date, the obvious source for this statement is Seneca, *Moral Epistles* CXXI.18–21, which argues that all animals have a naturally implanted knowledge of which other animals are dangerous to them. This is a very much closer parallel than the passage of Fulgentius (*Mythologiae* I.6) cited by *Riverside*, or the passage of Pliny (*Natural History* X.95.204) cited by Pearsall (*Variorum: Nun's Priest's Tale*, p. 227, where 45 is a mistake for 95).

3293–4 Boethius, author of the *Consolation of Philosophy*, also wrote a treatise on music (*De institutione musica*, ed. G. Friedlein (Leipzig, 1867); tr. by C. M. Bower as *Fundamentals of Music* (New Haven, CT, 1989)). This work 'became the basic text in music studied as one of the liberal arts of the quadrivium' in medieval universities (Bower, p. xiii).

3297 *to my greet ese*: That is, the fox has eaten them.

3312–16 *Burnel the Asse*: The ass Burnellus (or Brunellus) is the hero of the *Mirror for Fools*, a late twelfth-century Latin beast epic in elegiac verse, written by Nigel of Longchamp (formerly called Wireker), a monk of Christ Church, Canterbury (*Speculum Stultorum*, ed. J. H. Mozley and R. R. Raymo (Berkeley, CA, 1960), and tr. G. W. Regenos as *The Book of Daun Burnel the Ass* (Austin, TX, 1959); abridged tr. by J. H. Mozley, *A Mirror for Fools* (Oxford, 1961)). On the relation between the *Mirror for Fools* and NPT, see Headnote. The story referred to here is related to the ass by a travelling companion on the road to Paris (lines 1251–1502). A young boy named Gundulf, while chasing chickens out of the family barn, broke the leg of a chick with his stick. Brooding on this injury for six years, the now grown-up cock finally took his revenge by failing to crow on the day when the boy was due to go to town and be ordained to the priesthood, so that the family slept in and missed the ordination ceremony. The comic implication is that, just as human beings might read stories about their own kind, so animals read beast literature. There is even a suggestion, in the phrase 'his vers', that the *Mirror for Fools* might have been written by Burnellus the Ass, rather than about him.

3325–8 R. A. Pratt (*Speculum*, 41 (1966), 619–42, at pp. 635–6) compares these lines with a passage in the *Communiloquium* of John of Wales.

3329 'Ecclesiaste' usually refers to the biblical book of Ecclesiasticus (see WB 651 and n. and cf. n. to Mil 3530), but the verses that have been suggested as the subject of this reference (11:31; 12:10, 11, 16; 27:26) concern deception rather than flattery. K. Sisam (ed., *The Nun's Priest's Tale* (Oxford, 1927), pp. 52–3) suggested that 'Ecclesiaste' referred to the author of all the 'Solomonic' books of the Bible, and proposed Proverbs 29:5 (which is quoted at Mel 1179 among other warnings against flattery) as the text that Chaucer had in mind. Pearsall (*Variorum: Nun's Priest's Tale*, p. 234) suggests Proverbs 26:28, 28:23 as further possibilities.

3334 'Russell' means 'reddish', and is thus an appropriate name for the fox. In beast epic the fox is usually called Reynard, and it is the squirrel who is called 'Rousseau' or 'Rousel', and the name 'Rossel' is sometimes given to one of the fox's sons; see Pratt,

Speculum, 47 (1972), 652–3. Pratt suggests that in avoiding the name Reynard, Chaucer was trying to keep his own tale separate from the French Reynard-cycle and its many descendants.

3338 This comment on the inescapable nature of destiny is swiftly and comically belied by the fact that Chauntecleer escapes death with ease – whereupon the narrator substitutes a moralizing reflection on the sudden changeability of Fortune (3403–4). For a serious view of the relation of destiny and Fortune, as expounded in Boethius's *Consolation of Philosophy* and dramatized in Chaucer's more serious works, see n. to Kn 1663–9, and Mann, 'Chance and Destiny', esp. pp. 106–7.

3346 The Latin name for Friday is *dies Veneris* ('the day of Venus'); the English name depends on the identification of Venus with the Norse goddess Frig, wife of Woden. Cf. Kn 1534–9.

3347–51 *Gaufred*: Geoffrey of Vinsauf, author of a Latin treatise on rhetoric entitled the *Poetria Nova*, which was composed around 1210. One of Geoffrey's examples of apostrophe (lines 367–430, tr. Nims, pp. 29–31) is a lament on the death of Richard I (the Lionheart), king of England, who was fatally wounded by an arrow on Friday, 26 March 1199, while fighting in France (see J. Gillingham, *Speculum*, 54 (1979), 18–41). The lament apostrophizes the 'tearful day of Venus' ('O Veneris lacrimosa dies!') on which he met his doom. This section of the *Poetria Nova* was glossed, quoted and anthologized in the Middle Ages (see K. Young, *MP*, 41 (1944), 172–82).

3352 Since Richard did not die until eleven days after being wounded, on Tuesday, 6 April, this statement is technically incorrect.

3356–9 *Ilioun . . . Pirrus . . . Eneydos*: Ilium is the name given to the inner citadel at Troy; see n. to ML 289. Pyrrhus, son of Achilles, broke into the palace of Priam, king of Troy, and killed him. The account of this event in the *Aeneid* (II.469–558) describes the female shrieks and wails that accompanied it. Cf. ML 288 and n.

3363–8 The Hasdrubal in question is not the brother of Hannibal, but the Carthaginian leader who was defeated by Scipio Africanus the Younger in 146 BC. When Carthage was taken, he threw himself at Scipio's feet and asked for pardon; his wife reproached him for his cowardice and cast herself and her children into the flames that were consuming the city. Chaucer certainly knew Jerome's brief account of her suicide (*Against Jov.* I.43; cf. Fkl 1399 and n. to Fkl 1367–1456), and may also have read Valerius Maximus, *Memorable Doings and Sayings* III.2, ext.8.

3370–72 This (alleged) deed of Nero is also referred to at Mk 2479–81; see n. to Mk 2463–2550.

3375–82 The witness to a crime had a duty to 'raise the hue and cry' – that is, to call out and summon the neighbourhood to help catch the criminal (Hornsby, p. 140). 'Out!' and 'Harrow!' were both cries used in this context.

3380 *Riverside* includes 'and' in the exclamation, but this makes it rather ludicrous, as Pearsall notes (*Variorum: Nun's Priest's Tale*, p. 245).

3381 The pursuit of a fox who is making off with a cock or goose is a frequent subject in medieval English carvings and pictures; see K. Varty, *Reynard the Fox* (Leicester, 1967), pp. 37–41 (revised and expanded as *Reynard, Renart, Reinaert and Other Foxes in Medieval England: The Iconographic Evidence* (Amsterdam, 1999), pp. 36–48). A woman carrying a distaff (cf. NP 3384) is often depicted in these scenes.

3394–6 *Jakke Straw*: Jack Straw is named in several contemporary chronicles as one of the leaders of the Peasants' Revolt in 1381. The rebels killed all the Flemings they could find in London (cf. n. to Co 4357, and see R. B. Dobson, *The Peasants' Revolt of 1381* (London, 1970), pp. 162, 175, 188–8, 201, 206, 210), presumably because they blamed the interference of foreign financial interests for their own troubles. Since Chaucer was living in London at the time, he very probably witnessed much of the violence at first hand (Pearsall, *Life*, p. 146). For a discussion of his likely reactions, see G. Kane, in *Lexis and Texts in Early English: Studies Presented to Jane Roberts*, ed. C. J. Kay and L. M. Sylvester (Amsterdam and Atlanta, GA, 2001), pp. 161–71. The noise made by the rebels seems to have made a great impression on those who heard it; see S. Justice, *Writing and Rebellion: England in 1381* (Berkeley, CA, 1994), pp. 206–8. Ian Bishop suggests that Chaucer is here parodying Gower's *Vox Clamantis*, in which the Peasants' Revolt is presented as a furious rampage by various kinds of animals (*RES*, n.s. 30 (1979), 257–67, at pp. 263–4).

3415–16 The cock tricks the fox into forgetting that speech is not merely ideational, but has a physical aspect also. The contrast between these two aspects of speech is part of the larger interplay between the verbal and the physical that characterizes both beast fable and beast epic; see Mann, *Ysengrimus*, pp. 58–77, and *A la recherche du Roman de Renart*, ed. K. Varty, vol. I (New Alyth, Perth., 1988), pp. 135–62, esp. pp. 146–55.

3422   out of the yerd*] into this yerd El Hg. It is difficult to see how the El/Hg reading could have arisen, but sense rules it out.

3426–35   The cock-and-fox story is unusual in having *two* concluding morals: beast fables usually end in one moral, while the episodes of beast epic have none at all. Because of this narrative duality, which means that each animal is both trickster and tricked, this particular story resists the moral closure characteristic of beast fable, and can be adapted to the comic world of beast epic.

3441–2   The reference is to Romans 15:4. Cf. *RR* 15171–3, tr. Horgan, p. 235.

3443   The *Testament* of Jean de Meun ends with a similar exhortation to the reader to take the wheat and blow away the chaff (lines 2111–12). Cf. ML 701–2 and n., Pars 35–6, *LGW* G 312, 529.

3446   thy*] his El Hg. The switch from 'thy' in line 3444 to 'his' in the El/Hg version of line 3446 is puzzling; even more so is the parenthetical 'As seyth my lord' in line 3445. It is not clear which lord (human or divine?) is in question, and the third-person phrase oddly turns a direct address to God into something like a quotation. The reference may be to Christ's prayer in Gethsemane (Matthew 26:39, 42), but a marginal gloss in El and Hg reads '[El only: scilicet] dominus Archiepiscopus Cantuariensis' ('that is, the lord Archbishop of Canterbury'). As head of the Church, the Archbishop would be the Priest's ultimate superior, but attempts to find a similar prayer formula associated with the contemporary Archbishop, William Courtenay, have been unsuccessful. For discussion of the problems and various proposed solutions, see Pearsall, *Variorum: Nun's Priest's Tale*, pp. 257–8, and P. J. C. Field, *MÆ*, 71 (2002), 302–6. I have emended 'his' to 'thy' in order to achieve surface coherence with the minimum of interference.

THE NUN'S PRIEST'S EPILOGUE

3447–62   The epilogue appears in nine MSS (Manly and Rickert IV, 516), but not in El or Hg; the text given here is based on Cambridge, University Library, MS Dd.4.24. *Riverside* prints this epilogue in the text of *CT*, in square brackets; the Textual Notes (p. 1133) accept the general view that it is a link later cancelled by Chaucer and reworked into the Monk's Prologue (cf. NP 3451 with Mk 1945). Although these lines are generally of a much higher quality than the clearly spurious links produced by scribes who wished to fill gaps between the tales (see *Riverside* Textual Notes for examples), the conventionality and non-specificity ('another') of the last two lines have a distinctly scribal character, and it may be that the whole passage is a clever imitation of Chaucer's manner by an unusually talented scribe. For a full review of the various arguments advanced by scholars, see Pearsall, *Variorum: Nun's Priest's Tale*, pp. 87–91. Because of its doubtful authenticity, the Epilogue is set here in italics.

THE SECOND NUN'S PROLOGUE

As elsewhere in *CT*, Chaucer switches to rhyme royal for this religious tale (see n. to ML 96). The content of the Second Nun's Prologue is a composite of several elements, some with obvious sources, some not. The first part (lines 1–28) develops the conventional idea that 'the devil finds work for idle hands to do' (see next note). C. Brown, rejecting Skeat's suggestion that it was inspired by Jean de Vignay's introduction to his French translation of the *Golden Legend*, pointed out that 'similar remarks upon Idleness were frequently expressed by authors and translators when they took pen in hand', and went on to give examples (*MP*, 9 (1911), 1–16, at pp. 1–4). There follows an Invocation to Mary (29–84), the first part of which is largely based on Dante's *Paradiso*, XXXIII.1–21 (see nn. to SN 30–56). The interpretation of Cecilia's name in the last part of the Prologue (85–119) is taken, as a marginal gloss in El and Hg makes clear, from the life of Cecilia in the *Golden Legend* of Jacopo da Varazze (Jacobus de Voragine), called in the gloss 'Januensis', 'of Genoa', as at the opening of his work; Varazze is on the Genoese Riviera and Jacopo was arch-bishop of Genoa from 1292 to 1298.

1   *norice unto vices*: Proverbial. See the *Distichs of Cato* I.2, and for various formulations of this idea in English, see Whiting I6; cf. also the quotation of Ecclesiasticus 33:29 at Mel 1589.

2–3   In the *Romance of the Rose* (573–92, tr. Horgan, p. 11), the female door-keeper who admits the Lover into the garden of Pleasure (Deduit) is called Idleness (Oiseuse). Cf. Kn 1940 and Pars 714.

19   *seen*: This is the reading of El/Hg (and other MSS). Manly and Rickert and *Riverside* prefer the alternative reading 'syn', but this extends the sentence into the next stanza and makes the syntax over-complicated, as well as blurring the thought. The idea here is that even without the fear of death or hell, people

can see that idleness produces nothing and is parasitic on the
work of others.

27   In hagiographical and patristic writings, the roses conventionally
      signify martyrdom and the lilies chastity. See J. L. Lowes, *PMLA*,
      26 (1911), 315–23, and *PMLA*, 29 (1914), 129–33. Cf. SN
      220–21.

30   St Bernard of Clairvaux (*c.* 1090–1153) was known for his
      devotion to the Virgin; however, the invocation in lines 36–56
      is not based on any of his writings but on the hymn to Mary
      that Dante places in his mouth in *Paradiso* XXXIII.1–21. See
      following notes.

36   Cf. Dante, *Paradiso* XXXIII.1: 'Vergine madre, figlia del tuo
      figlio' ('Virgin mother, daughter of thy son'; tr. Singleton). The
      repetition of 'thou', which occurs throughout the Invocation but
      is specially noticeable in this stanza, is a stylistic pattern influ-
      enced by classical and biblical models; see P. M. Clogan, *Med-
      Hum*, n.s. 3 (1972), 213–40, at p. 222.

37   *welle of mercy*: The Latin equivalent of this phrase, 'fons pietatis',
      is a frequent appellation of Mary in Latin hymns (Salzer,
      Sinnbilder, pp. 323, 521; for further examples in Latin, French
      and Italian, see J. L. Lowes, *MP*, 15 (1917), 193–202, at p. 194
      and n. 4).

39   The line translates Dante, *Paradiso* XXXIII.2: 'umile e alta più
      che creatura'.

40–42 These lines echo Dante, *Paradiso* XXXIII.4–6: 'tu se' colei che
      l'umana natura | nobilitasti sì, che'l suo fattore | non disdegnò di
      farsi sua fattura' ('thou art she who didst so ennoble human
      nature that its Maker did not disdain to become its creature'; tr.
      Singleton).

43–5 Cf. Dante, *Paradiso* XXXIII.7–9: 'Nel ventre tuo si raccese
      l'amore, | per lo cui caldo ne l'etterna pace | così è germinato
      questo fiore' ('In thy womb was rekindled the Love under whose
      warmth this flower in the eternal peace has thus unfolded'; tr.
      Singleton). However, as C. Brown pointed out (*MP*, 9 (1911),
      6), the wording is closer to the opening of a poem attributed to
      Venantius Fortunatus (*Opera Poetica*, ed. F. Leo, (Berlin, 1881),
      p. 385): 'Quem terra pontus aethera | colunt adorant praedicant, |
      trinam regentem machinam | claustrum Mariae baiulat' ('Mary's
      cloister [her womb] bears the burden of the ruler of the threefold
      cosmos, whom earth, sea and air worship, adore and proclaim').

50–51 These lines echo Dante, *Paradiso* XXXIII.19–21: 'In te miser-
      icordia, in te pietate, | in te magnificenza, in te s'aduna | quan-

tunque in creatura è di bontate' ('In thee is mercy, in thee pity, in thee munificence, in thee is found whatever of goodness is in any creature'; tr. Singleton).

52 *sonne of excellence*: The Virgin was often called 'sun' in Latin hymns. See Salzer, *Sinnbilder*, pp. 394–9).

53–6 These lines render Dante, *Paradiso* XXXIII.16–18: 'La tua benignità non pur soccorre | a chi domanda, ma molte fïate | liberamente al dimandar precorre' ('Thy loving-kindness not only succors him who asks, but oftentimes freely foreruns the asking'; tr. Singleton).

lives leche: medical metaphors, including *vitae medica/medicina* ('doctor/medicine of life') were frequently applied to the Virgin. See Salzer, *Sinnbilder*, pp. 513–15.

58 *flemed wrecche*: See n. to SN 62. The idea that life on earth is an exile from one's heavenly home is fundamental to Boethius's *Consolation of Philosophy* (see esp. IV m.1), and appears in Chaucer's 'Balade de Bon Conseil' ('Truth'), 17–19.

59–61 See Matthew 15:21–8.

62 *sone of Eve*: The phrase is obviously unsuited to the female teller of this tale. The phrase 'exiled sons of Eve' occurs in the famous Marian anthem 'Salve regina' (see *SA²* I, 502–3), and also, as F. Tupper (*MLN*, 30 (1915), 5–12, at pp. 9–11) and C. Brown (ibid., 231–2) pointed out, in the Little Office of the Virgin (see n. to Pri 517), but although this is a likely source of Chaucer's phrase (and also for 'flemed wrecche' at SN 58), the use of the masculine singular still seems incongruous in context. It is likely that the phrase reflects the original composition of the life of St Cecilia as an independent work (see Headnote to SNT), and refers to Chaucer himself. When he inserted the life into *CT*, he presumably failed to notice the resulting anomaly.

64 James 2:17.

70 On Mary's mother Anne, see n. to ML 641.

71–3 The notion that the body was the prison of the soul derives from Greek thought, and was widely disseminated in both classical and biblical literature. See, for example, *Aeneid* VI.734; Prudentius, *Psychomachia* 904–7; Augustine, *Enarrationes in Psalmos* CXLI.18 (CCSL 40, p. 2058), and cf. G. Bauer, *Claustrum Animae. Untersuchungen zur Geschichte der Metapher vom Herzen als Kloster* (Munich, 1973), pp. 66–7. J. L. Lowes (*MP*, 15 (1917), pp. 196–7) sees the immediate source of these lines in Macrobius's *Commentary on the Dream of Scipio* (I.x.6 and I.xi.3, tr. Stahl, pp. 127, 130–31), since Macrobius also speaks of the 'contagion of the body' ('contagio corporis') in the same section of his commentary (I.xi.11, tr. Stahl, pp. 132–3. See also I.viii.8, tr. Stahl, p. 122). (The Latin passages are also reproduced in *SA*, pp. 666–7.) However, Servius's commentary on *Aeneid* VI also speaks of the body as both prison and contagion (Lowes, pp. 197–8).

75   *havene of refut*: See n. to ML 852.

78   *reden that I write*: This reference to reading and writing is inconsistent with the fictional supposition that the Prologue is orally delivered by the Second Nun to the listening pilgrims. Presumably it is another survival from the independent composition of this tale (see n. to SN 62).

85–119 As a marginal gloss in El and Hg makes clear, the etymological explanations in these lines are taken from the *Golden Legend* (see Headnote to SNPr, and, for a text and translation, *SA²* I, 504–5). They are based on Latin phrases approximating to Cecilia's name: 'hevenes lilye' translates *caeli lilia*; 'the wey to blinde' translates *caecis via*; 'hevene' and 'lia' represent *coelum* and *lya*; 'Wantinge of blindnesse' translates *caecitate carens*; 'hevene' and 'leos' represent *coelum* and *leos* (= Greek *laos*, 'people'). Such explanations of the name are more pious than accurate.

philosophres: The *Golden Legend* (see *SA²* I, 504–5) makes clear that this statement is taken from Isidore's *Etymologies* (III.xxxi.1): 'Caelum philosophi rotundum, volubile atque ardens esse dixerunt.'

THE SECOND NUN'S TALE

The legend of St Cecilia has no historical foundation, as H. Delehaye demonstrated (*Étude sur le légendier romain* (Brussels, 1936), pp. 73–88). No saint of this name is mentioned before the fifth century (well after the date of the Roman persecutions), when the story of her life was put together by the inventive author of the *Passio S. Caeciliae*, who drew on a number of conventional hagiographical motifs (the refusal of marriage, the refusal to worship Roman gods, conversion of pagans, the dialogue with a judge, conversion of a house into a church). Inscriptions in the catacombs of Praetextatus and Callixtus (see n. to SN 172) seem to have furnished the names of her martyred companions, Valerian, Tiburtius and Maximus; Caecilia herself, Delehaye suggests (pp. 84–6) may have been a Christian benefactress who founded the church in Trastevere that bears her name, and who thereby earned the honour of burial alongside martyrs and popes in the catacomb of Callixtus. The existence of a Roman bath (*calidarium*) next to the church seems to have suggested to the ingenious hagiographer the attempt to kill her by its means, and served as a spurious substantiation of the story (Delehaye, p. 84; see also n. to SN 515). The legend that the sixteenth-century statue of St Cecilia which now lies beneath the altar of her church represents the state of her body when her (purported) tomb was opened in 1599 is shown by Delehaye (pp. 88–96) to be equally apocryphal.

Chaucer's tale is drawn from two principal sources, both of them ultimately deriving from the *Passio S. Caeciliae*. The first part, from line 85 up to line 348, corresponds closely to the life of Cecilia in the *Golden Legend*, a collection of saints' lives compiled by the Dominican friar Jacopo da Varazze (Jacobus de Voragine), around 1260; this enormously popular work survives in over 1,000 manuscripts. The Latin text of this life is printed from a fourteenth-century English manuscript in *SA²* I, 504–17, with accompanying translation; for a critical edition of the whole work, see *Legenda Aurea*, ed. G. P. Maggioni, 2 vols. (Florence, 1998), II, 1180–87. Chaucer's source for the second part of the tale (line 349 to the end), as S. L. Reames demonstrated (*MP*, 87 (1990), 337–61), is an abridgement of the *Passio*, composed for liturgical use by the Roman curia and borrowed by the Franciscans (*SA²* I, 495), which survives in at least 20 manuscripts (text and translation in *SA²* I, 516–27). This abridgement is very much closer to the Second Nun's Tale than the text of the *Passio* contained in the fifteenth-century edition of Boninus Mombritius which was reproduced in *SA*, pp. 677–84, and its existence renders untenable the older view that in this part of the tale Chaucer was freely adapting and altering his source. In both parts of the tale, Chaucer follows his originals closely, as he himself indicates at lines 79–83. However, it is still necessary to explain why he should have switched from one source to the other. At the point where the shift is made, the *Golden Legend* has a long section describing in detail the interrogation of Valerian and Tiburtius by Almachius, and their conversation with Maximus. By following the abridgement at this point, Chaucer reduces this section to a summary (360–78), and so keeps the major focus on Cecilia and her altercation with the Roman prefect. This is in keeping with Chaucer's preference for female rather than male heroes in *CT* (see Mann, *Feminizing Chaucer*, p. 3).

'The lif ... of Seint Cecile' is mentioned in the list of Chaucer's works given in the Prologue to the *Legend of Good Women* (F 426, G 416), suggesting that he first wrote it as an independent work and later decided to incorporate it into *CT*. It is perhaps a mere coincidence that the name of the woman of whose 'raptus' (rape or abduction?) Chaucer was accused in 1380 was Cecily Champain (see C. Cannon, *Speculum*, 68 (1993), 74–94). G. H. Cowling (*Chaucer* (New York, 1927), p. 24) raised in passing the possibility of a connection between this puzzling incident and the Second Nun's Tale; for a recent reconsideration, see C. Cannon, *SAC*, 22 (2000), 67–92, at pp. 87–8. Another possibility, proposed by M. Giffin (*Studies on Chaucer and his Audience* (Hull, Quebec, 1956), pp. 31–40), is that the poem was prompted by the appointment of Adam Easton as Cardinal Priest of Santa Cecilia in Trastevere, at a date between December 1381 and December 1384. In 1383, Richard II and Queen Anne visited Norwich Cathedral Priory, where Easton had been a monk. Giffin suggests that Chaucer wrote the life of Cecilia for Richard II to present to the Benedictines of Norwich (p. 31); 'a poem honoring Easton's title of Santa Cecilia might have been persuasive toward obtaining the English cardinal's assistance in a difficult dispute with the papacy'. (See further J. C. Hirsh, *ChauR*, 12 (1977), 129–46, at pp. 129–30.)

129 *Valerian*: See Headnote.

134 *organs*: On the plural form of the word, and the type of organ referred to, see n. to NP 2851. This detail of the life of St Cecilia seems to have been the origin of the tradition that makes her the patron saint of music (see Farmer, *Dictionary of Saints*).

172 *Via Apia*: The Appian Way was (and is) a major Roman road, built in the fourth–third centuries BC, running from the city to Capua, Benevento and Brindisi. The section nearest Rome was lined on each side by the tombs of noble families. Underground are the catacombs, subterranean labyrinths hollowed out of the soft tufa rock, in which the early Christians buried their dead, and, according to legend, hid from their persecutors (see n. to SN 311–12). Cecilia is sending Valerian to make contact with the Christian community.

173 *but miles thre*: The Appian Way is not three miles away from Rome; it runs out of the city. Chaucer is apparently mistranslating the *Golden Legend*, which reads 'in tertium miliarium ab urbe' – that is, 'to the third milestone from the city'. The catacombs lie between the second and the third milestones.

177 Urban is later (SN 217) called a pope, and is thus presumably meant to be identified as Urban I (AD 222–30). However, Urban's pontificate 'fell wholly in the reign of Emperor Alexander Severus (222–35), which was free from persecution' (J. N. D. Kelly, *The*

Oxford Dictionary of Popes (Oxford and New York, 1986), p. 15). His association with the catacombs was perhaps suggested to the author of the *Passio S. Caeciliae* by a fragmentary epitaph to a 'bishop Urbanus' in the catacomb of Callixtus; an alternative tradition located the pope's burial-place in the catacomb of Praetextatus (Delehaye, pp. 80–81).

195 *bisy bee*: The phrase translates the *Golden Legend*'s 'apis argumentosa', but it is also proverbial in English; see Whiting B165, and cf. Mch 2422.

201 *An old man*: Probably St Paul, since the inscription he carries is close to Ephesians 4:5–6, but medieval liturgical texts suggest that he was also interpreted as 'a second angelic manifestation of Pope Urban' (*SA²* I, 499, 507 n.).

207–9 Cf. Ephesians 4:5–6.

220–21 See n. to SN 27.

242 *Tiburce*: See Headnote.

271–83 Chaucer is still translating the *Golden Legend*, which is quoting the Preface (a prayer introducing the central part of the mass) for St Cecilia's day according to the Ambrosian rite, so called because it was supposedly composed by St Ambrose, bishop of Milan (d. 347). See M. Henshaw, *MP*, 26 (1928), 15–16.

277 Valerians*] Cecilies El Hg. The emendation is supported by Ambrose's Preface (see preceding n.).

311–12 Legend has it that the early Christians used the catacombs to hide from their persecutors, but there is no historical evidence that this was in fact the case (J. Stevenson, *The Catacombs: Rediscovered Monuments of Early Christianity* (London, 1978), p. 24).

326–9 *Riverside* places a semi-colon at the end of line 327, but the Latin source shows that this line belongs syntactically with 328–9 (*SA²* I, 509:104, 511:105).

330 he goddes sone Hg] goddes sone El. Manly and Rickert and *Riverside* adopt the reading 'heigh', which has manuscript support, but 'he' is a 'harder' reading (on which see n. to Cl 508) and also closer to the Latin source, which reads 'Hic igitur filius Dei . . .' (*SA²* I, 511:105). For the construction, see Mustanoja, pp. 135–6.

337–41 The notion that the brain consisted of three separate cells, each with its own special function, was a common one (see n. to Kn 1376). V. A. Kolve argues that here 'engin' ('ingenium' in the source) represents the 'imaginative' or image-making faculty ('ymaginativa'), while 'intellect' represents the 'estimative' or judging faculty ('aestimativa' or 'logica'); see *Chaucer and the Imagery of Narrative* (Stanford, CA, 1984), pp. 380–81, n. 24. Memory stores the information derived from these two faculties. St Augustine compares the tripartite nature of the brain to the Trinity (*The Trinity* X.11–XII.4, tr. S. McKenna (Washington, DC, 1963), pp. 310–46).

362 *Almache*: The city prefect (*praefectus urbi*) of Rome was responsible for law and order in the city, and was directly answerable to the emperor (*Der Kleine Pauly. Lexikon der Antike*, 5 vols. (Stuttgart, 1964–75), s.v.). No prefect named Almachius is to be found in historical records (Delehaye, pp. 81–2).

369 Corniculars were subordinate officers who performed both clerical and military functions (*Der Kleine Pauly*, s.v. corniculum, cornicularii).

384–5 An echo of Romans 13:12.

386–8 An echo of 2 Timothy 4:7–8.

421–2 Almachius has already commanded Cecilia to be brought before him (see SN 410–13); S. L. Reames explains the duplication as a result of Chaucer switching back from his main source at this point, the Roman/Franciscan abridgement, to the *Golden Legend* (*MP*, 87 (1990), 346).

425 *a gentil womman born*: Cecilia's name would have been interpreted as an indication of her high social rank, since the *gens Caecilia* was one of the oldest families of Rome.

467 spareth] stareth El Hg. The Latin source at this point (*SA²* I, 525:171–2) reads 'Parcit et sevit, dissimulat et advertit' ('He [alternately] spares and rages, dissimulates and threatens') – presumably referring to Almachius's self-contradictory shift from aggressiveness to an attempt to persuade Cecilia to be reasonable and save herself. The Latin 'Parcit' supports the supposition that Chaucer wrote 'spareth' rather than 'stareth' (which is easily explicable as a variation to an easier reading), though Chaucer's rearrangement of the sentence alters the meaning slightly: 'Lo, he dissembles . . . he restrains himself [outwardly] and mentally rages.'

515 *a bath*: The author of the *Passio S. Caeciliae* probably conceived this as a Roman bath or hypocaust (a room with a space beneath the floor that was heated from conduits). As mentioned earlier (see Headnote), the building that became the Church of Santa Cecilia in Trastevere was adjacent to a bath of this type. Medieval illustrations of Cecilia's martyrdom showing her in a tub full of hot water reinterpret the bath in more familiar terms; see V. A.

Kolve, in *New Perspectives in Chaucer Criticism*, ed. D. M. Rose (Norman, OK, 1981), pp. 137–74.

545–6 The Roman/Franciscan abridgement here reads 'ut ... hanc domum meam in eternum ecclesie nomini consecrarem' ('so that I might ... dedicate this house of mine in perpetuity to the ownership of the church'; *SA²* I, 527:208–9). This detail was used by John Wyclif as evidence that lay persons could licitly perform minor sacraments, such as consecrations (Reames, *MP*, 87 (1990), 344). The *Golden Legend*, and many versions of the liturgy for St Cecilia's feast day, avoid the problem by reading 'consecrares' ('that you should consecrate . . .'; ibid., p. 344, nn. 20–22). Chaucer's use of the causative construction 'do werche' ('have made') 'can be understood as a very careful solution to the sticky problem', as Reames points out (ibid.).

550–53 The Church of St Cecilia in the district of Rome known as Trastevere ('across the Tiber') survives to the present day.

THE CANON'S YEOMAN'S PROLOGUE

Possibly because Chaucer was working on this tale shortly before his death, the Canon's Yeoman's Prologue and Tale are absent from Hg; the text given here is based on El.

The Canon and his Yeoman were evidently not part of Chaucer's original plan for *CT*, and their sudden intrusion on the pilgrim company, and on the by now settled pattern of tale-telling, is not easy to account for. Since there still remain a number of pilgrims who have not told a tale (such as the Yeoman, the Guildsmen and the Plowman), and in any case the plan outlined in the General Prologue is that each pilgrim should tell not one but four tales, Chaucer cannot have needed extra tellers. Chaucer's eighteenth-century editor Thomas Tyrwhitt supposed that 'some sudden resentment had determined Chaucer to interrupt the regular course of his work, in order to insert a satire against the alchemists' (quoted in Skeat, III, 493), but this is mere speculation, and there is in any case no reason why a tale about alchemy could not have been told by one of the existing pilgrims. Conversely, there is no obvious reason why Chaucer could not have revised the General Prologue to include another pilgrim, particularly in view of the fact that the total number he gives for the pilgrim company does not correspond with the number he names and describes (see n. to GP 24).

It is possible, as A. E. Hartung argued (*ChauR*, 12 (1977), 111–28) that the second part of the Canon's Yeoman's Tale, the story of the swindling alchemist-canon, was composed independently of *CT*, and that the first, 'autobiographical', part of the tale, along with the Prologue, was written later. The theory that the tale began life as a work independent of *CT* finds support in the fact that at lines 1409–25, the narrator consistently addresses alchemists as 'ye', suggesting that he does not consider himself as one of their number. The comparable use of the pre-existing 'lif . . . of Seint Cecile' as the Second Nun's Tale (see Headnote to SNT) suggests that at this stage of *CT* Chaucer might have been trying to save time by incorporating into the Canterbury collection works he had written earlier. Less likely is the suggestion made by P. Brown (*English Studies*, 64 (1983), 481–90), as a possible explanation for the 'gradual deterioration of literary quality from the Prologue through *prima pars* [= Part One] to *pars secunda* [= Part Two]', that Part Two may be by an imitator of Chaucer, or may be a story he had intended to rework but had not yet got around to. Despite the inferiority of Part Two to what precedes it, it seems unlikely to have been written by anyone but Chaucer, and the ending (CY 1453 ff.) is inspired.

H. G. Richardson (*Transactions of the Royal Historical Society*, 4th series, 5 (1922), 28–51, at pp. 38–40) drew attention to a case in the Plea Rolls for January 1375, in which a chaplain called William de Brumley confessed to having made four counterfeit pieces of gold, following the teaching given to him by William Shuchirch, canon of St George's chapel at Windsor. Hartung (p. 120) concurs with Manly's suggestion (*New Light*, pp. 244–8; Manly and Rickert IV, 521) that the apology to 'worshipful chanones religious' at CY 992 suggests that the canons of St George's (where Chaucer, in his capacity as Clerk of the King's Works, was overseeing repairs in the spring of 1390; see *Life-Records*, pp. 408–10), or the canons of one of the other collegiate churches in the London area, might have been the original audience of Part Two. However, there are similar direct addresses in *CT* (see, for example, Phys 72 ff., NP 3325 ff.), and the apology to a social group which might consider itself slandered by a narrative or remark, with a claim that it is only the guilty members of the group who are aimed at, is a conventional literary motif; there is no need therefore to interpret the address to canons as delivered in the flesh rather than on the page.

These problems by no means exhaust the difficulties of the Canon's Yeoman's Prologue and Tale. There is, for example, the question of whether the Canon of the Prologue and Part One is to be identified with the swindling canon of Part Two, even though the Yeoman firmly asserts that he is not (CY 1088–90). R. G. Baldwin's attempt to argue that they are identical is over-elaborate and generally unconvincing (*JEGP*, 61 (1962), 232–43), but he is right to point out (p. 234) that if the two canons are *not* identical, we have no warrant for thinking the first one to be guilty of the trickery of the second, and therefore cannot easily explain why the first one suddenly departs when his Yeoman begins to reveal his lack of success. The Yeoman's own sudden switch from boasting about his master's powers to withering scorn is equally hard to explain; he could have answered the Host's question as to why the Canon is so poorly dressed if he commands such wealth in the conventional way, by explaining that he disguises his riches in order to avoid exciting envy and enmity (cf. CY 1370–74). Another puzzle is why the Canon and his Yeoman needed to ride five miles at a gallop before overtaking a company, presumably travelling at walking-pace, which they had seen leaving the hostelry where they had all spent the night.

These puzzles suggest that the autobiographical mode in the Prologue and Tale is adopted not so much from an interest in personal psychology or history, as from a desire to give the paraphernalia and jargon of alchemy the immediacy of first-hand narration. If the General Prologue portraits immerse the reader in a series of specialized worlds founded in work (see Headnote to GP), the Canon's Yeoman's Prologue and Tale conjure up a specialized world *par excellence*, with its own discourse, tools, materials and beliefs. As with the clerk's removal of the rocks in the Franklin's Tale, it is hard to tell where advanced technology turns into magical sleight of hand.

556 'Blean Wood(s), forming the NE part of an extensive forest belt which once covered the greater part of Kent, formerly commenced at Boughton (*Boghtoun*) and reached almost to the walls of Canterbury; it still crosses W of Canterbury through parts of Harbledown' (Magoun, p. 32). Boughton is about five miles from Canterbury, and also somewhat less than five miles down the road from Ospring, a favourite overnight stop on the way to Canterbury (ibid., pp. 34, 119).

558 hadde a whit surplis*] wered a surplis El. The main point of mentioning the surplice seems to be identifying it as white, and thus indicating that its wearer is a canon (see n. to CY 573).

562 *yeman*: The term here simply denotes a personal servant; see L. Patterson, *SAC*, 15 (1993), 25–57, at p. 30, n. 14, and cf. n. to GP 101.

564–5 These lines are omitted in El (through eyeskip to the initial A of line 566?), but they seem authentically Chaucerian.

573 *som chanoun*: Canons were (and are) of two kinds: (1) secular canons, who (as their name implies) lived 'in the world' ('in saeculo'), serving a cathedral or collegiate church by singing the church services and looking after its upkeep; (2) regular canons, who (again, as their name implies) lived a communal life in conformity with the Rule of St Augustine (tr. R. Canning, with Introduction and Commentary by T. J. van Bavel (London, 1984)), or one of its derivatives. This Canon's clothing shows that he is a regular or Augustinian canon; he wears a black cloak and hood over a white surplice (under which is a black cassock, the 'oversloppe' of line 633), as was prescribed for canons going outside their convent (see M. P. Hamilton, *Speculum*, 16 (1941), 103–8); hence they were also often called 'black canons'. Like monks and friars, regular canons recited the eight daily services that make up the Divine Office (see n. to Mil 3655), but they differed from monks in that they were not vowed to strict claustration (see n. to GP 165), and from friars in that they were not vowed to mendicancy (see n. to GP 209).

611–12 The suspicion that there is a double meaning here (the Yeoman is willing to bet all he possesses because he in fact possesses nothing) is confirmed by lines 733–6, where he confesses himself destitute and in debt.

645–6 Proverbial; see Whiting E199, 200, 203 and Walther 19859.

669 *multiplye*: This is the term used to describe the final stage of the alchemist's work, the transmutation of metals, but it is also used of other alchemical processes, and 'some looseness of application can be detected in every period' (J. E. Grennen, *Classica et Mediaevalia*, 26 (1965), 306–33, at p. 321). 'To say that the word "multiply" is an important word in alchemy is to understate the case. There is hardly a treatise in which it does not figure prominently' (ibid., p. 320). See further Headnote to CYT.

688–9 *Catoun*: The reference is to the Latin proverb-collection known as the *Distichs of Cato* (see n. to Mil 3227), I.17: 'Ne cures, si quis tacito sermone loquatur: | conscius ipse sibi de se putat omnia dici' ('Pay no attention if someone speaks *sotto voce*; a self-conscious person thinks that he is the subject of every conversation').

704 *Riverside* puts a full stop at the end of this line, but it seems logically connected with 705.

THE CANON'S YEOMAN'S TALE

The Canon's Yeoman's Tale falls into two parts, designated 'prima pars' and 'pars secunda' by a rubric in El following line 972. It is not until Part Two that the narrative proper, the story of the tricks played by the swindling canon on the gullible priest, is reached. There are no known sources or close analogues for these particular instances of deception, though there are similar stories of alchemical confidence-tricks; see *SA*, pp. 688, 694–5, and *SA*² II.

Part One is not a tale at all but a long and confused description of alchemical practice. Alchemy in the Middle Ages was a serious pursuit, which 'can be seen as the *Prelude to Chemistry* and hence to modern science as a whole'; see Patterson, *SAC*, 15 (1993), p. 48. *Prelude to Chemistry: An Outline of Alchemy* is the title of a book by J. Read, 2nd edn (Cambridge, MA, 1966). The practical experiments that alchemists carried out contributed to knowledge of chemical elements and the possibilities for their modification; unfortunately, however, the theories on which alchemy was based were fundamentally mistaken, and the descriptions of its procedures in alchemical treatises were often deliberately mystifying.

Patterson (pp. 42–3) describes the principles of alchemy as follows:

The alchemical project relies on a radically monist view of the world. According to *The Visions of Zosimus*, a founding text of Western alchemy composed probably about 300 B.C.E., all natural generation, including animal, vegetable, and mineral, proceeds from 'one single nature reacting on itself, a single species.' . . . This monism was underwritten by a physics derived from Aristotle and then modified by Islamic science. For Aristotle, metals, like all other substances, consist of a prime matter 'formed' according to the proportion in which the four basic qualities – heat, cold, dryness, and moistness – are mixed. Minerals and metals are created through the interaction of the sun with water and with earth, interactions that generate either vaporous exhalations, which are cold and moist, or smoky exhalations, which are hot and dry. When shut in and compressed, these exhalations form all minerals and metals. Islamic alchemists subsequently identified the vaporous exhalation with sulfur, which was cold and moist, and the smoky exhalation with mercury, which was correspondingly hot and dry. Since these two 'spirits' were the constituent elements of all metals, transmutation could be accomplished by altering the proportions between them in any individual substance. Hence, as Albertus Magnus said, since 'nature could transform sulphur and mercury into metals by the aid of the sun and stars, it seemed reasonable that the alchemist should be able to do the same in his vessel.' Just as the human body becomes ill from an imbalance of the four elements (the humors), so does a metal: it can be 'cured' (that is, promoted from base to pure) by the addition of a medicine – an elixir – that readjusts the proportions of the four elements. In this sense the alchemist does not violate but perfects nature ... And the elixir that accomplishes this completion of nature's work is the philosopher's stone: it embodies the divine *pneuma* or *spiritus* from which the world is constituted, the quintessence that [a] late-medieval English text called 'Gods Prevetie'.

Compare Jean de Meun's account of alchemy in the *Romance of the Rose*, 16083–118 (tr. Horgan, pp. 248–9), which is prefaced by a reference to the transformation of fern ashes into glass (cited at Sq 253–5):

The same could be done with metals, if one could manage to do it, by removing impurities from the impure metals and refining them into a pure state; they are of similar complexion and have great affinities with one another, for they are all of one substance, no matter how Nature may modify it. Books tell us that they were all born in different ways, in mines down in the earth, from sulphur and quicksilver. And so, if anyone had the skill to prepare spirits in such a way that they had the power to enter bodies but were unable to fly away once they had entered, provided they found the bodies to be well purified, and provided the sulphur, whether white or red, did not burn, a man with such knowledge might do what he liked with metals. The masters of alchemy produce pure gold from pure silver, using things that cost almost nothing to add weight and colour to them; with pure gold they make precious stones, bright and desirable, and they strip other metals of their forms, using potions that are white and penetrating and pure to transform them into pure silver. But such things will never be achieved by those who indulge in trickery: even if they labour all their lives, they will never catch up with Nature.

Gower also gives a brief but accurate account of alchemy at *CA* IV.2457–2632.

For historical accounts of alchemy, see F. S. Taylor, *The Alchemists: Founders of Modern Chemistry* (New York, 1949), and E. J. Holmyard, *Alchemy* (Harmondsworth, 1957). For attitudes to alchemy in the medieval West, see W. H. L. Ogrine, *Journal of Medieval History*, 6 (1980), 103–32. Medieval alchemical treatises which may be conveniently consulted are *The Works of Geber, Englished by Richard*

Russell, 1678, ed. E. J. Holmyard (London, 1928), hereafter cited as *Geber* (the earliest manuscripts of the Latin text translated by Russell date from the thirteenth century, and it purportedly derives from an eighth-century Arabic original by Jabir ibn Hayyan, known as 'Geber' in the West); the translated extracts from Albertus Magnus in Grant, *Source Book*, pp. 586–603; and *Thomas Norton's Ordinal of Alchemy* (late fifteenth century), ed. J. Reidy, EETS o.s. 272 (London, 1975). Also useful is L. Abraham, *A Dictionary of Alchemical Imagery* (Cambridge, 1998). Although the Yeoman, as befits a mere layman (see CY 787), gives only a confused account of alchemical theory and practice, the tale nevertheless presents evidence of Chaucer's considerable knowledge of alchemy, as E. H. Duncan has shown in a detailed comparison with medieval alchemical treatises (*MP*, 37 (1940), 241–62: cited as 'Duncan' in subsequent notes).

Whatever Chaucer's attitude to the serious practice of alchemy, there is no doubt that the canon is an out-and-out trickster. The bewildering terminology that proliferates in the first part of the tale suggests that such trickery is facilitated by the specialized language of the craft ('termes'), which makes it impossible for the layman to distinguish science from gibberish. Language takes on a life of its own, constructing a kind of alternative reality which cannot be empirically tested and has to be taken on trust. 'Chaucer ... suggests that the multiplication of metals and the multiplication of words are analogous phenomena: the alchemist's nostalgia, from his world of confusion, proliferative materials, and opaque jargon, is in some part a longing for a world of transparent language before Babel' (J. Fyler, *ELH*, 55 (1988), 1–26, at p. 12; see also n. to CY 669). In contrast to the etymological explanation of Cecilia's name (SN 85–119 and n.), which seeks to demonstrate the unity of words and meaning, the Canon's Yeoman's Tale 'raises the problem of the verbal representation of truth with a special intensity and sophistication' (Patterson, p. 39; cf. pp. 32–3). The tale concludes with an anecdote that shows verbal definitions leading, not to understanding, but to an apparently endless chain of linguistic substitution which never makes contact with the physical world. In Patterson's words (p. 48), alchemy discloses 'not the secrets of nature but the guilty secrets of language'. For a poet, this notion of the power of words to create a substitute reality must have been empowering and disabling in roughly equal measure.

720–21 Seven years was the minimum term of service for apprentices; in lamenting that he has learned nothing during that time, the Yeoman 'echoes the frequent complaints by apprentices of the failure of their masters to teach them their craft' (Patterson, *SAC*, 15 (1993), p. 30, n. 14).

726 Although it is not independently attested until the late sixteenth century, the Yeoman is evidently referring to the proverb 'A man is a man though he have but a hose on his head' (see *Oxford Dictionary of English Proverbs*[3], pp. 504–5, and Tilley M244). Presumably one leg of a pair of hose made a warm piece of headgear for those who could not afford a hat.

750 ff. The Yeoman's account of his 'elvisshe craft' is 'a confused conglomeration of materials, animal, vegetable and mineral, of apparatus and of processes, coming helter-skelter from his bedazzled brain' (Duncan, p. 245). Nevertheless, comparison with medieval alchemical treatises makes it possible to piece together the processes in which many of these elements were involved, as Duncan explains. The alchemist's aim was to transmute a lower or baser metal to a higher one by altering the proportions of their constituent elements (see Headnote to CYT).

> In order that the work of transmutation might be carried out, two sorts of operations were required: one set designed to remove the impurities of the metals to be transmuted to a purer state, another set designed to supply the deficiencies, by means of an Elixir, Philosopher's Stone, or Medicine, which, joined to the outwardly purified lower metal, would raise it to the nature of the higher one.
>
> (Duncan, p. 243)

The first operation involves sublimation (referred to at 770, 774), which 'consists in heating a substance until it vaporizes and then condensing the vapour directly back to the solid state by rapid cooling' (Holmyard, *Alchemy*, p. 46; cf. *Geber*, pp. 74–5). The material to be sublimated is placed in the bottom of a vessel; the fire separates the 'impure' elements from the higher 'spiritual' ones, which are deposited as crystals in the cool upper part of the vessel (Read, *Prelude to Chemistry*, p. 138). The impure elements are assimilated into other substances (known as 'feces') – such as the burned bones and iron flakes mentioned at 759, or the salt mentioned at 762 – which are introduced into the pot at the same time as the metal to be purified. Also used as feces are chalk, alkali (impure sodium carbonate) and metal filings ('limaille'); see CY 806, 810, 853, and Duncan, p. 256. The vessel used for this process was a sublimatory (793), a solid vessel in two parts. The lower part was a large round dish or bowl made of earthenware (761), heavily glazed inside; the upper part was a conical lid made of glass (*Geber*, pp. 90–91; for an illustration of such a vessel, see *Geber*, p. 233, reproduced in Holmyard as Figure 8). The joins of the vessel were luted (cf. the reference to 'enluting' at 766) – that is, daubed with clay so as to make it airtight (Duncan, pp. 250–51). The clay made of human or horse's hair (812) was probably used for luting (Duncan, p. 257; cf. Holmyard, p. 49).

According to Duncan's analysis, over half the alchemical items mentioned by the Yeoman can be connected with the process mentioned at line 816, the 'citrination' of silver, which Duncan (p. 249), paraphrasing Geber's alchemical treatise, describes as follows: 'It is possible to transmute silver into gold, or at least to *color* it so that it looks like gold, by projecting upon the metal, or fusing into the metal, under extreme heat, the carefully prepared and refined substance of certain red- or yellow-colored compounds of sulphur or mercury.' (For the fundamental importance of sulphur and mercury in alchemical thinking, see Headnote to CYT.) The starting-point of the experiment is thus the 'five or sixe ounces ... of silver' mentioned at CY 756–7. The Yeoman refers to two 'medicines' suitable for the transmuting process: the first is 'sublimed mercurye' (774) – that is, a red powder produced from 'mercurye crude' (771–2) by 'calcening' or 'calcinacioun' (771, 804), the reduction of a substance to powder by heat. The second is 'orpiment' (759, 774), 'a yellow powder known to modern chemistry as the trisulphide of arsenic' (Duncan, p. 252); cf. the reference to arsenic at line 798.

Having 'sublimed' either or both of these materials twenty times or so, to ensure that his 'medicine' was pure, the alchemist would then have dissolved the resultant powder in liquid and mixed the solution with part of the dissolved silver, 'coagulated them, and projected the coagulate mass upon the remainder of the silver in flux, that is, molten' (Duncan, p. 258). The silver would then take on a 'citrine' colour and the experiment would be complete.

The alchemist's final task would be to test that the metal he had produced was really gold; Duncan (pp. 258–9), still following Geber, describes various tests of this sort which require the use of ashes (807), burned bones (759), urine (807) and bull's gall (797). See *Geber*, pp. 183, 186, 208.

762 According to Duncan (p. 251), there is no obvious reason why pepper should have been added to the pot, and it seems to owe

its presence to the fact that 'the mention of salt inevitably calls up pepper'. Maybe this is a private joke on Chaucer's part.

768 See n. to CY 922–9.

775 The porphyry stone was used as a hard surface on which materials could be ground with a pestle (Grant, *Source Book*, pp. 594, 597).

778–9 On the 'spirites', see n. to CY 820–24. The Yeoman is referring to the process of sublimation (see n. to CY 750 ff.); the spirits vaporize and then form crystals on the upper part of the sublimatory as they cool, while the impure, non-volatile elements remain in the lower part of the vessel.

790 These are metallic salts; for examples of their alchemical uses, see *Geber*, p. 209 ('bole armoniak'), pp. 191, 213, 221, 224 ('vertgrees'), and pp. 7, 72 ('boras').

792 The urinals presumably held the urine which was used in various alchemical processes; cf. CY 807 and n. A descensory was an iron or earthenware funnel with a grid at the top on which the material to be treated was placed; it was covered with a lid and placed in the furnace. The liquid products of the heating process then flowed down the funnel into a receiver (see Holmyard, *Alchemy*, p. 47; *Geber*, pp. 94–5 and illustration on p. 97).

794 *Cucurbites . . . alembikes*: These are the two parts of the vessel used for distillation. The 'cucurbite' was a gourd-shaped flask into which the material to be distilled was placed; on top was the 'alembike' or still-head, with a delivery spout down which the distilled liquid would run off into a waiting receiver. See Holmyard, *Alchemy*, pp. 47–8, and Figures 2 and 4.

797 *Watres rubifying*: Reddening and whitening inferior metals, so that they took on the colours of gold or silver (see n. to CY 750 ff.) was an important part of alchemical procedure. The 'reddening waters' were made by dissolving a calx (a powder produced by calcination of a metal or mineral) in water; the solution was then fused with the metal to be transmuted. See *Geber*, p. 168.

800 *Geber* (p. 55) dismisses the use of herbs in alchemy, but Arnold of Villanova (see n. to CY 1428–9) speaks (albeit sceptically) of a juice made from three herbs (one of which is 'lunary' or moonwort) which will transform quicksilver into gold (Duncan, p. 260). The other two herbs are not mentioned by Geber or Arnold.

804 For calcination, see n. to CY 750 ff. Geber says that a calcinatory furnace should be three feet by four feet, with walls six inches

thick. The materials to be calcined were placed in clay dishes or pans and set in the furnace (see *Geber*, p. 229, and for an illustration, p. 241).

805 The whitening *of* waters makes no sense in alchemical terms, and this phrase must refer to whitening *by* waters (see n. to CY 797, and for an account of methods for whitening copper and iron, see *Geber*, pp. 163–6). Possibly Chaucer had encountered the phrase 'waters albifying', and mistook the present participle for a verbal noun (see *Riverside* n.)

806 Egg whites were used to prepare an oil (*Geber*, p. 224).

807 *donge*: Hot horse-dung was piled around a glass vessel to give a gentle but steady heat; see *Geber*, pp. 14, 109, 263). Dried dung was also used to make the clay with which alchemical vessels were cemented together (Holmyard, *Alchemy*, p. 49).

pisse: As well as being used in 'cementing' (see n. to CY 817), urine was calcined to produce a salt (*Geber*, p. 206).

808 poketz*] pottes El. It is not immediately obvious what alchemical function might be served either by waxed bags ('poket' is the diminutive of 'poke', a bag) or by waxed pots, but 'poketz' seems likely to be the 'harder' reading (on which see n. to Cl 508).

808–13 In these lines the Yeoman lists numerous metallic salts discussed by Geber in the chapter on 'middle minerals' in his treatise *Of the Invention of Verity*: saltpetre, vitriol, salt tartar, salt alkali (made from 'unslaked lime'), glass alum (*Geber*, pp. 205–7). Their various uses in preparing metals for transmutation are described in chs. 6–23 of this short treatise (ibid., pp. 209–24).

812–13 On the clay, see n. to CY 750 ff. Oil of tartar is mentioned by Geber, p. 213.

813 *berm, wort*: Yeast and unfermented beer are surprising items in the list, since neither makes an appearance in Geber or in Arnold of Villanova (Duncan, p. 261).

814 *embibing*: Imbibing is the process of moistening or soaking a calx (a powder produced by calcination) with a chemical solution (see *Geber*, p. 216).

817 *cementing*: A process used in testing the quality of metals produced by transmutation; the 'cement' is 'a pasty mixture' placed over the sheets of metal, which are then heated in the furnace for three days; if the plates are 'cleansed from all *Impurity*' at the end of this time, they are to be deemed genuine (*Geber*, pp. 186, 262).

fermentacioun: According to A. J. Pernety, an eighteenth-century student of alchemy, fermentation is properly 'the rarefaction of a dense body by the interspersion of air in its pores; other writers regarded it as an animating or resuscitating process. The Philosopher's Stone was often pictured as a "ferment" which could insinuate itself between the particles of imperfect matter, thereby attracting to itself all the particles of its own nature' (Read, *Prelude to Chemistry*, pp. 139–40).

820–24 *foure spirites*: Quicksilver, trisulphide of arsenic (orpiment), sal ammoniac and sulphur (brimstone). Arnold of Villanova explains that they are called spirits 'because they flee from the fire and fly away in smoke' (Duncan, p. 245); that is, they vaporize easily.

bodies sevene: See next n.

825–9 The idea that each of the planets was connected with a metal goes back to Greek astrology; alchemists habitually used the planetary names to denote metals (Holmyard, *Alchemy*, p. 21).

837–8 *Riverside* punctuates with a full stop at the end of line 837 and a question-mark at the end of line 838, but they are best taken together: 'if that craft is so easy to learn, anyone who has some cash can become an alchemist'. See the quotation of these lines in *MED*, s.v. ascaunce 1b, punctuated as here.

853 On the use of the corrosive waters, see n. to CY 856.

854–5 Geber gives instructions for 'the *Ingenious Mollification* of *Hard Bodies*, and . . . the *Induration* (or *Hardening*) of the *Soft*, by way of *Calcination*' (*Geber*, p. 156; see also p. 119).

856 *abluciouns*: Geber explains that once a calx has been produced, it must be cleansed with 'Corrosive, Acute, or Harsh Things . . . by Grinding, Imbibing and Washing' (p. 10; cf. p. 167). He also gives instructions for the 'washing' of quicksilver in vinegar, to cleanse it of 'earthiness' (pp. 157–8).

863 *Elixir*: The effective agent in the alchemical production of gold and silver, the 'philosopher's stone'; see Headnote.

907 Duncan (pp. 253–4) suggests that the breaking of the pot might have been caused by the ground litharge (oxide of lead; line 775). If the canon had added this to the pot, and if the salt (762) had happened to be saltpetre (prescribed by Geber in a recipe for the 'citrination' of silver), bringing these two substances together 'in a closed vessel and exposed to heat would have resulted in the liberation of such quantities of heat by oxidation that an explosion would have occurred'.

922–9 Alchemical treatises laid great stress on the composition and regulation of the fire; see Duncan, p. 252.

961 Solomon's wisdom was proverbial; see Whiting S460.

962–5 These lines quote two familiar proverbs (see Whiting A155, G282, and cf. *HF* 272), but the immediate source is the *Liber Parabolarum* ('Book of Proverbs') of Alan of Lille (*c.* 1125–1202), a proverb-collection which was well known through its use as a school-text, in which they are found side by side (ed. O. Limone (Lecce, 1993), III.217–18): 'Non teneas aurum totum quod splendet ut aurum | nec pulchrum pomum quodlibet esse bonum' ('Don't think that everything that shines like gold is gold, and don't think that every beautiful apple is a good one'). A Latin gloss in the margin of El quotes the first few words of each of these lines. The Latin source supports the emendation of El's 'seineth' (presumably a misreading of 'semeth') to 'shineth'.

1048 *in good time*: *Riverside* explains this 'as a formula to avert evil consequences, similar to "touch wood"'. Cf. *MED* s.v. time 13a. The canon, that is, is expressing the hope that future events will not contradict his claim to be a reliable borrower.

1056 *Riverside* reads 'and if'; El's 'if that' is preferable, since the second half of the sentence is not a second offer but a substantiation of the first.

1066–7 Proverbial; see Whiting S167, and cf. *PF* 518.

1148 *A poudre*: The powder is, purportedly, the 'Elixir' or Philosopher's Stone by which the transmutation is to be effected (see Headnote to CYT). Even supposing it to be genuine, a medieval alchemist would have found ridiculous the idea that the transmutation of mercury could be achieved in one straightforward operation; it was precisely the multiplicity of operations involved that postponed the recognition of ultimate failure.

1160 ff. Chaucer does not describe the crucible or the fire in any detail, but since the coal is arranged 'above' the crucible as well as below it (CY 1152–3), we may assume that the crucible is closed with some kind of a cover or lid; since the trick depends on the silver enclosed in the hollow piece of beech-wood charcoal melting and dropping down into the crucible, we may assume that the lid had an opening in it. The replacement of the quicksilver by real silver depends on the fact that 'the melting point of silver is 962°C . . . whereas at 375°C (the boiling point of mercury) the mercury in the crucible would be volatilized, leaving only the silver to be poured into the mould' (P. F. Baum, *MLN*, 40 (1925), 152–4, at p. 154).

1185 *Seint Gile*: It is tempting to suppose that there is a pun on the ME word *gile* (modern English 'guile'), but the saint's name would have been pronounced with a soft 'g' and 'gile' with a hard one.

1207   *Goth walketh*: See n. to Mk 2194.

1224 ff. It is by no means clear why the canon has to make his mould the exact shape and size of an ounce of silver (presumably he could have poured the molten silver into a larger 'ingot'), and in doing so he runs the risk of detection by the priest. Perhaps it is meant to underline the exactness of the equivalence between the silver and the mercury it has replaced.

1234   The molten silver in the mould is put in a water-bath to cool and solidify it.

1238–9   These lines are omitted in El, but sound authentically Chaucerian.

1266–73 The second trick, like the first, depends on the volatilization of mercury at a lower temperature than the melting-point of silver; see n. to CY 1160 ff.

1308 ff. Disappointingly, instead of demonstrating even greater ingenuity than the first two tricks, the third depends on a simple sleight of hand. Presumably by now the priest is so convinced of the canon's powers that ingenuity is no longer required.

1342   Proverbial; see Whiting B292, F561 and 566, and cf. Kn 2437, Sh 38, 51.

1361   *fourty pound*: £40 was a huge sum of money; see n. to Sh 181.

1368–74 This combination of an insistence on secrecy with a willingness to reveal the secrets to a privileged elect is characteristic of alchemical treatises; the obscurity of their discourse is explained as due to the need to hide these weighty truths from the foolish and ignorant (see Grennen, *Classica et Mediaevalia*, 26 (1965), 309–11, and Patterson, *SAC*, 15 (1993), 39–42; cf. also n. to CY 1441–7).

1407–8   Proverbial; see Whiting C201, H53, M160.

1410   Proverbial; see Whiting L89, T211.

1411   Proverbial; though the examples given in Whiting T256 are post-medieval.

1413   *Bayard*: A traditional name for a horse (see Rv 4115). 'Blind Bayard' was a proverbial expression apparently denoting blundering pig-headedness (see *MED* s.v. baiard *n* (1), Whiting B71–3 and Rowland, *Blind Beasts*, pp. 127–8).

1428–9   Arnold of Villanova (1240–1311), a Catalan who taught at Montpellier in France, was the author of numerous medical and alchemical treatises. The 'Rosarye' is his *Rosarium philosophorum* ('Rosary of the Philosophers'), but the source for what follows is another treatise, entitled *De lapide philosophorum* ('On the Philosophers' Stone'); see J. L. Lowes, *MLN*, 28 (1913), 229, and next n.).

1431–40 The passage of Arnold of Villanova's *De lapide philosophorum* (ch. 4) quoted in CY 1431–2 appears at f. 304r of the edition of his works published at Lyons in 1532; it is reproduced in Lowes, *MLN*, 28 (1913), 229, and in *SA*, p. 698 (where 'sol' is a misprint for 'sole'). In translation, it runs:

> The pupil said, 'Why do the philosophers say that mercury does not die, unless he is killed by his brother?' The master said, 'The first of them who said so was Hermes, who said that the dragon never dies unless he is killed by his brother; he means that mercury never dies – that is, hardens – unless through his brother, that is, through Sol [gold] and Luna [silver].

As CY 1439 makes clear, mercury's 'brother' is sulphur; for the representation of metals in terms of family relations, see D. Finkelstein, *Archiv*, 207 (1970), 260–76, at pp. 265–7. The substance of this article is conveniently accessible in D. Metlitzki, *The Matter of Araby in Medieval England* (New Haven, CT, and London, 1977), pp. 80–92. E. H. Duncan (*MLN*, 57 (1942), 31–3) glosses the last sentence of the passage in Arnold by reference to the *Rosarium*, where Arnold says that Sol is the father of sulphur and Luna its mother, but the Latin reads 'id est', not 'quod est'. In any case, in Chaucer's rendering, the plural 'were' makes line 1440 refer to mercury and sulphur equally, and its meaning is even less clear.

'The symbolic designation of mercury as "dragon" . . . is only one of over sixty code words for quicksilver by which it was known to Arab alchemical writers' (Finkelstein, p. 263; see also Holmyard, *Alchemy*, p. 27 and ch. 7). The metaphor of 'killing' mercury derives from the etymological sense of the word 'mortify' (1431; cf. CY 1126), which in alchemy has the technical sense 'harden'; 'a widespread belief of the time was that mercury (*argentum vivum*) or *quick*silver differed from silver (*argentum*) only in that the mercury was *alive*, i.e., in fluid state. Hence, if you could kill mercury by stopping its fluidity or life, you would get ordinary silver' (J. W. Spargo, *SA*, pp. 688–9, n. 2).

1434 *Hermes*: Hermes Trismegistus ('Thrice-great Hermes') is the Greek name for Thoth, the Egpytian god of wisdom. A large corpus of texts, embodying occult teachings on religion, astrology and magic, circulated under his name. The work known as the *Tabula Smaragdina* (*The Emerald Table*, ed. R. Steele and D. W. Singer (London, 1928)), which consisted of a set of oracular utterances on natural principles, was referred to as an authority by medieval alchemists (see Holmyard, *Alchemy*, pp. 97–100).

1441–7 Chaucer is still quoting the *De lapide philosophorum* of Arnold of Villanova; see Duncan, *MLN*, 57 (1942), p. 32. The phrase 'the secree of secretes' is not a reference to the pseudo-Aristotelian *Secretum Secretorum* (which is not an alchemical treatise but a 'mirror for princes'); as used by Arnold, it merely means 'the greatest of secrets' (see K. Young, *MLN*, 58 (1943), 98–105). It represents 'the ritual injunction to secrecy from master to pupil and author to reader that characterizes all Arabic alchemical treatises' (Finkelstein, *Archiv*, 207 (1970), 271; see also 272–6. Cf. n. to CY 1368–74).

1448–71 The 'book *Senior*' is a Latin version of 'an Arabic alchemical treatise of the tenth century by "Sheikh" Muhammad ibn Umail at-Tamimi as-Sadiq, known to the West as "Senior Zadith filius Hamuel"' (Finkelstein, *Archiv*, 207 (1970), 268). In the Arabic original, the speakers in the dialogue are called Qalimus and Runus (J. Ruska, *Anglia*, 61 (1937), 136–7); in the Latin version they are King Solomon and an unidentified sage. As Finkelstein points out, Chaucer's substitution of Plato for Solomon is probably to be explained by the fact that the phrase 'and Plato said' ('Et dixit Plato ... Item dixit Plato') occurs twice, both in the Arabic source and in its Latin translation, immediately after the dialogue between Solomon and the sage (see below). 'The association of alchemical teaching with Plato is a common feature of alchemical literature' (Finkelstein, 269–70). In addition, annotations in a fourteenth-century MS (Cambridge, Trinity College, MS 112, ff. 39r and 40r) equate 'Senior' with 'Plato', and so indicate why Chaucer speaks of 'his [i.e., Plato's] book *Senior*' (*Riverside*, n. to CY 1448–71).

The Latin version of Ibn Umail's treatise was edited by H. E. Stapleton and M. Hidayat Husain and printed in *Three Arabic Treatises on Alchemy by Muhammad bin Umail*, ed. M. Turab 'Ali, *Memoirs of the Asiatic Society of Bengal*, 12 (Calcutta, 1933). The parts relevant to CYT are on pp. 180 and 183, and are also given in *SA*, pp. 697–8, but the latter text contains several misprints; the correct forms are given in parentheses in the following translation:

King Solomon said, 'Take the stone which is called Thitarios, which is a red, white, yellow, black stone which has many names and different colours.' ... The sage said, 'Identify it for me.' He said, 'It is the noble substance of magnesia, which all the philosophers praise.' He said, 'What is magnesia?' He replied, 'Magnesia is a congealed, composite water, which is antithetical to [*repugnat*] fire.' And Plato said, 'Everything is one ...' And this is the secret which they swore they would not reveal [*indicarent*] in any book. Nor will any of them declare [*declarabit*] it, attributing it to the glorious God, that he may reveal it to whom he wishes, and withhold it from whom he wishes ...

The scepticism of the disciple in CYT, which is evident in his comment that Plato's explanation is '*ignotum per ignocius*' (see n. to CY 1457), is absent from the Latin source, in which the dialogue is taken seriously, whereas in Chaucer it illustrates the failure of alchemical discourse to make contact with concrete reality. See further Headnote to CYT.

1454 *Titanos*: A Greek word, which, according to Liddell and Scott's *Greek Lexicon*, denotes a white earth – most probably gypsum, but also lime or chalk. The 'Thitarios' of the Latin source (see preceding n.) is a meaningless corruption; Chaucer presumably had access to a better text or better information.

1455 *Magnasia*: Probably magnesium oxide, a brilliant white powder. In alchemical terms, it is 'a name for the perfect white earth or matter of the Stone attained at the albedo, the quintessence' (Abraham, *Dictionary of Alchemical Imagery*, p. 121); for a quotation from a Greek alchemical treatise extolling the mystic properties of magnesia, see Holmyard, *Alchemy*, p. 31.

1457 *ignotum per ignocius*: The disciple is complaining that Plato explains the unknown ('ignotum') by means of something more unknown ('per ignocius'). The explanation is thus merely a process of verbal substitution rather than real illumination.

1467 Since Plato lived more than four centuries before Christ, this reference is highly anachronistic. The Latin original (see n. to CY 1448–71) refers only to 'God'.

THE MANCIPLE'S PROLOGUE

1–3 Although these lines imply that the 'litel toun' is well known, it is not easily identifiable. The most likely candidate is Harbledown, two miles north-west of Canterbury, but Up-and-Down

Field, in the parish of Thannington Without, and Bobbing, two miles west of Sittingbourne, have also been proposed (D. C. Baker, ed., *A Variorum Edition of the Works of Geoffrey Chaucer: The Manciple's Tale* (Norman, OK, 1984), pp. 79–80). On the Blean forest ('the Blee'), see n. to CY 556.

5   'Dun' denotes a dark-coloured horse; 'dun is in the mire' is a proverbial expression meaning 'things have come to a standstill' (see *MED* s.vv. don *n*, and mire *n* (1); Whiting D434).

6   *for preyere ne for hire*: This is an English version of the formulaic Latin expression 'nec prece nec precio' ('neither for entreaty nor for money').

11   On the possibility that the Cook is to be identified with a London cook called Roger of Ware, see Co 4336 and n.

14   *nat worth a botel hey*: Apparently proverbial. See Whiting B470.

24   *Chepe*: See nn. to GP 754, Co 4377 and Pard 564.

25   *Maunciple*: See n. to GP 567.

42   *justen atte fan*: 'A reference to a popular game demanding considerable agility. The "fan" was the fan, or vane, of the quintain, a crossbar pivoting atop a post. At one end of the crossbar was the fan, or vane, a board at which the player was to ride or run, like a jousting knight, and strike with a spear or stick in such a way and with such speed that he would be able to dodge the other end of the crossbar swinging around behind his head. To the other end of the crossbar was usually attached some heavy object, a club, a wooden sword, or a bag of sand, to encourage the agility of the player' (Baker, *Variorum: Manciple's Tale*, pp. 86–7). Presumably the Cook is lurching wildly from side to side as if he were making a desperate attempt to hit the 'fan'.

44–5 This appears to be 'a reference to one of the degrees of drunkenness that one might successively attain, signified by the fabulous behavior of four animals: the lamb, the lion, the ape and the swine' (Baker, *Variorum: Manciple's Tale*, p. 87). For literary references to this idea, see Skeat V, 436–8. The 'ape' stage seems to have manifested itself in playfulness of various kinds, of which playing with a straw is one (ibid.).

72   *Reclaime . . . lure*: These are hawking terms. To 'reclaim' a hawk is to call it back from flight by means of the lure (see n. to WB 415).

THE MANCIPLE'S TALE

The story of a talking bird which is punished for telling the truth about a wife's adultery is widespread in various forms (*SA*, p. 699). Chaucer certainly knew the version in Ovid's *Metamorphoses* (II.534–632), but this contains only the skeletal outline of the Manciple's Tale: the raven (despite being warned by the crow of the penalties of telling tales) informs Phoebus that his mistress Coronis is unfaithful. Overcome with anger, Phoebus kills Coronis with his bow and arrows; as she dies, she reveals that she is pregnant with his child. The repentant Phoebus tries in vain to revive her, and then builds a funeral pyre for her, but snatches the unborn child from her womb and gives it to the centaur Chiron for safe-keeping. (The child becomes Aesculapius, the god of medicine.) Meanwhile, the raven is changed from black to white (nothing is said of his losing the ability to sing). Chaucer omits the inset story told by the crow about its own punishment for truthtelling (and makes the crow, rather than the raven, the subject of the outer tale), and also omits any reference to the pregnancy. He prefaces the story with an account of the paradisal relations between the god and his talking bird, both of whom are distinguished by their verbal and musical skills, and he emphasizes the bleak loss of this paradisal harmony at the end of the tale, with the bird's blackness, loss of speech and separation from human contact. He also adds to the tale a number of moralizing reflections, on the ineradicability of nature, on 'newefangelnesse', on the relation between words and deeds, and on the virtue of holding one's tongue; for the sources of these passages, see nn. to Mcp 311–60.

Chaucer may have known the medieval French version of Ovid's story in the *Ovide moralisé* (most accessible in *SA*, pp. 702–9, or in *SA*[2] II), which expands the crow's warnings against talking too much, and concludes with a lengthy passage on the evils of gossip and slander. Gower's retelling of the story in *CA* (III.768–835), like the Manciple's Tale, omits the crow's advice to the raven and the pregnancy of Coronis, but it is not clear whether it predates or postdates Chaucer's version (on possible echoes of Gower, see n. to Mcp 318 ff.). Other tales that have been compared with this tale are the version of Ovid in Machaut's *Livre du voir dit* (ed. D. Leech-Wilkinson, tr. R. B. Palmer (New York and London, 1998), lines 7793–8130), and the rather different story in *The Seven Sages of Rome*, in which the unfaithful wife outwits the bird so that the husband kills it instead of her (ed. K. Brunner, EETS o.s. 191 (London, 1933), lines 2193–2292; cf. n.

to WB 232). Relevant sections of all these sources are printed in *SA*, pp. 699–722, and in *SA*[2] II; for a discussion, see Baker, *Variorum: Manciple's Tale*, pp. 4–11.

Whatever imaginative stimulus these different versions gave to Chaucer, his own moralizing additions, with their insistence on the delusions and dangers involved in rhetorical elaborations of any kind, give the Manciple's Tale a quite distinctive meaning, particularly when placed in context in *CT*; the tale's rejection of 'tidinges' (360) leads quite naturally into the Parson's rejection of 'fable' (Pars 31) and the ending of tale-telling altogether (see A. C. Spearing, in *The Cambridge Companion to Chaucer*, ed. P. Boitani and J. Mann, 2nd edn (Cambridge, 2003), 195–213, at p. 211).

109–10 *Phitoun*: Ovid gives a brief account of this exploit (*Metamorphoses* I.438–44), but he does not mention that the mighty snake (Python) was sleeping in the sun when it was slain.

116–18 For Amphion's construction of the walls of Thebes through the magical power of music, see nn. to Kn 1546 and Mch 1716.

131 In the Ovidian version of the story, the raven (who is replaced by the crow in McpT) is not caged, and flies about freely. The image of the caged (that is, domesticated or 'civilized') bird reappears in Mcp 163–74 (see n.).

143–5 In the Ovidian versions of the story, Phoebus and Coronis are lovers rather than a married couple. In these lines, Phoebus is assimilated to the jealous husband of fabliau, a surprising development after the romantic opening description of this 'flour of bachelrye' (125). Cf. Mil 3224, where the jealous husband is said, significantly, to keep his young wife 'in cage' (and see nn. to Mcp 131 and 163–74).

148–54 These lines translate part of Theophrastus's *Liber aureolus* (*Golden Book*), as quoted in Jerome, *Against Jov.* I.47. A gloss in the margin of Hg (but not El) quotes the Latin original and continues with the immediately succeeding lines: 'For necessity is an unreliable [*infida*; Hg's 'feda' is an error] keeper of chastity ... A beautiful woman is the object of desire, an ugly one is quick to desire. What many desire is difficult to guard.' Cf. WB 253–6, 265–8, and n. to WB 248–302.

160–62 A well-known version of this idea was the line in Horace's *Epistles* (I.x.24): 'Naturam expelles furca, tamen usque recurret' ('You can thrust Nature out with a pitchfork, but she'll always be back again'). This saying of Horace is quoted at *RR* 13987–94 (tr. Horgan, p. 216), in between the comparisons to the caged bird and the pampered cat which are used by Chaucer at Mcp 163–80.

163–74 This image of the ineradicability of Nature originates in Boethius, *Consolation of Philosophy* (*Boece* III m.2.21–31). However, in Boethius it refers to man's instinctual longing for the perfect bliss of heaven; more relevant to McpT is its use by Jean de Meun at *RR* 13911–36 (tr. Horgan, p. 215), where it illustrates women's inextinguishable desire for sexual freedom. See also next n.

Chaucer had already used the bird-in-the-cage simile as an illustration both of the power of Nature and of 'newfangelnesse' at Sq 607–20 (see n.); cf. Mcp 193–5.

175–80 This comparison with the natural world, like the preceding one, forms part of the speech of the Old Woman (La Vieille) in the *Romance of the Rose* (14009–22, tr. Horgan, p. 216), and is likewise used to illustrate the impossibility of restraining sexual appetite in women. It recalls the traditional tale of the cat and the candle (see E. Cosquin, *Romania*, 40 (1911), 371–430, 481–531, and W. L. Braekman and P. S. Macaulay, *NM*, 70 (1969), 690–702).

183–6 The comparison with the she-wolf's behaviour forms part of the Friend's advice to the Lover in *RR* (7731–6, tr. Horgan, p. 119); it was also a proverbial exemplum in wide circulation (see T. B. W. Reid, *MÆ*, 24 (1955), 16–19, and Whiting W448).

187–8 Given that the preceding examples are used by Jean de Meun and other writers to illustrate the sexual rapaciousness of women, it comes as a surprise to find Chaucer suddenly reversing the apparently inevitable direction of his remarks and insisting that they apply to men rather than women. For a comparable switch, see his insistence at the end of *Troilus and Criseyde* (V.1779–85) that the story of Criseyde's betrayal is meant to teach women to beware of male treachery (and see Mann, *Feminizing Chaucer*, pp. 15–17).

207–10 For the sources of this saying, see n. to GP 741–2. It is also quoted at *RR* 15161–2 (tr. Horgan, p. 235) where, however, the source is Sallust not Plato.

222 *Riverside* claims 'an obvious pun on "lay" meaning "to have sexual intercourse"', but there is no evidence for this use of the verb 'lay' in *MED*, and according to *OED* (Supplement), it is first recorded in the twentieth century and originates in US English. The literal meaning 'to place in a recumbent posture' (*MED*

2a) already has plenty of sexual connotations in this context, so that a pun might in any case be regarded as redundant.

226–34 *Alisandre*: The story of Alexander and the pirate (who gave this answer when asked to account for his depredations) was well known, and Chaucer could have encountered it in a number of places. See, for example, Augustine, *City of God* IV.4; John of Salisbury, *Policraticus* III.14; *Gesta Romanorum*, ed. H. Oesterley (Berlin, 1872), ch. 146.

243 The bird's jeering cry evidently implies the word 'cuckold' (ME *cokewold*); for this traditional implication of the cuckoo's call, see Jean de Condé, *La messe des oiseaux*, ed. J. Ribard (Geneva, 1970), lines 301–11, and the ME poem 'The Cuckoo and the Nightingale' attributed to John Clanvowe, *Middle English Debate Poetry*, ed. J. W. Conlee (East Lansing, 1991), p. 260.183–5.

256 *swive*: Both El and Hg avoid writing this word, though both had copied it on numerous earlier occasions (Mil 3850; Rv 4178, 4266, 4317; Co 4422; Mch 2378). Hg writes '&c', and El writes 'sw&c', adding the comment, 'Nota malum quid' ('Notice something bad').

275–7 Phoebus does not just repent his rashness, he convinces himself his wife was innocent. Cf. his words to the crow in Machaut, *Le livre du voir dit* (lines 8119–20; my translation): 'And it could be that she was innocent of this deed, and that you have lied to me.'

311–12 As T. F. Mustanoja pointed out (*Medieval and Linguistic Studies in Honor of Francis Peabody Magoun, Jr*, ed. J. B. Bessinger and R. P. Creed (London, 1965), pp. 250–54), these lines echo a Latin couplet found in Peter Abelard's admonitory poem to his son Astralabe (*PL* 178, col. 1764, lines 217–18): 'Nolo virum doceas uxoris crimen amatae, | Quod sciri potius quam fieri gravat hunc' ('Don't tell a man of the wrongdoing of his beloved wife, for it will hurt him more that the deed should be known than that it should be committed'). The couplet also circulated separately; see Walther 17154. Cf. the *Ovide moralisé*, lines 2542–6 (*SA*, p. 709):

> Nulz homs, por plere a son seignor,
> Ne doit de sa dame desdire,
> Et s'ele veult faire avoultire,
> Il ne s'i doit pas consentir
> N'encuser la . . .

('No man, to please his lord, should speak ill of his lady, and if she wants to commit adultery, he ought neither to consent to that nor accuse her . . .')

314–15 See Proverbs 21:23.

318 ff. *My sone*: This phrase is repeated numerous times from this point to the end of the tale. It is justified in context by the supposition that the Manciple is quoting his mother, but the effect is strongly reminiscent of wisdom literature (see Headnote to Mel), which is often cast in the form of a father's or teacher's address to a son or pupil. It has also been suggested that Chaucer is parodying Gower's *Confessio Amantis*, in which the 'father-confessor' Genius frequently addresses the Lover as 'my sone' (see R. Hazelton, *JEGP*, 62 (1963), 1–31, at p. 24, and Baker, *Variorum: Manciple's Tale*, p. 122).

319 Proverbial; see Whiting T373.

322–4 Proverbial, though other examples are post-medieval; see Tilley T424.

325–8 These lines paraphrase the *Distichs of Cato* I.12b: 'nam nulli tacuisse nocet, nocet esse locutum' ('For it harms no one to have kept silence; it is harmful to have spoken').

329–31 This maxim is found in the list of aphorisms in the preface to Gerard of Cremona's Latin translation of Ptolemy's *Almagest*; see K. Young, *SP*, 34 (1937), 1–7, at n. 32, and cf. n. to WB 180–83. It is cited at *RR* 7007–13 (tr. Horgan, p. 107).

332–4 This is a quotation from the *Distichs of Cato*, I.3: 'Virtutem primam esse puto, compescere linguam' ('I think that the first virtue is to restrain one's tongue'). As line 334 implies, this text was used as an elementary reader for young students learning Latin (see n. to Mil 3227). This proverb is also quoted in Albertano of Brescia, *Liber de doctrina dicendi et tacendi* I.23, and in *RR* 7023–7, 12149–53 (tr. Horgan, pp. 107, 187). Cf. *TC* III.292–4.

338 Proverbs 10:19; quoted in Albertano's *Liber de doctrina dicendi et tacendi* V.50, and also in the *Ovide moralisé*, line 2522. Cf. Whiting S608.

340–42 Cf. Psalm 56:5 (AV 57:4): 'and their tongue a sharp sword'. Cf. Whiting T385 and 388.

343 Apparently a reference to Proverbs 6:16–19.

344–5 *Salomon . . . David . . . Senekke*: Chaucer may have been thinking of the many quotations in Albertano of Brescia's *Liber de doctrina dicendi et tacendi* from 'Solomon' (that is, the biblical books of Proverbs, Ecclesiastes, Wisdom and Ecclesiasticus) and from Seneca's *Moral Epistles*, as well as works incorrectly attributed to Seneca, such as the *De moribus* and the *Formula honestae vitae* (see Headnote to Mel and n. to Mel 1071); for a list of examples, see the index of authors cited in P. Navone's edition (pp. 59–62). The Psalms are also cited twice, although David's name is not mentioned.

349–50 Cf. the Flemish proverb: 'Luttel onderwinds maakt groote rust' (J. Grauls and J. F. Vanderheijden, *Revue belge de philologie et d'histoire*, 13 (1934), 745–9).

355–6 An echo of Horace, *Epistles* I.xviii.71: 'semel emissum volat irrevocabile verbum' ('a word once uttered flies away and cannot be recalled'). Horace is quoted in Albertano, *Liber de doctrina dicendi et tacendi* I.40, and translated at *RR* 16515–16 (tr. Horgan, p. 255).

357–8 The idea that a secret is as if imprisoned while it is not revealed, but holds one imprisoned once it is spoken, is found in Albertano, *Liber de doctrina dicendi et tacendi* III.12. See also Whiting W626.

359–60 This is another quotation from the *Distichs of Cato* (I.12a): 'Rumores fuge neu studeas novus auctor haberi' ('Shun gossip and do not be keen to set it going'). The second line of the distich has already been quoted at Mcp 325–8 (see n.).

THE PARSON'S PROLOGUE

1–12 Both El and Hg read 'Ten' in line 5 instead of 'Foure', but the rest of the passage contains unequivocal indications that it is late afternoon. The error probably arose from a misreading of the arabic form for '4'(♃) as roman 'x' (Manly and Rickert IV, 528). On the practice of measuring time by shadow-lengths and the angular height of the sun above the horizon, see n. to ML 1–4. Chaucer's shadow is now eleven times one-sixth of his body height, and the sun has descended from the meridian ('south line'), its noon-time position, to less than 29° above the horizon. The date is not given, but an altitude of 28–29° at 4 p.m. fits 15–17 April; the zodiacal sign Libra would be rising in the east at this time. However, this interpretation cannot be reconciled with the date of 18 April given earlier in ML 5–6. Moreover, the Manciple's Prologue is timed in the morning (Mcp 16), and yet after the Manciple's short tale it seems that it is already late afternoon. The passage contains yet another difficulty: the 'mones exaltacioun' (that is, the section of the zodiac in which the moon exercised greatest influence) was not Libra (which belonged to Saturn), but Taurus (Eisner, *Kalendarium*, pp. 32–3). Scholars disagree on whether (a) Chaucer simply made a mistake, or (b) the text should be emended (see North, *Chaucer's Universe*, pp. 126–7). Another possibility is that Chaucer chose these details for their poetic resonances rather than for their astronomical accuracy. Thus 29° suggests the 29 pilgrims, the Moon suggests mutability, and Libra (the Scales) suggests the Last Judgement – all of which, together with the lengthening shadows and the approach of night, helps to create a sense that the pilgrimage and the tale-telling are drawing to their conclusion (Donaldson, *Chaucer's Poetry*, pp. 948–9). *CT* begins with a reference to Aries, the sign in which the sun rises and sets at the spring equinox; it ends with a reference to Libra, the sign in which the sun rises and sets at the autumnal equinox.

12   No village ('throop') is known to have existed between Harbledown (see n. to Mcp 1–3) and Canterbury.

16   The Host's comment implies that the original plan, that each pilgrim should tell four tales, has been abandoned; see GP 792–4 and n.

22   *vicary*: The legal holder of a parochial benefice was called a rector or parson; he had 'full freehold rights in the parochial revenues' (including the right to assign them to others). A vicar (as the name implies) was 'a replacement for a permanently absent rector' and received only 'a portion of the total income' (R. N. Swanson, *SAC*, 13 (1991), 41–80, at pp. 48–9). An absentee rector might be an individual who (for example) held another ecclesiastical post elsewhere (cf. GP 507–11 and n.), or was studying at university, but rectorships were also often nominally held by ecclesiastical foundations, such as monasteries or university colleges, and in such cases the parish was served by a perpetual vicarage. Since the Parson has the power to 'sette . . . his benefice to hire' (GP 507) – though he does not do so – it appears that he is not a vicar but a rector.

32–4 See 1 Timothy 1:4, 4:7, and 2 Timothy 4:4.

35–6 D. W. Robertson (*A Preface to Chaucer* (Princeton, NJ, 1962), pp. 58, 316–17) cites biblical and patristic parallels to the wheat/chaff metaphor (cf. NP 3443 and n.), but Chaucer also uses it in secular contexts; see ML 701–2, *LGW* G 312, 529.

39   *that*: In the case of two parallel subordinate clauses, 'that' is often used in the second clause as a substitute for the conjunction

in the first clause (here, 'if' in line 37), with the meaning of the
conjunction it replaces (see *MED* s.v. that *conj* 14a).

43   *rum, ram, ruf*: The Parson is alluding to medieval English alliterative verse, which is metrically structured by stress and alliteration
(rather than stress and rhyme). The most frequent type of line
has four stressed syllables, three of which are linked by alliteration. The Parson's comment in line 42 implies that alliterative
poetry flourished in the North; modern scholarship usually
associates it with the West of England (both the north-west and
south-west), but *Piers Plowman*, for example, which is a major
representative of the genre, has strong associations with London.
See T. Turville-Petre, *The Alliterative Revival* (Cambridge,
1977), pp. 29–36.

geste: see n. to Mel 933.

51   The vision of heaven as a transcendental form of the city of
Jerusalem derives from Revelation 21.

69–70 All manuscripts have these two lines in the position they
occupy here. However, *Riverside* (and other modern editions)
accepts Manly's suggestion (in his 1928 edition of *CT*) that they
should be placed at the end of ParsPr, on the assumption that
(my) line 70 refers to the Parson beginning to tell his tale. Against
this, E. Brown has argued in favour of the manuscript position,
on the grounds that normally Chaucer would explicitly signal a
shift of speaker such as the emendation hypothesizes (*ChauR*, 10
(1976), 236–42). Although the phrase 'And with that word'
usually refers to action accompanying or immediately following
on a completed speech, it sometimes introduces additional
speech, as here (cf. Phys 251–2, *TC* II.264–6).

THE PARSON'S TALE

The Parson's Tale is not (as it is often called) a sermon; it does not
conform to the rigid formal organization of medieval sermons. Rather,
it is a treatise on penitence. It proceeds in logical order from an
introductory discussion of penitence, contrition and confession, to an
account of the Seven Deadly Sins (including their sub-species) and the
virtues that counteract them, and concludes with a brief discussion of
satisfaction. The various sections of the work may be set out sche-
matically as follows:

    1. Penitence and Contrition (80–315)
    2. Confession and Types of Sin (316–86)

3. Pride (387–474)
     Humility (475–83)
4. Envy (484–514)
     Love (515–32)
5. Wrath (533–653)
     Meekness and Patience (654–76)
6. Sloth (677–727)
     Strength (728–38)
7. Avarice (739–803)
     Mercy and Pity (804–17)
8. Gluttony (818–30)
     Abstinence (831–5)
9. Lechery (836–914)
     Chastity (915–57)
10. Oral Confession (958–1028)
11. Satisfaction (1029–80)

The sources of the Parson's Tale are complex (for a full discussion, see *SA²* I, 529–34). The outer framework of the treatise (1, 2 and 11 above) derives from Book III of the *Summa de poenitentia et matrimonio* of Raymond of Pennaforte, a Dominican friar (pp. 437–502 in the edition of the *Summa* published at Rome in 1603; repr. Farnborough, 1967). Raymond's work was written in the early thirteenth century (probably 1225 x 1227) – that is, in the wake of the Fourth Lateran Council (1215), which made annual confession obligatory and so instigated the production of large numbers of penitential and confessional manuals. For a comparison of the Parson's Tale with other manuals of this sort, see L. W. Patterson, *Traditio*, 34 (1978), 331–80, at pp. 334–40 (cf. n. to Pars 956, and *SA²* I, 534–6).

Into this outer framework has been inserted the central section of the Parson's Tale, concerning the Seven Deadly Sins and the seven remedial virtues. The ultimate source for the material on the Sins is the *Summa de vitiis* (*c.* 1236) by another Dominican friar, William Peraldus. However, two abridged versions of the *Summa*, both produced in England in the third quarter of the thirteenth century, offer closer parallels to some parts of the Parson's Tale than the original. Both treatises are identified in modern scholarship by their first words, *Quoniam* and *Primo*. *Quoniam* rearranges the order of the Sins, and adds some extra material; *Primo* is a further abridgement of *Quoniam*. (See S. Wenzel, *Traditio*, 30 (1974), 351–78, for a detailed comparison of the Parson's Tale with these two treatises.) The sections of the Parson's Tale on the seven remedial virtues do not derive, directly or indirectly, from William's *Summa*, but have close parallels in a Latin treatise known as *Postquam*, which is preceded by the *Summa* in three of its nine manuscripts and by *Primo* in five others. (See the edition and translation of *Postquam* by S. Wenzel, *Summa virtutum de remediis anime* (Athens, GA, 1984), pp. 9, 12–30.) Illustrative samples of all these texts are given in *SA*² I, 536–611.

Wenzel favours the view that the combination, rearrangement, abridgement and occasional expansion of these various materials were carried out by Chaucer himself (see, e.g., *ChauR*, 16 (1982), 237–56, at p. 252). L. Patterson agrees with Wenzel on this (*Traditio*, 34 (1978), 340, n. 29), and argues (361–9) that four major instances of overlap with other passages of *CT* show that the Parson's Tale was composed after the other tales had been written and drew material from them (the overlapping passages are Pars 463, 763/WB 1158; Pars 600/Pard 631–2; Pars 938–9/Mch 1441–51; Pars 1008/Sum 2098). It is not, however, easy to see why, out of the whole of *CT*, Chaucer should have chosen to echo these particular passages in his final tale. If, on the other hand, he was translating an existing compilation (either in Latin or in French), it is easy to imagine him later using material from it at appropriate moments in the tales. The position of the Parson's Tale at the end of *CT* does not counteract this supposition. Chaucer could well have translated the work at an early date as an independent literary exercise (or an act of penance), have echoed some passages of it in writing the other tales (just as he echoed other works he had read or translated), and finally decided to use it as the conclusion to *CT*, perhaps to save himself time by using material already to hand. This view has been argued by A. E. Hartung, in *Literature and Religion in the Later Middle Ages: Philological Studies in Honor of Siegfried Wenzel*, ed. R. G. Newhauser and J. A. Alford (Binghamton, NY, 1995), pp. 61–80. Hartung too believes that Chaucer himself reworked the various sources of the Parson's Tale, and interprets a number of (apparently) sourceless passages which adopt a strong tone towards sexual sin as indicative of the fault for which Chaucer was atoning. However, the discrepancy in outlook between these passages and the attitude towards sexuality in the rest of Chaucer's works suggests strongly to me that they were already present in the treatise he was translating. The closeness

with which he follows his sources in his other prose translations (*Boece* and Melibee) supports this idea, and the relatively
recent discovery of a source for the Second Nun's Tale, which
accounts for sections previously thought to be original with
Chaucer, may be taken as an indication that the Parson's Tale
likewise could have had a source which is lost to us or still
awaiting discovery.

For other parallels between the Parson's Tale and the rest of
CT, see Patterson, p. 359 n. 75, and the notes below.

Rubric A quotation of Jeremiah 6:16 (the Vulgate Bible reads 'semitis',
not 'viis'). The Latin is translated in Pars 77–8. Wenzel (*ChauR*,
16 (1982), 251) cites a parallel linking of this text with the 'way
of penance' in a fifteenth-century sermon-collection.

75 *that no man wole perisse*: An echo of 2 Peter 3:9; God is said to
be patient, 'not willing that any should perish, but that all should
return to penance'. The following clause echoes 1 Timothy 2:4.

81–3 This outline applies to the outer framework of ParsT (the part
borrowed from Raymond of Pennaforte; see Headnote). For the
six topics mentioned, see Pars 84, 86, 95, 102, 107, and 1057.
The explanation of why Penitence is so called is obscured in
the translation: Raymond explains that the word derives from
'poenae tentio' ('the holding of sorrow'), which is represented by
the ME 'that halt himself in sorwe' (86).

84 Ps. Ambrose, *Sermo* XXV.1 (*PL* 17, col. 677).

85 Ps. Augustine, *De vera et falsa poenitentia* VIII.22 (*PL* 40, col.
1120).

87–8 These two sentences are not in Raymond of Pennaforte.

89 Isidore, *Sententiae* II.xvi.1 (CCSL 111, p. 128).

92 Cf. Gregory, *Moralia in Job* IV.xxvii.51–2 (CCSL 143,
pp. 194–7).

93 *er that sinne forlete hem*: That is, before old age deprives them
of the power of sinning. The idea derives from a sermon attributed to St Augustine (*Sermo* CCCXCIII, *PL* 39, col. 1715), and
became proverbial; see Phys 286 and n.

95–100 *three accions of penitence*: See Augustine (attrib.), *Sermo*
CCCLI.2–4 (*PL* 39, cols. 1537–43); the quotation in Pars 97
appears in col. 1537. The three types of penitence are (1) repentance of one's former life on baptism; (2) repentance of deadly
sin committed after baptism; (3) repentance of venial sin committed after baptism. In the Augustinian text, (2) and (3) appear in
reverse order.

101 Augustine, *Epistolae* CCLXV.8 (*PL* 33, col. 1089).

109 From a sermon on penitence, formerly attributed to St John Chrysostom; see R. M. Correale, *NQ*, 225 (1980), 101–2, and *SA²* I, 547, n. 3.

112–27 The image of the tree is not in Raymond's *Summa*. There is a close parallel to Pars 113–16 in an AN compilation of penitential material (*Compileison de seinte penance*; see *SA²* I, 568–9); the Latin version of this section of the *Compileison* begins with a quotation from the same ps.-Chrysostom sermon that is the source of Pars 109 (see preceding n.), and which calls penitence 'fructifera'. Wenzel (*ChauR*, 16 (1982), 241–3) suggests that this may be the ultimate source of the idea of penance as a 'fruit-bearing tree'.

115 Matthew 3:8 (spoken not by Christ but by John the Baptist).

116 Matthew 7:20.

118 F. Beer (*NQ*, 233 (1988), 298–301) suggests that 'grace' should be emended to 'egrece', corresponding to the first of the two qualities attributed to the seed in Pars 117 ('egre and hoot'; see Pars 120 for the second). As she recognizes, however, the word 'egrece' does not appear in the *MED*.

119 Proverbs 16:6.

125 Psalm 118:113 (AV 119:113).

126 Daniel 4:7–15 (AV 10–18); cf. Mk 2155–8, NP 3128 and n.

127 The reference is perhaps to Proverbs 28:13.

130 Unidentified.

131–2 Nicholas of Clairvaux, *Sermo in festo sancti Andreae* 8 (*PL* 184, cols. 1052–3); ps. Hugh of St Victor, *Miscellanea* VI.100 (*PL* 177, col. 857).

133 Raymond of Pennaforte's *Summa* likewise identifies six causes of contrition (see *SA²* I, 548–51), but only two of them (fear of judgement and hell, hope of forgiveness and heaven) offer a general parallel to the causes listed in ParsT.

134 Proverbs 12:4, Vulgate version (said of an unfaithful wife). The erroneous attribution to Job is in Raymond of Pennaforte's *Summa*. Both El and Hg read 'confessioun' here, but the biblical source confirms that 'confusioun' is correct.

135 Isaiah 38:15 (where the words are attributed to King Hezekiah).

136 Revelation 2:5.

138 The comparison with the dog returning to its vomit is biblical; see Proverbs 26:11 and 2 Peter 2:22.

141 Ezekiel 20:43.

142 John 8:34; spoken not by Peter but by Christ (but cf. 2 Peter 2:19).

143 Not in Ezekiel; the reference may be to Job 30:28 or Psalm 42:2 (AV 43:2).

144 Not traced in Seneca. The same attribution is found in Raymond of Pennaforte, whose Latin reads 'Si scirem deos ignoscituros, homines autem ignoraturos tamen abhorrerem peccatum' (*SA*² I, 549:30–31). Newhauser's notes (ibid.) cite an almost identical aphorism (with 'condonaturos' for 'ignoscituros') in a florilegium by Werner II of Küssenberg, abbot of Sankt Blasien, which is attributed only to 'philosophus' (*Libri deflorationum sive excerptionum* II.22, *PL* 157, col. 1205C). Werner, however, borrowed the aphorism along with the whole passage in which it occurs from the gospel commentary of Zachariah of Besançon (1145–50); see *PL* 186, col. 315D. The reference is perhaps to Cicero, *On Duties* III.ix.37: 'even though we may escape the eyes of gods and men, we must still do nothing that savours of greed or of injustice, of lust or of intemperance' (see also III.ix.38–9). This passage was incorporated into the *Moralium dogma philosophorum* (ed. J. Holmberg (Uppsala, 1929), p. 71), a twelfth-century moral treatise composed of excerpts from classical authors, principally Seneca and Cicero (this may be the reason for the misattribution). The influence of the *Moralium dogma* on the source(s) of ParsT was demonstrated by R. Hazelton (*Traditio*, 16 (1960), 255–74), but he did not notice this parallel.

145 Seneca, *Moral Epistles* LXV.21.

150 Augustine, *Sermo* IX.16 (CCSL 41, pp. 138–41).

156–7 Proverbs 11:22; cf. WB 784–5.

159–60 The quotation is a conflation of two passages; see Jerome, *Epistulae* LXVI.10 (CSEL 54, p. 660) and ps. Jerome, *Regula monachorum* 30 (*PL* 30, col. 417).

162 Romans 14:10.

166 Ps. Bernard, *Sermo ad praelatos in concilio* 5 (*PL* 184, col. 1098).

168 Cf. Proverbs 6:34–5.

169–73 Anselm, *Meditationes* I, printed in *SA*² I, 610–11.

174 Unidentified.

176–7 Job 10:20–22.

189 1 Samuel 2:30 (the words are not spoken by the prophet Jeremiah, but by an unnamed 'man of God').

191 Job 20:25 (Vulgate version).

193 Psalm 75:6 (Vulgate version).

195 Deuteronomy 32:24, 33.

198 Isaiah 14:11.

201 Micah 7:6.

204 Psalm 10:6 (AV 11:5).

208 An echo of Matthew 13:42 and 25:30.

209 Isaiah 24:9.

210 Isaiah 66:24.

214–15 Gregory, *Moralia in Job* IX.lxvi.100 (CCSL 143, p. 528, lines 24–6).

216 Revelation 9:6.

218 Cf. Wisdom 11:21.

220 Cf. Psalm 106:33–4 (AV 107:33–4), but the connection is loose.

221 Basil, *Homilia in Psalmum XXVIII* verse 7 (*Patrologiae Cursus Completus Series Graeca*, ed. J.-P. Migne (Paris, 1857–68), vol. 29, col. 298).

227 Proverbs 11:7.

229 Cf. Ecclesiasticus 1:17–18.

230 Unidentified.

236–7 Ezekiel 18:24.

238–9 Gregory, *Homiliae in Hiezechielem* I.xi.21 (CCSL 142, p. 178, lines 371–3).

248 The same line of French is quoted in Chaucer's short poem 'Fortune' (line 7).

253–4 The quotation from St Bernard is unidentified. It alludes to Luke 16:2 and 21:18.

256–9 Bernard of Clairvaux, *Sermo in quarta feria hebdomadae sanctae* 11 (*Opera*, V, 64).

261–2 Cf. Augustine, *De Genesi contra Manichaeos* II.11 (*PL* 34, cols. 204–5).

269 Unidentified.

274 Bernard of Clairvaux, *Sermo II In ramis palmarum* 4 (*Opera*, V, 48).

281 Isaiah 53:5.

284 *Jesus Nazarenus rex Judeorum*: Jesus of Nazareth, king of the Jews.

285 The etymology derives from Jerome's *Interpretation of Hebrew Names* (*Liber interpretationis hebraicorum nominum*; CCSL 72, p. 136, line 24).

286 Matthew 1:21.

287 Acts 4:12 (Peter speaking to the Jewish elders).

288 This etymology derives from Jerome's gloss on 'Nazareth' (CCSL 72, p. 137, lines 24–5): 'flos aut virgultum eius' ('a flower or its twig').

289–90 Revelation 3:20.

302–3 Ps. Augustine, *De vera et falsa poenitentia* IX.24 (*PL* 40, col. 1121).

304 Jonah 2:8 (AV 2:7).

307 Psalm 96:10 (AV 97:10).

309 Psalm 31:5 (AV 32:5). The gloss 'I purposed fermely' makes more sense in relation to the correct form of the biblical quotation: 'I said, "I will confess against myself my injustice to the Lord," and thou hast forgiven the wickedness of my sin.'

313 Cf. Ephesians 2:3–6.

318–19 It has been suggested that these lines confuse the 'conditions' of confession with the 'circumstances' of sin, but Wenzel, *ChauR*, 16 (1982), 239, gives an example of the two words used interchangeably in relation to sin.

322 Romans 5:12.

325–30 Genesis 3:1–7.

331–2 For the Augustinian identification of the three stages in the process of sin – suggestion, delight and consent – with the devil, Adam and Eve respectively, see *De Genesi ad Manichaeos* II.14 (*PL* 34, cols. 206–7). Cf. Augustine, *De sermone domini in monte* I.xii.34 (CCSL 35, pp. 36–7).

333 ff. Original sin is 'the hereditary sin incurred at conception by every human being as a result of the original sinful choice of the first man, Adam' (*New Catholic Encyclopedia* (New York, 1967)). The doctrine was developed by St Paul; see Romans 5:12–19.

336 The identification of the three types of temptation as 'the lust of the flesh and the lust of the eyes, and the pride of life' derives from 1 John 2:16, but was a medieval commonplace (see D. R. Howard, *The Three Temptations: Medieval Man in Search of the World* (Princeton, NJ, 1966), ch. 2).

342 Galatians 5:17.

343 Based on 2 Corinthians 11:23–7.

344 Romans 7:24.

345–6 Jerome, *Epistulae* XXII.7 (CSEL 54, p. 153).

348 James 1:14.

349 1 John 1:8.

351 *subjeccioun*: Richard de Wetheringsett's parallel list of the stages

in sinning (see next n.) has 'suggestio diaboli' here, and other manuscripts read 'suggestioun'. *MED* (s.v. 3) cites only one other example of 'subjeccioun' meaning 'suggestion'.

355 Based on Exodus 15:9 (from the song of triumph sung by Moses and the Israelites after the destruction of the pursuing Egyptians in the crossing of the Red Sea): 'The enemy said: I will pursue and overtake, I will divide the spoils, my soul shall have its fill: I will draw my sword, my hand shall slay them.' A treatise by Richard of Wetheringsett (early 13th c.) interprets the 'enemy' (*inimicus*) as the devil, and applies the quotation to the various stages in the process of falling into sin (Kellogg, *Chaucer, Langland*, pp. 339–42). Richard's list of the seven stages of sin corresponds closely to the six steps listed in Pars 350–54; he also uses the metaphor of the devil's bellows which appears in Pars 351 (Wenzel, *ChauR*, 16 (1982), 243–5).

358 Deadly or mortal sin incurs eternal damnation unless repented of; venial sins are less serious and do not deprive the soul of salvation.

362 See Whiting S397.

363 The metaphor of the leaky ship derives from Augustine; see *Epistulae* CCLXV.8 (CSEL 57, p. 646), *Tractatus in Ioannis Evangelium* XII.14 (CCSL 36, p. 129), and *Enarrationes in Psalmos* LXVI.7 (CCSL 39, p. 865).

368 A free rendering of Augustine, *De libero arbitrio* I.xvi.34 (CCSL 29, pp. 234–5, lines 14–21).

375 On sex as a marital 'debt', see WB 129–30 and n., and cf. Mch 2048, Pars 940.

381 The preceding list of venial sins derives from a sermon *In lectione apostolica*, attributed to St Augustine (*Sermo* CIV.3, *PL* 39, cols. 1946–7).

383–4 The parallel between charity consuming venial sin and a drop of water falling into a furnace has not been traced in Augustine but is found in a number of medieval writers and seems to have been something of a commonplace. For examples, see Peter Lombard, *Sententiae* IV.xxi.3 (*PL* 192, col. 896); Peter of Poitiers, *Sententiae* III.5 and III.25, where it is attributed to Augustine (*PL* 211, cols. 1055 and 1119); an anonymous *Commentarium in Septem Psalmos Poenitentiales* Psalm XXXI (*PL* 217, cols. 1007–8).

386 *Confiteor*: A prayer beginning 'confiteor domino meo' ('I confess to Almighty God').

387 On the history of the concept of the seven major sins, see M. W.

Bloomfield, *The Seven Deadly Sins* (State College, MI, 1952; repr. 1967).

388 The image of sin as a tree was conventional; see A. Katzenellen-bogen, *Allegories of the Virtues and Vices in Medieval Art* (London, 1939), pp. 63–8. The image also appears at Mch 1640–41.

406 *clappeth as a mille*: Proverbial. See Cl 1200 and Whiting C276, M557.

407 *kisse pax*: The Kiss of Peace, given first by the officiating priest and then passed from one member of the congregation to another, is part of the central ceremony of the Mass. In Chaucer's day, the Kiss was not given to one's neighbour, but to a 'pax-board', a wooden or metal plaque decorated with a picture of the Crucifixion or other religious subject, which was handed round in order of social rank. For examples of the violent quarrels which could occur if the order of rank was not properly observed, see E. Duffy, *The Stripping of the Altars: Traditional Religion in England 1400–1580* (New Haven, CT, 1992), pp. 126–7. Similar anxieties over precedence were felt in respect of the Offertory; see GP 450 and n.

413 See Luke 16:19.

414 Cf. Gregory, *Homiliae in Evangelia* XL.3 (CCSL 141, p. 399, lines 133–44); Gregory refers to the biblical passage alluded to in Pars 413 while condemning fine clothing in general terms, but does not say what is attributed to him here.

424 Medieval encyclopedias (e.g., Isidore, *Etymologies* XII.ii.31) report that apes rejoice when the moon is new and grow progess-ively more miserable as it wanes. D. Biggins suggests that the image here is of an ape bent over by grief, 'moving painfully on all fours, with its bare posterior conspicuously on view' (*MÆ*, 33 (1964), 200–203, at p. 202). This does not explain why a female ape is specified. B. Rowland suggests that the allusion is to the period of estrus (believed to be related to the phases of the moon), when the she-ape 'displays bright purple-red patches on her swollen hindquarters', and 'offers herself for copulation' (*ChauR*, 2 (1967), 159–65, at p. 164).

434 Zachariah 10:5.

435 Matthew 21:7.

442 Psalm 54:16 (AV 55:15).

443 See Genesis 31 and 47:7–10. El and Hg link Pharaoh with Jacob and Laban with Joseph, but it should clearly be the other way round.

445 *castelled with papir*: There is a similar reference to elaborate
food-coverings made out of paper, and decorated with gold paint,
in the ME poem 'Cleanness' (lines 1407–8). See R. W. Ackerman,
JEGP, 56 (1957), 410–17.

450 The notion of three types of divine gift derives from the *Somme
des vices et des vertus* of Frère Lorens; see its ME translations:
Dan Michel, *Ayenbite of Inwit*, ed. R. Morris, EETS o.s. 23
(London, 1866), pp. 23–5, and *The Book of Vices and Virtues*,
ed. W. N. Francis, EETS o.s. 217 (London, 1942), pp. 19–21.
Cf. Pard 295 and n.

462–3 Similar ideas are expressed at WB 1109–76 (cf. esp. Pars 463
and WB 1158), and in Chaucer's short poem, 'Gentilesse'.

467–8 Seneca, *On Mercy* I.iii.3 and I.xix.3.

470 Cf. Gregory, *Moralia in Job* XXXIII.xii.25 (CCSL 143B, p. 1695,
lines 119–24).

473 Cf. Cl 995–1001.

477 Cf. Bernard of Clairvaux, *De gradibus humilitatis et superbiae*
I.2 (*Opera*, III, 17).

484 *the philosophre*: R. C. Fox (*NQ*, 203 (1958), 523–4) suggests
the source is Aristotle's *Rhetoric* II.10. R. Newhauser (*SA²* I, 585,
n. 2) refers to two Latin translations of the *Rhetoric* (*Aristoteles
latinus* 31.1–2, ed. B. Schneider (Leiden, 1978), pp. 87 and 244,
and also to Boethius's Latin translation of Aristotle's *Topics* II.2
(*Aristoteles latinus* 5.1–3, ed. L. Minio-Paluello (Leiden, 1969),
p. 33). For Augustine's definition of envy, see n. to Phys 114–
17. Both writers speak only of pain at another's good fortune,
not joy at another's harm.

493–4 Wenzel cites a parallel to this idea in John of Grimestone's
Preaching Book (*Traditio*, 30 (1974), 359, n. 27).

502 John 12:4–6.

504 Luke 7:39.

515 Cf. Matthew 22:37–9, Mark 12:30–31, Luke 10:27.

526 Matthew 5:44.

532 The normal meanings of 'paas' ('step, pace', or 'passage, section')
do not seem to fit here. Wenzel (*ChauR*, 16 (1982), 245–8)
suggests that the word means 'way, progression, process',
implying that the remedial virtues are linked stages in the process
of spiritual healing, but in context the word does not seem to
carry so great a burden of meaning. Perhaps it should be emended
to 'caas', meaning 'category' (see *MED* s.v. cas 7d).

535 Augustine, *City of God* XIV.15 (CCSL 48, p. 438, lines 74–5).

536 *the philosophre*: Aristotle; see his *De anima* I.1, echoed by
      Seneca, *On Anger* II.xix.3 (see R. C. Fox, *MLN*, 75 (1960),
      101–2, and A. V. C. Schmidt, *NQ*, 213 (1968), 327–8).

539 Ecclesiastes 7:4 (AV 7:3): 'Anger is better than laughter'.

540 Psalm 4:5.

551 The tree is the juniper; see Isidore, *Etymologies* XVII.vii.35. The
      Hg text ends at this point, the remainder of the manuscript
      having been lost. The text printed for the rest of the tale is thus
      based on El only.

562 *oold wratthe*: The definition of hate as old wrath derives from
      Augustine, *Sermo* LVIII.vii.8 (*PL* 38, col. 397).

564–79 On homicide as the product of ire, cf. Sum 2009. The section
      on homicide is not in William Peraldus's *Summa de vitiis* (the
      ultimate source for the treatment of the sins in ParsT), but from
      Raymond of Pennaforte's penitential treatise (see D. R. Johnson,
      PMLA, 57 (1942), 51–6, and cf. Hartung, in *Literature and
      Religion*, ed. Newhauser and Alford, pp. 72–3). The confusion
      in enumerating the six types of spiritual manslaughter on which
      Johnson comments is in effect the result of Robinson's punctu-
      ation (carried over into *Riverside*), which fails to register that the
      biblical quotation in 568 is a mere parenthetical gloss on type 3.
      Johnson correctly notes, however, that having announced four
      types of manslaughter, ParsT defines three of them (by law, by
      necessity and by chance), but omits to say that the fourth is
      voluntary manslaughter, illustrated by various methods of
      infanticide.

565 1 John 3:15.

566 Cf. Proverbs 25:18.

568 Proverbs 28:15.

569 Gratian, *Decretum* I.lxxxvi.21 (*Corpus Iuris Canonici*, I, col.
      302).

582 Cf. Psalm 144:9 (AV 145:9).

588–90 Exodus 20:7; Matt 5:34–7.

591 Cf. Pard 472–5 and 629–59.

592 Jeremiah 4:2.

593 Ecclesiasticus 23:12.

597 Acts 4:12.

598 Philippians 2:10.

599 Cf. James 2:19.

600 Cf. Pard 631–2.

603 The reference is to various methods of divining the future or

casting spells. On scapulomancy, the practice of telling one's fortune from the cracks in the shoulder-bone of a sheep, see Rowland, *Blind Beasts*, pp. 149–52.

605 Divination by observing the flight of birds or the entrails of beasts was a common practice in Roman times. On geomancy, see n. to Kn 2045. On the gnawing of mice or rats as a bad omen, see Bächtold-Stäubli, VI, 47–8.

608–11 The definition of lying and the distinction between the various types derive ultimately from Augustine, *De mendacio* V and XXV (CSEL 41, pp. 419 and 444).

614 The saying attributed to Solomon does not appear in the Solomonic books of the Bible in this exact form, but it may be an inexact allusion to Proverbs 28:23 (cf. Mel 1705).

617 On the phrase 'to sing "*Placebo*"', meaning 'to flatter', see Sum 2075 and n.

619 *Malisoun . . . harm*: This sentence does not make good sense and is probably corrupt.
as seyth Seint Paul: 1 Corinthians 6:10.

623 *as Crist seyth in the gospel*: Matthew 5:22.

627 *after the habundance of the herte . . .*: Matthew 12:34.

629 Proverbs 15:4.

630 *seyth Seint Augustin*: The Latin equivalent at this point in William Peraldus's *Summa* is 'Nihil est similius actibus demonum quam litigare' (K. O. Petersen, *The Sources of the Parson's Tale* (Boston, 1901; repr. New York, 1973), p. 57), which is an echo of St Augustine's comment on the jeerers and scoffers among his fellow-students in Carthage: 'Nihil est illo actu similius actibus daemoniorum' (*Confessions* III.iii.6, CCSL 27, p. 29, line 25).
Seint Paul seyth: 2 Timothy 2:24.

631 Proverbs 27:15. Cf. WB 278–80 and n., Mel 1086.

633 Proverbs 17:1.

634 Colossians 3:18. Cf. WB 160–61.

639 According to 2 Samuel 17:14, the counsel given to Absalom, the rebellious son of King David, was good, but because God wished to destroy Absalom he caused him to ignore it.

640 The quotation does not come from the Bible, but from the *Summa* of William Peraldus, which is the ultimate source of this section of ParsT (see Headnote).

642 Cf. Proverbs 6:16–19 and Ephesians 2:14–16.

648 Cf. Matthew 12:36.

649 Ecclesiastes 5:2 (AV 5:3).

650 Previously unidentified, but this is quite a well-known story told

of Socrates: it is found in the florilegium attributed to 'Caecilius Balbus' (see n. to Mel 1178), ed. E. Woelfflin, XLIII.1 (p. 33); John of Salisbury's *Policraticus* V.6; the *Compendiloquium* of John of Wales III.iii.12 (*Summa De regimine vitae humanae . . .*, Argentorati [Strasbourg], 1518, f. cxx^v, col. b); Albertano of Brescia, *Liber de doctrina dicendi et tacendi* V.57 (ed. Navone, p. 38); Walter Burley's *De vita et moribus philosophorum* (see n. to WB 180–83), cap. XXX (ed. Knust, p. 124).

651 *Seint Paul*: Ephesians 5:4.

657 Cf. Paschasius Radbertus, *Expositio in Matheo* III.v.4 (CCCM 56, p. 285).

658 The definition 'homo est animal mansuetum natura' is found in Boethius's Latin translation of Aristotle's *Topics* V.1, 3 (*Aristoteles latinus* 5.1–3, ed. Minio-Paluello, pp. 86, 95). Cf. Boethius's translation of Aristotle's *On Interpretation*, 11 (*Aristoteles latinus* 2.1–2, ed. L. Minio-Paluello (Leiden, 1965), p. 23).

659 In *Postquam* (see Headnote), this sentence is attributed to Gregory; Wenzel (*Summa virtutum*, ch. 4, 140; p. 159 and n. on p. 346) identifies the source as Gregory's *Homiliae in Evangelia* XXXV.4 (CCSL 141, p. 324, lines 109–11).

660 *Moralium dogma philosophorum*, ed. Holmberg, p. 30, lines 9–10.

661 *seyth Crist*: Cf. Matthew 5:9.
      seyth the wise man: The quotation translates part of a popular Latin couplet (Walther 16974, cf. Whiting S865). 'Nobile vincendi genus est patientia. Vincit | qui patitur. Si vis vincere, disce pati' ('Patience is a noble form of conquering. He who suffers, conquers. If you wish to conquer, learn to suffer'). See also Fkl 773–8 and n., and R. Hazelton, *Speculum*, 35 (1960), 357–80, at pp. 367–8.

664 Proverbs 29:9.

670–73 The source of this anecdote has not been identified. It resembles Seneca's story of Socrates saying to his slave, 'I would beat you if I were not angry' (*On Anger* I.xv.3), and Boethius's story about the man who would have earned the right to call himself a philosopher by being patient under insults if he had not drawn attention to his own patience (*Boece* II pr.7.123–40).

678 This Augustinian definition properly applies to envy rather than sloth (see Pars 484, and n. to Phys 114–17).

679 The reference is probably to 2 Chronicles 19:7, rather than to any of the Solomonic books of the Bible.

680 Jeremiah 48:10 (with 'deceitfully', not 'negligently').

687 Cf. Revelation 3:16.

688 Proverbs 18:9.

690 William of Saint-Thierry, *Epistola ad fratres de monte dei* I.viii.23 (*PL* 184, col. 323).

692 *as seyth Seint Gregorye*: In *Quoniam*, which is the source here, the saying is likewise attributed to Gregory, but the quotation has not been traced in his works.

694 Previously unidentified, but for the idea, see Augustine, *Enarrationes in Psalmos* CXLIV.11 (CCSL 40, pp. 2096–7), and *Sermo* LXXXVII.8 (*PL* 38, col. 535).

696 Judas hanged himself in despair after betraying Christ; see Matthew 27:5.

700–703 Luke 15:7, 11–24; 23:42–3.

705 *Axe and have!*: an echo of Matthew 7:7.

709 Proverbs 8:17.

710 Ignorance is called the 'mother of errors' and 'nurse of vices' in Isidore of Seville's *Synonyma de lamentatione animae peccatricis* II.64 (*PL* 83, col. 860B–C), and the 'mother of vice' in John of Salisbury's *Policraticus* III.1.

712 Ecclesiastes 7:19 (AV differs).

714 For the idea that idleness is the gate to sin, see SN 2–3 and n.

716 Psalm 72:5 (AV 73:5).

723 Cf. Bernard of Clairvaux, *Sermones super Cantica Canticorum* LIV.8 (*Opera*, II, 107).

725 2 Corinthians 7:10.

731 The gloss is based on the etymology of 'magnanimitee': *magn(us)* ('great') and *animus* ('mind').

739 1 Timothy 6:10. Cf. Pard 333–4 and Mel 1130, 1840.

741 Augustine, *City of God* XIV.15 (CCSL 48, p. 438, lines 75–6).

748 Ephesians 5:5.

749 The same idea is found in Dante, *Inferno* XIX.112–14.

750–51 Exodus 20:3–4.

754–6 Augustine, *City of God* XIX.15 (CCSL 48, p. 682, lines 21–2), referring to Genesis 9:25–7; the text's reference to Book IX is an error.

759 Seneca, *Moral Epistles* XLVII.1.

761–2 Cf. Seneca, *Moral Epistles* XLVII.10, 11, 17, compared with this passage by H. M. Ayres, *RomR*, 10 (1919), 1–15, at p. 4. For the idea that death makes no distinction of social rank, cf. Kn 3030 and ML 1142.

764 Cf. Seneca, *Moral Epistles* XLVII.10.

766 Genesis 9:25–7.

768 The source here (*Quoniam*; see Headnote) cites Augustine at a slightly earlier point, which may be why this statement is attributed to him (Wenzel, *Traditio*, 30 (1974), 368, and n. in *Riverside*). It has not been traced.

773 Cf. Romans 13:1.

775–6 An allusion to Matthew 7:2, Luke 6:38.

782 *irreguler*: In canon law, the term applied to those disqualified in perpetuity from receiving or exercising holy orders (*Dictionnaire de droit canonique*, s.v. Irrégularités, section II).

783 See Acts 8:18–24.

788 *Damasie*: Pope Damasus I (366–84). The quotation is attributed to Damasus in the *Summa* of William Peraldus; it occurs in Gratian, *Decretum* II.i.vii.27 (*Corpus Iuris Canonici*, I, col. 438), in a section which is attributed to 'Pascalis papa', but cap. 25 is attributed to 'Damasus papa'.

792 One would expect 'shepherds' rather than 'lambs' in the first of these two sentences; cf. John 10:12.

793 Cf. Pard 591–4 and n.

797 The story of Susanna, falsely accused of adultery by two elders whose sexual advances she had rejected, is related in the non-canonical part of Daniel (Daniel 13).

801 *hurtinge of holy thinges*: The gloss is based on a false etymology of 'sacrilege': 'sacrum laedere' ('to harm the holy'). The true derivation is from 'sacrum' and 'legere' ('to gather up, steal').

806 *Moralium dogma philosophorum*, ed. Holmberg, p. 27, lines 17–18.

819 *corrumped al this world*: Cf. Pard 504. For the identification of Adam's sin as gluttony, see Sum 1915–17 and n., Pard 508–11 and n.

820 Philippians 3:18–19. Cf. Pard 529–33.

822 *sepulture of mannes resoun*: William Peraldus attributes this definition to Rabanus Maurus, while *Quoniam* attributes it to Ambrose (Wenzel, *Traditio*, 30 (1974), 370 and n. 78), but it has not been traced in either author. However, it does occur in the widely known *Alexandreis* of Walter of Châtillon (ed. Colker, I.171–2); cf. Pard 558–9 and n.

828–9 Gregory, *Moralia in Job* XXX.xviii.60 (CCSL 143B, p. 1531, lines 64–70). Cf. *SA*, pp. 742–4, 749–50.

830 The *South English Legendary* has a comparable (though not identical) description of temptation as the 'five fingers of the devil'; see G. M. Sadlek, in *The South English Legendary: A*

Critical Assessment, ed. K. P. Jankofsky (Tübingen, 1992), pp. 49–64. Cf. Pars 852–64.

831 *Galien*: The Greek physician Galen was held in the highest reverence as a medical authority in the Middle Ages. The idea that over-eating was responsible for many illnesses was common; see Rawcliffe, *Medicine*, pp. 39–40; cf. NP 2837–41 and *PPl* VI.256–71.

831–2 The source attributes this saying to (ps.) Augustine, *De vera innocentia*, which is a traditional title for Prosper of Aquitaine's *Sententiae*, but the quotation has not been traced (Wenzel, *Traditio*, 27 (1971), 433–53, at p. 445 and n. 35).

837 Exodus 20:14 (one of the Ten Commandments).

838 Deuteronomy 22:21 (stoning) and Leviticus 21:9 (burning). The 'old law' stipulates that a man and a bondswoman who have had sex should be beaten, but specifies that they should *not* be beaten to death (Leviticus 19:20).

839 On the flood, see Genesis 6:5–7, 17; the idea that lechery was its special cause arose from reading verses 1–4 as indicating the nature of the wickedness referred to in verse 5. For the destruction of Sodom and Gomorrah by fire from heaven, see 19:24–5.

841 Revelation 21:8.

842 See Genesis 2:18–25 and Matthew 19:5.

843 Ephesians 5:32.

844 Exodus 20:17 (the last of the Ten Commandments).

845 *seyth Seint Augustin*: *De sermone domini in monte* I.xii.36 (CCSL 35, p. 39, lines 837–8).
seyth Seint Mathew: Matthew 5:28.

850 *as seyth the prophete*: At the corresponding point in *Quoniam*, the idea that lechery destroys one's reputation is supported by quotations from Ecclesiasticus 9:10: 'Every woman that is a harlot, shall be trodden upon as dung in the way' (with the comment 'that is, she will be considered vile and abominable'), and Jeremiah 2:36 (where God is addressing Israel as a harlot who has abandoned him): 'How exceeding base art thou become' (see Wenzel, *Traditio*, 30 (1974), 372).

852–64 On the 'five fingers of the devil' see n. to Pars 830. The definition of the five stages in love-making (the so-called 'gradus amoris') was a well-known topos which appears in both erotic and religious literature; see L. J. Friedman, *RPh*, 19 (1965), 167–77.

853 The basilisk is a mythical beast which figures in medieval bestiaries; it was reputedly able to kill a man with a glance (*The*

Bestiary: A Book of Beasts, tr. T. H. White (New York, 1954), p. 168).

854 Ecclesiasticus 26:10 and 13:1.

859 See n. to Mch 1839–41.

864 For these infernal punishments, see Mark 9:44, 46, 48 (worms and fire); Matthew 13:42, 50 (wailing and fire); Job 20:25 (trampling by devils; cf. Pars 191).

867 Apparently a rather garbled allusion to Galatians 5:19–21.

869 The parable of the sower, whose seed brought forth varying quantities of fruit depending on where it fell (Matthew 13:8), was traditionally interpreted in terms of the varying degrees of heavenly reward allotted to chaste matrimony (thirtyfold), widowhood (sixtyfold), and virginity (a hundredfold). See, for example, Jerome, *Adv. Jov.* I.3.

871 For examples of the importance of virginity in medieval thinking about sexual crimes, see C. Saunders, *Rape and Ravishment in the Literature of Medieval England* (Cambridge, 2001), chs. 1 and 2.

874 The gloss renders the fanciful etymology of the word 'adulterium' which is given in the *Summa* of William Peraldus, 'ad alterius thorum accessio' (Wenzel, *Traditio*, 30 (1974), 373, n. 99).

875–85 *manye harmes*: Compare the four harms listed at Ecclesiasticus 23:33 as inflicted by an adulterous woman: (1) she has not followed God's law; (2) she has offended against her husband; (3) she has fornicated in adultery; (4) she has produced children by another man.

879 1 Corinthians 3:17.

880–81 Genesis 39:8–9.

883 Cf. Pars 842 and n.

887 Exodus 20:13–15.

888 *the olde lawe of God*: Leviticus 20:10.

889 John 8:11.

891 *hospitaliers*: The Knights Hospitallers were a religious order originally established in Jerusalem around the time of the First Crusade, and dedicated to the care of the sick poor. In following centuries, the order acquired bases all over western Europe.

895 2 Corinthians 11:14.

897 1 Samuel 2:12.

898 *withouten juge*: The biblical gloss on 'Belial' is 'absque iugo' ('without a yoke'). Skeat (V, 471) suggested that the mistake may have arisen from confusion of OF *joug* ('yoke') with *juge* ('judge'); this would imply that ParsT had a French source.

898–9 *free bole*: On the medieval custom by which the lord of the manor provided a bull to range at will with the village cows and impregnate them, see G. C. Homans, *RES*, 14 (1938), 447–9.

900 1 Samuel 2:13–17.

904 Jerome, *Adv. Jov.* I.49.

906 Tobit 6:17.

907 *affinitee*: In canon law, the relationship between persons connected to each other by marriage (and thus prohibited from marrying each other).

910 Sodomy was conventionally spoken of as the sin that could not be named. For a biblical allusion to it, see Romans 1:26–7.

911 *the sonne that shineth on the mixne*: Proverbial. See Whiting S891, and cf. Walther 29914a.

912–14 This list of four causes of nocturnal emission was traditional among scholastic theologians; the first two kinds were held to be sinless, unlike the third and fourth (see M. Müller, *Divus Thomas [Friburgensis]: Jahrbuch für Philosophie und spekulative Theologie*, 3rd series, 12 (1934), 442–97).

916 *two maneres*: A third category of chastity (virginity) is mentioned at Pars 948.

918 *a ful greet sacrement*: Ephesians 5:32. Cf. Mch 1319.

919 John 2:1–11.

920 See n. to Pars 939–40.

921 See Augustine, *De bono coniugali* XX–XXI (CSEL 41, pp. 213–14), and cf. Mch 1446–52.

922 Ephesians 5:22–32; 1 Corinthians 11:3.

925–9 Cf. Genesis 2:22; the interpretation given here is traditional (see Kelly, *Love and Marriage*, pp. 40–41).

927 For a competing appeal to 'experience', see WB 1 ff.

929 Ephesians 5:25.

930 1 Peter 3:1–4.

931 *the decree*: Gratian, *Decretum* II.xxxiii.v.17 (*Corpus Iuris Canonici*, I, col. 1255).

933 *Seint Jerome*: The quotation is not from St Jerome but from Cyprian, *De habitu virginum* XIII (CSEL 3.1, p. 197).
    Seint John: Revelation 17:4.

934 Gregory, *Homiliae in Evangelia* XL.3 (CCSL 141, p. 399, lines 136–8).

939–40 *thre thinges*: The three things that legitimate marital sex are traditional (see Kelly, *Love and Marriage*, pp. 254–61, and cf.

Mch 1441–55). On sex as a marital 'debt', see WB 129–30
and n. The fourth reason named here (940, 943) is not counted
in the 'three things' because it is not a legitimate one.

941 *the decree*: Possibly a reference to Gratian, *Decretum* II.xxxiii.v.1
(*Corpus Iuris Canonici*, I, col. 1250), but there said of a husband,
not of a wife.

946 On the practice of a husband and wife agreeing to abstain from
sex while remaining married, see D. Elliott, *Spiritual Marriage:
Sexual Abstinence in Medieval Wedlock* (Princeton, NJ, 1993).

947 An allusion to the story of the woman, traditionally identified
with Mary Magdalene, who anointed Christ's feet from a box of
precious ointment (Matthew 26:7, Luke 7:36–8).

948 For descriptions of virginity as 'the life of angels', see Augustine,
De sancta virginitate XXIV, LIV (CSEL 41, pp. 260, 300); *Sermo*
CXXXII.3 (*PL* 38, col. 736).

951 Cf. Whiting B506.

955 For Samson's disastrous susceptibility to feminine charms, see
nn. to WB 721–3 and Mk 2023–30. David's lust for Bathsheba
led him to bring about the death of her husband Uriah (2 Samuel
11:2–17). On Solomon's lechery, see WB 35–6 and n., Mch
2298. The trio were commonly cited as evidence of a fatal weakness for women.

956 *the Ten Comandementz*: Patterson (*Traditio*, 34 (1978), 334–
40) shows that ParsT is unusual in its concentration on purely
penitential material; other penitential manuals usually took the
opportunity to include a variety of didactic materials, such as
explanations of the Ten Commandments, the Lord's Prayer, the
seven sacraments, and so on.

957 ... *I lete to divines*: Cf. Kn 1323. According to Skeat (V, 472),
this sentence indicates that the speaker is a layman (i.e., Chaucer
rather than the Parson); it would thus support the theory that
ParsT was first composed as an independent work. A parish
priest might still, however, differentiate himself from professional theologians and defer to their authority; cf. Pars 1043.

958 The discussion of the second part of Penitence began much
earlier, at Pars 316, but it was interrupted by the section on the
Seven Deadly Sins and their remedies (387–955), which derives
from sources other than Raymond's *Summa* (see Headnote).
From this point on, ParsT is again following Raymond's work,
although not its exact order: the section of his *Summa* corresponding to Pars 960–78 succeeds the section corresponding to

Pars 982–1027 (see 1603 edition, pp. 463B–464A and 455B–462A, respectively). Within the latter section, the passages corresponding to Pars 1025–7 are also in a different position from the one they hold in ParsT.

959 Augustine, *Contra Faustum* XXII.27 (CSEL 25, p. 621).

960–78 This account of the different 'circumstances' that affect assessment of the gravity of a sin follows a standard list. Raymond's *Summa* (see *SA*² I, 555) quotes a hexameter couplet which serves as a mnemonic: 'Quis, quid, ubi, per quos, quotiens, cur, quomodo, quando | Quilibet observet, animae medicamina dando' ('Who, what, where, by means of whom, how often, why, how, when, should be considered by anyone administering medicine to the soul'); cf. Walther 25429a and 25431. 'How' and 'when' are here conflated in the seventh circumstance (976–8).

983 Isaiah 38:15 (cf. Pars 135 and n.)

985 Ps. Augustine, *De vera et falsa poenitentia* X.25 (*PL* 40, col. 1122).

986 Luke 18:13.

987 Unidentified.

988 1 Peter 5:6.

994 Matthew 26:75.

996 The woman sinner who anointed Christ's feet at dinner (Luke 7:36–8) was traditionally identified as Mary Magdalene (mentioned at Luke 8:2).

997 *obedient to the deeth*: An echo of Philippians 2:8.

1003 *wikked haste dooth no profit*: Cf. Mel 1054.

1008 This principle is appealed to by the sick man in SumT (see 2095–8). According to Patterson (*Traditio*, 34 (1978), 366–9), there are no parallels to this advice either in Raymond's *Summa* or in other penitential treatises.

1015 On Judas's despair, see n. to Pars 696. For Cain's declaration that his crime was too great to be pardoned by God, see Genesis 4:13 (Vulgate version): 'My iniquity is greater than that I may deserve pardon.'

1020 Augustine, *Sermo* CLXXXI.iv.5 (*PL* 38, col. 981).

1026 Ps. Augustine, *De vera et falsa poenitentia* X.25 (*PL* 40, col. 1122).

1027 Annual communion, preceded by confession, was prescribed by the Fourth Lateran Council in 1215.

1031 This list clearly alludes to the conventional 'seven works of mercy' (based on Matthew 25:35–40): (1) feeding the hungry; (2) giving drink to the thirsty; (3) clothing the naked; (4) harbouring the stranger; (5) visiting the sick; (6) ministering to prisoners; (7) burying the dead.

1033 *day of doome*: An allusion to Matthew 25:31–46.

1036-7 Matthew 5:14–16.

1039 Matthew 6:9–13.

1040-44 The three virtues of the Lord's Prayer are a commonplace in medieval religious manuals (see Petersen, *Sources of Parson's Tale*, p. 28, n. 1, and Wenzel, *ChauR*, 16 (1982), 238-9).

1047 Ps. Jerome, *Commentarius in Marcum* IX (*PL* 30, col. 616); incorporated into the *Glossa ordinaria*, Mark 9:28 (*PL* 114, cols. 214-15); ps. Jerome, *Regula monachorum* XIII (*PL* 30, col. 353).

1048 Matthew 26:41.

1052, 1055 For the twofold meaning of 'discipline' as 'teaching' and 'mortification of the flesh', see Wenzel, *ChauR*, 16 (1982), 239.

1054 Colossians 3:12.

1068 *as a shadwe on the wal*: Cf. Mch 1315 and n., Sh 9.

1069 Gregory, *Moralia in Job* XXXIV.xix.36 (*CCSL* 143B, p. 1759); *Dialogi* IV.44 (*PL* 77, col. 404).

1073 *the seconde wanhope*: The reference to 'the mercy of Crist' shows that it is still the first kind of despair that is under discussion; the second appears only at 1074.

CHAUCER'S RETRACTIONS

This concluding section, usually referred to as Chaucer's Retractions or Retractations, has been variously interpreted, as evidence of a death-bed repentance on Chaucer's part (D. Wurtele, *Viator*, 11 (1980), 335–59), as a literary convention (see O. Sayce, *MÆ*, 40 (1971), 230–48, and the examples collected in *SA²*), or as a literary fiction which represents the culmination of the move away from 'fable' initiated in the Manciple's Tale (see Headnote to McpT). For a balanced summary of older views, see J. D. Gordon, in *Studies in Medieval Literature in Honor of Professor Albert Croll Baugh*, ed. M. Leach (Philadelphia, PA, 1961), pp. 82–96 .

Yet another view has been proposed by C. A. Owen, Jr (*MÆ*, 63 (1994), 239–49) and M. F. Vaughan (in *Rewriting Chaucer*, ed. Prendergast and Kline, pp. 45–90). Drawing attention to the fact that in three manuscripts there is no dividing rubric between the end of the Parson's Tale and the Retractions, they argue that the Retractions are simply the conclusion to a treatise on penitence which Chaucer composed as an independent work, and which was turned into the last tale in *CT* by scribal editors after his death. This hypothesis also addresses two problems created by the separation between the Parson's Tale and the Retractions: (1) the reference to 'this litel tretis' (1081) implies a continuity of speaker, rather than the switch from the Parson to Chaucer indicated in the rubric; (2) the reference to *CT* in the Retractions (1086) is oddly self-referential if the latter are taken to be the conclusion to *CT*.

Against this argument, it can be said that there are several other instances in *CT* where the boundaries of life and literature are blurred in a comparable fashion (see ML 45–89, Mch 1685–7 and the whole Thopas–Melibee sequence). Chaucer's voice is in some sense blended with that of each pilgrim, so that the shift into his own persona in the Retractions is not necessarily felt as a decisive break. While it is quite possible that the treatise on penance was originally composed (or translated) as an independent project and later incorporated into *CT* (see Headnote to ParsT), it is equally possible that it was Chaucer himself who gave it its role as the Parson's Tale. The Parson's Prologue, which is unarguably Chaucerian, implies that a prose tale will follow, and it would be quixotic to suppose that it was a prose tale other than the one occupying that position in the manuscripts.

1083 Romans 15:4; also quoted at NP 3441–2.

1086 *The Book of the xxv Ladies*: This is evidently a reference to the *Legend of Good Women*, but this work contains only ten legends in the form in which we have it. MLPr suggests, however, that it once contained more (see n. to ML 61 ff.). This view is supported by later references to *LGW* in Lydgate's *Fall of Princes* (I, 330–36; ed. H. Bergen, vol. I, EETS e.s. 121 (London, 1924)) and Stephen Hawes's *Pastime of Pleasure* (lines 1326–7; ed. W. E. Mead, EETS o.s. 173 (London, 1928)), though in both cases the number of ladies is given as nineteen (as it is also in three MSS of *CT*).

1087 *The Book of the Leoun*: No work of Chaucer's with this title survives. It might have been a translation or adaptation of Machaut's *Dit dou lyon*, which is a symbolic love-poem (*Oeuvres*, ed. E. Hoepffner, vol. II (Paris, 1911), pp. 159–237), or (much less probably) of Deschamps's *Dit du lyon*, a satirical beast-tale (*Oeuvres*, ed. G. Raynaud, vol. VIII (Paris, 1893), pp. 247–338).

Rubric *compiled*: This word may be taken as a sign that Chaucer is stepping back into his fictional role as reporter of the narratives of his fellow-pilgrims. However, it could also reflect the late-medieval notion of *compilatio* as an organizing principle in book-making; see M. B. Parkes, in *Medieval Learning and Literature: Essays Presented to R. W. Hunt*, ed. J. J. G. Alexander and M. T. Gibson (Oxford, 1976), pp. 115–41.

Glossary

This glossary does not include words whose form is sufficiently close to modern English to make them easily recognizable, and whose meaning is unchanged (e.g. **cat, grene, cloistre**). Nor does it include words that occur only once (sometimes twice) in *CT*; these are glossed on the page at the point of their occurrence. Readers should note that the same word may appear under different parts of speech and that each of these usually has a separate entry; e.g. **lite** appears as a noun, adjective and adverb, each of which is separately glossed.

To save tedious searches through the glossary, words which are spelled in more than one way are entered under each spelling, with cross-references to variant forms; glosses which are appropriate to only one of the variant spellings are not repeated under the entry or entries for the other(s). Anyone who wishes to see the full range of meanings for a word in *CT* will therefore have to consult all the different spelling versions. Where the variant forms are alphabetically contiguous and would thus immediately follow each other in the glossary, or would be so close to each other as to be easily identifiable, they have been conflated into a single entry, with the variation indicated by brackets (e.g. **apai(e)d**). Phrases are often entered under more than one head-word (e.g. **make mury** is under both **make** and **mury**), also with the aim of reducing the amount of searching necessary for the reader. In phrases quoted within entries, a tilde (~) represents the headword, except where an inflected form of it is given in full. Alternative versions of phrases are separated by a slash; optional words are placed within parentheses; alternative phrases with the same meaning are separated by a comma.

Glosses are arranged in accordance with a broad intention to place the more important meanings of a word first, and to indicate by their sequence the links between one meaning and another. After each gloss, there is a reference which indicates the first occurrence of the word in that meaning in *CT*; additional occurrences are indicated by a plus sign (+).

Regular verb inflections, noun plurals, etc, are not entered as a general rule, but any forms which are likely to cause difficulty in identification are recorded, both under their own form and under the head-word to which they belong; occasionally the form which is likely to give difficulty is listed even though the head-word is not (e.g. **broght** is entered though **bringe** *v* is not). Verbs are entered in the infinitive form (without final -n), unless that does not occur in *CT*, in which case the inflected form or forms are given, accompanied by a gloss. Otherwise inflected forms are followed by a reference to the infinitive form, where the glosses will be found. Verbal forms designated singular past (*sg past*) are those appropriate to the first and third persons; where second-person forms are given, they are identified by a '2', and other forms by '*1/3*'. Verbal nouns ending in -ing are not usually given a separate entry if their meaning accords with that of the verb from which they are derived. Nouns and adverbs (e.g. **benignitee, benignely**) are not always entered when their meaning clearly matches that of the corresponding adjective (e.g. **benigne**).

Abbreviations

absol absolute	*inf* infinitive
acc accusative	*interj* interjection
adj adjective	*interrog* interrogative
adv adverb, adverbial	*introd* introducing
alch alchemy	*leg* legal
art article	*lit* literally
astr astrology, astronomy	*masc* masculine
comp comparative	*med* medicine
conj conjunction	*modE* modern English
contr contracted, contraction	*n* noun
dat dative	*nom* nominative
dem demonstrative	*num* numeral
esp especially	*obj* object
fem feminine	*ord* ordinal
fig figurative(ly)	o's one's
fut future	o.s. oneself
gen genitive	*p ppl* past participle
imp imperative	*past* past tense
impers impersonal	*pers* person
indef indefinite	*phil* philosophy

phr phrase
pl plural
poss possessive
prep preposition
pres present tense
pres ppl present participle
pron pronoun
provbl proverbial
refl reflexive

rel relative
sg singular
s.o., s.o's someone, someone's
s.th. something
subj subjunctive
superl superlative
v verb
vbl n verbal noun

a *prep* on Mil 3430, 3516, Sh
180+; in Kn 2934+; ~ *Goddes
half*, ~ *Goddes name* in
God's name GP 854,
WB 50+

a *interj* ah! Kn 1785,
WB 280+

aas (*French*) *n* (see also ***ambes
as***) the one-spot on a die;
lowest possible throw (hence
an emblem of bad luck)
Mk 2661

abaised, abaist *p ppl* (see also
abasshed) perplexed, afraid Cl
317; confused Cl 1108; embarrassed Cl 1011

abak *adv* back Mil 3736,
Th 827

abandone *v refl* (see also **abaundone, abawndone**) devote o.s.
Mel 1577

abasshed *p ppl* (see also **abaised,
abaist**) perplexed, disturbed
ML 568

abate *v* weaken Pars 730;
degrade Pars 191; destroy
Mk 2590

abaundone, abawndone *v* (see
also **abandone**) give up
Pars 694; give Pars 874;
refl devote o.s.
Pars 713

abegge, abeye *v* (see also **abye**)
pay for Rv 3938, Phys 100

abhominable *adj* detestable,
odious, cursed Sum 2006, Pard
471+

abhominacio(u)n *n* disgust Sum
2179, Pars 687; *pl* loathsome
practices ML 88

abide *v* wait (for) Kn 927, Mil
3123+; stay, remain
Kn 2554+; settle Mch 1588+;
last Pard 747; endure
Mel 985; abstain Fkl 1522;
3 sg contr pres **abit**; *p ppl*
abiden

aboght *p ppl of* **abye** *v*

abo(u)ghte *past of* **abye** *v*

aboute *adv* about Kn 2133,
WB 653+; around Kn 2493,
ML 15+; in turn Kn 890; all
round GP 621, Mil 3239;
round about GP 488+; *be* ~ be
intent on, strive Kn 1142+; *go*
~ be intent on, set o.s. to
Phys 158

aboute *prep* round, around
GP 158+; about Kn 2189+;
engaged in Fri 1449, Sh 303;
in attendance on Mch 1495;
go ~ be busy in, occupy o.s.
with Fri 1530, 1569

abraide *v* (see also **abreide**) start

up, wake suddenly Rv 4190,
NP 3008

abregge *v* shorten, reduce, curtail Kn 2999+

abreide *v* (see also **abraide**)
come to, recover consciousness
Cl 1061+

abusioun *n* deception ML 214;
perversion, abuse Pars 445

abye *v* (see also **abegge, abeye**)
pay for, suffer for Kn 2303,
Co 4393, Sum 2155+; *past*
abo(u)ghte; *p ppl* **aboght**

accident *n* non-essential characteristic, variable attribute
(*phil*) Pard 539; outward sign
Cl 607

accidie *n* sloth Pars 388+

ac(c)omplice *v* accomplish
Mel 1132+; perform Kn 2864;
fulfil Mel 1068+; complete
Mel 1336; satisfy Pars 943

ac(c)ord *n* agreement GP 838,
ML 244+; reconciliation Pars
992; concord, harmony
Fkl 791, Mel 1289+, (also
with sense of musical harmony) NP 2879; *by oon ~*
unanimously Mel 1296; *be of
oon ~* be in harmony Phys 25;
falle of (s.o.'s) *~* come to an
agreement with (s.o.)
Fkl 741

ac(c)orde *v* agree GP 818,
Kn 1214+; agree, match
GP 830, CY 638, Mcp 208; be
fitting GP 244; correspond,
harmonize Pri 547; be reconciled Mel 1675, (*refl*)
Mel 1782; *~ to* be in harmony
with, be compatible with
Fkl 798, Mel 1205+; *be*

acorded come to an agreement
Mil 3301+; be reconciled Pars
623; *falle acorded* come to an
agreement WB 812

acorda(u)nt *adj*: *~ to* in keeping
with GP 37, Sq 103+; in harmony with Mil 3363; in
accordance with Fkl 1290

acquitaunce *n* (see also **aquitaunce**) discharge Co 4411

acquite *v* acquit, release from a
charge Fri 1599+; *refl* behave
Cl 936; *acquiteth yow of* fulfil
ML 37

act *n* act WB 114+; *pl* recorded
deeds, chronicles NP 3136

adoun *adv* down GP 393+;
beneath, below Kn 2753,
2995, Mk 2464, Mcp 105;
underneath Kn 2023; at the
bottom CY 779

adrad *p ppl* afraid GP 605+

afer(e)d *p ppl* afraid, frightened
GP 628, Kn 1518+; suspicious
Rv 4095

affeccio(u)n *n* desire, inclination
Kn 1158, ML 568,
Mel 1173+; emotion, emotional disturbance Mil 3611;
affection, fondness Sh 336,
Pars 786; movement of the
spirit Pars 728; feeling Sq 55

afferme *v* establish, fix Kn 2349,
Mel 1056+; confirm Mel 1050;
support the validity of
NP 3125

affray *n* commotion Sum 2156,
Mk 2083; disturbance
ML 1137

affraye *v* harass Cl 455;
frighten, alarm ML 563, Sh
400+

afire *adv and predicative adj* on
fire WB 726+

after *adv* afterwards GP 162,
Kn 989+

after *prep* according to, in
accordance with GP 125+;
alike Kn 1781; in proportion
to Pri 657+; in conformity
with Cl 327, Sq 389+; after
Kn 1467+; ~ *oon* of the same
standard GP 341; *telle* ~ repeat
after GP 731; *sende* ~ send for
Kn 2762; *crye/calle* ~ call for
Pri 605, NP 3028

after *conj* after Kn 2522+

after-diner *n* afternoon, time following mid-day meal Fkl 918+

after-soper *n* evening, time following supper Sq 302+

again *adv* (see also **agein, ayein**)
back GP 801, Mil 3496+;
again Kn 991+; in return, in
answer Kn 1092+; *cacche* (o's)
contenaunce ~ recover o's composure Cl 1110; *paye* ~ pay
back Sh 291; *clappe* ~ close up
Sum 1699

again(s) *prep* (see also **agein(s),
ayein(s)**) against GP 66,
Kn 1787+; towards Kn 2680;
to meet ML 391, WB 1000+;
in return for Rv 4186, Pard
154, Pars 110+; in the presence of Pard 743, Mk 2512; in
front of Mch 2325; in anticipa-
tion of Mcp 301; with regard
to Pars 186, 1060; ~ *the sonne*
in the sun Sq 53+; ~ *somer* at
the approach of summer Sq
142; ~ *the day* towards day
NP 3078, CY 1342; ~ *the
even-tide* towards evening

NP 3072; ~ *the fir* under the
effect of the fire CY 1279

agaste *v* frighten Mk 2205,
NP 3088; *refl* become afraid
Kn 2424; *p ppl* **agast** afraid
Kn 2341+

agein *adv* (see also **again, ayein**)
in return, back, Kn 1197+; in
answer Kn 1152+; again
Kn 1488+; back Co 4380,
Mch 2403+; *quite* ~ pay back
CY 1025

agein(s) *prep* (see also **again(s),
ayein(s)**) against Mel 1586+

aggregge *v* (see also **agregge**)
aggravate Mel 1287

agilte *v* offend, transgress
(against) Mel 1818, Pars 131+;
do wrong Pars 150+; be guilty
WB 392; *p ppl* **agilt**

ago, ago(o)n *p ppl* gone,
departed Kn 1276+; ago
Kn 1813+; past Kn 2784; extinguished Kn 2336; over Phys
246; vanished Fkl 1204; dead
Cl 631

agregge *v* (see also **aggregge**)
increase, aggravate Pars 892+;
~ *muchel of* exaggerate
Mel 1019

agrief *adv: take* ~ (*of*) take
amiss, be upset by WB 191+

agrise *v* shudder Fri 1649; melt
ML 614; ~ *of* revolt from
Phys 280

al *adj and n* all Mil 3636,
ML 907+; everything
GP 319+; ~ *a* a whole GP 584,
CY 996; ~ *and som* the sum
total, the long and the short of
it Kn 2761, WB 91+; *alle and
some* one and all Kn 2187+;

at ~ at all WB 1078+; entirely
Fkl 936, Pard 633; in every
respect Mch 1222; *not at* ~ in
no way Sh 170

al *adv* entirely, completely
GP 683, Kn 1377+; ~ *on
highte* aloud Kn 1784; ~ *only*
only Mel 1472. Used to introduce a concessive clause, with
subject-verb order inverted
and verb in subjunctive form
(if it has one): although, even
if GP 734+; ~ *be that* although
GP 297+

al day, alday *adv* all day
Kn 1178+; constantly, all the
time, continually, always
Kn 1168+

alderfirst *adv* first of all Mch
1618+

alenge *adj* (see also **elenge**)
wretched, miserable WB 1199

ale-stake *n* 'a stake or post set
up before an alehouse, to bear
a garland, bush, or other sign,
or as a sign itself' (*OED*); an
inn-sign GP 667+

aleye *n* alley Pri 568; garden-
walk Mch 2324+

algate(s) *adv* at any rate Rv
3962, Sum 1811+; nevertheless
ML 520, Mch 2376+; anyway,
in any case Fri 1514, Sum
2037; in any/every way Fri
1431+; entirely SN 318;
always, continually GP 571,
WB 588+

alighte *v* dismount, alight
GP 722+; descend Cl 909, Pri
470; *p ppl* **alight**

alle *pl of* **al** *adj*: ~ *and some* one
and all Kn 2187+

aller *gen pl of* **al** *adj* GP 586+; *at
oure* ~ *cost* at the expense of
all of us GP 799

allia(u)nce *n* alliance Kn 2973+;
marriage Cl 357; relationship
created by marriage Sh 139

allye *n* kinsman WB 301, Mk
2403+

allye *v* make an alliance Mch
1414; ~ *in* (s.o's) *blood* marry
into (s.o's) family Rv 3945;
been allied have friends or connections Mk 2530

almes-dede *n* alms-giving
ML 1156+

almesse *n* alms, alms-giving,
charity ML 168+

als *adv* (see also **as**) as Rv
4177+; also Rv 4317+

also *adv* also GP 64+; as
GP 730, WB 1243, Cl 124+; in
asseverations: ~ *mote I thee/
thrive* as I hope to prosper
WB 1215+; ~ *wysly God
my soule blesse* as truly as
God may bless my soul
Mel 922

altercacioun *n* dispute, wrangling Mch 1473+

alway, alwey *adv* always, continually, all the time GP 185+; still
Rv 3888, WB 602, Pri 462+;
steadily Pars 11; in all circumstances WB 1113+; ~ *forther*
still further Rv 4222

ambes as (*French*) *n* (see also
aas) (in the game of dice) two
ones, a double ace (the lowest
possible score, and hence an
emblem of bad luck) ML 124

amende *v* improve (on)
Kn 2196, Mil 3799+; surpass,

excel Cl 1026, Sq 97+; correct, remedy, put right Kn 910+, *refl* Pars 305; increase Kn 3066

amendement *n* amendment, improvement Pars 443+; reparation Rv 4185; *do ~* make amends Pars 443

amenuse *v* diminish, reduce Pars 359+

amerciment *n* penalty, fine Pars 752+

amis *adj* wrong Mil 3736, Sum 2172

amis *adv* wrongly Mil 3181+; badly Fkl 1298+; wickedly Pard 642

amoneste *v* admonish Pars 76+; recommend Mel 1294

among(es) *prep* among, amongst GP 759+; in the midst of Kn 2939; in NP 3313; between Pard 812, 814; *~ al this* meanwhile Cl 785

amorwe *adv* next morning GP 822+; in the morning Mch 1214

amounte *v* mean Kn 2362+

an *prep* (see also **on** *prep*) on; *~ heigh* on high, up above Kn 1065, Mil 3571+

and *conj* and GP 3+; if GP 829, Kn 1214, 1821, Mch 2433, Mk 1950+; even if WB 387, Fkl 1471

angle *n* angle Sq 230; name given to four of the twelve 'houses' of the zodiac ML 304 (see n.), Sq 263

anhange *v* hang Phys 259+

a-night(es) *adv* at night, by night Kn 1042+

annexed *p ppl*: *~ (un)to* connected with WB 1147+

anon-right(es) *adv* at once, immediately Mil 3480+

ano(o)n *adv* at once, immediately, without delay GP 32+; *right ~* Kn 1408+

anoy *n* trouble Sh 130+; irritation, vexation (*of* at) Pars 678+; hardship Pars 720; harm Mel 1489

anoye *v* do harm, be harmful (to) Fkl 875+; disturb, trouble ML 492+; vex, irritate Mel 1044+; *be anoyed* be reluctant (to do s.th.) Pars 687

anoyous *adj* troublesome Mel 1243+; irritating Mel 1044; harmful Pars 365

anything *adv* at all Kn 2285, CY 1477

apai(e)d *p ppl* satisfied Pars 900; *wel ~* satisfied, pleased Mch 1512, Fkl 1548+; *holde* (o.s.) *~* be content Kn 1868+; *ivel(e) ~* dissatisfied, discontent, displeased Fri 1282+; sorry Mch 2392+

apaise *v* (see also **apese**, **appe(i)se**) appease Mel 1100

apalled *p ppl* (see also **appalled**) enfeebled Sh 102; lack-lustre Pars 723

ape *n* ape Rv 3935+; dupe, fool GP 706+; *putte an ~ in* (s.o's) *hood* make a fool of (s.o.) Pri 440

apeire *v* slander Mil 3147; harm Pars 1078

aperceive *v* perceive Cl 600+

apert *adv* openly, in public WB 1114+

aperteine, apertene *v* belong
Mel 1269+; ~ *(un)to* be fitting,
proper for Mel 981+; be connected with Mel 1335, Pars
410+; be a sign of Pars 1068;
concern Mel 1540+

apese *v* (see also **apaise**,
appe(i)se) alleviate Cl 433

apointe *v refl* decide Mch 1595;
be apointed have resolved
Mch 1616

apothecarye (see also **pothecar-
rye**) *n* pharmacist, druggist
GP 425+

appalled *p ppl* (see also **apalled**)
enfeebled, wan Kn 3053,
Sq 365

apparaille *n* clothes Cl 1208;
trappings Pars 432

apparail(l)e *v* prepare Mk
2607+; dress WB 343+; furnish Pars 462; *refl* prepare o.s.
Mel 1342+

apparaillinge *vbl n* preparation
Kn 2913+

apparence *n* illusion
Sq 218+

appe(i)se *v* (see also **apaise**,
apese) remedy Mcp 98; *refl*
grow calm Mel 1861

approche *v* approach Kn 2095+;
be involved Sq 556; ~ *to* have
sexual intercourse with
Pars 579

aquitaunce *n* (see also **acquitaunce**) deed, document in evidence of a transaction
Mil 3327

arace *v* tear away Cl 1103+

areest *n* confinement Kn 1310;
restraint Mch 1282; *make* ~
seize NP 2900

areste *v* stop GP 827+; seize
Fkl 1370

arette *v* (see also **arrette**) blame
(on), attribute (to) GP 726+

argument *n* argument ML 228+;
manipulation of logic Rv
4123+; 'angle or arc used in
calculating the position or
motion of a planet' (*MED*)
Fkl 1277 (see n.)

aright *adv* properly, correctly,
well Sq 336+; right Rv 4254;
exactly GP 267; indeed, assuredly Mk 1945+; rightly
GP 189; *it stondeth not* ~ all is
not well Mil 3426; *go* ~ to go
well Mil 3115+

arist *3 sg contr pres of* **arise** *v*

ark *n* arc, part of a circle from
one horizon to the other which
the sun appears to pass
through each day ML 2,
Mch 1795

armipotente *adj* mighty in battle
Kn 1982+

armoniak *n*: *bole* ~ Armenian
bole (a red clay) CY 790; *sal* ~
ammonium chloride CY 798+

arm(o)ure *n* armour ML 936+;
arms Th 819; armaments
Mel 1333

arn *3 pl pres of* **be** *v*

array *n* clothing, turn-out
GP 73+; equipment, accoutrements, fittings GP 73, Mk
2303+; gear CY 567; state,
condition Kn 1538, Mil 3477,
ML 299+; adornment, finery,
splendour Kn 1932+; pomp Cl
273; preparation Mil 3630, Cl
275+; appearance ML 775;
way of behaving WB 235;

treatment Cl 670; *put in ~ made* to look nice Cl 262

arraye *v* clothe, fit out Kn 1389, Mil 3689+; adorn Kn 2090+; prepare Cl 961, ML 252+; dispose, arrange Kn 2046, 2867; equip Fkl 1187; *be wel arrayed* be in a fine condition Kn 1801

arrette *v* (see also **arette**) impute (to) Kn 2729; *~ to/upon* attribute to, blame on Pars 580, 1082

arrive *v* touch land ML 469; arrive ML 386+

ars-metrik *n* arithmetic Kn 1898+, (?with pun on **ers**) Sum 2222

art *n* art, skill GP 476+; (one of) the liberal arts, as basis of university courses, subject of university study Mil 3191, 3209, Rv 4056, Cl 35; (specifically) logic Rv 4122; profession Mel 1014; body of knowledge Mch 1241; way of life Kn 2791; way Fri 1486; stratagem Kn 2445

art 2 *sg pres of* **be** *v*

artow *contr of* **art thow**

arwe *n* arrow GP 104+

as *adv and conj* (see also **als**) as GP 152+; such as WB 345; like ML 670+; as if GP 81+; that Kn 1858, WB 270+; since Kn 2810+; so WB 805; *~ by, ~ of, ~ to* as regards Cl 924, Sq 17+; *so ~ as* GP 39+; with concessive force: *~ many a yeer ~ it is passed henne* though many years have passed since then Rv 3889; in asseverations: *~ help me Crist* so help me Christ Sum 1949; redundant 'as' (no equivalent in *modE*) (1) in commands and wishes Kn 2302, Mil 3777, Cl 7+; (2) in expressions of time GP 87, WB 473, Mel 977+; *~ nouthe/now* at the moment, just now GP 462+; *~ swithe* at once, without delay, in a trice ML 637+; *~ in this cas* in this situation ML 305+; *~ who seyth* as if to say Mel 1084; *~ s/he that is/was* being, since s/he is/was GP 851, Fkl 1053+; *~ he that hath/hadde* having Kn 964, 1817; *~ he that* like someone who Kn 1261; as someone who Mch 2404+; as the one who Mel 1528+

ascaunce(s) (that) *conj* as if Sum 1745; if CY 838

ascende *v* (of the sun, a planet, or sign of the zodiac) to rise above the horizon Sq 264, NP 2857+

ascendent *n* 'that degree of the ecliptic or zodiac which is arising above the horizon at a given moment; . . . also, the attendant configuration of signs, houses and planets supposed to determine the fortune of a child born at the time of the degree's ascending [cf. WB 613] or to determine a propitious time for various operations [cf. ML 302]' (*MED*); astrological background WB 613; *lord of the ~* planet with influence connected with a particular ascendant ML 301–2; *fortune the ~*

choose a favourable ascendant
GP 417

ascensioun *n* rising above the
horizon of part of the equinoctial circle or celestial equator
NP 2855; increasing elevation
of the sun in the sky between
spring and summer NP 2956;
vaporization CY 778

aslake *v* grow calm, subside
Kn 1760, Mil 3553

asonder *adv* asunder, separated
GP 491+

assaut *n* assault Kn 989+

assay *n* test, trial WB 290, Cl
621+; attempt CY 1249+;
putte in ~ make trial of Cl
1138, test CY 1338

assaye *v* test, make trial (of)
WB 942, Cl 454+; try, attempt
Fkl 1567+; try out Kn 1811,
WB 286

assemble *v* assemble GP 717+;
copulate Pars 939+ (also *be
assembled*)

assemblee *n* assembly ML 403;
copulation Pars 907

assent *n* consent GP 852+;
opinion Mch 1532; *ful* ~
whole-hearted opinion
Kn 3075; *by oon* ~ by
common agreement GP 777+;
by noon ~ on no account
Kn 945; *be of* ~ be in league
(with) Fri 1359, Pard 758; *of
hir* ~ with her connivance
WB 234

assente *v* consent (to), approve
(of) GP 374, Kn 3092+; agree
Mch 1575, Phys 146+; yield,
submit Cl 494

assoil(l)e *v* absolve from sin

Pard 387+; resolve, explain
Mch 1654

assure *v* promise Cl 165+; guarantee Kn 926, 1924; reassure,
make confident Cl 93+; entrust
Mch 2191

asterte *v* escape Kn 1592+; elude
Fri 1314

astoned *p ppl* amazed Cl 337;
dismayed Kn 2361; stunned
Fkl 1339; rendered lifeless
Pars 233

astrologye *n* astronomy, study
of the stars Mil 3192+

astromye, astronomye *n* astronomy, study of the stars
GP 414+

asure *n* lapis lazuli, bright blue
stone Cl 254+

aswage *v* subside Mch 2082+;
subdue Mk 2644

aswowne *adv* in a swoon Mil
3823+

at *prep* at GP 20+; from CY
621; with GP 42, Th 785+; by
Sum 2095+; to Kn 2226, Mch
1489; *ten* ~ *the clokke* ten
o'clock ML 14; ~ *al* at all
WB 1078+; entirely Pard 633;
in every respect Mch 1222; ~ *o
word* in a word ML 428+; ~
his power to the best of his
ability Pars 306

atake *v* overtake CY 556+; *wel
~* well met Fri 1384

atempree *adj* (see also
attempree) moderate Pars 481

atemprely *adv* (see also **attemprely**) moderately, with
restraint Sh 262+

aton *adv* (see also **oon**) at one;
bringe ~ reconcile Cl 437

atones *adv* at once, instantly Mil
    3280+; together GP 765+; at a
    stroke Mil 3470, ML 670
attaine *v* (see also **atteine**) reach
    Mk 2584; ~ *to* achieve
    Pars 469
atte *contr of* **at the** (in set
    phrases): ~ *beste* in the very
    best way, to (o's) heart's con-
    tent GP 29; ~ *fulle* completely
    GP 651+; in full Rv 4133+; to
    the hilt Rv 3936; fairly and
    squarely Rv 4305; ~ *laste*
    finally GP 707+; ~ *le(e)ste* at
    least Mil 3683; ~ *ende* in the
    end WB 404
atteine *v* (see also **attaine**) attain,
    achieve Kn 1243, Fkl 775; ~ *to*
    achieve Mel 1206+; ~ *unto* suc-
    ceed in having Cl 447
attempera(u)nce *n* moderation
    Phys 46+
attempree *adj* (see also
    atempree) moderate, restrained
    Mel 988+
attemprely *adv* (see also
    atemprely) moderately, with
    restraint Sum 2053+
atwinne *adv* apart Mil 3589+
atwo *adv* in two, asunder Mil
    3569+
auctor *n* (see also **auctour**)
    writer NP 2984 (with plural
    meaning)
auctoritee *n* written testimony,
    authoritative book or passage
    Kn 3000, WB 1+; authority,
    influence, reliability Mel 1165,
    NP 2975; authority, power
    Pard 387+; *of* (o's) *owene* ~ on
    o's own responsibility Mch
    1597, Mel 1385

auctour *n* (see also **auctor**)
    author, writer WB 1212+; orig-
    inator Mcp 359, Pars 882
audience *n* hearing Cl 329+;
    audience, opportunity to be
    heard, a hearing Cl 104+;
    court hearing WB 1032, SN
    466; *in general/open* ~ in the
    hearing of everyone, publicly
    ML 673, Cl 790+
auditour *n* hearer Sum 1937;
    auditor GP 594
aught *n* (see also **oght**) anything
    GP 389+; *as adv* by any means
    ML 1034
auncestre *n* ancestor WB 1156+
aungel *n* angel Kn 1055+
auntre *v* take a chance on Rv
    4209; *refl* take a chance
    Rv 4205
auter *n* altar Kn 1905+
avail(l)e *v* help, be of use (to) Fri
    1366+; be sufficient Kn 2401;
    have power Kn 3040; *impers*
    be of use, benefit (to) Mil
    3385, ML 589, Mch 2107+;
    wher him mighte ~ where his
    profit might lie Fri 1324
ava(u)nce *v* improve (s.o's) pos-
    ition GP 246+; promote Pars
    786; *be avanced* win pro-
    motion Pard 410
ava(u)nt *n* boast GP 227+
ava(u)ntage *n* advantage
    Kn 1293+; benefit Kn 2447;
    greatest convenience ML 146;
    gain ML 216; profit CY 731,
    Pars 851; *do* (o's) ~ get o.s.
    into good favour ML 729
ava(u)nte *v refl* boast WB 403+
avaunting(e) *vbl n* boastfulness
    Rv 3884+

ava(u)ntour *n* boaster
NP 2917+

aventure *n* chance GP 25+;
chance event, occurrence
Kn 1235, Fkl 1483; accident
Kn 2703+; lot, fortune
ML 465, Fkl 940+; vicissi-
tude(s) Kn 2444, ML 1151;
notable event, strange happen-
ing GP 795, Cl 15+; *min/his ~*
what happened to me/him
Kn 1160+; *thin ~* what is to
happen to you Kn 2357; *by/of*
~ by chance Kn 1506+; *take*
(o's) *~* take o's chance, accept
the risk Kn 1186, WB 1224;
putte in ~ risk Mch 1877+; *be*
in ~ be at risk Pars 1068

avis *n* judgement, opinion
Kn 1868+; advice Mel 1786;
deliberation GP 786,
Mel 1252; *take* (o's) *~* take
thought Mel 1726, 1787

avise *v* consider Cl 797+; think
about Mel 1348; *refl* reflect,
take thought, consider Mil
3185, Rv 4188, ML 664+; *~*
upon ponder on Cl 238+; *be*
avised take thought, take care
Mil 3584, Co 4333+; *be avised*
of reflect on Pars 979; *wel*
avised wise Mel 1324; *yvele*
avised ill-considered Mcp 335

avisely *adv* with forethought
Mel 1298+

avisement *n* thought, reflection
Mch 1531+; *of ful ~* deliberately ML 86

avisioun *n* vision Sum 1858;
dream NP 3114+

avouter *n* (see also **avowtier**)
adulterer Fri 1372

avoutrye *n* (see also **avowtrye**)
adultery Fri 1306+

avow *n* vow, pledge Kn 2237+

avowtier *n* (see also **avouter**)
adulterer Pars 841+

avowtrye *n* (see also **avoutrye**)
adultery Pars 840+

await *n*: *ligge/sitte in ~* lie in
ambush Fri 1657+; *have/keep*
in ~ watch suspiciously Mk
2725+

awaite *v*: *~ on* watch Sum 2052;
wait for Mil 3642, Fkl 1299; *~*
after wait for Pri 586

away *adv* (see also **awey(e)**)
away Kn 2819+; gone Rv 4071

awe *n* fear GP 654; *have in ~*
fear Mk 2559; *putte in ~*
intimidate Mk 2685

a-werk(e) *adv*: *sette* (s.o.) *~* put
(s.o.) through the mill Co
4337, WB 215

awey(e) *adv* (see also **away**)
away Kn 1180+; gone
ML 609, Fkl 1064+

awook *sg past of* **awake** *v*

awreke(n) *p ppl* avenged Mil
3752+

axe *v* ask Kn 1347+; require Mil
3545+

axing(e) *n* request Kn 1826;
question SN 423

ay *adv* always Rv 4128+; all the
time Mil 3472, Rv 4030+; continually GP 646+; every time
GP 63; for ever ML 843; all
along Mil 3453; *~ ner and ner*
ever nearer and nearer
Rv 4304

ayein *adv* (see also **again**, **agein**)
again Kn 892+; back
Mch 2260

ayein(s) *prep* (see also **again(s)**,
   agein(s)) against Cl 320; set
   against Mil 3155; ~ *the sonne*
   in the sun Kn 1509

baar *1/3 sg past of* **bere** *v*
bacheler, bachiler *n* young man
   in knightly service, young
   knight GP 80, WB 883+;
   unmarried man Mch 1274;
   knight of lower rank than a
   knight banneret Kn 3085;
   holder of bachelor's degree
   Fkl 1126
bachelrye *n* knighthood Mcp
   125; knights in attendance
   Cl 270
bacin *n* basin WB 287+
bacoun *n* bacon, salt pork
   WB 217+
bad *sg past of* **bidde** *v*
baillif, bailly *n* agent of a lord
   GP 603+; officer of a court
   Fri 1392
baite *v* feed ML 466+
bakbite *v* slander, defame Pars
   1018+
bake-mete *n* pastry-dish, pie
   GP 343+
bala(u)nce *n* pair of scales Mk
   2586; *leye in* ~ wager, stake
   CY 611
balke *n* beam Mil 3626,
   Rv 3920
balled *adj* bald GP 198+
baly *n* (see also **bely**) belly
   Sum 2267
bane *n* slayer, destroyer
   Kn 1681; *be* (s.o's) ~ cause
   (s.o's) death Kn 1097+
bar *1/3 sg past of* **bere** *v*
bare *adj* bare Kn 1758+; bare-

headed GP 683; scanty, poor
   Fri 1480; simple Fkl 720;
   empty Co 4390; poor CY 732;
   ~ *of* devoid of Mch 1548; *in*
   my kirtel ~ stripped down to
   my tunic Fkl 1580
bare *2 sg past of* **bere** *v*
bareine *adj* barren, sterile
   Kn 1977+; destitute
   Kn 1244
baren *pl past of* **bere** *v*
barge *n* ship, boat GP 410+
barm *n* arms, lap Cl 551, Sq
   631+
baronage *n* nobility, peers of the
   realm Kn 3096+
barre *n* bar Kn 1075; ornamental metal strip GP 329,
   Pars 433
bataille *n* battle Kn 879+
bathe *adj* both (Northern form)
   Rv 4087+
baude, bawde *n* procurer, pimp
   Fri 1339+
bauderye, bawderye *n* gaiety
   Kn 1926; procuring, pimping
   Fri 1305
Bayard 'Dobbin' (a traditional
   horse's name, and thus used
   to designate any horse)
   Rv 4115+
be, bee *v* be; ~ *as* ~ *may* however it may be Mk 2129, CY
   935; *1 sg pres* am, *2 sg pres*
   art, *3 sg pres* is; *pl pres* been,
   be(n), beth, are, arn; *sg pres*
   subj be; *1/3 sg past* was; *2 sg*
   past were; *pl past* were(n); *1/3*
   sg past subj were; *sg imp* be; *pl*
   imp beeth; *p ppl* been, be(n),
   ybe(n)
bechen *adj*: ~ *cole* piece of

charcoal made from beech-wood CY 1160+

bede *v* offer Cl 360+

bede(n) *pl past of* **bidde** *v*

bedred(e) *adj* bedridden Sum 1769, Mch 1292

been *weak pl of* **bee** *n*

been *inf, pl pres and p ppl of* **be** *v*

beer *1/3 sg past of* **bere** *v*

beere *n* bier Kn 2871+

beest *n* (see also **best**) beast, animal Kn 1309+

beete *v* kindle, light Kn 2253+; repair Rv 3927; relieve Pars 421; *pl past* **betten**

beeth *pl imp of* **be** *v*

bekke *v* nod Pard 396+

bely *n* (see also **baly**) belly Pard 534; bellows Pars 351

ben *pl pres and p ppl of* **be** *v*

bench n bench, seat WB 247; counting-table Sh 358; ~ *of feet* footstool Pars 589

benedicite(e) (*Latin*) *interj* bless me, my goodness, heavens! Kn 1785+ (pronounced bèndistè, as a trisyllable)

benefice *n* an ecclesiastical living GP 291+

benigne *adj* gentle, gracious, kind GP 483+; mild Sq 52

benisoun *n* blessing Mch 1365+

berd *n* beard GP 270+; *make (s.o's)* ~ get the better of, outwit (s.o.) Rv 4096, WB 361

bere *n* bear Kn 1640+

bere *v* bear, carry Kn 1422+; give birth to ML 722+; endure, suffer Cl 85+; *refl* to bear o.s., behave, perform GP 87, NP 2872+; ~ *doun* overbear,

talk down Mil 3831+; ~ *adoun* overthrow Kn 2644; ~ *on honde* accuse (s.o. of s.th.) ML 620+; maintain, assert WB 232; ~ *wrong on honde* make false assertions against WB 226; *3 sg pres* **bereth**, *contr* **berth**; *1/3 sg past* **baar**, **bar**, **beer**; *2 sg past* **bare**; *pl past* **baren**; *p ppl* **(y)bore**, **(y)boren**, **(y)born**

bering(e) *n* bearing, behaviour Mch 1604+

bern(e) *n* barn Mil 3258+

berye *v* bury Pard 405, 884

best *n* (see also **beest**) beast, animal Kn 1976+; *pl* cattle, livestock Cl 201+

beste *superl adj* best GP 252+; *atte/at the* ~ in the very best way, to (o's) heart's content GP 29+; *with the* ~ superbly GP 387, among the finest ML 76; *for the* ~ in everyone's best interests, as the best plan GP 788+; *(as) for thy/oure/his* ~ in your/our/his best interests Sum 1986, Cl 1161, Sh 347

bet *comp adv* better GP 242+; *go* ~ go quickly Pard 667; *what wol ye* ~ *than wel* what more do you want Mil 3370+; ~ *than nevere is late* better late than never CY 1410

bete *v* beat Mil 3759, Rv 4308+; hammer, emboss Kn 979, Phys 14+; *pl past* **bette(n)**; *p ppl* **bet**, **bete(n)**, **ybet**, **ybete(n)**

beth *3 pers pl pres and pl imp of* **be** *v*

bette(n) *pl past of* **bete** *v*

betten *pl past of* **beete** *v*

beye *v* (see also **bye**) buy Pard
    845+; redeem WB 718, Cl
    1153+; *past* **boghte, boughte**;
    p ppl **boght, yboght**
bicam *sg past of* **bicome**
bicause *adv and conj* because
    GP 174+
bicome *v* become Fri 1644+; suit
    WB 603; *sg past* **bicam**
bidde *v* direct, order GP 187,
    Mil 3228, WB 28+; tell
    GP 787+; ask, request Mch
    1618+; pray Mil 3641, SN
    140; compel, urge Sq 348+; ~
    fare wel say goodbye Sh 320;
    3 sg contr pres **bit**; *sg past* **bad**;
    pl past **bede(n)**; *p ppl* **bode**
bide *v* wait Kn 1576+; stay,
    remain Rv 4237, Co 4399+; *sg
    past* **bood**
bifalle *v* befall, happen GP 19,
    Kn 1805+; *faire yow* ~ may
    you prosper Pars 68; *sg past*
    bifel, bifil; *past subj* **bifelle**;
    p ppl **bifalle**
bifo(o)re, biforn *prep* before, in
    front of GP 100+; *him* ~ in
    front of him Kn 1634+; *us* ~
    ahead of us CY 680
bifore, biforn *adv* before
    Kn 1224+; in front, at the
    front GP 377+; beforehand
    Kn 1665+; earlier Kn 1148+;
    in readiness, ahead GP 572
big *adj* strong GP 546+
bigan *1/3 sg past of* **biginne** *v*
bigeten *p ppl* engendered Mk
    1948+
bigile *v* deceive, trick Mil 3300+
biginne *v* begin GP 42+. Used as
    a weak auxiliary with an
    infinitive, as equivalent of a

simple present or past tense:
    e.g. *biginneth dawe* dawns Mk
    2682; *bigan areste* brought to
    a halt GP 827; *bigan to goon*
    went Kn 2271; *bigonne they to
    rise* they rose Mel 1043; *1/3 sg
    past* **bigan**; *2 sg past* **bigonne**;
    pl past **bigonne**; *p ppl*
    bigonne(n)
bigo(o)n *p ppl* (see also **wo-
    bigon**) beset, overwhelmed;
    him is wo ~ he is overcome
    with sadness Mil 3372; cf.
    ML 918, Fkl 1316; *wel* ~
    happy, in good spirits WB 606
bihe(e)ste *n* promise ML 37+
bihete *v* (see also **bihote**)
    promise Fkl 788+; *sg past*
    bihighte; *pl past* **bihighten**;
    p ppl **bihight**
bihinde *adv* behind, in the rear
    ML 427+; at the back Mil
    3239+; afterwards Mk 1988;
    left behind Pars 1010; to fol-
    low CY 1291
bihinde *prep* behind Kn 1050+
bihote *v* (see also **bihete**)
    promise Kn 1854
bihove *v impers* be necessary
    Mel 1170+; be fitting
    Mel 1655, Pars 83+; *bihoveth
    hire* she needs Sq 602; *bihov-
    eth me* I must Fkl 1359+
bihovely *adj* necessary, appropri-
    ate Pars 107+
bijape *v* trick, deceive Kn 1585+
biknowe *v* confess ML 886+;
    acknowledge Kn 1556+; *pl
    past* **biknewe**
bilde *v* (see also **builde**) build
    Mch 1279
bile(e)ve *v* believe Mil 3162+

bileve *n* belief, faith Fkl 1133+; creed Mil 3456

bille *n* petition Mch 1971, Phys 166 (see n.) +; letter Mch 1937+; ~ *of somonce* summons Fri 1586

binde *v* bind Kn 2414+; tie Rv 4060+; imprison Cl 1205; constrain Pars 686; *sg past* **bond, boond**; *pl past* **bounde**; *p ppl* **bounden, ybounde(n)**

binime *v* take away (from) Pars 335+

biquethe *v* bequeath Kn 2768+; *p ppl* **biquethe**

bireve *v* take away Sum 2111+; take away from Kn 1361+; rob, deprive (of) ML 83, Sum 2059+; *sg past* **birafte, birefte**; *p ppl* **biraft, bireved**

biseche *v* (see also **biseke**) beseech, entreat, ask Mil 3600+; *sg and pl past* **bisoght(e), bisoughte**

bisege *v* besiege Mel 1099+

biseke *v* (see also **biseche**) beseech, entreat, ask Kn 918+; ~ *to* entreat, beg Mel 1116+

bisette *v* bestow Mil 3715; employ Mil 3299; spend Sum 1952+; fix Pars 366; dispose, manage Kn 3012; ~ (o's) *wit* use (o's) head GP 279; *past* **bisette**; *p ppl* **biset**

biseye *p ppl*: *ivel* ~ of poor appearance Cl 965; *richely* ~ of splendid appearance Cl 984

bishrewe *v* curse WB 844+

biside *adv* in addition Kn 967+

biside(s) *prep* beside, near GP 402+

bisily *adv* diligently, carefully Kn 1883, Mil 3763+; earnestly GP 301, SN 342+; eagerly Rv 4006, ML 180+; intently ML 1095, Sq 88+

bisinesse *n* activity, labour Mil 3643, Mel 1591+; activity, occupation Mil 3654+; business Sh 225; diligence Cl 1008+; endeavour GP 520, Fkl 827; attentiveness WB 933; tasks, duties Cl 1015, Mch 1904; concern Mel 1637; trouble, anxiety Kn 1928, WB 1196, Mch 1577+; *do* (o's) ~ make an effort, do (o's) best, give (o's) attention to Kn 1007, Cl 592+; *in his* ~ occupied CY 1270

bisoght(e), bisoughte *past of* **biseche** *v*

bispet *p ppl* spat upon Pars 276+

bistowe *v* bestow (in marriage) Rv 3981; employ WB 113; spend Sh 419+

bisy *adj* busy GP 321+; diligent, assiduous Kn 2853+; active Kn 1491, Sh 318; concerned Kn 2442; solicitous, attentive Cl 603; earnest ML 188, Sum 1940; anxious, troubled Kn 2320, Cl 134+; ~ *inow* hard put Mch 1560

bisy(e) *v refl* bestir o.s., exert o.s. WB 209+

bit *3 sg contr pres of* **bidde** *v*

bitake *v* entrust Cl 161+; consign Mil 3750+; *sg past* **bitook**

bithenke, bithinke *v* imagine WB 772+; *refl* recollect, call to mind Co 4403, Mel 1445+

(with *on*, Pars 700); consider
Pars 352; *be bithoght of* have
thought of GP 767; *sg past*
bithoghte; *p ppl* bithoght

bitide *v* happen, befall, occur
Mil 3450+; ~ *what* ~ come
what may Th 874; *sg past*
bitidde; *p ppl* bitid

bitime(s) *adv* in good time
Kn 2575+; promptly, straightway CY 913+

bitok(e)ne *v* signify, symbolize
WB 851+

bitook *sg past of* bitake *v*

bitrayse *v* betray Mk 2380+

bitwix, bitwixe(n) *prep* between
GP 277+

biwail(l)e *v* bewail, lament
ML 26+

biwepe *v* weep for Pars 178+

biwreye *v* reveal Kn 2229+; disclose WB 948+; betray
WB 974+

blame *v* find fault with Rv 3863,
ML 106, Cl 78+; reproach
ML 372; blame Mil 3181,
WB 541+

blede *v* bleed GP 145+; *sg past*
bledde

blende *v* blind Mil 3808, Mch
2113, CY 1077+; *3 sg pres*
blent; *p ppl* (y)blent

blere *v* blear CY 730+; ~ (s.o.'s)
eye hoodwink s.o. Rv 3865+

blesse *v* (see also **blisse**) bless
Mil 3455, ML 1146+; wish
blessings on Mil 3218; protect,
guard Mil 3484, *refl* Mcp 321;
make the sign of the cross over
Cl 679; *refl* to cross o.s. Mil
3448+

blew *adj* blue GP 564+

blind *adj* blind Kn 1965+; dark
CY 658

blis *n* (see also **blisse**) joy, happiness NP 3166; festivity, ceremonial splendour ML 409;
heavenly bliss ML 33+;
worldes ~ worldly happiness
NP 3200

blisful *adj* blessed GP 17+; fortunate ML 726+; happy
WB 220+; fine, splendid
ML 403, NP 3197; lovely,
beautiful Mil 3247+

blisse *n* (see also **blis**) joy, happiness Kn 1230+; festivity, ceremonial splendour Kn 1684+;
heavenly bliss Sum 1857+

blisse *v* (see also **blesse**) bless
Pard 474+; make the sign of
the cross over Cl 552; *refl*
cross o.s. ML 449

blithe *adj* happy, glad, joyful
GP 846+

blive *adv* quickly, hastily
Kn 2697+

blondre *v* walk blindly CY
1414; act in the dark CY 670

blowe(n) *p ppl* proclaimed
Kn 2241; inflated SN 440

boce *n* (see also **boos**) bulge
Pars 423

bode *p ppl of* bidde *v*

body *n* body Kn 2283+; person
Rv 4172+; *my* ~ myself, I, me
ML 1185, WB 1061+

boes *3 sg pres of* bihove *v*
impers (Northern form); *him* ~
he must Rv 4027

boght *p ppl of* beye/bye *v*

boghte *past of* beye/bye *v*

boidekin *n* dagger Rv 3960+

boiste *n* box, jar Pard 307+

bokeler *n* small shield GP 112+

bokes *pl of* **book** *n*

boldely *adv* boldly WB 227+;
vigorously Fri 1303+; insol-
ently Pars 599; with assurance
Sq 581; without delay Mil
3433, NP 3020

bole *n* bull Kn 1699+; *free ~* a
bull free to roam with the herd
Pars 898+

bolt-upright *adv* flat on the back
Rv 4266+

bon *n* (see also **boon**) bone
WB 511+; *pl* bones GP 546;
dice (made of ivory) Pard 656

bond *sg past of* **binde** *v*

bonde *n and adj* bondsman, serf
Fri 1660, Pars 149; subject (to)
WB 378, Mk 2270; *~ of linage*
born in bondage Mel 1561

bonde-folk *n* bondsmen, tenants
Pars 754+

bonde-men *n pl* customary
tenants, bondsmen Pars 752+

bood *sg past of* **bide** *v*

book *n* book GP 185+; Bible
ML 662+; *pl* bokes

boold *adj* bold GP 458+; *~ of
speche* voluble GP 755

boon *n* (see also **bon**) bone
Kn 1177+; ivory NP 3399

boond *sg past of* **binde** *v*

boone *n* request Mch 1618+;
prayer Kn 2269+

boor *n* boar Kn 2070+; male pig
Sum 1829; *pl* bores

boos *n* (see also **boce**) boss
Mil 3266

boost *n* boast ML 401+; arro-
gance, pride Mk 2099, 2609,
SN 441; *crake ~* bluster
Rv 4001

boote *n* remedy GP 424+; good,
benefit WB 472, Mel 993; salvation Pri 466; *do ~* heal
Sq 154

boras *n* borax (used as ingredi-
ent of medicine for skin disease) GP 630; borax (used in
alchemy in treating base
metals) CY 790

bord *n* board, plank Mil 3440;
table GP 52, ML 430+; board,
food CY 1017; *biginne the ~*
sit at the head of table GP 52;
go to ~ lodge WB 528; *holde
to ~* keep as lodger Mil 3188;
into shippes ~ on board a ship
Mil 3585

bore *p ppl of* **bere** *v* (see also
boren, born, ybore(n), yborn)
born Kn 1542+; carried Sq
178+; borne Mil 3831

borel *n* (see also **burel**) coarse
woollen cloth WB 356; *~ men*
laymen Mk 1955

boren *p ppl of* **bere** *v* (see also
bore, born, ybore(n), yborn)
born WB 1153

bores *pl of* **boor** *n*

born *p ppl of* **bere** *v* (see also
bore, boren, ybore(n), yborn)
born Kn 1073+; borne, carried
GP 87+; borne, given birth to
Cl 444; *borne man* servant
from birth Mch 1790

borste *pl past of* **breste** *v*

borwe *n* security, pledge; *leye
(o's) feith to ~* pledge (o's)
word Kn 1622; *have heer my
feith to ~* I pledge my word
Fkl 1234; surety, guarantor
Mel 1807+; *Seint John to ~* in
farewell (*lit* 'under the protec-

tion of St John', an expression
used in saying farewell) Sq 596

borwe *v* borrow Co 4417+

botel *n* bottle, flask Sum 1931+

boterflye *n* butterfly Mch 2304+

botme *n* bottom NP 3101+

bounde *pl past of* **binde** *v*

bounden *p ppl of* **binde** *v*

bounte(e) *n* goodness, virtue
WB 1160, Cl 157+; good Pars
525+; kindness Mch 1917,
Mel 1189, Pars 466; worth,
excellence Cl 415, Pri 457; generosity Pars 284+; prowess, valour Mk 2114

bour *n* bedroom Mil 3367+;
lady's private room WB 300+

bowe *n* bow GP 108+; *dogge for
the* ~ hunting dog trained to
track game wounded by
archers Fri 1369, Mch 2014

bowes *pl of* **bowe** *n and also of*
bough *n*

box *n* box-tree Kn 2922; box-
wood NP 3398

boy *n* servant (usually young)
Pard 670; rascal, knave Fri
1322, 1563; boy Pri 562

braide *v* (see also **breide**): ~ *of
swough* suddenly recover consciousness WB 799

brak *sg past of* **breke** *v*

brast *sg past of* **breste** *v*

braun, braw(e)n *n* muscle
GP 546, NP 3455+; brawn,
cooked meat Sum 1750+

breche *n* (see also **breech**)
breeches NP 3448

brede *n* breadth, width
Kn 1970+

breech *n* (see also **breche**)
breeches Pard 948+

breek *sg past and past subj of*
breke *v*

breide *v* (see also **braide**) pull,
snatch ML 837; recover consciousness, start Sq 477; ~ *of
sleep* wake up suddenly Rv
4285; ~ *out of* (o's) *wit* lose
o's senses Fkl 1027

breke *v* break GP 551+; break
out of Kn 1468+; break into
Pars 879; put a stop to
Mel 1043, Mk 1927, Pars 24;
~ *forward* break an agreement
ML 40; ~ (o's) *day* fail to pay
punctually CY 1040; *sg past*
brak, breek; *past subj* **breek**;
p ppl **broke(n)**

bren *n* bran Rv 4053+

brend *p ppl of* **brenne** *v* pure,
refined Kn 2162, 2896; burned
NP 3365

brenne *v* (see also **brinne**) burn
Kn 2331+; *sg past* **brende,
brente**; *pl past* **brende(n)**; *p ppl*
(y)brend, (y)brent

brere *n* briar Kn 1532+

breste *v* break Kn 1980+; burst
Kn 2610+; *sg pres* **brest**; *sg
past* **brast**; *pl past* **borste,
broste**; *p ppl* **brosten**

bret-ful *adj* brimful, crammed
full GP 687+

bretherhede *n* brotherhood Fri
1399+; guild, religious fraternity GP 511

bribe *v* pilfer Co 4417; practise
extortion Fri 1378

brid *n* bird Kn 2929+; (as term
of endearment) sweetheart Mil
3699+; (as term of dis-
paragement) wretch, fiend
Pars 195

bright *adj* bright GP 104+;
resplendent, glorious
ML 841+; beautiful, fair
Kn 1427+

brighte *adv* brightly Kn 2425+

brimstoon *n* brimstone, sulphur
GP 629+

brinne *v* (see also **brenne**) burn
WB 52

broche *n* (see also **brooch**)
brooch Mil 3265

brode *pl and weak sg of* **brood**
adj broad, wide Kn 2136+;
arwes ~ arrows with broad
heads Mk 2258

brode *adv* broad, widely, spread
out Mil 3315+; with eyes wide
open CY 1420; plainly,
frankly GP 739

broght *p ppl of* **bringe** *v* brought

broghte(n) *past of* **bringe** *v*
brought

broke *v* (see also **brouke**):
broken harm mischief-making
Mch 1425 (see n.)

brond *n* firebrand, torch
Kn 2338+

brooch *n* (see also **broche**)
brooch, ornament GP 160+

brood *adj* broad, wide GP 471+;
pl and weak sg **brode**

broste *pl past of* **breste** *v*

brosten *p ppl of* **breste** *v*

brotel, brotil *adj* brittle, fragile
Mch 1279+

brouke *v* (see also **broke**) enjoy,
keep Mch 2308+

builde *v* (see also **bilde**) build
WB 655+; *sg past* **bulte**

bukke *n* male deer Th 756;
blowe the bukkes horn go and
twiddle o's thumbs Mil 3387

(*lit* to idle away time blowing a
goat's horn, like a shepherd)

bulle *n* papal bull, edict Cl 739+

bulte *sg past of* **builde** *v*

burdo(u)n *n* bass accompaniment GP 673 (?with a pun on
meaning 'staff'), Rv 4165

burel *n* (see also **borel**): ~ *folk*
laymen Sum 1872+; ~ *man*
uneducated man, man of
'homespun' learning Fkl 716

burgeis *n* citizen GP 369+

burned *p ppl* burnished, shining
Kn 1983+

burthe *n* birth Mel 1567; *roote
of a* ~ position of the heavens
at the time of (o's) birth (as a
basis of calculation in astrology) ML 314 (see n.)

bussh *n* thicket Kn 1517+; bush
Mch 2155+; *under the* ~ in the
woods Mk 2265

busshel *n* bushel Sum 1746+; *an
eighte busshels* the quantity of
eight bushels Pard 771

but *adv* only GP 120, ML 953+

but *quasi-prep* (with negative)
only, no more than WB 881;
nis but is only Kn 2847, Rv
4047; *nothing* ~ *for love* only
for love Kn 1754; *noghte* ~
ones only once Mk 2286; *I
nam* ~ *deed* I am as good as
dead Kn 1122+; *I nere* ~ *lost* I
would be ruined Sh 185

but *conj* but ML 215+; unless, if
. . . not Kn 2245, Sh 193+;
except WB 880+; that . . . not
Mch 1665; *but that* except
that NP 3283; that . . . not
Mel 1621

but if *conj* unless GP 656,

ML 636+; that ... not Mil
3300, Fkl 1611

buxom *adj* submissive, obedient
Mch 1287+

by *adv* nearby, close at hand
NP 3268; *faste* ~ near, close at
hand Kn 1476, 1688

by *prep* by GP 25+; in accordance with Pri 634; with respect
to, concerning, as regards
GP 244, Mil 3194, WB 229+;
~ *the morwe* in the morning
GP 334; ~ *wey of kinde* according to nature Pri 650; ~ *wey of
reson* on rational consideration ML 219; *faste* ~ close to
GP 719+

by and by *advbl phr* side by side
Kn 1011; alongside Rv 4143

by that *conj* by the time that CY
971+

bye *v* (see also **beye**) buy
Kn 2088, WB 287+; pay for
ML 420, WB 167+; *past*
boghte, boughte; *p ppl* **boght,
yboght**

caas *n* (1) (see also **cas** *n* (1))
law-suit, case GP 323; chance
Pars 574; event, circumstance
GP 585; case, situation, circumstances GP 655, 797,
Kn 1780+; *in no* ~ in no circumstances Mel 1527

caas *n* (2) (see also **cas** *n* (2))
quiver for arrows Kn 2358

cacche *v* catch, seize Kn 1214,
Rv 4105, Cl 674; take hold of
Kn 1399; pull Pri 671; obtain,
acquire, get GP 498; get (an
idea, thought etc) WB 306,
Pars 689+; feel, experience (a

mood, desire etc) ML 186,
Sum 2003, Cl 619, Mch
2134+; receive Mch 2357;
incite Pars 852; ~ *again* (o's)
contenaunce recover o's composure Cl 1110; ~ *a sleep* go to
sleep Rv 4227; ~ *whoso may*
catch as catch can, let him
obtain it who can WB 76; *sg
and pl past* **caughte**; *p ppl*
caught

caitif *n* (see also **kaitif**) captive,
prisoner Mk 2079; wretch
Kn 924, 1717, Pard 728; *as
adj* enslaved Kn 1552;
wretched Pars 271

cake *n* a flat cake or loaf
GP 668, Rv 4094+

cam *sg past of* **come** *v*

camuse *adj* turned-up, pug, snub
(nose) Rv 3934, 3974

cape *v* gaze, stare (= gape) Mil
3444+

capoun *n* capon, chicken Sum
1839, Pard 856

cappe *n* cap, hat, *esp* a small
head covering worn under the
hood GP 683, 685; *sette* (s.o's)
cappe make a fool of (s.o.)
GP 586, Mil 3143

capul *n* horse Rv 4088, 4105,
Sum 2150+

care *n* sorrow, grief Kn 2352,
ML 514+; distress, hardship,
misfortune Kn 1489, Sh 264,
Th 759+; trouble Mcp 54,
CY 769; *pl cares colde* suffer-
ing, anguish Fkl 1305,
SN 347

care *v* grieve, be sad, sorrow Cl
1212; care, worry about
WB 329, *refl* Mil 3298

careine *n* (see also caroine)
decaying corpse, carrion Pars
441; gangrenous flesh
Mk 2624

carf *sg past of* kerve *v* cut Mk
2457+; carved GP 100+

cariage *n* a technical term for a
lord's right to his tenant's cart
and horses for transportation;
upon ~ in the way of carriage-
service Fri 1570; any tax or
rent Pars 752

carl *n* man, fellow GP 545, Mil
3469, Fri 1568; knave, rascal
Pard 717

caroine *n* (see also careine)
corpse Kn 2013

cart(e) *n* cart Kn 2022; war-
chariot Kn 2041

carye *v* carry GP 130+

cas *n* (1) (see also caas *n* (1))
case, situation Kn 1411,
Fkl 1430+; event, incident Rv
3855, Cl 316+; chance, accident GP 844; cause, reason
Mcp 308; case, matter
Kn 2971, Mel 1156; law-suit,
case ML 36, Phys 163; *in/for
no ~* under no circumstances
WB 665, SN 149; *in oother ~*
in other circumstances Mk
2294; *as in this ~* in this situation ML 305+; *par ~* by
chance Pard 885; *upon ~* by
chance Mil 3661; *to dyen in
the ~* though death were the
result Cl 859; *sette ~* put the
case, assume for the sake of
argument Mel 1491+

cas *n* (2) (see also caas *n* (2))
quiver for arrows
Kn 2080, 2896

cast *n* (*fig* sense of 'throw') plot,
contrivance Kn 2468, Mil
3605; *at thilke ~* on that
occasion Mk 2287

caste *v* cast, throw Mil 3712, Co
4386 (dice), WB 729+; place,
put Mk 2714, CY 939+; leap
Mil 3330; reckon, calculate Sh
216; estimate Kn 2172; deliberate, reflect Kn 2854, ML 212+;
perceive CY 1414; decide on
Pard 880, Mk 2701; determine
(on), plan ML 406+; *~ up* lift
WB 1249; *~ of* take off
WB 783; *refl* decide Mel 1858,
NP 3075; *~ to* apply o.s. to
Mel 1591, CY 738; *3 sg contr
pres* cast

catel *n* property, possessions,
wealth, capital GP 373+; livestock GP 540

caughte *sg and pl past of*
cacche *v*

ceint *n* belt, sash GP 329,
Mil 3235

celle *n* monk's cell Mk 1972; a
subordinate monastery
GP 172; brain-cell (each 'cell'
being the seat of a particular
faculty); *~ fantastik* part of the
brain controlling ideas and the
imagination Kn 1376

centre *n* the fixed centre of a
circle Sq 22; *pl* table of
'centres' (concerned with the
angular relationship of a
planet to the centre of its
sphere or its eccentric)
Fkl 1277 (see n.)

ceptre *n* sceptre Mk 2144, 2373

certain, certein *adj* certain
GP 252a+; a certain quantity

of, some Kn 2967, ML 242,
Sh 404; fixed, settled GP 815,
Kn 2293+; sure, unfaltering
Fkl 866

certain, certein *adv* certainly,
surely Mil 3495, Pri 576+

certein *n* a certain number of
Mil 3193, Sh 334+; a certain
quantity of CY 776, 1024;
certainty Pars 1000

certes *adv* certainly, surely,
indeed Kn 875+

cesse *v* cease Cl 154, Sq 257+;
grow quiet, calm ML 1066

cetewale *n* zedoary (a spice)
Mil 3207, Th 761

chaar *n* (see also **char**) chariot
Kn 2138+

chace *v* harass, afflict Sq 457,
Pars 355+; ~ *out* drive out,
expel Sum 1916+; ~ *forth* pursue (narrative) Cl 341, 393;
chaced from deprived of
ML 366

chaffare *n* chaffer, trade, dealing
Co 4389, Sh 340+; goods, merchandise ML 138+, WB 521

chaier *n* litter, sedan chair
Mk 2613; professor's chair
Fri 1518

chalange, chalenge *v* challenge,
dispute WB 1200; claim
Fkl 1324

chamb(e)rere *n* maid, chambermaid WB 300, Cl 819+

chambre *n* private room, bedroom ML 721, Cl 263, 324,
Mch 1922+; marriage-
chamber SN 276; *fig* abode
ML 167; the department of a
great household concerned
with the lord's or lady's private

affairs Kn 1427, 1440; ~ *of
Venus* vagina WB 618

champio(u)n *n* champion Fri
1662, Pars 698+; athlete
GP 239

chano(u)n *n* canon, clergyman
living under canon rule CY
573+

chapitre *n* chapter of a book
NP 3065+; chapter, assembly
of members of a religious
house Sum 1945; ecclesiastical
court Fri 1361

chapman *n* merchant, trader
GP 397+

chapmanhede, -hode *n* business,
trade ML 143, Sh 238

char *n* (see also **chaar**) chariot
Mk 2610

charge *n* burden, harm, trouble
Kn 2287, Mel 1216+; duty, responsibility, charge Cl 163,
Phys 95; importance, significance Sq 359; charge, order Cl
193; *yeve in* ~ order Sh 432;
yeve/take ~ (*of*) be concerned
(about) Kn 1284, WB 321; *no*
~ no matter CY 749; *be in*
(o's) ~ be in o's power GP 733

charge *v* order, direct, charge
ML 802, Sum 1992+; *refl*
burden o.s. Pars 360; *charged*
laden, weighed down Fri 1539,
Mch 2211+

chargea(u)nt *adj* burdensome,
troublesome Mel 1243,
Pars 692

charitable *adj* loving, kind-
hearted GP 143; charitable
Sum 1795+; devout Sum 1940

charitee *n* charity Pars 519+; *out
of* ~ lacking brotherly love

GP 452, Kn 1623+; *in ~* in a
state of grace Pars 235; *par ~*
for charity Th 891; *for seinte ~*
for holy charity Kn 1721+

charme *n* spell, magic charm
Kn 1927+

chartre *n* charter, deed convey-
ing property Mil 3327,
Mch 2173

chaunce *n* chance, unexpected
event Kn 1752, ML 1045; luck
ML 125; number thrown at
dice Pard 653 (see n.); *good ~*
good luck Fkl 679+; *for no
maner ~* in no way, under no
circumstances SN 527; *par ~*
by chance Pard 606; as it happened GP 475

chaunge *v* change, alter, vary
GP 348, Kn 1538+; exchange
Pard 724

chaunte *v* sing Kn 2202, Mil
3367, Mch 1850

cheere *n* face, countenance
ML 396, Cl 238+; expression,
look GP 857, Kn 913+; appearance GP 728+; gesture Cl 535;
behaviour GP 139, 728, Cl
241+; demeanour Cl 778+;
mood, frame of mind Cl 7+;
good humour, happiness, joy
Kn 2683, Cl 1112; kindness,
hospitality ML 1002+; *make ~*
assume, display an expression
(of sorrow, humility, etc) Mil
3618, Cl 678, Mel 1187;
(*intransitive*) enjoy o.s., be in a
good mood Sh 327, 426, (*tran-
sitive*) entertain, treat hospitably GP 747, Rv 4132+; *make
wantown ~* to act wantonly
Mch 1846

chees *sg imp and sg past of*
chese *v*

cherice, cherisse *v* cherish, treat
affectionately Mch 1388, Sq
353, Fkl 1554; foster, favour
Mk 2520

cherl *n* serf, bondsman Kn 2459,
Pars 761, (*fig*) Pars 763; churl,
boor, ignoramus Mil 3169, Rv
3917+; man, fellow Pard 750

chese *v* choose Kn 1595, Mil
3181+; *sg imp* **chees**; *pl imp*
cheseth; *3 sg pres subj* **chese**;
sg past **chees**; *p ppl* **chosen**

cheste *n* (see also **chiste**) trunk,
box, strongbox WB 44b+; cof-
fin WB 502+

chevis(s)a(u)nce *n* borrowing or
lending money at interest; rais-
ing funds GP 282+; *make a ~*
raise a loan Sh 329

chide *v* scold, nag WB 223+;
chide, rebuke Sum 1893,
Mel 1707; complain, grumble
Rv 3999+; (of birds) screech
Sq 649; *3 sg contr pres* **chit**;
past **chidde**

chieftain (see also **chivetein**) *n*
leader, head Pars 387

chiertee *n* love, affection
WB 396, Fkl 881, Sh 336

child *n* young man, youth Mil
3325, Mk 2151, 2155; term
for a young knight Th 817,
830; *of a ~* from childhood
Cl 834

chinche *n* niggard, miser
Mel 1603, 1619

chirking *vbl n* creaking, grating
noise Kn 2004, Pars 605

chiste *n* (see also **cheste**) strong-
box WB 317

chit 3 *sg contr pres of* chide *v*

chivachee, chivachye *n* cavalry
expedition GP 85; feat of
horsemanship Mcp 50

chivalry(e) *n* the nobility (i.e.
knights and their superiors)
ML 235; cavalry, company of
knights Kn 878, Mk 2681;
knighthood Kn 982+; chivalry,
chivalrousness, gallant deeds,
valour Kn 865, 2106; *bere the
flour of* ~ be the best of
knights Th 902

chivetein *n* (see also chieftain)
leader Kn 2555

circumstaunce *n* circumstance,
aspect of a situation Pars 960;
pl manifestations Kn 1932;
details Kn 2788; conditions
Pars 692; *with every* ~ in full
detail ML 152; *with every* ~,
with alle circumstaunces with
every formality, with careful
attention to propriety
Kn 2263, ML 317; with every
care Cl 584; with full details
Pars 610+

clad *p ppl of* clothe *v*

cladde *sg past of* clothe *v*

cladden *pl past of* clothe *v*

clamb *sg past of* climbe *v*

clappe *v* clap Fkl 1203; knock
Fri 1581, 1584; clack, talk
noisily Cl 1200, NP 2781, Pars
406; ~ *to* shut, bang to Mil
3740, Mch 2159; ~ *again* close
up Sum 1699

clarioun *n* clarion (a slender-
tubed trumpet with clear, shrill
notes) Kn 2511, 2600

clarree *n* clary, a drink made of
wine, spiced and sweetened

with honey Kn 1471, Mch
1807, 1843

clatere *v* clatter, clash Kn 2359;
chatter, jabber Mel 1069

clatering(e) *vbl n* clattering
Kn 2492+; clanging Sum 1865

clause *n: in a* ~ briefly, in short
GP 715, Kn 1763, Mch 1430+

clawe *v* claw Sum 1731; scratch
(an itch) Co 4326; ~ (s.o.) *on
the galle* rub (s.o.) on a sore
spot WB 940

cleer *adj* (see also cler) clear,
bright Kn 1683+; bright,
gleaming Pri 681; shining
Kn 1062, SN 201; beautiful
Th 858

cleere *adv* (see also clere) clearly,
distinctly GP 170; loudly
Mch 1720

cleernesse *n* radiance, splendour
SN 111, 403, Pars 222

clene *adj* clean GP 504+; pure,
innocent Kn 2326, WB 97,
Mch 1264+; unmixed
ML 1183; elegant, shapely
WB 598; empty, cleared
Fkl 995

clene *adv* cleanly GP 133; handsomely, neatly GP 367; completely ML 1106, Sq 626, CY
625+

clennesse *n* purity, uprightness
GP 506+; chastity SN 160+

clepe *v* call, shout Mil 3432+;
say GP 643; call, name
GP 376, Kn 2730, Rv 3990+;
call, summon WB 147, Sq
331+; ~ *again* call back,
revoke Mcp 354

cler *adj* (see also cleer) clear;
bright, glittering Cl 779; pure

Pard 914+; glorious ML 451;
pl and weak sg **clere**

clere *adv* (see also **cleere**)
brightly Kn 2331, ML 11, SN
254; distinctly, resonantly
Mch 1845, Pri 655

clerk *n* member of the clergy,
cleric Pard 391; parish clerk
WB 548; an educated person,
scholar GP 480, Mil 3457+;
man of letters, writer Cl 32,
Mel 1107+; university student
GP 285, Mil 3143, Rv 4018,
Fkl 1105+

cley *n* clay CY 807, 812

cliket *n* latch-key Mch 2046+

climbe *v* climb Mil 3625+; *sg
past* **clamb**; *pl past* **clomben**;
p ppl **clombe(n)**

clinke *v* ring Pard 664; ~ *yow so
mery a belle* sound so lively a
note, provide such entertainment for you ML 1186

clippe *v* cut, clip (hair) Mil
3326+

cloist(e)rer *n* monk GP 259,
Mk 1939; canon Mil 3661

clombe(n) *p ppl of* **climbe** *v*

clomben *pl past of* **climbe** *v*

cloos *p ppl* closed, shut
NP 3332, Mcp 37; closed up
Mel 1621; secret Mel 1146,
CY 1369

clo(o)th *n* cloth, piece of cloth
GP 447, Kn 2158+; garment,
piece of clothing Kn 899+;
hanging, tapestry Kn 2277,
2281; *pl* bedclothes
Kn 1616

clothe *v* clothe, dress Sh 12+; *sg
past* **cladde**; *pl past* **cladden**;
p ppl **(y)clad**

clout *n* rag Pard 348; shred,
piece Mch 1953

clum *interj* hush! mum! Mil
3638+

cofre *n* coffer, chest GP 298,
ML 26+

cokes *pl of* **cook** *n*

cokewold *n* cuckold Mil 3152+

cokkes bones *phr* a euphemistic
substitution for 'Goddes
bones' Mcp 9, Pars 29

cokkow *n* cuckoo Kn 1810;
(with reference to the cuckoo
as a symbol of cuckoldry)
Kn 1930, Mcp 243

col-blak *adj* black as coal
Kn 2142+

cold *adj* (see also **coold**) cold
Kn 1575+; fatal NP 3256;
referring to cold as the dominant quality of Saturn
Kn 2443 (see n.); *cares colde*
suffering, anguish Fkl 1305,
SN 347

colde *v* turn, grow cold ML 879,
Fkl 1023

cole *n* coal Kn 2692+; charcoal
CY 809+; *bechen* ~ piece of
charcoal made from beech-
wood CY 1160+

colera, colere *n* choler, bile (one
of the four 'humours')
NP 2928, 2946

colerik *adj* (of persons) dominated by the humour of choler
NP 2955; irascible, choleric
GP 587; (of signs of the
zodiac) having the characteristics of choler (hot and dry)
Sq 51

colour *n* colour Kn 1038,
NP 2868+; complexion

Kn 2168, NP 3458+; specious
reason, pretext WB 399; false
appearance Sq 511; *colours (of
rethorik)* rhetorical figures,
stylistic embellishments Cl 16,
Sq 39, Fkl 726

colpons *n pl* separate pieces
Kn 2867; hanks, clusters
GP 679

colt *n* colt Mil 3263+; *have a coltes tooth* to have youthful
desires WB 602, Rv 3888

coma(u)nde *v* command, order
Kn 1695+

come *v* come GP 23+; ~ *by*
grasp, understand CY 1395;
get at WB 984; *3 sg pres*
cometh, *contr* **comth**; *sg past*
cam, **coom**; *pl past* **co(o)men**,
coome; *sg past subj* **coome**;
p ppl **come(n)**, **ycome(n)**

com(m)une *n* the commons, the
third estate Kn 2509, Cl 70;
right to use common land
Mch 1313

com(m)une *adj* common, general Pard 596+; unanimous,
ML 155, Pard 601+; widely
known Mel 1481, Mk 2246+;
public Pars 102+; general Sq
107; *in ~* on an equal footing
NP 3000; in general
Kn 1251+; ~ *profit* general
good Cl 431+

compaignable *adj* sociable, enter-
taining as a companion
NP 2872; sociable, gregarious
Sh 4

compaignye *n* company GP 24+;
followers Kn 2307, Pri 492;
entourage Cl 268; companionship Kn 2774, Pars 312;

relationships GP 461; *make ~
associate (with)* Mel 1330;
holde ~ (with) (s.o.) keep (s.o.)
company Fri 1521, Fkl 763,
Pars 584; *withouten any ~*
without a companion
Kn 2779+; *par ~* for company
Mil 3839; in accompaniment
Rv 4167; ~ *of man* sexual intercourse Kn 2311

compas *n* a circle Kn 1889; *the
trine ~* the threefold world
(heaven, earth, and sea)
SN 45

compe(e)r *n* companion, intimate GP 670, Co 4419

complaine *v* (see also **compleine**)
lament, bewail, mourn (for)
Mk 2377+

compleccioun *n* (see also **com-
plexio(u)n**) temperament or
character as produced by the
predominance of one of the
four 'humours' Pars 585

compleine *v* (see also **complaine**)
lament, bewail, mourn (for)
Kn 1072+

compleint(e) *n* lament, lamentation Kn 2862, Fkl 920+; a
plaintive poem, a lament Mch
1881, Fkl 948

complexio(u)n *n* (see also **compleccioun**) temperament or
character as produced by the
predominance of one of the
four 'humours' Kn 2475;
specifically, one of the four
temperaments attributed to the
predominance of one of the
four 'humours' GP 333 (see
n.), NP 2955; normal or
healthy condition (when the

humours are balanced)
Fkl 782; unhealthy condition
(when humours are unbal-
anced) NP 2924

complin *n* compline, the last of
the eight daily services sung by
monks and friars (see n. to Mil
3655) Pars 386; (jokingly
applied to the miller's family
snoring in concert) Rv 4171

composicioun *n* agreement
GP 848, Kn 2651; combi-
nation Sq 229

conceit(e) *n* mind, understanding CY 1078; notion, conception CY 1214

conclude *v* include SN 429; conclude Kn 1895+; sum up
Kn 1358; end CY 957; succeed
CY 773; make up o's mind,
make a decision Mch 1607

conclusio(u)n *n* conclusion Co
4328, Fkl 889+; outcome
Fkl 1014, SN 394; successful
result Fkl 1263, CY 672; fate
Kn 1869; purpose WB 115, Sq
492; goal WB 430; decision
Kn 1743, Mil 3402; principle,
doctrine Mil 3193; *for plat ~*
with finality, definitely
Kn 1845; *as in ~* in sum Mk
2634; *in ~* in conclusion Pard
454; in the end ML 215, 683;
take ~ decide Kn 2857

concubin *n* concubine Mk 2199;
mistress GP 650

condescende *v* proceed to Sq
407; *~ in especial* get down to
detail Mel 1234; *be con-
descended (on)* settle (on)
Mch 1605, Mel 1257

condicionel *adj* conditional, con-

tingent; *necessitee ~* see n. to
NP 3245–50

condicioun *n* condition; state
GP 38, ML 99+; condition,
proviso Sum 2132; status,
station ML 313, Pars 755;
aspect, feature Pars 1012; circumstance Pars 319; character
Kn 1431; characteristic Phys
41, Mel 1169

conferme *v* confirm, endorse
Mch 1508, Pars 842; support,
corroborate Kn 2350; prosecute, follow through
Mel 1222; *refl* resolve
Mel 1777; *confermed* securely
established Phys 136

conforme *v refl* acquiesce (in) Cl
546, Mel 1872

confort *n* comfort, relief
Kn 1248+; pleasure GP 773+

conforte *v* comfort Fkl 823;
encourage, spur on Pars 652

confounde *v* harass, beset, per-
plex ML 100, Pars 740+;
harm, destroy ML 362, Pars
529; lead into perdition
SN 137

confus *adj* confounded Kn 2230;
confused SN 463

confusioun *n* destruction, ruin
Kn 1545, Sum 1958+; dam-
nation Pard 499, Mk 1943; disgrace, shame Pars 187;
confusion Fkl 869

consail *n* (see also **conseil, counseil**): *werke by ~* follow advice,
act after consultation
Mil 3531

consaille *v* (see also **conseille**)
counsel, advise Cl 1200

conscience *n* moral sense,

awareness of right and wrong
GP 142, Mch 1635, Mel 1635,
SN 434+; feeling(s) GP 150,
ML 1136; scruples GP 398, Fri
1438+; *spiced* ~ (over-)fastidi-
ousness GP 526; *swete spiced*
~ see n. to WB 435

conseil *n* (see also **consail, counseil**) counsel, advice ML 425,
WB 82, Mch 1363+; decision,
plan GP 784, ML 436+; consultation Mel 1042; council,
group of advisers Kn 3096,
ML 204+; private matter(s),
secret(s) ML 777, WB 533+;
werke by ~ follow advice, act
after consultation Mil 3530,
Mch 1485+; *axe* ~ seek advice
Mch 1480, Mel 1010, 1156;
take ~ deliberate Mel 1120;
get advice NP 3253; *in* ~
secretly, in confidence Fri
1437, Mch 2431; *be* ~ be a
secret Pard 819; *shewe* (o's) ~
reveal intimate matters, confide in (s.o.) Sum 1849

conseille *v* (see also **consaille**)
counsel, advise Sh 129,
Mel 1026+

conseil(l)ing(e) *vbl n* advising
Mel 1097; consultation
Mel 1260; advice WB 67,
Mel 1061

consente *v* consent (to), agree,
acquiesce (in) Cl 537+; be consistent (with) Mel 1382+

conserve *v* keep, maintain, preserve Kn 2329, Mel 1203+

constable *n* governor of a royal
castle ML 522+

consta(u)nce *n* constancy, steadfastness, fortitude Cl 668+

constellacioun *n* the position of
a planet in relation to the
ascendant sign of the zodiac;
arrangement of the heavens
Kn 1088, Mch 1969, Sq 129;
(o's) horoscope, i.e. the 'constellacioun' at o's birth as
affecting o's character and fate
WB 616, Fkl 781

contena(u)nce *n* (see also **countenance**) countenance, outward
appearance, looks Cl 671,
ML 320, Sq 284, Sh 392; composure Cl 1110; behaviour,
bearing Cl 924, Sq 94+; way of
behaving Mch 2209; sign, gesture Mel 1037; gesture,
flourish Sh 8; *for* ~ for appearance's sake Co 4421; *make a* ~
pretend, act as if Pars 858;
enhaunce (o's) ~ become overbearing Pars 614

continue *v* continue CY 739+;
maintain Cl 1048; *been continued with* be accompanied
by Pars 1046

contrario(u)s *adj* rebellious, contrary WB 780, Mel 1059;
opposed WB 698, Mel 1121

contrarye *n* contrary, opposite
Mel 1017+; opponent, enemy
Kn 1859, NP 3280; difficulty
Pars 720; *doon a* ~ harm
Mel 1280

contrarye *v* antagonize, offend
Fkl 705; oppose, contradict
WB 1044, Mch 1497+

contree *n* country, land
Kn 864+; region Sum 1710+;
district GP 216+

contrefete *v* (see also **countrefete**) forge Cl 743

convenable *adj* (see also
  covenable) appropriate
  Pars 317
convenient *adj* suitable, appropriate Fkl 1278, Pars 421
converte *v* convert (in a religious
  sense) ML 574; turn back
  Kn 3037; change, turn
  Phys 212
conveye *v* escort Kn 2737, Cl
  391; introduce Cl 55
coold *adj* (see also **cold**) cold
  GP 420+
coom *sg past of* **come** *v*
coome *sg past subj of* **come** *v*
coome(n) *pl past of* **come** *v*
coost *n* shore, coast Fkl 995, Pri
  436; region, part of the world
  WB 922
coote *n* (see also **cote** *n* (2))
  tunic, dress (worn by both
  sexes, either alone or under a
  cloak or other overgarment)
  GP 103+
cope *n* cope, cowl, outer garment worn by religious
  orders and clerics GP 260,
  Mk 1949
coper *n* copper CY 829+
coppe *n* cup GP 134+; *drinke
  withouten* ~ to suffer intensely
  Fkl 942
corage *n* heart, spirit, disposition, temperament GP 11, Cl
  787, Sq 22+; inclination, desire
  Cl 907, Mch 1254+; valour,
  courage ML 939, Mk 2646,
  Pars 689; attention Mcp 164
corage(o)us *adj* courageous Mk
  2337; spirited, ardent Pars 585
corn *n* corn, wheat GP 562+;
  grain of wheat Pard 863+;

crop Mk 2035; *fig* the best,
  most important, part (as
  opposed to 'chaf') ML 702,
  Mk 1954
corny *adj* tasting strongly of
  malt Pard 315, 456
coro(u)ne *n* crown, wreath
  Kn 2290+
corpus (*Latin*) body; *Goddes* ~
  God's body Mil 3743; ~ *dominus* (ungrammatical Latin for
  corpus domini) God's body Pri
  435; ~ *Madrian* Madrian's
  body (a non-existent saint) Mk
  1892; ~ *bones* a confusion of ~
  domini and *Goddes bones*
  Pard 314, Mk 1906
correccioun *n* correction Pard
  404, Pars 60+; punishment
  Kn 2461+; authority, jurisdiction Fri 1329
corrupt *p ppl* corrupt ML 519;
  infectious Mch 2252; infected
  Pars 427; sexually experienced
  Pars 912; *be* ~ *for mede* be
  bribed Mk 2389, Pars 167
cors *n* body Mcp 67; person, self
  Pard 304, Th 908; corpse
  Pard 665
corven *p ppl of* **kerve** *v* cut
  Kn 2696; cut out Mil 3318
cosin *n* relation, kinsman Sh
  69+; first cousin Kn 2763; ~
  germain first cousin Mel 1368;
  be ~ *to* be akin to GP 742,
  Mcp 210
cosinage *n* kinship Sh 36+
cost *n* cost, expense GP 192+;
  lose (o's) ~ lose o's labour CY
  782+
costage *n* expenditure,
  expense(s), cost(s) WB 249,

Sh 372+; *doon* ~ spend money
Sh 45

costlewe *adj* costly, expensive
Pars 432+

cote *n* (1) cottage, hovel, hut
Kn 2457, Cl 398,
NP 2836

cote *n* (2) (see also coote) tunic,
dress (worn by both sexes,
either alone or under a cloak
or other overgarment) GP 564,
Cl 913

cote-armour, cote-armure *n* a
tunic embroidered or painted
with a knight's heraldic arms
and worn over his armour
Kn 1016, Th 866+

couche *v* cower Cl 1206; lay,
place Mil 3211, CY 1152+; ~
fir lay a fire Kn 2933; *couched*
ornamented, set (with jewels)
Kn 2161

co(u)ghe *v* cough, clear o's
throat Mil 3697+

counseil *n* (see also consail, conseil) counsellor Kn 1147;
secret, private matters GP 665,
Mil 3503+; *be of* (s.o.'s) ~ be
(s.o's) adviser, confidant
Kn 1141+

countenance *n* (see also con-
tena(u)nce): *for a* ~ as a pretence CY 1264

countour *n* lawyer, pleader in
court GP 359 (see n.); counting-house Sh 85+

countrefete *v* (see also contrefete) imitate GP 139, Phys
13+; make a copy of Mch
2121; counterfeit, forge
ML 746; borrow (learned
terms), affect Phys 51

countrewaite *v* guard (against)
Mel 1319, Pars 1005

coupable *adj* (see also cowpable)
guilty Mel 1541, Pars 571

cours *n* course GP 8, ML 704,
Mk 1996, SN 387+; charge in
tourney Kn 2549; *han a* ~ *at*
hunt Kn 1694

courser *n* a swift spirited horse,
charger Kn 952+

court *n* court GP 140+; courtyard Sq 171; manor-house
Sum 2162; ~ *Cristien* ecclesiastical court Pars 903

courtepy *n* short woollen jacket
GP 290, Fri 1382

coveite *v* covet, desire WB 266+

coveitise *n* covetousness, greed,
avarice, desire Rv 3884+

covenable *adj* (see also convenable) appropriate, suitable, fit
Mel 1592+

covenant *n* agreement Mch
2176; promise Kn 1924+; contract GP 600

covent *n* convent, a company living under religious rule Sum
1863, Pri 677+; a group of 13
friars Sum 2259

coverchief *n* kerchief, head cloth
or veil worn by women, usually made of fine material and
sometimes enriched with
jewels GP 453, ML 837,
WB 590, 1018

cow *n* cow Pard 354+; *pl* kyn

coward *adj* cowardly Pard 698,
Mel 1327, Mk 1910

cowpable *adj* (see also coupable)
blameworthy, sinful Pars 414

coy *adj* quiet, reticent; modest,
demure GP 119, Cl 2

craft *n* skill Fkl 909+; art
Kn 2409, Sq 185; subject, discipline Fkl 1127; trade, occupation GP 401, 692, Mil 3189,
CY 619; gild Co 4366; deceit,
trickery Mch 2016, Phys 84,
CY 621; trick Mk 2068;
konne ~ (*on*) have skill, be
skilled (in) Fri 1468,
Mch 1424

crafty *adj* skilled in a trade; ~
man craftsman Kn 1897; skilful CY 1290; learned CY
1253; crafty, cunning
CY 655

crake *v* sing lustily, bawl Mch
1850; ~ *boost* bluster Rv 4001

creat *p ppl* created Mel 1103,
Pars 218

creature *n* creature Kn 2395+;
created thing Kn 1247, SN
49+

creaunce *n* faith, belief
ML 340, 915

crea(u)nce *v* borrow money,
obtain credit Sh 289+

crepe *v* creep, crawl Mil 3441+;
sg past **creep**; *p ppl* **cropen**

crisp *adj* curly Kn 2165,
WB 304

Cristendom *n* Christianity
ML 351, SN 459+; baptism
ML 377, SN 208; Christen-
dom, Christian countries
GP 49

Crist(i)en *adj* Christian GP 55+;
as n ML 429+; *evene* ~ fellow
Christian Pars 395+

cristne *v* baptize, christen
ML 226+

crois *n* (see also **cros**) cross
GP 699, ML 450+

croked *p ppl* crooked, twisted
ML 560, Pard 761+

cropen *p ppl of* **crepe** *v*

cros *n* (see also **crois**) cross
Rv 4286

croslet, crosselet *n* crucible CY
793+

crouche *v* make the sign of the
cross over Mch 1707; ~ *from*
guard from (s.th. evil) by
making the sign of the cross
Mil 3479

cro(u)per *n* crupper, cover for a
horse's hindquarters CY 566+

crowde *v* push ML 801; drive
ML 296

crul *adj* curly GP 81, Mil 3314

crye *v* cry (out), call GP 636+;
entreat, beg (for) Mil 3288+;
announce, proclaim Kn 2731,
Sq 46; complain Cl 801; ~
(*out*) (*up*)*on* cry out against,
condemn Sq 650, Fkl 1496+

cultour *n* coulter, iron blade
fixed in front of the share in a
plough Mil 3763+

cura(a)t *n* parish priest GP 219,
Pars 1009

cure *n* care Cl 82+; heed, concern GP 303, WB 138; endeavour ML 188; care, effort
Kn 2853; custody, control Fri
1333, Phys 22; cure, healing
Fkl 1114, Mel 1270, SN 37;
honest ~ desire for decency
Pard 557; *have in* ~ have in
(o's) power ML 230; *do* ~ take
pains Kn 1007, WB 1074

curiositee *n* elaborateness Pars
446, 829

curious *adj* skilled, learned
GP 577; careful, solicitous

Sh 243; anxious Mch 1577;
skilfully made, elaborate
GP 196, WB 497, Pars 433;
complicated Sh 225; splendid
ML 402; abstruse, recondite
Fkl 1120

curs *n* curse, excommunication
GP 655+

curse *v* curse Mch 1308+; condemn Pars 745; excommuni-
cate GP 486

cursednesse *n* sinfulness, wickedness Pri 631, CY 1301+; sin,
wicked deed Pard 638, Pars
911; perversity, 'cussedness'
Mch 1239

cursing *vbl n* excommunication
GP 660, Fri 1587; cursing, pro-
fanity Pars 619+

curteis *adj* courtly, refined, con-
siderate, polite Fri 1287, Mch
1815, NP 2871+; gracious,
benevolent Mel 1760, Pars
246; respectful, deferential
GP 99, 250

curteisly *adv* courteously Sum
1802, Mel 1857; 'decently' (in
ironic sense) Rv 3997

curteisye *n* courtly behaviour,
good breeding, refined and con-
siderate conduct GP 46, 132,
ML 166, Mk 2496; courtesy,
refinement of manners Sum
1669, Mch 2309, Sq 95; kindness, benevolence ML 179; *for
youre* ~ kindly, if you please
Mil 3287

custume *n* custom WB 682, Mch
1889; customary rent or service Pars 567, 752

cut *n* lot determined by drawing
straws or sticks of different

length (lot falling on person
drawing longest or shortest)
GP 835+

daierye *n* dairy WB 871; dairy
herd GP 597

daliaunce *n* flirtation WB 260+;
sociable conversation, chatting
GP 211, CY 592; *do* ~ engage
in conversation Th 704

dame *n* lady (used of a woman
of rank or mistress of a household) Rv 3956+; mother Mil
3260, WB 576+

dampnacioun *n* damnation
Pard 500+; curse, ruin
WB 1067

dampne *v* condemn Kn 1175,
WB 70+; damn Phys 88+

dar *1/3 sg and 3 pl pres of* **durre**
v dare Kn 1151+; *2 sg pres*
darst; *1/3 sg past* **dorste**; *pl
past* **dorsten**

darreine *v* claim as rightfully o's
own Kn 1609, 1853; ~ *bataille*
engage in combat
Kn 1631, 2097

darst *2 sg pres of* **durre** *v*

dart *n* dart, arrow Kn 1564;
spear used as prize in a race
WB 75

date *n* time CY 1411; *of latter* ~
from more recent times
WB 765

daun *n* sir, lord, master (a title
given to dignitaries and
scholars) Kn 1379+

daunce *n* dance Sq 283+; *the
olde* ~ the ancient practice, the
business, all the old tricks
GP 476, Phys 79

daunger *n* resistance, opposition

Kn 1849; reluctance WB 521;
danger GP 402; *have in* ~ to
dominate, have in (o's) power
GP 663

daungerous *adj* haughty, aloof
GP 517; hard to please, fastidious Mil 3338, WB 1090,
Mel 939; niggardly WB 151,
514, Fri 1427

daunte *v* daunt, subdue Mk
2609, Pars 270; ~ *fro* frighten
away from WB 463

dawe *v* dawn, grow light
Kn 1676, Rv 4249+

daweninge *n* dawn; *in the* ~ at
dawn Rv 4234; *in a* ~ one day
at dawn NP 2882

dawes *pl of* **day** *n*

day *n* day GP 19+; days, lifetime
Cl 1136+; *breke* (o's) ~ fail to
make repayment CY 1040;
graunte dayes of allow time
for Fkl 1575; *al* ~ constantly,
all the time Kn 1168; (*up*)*on a*
~ one day GP 19, Kn 1414+;
upon a ~ in one day GP 703;
ful ofte a ~ many times in a
day Kn 1356, many times in
that day Kn 2623; *at* ~ *set* on
the appointed day Cl 774; *artificial* ~ light part of day, daytime ML 2; *al the longe* ~ all
day long Mil 3438; *pl* **dawes,
dayes**

deba(a)t *n* quarrel, dispute,
strife WB 822, Fri 1288+;
combat, war Kn 1754,
ML 130; *be at* ~ fall out, quarrel Mil 3230

debate *v* quarrel Pard 412; fight
Th 868

debonaire *adj* meek, gentle,

mild, humble Kn 2282,
NP 2871+

debonairetee *n* mildness, gentleness Pars 540+; kindness, graciousness Mel 1621, 1820,
Pars 467+

declare *v* tell, relate Kn 2766+;
explain, make clear Kn 3002,
ML 572+; make known, reveal
Kn 2356+; ~ *of* tell about
Mch 1687

declinacioun *n* declination, angular distance from the equinoctial, or celestial equator (*astr*)
Fkl 1033 (see n.); *hot* ~ sun's
greatest distance north of the
equinoctial, summer solstice
Fkl 1246; ~ *of Cancer* summer
solstice Mch 2223

decre(e) *n* decree, law
Kn 1167+; edict GP 640;
canon law Pars 931; legislation
Mk 2477

dede *n* deed, act GP 742+; result
Mel 1668; *in* ~ in reality, in
fact GP 659, Mk 2321+; in
action Mil 3591; *with the* ~ in
doing so WB 70; in the act
SN 157

dede *pl and weak sg of* **deed** *adj*

dedly *adv* to the death SN 476;
as death, deathly ML 822

deed *adj* dead GP 145+; *to been*
~ until death Kn 1343; *pl and
weak sg* **dede**

de(e)dly *adj* deadly Mel 1424+;
deathly, death-like Kn 913+;
dying, doomed Fkl 1040

deef *adj* deaf GP 446+; *pl* **deve**

deel *n* (see also **del**) part, bit;
every ~ every bit CY 1269 (see
also **everyde(e)l**); *never a* ~ not

a bit, not at all Kn 3064+; *a
ful greet* ~ to a great extent
GP 415; *by an hondred thousand* ~ a hundred thousandth
part Mcp 137

deele *v* (see also **dele**) have dealings (with) GP 247

deep *adj* deep Kn 3031+; mysterious Mel 1406; deep in mud
Fri 1541; *pl and weak sg*
depe

deere *adj* dear; noble, honoured
Kn 2260, SN 272; noble, pre-
cious Mil 3588, ML 237,
WB 827

deere *adv* dearly Kn 3100+

dees *n pl* (see also **dis**) dice Pard
623; game of dice Sq 690+

deeth *n* death Kn 964+; plague
GP 605

defame *n* (see also **diffame**) disgrace, dishonour Pard 612,
Mk 2548

defame *v* (see also **diffame**) disgrace Pars 645; accuse Pard
415; slander Mil 3147

defaute *n* lack Pars 181+; fault,
defect Sum 1810, Cl 1018+;
offence, sin Pard 370+; wickedness Mk 2528

defence *n* (see also **defense**)
resistance WB 467

defende *v* (see also **deffende**)
defend, protect Mel 1027+;
ward off Mel 1532; forbid
WB 60, Sum 1834+; prohibit
CY 1470; *refl* defend o.s.
ML 933+

defense *n* (see also **defence**)
defence Mel 1533, 1537;
stonde at ~ defend o.s.
Cl 1195

deffende *v* (see also **defende**)
defend, protect Pars 758+;
defend, excuse Pars 404, 584;
forbid Pars 332+

def(f)ye *v* reject, renounce Mil
3758, NP 3156; scorn Sh 402;
defy NP 3171

degree *n* step, tier Kn 1890+;
rank, social condition GP 40,
Kn 1434+; condition, state
Kn 1841+; degree, $\frac{1}{360}$th of a
circle (*astr*) Sq 386+; *in* (o's) ~
in order GP 744, Cl 263; *in no*
~ in no way Sq 198, Sh 171; *in
ech* ~ in every way WB 404;
after/at/in/to (o's) ~ according
to (o's) rank Kn 2192, 2856,
Mch 2027+; *lord at alle
degrees* lord to the highest
degree Mil 3724

dei(g)ne *v impers* seem worthy,
proper to (s.o.); (with negative
and dative pronoun) to refuse
(to do s.th.), scorn (the idea of
doing s.th.) Mk 2134, 2270,
NP 3181

deintee *n* delight, pleasure
ML 139+; luxury, delicacy
GP 346+; *telle* ~ *of*, *holde* ~ *of*
set store by WB 208, Pars 477;
have ~ *of* take pleasure in
Fkl 681

deintee *adj* excellent, choice
GP 168; delightful Cl 1112+;
(of food) delicious, sumptuous
Sq 70+

deintevous *adj* sumptuous,
delicious Cl 265+

deis *n* dais, platform
GP 370+

deitee *n* deity Pri 469; divine
power Fkl 1047; *thy/his* ~

thee/him (of gods) CY 1469,
Mcp 101

dekne *n* deacon SN 547,
Pars 891

del *n* (see also **deel**) part, bit;
every ~ every bit, everything,
all Kn 2091, Mil 3744+;
never(e) *a* ~ not a bit, not at all
WB 561+

dele *v* (see also **deele**) divide
Sum 2249; have dealings
(with) CY 1074; participate
(in) Pars 907; have sexual intercourse (with) Pars 908

deliberacioun *n* deliberation
Mel 1029+; *by* ~ with, after
deliberation Phys 139,
Pars 355

delicat *adj* delightful Cl 682; luxurious, fine Mch 1646, Pars
432; rich, choice Pars 828; sensual, voluptuous Cl 927, Mk
2471, Pars 835; sensitive
Pars 688

delice *n* pleasure, luxury Pard
547+

deliciously *adv* delightfully
Sq 79; luxuriously
Mch 2025; sumptuously
Pars 377

delit *n* delight, pleasure
GP 335+; sexual pleasure
Fkl 1396+

delitable *adj* delightful, pleasant
Cl 62+

delite *v* delight, take pleasure
(in) Cl 997, Mel 1158, Mk
2470+; *refl* take pleasure in,
enjoy Sum 2044+

delivere *v*: ~ (*fro/of/out of*) save,
rescue (from) ML 518+;
release (from) Kn 1769+

delivernesse *n* agility Mel 1165,
Pars 452

delve *v* dig (up) GP 536, Sq 638

dema(u)nde *n* question ML 472,
Mch 1870+

deme *v* judge, decide Mil 3194,
Mel 1030+; think, believe
Kn 1881, Mil 3161,
ML 1038+; order, direct
Mel 1855; adjudge, rule Phys
199; sentence Sum 2024, Phys
271; express an opinion Sq
261; ~ *to the badder ende*
adopt the worst interpretation
Sq 224

demoniak *n* madman Sum
2240, 2292

depardieux (*French*) *interj* certainly, indeed! ML 39,
Fri 1395

departe *v* separate, divide
Kn 1134+; break up WB 1049;
wean Cl 618; single out Pars
355; depart Kn 3060, Pars 593

departinge *vbl n* departure
ML 293; separation Kn 2774;
dividing Pars 425+

depe *pl and weak sg of* **deep** *adj*

depe *adv* deeply GP 129+; far
inside Mil 3442

depeint(ed) *p ppl* depicted
Kn 2049; painted Kn 2054;
stained Pard 950

dere *v* harm, injure Kn 1822+

derk *adj* (see also **dirk**) dark
Kn 2082+; obscure ML 481;
secret, deceptive Kn 1995+;
gloomy Fkl 844; inauspicious
(*astr*) ML 304

derne *adj* secretive, discreet Mil
3297; ~ *love* clandestine love,
secret passion Mil 3200+

descende *v* descend Rv 3984+;
dismount Fkl 1242; ~ *to the*
special get down to detail
Mel 1355

descharge *v* rid (s.o. of s.th.), get
rid of Pars 360+

descripcio(u)n *n* (see also **discripcioun**) definition Pars 741;
design Kn 2053

desdain, desdein *n* disdain, contempt SN 41+; *take in* ~ take
offence (at) GP 789; *have in* ~
be offended with Fkl 700

deserve *v* deserve Kn 964+; ~
unto deserve from (s.o.)
CY 1352

desherite *v* (see also **disherite**)
dispossess Mel 1751

deshonest *adj* (see also **dishonest**) dishonourable
Pars 777

desir(o)us *adj* desirous, eager
Kn 1674+; ~ *in armes* keen in
battle Sq 23

deslavee *adj* unbridled, unrestrained Pars 629+

desolat *adj* deserted, lonely Mch
1321; *holden* ~ socially
shunned Pard 598; ~ *of* lacking, destitute of ML 131+;
helpless WB 703

desordeinee *adj* inordinate Pars
818+

desordinat *adj* (see also **disordinat**) inordinate, excessive Pars
415+

desordinaunce *n* (see also **disordinaunce**) flouting of order
Pars 267

despeir *n* despair Kn 1245+

despeire *v refl* (see also **dispeire**)
despair Pars 698; *p ppl*

despeired in despair
Fkl 943+

despence *n* (see also **despense,
dispence, dispense**) means of
subsistence, living ML 105

despende *v* (see also **dispende**)
spend Rv 3983+; pass (time)
Mk 2310; waste Mel 931; dispense Pars 812; use Mch 1403

despense *n* (see also **despence,
dispence, dispense**) expense,
expenditure Kn 1928+

despise *v* despise ML 115+;
revile, chide Mel 1019, Mk
2669+

despit *n* disdain, malice, hostility
Kn 941+; spite, defiance
Kn 947, Sum 2154, Sq 650+;
humiliation, insult Mil 3752+;
resentment Sum 2061+; *have
in* ~ to despise Sum 1876+;
have ~ to resent WB 481; *have*
~ (to do s.th.) to disdain, resist
(doing s.th.) Fkl 1395+; *in* ~ *of*
in contempt of Pri 563+

despit(o)us *adj* contemptuous,
scornful GP 516, Pars 395+;
disobedient, recalcitrant
WB 761+; cruel, pitiless, fierce
Kn 1777+

despitously *adv* angrily, fiercely
Kn 1124+; cruelly, violently
ML 605+

desport *n* (see also **disport**) recreation, amusement, pleasure
Rv 4043+; pleasant or entertaining behaviour GP 137

destempred *p ppl* (see also **distempre**) unbalanced Pars 826

destourbe *v* hinder, prevent Pars
340+

destreine *v* (see also **distreine**)

bind Pars 269; restrain Mcp
161; constrain Pars 104+; distress, torment Kn 1455,
Fkl 820+

destroye, destruye *v* destroy, ruin
Kn 1330, Sum 1847+; harass,
ruin Pard 858+

dette *n* debt, obligation
GP 280+; that which spouses
owe to each other, sexual intercourse WB 130+

deve *pl of* deef *adj*

devel *n* devil Rv 3903+; *a*
(*twenty*) ~ *way/wey*(*e*) in the
devil's name Mil 3134+

devine *v* (see also **divine**) conjecture, guess Kn 2521, Sh 224;
imagine, believe NP 3266

devis *n* desire, pleasure GP 816;
at point ~ to perfection, to a T
Mil 3689+

devise *v* imagine, conceive
Kn 1254+; plan, contrive
Kn 1844+; construct, make
Kn 1901+; tell, say, describe
GP 34+; talk Sq 261; direct,
prescribe Kn 1416+; ~ *of* to
think about Mch 1586; *fressh
for to* ~ fresh, bright to see
Kn 1048

devisioun *n* (see also **divisioun**)
division, clan Kn 2024

devocioun *n* devotion,
devoutness Kn 2371+; prayer
Mil 3640

devoir *n* duty ML 38, Pars 764;
do (o's) ~ do o's best
Kn 2598+

deye *v* die Kn 3034+

diffame *n* (see also **defame**) disgrace, dishonour Cl 730; reputation Cl 540

diffame *v* (see also **defame**) slander, speak ill of Sum 2212

diffye *v* reject, renounce
Kn 1604, Mch 1310; scorn
Sum 1928

dighte *v* prepare, get ready
Kn 1630, Cl 974+; clothe
Kn 1041; garnish Mil 3205;
deal with, have sexual inter-
course with WB 398+; *refl* go
Mk 1914+; *p ppl* (**y**)**dight**

digne *adj* worthy GP 141+; suitable ML 778; honoured,
revered, noble Kn 2216,
ML 1175+; fine, proud
GP 517+

dignitee *n* worthiness, excellence
Rv 4270+; dignity, rank Cl
470+

diligence *n* diligence, industry
Sum 1818+; eagerness Cl
1185; *do* ~ take pains, endeavour Kn 2470, SN 79+; *do* (o's)
~ do (o's) utmost Pri 539+

dine *v* dine, eat dinner
ML 1083+; eat for dinner
Sum 1837

dirk *adj* (see also **derk**) dark
Fkl 1074+

dis *n pl* (see also **dees**) dice
Kn 1238+; dice-playing
Co 4392+

discipline *n* mortification of the
flesh Pars 1055; teaching Pars
1052; science, craft CY 1253

disclaundre *v* slander ML 674+

discomfite, disconfite *v* defeat,
rout Mel 1339+

disconfiture *n* defeat Kn 1008+

disconfort *n* dismay Kn 2010;
grief, distress Fkl 896+

discovere *v* reveal, disclose

Mel 1141+; expose
Mch 1942

discrecioun *n* judgement, discernment Kn 1779+; *have* ~ *to* have reached the age of adult reasoning Mk 2632; *by* ~ in moderation WB 622, Pars 861

discripcioun *n* (see also **descripcioun**) description Sq 580; definition Phys 117

discrive *v* describe Sq 40+; ~ *of* write about Mch 1737

disese *n* hardship, suffering, misfortune ML 616+; vexation Mcp 97; distress NP 2771

disherite *v* (see also **desherite**) disinherit, dispossess Kn 2926+

dishonest *adj* (see also **deshonest**) dishonourable, shameful Cl 876+; immodest, unchaste Mcp 214

disjoint *n* difficulty, strait Kn 2962+

disordinat *adj* (see also **desordinat**) inordinate, excessive Pars 422

disordinaunce *n* (see also **desordinaunce**) violation of order Pars 275, 277

disparage *v* degrade, disgrace Rv 4271+

dispeire *v refl* (see also **despeire**) despair Mch 1669; *p ppl* **dispeired** in despair Fkl 1084

dispence *n* (see also **despence, despense, dispense**) expense, expenditure Kn 1882+; *esy of* ~ parsimonious GP 441; *fre of* ~ generous in spending Cl 1209+

dispende *v* (see also **despende**) spend Pars 849; dispense, distribute Mel 1370; pass (time) Cl 1123

dispense *n* (see also **despence, despense, dispence**): *free of* (o's) ~ generous in spending Co 4388

displesa(u)nt *adj* offensive Pars 544+

displese *v* displease, be offensive to WB 128+

disport *n* (see also **desport**) entertainment, amusement, pleasure GP 775+; solace, source of pleasure Mch 1332+; *do* ~ (with *dat*) entertain, cheer up Mch 1924

disporte *v refl* amuse o.s. Mil 3660+

dispose *v* resolve, make up o's mind Cl 244, (with *herte* as *obj*) Fri 1659; direct, regulate Pars 336; *wel disposed* in good health Mcp 33; *be disposed* be of a mind to, intend Cl 639+

disposicioun *n* power, disposal Kn 2364, Mel 1765+; disposition Kn 1378, Mel 1136; influence (of a planet) Kn 1087, WB 701

dispreise *v* depreciate, disparage Mel 1071+

disputisoun *n* debate, argument, controversy Mch 1474+

dissimule *v* dissemble, pretend SN 466+

distempre *v* (see also **destempred**) anger, upset Sum 2195+

distreine *v* (see also **destreine**)

hold fast, retain Mel 1215; torment, oppress Kn 1816, Pars 752

divers *adj* diverse Rv 3857+; different Pars 489

divine *n* theologian Kn 1323+

divine *v* (see also **devine**) conjecture, speculate Kn 2515+

divinitee *n* divinity SN 316+; theology, divine learning Fri 1512+

divisioun *n* (see also **devisioun**) division, fragmentation Pars 1009+; dissension Kn 2476; distinction Kn 1780+

do *v* do, perform, carry out GP 78+; act, behave Rv 3881+; place CY 899; bring about Kn 2405; *do* followed by an infinitive: to cause s.th. to happen or to be done, e.g. *do fecche* have fetched ML 662; ~ *of* remove Kn 2676; ~ *up* raise Mil 3801; ~ *wey* take away Mil 3287; stop SN 487; ~ *no fors of* attach no importance to, not to care about WB 1234, Fri 1512+; be negligent of Pars 721; *for to doone* a fit thing to do Pars 62; *have do!* have done! get it over! Mil 3728; *pl imp* **dooth**; *sg past* **dide**; *pl past* **dide(n)**; *p ppl* **do**, **ydo(n)**, **(y)doon**

doctour *n* doctor GP 411; one of the Church Fathers, early Christian authorities on theology Fri 1648+

doctrine *n* doctrine Pars 676+; teaching Pri 499+; advice, instruction Mel 1232+; edifi-

cation Mel 935+; knowledge, wisdom Mel 1512

doghter *n* daughter Kn 2064+; *pl* **doghtren**, **doghtres**

doghty *adj* (see also **doughty**) bold, brave Sq 11+; excellent Sq 338

doke *n* duck Mil 3576+

domb *adj* dumb, speechless GP 774+

dome *n* (see also **doom**) *day of* ~ Judgement Day Pars 118+

domesman *n* judge Mk 2490+

dominacioun *n* power, rule, control Kn 2758+

dong(e) *n* dung GP 530+

doom *n* (see also **dome**) judgement GP 323, Cl 1000+; *swere in* ~ take an oath in court Pard 636+; *as to my* ~ in my opinion Fkl 677+

doon *p ppl of* **do** *v*

dooth *pl imp of* **do** *v*

dore *n* door GP 460+; *out atte* ~ out of doors Sum 1757+

dorste *sg past of* **durre** *v* dared Rv 3932+; sometimes used as equivalent to *pres subj* dare GP 454, Mcp 277+

dorste(n) *pl past of* **durre** v dared Mil 4009+; sometimes used as equivalent to *pres subj* dare NP 2918; ~ *han swore* could have sworn Cl 403

dostow *contr of* **dost thow**

dotard *adj* foolish, senile WB 291+

dote *v* be/become a fool Mch 1441+

doughty *adj* (see also **doghty**) bold, brave Mk 2312

doute *n* doubt GP 487+; fear

Pars 1023; apprehension
Fkl 1096; danger Mch 1721;
out of/withouten ~ doubtless,
certainly GP 487, Kn 1322+; *it
is no* ~ it is certain Sum 1712
doute *v* fear, be afraid (of)
Mel 1327+
dowaire, dowere *n* dowry Cl
807, 848
dowve *n* dove Kn 1962+
drad *p ppl of* **drede** *v*
dradde *sg past of* **drede** *v*
dradden *pl past subj of* **drede** *v*
draf *n* chaff Pars 35; ~-*sek* sack
of chaff or rubbish Rv 4206
drago(u)n *n* dragon WB 776+;
mercury (*alch*) CY 1435 (see
n.) +
drasty *adj* crude, trashy
Mel 923+
dra(u)ghte *n* draught, drink
GP 135+
drawe *v* draw Kn 2547, Mch
1817+; drag Kn 944+; pull Fri
1560+; pull out Rv 3892; lead,
attract GP 519+; carry
Kn 1416; bring Mil 3112+;
obtain Pars 549; derive CY
1440; drag behind a horse Pri
633; draw water Kn 1416; *refl*
come, go Sq 252+; ~ *cut* draw
lots GP 835+; ~ *to* approach
Mil 3633; resort to Sh 27; ~
unto incline to, fall in with Cl
314; get near to Fkl 965; ~ *in*
lead to Pars 1000; ~ (*in*)*to*
memorye recall, call to mind
Kn 2074, Mil 3112+; *sg past*
drogh, drough, drow; *p ppl*
(y)drawe, drawen
drede *n* fear Kn 1396+; anxiety
Sh 123+; doubt, uncertainty

Kn 2450+; danger Mel 1327;
have in ~ fear, venerate Mk
2162; *that/it is no* ~ there is no
doubt ML 869, WB 63+; *with-
outen/out of* ~ without doubt
ML 29+
drede *v* fear, be afraid of
Mel 1176+; *refl* be afraid
GP 660+; reverence Fkl 1312+;
doubt Kn 1593, SN 324; *pl
imp* **dreed**; *sg past* **dradde,
dredde**; *pl past subj* **dradden**;
p ppl **drad**
dred(e)ful *adj* (see also **dreedful**)
fearful, timorous Fkl 1309;
frightening, terrible ML 937+
dreed *pl imp of* **drede** *v*
dreedful *adj* (see also **dred(e)ful**)
fearful, timorous Kn 1479
dreint *p ppl of* **drenche** *v*
dreinte *sg and pl past of*
drenche *v*
dreme *v* dream NP 3012+,
(*impers*) Th 787
drenche *v* drown Mil 3521+;
sink Pars 363+; *sg and pl past*
dreinte; *p ppl* **dreint**
drery *adj* sad, sorrowful Cl 514+
dresse *v* place Cl 381; arrange,
prepare GP 106, Mil 3635; dispose Cl 1049; turn, turn o's
attention to Sq 290+, *refl* Mil
3468+; guide Mel 1118; deal
with, dispose of Mch 2361;
refl place o.s., take up o's position Kn 2594, Mil 3358; get
ready ML 265+; go, make (o's)
way ML 416+
dreye *adj* dry Kn 3024+
drinke *v* drink GP 635+; *sg past*
drank; *pl past* **dronke(n)**; *p ppl*
dronke(n), ydronke

drive *v* drive Kn 1859+; go,
  rush, be impelled forward
  ML 947, Sum 1694; subject
  Rv 4110; ~ *awey* while away
  Pard 628; ~ *forth hir weye*
  make her way ML 875;
  ~ *forth the world* live on
  Sh 231; ~ *a bargain* conclude a
  bargain Fkl 1230; *sg past*
  droof; *p ppl* **drive(n)**,
  ydriven

droghte *n* drought GP 2+

dronkelewe *adj* drunken,
  drunkard Sum 2043+

dronke(n) *pl past and p ppl of*
  drinke *v*

droof *sg past of* **drive** *v*

droppe *v* drip, leak Rv 3895+;
  sprinkle Kn 2884

dro(u)gh, drow *sg past of*
  drawe *v*

duc *n* duke Kn 860+

duetee *n* due, tax or rent owed
  to a lord or to the church Fri
  1352+; *with* ~ as is due, with
  propriety Kn 3060; *agains his*
  ~ contrary to what is due to
  him Pars 407

dulle *v* nullify Pars 233; distress,
  vex CY 1093+

dure *v* continue, last ML 1078+;
  remain Kn 1236+

dwelle *v* remain, stay, continue
  GP 512+; live Kn 2814+;
  reside Kn 2804

ech *adj and n* each, every; each,
  every one GP 39+; *upon* ~ *a*
  side on every side WB 256

echon(e), echoon *pron* each one,
  every one GP 820+

eek *adv and conj* (see also **eke**)

also, as well Kn 1967+; moreover, likewise WB 30

eelde *n* (see also **elde**) age, old
  age Rv 3885

eet *sg past of* **ete** *v*

effect *n* effect Pars 607+; purpose Kn 2851+; fulfilment, realization CY 1261+; essentials,
  main point (of a story)
  Kn 2207+; gist, purport
  Kn 2259+; significance, consequence Kn 2989, NP 3134;
  essence Sq 322; sum total Fri
  1451; *pl* feelings Kn 2228; *to*
  th'effect that to the end that
  Mel 1868; *to th'effect* to get to
  the point Kn 1189; *this is*
  th'effect this is the long and
  the short of it Kn 2366+;
  (*as*) *in* ~ in fact, actually
  GP 319+; in substance
  Cl 721

eft *adv* afterwards, again
  Kn 1669+

eftso(o)ne(s) *adv* immediately,
  without delay Mil 3489, Mk
  2596+; again, a second time
  ML 909, WB 808+; next time
  CY 933

egge *v* incite, instigate Mch
  2135, Pars 968

egre *adj* sharp, pungent
  Mel 1177, Pars 117; fierce
  Cl 1199

eighe *n* (see also **eye**) eye Sum
  2051, Fkl 1036

eile *v* ail, be the matter (with)
  Kn 1081+; ~ *at me* have
  against me Th 785

eir *n* air Kn 1246+

eise *n* (see also **ese**) ease
  Sum 2101

either *pron* (see also **outher**)
each Kn 2553+

eke *adv and conj* (see also **eek**)
also, as well ML 59+; more-
over, likewise GP 757+

elde *n* (see also **eelde**) age, old
age Kn 2447+

elder *comp adj* older Pri 530+

eldre *n* ancestor, predecessor
WB 1118+

elenge *adj* (see also **alenge**)
wretched, miserable Sh 222

elles, ellis *adv* else Kn 1151+;
otherwise GP 375+; ~ *God forbede* God forbid that it should
be otherwise CY 1046, 1064

elleswher(e) *adv* elsewhere
Kn 2113+

elvissh *adj* elvish, magical CY
751+; remote, otherworldly
Th 703

embassadour *n* ambassador
Pard 603+

embrace *v* (see also **enbrace**)
embrace Sum 1803+; grasp
Mel 1215+; have a hold on
Cl 412; bring it about
Mcp 160

empeire *v* impair, damage Mch
2198; make (things) worse
Mel 1019

empoisone *v* poison Kn 2460+

emprente *v* (see also **enprente**)
imprint Mch 2117+; impress,
fix Cl 1193

emprise *n* enterprise, task,
exploit Kn 2540+; adventurousness Mk 2667

empte *v* empty CY 741+

enbrace *v* (see also **embrace**)
embrace Th 701

encens *n* incense Kn 2277+

encense *v* burn or offer incense
SN 395+; cense Pars 407

encheso(u)n *n* cause, reason Sq
456+; *by* ~ *of* because of
Mel 1593

encline *v* incline, be inclined
ML 1082+; bow Mel 1501,
Mk 1902+; ~ *the eres to* lend
an ear to Mel 1180

encombre *v* hinder Pars 687;
bog down GP 508; burden,
trouble Kn 1718

encrees *n* increase, growth
GP 275+

encresce, encres(s)e *v* increase,
grow Kn 1338+; develop,
advance Mel 1276; *be
encressed* improve Cl 408, be
worth more Sh 81

ende *n* end GP 15+; outcome,
upshot WB 1070+; fate
Kn 1844, 1869; solution
ML 266; resolution Cl 188;
aim, purpose Kn 2259+; *this is
the* ~ this is the long and short
of it ML 145+; *atte* ~ in the
end WB 404; *word and* ~ from
beginning to end Mk 2721

endelong *prep* along, from end
to end of Kn 2678+

endite *v* write, compose GP 95+;
draft, draw up GP 325; accuse,
indict Mk 2668

endure *v* last, continue Kn 3014,
ML 231+; stay, remain
Kn 1185+; endure, bear
Kn 1091+

enforce *v* fortify, strengthen
Mel 958, Pars 730+; grow
stronger Mel 1165; *refl* try
Mel 1047+

enforme *v* inform Cl 738+

engendre *v* engender, beget, bring forth GP 4, 421, Kn 1375, WB 465+; procreate Mk 1958; be produced, arise Mel 1392, NP 2923

engendrure *n* procreation WB 128+; offspring Pars 562+

engin *n* imagination SN 339 (see n.) +; inventiveness Pars 453; contrivance Sq 184

enhaunce *v* raise, elevate, advance Kn 1434+

enjoine *v* enjoin, impose (on) Mel 1749+

enlumine *v* enlighten Pars 244; make illustrious Cl 33

enointe *v* anoint GP 199+; *p ppl* **enoint**

enprente *v* (see also **emprente**) imprint, fix Mch 2178

enquere *v* ask, enquire (for) Mil 3166+

ensample *n* (see also **exemple**) example GP 496+; exemplary anecdote, illustration Kn 2039+

enspire *v* (see also **inspire**) inspire, impart knowledge to CY 1470

entencioun *n* intention Cl 703+; meaning CY 1443

entende *v* intend Mch 1791; strive WB 1114+; ~ *unto* strive after WB 275; ~ *to* pay attention to, devote o.s. to Fri 1478+; attend Mch 1900

entente *n* intention, purpose, reason Kn 1000+; meaning Sq 4004; heart, (state of) mind, spirit ML 867, Fkl 1178+; *in ~ to* with the intention of Pars 800+; *to the ~ that* in order

that Mel 1868, CY 1306; *seye* (o's) ~ speak (o's) mind Sum 1733; *in hool* ~ wholeheartedly, without reservations Cl 861; *in good/with glad ~* with good will, kindly, cheerfully Kn 958+; *as to commune* ~ as far as the general meaning is concerned Sq 107; *doon* (o's) ~ take pains SN 6+; *sette* (o's) ~ (*on*) set o's heart on, be completely devoted to Fri 1374+; pay attention (to), take care (to) Pars 314, 932

ententif *adj* eager Mch 1288+; diligent, earnest Mel 1015+

entierly *adv* entirely, wholly Pars 675+

entisinge *vbl n* enticement, temptation Pars 353+

entraille *n* entrails, bowels Cl 1188, Pri 573

entremet(t)e *v refl* intervene, interfere WB 834+

envenime *v* poison WB 474+

er *adv* before, formerly Mil 3789+

er *prep* before Rv 4170+; ~ *this* before now Kn 1683+; ~ *that* before the expiration of Sum 1692

er (that) *conj* before GP 36+

erc(h)edekene *n* archdeacon, 'the chief administrative officer of an archbishop or bishop, who presided over the ecclesiastical court of the diocese' (*MED*) GP 655+

ere *n* ear WB 636+; *pl* **eres, eris**

ers *n* arse Mil 3734+

erst *adv* before GP 776,

NP 3281+; *adv and conj* ~ *er*
before Sum 2220+; *conj* ~ *than*
before Kn 1566; *adv phr* at ~
for the first time Cl 985+

eschawfe *v* heat Pars 537, 546;
inflame, become inflamed Pars
657, 916

eschew, eschu *adj* averse, loath
Mch 1812, Pars 971

eschewe, eschue *v* avoid, shun,
refrain from Kn 3043,
Mel 1172+

ese *n* (see also **eise**) ease, comfort Kn 969+; prosperity
NP 2772; hospitality Rv 4119;
pleasure Mch 1643; relief Mch
2115; *doon* ~ entertain, amuse
GP 768; help Cl 664+; comfort
Mch 1981; *in youre* ~ within
your means Sh 291

ese *v* entertain, accommodate
GP 29, Kn 2194; console
Kn 2670; soothe WB 929

esement *n* compensation Rv
4179+

esily *adv* easily Pars 1041;
comfortably GP 469, Cl 423,
Sq 115; softly Mil 3764; ~ *a*
pas slowly, in a leisurely way
Sq 388

espace *n* (see also **space**) time,
opportunity Mel 1029

espece *n* (see also **spece**) species,
particular kind Pars 448

especial *adj* (see also **special**)
special Pars 893; intimate
Mel 1166; *condescende in* ~
get down to detail Mel 1234

espiaille *n* spying Mel 1319;
body of spies Fri 1323

espirituel *adj* spiritual
Pars 79+

espye *n* spy, look-out Pard 755,
Mel 1026

espye *v* catch sight of, see, notice
Kn 1112+; observe, watch Cl
235, Mk 2068+; discover, find
out (*of*, about) Kn 1420,
ML 324+; detect Sh 184,
NP 3323+; seek to discover
ML 180, Mch 1257+; search
out Th 799

est *n* east ML 297+

est *adv* in or to the east, eastwards ML 949+; ~ *and west* in
all directions Pard 396

esta(a)t *n* (see also **staat**) state,
condition Kn 2196, Cl 610,
Mch 1283, Sh 232, Pars 681+;
station, rank GP 522, Kn 926,
956, Mk 2169+; social standing WB 821+; status Mch
1322; condition in life Mil
3229; social class, profession
GP 716; term of office Sum
2018; aspect (*astr*) Mch 1969;
in greet ~ in excellent condition GP 203; *save his* ~ preserve his standing Rv 3949;
have his ~, *be served in his* ~
be treated according to his
rank Cl 958, Pars 771; *kepe*
royal ~ maintain regal splendour Sq 26

estatlich, estatly *adj* dignified
GP 140+

estres *n pl* interior, recesses
Kn 1971, Rv 4295

esy *adj* easy Pars 1042; comfort-
able Mch 1264; lenient, kind
GP 223; moderate GP 441,
Mel 1500, 1856; ~ *fir* slow fire
CY 768

ete *v* eat Kn 947+; ~ *almesse* live

on charity Mel 1567; *sg past*
eet; *p ppl* ete(n)

eterne *adj* eternal, everlasting
Kn 1109+

Evangile, Evaungelie *n* Gospel
ML 666, Mel 1079

evene *adj* straight Mil 3316;
equal Kn 2588, Mel 1482;
impartial, just Kn 1864;
medium GP 83; calm,
untroubled Cl 811; ~
Cristen(e) *n* fellow Christian(s)
Pars 395+

evene *adv* evenly, equally
Kn 2593, Sum 2249; calmly,
coolly Kn 1523; exactly
Fkl 1069, CY 1200; just
ML 1143; ~ *joinant* im-
mediately adjoining
Kn 1060

evere *adv* ever GP 732,
Kn 1212+; perpetually Mk
2436; always, continually
GP 50, Mil 3444+; ~ *in oon*
always alike, continually Rv
3880+; *whan that* ~ whenever
WB 45; *wher that* ~ wherever
CY 733+; *al that* ~ whatever
Fkl 1256+

everemo, everemoore *adv* ever-
more, forever Kn 1229+; constantly, always Rv 3961,
NP 2815+; at all times GP 67;
every time CY 957; all the
time, continually WB 834+;
for ~ forever Kn 1032+;
always ML 760+; ~ *in oon* all
the time Mch 2086

everich *pron, adj and n* everyone
ML 531+; each, each one
GP 371, Kn 1186+; ~ *a* every
GP 733

everycho(o)n *pron* every one,
one and all GP 31+

everyde(e)l *n and adv* (see also
deel) everything Fkl 1288+;
entirely, completely Kn 1825,
Mch 1508+; in full Rv 4315+;
in every respect GP 368,
WB 162

exaltacioun *n* the position of a
planet in the zodiac where it
was thought to exert its greatest influence WB 702+

excellent *adj* excellent, outstanding ML 150+

excercise *v* exercise CY 750+;
put to good use Kn 1436; *refl*
discipline o.s. Pars 689

excite *v* incite, urge, prompt
Sum 1716, CY 744, Pars 973

excusacioun *n* justification,
excuse Pars 164, 680

excuse *v* exonerate, exculpate
ML 1059, Mch 2269+; excuse
GP 651+; *refl* excuse o.s.
WB 391+; be excused from
Pars 1042; *have me excused*
(*of*) forgive me (for) Sq 7+

execucioun *n* execution; *putte to*
~ carry into effect, enforce
Mel 1853; *doon* ~ carry out an
action Cl 522, Mcp 287;
execute (a sentence) Fri 1303

exemple *n* (see also **ensample**)
example GP 568

exercise *n* exercise NP 2839;
training Cl 1156

experience *n* experience
Kn 2445+; demonstration,
proof Cl 788

expert *adj* experienced
WB 174+; trained CY 1251; ~
of learned in GP 577

expounde, expowne *v* explain, interpret Pri 535, Mk 2156+; translate Pri 526

expres *adv* explicitly, clearly WB 27+; ~ *again*(*s*) directly opposed to Phys 182, Pars 587+

expresse *v* express Pri 476, Pars 1039; relate, describe Mch 2362, Mel 950+; declare Phys 170; utter Pri 485

ey *n* egg NP 2845, CY 806

eye *n* (see also **eighe**) eye GP 10+; *nether* ~ anus, arsehole Mil 3852; *at* ~ with o's own eyes Kn 3016+; to the eye Cl 1168+; *pl* **eyen**

fable *n* story, legend, fiction Sum 1760+

face *n* 'one of the three parts of ten degrees into which each sign of the zodiac was divided' (*MED*) Sq 50 (see n.), Fkl 1288

fader *n* father GP 100+; ancestor Cl 61; (*inflectionless gen*) father's GP 781+; ~ *kin* father's kin/family Rv 4038+

fadme *n* fathom, measure of length roughly equivalent to six feet Kn 2916+

faierye *n* (see also **fairye**) fairyland Mch 2227+; fairy WB 872; fairy creatures WB 859, Mch 2039; magic, enchantment Mch 1743

faille *n*: *withoute*(*n*) ~ without fail, doubtless Kn 1644, 1854; actually, truly CY 1163

fail(l)e *v* fail Kn 1610, 2798,

Mch 1632+; fall short Sh 415; lack Mk 2462; prove unsuccessful Pars 719; ~ *of* fail in WB 430, CY 671+; run out of Sh 248; fail to keep Sh 275; ~ *yow my thankes* be lacking in gratitude to you Sh 188

fain *adj* (see also **fawe**) glad, happy, pleased Kn 2437+; eager Mch 2017+

fain *adv* (see also **fein**) gladly GP 766, Kn 1257+

fainte *v* (see also **feinte**) enfeeble ML 926

fair *adj* (see also **feir**) fair, fine, beautiful, lovely GP 154+; *as n* beauty Sq 518

faire *adv* beautifully, elegantly GP 273+; finely, well GP 94, 124, Mil 3289+; neatly Kn 2594, Mil 3210+; courteously, kindly WB 222+; gently Kn 2697, WB 803+; carefully Mil 3568; becomingly, properly Sum 2286, NP 2872; exactly, right Kn 984, NP 3267; fairly Kn 2659; ~ *and wel* conscientiously GP 539; well Mil 3743; carefully CY 1113; fairly and squarely Rv 4069, 4226; willingly Kn 1826; cheerfully Rv 4062; ~ (*bi*)*falle you* God bless you NP 3460+

fairnesse *n* beauty Kn 1098+; gentleness GP 519

fairye *n* (see also **faierye**) fairyland Mch 2234+; magic contrivance, illusion Sq 201

falding *n* type of coarse woollen cloth GP 391, Mil 3212 (see

Hodges, *Chaucer and Costume*, pp. 155–60)

falle *v* fall GP 128+; be born Cl 990; befall, happen (to), come about GP 324, 585, Kn 1668, Mil 3733+; become WB 812; allow Sq 570; ~ *in* stray into Mel 1134; ~ *to* begin to Mil 3273; suit ML 149; ~ *unto* belong, be appropriate to Cl 259; ~ *in office* get employment Kn 1418; ~ *of* (s.o.'s) *acord* come to an agreement with (s.o.) Fkl 741; *as it wolde* ~ as chance determined NP 2995; *yfallen in* occurring in Pard 496; *sg past* **fil, fel**; *pl past* **fille(n)**; *3 sg past subj* **fille**; *p ppl* **falle(n)**, **yfalle(n)**

false *v* falsify, alter Mil 3175; ~ (o's) *trouthe* break o's word Sq 627

falshede *n* falseness, deceitfulness, treachery CY 979+

fame *n* reputation Kn 3055, Cl 940, Phys 111+; rumour, report, news ML 995, Cl 940+; *bringe in* ~ bring into repute Mil 3148

famulier *adj* intimate, at home GP 215, Sh 31; of o's own household, domestic Mch 1784

fand *sg past of* **finde** *v*

fantasye *n* fancy, delusion, imaginings Mil 3835, Mch 1577, 1610, Fkl 844; fancy, inclination Mil 3191, WB 516; (sexual) desire Mk 2285+; *after* (o's) ~ according to o's whim or desire WB 190+

fare *n* behaviour Sh 263; activity, goings-on Kn 1809; commotion ML 569; *make* ~ make a fuss Rv 3999

fare *v* go Kn 1395+; go away NP 2879; act, behave Kn 1261+; carry on WB 330; fare Mil 3457; live Sum 1881; ~ *with* (o.s.) behave Sq 461; ~ *by* act towards Pars 899; ~ *as/ lik* act, be like Rv 3871+; *it fareth* (*by*) it goes, turns out (with) Co 4408; *it fareth with it* is the case with Mch 1217; ~ *wel* do well Kn 2435, Sum 1773+; ~ *amis* fail Fkl 1298; ~ *the wors of* be the worse for Co 4350; *far(e)wel* (*sg imp*), *fareth wel* (*pl imp*) farewell Kn 1250, Mch 1688+; *lat him* ~ *wel* good luck to him WB 501; *how* ~ *ye* how are you Sum 1801+; *sg past* **ferde**; *pl past* **ferden**; *p ppl* **fare(n)**

faringe *pres ppl*: *wel-*~ good looking Fkl 932, Mk 1942

fast(e) *adv* fast, firmly Mil 3499, ML 509+; tightly Kn 2151, Mch 1821+; earnestly Kn 1266, Mil 3289, WB 652, SN 140, CY 1146+; diligently ML 839+; with vigour Mil 3306, NP 3087; vigorously Kn 2359, 2423, Mil 3341+; intently SN 245; busily Cl 598, 978; heartily WB 672, Mch 1769, Mcp 88; hard Kn 1535, 2558, 2946, Mk 2531+; deeply Rv 4194+; soundly Mch 1928; fast Kn 1469+; *as* ~ immediately CY 1105+; ~ *by* near, close at hand Kn 1476, 1688; (*prep*) close to GP 719+

faste *sg past of* **faste** *v*, to fast

faught *sg past of* **fighte** *v*

faukon, fawkon *n* falcon Sq 411+

fawe *adj* (see also **fain**) happy, eager WB 220

fay *n* (see also **fey**) faith, honour Mil 4034+

feble *adj* (see also **fieble**) feeble, weak Kn 1369+

feblesse *n* feebleness, weakness Pars 823+

fecche *v* fetch, bring GP 819+; carry off ML 1064+; *sg past* **fette**; *p ppl* **fet, yfet**

fee *n* fee GP 317+; property WB 630; ~ *simple* unrestricted ownership (*technically* tenure of land without limitation to any particular class of heirs) GP 319

feeld *n* field Kn 886+; field, ground (*heraldry*) Mk 2383

fe(e)le *v* feel Kn 2232+; ~ *wikkedly of* feel wickedly toward Pars 559, 581; perceive SN 155; know Fkl 727, CY 711

feeling(e) *vbl n* feeling WB 610+; skill NP 3293

feend *n* devil Rv 4288+

feendlich, feendly *adj* (see also **fendlich**) fiendish, monstrous ML 783+

feere *n* (see also **fere**) fear Kn 1333+

feeste *n* (see also **feste**) feast Kn 2197+

feet *n pl* feet GP 473+; *him to feete* at his feet ML 1104; *step on thy* ~ step on it Rv 4074

fein *adv* (see also **fain**) gladly Mch 1418

feine *v* invent GP 736, Fri 1378; counterfeit, forge Fri 1360, 1507; conceal Mel 1311; evade, shirk Cl 529; dissemble Sq 510+; simulate WB 417, Sq 524+; pretend (*often refl*) ML 351, Cl 513+; pretend to be (*refl with adj*) Phys 62; *feined* false, hypocritical GP 705, ML 362+

feinte *v* (see also **fainte**) become exhausted CY 753; flag, weaken Cl 970

feir *adj* (see also **fair**) fair, fine, beautiful Rv 3977+

feith *n* faith GP 62+; faithfulness, fidelity Cl 866+; pledge, promise, word Kn 1622, Sum 2139, Mel 1807+

feithful *adj* faithful Cl 310+; true Fri 1425; conscientious SN 24; ~ *man* true Christian Mk 1891

feithfully *adv* faithfully ML 461+; truly, assuredly Fri 1420, Cl 1066+; devotedly Cl 1111

fel *adj* fierce, cruel Kn 1559+; deadly Th 829

fel *sg past of* **falle** *v*

felawe *n* fellow, companion GP 395+; friend Kn 1192+

felaweshipe *n* company, companionship GP 26+; *make ~ with* keep company with Mel 1189

feld *p ppl of* **felle** *v*, to fell

felonye *n* crime Kn 1996+; ill will, malice Pars 543

fendlich *adj* (see also **feendlich, feendly**) fiendish, monstrous ML 751

fer *adj* distant, remote Th 718+;
comp **ferre** further Mil 3393;
superl **ferreste** furthest GP 494

fer *adv* far GP 388+; *wiltow ~
are you going* far Fri 1387;
comp **fer, ferre(r)** further
GP 48+; *~ ne ner* neither later
nor sooner Kn 1850; *as ~ as*
insofar as Kn 1648

ferde *sg past of* **fare** *v*

ferden *pl past of* **fare** *v*

fere *n* (see also **feere**) fear
Kn 2344+

fered *p ppl* afraid, frightened
NP 3386, CY 924

ferforth *adv*: *so ~* so far, to such
an extent (that) ML 572+; *as ~
as* as far as ML 19+

ferforthly *adv*: *so ~ that* to such
an extent that Kn 960; *as ~ as
evere were ye foled* as sure as
ever you were born Fri 1545

ferme *adj* firm Cl 663,
Mch 1499

ferre *comp of* **fer** *adj*

ferre(r) *comp of* **fer** *adv* further
GP 48+

ferreste *superl of* **fer** *adj*

ferthe *ord num* fourth ML 3+

ferther *adj* farther Mch 2226+

ferther *adv* further GP 36+

ferthing *n* farthing GP 255+; particle, small bit GP 134

fest *n* fist Rv 4275+

feste *n* (see also **feeste**) feast
Kn 883+; entertainment Pars
47; *make ~* relax, enjoy o.s. Sh
327; (*with obj*) make much of
Cl 1109, Sh 342

fet *p ppl of* **fecche** *v*

fetis *adj* neat, elegant GP 157,
Pard 478

fetisly *adv* neatly, elegantly
GP 124+

fette *sg past of* **fecche** *v*

fey *n* (see also **fay**) faith, honour
Kn 1126+

fieble *adj* (see also **feble**) feeble,
weak ML 306+

fiers *adj* brave, valiant
Kn 1598+; violent, cruel
Kn 2012+; dangerous ML 300

fighte *v* fight Kn 984+; *sg past*
faught; *pl past* **foghte(n)**; *p ppl*
foghten

figure *n* shape Fri 1459+; image
ML 187+; metaphor, figure of
speech GP 499, Cl 16; figure,
design Fkl 831; (stellar) configuration Kn 2035, 2043

fil *sg past of* **falle** *v*

fille *3 sg past subj of* **falle** *v*

fille(n) *pl past of* **falle** *v*

fin *n* end, conclusion ML 424+;
outcome Mk 2158; object
Mch 2106

fin *adj* fine, excellent GP 194+;
(of colours) pure, radiant
Kn 1039

final *adj* final Fkl 987; *cause ~*
ultimate cause, governing
purpose (*phil*) Mel 1401
(see n.) +

finally *adv* finally, at last
Kn 1204+; utterly, completely
Pars 276

finde *v* find GP 648+; provide
Kn 2413, ML 243; provide for
Pard 537; support, maintain
NP 2829; invent GP 736; *3 sg
contr pres* **fint** (**findes** Rv 4130,
Northern form); *sg past* **fand**,
fo(o)nd; *pl past* **founde, fond**;
p ppl **founde(n), yfounde**

fine *v* cease, stop WB 788, 1136

fint *3 sg contr pres of* **finde** *v*

fir *n* fire GP 624+; torch
Kn 2911; *wilde* ~, ~ *of Seint
Antony* skin disease, e.g. erysipelas (*med*) Mch 2252, Pars
427; Greek fire (inflammable
material used in warfare)
WB 373

firmament *n* sky Mch 2219+;
the sphere of the Primum
Mobile ML 295 (see n.)

firy *adj* fiery, burning Kn 1493+

fissh *n* fish GP 180+; Pisces
(*astr*) Sq 273

fit *n* part of a poem, section Th
888; bout, session Rv 4230,
WB 42; *ille* ~ unlucky time
Rv 4184

flambe *n* (see also **flawmbe**)
flame Mk 2163+

flatere *v* flatter WB 930+

flaugh *2 sg past of* **fle(e)** *v* (2)

flawmbe *n* (see also **flambe**)
flame Pars 353

fle(e) *v* (1) flee, retreat, run away
ML 121, WB 279+; escape
Kn 1170+; avoid, shun
Mel 1177+; fly Cl 119; ~ (o's)
way run away WB 798; *sg past*
fledde, fleigh; *pl past* **fledden**;
p ppl **fled**

fle(e) *v* (2) fly Mil 3806, Sq
122+; *1/3 sg past* **fleigh, fley**;
2 sg past **flaugh**; *pl past*
flowen

fle(e)te *v* float, drift Kn 1956+; *3
sg contr pres* **fleet**

fleigh *1/3 sg past of* **fle(e)** *v* (1)
and (2)

flekked *p ppl* flecked, streaked
Mch 1848, CY 565

fleme *v* banish Mcp 182; *p ppl*
flemed exiled SN 58

flesshly *adj* physical Pars 516+;
in the body, worldly Pars
204+; bodily, carnal Pars 276+

flesshly *adv* in the flesh Pars
202, 333; sexually, carnally Pri
585+

fley *1/3 sg past of* **fle(e)** *v* (2)

flood *n* flood Mil 3518+; flood
tide, high tide Sq 259,
Fkl 1059, Mk 2587+

florisshe *v* flourish, thrive
Mel 995; put out leaves or
flowers Pars 288, 636

flour *n* flower GP 4+; ~ *of il ending* the worst possible fate
Rv 4174

floure *v* flourish Cl 120, Phys 44

flowen *pl past of* **fle(e)** *v* (2)

flye *n* fly Co 4352+; insect
Pars 467

fnorte *v* snore, snort Rv 4163,
ML 790

foghte(n) *pl past and p ppl of*
fighte *v*

foine *v* lunge, thrust Kn 1654+

foison *n* abundance, plenty Mil
3165, ML 504

folily *adv* foolishly, rashly
Mel 1449+; wantonly, lecher-
ously Mch 1403

folwe *v* follow GP 528,
Kn 2682+; imitate Cl
1143, 1189

folye *n* folly ML 163+; foolish-
ness, something foolish
Kn 1798, Fkl 1131,
NP 3438+; sin, dissipation
Phys 64, Pard 464; lechery
Kn 1942, Rv 3880, Cl 236+

fond *sg and pl past of* **finde** *v*

fonde *v* try WB 479+; sound out
 ML 347

fo(o) *n* foe, enemy GP 63+;
 Cristes ~ the devil Mil 3782;
 weak pl **foon**

fool *n* fool Kn 1606+; sinner
 Pars 156

fool *adj* lecherous, lascivious
 Pars 853; ~ *wommen* prostitutes Pars 885

fool-large *adj* foolishly generous,
 spendthrift Mel 1599+

foom *n* foam Kn 1659; sweat
 CY 564+

foomen *n pl* enemies ML 718+

foon *weak pl of* **fo(o)** *n*

foond *sg past of* **finde** *v*

foore *n* trail, footsteps WB 110,
 Sum 1935

foot *n* foot Kn 1479+; feet
 Fkl 1315

for *prep* for GP 62+; because of,
 on account of Mk 2131+; by
 means of Sq 184; for fear of,
 against WB 964, Th 862, Mk
 2560, Pars 607; in spite of
 Kn 2745, WB 39, Mch 2330,
 Phys 129, CY 1396+; as, to be
 Phys 141, SN 457+; as regards
 GP 387, Cl 474; ~ *old* with
 age Kn 2142; ~ *dronken*
 because of being drunk Mil
 3120, Rv 4150; ~ *blak* for
 blackness Kn 2144; ~ *sik* for illness WB 394; ~ *drye* for dryness Sq 409; ~ *God* by God
 Mil 3526; ~ *min hood* by my
 hood CY 1334; ~ *any thing* at
 all costs GP 276; (*as*) ~ *me* as
 far as I am concerned
 Kn 1619, Mch 1554+; ~ *the*
 nones for the occasion

GP 379, Mil 3126+; as a rhyming tag, meaning little more
 than 'indeed' GP 523+

for (that) *conj* for, because
 GP 102+; in order that, so that
 Kn 2879, Mk 2715+; in the
 event that NP 3299

forage *n* dry fodder, winter
 food, hay Rv 3868+; fodder
 Th 783

forasmuche (as), for as muchel as
 conj inasmuch as Kn 1608, Sh
 33+

forbede *v* forbid Mil 3508+; *sg*
 past **forbad**; *p ppl* **forbode(n)**

forbere *v* bear, endure Mch
 2182; omit Kn 885; leave
 alone WB 665; forbear, refrain
 (from) Mel 1862+; ~ *his*
 wordes spare his language
 Mil 3168

forbode(n) *p ppl of* **forbede** *v*

forby *adv* past Phys 125+; *heer*
 ~ past this place Pard 668

force *n* (see also **fors**) force, violence Kn 1927+; *by* ~ of necess-
 ity Kn 2554, Phys 205; *what* ~
 what does it matter Mch 1295;
 na/no ~ no matter Rv 4176+

fordo *v* destroy, ruin Kn 1560+;
 p ppl **fordo, fordoon**

foreward *adv* (see also **forward**):
 first and ~ first of all Mch
 2187+

forfered *p ppl* afraid Kn 2930,
 Sq 527

forgaf *sg past of* **foryeve** *v*

forgat *sg past of* **foryete** *v*

forgeten *p ppl of* **foryete** *v*

forgo *v* forego, give up
 WB 315+; lose Mel 993+;
 refrain (from) Mch 2085

forlese *v* lose utterly Pars 789;
  p ppl **forlore, forlorn**

forlete *v* desert, abandon Pars
  972; cease Pars 250; renounce,
  leave off Pars 93+; lose Pard
  864, Pri 658

forlore, forlorn *p ppl of* **forlese** *v*
  wasted Fkl 1557; ruined,
  destroyed Mil 3505

forme *n* form, shape Fri 1471+;
  state Fkl 1161; manner, nature
  Sq 337; form, lair (of a hare)
  Sh 104; proper manner,
  etiquette Sq 100; *in* ~ properly,
  with decorum GP 305

forncast *p ppl* planned, premeditated NP 3217 (see n.),
  Pars 448

forneis *n* (see also **fourneis**) furnace GP 202+

fors *n* (see also **force**) importance; *no* ~ no matter
  ML 285+; *make/do no* ~ *of*
  attach no importance to Fri
  1512, NP 2941+; not to care
  WB 1234+; be negligent of
  Pars 721

forsake *v* forsake WB 644+;
  refuse, reject Mel 1557; *sg past*
  forsook; *p ppl* **forsake(n)**

forseide *p ppl* aforesaid
  Mel 1001+

forswering *n* perjury Pard 592+

forth *adv* forth, forward, out
  GP 825+; afterward
  Fkl 1081+; *tarien* ~ *the day*
  waste the day Kn 2820; *spekel*
  telle ~ proceed to speak, tell
  Kn 1336+; *do* ~ continue to do
  Cl 1015; *chace* ~ pursue, go on
  with Cl 341

forther *adv* forward Rv 4222;

further on Pars 701; ~ *moor*
  further on Kn 2069

forthermo, forthermoor(e) *adv*
  furthermore WB 783+

forther over *adv* moreover,
  besides, in addition Pard 648+

forthre *v* assist, support
  Kn 1137+

forthward *adv* forth ML 263+

forthy *adv* therefore Kn 1841+

for to *adv with inf particle* (used
  with infinitive) in order to
  GP 17+; although, even if; ~ *to*
  be deed even if I were to die Cl
  364; ~ *dien in the peine* even if
  we were to be tortured to
  death Kn 1133; ~ *gon to helle*
  even if I were to go to hell Sh
  137; as equivalent to **to**, a
  mere marker of the infinitive
  GP 13+

fortunat *adj* fortunate, prosperous Cl 1137+; blessed Cl 422;
  propitious Mch 1970

fortune *v* control the destiny of
  Kn 2377; ~ *the ascendent*
  choose a favourable ascendant
  (*astr*) GP 417

forward *n* agreement GP 33+

forward *adv* (see also **foreward**):
  first and ~ first of all Mel 1241

forwoot *3 sg pres of* **forwite** *v*
  have foreknowledge of
  NP 3234, 3248

forwrapped *p ppl* wrapped up,
  covered up Pard 718, Pars 320

foryete *v* forget Kn 1882+; ~
  (*o's*) *minde* lose (o's) memory
  ML 527; *sg past* **forgat**; *p ppl*
  forgeten, foryeten

foryeve *v* forgive (for) GP 743+;
  sg past **forgaf**

foryevenesse, foryifnesse *n* forgiveness Mel 1773+

fostre *v* rear, educate Rv 3946+; teach SN 539; look after Cl 222, Mch 1387; sustain, nourish Fkl 874; ~ *up* bring up ML 275, Cl 213+

fother *n* cart-load, load GP 530+

foul *adj* foul, dirty, defiled GP 501+; wretched, vile Kn 3061+; ugly, loathsome ML 764, WB 265+; terrible Sh 194, Mk 2083+; *for ~ ne fair* on no account ML 525; *thurgh ~ or fair* over rough and smooth Sq 121

foule *adv* shamefully, disgracefully WB 1069+; wickedly Fri 1312, Mcp 278; ~ *ysped* made a mess of it Rv 4220; ~ *moot thee falle* I hope you come to a bad end Mcp 40

fourneis *n* (see also **forneis**) furnace GP 559, Mk 2163, CY 804+

fow(e)l *n* bird GP 190+

fraine *v* (see also **freine**) ask, inquire Pri 600

franchise *n* freedom, being freeborn Pars 452; nobility, magnanimity, generosity Mch 1987, Fkl 1524+

frank *n* franc, French gold coin Sh 181+

frankelein *n* franklin, landowner, gentleman GP 331 (see n.) +

fredam, fredom *n* nobility, generosity, magnanimity GP 46, Kn 2791+

free *adj* free Kn 1292+; voluntary GP 852+; incapable of restriction Kn 1606, Fkl 767; unobstructed Pri 494; noble, gracious Kn 2386, Pri 467+; graceful, beautiful Phys 35; generous, liberal Co 4387, Cl 1209, Sh 43+; willing Pard 401

freend *n* friend GP 670+; kinsman Kn 992+

freine *v* (see also **fraine**) ask Mel 1832, SN 433

freletee *n* frailty, weakness WB 92, Pars 449+

frere *n* friar GP 208+

fressh *adj* fresh GP 90+; clean, gay Mk 2122+; gay, joyous, lively Kn 2386, WB 508, Cl 1173, Sh 177+

fressh *adv* freshly, newly Kn 2832, Sh 309; gaily Kn 1048

frete *v* eat, devour, gnaw Kn 2019+

fro, from *prep* from GP 15+; against Mil 3479+

fruit *n* fruit Rv 3872+; result, product, reward Kn 1282+; essential part, heart, kernel ML 411, Fri 1373, Mch 1270+

ful *adj* full GP 233+; whole Kn 3075+; *as n: atte fulle* completely GP 651+; in full Rv 4133+; to the hilt Rv 3936; fairly and squarely Rv 4305

ful *adv* very, completely GP 119, Phys 25+

fulfille *v* fill Kn 940, WB 859+; fulfil, carry out, accomplish Kn 1318+; *p ppl* **fulfild**

fume *n* vapour CY 1098; bodily 'exhalation' NP 2924

fumositee *n* vapour, exhalation (of the 'humours' in the body) Sq 358, Pard 567

fundement *n* foundation Sum 2103; arse, anus Pard 950

furlong *n* furlong Rv 4166+; ~ *way* time required to walk one furlong (?2½ minutes) Mil 3637+

fy *interj* fie! shame! Kn 1773+

ga *v* go (Northern form of **go** *v*) Rv 4037+; *p ppl* **gane** Rv 4077

gabbe *v* tell lies NP 3066; blab, gossip Mil 3510

gadre *v* gather Kn 1053+

gail(l)ard *adj* gallant, gay, gaily dressed Mil 3336, Co 4367

gail(l)er *n* gaoler Kn 1064+

gaine *v* avail, help Kn 1176+; ~ *agains* be effective against Kn 1787

gale *v* make an outcry WB 832, Fri 1336

galping(e) *pres ppl* yawning Sq 350, 354

galwes *n pl* gallows WB 658+

game *n* game GP 853+; joke Kn 1806, Co 4354, Fri 1279+; contest Kn 2108+; fun, amusement Kn 2286, Fri 1275+; plan, scheme Mil 3405; game of love Mk 2288; *someres* ~ Midsummer revels WB 648; *make* ~ frolic Mil 3259; *make* ~ *and glee* provide entertainment Th 840; *have a* ~ amuse o.s. Mk 2550; *it is no* ~ it's no laughing matter Sh 290; *in (his)* ~ in jest, jokingly Co 4355, Mk 1964+; *make ernest of* ~ take a joke seriously Mil

3186; *for ernest ne for* ~ on no account Cl 733; *bitwix ernest and* ~ half seriously and half playfully Mch 1594

gan *sg past of* **ginne** *v*

gane *p ppl of* **ga** *v*

gardinward *adv:* (*un*)*to the* ~ toward the garden Mil 3572, Fkl 1505

garnesoun, garnisoun *n* garrison Mel 1027; defence, protection Mel 1337+

gat *sg past of* **gete** *v*

gat-tothed *adj* having teeth set wide apart GP 468+

gaude *n* (see also **gawde**) trick Pard 389

gaure *v* stare, gaze Mil 3827+

gawde *n* (see also **gaude**) trick Pars 651

gay *adj* gay, light-hearted, lively Mil 3339, WB 508+; beautiful, handsome, fine GP 111, Mil 3254+; finely dressed GP 74+; melodious GP 296+; ~ *gerl* loose woman Mil 3769

gay(e) *adv* richly, finely Mil 3689, CY 1017

gea(u)nt *n* giant Th 807+

geere *n* (see also **gere**) clothes, dress GP 365; utensils GP 352; possessions ML 800

geeste *n* (see also **geste**) chronicle, story Mch 2284

general *adj* universal Kn 2969, Pars 163, 388; general Fkl 945+; ~ *reule* rule without exceptions Mel 1231; *in* ~ in a body, without exception ML 417; in general terms Kn 2285, Mel 1233

generally *adv* universally,

without exception WB 1037;
in general Mcp 328, Pars 371+

gent *adj* shapely Mil 3234;
noble Th 715

gentil *n* member of the gentry or
nobility Mil 3113, WB 1209+

gentil *adj* noble, nobly born
Kn 1753, WB 1153+; noble,
knightly GP 72, WB 1170+;
noble, kind (used ironically)
GP 567+; refined, sensitive
Kn 1043+; refined Mil 3360;
excellent GP 718, Pard 304+;
noble, well-bred Sq 195; gracious Cl 852

gentil(l)esse *n* nobility of birth
or rank WB 1109+; mark of
nobility Mk 2254; nobility,
largeness of soul, virtue
WB 1134, Fkl 1524+;
elegance, distinction Sq 426;
graciousness Kn 920, Mil
3382+; kindness NP 3296, CY
1054; refined behaviour
WB 260, Mch 1603; noble
behaviour Mil 3179, Sq 483;
for youre ~ out of courtesy
WB 1211+; *of his ~* out of
kindness Fkl 1574; *in al ~* in a
manner suited to noble birth
Cl 593

gentilly *adv* courteously
ML 1093+; considerately
Kn 3104; generously Fkl 1608;
honourably Fkl 674

gentrye *n* nobility of birth
WB 1152+; nobility WB 1146,
Pars 461+; mark of breeding
Pars 601

gerdone *v* reward, repay
Mel 1272+

gerdo(u)n *n* (see also **guerdoun**)

reward, recompense Cl 883+;
for al gerdons ?as you hope to
prosper Mel 1052

gere *n* (see also **geere**) clothes,
dress Kn 1016, Cl 372;
armour Kn 2180; equipment
Fkl 1276; things Rv 4016;
behaviour, moods
Kn 1372, 1531

gerl *n* girl Mil 3769; youngster
(of either sex) GP 664

gerland *n* garland, wreath
GP 666+

gesse *v* guess, suppose, estimate
GP 82+; suspect Fkl 1486;
imagine ML 622; *for to ~* in
everyone's estimation
Kn 2593

gest *n* guest Cl 338+; paying
guest Mil 3188

geste *n* (see also **geeste**) chronicle, story ML 1126, Mch
642+; ?alliterative verse
Mel 933

get *n* (see also **jet**) contrivance
CY 1277

gete *v* obtain for (s.o.) Pri 479+;
beget ML 715+; get, acquire,
obtain GP 704, Mil 3465+, *refl*
GP 291, 703, Mil 3620,
ML 647+; *3 sg pres* get, geteth;
sg past gat; *p ppl* gete(n),
ygeten

gif *conj* if (Northern form) Rv
4181+

gilt *n* offence, sin, wrongdoing
Kn 1765, Mch 2268,
Mel 1825+; guilt ML 637+; *in
the ~* in the wrong WB 387; *as
in my ~* through any fault of
mine Fkl 757

gilt(e)lees *adj* guiltless, innocent

ML 643+; *adv* unjustly
Kn 1312, ML 674+

gin *n* contrivance, device Sq
128+

gingle *v* jingle GP 170+

ginne *v* begin CY 1192+. Used
as a weak auxiliary with an
infinitive, as equivalent of a
simple present or past tense:
e.g. *ginneth gon* goes Rv 4064;
gan preye prayed GP 301; *gan
to sike* sighed Kn 1540;
gonnen to smite struck
Kn 1658; *sg past* **gan**; *pl past*
gonne(n)

gipoun *n* padded tunic worn
under a coat of chain-mail
GP 75; surcoat, tunic worn
over plate-armour Kn 2120
(see n.)

girdel *n* belt GP 358+; *wel his ~
underpighte* padded out his
belt well, filled his belly
ML 789

gise *n* manner, way Kn 1208+;
custom, practice Kn 993, Rv
4126+; fashion Kn 2125; *in his
~* in his own fashion ML 790;
at his owene ~ as he pleased/
pleases GP 663, Kn 1789

gite *n* gown, mantle Rv 3954,
WB 559

giterne *n* gittern, a lute-like
instrument Mil 3333
(see n.) +

glad *adj* glad, cheerful, happy
GP 811+; *upon thy glade
day* in your prosperity
ML 426

glade *v* gladden, cheer, comfort
Kn 2837, Cl 1107+; make bliss-
ful Cl 822; entertain, please

CY 598; *refl* rejoice, be glad
Sq 609

gladly *adv* gladly, with pleasure
GP 308+; willingly Sq 224;
habitually, customarily
NP 3224, Pars 612, 887; *be ~
wise* like to be wise Sq 376

gle(e)de *n* live coal, ember
Kn 1997+; fire Mil 3379,
ML 111+

glide *v* glide Kn 1575+; rise
Sq 373+; flow Fkl 1415; go
Th 904; *sg past* **glood**; *p ppl*
gliden

glorifye *v* glorify Pars 1037;
refl take pride in Pars 405,
757

glose *n* gloss, explanatory comment Sum 1792+; *withouten ~*
plainly, without word-spinning
Sq 166

glose *v* gloss, interpret
ML 1180, WB 26+; use
euphemisms Mch 2351;
beguile Mk 2140; blandish,
cajole, use fine words WB 509,
Mcp 34, Pars 45

glotonye *n* gluttony Pars 482+

gnawe *v* gnaw Mk 2448; champ
Kn 2507; *sg past* **gnow**

go *v* (see also **ga**) go GP 377+,
refl Mil 3434; walk Kn 968+;
live WB 269, Mk 1933; come
WB 931; play, sound Pard
331, NP 2852; *~ (un)to* proceed with CY 899, Mcp 237;
proceed to Pars 603; *~ biforn*
come first ML 704; anticipate
(prayers) Pri 478, SN 56; *so
moot(e) I (ride or) ~* as I live
Mil 3114, Sum 1942, Fkl 777;
goon is many a yere, go sithen

many yeres many years ago
ML 132, Kn 1521; *goon sithen
many a day* long ago Sq 536;
goon with childe pregnant, big
with child ML 720; *hadde ygo
unto* had devoted himself to
GP 286; *pl imp* go(o)th; *sg
past* yede; *p ppl* go, go(o)n,
ygo(n)

godsibb *n* (see also **gossib**)
relation by baptism, child of
o's godparent or parent of o's
godchild Pars 908+

gon *p ppl of* **go** *v*

gonne(n) *pl past of* **ginne** *v*

good *n* property, wealth
GP 581+; good, benefit, blessing WB 231+; profit Fri 1453

good(e) man *n phr* (see also
goodman) good man, excellent
man GP 477+; master of the
house, householder Sum 1768,
Sh 29+

goodlich, goodly *adj* good, excellent NP 2820; courteous, kind
Mel 1731+; pleasant NP 2779;
handsome Sq 623

goodly *adv* excellently
Mel 1780; courteously, kindly
Mel 1875; gladly GP 803; well
Mel 1230; *as a man may* ~ as
he possibly can Mel 1670; *as* ~
as as well as Mch 1935

goodman *n* (see also **good(e)
man**) master of the house,
householder Pard 361

goodnesse *n* goodness ML 158+;
good Mel 1692+; *turne to* ~ be
beneficial to Pars 470; *youre* ~
your excellency Mel 1744

goon *p ppl of* **go** *v*

goore *n* gore, inset panel in a

skirt (to make it flare out)
Mil 3237; coat, gown Th 789

goost *n* soul, spirit Kn 2768,
Mil 3646+; damned soul,
ghost GP 205, Mk 1934+;
Holy Ghost Pri 470+

goostly *adj* spiritual Pars 392+

goot *n* goat GP 688+

go(o)th *pl imp of* **go** *v*

gossib *n* (see also **godsibb**) intimate friend WB 243+

gourde *n* bottle, flask Mcp 82,
91

governa(u)nce *n* government
Pard 600+; control, authority
ML 287, Cl 23+; management
WB 814+; controlling policy
or plan Kn 1313, Fkl 866; care
Phys 73, Mel 1270, NP 2865;
self-control Fkl 786; demeanour, behaviour GP 281, Mch
1603+; conduct Cl 994; control, regulation Sq 311; *have* ~
of rule over Mk 2060; *in* ~
under his control Sum 1894

governe *v* rule, control, hold
sway over Kn 1303,
WB 1237+; administer, manage Cl 322, Sh 244; *refl* act,
behave Mel 1002+; *governeth
yow of* regulate Sh 261

governinge *vbl n* control
GP 599; *pl* authority Phys 75

governour *n* ruler, governor
Kn 861+; leader GP 813;
official, administrator Mk
1940; keeper Fkl 1031

grace *n* (see also **gras** *n* (2))
grace Kn 2400, 3069, Mil
3560+; favour GP 88, 573,
Kn 1120+; mercy, pardon
Kn 1828, ML 647+; good

fortune Kn 1245, Pard 783,
NP 3159+; *pl* thanks
Mel 1804; *of* ~ as a favour Sq
161; *for his* ~ by his grace Sh
166; *of youre* ~ graciously,
kindly Kn 3080; *don a* ~ grant
a favour Kn 1874; *aventure or*
~ chance or good fortune
Fkl 1508; *harde* ~ ill luck CY
665; *sory* ~ misfortune
WB 746; *with harde/sory* ~
bad luck to him/you Sum
2228, Pard 717, 876; *sauf/*
save your ~ with respect
Mel 1070+

gracious *adj* gracious Mel 1821;
attractive, alluring Mil 3693;
beautiful Cl 613

grain *n* (see also **grein**): *in* ~ fast
dyed Th 727

grant merci (*French*) *phr* (see
also *graunt merci*) many
thanks CY 1380

gras *n* (1) grass Rv 3868+; plant
WB 774, Sq 153

gras *n* (2) (see also **grace**) grace
Th 831

graunge *n* monastery's farm Mil
3668, Sh 66

graunte *v* grant GP 786,
Kn 1620+; allow Mel 988+;
consent WB 1013, ML 1093+;
agree GP 810+; admit WB 85,
Mel 1261; appoint Cl 179+; ~
dayes of allow time for
Fkl 1575

graunt merci (*French*) *phr* (see
also *grant merci*) many thanks
Fri 1403+

grave *v* bury WB 496+; engrave,
carve Mil 3796, Fkl 830+;
p ppl (**y**)**grave**

grece *n* (see also **gresse**) grease,
fat GP 135+

gree *n* (1) degree Mch 1375; victory Kn 2733

gre(e) *n* (2) good will, favour;
receive in ~ look favourably on
ML 259; accept willingly
Cl 1151

gre(e)t *adj* great GP 84+; large
GP 559+; thick Kn 1076;
coarse Mch 1422; abundant
Phys 37; *pl and weak sg* **grete**;
comp **gretter**; *superl* **gretteste**

grein *n* (see also **grain**) grain
GP 596+; seed Pri 662+; carda-
mom Mil 3690; scarlet dye
NP 3459; *dye in* ~ fast dye
Sq 511

greithe *v* prepare Mk 2594; *refl*
get ready Rv 4309

gresse *n* (see also **grece**) oil, fat
Phys 60

grete *pl and weak sg of* **greet** *adj*

grete *v* greet ML 1051+; *sg past*
grette

gretter *comp adj* greater
Kn 863+; larger GP 197

gretteste *superl adj* greatest
GP 120+; largest Mel 1050

greva(u)nce *n* injury, harm
Mel 1486, Pars 662+; griev-
ance Mk 2513; sorrow
Fkl 941+

greve *n* thicket Kn 1641; bush
Kn 1495, 1507

greve *v* harm, injure, hurt
ML 352, WB 1205+; anger,
displease, vex Sum 2181, Pri
448+; *refl* be angry Rv 3859+;
take offence Rv 3910+; *noght*
greveth us we do not begrudge
Kn 917

grevous *adj* grievous Kn 1010+;
serious Pars 449; difficult Pars
529; hostile Pars 641

grevously *adv* grievously
Mel 1001+; gravely Pars 914;
strenuously Pars 667

grief *n* trouble Sum 2174+;
injury, grievance Mel 1545

grinde *v* grind Kn 2549, Rv
4032+; *3 sg contr pres* **grint**; *sg
past* **grinte**; *p ppl* **grounden,
ygrounde**

grisly *adj* horrible, dreadful, terrible Kn 1363+; frightful Pars
177, 223

grope *v* grope Rv 4217+; ques-
tion, examine, probe GP 644,
Sum 1817; ~ *after* search for
CY 679

grote *n* groat, silver coin worth
four pennies Sum 1964+

ground *n* ground Kn 2427+; texture, material GP 453

grucche *v* murmur, grumble (at)
Kn 3045+; ~ *of/again(s)* be dis-
satisfied at, grumble at
Kn 3062, Pars 500+

grucching(e) *vbl n* grumbling,
murmuring WB 406+

gruf *adv* headlong, face down-
ward Kn 949+

guerdoun *n* (see also **gerdo(u)n**)
reward, recompense Sum 1878

gye *v* lead, guide Mch 1429, Mk
2397; rule, govern Kn 1950,
Cl 75+; protect, keep Kn 2786,
SN 136+

habergeoun *n* (see also **hau-
bergeo(u)n**) mail-coat GP 76

habit *n* clothing WB 342+;
bodily condition Kn 1378

habounde *v* abound Mch 1286+

habunda(u)nce *n* abundance,
plenty Sum 1723+

habunda(u)nt *adj* abundant
Cl 59+

haf *sg past of* **heve** *v*

haire *n* (see also **heire**) hair-shirt
SN 133

hait *interj* (see also **heit**) gee up!
come on! Fri 1543

halden *p ppl of* **holde** *v* (Northern form)

half *n* side Mil 3481; behalf; *a
Goddes* ~ in God's name
WB 50

haliday *n* (see also **haly day**)
holy day, feast day (including
Sunday) Mil 3309+

halke *n* corner, cranny Fkl 1121;
hiding-place SN 311

hals *n* neck ML 73+

halt *3 sg pres of* **holde** *v*

halwe *n* saint ML 1060+; shrine
of a saint GP 14+

halwe *v* sanctify, hallow Pars
919; consecrate SN 551+

haly day *n* (see also **haliday**)
holy day, feast day Pars 667

han *inf and pl pres of* **have** *v*

hange *v* (see also **honge**) hang
Mil 3565+; *sg past* **he(e)ng**; *pl
past* **henge, honge(d)**; *p ppl*
hanged

hap *n* chance Mch 2057+; luck
Mk 2738+

happe *v* happen, come about
GP 585+; *impers* happen,
befall Kn 1189, Fri 1401+

happy *adj* fortunate Mel 1558+

hardily *adv* confidently, boldly
Rv 4009, Mch 2273; certainly,
indeed GP 156+

hardinesse *n* bravery, courage
Kn 1948+; boldness, confi-
dence WB 612, Cl 93,
Mel 1318+; arrogance
Pars 438

hardnesse *n* hardness, cal-
lousness Pars 486; hardship
Pars 686

hardy *adj* bold, stout-hearted,
brave GP 405+; rash Cl 1180

harlot *n* rogue GP 647, Rv
4268+; lecher Pars 885; fellow,
servant Sum 1754

harlotrye *n* sexual immorality,
lechery GP 561, Mch 2262+;
wickedness Fri 1328; dirty
story Mil 3145+

harm *n* harm, injury Mil 3830+;
sickness GP 423, ML 479; sorrow, pain Kn 2229, ML 99+; a
pity GP 385+

harnais, harneis *n* (suit of)
armour Kn 1006+; harness Mil
3762+; fittings, ornaments
Kn 2896; details Pars 974;
equipment WB 136

harrow *interj* help! Mil 3286+;
alas! Pard 288

harwe *v* plunder, harrow (hell)
Mil 3512, Sum 2107

harye *v* drag Kn 2726, Pars 171

hasard *n* dice-playing Pard 465+

hasardour *n* gambler, gamester
Pard 596+

hasardrye *n* gambling Pard 590+

haste *v* hurry on Phys 159;
hasten Mel 1054, *refl*
Kn 2052+

hastif *adj* hasty, speedy Cl 349+;
sudden Pars 541; urgent Mil
3545; eager, impetuous
Mch 1805

hastifnesse *n* hastiness, impetuos-
ity Mel 1133+

hastilich(e), hastily *adv* speedily,
quickly Kn 1714, ML 1047+;
soon, without delay Cl 140,
Mch 1411, 2122, Sh 109+;
eagerly, willingly Kn 1514,
Pars 675; hastily, rashly
Mel 1341+; suddenly
CY 1282

hate *n* hatred Kn 1671+; object
of hatred Pars 137

haubergeo(u)n *n* (see also
habergeoun) mail-coat
Kn 2119+

hauberk *n* coat of mail
Kn 2431+; plate-armour
(covering the chest) Th 863

haunt *n* haunt, territory
GP 252b, Th 811; *have an ~ of*
be expert in GP 447

haunte *v* haunt, visit Pars 885;
practise, indulge in Co 4392+

hautein *adj* proud Pars 614;
loud Pard 330

have *v* have GP 224+; keep Cl
201, Pard 725; preserve
Kn 2714; hold Kn 1448,
Fkl 700, Mel 1195, Mk
2588+; take CY 1187; *refl*
behave Mel 1575; *inf* **han**,
have; *1 sg pres* **have**; *2 sg pres*
hast; *3 sg pres* **hath** (has Northern form Rv 4027); *pl pres*
have, han; *sg imp* **have**; *pl imp*
haveth; *3 sg pres subj* **have**;
1/3 sg past **had, hade, hadde**; *2
sg past* **haddest**; *pl past*
hadden; *p ppl* **(y)had**

hawe *n* haw, hawthorn berry
WB 659; *~-bake* baked haws,
i.e. meagre fare ML 95

he *3 pers sg masc pron* he
GP 44+; ~ . . . ~ this one . . .
that one Kn 2519+

hed(d)e, heed *n* (see also **heved**)
head GP 109+; *(up)on* (o's) ~
on pain of death Kn 1344+;
maugree (o's) ~ in spite of all
(one) can do, irrespective of
(o's) wishes Kn 1169+; *after
thin owene* ~ according to
your own judgement Mil
3528; *putte forth his* ~ show
himself SN 312

he(e)d(e) *n* heed; *take* ~ *(of)* pay
attention to GP 303, Sum
1901+; be concerned for
Mk 2388

heeld *sg past of* **holde** *v*

heele *n* (see also **hele**) health
Sum 1946+; happiness, prosperity Kn 1271+

heelp *sg past of* **helpe** *v*

heeng *sg past of* **hange** *v*

heep *n* heap Kn 944+; crowd,
large number, multitude
GP 575, Mch 2429+

heer *n* hair GP 589+

heeragains *adv* in opposition to
this Kn 3039; in response to
this Pars 668

heerbiforn *adv* (see also
her(e)biforn) previously
Fkl 1535+

heere *v* (see also **here** *v*) hear
GP 169+; listen (to) Phys 173+

heerof *adv* (see also **hereof**,
herof) about this Pars 287

heerto *adv* (see also **herto**) for
this ML 243

heeste *n* (see also **heste**) command WB 74

heet *sg past of* **hote** *v*

heete *n* (see also **hete**) heat CY
578, Pars 120+

heete *1 sg pres and 3 sg pres
subj of* **hote** *v*

heeth *n* heath GP 6+; heather
Mil 3262

heigh *adj* (see also **hey, hy**) high
GP 316, WB 1167+; lofty,
exalted Kn 2989, Pars 598+;
great Kn 1798, 2913,
ML 162+; prominent
Kn 2167; solemn ML 675+;
admirable, noble Kn 2537,
WB 1160, Fkl 773+; severe
ML 795, 963; ~ *sentence* great
wisdom GP 306, Mch 1507,
Mk 2748; ~ *style* elevated style
Cl 18; *in* ~ *and lo(u)gh* in
everything GP 817+; ~ *and
lough* everybody ML 1142; *an*
~ *up* high, aloft Kn 1065+

heigh(e) *adv* (see also **hye**) high
Rv 4322+; loudly Kn 2661

heighnesse *n* (see also **heynesse**)
high rank Pars 190

heire *n* (see also **haire**) hair-shirt
Pars 1052+; ~ *clowte* hair-
cloth Pard 736

heit *interj* (see also **hait**) gee up!
come on! Fri 1561

helde *v* (see also **holde**) own,
keep WB 272

hele *n* (see also **heele**) health
Kn 3102, Pars 831

hele *v* (1) heal Kn 2706+

hele *v* (2) conceal WB 950+

help *n* help Kn 2400+; helper,
supporter Pri 534, Mel 1104+

helpe *v* help GP 258+; ~ *of* cure
of GP 632; *ther helpeth noght*
there's no help for it Kn 3033;
noght helpeth it it's no use

NP 2802; *sg past* heelp; *p ppl*
holpe(n)

hem *acc and dat pl of 3 pers
pron* them GP 11+; *refl* themselves Kn 2594+

hemself, hemselven *3 pers pl refl
pron* themselves WB 761+

hende *adj* handsome WB 628;
polite Fri 1286; courtly,
affable (semi-ironically) Mil
3199+

heng *sg past of* hange *v*

henge *pl past of* hange *v*

henne *adv* hence, from here
Kn 2356+; thereafter
Rv 3889

hennesforth *adv* henceforth Sq
658+

hente *v* seize, take hold of
Kn 904+; take Kn 957,
ML 1144+; take away, sum-
mon GP 698; catch Kn 1581,
Mil 3347+; acquire, get
GP 299; *past* hente; *p ppl*
(y)hent

heraud *n* herald Kn 1017+

herbergage *n* lodgings Co
4329+; home Cl 201; accommodation NP 2989

herberwe *n* lodgings, accommodation GP 765+; position
Fkl 1035; shelter Pars 1031;
harbours GP 403

here (1) *3 pers sg fem pron, acc/
dat* (see also hir(e)(2)) her
Kn 1421, ML 460+

here (2) *3 pers pl poss pron* (see
also hir(e) (2)) their WB 44b

here *v* (see also heere) hear
Kn 914+; listen (to) WB 828+

her(e)biforn *adv* (see also heerbiforn) previously Kn 1584+

hereof *adv* (see also heerof,
herof) about this Pars 984

heres, heris *n pl* hair GP 555+

herie *v* praise ML 872+; worship
Mk 2229+

heritage *n* inheritance ML 366+

herke *v* listen (to) ML 425+

herkne *v* listen (to), hear
GP 788+; ~ *after* listen out for
Sq 403

herne *n* out-of-the-way place
Fkl 1121+

herof *adv* (see also heerof,
hereof) of this, about this Mch
1683+

hert *n* hart, stag Kn 1675+

herte *n* heart GP 150+; ~-*blood*
heart's blood Kn 2006+;
~-*roote* the bottom of o's heart
WB 471; ~-*spoon* midriff
Kn 2606

hertely *adv* heartily, sincerely
GP 762+

hertly *adj* heartfelt, sincere Cl
176+

herto *adv* (see also heerto) to
this Mel 1291

herupon *adv* on this point Sh
141; thereupon Cl 190

heryinge *vbl n* praise, worship
Pri 459+

heste *n* (see also heeste) order,
command, decree Kn 2532+;
promise Fkl 1064

hete *n* (see also heete) heat Phys
38+

hete *1 sg pres of* hote *v*

hethenesse *n* heathen countries
GP 49+

heve *v* raise, lift Kn 2428, Pars
858+; heave GP 550+; *sg past*
haf

heved *n* (see also **hed(d)e**, **heed**) head Th 842+

hevene *n* heaven(s) GP 519+; ~ *king* heaven's king Mil 3464+

hevinesse *n* sorrow, grief Kn 1454+; resentment, rancour Cl 432, Mel 1748; drowsiness Mcp 22; sluggishness Pars 686

hevy *adj* heavy Mel 1214+; weighty, grave Mel 1022+; sorrowful, sad Fkl 822+; sluggish Pars 677+; *to ~ or to hoot* too heavy or too hot (to carry away) (*provbl expression*) Fri 1436

hewe *n* colour, complexion GP 394+; appearance Fri 1622+

hewed *p ppl* coloured Fkl 1245+

hey *n* hay Mil 3262+; grass Mk 2172+

hey *adj* (see also **heigh**, **hy**) high Mel 1819+; lofty Pars 469

heynesse *n* (see also **heighnesse**) high rank, honour Pars 336+

hide *v* hide, conceal Kn 1477+; be hidden Sq 141; *3 sg pres* **hideth**, **hit**; *sg past* **hidde**; *p ppl* **(y)hid**

hider *adv* hither GP 672+

hiderward *adv* this way (to or toward the speaker) Sh 426+

hidous *adj* hideous, dreadful Kn 1978+

hie *n* haste Kn 2979+

hie *v* hasten, hurry Kn 2274+, *refl* Sh 210+; bring quickly Sq 291

hierde *n* herdsman GP 603; shepherd SN 192

hight *p ppl of* **hote** *v*

highte *n* height; *on ~* aloft, on high Kn 2607+; aloud Kn 1784

highte *sg and pl past of* **hote** *v*, *used as present* be called Kn 1557+

him *3 pers masc pron, acc/dat sg* him GP 284+; *refl* himself GP 87+

himself, himselve(n) *3 pers sg masc refl pron* himself GP 184+

hindre *adj* hinder, rear Pars 424+

hine *n* farm labourer GP 603, Pard 688

hire *n* payment, wages GP 538+; *sette to ~* farm out GP 507; *quite youre ~* repay you WB 1008

hir(e) (1) *3 pers sg fem pron* (see also **here** *pron* (1)) (1) *poss* her GP 119+, (2) *acc/dat* her GP 163+; from her WB 967; for herself WB 210

hir(e) (2) *3 pers pl pron, poss and gen* (see also **here** *pron* (2)) their GP 32+; of them; *~ aller* of them all GP 586; *~ bothe* of both of them ML 221; *~ thankes* willingly Kn 2114+

hir(s) *3 pers pron, gen pl* theirs Sum 1926

hirself, hirselve(n) *3 pers sg fem refl pron* herself Mil 3543+

his *3 pers sg pron, poss and gen* (1) *masc* his GP 55+; of him SN 138; *~ thankes* willingly Kn 1626+; (2) *neut* its GP 8, Kn 1036+; *pl* **hise**

hit *3 sg contr pres of* **hide** *v*

hold *n* (see also **hoold**) possession Sq 167

holde *v* (see also **helde**) hold
GP 783, Kn 1949+; keep
Kn 2098, Sum 2197+; keep to,
remain in Kn 2525, ML 721+;
retain Phys 182; bring to bay,
check Mel 1326; remember
Pard 438; regard, consider
GP 141, WB 572+; *refl* keep
o.s., remain Mel 1037+; consider o.s. Kn 1868+; ~ *compaignye* (*with* s.o.) keep (s.o.)
company Fri 1521+; ~ (o's)
wey take (o's) course, make
(o's) way Kn 1506+; *be
holde(n)* be obliged WB 135,
Mel 1703+; be obligated
Kn 1307; *3 sg pres* **holdeth,
halt**; *sg imp* **hoold**; *pl imp*
hoold, holdeth; *sg past* **heeld**;
pl past **helde(n)**; *p ppl*
holde(n), yholde (Northern
form **halden**)

holour *n* lecher WB 254+; lover
Pars 878

holpe(n) *p ppl of* **helpe** *v*

holwe *adj* hollow Kn 1363+;
lean, hungry GP 289

hom *adv* (see also **hoom**) home,
homewards GP 400+

homicide *n* murder Sum 2009+;
murderer Mch 1994, Pard
893+

homly *adj* domestic, belonging
to o's home Mch 1785+;
homely, simple Sum 1843

hond *n* hand GP 193+; *of* (o's) ~
with respect to fighting ability
Kn 2103, ML 579; *holde up*
(o's) ~ promise GP 783; *bere
on* ~ accuse (s.o. of s.th.)

ML 620+; maintain, assert
WB 232; *bere wrong on* ~
make false assertions WB 226;
have in ~ have in (o's) control
WB 211+; *have on* ~ be occupied with WB 451+

honeste *adj* honourable, noble,
creditable, worthy of respect
WB 1183+; proper, seemly
GP 246+; beautiful, fine
Mch 2028

honestee *n* propriety, decorum,
decency Fri 1267+; chastity,
purity Phys 77+

honestetee *n* honour Cl 422;
decency Pars 429; beauty,
pleasingness Pars 431+

honestly *adv* with reverence SN
549+; suitably, properly
Kn 1444, Sh 244; richly, finely
Mch 2026

honge *v* (see also **hange**) hang
Kn 2410+

honge(d) *pl past of* **hange** *v*

hon(o)ure *v* honour, show
respect to GP 50, Kn 2407+;
celebrate Sum 1719

hony *n* honey Kn 2908+

hool *adj* whole, healthy
GP 533+

hool *adv* wholly Fkl 1450;
soundly Mch 1538

hoold *n* (see also **hold**) castle
ML 507; house Mch 1306; possession WB 599, Fri 1607;
have in ~ possess NP 2874

hoold *sg and pl imp of* **holde** *v*

hoolly *adv* wholly, entirely
GP 599+; *al* ~ absolutely all
Sum 2096

hoom *adv* (see also **hom**) home,
homewards Kn 1026+

hoor *adj* hoary, white-haired Rv
3878+

hoord *n* (see also **hord**) hoard,
store Mil 3262+

hoost *n* (1) host, army Kn 874+

hoost(e) *n* (2) host, landlord
GP 747+

hoot *adj* hot GP 394+; pungent
CY 887; ardent, lascivious
GP 626; fresh, recent GP 687;
difficult Mch 2126; *pl and
weak sg* **hote**

hoote *adv* (see also **hote**) hotly,
passionately GP 97+

hope *v* hope Mil 3725+; believe,
fear Rv 4029

hoper *n* hopper (of a mill) Rv
4036+

hoppe *v* dance Rv 3876+

hord *n* (see also **hoord**) hoard,
store Co 4406+

horrible *adj* horrible, frightful
Kn 1451+; foul, heinous Pard
379+; hideous, loathsome
ML 751+

hors *n* horse GP 94+; *as pl*
horses GP 74+

hose *n* legging, stocking
GP 456+; *pl* **hosen, hoses**

hostelrye *n* inn GP 23+

hostile(e)r *n* inn-keeper
GP 241+; servant at an inn
Pars 440

hote *pl and weak sg of* **hoot** *adj*

hote *adv* (see also **hoote**) hotly
ML 586

hote *v* be called WB 144;
promise Kn 2398, 2472,
ML 334, Cl 496+; *his name
was hoten* his name was Rv
3941; *1 sg pres* **he(e)te**; *3 sg
pres subj* **heete**; *sg past* **heet**; *sg*
and pl past **highte**; *p ppl* **hoten**
(= called); **hight** (= promised)

housbondrye *n* household affairs
Rv 4077, Mch 1380; thrifty
housekeeping Mch 1296,
NP 2828; household goods
WB 288

how that *conj* although Pars
631+

humblesse *n* humility Kn 1781+

humour *n* bodily fluid (one of
four) determining a person's
physical 'complexion' (see n.
to GP 333)

hunte *n* hunter, huntsman
Kn 1678+

hy *adj* (see also **heigh, hey**) high
Kn 897+; exalted Mk 2696;
great Mch 1222, Mel 1876+;
noble Mk 2645; holy Mch
1660; *hye God* great God
WB 1173+; *hye weye* high
road Kn 897; *hye bord* high
table Sq 98; *hyer hond* upper
hand GP 399

hye *adv* (see also **heigh(e)**) high
GP 271+; into high position
Rv 3981

ich *1 pers sg pron* (see also **ik**) I
Mil 3277+

idel *adj* vain, empty Pars 740;
thoughtless, frivolous Pard
638, Pars 165+; lazy, idle
Kn 2505+; *(as quasi-n) in ~* in
vain Fkl 867, Pard 642+

idelnesse *n* idleness Kn 1940+

idolastre *n* idolater Mch 2298+

ifeere *adv* together ML 394+

ifinde *v* find Sq 470, Fkl 1153

ihe(e)re *v* hear Mil 3176,
Mch 2154

ik *1 pers sg pron* (see also **ich**) I
Rv 3864+

iknowe *v* know Fri 1370,
Fkl 887

il *adj* (see also **ille**) ill, unfortunate Rv 4174; unlucky
Rv 4184

iliche, ilike *adv* alike, equally
Kn 2526+; unvaryingly Cl
602+

ilik(e) *adj* like GP 592, Kn 1539;
alike Kn 2734

ilke *adj* same, very GP 64+

ille *adj* (see also **il**) bad, incompetent Rv 4045

illusioun *n* illusion, deception
Fkl 1134+; *do ~* deceive
CY 673

imaginacioun *n* fantasy, hallucination Mil 3612; assumption
Kn 1094; ingenuity Sum 2218;
scheming, craftiness NP 3217
(see n.)

imagine *v* imagine Pars 693;
deduce ML 889; plot Pars 448;
wonder Cl 598

impresse *v* become fixed Mch
1578+

impressioun *n* effect on the mind
or emotions Sq 371; *take ~*
receive a mental image Mil
3613+

in *n* lodgings Kn 2436+; house,
home Mil 3547+

in *prep* in GP 3+ (spelled **inne** at
the end of a relative clause);
into Rv 4094; on, upon Mch
2137, Mk 2582+; for, because
of Mel 977; against Pars 695

indulgence *n* mercy Mel 1774;
of ~ as a concession WB 84

in-feere *adv* together ML 328+

infortune *n* misfortune Mk
2401; malign influence (of a
planet) Kn 2021

inne *prep* (see **in** *prep*)

inogh, inowe *adj* sufficient,
adequate GP 373, Kn 1613+;
plentiful, abundant, plenty of,
lots of Kn 2836, WB 332+

ino(u)gh, inowe *n* enough, sufficient Mil 3149, ML 872+

ino(u)gh, inow(e) *adv* enough,
sufficiently Kn 888+; very,
extremely Cl 209, Mel 1836;
copiously, a great deal Mch
1781; plentifully Mk 2045;
wel ~ very well Mch 2344+;
right ~ amply Kn 1233+; *not
but ~* quite enough CY 601;
deere ~ a jane not worth a halfpenny Cl 999; *deere ~ a leek*
not worth a leek CY 795

inpacience *n* impatience Pars
276+; irritability Mel 1544;
stubbornness Pars 391

inpacient *adj* impatient, resent-
ful Mel 1540+; stubborn
Pars 401

inportable *adj* unendurable Cl
1144+

inpossible *n* impossibility
WB 688+

inpossible *adj* impossible
Fkl 1549+

inspire *v* (see also **enspire**) blow
on, breathe life into GP 6

into *prep* into GP 23+; on to Mil
3471; to GP 692, Pard 722+;
toward ML 840, Fkl 863; to,
until Mel 1233, SN 552

inward *adv* in Rv 4079;
inwardly Mel 1645+

inwith *prep* within, in ML 797+

ipocras *n* 'a kind of cordial, made of red wine, spices, sugar, etc, strained through cloth bags' (*MED*) Mch 1807, Pard 306

iren *n* iron GP 500+; specifically, iron of an axe WB 906

irous *adj* angry, irascible Sum 2014+

is *sg pres of* be *v* is GP 4+; (in Northern speech) am Rv 4031+; art Rv 4089

ivel *adj* bad, wicked Mil 3173+; *as n* evil Pri 632+

ivel(e) *adv* ill, badly Mil 3715, Cl 460+; wickedly, badly Rv 4320+; little Kn 1127; ~ *apaid* dissatisfied, discontent Fri 1282+

iwys *adv* indeed, surely, certainly Mil 3277+

jalous *adj* jealous Kn 1840+; malicious Kn 1329

jalousye *n* jealousy Kn 1299+; zeal, fervour Pars 539

jane *n* a small Genoese coin (worth about a halfpenny) Th 735; *deere inow a* ~ not worth a halfpenny Cl 999

jangle *v* chatter ML 774; chatter, gossip Sq 220+

jangler(e) *n* gossip, tale-teller Mcp 343, 348; loudmouth, story-teller GP 560

jangleresse *n* gossip Mel 1085; sharp-tongued woman, nagger, scold WB 638+

jangles *n pl* idle chatter Fri 1407+

jape *n* joke Mil 3390+; trick GP 705, WB 242+; (piece of) foolishness Sum 1961; delusion NP 3091

jape *v* joke Fri 1513+; trick, deceive Kn 1729; mock Mch 1389

japere *n* buffoon Pars 651+; trifler Pars 89

japerye *n* jest Mch 1656; buffoonery Pars 651

jet *n* (see also **get**) fashion GP 682

jewel *n* (see also **juel**) jewel Cl 869; precious object, treasure Sq 341

Jewerye *n* (see also **Juerye**) Jewish quarter Pri 489+

jogelour *n* conjurer Fri 1467+

joine *v* join Mk 2493+

jolif, joly *adj* spirited, gallant Mil 3339+; lively Rv 4155, WB 456+; gay, cheerful Mil 3671+; fine, handsome, beautiful Mil 3316, Rv 3931, WB 860+; frisky, lively Mil 3263, Pard 453; lusty, randy Mil 3355+; jovial, pleasure-loving Sum 1727; noble, fair CY 583; *my* ~ *body* my own self, my fine person ML 1185, Sh 423

jolitee *n* pleasure WB 470+; fun, gaiety CY 600; festivity Sq 278, 344; sport Kn 1807; love, sexual desire Th 843; attractiveness, handsomeness GP 680, Mcp 197

joly *adj* see **jolif**

jolynesse *n* gaiety Sq 289; gallantry, spirit WB 926

jubbe *n* jar, container for liquid Mil 3628+

juel *n* (see also **jewel**) precious object Kn 2945

Juerye *n* (see also **Jewerye**) Jewish quarter Pri 551

juge *n* judge GP 814+; umpire Kn 1712+

jug(g)e *v* judge Phys 228+

jug(g)ement *n* judgement GP 778, ML 1038+; power, jurisdiction Mel 1753; order ML 688

juise *n* (see also **juwise**) punishment ML 795

jupartye *n* risk, danger Fkl 1495+

juste *v* joust, tilt in a tournament GP 96+

justice, justise *n* justice Mel 1409+; judge GP 314, ML 665+; jurisdiction Pard 587

juwise *n* (see also **juise**) sentence, punishment Kn 1739

kaitif *n* (see also **caitif**) wretch Pars 214; captive Pars 471; *as adj* miserable, wretched Pars 344

kan *1/3 sg and pl pres of* **konne** *v*

kanst *2 sg pres of* **konne** *v*

kanstow *contr of* **kanst thow**

keene *adj* (see also **kene**) sharp Kn 2876; brave Mk 2249

keep *n* (see also **kepe**): *take ~* take note GP 503+; be on o's guard Kn 2688; *take ~ of* concern o.s., bother about GP 398+; pay attention to Pard 352; take (s.th.) in Cl 1058; *take ~ upon* observe, take (s.th.) in Mch 2398

kembe *v* comb Kn 2143+

kemelin *n* (see also **kimelin**) trough (used in cooking or brewing) Mil 3548

kene *adj* (see also **keene**) sharp GP 104+; strong Mch 1759

kepe *n* (see also **keep**): *take ~ (of/to)* take note (of), pay attention (to), be careful Mch 1309+; concern o.s., bother about WB 214+

kepe *v* keep GP 852+; observe, honour WB 710+; take care GP 130; take care of, look after GP 593, ML 717+; protect, preserve Kn 2302+; save WB 1056; watch over GP 415; guard, keep confined WB 360, Mcp 144+; care, wish Kn 2238+; govern, rule ML 577+; *refl* govern o.s., behave Phys 106+; *~ of* care about Sh 403; *~ (o's) tonge* guard o's tongue Mcp 315+; *~ fro* guard against ML 454+; abstain from Mch 1640; *refl* guard o.s. against NP 3116+

kepere *n* guardian Kn 2328+; keeper, monk in charge of a monastic cell GP 172

keping(e) *vbl n* keeping, preserving Mel 1639+; guarding Mil 3851+; protection Mel 1302+

kerve *v* cut Kn 2013, 2696, Sq 158+; carve GP 100+; *sg past* **carf**; *p ppl* **corven, ycorve(n), ykorven**

kerver(e) *n* carver Kn 1899+

kesse *v* (see also **kisse**) kiss Cl 1057, Sq 350; *sg past* **keste**

kid *p ppl of* **kithe** *v*

kike *v* gaze Mil 3445+

kimelin *n* (see also **kemelin**)
trough (used in cooking or
brewing) Mil 3621

kinde *n* nature, natural character Kn 2451, WB 1149+; creation SN 41; family, birth
WB 1101, SN 121+; sperm,
sexual fluid Pars 965; *by/of ~*
by nature Fkl 768, NP 2952+;
of propre ~ by their very
nature Sq 610; *by ~* customarily, normally CY 659; *of ~*
by virtue of (o's) profession
Sum 1706; *by wey of ~* in the
course of nature Pri 650+;
sette hem in hir ~ classify them
according to their nature
CY 789

kinde *adj* loving, affectionate,
kind WB 823+; pleasant
GP 647

kindely *adv* by nature WB 402;
kindly Sh 353

kinrede *n* kindred Kn 1286+

kirtel *n* jacket, tunic
Mil 3321+

kisse *v* (see also **kesse**) kiss
Kn 1759, Mil 3284+; *sg and pl
past* **kiste**; *p ppl* **kist**

kit *p ppl of* **kutte** *v*

kithe *v* show, display Fri 609+;
perform ML 636+; *p ppl*
kithed, kid

kitte *sg past of* **kutte** *v*

knave *n* boy ML 715+; servant
Mil 3431+; commoner, some-
one low-born WB 1190, Pars
188; villain, rogue WB 253,
Pars 433; fighter on foot
Kn 2728

kneding-trogh, -tub *n* kneading-
trough Mil 3548+

knee *n* (see also **knowe**) knee
GP 391+; *bifore the
erchedeknes ~* before the archdeacon Fri 1588

knitte *v* knit, tie, join, unite
Kn 1128, Rv 4083+; agree
Fkl 1230; *refl* attach o.s.
Mel 1614; be in conjunction
ML 307; *p ppl* **knit**

knotte *n* knot GP 197+; nub,
main point Sq 401+

knowe *n* (see also **knee**) knee
Fkl 1025+

knowe *v* know GP 382+; be intimate with Pri 585; acknowledge Mk 2218+; *~ of* know
about Kn 1815+; *~ for* know
to be WB 320+; *sg past*
knew(e); *pl past* **knew,
knewe(n)**; *p ppl* **knowe(n),
yknowe(n)**

knoweleche, knoweliche *n* knowledge Pars 75+; acquaintance
Sh 30

knoweleche, knoweliche *v*
acknowledge Mel 1745+

knowe(n) *p ppl of* **knowe** *v*

knowing(e) *vbl n* knowledge Sq
301+

konne *v* can, be able/capable,
know how (to do s.th.) GP 94,
652, WB 386, NP 2911+;
know (about), understand, be
versed in GP 110, 210, 476,
Mil 3200+; know Mil 3126,
WB 56+; learn Pri 540+; *~ on*
know about ML 47+; *~ red*
have a plan or suggestion Mch
1668; *~ no bettre reed* know
no better remedy Mk 2549; *~
(o's) good* know what is advantageous, have sense WB 231,

ML 1169; ~ *thank* owe thanks
Kn 3064; *1/3 sg and pl pres*
kan; *2 sg pres* kanst; *pl pres*
konne(n); *sg pres subj* konne;
sg past koude, kouthe; *pl past*
koude(n); *p ppl* koud, kouth
konning(e) *n* ability, skill
ML 1099, Sq 35+; intelligence,
wisdom Mel 1739,
Pars 399
koud *p ppl of* konne *v*
koude *sg past of* konne *v*
koude(n) *pl past of* konne *v*
kouth *p ppl of* konne *and adj*
known Pars 766; made known
Cl 942; renowned, famous
GP 14
kouthe *sg past of* konne *v*
kutte *v* cut Pard 954+; *past*
kitte; *p ppl* kutted, kit
kyn *pl of* cow *n*

laas *n* cord GP 392+; net
Kn 1817+
labour *n* labour Kn 2913+; *do*
(o's) ~ make an effort, do o's
best Kn 2193, ML 381+
lad *p ppl of* lede *v*
ladde *sg and pl past of* lede *v*
lady *n* lady GP 839+; lady's
GP 88+
laft *p ppl of* leve *v* (1)
lafte *sg and pl past of* leve *v* (1)
lak(ke) *n* lack, deficiency Mch
2271+; fault, failure Sum
2139; *finde* ~ find fault
NP 2844; ~ *of sacramentz* failure to receive the sacraments
Fri 1308; *do that* ~ commit
that fault Mch 2199
lakke *v* be lacking Kn 2280+;
miss CY 1419; fail in CY 672;

impers: *me/him lakketh* I/he
lack(s) GP 756, Sum 2109+
lampe *n* '? a lamp-shaped vessel
similar in function to a bell-
jar' (*MED*) (*alch*) CY 764;
'? vessel used for heating substances' (*MED*) (*alch*)
CY 802
lang *adj* (see also **long**) long
(Northern form) Rv 4175
langour *n* illness, sickness
Fkl 1101; suffering Mk 2407;
languor Pars 723
langwiss(h)e *v* suffer Mch 1867+
lappe *n* lap, skirt GP 686+;
sleeve SN 12; fold of a garment Cl 585
large *n*: *at* (o's) *large* at large, at
liberty Kn 1283+; unrestricted,
unencumbered Kn 2288
large *adj* generous Mel 1760+;
free Fkl 755; lavish, extravagant Sh 431+; large, broad,
wide GP 472, Kn 886+; great
Mch 1223+; ample Mil 3497;
big GP 753+
large *adv* fully Sq 360; broadly
GP 734
largely *adv* fully Pars 532;
broadly Pars 804; ~ *of gold a*
fother a good heap of gold
Kn 1908; *a journee* ~ a good
day's journey Kn 2738
largesse *n* generosity, liberality
Sh 22+
lasse *n* less Mil 3519+
lasse *comp adj* (see also **lesse**)
lesser Kn 1756+; shorter Pard
865; less WB 335+
lasse *comp adv* less Pars 358+;
the ~ the less Mel 1454+
laste *v* last Kn 2557+; extend

Cl 266; *3 sg contr pres* **last**; *sg and pl past* **laste, lasted**

lasting(e) *pres ppl* lasting, constant Kn 3072+

lat *sg and pl imp of* **lete** *v*

late *adv* late Rv 4196+; lately, recently GP 77+

late *v* (see also **lete**) let (blood) Mil 3326+

late(n) *p ppl of* **lete** *v*

latoun *n* brass (an alloy of copper, tin and other metals) GP 699+

latter *comp adj* latter NP 3205; later, more recent WB 765+

laude *n* praise, honour Fri 1353+

laughe *v* laugh GP 474+; *sg past* lo(u)gh; *pl past* lough(e); *p ppl* laughen

launcegay *n* light lance Th 752+

launde *n* glade, clearing Kn 1691+

laurer *n* laurel Kn 1027+

laus *adj* (see also **loos**) loose Rv 4064

laxatif *n* laxative, purgative Kn 2756+

lay *n* (1) lay, song Fkl 710+

lay *n* (2) law ML 376+

laye *v* (see also **legge, leye**) lay Rv 4021+

lazar *n* leper GP 242+

lecchour *n* (see also **lechour**) lecher Fri 1371+

leche *n* physician, healer Rv 3904+

lechour *n* (see also **lecchour**) lecher WB 242+

lede *v* lead Kn 1446+; bring ML 357+; carry GP 530+; rule ML 434+; *3 sg contr pres* let;

sg and pl past **ladde**; *pl past* **ledde**; *p ppl* **(y)lad**

ledene *n* language, tongue Sq 435+

leed *n* lead SN 406+; cauldron GP 202

leef *adj* (see also **lief**) dear, precious CY 1467; beloved Mk 2052; desirable Pard 760; *hadde as ~ as* would as soon (do s.th.) as Fri 1574; *as n* dear one, love NP 2879; *pl and weak sg* **le(e)ve**

leefful *adj* (see also **leveful**) lawful Pars 41+

leene *adj* (see also **lene**) lean, thin GP 287

leep *sg past of* **lepe** *v*

leere *v* (see also **lere**) learn (about) ML 181+

lees *n* leash SN 19; *renne in o ~* run on one leash Pars 387

leest *adv* least Mk 2142, 2526

leest(e) *superl adj* (see also **leste**) least Kn 1701+; least important Sh 46; *at the ~ way/weye* at least, at any rate Kn 1121, WB 73+; *at the/atte ~* at least, at any rate Mil 3683, WB 73+; *the meeste and the ~* the most and the least important Kn 2198+

leet *sg imp and 3 sg past of* **lete** *v*

leeve *n* (see also **leve**) leave, permission Sum 1823

leeve *pl and weak sg of* **leef, lief** *adj* dear Kn 1136+; *as n* dear one Mil 3393

leeve *v* (see also **leve** *v* (3)) believe Mel 1754

legende *n* life-story (of saint)

NP 3121, SN 25+; collection
of lives ML 61; story Mil
3141, WB 686+

legge *v* (see also **laye, leye**) lay
Mil 3269, Rv 3937

leid *p ppl of* **leye** *v*

leide *sg past of* **leye** *v*

leide(n) *pl past of* **leye** *v*

lein *p ppl of* **lie** *v* (1)

leiser *n* chance, opportunity Mil
3293+; power Fkl 977; time
Kn 1188+; leisure WB 683+;
by ~ without haste Mel 1031+

leit *n* flame Pars 954; *thonder-~*
lightning Pars 839

lemaille *n* (see also **limaille**)
metal filings CY 1197

lemman *n* lover, mistress, sweetheart Mil 3278+

lendes *n pl* hips Mil 3237; buttocks Mil 3304

lene *adj* (see also **leene**) lean,
thin GP 591+

lene *v* lend GP 611+; give
Kn 3082

lenger *comp adj* longer GP 821+

lenger *comp adv* longer
Kn 1576+; *ever* ~ *the moore*
the longer, the more Cl 687+;
ever ~ *the wers* the longer, the
worse Rv 3872

lengthe *n* length Kn 1970+;
height GP 83, ML 934+

leo(u)n *n* lion Kn 1598+; *the
sign of the* ~ the sign of Leo
in the zodiac Kn 2462,
Fkl 1058

lepe *v* leap, jump, spring
Kn 2687+; bound Co 4378+;
sg past **leep**

lere *v* (see also **leere**) learn
ML 630+

lerne *v* learn GP 308+; study Mk
2309; teach CY 748+

lerned *adj* learned, educated
GP 480+

lerninge *n* learning GP 300+;
instruction SN 184; knowledge
SN 353

lese *v* lose Kn 1215+; *p ppl* **lorn**

lesing *n* lie Kn 1927+; *make a* ~
tell a lie, practise deceit
Mel 1067+

lesing(e) *vbl n* losing, loss
Kn 1707+; *for* ~ for fear of losing Mk 2560

lesse *comp adj* (see also **lasse**)
lesser ML 959+; less
Mel 1498

lest *n* (see also **list** and cf. **lust**)
pleasure, enjoyment GP 132;
desire Kn 2984; whim, fancy
Cl 619

lest *3 sg contr pres of* **leste** *v*

leste *superl adj* (see also **leeste**)
least Mel 1324; *at the/atte* ~ at
least Fkl 697; at any rate
Fkl 1542

leste *v impers* (see also **liste,
luste**) please GP 750+ (e.g.
yow lest it pleases you = you
desire/choose); *3 sg contr pres*
lest; *sg contr past* **leste**; *3 sg
pres subj* **leste**

let (1) *3 sg contr pres of* **lede** *v*

let (2) *p ppl of* **lette** *v*

lete *v* (see also **late** *v*) let, allow
GP 128+; leave GP 508,
Kn 873+; leave off Mil 3311+;
abandon ML 325+; let out
Sum 2149+; lose SN 406+;
with inf have (s.th.) done,
cause to be done: e.g. *leet crye*
had proclaimed Kn 2731; *leet*

bringe had brought Kn 2889+;
~ *do* (*with inf*) to have s.th.
done, cause to be done Sq 45+;
(*with inf*) suppose one were to
... WB 1141+; *lat be* leave off,
give up Mil 3285+; lay aside
GP 840+; *lat* (*it*) *go*(*on*) let it
pass CY 1475; no matter
WB 476; *sg imp* lat, leet; *pl
imp* lat; *sg past* leet; *pl past*
lete; *p ppl* late(n), lete

lette *v* hinder, prevent (from)
Kn 1892, WB 839+; delay
Kn 889+; postpone NP 3084+;
be hindered Mel 1401; ~ *of*
hinder in (doing s.th.)
Mel 926, Sh 86; ~ *of* deprive
of Mch 1677; refrain from
Kn 1317; *sg past* lette(d); *p ppl*
let

lett(e)rure *n* learning Mk 2296;
literacy Mk 2496+

lettre *n* letter ML 728+; document Fri 1364, Sum 2128; writing Mk 2208, SN 202,
Pars 1021

letuarye *n* medicine, potion
GP 426+

leve *n* (see also **leeve**) leave, permission Kn 1064+; leave (to
go) Kn 1217+

leve *pl and weak sg of* leef, lief
adj

leve *v* (1) leave Kn 1614+; leave
off, stop Co 4414, Cl 250+;
omit, neglect GP 492+; abandon, renounce SN 287+; *pl
imp* leveth; *sg and pl past*
lafte, lefte; *p ppl* laft, left,
ylaft

leve *v* (2) grant, allow Fri 1644+

leve *v* (3) (see also **leeve**) believe

Kn 3088+; ~ *on* trust in Cl
1001; *pl imp* leveth

leveful *adj* (see also **leefful**) lawful, legitimate Rv 3912+

levere *comp adj* dearer Sq 572;
me/him (etc.) *was/were* ~ I/he
(etc.) would rather, would prefer GP 293+; *have* ~ prefer
WB 168+; *I hadde* ~ I'd rather
(have it) Mk 1893+; *him/hir*
(etc.) *had* ~ he/she (etc.) would
rather (have) Mil 3541+

levesel *n* arbour of leaves Rv
4061; bunch of leaves used as
a tavern sign Pars 411

lewed *adj* uneducated, ignorant
GP 574, ML 315+; stupid Mch
2275, Fkl 1494+; coarse, crude
Mil 3145, Mch 2149+; lay
Pard 392; ~ *man* layman
GP 502+

lewedly *adv* incompetently,
stupidly ML 47+

lewednesse *n* ignorance Sq 223;
incompetence, stupidity
Mel 921; sinfulness Sum 1928

leye *v* (see also **laye, legge**) lay,
place GP 81+; lay, wager Rv
4009+; lay out CY 783; *refl*
lay o.s., lie Kn 1384+; ~ *on* set
to work Kn 2558+; ~ *forth* produce ML 213; ~ *adoun* destroy
Mk 2099+; *sg past* leide; *pl
past* leide(n); *p ppl* (y)leid

licence *n* permission, leave
WB 855+

liche *adj* (see also **lik**) like Sq 62

licoris *n* (see also **likoris**) liquorice Mil 3207+

licour *n* liquid, sap GP 3; liquor
Pard 452

lie *v* (1) (see also **ligge**) lie

GP 538+; lodge, stay, spend the night GP 20+; ~ *to wedde* be a pledge, act as bail Kn 1218; *3 sg and pl pres* lith; *sg past* lay; *pl past* layen; *p ppl* lein

lie *v* (2) lie, tell a lie GP 763+; *2 sg pres* lixt

lief *adj* (see also leef) dear, beloved Cl 479+; prized, valued Sq 341; ~ *were me* I should like Sh 159; *be him/hir* ~ *or looth* whether he/she likes it or not Kn 1837+; ~ *to gabbe* fond of gossiping Mil 3510

liege *n* (see also lige) vassal, subject ML 240

lif *n* (see also live (*dat*)) life GP 71+; *olde* ~ old age Phys 72; *his* ~ in his life Mch 1731; *evere his* ~ all his life Mk 2179; *(for/to) terme of (al) his* ~ for the rest of his life Kn 1029, WB 644+; *the terme of al thy* ~ for the rest of your life WB 820; *terme of alle hir lives* all their lives long Fri 1331

lige *n* (see also liege) vassal, subject Cl 67+

lige *adj* liege (entitled to allegiance) WB 1037+; liege (owing allegiance) Cl 310

ligge *v* (see also lie *v* (1)) lie Kn 1011+

light *adj* light Kn 2120+; cheerful, merry, light-hearted Kn 1783, Mil 3671+; easy Mel 1040, CY 838

lighte *v* (1) light WB 334+; light up, illuminate Kn 2426+; give light to Pars 1036; shine Pars 1037; *sg past* lighte

lighte *v* (2) cheer, gladden Pri 471; be cheered, be lightened Sq 396+; dismount ML 786+; descend Fkl 1248; *sg past* lighte

lightly *adv* quickly Kn 1461+; easily Rv 4099, WB 517+; cheerfully, joyfully Kn 1870; lightly Sq 390; carelessly, frivolously Pars 1024

lightnesse *n* agility Mil 3383; frivolousness Pars 379

ligne *n* (see also line) line (of descent) Kn 1551

lik *adj* (see also liche) like GP 259+; comparable ML 1077; alike Pars 631; likely (to be) Mil 3226

like *v* please, be pleasing to GP 777, Kn 1847+; often *impers*, with *dat personal pron*: *if yow liketh* if it pleases you; dative case sometimes implicit with nouns: *God liketh* it pleases God; with two datives: *us liketh yow* you please us Cl 106

likerous *adj* amorous WB 752; flirtatious Mil 3244; lecherous WB 466, Mcp 189; gluttonous, luxurious WB 466, Cl 214+; delectable Mil 3345; eager, keen Fkl 1119

likerousnesse *n* lecherousness, lasciviousness WB 611, Pars 430+; gluttony Pars 377; greed Pars 741; unruliness, unlicensed behaviour Phys 84

liking(e) *n* liking ML 767;

pleasure WB 736+; desire, will
Cl 320+; *at youre* ~ to your liking Pard 458

liklihede *n*: *by* ~ probably, in all
probability Cl 448+

likne *v* liken, compare GP 180+

liknesse *n* likeness Pars 212;
image Pars 544+; story, parable Kn 2842

likoris *n* (see also **licoris**) liquorice Mil 3690

lim *n* (1) limb Kn 2135+;
member Pars 136

lim *n* (2) lime CY 806; mortar
Fkl 1149+

limaille *n* (see also **lemaille**)
metal filings CY 853+

limitour *n* friar whose begging
and spiritual activities took
place within the fixed territorial limits assigned to his convent GP 209 (see n.) +

linage *n* lineage, family, kindred
Kn 1110+; offspring Pars 920

linde *n* linden, lime Kn 2922; *as
light as leef on* ~ as light-
hearted as a leaf on the tree
(*provbl*) Cl 1211

line *n* (see also **ligne**) line (of
descent) WB 1135+; *the south
~ meridian* (line from the
centre of the earth to the zenith) Pars 2 (see n.)

list *n* (see also **lest** and cf.
lust) pleasure, enjoyment
WB 633

liste *v impers* (see also **leste**,
luste) please GP 583+ (e.g.
yow list = it pleases you, you
desire/choose); (*used personally*) want, be pleased to
Fkl 689+; *3 sg contr pres* list;

sg contr past liste; *3 sg pres
subj* liste

listes *n pl* lists, enclosed area
used for jousting or armed
combat GP 63+

listeth *pl imp* listen Th 712, 833

listow *contr of* **liest thow**

litarge *n* lead monoxide, litharge
GP 629+

lite *n* little ML 109+; *a* ~ a little,
somewhat Rv 3863+; a short
time, a little while Kn 1334+;
but a ~ only a little ML 352+

lite *adj* little, small Kn 1193+;
much and ~ great and small
GP 494

lite *adv* little Kn 1520+; *thow
knowest it* ~ you don't know it
Kn 1723; ~ *and* ~ little by little
Sum 2235

lith *3 sg and pl pres of* **lie** *v* (1)

live *dat of* **lif** *n*: *on* ~ alive
Kn 3039+; *hire* ~ in their
lives WB 392; *so wel was him
on* ~ so happy was his life
WB 43

lives *adv as adj* living, alive
Kn 2395+

living(e) *n* life SN 322; way of
life WB 1122+; food Cl 227

lixt *2 sg pres of* **lie** *v* (2)

logged *p ppl* lodged
NP 2996+

logh *adj* (see also **loue, lough,
lowe**) low ML 993+

logh *sg past of* **laughe** *v*

loke *v* (1) lock WB 317; *p ppl*
loken

loke *v* (2) (see also **looke**) look
Kn 1124+; see Kn 3073; ~ *on*
look at Mil 3344

loking *n* (see also **looking**)

favourable looks Mel 1142;
aspect (*astr*) Kn 2469

lokkes *n pl* locks (of hair)
GP 81+

Loller *n* Lollard ML 1173 (see
n.) +

lond *n* land GP 579+; country
GP 400+; *fineste of a* ~ finest
in the country GP 194; *upon* ~
in the country GP 702; *in
londe* to the country, away
NP 2879; as a line-filler
(see Headnote to Th)
Th 887

lone *n* loan Sh 295; gift
Sum 1861

long *adj* (see also **lang**) long
GP 93+; high Kn 1984; tall
Kn 1424, Mil 3264

longe *v* (1) long, desire GP 12+;
impers: *longeth me* I long
Mch 2332

longe *v* (2) belong Kn 2278+; ~
to befit Mch 2024+; *longing(e)
for* belonging to Mil 3209+

looke *v* (see also **loke**) look
GP 289, ML 532+; look at
Pard 578; take care (to do
s.th.) Mil 3549+; see
WB 1113+; gaze, stare
ML 1095, Sum 2170; ~ *in/on/
upon* look at, gaze on
Kn 1499, Mil 3515,
Cl 413+

looking *n* (see also **loking**) gaze,
look Kn 2171+; glance Pars
853; expression Cl 514; looks
Sq 285, Pars 936

loore *n* (see also **lore**) teaching
GP 527, ML 761+; advice,
counsel Mil 3527, ML 342+;
knowledge ML 4, Cl 788+; wis-

dom Cl 87; skill NP 3350;
practice Phys 70

loos *n* reputation, fame
Mel 1644+

loos *adj* (see also **laus**) loose
Rv 4138+

looth *adj* hateful, disliked Mil
3393; unpleasant, disagreeable
GP 486+; *me/him were* ~ I/he
should/would not wish to, I/he
should/would be reluctant to
GP 486, ML 91+; *be him/hir
lief or* ~ whether he/she likes it
or not Kn 1837+

lordinges *n pl* sirs (conventional
address to the audience in narrative verse) GP 761+

lordshipe *n* rule, power
Kn 1625, Fkl 743+; rank, authority Cl 797+; position of
power or high social status
Mel 2665+; patronage, protection Kn 1827; ruler
Pars 568

lore *n* (see also **loore**) knowledge, wisdom ML 1168

lorn *p ppl of* **lese** *v* lost Rv
4075+; ruined, destroyed Mil
3536+; killed, dead Mk 2040

los *n* loss Kn 2543+

loue *adj* (see also **logh, lough,
lowe**): ~ *coler* low-cut collar
Mil 3265

lough *adj* (see also **logh, loue,
lowe**) low, socially inferior
Pars 771; *in heigh and* ~ in
everything GP 817

lough *sg past of* **laughe** *v*

lough(e) *pl past of* **laughe** *v*

loute *v* bow Mel 1187+

lowe *adj* (see also **logh, loue,
lough**) low GP 107+; low, soft

Kn 2433; humble, socially
inferior WB 1101+; meek
Mel 1823

lowe *adv* low Kn 1111+; softly
Sq 216; humbly Kn 1405;
meekly, obediently Mch 2013

lucre *n* profit Pri 491+

lulle *v* rock, soothe (baby)
ML 839; cuddle, caress
Cl 553, Mch 1823

lure *n* device with which a hawk
is lured back to its owner's
hand Fri 1340 (see n. to
WB 415) +

lust *n* (cf. **lest, list**) pleasure,
enjoyment GP 192, Kn 3066+;
desire, wish Kn 2478+; pleasure, will ML 762, Cl 352+;
sexual desire WB 416+; sexual
pleasure WB 927+; source of
joy Kn 1250; appetite for pleasure WB 611; appetite Mcp
181; *pl* physical attractions
Mch 1679

luste *v impers* (see also **leste,
liste**) please Kn 1950+ (e.g.
yow lust = it pleases you, you
desire/choose); *3 sg contr pres*
lust

lustiheed *n* gaiety Sq 288; joy,
delight Mcp 274

lustily *adv* gaily Kn 1529+; entertainingly Pars 21

lusty *adj* lively, spirited GP 80,
WB 605+; gallant Kn 2111+;
cheerful, gay Kn 1513+; pleasant, delightful Kn 2176, 2484,
Mch 1395+; pleasure-loving
WB 553, Sq 272+; pleasing,
fine Kn 2116+; eager, keen Rv
4004, CY 1345

luxurye *n* lust, lechery

ML 925+; self-indulgence
Pars 446

maad *p ppl of* **make** *v*

maat *adj* helpless Kn 955,
ML 935

mace *n* mace, club Kn 2124+

madde *v* be mad, be deranged
Mil 3156, 3559

magestee *n* majesty Rv 4322+

magik *n* magic GP 416+

magnanimitee *n* lofty-
mindedness SN 110; fortitude
Pars 731

magnificence *n* stout-
heartedness, fortitude SN 50,
Pars 736; magnificence, glory
ML 1000+

maide *n* maiden, girl GP 69+; virgin Kn 1171, WB 79+; (serv-
ing) maid Mil 3417+; ~ *child*
girl child Cl 446+

maiden *n* maiden, girl Mil
3202+; virgin Kn 2305+

maidenhed(e), maidenhode *n*
maidenhood, virginity
Kn 2329+

maintene *v* maintain Cl 1171;
uphold Kn 1441; support, sustain Mel 1650, Pars 774; persist in Kn 1778

maister *n* master GP 837+;
learned man, scholar, someone
educated at university (i.e. a
Master of Arts) GP 261, Fri
1300+; teacher Mk 2495+; ~
strete main street Kn 2902; ~
tour principal tower Sq 226

maistresse *n* mistress Cl 823;
governess Sq 374+

maistrye *n* dominance, mastery,
control WB 1040+; strength,

power Mk 2392; skill, skilfulness Mil 3383, WB 818;
tour de force, demonstra-
tion of skill CY 1060; *for
the* ~ in the highest degree
GP 165

make *n* mate, spouse, wife or
husband ML 700+; opposite
number Kn 2556

make *v* make GP 9+; build
Kn 1901, Sum 2099+; prepare
Fkl 1212, Pars 829; compose,
write (*of*, about) GP 95,
ML 57, 96, Mch 1996+; draw
up (document) GP 325, Mil
3327, WB 424+; utter Mch
2318; hold (feast, revel etc)
Kn 2717, ML 353+; tell (lie)
Mel 1067+; put Mk 2483; put
into effect Sh 329+; cause,
bring (s.th.) about Kn 3035,
WB 872, Sum 1833+; ~ *up*
build Kn 1884; ~ *to* cause
(s.th. to be done) Mk 2067; ~
disport/game provide amusement GP 775, Co 4382+; ~
game frolic Mil 3259; ~ *mury*
entertain GP 802; ~ *solas* give
relief Th 782; ~ *remem-
braunce/memorye* record, call
to mind Mch 2284, Mk 1974;
~ *fors* care about Mcp 68; ~ *a
vanisshinge* vanish Kn 2360; ~
it straunge be fussy about Rv
3980; play hard to get, show
reluctance Fkl 1223; ~ *it tough*
make a meal of it, make a performance of it Sh 379; ~ *it wis*
deliberate, hesitate GP 785; ~
(s.o's) *berd* get the better of
s.o. Rv 4096, WB 361; *sg past*
made, maked; *pl past*

made(n); *p ppl* **(y)maad,
(y)maked**

maladye *n* malady, sickness, illness GP 419+; pain, suffering
Pars 1001

male *n* bag, pouch GP 694+

malencolye *n* 'one of the four
humours, black bile' (*MED*)
NP 2933, 2946; melancholy,
bile, spleen WB 252

malice *n* hatred, ill-will
ML 363+; wickedness Sq
562+; misfortune Co 4338

malisoun *n* curse CY 1245+

man *pron indef* (see also **men**)
one, anyone Sum 2002+

manace *n* menace Kn 2003+

manace *v* threaten Cl 122+

manciple *n* (see also **maunciple**)
'officer or servant who buys
provisions for a college, inn of
court, or other institution'
(*MED*) Mcp 25+

mandement *n* writ, summons
Fri 1284+

maner(e) *n* kind, sort (not
always followed by *of*) GP 71,
Kn 1875+; manner Kn 876, Sq
337+; way, manner Mil 3328,
ML 321+; bearing, manner
GP 140+; style Mch 1881, Mk
1991; circumstances ML 880;
cause, reason Phys 264; custom Phys 120; *in* ~ *of* in the
nature of Pars 963; *in alle* ~ in
any way Pars 589

manhede, manhode *n* valour
Kn 1285, Mk 2671; courtesy,
good manners GP 756,
Mcp 158

manly *adj* manly Kn 2130+;
courteous, well-bred Pars 601;

with ambiguous reference to
both the above senses: GP 167,
Mch 1911

manly *adv* bravely, boldly
Kn 987+

mannissh *adj* masculine
ML 782; human Mel 1264; *as
adv* like a man; ~ *wood*
virago-like Mch 1536

mansio(u)n *n* 'a temporary seat
of a solar planet or of the sun
in a sign of the zodiac' (*MED*)
Kn 1974+; a daily position of
the moon Fkl 1130 (see n.) +

manslaughtre *n* manslaughter
Pard 593+

mantel *n* mantle, robe GP 378;
foot-~ over-skirt coming down
to the feet (to protect the dress
in riding) GP 472

many(e) *adj* many GP 60+; ~
oon many a one GP 317+

marbul *n* marble Kn 1893+

marchal *n* marshal, official in a
noble household in charge of
ceremonies, service, etc.
GP 752+

marchandise *n* merchandise Sh
345, Pars 779; trading, com-
merce Pars 777+

marcha(u)nt *n* merchant
GP 270+

mark *n* (1) (see also **merk**) mark,
sign WB 619+; race, kind
WB 696

mark(e) *n* (2) mark, monetary
unit equivalent to ⅔ of £1 Pard
390+

markis *n* marquis Cl 64+

markisesse *n* marchioness Cl
283+

matere *n* (see also **matire**) mat-

ter, affair, business Kn 1417,
ML 205+; subject, theme
ML 322+; material Mil 3175;
subject, question Kn 1259,
WB 910+; (tree-)trunk (?with
secondary reference to
'material, content') Mel 1209;
(literary) enterprise GP 727,
Mk 1984, Pars 28; cause,
reason Mel 1536+; matter,
substance Pars 333; fuel
Pars 137; materials, ingredients CY 1232; *scole-~* questions for scholastic debate
Fri 1272

material *adj* material Mel 1398
(see n.); solid Pars 576; earthly
Pars 182

matire *n* (see also **matere**)
material, ingredients CY 770+

matrimoi(g)ne *n* matrimony
Kn 3095+

maugree *prep* in spite of
Kn 1607+; ~ (o's) *heed* in spite
of all (one) can do, irrespective
of (o's) wishes Kn 1169+; ~
hir/thine eyen in spite of them-
selves/yourself Kn 1796,
WB 315

maumetrie *n* (see also **mawmettrie**) Mohammedanism, paganism ML 236

maunciple *n* (see also **manciple**)
'officer or servant who buys
provisions for a college, inn of
court, or other institution'
(*MED*) GP 567+

mawe *n* stomach, belly
ML 486+; gullet ML 1190

mawmet *n* idol Pars 749+

mawmettrie *n* (see also
maumetrie) idolatry Pars 750

may _1/3 pres sg and pres pl of_
  mowe _v_
mayst _2 pres sg of_ mowe _v_
maystow _contr of_ mayst thow
maze _v_ confuse, bewilder
  ML 526+; be confused
  Mch 2387
mede _n_ (1) (see also meeth)
  mead Th 852
mede _n_ (2) (see also meede _n_ (1))
  meadow WB 861+
mede _n_ (3) (see also meede _n_ (2))
  payment Mil 3380; reward
  Pars 595+; bribery Mk 2389+;
  recompense Cl 885; _quite_
  (s.o's) ~ reward s.o. GP 770
medicine _n_ medicine Mch
  2380+; transmuting agent
  (_alch_) Sq 244
medle _v_ mix Pars 122; meddle
  Mel 1541+; _refl_ ~ _of_ interfere
  with Mel 1544
meede _n_ (1) (see also mede _n_ (2))
  meadow GP 89
meede _n_ (2) (see also mede _n_ (3))
  bribery Phys 133
meel _n_ (see also mel) meal
  ML 466+
meene _n_ (see also mene) agent
  Fri 1484; intermediary
  Pars 990
meest _superl adj_ (see also moost)
  greatest Kn 2198, Cl 131+
meete _adj_ (see also mete) fitting
  Kn 2291
meete _v_ (see also mete _v_ (2))
  meet Kn 1524+; _sg and pl past_
  mette; _p ppl_ met, ymet(te)
meeth _n_ (see also mede _n_ (1))
  mead Kn 2279+
mei(g)nee _n_ household Kn 1258,
  Sum 2045+; servants Sum

2156; retinue Co 4381, Sq
391+; army, troops Mk 2342,
Mcp 228, 231; followers
NP 3394; company Mch 2436,
Pars 894
meke _adj_ meek, humble GP 69+
mel _n_ (see also meel) meal
  Sum 1774
mele _n_ meal, ground corn Rv
  3939+
memorye _n_ memory Kn 1906+;
  _be in_ ~ be conscious Kn 2698;
  have in ~ remember, consider
  Mch 1669; _worthy to_ ~ memorable Mch 2244; _make_ ~
  record Mk 1974; _drawe (in)to_
  ~ recall, call to mind Kn 2074,
  Mil 3112+
men _pron indef_ (see also man)
  one, anyone (_with sg v_ (from
  man with reduced stress))
  GP 149, Kn 2777, Mil 3392+
mencioun _n: make_ ~ relate,
  report, commemorate Kn 893+
mendinant _n_ mendicant, friar
  Sum 1906, 1912
mene _n_ (see also meene) instrument, agent Mch 1671; go-
  between Mil 3375; _pl_ means,
  ways ML 480+; _the_ ~ the
  golden mean, moderation
  Pars 833
mene _adj_: ~_-time_, ~_-while(s)_
  meantime ML 546+
mene _v_ mean GP 793+; ~ _by_
  speak about Kn 1673
merite _n_ merit SN 33+; reward
  Phys 277, Pars 529; ~ _of_ credit
  for Pars 941
merk _n_ (see also mark _n_ (1))
  image, mould Fkl 880
mervaille, merveille _n_ marvel,

wonder Cl 248, Fkl 1344+;
miracle ML 502, 677; marvel-
lousness Cl 1186; ~ of astonishment, wonder at Mil 3423, Sq
87; no ~ no wonder Mel 1546

merveillous adj wonderful Pri
453; magical Fkl 1206;
strange, astonishing Cl 454,
CY 629

mery(e) adj (see also **mirye,
mury(e)**) pleasant NP 2966;
clinken so ~ a belle sound so
lively a note (lit ring so fine a
bell) ML 1186

meschaunce n (see also **mischaunce**) mischance, calamity,
bad luck Kn 2009, ML 610,
WB 407+; misfortune, trouble
ML 944, Mk 2014+; wrong-
doing Phys 80; evil Fkl 1292;
with ~ curse him Co 4412,
Sum 2215+, curse her
ML 896, curse it Mcp 193;
God yeve (s.o.) ~ a curse on
(s.o.) ML 602+

mescheef, meschief n misfortune,
affliction, trouble GP 493+;
calamity WB 248+; injury,
harm Kn 1326; at ~ at a disadvantage, defeated Kn 2551

message n message Sq 99, SN
188+; errand ML 1087; messenger ML 144, Cl 738+

messager n messenger ML 724+;
harbinger Kn 1491+

mesurable adj temperate,
restrained, moderate GP 435+

mesure n moderation Cl 622+;
restraint, modesty Phys 47;
measure Cl 256, Pars 776; measuring Pars 799; out of ~
immoderate, immoderately

Mel 1416+; by/with ~ in moderation Mel 1605, Mk 2299+

met p ppl of **meete** v and **mete** v
(1)

mete n food GP 136+; meal,
dinner GP 127, ML 1014+;
meat Sum 2244

mete adj (see also **meete**) fit
Kn 1631

mete v (1) impers dream Mil
3684+; personal dream
WB 577+; sg past **mette**; p ppl
met

mete v (2) (see also **meete**) meet
Co 4374, CY 706

mette sg past of **meete** v and
mete v (1)

mewe n (see also **muwe**) cage
(properly, one where hawks
are placed while moulting) Sq
643+

middle n middle NP 3048+;
waist Mch 1602

might n power Kn 1856, Fri
1492+; capacity Rv 3879, Fri
1661, Pard 468+; ability
GP 538+; al my/thy ~ all that I
am/you are capable of
Kn 1607+; do (o's) ~ do all
one can Kn 960+

mighte 1/3 sg and pl past of
mowe v

mighten pl past of **mowe** v

mightily adv vigorously
ML 921, Mk 2327+; violently
Mil 3475; completely
Mk 2592

mighty adj mighty, powerful
Kn 1673+; strong Kn 1423,
Mil 3497; great GP 108,
Kn 2611; vigorous, able-
bodied Mk 1951

min *poss adj and pron* (used before vowel or h-) my, mine GP 782+

minde *n* mind Kn 1402+; remembrance, memory ML 1127, Cl 849, Mch 2390+; *have ~ on* remember ML 908; *be in ~* be remembered Fkl 878, Pri 653; *have in ~* remember Sq 109, Fkl 1154+; *forgete (o's) ~* lose o's memory ML 527

minestral *n* minstrel Sq 78+

ministre *n* servant Kn 1663+; officer, official NP 3043, SN 411+

minstralcye *n* music Kn 2197+; musical ability Mcp 251; musical instrument(s) Mcp 113, 267; revelry, fun Co 4394

miracle *n* miracle ML 477+; wonder Kn 2675; *pleyes of miracles* miracle-plays WB 558

mirily *adv* (see also **murily**) merrily Sh 110; pleasantly, enjoyably WB 330; cheerfully Th 698; happily NP 3267; sweetly NP 3272+; appositely WB 1192

mirour *n* mirror Kn 1399+

mirthe *n* (see also **murthe**) happiness Mch 1739, CY 1287+; enjoyment, merriment, fun Rv 4005, ML 410+; entertainment GP 759+; pleasantness NP 3157; pleasure Mil 3654, Sh 318, 375; good time WB 399; *do ~* entertain GP 766

mirye *adj* (see also **mery(e)**, **mury(e)**) pleasant Mel 964+; cheerful Mk 1924, NP 2968+; happy NP 3259; entertaining Pard 316, NP 3449+; humorous Rv 4128; sweet-sounding NP 2851+; *make ~* enjoy o.s. CY 1195

mirye *adv* (see also **murye**) happily Mch 2218+; pleasantly Mch 2326, NP 3071

misaventure *n* misfortune ML 616+; *with ~* bad luck to you Fri 1334

mischaunce *n* (see also **meschaunce**): *with ~* curse it Fri 1334; *God yeve hem ~* God curse them Fkl 1374

misdo *v* do wrong (to) Mel 1708, Mk 1922, Pars 85

misdoer *n* wrongdoer, criminal Mel 1441+

miseise *n* (see also **misese**) suffering, misery Pars 186+

misericorde *n* mercy, pity, charity Sum 1910+

misese *n* (see also **miseise**) suffering, distress Pars 177, 806

misgo(n), **misgoon** *p ppl* gone the wrong way, gone astray Rv 4218+

mishappe *v* be unfortunate, meet with misfortune (*personal*) Mel 1696, (*impers*) Kn 1646; miscarry CY 944

missaye *v* (see also **misseye**) say something wrong, speak out of turn Mch 2391

misse *v* miss, notice as absent Rv 4216; fail Mil 3679; *~ of* fail to find Fri 1416; lack Sh 352

misseye *v* (see also **missaye**) speak ill of, insult Pars 379; say something wrong Mcp 353

mistake *v refl* do wrong, err
Mel 1690, 1818

mister *n* trade GP 613; plight
Kn 1340; *what ~ men* what
kind of men Kn 1710

mitain, mitein *n* mitten, glove
Pard 372, 373

mite *n* mite, farthing Kn 1558+

mo *n* more GP 576+; others Cl
1039, Mch 2113; *withoute ~*
alone SN 207

mo *adj* more (in number)
GP 808+; besides Kn 2430+;
many another ~ many another
besides Kn 2071+; *othere ~*
others besides Mil 3183+; *no
wight ~* no one else Mch 2157;
times ~ at other times too
Cl 449

mo *adv* any more WB 864; more
Sh 413

moder *n* mother Mil 3795+

moebles *n pl* (movable) property
Mch 1314, SN 540

moerdre *n* (see also **mordre**) murder Kn 1256

moeve *v* move, incite, prompt
Pars 128+; sway, trouble
ML 1136; stir up Mel 1028+

moevere *n* mover Kn 2987+

moeving(e) *n* impulse Mel 1239,
Pars 355+; agitation Pars 537;
Firste ~ Primum Mobile (outermost moving sphere) ML 295
(see n.)

moiste *adj* moist GP 420+; supple GP 457; new Pard 315,
Th 764

moment *n* moment Kn 2584; (in
medieval reckoning) the fortieth or fiftieth part of an hour
Pars 254

mone *n* lamentation Kn 1366+;
plea ML 656

monstre *n* monster Mch 2062+;
prodigy Fkl 1344

montai(g)ne *n* (see also **monteine**) mountain ML 24+

montaunce *n* (see also
mountaunce) amount Pard
863; value Mcp 255

monteine *n* (see also **mon-
tai(g)ne**) mountain Mk 2627

mood *n* anger Kn 1760; frame
of mind, mood Phys 126

moore *comp adj* more GP 304,
Kn 2429+; in addition
WB 584; greater Kn 2824, Rv
3858, Cl 916+; *the ~ part* the
majority Mch 1231+; *quasi-n*
more Kn 2850+; *bothe lasse
and ~* both the greater and the
less, (people) of all ranks
Kn 1756, ML 959+; *withoute
~* alone, without anything else
Kn 2316+; *withouten any ~*
without more ado Kn 1541,
Mch 1939

moore *comp adv* more
GP 219+

mooreover *adv* moreover, in
addition Mel 1066+; *and yet ~*
and that is not all Kn 2801

moorne *v* (see also **morne**)
grieve, sorrow Fkl 819; mourn
Kn 2968, ML 621; long, yearn
Mil 3706, Th 743; *~ after*
yearn for Mil 3704

moost *superl adj* (see also **meest**)
greatest GP 303, 798,
Kn 895+; most Sq 361,
Mel 1048, Pars 1039

moost(e) *superl adv* (see also
moste) mostly, chiefly

GP 561+; most Kn 2203+;
above all Kn 2407, Cl 932+

moot *1/3 sg pres of* **mote** *v*

mo(o)te *sg pres subj of* **mote** *v*

moote(n) *pl pres of* **mote** *v*

moralitee *n* morality Sum
2046+; ethical wisdom Mk
2497; moral significance
NP 3440; *pl* moral qualities
Pars 463

mordre *n* (see also **moerdre**) murder Pri 576+

mordre *v* murder WB 801+

mordrere, mordrour *n* murderer
Cl 732+

morne *n* morning; ~ *milk* morning milk GP 358+

morne *v* (see also **moorne**)
grieve WB 848

morsel *n* mouthful, piece of food
GP 128+; ~ *breed* mouthful of
bread Mk 2434

mortefye, mortifye *v* deprive of
life Pars 233+; harden CY
1126, 1431 (see n.)

morwe *n* morning GP 334+;
next day Kn 1629+; *by the* ~
in the morning GP 334+

morweninge *n* morning
Kn 1062+

morwe-tide *n* morning Mch
2225+

most *2 sg pres of* **mote** *v*

moste *superl adv* (see also
moost(e)) most Mel 1857

moste *sg past of* **mote** *v* (*also
used as pres* (*pl* **mosten**)) (1) *as
past*: might Cl 550; had to
GP 712, 847, Kn 1477+;
(*elliptically*) had to go Sq 604;
would have to Kn 3088, Sq
38, 280, Mk 2042; were

bound to Mch 2102; (2) *as
pres*: must Mil 3297,
ML 282+; *impers*: *us moste* we
must CY 946

mote *v* (see also **moste**) may
GP 232, 832, Mil 3114, 3675,
Rv 3918+; must GP 732, 735,
738, 742, Kn 885+; (*elliptically*) must go ML 294; *1/3 sg
pres* **moot**; *2 sg pres* **most**; *pl
pres* **mote(n), moote(n)**; *sg pres
subj* **mo(o)te**; *sg past* **moste**; *pl
past* **mosten**

moththes *n pl* moths WB 560+

motif *n* proposition Mch 1491;
impression ML 628

mountaunce *n* (see also **montaunce**) value Kn 1570

mowe *v* can GP 169, 230,
Kn 2449+; may GP 246, Rv
3886, Sum 1722+; be able to
Mel 1466; have the power
WB 1097, Sum 2175+; *be as
be may* be it as it may Mil
3783+; (*al*) *that ye/he may* as
best you/he can Rv 4033, Phys
159; *1/3 sg pres* **may**; *2 sg pres*
mayst; *pl pres* **mowe(n), may**;
1 pl pres **mow**; *2 sg pres subj*
mowe; *1/3 sg past* **mighte**; *2 sg
past* **mightest**; *pl past*
mighte(n)

mowle *v* grow mouldy Rv 3870,
ML 32

muche *adj* great GP 494,
WB 1079+; much Kn 1808+;
many NP 2770; ~ *thing* many
a thing Fri 1273; *quasi-n* much
GP 211+

muche *adv* much GP 132,
Kn 1116+; greatly Mel 992+

muchel *adj* great Kn 870+; much

Kn 1359+; many Mel 1654+; ~
thing many things WB 1004;
as n much Mch 1241; *for as ~
as* forasmuch as Sh 33+; *in so
~ to* that extent Mel 1454; *in
as ~ as* as far as Mel 1670

muchel *adv* greatly GP 258+;
much Kn 2850+

mullok *n* rubbish CY 938, 940;
rubbish-heap Rv 3873

multiplye *v* multiply, increase
WB 28, Pard 365+; increase
gold and silver by transmutation of baser metals (*alch*) CY
669+

murily *adv* (see also **mirily**)
sweetly Pri 553; cheerfully
Sh 301

murmur(e) *n* grumbling, complaint Kn 2459, WB 406, Cl
628+

murmure *v* grumble Pars 507;
murmur Sq 204

murthe *n* (see also **mirthe**) enjoyment, merriment Cl 1123

mury(e) *adj* (see also **mery(e)**,
mirye) pleasant GP 764, Sum
1774+; cheerful, jovial
GP 757+; happy Kn 1386,
Mch 1348+; glad Kn 2562,
ML 615; beautiful, fine
Kn 1499; sweet-sounding
GP 235, Mil 3218, Th 834+;
entertaining Cl 9, 15,
NP 2817; enjoyable Rv 4230,
WB 42; *make ~* entertain
GP 802; *~ men* followers
Th 839

murye *adv* (see also **mirye**) happily, merrily Mil 3575+

muwe *n* (see also **mewe**) coop
(for fattening poultry) GP 349

na *adj* (see also **no**) no (Northern form) Rv 4026+

nacio(u)n *n* nation GP 53,
ML 268+; family WB 1068

nadde *contr of* **ne hadde**

naddre *n* (see also **neddre**)
adder, snake Pars 331

naile *v* nail Cl 29+; fetter Cl
1184; fasten (spear-heads)
with nails Kn 2503

naked *adj* naked Kn 1956+;
weak SN 486

nam *contr of* **ne am**

nameliche, namely *adv* especially, in particular Kn 1268+

namo *n and adj* no more
GP 101+; no one else
Kn 1589+; no others GP 544

namoore *n, adj and adv* no more
GP 98+

nan *adj* (see also **non, noon**) no
(Northern form) Rv
4185, 4187

narwe *adj* narrow GP 625+;
small, cramped NP 2822

narwe *adv* closely Mil 3224;
tightly Sum 1803; closely, carefully Mch 1988

nas *contr of* **ne was**

nat *adv* not GP 246+

n'at *contr of* **ne at**

nathelees *adv* nevertheless
GP 35+

nativitee *n* birth Sq 45+

natural *adj* (see also **nature(e)l**):
~ vertu see n. to Kn 2743–57

nature *n* nature GP 11+; sperm,
sexual fluid Pars 577

nature(e)l *adj* (see also **natural**)
natural WB 1144+; *magik ~*
natural or 'white' magic, 'that

which did not involve recourse
to the agency of personal
spirits' (*OED*), 'the knowledge
of hidden natural forces (e.g.
magnetism, stellar influence),
and the art of using these in
calculating future events, cur-
ing disease, etc' (*MED*)
GP 416+; *day* ~ a 24-hour day
Sq 116

naught *n* nothing GP 756+

naught *adv* not Kn 2068+

nave *n* hub Sum 2266+

nay *adv* nay, no Kn 1126+; *it is
na* ~ it cannot be denied Rv
4183+

ne *adv* not GP 70+

ne *conj* nor GP 179+; *ne . . . ne*
neither . . . nor Mil 3110

nece *n* female relative, kins-
woman WB 383+

necessaries *n pl* necessities
ML 711, 871

necessitee *n* necessity Kn 3042;
simple ~, ~ *condicionel* see n.
to NP 3246–50

neddre *n* (see also **naddre**)
adder, snake Mch 1786

nede *n* (see also **neede**) need,
necessity Kn 2505+; business
Mil 3632+; exigency, difficulty, trouble Mch 1631,
Mel 1674+; disaster Mk 2386;
~ *is* there is need, it is necessary Kn 2505+; *thee/yow were
nede* you would need Sh 109,
NP 3453; *it is no* ~ there is no
need Cl 461; ~ *has na peere*
necessity has no fellow Rv
4026; *he has his nedes sped* he
has got what he wanted
Rv 4205

nede *adv* necessarily Cl 531+

nede *v* be necessary GP 462+;
need Pars 700; *him neded* he
needed Rv 4020+; *ther nedeth*
it is necessary Kn 1746+; *what
nedeth (it)* why is it necessary
Sq 298+; *what nedeth thee*
why do you need to (do s.th.)
WB 316

nedeful *adj* needy ML 112+;
needful Mel 1643

nedelees *adv* needlessly Cl 455+

nedely *adv* of necessity, necessarily WB 968+

nedes *adv* of necessity, necessarily Kn 1169+

neede *n* (see also **nede** *n*) need,
necessity GP 304

neer *adv* (see also **ner**) near
GP 839+; nearer Kn 968, CY
721+

neigh *adv* (see also **ney**, **ny**) near
Kn 1489+; closely GP 588;
nearly GP 732+; *wel* ~ very
nearly, almost Sq 431+

nempne *v* name ML 507+

ner *adv* (see also **neer**) near,
nearer Rv 4304+; *take him so*
~ placed him in a position of
such intimacy Kn 1439; *fer ne*
~ neither later nor sooner
Kn 1850

nere *contr of* **ne were**; ~ *min
extorcioun* were it not for my
extortion Fri 1439

nether *adj* lower; ~ *eye* anus,
arse-hole Mil 3852; ~ *purs*
balls, testicles WB 44b

nevene *n* name CY 821; speak
of CY 1473

nevere *adv* never, at no time
GP 70+; not, not at all SN 15;

~ *so* ever so GP 734+; ~ *no(o)n*
none Cl 1033+

neveremo *adv* nevermore
Kn 1346+; never WB 1099,
Mch 1676+

neverthemo, never the moore
adv (emphatically) neither
Mch 2089; (not) at all
WB 691+

newe *adj* new, fresh GP 457+;
modern GP 176; unfamiliar,
unusual ML 138; *of ~* recently
Fri 1342+; for the first time
CY 1042

newe *adv* newly, freshly
GP 365+; recently Mil 3221+;
~ to beginne to be created for
the first time GP 428; *al ~* all
over again Sh 378; *ay ~* over
and over again, continually
Mch 2204; *alwey ~ and ~*
again and again Pard 929

newefangel *adj* fond of novelty
Sq 618, Mcp 193

next *adj* next, following
Kn 2367+; nearest ML 398,
Mch 2201, Pri 624; nearest to
Pars 987; *the nexte way* the
quickest way Kn 1413+

next *adv* next Pri 450+

ney *adv* (see also **neigh, ny**)
almost Pars 345

nice *adj* foolish, silly Rv 3855,
ML 1088+; ludicrous Rv
3855; scrupulous GP 398

nicetee *n* stupidity, folly Rv
4046, SN 463+; *do his ~* have
his fun WB 412

nigard *n* niggard, miser
WB 333+

night *n* night GP 10+; *at quarter
~* a quarter of the way through

the night Mil 3516; *as pl*
nights Sum 1885, NP 2873

nil(le) *contr of* **ne wil(le)**

n'in *contr of* **ne in**

nis *contr of* **ne is**

niste *contr of* **ne wiste**

no *adj* (see also **na**) no GP 48+

noble *n* a gold coin, worth 6s 8d
($\frac{1}{3}$ of £1) Mil 3256+ (see Grierson, *Coins* p. 156)

noblesse *n* nobility, excellence
ML 185+; honour WB 1167,
Cl 468+

nobleye *n* honour, splendour Cl
828, Sq 77; nobility, nobles
SN 449

noght *n* nothing GP 768+

noght *adv* not GP 107+; *~ but
for* only because WB 645

noise *n* noise Kn 2492+; quar-
rel(ling) Mel 1485+

nolde *contr of* **ne wolde**

nombre *n* number GP 716+

non *adj* (see also **nan, noon**)
(used before vowel or h-) no
Kn 1787+

non *adv* (see also **noon**): *or ~* or
not Fkl 778

nones, nonis *n*: *for the ~* for the
purpose, for/on the occasion
GP 379, Kn 879, Mil 3126+;
as a rhyming tag meaning little
more than 'indeed' GP 523+

nonne *n* nun GP 118+

noon *pron* none GP 524+

noon *adj* (see also **nan, non**) no
WB 269+

noon *adv* (see also **non**) no Sq
387; *or ~* or not Sum 2069+

noot *contr of* **ne woot**

norice *n* nurse WB 299+

norice, noriss(h)e *v* nurse,

nourish Pars 509, 613; nourish, foment Mel 1014; foster,
cherish Mel 1445+; bring up,
rear, educate Rv 3948, Cl 399,
Mel 1511

noriss(h)inge *vbl n* growth
Kn 3017; nourishing, nourish-
ment GP 437+; upbringing
Cl 1040

nosethirles *n pl* nostrils
GP 557+

notable *adj* well-known, historically attested Mch 2241, Pri
685+

note *n* note, tune GP 235, Mil
3217, Pri 521+

nothing *pron* nothing Kn 2016+;
for ~ not at all WB 1121

nothing *adv* not at all, in no
respect Kn 1519, ML 575+; *~*
but only Kn 1754, Mch 1926+

notifye *v* proclaim ML 256;
make known Pars 430+

now *adv* now GP 573+; *~ and ~*
from time to time Sq 430; *as ~*
just now Sq 652

nowher *adv* nowhere GP 251+

ny *adj* near, close Mil 3392+;
immediate Mel 1395

ny *adv* (see also **neigh, ney**) near
WB 931+; nearly, closely
Mel 1545; almost Mch 1775+;
wel ~ very nearly, almost
Kn 1330+

o *num adj and pron* (see also **on,
oo, oon**) one GP 738,
Kn 1891+; *that ~ man* one
man NP 3076; *at ~ word* in a
word CY 1360

obeisa(u)nce *n* obedience,
respectfulness Kn 2974, Cl

230, Sq 93+; *do your ~* obey
you Cl 24+; *do his obeisaunces*
pay respectful attentions
Sq 515

obeisa(u)nt *adj* obedient Cl 66+

obeye *v* obey WB 1255+; *~ to*
obey, submit to Cl 194,
Mel 1550+; *refl ~ to* submit to
Mel 1684

obligacioun *n* pledge Mel 1767+

oblige *v* bind Mel 1747+

observa(u)nce *n* observance (of
law), duty Kn 1316, Mch
1548; rite, ceremony Kn 2264;
procedure, practice Fkl 1291;
attention Mch 1564; *do ~* take
care Pars 747; *do his/thy ~ ,
kepe hir observaunce(s)* follow
custom, pay tribute to the
occasion Kn 1045, 1500,
Fkl 956; *kepeth hise observaunces* pays attentions
Sq 516

observe *v* sanction Pri 631;
observe Pars 947; take note of
Pars 303; take care Pars 429

occasio(u)n *n* cause, stimulus
WB 740, Pars 338+; *occasions
of* opportunities for Phys 66

occident *n* west ML 297; West
(Europe) Mk 2674

of *adv* off Kn 2676, Mil 3811,
Mk 2558+; *com ~* come on,
get on with it, hurry up Mil
3728, Rv 4074+

of *prep* of GP 2+; from Rv
4253, WB 636, Cl 834, Sq
476, Fkl 1183, Th 923,
Mel 1873+; by Rv 3959,
WB 661, 706, Mch 2436,
Fkl 768, Pard 449, CY 748+;
for Sum 1868, Fkl 718,

Sh 280, Mel 1019, Mk 1990+;
with GP 345, Kn 1888,
WB 1185, NP 3251; as to,
about, concerning ML 90,
Mch 2216, Fkl 1179,
Mel 1083, NP 3329+; during
GP 87, Mil 3415, ML 510; at
Rv 4046; some GP 146; some
of WB 187, Pard 910+; *con-
sentant* ~ accessory to
Phys 276

offence *n* (see also **offense**)
harm, injury Kn 1083, Sum
2058+; offence ML 1138

offende *v* injure, do harm to,
hurt Kn 909+; wound
Kn 3065

offense *n* (see also **offence**)
harm, injury Cl 1197; offence
Mel 1748+

office *n* job, business Fri 1421,
1428; duty, business
Mel 1269, CY 924; secular
employment GP 292; service
Kn 1418, Pars 438; role Fri
1297; employments Mk 2256;
function, operation WB 127,
1137, 1144; office Fri 1577;
office, (religious) service
Kn 2836+; *houses of* ~ offices,
kitchen and pantries Cl 264

officer *n* officer Kn 1712+; servant Kn 2868, Cl 190, Pard
480+; official SN 497; office-
holder in a monastery Sh 65,
Mk 1935

offringe *n* offertory, collection
of alms in church GP 450+

ofte *adj* frequent Pars 233+;
many GP 485+; ~ *time*, ~ *sithe*
often GP 52+

ofte *adv* often GP 55+

ofter *comp adv* oftener Cl 215+

oght *n* (see also **aught**) anything
Fkl 1469, CY 836, 1333; *as
adv* at all Kn 3045, Pri 602,
CY 597

oghte *v* (see also **oughte**) ought
GP 505+; *impers*: *us* ~ we
ought Mel 998+; *him* ~ he
ought Mel 1213+

oinement *n* ointment GP 631+

okes *pl* of **ook** *n*

on *pron* (see also **o, oo, oon**):
many ~ many a one WB 680

on *prep* (see also **an**) on GP 12+;
in GP 501, Kn 944, 2866, Rv
3993, ML 348, Mch 2370+; to
Mch 2150; at Sq 348; at,
about Sq 258+; as regards
Mch 1424+; by Sq 29; over,
against GP 594; (*a*)*waitinge* ~
waiting for Mil 3642, Fri
1376; *konne* ~ know about Sq
3, Fkl 786+; ~ *reste* at rest
Sq 379

one *v* unite Sum 1968, Pars 193

ones, onis *adv* once Kn 1034,
WB 10+; *at* ~ at once, at one
time GP 765+

on-lofte *adv* above, in heaven
ML 277; flourishing Cl 229

oo *num adj and pron* (see also **o,
on, oon**) one GP 304,
Kn 2733+

ook *n* oak Kn 1702+; *pl* **okes**

oon *num adj and pron* (see also
o, on, oo) one GP 148+; someone Mil 3817, Rv 4290; alike,
the same thing Sq 537; single
WB 66; alike, the same Cl 711,
Pard 333+; *many* ~ many a
one GP 317+; *after* ~ of the
same standard GP 341;

equally, the same way Kn
1781; *evere in* ~ ever alike, con-
stantly Kn 1771, Rv 3880,
WB 209+; *at* ~ in agreement
Rv 4197; *in* ~ in the same way
Fri 1470; *that* ~ the one, one
Kn 1013+; ~ *and* ~ one by one
GP 679; ~ *and oother* all and
sundry, this person and that
Kn 2573; ~ *the faireste* the
most beautiful Cl 212,
Fkl 734

ooth *n* oath GP 120+; *pl* **othes**

oother *adj* (see also **other**) other
GP 461; the other GP 427,
Kn 899+; *that* ~ the other
GP 113, Kn 1014+; *noon* ~
none other Mch 2323; not
otherwise Kn 1085+; no other
way Kn 1182; *pl* **oothere**

ootherwey(e)s, ootherwise *adv*
otherwise Cl 1072,
Mel 1065+; in some other way
Mch 1534

operacioun *n* function
WB 1148; effect Fkl 1129;
operation, business Sq 130,
Fkl 1290

oppose *v* lay to (s.o's) charge Fri
1597; interrogate SN 363

oppresse *v* crush, suppress SN 4;
encumber Mel 1216; ravish,
violate Fkl 1385+

oppressioun *n* oppression Sum
1990; rape, violation WB 889

or *conj* (1) or GP 296+

or *conj* (2) before Kn 1548,
ML 289+

ordeine *v* ordain, decree Pars
771+; arrange, prepare
ML 415, CY 1277+; arrange,
settle Mel 1056+; order, regu-

late Pars 218+; provide
Kn 2253; appoint Sq 177

ordinaunce *n* arrangement(s),
plan(s) ML 250, 805,
Mel 1068, Pars 19; order Cl
961, Pars 177, 260; provision
ML 961, Fkl 903; disposal,
control ML 763, 992,
Mel 1725; order, decree Mil
3592, SN 445+; *by* ~ in due
order Kn 2567, Mel 1113;
according to the principle of
order Pars 922; *biset his* ~
ordered his plan Kn 3012

ordre *n* order Kn 3003+;
(religious) order GP 214+; *by*
~ in order Kn 1934+

ordred *p ppl* ordained, in orders
Pars 782+

ordure *n* filth, dirt Pars 157+

orient *n* east Kn 1496; East
(Asia) Mk 2314+

orisonte *n* horizon Mch 1797+

oriso(u)n *n* prayer Kn 2261,
ML 537+

orpiment *n* orpiment, yellow
arsenic CY 759+

Osanne *interj* Hosanna!
ML 642+

otes *n pl* oats Sum 1963+

other *adj* (see also **oother**) other
Kn 1136; the other Kn 1651+;
pl **othere** other GP 759+;
others Kn 2885, Mk 2154+; ~
two another two GP 794

othes *pl of* **ooth** *n*

oughte *v impers* (see also **oghte**):
hem oughten they ought
Mel 1731

ounce *n* ounce CY 756+; *by*
ounces in thin clusters GP 677

out *interj* help! Mil 3286+

out(e) *adv* out GP 45+

oute *v* display, expose
WB 521+

outher *conj* (see also **either**)
either Kn 1485+; or Sum
1828; ~ . . . ~ either . . . or
CY 1149

outherwhile *adv* sometimes
Mel 1543, 1667

out of *prep* out of GP 181+;
bereft of GP 452+; without
GP 487, SN 46+

outrage *n* excess, disorder, fury
Kn 2012, Pars 834; injury, violence Mel 1525+; crime, evil
deed Mel 1438+

outrageous *adj* excessive, unrestrained Mch 2087, Mel 990,
Pars 558+; outrageous, enormous Mel 1824+; superfluous,
extravagant Pars 412+; extraordinary Pars 470; impudent
Pars 992

outrely *adv* utterly, completely,
wholly Kn 1563+; in the
extreme Cl 335; emphatically,
plainly Kn 1154, Cl 768,
Mel 1020; superlatively
GP 237; *al* ~ to the utmost
degree, completely, absolutely
WB 664+

outward *adv* outwardly
Mel 1645+

over *adv* over Mil 3177+; too
Mel 1576+ (also with *adjs*:
*over-greet, over-hard, over-
lowe* etc.)

over *prep* over Kn 1693+; above
ML 277+; besides Kn 1563+;
over, more than Pard 687;
beyond Kn 2998, Pard 468+

overal *adv* everywhere GP 216+;
anywhere Kn 1207, Sum 2084;
on all sides WB 264+

over-muchel *adj and adv* too
much Mel 1467+

oversprede *v* spread over, over-
spread GP 678+; *past* **overspradde**

owe *v* owe WB 425+; own Pard
361; ought Mel 1501

owene *adj* own GP 213+

owher *adv* anywhere GP 653+

paas *n* (see also **pas**) pace
Kn 2901; (of a horse) walking-
speed WB 838 (see n.), CY
575; ?passage, section Pars
532 (see n.); *a* ~ at walking-
speed, at a footpace Kn 2217+;
a sory ~ with dejected steps
Mil 3741; *a softe* ~ at a
relaxed speed, at a leisurely
pace Mil 3760+; *a sturdy* ~
with determined strides, at a
great rate Sum 2162; *a strong*
~ a tight corner, a critical situation Mel 1445; *pl* **paces**

pace *v* (see also **passe**) pass, go,
proceed GP 36, 175,
Kn 1602+; depart Cl 1092; die
Sq 494; surpass, exceed
GP 574; ~ *of* pass over
ML 205; ~ *forby* pass by
Pri 569

pacience *n* patience WB 436+;
take in ~ accept patiently
Kn 1084+

pacient *n* patient GP 415+

pacient *adj* patient GP 484+

page *n* page, attendant Kn 1427;
commoner, peasant Kn 3030,
Fkl 692+; servant Mil 3376+;
boy Rv 3972

paid *p ppl* paid Sh 366; satisfied, content WB 1185

paine *n* (see also **peine**) pain, suffering Mk 2589; *do* (o's) ~ take pains, do o's utmost Fkl 730

paire *n* (see also **peire**) pair Co 4386+

palais, paleis *n* mansion Mch 2415; palace Kn 2199+

palfrey *n* palfrey, saddle-horse GP 207+

pan *n* skull, head Kn 1165+

panade *n* a kind of large knife Rv 3929+

panne *n* pan Rv 3944, Fri 1614+

papejay *n* (see also **papinjay, popinjay**) popinjay, parrot Mch 2322

paper *n* (see also **papir**) accounts, papers Co 4404

papinjay *n* (see also **papejay, popinjay**) popinjay, parrot Sh 369

papir *n* (see also **paper**) paper Pars 445

par (*French*) *prep* by; ~ *amour* as a lover Kn 1155, with passion Th 743; ~ *compaignye* for company Mil 3839+; in accompaniment Rv 4167; ~ *ma fay* on my word Th 820; ~ *chariitee* for charity Th 891; ~ *chaunce* by chance Pard 606; as it happened GP 475; ~ *cas* by chance Pard 885

parage *n* lineage, descent WB 250+

paramour, paramours *n* love, amorousness Mil 3354, Co 4372+; mistress Mil 3756, WB 454+; lover Fri 1372

paramour(s) *adv*: *love* ~ be in love Kn 1155, 2112

paraunter, paraventure *adv* (see also **peraventure**) perhaps Rv 3915, ML 190+; by chance Cl 234+; for example Pars 1019

parcel *n* piece, part Fkl 852+

pardee *interj* by God! indeed, assuredly GP 563+

pardo(u)n *n* pardon Mel 1773+; indulgence(s) GP 687, Pard 920+

pardurable *adj* (see also **perdurable**) lasting, permanent Mel 1509+; everlasting Pars 669

parementz *n pl* rich clothing Kn 2501; tapestries; *chambre of* ~ state room (hung with tapestries) Sq 269

parfay, parfey *interj* by my faith, truly! Mil 3681+

parfit *adj* (see also **perfit**) perfect, complete GP 72+

parfo(u)rme, parfourne *v* (see also **perfourne**) perform Mch 2052, Mel 1212+; put into effect Sh 317+; fulfil Mk 1947, Mcp 190; complete Sum 2104, Mch 1795; celebrate Pri 456+

parisshen *n* parishioner GP 482+

parlement *n* deliberation, decision Kn 1306; conference, council Kn 2970, 3076

part(e) *n* part Kn 2824+; share Kn 1178+; side Kn 2185; side, party Kn 2446+; *have* ~ *of* have an interest in, have a concern for Kn 2792; have a share in Co 4394, Cl 650, Pars 792;

have ~ *on* take Sh 218; *an hundred* ~ a hundred times Sum 2062; *by twenty thousand* ~ multiplied twenty thousand times Sq 553

parte *v* part Co 4362; depart, go Pard 649, 752; share, divide Fri 1534, Sum 1967+

particuler *adj* specialized Cl 35+

partie, party *n* part, portion Kn 3008, ML 17, Mel 1035+; side, party Mel 1014+; quarter Mel 1370; partial judge, partisan Kn 2657

pas *n* (see also **paas**) footpace, walking-speed GP 825; *pl* steps, motion ML 306; *esily a* ~ slowly, in a leisurely way Sq 388; *a ful gret* ~ quickly Phys 164

passe *v* (see also **pace**) pass, go Kn 1033+; pass (over) GP 464; proceed Kn 1461, NP 2939; pass by, come to an end, disappear Mil 3578, Mch 1315+; get through, get out of Mel 1445; exceed Kn 2885+; surpass GP 448, Mch 1504+; ~ *of* pass over Sq 288; ~ *awey* pass on from Mk 1923; ~ *forth* go on, continue Mil 3370, 3419; ~ *over* move on, skip over Mch 2115+

passing *adj* excessive Mch 1225; excellent CY 614

passio(u)n *n* emotion ML 1138; suffering, martyrdom SN 26+; (*Cristes*) ~ (Christ's) passion Mil 3478+

pasture *n* pasture Mch 1313+; (act of) feeding NP 3185

patente *n* letters patent GP 315 (see n.); ecclesiastical licence Pard 337

pavement *n* (paved or tiled) floor ML 85+

payen *n* pagan ML 534+

pece *n* piece Sh 136+

pecok *n* peacock GP 104+

pees *n* peace GP 532+; *holde in* ~ cease ML 228

peine *n* (see also **paine**) pain, suffering Kn 1297+; torture Kn 1133; penalty Fri 1314; punishment Mel 1749+; endeavour Sq 509; difficulty Mel 1404; *up(on)* ~ *of* on pain of Kn 1707+; *sette* ~ *in* take trouble with CY 1398; *do* (*o's*) ~ endeavour, take pains Mcp 330

peine *v* torment, torture Mk 2604, Pars 213+; *refl* try, make an effort GP 139, ML 320+

peinte *v* paint Kn 1934+; embellish Pars 610+

peire *n* (see also **paire**) pair GP 473; set GP 159, Sum 1741; *a* ~ *plates* a set of plate armour Kn 2121

peitrel *n* breast-plate, straps going from the saddle round the horse's chest CY 564, Pars 433

pena(u)nce *n* penance GP 223+; purgatory Sum 1724; suffering, distress, sorrow Kn 1315, ML 286+; punishment SN 446+

penible *adj* assiduous Sum 1846, Mk 2300; devoted Cl 714

peny *n* penny Fri 1575+; money Rv 4119; *pl* **pens** pence Fri 1576+

peple *n* people GP 706+

peraventure *adv* (see also **paraunter, paraventure**) perhaps Pard 935+

perce *v* pierce GP 2+

perdurable *adj* (see also **pardurable**) everlasting Pars 75+

perfit *adj* (see also **parfit**) perfect, true Pars 938

perfourne *v* (see also **parfo(u)rme, parfourne**) perform Mel 1066+; put into action Pars 529; ~ *up* make up, complete Sum 2261

peril *n* peril Rv 3932+; *upon my* ~ may I be damned otherwise WB 561

perilous *adj* dangerous Rv 3961+

peris *pl of* **pere** *n* pears Mch 2331+

perisse *v* perish Pars 75+; be ruined Phys 99; *is perissed* perished Pars 579

perree, perrye *n* jewellery Kn 2936, WB 344+

pers *n* blue, blue cloth GP 439, 617

persevere *v* persevere WB 148; last Pard 496

person(e), persoun *n* person GP 521+; parson GP 478, Rv 3943, Fri 1313+

pertinacye *n* obstinacy Pars 391+

philosofre, philosophre *n* philosopher GP 297 (punning on 'alchemist'), ML 25+; alchemist CY 837+; astrologer, magician ML 310, Fkl 1561+

philosophye *n* philosophy GP 295, Rv 4050+; alchemy, science CY 1058+

physik *n* physic, medicine GP 411+; the medical art Pars 913

pich *n* pitch, tar Mil 3731+

pie *n* magpie Rv 3950+

pietous *adj* (see also **pitous**) merciful Sq 20

pike *v* pick WB 44a; pick over CY 941; clean, make neat Mch 2011

pile *v* plunder, fleece Fri 1362+

piled *p ppl* sparse, scrubby GP 627; bald Rv 3935, 4306

piler *n* pillar Kn 1993+

pilour *n* spoiler, scavenger Kn 1007+

pinche *v* pleat GP 151; ~ *at* carp at, find fault with GP 326+

pine *n* suffering, distress Kn 1324+; punishment Mk 2230; torment Sq 448

pine *v* torture Kn 1746+

pipe *v* pipe Rv 3876+; play the bagpipes Rv 3927; whistle Kn 1838

pirie *n* pear-tree Mch 2217+

pistel *n* Epistle Cl 1154; message WB 1021

pit *n* pit Mil 3460, Pri 571+; grave Mch 1401+

pitee *n* pity, tenderness, sympathy Kn 920+; grief, distress ML 292; lamentation Kn 2833; cause for pity Kn 1751+

pitous *adj* (see also **pietous**) compassionate, merciful, tender

Kn 953+ (in GP 143 with play
on meaning 'devout'); pitiable,
pitiful, sorrowful Kn 955+;
pious, devout Kn 2371+

pitously *adv* with pity, merci-
fully ML 835, Sq 440+; pitiably, miserably, pitifully
Kn 949+; devoutly, reverently
Kn 2263

place *n* (see also **plas**) place
GP 623+; arena Kn 1895+;
house GP 607, Sum 1768+;
building Kn 1971+; manor Sh
273; rank WB 1164; *in the ~*
on the spot Mch 1991+

plain *adj* plain Kn 1091+;
smooth, level Mcp 229

plain *adv* (see also **plein** *adv* (2))
plainly ML 219+

plain(e) *n* plain ML 24,
Cl 59+

plas *n* (see also **place**) place
Th 781

plat *adj* blunt, plain Kn 1845;
flat Sq 164, Pri 675; *as n* flat
(side) Sq 162

plat *adv* bluntly, plainly
ML 886+

plate *n* armour-plating Kn 2121,
Th 865; plate Pars 433

platly *adv* plainly, directly Pars
485, 1022

plein *adj* plain, unadorned
Fkl 720, Phys 50; full, complete GP 315+; ~ *bataille* open
war Kn 988; ~ *entente* whole
purpose Kn 1487+

plein *adv* (1) completely, entirely
GP 327

plein *adv* (2) (see also **plain**)
plainly GP 790+

pleine *v* lament, bewail, be sorry

Kn 1320+; express o's unhappiness Cl 97, Fkl 1317; complain
WB 387+, *refl* WB 336; ~
(up)on complain of Kn 1251+;
make a complaint against Fri
1313, Phys 167

pleinly *adv* (1) plainly GP 727+
pleinly *adv* (2) fully Kn 1733+
pleint(e) *n* lament, lamentation
ML 66, Fkl 1029+
plesa(u)nce *n* pleasure, delight
Kn 1571+; desire, will Cl
305+; attentiveness, courtesy
Sq 509, Mcp 157; complaisance Cl 792; *in thy ~* to please
you Kn 2409; *do ~* give pleasure Mch 1563+; do a favour
Mch 1612; serve, attend Cl
1111; do (a) service Fkl 1199+
plesa(u)nt *adj* pleasant GP 222;
pleasing, agreeable Cl 991,
Mch 1621+; affable GP 138
plese *v* please GP 610+; indulge
in pleasure with Mch 1680;
satisfy the demands of
Cl 216
pley *n* play, fun Kn 1125, Mil
3773+; play WB 558; game Cl
10+; games Kn 2964; joke Fri
1548; *sooth ~ quade ~* a true
joke is a bad joke Co 4357;
amusement, sport Pard 627;
(in sexual sense) Sh 117
pleye *v* play GP 236+; joke
GP 758, Kn 1127+; make
sport Mk 2081; amuse o.s.,
have fun, take recreation, have
a holiday GP 772, Kn 1195+
(*also refl*); (in a sexual sense)
Mil 3273, Rv 3867+ (this
sense sometimes latent in other
quotations)

pleying(e) *vbl n* amusement
Kn 1061; love-play Mch 1854

plight *p ppl* plucked WB 790;
pulled Mk 2049

plighte *v* pledge WB 1009+

plighte *past* snatched, pulled
ML 15

plit *n* situation Pars 762; condition Mch 2335, Mel 1148+

plowman *n* ploughman GP 529+

plye *v* bend Cl 1169; mould
Mch 1430

poetrye *n* poetry Cl 33; *pl*
poems Sq 206

poinaunt *adj* piercing, stinging
Pars 130+; sharp, pungent
GP 352+

point *n* point GP 114+; object
Kn 1501; full-stop CY 1480;
particle, fraction Kn 2766;
detail NP 3022; state Pars 921;
lace Mil 3322 (see n.); ~ *for* ~
every detail Cl 577; *fro* ~ *to* ~
in every detail Phys 150+; *in
good* ~ in good condition
GP 200; *at* ~ *devis* to perfection, to a T Mil 3689+; *be in* ~
to be on the point of ML 331+

poke *n* bag Mil 3780+

pomely *adj* dappled GP 616+

pompous *adj* splendid, magnificent Mk 2471; arrogant, vainglorious Mk 2555

poore *adj* (see also **povre**) poor
WB 109+

popinjay *n* (see also **papejay,
papinjay**) popinjay, parrot
Th 767

port *n* bearing, manner
GP 69, 138

portehors *n* (portable) breviary
Sh 131 (see n.) +

pose *n* cold in the head Mcp 62;
on the ~ suffering from a cold
Rv 4152+

positif *adj* customary, conventional Kn 1167 (~ *lawe*, the
law specific to an individual
society, as distinguished from
the 'natural law' which governs human kind as a whole)

possessioun *n* possession
Kn 2242+; possessions, wealth
WB 1147+

potage *n* soup Pard 368+

pothecarye *n* (see also **apothecarye**) pharmacist, druggist
Pard 852

poudre *n* powder CY 760+

poupe *v* (see also **powpe**) blow,
toot Mcp 90

poure *v* look closely, gaze Sum
1738, Mch 2112+; ~ *upon*
gaze intently at WB 295+;
pore over, study earnestly
GP 185

povereste *superl adj* (see also
povrest) poorest Pard 449+

povre *adj* (see also **poore**) poor
GP 225+

povreliche, povrely *adv* poorly,
meanly Kn 1412, Cl 213+

povrest *superl adj* (see also **povereste**) poorest Cl 205

powpe *v* (see also **poupe**) blow,
toot NP 3399

practik, praktike *n* practice
WB 44d; practices, behaviour
WB 187

pray(e) *n* (see also **preye**) prey
Kn 2015+

praye *v* (see also **preye**) pray
WB 826+; ask GP 725+

prayere *n* (see also **preyere**)

prayer Kn 2226+; request,
entreaty Kn 1204+

preche *v* preach GP 481+

preci(o)us *adj* precious, valuable
WB 338+; fastidious, refined
Mch 1962; fastidious, hard to
please WB 148

predicacioun *n* preaching
ML 1176+

preef *n* (see also **preeve, preve**)
test, trial Mcp 75; *good ~* success CY 1379; *with ivel ~* bad
luck to you WB 247

prees *n* crowd, throng ML 393+;
danger, distress Mk 2137

prees(s)e *v* crowd, throng
Kn 2530+; *~ on* urge WB 520

preest *n* (see also **prest**) priest
GP 501+

preeve *n* (see also **preef, preve**)
experience NP 2983; *~ demonstratif* proof based on logic,
demonstrative proof
Sum 2272

preeve *v* (see also **preve, prove**)
prove Mch 1330

preise *v* praise WB 294+; value,
prize Mch 1854; *to ~* to be
praised Phys 42+

preisinge *vbl n* praising, praise
Pars 454+; honour, glory
Pars 949

prentis *n* apprentice Co 4365+

prescience *n* prescience, foreknowledge Kn 1313+

presence *n* presence Kn 927+; *in
~* in company Cl 1207; *in
heigh ~* in solemn assembly
ML 675

presse *n* press, clamp GP 81; cupboard, closet GP 263,
Mil 3212

prest *n* (see also **preest**) priest
ML 1166

preve *n* (see also **preef, preeve**)
test, trial Cl 787

preve *v* (see also **preeve, prove**)
prove GP 485+; test Cl 699+;
find out Mel 1437; turn out Cl
1000, CY 645; succeed CY
1212; *~ wel* be very evident
Mch 2425

preye *n* (see also **pray(e)**) prey
Fri 1455+

preye *v* (see also **praye**) pray
GP 301+; ask, request, beg
GP 811, Kn 1483+

preyere *n* (see also **prayere**)
prayer(s) GP 231, Mil 3587+;
request Fri 1489+

prike *v* (see also **prikke**) prick
Mch 1635; urge, stimulate
GP 11+; spur, ride Kn 2678+;
pierce, stab Fri 1594; goad Cl
1038; thrust Rv 4231

priking(e) *vbl n* riding, galloping
Kn 2599+; tracking the hare
GP 191 (?with pun on sexual
sense of word)

prikke *n* prick, sting Pars 468;
stab, jab Kn 2606; point, condition ML 119+

prikke *v* (see also **prike**) prick
Mel 1326

prime *n* 9 o'clock in the morning (see North, *Chaucer's Universe*, pp. 110–11) Kn 2189+;
~ large fully 9 o'clock Sq 360;
half wey ~ half-way between 6
and 9 a.m., 7.30 a.m. Rv 3906

primer *n* a lay person's
devotional manual, also used
as an elementary reading book
Pri 517 (see n.) +

pris *n* price GP 815; value
WB 523+; renown, glory
Kn 2241+; reputation GP 67;
praise Cl 1026+; excellence
Fkl 911; *of* ~ excellent Th 897;
bere the ~ surpass everyone
GP 237; *holde in gret* ~ esteem
highly Fkl 934

privee *n* privy, lavatory Mch
1954+

privee *adj* secret Kn 2460+; private WB 620+; discreet, secretive Mil 3201+; intimate
ML 204+; sly, furtive Pard
675; ~ *man* intimate, confidant
Cl 519; ~ *membres* privy
members, private parts Pars
425+

privee *adv* privately WB 1114+

prively *adv* secretly, privately
GP 609+; inwardly Fkl 741

privitee *n* personal affairs
Kn 1411; secret(s) Mil 3164+;
secrecy Mil 3623+; private,
privacy Mil 3493+; private
environment Co 4334; private
parts Mk 2715; *in hir* ~
secretly ML 548

proces *n* process Kn 2967+;
narrative Sq 658; series of
events Mk 2321

professioun *n* profession, taking
of vows on entering a religious
order Sum 1925+

profre *v* offer Kn 1415+; *refl*
offer o.s. Mil 3289

pronounce *v* announce Pard
335; tell CY 1299

proporcioun *n* proportion Pars
9; proportionate reckoning
Fkl 1286; part, portion
CY 754

propre *adj* own GP 540+;
proper Pard 417+; handsome,
good-looking Mil 3345; fine
Rv 3972+; characteristic Sq
610+

proprely *adv* correctly, properly
Kn 1459+; literally GP 729; in
particular Kn 2787; hand-
somely Mil 3320; characteristically WB 224, 1191

propretee *n* attribute, characteristic Mel 1174+

prove *v* (see also **preeve**, **preve**)
prove Kn 3001+; ~ *wel* be very
evident GP 547

provost *n* chief magistrate Pri
616+

prow *n* profit, benefit Pard 300+

prye *v* pry Sum 1738+; gaze Mil
3458, CY 668

publisse *v* make public, report
Cl 415, 749

pulle *v* pull Kn 1958+; pluck
GP 177, Mil 3245+; ~ *a finch*
cheat a dupe GP 652

purchace, purchase *v* acquire,
obtain Pars 742+; obtain, get
CY 1405; provide ML 873;
bring about Mel 1680+;
acquire possessions, get rich
GP 608

purchas *n* profit (*esp* what one
picks up in an irregular way)
GP 256+

purchasing *vbl n* gain, profit Fri
1449; conveyancing GP 320

pure *adj* pure SN 48+; very
Kn 1279

pured *p ppl* refined, pure
WB 143, Fkl 1560

purge *v* purge NP 2953+; evacuate, discharge WB 134+

purpos *n* purpose, proposal, resolution Kn 2542+; matter in hand ML 170+; *come to ~* become relevant Sq 653; *it cam him to ~* he decided Sq 606; *be in ~* intend Rv 3978

purpose *v* intend Fkl 1458, Mel 1055+, *refl* Mel 1834; resolve Cl 706

purs *n* purse GP 656+; *nether ~* balls, testicles WB 44b

pursue *v* chase, pursue Pars 355; persecute Pars 526; sue Mel 1694

purtreiture *n* picture, painting Kn 1915+

purtreye *v* draw, paint GP 96; picture to o.s. Mch 1600

purve(i)a(u)nce *n* foresight, providence, ordinance Kn 1252+; arrangements, preparations Mil 3566, ML 247+; provision WB 570, Pars 685

purveye *v* provide WB 591+; prepare Pars 1003

putte *v* put Kn 988+; suppose Mel 1477; *3 sg contr pres* put

quade *adj* bad; *sooth pley ~ pley* a true joke is a bad joke Co 4357; *a thousand last ~ yeer* a wagonload of misery (*lit* a thousand cartloads of bad years) Pri 438

quake *v* quake, tremble Kn 1576, Mil 3614+; *sg past* quook; *p ppl* quaked

quarter *n* quarter ML 798+; *at ~ night* a quarter of the way through the night, 9 p.m. Mil 3516

queint *p ppl of* **quenche** *v*

queinte *n* female genitals Mil 3276 (see n.), WB 332+

queinte *adj* clever, subtle Mil 3275, Rv 4051+; ingenious, curious Mil 3605, Sq 234+; strange, odd Kn 1531+; elaborate, esoteric ML 1189, CY 752

queinte *past of* **quenche** *v*

queintise *n* cunning Pars 733; elaboration, elegance Pars 932

quelle *v* kill, destroy Pard 854+

quenche *v* quench Kn 2321+; be quenched, go out Kn 2334+; *past* queinte; *p ppl* (y)queint

questioun *n* question Kn 1347+; discussion Kn 2514

quik *adj* alive, living Kn 1015+; lively Sq 194; vigorous, pithy GP 306; *quikkest* busiest Fkl 1502

quike *v* bring to life SN 481+; come to life Pars 235+; kindle Kn 2335, Fkl 1050+

quit *adj* free Fkl 1363+

quite *v* release, set free Kn 1032; repay, requite, pay back Mil 3119+; pay GP 770; pay for Mk 2374; *refl* acquit o.s., do o's part Fkl 673

quod *past* said GP 788+

quook *sg past of* **quake** *v*

rad *p ppl of* **rede** *v*

radde *sg past of* **rede** *v*

rafte *sg past of* **reve** *v*

rage *n* rage Kn 2011+; blast of wind Kn 1985; anguish Fkl 836

rage *v* play, banter, frolic

GP 257, Mil 3273+ (with
sexual connotations)

ragerye *n* high spirits, playfulness WB 455, Mch 1847

rakel *adj* hasty, rash Mcp 278+

rasour *n* razor Kn 2417+

rathe *adv* early Mil 3768+

rather *comp adv* rather, sooner
GP 487, Kn 1153, ML 335+

raughte *past of* **reche** *v* reached
Kn 2915, Mil 3696+; ~ *after*
reached for GP 136

raunceon, raunsoun *n* ransom
Kn 1024+

ravise, ravisshe *v* ravish, seduce
Pri 469; carry off, carry away
Sum 1676+; delight, enrapture
Mch 1750+

real *adj* regal, kingly Th 847,
NP 3176+

realtee *n* (see also **royaltee**)
pomp, magnificence Cl 928

reawme *n* (see also **reme**) realm
Sh 116+

recche *v* (see also **rekke**) care,
mind Kn 1398+; ~ *of* care
about, take notice of Mil
3772+; *impers* trouble, concern Cl 685; *past* **roghte**

recchelees *adj* careless, negligent
GP 179, ML 229+; inconsider-
ate, unresponsive Cl 488; heedless Mcp 279

recchele(e)snesse *n* thought-
lessness, carelessness
Pars 111+

receit *n* formula CY 1353+

receive *v* receive, accept
ML 259+; *received* acceptable
ML 307

reconforte *v* comfort, console
Mel 978; encourage Mel 1660;

refl take heart, be consoled
Kn 2852

record *n* reputation, account
Sum 2049; *of* ~ recorded, evi-
denced Sum 2117

recorde *v* witness, bear witness
(to), confirm Kn 1745,
Mel 1079; *impers* remember
GP 829

red *p ppl of* **rede** *v*

redde *sg past of* **rede** *v*

redden *pl past of* **rede** *v*

rede *pl and weak sg of* **reed** *adj*

rede *v* read GP 709+; advise,
suggest Kn 3068+; ~ *of* teach
about Fri 1518; *sg past* **radde**,
redde; *pl past* **redden**; *p ppl*
rad, red

redily *adv* promptly Kn 2276+

redresse *v* amend, set right
WB 696, Cl 431; restore
Fkl 1436; *refl* direct o.s.
Pars 1039

reed *n* advice Mil 3527+; plan,
course of action Kn 1216+;
counsel, adviser GP 665

reed *adj* red GP 90+; *pl and
weak sg* **rede**

refreine *v* curb, restrain Pars
294+; *refl* restrain o.s.
Pars 382

refresshinge *vbl n* refreshment
Pars 78+

reft *p ppl of* **reve** *v*

refut *n* refuge ML 546+

regard *n*: *at* ~ *of* in comparison
with Pars 180+; *in* ~ *of* with
respect to Pars 477; *as to* ~ *of*
with reference to Pars 399

regne *n* kingdom, realm
Kn 866+; rule, sovereignty,
power Kn 1624+

regne *v* reign, rule ML 816+

reherce, reherse *v* repeat, recount
GP 732+; describe Fri 1296+;
list, enumerate Pars 239+

rein *n* rain GP 492+

reine *n* rein Kn 904+

reise *v* raise WB 705+; ~ *up* collect Fri 1390

rejoise *v* rejoice Mel 989; *refl*
rejoice, take pleasure Cl 145+

rejoisinge *vbl n* joy, cause for
rejoicing Mcp 246+

rekene *v* (see also **rekne**) calculate GP 401; enumerate
Kn 1933+; settle accounts, calculate Sh 78+; count, reckon
WB 367; value Sq 427

rekeninge *vbl n* account
GP 600+; bill GP 760

rekke *v* (see also **recche**) care,
mind Kn 2257+; ~ *of* care
about, take notice of CY 698+;
impers trouble, concern; *what
rekketh me* what do I care
WB 53+

rekne *v* (see also **rekene**) render
an account ML 110; evaluate,
consider ML 158

rele(e)sse *v* release Mk 2177+;
release, relinquish Fkl 1533;
remit, forgive Fkl 1613+;
discharge from ML 1069,
Cl 153

releve *v* recompense Rv 4182+;
help, assist Mel 1490; rescue
Pars 945

religioun *n* religion SN 427;
religious order, monastic life
Mk 1944+; *man of* ~ man in
holy orders GP 477

religious *adj* in a religious order
Mk 1960+

reme *n* (see also **reawme**) realm
NP 3136

remembre *v* remember
ML 1057; remind Fkl 1243; ~
(*up*)*on/of* remember Mch
1898, Fkl 1542, Pars 133+,
refl Mch 1898+; *impers*: *it
remembreth me* I remember
WB 469

remena(u)nt *n* rest, remainder
GP 724+

remeve, remewe, remoeve *v*
remove Sq 181, Fkl 993+;
move Fkl 1205

rende *v* tear Kn 990+; split
NP 3101; *past* **rente**; *p ppl*
yrent

reneye *v* renounce, abjure
ML 340+

renne *v* run GP 8, Kn 2868+;
come quickly Kn 1761+; ~ *in*
incur CY 905; ~ *for* run in
favour of ML 125; *sg past* **ran**;
pl past **ronne(n)**; *p ppl* **ronne,
yronne(n)**

renovelle *v* renew Mel 1845+; be
renewed Pars 1027

rente *n* revenue, income
GP 256+; toll, tribute
ML 1142

rente *past of* **rende** *v*

repair *n* visiting, flocking of
people WB 1224+

repaire, repeire *v* return
ML 967+; revert Sq 608; go,
resort to NP 3220

repente *v* repent Mel 1135+, *refl*
ML 378+; *impers*: *repented me*
I repented WB 632

repleccioun *n* (see also
replexion) repletion, surfeit
NP 2837

replenisse *v* replenish, fill Pars 920+

replet *adj*: ~ *of* filled with Pard 489+

replexion *n* (see also **replecci-oun**) repletion, surfeit NP 2923

replye *v*: ~ *again* object to Mch 1609+

repreeve *n* (see also **repreve**) reproof WB 16

reprevable *adj* reprehensible, blameworthy Pard 632+

repreve *n* (see also **repreeve**) shame, disgrace WB 84+; reproach Mch 2204+; reprimand Mch 2263; insult Pars 258

repreve *v* blame, reprove Mel 1032+; insult, taunt Pars 623+; ~ *of* reproach with, reprove for WB 937+

reprevinge *vbl n* reproach, taunting Pars 556+

requere *v* ask of WB 1010+; request Mel 1737; ~ *of* ask for, request Mel 1683

reso(u)n *n* reason Cl 25, Mel 979+; reason, argument ML 213+; explanation, account Mil 3844; reasonableness Fkl 833; what is right GP 37; remark, statement GP 274; *as is/was* ~ as is/was right GP 847, Sum 2277+; ~ *was* it was right Mch 1768; *as fer as* ~ *fil* as far as was reasonable Sq 570; *by* ~ with reason Pard 458+; *by* ~ *of* because of Mel 1023; *by wey of* ~ on rational consideration

ML 219; according to reason, rationally Pars 707+

resoune, resowne *v* resound, echo Kn 1278, Sq 413

respit *n* delay Kn 948+; respite SN 543+

reste *n* rest GP 820+; *in/on/to* ~ at rest GP 30, WB 428, Sq 379

reste *v* rest Kn 2621+; *refl* rest o.s. Mch 1926; cease CY 859

restreine *v* restrain Mel 1092+, *refl* restrain o.s. Mk 2606+; ~ *of* restrain from Mel 1492

retenue *n* retinue Cl 270; *of* ~ in service Kn 2502; *at his* ~ in his service Fri 1355

rethor *n* rhetorician, master of eloquence Sq 38+

rethorik *n* rhetoric Fkl 719+; eloquence Cl 32

reto(u)rne *v* return ML 986+

reule *n* (see also **rewle**) rule Mel 1166+; (monastic) rule GP 173

reule *v* (see also **rule**) rule GP 816+

reve *n* reeve GP 542+

reve *v* seize Kn 2015; take away Mk 2098, SN 376+; plunder, steal Pars 758; rob Rv 4011; deprive of Fkl 1017, Pars 561+; ravish WB 888; *sg past* **rafte**; *p ppl* reft, yraft

revelour *n* reveller Co 4371+

reverence *n* reverence, respect GP 141+; honour Pri 473; *bere/do* (*a*) ~ show respect, do honour (to) Kn 2531+; *at* ~ *of* in honour of SN 82+

reverence *v* show respect (to) CY 631, Pars 403

revers *n* reverse, contrary Sum
2056, NP 2977

reward *n* regard, heed
Mel 1259+; *take litel/no ~*
have little/no concern
Mel 1371+

rewe *n* row Kn 2866; *by ~* in a
row WB 506

rewe *v* have pity Kn 1863+; be
sorry Mil 3530+; do penance
for CY 997; *impers:* (*it*) *me*
reweth (*of*) I am sorry (for)
Mil 3462+

rewful *adj* (see also **ruful**) pitiable ML 854

rewle *n* (see also **reule**) rule
Pars 217

ribaudye *n* ribaldry, obscenity
Rv 3866+

ribibe *n* hag Fri 1377 (metaphorical use of 'ribible'; see next
entry)

ribible *n* (see also **rubible**)
rebeck, two-stringed fiddle
Co 4396

riche *adj* rich GP 248+; splendid, sumptuous GP 296,
Kn 2525+

riche *adv* richly GP 609+; mag-
nificently, splendidly
Kn 2577+

richesse *n* riches, wealth
Kn 1255+

ride *v* ride GP 27+; go on
expeditions GP 45; mount
(sexual sense) NP 3168;
3 sg contr pres **rit**; *sg past*
rood; *pl past* **riden**; *p ppl*
riden

riding(e) *vbl n* riding Pars 432+;
procession Co 4377

right *n* right, justice Kn 3089+;

(*up*) *at alle rightes* in every
respect Kn 1852+

right *adv* straight, directly
Kn 1691+; just, exactly
GP 257+; certainly GP 659+;
very GP 288+; wholly GP 804;
fully Cl 243; clearly Mil 3583;
~ naught not at all WB 582+;
~ tho at that very minute Cl
544; *~ anoon* straight away
Kn 965; *~ in the cradel* in the
very cradle Kn 2019; *~ of the*
same of the very same
Kn 2904; (used as an intensi-
fier before adverbial clauses)
exactly, precisely, just GP 661,
WB 791+

rightful *adj* just Kn 1719+;
rightful Pars 545; proper
Pars 825

rightwisnesse *n* righteousness
Sum 1909+

ringe *v* ring, sound, resound
Kn 2359+; *sg past* **rong**

riot *n* debauchery, dissipation
Co 4392+

riotour *n* profligate, debauchee
Pard 661+

riotous *adj* dissolute Co 4408;
quarrelsome Mel 1087

ripe *adj* ripe Rv 3875+; mature
Cl 220+

rise *v* rise GP 33+; *3 sg contr*
pres **rist**; *sg and pl past* **roos**;
p ppl **risen**

rit *3 sg contr pres of* **ride** *v*

rive *v* stab Mch 1236+

river *n* river Kn 3024+; river-
bank (used for hawking)
Fkl 1196; hawking WB 884,
Th 737

robbour *n* robber Mk 2628+

rode *n* complexion Mil 3317+
rody *adj* ruddy, red Sq 385+
rogh *adj* (see also **rough, rowe**)
   rough Mil 3738
roghte *past of* **recche** *v and*
   rekke *v*
rolle *v* (see also **roule**) roll
   GP 201, Kn 2614; revolve,
   turn over Sum 2217+
romble *v* (see also **rumble**)
   make a rumbling noise
   Mk 2535
rome *v* roam, wander about
   Kn 1065+, *refl* Fkl 843; make
   o's way Mil 3694
rong *sg past of* **ringe** *v*
ronne(n) *pl past and p ppl of*
   renne *v*
rood *sg past of* **ride** *v*
roos *sg and pl past of* **rise** *v*
rooste *v* roast GP 147+; *sg past*
   rosted; *p ppl* **ro(o)sted**
roote *n* root GP 434+; foot (of
   mountain) Cl 58; position of
   the heavens at a specific
   moment in time (used as a
   basis for astrological calculations) ML 314 (see n.),
   Fkl 1276 (see n.)
rore *v* roar Kn 2881+
rosted *sg past and p ppl of*
   rooste *v*
rote *n* rote; *by* ~ by heart
   GP 327+
roten *adj* rotten Rv 3873+
rough *adj* (see also **rogh, rowe**)
   rough Fri 1622
roule *v* (see also **rolle**):
   ~ *aboute* roam, gad about
   WB 653
round(e) *adv* loudly Pard 331;
   gently, easily Th 886

roune *v* (see also **rowne**) whisper
   Fri 1572
route *n* company, band, train
   GP 622, Kn 889+
route *v* snore Mil 3647, Rv
   4167+
routhe *n* pity Kn 2392+; pitiful
   sight Cl 562; *it was* ~ it was
   pitiable Kn 914+; *make* ~
   lament Rv 4200
rowe *adj* (see also **rogh, rough**)
   rough, savage CY 861
rowm *adj* roomy Rv 4126+
rowne *v* (see also **roune**) whisper
   WB 241+; tell Th 835
royaltee *n* (see also **realtee**)
   pomp, magnificence
   ML 418, 703
rubible *n* (see also **ribible**)
   rebeck, two-stringed fiddle Mil
   3331 (see n.)
rude *adj* rough, coarse, uncultivated WB 1172, Cl 750+;
   uneducated Mil 3227
rudeliche, rudely *adv* coarsely
   GP 734; untidily Cl 380
ruful *adj* (see also **rewful**) sad
   Kn 2886
ruine *n* toppling, falling
   Kn 2463, Mel 1564
rule *v* (see also **reule**) rule
   Kn 1672; *refl* ~ *after* be guided
   by/according to Cl 327,
   Pars 592
rumbel *n* (see also **rumbul**)
   rumble, murmur Kn 1979
rumble *v* (see also **romble**) make
   a rumbling noise CY 1322
rumbul *n* (see also **rumbel**)
   rumour Cl 997
rym *n* rhyme ML 96, WB 1127+
ryme *v* rhyme, versify Kn 1459+

sad *adj* satiated, weary CY 877;
steadfast, firm, settled, constant Cl 602, 754, 1047, Mcp
275+; unshaken, steady Cl
552, 693; sober, serious Cl
220, 237, 1002, Mch 1399+;
dignified, grave Kn 2985,
ML 135; sure, reliable
Mcp 258

sadly *adv* firmly, closely
Kn 2602, Sum 2264; tightly Cl
1100; heavily ML 743; seriously, soberly Sh 76; steadfastly, resolutely Mel 1222,
Pars 124

sadnesse *n* steadfastness, constancy Cl 452; seriousness,
soberness Mch 1591+

sal *1/3 sg pres of* shal *v* shall
(Northern form) Rv 4043+

sal armoniak *n* ammonium chloride CY 798+

salewe, salue *v* salute, greet
Kn 1492+

salvacioun *n* (see also savacioun)
salvation Mch 1677; preservation Mel 1171

sangwyn *adj* sanguine (one of
the four 'complexions')
GP 333; ruddy Kn 2168; as *n*
red (cloth) GP 439

sapience *n* wisdom WB 1197+;
pl kinds of intelligence SN 338

sarmon *n* (see also sermon) sermon Mel 1044

sauf *adj* (see also save) safe,
secure ML 343+; saved Fri
1500; ~ *your grace* with
respect Mel 1688

saufly *adv* safely, confidently
WB 878+

saugh *sg past of* se(e) *v*

sautrye *n* (see also sawtrye) psaltery, a kind of zither GP 296
(see n.) +

savacioun *n* (see also salvacioun)
salvation WB 621+

save *n* a decoction of herbs
Kn 2713, Sq 639

save *adj* (see also sauf): ~ *your
grace* with respect Mel 1070+

save *v* save Kn 2563+; protect
Cl 441, Mel 1026+; preserve
Cl 1089, Sq 531, Fkl 1478;
keep Phys 200; ward off
Pars 1047

save *prep* except GP 683,
Kn 1410+

save *conj* except (that) WB 998+

saving(e) *prep* except Kn 2838+;
without prejudice to Mch
1766+

savour *n* taste, savour Sum
2196+; smell, aroma Kn 2938,
Sum 2226+

savoure *v* taste WB 171+; relish
Pars 829

saw *1–3 sg past of* se(e) *v*

sawe *n* saw, saying Kn 1163+;
speech Kn 1526, CY 691+

sawe *1/3 sg and pl past of* se(e) *v*

sawtrye *n* (see also sautrye) psaltery, a kind of zither Mcp 268

say *1/3 sg past of* se(e) *v*

saye *v* (see also seye) say, tell
GP 70+

sayen *pl past of* se(e) *v*

sayn *p ppl of* se(e) *v*

scape *v* escape Kn 1107+

scarsitee *n* parsimony Mel 1600;
scarcity CY 1393

scarsly *adv* scarcely, with difficulty Sh 228+; frugally GP 583

scathe *n* a pity GP 446, Cl 1172

science *n* knowledge, learning
GP 316+; craft, skill CY 721+;
branch of learning Pri 476

sclaundre *n* (evil) report Cl
722+; slander, disgrace Sh
183+

sclaundre *v* slander CY 695+

sclendre *adj* (see also **sklendre**)
slender, thin GP 587

scole *n* school Pri 495+; school,
fashion GP 125, Mil 3329;
'the schools', university
WB 528, Fri 1277, Sum
2186+; *~-termes* school-terms,
learned formulae Mch 1569;
~-matere questions for scholastic debate Fri 1272

scoler *n* scholar GP 260+

scoleye *v* study GP 302, WB 44f

scrippe *n* small bag, knapsack
Sum 1737+

seche *n* (see also **seke**) seek,
search for WB 909; explore
ML 521; pursue CY 1442; *was
nat longe for to ~* didn't have
to be requested for long
GP 784

secree *n* secret, private affairs
Mel 1141, Mk 2021+; secrets
Fri 1341+; mystery CY 1447

secree *adj* secret, secretive Mch
1937; secret, concealed
Fkl 1109+; hidden, mysterious
Sum 1871; discreet, close-
mouthed, reticent WB 946+;
private SN 178; *~ places* private parts Pars 576

secre(e)ly *adv* secretly Cl 763+;
discreetly Mel 1143+

secte *n* sect, faith Sq 17; sex
Cl 1171

seculer *n* layman NP 3450+

seculer *adj* secular, lay Mch
1251+

see *n* sea GP 276+

se(e) *v* see GP 831+; watch over,
protect ML 156+; inspect Sh
66; *lat ~* show Kn 3083; let it
be seen, let us see Mil 3116+;
1/3 sg past saugh, saw(e), say,
seigh, sey, sy; *2 sg past* saw; *pl
past* sawe, say(en), sey, syen;
p ppl sayn, se(e)ne, seighen,
seye, ysene, (y)seyn

seek *adj* (see also **sik**) sick, ill
GP 18

seet *sg past of* **sitte** *v*

seeth *sg past of* **sethe** *v*

seidestow *contr of* **seidest thow**

seigh *sg past of* **se(e)** *v*

seighen *p ppl of* **se(e)** *v*

seil(l)e *v* sail Fkl 851+

seind *p ppl of* **senge** *v* grilled
NP 2845

seinte *adj* holy Kn 1721, SN
553+; *~ Trinitee* the holy
Trinity Sum 1824

seintuarye *n* sanctuary, church
Pars 781; relic, sacred object
Pard 953

seke *v* (see also **seche**) seek, go
in quest of GP 13+; search for
WB 650+; explore, search
ML 127+; examine, consult
Co 4404, ML 60, NP 3136+;
to seken to be sought for CY
874; *~ aboute* find out, settle
Pri 443; *~ after* search for
Kn 1266; *~ upon* attack Fri
1494; *to seken up and down*
however far one searched
Kn 2587+; *past* so(u)ghte;
p ppl soght

selde *adv* seldom Kn 1539+

self *adj* self-same Kn 2584+;
very ML 115; *weak sg* selve

sely *adj* simple, innocent, poor
Mil 3404+; blessed WB 132

semblable *adj* similar, like Mch
1500+

sembla(u)nt *n* semblance, appearance Cl 928+; *make* ~ allow to
appear Mel 1149; make a
show (of), pretend Mel 1687+

seme *v* seem, appear GP 39+;
hem semed it seemed to them
(that) Sq 56

semely *adj* beautiful, lovely,
handsome Kn 1960+; fine
GP 751

semely *adv* becomingly, properly
GP 123, 136; pleasingly
GP 151

sende *3 sg past of* sende *v*

sene *p ppl of* se(e) *v*; *as adj* visible GP 134, Kn 2298+

senge *v* singe WB 349; *p ppl*
seind

sengle *adj* single Mch 1667+

sensualitee *n* bodily nature, the
faculty governing the senses
Pars 261+

sent *3 sg contr pres of* sende *v*

sentence *n* sense, significance
Mch 2288; (serious) meaning,
subject, teaching GP 798+; subject Pri 563, NP 3214+; content, substance Phys 157,
Mel 946+; judgement, decision
Kn 2532+; opinion, way of
thinking Kn 3002+; maxim,
saying ML 113+; text Fri
1518; wisdom NP 3350; *heigh*
~ great wisdom GP 306, Mch
1507, Mk 2748

sepulture *n* burial Kn 2854+;
tomb Pard 558+

serche *v* explore Mel 1407;
scour WB 867

sergeant *n* servant Cl 519+; city
officer SN 361; ~ *of the lawe*
serjeant at law, member of a
superior order of barristers
GP 309 (see n.)

sermon *n* (see also sarmon) sermon Sum 1789; *pl* writings
ML 87

sermoning *vbl n* talk, speech Mil
3597+; lecturing Kn 3091

servage *n* servitude, bondage
Kn 1946+

serve *v* serve GP 187+; deal
with, act by Kn 963, Cl 640+;
~ *of* be of use for Mcp 339;
served his entente furthered his
purpose Sq 521

servisable *adj* willing to serve,
attentive GP 99+

servitute *n* servitude Cl 798+

seso(u)n *n* season GP 19+

set *p ppl of* sette *v* seated
Kn 2528+; set GP 132+; *at day*
~ on the appointed day Cl 774

set *3 sg contr pres of* sette *v*

sete *n* seat Kn 2580+

seten *pl past and p ppl of* sitte *v*

sethe *v* boil, stew GP 383+; *sg
past* seeth; *p ppl* sode(n)

sette *v* set, place GP 132+; put
GP 507+; seat GP 748+;
arrange GP 815+; cast Cl 233;
adorn Cl 382; estimate, value
(at the rate of) Kn 1570, Mil
3756+; *refl* seat o.s. Kn 1541+;
sette him up sat up Mil 3819;
~ *cas* put the case, assume for
the sake of argument

Mel 1491+; *sette* (o's) *entente*
(*on*) set (o's) heart on, be completely devoted to Fri 1374+;
pay attention (to), take care
(to) Pars 314, 931; ~ (s.o's)
cappe make a fool of (s.o.)
GP 586+; ~ (s.o's) *howve*
make (s.o.) look ridiculous,
mock (s.o.) Rv 3911; ~ *a-werk*
set to work Co 4337; *yset in*
grounded in Cl 409; *3 sg contr
pres* set; *sg past* sette; *pl past*
sette(n); *p ppl* (y)set

seur *adj* sure Mel 1452+

seuretee *n* (see also **suretee**)
pledge, surety Kn 1604+;
security ML 243+; safe-
guard, source of security
Pard 937; confidence
Pars 735

sewe *v* follow Mel 1429+

sextein *n* sexton or sacristan
(officer of a religious house
who looks after buildings,
ornaments, vestments, etc)
Sum 1859+

sey *sg past of* se(e) *v*

seye *v* (see also **saye**) say, tell
GP 178+; *be for to* ~ mean, signify Mil 3605+

seye *p ppl of* se(e) *v*

seyn *p ppl of* se(e) *v*; *inf of*
seye *v*

seystow *contr of* seyest thow
Kn 1125+

seyth *3 sg pres of* seye *v*

shadde *sg past of* shede *v*

shal *v* must, be obliged to
GP 792, 853, Kn 1391+; (as
an auxiliary used to form the
future tense) shall, will
Kn 2764, ML 98, WB 177+;

(with ellipsis of verb of
motion) shall/must go
ML 279, Fri 1636+. Special
uses of *sholde*: (1) in formation of future in the past:
would GP 249, 689, Kn 2078,
2662, ML 587, Cl 247+; was
to Cl 261, Mk 2701,
NP 3142+; was about to Pri
658+; (2) modal uses: in conditional sentences (expressed
or implied) would GP 648,
Sum 1944, Fkl 775, Phys
145+; meaning 'should, ought
to' GP 184, Mil 3454, Rv
3966, ML 44+; meaning 'were
to' Kn 1170, Cl 245, Sq 40,
Fkl 931, Pard 451+; meaning
'was likely to' GP 249; meaning 'was about to' Kn 1980;
(in questions) should
Kn 1967+; is likely to ML 337;
1/3 sg pres shal; *2 sg pres*
shalt; *pl pres* shal, shulle(n),
shul(n); *sg pres subj* shul; *1/3
sg past* sholde; *2 sg past* sholdest; *pl past* sholde(n)

shaltow *contr of* shalt thow

shame *v* make ashamed
ML 101+

shap *n* shape Kn 1889+; figure
Mk 2254

shape *v* create WB 139, Cl 903;
contrive, devise Mil 3403,
ML 210+; bring about, ensure
Kn 2541, Mch 1632+; prepare
ML 249, Mch 1408+; form Th
700+; decree, destine, ordain
Kn 1225+; determine
Kn 1108+; appoint, allot
ML 253; direct Cl 783; *refl* set
o.s., get ready, prepare

GP 772+; determine, plan
ML 142, Fri 1538+; take steps
Mel 1607; *sg past* **shoop;** *pl
past* **shopen;** *p ppl* **shape(n),
yshape(n)**

sharp *adj* sharp GP 114+; fierce,
violent Kn 1287+; rough,
jagged Kn 1978; unpleasant
Co 4328

sharp *adv* sharply Kn 2549+

sharply *adv* peremptorily
GP 523, Cl 1192+

shave *p ppl* shaven GP 588+

shawe *n* copse, wood Co 4367,
Fri 1386

shede *v* shed Mk 2257; fall Mk
2731; ~ (o's) *nature* emit seminal fluid Pars 577; *sg past*
shadde, shedde

sheeld *n* shield Kn 2122+; *écu*
GP 278 (see n.), Sh 331 (see
n.) +

sheene *adj* (see also **shene**)
beautiful Kn 972

sheete *v* (see also **shete**) shoot
Rv 3928

shende *v* destroy, ruin Co 4410,
ML 927+; injure, damage
Kn 2754+; *be* (y)*shent* suffer,
be punished Fri 1312, Pri 541;
3 sg contr pres **shent;** *p ppl*
(y)shent

shene *adj* (see also **sheene**)
bright, shining GP 115+;
beautiful, fair, radiant
Kn 1068+

shent *3 contr pres sg and p ppl
of* **shende** *v*

shepne *n* (see also **shipne**) shippen, cattle-shed Kn 2000

shere *n* shears, scissors
Kn 2417+; *pl* **sheres, sheris**

shere *v* shear Mk 2067; *p ppl*
shore, yshorn

sherte *n* shirt Kn 1566,
WB 1186+

shet *p ppl of* **shette** *v*

shete *v* (see also **sheete**) shoot
Pars 574+

shette *v* shut, close Kn 2597,
Mil 3499+; close, fasten up
ML 1056, SN 517; *sg and pl
past* **shette;** *p ppl* **shet, yshette**

shewe *v* show Kn 2677+;
explain, expound Kn 2536, Cl
90+; declare, express Phys
179, Pri 459; appear, seem
Mel 1196; appear, be revealed
Pars 330+; *refl* show o.s. CY
916+; ~ *confessioun* make confession Sum 2093

shifte *v* apportion, distribute
WB 104; assign SN 278

shilde *v* prevent, forbid Mil
3427+; protect Mch 1787+

shine *n* shin GP 386+

shipman *n* sailor GP 388+

shipne *n* (see also **shepne**)
shippen, cattle-shed
WB 871

sho *n* (see also **shoo**) shoe
GP 253+

shode *n* crown of the head
Kn 2007; parting (of hair)
Mil 3316

sholde *1/3 sg past of* **shal** *v*

sholde(n) *pl past of* **shal** *v*

sholdest *2 sg past of* **shal** *v*

shoo *n* (see also **sho**) shoe Mil
3318+; *pl* shoes, **shoon**

shoon *sg past of* **shine** *v*

shoop *sg past of* **shape** *v*

shopen *pl past of* **shape** *v*

shore *p ppl of* **shere** *v*

shorte *v* shorten GP 791+

shortly *adv* briefly, in short
GP 30+; quickly, in a short
time Kn 2052, Mil 3636

shot *n* missile, arrow Kn 2544,
NP 3349

shot-windowe *n* casement
window Mil 3358+

shour *n* shower Mil 3520+

shove *p ppl* driven, moved away
Fkl 1281

shrewe *n* rascal, villain, wretch
Rv 3907+; shrew Mch 1222+

shrewe *v* curse WB 446+

shrewed *adj* wicked WB 54+

shrewednesse *n* wickedness,
maliciousness WB 734+

shrift(e) *n* confession Sum
1818+; profession of faith
SN 277

shrighte *past* shrieked, cried
Kn 2817+

shrive *v refl and passive* be confessed, make confession
GP 226+; *p ppl* **shriven,
yshrive(n)**

shul *pl pres and sg pres subj of*
shal *v*

shulder *n* shoulder Kn 2163+; *pl*
shuldres

shulder-bo(o)n *n* shoulder-bone
Pard 350+

shulle(n), shuln *pl pres of* **shal** *v*

sib *adj* related, of kin
Mel 1375+

side *n* side GP 112+; part
SN 475

sighte *past of* **sike** *v*

signe *n* sign, token GP 226+;
'one of the twelve equal dimen-
sions of the zodiac' (*OED*)
Kn 2462+

sik *n* sigh Kn 1920, Sq 498

sik *adj* (see also **seek**) sick, ill
GP 245+: *for ~* for illness
WB 394

sike *v* sigh Kn 1540+; *past*
sighte, siked

siker *adj* sure Kn 3049+; safe
Mch 1390+; steady Sum 2069;
firm Mch 1708; dependable,
reliable Mel 1374+

siker *adv* surely WB 465+

sikerlik, sikerly *adv* certainly,
assuredly, for certain GP 137,
Cl 184+

sikernesse *n* security, stability
ML 425+

similitude *n* counterpart, equal
Mil 3228, Sq 480; description
SN 431

simonye *n* simony, 'the practice
of buying or selling ecclesiastical preferments, benefices, or
emoluments' (*OED*)
Fri 1309+

sin *prep and conj* since
GP 853+; *~ that* since (the
time when) GP 601+; since,
because, seeing that
Kn 1273+

singe *v* sing GP 236+; crow Rv
4233; squeal, cry out Fri
1311+; *1/3 sg past* **sang,
so(o)ng**; *2 sg past* **songe**; *pl
past* **songe(n)**; *3 sg past subj*
songe; *p ppl* **songe(n), ysonge**

singuler *adj* single, individual
CY 997, Pars 300; *~ persone*
private individual Mel 1435

sinke *v* sink Kn 951+; *sg past*
sank; *p ppl* **sonken**

sire *n* master GP 355, WB 713+;
father Rv 4246+

sirurgien *n* surgeon Mel 1005+

sit *3 sg contr pres of* **sitte** *v*

sith *adv* (see also **sitthe**) since, afterwards Rv 3893+

sithe *n* time GP 485+; *ofte ~* often Kn 1877+

sithen *adv* afterwards Kn 2617+; ago: *go(on) ~ many a day/ many yeres* long ago Kn 1521, Sq 536

sith(en) (that) *conj* since Kn 930+

sitte *v* sit GP 94+; befit, be suitable for (*with dat*) Mch 2315+; *it sit wel* it is befitting, right Mch 1277; *ivele it sit* it is improper, wrong Cl 460; *3 sg contr pres* **sit**; *sg past* **sat**, **seet**; *pl past* **seten**; *p ppl* **seten**

sitthe *adv* (see also **sith**) afterwards Mk 2723

sixte *adj* sixth WB 45+

skile *n* reason, justice Mel 1810; reasoning, argument Sq 205, Mel 1870; *~ (it) is/was* it is/was reasonable, proper ML 708+

skilful *adj* reasonable, rational ML 1038+

skippe *v* skip, gambol Mil 3259; spring, leap Mch 1672, Fkl 1402+; pass Pars 361

sklendre *adj* (see also **sclendre**) slender, slight Cl 1198+; scanty NP 2833

slake *v* fail Cl 137; weaken, tire Cl 705+; abate Fkl 841; decrease Cl 802; relieve Cl 1107

slakke *adj* slack Mch 1849; slow, tardy Kn 2901, Sh 413

sle(e) *v* slay, kill GP 63+; pierce Kn 1118, Fkl 893+; destroy ML 301; extinguish Mk 2732; *3 sg pres* **sleeth**; *sg past* **slough**, **slow**; *pl past* **slowe**; *p ppl* **slawe(n)**, **(y)slain**, **yslawe**

sleep *sg past of* **slepe** *v*

sleepe *pl past of* **slepe** *v*

sleigh *adj* (see also **sly(e)**) shrewd, clever Mil 3201; cunning, wily Rv 3940

sleighly *adv* (see also **slyly**) secretly Kn 1444; cunningly, stealthily Sum 1994

sleighte *n* (see also **slighte**) cunning, trickery GP 604+; trick, stratagem Mch 2126+; cleverness, intellectual ingenuity Kn 1948, Rv 4050+; ingenuity, skill Cl 1102

slepe *v* sleep GP 10+; *sg past* **sleep**, **slepte**; *pl past* **sleepe**, **slepen**

slepestow *contr of* **slepest thow**

slewthe *n* (see also **slouthe**) sloth, laziness Pars 388

slide *v* slide, slip (away) Cl 82+; pass away Fkl 924; *3 sg contr pres* **slit**

slighte *n* (see also **sleighte**) cunning, trickery Phys 131

slik *adj* (see also **swilk**) such (Northern form) Rv 4170+

slit *3 sg contr pres of* **slide** *v*

slogardye *n* slothfulness, laziness Kn 1042+

slough *n* (see also **slow**) slough, mire NP 2798

slough *sg past of* **sle(e)** *v*

slouthe *n* (see also **slewthe**) sloth, laziness ML 530+

slow *n* (see also **slough**) slough, mire Fri 1563+

slow *sg past of* **sle(e)** *v*

slowe *pl past of* **sle(e)** *v*

sly(e) *adj* (see also **sleigh**) clever, cunning Sq 672+; wily, deceitful Mch 1786+; skilful Mch 1692, Sq 230; insidious, subtle SN 10; *as n* rogue Mil 3392

slyly *adv* (see also **sleighly**) secretly, stealthily Pard 792+

smal *adj* slender Mil 3234, WB 261, Cl 380+; narrow GP 329, NP 2905; thin NP 3308; little, small GP 9+; trivial WB 952+; fine GP 158, Pars 197; weak, thin GP 688; high-pitched Mil 3360; lowly Mch 1625

smal(e) *adv* finely Mil 3245+; little WB 592+; in close-fitting clothes Mil 3320

smert *adj* stinging Kn 2225; bitter, keen, severe Kn 2392, 2766, Sq 480+; hot CY 768

smert(e) *n* pain Mil 3813, Mk 2606+

smerte *adv* sharply, severely GP 149, Cl 629, Pard 413

smerte *v impers* give pain, hurt GP 230, 534, Mk 2713+; *him/ me* ~ he/I suffer(ed) GP 230+; *personal* suffer, feel pain Sum 2092+; *3 sg pres subj* **smerte**; *past* **smerte**

smite *v* strike Kn 1220+; ~ *of* cut off Phys 226+; *3 sg contr pres* **smit**; *sg past* **smoot**; *p ppl* **smiten**

smok *n* smock, shift Mil 3238+

smoot *sg past of* **smite** *v*

snibbe *v* rebuke, reprimand GP 523+

snowte *n* snout Sh 405+

so *adv* so GP 55+; to such an extent GP 11+; in such a way GP 31+; such (a) GP 88, Kn 907+; ~ *as* as GP 39+; *if* ~ *be/were, if* ~ *falle* if it is/were the case Kn 1211+; in asseverations: ~ *have I joye or blis* on my hope of bliss WB 830; ~ *moote I ride or go,* ~ *moot I goon* as I live Sum 1942, Fkl 777; ~ *thee'ch/thee'k/moot I thee* as I may prosper Rv 3864, WB 361+; introducing a wish Mch 2253

so (that) *conj* provided that Kn 2237, WB 125+

sobre *adj* sober, grave, serious ML 97+; sober, temperate Sum 1902+

socour *n* succour, help Kn 918+

sodein *adj* sudden ML 421+

sodeinliche, sodeinly *adv* suddenly Kn 1118+; without delay, directly Mch 1409, Mel 1009+

sode(n) *p ppl of* **sethe** *v*

softe *adj* soft GP 153+; weak, gentle Phys 101; *a* ~ *paas* slowly, calmly Mil 3760+

softe *adv* gently Kn 1021+; quietly Kn 1773, Mil 3649+; unobtrusively Mil 3410; peacefully Sh 93; comfortably Mch 1947

softely *adv* quietly Cl 323+; stealthily Rv 4058+; gently Sq 636; calmly Pri 672; slowly Th 886; tenderly SN 408; comfortably Pars 835

soght *p ppl of* **seke** *v*

soghte *past of* **seke** *v*

soj(o)urne *v* stay, dwell
ML 148+

sola(a)s *n* comfort Pars 206+;
pleasure, delight, fun Mil
3200+; entertainment GP 798;
powers of entertaining Mil
3335; relief Th 782

solempne *adj* sumptuous, splendid, ceremonious ML 387, Cl
1125, Sq 61; festive Sq 111;
formal, ritual Pars 102+;
important GP 364; cheerful/
dignified (punning) GP 209

solempnely *adv* ceremoniously,
with pomp, splendidly
ML 317+; imposingly, with
dignity GP 274; earnestly
SN 272

solempnitee *n* ceremony, festivity, pomp Kn 870+; celebra-
tion Phys 244

som *adj and pron* some
GP 640+; ~ . . . ~ one . . .
another Kn 1255+; *al and* ~
the long and the short of it
Kn 2761+; *alle and some* one
and all Kn 2187+; *pl* **som(m)e**

somdel *adv* somewhat, rather
GP 174+; partly Kn 2170; in
some degree Rv 3911

somme *n* sum (of money)
Fkl 1220+

somnour *n* 'an officer who summoned delinquents before the
ecclesiastical courts' (Skeat)
GP 543+

som(o)ne *v* summon Fri 1347+;
encourage, invite
Mel 1462, 2662

somtime *adv* sometimes Mil

3332+; once, at one time
GP 65+; at a certain time,
occasionally Kn 1668; at some
time, one day Kn 3024,
ML 110+

sond *n* sand Mil 3748+

sonde *n* message ML 388+; messenger SN 525; sending Sh 219;
what is sent, dispensation, ordinance ML 523+

sondry *adj* various, different
GP 14+

sone *n* son GP 79+

sone *adv* (see also **soone**)
straightway Mil 3150,
CY 1289

songe *2 sg past, pl past, 3 sg
past subj and p ppl of* **singe** *v*

songen *pl past and p ppl of*
singe *v*

sonken *p ppl of* **sinke** *v*

sonne *n* sun GP 7+

soone *adv* (see also **sone**) speedily, without delay Kn 1022+;
straightway Pars 61; soon
Kn 1467+

so(o)ng *1/3 sg past of* **singe** *v*

soor *adj* severe, grievous
Kn 1755+; painful, suffering
Kn 2804; bitter ML 758;
aching Kn 2220+

soor(e) *n* suffering, torment
Kn 1454+; disease Pard 358

soore *adv* (see also **sore**) painfully GP 230+; severely
Kn 1115+; bitterly GP 148+;
deeply Kn 1518+; vigorously
Rv 4229+; hard, earnestly Sum
1784+; seriously NP 3109; ill
Cl 85

soote *adj* (see also **swo(o)te**)
sweet GP 1+

sooth *n* (see also **sothe**) truth
GP 284+

sooth *adj* true Mil 3391+; truthful Sq 21; *as adv* truly
Kn 1521+; *pl* **sothe**

soothfastnesse *n* (see also **sothfastnesse**) truth
Mel 1175+; truthfulness, loyalty Cl 934

soothly *adv* truly GP 117+

sop *n* piece of bread dipped in wine GP 334, Mch 1843

sope(e)r *n* supper, evening meal GP 348, Fkl 1189+

sophime *n* sophism, question of logic Cl 5; sophistry Sq 554

sore *adv* (see also **soore**) painfully, severely Kn 1394+; bitterly WB 632; deeply Mil 3462+

sort *n* (1) destiny, fate GP 844; casting of lots Pars 605

sort *n* (2) sort, kind Rv 4044; company, band ML 141

sorwe *n* sorrow Kn 951+; *with ~* curse him Co 4412; bad luck to you WB 308; more's the pity NP 3253

sorwe *v* sorrow, grieve Kn 2652+

sorweful *adj* sorrowful Kn 1070+

sory *adj* painful Th 759; dismal Kn 2004+; sad, mournful Kn 2010+; sorry Mel 1879+; wretched ML 466+; *~ grace* misfortune WB 746; *with ~ grace* bad luck to you/him Pard 717+; *a ~ paas* with dejected steps Mil 3741

soster *n* (see also **suster**) sister Mil 3486

sothe *n* (see also **sooth**) truth GP 845+; *for ~* in truth GP 283+

sothe *pl of* **sooth** *adj*

sothfastnesse *n* (see also **soothfastnesse**) truth Cl 796+

sotilly *adv* (see also **subtilly**) cleverly, skilfully WB 956

soughte *past of* **seke** *v*

souke *v* (see also **sowke**) suck Cl 450+

soun *n* sound GP 674+

soupe *v* eat supper Rv 4146+

souple *adj* supple GP 203; compliant Mk 2500

sourde *v* arise Pars 448+

sours *n* source Cl 49; swift upward flight Sum 1938+

south *adj*: *~ line* the meridian, a notional line passing from north to south through the zenith (the point directly overhead any given location) Pars 2 (see n.)

soutiltee *n* (see also **subtil(i)tee**) trick WB 576; skill CY 1371

soverain, soverein *n* lord, sovereign Mel 1438+; superior CY 590

soverain, soverein *adj* excellent, outstanding GP 67+; principal, greatest Kn 1974+; supreme ML 1089, Fkl 1552+; highest, total Cl 112; supreme, unqualified Phys 136, Mel 1078+; sovereign WB 1048+

soverainetee, soverein(e)tee *n* supremacy, mastery WB 818, Cl 114+; lordly authority, rule Pars 774

sovereinly *adv* pre-eminently

NP 3362; handsomely
Mel 1272

sowdan *n* sultan ML 177+

sowdanesse *n* sultaness
ML 358+

sowed *p ppl* sewn GP 685+

sowke *v* (see also **souke**) suck
Rv 4157; squeeze out Co 4416

sowne *v* sound GP 565+; play
(instrument) Sq 270; harp on
GP 275; echo Sq 105; tend Mk
2158; ~ *in(to)* be consistent
with, tend towards, conduce to
GP 307, Sq 517+

space *n* (see also **espace**) time
GP 87, Kn 1896, Mil 3596+;
while Kn 2982+; leisure, opportunity GP 35, Sq 493+; length
ML 577; space, extent Rv
4124+; *the metes* ~ the course
of the meal ML 1014; *in time
and* ~ in due time SN 355;
heeld the ~ followed the custom GP 176

spak *1–3 sg past of* **speke** *v*

sparcle *n* (see also **sparkle**) spark
Th 905

spare *v* refrain, leave off
GP 192+; hold back Fri
1543+; omit, fail Kn 1396+;
spare, have mercy on
WB 421+; save Mch 1297;
refl hold (o.s.) aloof
Rv 3966

sparhauk(e) *n* sparrow-hawk Th
767+

sparkle *n* (see also **sparcle**) spark
Rv 3885

sparre *n* rafter, beam Kn 990+

sparwe *n* sparrow GP 626+

spece *n* (see also **espece**) species,
kind Kn 3013+

speche *n* speech GP 307+;
expression Mcp 205

special *adj* (see also **especial**)
special Pars 894+; particular
Mel 1355, Pars 488; *in* ~
specially, in particular
GP 444+; *descende to the* ~ get
down to detail Mel 1355

specially *adv* in particular
GP 15+; in detail Sh 343+;
specially Pars 894, 1044

spede *v* (see also **speede**) prosper, further, assist GP 769+;
accomplish Rv 4205+; be successful Mch 1632; hasten,
hurry Mil 3649+; *refl* make
haste, hurry Kn 1217, Mil
3562+; *foule ysped* come off
badly Rv 4220; *sg and pl imp*
speed; *sg and pl past* spedde;
p ppl (y)sped

spedily *adv* speedily Sh 252+

speed *sg and pl imp of* **spede** *v*

speede *v* (see also **spede**) be successful Phys 134

speeke *3 sg pres subj of* **speke** *v*

speeke(n) *pl past of* **speke** *v*

speere *n* sphere Fkl 1280+

speke *v* speak, talk, say
GP 142+; *3 sg pres subj*
speeke; *1–3 sg past* spak; *pl
past* speeke(n), speke; *p ppl*
spoke(n), yspoken

spere *n* spear GP 114+

spette *pl past of* **spitte** *v*

spice *n* spice Mch 1770+;
species, kind Pars 83+

spiced *p ppl* spiced Mil 3378;
fastidious, over-scrupulous
GP 526; *swete* ~ *conscience* see
n. to WB 435

spicerye *n* spices Kn 2935+

spille v die, perish Mil 3278+;
destroy, put to death WB 898,
ML 857+; ruin WB 388+;
waste Mcp 153; shed Pars 571;
let fall Pars 965; p ppl spilt

spitously adv sharply, vehemently Mil 3476; mercilessly
WB 223

spitte v spit Pard 421+; pl past
spette, spitte

spoke(n) p ppl of speke v

spore n spur GP 473+

sporne v stumble Rv 4280;
spurn, kick Sq 616

spousaille n wedding, marriage
Cl 115+

spouse v marry Cl 3+

sprede v spread Kn 2903+; sg
past spradde; p ppl (y)sprad,
yspred

spreind p ppl of springe v (2)

springe v (1) spring Kn 1871+;
(of day) dawn, break GP 822+;
grow, sprout Kn 2173+;
spread abroad Kn 1437+; ~ of
arise, originate from ML 889+;
sg past sprang, sprong; p ppl
spronge(n)

springe v (2) sprinkle, scatter
Kn 2169, ML 1183+; mingle
ML 422; p ppl (y)spreind

springing n source Cl 49; origin
Pars 322

sprong sg past of springe v (1)

spronge(n) p ppl of springe v (1)

squier n squire GP 79+

staat n (see also esta(a)t) state
GP 572

stal sg past of stele v

stalke n stalk Kn 1036+; piece of
straw Rv 3919; uprights (of a
ladder) Mil 3625

stalke v steal, move stealthily
Kn 1479+, refl Cl 525

stande v (see also stonde) stand
Mil 3677+; be, be the case Sh
114+; ~ in/on consist in Mch
2022, Pars 107+; 3 sg contr
pres stant

stape(n) p ppl advanced Mch
1514, NP 2821

starf sg past of sterve v

stark adj strong, robust Mch
1458; fierce Mk 2370

stature n height GP 83; build
Cl 257

statut n statute, law GP 327+;
obligation WB 198

staves pl of staf n staves, sticks
Kn 2510+

stede n place Mel 1090; in ~ of
instead of, in the place of
GP 231+; stande in ~ avail
Mel 1090

stedefast adj steadfast Cl 564+

sted(e)fastly adv steadfastly
WB 947+; firmly, in earnest
Cl 1094; resolutely
SN 474

sted(e)fastnesse n steadfastness,
constancy Cl 699+

steere n helm, rudder
ML 448, 833

steerne adj (see also sterne,
stierne) severe, grim Cl 465

stele v steal GP 562+; creep,
move stealthily Mil 3786+, refl
Pard 610; sg past stal; p ppl
stole(n), stoln

stente v (see also stinte) cease
Kn 903+; end Kn 2442; stop
Kn 1368; forbear Mk 2735; ~
of desist from Cl 734; sg past
stente; p ppl stent

stepe *adj* prominent
GP 201, 753

sterne *adj* (see also **steerne, stierne**) resolute, brave, bold
Kn 2154, 2441; terrible
Kn 2610

sterre *n* star GP 268+; ~ *of day*
the morning star ML 852

sterte *v* (see also **stirte**) leap,
spring Kn 952+; rush
NP 3047; start (from sleep)
Kn 1044+; plunge Kn 1514;
escape WB 573; quiver
Kn 1762; *refl* leap, spring
Kn 1579; *sg and pl past* **sterte**;
p ppl **ystert**

sterve *v* die, perish Kn 1144+; *sg*
past **starf**; *pl past* **storven**;
p ppl **ystorve**

stevene *n* (1) voice Kn 2562+;
tongue Sq 150

stevene *n* (2) appointment,
rendezvous Kn 1524+

stewe *n* (see also **stive**) brothel
Pard 465

stibourne *adj* obstinate, fierce
WB 456, 637

stierne *adj* (see also **steerne,**
sterne) stern, severe Pars 170

stif *adj* stiff Sum 2267; sturdy,
powerful GP 673

stike *v* stick, be embedded Rv
3877+; stab ML 430+; thrust
Kn 1565; spear Pard 556;
pierce Phys 211

stikke *n* stick Kn 2934+; paling
NP 2848

stille *adj* quiet, silent Kn 2535,
Cl 2+; still Mel 1219; undis-
turbed Cl 891, Fkl 1472+;
secret Mel 1146

stille *adv* quietly Kn 1003+;
silently WB 1034, Cl 293; still
Mil 3637, Rv 4199+; calmly
ML 720; secretly Cl 1077; constantly Cl 580, Pard 725

stille *v* calm, appease
Mel 1487, 1514

stinte *v* (see also **stente**) cease,
come to an end ML 413+;
stop, leave off Kn 2811+; stop,
put an end to Kn 2348+; stand
still Fri 1558; ~ *of* cease to
speak of Kn 1334+; desist
from, leave off Cl 703+; *p ppl*
(y)stint

stiropes *n pl* stirrups ML 1163+

stirte *v* (see also **sterte**) leap,
spring Mil 3824+; start (from
sleep) Cl 1060; rush NP 3377;
slip (in) Mch 2153; *sg past*
stirte; *pl past* **stirte(n)**; *p ppl*
stirt

stive *n* (see also **stewe**) brothel
Fri 1332

stiward *n* steward GP 579+

stode(n) *pl past of* **stonde** *v*

stole(n), stoln *p ppl of* **stele** *v*

stomak *n* appetite Sum 1847;
emotion, compassion
Fri 1441

stonde *v* (see also **stande**) stand
GP 88+; stand still Fri 1541;
be, be the case Kn 1322, Cl
346+; be left alone Sh 220; be
on view (as a prize) Th 741; ~
again withstand Fri 1488; ~ *at*
abide by GP 778+; ~ *by* make
good, validate WB 1015+; ~ *in*
consist in Pars 451; ~ *(un)to*
submit to Mil 3830, Pars 60+;
~ *in grace* be in, enjoy (s.o.'s)
favour GP 88+; *it stondeth nat*
aright matters are not well

Mil 3426; *sg past* **stood**; *pl past* **stode(n)**, **stoode(n)**

stongen *p ppl of* **stinge** *v*

stoon *n* stone GP 774+; jewel, precious stone GP 699+; ball, testicle NP 3448

stoor *n* livestock GP 598+; hoard, store Sum 2159, Cl 17; *telle* ~ *of* set store by, take account of WB 203+

storven *pl past of* **sterve** *v*

storye *n* history, legend GP 709, Kn 859+; story Sq 655, NP 3211

stot *n* farm-horse GP 615; bawd, whore Fri 1630

stounde *n* time WB 286; while Rv 4007; moment Cl 1098; *o* ~ *for an instant* Kn 1212; *in a* ~ at one time Rv 3992; in a short while ML 1021

stoupe *v* stoop Mch 2348+; bend down Fri 1560+

stout *adj* strong, powerful GP 545; brave, valiant Kn 2154; menacing Kn 2134

strange *adj* (see also **straunge**) distant, formal Sh 263

straughte *pl past of* **strecche** *v*

straunge *adj* (see also **strange**) foreign GP 13, 464, Kn 2718+; alien ML 700; stranger, of different family Cl 138, Mch 1440+; stranger, unknown Sq 89+; external, adventitious WB 1161; exotic Sq 67; *make it* ~ be fussy about Rv 3980; play hard to get, show reluctance Fkl 1223

straungenesse *n* estrangement Sh 386; rarity Pars 414

strawe *v* strew, cover the floor of Sq 613+

strecche *v* stretch, extend Kn 2916, *refl* Mel 1825+; *pl past* **straughte**

stree *n* straw Kn 2918+

streem *n* (see also **strem**) stream Rv 3895+; river ML 23+; current GP 402; ray, beam Kn 1495+; *pl* **stremes**

streight *adv* directly GP 671+; immediately Kn 1650; straight Mil 3316

streine *v* constrain, force Cl 144, NP 3244+; clasp, squeeze Mch 1753; press, strain Pard 538

streit *adj* narrow Kn 1984; strict, rigorous GP 174; confined, restricted in space Rv 4122; scanty Fri 1426+; *his streite swerd* his drawn sword NP 3357

streite *adv* tightly GP 457; strictly, securely Mch 2129

strem *n* (see also **streem**) stream, river GP 464; ray Mk 2754

strenger *comp adj* stronger Pard 825+

strengthe *n* strength GP 84+; force Kn 2399+; fortitude Pars 728; power Mk 2058

strepe *v* strip Kn 1006+

strete *n* street Kn 2902+

strif *n* strife, dissension, quarrel Kn 1187+

strive *v* strive, struggle Kn 1177+; vie, contend Kn 1038; *sg past* **stroof**

striving *n* striving Sum 1998; strife, quarrelling Pard 550+

strogle *v* (see also **strugle**) struggle Pard 829

strokes *pl of* **strook** *n*

strond *n* strand, shore ML 825+; country GP 13

strong *adj* strong GP 239+; powerful, mighty Kn 2373+; flagrant, out-and-out Pard 789; brazen Mch 2367; ~ *of* strong in, well provided with Phys 4, 135; *a ~ paas* a tight corner, a difficult situation Mel 1445

stroof *sg past of* **strive** *v*

strook *n* stroke, blow Kn 1701+; *pl* **strokes**

strugle *v* (see also **strogle**) struggle Mch 2374+

studye *n* study GP 303+; reverie Kn 1530

studye *v* study GP 184+; meditate Cl 5+; deliberate GP 841, Mch 1955; take pains Mel 1487; ~ *to* take thought for Pars 1090

sturdy *adj* sturdy Sum 1754; rebellious WB 612; stern, harsh Cl 698, 1049; *a ~ paas* with determined strides, at a great rate Sum 2162

subget *n* (see also **subgit**) subject Cl 482+

subget *adj* subject Pars 263+

subgit *n* (see also **subget**) subordinate Sum 1990

subjeccioun *n* subjection ML 270+; suggestion Pars 351

substa(u)nce *n* possessions, goods, wealth GP 489+; raw material, capacity NP 2803; substance, 'that which under-

lies phenomena' (*OED*) (*phil*) Pard 539

subtil *adj* slender, fine Kn 2030; cunningly made, intricate Kn 1054; skilful Kn 2049, Fkl 1141; cunning Phys 141+; subtle, clever Mil 3275, ML 213+; secret, covert Cl 737, Sq 285+; oblique, devious Mch 1767

subtil(i)tee *n* (see also **soutiltee**) trickery Fri 1420+; cunning, treachery Cl 691, Sq 140+; cleverness, sagacity Sum 2290; skill NP 3319, CY 620+; lore, mumbo-jumbo CY 844

subtilly *adv* (see also **sotilly**) cunningly, cleverly GP 610+; skilfully WB 499+; subtly Mel 1311; surreptitiously Mch 2003; artfully Mch 2274+; treacherously Sum 1995+; insidiously Pard 565

suffisantly *adv* adequately Mel 1302+

suffisa(u)nce *n* sufficiency, competence GP 490+; satisfaction, contentment NP 2839+; *worldly* ~ source of contentment in this world Cl 759

suffisa(u)nt *adj* sufficient, adequate Kn 1631+; competent, capable Cl 960, Mch 1458+; satisfactory WB 910+; appropriate Mel 1032

suffise *v* suffice, be adequate Rv 4125+; satisfy WB 1235; *impers* be enough Kn 1953+; *suffiseth thee/him* it is enough for you/him Mil 3549+; ~ *unto* satisfy Mch 1999

suffra(u)nce *n* patience,

forbearance Cl 1162, Fkl 788+; endurance Pars 1056; permission, licence Pars 625

suffre *v* allow GP 649+; submit to Cl 537+; suffer, endure Kn 1219+; forbear Mel 1217+

suggestioun *n* charge Mk 2417; prompting, temptation Pars 331+

suite *n* (see also **sute**): *of the same ~* of the same cloth Kn 2873

superfluitee *n* superfluity, excess GP 436+; excess, extravagance Pard 471+

suppose *v* believe, think (with a stronger emphasis on believing than in *modE*) Sum 1791+; imagine, conceive WB 786

supposing(e) *n* supposition Mel 1402; assumption CY 873; belief, opinion; *to my ~* as I believe Cl 1041

suretee *n* (see also **seuretee**) certainty, assurance WB 903; security WB 911

surplis *n* surplice Mil 3323+

surquid(r)ye *n* presumptuousness, over-ambition Pars 403; over-confidence Pars 1067

suspecioun *n* suspicion ML 682+

suspect *n* suspicion Phys 263; *have in ~* be suspicious of Mel 1195+; *be in ~ of* be suspicious of Cl 905

sustena(u)nce *n* means of subsistence, livelihood Co 4422; sustenance, nourishment Sum 1844+

sustene *v* sustain, support Kn 1993+; endure ML 847+

suster *n* (see also **soster**) sister Kn 871+

sute *n* (see also **suite**): *be of the same ~* match, be of the same cloth Mil 3242

swa *adv* so (Northern form) Rv 4030+

swain *n* servant Rv 4027; youth Th 724

swal *sg past of* **swelle** *v*

swappe *v* strike Cl 586, SN 366; drop Cl 1099; *sg imp* **swap**; *sg past* **swapte**

swatte *sg past of* **swete** *v*

sweete *adj* (see also **swete**) sweet GP 5+; alluring GP 265

swelte *v* faint Mch 1776; grow faint Kn 1356, Mil 3703; *sg past* **swelte**

swelwe *v* (see also **swolwe**) swallow Cl 1188

swerd *n* sword GP 112+

swere *v* swear GP 454+; *althogh he hadde it sworn* although he had sworn the contrary WB 640; *sg past* **swoor**; *pl past* **swore(n)**; *p ppl* (y)**swore**, (y)**sworn**

swering(e) *n* swearing Pard 631+

swete *adj* (see also **sweete**) sweet Kn 2427+

swete *adv* sweetly Mil 3305+

swete *v* sweat Mil 3702+; *sg past* **swatte**

swetnesse *n* sweetness Pri 555+

swevene *n* dream Mk 2740+

swich *adj and pron* such GP 3+

swilk *adj* (see also **slik**) such (Northern form) Rv 4130+

swin *n* swine GP 598; pig, hog ML 745+; boar Fkl 1254

swink *n* labour, toil GP 188+

swinke *v* labour, toil GP 186+; produce by labour SN 21; *p ppl* **swonken, yswonke**

swithe *adv* quickly, with all speed ML 730+; *as ~* at once, without delay, in a trice ML 637+;

swive *v* lay, fuck Mil 3850+

swogh *n* (see also **swough** *n* (2)) sigh Mil 3619

swolwe *v* (see also **swelwe**) swallow Mel 1618+

swonken *p ppl of* **swinke** *v*

swoor *sg past of* **swere** *v*

swo(o)te *adj* (see also **soote**) sweet Kn 2860+

swore, sworn *p ppl of* **swere** *v*

swore(n) *pl past of* **swere** *v*

swough *n* (1) (see also **swow**) swoon WB 799+

swough *n* (2) (see also **swogh**) sough, sighing sound Kn 1979

swow *n* (see also **swough** *n* (1)) swoon Sq 476+

swowne *v* faint Kn 913+

swowning(e) *n* swoon, faint Cl 1080+

sy *sg past of* **se(e)** *v*

syen *pl past of* **se(e)** *v*

taa *v* take (Northern form) Rv 4129+

taak *imp of* **take** *v*

taas *n* heap, pile Kn 1005+

table *n* table GP 100+; (writing)-tablet Kn 1305, Sum 1741+; (astronomical) table Fkl 1273 (see n.); *be at ~* be a lodger CY 1015; *pl* backgammon Fkl 900, Pars 793

tail(l)age *n* tax, forced levy Pars 567, 752

taille *n* tally, a scored wooden stick kept by a creditor as a record of sums owing GP 570, Sh 416 (see n.)

take *v* take GP 34+; capture Kn 1866+; place Kn 1439; catch, surprise Mch 2268+; understand Kn 2266, WB 77+; give, hand over ML 717, Sh 294+; *~ at* take to Kn 2226; *refl* devote o.s. to Th 795+; *~ (o's) aventure* take (o's) chance, accept the risk Kn 1186, WB 1224; *~ for the beste* adopt as the best course Kn 1847; *~ impressioun* receive a mental image Mil 3613; *3 sg contr pres* **tath**; *sg and pl imp* **taak**; *pl imp* **taketh**; *sg past* **took**; *pl past* **toke(n)**, **took, tooke(n)**; *1/3 sg past subj* **tooke**; *p ppl* **take(n)**, **ytake(n)**

tale *n* tale GP 36+; speech, words Kn 1577+; reckoning, account WB 262; *telle ~ of* take account of NP 3118; give an account of GP 330

tale *v* talk GP 772; speak, utter Pars 378

talent *n* desire, inclination Pard 540, Mel 1249+; mood, passion ML 1137

tappe *n* bung, stopper Rv 3890+

tappestere *n* barmaid GP 241+

tare *n* tare, weed (i.e. something worthless) Kn 1570+

targe *n* shield GP 471+

tartre *n* tartar GP 630+

tarye *v* protract, prolong
Kn 2820, Rv 3905; delay, hold
up Mch 1696, Sq 73+; put
off, keep waiting Sq 402,
Mk 2273; delay, wait
Mil 3409+

taryinge *n* delay GP 821+

tath *3 sg contr pres of* **take** *v*

taverner *n* tavern-keeper Pard
685+

teche *v* teach GP 308+; ~ *to*
direct to Fri 1326, NP 2949;
sg past **taughte**; *p ppl*
(y)taught

teer(e) *n* (see also **tere**) tear
ML 537, Cl 1104+

teine *n* strip, rod CY 1225+

telle *v* tell GP 83+; describe,
relate ML 1070+; speak
Kn 1000+; say Kn 1534,
ML 783+; say, mention
Kn 1148+; enumerate, list
Kn 2813, CY 754+; ~ *of*
esteem, value Mk 2486; ~
stoor of set store by, make
account of WB 203+; ~ *tale of*
make/take account of GP 330,
NP 3118; ~ *deintee of* set store
by WB 208; ~ *after* repeat
after GP 731; *sg past* **tolde**; *pl
past* **tolde(n)**; *p ppl* **to(o)ld**,
yto(o)ld

temple *n* temple Kn 928+; Inn of
Court GP 567

temporal, temporel *adj* temporal,
worldly ML 107, WB 1132+

tempre *v* blend CY 901, 926

tendre *adj* tender GP 7+

tercelet *n* male falcon (so named
because it is one-third smaller
than the female) Sq 504+

tere *n* (see also **teer(e)**) tear
Kn 1280+

terme *n* condition, state
Kn 3028; 'a division of the
zodiac defining a period within
which the influence of a planet
is heightened' (*MED*)
Fkl 1288; *pl* words,
expressions GP 639+; jargon,
technical language Pard 311,
pl ML 1189, Cl 16+; *in termes*
word-perfect, in the correct jargon GP 323; (*for/to*) ~ *of* (*al*)
his lif for the rest of his life
Kn 1029, WB 644+

terve *v* flay CY 1274; fleece
CY 1171

text *n* text GP 177+; precept,
axiom ML 45+; *pl* moral
reflections, adages Mcp 236

textuel *adj* learned, good at
exact quotation Mcp 235+

thakke *v* pat, slap Mil 3304,
Fri 1559

than *adv* (see also **thanne**) then
GP 12+

thank *n* thanks GP 613+; praise
Pars 1035; *kan* ~ owe thanks
Kn 1808, 3064; *hir/his
thankes* willingly, gladly
Kn 1626+

thanne *adv* (see also **than**) then
GP 535+

thar *v impers* need; *him* ~ he
needs Rv 4320; *thee* ~ you
need WB 329+; *personal*
Mel 1068

that *rel pron* that GP 44+;
that which WB 781+; on
which ML 262; when
Mil 3422

that *dem pron* that GP 102+;

~ *oon* . . . ~ *oother* the one . . .
the other Rv 4013

that *conj* (unfamiliar uses only)
~ *he kan* as well as he can Fkl
1262; ~ *ye may* as best you
can Rv 4033; ~ *he mighte* as
best he could ML 1036

the(e) 2 *sg pron, acc/dat form*
thee Kn 1083+

the(e) *v* thrive, prosper Sum
2207+; *so thee'k, so thee'ch,
so moot I* ~, *also mote I* ~ etc.
as I prosper Rv 3864, WB 361,
532, Pard 947+

theef *n* thief Mil 3791+; criminal, villain Kn 1325, ML 915,
WB 800+

theigh *conj* (see also **thogh,
though**) (even) if WB 53,
Fri 1327

thenche, thenke *v* (see also
thinke) think Mch 2165+;
imagine Mil 3253, Mch 1503;
intend Cl 641, Pars 671; consider WB 1165, Mch 2165+; ~
on remember, have in mind
Mil 3478+; *sg past* **tho(u)ghte**;
pl past **thoghten**

thenne *adj* (see also **thinne**):
thurgh thikke and ~ through
thick and thin Rv 4066

thennes *adv* thence, (away) from
there ML 510+; *fro* ~ thence,
from there ML 308+; *from* ~
from the place SN 66

ther *adv* there GP 43+; where
GP 34, 547, Kn 892+; whereas
Kn 1272, WB 1213+; to such a
place Kn 2809; in so far as Fri
1366; when WB 128+; (introducing a wish) ~ *Mars his
soule gye* may Mars guide his

soul Kn 2815; cf. ML 602, Fri
1561+

theraboute *adv* about that place
Kn 937; about it Sum 1837;
on it CY 832

therbifo(o)re, therbiforn *adv*
beforehand Kn 2034, Cl 689+;
previously Rv 3997, WB 631+

therbiside *adv* near that place
Kn 1478+

therby *adv* by that WB 20; by it
WB 1015, Fri 1600+; about it
Sum 2204; by that means Mil
3693, ML 520+; through it Sq
582, CY 722+; because of that
Sum 1878; *come* ~ come by it,
get possession of it WB 984;
get at it Fkl 1115

ther(e)as *adv* where GP 34,
Kn 1058+; whereas WB 1177;
in so far as Cl 848

therfore *adv* therefore, for that
reason GP 189+; for it
GP 809, Kn 1808; on that
account Cl 445, 731; for that
purpose Sq 177

therinne *adv* therein, in it, in
that Mil 3551+; in which
Th 755

therof *adv* of that GP 462; of it
Phys 282, Mel 1040+; by it
Kn 2990; thereby Pars 314;
about that Mil 3298, Rv
4000+; as to that, concerning
that Mil 3783, WB 65+; from
that Mel 1389; for that Cl
644+; ~ *no fors* never mind
about that Mch 2430+

theron *adv* on it GP 160; on that
subject ML 1033; in that,
therein Mch 2346; about it
Sq 3

therout(e) *adv* out of it, thence
Kn 1985; outside CY 1136;
out of doors Mk 2172

therto *adv* besides, moreover,
also GP 48+; to it Mel 1205,
1206, Mk 2238+; for it
Kn 2109, Mch 2439,
Mel 1346; for that purpose Pri
567; of it Fkl 1330

therupon *adv* thereupon
GP 819; over that
Mil 3323

therwith *adv* with it, with them,
with that GP 678, Mil 3777+;
thereupon, forthwith Kn 1299,
Mil 3480+; meanwhile
Kn 2878, Mk 2430, Pars 10;
besides, in addition Sq 194,
Mk 2299+; for that reason
NP 2876

therwithal *adv* with it GP 566;
with that, thereupon Kn 1078,
Mel 1006; besides, in addition,
also Mil 3233, WB 509+

thewes *n pl* qualities Cl 409+

thider *adv* thither, there
Kn 1263+; ~ *as* where Pard
749+

thikke *adj* thick Kn 1056+; thick-
set GP 549, Rv 3973; *thurgh ~
and thenne* through thick and
thin Rv 4066

thikke *adv* thickly Mil 3322+; ~
as they may goon as thickly-
crowded as they can walk
Kn 2510

thilke *dem adj and pron* the
same, that GP 182+

thin *possess adj and pron* thy,
your (used before vowel or h-)
Kn 951+; *thine* your servants
Kn 2381

thing *n* thing GP 644+; subject,
matter GP 736, Kn 885+;
affair, business Mil 3494+;
property, substance, pos-
sessions GP 490, WB 1132, Cl
504+; deed, document GP 325;
charge Fri 1597; creature
Mch 1429+; *for any ~* at all
costs GP 276; *pl* prayers,
devotions WB 876, Sh 91;
compositions Sq 78;
business affairs Sh 217,
NP 3089

thinke *v* (see also **thenche,
thenke**) think Kn 1643,
WB 201+; imagine GP 346+;
consider Kn 1606+; intend Cl
144, Pard 442+; seem GP 37,
Kn 1867, Cl 908+; ~ *(up)on*
remember, have in mind Mil
3701+; *sg past* **tho(u)ghte**; *pl
past* **thoghten**

thinne *adj* (see also **thenne**)
poor, feeble Mch 1682,
CY 741

this *contr of* this is

thise *pl of* this *dem adj and pron*
these Kn 1531+

tho *dem adj and pron* those
GP 498+; they Mil 3246; them
WB 370+

tho *adv* then Kn 993+

thogh *conj* (see also **theigh,
though**) though, although
GP 230+; even if GP 253,
Kn 1170+

thoght *n* thought GP 479+;
mind, heart Kn 2232,
WB 1083, Mch 2178; imagination Mch 1586+; anxiety, sorrow Fkl 822, 1084, Pri 589;
intention SN 327

thoghte *sg past of* thenche, thenke, thinke *v*

thoghten *pl past of* thenche, thenke, thinke *v*

thoghtful *adj* prudent, thoughtful Cl 295; moody Pars 677

thombe *n* thumb GP 563+

thonder *n* thunder GP 492+

thonder-dent, -dint *n* thunderclap Mil 3807; thunderbolt WB 276

thonke *v* thank Kn 1876+

though *conj* (see also theigh, thogh) though, although GP 68+; even if Kn 1321+

thral *n* thrall, subject, servant WB 155+

thral *adj* enthralled, enslaved Kn 1552+

thraldom *n* servitude, bondage ML 286+

thraste *pl past of* threste *v*

threed *n* thread Kn 2030+

thre(e)dbare *adj* threadbare GP 260+

thresshfold *n* threshold Mil 3482+

threste *v* thrust Kn 2612+; *sg past* threste; *pl past* thraste

thridde *adj* third Kn 1463+

thries *adv* thrice, three times GP 63+

thrift *n* prosperity, good fortune CY 739+; *by my* ~ as I prosper Rv 4049

thriftily *adv* properly, in a seemly fashion GP 105, Mil 3131; politely Fkl 1174

thrifty *adj* decent, good, respectable ML 46+; excellent, worthy Mch 1912; highquality ML 138

thritty *adj* thirty Sh 26+

thrive *v* thrive, prosper Mil 3675+; ~ *of* succeed in CY 1478; *so mote I* ~, *also evere moot I* ~, *so* ~ *I*, *also mote I* ~ as I prosper Mil 3675+

throop *n* village WB 871, Cl 199+; *pl and gen sg* thropes

throte *n* throat Kn 2013+; gullet Pard 517

throwe *n* (space of) time, while ML 953+; *many a* ~ many times CY 941

throwe *v* throw ML 85+; cast, drive Cl 453; *p ppl* ythrowe

thurgh *prep* through Kn 920+; on account of, through the agency of Kn 1328, Sq 11+

thurghout *prep* throughout Kn 1432+; through Kn 1096, ML 464+; straight through, right through Sq 237+

thurrok *n* the bilge of a ship Pars 363, 715

thurst *n* thirst ML 100+

tide *n* tide GP 401, ML 1134; duration of a tide's ebb and flow ML 520, 798; time Sq 142, NP 3096+

tide *v* betide, befall ML 337; *ther tides me na reste* I shall meet with no rest Rv 4175

tidinge *n* event ML 726; news Cl 901; *pl* news, reports, accounts ML 129+

tigre *n* tiger Kn 1657+

tikle *v* tickle, gratify WB 395, 471

til *prep*, *adv and conj* to (normally used before vowel or h-) GP 180+; (before a consonant as a Northernism) Rv 4110;

until GP 698+; ~ *and fra* to
and fro Rv 4039

tipet *n* hanging part of a sleeve
GP 233; hanging part of a
hood Rv 3953

to *adv* too ML 420+

to *adv and prep* to GP 2+; as
Kn 1289, Cl 793+; for,
towards Kn 2224+; for Mk
2230; at GP 30; ~ *wedde*, ~
borwe as a pledge, as security
Kn 1218+

to-breke *v* break Rv 3918+;
break in pieces CY 907;
bash in Rv 4277; *p ppl*
to-broke

to-breste *v* dash to pieces, shatter Kn 2611+; *p ppl* **to-brosten**

togh *adj* (see also **tough**) tough,
strong Kn 1992

togidre(s) *adv* together GP 824,
Kn 2625+

to-hewe *v* hack to pieces
Kn 2609+; *p ppl* **to-hewe**

toke(n) *pl past of* **take** *v*

tokening(e) *n* token, sign; *in* ~ as
a sign CY 1153+

to-morn *adv* tomorrow, in the
morning WB 1245+

tonge *n* tongue GP 265+; speech
Kn 1438, Pard 557; language
Mk 2307; power of expression
Sq 35

tonne *n* barrel, cask Rv 3894+;
~-*greet* as thick as a barrel
Kn 1994

too *n* toe Kn 2726+; *weak pl*
toon

tooke *1/3 sg past subj of* **take** *v*

tooke(n) *pl past of* **take** *v*

toold *p ppl of* **telle** *v*

toon *weak pl of* **too** *n*

toord *n* (see also **tord**) turd
Pard 955

top *n* hair GP 590, Phys 255+;
top, summit Kn 2915

tord *n* (see also **toord**) turd
Mel 930

to-rende *v* tear in pieces Cl
1012, Phys 102+; *past* **to-
rente**; *p ppl* **to-rent**

tormente *v* torment, torture
Kn 1314, ML 885+

tormentour *n* tormentor,
executioner ML 818+

torne *v* (see also **tourne, turne**)
turn NP 3214

to-tere *v* tear to pieces Pard
474+; *sg past* **totar**; *p ppl*
to-tore

touche *v* touch Rv 3932+; concern, affect Mil 3494, Mk
2094+; concern, be about Mil
3179; discuss Fri 1271, Pars
612+; reach Kn 2561; ~ *to*
relate to Mel 1299

touchinge *pres ppl* concerning
Sum 1988+

tough *adj* (see also **togh**): *make
it* ~ make a meal of it, make a
performance of it Sh 379

toun *n* (see also **town**) town
GP 217+

tour *n* tower Kn 1030+

tourne *v* (see also **torne, turne**)
turn WB 988

tourneyinge *n* (see also **turneyinge**) tournament Kn 2720

toute *n* rump, arse Mil
3812, 3853

towaille *n* towel Mk 2745+

toward *prep* toward, to GP 27+;
for Cl 778

town *n* (see also **toun**) town

Sum 2294+; *of* ~ from the
town Mil 3380; *in* ~ among
men Th 793

trad *sg past of* **trede** *v*

traisoun *n* (see also **treso(u)n**)
treason, treachery NP 3117+

traitour *n* traitor Kn 1131+

translacioun *n* translation SN
25+

trapped *p ppl* covered with trappings Kn 2157+

traunce *n* trance Kn 1572+

travail(l)e *n* labour, toil, effort
Kn 2406+; oppression, trouble
Mil 3646; *do* (o's) ~ exert o.s.
Cl 1210

travaille *v* labour, exert o.s. Fri
1365+; suffer Pars 985

trecherye *n* treachery NP 3330+

trede *v* tread Sum 2002+; mount
(in a sexual sense) NP 3178; *3
sg contr pres* **tret**; *sg past* **trad**;
p ppl **treden**

tredefoul *n* mounter of birds (in
sexual sense) Mk 1945,
NP 3451

treden *p ppl of* **trede** *v*

tree *n* tree GP 607+; cross Mil
3767+; wood WB 101,
Cl 558

tregetour *n* conjurer Fkl 1141+

trental *n* a set of thirty requiem
masses Sum 1717, 1724

tresor *n* treasure, valuables
ML 442+

treso(u)n *n* (see also **traisoun**)
treason, treachery Kn 2001+

trespa(a)s *n* offence, fault,
wrong Kn 1764+

trespace, trespas(s)e *v* do wrong
Pard 741+; do offence, injury
Mch 1828, Pard 416+; trans-

gress Mk 2180+; commit
Mel 1884+

trespassour *n* offender
Mel 1358+

tresse *n* braid, plait Kn 1049; *pl*
locks Mch 2308+

tret *3 sg contr pres of* **trede** *v*

trete *v* treat Pars 582; tell Pard
630; ~ *of* tell Mk 2311; speak
about, discuss Sq 220+; negotiate Mel 1798; ~ *of folye*
engage in foolish behaviour
Phys 64

tretice, tretis *n* negotiation
ML 233; (marriage) treaty Cl
331; treatise, work Mel 957,
Pars 957+

trewe *adj* loyal, honest, faithful
GP 531, Kn 959+; just
Kn 1864+; righteous, reliable
Mil 3529; true Cl 855,
Mel 1152+; genuine Pard 930;
as n pl the faithful ML 456

trewely *adv* truly GP 707+; faithfully GP 481, Kn 1137+; honestly Rv 4133; sincerely
Pars 1045

triacle *n* salve, antidote
ML 479; medicinal potion
Pard 314

tribulacio(u)n *n* tribulation
WB 156+

trille *v* turn Sq 316+

trippe *v* dance, frisk Mil 3328,
Sq 312

triste *v* trust ML 832+

trogh *n* trough Mil 3548+

trompe *n* trumpet GP 674+

trone *n* throne Kn 2529+

trouble *adj* disturbed, troubled
Cl 465+; confused Pars 824;
muddy Pars 816

trouble *v* disturb, plague
WB 363+

troubled *p ppl* troubled
Mel 1001+; clouded
Mel 1701, SN 72

trouthe *n* loyalty, fidelity, honesty, integrity GP 46+; honour,
word GP 763, Kn 1610+; faith
WB 1009+; promise, pledge
Fri 1404+; truth Mel 1069+

trowe *v* believe, think, suppose
GP 155+; believe Kn 1520,
Sum 1985+; believe (in), trust
SN 171+

tukked *p ppl* (see also ytukked)
with gown tucked up GP 621

turne *v* (see also torne, tourne)
turn Kn 1327+; revolve
Kn 2454; roll Kn 1238; over-
turn NP 3403; throw (dice)
Kn 1238; turn on a lathe Rv
3928; *refl* turn over NP 3010;
turn away Fkl 1011; be converted Pars 772; ~ *again* turn
back, return ML 23+

turneyinge *n* (see also tourneyinge) tournament Kn 2557

turtel, turtle *n* turtle-dove Mil
3706, Mch 2080, 2139

tweine *adj* (see also tweye) two
Kn 1134+

twelf *adj* twelve GP 651+;
~-*month(e)* twelvemonth, year
GP 651+

tweye *adj* (see also tweine) two
GP 704+

twies *adv* twice Co 4348+

twinne *v* sunder, sever ML 517;
depart Sq 577, SN 182; go
GP 835; escape Mk 2005; ~
from forsake, renounce
Pard 430

twiste *n* branch Mch 2349,
Sq 442

twiste *v* squeeze, wring Mch
2005, Sq 566; torment
WB 494; *sg past* twiste

tyraunt *n* tyrant Kn 961+

unavised *adj* rash, thoughtless
Mcp 280; unpremeditated
Pars 449

unbokele *v* unbuckle Mil 3115,
Sq 555+

unbounde(n) *p ppl* unbound, set
loose Mch 1226+

uncovenable *adj* unfitting Pars
431, 631

under *prep and adv* under
GP 105+; below Kn 1981; by,
beside WB 990, Fri 1380+;
behind the back of Mcp 198; ~
the yerde in tutelage Sh 97;
adv underneath Sq 519,
SN 518

understonde *v* understand
GP 746+; *p ppl* under-
stonde(n)

undertake *v* undertake Sq 36+;
take on an enterprise GP 405;
warrant, guarantee GP 288+

undigne *adj* unworthy Cl 359+

undiscreet *adj* undiscerning, ill-
judging Cl 996, NP 3434

undo *v* open, unfasten (a door
or window) Mil 3727, 3765

undren *n* sometime in the morning later than 9 a.m. (the particular time indicated varied in
the course of the Middle
Ages); probably 'mid-morning'
(around 10.30) Cl 260+

unhappy *adj* unlucky, unfortunate ML 306, CY 1084

unitee *n* unity Mch 1334+

unkinde *adj* unnatural ML 88; ungrateful Pard 903, Pars 970

unkindely *adv* unnaturally Pard 485; ungratefully Pars 154

unknowe(n) *adj* unknown GP 126+

unkonninge *n* stupidity Mel 1876; lack of skill Pars 1082

unkouth *adj* curious, strange, unusual (in good sense) Kn 2496, Sq 284

unleveful *adj* unlawful Pars 593, 777

unlik *adj* unlike Cl 156+

unmesurable *adj* immeasurable, immense ML 934; immoderate, inordinate Pars 813+

unnethe(s) *adv* with difficulty, hardly, scarcely Mil 3121, ML 1050+

unreste *n* unrest, disquiet WB 1104; disturbance, vexation Fri 1495, Cl 719

unsavory *adj* distasteful Pars 510, 723

unsely *adj* unfortunate Rv 4210; miserable SN 468

unto *prep* unto, to GP 71+; until Kn 2412+

unto(o)ld *p ppl* uncounted, innumerable Mil 3780; untold Pars 1010

untressed *p ppl* unplaited, loose Kn 2289+

untrewe *adj* faithless, false Cl 995+

untrouthe *n* falsehood, treachery ML 687; unfaithfulness Mch 2241

unwar *adj* unexpected ML 427, Mk 2764

unwar *adv* unwittingly Pars 885; unexpectedly Fkl 1356

unwemmed *p ppl* spotless, undefiled ML 924+

unwiting *pres ppl* not knowing CY 1320; ~ *of* unknown to Fkl 936

unyolden *p ppl* without having surrendered Kn 2642, 2724

up *adv* (see also uppe) up GP 681+; open (outwards) Mil 3801

up *prep*: ~ *peine of* on pain of (death) Kn 1707+; ~ *peril of* I swear by (my life, soul, etc) Sum 2271, Mch 2371+

uppe *adv* (see also up) open (outwards) Sq 615

upright(e) *adj* upright Kn 1387+; upright, straight Mil 3264; stretched full length, flat on o's back Rv 4194+; upwards, pointing upwards Kn 2008, Mil 3444, Sum 2266

up-so-doun, up-so-down *adv* upside down Kn 1377+

urinal *n* glass vessel employed to receive urine Pard 305+

usage *n* custom Sum 2278+; rules, practice GP 110; experience Kn 2448; the exercise Pars 690; *as is/was* ~ as is/was customary ML 998+; *have in* ~ be accustomed (to) Pri 506; *in* ~ in use Pri 527; *of* ~ from habit Pard 899+

usa(u)nt *adj* accustomed, given (to) Rv 3940, Pars 821

use *v* use WB 137+; practise ML 44, Fkl 1293, Pard 428+;

exercise Pars 669; indulge in
Mch 1678; accustom Pars 245;
have sexual intercourse with
Pars 375; enjoy Kn 2385

us self, us selve(n) *refl pron* ourselves WB 812, Cl 108+

usure *n* usury Fri 1309+

vanitee *n* vanity, emptiness, foolishness NP 2922+; folly Mil
3835, Sum 2208+; idle tale
Pars 378

varia(u)nce *n* difference, change
Pars 427; variation Cl 710

vein *adj* vain, worthless
Kn 2240+; deluded, empty
Kn 1094

veine *n* vein CY 1241; (in
plants) sap-vessel GP 3

venerye *n* hunting GP 166,
Kn 2308

venge *v* avenge Mel 1371+; *refl*
take revenge Mel 1280+

venim *n* venom, poison
Kn 2751+

venimus *adj* venomous, poisonous Mk 2105+

venquisse, venquisshe *v* vanquish, conquer ML 291,
Mel 1090+

vernage *n* a strong and sweet
kind of white Italian wine Mch
1807, Sh 71

verrailiche, verraily *adv* truly,
really, without a doubt
Kn 1174+; indeed ML 927

verray *adj* real, true GP 72+;
very WB 888, Fri 1393+;
downright Mel 921; ~ *fool*
fool that you are Kn 1606

vers *n* line Pri 522; verse
Mel 1107+

vertu(e) *n* GP 4, power
Kn 2249, 2749, Sq 146+;
ability, powers Kn 1436+; virtue GP 307, ML 164+; *by ~ of*
in consequence of WB 616+;
make ~ of necessitee to make
the best of what is unavoidable
Kn 3042; to bear cheerfully
what is unavoidable Sq 593;
expulsif ~ 'the natural faculty
of expelling . . . from the body
. . . toxic and superfluous matter' (*MED*) Kn 2749; *retentif ~*
'the natural faculty to retain
and control bodily effluents'
(*MED*) Pars 913; *natural ~* see
n. to Kn 2743–56; *naturel ~*
natural ability Pars 452

vessel *n* vessel WB 100+; vessels,
plate Mk 2148+

vestiment *n* robe Kn 2948,
Sq 59

viage *n* journey GP 723+; voy-
age ML 259+; expedition
GP 77; enterprise, undertaking
ML 259, Fri 1569, Sh 371

vice *n* vice ML 323+; fault,
defect WB 282+; deformity
WB 955

vigilie *n* watch kept on the eve
of a funeral or religious festival GP 377, WB 556 (see n.)

vileins *adj* base WB 1158, Mcp
183; offensive, rude Fri 1268;
wicked Pars 556, 627; shameful Pars 631+; surly,
ungracious Mel 1503

vileinsly *adv* meanly, vilely
Pars 154; shamefully
Pars 279

vileinye *n* discourtesy GP 70,
Pard 740; boorishness,

coarseness, lack of manners
GP 726+; disgrace, shame
Kn 2729, Mch 2310+; injury
Rv 4191, Mel 1357+; shameful act, wickedness WB 962+;
wrong Mch 1791+; servitude,
degradation Pars 142; *do* ~ *to*
dishonour Kn 942, Fkl 1404;
seye/speke ~ *of* speak ill of
WB 34, 53; *in* ~ in a shameful
way SN 156, Pars 857

vinolent *adj* bibulous WB 467;
wine-filled Sum 1931

violence *n* violence Fri 1431+;
act of violence Pars 802; force,
strength CY 908

visage *n* face GP 109+; *make
good* ~ put up a good front
Sh 230

vitaille *n* food, provisions
GP 248+; produce, fruits of
the earth Cl 59

vitaille *v* stock with food Mil
3627+

voide *v* evacuate, clear out
Kn 2751; clear Mch 1815;
vacate, leave clear Cl 806;
send away, dismiss Cl 910,
CY 1136; remove Sq 188,
Fkl 1150+

vois *n* voice GP 688+; opinion,
report ML 155, 169;
expression of approval Mch
1592; rumour, report Cl 629;
with o ~ unanimously
Mel 1765+

voluper *n* cap Mil 3241; night-
cap Rv 4303

vouchesauf *v* vouchsafe, grant,
agree GP 807+; condescend, be
so good as to ML 1083, Mch
2341+

waar *adj* (see also **war**) aware
Mel 1389

wade *v* wade Sum 2084; go Mk
2494; ~ *out of* move away
from, escape from Mch 1684

waik *adj* weak Kn 887+

wail(l)e *v* wail Kn 931+

waimentinge *n* lamentation, wailing Kn 902+

waite *v* lie in wait ML 582, SN
9+; watch, observe ML 593, Cl
708, Sq 88+; look, see
WB 517; watch for Mil 3302,
Fkl 1263+; take precautions,
be watchful GP 571, Mil
3295+; watch for a chance to
Kn 1222, Mk 2141; expect
ML 246, Pars 403+; expect the
time (when) Mch 2096; await
Kn 929; ~ *after* look for,
expect GP 525, ML 467+; ~
on watch out for Fri 1376

waive *v* (see also **weive**) reject,
refuse Pars 353

wake *v* stay awake Mil 3354+;
keep watch Fri 1654, Sum
1847+; stir up, rouse
ML 1187; awake Kn 1393,
Mch 2397+; *sg past* **wook**

wakinge *vbl n* period of wakefulness ML 22; watching, vigil
Pars 257+

wal *n* wall Kn 1060+

walwe *v* roll about, thrash about
Rv 4278, WB 1085+; roll,
surge Mil 3616

wan *adj* dark Kn 2456; pale Mil
3828; livid, leaden-coloured
CY 728

wan *sg past of* **winne** *v*

wanhope *n* despair Kn 1249+

wante *v* need Mel 1026; be lacking Mel 1048, Mcp 338+; *him wanted/wanteth* he lacked/lacks Mel 1046, 1080

wanting(e) *vbl n* lack Kn 2665+

wantown(e) *adj* jovial (with pun on 'wanton') GP 208; wanton, lascivious, playful Cl 236, Mch 1846

wantownenesse *n* affectation, conscious charm GP 264; wantonness ML 31

war *adj* (see also **waar**) prudent GP 309, Sh 365; aware Mil 3735, CY 1079+; in the know Mil 3604; cautious, wary SN 13; *be ~* take note, notice GP 157, Kn 896+; *be ~ (from/ of)* be wary, beware (of) Kn 1218+; *be ~ (by)* take warning (from) WB 180, Fri 1656+; take care Phys 97

warante *v* (see also **warente**) warrant Mil 3791

ward *n* guardianship, keeping Phys 201, Pars 880

wardein *n* warden Rv 3999+; guardian WB 1216

ware *n* wares, merchandise ML 140+

ware *v* beware of, guard against Sum 1903+; *refl* GP 662+; look out, make way Th 699

warente *v* (see also **warante**) safeguard Pard 338

warice, warisshe *v* recover Mel 982; cure Fkl 856+; save Pard 906

warmnesse *n* heat Mch 2221; warmth Mel 1185

warne *v* warn, caution Mil 3583+; notify, tell ML 1184,

Cl 642+; summon, invite Mel 1462

warnestore *v* fortify Mel 1297+

wasshe *v* wash ML 356+; *sg past* wessh(e); *p ppl* wasshe(n)

wast *n* waste WB 500+

waste *v* waste, squander Co 4416+; destroy Kn 3020+; wear out Kn 3023; pass away ML 20; *~ awey* die away Sum 2235

wawe *n* wave Kn 1958+

wax *sg and pl past of* **wexe** *v*

way *n* (see also **wey(e)**) way Kn 1413+; *the righte ~* the direct route Kn 2739+; *the nexte ~* the quickest way Kn 1413; *a mile ~* (by) the time taken to walk a mile (20 minutes or so) Sh 276; *a furlong ~* time required to walk one furlong, (?2½ minutes) Mil 3637+; *go (o's) ~* leave, go away ML 373; *at the leeste ~* at least Fkl 1417; *a twenty devel ~* devil take it Rv 4257

wedde *n dat* pledge; *to ~* as pledge, as security Kn 1218, Sh 423

wede *n* clothing Kn 1006; dress, garment Cl 863

weder *n* weather Sum 2253+; storm ML 873

weel *adv* (see also **wel, wele**) well Kn 926+

weep *sg imp and sg past of* **wepe** *v*

weet *adj* wet Kn 1280, Rv 4107+; *pl and weak sg* **wete**

weex *sg past of* **wexe** *v*

weilaway, weilawey *interj* alas! Kn 938+; *so ~* alas ML 370+

weive *v* (see also **waive**) shun,
avoid WB 1176; give up, abandon Mel 1066+; reject
Mel 1208, Mcp 178+; ~ *fro(m)*
cast aside, forsake, deviate
from Mch 1483+; remove ML
308

wel *adv* (see also **weel, wele**)
well GP 29+; fully GP 24, Mil
3637, Sq 383; in detail Mil
3784; (with adjectives) much
GP 256+; very GP 614, Mil
3701+; *be* ~ be in a good position ML 308+; ~ *smellinge*
beautifully scented Kn 1961; ~
ny very nearly Kn 1330+; ~
unnethe(s) hardly Fkl 736, Mk
2421; ~ *was him* he was satisfied, happy Kn 2109,
NP 2876+

welde *v* govern, control
WB 271, Mk 2010+; manipu-
late, deal with Mk 2262; have
the use of Sum 1947; *sg past*
welded, welte

wele *n* wealth, riches ML 122+;
welfare, prosperity, happiness
Kn 1272+; splendour Kn 895;
been in hir ~ are in their
element Kn 2673

wele *adv* (see also **weel, wel**)
well Kn 2231

weleful *adj* fortunate, prosperous Mel 1317; blessed, joy-
giving ML 451

welked *p ppl* withered, faded
WB 277, Pard 738

welkne *n dat* sky Cl 1124,
Mk 2731

welle *n* well Kn 1533+; source
Kn 3037, ML 323+; spring Cl
48, Th 915+; fount Pri 656+

wel neigh, wel ny *adv* very
nearly, almost Kn 1330+

welte *sg past of* **welde** *v*

wenche *n* girl, lass Mil 3254, Rv
3973+; serving-maid Mil
3631+; whore Fri 1355+; mistress WB 393+

wende *v* go, travel GP 16+;
move Kn 2965; depart
Kn 999, ML 265+; pass away
Kn 3025; *refl* go Kn 2270+;
leave, set out WB 915; ~ (o's)
weye depart, set out WB 918,
Mch 1945+; *p ppl* **went**

wene *v* think, suppose, believe,
imagine Kn 1269+; reckon
Kn 1804; expect Mil 3813, Rv
4320, Mch 1280+

went *p ppl of* **wende** *v*

wepe *v* weep GP 144+; *sg imp*
weep; *sg past* weep, wepte; *pl
past* wepen, wepten; *p ppl*
wept, wopen

wepne *n* weapon Kn 1591+

werche *v* (see also **werke** *v* (1),
wirche) work Mil 3664+; operate, function Kn 2759; make
SN 545; perform CY 1155; do
good works Sum 2114

were *v* wear GP 75+; *sg past*
wered; *p ppl* wered

were *1/3 sg past subj of* **be** *v*

were(n) *pl past of* **be** *v*

werk *n* work Mil 3311+;
deed(s), practice GP 479,
ML 928+; workmanship Th
864; behaviour Fkl 1106; activity Mcp 241; *pl* works, deeds
Mil 3308+

werke *v* (1) (see also **werche,
wirche**) do GP 779+; act
GP 497, Mil 3527+; make,

fashion, construct Kn 1913+;
create Kn 3099+; work CY
604; operate Pars 726; proceed
Mil 3131; practise Mil 3308+;
labour Mch 1965; cause
Kn 2072, 2624; contrive
ML 619, Mch 1692; perform
Fkl 733, CY 359+; commit
ML 856; *sg past* **wro(u)ghte**;
p ppl **(y)wroght**

werke *v* (2) ache Rv 4030

werker(e) *n* doer Sum 1937,
Mk 2386

werking(e) *n* (see also **wirk-
ing(e)**) work Mel 1596, CY
622+; action Mel 1400; deed
Mcp 210, Pars 82; performance Pars 240

werre *n* war GP 47+; attack
Kn 1287; fight Kn 2100; conflict, strife WB 390, Fkl 757

werreye *v* make war (on)
Kn 1484+; attack Pars 401+

werse *comp adj* (see also
wors(e)) worse Mil 3174

wers(e) *comp adv* (see also
wors(e)) worse Mil 3733+

wery *adj* weary Rv 4107+; tiring
worse Mil 3643

wesele *n* weasel Mil 3234+

wessh(e) *sg past of* **wasshe** *v*

wete *pl and weak sg of* **weet** *adj*
wet Kn 1280+; *as n* moisture
CY 1187

wether *n* sheep, ram Mil
3249, 3542

wex *n* (bees)wax GP 675+

wexe *v* increase, grow Kn 2078,
WB 28+; become, grow, be
Kn 1362, 3024, Mel 1475+;
(of moon) wax Kn 2078+; *sg*

past wax, we(e)x; *pl past* wax;
p ppl **woxe(n), ywoxen**

wey *adv*: *do* ~ take away Mil
3287; lay aside SN 487

wey(e) *n* (see also **way**) way
GP 34+; *hye* ~ high-road
Kn 897; *the righte* ~ the direct
route Cl 273; *the nexte* ~ the
quickest way Kn 2365+; *bi the*
~ along the road GP 780+; en
route GP 467; *go (o's)* ~ proceed Kn 2560; leave, go away
Mil 3133+; *every* ~ in every
direction SN 108; *by any* ~ at
all costs Pars 628; *a furlong* ~
a little while (time taken to
walk a furlong) Rv 4199+; *at
the leeste* ~ at least Kn 1121+;
a (twenty) devel ~ in the devil's
name Mil 3134+; *by* ~ *of* in
terms of, in the course of,
according to Kn 1291,
ML 219+; *go out of the* ~
retire from the public eye Sh
234; *noon oother weyes* in no
other way Pard 412

weye *v* weigh GP 455+; be of
weight Mk 2233, Pars 367;
value, estimate Kn 1781

whan (that) *conj* when GP 1+

what *adj* what, which GP 40,
Kn 2945+; what kind of Mcp
247; whatever, whichever Cl
165+

what *adv and conj* why GP 184,
Kn 1380, ML 56+; in what
way, how Kn 1307+; ~ . . . ~,
~ *for . . . and (for)* partly with
. . . partly with Kn 1453, Rv
3967+

what *interj* what! WB 167+

what how *interj* (call to attract attention) hello! Mil 3437+

whatso *pron* whatever GP 522+

wheither *pron and conj* which (of two) WB 1227+; whichever (of two) Kn 1856+; whether GP 570+; (introducing direct question, not to be translated) Sum 2069

whelp(e) *n* puppy GP 257; cub Kn 2627; dog Sq 491, NP 2932+

whennes *adv and conj* whence Cl 588+

wher *conj* (2) *contr of* **wheither** whether Kn 1101+; (introducing direct question, not to be translated) Kn 1125, Mk 1929

wher(e) *adv and conj* (1) where Kn 897+; wherever Kn 2252, Pard 748+; whereas CY 727

wher(e)as *rel adv and conj* where Kn 1113, ML 647+; when Mel 1544; in which Mel 1331; whereas Mel 1253; although Mk 2157

whereso *adv and conj* (see also **wherso** *conj* (1)) wherever Mk 2638

wherfore *adv* wherefore, because of which Kn 2541+; for which Kn 1568; on what account ML 1049; on any account Phys 216

wherof *adv* from what, whence WB 72, Pars 450; at which CY 1035; of what CY 1148; for what Mcp 339, Pars 308

wherso *adv and conj* (1) (see also **whereso**) wherever Rv 4238, Sq 118, Mcp 361

wherso *conj* (2) whether ML 294+

wherto *interrog adv* why, for what purpose Mel 1612+

wherwith *interrog and rel adv* with what WB 131; with which Pars 468; (with ellipsis of antecedent object) that with which, the means with which GP 302, Sum 1718

whete *n* wheat Rv 3988+

which *interrog and rel adj and pron* which GP 4, Kn 2686+; of what kind GP 40; whichever GP 796; who(m) WB 537+; what Mch 2421; what a WB 39; ~ *a* what a Kn 2675+

whider *adv* whither, where Cl 588+

whil *conj* while GP 35+

while *n* while Kn 1437+; time Mil 3299+; *quite* (s.o's) ~ *pay* (s.o.) back ML 584; *allas the* ~, *so weilawey the* ~ alas the day ML 370, Cl 251

whiles *conj* (see also **whils**) while Fkl 1118, Pard 439+; *in the mene-*~ meanwhile ML 668

whilom *adv* formerly, at one time, once upon a time GP 795+; *as adj* former Mk 2076

whils *conj* (see also **whiles**) while CY 1139+

whit *adj* white GP 90+; fair Mch 2144

whoso *pron* whoever Mil 3176, WB 76+

wid *adj* wide GP 28+

wide *adv* widely Fri 1524+

widwe *n* widow GP 253+

wif *n* woman GP 445, 449, Phys 71+; wife Kn 932+; landlady CY 1015

wifhod(e) *n* wifehood, wifeliness ML 76+; the married state WB 149

wiflees *adj* wifeless Mch 1236, 1248

wifly *adj* wifely Cl 429+

wight *n* person GP 71+; creature Mil 3484, Rv 4236+; supernatural being Mil 3479; *any ~* anyone Kn 1425+; *every ~* everybody GP 842+; *no ~* no one GP 280+; *a litel ~* for a short time Rv 4283

wight *adj* agile, swift Rv 4086; strong Mk 2267

wighte *n* weight Kn 2145+

wike *n* (see also **wowke**) week Kn 1539+

wiket *n* wicket-gate Mch 2045+

wikke(d) *adj* wicked Kn 1580+; evil, bad Kn 1087+; wretched ML 118; bad, poor Rv 4201

wil *n* (see also **wille**) will Kn 1104+; desire, inclination Rv 3877+; wish, pleasure, will WB 897+; intention, determination Cl 509

wil *1/3 sg and pl pres of* **wille** *v*

wilde fir *n* destructive fire, conflagration Rv 4172+; inflammable material used in warfare WB 373; artificial flames (reference to some kind of *flambé-* ing process) Pars 445

wilfully *adv* willingly, voluntarily Pard 441, Mel 1422+; purposely Mel 1236

wilfulnesse *n* self-will, wilfulness Kn 3057; determination, resolution Mel 1361+

wille *n* (see also **wil**) will Kn 2536+; desire, inclination Kn 1317+; wish, pleasure, will Kn 2387+

wille *v* wish, desire, want GP 276, Kn 889, 2107, WB 307, Cl 721, Pri 653, NP 3251+; wish, be willing to GP 805, Kn 1416, ML 857+; (as an auxiliary used to form the future tense) will GP 42+; (with ellipsis of verb of motion) will go Fri 1387, Sq 617+; have a mind to Th 868; intend GP 27, Mch 1405; is liable to, is capable of Mk 1911. Special uses of *wolde*: (1) in describing habitual actions: would, used to GP 144+; (2) in formation of future in the past: would GP 813, Kn 954+; (3) modal uses: in conditional sentences (expressed or implied): would GP 374, Kn 876+; meaning 'would like to' GP 766, Kn 2242+; meaning 'would like (that)' Rv 3962, Pard 952+; meaning 'were to' Kn 1473+; meaning 'were willing to' Mch 2341+; meaning 'could wish' ML 161+; (*as/so*) *wolde God* would to God (that) WB 37+; *1/3 sg pres* **wil**, **wol(e)**; *2 sg pres* **wilt**, **wolt**; *pl pres* **wil**, **wol(e)**, **wolen**; *imp* **wille**; *1/3 sg past* **wolde**; *2 sg past* **woldest**; *pl past* **wolde(n)**; *p ppl* **wold**

wilne *v* desire, wish Kn 1609+
wiltow *contr of* **wilt thow**
win *n* wine GP 334+
winde *v* twist, turn WB 1102;
  wrap up Cl 583; envelop,
  enfold SN 42; wind Rv 3953;
  refl weave about CY 980;
  p ppl **wounde**
winke *v* shut (o's) eyes
  NP 3306+; wink, summon by
  a glance Sq 348
winne *v* gain, acquire, get
  GP 442+; obtain, win
  Kn 1486+; win Kn 891+;
  profit, make a profit GP 427,
  Fri 1421+; capture GP 51,
  Sum 2082+; conquer, overcome Kn 980, Mk 2359+; ~ *on*
  get the better of GP 594; *for al*
  this world to ~ even to gain
  the whole world WB 961; *sg*
  past **wan**; *p ppl* **wonne(n)**,
  ywonne
winning *n* gain(s), profit
  GP 275+
winter *n* winter Mch 2140+;
  year ML 197, WB 600+
wirche *v* (see also **werche, werke**
  v (1)) work Mil 3430+; per-
  form Mil 3308, ML 566; act
  Mch 1383; do good works
  Sum 1978
wirking(e) *n* (see also **werk-**
  ing(e)) behaviour WB 698,
  Cl 495+; calculation
  Fkl 1280
wis *adj* wise GP 68+; *make it* ~
  deliberate, hesitate GP 785; *pl*
  the wise wise men, the wise
  Mil 3598+
wise *n* fashion, manner, way
  Kn 1338+; *in every maner(e)* ~

in every respect Cl 605, Sh
  245+; *in alle* ~, *in alle maner* ~
  at all costs Sh 61, 346; *in no*
  maner ~ in any way, at all Sum
  1898; *in which manere* ~ in
  what way Phys 279
wisely *adv* wisely, sagely
  Kn 2851+
wisse *v* guide, instruct
  WB 1008+
wist *p ppl of* **wite** *v* (1)
wiste *sg past of* **wite** *v* (1)
wisten *pl past of* **wite** *v* (1)
wit *n* (see also **witte**) intellectual
  capacity, understanding
  GP 746, Mil 3227+; intelligence, cleverness GP 279, 574,
  Sum 2291+; cunning
  WB 400+; ingenuity Kn 2195;
  mind Kn 1456+; reason Mil
  3135, ML 609+; reasoning
  ML 888; wisdom Mch 2245,
  Pard 326+; display of wisdom
  Rv 3901; strategy, course of
  action Cl 459, Fri 1479;
  opinion WB 41+; *took his* ~
  derived his opinion ML 10; *as*
  fer as I have ~ as far as my
  understanding holds Fkl 985;
  pl mental faculties, reason Mil
  3559+; *five* ~ five senses
  Mel 1424+
wite *v* (1) know GP 224, 389,
  Kn 1260+; find out, learn Fri
  1450+; *1/3 sg pres* **wo(o)t**; *2 sg*
  pres **woost**; *pl pres* **woot**,
  wite(n); *sg past* **wiste**; *pl past*
  wisten; *p ppl* **wist**
wite *v* (2) blame (on) Mil
  3140+; ~ *of* blame for
  Mk 2670
with *prep* with GP 31+; by

GP 511, Kn 2018, 2022, ML 475+

withal(le) *adv* besides, in addition, moreover GP 127+

withdrawe *v* remove, take away CY 1423, Pars 802+; withhold WB 617, Pars 377+; go away Pars 449; *refl* remove o.s. Pars 143+

withholde *v* retain, maintain GP 511; retain, engage (s.o's services) Mel 1012, 2423; hold back Mk 1996+; keep Pars 1041; keep in bondage SN 345; *p ppl* withholde(n)

withinne *prep* in, within Kn 1300+; *adv* inside, inwardly Mil 3240, WB 943

withoute *adv* outside Kn 1888+

withoute(n) *prep* without GP 343+; besides GP 461

withseye *v* gainsay GP 805, Pars 507+; deny SN 447+

withstonde *v* withstand, resist Fri 1497+; *3 sg pres* withstand-eth; *p ppl* withstonden

witing *vbl n* knowledge Kn 1611+

witingly *adv* knowingly, con-sciously Pars 401+

witnesse *v* bear witness (to) Mel 1459+; take as witness SN 277; ~ *on* (s.o.) take (s.o.) as witness/as an example WB 951+

witte *n* (see also **wit**) understand-ing, intellectual capacity Fri 1480

wive *v* take a wife Cl 140+

wlatsom *adj* loathsome Mk 2624, NP 3053

wo *n* grief, sorrow Kn 919+; dis-tress, misery, affliction Kn 1030+; lamentation Kn 900, Mk 2492+; pain SN 521; ~ *was this king/knight* this king/knight was sorrowful ML 757, WB 913+; ~ *is me* sor-row overcomes me ML 817; ~ *was his cook* it was the worse for his cook GP 351; ~ *were us* we should be in a miserable situation Cl 139; *do/werke* ~ inflict misery on, do harm to Kn 2072, 2624, Fri 1310+; *make* ~ lament Rv 4200+

wo-bigon *adj* (see also **bigo(o)n**) overwhelmed with suffering/ sorrow Mil 3658

wode *n* wood Kn 1422+

wol *1/3 sg and pl pres of* **wille** *v*

wold *p ppl of* **wille** *v*

wolde *1/3 sg past of* **wille** *v*

wolde(n) *pl past of* **wille** *v*

woldest *2 sg past of* **wille** *v*

wole *1/3 sg pres of* **wille** *v*

wole(n) *pl pres of* **wille** *v*

wolle *n* wool Mil 3249+

wolt *2 sg pres of* **wille** *v*

woltow *contr of* **wolt thow**

wombe *n* stomach Rv 4290+; womb Cl 877+

wommanhede *n* womanliness Kn 1748, ML 851+

wommanly *adj* womanly Kn 3083+

wonder *n* wonder GP 502+; astonishment, wonderment Cl 1058+; puzzlement Sq 199; miracle Pri 673, SN 359; mar-vel ML 182, Mch 2123; ~ *is/ was* it is/was wonderful Sh 23, Th 692+

wonder *adj* wonderful, wondrous Kn 2073, ML 1045+

wonder *adv* wonderfully, exceedingly, very GP 483, Kn 1654+

wonderly *adv* wonderfully GP 84+

wondre *v* wonder, marvel Kn 1445, Cl 335+; ~ *(up)on* wonder about, marvel at Cl 358, Sq 258+

wone *n* custom GP 335+

wone *v* live, dwell GP 388, Kn 2927+; live, exist SN 332

wones *pl of* **woon** *n*

wonne(n) *p ppl of* **winne** *v*

wont *p ppl* accustomed Kn 1195+

wood *adj* mad, insane GP 184+; furious, raging Kn 1329+; angry Mil 3394, WB 664+

woodnesse *n* madness Kn 2011+

wook *sg past of* **wake** *v*

woon *n* place Th 801; *pl* **wones** buildings Sum 2105

woost 2 *sg pres of* **wite** *v* (1)

woot 1/3 *sg pres and pl pres of* **wite** *v* (1)

wopen *p ppl of* **wepe** *v*

word *n* word GP 304+; speech, utterance GP 856, Kn 1112+; *at o* ~ in a word ML 428+; ~ *and ende* from beginning to end Mk 2721

world *n* world GP 176+; the population NP 3345; *worldes* (*gen*) used as equivalent to adj 'worldly' NP 3200

worm *n* worm Cl 880+; grub WB 376, 560; serpent Phys 280; reptile Pard 355

wors(e) *comp adj* (see also

werse) worse Kn 1224, Pars 614+

wors(e) *comp adv* (see also **wers(e)**) worse Co 4350+

worship *n* honour Kn 1904+; dignity, good repute Fkl 962+; credit Sh 13+; source of credit Mel 1485; veneration Pri 654

worshipe *v* honour, respect Cl 166; honour, venerate Kn 2251, Pri 511+

worshipful *adj* honourable, noble Kn 1435, Mel 1765+; deserving of respect Cl 401+

wortes *n pl* greens, herbs Cl 226+

worthinesse *n* excellence, nobility, worth GP 50+; prowess Kn 2592; dignity, reverence Sum 2260; *youre* ~ your honour Cl 824

worthy *adj* noble, excellent, full of worth GP 43+; respectable, of dignity, of good standing GP 217+; many uses are deliberately ambiguous as to which of these two meanings is uppermost: e.g. GP 243, 269, Mch 1246+; redoubtable GP 47, ML 579, Mk 2249+; worthy, suitable GP 579+

wostow *contr of* **woost thow**

wowe *v* woo Mil 3372+

wowke *n* (see also **wike**) week Fkl 1161

woxe(n) *p ppl of* **wexe** *v*

wrastle *v* wrestle GP 548, Kn 2961+

wrathe *v* (see also **wratthe**) anger, provoke Mcp 80+

wratthe *n* wrath, anger Pars 335+

wratthe *v refl* (see also **wrathe**)
become angry Pars 1013

wraw(e) *adj* angry Mcp 46; peevish Pars 677

wrecche *n* wretch Kn 931+; exile
SN 58; miser Mel 1603

wrecche, wrecched *adj* wretched
Kn 921+

wrecchednesse *n* wretchedness,
misery ML 941+; wickedness,
folly Rv 3897, Fkl 1271+; baseness, base act Fkl 1523; vile/
contemptible things Mcp 171,
Pars 34

wreche *n* vengeance ML 679+

wreke *v* avenge, revenge
Kn 961, WB 809+; wreak, give
vent to Mk 2597; *refl* avenge
o.s., take vengeance Sq 454,
Pard 857+; *p ppl* **wreke(n)**

wreye *v* reveal Mil 3503,
Fkl 944; betray Mil 3507

wrighte *n* worker in wood, carpenter GP 614, Mil 3143

wringe *v* pinch WB 942, Mch
1553; wring (the hands)
ML 606, Cl 1212; wring out
Th 776; *sg past* **wrong**

write *v* write GP 96+; proclaim,
indicate Rv 3869; *3 sg contr
pres* **writ**; *sg past* **wroot**; *pl
past* **writen**; *past subj* **write**;
p ppl **write(n), ywrite(n)**

wroght *p ppl of* **werke** *v* (1)
worked GP 367+; painted
Kn 1919; made Kn 1983+;
created Mk 2008+; fashioned
Kn 2497

wroghte *sg past of* **werke** *v* (1)

wrong *sg past of* **wringe** *v*

wroot *sg past of* **write** *v*

wrooth *adj* angry GP 451,

Kn 1179+; *pl and weak sg*
wrothe

wroughte *sg past of* **werke** *v* (1)

wrye *v* (1) cover Kn 2904, Sum
1827+; *p ppl* **ywrye**

wrye *v* (2) ~ *awey(ward)* turn
away Mil 3283, Mcp 262

wys *adv* certainly, surely
Kn 2786, Fkl 1470+

wys(e)ly *adv* assuredly, for sure
Rv 3994, Mch 2114; earnestly
Fkl 789; heavily Rv 4162; (in
oaths and asseverations) *as ~
as* as surely as, inasmuch as
Kn 2234; *(al)so ~* (may s.o.)
surely (do s.th.) ML 1061+

Regular (weak) *p ppl* forms
beginning with y have not generally been entered; they
should be sought under their
second letter in the main entry
for the verb (e.g. **ydight** under
dighte *v*).

yaf *sg and pl past of* **yeve** *v*

yate *n* gate Cl 1013+

yave(n) *pl past of* **yeve** *v*

ybe(n) *p ppl of* **be** *v* been Mch
2401+

ybet, ybete(n) *p ppl of* **bete** *v*
beaten Mil 3759+; hammered,
embossed Kn 979+

yblent *p ppl of* **blende** *v*

yboght *p ppl of* **beye/bye** *v*

ybore(n), yborn *p ppl of* **bere** *v*
(see also **bore, boren, born**)
born Kn 1019, Cl 158+;
borne, carried GP 378+;
borne, given birth to Cl 443

ybounde(n) *p ppl of* **binde** *v*

ybrend, ybrent *p ppl of* **brenne** *v*
burned Kn 946+

yclad *p ppl of* **clothe** *v*

ycome(n) *p ppl of* **come** *v*

ycorve(n) *p ppl of* **kerve** *v*

ydo, ydo(o)n *p ppl of* **do** *v* done
Kn 1025+; finished, over
Kn 2534, WB 574+; per-
formed SN 386; placed CY
899; *of* ~ taken off Kn 2676

ydriven *p ppl of* **drive** *v*

ydronke *p ppl of* **drinke** *v*

ye *2 pers pron (nom pl)* you
GP 780+

ye *adv* yea, yes Mil 3455+

yede *sg past of* **go** *v* went CY
1141; came CY 1281

yeer *n (see also* **yer***)* year
GP 347+; *as pl* years
GP 82+

yeerd *n (see also* **yerd(e)** *n (1))*
enclosure, yard NP 2847+

yelde *v* pay WB 130+; reward
Sum 1772, 2177; give back,
restore Phys 189, Mel 1292;
give Sum 1821, Pars 378+;
relinquish, give up Kn 3052,
Cl 843; deliver up WB 912;
p ppl **yolden**

yelle *v* shout Kn 2672: yell
NP 3389

yeman *n* yeoman, 'a servant or
attendant in a royal or noble
household, . . . ranking
between a sergeant and a
groom or between a squire and
a page' (*OED*) GP 101, Fri
1380+; servant or attendant on
an (ecclesiastical) official Fri
1524, CY 562+; 'a man holding a small landed estate; a
freeholder under the rank of a
gentleman; hence *vaguely*, a
commoner or countryman of

respectable standing' (*OED*)
Mil 3270; men of the above
rank serving in battle
Kn 2509, 2728

yer *n (see also* **yeer***)* year
Kn 1458+

yerd(e) *n (1) (see also* **yeerd***)*
yard, garden Sum 1798,
Fkl 1251; enclosure, yard
NP 2951+

yerde *n (2)* stick, rod GP 149,
Pars 670+; staff Kn 1387;
under youre ~ under your authority Cl 22; *under the* ~ in
tutelage Sh 97; yard Kn 1050

yerne *adv* eagerly WB 993;
busily Pard 398

yet *adv and conj (see also* **yit***)*
yet GP 70+; still Kn 2307+;
always Pard 425; in addition,
besides GP 612, Kn 2005+;
moreover Mch 2246+; *~today*
even now Fkl 1473; ~ *now* in
addition Kn 938, 1156

yeve *v (see also* **yive***)* give
GP 223+; grant Mch 2377,
Pars 442+; ~ *again* return Mil
3773; ~ *up* utter Mch 2364; *sg
past* yaf; *pl past* yaf, yave(n);
p ppl yeve(n)

yfalle(n) *p ppl of* **falle** *v* fallen
GP 25, Mil 3460; ~ *in* occur-
ring in Pard 496; *thing* ~ occurrence CY 1043

yfet *p ppl of* **fecche** *v*

yfounde *p ppl of* **finde** *v*

ygeten *p ppl of* **gete** *v*

ygo(n) *p ppl of* **go** *v*

ygrave *p ppl of* **grave** *v*

ygrounde *p ppl of* **grinde** *v*

yhent *p ppl of* **hente** *v*

yholde *p ppl of* **holde** *v* held

Kn 2958; considered
Kn 2374+; *hir wey* ~ taken her
course Mch 1932

yif *sg and pl imp of* **yive** *v*

yifte *n* gift Kn 2198+

yis *adv* yes Mil 3369+

yit *adv* (see also **yet**) yet Cl 120;
in the future Fkl 688; then
NP 3408; *as* ~ still Cl 120; so
far Fkl 1577

yive *v* (see also **yeve**) give
GP 225+; *sg and pl imp* **yif**

yknowe(n) *p ppl of* **iknowe** *and*
knowe *v*

ykorven *p ppl of* **kerve** *v*

ylad *p ppl of* **lede** *v*

ylaft *p ppl of* **leve** *v* (1)

yleid *p ppl of* **leye** *v*

ymaad, ymaked *p ppl of* **make** *v*

ymet(te) *p ppl of* **meete** *v*

yolden *p ppl of* **yelde** *v*

yond *adv* yonder, over there
Kn 1099+; far away Cl 1199

yong *adj* young GP 7+

yo(o)re *adv* for a long time Rv
4230+; formerly, before
ML 174+; long ago Rv 3897+;
of time ~ for a long time
Fkl 963; *times* ~ times gone by
Cl 1140; ~ *ago(on)* long ago
Kn 1813+

your(e) *poss pron* your
GP 804+; *absol* yours
CY 1248

yow 2 *pers pl pron, acc/dat* you
GP 34+

ypocrisye *n* hypocrisy Pard 410+

ypocrite *n* hypocrite Sq 514+

yqueint *p ppl of* **quenche** *v*

yraft *p ppl of* **reve** *v*

yrent *p ppl of* **rende** *v*

yronne(n) *p ppl of* **renne** *v* run
GP 8+; clustered Kn 2165

ysene *p ppl of* **se(e)** *v*

yset *p ppl of* **sette** *v*

yseyn *p ppl of* **se(e)** *v*

yshape(n) *p ppl of* **shape** *v*

yshave *p ppl* shaved, shaven
GP 690+

yshent *p ppl of* **shende** *v*

yshette *p ppl of* **shette** *v* shut
ML 560+

yshorn *p ppl of* **shere** *v*

yshrive(n) *p ppl of* **shrive** *v*

yslawe *p ppl of* **sle(e)** *v* slain,
killed Kn 943+

ysonge *p ppl of* **singe** *v*

yspoken *p ppl of* **speke** *v*

ysprad, yspred *p ppl of*
sprede *v*

yspreind *p ppl of* **springe** *v* (2)

ystorve *p ppl of* **sterve** *v* dead

yswonke *p ppl of* **swinke** *v*

yswore, ysworn *p ppl of* **swere** *v*
sworn Kn 1132+

ytake(n) *p ppl of* **take** *v*

ythrowe *p ppl of* **throwe** *v*

yto(o)ld *p ppl of* **telle** *v*

ytukked *p ppl* (see also **tukked**)
with gown tucked up
Sum 1737

ywonne *p ppl of* **winne** *v*

ywoxen *p ppl of* **wexe** *v*

ywrite(n) *p ppl of* **write** *v*

ywroght *p ppl of* **werke** *v* (1)
made WB 117; worked
GP 196, Th 864; created
Mch 1324

THE STORY OF PENGUIN CLASSICS

Before 1946 ...'Classics' are mainly the domain of academics and students, without readable editions for everyone else. This all changes when a little-known classicist, E. V. Rieu, presents Penguin founder Allen Lane with the translation of Homer's *Odyssey* that he has been working on and reading to his wife Nelly in his spare time.

1946 *The Odyssey* becomes the first Penguin Classic published, and promptly sells three million copies. Suddenly, classic books are no longer for the privileged few.

1950s Rieu, now series editor, turns to professional writers for the best modern, readable translations, including Dorothy L. Sayers's *Inferno* and Robert Graves's *The Twelve Caesars*, which revives the salacious original.

1960s The Classics are given the distinctive black jackets that have remained a constant throughout the series's various looks. Rieu retires in 1964, hailing the Penguin Classics list as 'the greatest educative force of the 20th century'.

1970s A new generation of translators arrives to swell the Penguin Classics ranks, and the list grows to encompass more philosophy, religion, science, history and politics.

1980s The Penguin American Library joins the Classics stable, with titles such as *The Last of the Mohicans* safeguarded. Penguin Classics now offers the most comprehensive library of world literature available.

1990s The launch of Penguin Audiobooks brings the classics to a listening audience for the first time, and in 1999 the launch of the Penguin Classics website takes them online to a larger global readership than ever before.

The 21st Century Penguin Classics are rejacketed for the first time in nearly twenty years. This world famous series now consists of more than 1300 titles, making the widest range of the best books ever written available to millions – and constantly redefining the meaning of what makes a 'classic'.

The Odyssey continues ...

The best books ever written

PENGUIN (🐧) CLASSICS

SINCE 1946

Find out more at www.penguinclassics.com